THE COMPLETE SHORT STORIES AND SKETCHES
OF STEPHEN CRANE

THE COMPLETE
SHORT STORIES & SKETCHES
OF STEPHEN CRANE

EDITED WITH AN INTRODUCTION
BY THOMAS A. GULLASON

DOUBLEDAY & COMPANY, INC.

GARDEN CITY, NEW YORK

For BETTY and EDWARD

PREFACE

Stephen Crane is as glamorous a figure as ever. He is still fondly remembered as the "genius" of his generation, and the "wonder boy" of American literature. But mainly because of his bizarre life, and Thomas Beer's impressionistic interpretation of it in *Stephen Crane* (1923), the critical emphasis—in fact, the craze—has been on his biography. John Berryman's *Stephen Crane* (1950), *Stephen Crane: Letters* (1960), and Lillian Gilkes' *Cora Crane* (1960) have stimulated further speculations into the nature and color of Crane's soul, so that at least two new biographies are now in preparation.

Far less attention has been paid to Crane as a creative artist. Only his poetry has been carefully studied by Daniel Hoffman in *The Poetry of Stephen Crane* (1957); and only in the last dozen years has there been a concerted effort to study his fiction. Even here, many critics—rightly awed by the fact that Crane wrote brilliantly about the Civil War without having seen it—have been lost in source studies and backgrounds to the war tales, especially *The Red Badge of Courage*. While all these studies are of value, Crane's place in American letters, whether as a short story writer or as a novelist, is still really insecure, because it has not been amply studied.

There is another, more major reason for Crane's literary neglect: simply, the unavailability of his complete works. Though a handsome twelve-volume edition of Crane's output was collected, *The Work of Stephen Crane* (1925–27), it was published in a limited edition of 750 copies. Besides this, the collection was far from complete. Most students of Crane, then, have had to depend on the anthologies, some of them now out of print, which selected only the best of Crane, like "The Open Boat," "The Blue Hotel," and "The Bride Comes to Yellow Sky." *The Red Badge* has always been easily obtainable; and recently *Maggie* has appeared in several editions.

But the bulk of Crane is still to be found only in the twelve-volume *Work*. The *Work* forsakes a chronological approach in order to present Crane in as attractive a manner as possible—namely, by the technique of contrast. For example, the first volume includes *The Red Badge* and "The Veteran," to show Henry Fleming during and after the Civil War. The second volume, *Tales of Two Wars,* contrasts Crane's prewar stories, like "The Little Regiment," with his Cuban war sketches, like "The Second Generation." In the third volume, *The Third Violet* is contrasted with

"The Monster," when the latter story, because of its setting, characters, and themes more properly belongs with *Whilomville Stories* (volume five). In the ninth volume, *Wounds in the Rain,* Cuban sketches are placed alongside non-Cuban ones, like " 'Ol' Bennet' and the Indians," with the result that Crane's unity and purpose is destroyed; originally, in 1900, Crane published only Cuban sketches in *Wounds.* His last novels, *Active Service* and *The O'Ruddy,* are in volumes four, seven, and eight; his earliest novel, *Maggie,* is found in volume ten. While the principle of contrast does dramatize and heighten differences in the fiction, it baffles the reader, for he is never sure of any development or any clear and significant changes in Crane's art.

This dilemma appears in the work of many authors. Recently, Edmund Wilson complained about Constance Garnett's collection of Chekhov's stories, and its lack of chronology. Chekhov's earliest stories were placed alongside his later, more serious ones; the result, says Mr. Wilson: ". . . garbling of Chekhov's development is one of the causes for the frequent complaints on the part of English-speaking critics that they cannot make out what he is driving at." The case with Crane may not be this serious, but Crane certainly was "driving at" far more than the war theme (which includes the psychology of fear, courage, and cowardice); yet this is the dominant image we have of his fiction.

In this collection, I have tried to fix the Crane chronology as accurately as possible. One will probably come to a long-standing conclusion: that "The Open Boat," "The Blue Hotel," "The Bride Comes to Yellow Sky," "The Monster," and "Death and the Child" are his best work. But with chronology one can get a surer insight into the workings of Crane's art and his subjects, and the puzzles in one story may be solved by what preceded it or followed it. With biographical aid—vigorously debunked by many "new critics" and vigorously defended by Leon Edel in his *Literary Biography*—one can more clearly explain Crane's rapid development as an artist, his erratic performances, and his major successes.

There are some hazards in attempting a chronological as well as a complete approach to a writer's art. The best of Crane becomes dwarfed, for his frequent potboilers cheapen the significance of his rich talent. On the other hand, there is always the fascination of watching a writer groping, experimenting, questing for his best self—or his "one good tune," as Alberto Moravia puts it. When the final accounting of Crane's output is made, one realizes that he has only a handful of masterpieces; the same is true of many others, like Ernest Hemingway, Sherwood Anderson, and William Faulkner. Crane also has—and this fact is often ignored—a goodly number of above average stories: "The Pace of Youth," "A Desertion," "An Experiment in Misery," "A Dark Brown Dog," "The Men in the Storm," "A Mystery of Heroism," "One Dash—Horses," "The Little Regiment," "His New Mittens," "The Price of the Harness," "Virtue in War," "An Episode of War," "Shame," "The Upturned Face," and "The Knife." Furthermore, one is amazed at the modernity of Crane's art—a comparative study of "The Blue Hotel" with Hemingway's "The Killers" shows this—and it can be seen even more clearly by comparing Crane's stories with those by his contemporaries: Mark Twain, Frank Norris, Hamlin Garland, and William Dean Howells.

There are various other problems in compiling a volume of this type. Dating stories can be a simple, mechanical matter, but some of Crane's stories were unpublished and therefore undated. Crane's existing letters do not supply enough clues. In such cases, one is forced to depend on style and subject matter to determine the period in which these stories were written. A larger confusion becomes apparent when one realizes that Crane often published a story in several newspapers and magazines (not necessarily in the same year) before collecting it, sometimes, into a book. To locate the first appearance of a story becomes a calculated risk, especially since some of them were published in such unlikely places as *The Plumbers' Trade Journal;* here I have relied mainly on the painstaking bibliographical work of Ames Williams and Vincent Starrett. Moreover, Crane wrote some stories as part of a continuing series, and though they were not published in the same year or period, I have often kept them as one unit within that year or period and forsaken chronology temporarily. I did not always group them closely, for this would have destroyed the general chronology. Tales gathered (sometimes by myself) as *The Little Regiment, The Sullivan County Sketches, Midnight Sketches, Whilomville Stories,* the Tommie series, and *Wounds in the Rain* can be read individually. But *Spitzbergen Tales* ("The Kicking Twelfth," "The Shrapnel of Their Friends," "And If He Wills, We Must Die," "The Upturned Face") and *Wyoming Valley Tales* ("The Battle of Forty Fort," "The Surrender of Forty Fort," " 'Ol' Bennet' and the Indians") do have closer connections, and Crane's purpose and design would be destroyed if they were not read as self-contained units. Further biographical facts may call for some revisions in my present dating. Crane, or his editors, also changed the titles of some of the stories; wherever necessary, I have presented one alternate title, though one story, "A Freight Car Incident," has four different titles.

The fate of *Last Words* (1902) suggests that extreme caution must be used with regard to dating. For years, most critics presumed that this posthumous collection was Crane's last work, when in reality it included much of his earliest. Recently a story in that collection, "Why Did the Young Clerk Swear?," was located in *Truth* (March 18, 1893). Another story,

"The Reluctant Voyagers," first published in February 1900, in the New York *Press*, belongs to an earlier period; Corwin Linson saw the completed manuscript in 1893. There are other examples of this problem. Thomas Beer and a recent critic, Hans Arnold, are sure that the *Wyoming Valley Tales* were written in 1892. In his letters, however, Crane mentions readying these tales for his agent in 1899; here I have kept the later date. Even though "An Eloquence of Grief," "The Auction," "A Poker Game," and others were not published until 1898 and later, they belong with Crane's New York sketches, most of which were written between 1893 and 1896. Crane said in November, 1896: "There are some 15 or 20 short sketches of New York street life and so on which I intended to have published in book form under the title of *Midnight Sketches*." Two other stories seem to belong to the period of the New York sketches; but Cora Crane completed "The Man from Duluth," and she may have revised "A Man by the Name of Mud." Whenever I had definite evidences, I have sometimes ignored publishing dates in order to get the "real" chronology.

Usually when more than a year elapsed between completion and publication, I have used the "completion" date. This "completion" date approach has its dangers, especially with Crane. For example, he was trying to sell "The Blue Hotel" in February 1898, but this was probably the shortened version and not the complete tale that was published in November and December 1898. Though "The Revenge of the *Adolphus*" was completed in February 1899, and sent to his agent (and not published until September 1899), Crane was asking for advice in regard to nautical terms used in the tale as late as May 1899. "A Man and Some Others" was completed in the fall of 1896, but Crane probably had to make some changes before Gilder would publish it in February 1897. "The Monster" was "completed" in September 1897, but it was hard to sell because of its subject, and Crane may have had to make some changes before it was published in August 1898.

Following each story, I have presented the initial publishing or completion date. Several times, I have included more than one date because some stories appeared in installments in the newspapers. In some instances, I have used a question mark after the date to show that the story was never published and/or that I have relied on biographical evidences, letters, style, and subject to fix the real time of writing. In other instances, I have two different sets of dates, one of which is in brackets. This means that though the story was published later—a few of *The Sullivan County Sketches*, several of the New York sketches, and so on—it was completed at an earlier date; here again, I have relied on biography, letters, and subject and style.

In the bracketed materials, following the date, I have listed the first-known publication history of each story. However, many of the first appearances of Crane's stories, in the newspapers, are abridgments; the complete texts are often found in volume form only. In a few cases I did not list page references, because the magazines or newspapers could not be traced; but the dates are authoritative. Only in one case, "Dan Emmonds," I have bracketed the month and the year in which the story was first mentioned in a letter; Crane said that he wrote the story earlier than 1896. At the beginning of two stories—"The Man from Duluth" and "The Squire's Madness"—I have indicated that Cora Crane finished them; she may have changed or completed other materials in *Last Words*. At the beginning of others, I have indicated stories that were written as part of a series or group and often collected under one title, like *Whilomville Stories*.

Another task was to separate fact from fiction, for Crane was a practicing journalist who wrote for many American and English newspapers. *Last Words* includes much non-fiction: "London Impressions," "Minetta Lane," "Roof Gardens," "The Assassins in Modern Battles," "In the Broadway Cars," "Ballydehob," and "The Royal Irish Constabulary." The *Work* repeats several of these—"London Impressions," "Ballydehob," "The Royal Irish Constabulary"—and adds at least one more, "The Scotch Express." Two others, "A Prologue" (*Work*) and "At Clancy's Wake" (*Last Words*), are really playlets. There are several borderline cases. These include, among others, the autobiographical reminiscences "War Memories" and "Marines Signaling Under Fire at Guantanamo," both of which convey the atmosphere of *Wounds* but lack the movement of a real short story. Then others seem to be feature articles and human interest stories, which have been dressed up by Crane's fictional method. Many of these are clearly non-fiction: "Nebraska's Bitter Fight for Life," "The Devil's Acre," "Ghosts on the Jersey Coast," "The Ghostly Sphinx of Metedeconk," "The Wreck of the *New Era*," "Yellow Undersized Dog," and others. Still others have passed into the realm of fiction: "In a Park Row Restaurant," "Mr. Binks' Day Off," "A Lovely Jag in a Crowded Car," and more. In these newspaper sketches one can see Crane using the news medium to test his fictional craft. He creates characters, usually a "stranger" with Crane himself as reporter; much dialogue is used, along with an impressionistic and dramatic style. What results is Crane's own inimitable subjective manner of arriving at journalism's objective demands: Who? What? When? Where? How? Why? Sometimes, then, his fictional approach so buries the facts that a special feature article can pass for a sketch or story.

Besides feature articles, Crane also wrote many war dispatches (now being collected), and historical sketches gathered as *Great Battles of the World* (1901). The wonder of all this is how Crane could find time for serious fiction when **he** was continually involved in hack work. Yet somehow these transitory pieces—news features, travel sketches, war dispatches —became exercises in fictional style and subject; many a seed idea or source for a Crane story can be found in these non-fictions.

The collating of texts was probably the most demanding job. Many of Crane's original manuscripts are not available, and even when they are, they differ in wording and punctuation from the published versions. Though Crane was never as bad as Balzac—who changed his materials endlessly—he made brief yet constant alterations in a story as it went through several appearances in newspapers, magazines, and finally into a volume. All the stories in this collection have been checked against the first printings and, in some cases, against manuscripts in Crane's or Cora Crane's handwriting. Most often I have used the last printed version (during Crane's lifetime) of the stories. The early version of "The Price of the Harness" (*Cosmopolitan*), reprinted in some anthologies, includes an overstated ending; Crane eliminated this when he reprinted the story in *Wounds*. I have kept Crane's profanity, his dialect patterns (ses for says, 'ain't for ain't), and his sentence lengths, all of which were altered or eliminated by various editors.

Some interesting discoveries become apparent in the collating of texts. "The Bride Comes to Yellow Sky," in its original appearance in *McClure's Magazine* (1898), has (in places) the typical Hemingway style: short, staccato sentences. Some modern editors have resorted to commas and semicolons to lengthen these sentences. By doing this, they have sometimes destroyed Crane's understated effects. Other stories show similar alterations in sentence length.

Though one cannot always be certain that some changes—from newspaper and magazine to book—were made by Crane, they suggest his style, so that one realizes that at times Crane was a careful student of revision. In one of his earliest stories, "An Ominous Baby," he shortened "swallowing cavern" to "cavern" for better effect. The same is true of "The Men in the Storm," where its original opening in the *Arena* "At about three o'clock of the February afternoon. . . ." was deleted, and the story subsequently began: "The blizzard began to swirl great clouds of snow along the streets. . . ." Often in succeeding appearances of a story, Crane deleted words and phrases that blurred his usually taut design. A case in point is "An Experiment in Misery." In its original appearance (April 22, 1894), it had an opening aimed specifically for a newspaper audience; for it read like a feature article. When he trimmed the opening (and made the ending briefer) for its reappearance in *The Open Boat and Other Stories* (London, 1898), it became all story. Crane probably would have trimmed "An Experiment in Luxury" too if he had reprinted it in a volume. The reverse is true of some stories, like "The Upturned Face." Its version in *Ainslee's Magazine* (March 1900) is briefer than its later appearance in *Last Words*. Probably Crane (or Cora?) realized that his earlier version was too cryptic, and so some additions, sometimes sentences, were made to show further ironic and emotional responses in the story.

Some revisions were the work of editors. And these reveal Crane's life-long war with censorship and with his genteel world. In "The Price of the Harness" (*Cosmopolitan*) Crane's intended "Jesus" became "Hell"; a whole sentence, "He laid his face to his rifle as if it were his mistress," was dropped out, and later it was included in *Wounds*. In "A Man and Some Others" (*Century Magazine*), the word "Hell" was deleted, and the delicate "g——" replaced Crane's intended "Gawd!" In "The Second Generation" (*The Saturday Evening Post*), "damned" was deleted. There were many other cases of this to indicate the pressures on Crane, which may have temporarily frustrated his natural style and his modern subjects.

English editors, supposedly much more liberal in the 1890s, were also toying with Crane's language, sometimes with comic results. In "Twelve O'Clock" (*Pall Mall Magazine*) "spittoons" became "receptacles," and "God-damn" became "——." In "And If He Wills, We Must Die" (*Illustrated London News*) "damned" became "darned," "damn it" became "curse it." In "The Revenge of the *Adolphus*" (*Strand Magazine*) "Gawd" became "Jove," "damned" became "blessed" and "damn," "hang."

One can anticipate further discoveries of manuscripts, but for the moment this volume is the most complete collection of Crane's short fiction. I have not included any fragments of short stories, many of which are now in the possession of Special Collections at Columbia University. These include, among others, "Art in Kansas City," "The Fire Tribe and the White Face," "A Flurry of Condensed Milk," and "In the Country of Rhimers and Writers." They are all of some interest. Nor have I included the generous gifts of Clifton Waller Barrett—"Brer Washington's Consolation" and "The Ideal and the Real." Both stories have missing passages, and imaginative guesswork could not solve them. In all, two stories in this collection ("Dan Emmonds" and "The Camel") have never been published; twenty-one others have never been collected in book form; and one other has never been published in the United States.

I owe a deep debt of gratitude to many people, individually and collectively, who helped to make this volume possible. I want to take this opportunity to thank the following: Mr. Harold Kuebler of Doubleday, for his interest, which brought this project into being; Alfred A. Knopf, Inc., copyright holders of Crane's work, for allowing me to reprint these stories; Ronald Baughman, Head of Special Collections at Columbia University, for granting me permission to reprint Crane's unpublished stories; Mr. Clifton Waller Barrett, for contributing greatly to the progress of

Crane scholarship; and Vice-President Ernest Hartung and the University Research Committee of the University of Rhode Island, for grant-in-aid funds.

I owe special thanks to Mr. Robert H. Rhodes, in charge of interlibrary loans at the University of Rhode Island, for his patient help in acquiring many materials. I wish to express my thanks also to the library staffs of Wisconsin, Dartmouth, University of Virginia, New York Public Library, Yale, Harvard, Princeton, Syracuse University, Huntington Library, Free Public Library of Philadelphia, and the Detroit Public Library.

Finally, I want to acknowledge my indebtedness to all previous Crane scholarship, especially the following: Ames W. Williams and Vincent Starrett, *Stephen Crane: A Bibliography* (1948); *Stephen Crane: An Exhibition of His Writings* (1956), arranged and described by Joan H. Baum; Maurice Beebe and Thomas A. Gullason, "Criticism of Stephen Crane: A Selected Checklist with an Index to Studies of Separate Works," *Modern Fiction Studies* (Autumn, 1959).

University of Rhode Island
Kingston, Rhode Island

CONTENTS

INTRODUCTION

Stephen Crane's literary reputation is based mainly on his Civil War novel, *The Red Badge of Courage* (1895), and periodic world wars have helped to perpetuate this condition. This has handicapped Crane's real importance in at least three ways: it implies that he had only one theme—war; it minimizes his significance as a short story writer; and it suggests that anything he wrote after 1895 was anticlimactic. In reality, Stephen Crane dealt with a variety of themes; he was consistently drawn to short fiction; and his best writing was done in this medium, between 1897 and 1900, the years of "The Open Boat," "The Blue Hotel," "The Bride Comes to Yellow Sky," "The Monster," "Death and the Child," "The Price of the Harness," "An Episode of War," "The Upturned Face," and *Whilomville Stories.* Ernest Hemingway, with whom Crane has often been compared, had a similar fate. Almost always Hemingway was identified with his novels—*A Farewell to Arms, The Sun Also Rises,* and *For Whom the Bell Tolls*—though his major achievement was in the realm of the short story.

Countless other practitioners of both short and long fiction have, in the end, been judged mainly by their novels. Generally, critics and readers look upon the short story as something light, ephemeral, narrow, insubstantial—a spare-time art. The editor of *The Critic,* in 1887, went so far as to say: "As a rule, the short story is produced in youth, while the novel is a product of experience." Nonetheless, America has had a long and distinguished list of short story writers, though the very few essays and books of criticism on the theory and practice of short fiction clearly indicate that it is still not taken seriously. By contrast, there has been an avalanche of books on the novel and novelists. In his *Modern Short Story* (1941) H. E. Bates, the distinguished writer and critic, admits: "The short story, though much practised, is still a misunderstood and neglected form in the mind of the public." The judgment of William Faulkner (and other novelists) may one day create a healthier climate: ". . . the short story . . . is the most demanding form after poetry." For like poetry, the short story is brief and seems transitory, but it can have rich and momentous implications.

Though Stephen Crane did not begin his literary career as a poet, he felt that his best work was done in his volume of poems, *The Black Riders* (1895). He was fond of its "ethical sense" which reflected his "ideas of life as a whole"; specifically, the volume contained abstracts of the ideas of his fiction. But Crane probably realized that in his verse he sounded too much like a preacher reading sermons (he despised "preaching" in art) and that he was too cryptic. The endless parodies of his work, and the lack of a wide, appreciative audience made him return to poetry only once more, in 1899, with *War Is Kind*. Still, the best features of his poetic technique were carried over into his fiction so that Crane is, as Carl Van Doren once stated, a "kind of poet among storytellers."

Devoting himself primarily to prose fiction, Crane wrote other novels besides *The Red Badge*: *Maggie* (1893), *George's Mother* (1896), *The Third Violet* (1897), *Active Service* (1899), and *The O'Ruddy* (1903). Most of these were short novels, and even here Crane had a psychological block against length. He was still attracted to the brevity of his poems. A reader of Edgar Allan Poe's work, he may have been influenced by Poe's theories on length versus brevity, as seen in "The Poetic Principle" and "The Philosophy of Composition." Crane rightly sensed that he functioned best in short episodes and dramatic scenes, where he gained in concentration, in taut power, and in unity (the "totality of effect or impression"). Usually in his longer novels, especially *Active Service* and *The O'Ruddy*, Crane lost his sustained control, and his effects were sprawling and melodramatic. The reverse was true of *The Third Violet*, where many scenes in the novel "were too compressed."

Crane had a perpetual warfare with the novel form. Tolstoy's *Anna Karenina* and *War and Peace* he considered too long, especially the latter, which he felt could have been done in "one third of the time. . . . It goes on and on like Texas." Zola's novels bored him, particularly the length of *Nana*; and in a general summary of this work, he said: "He hangs one thing to another and his story goes along but I find him pretty tiresome." He was critical of the long novels of Mark Twain; he thought Thomas Hardy overtreated his materials, and that Henry James was too "diffuse." Even his own *Red Badge* Crane considered too long. His ideal was simply this: "I like my art straight"; and he could have added, "I like it brief." The reality was that he defeated himself in his lengthy novels. Two of Crane's ardent champions saw this waste of talent. Edward Garnett said bluntly: "Crane ought never to have essayed the form of the novel." And H. L. Mencken believed that Crane's method "was grossly ill-adapted to the novel," for he "had no literary small talk." This was one of many contradictions in Crane's art and life. He instinctively understood the pitfalls of length, but because he knew that writing novels meant the possibility of more money and a larger audience, he wrote potboilers like *Active Service* (coaxed along by Harold Frederic) and *The O'Ruddy* to capitalize on the public's hunger for romances.

Along with his theory of brevity, Crane was impressed by the rich tradition of the short story and by the growing number of magazines in the 1890s which provided a ready market. Rudyard Kipling, whose stories were very popular in the 1880s and 1890s, won a temporary convert in Crane, who later renounced his "clever" school of writing in 1892. Ambrose Bierce's *Tales of Soldiers and Civilians* (1891) excited him, and pointing specifically to "An Occurrence at Owl Creek Bridge," Crane said: "Nothing better exists. That story contains everything." He knew Maupassant's work (at least through Henry James's critical essays), Bret Harte's early California sketches, and Mark Twain's Western tales. His close friendship with Hamlin Garland may have led Crane to the Midwesterner's *Main-Travelled Roads* (1891). Finally, the largest single inspiration on Crane seems to have been Poe. Thomas Beer mentions that "Crane liked Poe's rhythmic prose as a boy." And in 1895, when Willa Cather met Crane in Lincoln, Nebraska, she found him "reading a little volume of Poe that he carried in his pocket." Often accused of a lack of bookishness by the critics, Crane was really secretive about his reading habits. In his own library, Crane had novels and tales by Kipling, Henry Fielding, Harold Frederic, Henry James, and Sir Walter Scott, not to mention works by members of his own family; and he knew the writings of William Dean Howells, Balzac, Dostoevsky, and others. Whenever he was engaged in literary discusssions relating to influences on his work, he feigned ignorance of authors, especially French. On one occasion, when asked about Stéphane Mallarmé, he said: "I don't know much about Irish authors." In the little-known story "Why Did the Young Clerk Swear?" (1893), the hero becomes disenchanted with a French romantic novel.

Before Crane turned to fiction, he seemed destined to join a family of journalists. His father, the minister Jonathan Townley Crane, wrote for religious periodicals; his mother served as a reporter for the Philadelphia *Press* and the New York *Tribune;* and his older brothers Townley and Wilbur were correspondents for the *Tribune.* By 1888, at the age of sixteen, young Crane assisted his brother Townley during the summer months at Asbury Park, and by 1891 and 1892 he was contributing his own pieces to the newspapers. However, in 1892, Crane's promising career with the *Tribune* ended (both he and his brother Townley were presumably fired) when he wrote a dispatch, "On the New Jersey Coast" (August 21), that read like a caustic editorial. With his sardonic irony, he mocked bourgeois values, Asbury Park itself, and labor, represented by the parading members of the Junior Order of United American Mechanics. From this experience Crane must have developed one of his pet theories— "Preaching is fatal to art in literature"; "An artist has no business to preach." Later, whether in feature articles or short fiction, Crane sometimes went to extremes: he preached as though from a pulpit, for he was the son of a Methodist minister; he detached himself so completely that his implied moral in *Maggie*, for example, was not understood, and he was charged instead with "cruelty."

It was Willis Johnson, day editor of the *Tribune* and a friend of Crane's father, who advised the young man to devote all his time to fiction, for news reporting was not the place for his "subtle rhetorical tricks." Though Crane accepted his advice and began to produce more fiction, he never gave up journalism altogether. Crane had jobs, some quite brief, on other New York newspapers: the *Sun, Press, Herald, Journal,* and *World.* Practicing journalists quickly realized that Crane had little interest in factual news as such and less interest in the demands of his copy editors. Often editors, like Curtis Brown, thought his few contributions were "queer." On rare occasions was his reportage found satisfactory. Hamlin Garland was pleased with Crane's accurate account of his lecture on William Dean Howells (New York *Tribune,* August 18, 1891).

Nonetheless, Stephen Crane's "romance" with journalism was lifelong. In his first literary essay, "Henry M. Stanley," written in 1890, Crane idealized Stanley, once correspondent for the New York *Herald,* as a symbol of the brave adventurer, the soldier of fortune, and the Christian gentleman. Years later during the Spanish-American War of 1898, Crane, as war correspondent, displayed these very same traits. He wanted to prove himself both as a man and as a reporter. Many other fiction writers, like Bret Harte, Rudyard Kipling, and Theodore Dreiser had a "romance" with journalism. However, Crane's time, the 1890s in New York, was the most sensational period in newspaper history. It was the era of yellow journalism, of Joseph Pulitzer, and of William Randolph Hearst. Newspaper work was a "battling apprenticeship" for Crane, but it was worth it.

Many critics, however, have argued as sincerely as Amy Lowell—"Crane was the last man in this world who should have attempted newspaper writing"—but Crane did not waste his newspaper experience. In his feature articles he gradually refined his rhetorical devices and his impressionistic manner. One episode in 1898 suggested this. An editor, about to release a Crane dispatch, said: "I dropped a few adjectives here and there, Steve. This has to be *news*, sent at cable rates. You can save your flubdub and shoot it to New York by mail. What I want is the straight story of the fight." In his day-to-day routine as a reporter, Crane also found readymade subjects for his real fiction. He became a student of the American scene and a shrewd social critic. He watched the mannerisms of the people in the Bowery; he listened to their speech patterns; he "felt" their suffering. He saw the wealth of the few and the poverty of the many, and this gave him deeper insight into the terrors of environment and the need for reform. Some of his "protest" stories include "An Experiment in Misery," "An Ominous Baby," and "An Experiment in Luxury." His literary philosophy—

partly naturalistic—developed from his close observation of the violent and subhuman life of the slum dwellers. This revealed more clearly than ever before his humanitarianism, a trait which he admired in his favorite author, Tolstoy. Like Walt Whitman, he too felt a kinship for the oppressed: the prostitute, the dope addict, and the hobo. These New York experiences were probably responsible for turning him to socialism for two weeks, but "when a couple of Socialists assured me I had no right to think differently from any other Socialist and then quarreled with each other about what Socialism meant, I ran away."

Crane's education through New York journalism made him report mentally to himself, and then, after a period of reflection, he rendered the crimes and punishments of city life in his fiction. To a fellow journalist, Arthur Oliver, he demonstrated how an artist could get to the "real thing." Crane scooped up a handful of sand and tossed it to the sea breezes of Asbury Park and said, "Treat your notions like that . . . Forget what you think about it and how you feel about it." Crane's fascination with the psychology of "feeling" could be seen in other places. To Corwin Linson, he complained about Century's *Battles and Leaders of the Civil War* which he studied as possible background for his *Red Badge*: "I wonder that *some* of these fellows don't tell how they *felt* in those scraps! They spout eternally of what they *did*, but they are as emotionless as rocks!" On another occasion Linson, wondering why Crane did not wear heavier clothing as he stood in a breadline getting the "atmosphere" for "The Men in the Storm," heard his friend remark, "How would I know how those poor devils felt if I was warm myself?" Through journalism Crane tested and retested one of the keys of his aesthetic credo. Ambrose Bierce knew the essence of Crane's art when he said, "This young man has the power to feel."

But this did not mean that Crane had no interest in the *what*, in everyday events. He had a very keen sense for what was newsworthy. In 1893, for example, he requested Linson to return the only copy of his tale, "An Ominous Baby," for "during these labor troubles—is the best possible time to dispose of it." And to the magazine editor Mr. McClure he wrote, in 1896: "By the way I would like to go to the scene of the next street-car strike." Some of his fiction, like "A Gray Sleeve," seemed aimed at the trite tastes of the sentimental reader; others, like "The Second Generation," drew upon the topical issues of the day. Still others, like the unpublished "Vashti in the Dark," which dealt with rape, and "The Monster" were examples of the way the boldness and sensationalism of yellow journalism rubbed off on Crane. He could have become the ideal newspaperman, but on *his* terms (he was later considered the best of the war correspondents in Cuba). He had the right temperament: "Humanity was a much more interesting study. When I ought to have been at recitations [at Syracuse University] I was studying faces on the streets, and when I ought to have been studying my next day's lessons I was watching the trains roll in and out of Central Station." Crane used these facts of humanity for his own inimitable ends.

Another phase of journalism—dramatic criticism—indirectly hinted at a significant development in Crane's fictional manner. As late as September 1895, Crane felt certain that he would become the drama critic of the Philadelphia *Press,* but he was not hired. Disappointed, Crane still had a keen interest in the theater, and living in New York, he had seen productions of Hauptmann's *Hannele* and Herne's *Shore Acres.* In his own work he created short playlets: "A Prologue," "At Clancy's Wake," and the unpublished "Greed Rampant." In many of his stories he alluded to the theater, to melodrama, and to the romantic and tragic scenes which involved the hero or heroine. One of his earliest efforts, the satiric, dramatic sketches "A Foreign Policy, in Three Glimpses" (1891), suggested his later reading play, *The Blood of the Martyr* (1898), which was similar in tone and purpose. Only one of Crane's plays was meant to be acted, and this was the charity affair *The Ghost* (1898), a collaborative effort with nine friends. Crane had endless other dramatic projects but none of them materialized. He urged Joseph Conrad to collaborate with him on a play to be named *The Predecessor;* he talked over an idea with Clyde Fitch; he tried to interest someone in a stage adaptation of his short story, "The Upturned Face." Several of his unpublished and incomplete plays (in the possession of Special Collections, Columbia University) include one set in "Old France," another in Cuba, and a third in the American West ("The Fire Tribe and the Paleface" seems to be an adaptation of his unpublished story, "The Fire Tribe and the White Face"). Like Chekhov, Crane continually thought in terms of "staging" his fiction. A close study of "The Open Boat," among others, shows that Crane experimented and enriched his materials with the aid of dramatic techniques. For in this story, Crane was more anxious to render rather than to report; he was far more concerned in the dramatic, not the narrative level; and he focused on dialogue and on a series of crisis scenes and episodes to achieve a remarkable sense of immediacy.

Crane's adventures in journalism do not, however, explain enough of the backgrounds of his literary life. His family world makes clear many of the themes in his work, and, in turn, helps to give a clearer perspective on his art. With his father a Methodist minister and his mother the daughter of one, Crane developed rebellious instincts quite early. Though he loved his father and once called him "a great, fine, simple mind," he could not always tolerate his conservatism. In works such as *Popular Amusements*

(1869) and *Arts of Intoxication* (1870), Jonathan Crane warred against gambling, profanity, cigarette and opium smoking, alcohol, baseball, dancing, novels, and the theater (which suggested "indecency" and the "brothel"). The war was carried to the pious climate of Asbury Park and Ocean Grove where young Crane spent part of his boyhood, and where Methodist leaders tried to prohibit dancing, gambling, alcohol, and the sale of newspapers on Sundays. But sins were in evidence, and Crane observed. In his own actions, he seemed to purposely sin against the complaints of the father, which later became subjects and conflicts in his fiction. At Hudson River Institute in New York (1888–90), he probably worked hard to earn the nickname, "the minister's wild son." Though there was no proof that he ever took opium, Crane knew of the habit (the term "yen nock" in "Yen-Nock Bill and His Sweetheart" refers to the opium pipe) and he wrote an article, "Opium's Varied Dreams" (May, 1896). He played baseball and football; he cursed; he smoked cigarettes; he gambled. Often he was linked with prostitutes, and eventually eloped with the madam of the Hotel de Dream, Cora Taylor. Theodore Roosevelt's summary of Crane's reputation in the 1890s was widely accepted: "He was a man of bad character and he was simply consorting with loose women." By reveling in sin and damnation, Crane was warring against his father and a genteel age.

Crane's mother had a more troubling effect on him. Daughter of George Peck, a well-known Methodist clergyman (other members of the Peck clan were also clergymen), Mary Crane's Calvinistic upbringing, with its belief in natural depravity and in the hell-fire and day-of-doom philosophy, only instilled fear and horror in young Crane and then finally open rebellion. His volumes of poetry chart this rebellion. Forced to attend religious meetings at Ocean Grove, Crane once termed Methodism a "holy show"; and after his father's death in 1880, matters became worse. Now his mother "lived in and for religion." In November 1899, Crane reflected on those earlier times: "My brother Will used to try and argue with her on religious subjects such as hell but he always gave it up. Don't understand that mother was bitter or mean but it hurt her that any of us should be slipping from Grace and giving up eternal damnation or those things. You could argue just as well with a wave." At least on one occasion, when Crane was fourteen, his growing rebellion against religion took on the air of a grotesque comedy. He surprised his mother by agreeing to go to a prayer meeting—only after he had been made "ecstatic" by some wine given to him by an organ grinder. Crane later used this incident with ironic force in *George's Mother*. There are many other references to religion in Crane's fiction, often through imagery, to show his long-standing battle with his Methodist background and with the Bible, which he studied at home and in the schools he attended. Frank Noxon remembered Crane saying that he had "had such a dose of piety in his youth that the reaction was unfavorable to religious consecration in later years." For these reasons, Crane baldly posed one of the tragedies of his life by asking another: ". . . is there any place exactly suited to a minister's son?"

Another contradiction comes to light, for Crane's parents were also crusading humanitarians, and this exactly suited their youngest son. His father had forsaken Presbyterianism for Methodism, because he was disturbed about "a point in its dogma: did the souls of unbaptized infants go to hell?" He had doubts about the "intentions of missionaries" overseas, and the "sanctity of small towns." A Methodist employer had fired a boy because he denied hell, and Jonathan Crane tried to save the boy's job. Mary Crane had a similar nature. Despite criticism, she took care of a girl who "had an accidental baby." She fought the sale of alcohol to children, and tried to win a wider franchise for women by attempting to get them placed on school boards. These qualities became part of young Crane's rebellion and explains, partially, why he was attracted to Cora Taylor, also a champion of causes (for example, she aided the orphaned Frederic children). This sense of social purpose, later to be found in Crane's fiction, was part of the everyday world of his parents. In the opening pages of *Arts of Intoxication,* Jonathan Crane implied his deep sense of service: "Italy, France, Germany, England, and the United States are laboring beneath a mountain weight of crime, poverty, suffering, and wrong of every description, and no nation on either continent is fully awake to the perils of the hour."

The intellectual life of his parents suggests that Stephen Crane had a rich, though private, education. His father was a graduate of the College of New Jersey (later Princeton University) and his mother graduated from the City College of New York. Though their youngest son never paid much attention to formal education at Claverack (Hudson River Institute), Lafayette College, and Syracuse University, he had a substantial informal one. His story "Uncle Jake and the Bell Handle," written when he was fourteen, shows his precocious way with language. As Thomas Beer once demonstrated, Crane could use difficult words with ease very early—words like irascible, pyrotechnic, impartial, and memorial. He even invented words, like "higgle." The major share of his father's library was left to him, and as late as 1900, H. G. Wells noted that young Crane cherished his father's books and those by other relatives.

A review of Jonathan Crane's works proves him to have been a veritable encyclopedia of knowledge. He had a strong preference for classical literature and for history. In his volumes he refers to Homer, Alexander, Caesar, the Biblical wars, Herodotus, the Crusades, an English victory in India, the battle at Vera Cruz, the war of 1674 between France and the several powers of Europe, the American Revolution, the Civil War, and Harpers Ferry. This in turn explains his son's obsession with war and with history. Never having witnessed a battle, Jonathan Crane could say to the readers of his pious works: "Let us again recur to military life for illustration." *Arts of Intoxication* and *Popular Amusements* begin with scenes of conflict; and there are scattered passages which refer to the illusions and the tragic ironies of battle (in one case, the Civil War), the psychological responses of a human being under the stress of combat, and animal imagery (the "panther-like yell of assault"). All these are reflected in one way or another in his son's fiction.

The distinguished war record of earlier Cranes gave Jonathan Crane added incentive to refer to war in his religious tracts. His youngest son, Stephen, gave a prideful summary, in 1896, of the achievements of his ancestors: one had commanded the Sixth New Jersey Infantry during the Revolution; another had been a commander in the Navy; and still another, after being captured by the Hessians, had been brutally treated and then killed. This record, along with their father's possible urging, made some of the children students of military life. One son, William, became an expert "in the strategy of Chancellorsville and Gettysburg"; another son gave Harry Castleman's romantic war tales as gifts to young Crane; and Crane himself was a lieutenant, then a captain in military training at Claverack. Years later Harvey Wickham recalled a day at Claverack when he dropped his gun during a prize drill and his superior, Crane, after calling him "Idiot! Imbecile!" added: "You were fairly decent up to the last minute. And then to drop your gun! Such a thing was never heard of." During his short life, young Crane often displayed a similar fanatic pride in things relating to military life.

In other ways, Crane was close to the mementos and visions of war. In 1896, a literary critic visited Crane's apartment and was surprised to find that a wall was relieved at intervals by "war trophies." Crane read football articles in the newspapers with glee, because "That's like war!" He told Hamlin Garland on one occasion that all his knowledge of battle was gained on the football field: "The psychology is the same. The opposite team is an enemy tribe." Two of his football articles, "Harvard University Against the Carlisle Indians" (November 1, 1896) and "How Princeton Met Harvard at Cambridge . . ." (November 8, 1896), described the games as though they were raging battlefields. In England in 1898, Crane asked his brother William, in the United States, to keep his Claverack swords. One reason for his sardonic irony in relation to the parading Junior Order of United American Mechanics was because they "had no ideas of marching." In May 1899, he complained about Captain Rowan, the "hero" of "A Message to Garcia": ". . . he wore a yachting cap as part of his uniform which was damnable." No wonder Crane once told Willa Cather that war was "a native product," because he had been imagining battles and military life since his "knickerbocker days."

The examples of Crane's parents and his ancestors made him a student of classical literature and history, past and present. Yet most critics, like Carl Van Doren, were certain that the "Civil War was as far back in time as his imagination went with any passionate knowledge." A school companion knew that Crane "reveled in the classics of Greece and Rome" and that Plutarch's *Lives* was his "constant companion." And history was Crane's favorite subject. His mother encouraged him to read *Harper's History of the Rebellion.* One friend at Syracuse University remembered that his knowledge of history was "considerable"; and while there he took Dr. Little's course on the French Revolution. He was a student of Cromwellian days peopled with Roundheads and Royalists and of Queen Anne's time; this was suggested by his lost tale, "Siege," and *The O'Ruddy.* In his own library, he had May's *Constitutional History of England,* Sterling's *Russia Under Nicholas the First,* Robertson's *History of Scotland,* and George Peck's (Crane's grandfather) *Wyoming,* which dealt with the American Revolution. In August 1899, Crane, who had plans for a new work of historical fiction, sent a letter to the New Jersey Historical Society inquiring about facts relating to the American Revolution.

Another charge made by Carl Van Doren, and echoed by others, was that Crane was "as ignorant as an American diplomat of history and political conditions." Crane's sense for present history was as acute as his understanding of the past. In "The King's Favor," he dealt with a real incident which involved King Cetewayo, a Zulu chief, and British imperialism. In "A Foreign Policy, in Three Glimpses," he dramatized the Afghanistan troubles of 1884, the Fiji Island raids by the British in 1874, and the U.S.-Chilean friction of 1891. In "The Monster" he mentioned the Armenian massacres, and in *The Blood of the Martyr* he satirized German imperialism in China during the 1890s. Continually (often in his war dispatches) Crane referred to the policies and actions of the major powers: Great Britain, France, Germany, Russia, Spain, Italy, and the United States.

This sense of the past and present plays a significant role in his fiction. Crane makes many allusions to historical figures and subjects: to Romans, the Huns, Xenophon's *Anabasis,* Napoleon, Washington at the Battle of Long Island, the French Revolution, the history of Cortez and the Aztecs, a Roman mob in Nero's time, Waterloo, and the American Revolution. Several times Crane alludes to Homer, the Greek sense of tragedy, and to the knights of the Middle Ages. These only hint at his fuller knowledge.

Crane used these historical images frequently for mock epic purposes—to heighten, sometimes with comic irony, the isolated hero and his pathetic cosmic struggle; and at other times to symbolize the tragic struggle of man through the ages. In *Maggie,* he wrote: "The two little boys, fighting in the mode of four thousand years ago, did not hear the warning." In *The Red Badge:* "He had long despaired of witnessing a Greeklike struggle. . . . Tales of great movements shook the land. They might not be distinctly Homeric, but there seemed to be much glory in them." In "An Explosion of Seven Babies," Crane drew upon the past for mock epic effect: "His [the little man's] chosen course lay directly toward the seven babies who, in their anxiety to view the combat, had risen from the bench and were standing ready as a Roman populace to signify the little man's death by rubbing their stomachs." This points to another obvious contradiction in Crane's aesthetic credo. On the one hand, he was a ruthless student of firsthand observation, the factual reporter seeing and testing and reflecting before he wrote his fiction; on the other hand, he ignored the facts of observation, and depended on his imagination and on his reading to recreate unobserved things like the Civil War.

Like his father, Crane also warred against the prevailing romanticism of the times, though not always consistently in his biographical and literary life. Jonathan Crane generally felt that fiction was "counterfeit coin," and that one should read only the Bible, history, and current events. He admitted in *Popular Amusements,* however, that "there are some few works of fiction which are well written and true to nature, and which inculcate the right and condemn the wrong." He wanted fiction to instruct, "to raise him [the reader] to the height of a great purpose." He was hostile to the romantic effects on readers: "In fact, Cinderella of the old nursery story is the true type of thousands of our novel-readers. They live a sort of double life—one in their own proper persons, and in their real homes; the other as ideal lords and ladies in dream-land." Young Crane had the urge to great purpose in his fiction; and most of his fiction was anti-romantic.

A special gift of Jonathan Crane's appears in his son's fiction. Usually linked with violence and death, Stephen Crane inherited from his minister-father a playful sense of humor. Edith Crane remembered that her grandfather "had a great sense of humor, and was so noted for it that a movement was once made to publish a book of his witticisms." Clarence Peaslee, a roommate of young Crane's at Syracuse, also knew that Jonathan Crane was "a noted wit, which was particularly evident in debate and private conversation." Most critics, however, find Stephen Crane's work humorless; and a few find only sporadic examples. Melvin Schoberlin says that the only amusing scene in Crane's fiction is found in "The Carriage-Lamps." Crane's comedy is frequently missed, for seemingly somber tales

like *The Sullivan County Sketches* (1892) are really playful hoaxes.
Throughout his work one can find many comic situations; the most con-
sistent and fullest examples are in *Whilomville Stories* (1900). Sometimes
Crane's comedy takes on grim and grotesque overtones, as in "The Blue
Hotel"; here the comic "relief" adds to the ironies and enriches the final
violence and terror of the story.

The dominant strain in Crane's life and art—violence and death—is
suggested by his reactions against his mother's religion of hell and by his
wearing experiences in New York, the American West, Greece, and Cuba.
Thomas Beer's classic remark—"Let it be stated that the mistress of this
boy's mind was fear"—is too narrow to encompass the variety of sensations
Crane personally felt and analyzed. He studied other emotional responses
like shame, anger, cowardice, foolhardiness, and courage; and he observed
these within an individual or sometimes as the individual clashed with his
group world. These emotions, when added up, demonstrate his fascination
with the whole inner life of man, which he translated concretely by the
physical crises in his stories.

Crane's own biographical life supplied him with many of these tensions. As a child, he was fearful of riding a "savage" horse until his
mother insisted on a display of courage. He was terrorized by dreams of
black riders charging up from the sea. His father's death left him embittered. Once, near Asbury Park, he saw a white girl stabbed by her Negro
lover, and he went home in a state of shock. At Lafayette College the
upperclassmen battered down his door during a hazing incident, and found
him "petrified with fear . . . in one corner of the room with a revolver in
his hand." During his Western adventures he barely escaped death at the
hands of a notorious bandit; this incident was recounted in "One Dash—
Horses."

All these experiences are related to Crane's mystic attraction to death.
To Karl Harriman, he made a prediction, which he also made to others:
he would not live beyond thirty-one. During his short life, he seemed to
abuse his body in order to prove his point. In his New York days he often
went hungry. The ordeal on the *Commodore,* which Crane recreated in
"The Open Boat," further sapped his strength. Then his sojourn as a war
correspondent in Greece and Cuba completely ruined his health. At least
once in Cuba he stood up in the line of enemy fire as though he sought
death.

The terrors of the group environment he felt keenly as a young boy in
the small towns of New York and New Jersey. Here he became sensitive
to insult and injury. His mother had insisted on preserving his Lord Fauntleroy curls until his brother Edmund saved him from disgrace; this incident later appeared in "The Angel Child." The small-town mind he saw

epitomized by hypocritical old matrons, or, as he termed them, "feminine mules." Though he once stated that "the mob has no courage," he was always aware of group pressure, and sometimes found little comfort in the terrors of loneliness and isolation. The words "lonely" and "doomed" recur frequently in his letters. At times, Crane warred against the group by siding with the outcasts and with the oppressed. At Claverack he joined with the underdog Cuban students against the "collective Goliath." At Syracuse University, he "found it hard to conform to campus ideals." In New York City he defended prostitutes against the rough treatment by the police and sent a telegram to Theodore Roosevelt, then police commissioner. It was no surprise that in several inscriptions of *Maggie* he noted that ". . . environment is a tremendous thing in the world and frequently shapes lives regardless."

The most curious contradiction in Crane's life and art is seen in his relation to romance and reality. Karl Harriman, a guest at Brede Place, England, once reflected: "It is odd that a notorious realist should live amid such romance." While Crane championed the poverty-stricken slum dwellers of New York and complained of the smugness of the rich, he later seemed aloof to the sufferings of the poor by attempting to live the life of an "Elizabethan baron" at Brede Place. He idealized military correctness in dress and behavior, yet he often looked like a hobo. When Willa Cather met him she was confused by the gloves he wore, "which seemed rather a contradiction," because his general attire was slovenly. He followed wars as though he had an unending romance with disaster, yet he relished the quiet, rural life at Hartwood, New York. He wooed genteel young women like Helen Trent and Nancy Crouse, and his letters were full of romantic notions. But his reality was the prostitute. He could not tolerate the sentimentality of Robert Louis Stevenson and Frances Burnett (the creator of *Little Lord Fauntleroy*), but he was touched by sentiment, as seen in his review of Ouida's *Under Two Flags,* and in some of his own fiction. His ideal in writing was to get as close to reality as possible, in the best naturalistic fashion; to prove his point, he slept in a flophouse to get the atmosphere for "An Experiment in Misery." Yet many of his stories were products of his own private reflections. All these factors relating to Crane's biographical life illuminate his fictional themes and his attitude toward them.

Many other sources besides his family world have been advanced. While Crane's works are not always "deep," they do make one raise John Berryman's query: "Who knows how many origins a deep work has?" The countless literary source studies often relate to *Maggie* and *The Red Badge,* but the themes, characters, and style of these two novels are common to his short fiction as well. Several critics are convinced that European back-

grounds explain the models of Crane's works. For *Maggie* and its naturalism, and presumably the naturalism of his short stories, critics have gone to
Zola's *L'Assommoir.* For *The Red Badge* critics, like V. S. Pritchett, feel
certain that the novel came in on the Tolstoy "wave" of *War and Peace*
and *Sebastopol;* and that "but for Tolstoy it would never have been written." Still others are convinced of the major influence of Zola's *La Débâcle*
on *The Red Badge.*

   The American sources are lengthier, especially for *The Red Badge.*
Critics have mentioned *Corporal Si Klegg,* Century's *Battles and Leaders,*
Harper's History, Kirkland's *Captain of Company K,* the drawings of
Winslow Homer, Ambrose Bierce, Walt Whitman's *Specimen Days,* General Van Petten, Rudyard Kipling, the oral tales of Civil War veterans,
and many others. Recently, Marcus Cunliffe tried to prove that Crane's
sources for *Maggie* were in the main American: Crane's New York, the
social consciousness of the magazine *Arena,* Charles Loring Brace's *The
Dangerous Classes of New York,* and Thomas De Witt Talmage's sermons.
Besides all this, Crane knew Jacob Riis, the famous social reformer; he re-
ported his lecture on slum life at Asbury Park (July 24, 1892). And Riis's
How the Other Half Lives (1891) forecasts the atmosphere and tone of
Maggie. Crane's early champions, Hamlin Garland and William Dean
Howells, were both vitally concerned with social questions, and both
talked to Crane with some frequency in the early 1890s. In fact, Garland
suggested the "protest" story "The Men in the Storm" to Crane, and then
the *Arena* as publisher, for this magazine was noted for reform articles on
poverty, sweatshops, slum clearance, child labor, and alcoholism. If one
acknowledges the importance of his biographical life and of these native
American sources, Stephen Crane (not Mark Twain, who was really quite
preoccupied with European civilization) is our first thoroughly American
writer. Moreover, Maxwell Geismar's conclusion—that Crane's ignorance
of the world around him restricted his art—should be challenged. Stephen
Crane was remarkably knowledgeable about the world, and this helped to
widen the art and life of his fiction.

   Whatever sources he used, Stephen Crane's literary reputation was ad-
versely affected by his bohemian life and by his modern style of writing.
At one time or another he was labeled a dope addict and a syphilitic. He
was continually linked with prostitutes, and his life at Brede Place was
likened to a "Babylonian orgy." The New York City police hounded him
until he forsook the city, and spent his last years in England. Hamlin
Garland, for one, was disillusioned by his protégé's behavior, and their
later relations were lukewarm. The subjects of some of his early fiction—
prostitution, alcoholism, dope addiction—reinforced the charges leveled
against Crane.

But Crane's style, not his subjects, made his literary rise difficult. The same year *Maggie* was published and poorly received there appeared *The Heavenly Twins*, which hinted at the then shocking problem of venereal disease. *The Heavenly Twins*, however, was protected by its romantic style. Crane's ironic-impressionistic method in *Maggie*, and not the subject of prostitution, so bewildered the editors they missed his compassion completely. Mark Twain may have sounded the note of irony in American literature, but it was not modern like Crane's, whose abrupt, disconnected, flat statements and darting, rapierlike ironies seemed too arty and too hating. Crane had to wait until the 1920s before he could be understood at all on his own terms. He was too modern in other ways: his impressionism seemed to be an affectation and made no sense; his symbolism was ignored; his stories lacked the conventional plot; and his curse words were unacceptable (they were usually deleted by his American publishers). To illustrate the conservatism of the decade, one need only point to Frances Willard who censured Richard Gilder for allowing the word "rape" in his *Century Magazine*. Later, Gilder, as Crane's own publisher, complained about "swearing in fiction" as late as October 1896.

Realism was making some headway in the 1890s, but Crane's art was too extreme even for his fellow realists and literary fathers, Garland and Howells. While he confessed that his "little creed of art" was "identical with the one of Howells and Garland," and that this "readjustment of his point of view" was concluded in 1892, Crane was too radical and too progressive for them. Garland was shocked by one of Crane's projects, the novel *Flowers of Asphalt* (never completed), about a boy prostitute. He praised *Maggie*, but felt that Crane studied only the worst elements of slum life and ignored "the families living on the next street, who live lives of heroic purity and helpless hardship." Howells also seemed worried by Crane's boldness. He mentioned Crane's attention to the "grimy truth," and he was concerned about his use of profanity. In his estimate of Crane's art in 1902, Howells indicated a gap between his credo and Crane's, and that, like Garland, he did not fully understand Crane's talent: ". . . *Maggie* remains the best thing he did . . . while *The Red Badge of Courage* and the other things that followed it, were the throes of an art failing with materials to which it could not render an absolute devotion from absolute knowledge." Crane was almost singlehandedly carrying on the *real* battle of modernism in literature.

Today in the 1960s, though his literary reputation is finally secure, Stephen Crane is still plagued by a variety of legends. Several critics repeatedly stress one fact: Crane began at the peak of his writing career, and he had no need to improve. He did not, however, come into life "fully armed." He had a very brief apprenticeship during his fiction writing career, which began in 1891 and ended in 1900. His news dispatches from Asbury Park, his earliest New York sketches, and *The Sullivan County Sketches* gave him something that resembled a training period. The eleven *Sullivan County Sketches* are especially significant because they present on a miniature scale the characteristic hero, theme, structure, panorama, and style of much of his later fiction. These include the grotesque and anonymous anti-hero, the "little man"; the theme of crime and punishment, where the little man is repeatedly punished for his "crime" of egotism; the ironic structure of the sketches, which usually end in anti-climax; the larger panorama, the world of nature, which underscores the smallness of man and his isolation; and finally the impressionistic style and the animal imagery, which color and objectify the primitive emotion or emotions under study. But Crane, in these sketches, was too imitative and too self-conscious. He tried to be "clever," like Kipling; he parodied Poe's horror stories. There is a great distance, then, in art, substance, and individuality between these sketches and "The Blue Hotel."

A related problem, stressed by some critics, is that because Crane wrote enough to fill twelve volumes in nine years he wrote too hastily—he was a hack. Crane encouraged this view, for he mentions that he wrote *Maggie* in a few days, *The Red Badge* in ten days, and "The Monster" in a week. His unpublished notebook, the manuscript versions of the tales, and the changes made on a single work as it appeared in a newspaper, magazine, and in a book indicate that Crane continually revised and corrected some of his work. Yet Conrad, who watched Crane write, insisted that his friend did not need to rewrite. Crane's manner of writing poetry adds to this myth. Hamlin Garland recalled with amazement how Crane turned on his "poetic spout" and produced complete poems at a moment's notice: "That's the way they come—in little rows, all made up, ready to put down on paper." Then, too, the fact that Crane was driven by the need of money supposedly forced him to write so quickly that ideas never ripened in his mind. Up to a point this is true. In his last years in England he borrowed hastily from his grandfather's *Wyoming*. Here is a passage from *Wyoming*:

Just at that moment the only two Indians remaining alive took to their heels, when Mr. Bennett, who could throw a tomahawk with the precision and force of any red-skin on the frontier, picked up a tomahawk and let it slip, and it stuck in the back of one of them. The Indian turned round, being at about the distance of forty feet, and hollowed out "whoo," and his blanket fell from his shoulders, and the hatchet was left with it on the ground, he running off naked.

Here is Crane's version in " 'Ol' Bennet' and the Indians":

The scream of the watchman instantly aroused the other warriors, who, as they scrambled in their blankets, found over them a terrible white-lipped creature with an axe—an axe, the most appallingly brutal of weapons. Hammond buried his weapon in the head of the leader of the Indians even as the man gave out his first great cry. The second blow missed an agile warrior's head, but caught him in the nape of the neck, and he swung, to bury his face in the red-hot ashes at the edge of the fire. . . . Well, this slaughter continued in the red glare of the fire on the lonely mountainside until two shrieking creatures ran off through the trees, but even then my father [Ol' Bennet] hurled a tomahawk with all his strength. It struck one of the fleeing Indians on the shoulder. His blanket dropped from him, and he ran on practically naked.

Crane's confessions to Willa Cather in 1895 gave insight into his literary methods. To her he admitted that while the writing of a story was brief, it took months before "he could get any sort of personal contact with it, or feel any potency to handle it." Referring to *The Red Badge*, he said he wrote the novel in nine days but that he "had been unconsciously working the detail of the story through most of his boyhood." He said he led a "double life," writing in "the first place the matter that pleased himself, and doing it very slowly; in the second place any sort of stuff that would sell." Many stories seem hastily written or written to a kind of formula: "A Christmas Dinner Won in Battle," "Stories Told by an Artist," "An Indiana Campaign," "The Reluctant Voyagers," "A Gray Sleeve," "Three Miraculous Soldiers," and others. His best stories, like "The Bride Comes to Yellow Sky" and "The Blue Hotel," really mattered to Crane.

Another complaint is that Crane could not construct a plot. Yet Clarence Peaslee recalled: "It was his delight to block out the plot of a story and then tell his friends about it, putting it in various lights and constructions, and then asking which was more effective." His plots are there, but they are obscured by style and method. In "The Bride Comes to Yellow Sky," the reader is aware of four sharply defined episodes, which seem unconnected, but which are connected by the jarring ironies. Crane wanted to contrast two environments—the old West and the new—and to bring the two perspectives into sharper focus he depended on episodic structure; this technique—this arrangement—is common to much of his fiction. Like Chekhov, Crane's intention in his stories was to study the mood of a man's soul in relation to a crisis situation; the events of his stories explain the emotional state and reaction of his characters. Crane bridges his episodic structures by means of mood. He worked in terms of episodes because he was anxious to dramatize scenes or to sketch in a situation. Many of his stories are in fact called "sketches" or "scenes."

By using other devices from the other arts, like painting, Crane buried plot further and so enriched the form of the short story. The technique of impressionism he seems to have learned from his friends at the Art Students' League in New York; Hamlin Garland espoused the theories of French impressionism as early as the 1880s; and there was available in English a book of sketches by French symbolists and impressionists, *Pastels in Prose* (1890). A few of Crane's stories—"The Silver Pageant," "Stories Told by an Artist," and *The Third Violet*—reveal his attraction to art and the artist. Both Conrad and Garnett were convinced that Crane was the "complete impressionist." Like Conrad, Crane was anxious to make one "feel" and to make one "see." He wanted to convey the sensations produced on the sensibility of his characters, and like the impressionist painters, he sketched the "fluid play of light" on his heroes, as he interpreted aspects of their natures. In "War Memories," Crane studied the figure of a man: "He was naked save for a breech clout, and so close, so clear was the ecclesiastic suggestion that one's mind leaped to a fantasy that this thin, pale figure had just been torn down from a cross. The flash of the impression was like light, and for this instant it illumined all the dark recesses of one's remotest idea of sacrilege, ghastly and wanton. I bring this to you merely as an effect, an effect of mental light and shade, if you like; something done in thought similar to that which the French impressionists do in color; something meaningless and at the same time overwhelming, crushing, monstrous." By using color imagery and color contrasts, Crane approximated the painter's attempt to merge objects with their surroundings and at the same time to capture the separateness and the fast-changing face of life. To Crane, the universe was abrupt, indefinite, and chaotic, and he caught this rhythm in the movement of his impressionistic prose.

A recent critic, Robert Hough, notes the influence of Goethe's *Theory of Colors* (1810). In one place, Crane had mentioned his interest in Goethe's theories. Crane, then, learned about the psychology of colors not only from impressionism but also from Goethe, who demonstrated how colors created certain states of feeling, how they defined a situation, and how they helped to paint dramatic and panoramic effects. Most important, colors to Goethe and to Crane became useful as symbols: dull yellow was linked to decay and death; red to high tension; cold colors to darkness and violence. In his fiction, Crane hints at the relevance of colors as symbols. In "When Every One Is Panic Stricken," there "glared [from the fire in the basement] a deep and terrible hue of red, the color of satanic wrath, the color of murder." In "The Blue Hotel" the "covered land was blue with the sheen of an unearthly satin. . . ."

In still another way, Crane lessened the value of a mechanical plot. As he painted striking yet isolated scenes, Crane made each episode become part of a moving picture, so that his art is properly linked with cinematic techniques. In "The Blue Hotel" the Easterner's "mind, like a film, took lasting impressions of three men—the iron-nerved master of the ceremony; the Swede, pale, motionless, terrible; and Johnnie, serene yet ferocious, brutish yet heroic." Crane depended on rapid movement, on change, on gnarled and disconnected effects, and on indirect and understated gestures. His vision was scenic; and his lack of transitions suggested the chaos and dislocations in the life of his fictions. What Crane succeeded in doing, then, by imposing the various arts on to the plot, was to prove that the short story could be a fluid and flexible medium of expression. By itself, plot hampered Crane.

Another charge leveled against Crane is that he cannot create characters. In his best stories his people are often thought of in general terms, like the soldier, the cook, and the correspondent. If they do have names, they have common ones, like Billie, Henry, and Jimmie. While the characters seem wooden and one-dimensional, Crane keeps them typical and anonymous because he is interested in the dual nature of man. He translates the inner effects on a character as he faces a crisis situation, usually death; at the same time, Crane contrasts this inner tension with the character's outer self, usually a static and confident portrait. By this method, Crane posits the appearance-reality motif: man as he thinks he is; and man as he really is. Then follows the struggle—the war—between man's will and courage, and the world of chance, fate, and nature. Sometimes man is victorious; and even when he loses, he has at least accepted a challenge to his dignity. The Crane hero, then, is left anonymous and typical in order to mirror symbolically the isolated and grotesque life of man who is warped by his own ego or temporarily frustrated or rendered helpless by his illusions, by his environment, and by nature.

Critics have felt safest with the themes of Crane's fiction. They have mentioned many plausible ones: the initiation theme; the discovery of self; ideals versus realities; death and rebirth; the moral problem of conduct; the theme of absurdity; themes relating to courage, cowardice, loyalty, isolation, and disenchantment; the search for social acceptance; and others. One ironic theme, however, dominates Crane's short fiction from the very first: crime and punishment. Sometimes he renders this theme comically, as in his first story "Uncle Jake and the Bell Handle." Uncle Jake commits a "crime" by pulling a bell handle; until he returns home, he suffers punishment. Throughout *The Sullivan County Sketches*, the little man commits the "crime" of egotism, and is punished for it by having his ego deflated by a madman, a woman, a hungry dog, a bear, and others. In other tales the theme of crime and punishment leads to pathos and to tragedy. In "The Monster" Henry Johnson and Dr. Trescott commit a "crime" of humanity, and they are punished by an inhuman community. There is the "crime" of poverty in "An Ominous Baby" and in "An Experiment in Misery"; as the poor receive their undeserved punishments, they are contrasted to the indifference of the well-to-do, who reflect the general indifference of American capitalism. The ending of "An Experiment in Misery" exposes the real crime: "And in the background a multitude of buildings, of pitiless hues and sternly high, were to him [the outcast] emblematic of a nation forcing its regal head into the clouds, throwing no downward glances; in the sublimity of its aspirations ignoring the wretches who may flounder at its feet." In "His New Mittens" Horace commits a crime by wetting his mittens, and after he is punished by his mother and his aunt, he punishes them in turn by running away. In "The Open Boat" and "The Blue Hotel" this theme reaches a highly complex level. The social environment, and not the gambler, should be punished for the crime of killing the Swede in "The Blue Hotel." Nature's crime of indifference has led to the unnecessary punishment of the oiler in "The Open Boat."

Generally, the story patterns are consistent too. They begin quietly, often in the world of nature, which suggests peace and harmony. Suddenly, from nowhere, a crisis occurs, and until the end of the story the situation is explosive and disastrous, reflecting the true nature of things. The movement in a Crane story, then, is from peace to war. The characters themselves chart this chaos. In "An Explosion of Seven Babies" the little man "touched some hidden spring in his being and went off like a firework." In "The Blue Hotel" the Swede "fizzed like a firewheel." As the Crane hero goes off like a firework, he opens up his inner life.

Crane's other uses of imagery further heighten the ironies of his essentially tragic vision. Often, as he tells a serious or comic story, Crane suggests the solemn, austere pomp and glory of the Bible: "Soon it came to pass. . . ." ("A Tent in Agony"); "Now it came to pass. . . ." ("Uncle Jake and the Bell Handle"); "And it was written. . . ." ("A Great Mistake"); "They were fearful he had met his time" ("The Holler Tree"). He also refers to Biblical materials directly: Daniel, Resurrection morn, the priest, and the altar. On the one hand, this tone and this imagery most often relate to the mock-epic scope of Crane's fiction; on the other, they show, in "An Experiment in Misery," the emptiness of things—life as a wasteland. Religious imagery, ironically employed, enriches Crane's themes.

Nor is it unusual that many of Crane's stories take place in the dark or at midnight. At one time, Crane wanted to publish fifteen or twenty of his New York sketches under the title *Midnight Sketches*. The power of blackness intrigued him. It became the symbol of terror, violence, and "the portals of death." In "The Duel That Was Not Fought" the time is midnight, the prelude to the potential disaster in the story. "An Experiment in Misery" takes place at night; "daylight was commonplace and uninteresting." In "When Every One Is Panic Stricken" the stranger "was imparting some grim midnight reflections upon existence. . . ."

In Crane's work, theme, character, structure, and imagery take on symbolic overtones, and though many critics refuse to accept it, Crane's best stories make full use of symbols and emblems. References to the West, the sea, and nature in some of his lesser stories and feature articles expand in meaning and complexity in the later fiction. Before his famous statement on nature in "The Open Boat," Crane, in a feature article "Nebraska's Bitter Fight for Life" (February 24, 1895), saw "this terrible and inscrutable wrath of nature. It was as if upon the massive altar of the earth, their homes and their families were being offered in sacrifice to the wrath of some blind and pitiless deity." In "Mr. Binks' Day Off" he thought again in these terms: "It [the song of the trees] was filled with an infinite sorrow—a sorrow for birth, slavery, death. It was a wail telling the griefs, the pains of all ages. It was the symbol of agonies. It celebrated all suffering. . . . It is the universal voice raised in lamentations." In "One Dash—Horses" the blanket before an adobe wall "was to Richardson a horrible emblem." In "Death and the Child" a single sentence leads to the meaningful level of the story: "It was as simple as some powerful symbol."

Even before Crane left New York for the West or "The Open Boat" experience, he saw the power of these environments and eventually described them in symbolic terms. The country environment is contrasted to the urban environment in "Uncle Jake and the Bell Handle"; here, Uncle Jake's innocence is thwarted by advanced civilization. The city environment is likened to battle and the country to peace in "Mr. Binks' Day Off." The sketches "Billie Atkins Went to Omaha," "In a Park Row Restaurant," "The Duel That Was Not Fought," "A Freight Car Incident," and "A Christmas Dinner Won in Battle" all prepare for, in brief compass, Western civilization, and the issues and conflicts which accumulate in "The Blue Hotel." A seemingly offhand remark in "Coney Island's Failing Days"—"the sea always make me feel that I am a trivial object"—is a first stage, along with "The Reluctant Voyagers," in suggesting the sea's symbolic role in "The Open Boat." Continually Crane contrasts environments in his stories for ironic and tragic effects: the poor versus the middle class in the New York sketches; the Easterner versus the Westerner; and the land versus the sea.

Moving in so many environments, Crane individualized them and his characters mainly through his ever present use of dialect. In "The Blue Hotel" Pat Scully's speech "was always a combination of Irish brogue and idiom, Western twang and idiom, and scraps of curiously formal diction taken from the storybooks and newspapers." Crane's Negroes in *Whilomville Stories* and in "The Monster," the Irish in "An Old Man Goes Wooing," the Bowery dialect, the speech patterns of the adults and the children from rural communities—all these demonstrate another way in which Crane achieved his sense of immediacy.

While the stories do have these distinguishing features, there are definite changes in Crane's art and themes. In the beginning in 1891, with "Uncle Jake and the Bell Handle," "The Camel," "A Foreign Policy, in Three Glimpses," and "The King's Favor," Crane is playful, humorous, and satiric. He is depending mainly on anecdotes and topical issues, like Maine's prohibition and British imperialism. His stories are really sketches, scenes, and personal (sometimes too personal) impressions. There is little plot interest, and less evidence of his later impressionistic style. In *The Sullivan County Sketches* in 1892, Crane is still too theatrical and too self-conscious. While he imitates both Kipling and Poe, he displays his typical and individualized impressionistic style. He is now thinking of stories or sketches in groups. Each scene or sketch of Sullivan County becomes a part of a whole series, a panoramic study of camping life. But on the whole, Crane's language in these sketches is too stilted and bombastic; and his plots are too boyish and full of pranks.

In this same year, Crane wrote his first city sketch, "Travels in New York: The Broken-Down Van," and here he was laying the groundwork for his Bowery novels, *Maggie* and *George's Mother*. A story in 1893, "A Desertion," is an episode straight out of *Maggie*, and underlines a distinct change in Crane's art. The social problems of the city affected him so deeply that the boyish hoaxes of *The Sullivan County Sketches* are nowhere in evidence. During this period, however, Crane was so solemn that the preaching urge of "On the New Jersey Coast" returns in "An Experiment in Misery," "The Men in the Storm," "An Experiment in Luxury," and elsewhere. "An Experiment in Luxury," especially, shows that Crane had not separated himself fully from journalism, for he reports and does not render his story. Like *The Sullivan County Sketches*, the New York City sketches should be viewed as a group, as scenes of city life. The best tales of this social phase of Crane's career are "An Experiment in Misery" and "The Men in the Storm." Both demonstrate that social problems sobered him up; serious issues made him take himself and his art seriously. But he was too serious and too self-conscious about his social causes; he still did not have complete control of himself and his materials. At least he was no longer clever and imitative. He was now the individualistic writer who saw the everyday social problems in symbolic terms.

With the serialization of *The Red Badge* in December 1894, Crane turned to war fiction. His earlier sketches had already sounded this theme. In "Uncle Jake and the Bell Handle" the uncle says: "To see this innocent country plunged in to er civil war by the hand of an ignorant old man would be terr'ble." The eleven *Sullivan County Sketches*, besides representing the themes of his war stories, contain the animal imagery and the combat pictures so familiar to *The Red Badge*. In "Mr. Binks' Day Off" Crane says, "The sense of a city is battle." The prewar stories, collected as *The Little Regiment* (1896), are a curious blending of romantic and realistic materials. They prove again that Crane had not fully declared his independence as an artist; and he was still experimenting with style and subject. "A Gray Sleeve" and "Three Miraculous Soldiers" are clearly imitative of the popular romances of the day. "A Mystery of Heroism" and "The Little Regiment" are distillations of *The Red Badge;* they are the best tales in the collection. In "A Mystery of Heroism," the most successful of the tales, the hero "had been blindly led by quaint emotions, and laid himself under an obligation to walk squarely up to the face of death." Here Crane maintains a perfect balance between the trivial and ironical adventure of Collins, and the large scale war and havoc surrounding him. The terrifying pathos of the story is rendered powerfully by means of understatement; the anticlimactic close is not a clever trick, as it was in *The Sullivan County Sketches:* it illuminates the riddle of heroism.

Far less attention has been given to Crane's later war stories, most of which are collected in *Wounds in the Rain* (1900). Actually these stories are superior to the prewar ones. Real war saved Crane from sterile repetitions of *The Red Badge*. Real war gave him a variety of new themes —some humorous ("The Sergeant's Private Madhouse," "The Lone Charge of William B. Perkins"); it made him become more objective and more sensitive to the tensions and pressures and moods of combat. His satire was broader, as it revealed the individual and the social world; and his psychological penetration was more acute and less pretentious. The real experience of war taught Crane more about proportion, emphasis, restraint, contrast, and naturalness. A comparison between *The Red Badge* and *The Little Regiment* on the one hand and his real war stories on the other shows that earlier Crane was lost in imaginative and artificial guesswork, and that he was depending on a good deal of bombast, on overwriting—demonstrated by his rhetoric and the outpourings of images and colors—to approximate the emotions of men in combat. Fred Pattee raises a crucial question about impressionism, and it explains Crane's problem with style during *The Red Badge* phase:" If *every* detail has been made vivid it becomes like music played wholly in *fortissimo;* if every epithet and color stroke has been heightened to its extreme the result is monotony. There is no contrast; the straining is too evident. . . ."

In the best of Crane's later war stories—"Death and the Child," "The Price of the Harness," "An Episode of War," "The Upturned Face"— Crane's style is flat because he is studying his subjects, like "naked duty" and "the simple, majestic commonplace," in a low key. A statement at the close of "War Memories" spells out Crane's new manner: "The episode was closed. And you can depend upon it that I have told you nothing at all, nothing at all, nothing at all." His impressionism is now subdued for better effect; he is more direct and more dependent on understatement. In fact, "An Episode of War" and "The Upturned Face" are amazing forecasts of Hemingway's style and subject. Crane captures the stark tragedies of war in "The Price of the Harness," "An Episode of War," and "The Upturned Face." With a maturer vision and a maturer style he strips his materials to the barest essentials and by this achieves a more powerful impact. Other stories in *Wounds in the Rain* prove that when Crane is rooted in topical newspaper issues his craft weakens. "This Majestic Lie," for example, grew out of his news dispatch, "Grocer's Blockade"; "The Lone Charge of William B. Perkins" was based on the actions of a news reporter, Ralph Paine.

Of the Western tales, the outstanding ones are "The Blue Hotel," "The Bride Comes to Yellow Sky," and "One Dash—Horses." Though Crane has been accused of not picturing society enough, he does in these stories display a characteristic trait. Individuals—the Easterner, the drummer, and others—come to represent various sections of the country, even though the tales are localized in the West. Eastern culture and the West's new environment clash with the old image of Western primitivism. This is the meeting ground of these stories. And Crane uses this world of nature in the raw to display the elemental struggles of man in spite of the civilization that has touched both East and West. He recreates this conflict of the old and the new West in a playful manner in "The Bride Comes to Yellow Sky." He studies the lawlessness in primitive Mexico in "One Dash—Horses," where Richardson must depend on his ingenuity in order to survive. In "The Blue Hotel," the West becomes the center of the cosmic struggle of man as he faces his primitivism, his civilization, and the absurdity of life. All these tales are tense and dramatic, where Crane renders in sharply edged episodes the responses to the terribleness of death and the mystery of life.

The last substantial body of short fiction by Crane are the fourteen pieces that make up *Whilomville Stories* (1900). Though most contemporary critics look upon them as second-rate, they are highly significant. They prove that even though Crane was debt-ridden and dying of tuberculosis, he had control of his writing gifts to the very end. In these stories he returns to the boyish exuberance and the pranks of *The Sullivan County Sketches,* but there is a great difference. Here his aim is to recollect the days of childhood for an adult audience. Like *The Sullivan County Sketches* and the New York sketches, these tales are intended as a series of scenes or views of small town life, with children playing the major roles. The theme and design of the collection is stated in "His New Mittens" (which was not included in *Whilomville Stories*): "They [the boys] sang these lines to cruel and monotonous music which is as old perhaps as American childhood, and which it is the privilege of the emancipated adult to completely forget." What Crane does is to bring to life the adult's former boyhood world, with all of its cruelty, pity, and humor. These stories, then, are meant for the adult reader, not for children. The pattern of each story is suggested by a remark Crane once made about children. They were, he said, "like breakers on a beach. They do something and that is all there is in it." Each story has this rhythm of movement. And with his acute psychological insight, Crane touches the "innards of the actual boy" in these stories.

From the very beginning of his career, Crane was fascinated by the actions and reactions of children. He used child imagery in his adult works, like *The Red Badge.* Here are a few examples: "A mounted officer displayed the furious anger of a spoiled child"; "He was like a babe which, having wept its fill, raises its eyes and fixes them upon a distant toy." To understand the pressures of adult conflict, Crane often went to the child's world of innocence, where he could see openly revealed the full gamut of human emotions usually masked by adults. At the end of his career, Crane returned to the child's world and studied it from an adult's perspective.

The best of the *Whilomville Stories* are "His New Mittens," "The Knife," and "Shame." Again, as in *Wounds in the Rain,* Crane is no longer straining for effects, and the cleverness, the bombast, and the rhetorical flights of his early writings are missing. He is natural and unaffected, direct and subdued as he transcribes the conflicts in the small town. With his remarkable ear for the speech patterns of children and their romantic nonsense (reminiscent of Tom Sawyer's antics), Crane with careful control recreates the delicate feelings, the insults, the injuries, the comedy, and the pathos of childhood and rural life. While he often draws upon sentimental materials—puppy love, social ostracization—Crane maintains a cool and detached tone.

Crane's most ambitious stories, and at the same time his greatest, are Greek—Greek in the sense of being like classical tragic drama. These stories include "The Open Boat," "The Blue Hotel," "The Monster," and "Death and the Child." All are struggles of endurance, where man tests himself and his meaning against his environment, chance, fate, and nature. Like Greek tragedy, these stories begin in order and end in chaos or death. And the major characters (not always heroic) are pitted against an epiclike background, where they dramatize the clash of man's primitive instincts and his civilized ideals. To Crane, man is lost, but he can find meaning in brotherhood ("The Open Boat") and in courage ("The Monster"). But there is terror and absurdity in Crane's vision also. In "Death and the Child," Peza's horror and isolation are symbolized by the choric child who says: "Are you a man?" In "The Blue Hotel" there is the fearsome and grinding power of inevitability and destruction. Crane's earlier group scenes of camping life, war, New York life, and country life are now transformed and expanded onto an epic canvas. Besides this, Crane uses his poetic skills—symbolism, imagery, incremental repetitions, and variations on a theme—to poetize his stories. His impressionistic style and his cinematic and dramatic gifts are at their peak, as well as his tragic vision. Here was Crane's best forte, and it was between 1897 and 1900.

How did Crane find his best self—his Greek manner? It was an erratic and cumulative process. For as he was writing his finest achievements between 1897 and 1900 he was still turning out mediocre work. A turning point in Crane's career was his New York phase. At this time he was struggling with form and substance. His own romantic notions of life and his dependence on earlier writers frustrated his own native development. Temporarily lost in clever parody, he gradually received his shock of recognition and broke away from the dead materials of the past. The present reality of slum life clashed with his romantic ideals and produced his original New York sketches. The same process was repeated in his other work. With *The Red Badge* and *The Little Regiment*, he was straining to bring to life a world he had never seen; he was too dependent on earlier legends and tales. And though the fabric of all his fiction was created by the contrast and combat of his romantic illusions with the grim reality, Crane had to wait for reality in order to write freely and naturally. Crane continually sought "the real thing," and when he found it in New York, Greece, and Cuba, he found his artistic independence. Gradually, he also refined and blended the poetic, cinematic, symbolic, dramatic, impressionistic, and tragic techniques which appear in his best work. Finally, as Crane focused on man and his struggles with the forces surrounding him, he slowly moved away from static portrayals and created the image of man in larger and more human terms; and as he controlled his preachings he showed, like Tolstoy, that he was devoted to the religion of man in spite of the enigma of the universe.

Stephen Crane's place in American literature may be secure, but it is not to be envied. The literary historians have labeled him pioneer, herald, precursor, harbinger, and forerunner of naturalism and modernism. But this makes one view Crane in the past tense only. His great stories are as modern as ever. His themes and his art are as living as those of Ernest Hemingway, who was deeply influenced by him. His talents in the short story field are more far-ranging than most American authors. While he was a student of war, Crane dealt with love, death, childhood, nature, the small town, city life, the American West, the international scene, philosophy (through his fables), and the universe. He was satirist, folk humorist, fabulist, social critic, painter, epic poet, and tragedian. Though he is still called a realist, naturalist, symbolist, impressionist, and existentialist, Crane cannot truly be labeled. Like John Steinbeck, he continually experimented and sought new techniques, new styles, and new themes as he moved from one phase of his career to another. In the end, Stephen Crane is—now—an original and vibrant talent and one of America's greatest short story writers.

THE COMPLETE SHORT STORIES AND SKETCHES
OF STEPHEN CRANE

SKETCHES FROM LIFE:
UNCLE JAKE AND THE BELL HANDLE*

Uncle Jake was called a good, old soul. In fact, there was not a better, kinder man in the whole county than old Uncle Jake and when he was going to the city to sell his turnips and buy any amount of sugar, molasses, starch and such things, he promised his twenty-eight-year-old niece that she should go down to the city with him and he would "take her round," he said, in a lordly way. This, considering that he had only been to the city once before himself, was a very generous offer and Sarah was very glad to have an uncle who was so worldly minded and knew all about the big cities and all that.

So the next day at sunrise Uncle Jake dressed himself in his best suit of black clothes and Sarah arrayed her angular form in her best calico gown, and put on her cotton mitts and the lilac sunbonnet with the sunflowers on it. After surveying his niece with a good deal of pride and some misgivings about the city men, whom he thought might be likely to steal such a lovely creature, he kissed his wife good-bye as if he were going to Europe for ten years, clambered upon the high seat of his wagon, pulled Sarah up beside him as if she had been a bundle of straw, flourished his whip, smiled blandly and confidently upon his wife, the two hired men and a neighbor's boy, and drove away.

The two large fat horses walked up hill and trotted down dale and Uncle Jake's white beard blew about in the wind, first over one cheek and then over the other, as he sat upon the high seat with his legs braced, pulling the horses' heads this way and that. As the sun commenced to get warm, Sarah put up the big cotton umbrella over the lilac sunbonnet with the sunflowers, the dusty wheels rattled, the turnips in the wagon bobbed and rolled about as if each one was possessed of a restless devil, and Uncle Jake, and Sarah, and the turnips and the sunbonnet rode gaily toward the city.

Soon the houses began to appear closer together, there were more tin cans and other relics strewn about the roadside, they began to get views of multitudes of backyards, with wet clothes on the lines; grimy, smoky factories; stockyards filled with discordant mobs of beasts; whole trains of freight cars, standing on side tracks; dirty children, homeless dogs and wandering pigs. To Uncle Jake's experienced eye, this denoted that they were entering the city.

    * By permission of Alfred A. Knopf, Inc. Hitherto unpublished in book form.

Beer saloons commenced to loom up occasionally with men standing in front of them who wore their hats over their right eyes, or their left eyes, or their ears, or whichever member they deemed it proper, as gentlemen of leisure and of sporting proclivities. Old Uncle Jake nodded benignly at these gentlemen, whom he doubtless thought had heard he was coming to town and had "knocked off" work to see him go past, while the gentlemen nearly swallowed their tobacco in their amazement at the white-haired old "duck" but recovering themselves winked bleared eyes and bowed red noses at the lilac bonnet with the sunflowers but that was immediately focussed on somebody's wash line in the backyard opposite, where, it seemed half of the men of the family were given over to wearing red nether garments and the other half were partial to white, thereby imparting a picturesque and lurid appearance to the line of clothes dangling in the breeze. They reached the Main Street of the town and Uncle Jake sold his turnips to a dealer who beat the old man down considerably by lying to him about "market prices". They spent the morning in going about to the different stores buying their supplies. Uncle Jake would take his niece by the hand and enter a store, calling the first clerk he saw "Mr. Jones and Co." or whatever name he saw on the sign board. After cordially shaking him by the hand, he would introduce his little niece Miss Sarah Bottomley Perkins and announce that she "was only twenty-eight years, seven months and—how many days Saree? Don't know? Well, never mind. Well, sir, crops was never better than this year, by George, sir." Had Mr. Jones and Co. noticed the amazin' manner in which cucumber pickles grew this year or the astounding manner in which early pumpkins came up? No? Well, well, he hoped he would see Mr. Jones and Co. in a year or two. But he couldn't say. His wife, poor critir, had the most astonishing case of plumbago that had been in Green County since '58 when old Bill William's wife's second cousin took down with it. Well, he supposed he must be going. The best of friends must part. If Mr. Jones and Co. ever kim out in Green County he knew he had a place at old Jake Perkinses board: "Good-bye, my boy. Heaven bless you."

Then the old gentleman would buy three yards of calico or seven pounds of brown sugar maybe, and bidding an affectionate good-bye to the clerk, take his niece by the hand and leave, waving his hand back at the store, while in sight to the eminent danger of a collision between the fat horses and the street cars.

Uncle Jake spent the morning this way. Some of the clerks, understanding the old man and being gentlemen, listened politely and deferentially to his ramblings, while others who were not troubled that way, snickered behind his back at the other clerks, and pointed their fingers at him, while the old man beamed a world of peace and good will toward all men through the glasses of his spectacles.

At noon, they put up the fat horses at a livery stable whose proprietor charged Uncle Jake fifty cents more than he did anyone else, merely on principle. They went to a hotel and were ushered into the parlor to await the summons of the dinner gong.

Uncle Jake and his niece walked about the spare hotel parlor and were both filled with amazement at what they deemed its magnificence. Uncle Jake's curiosity was immense. He wandered about the room, running his hands over the picture frames and feeling of the upholstery of the chairs.

In an evil hour, he came upon the bell handle.

It was an old-fashioned affair arranged in a sort of brass scoop or cup from which projected the long handle. He looked at it for some time and wondered what it was for. He pressed on it and no tap commenced to flow ginger-pop. Finally he pulled it.

Now it came to pass that, at precisely that moment, a waiter of the hotel made a terrific onslaught on a gong that was sure to make any horses in the vicinity run away and awaken all the late sleepers for blocks around.

Uncle Jake's pull on the bell handle and the sound of the gong were identical.

"Good Lord! what have I did? Holy Mackerel! I have gone and done it!"

With these words, Uncle Jake sank, pale-faced, back on a chair like a man who has been stricken down with a stuffed club. The old man's hair stood on end. He was "done up," as he expressed it. His manner conveyed a sense of terror to his niece who seemed inclined to fill the air with her lamentations but suppressed herself enough to cry "Oh! uncle! uncle! what have you done," asking him the same momentous question he had asked himself a moment before.

"Done, Sarah? Done? Oh, sufferin' Susan, that I should live to see this day! Done! I've called out the fire department, or the police force or the ambulance corps or something else that's awful! Oh! miserable man! maybe it's the insurance agents or the Board of Health and this poor old carcass will never get home alive." His violent agitation made the innocent maiden still more bent on howling but her uncle stopped her as before.

"S-s-s-h! Sar-ee! S-s-s-h! My pore girl, you now see your old uncle as a fergitive from justice, a critir hounded by the dogs of the law! S-s-s-h! Make no sound er they'll be down on us like a passel of wolves!"

Impressed by her uncle's manner, Sarah kept quiet while the old man went about the room on his tiptoes, peering out the window in momentary expectation of seeing the police force, the ambulance corps, and the fire department come up the street.

"Thank goodness, Sar-ee, that the militia can't be called out on such short notice and they'll have time to find out that it is a mistake. To see this innocent country plunged in to er civil war by the hand of an ignorant old man would be terr'ble." The old man peeped out the door and says "Come Sar-ee! S-s-sh! The minions of the law may be on our track any minute!"

Out they went into the street, hand in hand, giving cautious glances about and starting at any sudden sound. Every eye seemed to them to be full of suspicion. When they would see a policeman, they would turn up an alley or a side street. The city was very quiet and the blue buttons were out in full force, so the "fergitive from justice" and his companion went around a good many corners. When they arrived at the livery stable, their route from the hotel, if it could be mapped, would look like a brain-twisting Chinese puzzle. They hurried the hostlers and Uncle Jake's hand shook the reins up and down as if he were knocking flies off the fat horses.

They drove down byways until they reached their road home, where the fat horses were surprised into making the exertion of their lives.

Uncle Jake and Sarah cast many fearful glances behind them until they were safe in the shelter of the old barnyard.

There with fat horses breathing heavily beside him, the cows looking solemnly over the fence and all the delights of his old heart about him, he made a vow never again to touch "no bell handles nor pull out no plugs agin, as long as I live, bein's as how my gray hairs were like to be lowered in sorrer this blessed day."

1885
[*Bulletin of the New York Public Library,*
Vol. 64 (May, 1960), pp. 275-278.]

THE KING'S FAVOR

The lives of all musicians do not glide on in a quiet flow of melody and unpaid music bills. It is popularly supposed that a musician is a long-haired individual who does nothing more exciting than fall in love with his loveliest pupil, dine on mutton chops and misery all his life; and finally become famous as a composer, after the name on his tombstone has been nearly obliterated by the moss and mold of years.

Mr. Albert G. Thies, a prominent New York tenor, proves by his history that such is not always the case. He has had adventures in many strange lands. The crowned heads of Europe and the furred backs of Africa have both taken a hand in chasing him from their dominions; the first, as an alleged political conspirator; the second, as a choice morsel of diet. He has sung before crowned heads and before heads in dilapidated old hats; before the gilded, tasseled boots of the German hussar and the ponderous, wooden sabots of the Hollandese peasant. In fact, he has had as varied an existence as a soldier of fortune. The frozen ice fields of the North have made him cold and the scorched sands of the desert have made iced lemonade an absolute necessity.

About four years ago, Mr. Thies was giving a series of evenings of song in the principal cities of the British colonies in South Africa. In the height of a successful season, he was told that old King Cetewayo, the famous Zulu chief, had sent a request for a private musicale. The king was then a prisoner in the hands of the British. His dark-skinned *impis* had gone down, the red and purple of the waving plumes had fallen beneath the Enfield rifles of the scarlet-coated visitors from the sea. Cetewayo's captors did all in their power to make his captivity as comfortable as possible. He, with his wives, occupied a large and commodious farmhouse, and was dealt out liberal allowances of provisions and supplies by the government. They even possessed a piano, though of course, it was of no use except as a means of recreation and wholesome amusement to the fair Mursala, one of the king's wives. She was very muscular; she was six feet two inches high; and she played the piano by main strength. The hand-organ grinders of America, playing different tunes in chorus, would have felt insignificant if they could have listened to Mrs. Cetewayo. Her mode of amusement caused some discomfort in the family circle. If the three others had shown a like propensity for contrasting their dark fingers with the ivory keys, I fear there would have been direful murder done in that household. But the king had paid sixteen cows for Mursala, so she was a valuable piece of property; she had an intrinsic worth; a face value, although the last would never be noted except by a Zulu in an advanced stage of barbarism. And she must be allowed to disturb the entire vicinity without reproach, or she might take herself off to the dim recesses of her native jungle; and her dark fingers never more mingle in the wool of her imperial lord and master; and he be at a dead loss in cows.

Mr. Thies, accompanied by an English friend and a Hottentot interpreter, appeared before the king. Cetewayo sat on the floor, in front of his four wives. He arose and received the singer with gracious dignity. After they had exchanged the usual compliments, through the interpreter, Mr. Thies went to the piano. Mursala had caused sad havoc in the instrument, but the singer did not allow that to disconcert him. He sang numbers of songs. He did not choose highly classical music, but sang the simple English ballads and American popular songs. The interpreter explained the words of each number after it was rendered. The king was delighted. He demanded to hear some of the pieces over and over again.

For the last of the program Mr. Thies chose an inspiring war song. There was no need of an interpreter then; the king recognized at once the sounds of battle, the clatter and din of war, and the cries of victory.

His eyes, grown sullen and downcast from years of captivity, again flashed, and his chest heaved. He was again a great chief, leading his hundreds of brown-bodied warriors, snake-like through the rustling grass to where the red coats and bayonets of the stolid, calm Britons glimmered and shone in the sunlight. He heard the swift rush of hundreds of naked feet, as his warriors swept down on the immovable British square, and writhed and twisted about it like a monstrous serpent. He heard the low muttered war chant of his followers, sounding to his enemies in the distance as the most ominous and dreadful of forebodings; the great wild cry of the battle as his swarthy demons dyed their spears in the white man's blood; the yells and curses of the Britons as they went down, blanched and pale and bloody, to death. He saw the ghastly faces and gory bodies of his enemies lie thick amongst the brown grass.

When the music ceased, he drew a long deep breath. He associated closely the singer, his own thoughts of battle, and the music. He stood up and extended the royal hand. "Thou art a great warrior, oh, son of a wise father. Come with me, and we two will drive these English dogs into the sea."

Mr. Thies modestly declined to drive his half of several millions of people into anything.

The king was surprised that a great warrior who could stir people's hearts in such a manner would not accept the partnership. He thought he could get his people to rise once more for one great final struggle could they but hear the inspiring voice of this mighty warrior from an unknown land, whose warriors had defeated the redcoats in many battles. But he did not allow his disappointment to affect his attitude toward his guest. The musician stood high in the king's favor.

Suddenly a thought struck his imperial majesty. He would confer upon the great stranger the highest honor known to his race.

"Hearken, oh warrior, son of many warriors, the fallen king loves you," said Cetewayo, waving his hand graciously, "I, even I, king of the Zulus. And it becomes a great king to give honor to his friend, aye, even to as much as twenty cows. Then, oh great stranger, take Mursala, my wife, to be your wife, to follow you to the land of the setting sun and keep your hut and tend your cows until she die."

When the interpreter put the king's kindness and condescension into

English, a solemn hush fell upon the two white men. The king and his four wives gazed expectantly.

The silence was horrible. Mr. Thies moved his feet restlessly and felt very uncomfortable. The Englishman, with his head down, laughed in an insane manner.

The king detected the giggle. He stood up and glanced fiercely at them. Was this the way to treat the gift of a monarch? His brow grew dark. He was a prisoner but he looked formidable. Standing six-feet-four-inches high, his massive shoulders and long, sinewy arms showed him to be indeed the king who had led his people in so many desperate battles. The two friends felt that it was an evil hour for them. They turned to the interpreter and implored him, by all he held sacred, to smooth the thing over some way and let them escape the royal displeasure. They begged him to make it known to Cetewayo that an American gentleman's views on connubial bliss were a little queer and old-fashioned, and differed from the prevailing modes of the jungle elite. Mr. Thies urged him to thank the monarch heartily and say that it would be Mr. Thies' pleasure to send a red and white sun-umbrella and a toy pistol to the king, from Capetown, the moment of his arrival there. The Englishman expressed his great desire to forward a pair of suspenders and an opera glass by the first Hottentot express. The king could not be propitiated by these munificent offers. He smiled faintly. The two friends saw their advantage and followed it up with the promise of a jackknife and a bottle of red ink. The great monarch smiled decidedly and irrevocably. When Mr. Thies heaped on, so to speak, a pack of cards and a silk handkerchief, the Englishman responding with a dozen clay pipes and a banjo, his imperial majesty became gleeful. They commenced to feel safe. The king grew cheerful and pleasant. His conversation became as courtly and affable as it had been in the first part of the interview. They considered it a good time to retreat and so made their adieus. The king seemed very sorry to have Mr. Thies leave. He inquired anxiously if he could not be counted on to change his mind about the insurrection scheme. Mr. Thies, however, assured him that no considerations could induce him to devote his talents to the extermination of the whites of Africa. So the old king bowed his head as if his last hope of revenge was taken from him, and reluctantly bade adieu. The two whites backed out the door. The last sight of Cetewayo was as he sat calm and immovable, with his stern old face set with the rigidity of a bronze cast, only the eyes seeming to say that his hope of being once more the ruler of a nation was gone forever.

When they reached the open air, Mr. Thies heaved a sigh which is said to have shaken the more tender of the young sprouts on certain of the banyan trees, adjacent to him. Mursala, mayhap, pressed her face against the pane, and bade a sad farewell as the horses clattered down the road.

Mr. Thies always speaks of this adventure as the narrowest escape of his life. Daniel, mingling in a social way with the denizens of the den, could never have experienced the sensations that the singer did, as he stood before the king and felt, somehow, that he must refuse the royal gift.

Mr. Thies returned to America safely and was very glad to put several thousand miles of water between him and the lovely Zulu. He has resolved upon a course of action when called to sing before savage kings. He will send a little circular with a blank to be filled in. The questions will be something as follows: 1—"Are you married?" 2—"How many?" 3—"Have you a natural affection for your wife?" 4—"Could any offer induce you to part with one?"

These questions being answered satisfactorily, Mr. Thies feels that he can trust himself.

May 11, 1891
[_The University Herald_, Syracuse, New York,
Vol. 19, pp. 128–131.]

A FOREIGN POLICY, IN THREE GLIMPSES:
FIRST GLIMPSE*

I

Lonely Isle, white sands, and green palms glimmer in the rays of a tropical sun. From the countless flowers, a heavy perfume, incense burned upon the altar of the earth, rises toward Heaven. Brown-bodied natives swarm in and out of the cone-shaped huts. In the shady dells, merry maidens toss blossoms to and fro; in the surf, young men, gaily laugh as they breast the white-crested waves; upon the beach, fat little boys play games and settle infantile disputes. A sail, a dead black upon its shady and visible side, rears slowly above the horizon and seems to peer at the island. The natives perceive the sail and gather upon the beach to discuss it. It grows larger and larger until a small schooner comes to an anchor outside where the waves roar upon the reef. A boat puts off toward the crowd of wondering natives. It finally bumps upon the beach and men with white faces step out. The innocent, guileless natives give a cordial welcome. The strangers offer valuable glass beads and calico remnants for the products of Lonely Isle. The natives accept with alacrity, amazed

* By permission of Alfred A. Knopf, Inc. Hitherto unpublished in book form.

at the sight of so much wealth and the simplicity of the white strangers. The traders laugh in their beards and gleefully swindle the natives. They camp upon the beach, awaiting the time when their vessel shall be filled, like a voracious animal, with spoil from the island.

All goes well for a few days. Then a shriek rings over the white sands and up to the blue sky above Lonely Isle. It is a woman's voice. A white hand grasps her throat and as she attempts to repeat her cry, her mouth is stuffed with a pocket handkerchief. The male natives gather around the traders and their chief says quietly: "You must give up the girl, white men." The only audible reply is: "Lookut 'is bloomin' chieflets. Hi say, where did you git them pants, now."

The sturdy natives gaze darkly upon the strangers. There is a discussion which ends in an altercation. There are blows exchanged. The girl kills herself with a dirk from a trader's girdle and the white men retreat leaving their leader dead upon the sand. The ship becomes a black speck and topples off the horizon.

II

Two black-hulled British gunboats are at anchor off Lonely Isle. A crowd of natives watch them curiously from the shore. Suddenly, a signal is run up to the masthead of the foremost gunboat, a streak of fire flashed from her bow, there is a thundering roar and a shell shrieks as it falls among the cone-shaped huts of the island. The natives die around in the grass as flash upon flash leaps from the sides of the man-of-war. After a couple of score are killed in this manner, the marines land and kill a few more with the bayonet. While they are thus employed, a group of chiefs advance from the shelter of the woods, holding up their hands in token of peace. The captain of the marines who, while smoking a short brier-wood, is engaged in thoughtfully prodding a writhing native, with a sword, looks casually up and observes them. The native seizes the opportunity to crawl behind a bunch of grass and die.

"Most noble king," says the principal chief to the captain. "We have come to ask why all this wanton slaughter for a brute who had committed an indignity upon one of our maidens and thus deserved his fate. Two score of our people lie cold in death." "Why, my friend," replies the captain, "British interests must be protected—oh, I say, now where's my native? This won't do, you know. He wriggled his legs great." The captain looks about for his writhing victim but, as mentioned, the native had quietly died behind the bunch of grass. "This won't do, you know. I've been regularly jewed out of some fun. I shall report this matter to my commanding officer."

"Most noble and powerful chieftain," continues the chief, "you hold our poor lives in your cannon's mouth but we would crave, noble sir, that you produce for our inspection those British interests, you mention."

"Oh, that's all right, old ten-pin, British interests must be protected you know."

Slightly exasperated, the venerable chief says: "You confounded insolent, insignficant little prig, I'd like to bat you one with my war club. What we want to know is, why in Heaven's name don't you go away? Ain't you satisfied, dern you? You have killed forty of us for a bloody-handed villain who reeked of no law but might. And, now why don't you get out? We don't want you! See? Get out, that's all we ask. Hear?"

To this the captain calmly replies, as he borrows a match from his first sergeant and scratches it on the head of a dead native: "My friend, I think I have already informed you that British interests must be protected."

"But," frenziedly cries the chief, "where in the devil's name are the British interests? And, if so, where are our interests?"

"British interests, b'gad, must be protected if we die for it," cry the sturdy soldiery as they go into permanent camp.

III

It has been flashed to London that, "owing to the murder of Europeans it has been found necessary to occupy Lonely Isle with a British force, powerful enough to cope with the natives and afford adequate protection to foreign residents." In less than four hours after the receipt of this dispatch, there are thirteen companies organized for carrying on commerce with Lonely Isle. The representatives of these companies swoop down on the doomed native; they improve him, they rescue him, they enlighten him, they dicker with him and they beat him out of his senses, they rob him, they convert him and when they get through with him, he has been manipulated out of everything but his blackened conscience and his toe-nails. He gets uproariously drunk on the worst rum England can produce, and through the storm doors of his clouded mind he has an impression that he will strike for liberty about twice a month.

He does so. There's a howl from Lonely Isle. "Oh I say now this won't do, you know. British interests predominate here and we must have protection you know."

Gunboats arrive again and kill all natives in sight. After which the British government puzzles over the Lonely Isle question. "How can we afford sufficient protection to our interests in Lonely Isle without annexing it? Why it can't be done! Of course, it can't: the only way to advance civilization and protect British interests is to annex Lonely Isle." "But what is to become of the poor native? He owns it, you know. I don't see what right—" "Oh, damn the native! British interests must be protected, you know."

A FOREIGN POLICY, IN THREE GLIMPSES: SECOND GLIMPSE

The Czar of Russia to the British Lion in 1884: "By Jim, I have ideaovitch to cutski your throatovitch."
The Lion: "What's that? Oh, I say, Mr. Czar you didn't mean me, did you?"
The Czar: "Damnovitch, if I didn'ski, by Jim!"
The Lion: "Oh, I say now, I am really sorry, you know. I didn't mean it, you know."
The Czar: "Anyway, I believeovitch I'll breakski your faceovitch, you damnovitch cusski."
The Lion: "Oh, my dear, dear sir, you are mistaken, indeed, indeed you are. You have no idea how I hate to fight when my opponent is as big as you are. I am the most peaceable animal on earth in a case like this. I will not fight unless you insist on it and knock me down three times. Forgive me this once and I'll never do so no more, s'elp me Gawd."

A FOREIGN POLICY, IN THREE GLIMPSES: THIRD GLIMPSE

Chorus from British Newspapers in 1892: "The attitude of the United States in the trouble with Chile is disgusting to all mankind. Never in history did a nation of the world give such an exhibition of the brutal coward and bully as is now afforded us by the ignorant, petty, and vainglorious government at Washington. America's policy all along has been that of a stupid, big, fat and conceited republic which attempts to browbeat and coerce a little but liberty-loving, truthful and virtuous rival. America would never dare to assume such an attitude toward a nation of any importance, but her silly, vain president seeks a little insignificant country to bluster to and strut before. Language fails us—God save the queen, b'gad."

May, 1891?
[Bulletin of the New York Public Library,
Vol. 61 (January, 1957), pp. 43–46.]

THE CAMEL*

"No man," observed my Uncle Clarence musingly, "likes to find grass in his whiskey and this is why, during all that journey, I did not allow the camel to eat anything. When I first made up my mind to travel in the State of Maine I set about contriving some scheme to provide myself with proper nourishment during the trip without shocking the delicate nerves of the people of Maine who, one and all, men, women, and children, bitterly loathe even a furtive suggestion of whiskey. As far as the frontier of Maine the camel carried on his back three cases of soda and one dozen bottles of the best Scotch. I had thought of bringing lemons, sugar and cloves for use in cold weather but I was told these articles could be purchased in Maine if the intention of the purchaser was concealed from the grocer. At the frontier, I, with the aid of a wonderful mechanism, injected the whiskey into one of the camel's stomachs; and into the other stomach I injected the soda water, afterward hiding the mechanism in my boots since, as the mechanism had injected the nourishment into the camel, it was also to be employed in getting it out again. Then seizing the camel by its halter I walked boldly into Maine.

There was a town at no great distance and I went at once to the principal hotel for luncheon, placing my camel in the care of the hostler somewhat to his surprise. The town was rather enlivened, and upon asking the cause of the gala aspect, I was told that the cornerstone of a new church was to be laid in the afternoon and it had been made the occasion for no inconsiderable celebration. The clergy of the whole county were to be in attendance with all the prominent laymen. After luncheon I strolled out to witness this interesting ceremony. There was a great concourse of people and a band ready to play in the proper intervals, and under the trees were long tables heavy with refreshments. On a decorated stand were gathered the flower of the county's clergy.

Now I had been careless about one thing. I esteem myself as a thoughtful person but in contriving my receptacle for whiskey and soda, I had taken no thought of a possible effect upon the camel. The chief orator of the day was bestowing his ringing eloquence upon us, and the vast crowd was breathlessly intent upon each word when I heard shouts of alarm and amazement from the crowd; and upon turning my eyes toward the middle of the uproar I perceived my camel making his way toward the speaker's stand. He was smiling with an expression of foolish good

* By permission of Alfred A. Knopf, Inc. Hitherto unpublished.

nature and his legs were spraddling out in his drunken attempt to keep himself erect. The chief orator of the day cut a burning sentence in the middle, gave a shriek whoop and fell backwards, disappearing amid the crash of lumber and the tearing of bunting.

As near as I remember now it was the first time I had seen a clergyman climb a tree. I was astonished at their agility. It seemed but a moment before the trees were black with clergymen. The band fled in a body leaving a broad wake of musical instruments. My agitation had been so extreme that I was not capable of following events with my usual clearness but presently I seemed to be alone with the camel and the cornerstone. When I indignantly approached the brute I found him munching the bass drum which a thoughtless bandsman had failed to take with him. From the trees above me resounded cries and moans. The committee of well-known citizens who escorted me and the camel over the frontier on the evening of that same day courteously informed me that they only carried their shotguns as a protection against the cold night air.

1891?

DAN EMMONDS*

As soon as my father set foot in America he became a very great success, and it was not long before he sent for my mother and me. I was very glad to get to New York and I became a fine man in a very little time, occupying myself in the saloon and in other gentlemanly amusements. But in truth my father never extremely admired me for some reason or another. "You should have been the son of a big brewer, Dan," he often said to me. "A poor little saloon keeper like me is dazzled by you. However, the business is coming on, and I hope one day to be able to maintain you properly."

At last I conducted some affairs for my father in a particularly clever manner and upon learning of it he declared that it was a great pity it was no longer the fashion to send youths out as cabin boys so that sea captains might give them instruction and that he much feared he would have to pay my fare on some distant voyage in order that his commercial ventures might have opportunity to get strong again. I told him at once that I regarded a sea voyage as a fine thing in an educational way and no doubt I would return greatly benefited. I had always a great passion for the sea.

My father looked upon my acquiescence with suspicion, and for a long time I could see him debate in regard to the wisdom of sending me. "By

* By permission of Alfred A. Knopf, Inc. Hitherto unpublished.

the paper," said he, "there's some opportunity for mischief here. I must examine it further."

At last, however, I conducted some more business for my father, and at its conclusion he said he had no doubt but that a sea voyage would be a great thing. Accordingly he obtained for me a passage on the ship *Susan L. Terwilleger,* which was about to begin a long voyage to Melbourne. The time up to my going on board was without incident save when my father detected two cases of sherry and one of port in my baggage. Having taken them in charge he parted from me with a tender smile.

For two or three hours, I occupied myself in bidding farewell to New York harbor which in the morning light was a broad gold cloth. As I hung upon the rail I occasionally turned to watch the captain and the mates who were motioning and swearing in all directions until no one knew his own business. Up in front, a crowd of ragged sailors were running this way and that way and hauling into view a number of dirty sails.

At last after great labor we got the ship out to the breeze and Sandy Hook was no more than a little strip of sand. It was then the sails began to drag the ship forward and the old thing reeled and swayed. I discovered that I was afloat on what has always been called the deep blue sea.

I need not weary you with any details of the first part of the voyage excepting to say that the captain's rum and tobacco were good, and he was a first-class companion with a bottle between him and me. We became great philosophers and conversed deeply upon many things that were not usually understood, cocking up our legs and puffing and letting the ship go to ruin.

But when we were almost to Australia there came a terrible storm and our ship got the worst beating at the hands of the sea that has happened since Robinson Crusoe's ships used to sail up and down mountains. Salt water surged on the deck here and there and from side to side until it was all I could do to keep my mouth from getting full of it. I hung near the captain's rum and prayed for land. As for the officers and crew, they were greatly frightened. They swathed themselves in oil clothes, and went about bawling at each other when only six feet apart. They could only console themselves with thinking of what they might tell of it afterward.

The great wind blew the poor helpless vessel for many miles in one direction, and then blew it violently in another. In truth the wind never paused to reflect where to hurl us, but merely hurled us in all directions until the captain did not know whether he was upon his own quarterdeck or in his father's barnyard on the old farm in Connecticut, of which he had often told me. And as for me, I might have been standing on my head in the middle of the main street of Dublin for all I knew to the contrary. The quantity of rum I consumed makes me ashamed to think of it.

"Captain," said I, "I'm no great hand at courage, and I particularly request you will not allow the ship to founder before I have at least two hours steady work at the bottle."

"Drink fast, my lad," the captain replied. "It is a good thing you have not the head of my old friend Jerry Martin of Portland who required four days of hard lifting at the glass before he could grow indifferent to the death of his second wife whom he disliked exceedingly. Drink fast or you will leave behind you that which will be a hard thing to leave in any such senseless tub as this."

I obeyed the captain's order until it was a matter of indifference to me if the ship turned handsprings and, as a matter of truth, that is what she did presently. Six sailors were spilled to starboard at one lurch. Their screams were so dreadful to me that I ran for the cabin. I was resolved to do great things, only the captain and all three of the mates were there before me.

When night came it was as if a black cloth had been thrown over a dog and the convulsions of our poor ship was a dreadful thing. We were blind with the spray, and drenched to the skin, and we felt that if we all died presently it would relieve us from a great anxiety. The captain himself said that anyhow we should have been drowned hours before, speaking from the standpoint of a scientific seaman. Some of the men came near us and the second-mate, who was an old officer of the navy, was quite civil to them. It was then I made up my mind that the hour of our destruction was at hand.

Sure enough at that moment our ship gave a great groaning cry and flew into a thousand pieces. I remember that the flashing white waves looked like teeth when they swallowed me. I sank over two hundred feet in the sea, and I reflected upon twenty ways in which I might have conducted my father's business in New York. When I thrust my head out of water there was nothing to be seen of ship nor companions. However, a hen coop that had been lashed to the galley flew past me on a high wave, and I had sufficient wit left in me to grasp the slats.

I need not describe to you how fearfully the storm raged nor how hard I clung to the hen coop. Eventually the winds abated, and I saw that I was alone upon the sea with no company but the hen coop and the dead body of a pig named Bartholomew, who had been a great favorite with the ship's cook.

I propelled the coop with great difficulty over to the floating body of the pig, for I thought that if the coop failed me, I could use the pig, and if the pig disappeared, I would still have the coop. Anything was better than being left out there with nothing.

Presently the sun broke clear and mild from the clouds with a great air of innocence as if he had never been gone when the captain wanted him, and I saw a fair blue streak on the horizon which I knew to be land. "It's just as I expected," I said out loud. "But here's the point—I don't know how to get to you, miserable undiscovered country that you are."

I first tried pushing the coop away from the pig, and then dragging the pig up and so on, but I soon tired of this mode of traveling, for the pig lay like a block of marble in the water, and I despaired of reaching the island in less than nine years. But it was at this moment that I descried a small boat, something like a fishing smack, skimming over the water quite near to me. It had been previously hidden by the huge waves, for it was so low in the water that I couldn't have perceived a lighthouse many feet away.

I set up a great howl when I discovered the smack and she went in stays with a shiver and shake as if my cry from the sea had startled half the life out of her. She came toward me then like a bird, and it was not long before I could see a row of heads hanging over the side, staring at me and conversing. The craft was so well sailed that she pulled up within ten feet of me, and lay with her nose to the wind as quiet as my own hen coop. The men in her were all copper as a doorplate, and had straight black hair, very peculiar. Some of them that I saw running were dressed in little kilts.

We eyed each other for a minute and then, sure as I am alive, they of a sudden burst into cheers and began to hug each other for joy. I was too amazed to speak. You would have thought they had found a diamond floating upon the water. I did not suppose I was truly the reason of their celebration until they dragged me over the side, and fairly went into convulsions over me.

I began to think how to treat these strange people, for I knew that I must pay my respects to everything I could see, and be very circumspect and wise upon all religious matters. So, as soon as I could get enough liberty I bowed politely to them and said: "The height of good living to you all, gentlemen, and may you know that there is nothing I admire so much as I do you. First of all, I pay my respects to your old venerable king if you have one; if not, to your beautiful maiden queen and to the aged high priest with the long whiskers, if there be such among you. I wish you to know that I am a man of peace and am arrived here against my wishes and with no plan of any kind against you. I beseech you to observe that my only object in coming here is to get away again as soon as possible. More power be with me. But, above all, gentlemen—and now heed me closely here—I am a man of great liberality in religious matters, and am willing to worship anything from fire and the sun to a large stone kitten if it will be a comfort to the people of the country. Furthermore I am a quiet and modest citizen of the city of New York, and have no desire to hobnob with your king nor your queen, nor your high priests for that matter, as it breeds trouble in countries of this kind. If you have a small detached house with a bit of a garden, maybe, in the outskirts of your beautiful white city, I would pay what rent I am able, and try to live at peace with those about me until I can regain my own country. May the light of the sun illumine the faces of your clay gods when they look at you—that is to say, if you have clay gods. If you have not, I can only say that what you do have must needs be right in my opinion, since you are enlightened citizens of this great country while I am only a citizen of New York City, and not up to the average when there."

This was a pretty neat speech, and it was not until the conclusion of it that I began to wonder whether a man of them understood me. However, when I looked at them, they were all smiling in clear delight, and I could see that my eloquence had been no less than music to them. They lay back as if they had just been listening to me playing on a harp.

I was a trifle bewildered by such great appreciation. "What's this," said I to myself. "This might do me harm. They will never part with me if I turn out to be a valuable popular amusement."

I reflected for a time and they all sat around like images waiting for me to speak. Finally I saw there was no good in pondering. I must wait until the situation came out more. So I sat there.

Presently they turned the boat and headed for the island. She flew like a duck, with those coppery fellows dancing for joy, and seeming anxious to tell their friends. "Well," said I to myself, as the island in front began to grow large, "here you are, my boy, with nothing to back you, now that you have left Bartholomew and the chickens. Devil knows what kind of a stew you will make for these grinning barbarians." I was greatly frightened. "Good fortune be with you, Bartholomew," said I addressing the distance. "You are better off than I am indeed, if I am going to be killed after taking this long troublesome voyage."

1891?
[March, 1896]

FOUR MEN IN A CAVE*

LIKEWISE FOUR QUEENS, AND A SULLIVAN COUNTY HERMIT

The moon rested for a moment on the top of a tall pine on a hill.

The little man was standing in front of the campfire making orations to his companions.

"We can tell a great tale when we get back to the city if we investigate this thing," said he, in conclusion.

They were won.

The little man was determined to explore a cave, because its black mouth had gaped at him. The four men took lighted pineknots and clambered over boulders down a hill. In a thicket on the mountainside lay a little tilted hole. At its side they halted.

"Well?" said the little man.

They fought for last place, and the little man was overwhelmed. He tried to struggle from under by crying that if the fat, pudgy man came after, he would be corked. But he finally administered a cursing over his shoulder and crawled into the hole. His companions gingerly followed.

A passage, the floor of damp clay and pebbles, the walls slimy, green-mossed, and dripping, sloped downward. In the cave atmosphere the torches became studies in red blaze and black smoke.

"Ho!" cried the little man, stifled and bedraggled, "let's go back." His companions were not brave. They were last. The next one to the little man pushed him on, so the little man said sulphurous words and cautiously continued his crawl.

Things that hung seemed to be on the wet, uneven ceiling, ready to drop upon the men's bare necks. Under their hands the clammy floor seemed alive and writhing. When the little man endeavored to stand erect the ceiling forced him down. Knobs and points came out and punched him. His clothes were wet and mud-covered, and his eyes, nearly blinded by smoke, tried to pierce the darkness always before his torch.

"Oh, I say, you fellows, let's go back!" cried he. At that moment he caught the gleam of trembling light in the blurred shadows before him.

"Ho!" he said, "here's another way out."

The passage turned abruptly. The little man put one hand around the corner, but it touched nothing. He investigated and discovered that the little corridor took a sudden dip down a hill. At the bottom shone a yellow light.

* *The Sullivan County Sketches.*

The little man wriggled painfully about and descended feet in advance. The others followed his plan. All picked their way with anxious care. The traitorous rocks rolled from beneath the little man's feet and roared thunderously below him. Lesser stones, loosened by the men above him, hit him on the back. He gained a seemingly firm foothold and, turning halfway about, swore redly at his companions for dolts and careless fools. The pudgy man sat, puffing and perspiring, high in the rear of the procession. The fumes and smoke from four pine-knots were in his blood. Cinders and sparks lay thick in his eyes and hair. The pause of the little man angered him.

"Go on, you fool," he shouted. "Poor, painted man, you are afraid!"

"Ho!" said the little man, "come down here and go on yourself, imbecile!"

The pudgy man vibrated with passion. He leaned downward. "Idiot—!"

He was interrupted by one of his feet which flew out and crashed into the man in front of and below him. It is not well to quarrel upon a slippery incline when the unknown is below. The fat man, having lost the support of one pillar-like foot, lurched forward. His body smote the next man, who hurtled into the next man. Then they all fell upon the cursing little man.

They slid in a body down over the slippery, slimy floor of the passage. The stone avenue must have wibble-wobbled with the rush of this ball of tangled men and strangled cries. The torches went out with the combined assault upon the little man. The adventurers whirled to the unknown in darkness. The little man felt that he was pitching to death, but even in his convolutions he bit and scratched at his companions, for he was satisfied that it was their fault. The swirling mass went some twenty feet and lit upon a level, dry place in a strong, yellow light of candles. It dissolved and became eyes.

The four men lay in a heap upon the floor of a gray chamber. A small fire smoldered in a corner, the smoke disappearing in a crack. In another corner was a bed of faded hemlock boughs and two blankets. Cooking utensils and clothes lay about, with boxes and a barrel.

Of these things the four men took small cognizance. The pudgy man did not curse the little man, nor did the little man swear in the abstract. Eight widened eyes were fixed upon the center of the room of rocks.

A great, gray stone, cut squarely like an altar, sat in the middle of the floor. Over it burned three candles in swaying tin cups hung from the ceiling. Before it, with what seemed to be a small volume clasped in his yellow fingers, stood a man. He was an infinitely sallow person in the brown-checked shirt of the plows and cows. The rest of his apparel was boots. A long gray beard dangled from his chin. He fixed glinting, fiery eyes upon the heap of men and remained motionless. Fascinated, their tongues cleaving, their blood cold, they arose to their feet. The gleaming glance of the recluse swept slowly over the group until it found the face of the little man. There it stayed and burned.

The little man shriveled and crumpled as the dried leaf under the glass.

Finally, the recluse slowly, deeply spoke. It was a true voice from a cave, cold, solemn, and damp.

"It's your ante," he said.

"What?" said the little man.

The hermit tilted his beard and laughed a laugh that was either the chatter of a banshee in a storm or the rattle of pebbles in a tin box. His visitors' flesh seemed ready to drop from their bones.

They huddled together and cast fearful eyes over their shoulders. They whispered.

"A vampire!" said one.

"A ghoul!" said another.

"A Druid before the sacrifice," murmured another.

"The shade of an Aztec witch doctor," said the little man.

As they looked, the inscrutable face underwent a change. It became a livid background for his eyes, which blazed at the little man like impassioned carbuncles. His voice arose to a howl of ferocity. "It's your ante!" With a panther-like motion he drew a long, thin knife and advanced, stooping. Two cadaverous hounds came from nowhere and, scowling and growling, made desperate feints at the little man's legs. His quaking companions pushed him forward.

Tremblingly he put his hand to his pocket.

"How much?" he said, with a shivering look at the knife that glittered.

The carbuncles faded.

"Three dollars," said the hermit in sepulchral tones which rang against the walls and among the passages, awakening long-dead spirits with voices. The shaking little man took a roll of bills from a pocket and placed three ones upon the altar-like stone. The recluse looked at the little volume with reverence in his eyes. It was a pack of playing cards.

Under the three swinging candles, upon the altar-like stone, the gray beard and the agonized little man played at poker. The three other men crouched in a corner and stared with eyes that gleamed with terror. Before them sat the cadaverous hounds licking their red lips. The candles burned low and began to flicker. The fire in the corner expired.

Finally, the game came to a point where the little man laid down his hand and quavered: "I can't call you this time, sir. I'm dead broke."

"What?" shrieked the recluse. "Not call me? Villain! Dastard! Cur! I have four queens, miscreant!" His voice grew so mighty that it could not fit his throat. He choked, wrestling with his lungs for a moment. Then the power of his body was concentrated in a word: "Go!"

He pointed a quivering, yellow finger at a wide crack in the rock. The little man threw himself at it with a howl. His erstwhile frozen companions felt their blood throb again. With great bounds they plunged after the little man. A minute of scrambling, falling, and pushing brought them to open air. They climbed the distance to their camp in furious springs.

The sky in the east was a lurid yellow. In the west the footprints of departing night lay on the pine trees. In front of their replenished campfire sat John Willerkins, the guide.

"Hello!" he shouted at their approach. "Be you fellers ready to go deer-huntin'?"

Without replying, they stopped and debated among themselves in whispers.

Finally, the pudgy man came forward.

"John," he inquired, "do you know anything peculiar about this cave below here?"

"Yes," said Willerkins at once. "Tom Gardner."

"What?" said the pudgy man.

"Tom Gardner."

"How's that?"

"Well, you see," said Willerkins slowly, as he took dignified pulls at his pipe, "Tom Gardner was once a fambly man, who lived in these here parts on a nice leetle farm. He uster go away to the city orften, and one time he got a-gamblin' in one of them there dens. He went ter the dickens right quick then. At last he kum home one time and tol' his folks he had up and sold the farm and all he had in the worl'. His leetle wife, she died then. Tom, he went crazy, and soon after—"

The narrative was interrupted by the little man, who became possessed of devils.

"I wouldn't give a cuss if he had left me 'nough money to get home on, the doggoned, gray-haired red pirate," he shrilled, in a seething sentence. The pudgy man gazed at the little man calmly and sneeringly.

"Oh, well," he said, "we can tell a great tale when we get back to the city after having investigated this thing."

"Go to the devil!" replied the little man.

July 3, 1892
[New York *Tribune*, part 2, p. 14.]

TRAVELS IN NEW YORK:
THE BROKEN-DOWN VAN

The gas lamps had just been lit and the two great red furniture vans with impossible landscapes on their sides rolled and plunged slowly along the street. Each was drawn by four horses, and each almost touched the roaring elevated road above. They were on the uptown track of the surface road—indeed the street was so narrow that they must be on one track or the other.

They tossed and pitched and proceeded slowly, and a horse car with a red light came up behind. The car was red, and the bull's-eye light was red, and the driver's hair was red. He blew his whistle shrilly and slapped the horse's lines impatiently. Then he whistled again. Then he pounded on the red dashboard with his car-hook till the red light trembled. Then a car with a green light crept up behind the car with the red light; and the green driver blew his whistle and pounded on his dashboard; and the conductor of the red car seized his strap from his position on the rear platform and rung such a rattling tattoo on the gong over the red driver's head that the red driver became frantic and stood up on his toes and puffed out his cheeks as if he were playing the trombone in a German streetband and blew his whistle till an imaginative person could see slivers flying from it, and pounded his red dashboard till the metal was dented in and the car-hook was bent. And just as the driver of a newly-come car with a blue light began to blow his whistle and pound his dashboard, and the green conductor began to ring his bell like a demon, which drove the green driver mad and made him rise up and blow and pound as no man ever blew or pounded before, which made the red conductor lose the last vestige of control of himself and caused him to bounce up and down on his bell strap as he grasped it with both hands in a wild, maniacal dance, which of course served to drive uncertain Reason from her tottering throne in the red driver, who dropped his whistle and his hook and began to yell, and ki-yi, and whoop harder than the worst personal devil encountered by the sternest of Scotch Presbyterians ever yelled and ki-yied and whooped on the darkest night after the good men had drunk the most hot Scotch whiskey; just then the left-hand forward wheel on the rear van fell off and the axle went down. The van gave a mighty lurch and then swayed and rolled and rocked and stopped; the red driver applied his brake with a jerk and his horses turned out to keep from being crushed between car and van; the other drivers applied their brakes with a jerk and their horses turned out; the two cliff dwelling men on the shelf halfway up the front of the stranded van began to shout loudly to their brother cliff dwellers on the forward van; a girl, six years old, with a pail of beer crossed under the red car horses' neck; a boy, eight years old, mounted the red car with the sporting extras of the evening papers; a girl, ten years old, went in front of the van horses with two pails of beer; an unclassified boy poked his finger in the black grease in the hub of the right-hand hind van wheel and began to print his name on the red landscape on the van's side; a boy with a little head and big ears examined the white rings on the martingales of the van leaders with a view of stealing them in the confusion; a sixteen-year-old girl without any hat and with a roll of half-finished vests under her arm crossed the front platform of the green car. As she stepped up on to the sidewalk a barber from a ten-cent shop said "Ah! there!" and she answered "smarty!" with withering scorn and went down a side street. A few drops of warm summer rain began to fall.

Well, the van was wrecked and something had got to be done. It was on the busiest car track on Manhattan Island. The cliff dwellers got down in some mysterious way—probably on a rope ladder. Their brethren drove their van down a side street and came back to see what was the matter.

"The nut is off," said the captain of the wrecked van.

"Yes," said the first mate, "the nut is off."

"Hah," said the captain of the other van, "the nut is off."

"Yer right," said his first mate, "the nut is off."

The driver of the red car came up, hot and irritated. But he had regained his reason. "The nut is off," he said.

The drivers of the green and of the blue car came along. "The nut," they said in chorus, "is off."

The red, green and blue conductors came forward. They examined the situation carefully as became men occupying a higher position. Then they made this report through the chairman, the red conductor:

"The nut is gone."

"Yes," said the driver of the crippled van, who had spoken first, "yes, the damned nut is lost."

Then the driver of the other van swore, and the two assistants swore, and the three car drivers swore, and the three car conductors used some polite but profane expressions. Then a strange man, an unknown man and an outsider, with his trousers held up by a trunkstrap, who stood at hand, swore harder than any of the rest. The others turned and looked at him inquiringly and savagely. The man wriggled nervously.

"You wanter to tie it up," he said at last.

"Wot yo' goin' to tie it to, you cussed fool?" asked the assistant of the head van scornfully, "a berloon?"

"Ha, ha!" laughed the others.

"Some folks make me tired," said the second van driver.

"Go and lose yourself with the nut," said the red conductor severely.

"That's it," said the others. "Git out, 'fore we t'row you out."

The officiously profane stranger slunk away.

The crisis always produces the man.

In this crisis the man was the first van driver.

"Bill," said the first van driver, "git some candles." Bill vanished.

A car with a white light, a car with a white and red light, a car with a white light and a green bar across it, a car with a blue light and a white circle around it, another car with a red bull's-eye light and one with a red flat light had come up and stopped. More are coming to extend the long line. The elevated trains thundered overhead, and made the street tremble. A dozen horse cars went down on the other track, and the drivers made derisive noises, rather than speaking derisive words at their brother van-bound drivers. Each delayed car was full of passengers, and they craned their necks and peppery old gentlemen inquired what the trouble was, and a happy individual who had been to Coney Island began to sing.

Trucks, mail-wagons, and evening paper carts crowded past. A jam was imminent. A Chatham Square cab fought its way along with a man inside wearing a diamond like an arc light. A hundred people stopped on either sidewalk; ten per cent of them whistled "Boom-de-ay." A half dozen small boys managed to just miss being killed by passing teams. Four Jews looked out of four different pawnshops. Pullers-in for three clothing stores were alert. The ten-cent barber eyed a Division Street girl who was a millinery puller-in and who was chewing gum with an earnest, almost fierce, motion of the jaw. The ever-forward flowing tide of the growlers flowed on. The men searched under the slanting rays of the electric light for the lost nut, back past a dozen cars; scattering drops of rain continued to fall and a hand organ came up and began an overture.

Just then Bill rose up from somewhere with four candles. The leader lit them and each van man took one and they continued the search for the nut. The humorous driver on a blue car asked them why they didn't get a firefly; the equally playful driver of a white car advised them of the fact that the moon would be up in the course of two or three hours. Then a gust of wind came and blew out the candles. The hand-organ man played on. A dozen newsboys arrived with evening paper extras about the Presidential nomination. The passengers bought the extras and found that they contained nothing new. A man with a stock of suspenders on his arm began to look into the trade situation. He might have made a sale to the profane man with the trunkstrap but he had disappeared. The leader again asserted himself.

"Bill," he shouted, "you git a lager beer-keg." Bill was gone in an instant.

"Jim," continued the leader, in a loud voice, as if Jim were up at the sharp end of the mainmast and the leader was on the deck, "Jim, unhitch them hosses and take out the pole."

Jim started to obey orders. A policeman came and walked around the van, looked at the prostrated wheel, started to say something, concluded not to, made the hand-organ man move on, and then went to the edge of the sidewalk and began talking to the Division Street girl with the gum, to the infinite disgust of the cheap barber. The trunkstrap man came out of a restaurant with a sign of "Breakfast, 18 cents; Dinner, 15 cents," where he had been hidden, and slunk into the liquor store next door with a sign of "Hot spiced rum, 6 cents; Sherry with a Big Egg in it, 5 cents." At the door he almost stepped on a small boy with a pitcher of beer so big that he had to set it down and rest every half block.

Bill was now back with the keg. "Set it right there," said the leader. "Now you, Jim, sock that pole under the axle and we'll h'ist 'er up and put the keg under."

One of the horses began kicking the front of the van. "Here, there!" shouted the leader and the horse subsided. "Six or seven o' you fellers git under that pole," commanded the leader, and he was obeyed. "Now all together!" The axle slowly rose and Bill slipped under the chime of the keg. But it was not high enough to allow the wheel to go on. "Git a paving block," commanded the leader to Bill. Just then a truck loaded with great, noisy straps of iron tried to pass. The wheels followed the car track too long, the truck struck the rear of the van and the axle went down with a crash while the keg rolled away into the gutter. Even great leaders lose their self-control sometimes; Washington swore at the Battle of Long Island; so this van leader now swore. His language was plain and scandalous. The truckman offered to lick the van man till he couldn't walk. He stopped his horses to get down to do it. But the policeman left the girl and came and made the truckman give over his warlike movement, much to the disgust of the crowd. Then he punched the suspender man in the back with the end of his club and went back to the girl. But the second delay was too much for the driver of the green car, and he turned out his horses and threw his car from the track. It pitched like a skiff in the swell of a steamer. It staggered and rocked and as it went past the van plunged into the gutter and made the crowd stand back, but the horses strained themselves and finally brought it up and at last it blundered on to its track and rolled away at a furious rate with the faces of the passengers wreathed in smiles and the conductor looking proudly back. Two other cars followed the example of the green and went lumbering past on the stones.

"Tell them fellers we'll be out of their way now in a minute," said the leader to the red conductor. Bill had arrived with the paving block. "Up with 'er, now," called the leader. The axle went up again and the keg with the stone on top of it went under. The leader seized the wheel himself and slipped it on. "Hitch on them hosses!" he commanded, and it was done. "Now, pull slow there, Bill," and Bill pulled slow. The great red car with the impossible landscape gave a preliminary rock and roll, the wheel which had made the trouble dropped down an inch or two from the keg and the van moved slowly forward. There was nothing to hold the wheel on and the leader walked close to it and watched it anxiously. But it stayed on to the corner, and around the corner, and into the side street. The red driver gave a triumphant Ki-yi and his horses plunged forward in their collars eagerly. The other drivers gave glad Ki-yis and the other horses plunged ahead. Twenty cars rolled past at a fast gait. "Now, youse fellys, move on!" said the policeman, and the crowd broke up. The cheap barber was talking to a girl with one black eye, but he retreated to his shop with the sign which promised "bay rum and a clean towel to every customer." Inside the liquor store the trunkstrap man was telling a man with his sleeves rolled up how two good men could have put their shoulders under the van and h'isted it up while a ten-year-old boy put on the wheel.

July 10, 1892
[New York *Tribune*, part 1, p. 8.]

THE OCTOPUSH*

A SULLIVAN COUNTY NOCTURNE

[The Fishermen]

Four men once upon a time went into the wilderness seeking for pickerel. They proceeded to a pond which is different from all other sheets of water in the world, excepting the remaining ponds in Sullivan County. A scrawny stone dam, clinging in apparent desperation to its foundation, wandered across a wild valley. In the beginning, the baffled waters had retreated into a forest. In consequence, the four men confronted a sheet of water from which there upreared countless gray, haggard tree trunks. Squat stumps, in multitudes, stretched long, lazy roots over the surface of the water. Floating logs and sticks bumped gently against the dam. All manner of weeds throttled the lilies and dragged them down. Great pine trees came from all sides to the pond's edge.

* *The Sullivan County Sketches.*

In their journey, the four men encountered a creature with a voice from a tomb. His person was concealed behind an enormous straw hat. In graveyard accents, he demanded that he be hired to assist them in their quest. They agreed. From a recess of the bank he produced a blunt-ended boat, painted a very light blue with yellow finishings, in accordance with Sullivan aesthetics. Two sculls, whittled from docile pine boards, lay under the seats. Pegs were driven into the boat's side, at convenient rowlock intervals. In deep, impressive tones, the disguised individual told the four men that, to his knowledge, the best way to catch pickerel was to "kidder fur 'em from them there stumps." The four men clambered into the beautiful boat, and the individual maneuvered his craft until he had dealt out to four low-spreading stumps, four fishers. He thereupon repaired to a fifth stump, where he tied his boat. Perching himself upon the stump-top, he valiantly grasped a mildewed corncob between his teeth, ladened with black, eloquent tobacco. At a distance it smote the senses of the four men.

The sun gleamed merrily upon the waters, the gaunt, towering tree trunks, and the stumps lying like spatters of wood which had dropped from the clouds. Troops of blue and silver darning needles danced over the surface. Bees bustled about the weeds which grew in the shallow places. Butterflies flickered in the air. Down in the water, millions of fern branches quavered and hid mysteries. The four men sat still and skiddered. The individual puffed tremendously. Ever and anon, one of the four would cry ecstatically, or swear madly. His fellows, upon standing to gaze at him, would either find him holding a stout fish, or nervously struggling with a hook and line entangled in the hordes of vindictive weeds and sticks on the bottom. They had fortune, for the pickerel is a voracious fish. His only faults are in method. He has a habit of furiously charging the fleeting bit of glitter and then darting under a log or around a corner with it.

At noon, the individual corralled the entire outfit upon a stump, where they lunched while he entertained them with anecdote. Afterward, he redistributed them, each to his personal stump. They fished. He contemplated the scene and made observations which ran across the water to the four men in bass solos. Toward the close of the day, he grew evidently thoughtful, indulging in no more spasmodic philosophy. The four men fished intently until the sun had sunk down to some treetops and was peering at them like the face of an angry man over a hedge. Then one of the four stood up and shouted across to where the individual sat enthroned upon the stump.

"You had better take us ashore, now." The other three repeated. "Yes, come take us ashore."

Whereupon the individual carefully took an erect position. Then, waving a great yellow-brown bottle and tottering, he gave vent to a sepulchral roar.

"You fellersh—hic—kin all go—hic—ter blazersh."

The sun slid down and threw a flare upon the silence, coloring it red. The man who had stood up drew a long, deep breath and sat down heavily. Stupefaction rested upon the four men.

Dusk came and fought a battle with the flare before their eyes. Tossing shadows and red beams mingled in combat. Then the stillness of evening lay upon the waters.

The individual began to curse in deep maudlin tones. "Dern fools," he said. "Dern fools! Why dontcher g'home?"

"He's full as a fiddler," said the little man on the third stump. The rest groaned. They sat facing the stump whereon the individual perched, beating them with mighty oaths. Occasionally he took a drink from the bottle. "Shay, you'm fine lot fellers," he bellowed, "why blazersh dontcher g'home?"

The little man on the third stump pondered. He got up finally and made oration. He, in the beginning, elaborated the many good qualities which he alleged the individual possessed. Next he painted graphically the pitiful distress and woe of their plight. Then he described the reward due to the individual if he would relieve them, and ended with an earnest appeal to the humanity of the individual, alleging, again, his many virtues. The object of the address struggled to his feet and in a voice of faraway thunder, said: "Dern fool, g'home." The little man sat down and swore crimson oaths.

A night wind began to roar, and clouds bearing a load of rain appeared in the heavens and threatened their position. The four men shivered and turned up their coat collars. Suddenly it struck each that he was alone, separated from humanity by impassable gulfs. All those things which come forth at night began to make noises. Unseen animals scrambled and flopped among the weeds and sticks. Weird features masqueraded awfully in robes of shadow. Each man felt that he was compelled to sit on something that was damply alive. A legion of frogs in the grass by the shore and a host of toads in the trees chanted. The little man started up and shrieked that all creeping things were inside his stump. Then he tried to sit facing four ways, because dread objects were approaching at his back. The individual was drinking and hoarsely singing. At different times they labored with him. It availed them nought. "G'home, dern fools." Among themselves they broached various plans for escape. Each involved a contact with the black water, in which were things that wriggled. They shuddered and sat still.

A ghostlike mist came and hung upon the waters. The pond became a graveyard. The gray tree trunks and dark logs turned to monuments and crypts. Fireflies were wisp-lights dancing over graves, and then, taking regular shapes, appeared like brass nails in crude caskets. The individual began to gibber. A gibber in a bass voice appalls the stoutest heart. It is the declamation of a genie. The little man began to sob; another groaned; and the two remaining, being timid by nature, swore great lurid oaths which blazed against the sky.

Suddenly the individual sprang up and gave tongue to a yell which raised the hair on the four men's heads and caused the waters to ruffle. Chattering, he sprang into the boat and, grasping an oar, paddled frantically to the little man's stump. He tumbled out and cowered at the little man's feet, looking toward his stump with eyes that saw the unknown.

"Stump turned inter an octopush. I was asettin' on his mouth," he howled.

The little man kicked him.

"Legs all commenced move, dern octopush!" moaned the shrunken individual.

The little man kicked him. But others cried out against him, so directly he left off. Climbing into the boat, he went about collecting his companions. They then proceeded to the stump whereon the individual lay staring wild-eyed at his "octopush." They gathered his limp form into the boat and rowed ashore. "How far is it to the nearest house?" they demanded savagely of him. "Four miles," he replied in a voice of cave-damp. The four men cursed him and built a great fire of pine sticks. They sat by it all night and listened to the individual who dwelt in phantom shadows by the water's edge dismally crooning about an "octopush."

July 10, 1892
[New York *Tribune,* part 2, p. 17.]

A GHOUL'S ACCOUNTANT*

THE STORY OF A SULLIVAN COUNTY PRODUCE DEAL

In a wilderness sunlight is noise. Darkness is a great, tremendous silence, accented by small and distant sounds. The music of the wind in the trees is songs of loneliness, hymns of abandonment, and lays of the absence of things congenial and alive.

Once a campfire lay dying in a fit of temper. A few weak flames struggled cholerically among the burned-out logs. Beneath, a mass of angry, red coals glowered and hated the world. Some hemlocks sighed and sung,

* *The Sullivan County Sketches.*

and a wind purred in the grass. The moon was looking through the locked branches at four imperturbable bundles of blankets which lay near the agonized campfire. The fire groaned in its last throes, but the bundles made no sign.

Off in the gloomy unknown a foot fell upon a twig. The laurel leaves shivered at the stealthy passing of danger. A moment later a man crept into the spot of dim light. His skin was fiercely red and his whiskers infinitely black. He gazed at the four passive bundles and smiled a smile that curled his lips and showed yellow, disordered teeth. The campfire threw up two lurid arms and, quivering, expired. The voices of the trees grew hoarse and frightened. The bundles were stolid.

The intruder stepped softly nearer and looked at the bundles. One was shorter than the others. He regarded it for some time motionless. The hemlocks quavered nervously and the grass shook. The intruder slid to the short bundle and touched it. Then he smiled. The bundle partially upreared itself, and the head of a little man appeared.

"Lord!" he said. He found himself looking at the grin of a ghoul condemned to torment.

"Come," croaked the ghoul.

"What?" said the little man. He began to feel his flesh slide to and fro on his bones as he looked into this smile.

"Come," croaked the ghoul.

"What?" the little man whimpered. He grew gray and could not move his legs. The ghoul lifted a three-pronged pickerel spear and flashed it near the little man's throat. He saw menace on its points. He struggled heavily to his feet.

He cast his eyes upon the remaining mummy-like bundles, but the ghoul confronted his face with the spear.

"Where?" shivered the little man.

The ghoul turned and pointed into the darkness. His countenance shone with lurid light of triumph.

"Go!" he croaked.

The little man blindly staggered in the direction indicated. The three bundles by the fire were still immovable. He tried to pierce the cloth with a glance and opened his mouth to whoop, but the spear ever threatened his face.

The bundles were left far in the rear, and the little man stumbled on alone with the ghoul. Tangled thickets tripped him, saplings buffeted him, and stones turned away from his feet. Blinded and badgered, he began to swear frenziedly. A foam drifted to his mouth, and his eyes glowed with a blue light.

"Go on!" thunderously croaked the ghoul.

The little man's blood turned to salt. His eyes began to decay and refused to do their office. He fell from gloom to gloom.

At last a house was before them. Through a yellow-papered window shone an uncertain light. The ghoul conducted his prisoner to the uneven threshold and kicked the decrepit door. It swung groaning back, and he dragged the little man into a room.

A soiled oil lamp gave a feeble light that turned the pineboard walls and furniture a dull orange. Before a table sat a wild, gray man. The ghoul threw his victim upon a chair and went and stood by the man. They regarded the little man with eyes that made wheels revolve in his soul.

He cast a dazed glance about the room and saw vaguely that it was disheveled as from a terrific scuffle. Chairs lay shattered, and dishes in the cupboard were ground to pieces. Destruction had been present. There were moments of silence. The ghoul and the wild, gray man contemplated their victim. A throe of fear passed over him, and he sank limp in his chair. His eyes swept feverishly over the faces of his tormentors.

At last the ghoul spoke.

"Well!" he said to the wild, gray man.

The other cleared his throat and stood up.

"Stranger," he said, suddenly, "how much is thirty-three bushels of pertaters at sixty-four an' a half a bushel?"

The ghoul leaned forward to catch the reply. The wild, gray man straightened his figure and listened. A fierce light shone on their faces. Their breaths came swiftly. The little man wriggled his legs in agony.

"Twenty-one, no two, six and—"

"Quick!" hissed the ghoul, hoarsely.

"Twenty-one dollars and twenty-eight cents and a half," laboriously stuttered the little man.

The ghoul gave a tremendous howl.

"There, Tom Jones, dearn yer!" he yelled, "what did I tell yer! hey? Hain't I right? See? Didn't I tell yer that?"

The wild, gray man's body shook. He was delivered of a frightful roar. He sprang forward and kicked the little man out of the door.

July 17, 1892
[New York *Tribune,* part 2, p. 17.]

THE BLACK DOG*

A NIGHT OF SPECTRAL TERROR

There was a ceaseless rumble in the air as the heavy raindrops battered upon the laurel thickets and the matted moss and haggard rocks beneath. Four water-soaked men made their difficult ways through the drenched forest. The little man stopped and shook an angry finger at where night was stealthily following them. "Cursed be fate and her children and her children's children! We are everlastingly lost!" he cried. The panting procession halted under some dripping, drooping hemlocks and swore in wrathful astonishment.

"It will rain for forty days and forty nights," said the pudgy man, moaningly, "and I feel like a wet loaf of bread, now. We shall never find our way out of this wilderness until I am made into a porridge."

In desperation, they started again to drag their listless bodies through the watery bushes. After a time, the clouds withdrew from above them, and great winds came from concealment and went sweeping and swirling among the trees. Night also came very near and menaced the wanderers with darkness. The little man had determination in his legs. He scrambled among the thickets and made desperate attempts to find a path or road. As he climbed a hillock, he espied a small clearing upon which sat desolation and a venerable house, wept over by wind-waved pines.

"Ho," he cried, "here's a house."

His companions straggled painfully after him as he fought the thickets between him and the cabin. At their approach, the wind frenziedly opposed them and skirled madly in the trees. The little man boldly confronted the weird glances from the crannies of the cabin and rapped on the door. A score of timbers answered with groans, and, within, something fell to the floor with a clang.

"Ho," said the little man. He stepped back a few paces.

Somebody in a distant part started and walked across the floor toward the door with an ominous step. A slate-colored man appeared. He was dressed in a ragged shirt and trousers, the latter stuffed into his boots. Large tears were falling from his eyes.

"How-d'-do, my friend?" said the little man, affably.

"My ol' uncle, Jim Crocker, he's sick ter death," replied the slate-colored person.

"Ho," said the little man. "Is that so?"

* *The Sullivan County Sketches.*

The latter's clothing clung desperately to him and water sogged in his boots. He stood patiently on one foot for a time.

"Can you put us up here until tomorrow?" he asked, finally.

"Yes," said the slate-colored man.

The party passed into a little unwashed room, inhabited by a stove, a stairway, a few precarious chairs, and a misshapen table.

"I'll fry yer some po'k and make yer some coffee," said the slate-colored man to his guests.

"Go ahead, old boy," cried the little man cheerfully from where he sat on the table, smoking his pipe and dangling his legs.

"My ol' uncle, Jim Crocker, he's sick ter death," said the slate-colored man.

"Think he'll die?" asked the pudgy man, gently.

"No!"

"No?"

"He won't die! He's an ol' man, but he won't die, yit! The black dorg hain't been around yit!"

"The black dog?" said the little man, feebly. He struggled with himself for a moment.

"What's the black dog?" he asked at last.

"He's a sperrit," said the slate-colored man in a voice of somber hue.

"Oh, he is? Well?"

"He haunts these parts, he does, an' when people are goin' to die, he comes and sets and howls."

"Ho," said the little man. He looked out of the window and saw night making a million shadows.

The little man moved his legs nervously.

"I don't believe in these things," said he, addressing the slate-colored man, who was scuffling with a side of pork.

"Wot things?" came incoherently from the combatant.

"Oh, these—er—phantoms and ghosts and what not. All rot, I say."

"That's because you have merely a stomach and no soul," grunted the pudgy man.

"Ho, old pudgkins!" replied the little man. His back curved with passion. A tempest of wrath was in the pudgy man's eye. The final epithet used by the little man was a carefully-studied insult, always brought forth at a crisis. They quarreled.

"All right, pudgkins, bring on your phantom," cried the little man in conclusion.

His stout companion's wrath was too huge for words. The little man smiled triumphantly. He had staked his opponent's reputation.

The visitors sat silent. The slate-colored man moved about in a small personal atmosphere of gloom.

Suddenly, a strange cry came to their ears from somewhere. It was a low, trembling call which made the little man quake privately in his shoes. The slate-colored man bounded at the stairway and disappeared with a flash of legs through a hole in the ceiling. The party below heard two voices in conversation, one belonging to the slate-colored man, and the other in the quavering tones of age. Directly, the slate-colored man reappeared from above and said: "The ol' man is took bad for his supper."

He hurriedly prepared a mixture with hot water, salt, and beef. Beef-tea, it might be called. He disappeared again. Once more the party below heard, vaguely, talking over their heads. The voice of age arose to a shriek.

"Open the window, fool! Do you think I can live in the smell of your soup?"

Mutterings by the slate-colored man and the creaking of the window were heard.

The slate-colored man stumbled down the stairs, and said with intense gloom, "The black dorg'll be along soon."

The little man started, and the pudgy man sneered at him. They ate a supper and then sat waiting. The pudgy man listened so palpably that the little man wished to kill him. The wood-fire became excited and sputtered frantically. Without, a thousand spirits of the winds had become entangled in the pine branches and were lowly pleading to be loosened. The slate-colored man tiptoed across the room and lit a timid candle. The men sat waiting.

The phantom dog lay cuddled to a round bundle, asleep down the roadway against the windward side of an old shanty. The specter's master had moved to Pike County. But the dog lingered as a friend might linger at the tomb of a friend. His fur was like a suit of old clothes. His jowls hung and flopped, exposing his teeth. Yellow famine was in his eyes. The wind-rocked shanty groaned and muttered, but the dog slept. Suddenly, however, he got up and shambled to the roadway. He cast a long glance from his hungry, despairing eyes in the direction of the venerable house. The breeze came full to his nostrils. He threw back his head and gave a long, low howl and started intently up the road. Maybe he smelled a dead man.

The group around the fire in the venerable house were listening and waiting. The atmosphere of the room was tense. The slate-colored man's face was twitching and his drabbed hands were gripped together. The little man was continually looking behind his chair. Upon the countenance of the pudgy man appeared conceit for an approaching triumph over the little man, mingled with apprehension for his own safety. Five pipes glowed as rivals of a timid candle. Profound silence drooped heavily over them. Finally the slate-colored man spoke.

"My ol' uncle, Jim Crocker, he's sick ter death."

The four men started and then shrank back in their chairs.

"Damn it!" replied the little man, vaguely.

Again there was a long silence. Suddenly it was broken by a wild cry from the room above. It was a shriek that struck upon them with appalling swiftness, like a flash of lightning. The walls whirled and the floor rumbled. It brought the men together with a rush. They huddled in a heap and stared at the white terror in each other's faces. The slate-colored man grasped the candle and flared it above his head. "The black dorg," he howled, and plunged at the stairway. The maddened four men followed frantically, for it is better to be in the presence of the awful than only within hearing.

Their ears still quivering with the shriek, they bounded through the hole in the ceiling and into the sick room.

With quilts drawn closely to his shrunken breast for a shield, his bony hand gripping the cover, an old man lay with glazing eyes fixed on the open window. His throat gurgled and a froth appeared at his mouth.

From the outer darkness came a strange, unnatural wail, burdened with weight of death and each note filled with foreboding. It was the song of the spectral dog.

"God!" screamed the little man. He ran to the open window. He could see nothing at first save the pine trees, engaged in a furious combat, tossing back and forth and struggling. The moon was peeping cautiously over the rims of some black clouds. But the chant of the phantom guided the little man's eyes, and he at length perceived its shadowy form on the ground under the window. He fell away gasping at the sight. The pudgy man crouched in a corner, chattering insanely. The slate-colored man, in his fear, crooked his legs and looked like a hideous Chinese idol. The man upon the bed was turned to stone, save the froth, which pulsated.

In the final struggle, terror will fight the inevitable. The little man roared maniacal curses and, rushing again to the window, began to throw various articles at the specter.

A mug, a plate, a knife, a fork, all crashed or clanged on the ground, but the song of the specter continued. The bowl of beef-tea followed. As it struck the ground the phantom ceased its cry.

The men in the chamber sank limply against the walls, with the unearthly wail still ringing in their ears and the fear unfaded from their eyes. They waited again.

The little man felt his nerves vibrate. Destruction was better than an-

other wait. He grasped a candle and, going to the window, held it over his
head and looked out.

"Ho!" he said.

His companions crawled to the window and peered out with him.

"He's eatin' the beef-tea," said the slate-colored man, faintly.

"The damn dog was hungry," said the pudgy man.

"There's your phantom," said the little man to the pudgy man.

On the bed, the old man lay dead. Without, the specter was wagging its
tail.

July 24, 1892

[New York *Tribune,* part 2, p. 19.]

KILLING HIS BEAR*

A WINTER TRAGEDY WITH THREE ACTORS

In a field of snow some green pines huddled together and sang in quavers
as the wind whirled among the gullies and ridges. Icicles dangled from
the trees' beards, and fine dusts of snow lay upon their brows. On the
ridge-top a dismal choir of hemlocks crooned over one that had fallen.
The dying sun created a dim purple and flame-colored tumult on the
horizon's edge and then sank until level crimson beams struck the trees.
As the red rays retreated, armies of shadows stole forward. A gray, ponderous stillness came heavily in the steps of the sun. A little man stood
under the quavering pines. He was muffled to the nose in fur and wool,
and a hideous cap was pulled tightly over his ears. His cold and impatient
feet had stamped a small platform of hard snow beneath him. A black-
barreled rifle lay in the hollow of his arm. His eyes, watery from incessant
glaring, swept over the snowfields in front of him. His body felt numb and
bloodless, and soft curses came forth and froze on the icy wind. The
shadows crept about his feet until he was merely a blurred blackness, with
keen eyes.

Off over the ridges, through the tangled sounds of night, came the yell
of a hound on the trail. It pierced the ears of the little man and made his
blood swim in his veins. His eyes eagerly plunged at the wall of thickets
across the stone field, but he moved not a finger or foot. Save his eyes, he
was frozen to a statue. The cry of the hound grew louder and louder, then
passed away to a faint yelp, then still louder. At first it had a strange vindictiveness and bloodthirstiness in it. Then it grew mournful as the

* *The Sullivan County Sketches.*

wailing of a lost thing, as, perhaps, the dog gained on a fleeing bear. A hound, as he nears large game, has the griefs of the world on his shoulders, and his baying tells of the approach of death. He is sorry he came.

The long yells thrilled the little man. His eyes gleamed and grew small, and his body stiffened to intense alertness. The trees kept up their crooning, and the light in the west faded to a dull red splash, but the little man's fancy was fixed on the panting, foam-spattered hound, cantering with his hot nose to the ground in the rear of the bear, which runs as easily and as swiftly as a rabbit, through brush, timber, and swale. Swift pictures of himself in a thousand attitudes under a thousand combinations of circumstances, killing a thousand bears, passed panoramically through him.

The yell of the hound grew until it smote the little man like a call to battle. He leaned forward, and the second finger of his right hand played a low, nervous pat-pat on the trigger of his rifle. The baying grew fierce and bloodcurdling for a moment, then the dog seemed to turn directly toward the little man, and the notes again grew wailing and mournful. It was a hot trail.

The little man, with nerves tingling and blood throbbing, remained in the shadows like a fantastic bronze figure with jeweled eyes swaying sharply in its head. Occasionally he thought he could hear the branches of the bushes in front swish together. Then silence would come again.

The hound breasted the crest of the ridge, a third of a mile away, and suddenly his full-toned cry rolled over the tangled thickets to the little man. The bear must be very near. The little man kept so still and listened so tremendously that he could hear his blood surge in his veins. All at once he heard a swish-swish in the bushes. His rifle was at his shoulder and he sighted uncertainly along the front of the thicket. The swish of the bushes grew louder. In the rear the hound was mourning over a warm scent.

The thicket opened and a great bear, indistinct and vague in the shadows, bounded into the little man's view and came terrifically across the open snowfield. The little man stood like an image. The bear did not shamble nor wobble; there was no awkwardness in his gait; he ran like a frightened kitten. It would be an endless chase for the lithe-limbed hound in the rear.

On he came, directly toward the little man. The animal heard only the crying behind him. He knew nothing of the thing with death in its hands standing motionless in the shadows before him.

Slowly the little man changed his aim until it rested where the head of the approaching shadowy mass must be. It was a wee motion, made with steady nerves and a soundless swaying of the rifle barrel; but the bear heard, or saw, and knew. The animal whirled swiftly and started in a new direction with an amazing burst of speed. Its side was toward the little man now. His rifle barrel was searching swiftly over the dark shape. Under the foreshoulder was the place. A chance to pierce the heart, sever an artery, or pass through the lungs. The little man saw swirling fur over his gun barrel. The earth faded to nothing. Only space and the game, the aim and the hunter. Mad emotions, powerful to rock worlds, hurled through the little man, but did not shake his tiniest nerve.

When the rifle cracked, it shook his soul to a profound depth. Creation rocked and the bear stumbled.

The little man sprang forward with a roar. He scrambled hastily in the bear's track. The splash of red, now dim, threw a faint, timid beam of a kindred shade on the snow. The little man bounded in the air.

"Hit!" he yelled, and ran on. Some hundreds of yards forward he came to a dead bear with his nose in the snow. Blood was oozing from a wound under the shoulder, and the snow about was sprinkled with blood. A mad froth lay in the animal's open mouth, and his limbs were twisted from agony.

The little man yelled again and sprang forward, waving his hat as if he were leading the cheering of thousands. He ran up and kicked the ribs of the bear. Upon his face was the smile of the successful lover.

July 31, 1892
[New York *Tribune*, part 2, p. 18.]

THE CAPTAIN

He is the skipper of a catboat and a member of the village fire department. He always wears two uniforms, to be prepared for an emergency. When he goes to a fire he wears his yachting dress; when he is in command of his gallant ship, the *Anna*, he still wears his fire department uniform. The uniform which marks him as the skipper of the *Anna* is a straw hat—a most wonderful straw hat, of sunburned yellow, with a rusty ribbon around it and a piece of twine, a peak-halyard, so to speak, running from it to a buttonhole of his coat. That is all there is to the uniform of the commander. But as for the uniform of the fireman that is a different thing. He wears it on his left breast; it is shield-shaped, it is of tin, and on it are red letters designating the name of his engine company. That is all there is of it, but it is quite enough. He is a thin man with a mustache that may be gray from salt encrustation, or "windburn," or age. At any rate it is gray and if it is not handsome it is at least a mustache. As for the rest of his face his cheek, if you speak of him as the commander of a vessel, is weather-beaten; if as the member of a fire department, burned—you might almost say scorched. His name—perhaps it is Maltravers; perhaps it is De Courcey; perhaps it is only Smith, or Jones, but whatever it is he is first, last and all the time "the Captain."

The Captain is a wit. His wit does not cut or even sparkle. It isn't that kind of wit. It's too dignified. It comes on slowly, to preserve the nautical connection of this sketch, with a full spread of canvas, but making little headway. It does not come about, or tack or reef, or do anything else that a racing yacht in command of a young and ambitious captain might be expected to do. His wit just runs slowly before the wind, comes into collision with you in a dull, heavy fashion, swings clear and drifts away until the sails fill again.

It is a most remarkable and mysterious wit, expressed at regular intervals and in a long drawl. You have to take in sail generally to meet it, for if you are bowling along you will cross the bows; there will not be any collision; you will not feel the bump of its square bows and—you will not know that you have been cruising in the same waters with the Captain's wit.

The wind is blowing freshly up the sound. The sky is as clear as the hollow of a bluebell. The water has that dark sparkle, which is neither green nor blue nor black—the flash of a darkly tinted jewel. The breeze throws thin wafers off the crests of the waves and tosses them lightly against your cheek, cool and damp and refreshing, like the spray of violet water. There is not a mark in the sweep of the sky. There is not a shadow on the swinging water of the Sound, save the dancing reflection of the *Anna's* sail. There is only clearness in the air, and the wind comes up between the green shores with freshening force.

"Captain," says the young woman from Baltimore, the young woman with a soft voice and the slightest Southern accent, "is a squall coming?"

The Captain, without the quiver of a muscle, with no gleam in his watery eye, with no play around the corner of his mouth, looks up at his peak, glances down the Sound, off to the east, up to the peak again, and then takes a tighter hold on his tiller. For a moment he is thoughtful, and then he breaks the trying silence.

"Yes, Miss," he says, in his fearfully long drawl, "there is."

"Oh!" cries the Baltimore girl, "I'm so glad. From which direction is it coming?"

The Captain looks up and studies the top of his mast.

"It's coming," he says, with agonizing deliberation, "from my house. My baby ain't missed a chance to squall in three months!"

Then the Baltimore girl gives a little laugh, a pretty enough laugh to win any man's approval, and says: "Captain, what a fine sailor you are, to be sure!"

"I was raised on the water," says the Captain solemnly.

"That is a handsome badge you have, Captain," says the young woman from Philadelphia. "May I look at it?"

The Captain gives a startled glance, unpins the clasp slowly, hands over his fire department uniform in a pained, doubtful way, and anxiously watches her turn it over in her hand.

"It's handsome," she says.

"It's pretty likely," he answers, with pardonable pride.

"And do you go to fires?"

"Always when I'm ashore."

"Captain," with the most marked admiration for his greatness, "did you ever put out a fire?"

"No-o-o," with his magnificent drawl.

"Why?"

"Always git there too late."

Then comes a long pause, in which the uniform is returned to the member of the fire department.

"And I never started a fire either," says the captain after a silence on his part for five minutes.

"How is that, Captain?"

"I mean never since I was married," he replies. "She—my wife—does that," and a faint smile cracks his dry cheeks.

The wind is strong enough now to make the boat leap like a racehorse. She occasionally takes a dive and throws bucketfuls of water on the deck. Every one is getting wet. The young woman from New York gets fairly drenched over the shoulders and head. Perhaps it is because she has pretty hair; perhaps it is because no woman likes to have her hair soaked in salt water; but, however that may be, she unfastens her hair and it tumbles about her shoulders, a mass of dark brown, with threads of it blown across her cheek and throat and drops glistening where the water in the dark curls is struck by the slanting sun.

"How do I look, Captain," she asks, putting her elbows on her knees and laying a hand on each cheek so that she can lean forward and look into his face with dark, flashing, and tantalizing eyes.

"Look like the gypsies that camp in the woods back of our house," he says, carefully measuring his words.

"They're pretty, aren't they?" asks the 'smart young man' from nowhere.

"Well," answers the captain-fireman cautiously, "they're wild, you know."

Then the young woman thinks that her hair is dry and puts it up again.

"What do you think of it now, Captain?" she asks.

No answer.

"What do you think of my hair now, Captain?" she repeats.

The Captain looks up and glances at his host.

"You done pretty well," he says.

"You like it then!"

"Oh, ye-e-s, I like it. I ain't h-a-a-rd to please."

The Baltimore girl thinks she would like to fish and asks the Captain with her most fascinating accent, just touched with her Southern softness, if she may.

"Yes," says the son of the sea, "take that boat hook and that piece of string. Then put a bent pin on the string and fish."

"What do you think I'll catch?" she says, flashing a bewildering smile on him.

"Well," he answers in a low voice, but with ineffable scorn, "you might catch some of those young men. Ain't any of 'em heavy enough to break your line."

The *Anna* is in the harbor now and every one is getting ready to go ashore in the small boats.

"Good-bye, Captain," says the Philadelphia girl, "I hope we can go out again tomorrow."

The party is in the small boats and halfway to shore, so that in the twilight on his craft as he moves about the deck, the Captain looks like a phantom sailor. Then he places his hand to his mouth and halloos with his comfortable drawl.

"Oh, Miss," he cries out. His voice, coming across the now still air as the oars strike the smooth waters of the harbor, is pleasing in its tones and fulness. "Oh, Miss, there'll be two squalls tomorrow, one up to the house, one out on the Sound," and his chuckle, which comes floating after the echo of his words, smacks of the sea and its freshness.

August 7, 1892

[New York *Tribune*, part 2, p. 19.]

A TENT IN AGONY*

Four men once came to a wet place in the roadless forest to fish. They pitched their tent fair upon the brow of a pine-clothed ridge of riven rocks whence a boulder could be made to crash through the brush and whirl past the trees to the lake below. On fragrant hemlock boughs they slept the sleep of unsuccessful fishermen, for upon the lake alternately the sun made them lazy and the rain made them wet. Finally they ate the last bit of bacon and smoked and burned the last fearful and wonderful hoecake.

Immediately a little man volunteered to stay and hold the camp while the remaining three should go the Sullivan county miles to a farmhouse for supplies. They gazed at him dismally. "There's only one of you—the devil make a twin," they said in parting malediction, and disappeared down the hill in the known direction of a distant cabin. When it came night and the hemlocks began to sob, they had not returned. The little man sat close to his companion, the campfire, and encouraged it with logs. He puffed fiercely at a heavily-built brier, and regarded a thousand shadows which were about to assault him. Suddenly he heard the approach of the un-known, crackling the twigs and rustling the dead leaves. The little man arose slowly to his feet; his clothes refused to fit his back; his pipe dropped from his mouth; his knees smote each other. "Hah!" he bellowed hoarsely in menace. A growl replied, and a bear paced into the light of the fire. The little man supported himself upon a sapling and regarded his visitor.

The bear was evidently a veteran and a fighter, for the black of his coat had become tawny with age. There was confidence in his gait and arro-gance in his small, twinkling eyes. He rolled back his lips and disclosed his white teeth. The fire magnified the red of his mouth. The little man had never before confronted the terrible, and he could not wrest it from his breast. "Hah!" he roared. The bear interpreted this as the challenge of a gladiator. He approached warily. As he came near, the boots of fear were suddenly upon the little man's feet. He cried out and then darted around the campfire. "Ho!" said the bear to himself, "this thing won't fight—it runs. Well, suppose I catch it." So upon his features there fixed the animal look of going—somewhere. He started intensely around the campfire. The little man shrieked and ran furiously. Twice around they went.

The hand of heaven sometimes falls heavily upon the righteous. The bear gained.

The Sullivan County Sketches.

In desperation the little man flew into the tent. The bear stopped and sniffed at the entrance. He scented the scent of many men. Finally he ventured in.

The little man crouched in a distant corner. The bear advanced, creeping, his blood burning, his hair erect, his jowls dripping. The little man yelled and rustled clumsily under the flap at the end of the tent. The bear snarled awfully and made a jump and a grab at his disappearing game. The little man, now without the tent, felt a tremendous paw grab his coattails. He squirmed and wriggled out of his coat, like a schoolboy in the hands of an avenger. The bear howled triumphantly and jerked the coat into the tent and took two bites, a punch, and a hug before he discovered his man was not in it. Then he grew not very angry, for a bear on a spree is not a black-haired pirate. He is merely a hoodlum. He lay down on his back, took the coat on his four paws and began to play uproariously with it. The most appalling, bloodcurdling whoops and yells came to where the little man was crying in a treetop and froze his blood. He moaned a little speech meant for a prayer and clung convulsively to the bending branches. He gazed with tearful wistfulness at where his comrade, the campfire, was giving dying flickers and crackles. Finally, there was a roar from the tent which eclipsed all roars; a snarl which it seemed would shake the stolid silence of the mountain and cause it to shrug its granite shoulders. The little man quaked and shriveled to a grip and a pair of eyes. In the glow of the embers he saw the white tent quiver and fall with a crash. The bear's merry play had disturbed the center-pole and brought a chaos of canvas about his head.

Now the little man became the witness of a mighty scene. The tent began to flounder. It took flopping strides in the direction of the lake. Marvelous sounds came from within—rips and tears, and great groans and pants. The little man went into giggling hysterics.

The entangled monster failed to extricate himself before he had frenziedly walloped the tent to the edge of the mountain. So it came to pass that three men, clambering up the hill with bundles and baskets, saw their tent approaching.

It seemed to them like a white-robed phantom pursued by hornets. Its moans riffled the hemlock twigs.

The three men dropped their bundles and scurried to one side, their eyes gleaming with fear. The canvas avalanche swept past them. They leaned, faint and dumb, against trees and listened, their blood stagnant. Below them it struck the base of a great pine tree, where it writhed and struggled. The three watched its convolutions a moment and then started terrifically for the top of the hill. As they disappeared, the bear cut loose with a mighty effort. He cast one disheveled and agonized look at the white thing, and then started wildly for the inner recesses of the forest. The three fear-stricken individuals ran to the rebuilt fire. The little man reposed by it calmly smoking. They sprang at him and overwhelmed him with interrogations. He contemplated darkness and took a long, pompous puff. "There's only one of me—and the devil made a twin," he said.

December, 1892

[*The Cosmopolitan*, Vol. 14, pp. 241–244.]

THE CRY OF A HUCKLEBERRY PUDDING*

A DIM STUDY OF CAMPING EXPERIENCES

A great blaze wavered redly against the blackness of the night in the pines. Before the eyes of his expectant companions, a little man moved with stately dignity as the creator of a huckleberry pudding.

"I know how to make'm," he said in a confident voice, "just exactly right."

The others looked at him with admiration as they sat down to eat.

After a time, a pudgy man whose spoon was silent, said: "I don't like this much."

"What?" cried the little man, threateningly.

"I don't seem to get on with it," said the pudgy man. He looked about for support in the faces of his companions. "I don't like it, somehow," he added slowly.

"Fool!" roared the little man, furiously. "You're mad because you didn't make it. I never saw such a beast."

The pudgy man wrapped himself in a great dignity. He glanced suggestingly at the plates of the two others. They were intact.

"Ho," cried the little man, "you're all idiots."

He saw that he must vindicate his work. He must eat it. He sat before them and, with ineffable bliss lighting his countenance, ate all of the huckleberry pudding. Then he laid aside his plate, lighted his pipe, and addressed his companions as unappreciative blockheads.

The pipe, the fire, and the song of the pines soothed him after a time, and he puffed tranquilly. The four men sat staring vacantly at the blaze until the spirits of the tent at the edge of the fire circle, in drowsy voices, began to call them. Their thoughts became heavily fixed on the knee-deep bed of hemlock. One by one they arose, knocked ashes from their pipes, and treading softly to the open flaps, disappeared. Alone, the camp-

* *The Sullivan County Sketches.*

fire spluttered valiantly for a time, opposing its music to the dismal crooning of the trees that accented the absence of things congenial and alive. A curious moon peered through locked branches at imperturbable bundles of blankets which lay in the shadows of the tent.

The fragrant blackness of the early night passed away, and gray ghostmists came winding slowly up from the marshes and stole among the wet tree trunks. Wavering leaves dotted with dewdrops glowed in a halflight of impending dawn. From the tent came sounds of heavy sleeping. The bundles of blankets clustered on the hemlock twigs.

Suddenly from off in the thickets of the gloom, there came a cry. It seemed to crash on the tent. It smote the bundles of blankets. There was instant profound agitation, a whirling chaos of coverings, legs, and arms; then, heads appeared. The men had heard the voice of the unknown, crying in the wilderness, and it made their souls quaver.

They had slumbered through the trees' song of loneliness and the lay of isolation of the mountain grass. Hidden frogs had muttered ominously since nightfall, and distant owls, undoubtedly perched on lofty branches and silhouetted by the moon, had hooted. There had been an endless hymning by leaves, blades, and unseen live things, through which these men, who adored Wagner, had slept.

But a false note in the sounds of night had convulsed them. A strange tune had made them writhe.

The cry of the unknown instantly awoke them to terror. It is mightier than the war yell of the dreadful, because the dreadful may be definite. But this whoop strikes greater fear from hearts because it tells of formidable mouths and great, grasping claws that live in impossibility. It is the chant of a phantom force which imagination declares invincible, and awful to the sight.

In the tent, eyes aglitter with terror gazed into eyes. Knees softly smote each other, and lips trembled.

The pudgy man gave vent to a tremendous question. "What was that?" he whispered.

The others made answer with their blanched faces. The group, waiting in the silence that followed their awakening, wriggled their legs in the agony of fright. There was a pause which extended through space. Comets hung and worlds waited. Their thoughts shot back to that moment when they had started upon the trip, and they were filled with regret that it had been.

"Oh, goodness, what was that?" repeated the pudgy man, intensely.

Suddenly, their faces twitched and their fingers turned to wax. The cry was repeated. Its burden caused the men to huddle together like drowning kittens. They watched the banshees of the fog drifting lazily among the trees. They saw eyes in the gray obscurity. They heard a thousand approaching footfalls in the rustling of the dead leaves. They groveled.

Then, they heard the unknown stride to and fro in the forest, giving calls, weighted with challenge, that could make cities hearing, fear. Roars went to the ends of earth, and snarls that would appall armies turned the men in the tent to a moaning mass with forty eyes. The challenges changed to wailings as of a fever-torn soul. Later, there came snorts of anger that sounded cruel, like the noise of a rampant bull on a babies' playground. Later still, howls, as from an abandoned being, strangling in the waters of trouble.

"Great Scott!" roared the pudgy man, "I can't stand this."

He wriggled to his feet and tottered out to the dying fire. His companions followed. They had reached the cellar of fear. They were now resolved to use weapons on the great destruction. They would combat the inevitable. They peered among the trees, wherefrom a hundred assaulting shadows came. The unknown was shrieking.

Of a sudden, the pudgy man screamed like a wounded animal.

"It's got Billie," he howled. They discovered that the little man was gone.

To listen or to wait is the most tense of occupations. In their absorption they had not seen that a comrade was missing.

Instantly, their imaginations perceived his form in the clutch of a raging beast.

"Come on," shouted the pudgy man. They grasped bludgeons and rushed valiantly into the darkness. They stumbled from gloom to gloom in a mad rush for their friend's life. The keynote of terror kept clanging in their ears and guided their scrambling feet. Tangled thickets tripped them. Saplings buffeted heroically, and stones turned away. Branches smote their heads so that it appeared as if lightning had flapped its red wings in their faces.

Once, the pudgy man stopped. The unknown was just ahead.

The dim lights of early dawn came charging through the forest. The gray and black of mist and shadow retreated before crimson beams that had advanced to the treetops.

The men came to a stand, waving their heads to glance down the aisles of the wilderness.

"There he is," shouted the pudgy man. The party, rushing forward, came upon the form of the little man, quivering at the foot of a tree. His blood seemed to be turned to salt. From out his wan, white face his eyes shone with a blue light. "Oh, thunderation," he moaned. "Oh, thunderation."

"What!" cried his friends. Their voices shook with anxiety.

"Oh, thunderation," repeated he.

"For the love of Mike, tell us, Billie," cried the pudgy man, "what is the matter."

"Oh, thunderation," wailed the little man. Suddenly he rolled about on the ground and gave vent to a howl that rolled and pealed over the width of the forest. Its tones told of death and fear and unpaid debts. It clamored like a song of forgotten war, and died away to the scream of a maiden. The pleadings of fire-surrounded children mingled with the calls of wave-threatened sailors. Two barbaric tribes clashed together on a sunburnt plain; a score of barekneed clansmen crossed claymores amid gray rocks; a woman saw a lover fall; a dog was stabbed in an alley; a steel knight bit dust with bloody mouth; a savage saw a burning home.

The rescuing party leaned weakly against trees. After the little man had concluded, there was a silence.

Finally, the pudgy man advanced. He struggled with his astonished tongue for a moment. "Do you mean to say, Billie," he said at last, "that all that tangled chaos emanated from you?"

The little man made no reply, but heaved about on the ground, moaning: "Oh, thunderation."

The three men contemplating him suddenly felt themselves swell with wrath. They had been terrorized to no purpose. They had expected to be eaten. They were not. The fact maddened them. The pudgy man voiced the assembly.

"You infernal little jay, get up off'n the ground and come on," he cried. "You make me sick."

"Oh, thunderation," replied the little man.

The three men began to berate him. They turned into a babble of wrath.

"You scared us to death."

"What do you wanta holler that way for?"

"You're a bloomin' nuisance. For heaven's sake, what are you yellin' about?"

The little man staggered to his feet. Anger took hold of him. He waved his arms eloquently.

"That pudding, you fools," he cried.

His companions paused and regarded him.

"Well," said the pudgy man, eventually, "what in blazes did you eat it for then?"

"Well, I didn't know," roared the other, "I didn't know that it was that way."

"You shouldn't have eaten it, anyhow. There was the sin. You shouldn't have eaten it anyway."

"But I didn't know," shouted the little man.

"You should have known," they stormed. "You've made idiots of us. You scared us to death with your hollerin'."

As he reeled toward the camp, they followed him, railing like fishwives. The little man turned at bay.

"Exaggerated fools," he yelled. "Fools, to apply no salve but moral teaching to a man with the stomachache."

December 23, 1892

[*The University Herald*, Syracuse, New York, Vol. 21, pp. 51–54.]

AN EXPLOSION OF SEVEN BABIES*

A SULLIVAN COUNTY EPISODE

A little man was sweating and swearing his way through an intricate forest. His hat was pushed indignantly to the far rear of his head, and upon his perspiring features there was a look of conscious injury.

Suddenly he perceived ahead of him a high stone wall against which waves of bushes surged. The little man fought his way to the wall and looked over it.

A brown giantess was working in a potato patch. Upon a bench, under the eaves of a worn-out house, seven babies were wailing and rubbing their stomachs.

"Ho!" said the little man to himself. He stood, observant, for a few moments. Then he climbed painfully over the wall and came to a stand in the potato patch. His eyes wandered to the seven babies wailing and rubbing their stomachs. Their mournful music fascinated him.

"Madam," he said, as he took off his hat and bowed, "I have unfortunately lost my way. Could you direct—" He suddenly concluded: "Great Scott!"

He had turned his eyes from the seven babies to the brown giantess and saw upon her face the glare of a tigress. Her fingers were playing convulsively over her hoe handle, and the muscles of her throat were swollen and wriggling. Her eyes were glowing with fury. She came forward with the creeping motion of an animal about to spring.

The little man gave a backward leap. Tremendous astonishment enwrapped him and trepidation showed in his legs.

"G-good heavens, madam," he stuttered. He threw up one knee and held

* *The Sullivan County Sketches.*

his spread fingers before his face. His mouth was puckered to an amazed whistle.

The giantess stood before him, her hands upon her hips, her lips curled in a snarl. She followed closely as the little man retreated backward step by step toward the fence, his eyes staring in bewilderment.

"For the love of Mike, madam, what ails you?" he spluttered. He saw here an avenger. Wherefore he knew not, but he momentarily expected to be smitten to a pulp.

"Beast!" roared the giantess, suddenly. She reached forth and grasped the arm of the palsied little man, who cast a despairing glance at the high stone wall.

She twisted him about and then, raising a massive arm, pointed to the row of seven babies, who, as if they had gotten a cue, burst out like a brass band.

"Well, what the devil—" roared the little man.

"Beast!" howled the giantess. "It made'm sick! They ate ut! That dum flypaper!"

The babies began to frantically beat their stomachs with their fists.

"Villain!" shrieked the giantess. The little man felt the winding fingers crush the flesh and bones of his arm. The giantess began to roar like a dragon. She bent over and braced herself. Then her iron arms forced the little man to his knees.

He knew he was going to be eaten. "Gawd," he moaned.

He arrived at the critical stage of degradation. He would resist. He touched some hidden spring in his being and went off like a firework. The man became a tumult. Every muscle in his body he made perform a wriggling contortion. The giantess plunged forward and kneaded him as if he were bread unbaked.

From over the stone wall came the swishing sound of moving bushes, unheard by the combatants. Presently the face of a pudgy man, tranquil in its wrinkles, appeared. Amazement instantly smote him in his tracks and he hung heavily to the stones.

From the potato patch arose a cloud of dust, pregnant with curses. In it he could dimly see the little man in a state of revolution. His legs flashed in the air like a pinwheel. The pudgy man stared with gleaming eyes at the kaleidoscope. He climbed upon the wall to get a better view. Some bellowing animal seemed to have his friend in its claws.

It soon became evident to the little man that he could not eternally revolve and kick in such a manner. He felt his blood begin to dry up and his muscles turn to paste. Those talons were squeezing his life away. His mangled arms were turning weak. He was about to be subdued.

But here the pudgy man, in his excitement, performed the feat of his life. He fell off the wall, giving an involuntary shout, and landed with a flop in the potato patch.

The brown giantess snarled. She hurled the little man from her and turned, with a toss of her disheveled locks, to face a new foe. The pudgy man quaked miserably and yelled an unintelligible explanation or apology or prayer. The brow of the giantess was black, and she strode with ferocious menace toward him.

The little man had fallen in a chaotic mass among the potato hills. He struggled to his feet. Somehow, his blood was hot in his veins, and he started to bristle courageously in reinforcement of his friend. But suddenly he changed his mind and made off at a high speed, leaving the pudgy man to his fate.

His unchosen course lay directly toward the seven babies who, in their anxiety to view the combat, had risen from the bench and were standing ready as a Roman populace to signify the little man's death by rubbing their stomachs. Intent upon the struggle, they had forgotten to howl.

But when they perceived the headlong charge of the little man, they, as a unit, exploded. It was like the sudden clang of an alarm bell to the giantess. She wheeled from the pudgy man, who climbed the wall, fell off in his haste into the bushes on the other side, and, later, allowed but the top of his head to appear over the top of it.

The giantess perceived the little man about to assault her seven babies, whose mouths were in a state of eruption. She howled, grabbed a hoe from the ground, and pursued.

The little man shied from the protesting babies and ran like a greyhound. He flung himself over a high fence. Then he waited. Curiosity held him. He had been mopped and dragged, punched and pounded, bitten and scratched. He wished to know why.

The brown giantess, mad with rage, crashed against the fence. She shook her huge fist at the little man.

"Drat yeh!" she roared.

She began to climb the fence. It is not well to behold a woman climb a fence. The little man yelled and ran off.

He stumbled and fell through a brush lot, and bounced terrifically into the woods. As he halted to get breath, he heard, above the sound of the wind laughing in the trees, a final explosion by the seven babies, as, perhaps, they perceived the brown giantess returning empty-handed to the worn-out house.

As the little man went on into the woods, he perceived a crouching figure with terror-gleaming eyes. He whistled and drew near it. Directly, the little man, bedraggled, dirt-stained, bloody, and amazed, confronted the pudgy man, perspiring, limp, dust-covered, and astonished. They gazed at each other profoundly.

Finally the little man broke the silence.

"Devilish mysterious business," he said, slowly. The pudgy man had a thousand questions in his eyes.

"What in Heaven's name, Billie—" he blurted.

The little man waved his hand. "Don't ask me. I don't know anything about it."

"What?"

"No more'n a rabbit. She said something about flypaper and the kids, that's all I know."

The pudgy man drew a long breath. "Great Lord," he said. They sat down on a log and thought.

At last, the little man got up and yawned. "I can't make head nor tail of the bloomin' business," he said, wearily. They walked slowly off through the day-gloom of the woods. "I wish she hadn't called me a beast. I didn't like that," added the little man, musingly, after a time.

In a shady spot on a highway, they found their two companions, who were lazily listening to a short stranger who was holding forth at some length and with apparent enthusiasm. At the approach of the little man and the pudgy man, the short man turned to them with a smile.

"Gentlemen," he said, "I have here a wonder of the age, which I wish to present to your intelligent notice. Smither's Eternal Fly Annihilating Paper is—"

The little man frothed at the mouth and cursed. Before his comrades could intervene he sprang forward and kicked the short man heavily in the stomach.

1892?

[*The Home Magazine,* Vol. 16 (January, 1901), pp. 77–80.]

THE MESMERIC MOUNTAIN*

A TALE OF SULLIVAN COUNTY

On the brow of a pine-plumed hillock there sat a little man with his back against a tree. A venerable pipe hung from his mouth, and smoke-wreaths curled slowly skyward. He was muttering to himself with his eyes fixed on an irregular black opening in the green wall of forest at the foot of the

---

* *The Sullivan County Sketches.*

hill. Two vague wagon ruts led into the shadows. The little man took his pipe in his hands and addressed the listening pines.

"I wonder what the devil it leads to," said he.

A gray, fat rabbit came lazily from a thicket and sat in the opening. Softly stroking his stomach with his paw, he looked at the little man in a thoughtful manner. The little man threw a stone, and the rabbit blinked and ran through an opening. Green, shadowy portals seemed to close behind him.

The little man started. "He's gone down that roadway," he said, with ecstatic mystery, to the pines. He sat a long time and contemplated the door to the forest. Finally, he arose, and awakening his limbs, started away. But he stopped and looked back.

"I can't imagine what it leads to," muttered he. He trudged over the brown mats of pine needles to where, in a fringe of laurel, a tent was pitched and merry flames caroused about some logs. A pudgy man was fuming over a collection of tin dishes. He came forward and waved a plate furiously in the little man's face.

"I've washed the dishes for three days. What do you think I am—" He ended a red oration with a roar: "Damned if I do it any more."

The little man gazed dim-eyed away. "I've been wonderin' what it leads to."

"What?"

"That road out yonder. I've been wonderin' what it leads to. Maybe some discovery or something," said the little man.

The pudgy man laughed. "You're an idiot. It leads to ol' Jim Boyd's over on the Lumberland Pike."

"Ho!" said the little man, "I don't believe that."

The pudgy man swore. "Fool, what does it lead to, then?"

"I don't know just what, but I'm sure it leads to something great or something. It looks like it."

While the pudgy man was cursing, two more men came from obscurity with fish dangling from birch twigs. The pudgy man made an obviously herculean struggle, and a meal was prepared. As he was drinking his cup of coffee, he suddenly spilled it and swore. The little man was wandering off.

"He's gone to look at that hole," cried the pudgy man.

The little man went to the edge of the pine-plumed hillock and, sitting down, began to make smoke and regard the door to the forest. There was stillness for an hour. Compact clouds hung unstirred in the sky. The pines stood motionless, and pondering.

Suddenly the little man slapped his knee and bit his tongue. He stood up and determinedly filled his pipe, rolling his eye over the bowl to the doorway. Keeping his eyes fixed, he slid dangerously to the foot of the hillock and walked down the wagon ruts. A moment later he passed from the noise of the sunshine to the gloom of the woods.

The green portals closed, shutting out live things. The little man trudged on alone.

Tall tangled grass grew in the roadway, and the trees bent obstructing branches. The little man followed on over pine-clothed ridges and down through water-soaked swales. His shoes were cut by rocks of the mountains, and he sank ankle-deep in mud and moss of swamps. A curve just ahead lured him miles.

Finally, as he wended the side of a ridge, the road disappeared from beneath his feet. He battled with hordes of ignorant bushes on his way to knolls and solitary trees which invited him. Once he came to a tall, bearded pine. He climbed it, and perceived in the distance a peak. He uttered an ejaculation and fell out.

He scrambled to his feet and said: "That's Jones's Mountain, I guess. It's about six miles from our camp as the crow flies."

He changed his course away from the mountain, and attacked the bushes again. He climbed over great logs, golden-brown in decay, and was opposed by thickets of dark-green laurel. A brook slid through the ooze of a swamp; cedars and hemlocks hung their sprays to the edges of pools.

The little man began to stagger in his walk. After a time he stopped and mopped his brow.

"My legs are about to shrivel up and drop off," he said. ". . . Still, if I keep on in this direction, I am safe to strike the Lumberland Pike before sundown."

He dived at a clump of tag-alders and, emerging, confronted Jones's Mountain.

The wanderer sat down in a clear place and fixed his eyes on the summit. His mouth opened widely, and his body swayed at times. The little man and the peak stared in silence.

A lazy lake lay asleep near the foot of the mountain. In its bed of watergrass some frogs leered at the sky and crooned. The sun sank in red silence, and the shadows of the pines grew formidable. The expectant hush of evening, as if something were going to sing a hymn, fell upon the peak and the little man.

A leaping pickerel off on the water created a silver circle that was lost in black shadows. The little man shook himself and started to his feet, crying: "For the love of Mike, there's eyes in this mountain! I feel 'em! Eyes!"

He fell on his face.

When he looked again, he immediately sprang erect and ran.

"It's comin'!"

The mountain was approaching.

The little man scurried, sobbing, through the thick growth. He felt his brain turning to water. He vanquished brambles with mighty bounds. But after a time he came again to the foot of the mountain.

"God!" he howled, "it's been follerin' me." He groveled. Casting his eyes upward made circles swirl in his blood. "I'm shackled, I guess," he moaned.

As he felt the heel of the mountain about to crush his head, he sprang again to his feet. He grasped a handful of small stones and hurled them. "Damn you!" he shrieked loudly. The pebbles rang against the face of the mountain.

The little man then made an attack. He climbed with hands and feet wildly. Brambles forced him back and stones slid from beneath his feet. The peak swayed and tottered, and was ever about to smite with a granite arm. The summit was a blaze of red wrath.

But the little man at last reached the top. Immediately, he swaggered with valor to the edge of the cliff. His hands were scornfully in his pockets.

He gazed at the western horizon, edged sharply against a yellow sky. "Ho!" he said. "There's Boyd's house and the Lumberland Pike."

The mountain under his feet was motionless.

1892?

[*Last Words*. London: Digby, Long & Co. (March, 1902), pp. 225–230.]

THE HOLLER TREE*

A SULLIVAN COUNTY SKETCH

As they went along a narrow woodpath, the little man accidentally stumbled against the pudgy man. The latter was carrying a basket of eggs, and he became angry.

"Look out, can't you! Do you wanta break all these eggs? Walk straight —what's the matter with you?" he said and passed on.

The little man saved his balance with difficulty. He had to keep from spilling a pail of milk. "T'blazes with your old eggs," he called out.

The pudgy man spoke over his shoulder. "Well, you needn't have any when we get to camp, then," he said.

"Who wants any of your infernal old eggs. Keep your infernal old eggs," replied the little man.

* *The Sullivan County Sketches.*

The four men trudged on into the forest until presently the little man espied a dead tree. He paused. "Look at that tree," he said.

They scrutinized it. It was a tall, gaunt relic of a pine that stood like a yellow warrior still opposing an aged form to blows in storm-battles.

"I bet it's got lots of nests in it and all sorts of things like that," murmured the little man. The pudgy man scoffed. "Oh, fudge," he said.

"Well, I bet it has," asserted the other.

The four men put down their loads of provisions and stood around and argued.

"Yes, I bet it's a cornerstone with an almanac in it and a census report and a certified list of the pew-holders," said the pudgy man to the little man.

The latter swore for some time. "Put up even money," he demanded in conclusion. "Put up even money."

"Look out—you'll kick over the eggs," replied the pudgy man.

"Well, put up even money. You daren't."

The pudgy man scornfully kicked a stone. "Oh, fudge. How you going to prove it? Tell me that."

The little man thought. "Well," he said, eventually, "I'll climb up. That's how."

The pudgy man looked at the tree and at the little man. He thought. "I'll cover you," he suddenly decided.

The little man laid down his pipe, tightened his belt, and went off and looked at the tree.

"Well—" he began, coming back.

"Go on and climb it," said the pudgy man. "You said you'd climb it." The little man went off and looked at the tree again. "Well, I will," he said, finally. The pudgy man giggled. The little man tightened his belt more. He approached and put both arms around the tree.

"Say," he said, turning round. "You—I—"

"Go on and climb it," interrupted the pudgy man. "You said you'd climb it."

The little man began to climb schoolboy fashion. He found many difficulties. The wood crumbled and rubbed into his clothes. He felt smeared. Besides, there was a horrible strain upon his legs.

When about halfway, he ceased wriggling and turned his head cautiously. "Say—"

The three men had been regarding him intently. They then burst out. "Go on! Go on! You've got that far—what's the use of stopping? I believe you're gettin' scared! Oh, my!"

He swore and continued up. Several times he seemed about to fall in a lump. The three below held their breath.

Once, he paused to deliver an oration and forgot his grip for a moment. It was near being fatal.

At last, he reached the top. "Well?" said the pudgy man. The little man gazed about him. There was a somber sea of pines, rippling in a wind. Far away, there was a little house, and two yellow fields.

"Fine scenery up here," he murmured.

"Oh, bother," said the pudgy man. "Where's your nests and all that? That's what I wanta know."

The little man peered down the hollow trunk. "They're in there."

The pudgy man grinned. "How do you know?"

The little man looked down the hole again. "It's all dark," he said.

The pudgy man complacently lit a fresh pipe. "Certainly, it is," he remarked. "You look great up there, don't you? What you goin' to do now, eh?"

The little man balanced himself carefully on the ragged edge and looked thoughtfully at the hole. "Well, I might slide down," he said in a doubtful voice.

"That's it," cried the other. "That's what you wanta do! Slide down!"

"Well," said the little man, "it looks pretty dangerous."

"Oh, I see! You're afraid!"

"I ain't!"

"Yes, you are, too! Else why don't you slide down?"

"Well, how th' devil do I know but what something's down there?" shouted the little man in a rage.

His companion replied with scorn. "Pooh! Nothin' but a hollow tree! You're afraid of the dark!"

"You must take me for a fool! What th' blazes do I wanta be slidin' down every hollow tree I see for?"

"Well, you climbed up, didn't you? What are you up there for? You can't find your little nests and things just settin' there an' cursin', can you? You're afraid, I bet!"

"You make—"

"Oh, yes, you are. You know you are."

The little man flung his legs over and slid down until only his head and his gripping fingers appeared. He seemed to be feeling about with his feet.

"There's nothing to climb down with," he said, finally.

"Certainly not. Did you hope for a stairway? You're afraid."

The little man's face flushed and his eyes grew like beads. He glared from out of the hole.

"I am not, you big—"

"Oh, yes, you are. Anyone can see it."

"Thunderation, you're th'—"

"Oh, come, Billie, either climb down th' outside or slide down th' inside. There's no use of you sittin' up there, you know, if you ain't going to do something. You're afraid, that's what."

"I tell you I ain't. What th' devil—?"

"Oh, yes, you are, too. You're pale with fright, Billie. We can see it down here. Oh, my! I'm surprised."

The little man raised a fist. "Thunder and blazes—"

He vanished down the hole.

The wood had crumbled and broken under the strain of the one hand. Hollow sounds of scratchings and thumpings came to the ears of his three companions. In agitation they ran about the vibrating trunk and called to their comrade in many voices. They were fearful he had met his time.

Presently, they heard a muffled noise of swearing. They listened. Down near the ground, the little man was cursing under forced draft. The old tree shook like a smokestack.

The pudgy man approached and put near his ear.

"Billie!"

"What?"

"Are you inside the tree?"

The little man began to kick and clamor. His voice came in a dull roar. "Certainly I'm inside the tree. Where th' devil did you suppose I was? What th'—?"

His voice died away in smothered thunder.

"Well, but, Billie," asked the pudgy man anxiously, "how you going to get out?"

The little man began to rage again. "What a fool you are. I don't know how I'm going to get out. Don't suppose I've got plans made already, do you?"

"Well, I guess you'll have to climb," mused the pudgy man. "That's the only way, and you can't stay in there forever, you know."

The little man made some efforts. There was a sound of rending clothes. Presently he ceased.

"It's no go," he announced.

The three men sat down and debated upon theories.

Finally the little man began to roar at them and kick his prison wall. "Think I wanta stay in here while you fellows hold arguments for a couple of hours? Why th' thunder don't you do something instead of talking so much? What do you think I am anyway?"

The pudgy man approached the tree. "You might as well keep quiet," he said in a grim voice. "You're in there and you might as well keep quiet—"

The little man began to swear.

"Stop your howling," angrily cried the pudgy man. "There's no use of howlin'."

"I won't! It's your fault I'm in here. If it hadn't been for you, I wouldn't'a climbed up."

"Well, I didn't make you fall down inside, anyway. You did that yourself."

"I didn't either. You made me tumble, old pudgkins. If you had minded your own business it would have been all right. It's your stupidity that's got me in here."

"It was your own, you little fool. I—"

The little man began to rave and wriggle. The pudgy man went very near to the tree and stormed. They had a furious quarrel. The eloquence of the little man caused some tremors in the tree, and presently it began to sway gently.

Suddenly, the pudgy man screamed. "You're pushin' th' tree over on me." He started away. The trunk trembled, and tottered, and began to fall. It seemed like a mighty blow aimed by the wrathful little man at the head of the fleeing pudgy man.

The latter bounded, light as a puff ball, over the ground. His face was white with terror. He turned an agonized somersault into a thicket, as the tree, with a splintering cry, crashed near his heels. He lay in a bush and trembled.

The little man's legs were wagging plaintively from the other end of the trunk. The two remaining men rushed forward with cries of alarm and began to tug at them. The little man came forth, finally. He was of deep bronze hue from a coating of wet dead wood. A soft bed of it came with him. They helped him to his feet. He felt his shoulders and legs with an air of anxiety. After a time, he rubbed the crumbles from his eyes and began to stagger and swear softly.

Suddenly, he perceived the pudgy man lying pale in the bush. He limped over to him.

The pudgy man was moaning. "Lord, it just missed me by 'bout an inch."

The little man thoughtfully contemplated his companion. Presently, a smile was born at the corner of his mouth and grew until it wreathed his face. The pudgy man cursed in an unhappy vein as he was confronted by the little man's grins.

The latter seemed about to deliver an oration, but, instead, he turned and, picking up his pail of milk, started away. He paused once and looked back. He pointed with his forefinger.

"There's your eggs—under the tree," he said.

He resumed his march down the forest pathway. His stride was that of a proud grenadier.

1892?

[*The Golden Book Magazine*, Vol. 19 (February, 1934), pp. 188–191.]

ACROSS THE COVERED PIT*

The Rev. C. H. Hoovey, D.C. of Connecticut, had the grave and reverent look which betokens his profession. To see the gentleman dressed in shining black in his pulpit on Sunday, one could never imagine that the devout preacher of the gospel was one of the most daring cave explorers in this country. Yet all the noted caverns of this country have been visited by him. No cavern looks so gloomy and forbidding but the doctor feels his boyish spirit of adventure seize him, and he longs to tread its dark mysteries and explore its unknown recesses. The unbroken region beyond the mouth of the Covered Pit in Manmoth Cave was a bugbear to him. To any one's knowledge, the mass of tangled slippery slabs that was heaped over the mouth of the pit, had never been tread on. As authorities had forbidden any one to cross this dangerous place, its strength had never been tested. It might be strong enough to allow a train of cars to cross it, and again, the weight of a cat might cause the whole mass to tumble to the unknown depth. The doctor had been to the edge of the pit several times. He would look at the huge patches of darkness that showed between the slabs which seem to have been thrown loosely over the mouth of the whole by a giant hand, and then glance at the dim outline of a wide tunnel which led along from the other side of the pit.

A wistful look would come into his eyes, as he would wonder about that unknown land. He would speculate for a while on the length and number of caverns and passages contained and then return to his hotel and dream of a large interrogation point framed in the mouth of the dark tunnel. It finally became too much for the doctor, and he attempted to bribe the guides by offering sums which came little short of being fabulous. Not one of them, however, would go with him.

At last, William, the famous colored guide, showed signs of his love of money predominating over his love of life, and the doctor worried the poor darkey until he won his reluctant consent to accompany him. The two provided themselves with the necessary articles and, one day, made their way stealthily along the passages toward the Covered Pit.

* By permission of Alfred A. Knopf, Inc. Hitherto unpublished in book form. Part of *The Sullivan County Sketches*.

The uniqueness of the doctor's scheme is apparent at once. As the authorities had forbidden it, they must steal into the cave without their knowledge and consequently their fate would be unknown. No one would ever know what became of Dr. Hoovey and William. The Covered Pit would withhold its story of the tragedy until the Resurrection Morn. A few pleasant thoughts like these crowded into the doctor's brain as he made his way along the cavern. He was half constrained to turn back and, at least, leave a letter telling where he had gone. He was half minded to turn back, anyhow. But there was William trudging stolidly along ahead of him and the doctor settled his nerves and pushed on.

They arrived at the edge of the pit and stood together trying to pierce the gloom in the openings between the slabs.

"It will make a right big grave," said William contemplating the pit. The doctor started but kept silent.

The two adventurers sat down on a boulder and made deliberate plans covering any casualty that might occur. It was also decided with no indecent haggling whatever that William should go first.

The guide tightened everything about him, and placed his torch in his hat that he might have both hands free.

Getting down on his hands and knees, he commenced to make his way like a cat on very tender ice. It was a moment of supreme suspense to both. The guide's labored breathing was plainly audible as he slowly moved along. The doctor shut his eyes at times and waited with almost a desire, the tension was so terrible, for the sudden grinding noise; then, the awful roar that would announce to him that the covering had fallen. But William's light gleamed on the other side and he was safe. It was now the doctor's turn. William shouted a few directions about the bad places. Then the doctor started. On his hands and knees as the guide had been, the doctor would thrust one hand forward, and finding a firm place, would bring the other one forward. Some of the slabs slanted frightfully and were damp and slippery. The doctor's life depended on the grip of his fingers.

When about halfway across, the doctor's hand loosened a slab ahead of him which had no connection with the structure of the cover but simply lay on one of the others.

With an awful sound the stone slid off the lower slab and plunged down into the pit. The explorer gave himself up for lost. As the movement of the stone was communicated to the slab on which he crouched, he thought he was gone. A second later when the sounds ceased he could hardly believe that he was still on the cover.

The sensations of the poor guide can only be imagined. Let alone the depressing effects on one's spirits that the horrible death of a companion in the bowels of the earth would have, the guide would be in a sorry plight, indeed. With the doctor and the cover at the bottom of the pit, he was alive in his tomb.

His bridge was burned behind him. His only known means of exit was across the covering to the pit, and if the cover broke, William was in a bad way. The darkey's teeth chattered as he heard the sound of the falling slab.

But the torch still flickered out over the pit and began to come nearer and nearer. A few more minutes of suspense and the doctor of divinity and the ignorant guide clutched each other's hands in the most affectionate manner possible.

The explorers proceeded along the tunnel. They were then on ground trod by no man before and the doctor was in his glory. They spent two days in the new regions and had some startling adventures but returned safely across the Covered Pit. When the sunlight beamed on their delighted visions, they looked at each other for a moment without speaking. Then the doctor remarked that he guessed he wouldn't explore any more caves for a while and William said he reckoned he needed a vacation, too.

1892?

[*Bulletin of the New York Public Library,*
Vol. 61 (January, 1957), pp. 39–41.]

WHY DID THE YOUNG CLERK SWEAR?
OR, THE UNSATISFACTORY FRENCH

All was silent in the little gents' furnishing store. A lonely clerk with a blond mustache and a red necktie raised a languid hand to his brow and brushed back a dangling lock. He yawned and gazed gloomily at the blurred panes of the windows.

Without, the wind and rain came swirling round the brick buildings and went sweeping over the streets. A horse-car rumbled stolidly by. In the mud on the pavements, a few pedestrians struggled with excited umbrellas.

"The deuce!" remarked the clerk. "I'd give ten dollars if somebody would come in and buy something, if 'twere only cotton socks."

He waited amid the shadows of the gray afternoon. No customers came. He heaved a long sigh and sat down on a high stool. From beneath a stack of unlaundered shirts he drew a French novel with a picture on the cover. He yawned again, glanced lazily toward the street, and settled himself as comfortable as the gods would let him upon the high stool.

He opened the book and began to read. Soon it could have been noticed that his blond mustache took on a curl of enthusiasm, and the refractory locks on his brow showed symptoms of soft agitation.

"Silvere did not see the young girl for some days," read the clerk. "He was miserable. He seemed always to inhale that subtle perfume from her hair. At night he saw her eyes in the stars.

"His dreams were troubled. He watched the house. Heloise did not appear. One day he met Vibert. Vibert wore a black frock coat. There were wine stains on the right breast. His collar was soiled. He had not shaved.

"Silvere burst into tears. 'I love her! I love her! I shall die!' Vibert laughed scornfully. His necktie was second-hand. Idiotic, this boy in love. Fool! Simpleton! But at last he pitied him. 'She goes to the music teacher's every morning, silly.' Silvere embraced him.

"The next day Silvere waited at the street corner. A vendor was selling chestnuts. Two gamins were fighting in an alley. A woman was scrubbing some steps. This great Paris throbbed with life.

"Heloise came. She did not perceive Silvere. She passed with a happy smile on her face. She looked fresh, fair, innocent. Silvere felt himself swooning. 'Ah, my God!'

"She crossed the street. The young man received a shock that sent the warm blood to his brain. It had been raining. There was mud. With one slender hand Heloise lifted her skirts. Silvere, leaning forward, saw her—"

A young man in a wet mackintosh came into the little gents' furnishing store.

"Ah, beg pardon," said he to the clerk, "but do you have an agency for a steam laundry here? I have been patronizing a Chinaman down th' avenue for some time, but he—what? No? You have none here? Well, why don't you start one, anyhow? It'd be a good thing in this neighborhood. I live just 'round the corner, and it'd be a great thing for me. I know lots of people who would—what? Oh, you don't? Oh!"

As the young man in the wet mackintosh retreated, the clerk with a blond mustache made a hungry grab at the novel. He continued to read: "Handkerchief fall in a puddle. Silvere sprang forward. He picked up the handkerchief. Their eyes met. As he returned the handkerchief, their hands touched. The young girl smiled. Silvere was in ecstasies. 'Ah, my God!'

"A baker opposite was quarreling over two sous with an old woman. A gray-haired veteran with a medal upon his breast and a butcher's boy were watching a dogfight. The smell of dead animals came from adjacent slaughterhouses. The letters on the sign over the tinsmith's shop on the corner shone redly like great clots of blood. It was hell on roller skates."

Here the clerk skipped some seventeen chapters descriptive of a number of intricate money transactions, the moles on the neck of a Parisian dressmaker, the process of making brandy, the milk-leg of Silvere's aunt, life in the coalpits, and scenes in the Chamber of Deputies. In these chapters the reputation of the architect of Charlemagne's palace was vindicated, and it was explained why Heloise's grandmother didn't keep her stockings pulled up.

Then he proceeded: "Heloise went to the country. The next day Silvere followed. They met in the fields. The young girl had donned the garb of the peasants. She blushed. She looked fresh, fair, innocent. Silvere felt faint with rapture. 'Ah, my God!'

"She had been running. Out of breath, she sank down in the hay. She held out her hand. 'I am so glad to see you.' Silvere was enchanted at this vision. He bent toward her. Suddenly he burst into tears. 'I love you! I love you! I love you!' he stammered.

"A row of red and white shirts hung on a line some distance away. The third shirt from the left had a button off the neck. A cat on the rear steps of a cottage near the shirts was drinking milk from a platter. The northeast portion of the platter had a crack in it.

"'Heloise!' Silvere was murmuring hoarsely. He leaned toward her until his warm breath moved the curls on her neck. 'Heloise!' murmured Jean."

"Young man," said an elderly gentleman with a dripping umbrella to the clerk with a blond mustache, "have you any nightshirts open front and back? Eh? Nightshirts open front and back, I said. D'you hear, eh? *Nightshirts open front and back!* Well, then, why didn't you say so? It would pay you to be a trifle more polite, young man. When you get as old as I am, you will find out that it pays to—what? I didn't see you adding any column of figures. In that case I'm sorry. You have no nightshirts open front and back, eh? Well, good day."

As the elderly gentleman vanished, the clerk with a blond mustache grasped the novel like some famished animal. He read on: "A peasant stood before the two children. He wrung his hands. 'Have you seen a stray cow?' 'No,' cried the children in the same breath. The peasant wept. He wrung his hands. It was a supreme moment.

"'She loves me!' cried Silvere to himself, as he changed his clothes for dinner.

"It was evening. The children sat by the fireplace. Heloise wore a gown of clinging white. She looked fresh, fair, innocent. Silvere was in raptures. 'Ah, my God!'

"Old Jean, the peasant, saw nothing. He was mending harness. The fire crackled in the fireplace. The children loved each other. Through the open door to the kitchen came the sound of old Marie shrilly cursing the geese who wished to enter. In front of the window, two pigs were quarreling over a vegetable. Cattle were lowing in a distant field. A hay wagon creaked slowly past. Thirty-two chickens were asleep in the branches of a tree. This subtle atmosphere had a mighty effect upon Heloise. It was beating down her self-control. She felt herself going. She was choking.

"The young girl made an effort. She stood up. 'Good night, I must go.' Silvere took her hand. 'Heloise,' he murmured. Outside, the two pigs were fighting.

"A warm blush overspread the young girl's face. She turned wet eyes toward her lover. She looked fresh, fair, innocent. Silvere was maddened. 'Ah, my God!'

"Suddenly the young girl began to tremble. She tried vainly to withdraw her hand. But her knee—"

"I wish to get my husband some shirts," said a shopping woman with six bundles. The clerk with a blond mustache made a private gesture of despair, and rapidly spread a score of differently patterned shirts upon the counter. "He's very particular about his shirts," said the shopping woman. "Oh, I don't think any of these will do. Don't you keep the Invincible brand? He only wears that kind. He says they fit him better. And he's very particular about his shirts. What? You don't keep them? No? Well, how much do you think they would come at? Haven't the slightest idea? Well, I suppose I must go somewhere else, then. Um—good day."

The clerk with the blond mustache was about to make further private gestures of despair, when the shopping woman with six bundles turned and went out. His fingers instantly closed nervously over the book. He drew it from its hiding place, and opened it at the place where he had ceased. His hungry eyes seemed to eat the words upon the page. He continued: "—struck cruelly against a chair. It seemed to awaken her. She started. She burst from the young man's arms. Outside, the two pigs were grunting amiably.

"Silvere took his candle. He went toward his room. He was in despair. 'Ah, my God!'

"He met the young girl on the stairs. He took her hand. Tears were raining down his face. 'Heloise!' he murmured.

"The young girl shivered. As Silvere put his arms about her, she faintly resisted. This embrace seemed to sap her life. She wished to die. Her thoughts flew back to the old well and the broken hayrakes at Plassans.

"The young girl looked fresh, fair, innocent. 'Heloise!' murmured Silvere. The children exchanged a long, clinging kiss. It seemed to unite their souls.

"The young girl was swooning. Her head sank on the young man's shoulder. There was nothing in space except these warm kisses on her neck. Silvere enfolded her. 'Ah, my God!' "

"Say, young feller," said a youth with a tilted cigar to the clerk with a blond mustache, "where th'ell is Billie Carcart's joint round here? Know?"

"Next corner," said the clerk, fiercely.

"Oh, th'ell," said the youth, "yehs needn't git gay. See! When a feller asts a civil question yehs needn't git gay. See! Th'ell."

The youth stood and looked aggressive for a moment. Then he went away.

The clerk seemed almost to leap upon the book. His feverish fingers twirled the pages. When he found his place he glued his eyes to it. He read:

"Then a great flash of lightning illumined the hallway. It threw livid hues over a row of flowerpots in the window seat. Thunder shook the house to its foundation. From the kitchen arose the voice of old Marie in prayer.

"Heloise screamed. She wrenched herself from the young man's arms. She sprang inside her room. She locked the door. She flung herself face downward on the bed. She burst into tears. She looked fresh, fair, innocent.

"The rain, pattering upon the thatched roof, sounded, in the stillness, like the footsteps of spirits. In the sky toward Paris there shone a crimson light.

"The chickens had all fallen from the tree. They stood, sadly, in a puddle. The two pigs were asleep under the porch.

"Upstairs, in the hallway, Silvere was furious."

The clerk with a blond mustache gave, here, a wild scream of disappointment. He madly hurled the novel with the picture on the cover from him. He stood up and said: "Damn!"

March 18, 1893
[Truth, Vol. 12, pp. 4–5.]

THE PACE OF YOUTH*

I

Stimson stood in a corner and glowered. He was a fierce man and had indomitable whiskers, albeit he was very small.

"That young tarrier," he whispered to himself. "He wants to quit makin' eyes at Lizzie. This is too much of a good thing. First thing you know, he'll get fired."

His brow creased in a frown, he strode over to the huge open doors and looked at a sign. "Stimson's Mammoth Merry-Go-Round," it read, and the glory of it was great. Stimson stood and contemplated the sign. It was an enormous affair; the letters were as large as men. The glow of it, the grandeur of it was very apparent to Stimson. At the end of his contemplation,

---

* *Midnight Sketches.*

he shook his head thoughtfully, determinedly. "No, no," he muttered. "This is too much of a good thing. First thing you know, he'll get fired."

A soft booming sound of surf, mingled with the cries of bathers, came from the beach. There was a vista of sand and sky and sea that drew to a mystic point far away in the northward. In the mighty angle, a girl in a red dress was crawling slowly like some kind of spider on the fabric of nature. A few flags hung lazily above where the bathhouses were marshaled in compact squares. Upon the edge of the sea stood a ship with its shadowy sails painted dimly upon the sky, and high overhead in the still, sun-shot air a great hawk swung and drifted slowly.

Within the merry-go-round there was a whirling circle of ornamental lions, giraffes, camels, ponies, goats, glittering with varnish and metal that caught swift reflections from windows high above them. With stiff wooden legs, they swept on in a never-ending race, while a great orchestrion clamored in wild speed. The summer sunlight sprinkled its gold upon the garnet canopies carried by the tireless racers and upon all the devices of decoration that made Stimson's machine magnificent and famous. A host of laughing children bestrode the animals, bending forward like charging cavalrymen, and shaking reins and whooping in glee. At intervals they leaned out perilously to clutch at iron rings that were tendered to them by a long wooden arm. At the intense moment before the swift grab for the rings one could see their little nervous bodies quiver with eagerness; the laughter rang shrill and excited. Down in the long rows of benches, crowds of people sat watching the game, while occasionally a father might arise and go near to shout encouragement, cautionary commands, or applause at his flying offspring. Frequently mothers called out: "Be careful, Georgie!" The orchestrion bellowed and thundered on its platform, filling the ears with its long monotonous song. Over in a corner, a man in a white apron and behind a counter roared above the tumult: "Popcorn! Popcorn!"

A young man stood upon a small, raised platform, erected in the manner of a pulpit, and just without the line of the circling figures. It was his duty to manipulate the wooden arm and affix the rings. When all were gone into the hands of the triumphant children, he held forth a basket into which they returned all save the coveted brass one, which meant another ride free and made the holder very illustrious. The young man stood all day upon his narrow platform, affixing rings or holding forth the basket. He was a sort of general squire in these lists of childhood. He was very busy.

And yet Stimson, the astute, had noticed that the young man frequently found time to twist about on his platform and smile at a girl who shyly sold tickets behind a silvered netting. This, indeed, was the great reason of Stimson's glowering. The young man upon the raised platform had no manner of licence to smile at the girl behind the silvered netting. It was a most gigantic insolence. Stimson was amazed at it. "By Jiminy," he said to himself again, "that fellow is smiling at my daughter." Even in this tone of great wrath it could be discerned that Stimson was filled with wonder that any youth should dare smile at the daughter in the presence of the august father.

Often the dark-eyed girl peered between the shining wires, and, upon being detected by the young man, she usually turned her head away quickly to prove to him that she was not interested. At other times, however, her eyes seemed filled with a tender fear lest he should fall from that exceedingly dangerous platform. As for the young man, it was plain that these glances filled him with valor, and he stood carelessly upon his perch, as if he deemed it of no consequence that he might fall from it. In all the complexities of his daily life and duties he found opportunity to gaze ardently at the vision behind the netting.

This silent courtship was conducted over the heads of the crowd who thronged about the bright machine. The swift, eloquent glances of the young man went noiselessly and unseen with their message. There had finally become established between the two in this manner a subtle understanding and companionship. They communicated accurately all that they felt. The boy told his love, his reverence, his hope in the changes of the future. The girl told him that she loved him, that she did not love him, that she did not know if she loved him, that she loved him. Sometimes a little sign saying "Cashier" in gold letters, and hanging upon the silvered netting, got directly in range and interfered with the tender message.

The love affair had not continued without anger, unhappiness, despair. The girl had once smiled brightly upon a youth who came to buy some tickets for his little sister, and the young man upon the platform, observing this smile, had been filled with gloomy rage. He stood like a dark statue of vengeance upon his pedestal and thrust out the basket to the children with a gesture that was full of scorn for their hollow happiness, for their insecure and temporary joy. For five hours he did not once look at the girl when she was looking at him. He was going to crush her with his indifference; he was going to demonstrate that he had never been serious. However, when he narrowly observed her in secret he discovered that she seemed more blithe than was usual with her. When he found that his apparent indifference had not crushed her he suffered greatly. She did not love him, he concluded. If she had loved him she would have been crushed. For two days he lived a miserable existence upon his high perch. He consoled himself by thinking of how unhappy he was, and by swift, furtive glances at the loved face. At any rate he was in her presence, and he could get a good view from his perch when there was no interference by the little sign, "Cashier."

But suddenly, swiftly, these clouds vanished, and under the imperial blue sky of the restored confidence they dwelt in peace, a peace that was satisfaction, a peace that, like a babe, put its trust in the treachery of the future. This confidence endured until the next day, when she, for an unknown cause, suddenly refused to look at him. Mechanically he continued his task, his brain dazed, a tortured victim of doubt, fear, suspicion. With his eyes he supplicated her to telegraph an explanation. She replied with a stony glance that froze his blood. There was a great difference in their respective reasons for becoming angry. His were always foolish, but apparent, plain as the moon. Hers were subtle, feminine, as incomprehensible as the stars, as mysterious as the shadows at night.

They fell and soared, and soared and fell in this manner until they knew that to live without each other would be a wandering in deserts. They had grown so intent upon the uncertainties, the variations, the guessings of their affair that the world had become but a huge immaterial background. In time of peace their smiles were soft and prayerful, caresses confided to the air. In time of war, their youthful hearts, capable of profound agony, were wrung by the intricate emotions of doubt. They were the victims of the dread angel of affectionate speculation that forces the brain endlessly on roads that lead nowhere.

At night, the problem of whether she loved him confronted the young man like a specter, looming as high as a hill and telling him not to delude himself. Upon the following day, this battle of the night displayed itself in the renewed fervor of his glances and in their increased number. Whenever he thought he could detect that she too was suffering, he felt a thrill of joy.

But there came a time when the young man looked back upon these contortions with contempt. He believed then that he had imagined his pain. This came about when the redoubtable Stimson marched forward to participate.

"This has got to stop," Stimson had said to himself, as he stood and watched them. They had grown careless of the light world that clattered about them; they were become so engrossed in their personal drama that the language of their eyes was almost as obvious as gestures. And Stimson, through his keenness, his wonderful, infallible penetration, suddenly came into possession of these obvious facts. "Well, of all the nerve!" he said, regarding with a new interest the young man upon the perch.

He was a resolute man. He never hesitated to grapple with a crisis. He decided to overturn everything at once, for, although small, he was very fierce and impetuous. He resolved to crush this dreaming.

He strode over to the silvered netting. "Say, you want to quit your everlasting grinning at that idiot," he said, grimly.

The girl cast down her eyes and made a little heap of quarters into a stack. She was unable to withstand the terrible scrutiny of her small and fierce father.

Stimson turned from his daughter and went to a spot beneath the platform. He fixed his eyes upon the young man and said: "I've been speaking to Lizzie. You better attend strictly to your own business or there'll be a new man here next week." It was as if he had blazed away with a shotgun. The young man reeled upon his perch. At last he in a measure regained his composure and managed to stammer: "A—all right, sir." He knew that denials would be futile with the terrible Stimson. He agitatedly began to rattle the rings in the basket and pretend that he was obliged to count them or inspect them in some way. He, too, was unable to face the great Stimson.

For a moment, Stimson stood in fine satisfaction and gloated over the effect of his threat. "I've fixed them," he said complacently, and went out to smoke a cigar and revel in himself. Through his mind went the proud reflection that people who came in contact with his granite will usually ended in quick and abject submission.

II

One evening, a week after Stimson had indulged in the proud reflection that people who came in contact with his granite will usually ended in quick and abject submission, a young feminine friend of the girl behind the silvered netting came to her there and asked her to walk on the beach after "Stimson's Mammoth Merry-Go-Round" was closed for the night. The girl assented with a nod. The young man upon the perch holding the rings saw this nod and judged its meaning. Into his mind came an idea of defeating the watchfulness of the redoubtable Stimson.

When the merry-go-round was closed and the two girls started for the beach, he wandered off aimlessly in another direction, but he kept them in view, and as soon as he was assured that he had escaped the vigilance of Stimson he followed them.

The electric lights on the beach made a broad band of tremoring light, extending parallel to the sea, and upon the wide walk there slowly paraded a great crowd, intermingling, intertwining, sometimes colliding. In the darkness stretched the vast purple expanse of the ocean, and the deep indigo sky above was peopled with yellow stars. Occasionally out upon the water a whirling mass of froth suddenly flashed into view, like a great ghostly robe appearing, and then vanished, leaving the sea in its darkness, from whence came those bass tones of the water's unknown emotion. A wind, cool, reminiscent of the wave wastes, made the women hold their wraps about their throats, and caused the men to grip the rims of their straw hats. It carried the noise of the band in the pavilion in gusts. Sometimes people unable to hear the music glanced up at the pavilion and were reassured upon beholding the distant leader still gesticulating and bobbing, and the other members of the band with their lips glued to their instruments. High in the sky soared an unassuming moon, faintly silver.

For a time the young man was afraid to approach the two girls; he followed them at a distance and called himself a coward. At last, however, he saw them stop on the outer edge of the crowd and stand silently listening to the voices of the sea. When he came to where they stood, he was trembling in his agitation. They had not seen him.

"Lizzie," he began. "I—"

The girl wheeled instantly and put her hand to her throat. "Oh, Frank, how you frightened me," she said—inevitably.

"Well, you know I—I—" he stuttered.

But the other girl was one of those beings who are born to attend at tragedies. She had for love a reverence, an admiration that was greater the more she contemplated the fact that she knew nothing of it. This couple, with their emotions, awed her and made her humbly wish that she might be destined to be of some service to them. She was very homely.

When the young man faltered before them, she, in her sympathy, actually overestimated the crisis, and felt that he might fall dying at their feet. Shyly, but with courage, she marched to the rescue. "Won't you come and walk on the beach with us?" she said.

The young man gave her a glance of deep gratitude which was not without the patronage which a man in his condition naturally feels for one who pities it. The three walked on.

Finally, the being who was born to attend at this tragedy said that she wished to sit down and gaze at the sea, alone. They politely urged her to walk on with them, but she was obstinate. She wished to gaze at the sea, alone. The young man swore to himself that he would be her friend until he died.

And so the two young lovers went on without her. They turned once to look at her.

"Jennie's awful nice," said the girl.

"You bet she is," replied the young man, ardently.

They were silent for a little time.

At last the girl said: "You were angry at me yesterday."

"No, I wasn't."

"Yes, you were, too. You wouldn't look at me once all day."

"No, I wasn't angry. I was only putting on."

Though she had, of course, known it, this confession seemed to make her very indignant. She flashed a resentful glance at him. "Oh, were you, indeed?" she said with a great air.

For a few minutes she was so haughty with him that he loved her to madness. And directly this poem, which stuck at his lips, came forth lamely in fragments.

When they walked back toward the other girl and saw the patience of her attitude, their hearts swelled in a patronizing and secondary tenderness for her.

They were very happy. If they had been miserable they would have charged this fairy scene of the night with a criminal heartlessness; but as they were joyous, they vaguely wondered how the purple sea, the yellow stars, the changing crowds under the electric lights could be so phlegmatic and stolid.

They walked home by the lakeside way, and out upon the water those gay paper lanterns, flashing, fleeting, and careering, sang to them, sang a chorus of red and violet, and green and gold; a song of mystic bands of the future.

One day, when business paused during a dull sultry afternoon, Stimson went uptown. Upon his return he found that the popcorn man, from his stand over in a corner, was keeping an eye upon the cashier's cage, and that nobody at all was attending to the wooden arm and the iron rings. He strode forward like a sergeant of grenadiers.

"Where in thunder is Lizzie?" he demanded, a cloud of rage in his eyes.

The popcorn man, although associated long with Stimson, had never got over being dazed. "They've—they've—gone round to th'—th'—house," he said with difficulty, as if he had just been stunned.

"Whose house?" snapped Stimson.

"Your—your house, I s'pose," said the popcorn man.

Stimson marched round to his home. Kingly denunciations surged, already formulated, to the tip of his tongue, and he bided the moment when his anger could fall upon the heads of that pair of children. He found his wife convulsive and in tears.

"Where's Lizzie?"

And then she burst forth—"Oh—John—John—they've run away, I know they have. They drove by here not three minutes ago. They must have done it on purpose to bid me good-bye, for Lizzie waved her hand sad-like; and then, before I could get out to ask where they were going or what, Frank whipped up the horse."

Stimson gave vent to a dreadful roar. "Get my revolver—get a hack—get my revolver, do your hear?—what the devil—" His voice became incoherent.

He had always ordered his wife about as if she were a battalion of infantry, and despite her misery the training of years forced her to spring mechanically to obey; but suddenly she turned to him with a shrill appeal. "Oh, John—not—the—revolver."

"Confound it, let go of me," he roared again, and shook her from him.

He ran hatless upon the street. There were a multitude of hacks at the summer resort, but it was ages to him before he could find one. Then he charged it like a bull. "Uptown," he yelled, as he tumbled into the rear seat.

The hackman thought of severed arteries. His galloping horse distanced a large number of citizens who had been running to find what caused such contortions by the little hatless man.

It chanced, as the bouncing hack went along near the lake, Stimson gazed across the calm gray expanse and recognized a color in a bonnet and a poise of a head. A buggy was traveling along a highway that led to Sorington. Stimson bellowed: "There—there—there they are—in that buggy."

The hackman became inspired with the full knowledge of the situation. He struck a delirious blow with the whip. His mouth expanded in a grin of excitement and joy. It came to pass that this old vehicle, with its drowsy horse and its dusty-eyed and tranquil driver, seemed suddenly to awaken, to become animated and fleet. The horse ceased to ruminate on his state, his air of reflection vanished. He became intent upon his aged legs and spread them in quaint and ridiculous devices for speed. The driver, his eyes shining, sat critically in his seat. He watched each motion of this rattling machine down before him. He resembled an engineer. He used the whip with judgment and deliberation as the engineer would have used coal or oil. The horse clacked swiftly upon the macadam, the wheels hummed, the body of the vehicle wheezed and groaned.

Stimson, in the rear seat, was erect in that impassive attitude that comes sometimes to the furious man when he is obliged to leave the battle to others. Frequently, however, the tempest in his breast came to his face and he howled: "Go it—go it—you're gaining; pound 'im! Thump the life out of 'im; hit 'im hard, you fool." His hand grasped the rod that supported the carriage top, and it was clenched so that the nails were faintly blue.

Ahead, that other carriage had been flying with speed, as from realization of the menace in the rear. It bowled away rapidly, drawn by the eager spirit of a young and modern horse. Stimson could see the buggy-top bobbing, bobbing. That little pane, like an eye, was a derision to him. Once he leaned forward and bawled angry sentences. He began to feel impotent; his whole expedition was a tottering of an old man upon a trail of birds. A sense of age made him choke again with wrath. That other vehicle, that was youth, with youth's pace; it was swift-flying with the hope of dreams. He began to comprehend those two children ahead of him, and he knew a sudden and strange awe, because he understood the power of their young blood, the power to fly strongly into the future and feel and hope again, even at that time when his bones must be laid in the earth.

The dust rose easily from the hot road and stifled the nostrils of Stimson.

The highway vanished far away in a point with a suggestion of intolerable length. The other vehicle was becoming so small that Stimson could no longer see the derisive eye.

At last the hackman drew rein to his horse and turned to look at Stimson. "No use, I guess," he said.

Stimson made a gesture of acquiescence, rage, despair. As the hackman turned his dripping horse about, Stimson sank back with the astonishment and grief of a man who has been defied by the universe. He had been in a great perspiration, and now his bald head felt cool and uncomfortable. He put up his hand with the sudden recollection that he had forgotten his hat.

At last he made a gesture. It meant that at any rate he was not responsible.

1893?

[New York *Press,* January 18 and 19, 1895, p. 7, each issue.]

THE RELUCTANT VOYAGERS

I

Two men sat by the sea waves.

"Well, I know I'm not handsome," said one gloomily. He was poking holes in the sand with a discontented cane.

The companion was watching the waves play. He seemed overcome with perspiring discomfort, as a man who is resolved to set another man right.

Suddenly his mouth turned into a straight line. "To be sure you are not," he cried vehemently. "You look like thunder. I do not desire to be unpleasant, but I must assure you that your freckled skin continually reminds spectators of white wallpaper with gilt roses on it. The top of your head looks like a little wooden plate. And your figure—heavens!"

For a time they were silent. They stared at the waves that purred near their feet like sleepy sea-kittens.

Finally the first man spoke. "Well," said he, defiantly, "what of it?"

"What of it!" exploded the other. "Why, it means that you'd look like blazes in a bathing suit."

They were again silent. The freckled man seemed ashamed. His tall companion glowered at the scenery.

"I am decided," said the freckled man suddenly. He got boldly up from the sand and strode away. The tall man followed, walking sarcastically and glaring down at the round, resolute figure before him.

A bath clerk was looking at the world with superior eyes through a hole in a board. To him the freckled man made application, waving his hands over his person in illustration of a snug fit. The bath clerk thought profoundly. Eventually, he handed out a blue bundle with an air of having phenomenally solved the freckled man's dimensions.

The latter resumed his resolute stride.

"See here," said the tall man, following him, "I bet you've got a regular toga, you know. That fellow couldn't tell—"

"Yes, he could," interrupted the freckled man, "I saw correct mathematics in his eyes."

"Well, supposin' he has missed your size. Supposin'—"

"Tom," again interrupted the other, "produce your proud clothes and we'll go in."

The tall man swore bitterly. He went to one of a row of little wooden boxes and shut himself in it. His companion repaired to a similar box.

At first he felt like an opulent monk in a too small cell, and he turned round two or three times to see if he could. He arrived finally into his bathing dress. Immediately he dropped gasping upon a three-cornered bench. The suit fell in folds about his reclining form. There was silence, save for the caressing calls of the waves without.

Then he heard two shoes drop on the floor in one of the little coops. He began to clamor at the boards like a penitent at an unforgiving door.

"Tom," called he, "Tom—"

A voice of wrath, muffled by cloth, came through the walls. "You go t' blazes!"

The freckled man began to groan, taking the occupants of the entire row of coops into his confidence.

"Stop your noise," angrily cried the tall man from his hidden den. "You rented the bathing suit, didn't you? Then—"

"It ain't a bathing suit," shouted the freckled man at the boards. "It's an auditorium, a ballroom, or something. It ain't a bathing suit."

The tall man came out of his box. His suit looked like blue skin. He walked with grandeur down the alley between the rows of coops. Stopping in front of his friend's door, he rapped on it with passionate knuckles.

"Come out of there, y' ol' fool," said he, in an enraged whisper. "It's only your accursed vanity. Wear it anyhow. What difference does it make? I never saw such a vain ol' idiot!"

As he was storming the door opened, and his friend confronted him. The tall man's legs gave way, and he fell against the opposite door.

The freckled man regarded him sternly. "You're an ass," he said. His back curved in scorn. He walked majestically down the alley. There was pride in the way his chubby feet patted the boards. The tall man followed, weakly, his eyes riveted upon the figure ahead.

As a disguise the freckled man had adopted the stomach of importance. He moved, with an air of some sort of procession, across a boardwalk, down some steps, and out upon the sand.

There was a pug dog and three old women on a bench, a man and a maid with a book and a parasol, a seagull drifting high in the wind, and a distant, tremendous meeting of sea and sky. Down on the wet sand stood a girl being wooed by the breakers.

The freckled man moved with stately tread along the beach. The tall man, numb with amazement, came in the rear. They neared the girl.

Suddenly the tall man was seized with convulsions. He laughed, and the girl turned her head.

She perceived the freckled man in the bathing suit. An expression of wonderment overspread her charming face. It changed in a moment to a pearly smile.

This smile seemed to smite the freckled man. He obviously tried to swell and fit his suit. Then he turned a shriveling glance upon his companion, and fled up the beach. The tall man ran after him, pursuing with mocking cries that tingled his flesh like stings of insects. He seemed to be trying to lead the way out of the world. But at last he stopped and faced about.

"Tom Sharp," said he, between his clenched teeth, "you are an unutterable wretch! I could grind your bones under my heel!"

The tall man was in a trance, with glazed eyes fixed on the bathing dress. He seemed to be murmuring: "Oh, good Lord! Oh, good Lord! I never saw such a suit!"

The freckled man made the gesture of an assassin. "Tom Sharp, you—"

The other was still murmuring: "Oh, good Lord! I never saw such a suit! I never—"

The freckled man ran down into the sea.

II

The cool, swirling waters took his temper from him, and it became a thing that is lost in the ocean. The tall man floundered in, and the two forgot and rollicked in the waves.

The freckled man, in endeavoring to escape from mankind, had left all save a solitary fisherman under a large hat, and three boys in bathing dress, laughing and splashing upon a raft made of old spars.

The two men swam softly over the ground swells.

The three boys dived from their raft, and turned their jolly faces shoreward. It twisted slowly around and around, and began to move seaward on some unknown voyage. The freckled man laid his face to the water and swam toward the raft with a practiced stroke. The tall man followed, his bent arm appearing and disappearing with the precision of machinery.

The craft crept away, slowly and wearily, as if luring. The little wooden plate on the freckled man's head looked at the shore like a round brown eye, but his gaze was fixed on the raft that slyly appeared to be waiting. The tall man used the little wooden plate as a beacon.

At length the freckled man reached the raft and climbed aboard. He lay down on his back and puffed. His bathing dress spread about him like a dead balloon. The tall man came, snorted, shook his tangled locks, and lay down by the side of his companion.

They were overcome with a delicious drowsiness. The planks of the raft seemed to fit their tired limbs. They gazed dreamily up into the vast sky of summer.

"This is great," said the tall man. His companion grunted blissfully.

Gentle hands from the sea rocked their craft and lulled them to peace. Lapping waves sang little rippling sea-songs about them. The two men issued contented groans.

"Tom," said the freckled man.

"What?" said the other.

"This is great."

They lay and thought.

A fish hawk, soaring, suddenly turned and darted at the waves. The tall man indolently twisted his head and watched the bird plunge its claws into the water. It heavily arose with a silver gleaming fish.

"That bird has got his feet wet again. It's a shame," murmured the tall man sleepily. "He must suffer from an endless cold in the head. He should wear rubber boots. They'd look great, too. If I was him, I'd—Great Scott!"

He had partly arisen, and was looking at the shore. He began to scream. "Ted! Ted! Ted! Look!"

"What's matter?" dreamily spoke the freckled man. "You remind me of when I put the bird-shot in your leg." He giggled softly.

The agitated tall man made a gesture of supreme eloquence. His companion upreared and turned a startled gaze shoreward.

"Lord!" he roared, as if stabbed.

The land was a long brown streak with a rim of green, in which sparkled the tin roofs of huge hotels. The hands from the sea had pushed them away. The two men sprang erect, and did a little dance of perturbation.

"What shall we do? What shall we do?" moaned the freckled man, wriggling fantastically in his dead balloon.

The changing shore seemed to fascinate the tall man, and for a time he did not speak.

Suddenly he concluded his minuet of horror. He wheeled about and faced the freckled man. He elaborately folded his arms. "So," he said, in slow, formidable tones. "So! This all comes from your accursed vanity, your bathing suit, your idiocy! You have murdered your best friend!" He turned away.

His companion reeled as if stricken by an unexpected arm. He stretched out his hands. "Tom, Tom," wailed he, beseechingly, "don't be such a fool." The broad back of his friend was occupied by a contemptuous sneer.

Three ships fell off the horizon. Landward, the hues were blending. The whistle of a locomotive sounded from an infinite distance as if tooting in heaven.

"Tom! Tom! My dear boy," quavered the freckled man, "don't speak that way to me."

"Oh, no, of course not," said the other, still facing away and throwing the words over his shoulder. "You suppose I am going to accept all this calmly, don't you? Not make the slightest objection? Make no protest at all, hey?"

"Well, I—I—" began the freckled man.

The tall man's wrath suddenly exploded. "You've abducted me! That's the whole amount of it! You've abducted me!"

"I ain't," protested the freckled man. "You must think I'm a fool."

The tall man swore and, sitting down, dangled his legs angrily in the water. Natural law compelled his companion to occupy the other end of the raft.

Over the waters little shoals of fish spluttered, raising tiny tempests. Languid jellyfish floated near, tremulously waving a thousand legs. A row of porpoises trundled along like a procession of cogwheels. The sky became grayed save where, over the land, sunset colors were assembling.

The two voyagers, back to back and at either end of the raft, quarreled at length.

"What did you want to follow me for?" demanded the freckled man in a voice of indignation.

"If your figure hadn't been so like a bottle, we wouldn't be here," replied the tall man.

III

The fires in the west blazed away, and solemnity spread over the sea. Electric lights began to blink like eyes. Night menaced the voyagers with a dangerous darkness, and fear came to bind their souls together. They huddled fraternally in the middle of the raft.

"I feel like a molecule," said the freckled man in subdued tones.

"I'd give two dollars for a cigar," muttered the tall man.

A V-shaped flock of ducks flew toward Barnegat, between the voyagers and a remnant of yellow sky. Shadows and winds came from the vanished eastern horizon.

"I think I hear voices," said the freckled man.

"That Dollie Ramsdell was an awfully nice girl," said the tall man.

When the coldness of the sea night came to them, the freckled man found he could by a peculiar movement of his legs and arms encase himself in his bathing dress. The tall man was compelled to whistle and shiver. As night settled finally over the sea, red and green lights began to dot the blackness. There was mysterious shadows between the waves.

"I see things comin'," murmured the freckled man.

"I wish I hadn't ordered that new dress suit for the hop tomorrow night," said the tall man reflectively.

The sea became uneasy and heaved painfully, like a lost bosom when little forgotten heart bells try to chime with a pure sound. The voyagers cringed at magnified foam on distant wave crests. A moon came and looked at them.

"Somebody's here," whispered the freckled man.

"I wish I had an almanac," remarked the tall man, regarding the moon.

Presently they fell to staring at the red and green lights that twinkled about them.

"Providence will not leave us," asserted the freckled man.

"Oh, we'll be picked up shortly. I owe money," said the tall man. He began to thrum on an imaginary banjo. "I have heard," said he, suddenly, "that captains with healthy ships beneath their feet will never turn back after having once started on a voyage. In that case we will be rescued by some ship bound for the golden seas of the south. Then, you'll be up to some of your confounded devilment, and we'll get put off. They'll maroon us! That's what they'll do! They'll maroon us! On an island with palm trees and sun-kissed maidens and all that. Sun-kissed maidens, eh? Great! They'd—"

He suddenly ceased and turned to stone. At a distance a great green eye was contemplating the sea wanderers.

They stood up and did another dance. As they watched the eye grew larger.

Directly the form of a phantom-like ship came into view. About the great green eye there bobbed small yellow dots. The wanderers could hear a far-away creaking of unseen tackle and flapping of shadowy sails. There came the melody of the waters as the ship's prow thrusted its way.

The tall man delivered an oration. "Ha!" he exclaimed, "here come our rescuers. The brave fellows! How I long to take the manly captain by the hand! You will soon see a white boat with a star on its bow drop from the side of yon ship. Kind sailors in blue and white will help us into the boat and conduct our wasted frames to the quarter-deck, where the handsome, bearded captain, with gold bands all around, will welcome us. Then in the hard-oak cabin, while the wine gurgles and the Havanas glow, we'll tell our tale of peril and privation."

The ship came on like a black hurrying animal with froth-filled maw. The two wanderers stood up and clasped hands. Then they howled out a wild duet that rang over the wastes of sea.

The cries seemed to strike the ship. Men with boots on yelled and ran about the deck. They picked up heavy articles and threw them down. They yelled more. After hideous creakings and flappings, the vessel stood still.

In the meantime the wanderers had been chanting their song for help. Out in the blackness they beckoned to the ship and coaxed.

A voice came to them. "Hello," it said.

They puffed out their cheeks and began to shout. "Hello! Hello! Hello!"

"Wot do yeh want?" said the voice.

The two wanderers gazed at each other, and sat suddenly down on the raft. Some pall came sweeping over the sky and quenched their stars.

But almost immediately the tall man got up and bawled miscellaneous information. He stamped his foot and, frowning into the night, swore threateningly.

The vessel seemed fearful of these moaning voices that called from a hidden cavern of the water. And now one voice was filled with a menace. A number of men, with enormous limbs that threw vast shadows over the sea as the lanterns flickered, held a debate and made gestures.

Off in the darkness, the tall man began to clamor like a mob. The freckled man sat in astounded silence, with his legs weak.

After a time one of the men of enormous limbs seized a rope that was tugging at the stern and drew a small boat from the shadows. Three giants clambered in and rowed cautiously toward the raft. Silver water flashed in the gloom as the oars dipped.

About fifty feet from the raft the boat stopped. "Who er you?" asked a voice.

The tall man braced himself and explained. He drew vivid pictures, his twirling fingers illustrating like live brushes.

"Oh," said the three giants.

The voyagers deserted the raft. They looked back, feeling in their hearts a mite of tenderness for the wet planks. Later, they wriggled up the side of the vessel and climbed over the railing.

On deck they met a man. He held a lantern to their faces. "Got any chewin' tewbacca?" he inquired.

"No," said the tall man, "we ain't."

The man had a bronzed face and a solitary whisker. Peculiar lines about his mouth were shaped into an eternal smile of derision. His feet were bare, and clung handily to crevices. Fearful trousers were supported by a piece of suspender that went up the wrong side of his chest and came down the right side of his back, dividing him into triangles.

"Ezekiel P. Sanford, capt'in, schooner *Mary Jones*, of N'yack, N.Y., boun' from Little Egg Harbor, N.J., to Athens, N.Y., genelmen," he said.

"Ah!" said the tall man, "delighted, I'm sure."

There were a few moments of silence. The giants were hovering in the gloom and staring.

Suddenly astonishment exploded the captain. "Wot th' devil—" he shouted, "wot th' devil yeh got on?"

"Bathing suits," said the tall man.

IV

The schooner went on. The two voyagers sat down and watched. After a time they began to shiver. The soft blackness of the summer night passed away, and gray mists writhed over the sea. Soon lights of early dawn went charging across the sky, and the twin beacons on the highlands grew dim and sparkled faintly, as if a monster were dying. The dawn penetrated the marrow of the two men in bathing dress.

The captain used to pause opposite them, hitch one hand in his suspender, and laugh. "Well, I be dog-hanged," he frequently said.

The tall man grew furious. He snarled in a mad undertone to his companion. "This rescue ain't right. If I had known—"

He suddenly paused, transfixed by the captain's suspender. "It's goin' to break," cried he, in an ecstatic whisper. His eyes grew large with excitement as he watched the captain laugh. "It'll break in a minute, sure."

But the commander of the schooner recovered, and invited them to drink and eat. They followed him along the deck, and fell down a square black hole into the cabin.

It was a little den, with walls of a vanished whiteness. A lamp shed an orange light. In a sort of recess two little beds were hiding. A wooden table, immovable, as if the craft had been built around it, sat in the middle of the floor. Overhead the square hole was studded with a dozen stars. A foot-worn ladder led to the heavens.

The captain produced ponderous crackers and some cold boiled ham. Then he vanished in the firmament like a fantastic comet.

The freckled man sat quite contentedly, like a stout squaw in a blanket. The tall man walked about the cabin and sniffed. He was angered at the crudeness of the rescue, and his shrinking clothes made him feel too large. He contemplated his unhappy state.

Suddenly, he broke out. "I won't stand this, I tell you! Heavens and earth, look at the—say, what in the blazes did you want to get me in this thing for, anyhow? You're a fine old duffer, you are! Look at that ham!"

The freckled man grunted. He seemed somewhat blissful. He was seated upon a bench, comfortably enwrapped in his bathing dress.

The tall man stormed about the cabin. "This is an outrage! I'll see the captain! I'll tell him what I think of—"

He was interrupted by a pair of legs that appeared among the stars. The captain came down the ladder. He brought a coffeepot from the sky.

The tall man bristled forward. He was going to denounce everything. The captain was intent upon the coffeepot, balancing it carefully, and leaving his unguided feet to find the steps of the ladder.

But the wrath of the tall man faded. He twirled his fingers in excitement, and renewed his ecstatic whisperings to the freckled man. "It's going to break! Look, quick, look! It'll break in a minute!" He was transfixed with interest, forgetting his wrongs in staring at the perilous passage.

But the captain arrived on the floor with triumphant suspenders. "Well," said he, "after yeh have et, maybe ye'd like t'sleep some! If so, yeh can sleep on them beds."

The tall man made no reply, save in a strained undertone. "It'll break in about a minute! Look, Ted, look quick!"

The freckled man glanced at a little bed on which were heaped boots and oilskins. He made a courteous gesture.

"My dear sir, we could not think of depriving you of your beds. No, indeed. Just a couple of blankets if you have them, and we'll sleep very comfortably on these benches."

The captain protested, politely twisting his back and bobbing his head. The suspenders tugged and creaked. The tall man partially suppressed a cry, and took a step forward.

The freckled man was sleepily insistent, and shortly the captain gave over his deprecatory contortions. He fetched a pink quilt with yellow dots on it to the freckled man, and a black one with red roses on it to the tall man.

Again he vanished in the firmament. The tall man gazed until the last remnant of trousers disappeared from the sky. Then he wrapped himself up in his quilt and lay down. The freckled man was puffing contentedly, swathed like an infant. The yellow polka dots rose and fell on the vast pink of his chest.

The wanderers slept. In the quiet could be heard the groanings of timbers as the sea seemed to crunch them together. The lapping of water along the vessel's side sounded like gaspings. A hundred spirits of the wind had got their wings entangled in the rigging and, in soft voices were pleading to be loosened.

The freckled man was awakened by a foreign noise. He opened his eyes and saw his companion standing by his couch.

His comrade's face was wan with suffering. His eyes glowed in the darkness. He raised his arms, spreading them out like a clergyman at a grave. He groaned deep in his chest.

"Good Lord!" yelled the freckled man, starting up. "Tom, Tom, what's th' matter?"

The tall man spoke in a fearful voice. "To New York," he said, "to New York in our bathing suits."

The freckled man sank back. The shadows of the cabin threw mysteries about the figure of the tall man, arrayed like some ancient and potent astrologer in the black quilt with the red roses on it.

v

Directly the tall man went and lay down and began to groan.

The freckled man felt the miseries of the world upon him. He grew angry at the tall man for awakening him. They quarreled.

"Well," said the tall man, finally, "we're in a fix."

"I know that," said the other, sharply.

They regarded the ceiling in silence.

"What in the thunder are we going to do?" demanded the tall man, after a time. His companion was still silent. "Say," repeated he, angrily, "what in the thunder are we going to do?"

"I'm sure I don't know," said the freckled man in a dismal voice.

"Well, think of something," roared the other. "Think of something, you old fool. You don't want to make any more idiots of yourself, do you?"

"I ain't made an idiot of myself."

"Well, think. Know anybody in the city?"

"I know a fellow up in Harlem," said the freckled man.

"You know a fellow up in Harlem!" howled the tall man. "Up in Harlem! How the dickens are we to—Say, you're crazy!"

"We can take a cab," cried the other, waxing indignant.

The tall man grew suddenly calm. "Do you know any one else?" he asked, measuredly.

"I know another fellow somewhere on Park Place."

"Somewhere on Park Place," repeated the tall man in an unnatural manner. "Somewhere on Park Place." With an air of sublime resignation he turned his face to the wall.

The freckled man sat erect and frowned in the direction of his companion. "Well, now, I suppose you are going to sulk. You make me ill! It's the best we can do, ain't it? Hire a cab and go look that fellow up on Park—What's that? You can't afford it? What nonsense! You are getting—Oh! Well, maybe we can beg some clothes of the captain. Eh? Did I see 'im? Certainly I saw 'im. Yes, it is improbable that a man who wears trousers like that can have clothes to lend. No, I won't wear oilskins and a sou'-wester. To Athens? Of course not! I don't know where it is. Do you? I thought not. With all your grumbling about other people, you never know anything important yourself. What? Broadway? I'll be hanged first. We can't get off at Harlem, man alive. There are no cabs in Harlem. I don't think we can bribe a sailor to take us ashore and bring a cab to the dock, for the very simple reason that we have nothing to bribe him with. What? No, of course not. See here, Tom Sharp, don't you swear at me like that. I won't have it. What's that? I ain't, either. I ain't. What? I am not. It's no such thing. I ain't. I've got more than you have, anyway. Well, you ain't doing anything so very brilliant yourself—just lyin' there and cussin'." At length the tall man feigned to prodigiously snore. The freckled man thought with such vigor that he fell asleep.

After a time he dreamed that he was in a forest where bass drums grew on trees. There came a strong wind that banged the fruit about like empty pods. A frightful din was in his ears. He awoke to find the captain of the schooner standing over him.

"We're at New York now," said the captain, raising his voice above the thumping and banging that was being done on deck, "an' I s'pose you fellers wanta go ashore." He chuckled in an exasperating manner. "Jes' sing out when yeh wanta go," he added, leering at the freckled man.

The tall man awoke, came over, and grasped the captain by the throat. "If you laugh again I'll kill you," he said.

The captain gurgled and waved his legs and arms.

"In the first place," the tall man continued, "you rescued us in a deucedly shabby manner. It makes me ill to think of it. I've a mind to mop you 'round just for that. In the second place, your vessel is bound for Athens, N.Y., and there's no sense in it. Now, will you or will you not turn this ship about and take us back where our clothes are, or to Philadelphia, where we belong?" He furiously shook the captain. Then he eased his grip and awaited a reply.

"I can't," yelled the captain, "I can't. This vessel don't belong to me. I've got to—"

"Well, then," interrupted the tall man, "can you lend us some clothes?"

"Hain't got none," replied the captain, promptly. His face was red, and his eyes were glaring.

"Well, then," said the tall man, "can you lend us some money?"

"Hain't got none," replied the captain, promptly. Something overcame him and he laughed.

"Thunderation," roared the tall man. He seized the captain, who began to have wriggling contortions. The tall man kneaded him as if he were biscuits. "You infernal scoundrel," he bellowed, "this whole affair is some wretched plot, and you are in it. I am about to kill you."

The solitary whisker of the captain did acrobatic feats like a strange demon upon his chin. His eyes stood perilously from his head. The suspender wheezed and tugged like the tackle of a sail.

Suddenly the tall man released his hold. Great expectancy sat upon his features. "It's going to break," he cried, rubbing his hands.

But the captain howled and vanished in the sky.

The freckled man then came forward. He appeared filled with sarcasm. "So!" said he. "So, you've settled the matter. The captain is the only man in the world who can help us, and I dare say he'll do anything he can now."

"That's all right," said the tall man. "If you don't like the way I run things, you shouldn't have come on this trip at all."

They had another quarrel.

At the end of it they went on deck. The captain stood at the stern addressing the bow with opprobrious language. When he perceived the voyagers he began to fling his fists about in the air.

"I'm goin' to put yeh off," he yelled. The wanderers stared at each other.

"Hum," said the tall man.

The freckled man looked at his companion. "He's going to put us off, you see," he said, complacently.

The tall man began to walk about and move his shoulders. "I'd like to see you do it," he said, defiantly.

The captain tugged at a rope. A boat came at his bidding.

"I'd like to see you do it," the tall man repeated, continually. An imperturbable man in rubber boots climbed down into the boat and seized the oars. The captain motioned downward. His whisker had a triumphant appearance.

The two wanderers looked at the boat. "I guess we'll have to get in," murmured the freckled man.

The tall man was standing like a granite column. "I won't," said he. "I won't! I don't care what you do, but I won't!"

"Well, but—" expostulated the other. They held a furious debate.

In the meantime the captain was darting about making sinister gestures, but the back of the tall man held him at bay. The crew, much depleted by the departure of the imperturbable man into the boat, looked on from the bow.

"You're a fool," the freckled man concluded his argument.

"So?" inquired the tall man, highly exasperated.

"So? Well, if you think you're so bright, we'll go in the boat, and then you'll see." He climbed down into the craft and seated himself in an ominous manner at the stern. "You'll see," he said to his companion, as the latter floundered heavily down. "You'll see!"

The man in rubber boots calmly rowed the boat toward the shore. As they went, the captain leaned over the railing and laughed. The freckled man was seated very victoriously.

"Well, wasn't this the right thing after all?" he inquired in a pleasant voice. The tall man made no reply.

VI

As they neared the dock something seemed suddenly to occur to the freckled man. "Great heavens," he murmured. He stared at the approaching shore. "My, what a plight, Tommy," he quavered.

"Do you think so?" spoke up the tall man. "Why, I really thought you liked it." He laughed in a hard voice. "Lord, what a figure you'll cut."

This laugh jarred the freckled man's soul. He became mad. "Thunderation, turn the boat around," he roared. "Turn 'er round, quick. Man alive, we can't—turn 'er round, d'ye hear?"

The tall man in the stern gazed at his companion with glowing eyes. "Certainly not," he said. "We're going on. You insisted upon it." He began to prod his companion with words.

The freckled man stood up and waved his arms.

"Sit down," said the tall man. "You'll tip the boat over."

The other man began to shout.

"Sit down," said the tall man again.

Words bubbled from the freckled man's mouth. There was a little torrent of sentences that almost choked him. And he protested passionately with his hands.

But the boat went on to the shadow of the docks. The tall man was intent upon balancing it as it rocked dangerously during his comrade's oration. "Sit down," he continually repeated.

"I won't," raged the freckled man. "I won't do anything." The boat wobbled with these words. "Say," he continued, addressing the oarsman, "just turn this boat round, will you? Where in the thunder are you taking us to, anyhow?"

The oarsman looked at the sky and thought. Finally he spoke. "I'm doin' what the cap'n sed."

"Well, what in th' blazes do I care what the cap'n said?" demanded the freckled man. He took a violent step. "You just turn this round or—"

The small craft reeled. Over one side water came flashing in. The freckled man cried out in fear, and gave a jump to the other side. The tall man roared orders, and the oarsman made efforts. The boat acted for a moment like an animal on a slackened wire. Then it upset.

"Sit down," said the tall man, in a final roar, as he was plunged into the water. The oarsman dropped his oars to grapple with the gunwale. He went down saying unknown words. The freckled man's explanation or apology was strangled by the water.

Two or three tugs let off whistles of astonishment, and continued on their paths. A man dozing on a dock aroused and began to caper. The passengers of a ferryboat all ran to the near railing.

A miraculous person in a small boat was bobbing on the waves near the piers. He sculled hastily toward the scene. It was a swirl of waters in the midst of which the dark bottom of the boat appeared, whale-like.

Two heads suddenly came up.

"839," said the freckled man, chokingly. "That's it! 839!"

"What is?" said the tall man.

"That's the number of that feller on Park Place. I just remembered."

"You're the bloomingest—" the tall man said.

"It wasn't my fault," interrupted his companion. "If you hadn't—" He tried to gesticulate, but one hand held to the keel of the boat, and the other was supporting the form of the oarsman. The latter had fought a battle with his immense rubber boots and had been conquered.

The rescuer in the other small boat came fiercely. As his craft glided up, he reached out and grasped the tall man by the collar and dragged him into the boat, interrupting what was, under the circumstances, a very brilliant flow of rhetoric directed at the freckled man. The oarsman of the wrecked craft was taken tenderly over the gunwale and laid in the bottom of the boat. Puffing and blowing, the freckled man climbed in.

"You'll upset this one before we can get ashore," the other voyager remarked.

As they turned toward the land they saw that the nearest dock was lined with people. The freckled man gave a little moan.

But the staring eyes of the crowd were fixed on the limp form of the man in rubber boots. A hundred hands reached down to help lift the body up. On the dock some men grabbed it and began to beat it and roll it. A policeman tossed the spectators about. Each individual in the heaving crowd sought to fasten his eyes on the blue-tinted face of the man in the rubber boots. They surged to and fro, while the policeman beat them indiscriminately.

The wanderers came modestly up the dock and gazed shrinkingly at the throng. They stood for a moment, holding their breath to see the first finger of amazement leveled at them.

But the crowd bent and surged in absorbing anxiety to view the man in rubber boots, whose face fascinated them. The sea wanderers were as though they were not there.

They stood without the jam and whispered hurriedly.

"839," said the freckled man.

"All right," said the tall man.

Under the pommeling hands the oarsman showed signs of life. The voyagers watched him make a protesting kick at the legs of the crowd, the while uttering angry groans.

"He's better," said the tall man, softly; "let's make off."

Together they stole noiselessly up the dock. Directly in front of it they found a row of six cabs.

The drivers on top were filled with a mighty curiosity. They had driven hurriedly from the adjacent ferry-house when they had seen the first running sign of an accident. They were straining on their toes and gazing at the tossing backs of the men in the crowd.

The wanderers made a little détour, and then went rapidly toward a cab. They stopped in front of it and looked up.

"Driver," called the tall man, softly.

The man was intent.

"Driver," breathed the freckled man. They stood for a moment and gazed imploringly.

The cabman suddenly moved his feet. "By Jimmy, I bet he's a goner," he said, in an ecstasy, and he again relapsed into a statue.

The freckled man groaned and wrung his hands. The tall man climbed into the cab.

"Come in here," he said to his companion. The freckled man climbed in, and the tall man reached over and pulled the door shut. Then he put his head out the window.

"Driver," he roared, sternly, "839 Park Place—and quick."

The driver looked down and met the eye of the tall man. "Eh?—Oh—839? Park Place? Yessir." He reluctantly gave his horse a clump on the back. As the conveyance rattled off, the wanderers huddled back among the dingy cushions and heaved great breaths of relief.

"Well, it's all over," said the freckled man, finally. "We're about out of it. And quicker than I expected. Much quicker. It looked to me sometimes that we were doomed. I am thankful to find it not so. I am rejoiced. And I hope and trust that you—well, I don't wish to—perhaps it is not the proper time to—that is, I don't wish to intrude a moral at an inopportune moment, but, my dear, dear fellow, I think the time is ripe to point out to you that your obstinacy, your selfishness, your villainous temper, and your various other faults can make it just as unpleasant for your own self, my dear boy, as they frequently do for other people. You can see what you brought us to, and I most sincerely hope, my dear, dear fellow, that

I shall soon see those signs in you which shall lead me to believe that you have become a wiser man."

1893?
[New York *Press*, Sunday Magazine, February 11,
pp. 6–11, 13; February 18, pp. 3–6, 1900.]

A DESERTION*

The yellow gaslight that came with an effect of difficulty through the dust-stained windows on either side of the door gave strange hues to the faces and forms of the three women who stood gabbling in the hallway of the tenement. They made rapid gestures, and in the background their enormous shadows mingled in terrific conflict.

"Aye, she ain't so good as he thinks she is, I'll bet. He can watch over 'er an' take care of 'er all he pleases, but when she wants t' fool 'im, she'll fool 'im. An' how does he know she ain't foolin' 'im now?"

"Oh, he thinks he's keepin' 'er from goin' t' th' bad, he does. Oh, yes. He ses she's too purty t' let run 'round alone. Too purty! Huh! My Sadie—"

"Well, he keeps a clost watch on 'er, you bet. On'y las' week, she met my boy Tim on th' stairs, an' Tim hadn't said two words to 'er b'fore th' ol' man begins to holler, 'Dorter, dorter, come here, come here!' "

At this moment a young girl entered from the street, and it was evident from the injured expressions suddenly assumed by the three gossipers that she had been the object of their discussion. She passed them with a slight nod, and they swung about into a row to stare after her.

On her way up the long flights the girl unfastened her veil. One could then clearly see the beauty of her eyes, but there was in them a certain furtiveness that came near to marring the effect. It was a peculiar fixture of gaze, brought from the street, as of one who there saw a succession of passing dangers, with menaces aligned at every corner.

On the top floor, she pushed open a door and then paused on the threshold, confronting an interior that appeared black and flat like a curtain. Perhaps some girlish idea of hobgoblins assailed her then, for she called in a little breathless voice, "Daddie!"

There was no reply. The fire in the cooking stove in the room crackled at spasmodic intervals. One lid was misplaced, and the girl could now see that this fact created a little flushed crescent upon the ceiling. Also,

* *Midnight Sketches.*

a series of tiny windows in the stove caused patches of red upon the floor. Otherwise, the room was heavily draped with shadows.

The girl called again, "Daddie!"

Yet there was no reply.

"Oh, Daddie!"

Presently she laughed as one familiar with the humors of an old man. "Oh, I guess yer cussin' mad about yer supper, dad," she said, and she almost entered the room, but suddenly faltered, overcome by a feminine instinct to fly from this black interior, peopled with imagined dangers.

Again she called, "Daddie!" Her voice had an accent of appeal. It was as if she knew she was foolish but yet felt obliged to insist upon being reassured. "Oh, daddie!"

Of a sudden a cry of relief, a feminine announcement that the stars still hung, burst from her. For, according to some mystic process, the smoldering coals of the fire went aflame with sudden, fierce brilliance, splashing parts of the walls, the floor, the crude furniture, with a hue of blood-red. And in this dramatic outburst of light, the girl saw her father seated at a table with his back turned toward her.

She entered the room, then, with an aggrieved air, her logic evidently concluding that somebody was to blame for her nervous fright. "Oh, yer on'y sulkin' 'bout yer supper. I thought mebbe ye'd gone somewheres."

Her father made no reply. She went over to a shelf in the corner, and, taking a little lamp, she lit it and put it where it would give her light as she took off her hat and jacket in front of the tiny mirror. Presently she began to bustle among the cooking utensils that were crowded into the sink, and as she worked she rattled talk at her father, apparently disdaining his mood.

"I'd 'a' come home earlier t'night, dad, on'y that fly foreman, he kep' me in th' shop till half-past six. What a fool! He came t' me, yeh know, an' he ses, 'Nell, I wanta give yeh some brotherly advice.' Oh, I know him an' his brotherly advice. 'I wanta give yeh some brotherly advice. Yer too purty, Nell,' he ses, 't' be workin' in this shop an' paradin' through th' streets alone, without somebody t' give yeh good brotherly advice, an' I wanta warn yeh, Nell. I'm a bad man, but I ain't as bad as some, an' I wanta warn yeh.' 'Oh, g'long 'bout yer business,' I ses. I know 'im. He's like all of 'em, on'y he's a little slyer. I know 'im. 'You g'long 'bout yer business,' I ses. Well, he sed after a while that he guessed some evenin' he'd come up an' see me. 'Oh, yeh will?' I ses. 'Yeh will? Well, you jest let my ol' man ketch yeh comin' foolin' 'round our place. Yeh'll wish yeh went t' some other girl t' give brotherly advice.' 'What th' 'ell do I care fer yer father?' he ses. 'What's he t' me?' 'If he throws yeh downstairs, yeh'll care for 'im,' I ses. 'Well,' he ses, 'I'll come when 'e ain't in, b' Gawd; I'll come when 'e ain't in.' 'Oh, he's allus in when it means takin' care a' me,' I ses. 'Don't yeh fergit it either. When it comes t' takin' care o' his dorter, he's right on deck every single possible time.' "

After a time, she turned and addressed cheery words to the old man. "Hurry up th' fire, daddie! We'll have supper pretty soon."

But still her father was silent, and his form in its sullen posture was motionless.

At this, the girl seemed to see the need of the inauguration of a feminine war against a man out of temper. She approached him breathing soft, coaxing syllables. "Daddie! Oh, Daddie! O-o-oh, Daddie!"

It was apparent from a subtle quality of valor in her tones that this manner of onslaught upon his moods had usually been successful, but tonight it had no quick effect. The words, coming from her lips, were like the refrain of an old ballad, but the man remained stolid.

"Daddie! My Daddie! Oh, Daddie, are yeh *mad* at me—really, truly *mad* at me?"

She touched him lightly upon the arm. Should he have turned then he would have seen the fresh, laughing face, with dew-sparkling eyes, close to his own.

"Oh, Daddie! My Daddie! Pretty Daddie!"

She stole her arm about his neck, and then slowly bent her face toward his. It was the action of a queen who knows that she reigns notwithstanding irritations, trials, tempests.

But suddenly, from this position, she leaped backward with the mad energy of a frightened colt. Her face was in this instant turned to a gray, featureless thing of horror. A yell, wild and hoarse as a brute cry, burst from her. "Daddie!" She flung herself to a place near the door, where she remained, crouching, her eyes staring at the motionless figure, spattered by the quivering flashes from the fire. Her arms extended, and her frantic fingers at once besought and repelled. There was in them an expression of eagerness to caress and an expression of the most intense loathing. And the girl's hair, that had been a splendor, was in these moments changed to a disordered mass that hung and swayed in witch-like fashion.

Again a terrible cry burst from her. It was more than the shriek of agony—it was direct, personal, addressed to him in the chair, the first word of a tragic conversation with the dead.

It seemed that when she had put her arm about its neck, she had jostled the corpse in such a way that now she and it were face to face. The attitude expressed an intention of arising from the table. The eyes, fixed upon hers, were filled with an unspeakable hatred.

The cries of the girl aroused thunders in the tenement. There was a loud slamming of doors, and presently there was a roar of feet upon the boards of the stairway. Voices rang out sharply.

"What is it?"

"What's th' matter?"

"He's killin' 'er!"

"Slug 'im wit' anythin' yeh kin lay hold of, Jack."

But over all this came the shrill shrewish tones of a woman. "Ah, th' damned ol' fool, he's drivin' 'er inteh th' street—that's what he's doin'. He's drivin' 'er inteh th' street."

1893?

[*Harper's Magazine*, Vol. 101 (November, 1900), pp. 938–939.]

AN EXPERIMENT IN MISERY*

It was late at night, and a fine rain was swirling softly down, causing the pavements to glisten with hue of steel and blue and yellow in the rays of the innumerable lights. A youth was trudging slowly, without enthusiasm, with his hands buried deep in his trousers pockets, toward the downtown places where beds can be hired for coppers. He was clothed in an aged and tattered suit, and his derby was a marvel of dust-covered crown and torn rim. He was going forth to eat as the wanderer may eat, and sleep as the homeless sleep. By the time he had reached City Hall Park he was so completely plastered with yells of "bum" and "hobo," and with various unholy epithets that small boys had applied to him at intervals, that he was in a state of the most profound dejection. The sifting rain saturated the old velvet collar of his overcoat, and as the wet cloth pressed against his neck, he felt that there no longer could be pleasure in life. He looked about him searching for an outcast of highest degree that they two might share miseries, but the lights threw a quivering glare over rows and circles of deserted benches that glistened damply, showing patches of wet sod behind them. It seemed that their usual freights had fled on this night to better things. There were only squads of well-dressed Brooklyn people who swarmed toward the bridge.

The young man loitered about for a time and then went shuffling off down Park Row. In the sudden descent in style of the dress of the crowd he felt relief, and as if he were at last in his own country. He began to see tatters that matched his tatters. In Chatham Square there were aimless

* *Midnight Sketches.*

men strewn in front of saloons and lodging houses, standing sadly, patiently, reminding one vaguely of the attitudes of chickens in a storm. He aligned himself with these men, and turned slowly to occupy himself with the flowing life of the great street.

Through the mists of the cold and storming night, the cable cars went in silent procession, great affairs shining with red and brass, moving with formidable power, calm and irresistible, dangerful and gloomy, breaking silence only by the loud fierce cry of the gong. Two rivers of people swarmed along the sidewalks, spattered with black mud, which made each shoe leave a scar-like impression. Overhead, elevated trains with a shrill grinding of the wheels stopped at the station, which upon its leg-like pillars seemed to resemble some monstrous kind of crab squatting over the street. The quick fat puffings of the engines could be heard. Down an alley there were somber curtains of purple and black, on which street lamps dully glittered like embroidered flowers.

A saloon stood with a voracious air on a corner. A sign leaning against the front of the doorpost announced "Free hot soup tonight!" The swing doors, snapping to and fro like ravenous lips, made gratified smacks as the saloon gorged itself with plump men, eating with astounding and endless appetite, smiling in some indescribable manner as the men came from all directions like sacrifices to a heathenish superstition.

Caught by the delectable sign, the young man allowed himself to be swallowed. A bartender placed a schooner of dark and portentous beer on the bar. Its monumental form upreared until the froth atop was above the crown of the young man's brown derby.

"Soup over there, gents," said the bartender affably. A little yellow man in rags and the youth grasped their schooners and went with speed toward a lunch counter, where a man with oily but imposing whiskers ladled genially from a kettle until he had furnished his two mendicants with a soup that was steaming hot, and in which there were little floating suggestions of chicken. The young man, sipping his broth, felt the cordiality expressed by the warmth of the mixture, and he beamed at the man with oily but imposing whiskers, who was presiding like a priest behind an altar. "Have some more, gents?" he inquired of the two sorry figures before him. The little yellow man accepted with a swift gesture, but the youth shook his head and went out, following a man whose wondrous seediness promised that he would have a knowledge of cheap lodging houses.

On the sidewalk he accosted the seedy man. "Say, do you know a cheap place to sleep?"

The other hesitated for a time, gazing sideways. Finally he nodded in the direction of the street. "I sleep up there," he said, "when I've got the price."

"How much?"

"Ten cents."

The young man shook his head dolefully. "That's too rich for me."

At that moment there approached the two a reeling man in strange garments. His head was a fuddle of bushy hair and whiskers, from which his eyes peered with a guilty slant. In a close scrutiny it was possible to distinguish the cruel lines of a mouth which looked as if its lips had just closed with satisfaction over some tender and piteous morsel. He appeared like an assassin steeped in crimes performed awkwardly.

But at this time his voice was tuned to the coaxing key of an affectionate puppy. He looked at the men with wheedling eyes, and began to sing a little melody for charity. "Say, gents, can't yeh give a poor feller a couple of cents t' git a bed? I got five, an' I gits anudder two I gits me a bed. Now, on th' square, gents, can't yeh jest gimme two cents t' git a bed? Now, yeh know how a respecterble gentlem'n feels when he's down on his luck, an' I——"

The seedy man, staring with imperturbable countenance at a train which clattered overhead, interrupted in an expressionless voice: "Ah, go t' hell!"

But the youth spoke to the prayerful assassin in tones of astonishment and inquiry. "Say, you must be crazy! Why don't yeh strike somebody that looks as if they had money?"

The assassin, tottering about on his uncertain legs, and at intervals brushing imaginary obstacles from before his nose, entered into a long explanation of the psychology of the situation. It was so profound that it was unintelligible.

When he had exhausted the subject, the young man said to him: "Let's see th' five cents."

The assassin wore an expression of drunken woe at this sentence, filled with suspicion of him. With a deeply pained air he began to fumble in his clothing, his red hands trembling. Presently he announced in a voice of bitter grief, as if he had been betrayed: "There's on'y four."

"Four," said the young man thoughtfully. "Well, look-a-here, I'm a stranger here, an' if ye'll steer me to your cheap joint I'll find the other three."

The assassin's countenance became instantly radiant with joy. His whiskers quivered with the wealth of his alleged emotions. He seized the young man's hand in a transport of delight and friendliness.

"B' Gawd," he cried, "if ye'll do that, b' Gawd, I'd say yeh was a damned good fellow, I would, an' I'd remember yeh all m' life, I would, b' Gawd, an' if I ever got a chance I'd return the compliment"—he spoke with drunken dignity—"b' Gawd, I'd treat yeh white, I would, an' I'd allus remember yeh."

The young man drew back, looking at the assassin coldly. "Oh, that's all right," he said. "You show me th' joint—that's all you've got t' do."

The assassin, gesticulating gratitude, led the young man along a dark street. Finally he stopped before a little dusty door. He raised his hand impressively. "Look-a-here," he said, and there was a thrill of deep and ancient wisdom upon his face, "I've brought yeh here, an' that's my part, ain't it? If th' place don't suit yeh, yeh needn't git mad at me, need yeh? There won't be no bad feelin', will there?"

"No," said the young man.

The assassin waved his arm tragically, and led the march up the steep stairway. On the way the young man furnished the assassin with three pennies. At the top a man with benevolent spectacles looked at them through a hole in a board. He collected their money, wrote some names on a register, and speedily was leading the two men along a gloom-shrouded corridor.

Shortly after the beginning of this journey the young man felt his liver turn white, for from the dark and secret places of the building there suddenly came to his nostrils strange and unspeakable odors, that assailed him like malignant diseases with wings. They seemed to be from human bodies closely packed in dens; the exhalations from a hundred pairs of reeking lips; the fumes from a thousand bygone debauches; the expression of a thousand present miseries.

A man, naked save for a little snuff-colored undershirt, was parading sleepily along the corridor. He rubbed his eyes and, giving vent to a prodigious yawn, demanded to be told the time.

"Half-past one."

The man yawned again. He opened a door, and for a moment his form was outlined against a black, opaque interior. To this door came the three men, and as it was again opened the unholy odors rushed out like fiends, so that the young man was obliged to struggle as against an overpowering wind.

It was some time before the youth's eyes were good in the intense gloom within, but the man with benevolent spectacles led him skillfully, pausing but a moment to deposit the limp assassin upon a cot. He took the youth to a cot that lay tranquilly by the window, and showing him a tall locker for clothes that stood near the head with the ominous air of a tombstone, left him.

The youth sat on his cot and peered about him. There was a gas jet in a distant part of the room, that burned a small flickering orange-hued flame. It caused vast masses of tumbled shadows in all parts of the place, save where, immediately about it, there was a little gray haze. As the young man's eyes became used to the darkness, he could see upon the cots that thickly littered the floor the forms of men sprawled out, lying in death-like silence, or heaving and snoring with tremendous effort, like stabbed fish.

The youth locked his derby and his shoes in the mummy case near him, and then lay down with an old and familiar coat around his shoulders. A blanket he handled gingerly, drawing it over part of the coat. The cot was covered with leather, and as cold as melting snow. The youth was obliged to shiver for some time on this affair, which was like a slab. Presently, however, his chill gave him peace, and during this period of leisure from it he turned his head to stare at his friend the assassin, whom he could dimly discern where he lay sprawled on a cot in the abandon of a man filled with drink. He was snoring with incredible vigor. His wet hair and beard dimly glistened, and his inflamed nose shone with subdued luster like a red light in a fog.

Within reach of the youth's hand was one who lay with yellow breast and shoulders bare to the cold draughts. One arm hung over the side of the cot, and the fingers lay full length upon the wet cement floor of the room. Beneath the inky brows could be seen the eyes of the man, exposed by the partly opened lids. To the youth it seemed that he and this corpse-like being were exchanging a prolonged stare, and that the other threatened with his eyes. He drew back, watching his neighbor from the shadows of his blanket edge. The man did not move once through the night, but lay in this stillness as of death like a body stretched out expectant of the surgeon's knife.

And all through the room could be seen the tawny hues of naked flesh, limbs thrust into the darkness, projecting beyond the cots; upreared knees, arms hanging long and thin over the cot edges. For the most part they were statuesque, carven, dead. With the curious lockers standing all about like tombstones, there was a strange effect of a graveyard where bodies were merely flung.

Yet occasionally could be seen limbs wildly tossing in fantastic nightmare gestures, accompanied by guttural cries, grunts, oaths. And there was one fellow off in a gloomy corner, who in his dreams was oppressed by some frightful calamity, for of a sudden he began to utter long wails that went almost like yells from a hound, echoing wailfully and weird through this chill place of tombstones where men lay like the dead.

The sound, in its high piercing beginnings that dwindled to final melancholy moans, expressed a red and grim tragedy of the unfathomable possibilities of the man's dreams. But to the youth these were not merely the shrieks of a vision-pierced man: they were an utterance of the meaning of the room and its occupants. It was to him the protest of the wretch who feels the touch of the imperturbable granite wheels, and who then cries with an impersonal eloquence, with a strength not from him, giving voice to the wail of a whole section, a class, a people. This, weaving into the young man's brain, and mingling with his views of the vast and somber shadows that, like mighty black fingers, curled around the naked bodies, made the young man so that he did not sleep, but lay carving the biographies for these men from his meager experience. At times the fellow in the corner howled in a writhing agony of his imaginations.

Finally a long lance-point of gray light shot through the dusty panes of the window. Without, the young man could see roofs drearily white in the dawning. The point of light yellowed and grew brighter, until the golden rays of the morning sun came in bravely and strong. They touched with radiant color the form of a small fat man who snored in stuttering fashion. His round and shiny bald head glowed suddenly with the valor of a decoration. He sat up, blinked at the sun, swore fretfully, and pulled his blanket over the ornamental splendors of his head.

The youth contentedly watched this rout of the shadows before the bright spears of the sun, and presently he slumbered. When he awoke he heard the voice of the assassin raised in valiant curses. Putting up his head, he perceived his comrade seated on the side of the cot engaged in scratching his neck with long fingernails that rasped like files.

"Hully Jee, dis is a new breed. They've got can openers on their feet." He continued in a violent tirade.

The young man hastily unlocked his closet and took out his shoes and hat. As he sat on the side of the cot lacing his shoes, he glanced about and saw that daylight had made the room comparatively commonplace and uninteresting. The men, whose faces seemed stolid, serene, or absent, were engaged in dressing, while a great crackle of bantering conversation arose.

A few were parading in unconcerned nakedness. Here and there were men of brawn, whose skins shone clear and ruddy. They took splendid poses, standing massively like chiefs. When they had dressed in their ungainly garments there was an extraordinary change. They then showed bumps and deficiencies of all kinds.

There were others who exhibited many deformities. Shoulders were slanting, humped, pulled this way and pulled that way. And notable among these latter men was the little fat man who had refused to allow his head to be glorified. His pudgy form, built like a pear, bustled to and fro, while he swore in fishwife fashion. It appeared that some article of his apparel had vanished.

The young man attired himself speedily, and went to his friend the assassin. At first the latter looked dazed at the sight of the youth. This face seemed to be appealing to him through the cloud wastes of his memory. He scratched his neck and reflected. At last he grinned, a broad smile gradually spreading until his countenance was a round illumination. "Hello, Willie," he cried cheerily.

"Hello," said the young man. "Are yeh ready t' fly?"

"Sure." The assassin tied his shoe carefully with some twine and came ambling.

When he reached the street the young man experienced no sudden relief from unholy atmospheres. He had forgotten all about them, and had been breathing naturally, and with no sensation of discomfort or distress.

He was thinking of these things as he walked along the street, when he was suddenly startled by feeling the assassin's hand, trembling with excitement, clutching his arm, and when the assassin spoke, his voice went into quavers from a supreme agitation.

"I'll be hully, bloomin' blowed if there wasn't a feller with a nightshirt on up there in that joint."

The youth was bewildered for a moment, but presently he turned to smile indulgently at the assassin's humor. "Oh, you're a damned liar," he merely said.

Whereupon the assassin began to gesture extravagantly and take oath by strange gods. He frantically placed himself at the mercy of remarkable fates if his tale were not true. "Yes, he did! I cross m' heart thousan' times!" he protested, and at the moment his eyes were large with amazement, his mouth wrinkled in unnatural glee. "Yessir! A nightshirt! A hully white nightshirt!"

"You lie!"

"No, sir! I hope ter die b'fore I kin git anudder ball if there wasn't a jay wid a hully, bloomin' white nightshirt!"

His face was filled with the infinite wonder of it. "A hully white nightshirt," he continually repeated.

The young man saw the dark entrance to a basement restaurant. There was a sign which read "No mystery about our hash!" and there were other age-stained and world-battered legends which told him that the place was within his means. He stopped before it and spoke to the assassin. "I guess I'll git somethin' t' eat."

At this the assassin, for some reason, appeared to be quite embarrassed. He gazed at the seductive front of the eating place for a moment. Then he started slowly up the street. "Well, good-bye, Willie," he said bravely.

For an instant the youth studied the departing figure. Then he called out, "Hol' on a minnet." As they came together he spoke in a certain fierce way, as if he feared that the other would think him to be charitable. "Look-a-here, if yeh wanta git some breakfas' I'll lend yeh three cents t' do it with. But say, look-a-here, you've gotta git out an' hustle. I ain't goin' t' support yeh, or I'll go broke b'fore night. I ain't no millionaire."

"I take my oath, Willie," said the assassin earnestly, "th' on'y thing I really needs is a ball. Me t'roat feels like a fryin' pan. But as I can't get a ball, why, th' next bes' thing is breakfast, an' if yeh do that for me, b' Gawd, I say yeh was th' whitest lad I ever see."

They spent a few moments in dexterous exchanges of phrases, in which they each protested that the other was, as the assassin had originally said, "a respecterble gentlem'n." And they concluded with mutual assurances that they were the souls of intelligence and virtue. Then they went into the restaurant.

There was a long counter, dimly lighted from hidden sources. Two or three men in soiled white aprons rushed here and there.

The youth bought a bowl of coffee for two cents and a roll for one cent. The assassin purchased the same. The bowls were webbed with brown seams, and the tin spoons wore an air of having emerged from the first pyramid. Upon them were black moss-like encrustations of age, and they were bent and scarred from the attacks of long-forgotten teeth. But over their repast the wanderers waxed warm and mellow. The assassin grew affable as the hot mixture went soothingly down his parched throat, and the young man felt courage flow in his veins.

Memories began to throng in on the assassin, and he brought forth long tales, intricate, incoherent, delivered with a chattering swiftness as from an old woman. "—great job out 'n Orange. Boss keep yeh hustlin', though, all time. I was there three days, and then I went an' ask 'im t' lend me a dollar. 'G-g-go ter the devil,' he says, an' I lose me job.

"South no good. Damn niggers work for twenty-five an' thirty cents a day. Run white man out. Good grub, though. Easy livin'.

"Yas; useter work little in Toledo, raftin' logs. Make two or three dollars er day in the spring. Lived high. Cold as ice, though, in the winter.

"I was raised in northern N'York. O-o-oh, yeh jest oughto live there. No beer ner whiskey, though, way off in the woods. But all th' good hot grub yeh can eat. B' Gawd, I hung around there long as I could till th' ol' man fired me. 'Git t' hell outa here, yeh wuthless skunk, git t' hell outa here, an' go die,' he ses. 'You're a hell of a father,' I ses, 'you are,' an' I quit 'im."

As they were passing from the dim eating place, they encountered an old man who was trying to steal forth with a tiny package of food, but a tall man with an indomitable mustache stood dragon-fashion, barring the way of escape. They heard the old man raise a plaintive protest. "Ah, you always want to know what I take out, and you never see that I usually bring a package in here from my place of business."

As the wanderers trudged slowly along Park Row, the assassin began to expand and grow blithe. "B' Gawd, we've been livin' like kings," he said, smacking appreciative lips.

"Look out, or we'll have t' pay fer it t'-night," said the youth with gloomy warning.

But the assassin refused to turn his gaze toward the future. He went with a limping step, into which he injected a suggestion of lamblike gambols. His mouth was wreathed in a red grin.

In City Hall Park the two wanderers sat down in the little circle of benches sanctified by traditions of their class. They huddled in their old garments, slumbrously conscious of the march of the hours which for them had no meaning.

The people of the street hurrying hither and thither made a blend of black figures, changing, yet frieze-like. They walked in their good clothes as upon important missions, giving no gaze to the two wanderers seated upon the benches. They expressed to the young man his infinite distance from all that he valued. Social position, comfort, the pleasures of living were unconquerable kingdoms. He felt a sudden awe.

And in the background a multitude of buildings, of pitiless hues and sternly high, were to him emblematic of a nation forcing its regal head into the clouds, throwing no downward glances; in the sublimity of its aspirations ignoring the wretches who may flounder at its feet. The roar of the city in his ear was to him the confusion of strange tongues, babbling heedlessly; it was the clink of coin, the voice of the city's hopes, which were to him no hopes.

He confessed himself an outcast, and his eyes from under the lowered rim of his hat began to glance guiltily, wearing the criminal expression that comes with certain convictions.

April 22, 1894
[New York *Press*, part 3, p. 2.]

AN EXPERIMENT IN LUXURY

"If you accept this invitation you will have an opportunity to make another social study," said the old friend.

The youth laughed. "If they caught me making a study of them they'd attempt a murder. I would be pursued down Fifth Avenue by the entire family."

"Well," persisted the old friend who could only see one thing at a time, "it would be very interesting. I have been told all my life that millionaires have no fun, and I know that the poor are always assured that the millionaire is a very unhappy person. They are informed that miseries swarm around all wealth, that all crowned heads are heavy with care, and—"

"But still—" began the youth.

"And, in the irritating, brutalizing, enslaving environment of their poverty, they are expected to solace themselves with these assurances," continued the old friend. He extended his gloved palm and began to tap it impressively with a finger of his other hand. His legs were spread apart in a fashion peculiar to his oratory. "I believe that it is mostly false. It is true that wealth does not release a man from many things from which he would gladly purchase release. Consequences cannot be bribed. I suppose that every man believes steadfastly that he has a private tragedy which makes him yearn for other existences. But it is impossible for me to believe that these things equalize themselves; that there are burrs under all rich cloaks and benefits in all ragged jackets, and the preaching of it seems wicked to me. There are those who have opportunities; there are those who are robbed of—"

"But look here," said the young man; "what has this got to do with my paying Jack a visit?"

"It has got a lot to do with it," said the old friend sharply. "As I said, there are those who have opportunities; there are those who are robbed—"

"Well, I won't have you say Jack ever robbed anybody of anything, because he's as honest a fellow as ever lived," interrupted the youth, with warmth. "I have known him for years, and he is a perfectly square fellow. He doesn't know about these infernal things. He isn't criminal because you say he is benefited by a condition which other men created."

"I didn't say he was," retorted the old friend. "Nobody is responsible for anything. I wish to Heaven somebody was, and then we could all jump on him. Look here, my boy, our modern civilization is—"

"Oh, the deuce!" said the young man.

The old friend then stood very erect and stern. "I can see by your frequent interruptions that you have not yet achieved sufficient pain in life. I hope one day to see you materially changed. You are yet—"

"There he is now," said the youth, suddenly. He indicated a young man who was passing. He went hurriedly toward him, pausing once to gesture adieu to his old friend.

The house was broad and brown and stolid like the face of a peasant. It had an inanity of expression, an absolute lack of artistic strength that was in itself powerful because it symbolized something. It stood, a homely pile of stone, rugged, grimly self-reliant, asserting its quality as a fine thing when in reality the beholder usually wondered why so much money had been spent to obtain a complete negation. Then from another point of view it was important and mighty because it stood as a fetish, formidable because of traditions of worship.

When the great door was opened the youth imagined that the footman who held a hand on the knob looked at him with a quick, strange stare. There was nothing definite in it; it was all vague and elusive, but a suspicion was certainly denoted in some way. The youth felt that he, one of the outer barbarians, had been detected to be a barbarian by the guardian of the portal, he of the refined nose, he of the exquisite sense, he who must be more atrociously aristocratic than any that he serves. And the youth, detesting himself for it, found that he would rejoice to take a frightful revenge upon this lackey who, with a glance of his eyes, had called him a name. He would have liked to have been for a time a dreadful social perfection whose hand, waved lazily, would cause hordes of the idolatrous imperfect to be smitten in the eyes. And in the tumult of his imagination he did not think it strange that he should plan in his vision to come around to this house and with the power of his new social majesty, reduce this footman to ashes.

He had entered with an easy feeling of independence, but after this incident the splendor of the interior filled him with awe. He was a wanderer in a fairy land, and who felt that his presence marred certain effects. He was an invader with a shamed face, a man who had come to steal certain colors, forms, impressions that were not his. He had a dim thought that some one might come to tell him to begone.

His friend, unconscious of this swift drama of thought, was already upon the broad staircase. "Come on," he called. When the youth's foot struck from a thick rug and changed upon the tiled floor he was almost frightened.

There was cool abundance of gloom. High up stained glass caught the sunlight, and made it into marvelous hues that in places touched the dark walls. A broad bar of yellow gilded the leaves of lurking plants. A softened crimson glowed upon the head and shoulders of a bronze swordsman, who perpetually strained in a terrific lunge, his blade thrust at random into the shadow, piercing there an unknown something.

An immense fireplace was at one end, and its furnishings gleamed until it resembled a curious door of a palace, and on the threshold, where one would have to pass a fire burned redly. From some remote place came the sound of a bird twittering busily. And from behind heavy portieres came a subdued noise of the chatter of three, twenty or a hundred women.

He could not relieve himself of this feeling of awe until he had reached his friend's room. There they lounged carelessly and smoked pipes. It was an amazingly comfortable room. It expressed to the visitor that he could do supremely as he chose, for it said plainly that in it the owner did supremely as he chose. The youth wondered if there had not been some domestic skirmishing to achieve so much beautiful disorder. There were various articles left about defiantly, as if the owner openly flaunted the feminine ideas of precision. The disarray of a table that stood prominently defined the entire room. A set of foils, a set of boxing gloves, a lot of illustrated papers, an inkstand and a hat lay entangled upon it. Here was surely a young man, who, when his menacing mother, sisters or servants knocked, would open a slit in the door like a Chinaman in an opium joint, and tell him to leave him to his beloved devices. And yet, withal, the effect was good, because the disorder was not necessary, and because there are some things that when flung down, look to have been flung by an artist. A baby can create an effect with a guitar. It would require genius to deal with the piled up dishes in a Cherry Street sink.

The youth's friend lay back upon the broad seat that followed the curve of the window and smoked in blissful laziness. Without, one could see the windowless wall of a house overgrown with a green, luxuriant vine. There was a glimpse of a side street. Below were the stables. At intervals a little fox terrier ran into the court and barked tremendously.

The youth, also blissfully indolent, kept up his part of the conversation on the recent college days, but continually he was beset by a stream of subconscious reflection. He was beginning to see a vast wonder in it that they two lay sleepily chatting with no more apparent responsibility than rabbits, when certainly there were men, equally fine perhaps, who were being blackened and mashed in the churning life of the lower places. And all this had merely happened; the great secret hand had guided them here and had guided others there. The eternal mystery of social condition exasperated him at this time. He wondered if incomprehensible justice were the sister of open wrong.

And, above all, why was he impressed, awed, overcome by a mass of materials, a collection of the trophies of wealth, when he knew that to him their dominant meaning was that they represented a lavish expenditure? For what reason did his nature so deeply respect all this? Perhaps his ancestors had been peasants bowing heads to the heel of appalling pomp of princes or rows of little men who stood to watch a king kill a flower with his cane. There was one side of him that said there were finer things in life, but the other side did homage.

Presently he began to feel that he was a better man than many—entitled to a great pride. He stretched his legs like a man in a garden, and he thought that he belonged to the garden. Hues and forms had smothered certain of his comprehensions. There had been times in his life when little voices called to him continually from the darkness; he heard them now as an idle, half-smothered babble on the horizon edge. It was necessary that it should be so, too. There was the horizon, he said, and, of course, there should be a babble of pain on it. Thus it was written; it was a law, he thought. And, anyway, perhaps it was not so bad as those who babbled tried to tell.

In this way and with this suddenness he arrived at a stage. He was become a philosopher, a type of the wise man who can eat but three meals a day, conduct a large business and understand the purposes of infinite power. He felt valuable. He was sage and important.

There were influences, knowledges that made him aware that he was idle and foolish in his new state, but he inwardly reveled like a barbarian in his environment. It was delicious to feel so high and mighty, to feel that the unattainable could be purchased like a penny bun. For a time, at any rate, there was no impossible. He indulged in monarchical reflections.

As they were dressing for dinner his friend spoke to him in this wise: "Be sure not to get off anything that resembles an original thought before my mother. I want her to like you, and I know that when any one says a thing cleverly before her he ruins himself with her forever. Confine your talk to orthodox expressions. Be dreary and unspeakably commonplace in the true sense of the word. Be damnable."

"It will be easy for me to do as you say," remarked the youth.

"As far as the old man goes," continued the other, "he's a blooming good fellow. He may appear like a sort of a crank if he happens to be in that mood, but he's all right when you come to know him. And besides he doesn't dare do that sort of thing with me, because I've got nerve enough to bully him. Oh, the old man is all right."

On their way down the youth lost the delightful mood that he had enjoyed in his friend's rooms. He dropped it like a hat on the stairs. The splendor of color and form swarmed upon him again. He bowed before the strength of this interior; it said a word to him which he believed he should despise, but instead he crouched. In the distance shone his enemy, the footman.

"There will be no people here tonight, so you may see the usual evening row between my sister Mary and me, but don't be alarmed or uncomfortable, because it is quite an ordinary matter," said his friend, as they were about to enter a little drawing room that was well apart from the grander rooms.

The head of the family, the famous millionaire, sat on a low stool before the fire. He was deeply absorbed in the gambols of a kitten who was plainly trying to stand on her head that she might use all four paws in grappling with an evening paper with which her playmate was poking her ribs. The old man chuckled in complete glee. There was never such a case of abstraction, of want of care. The man of millions was in a far land where mechanics and bricklayers go, a mystic land of little, universal emotions, and he had been guided to it by the quaint gestures of a kitten's furry paws.

His wife, who stood near, was apparently not at all a dweller in thought lands. She was existing very much in the present. Evidently she had been wishing to consult with her husband on some tremendous domestic question, and she was in a state of rampant irritation, because he refused to acknowledge at this moment that she or any such thing as a tremendous domestic question was in existence. At intervals she made savage attempts to gain his attention.

As the youth saw her she was in a pose of absolute despair. And her eyes expressed that she appreciated all the tragedy of it. Ah, they said, hers was a life of terrible burden, of appalling responsibility; her pathway was beset with unsolved problems, her horizon was lined with tangled difficulties, while her husband—the man of millions, continued to play with the kitten. Her expression was an admission of heroism.

The youth saw that here at any rate was one denial of his oratorical old friend's statement. In the face of this woman there was no sign that life was sometimes a joy. It was impossible that there could be any pleasure in living for her. Her features were as lined and creased with care and worriment as those of an apple woman. It was as if the passing of each social obligation, of each binding form of her life had left its footprints, scarring her face.

Somewhere in her expression there was terrible pride, that kind of pride which, mistaking the form for the real thing, worships itself because of its devotion to the form.

In the lines of the mouth and the set of the chin could be seen the might of a grim old fighter. They denoted all the power of machination of a general, veteran of a hundred battles. The little scars at the corners of her eyes made a wondrously fierce effect, baleful, determined, without regard somehow to ruck of pain. Here was a savage, a barbarian, a spear woman of the Philistines, who fought battles to excel in what are thought to be the refined and worthy things in life; here was a type of Zulu chieftainess who scuffled and scrambled for place before the white altars of social excellence. And woe to the socially weaker who should try to barricade themselves against that dragon.

It was certain that she never rested in the shade of the trees. One could imagine the endless churning of that mind. And plans and other plans coming forth continuously, defeating a rival here, reducing a family there, bludgeoning a man here, a maid there. Woe and wild eyes followed like obedient sheep upon her trail.

Too, the youth thought he could see that here was the true abode of conservatism in the mothers, in those whose ears displayed their diamonds instead of their diamonds displaying their ears, in the ancient and honorable controllers who sat in remote corners and pulled wires and respected themselves with a magnitude of respect that heaven seldom allows on earth. There lived tradition and superstition. They were perhaps ignorant of that which they worshiped, and, not comprehending it at all, it naturally followed that the fervor of their devotion could set the sky ablaze.

As he watched, he saw that the mesmeric power of a kitten's waving paws was good. He rejoiced in the spectacle of the little fuzzy cat trying to stand on its head, and by this simple antic defeating some intention of a great domestic Napoleon.

The three girls of the family were having a musical altercation over by the window. Then and later the youth thought them adorable. They were wonderful to him in their charming gowns. They had time and opportunity to create effects, to be beautiful. And it would have been a wonder to him if he had not found them charming since making themselves so could but be their principal occupation.

Beauty requires certain justices, certain fair conditions. When in a field no man can say: "Here should spring up a flower; here one should not." With incomprehensible machinery and system, nature sends them forth in places both strange and proper, so that, somehow, as we see them each one is a surprise to us. But at times, at places, one can say: "Here no flower can flourish." The youth wondered then why he had been sometimes surprised at seeing women fade, shrivel, their bosoms flatten, their shoulders crook forward, in the heavy swelter and wrench of their toil. It must be difficult, he thought, for a woman to remain serene and uncomplaining when she contemplated the wonder and the strangeness of it.

The lights shed marvelous hues of softened rose upon the table. In the encircling shadows the butler moved with a mournful, deeply solemn air. Upon the table there was color of pleasure, of festivity, but this servant in the background went to and fro like a slow religious procession.

The youth felt considerable alarm when he found himself involved in conversation with his hostess. In the course of this talk he discovered the great truth that when one submits himself to a thoroughly conventional conversation he runs risks of being most amazingly stupid. He was glad that no one cared to overhear it.

The millionaire, deprived of his kitten, sat back in his chair and laughed at the replies of his son to the attacks of one of the girls. In the rather good wit of his offspring he took an intense delight, but he laughed more particularly at the words of the son.

Indicated in this light chatter about the dinner table there was an existence that was not at all what the youth had been taught to see. Theologians had for a long time told the poor man that riches did not bring

happiness, and they had solemnly repeated this phrase until it had come
to mean that misery was commensurate with dollars, that each wealthy man
was inwardly a miserable wretch. And when a wail of despair or rage
had come from the night of the slums they had stuffed this epigram down
the throat of he who cried out and told him that he was a lucky fellow.
They did this because they feared.

The youth, studying this family group, could not see that they had great
license to be pale and haggard. They were no doubt fairly good, being
not strongly induced toward the bypaths. Various worlds turned open doors
toward them. Wealth in a certain sense is liberty. If they were fairly
virtuous he could not see why they should be so persistently pitied.

And no doubt they would dispense their dollars like little seeds upon
the soil of the world if it were not for the fact that, since the days of the
ancient great political economist, the more exalted forms of virtue have
grown to be utterly impracticable.

April 29, 1894
[New York *Press*, part 3, p. 2.]

AN OMINOUS BABY*

A baby was wandering in a strange country. He was a tattered child with
a frowsled wealth of yellow hair. His dress, of a checked stuff, was soiled,
and showed the marks of many conflicts, like the chain shirt of a warrior.
His suntanned knees shone above wrinkled stockings, which he pulled up
occasionally with an impatient movement when they entangled his feet.
From a gaping shoe there appeared an array of tiny toes.

He was toddling along an avenue between rows of stolid brown houses.
He went slowly, with a look of absorbed interest on his small flushed face.
His blue eyes stared curiously. Carriages went with a musical rumble over
the smooth asphalt. A man with a chrysanthemum was going up steps.
Two nursery maids chatted as they walked slowly, while their charges
hobnobbed amiably between perambulators. A truck wagon roared thunderously in the distance.

The child from the poor district made his way along the brown street
filled with dull gray shadows. High up, near the roofs, glancing sunrays
changed cornices to blazing gold and silvered the fronts of windows. The
wandering baby stopped and stared at the two children laughing and playing in their carriages among the heaps of rugs and cushions. He braced
his legs apart in an attitude of earnest attention. His lower jaw fell, and

* Tommie Series. Also *Midnight Sketches.*

disclosed his small, even teeth. As they moved on, he followed the carriages with awe in his face as if contemplating a pageant. Once one of the babies, with twittering laughter, shook a gorgeous rattle at him. He smiled jovially in return.

Finally a nursery maid ceased conversation and, turning, made a gesture of annoyance. "Go 'way, little boy," she said to him. "Go 'way. You're all dirty."

He gazed at her with infant tranquillity for a moment, and then went slowly off, dragging behind him a bit of rope he had acquired in another street. He continued to investigate the new scenes. The people and houses struck him with interest as would flowers and trees. Passengers had to avoid the small, absorbed figure in the middle of the sidewalk. They glanced at the intent baby face covered with scratches and dust as with scars and with powder smoke.

After a time, the wanderer discovered upon the pavement a pretty child in fine clothes playing with a toy. It was a tiny fire engine, painted brilliantly in crimson and gold. The wheels rattled as its small owner dragged it uproariously about by means of a string. The babe with his bit of rope trailing behind him paused and regarded the child and the toy. For a long while he remained motionless, save for his eyes, which followed all movements of the glittering thing. The owner paid no attention to the spectator, but continued his joyous imitations of phases of the career of a fire engine. His gleeful baby laugh rang against the calm fronts of the houses. After a little the wandering baby began quietly to sidle nearer. His bit of rope, now forgotten, dropped at his feet. He removed his eyes from the toy and glanced expectantly at the other child.

"Say," he breathed softly.

The owner of the toy was running down the walk at top speed. His tongue was clanging like a bell and his legs were galloping. He did not look around at the coaxing call from the small tattered figure on the curb.

The wandering baby approached still nearer, and presently spoke again. "Say," he murmured, "le' me play wif it?"

The other child interrupted some shrill tootings. He bent his head and spoke disdainfully over his shoulder. "No," he said.

The wanderer retreated to the curb. He failed to notice the bit of rope, once treasured. His eyes followed as before the winding course of the engine, and his tender mouth twitched.

"Say," he ventured at last, "is dat yours?"

"Yes," said the other, tilting his round chin. He drew his property suddenly behind him as if it were menaced. "Yes," he repeated, "it's mine."

"Well, le' me play wif it?" said the wandering baby, with a trembling note of desire in his voice.

"No," cried the pretty child with determined lips. "It's mine. My ma-ma buyed it."

"Well, tan't I play wif it?" His voice was a sob. He stretched forth little covetous hands.

"No," the pretty child continued to repeat. "No, it's mine."

"Well, I want to play wif it," wailed the other. A sudden fierce frown mantled his baby face. He clenched his fat hands and advanced with a formidable gesture. He looked some wee battler in a war.

"It's mine! It's mine," cried the pretty child, his voice in the treble of outraged rights.

"I want it," roared the wanderer.

"It's mine! It's mine!"

"I want it!"

"It's mine!"

The pretty child retreated to the fence, and there paused at bay. He protected his property with outstretched arms. The small vandal made a charge. There was a short scuffle at the fence. Each grasped the string to the toy and tugged. Their faces were wrinkled with baby rage, the verge of tears. Finally, the child in tatters gave a supreme tug and wrenched the string from the other's hands. He set off rapidly down the street, bearing the toy in his arms. He was weeping with the air of a wronged one who has at last succeeded in achieving his rights. The other baby was squalling lustily. He seemed quite helpless. He wrung his chubby hands and railed.

After the small barbarian had got some distance away, he paused and regarded his booty. His little form curved with pride. A soft, gleeful smile loomed through the storm of tears. With great care he prepared the toy for traveling. He stopped a moment on a corner and gazed at the pretty child, whose small figure was quivering with sobs. As the latter began to show signs of beginning pursuit, the little vandal turned and vanished down a dark side street as into a cavern.

May, 1894
[*The Arena*, Vol. 9, pp. 819-821.]

A GREAT MISTAKE*

An Italian kept a fruit stand on a corner where he had good aim at the people who came down from the elevated station, and at those who went along two thronged streets. He sat most of the day in a backless chair that was placed strategically.

There was a babe living hard by, up five flights of stairs, who regarded this Italian as a tremendous being. The babe had investigated this fruit stand. It had thrilled him as few things he had met with in his travels had thrilled him. The sweets of the world had lain there in dazzling rows, tumbled in luxurious heaps. When he gazed at this Italian seated amid such splendid treasures, his lower lip hung low and his eyes, raised to the vendor's face, were filled with deep respect, worship, as if he saw omnipotence.

The babe came often to this corner. He hovered about the stand and watched each detail of the business. He was fascinated by the tranquillity of the vendor, the majesty of power and possession. At times he was so engrossed in his contemplation that people, hurrying, had to use care to avoid bumping him down.

He had never ventured very near to the stand. It was his habit to hang warily about the curb. Even there he resembled a babe who looks unbidden at a feast of gods.

One day, however, as the babe was thus staring, the vendor arose and, going along the front of the stand, began to polish oranges with a red pocket handkerchief. The breathless spectator moved across the sidewalk until his small face almost touched the vendor's sleeve. His fingers were gripped in a fold of his dress.

At last, the Italian finished with the oranges and returned to his chair. He drew a newspaper printed in his language from behind a bunch of bananas. He settled himself in a comfortable position, and began to glare savagely at the print. The babe was left face to face with the massed joys of the world. For a time he was a simple worshiper at this golden shrine. Then tumultuous desires began to shake him. His dreams were of conquest. His lips moved. Presently into his head there came a little plan. He sidled nearer, throwing swift and cunning glances at the Italian. He strove to maintain his conventional manner, but the whole plot was written upon his countenance.

At last he had come near enough to touch the fruit. From the tattered

* Tommie Series. Also *Midnight Sketches*.

skirt came slowly his small dirty hand. His eyes were still fixed upon the vendor. His features were set, save for the underlip, which had a faint fluttering movement. The hand went forward.

Elevated trains thundered to the station and the stairway poured people upon the sidewalks. There was a deep-sea roar from feet and wheels going ceaselessly. None seemed to perceive the babe engaged in a great venture.

The Italian turned his paper. Sudden panic smote the babe. His hand dropped, and he gave vent to a cry of dismay. He remained for a moment staring at the vendor. There was evidently a great debate in his mind. His infant intellect had defined this Italian. The latter was undoubtedly a man who would eat babes that provoked him. And the alarm in the babe when this monarch had turned his newspaper brought vividly before him the consequences if he were detected. But at this moment the vendor gave a blissful grunt and, tilting his chair against a wall, closed his eyes. His paper dropped unheeded.

The babe ceased his scrutiny and again raised his hand. It was moved with supreme caution toward the fruit. The fingers were bent, claw-like, in the manner of great heart-shaking greed. Once he stopped and chattered convulsively, because the vendor moved in his sleep. The babe, with his eyes still upon the Italian, again put forth his hand, and the rapacious fingers closed over a round bulb.

And it was written that the Italian should at this moment open his eyes. He glared at the babe a fierce question. Thereupon the babe thrust the round bulb behind him, and, with a face expressive of the deepest guilt, began a wild but elaborate series of gestures declaring his innocence. The Italian howled. He sprang to his feet, and with three steps overtook the babe. He whirled him fiercely, and took from the little fingers a lemon.

1894?

[*The Philistine*, Vol. 2 (March, 1896), pp. 106–109.]

A DARK BROWN DOG*

A child was standing on a street corner. He leaned with one shoulder against a high board fence and swayed the other to and fro, the while kicking carelessly at the gravel.

Sunshine beat upon the cobbles, and a lazy summer wind raised yellow dust which trailed in clouds down the avenue. Clattering trucks moved with indistinctness through it. The child stood dreamily gazing.

* Tommie Series. Also *Midnight Sketches.*

After a time, a little dark brown dog came trotting with an intent air down the sidewalk. A short rope was dragging from his neck. Occasionally he trod upon the end of it and stumbled.

He stopped opposite the child, and the two regarded each other. The dog hesitated for a moment, but presently he made some little advances with his tail. The child put out his hand and called him. In an apologetic manner the dog came close, and the two had an interchange of friendly pattings and waggles. The dog became more enthusiastic with each moment of the interview, until with his gleeful caperings he threatened to overturn the child. Whereupon the child lifted his hand and struck the dog a blow upon the head.

This thing seemed to overpower and astonish the little dark brown dog, and wounded him to the heart. He sank down in despair at the child's feet. When the blow was repeated, together with an admonition in childish sentences, he turned over upon his back, and held his paws in a peculiar manner. At the same time with his ears and his eyes he offered a small prayer to the child.

He looked so comical on his back, and holding his paws peculiarly, that the child was greatly amused and gave him little taps repeatedly, to keep him so. But the little dark brown dog took this chastisement in the most serious way, and no doubt considered that he had committed some grave crime, for he wriggled contritely and showed his repentance in every way that was in his power. He pleaded with the child and petitioned him, and offered more prayers.

At last the child grew weary of this amusement and turned toward home. The dog was praying at the time. He lay on his back and turned his eyes upon the retreating form.

Presently he struggled to his feet and started after the child. The latter wandered in a perfunctory way toward his home, stopping at times to investigate various matters. During one of these pauses he discovered the little dark brown dog, who was following him with the air of a footpad.

The child beat his pursuer with a small stick he had found. The dog lay down and prayed until the child had finished and resumed his journey. Then he scrambled erect and took up the pursuit again.

On the way to his home the child turned many times and beat the dog, proclaiming with childish gestures that he held him in contempt as an unimportant dog, with no value save for a moment. For being this quality of animal the dog apologized and eloquently expressed regret, but he continued stealthily to follow the child. His manner grew so very guilty that he slunk like an assassin.

When the child reached his doorstep, the dog was industriously ambling a few yards in the rear. He became so agitated with shame when he again confronted the child that he forgot the dragging rope. He tripped upon it and fell forward.

The child sat down on the step, and the two had another interview. During it the dog greatly exerted himself to please the child. He performed a few gambols with such abandon that the child suddenly saw him to be a valuable thing. He made a swift, avaricious charge and seized the rope.

He dragged his captive into a hall and up many long stairways in a dark tenement. The dog made willing efforts, but he could not hobble very skillfully up the stairs because he was very small and soft, and at last the pace of the engrossed child grew so energetic that the dog became panic-stricken. In his mind he was being dragged toward a grim unknown. His eyes grew wild with the terror of it. He began to wiggle his head frantically and to brace his legs.

The child redoubled his exertions. They had a battle on the stairs. The child was victorious, because he was completely absorbed in his purpose, and because the dog was very small. He dragged his acquirement to the door of his home, and finally with triumph across the threshold.

No one was in. The child sat down on the floor and made overtures to the dog. These the dog instantly accepted. He beamed with affection upon his new friend. In a short time they were firm and abiding comrades.

When the child's family appeared, they made a great row. The dog was examined and commented upon and called names. Scorn was leveled at him from all eyes, so that he became much embarrassed and drooped like a scorched plant. But the child went sturdily to the center of the floor and, at the top of his voice, championed the dog. It happened that he was roaring protestations, with his arms clasped about the dog's neck, when the father of the family came in from work.

The parent demanded to know what the blazes they were making the kid howl for. It was explained in many words that the infernal kid wanted to introduce a disreputable dog into the family.

A family council was held. On this depended the dog's fate, but he in no way heeded, being busily engaged in chewing the end of the child's dress.

The affair was quickly ended. The father of the family, it appears, was in a particularly savage temper that evening, and when he perceived that it would amaze and anger everybody if such a dog were allowed to remain, he decided that it should be so. The child, crying softly, took his friend off to a retired part of the room to hobnob with him, while the father quelled a fierce rebellion of his wife. So it came to pass that the dog was a member of the household.

He and the child were associated together at all times save when the child slept. The child became a guardian and a friend. If the large folk kicked the dog and threw things at him, the child made loud and violent objections. Once when the child had run, protesting loudly, with tears raining down his face and his arms outstretched, to protect his friend, he had been struck in the head with a very large saucepan from the hand of his father, enraged at some seeming lack of courtesy in the dog. Ever after, the family were careful how they threw things at the dog. Moreover, the latter grew very skillful in avoiding missiles and feet. In a small room containing a stove, a table, a bureau, and some chairs, he would display strategic ability of a high order, dodging, feinting, and scuttling about among the furniture. He could force three or four people armed with brooms, sticks, and handfuls of coal to use all their ingenuity to get in a blow. And even when they did, it was seldom that they could do him a serious injury or leave any imprint.

But when the child was present these scenes did not occur. It came to be recognized that if the dog was molested, the child would burst into sobs, and as the child, when started, was very riotous and practically unquenchable, the dog had therein a safeguard.

However, the child could not always be near. At night, when he was asleep, his dark brown friend would raise from some black corner a wild, wailful cry, a song of infinite loneliness and despair, that would go shuddering and sobbing among the buildings of the block and cause people to swear. At these times the singer would often be chased all over the kitchen and hit with a great variety of articles.

Sometimes, too, the child himself used to beat the dog, although it is not known that he ever had what could be truly called a just cause. The dog always accepted these thrashings with an air of admitted guilt. He was too much of a dog to try to look to be a martyr or to plot revenge. He received the blows with deep humility, and furthermore he forgave his friend the moment the child had finished, and was ready to caress the child's hand with his little red tongue.

When misfortune came upon the child, and his troubles overwhelmed him, he would often crawl under the table and lay his small distressed head on the dog's back. The dog was ever sympathetic. It is not to be supposed that at such times he took occasion to refer to the unjust beatings his friend, when provoked, had administered to him.

He did not achieve any notable degree of intimacy with the other members of the family. He had no confidence in them, and the fear that he would express at their casual approach often exasperated them exceedingly. They used to gain a certain satisfaction in underfeeding him, but finally his friend the child grew to watch the matter with some care, and when he forgot it, the dog was often successful in secret for himself.

So the dog prospered. He developed a large bark, which came wondrously from such a small rug of a dog. He ceased to howl persistently at night. Sometimes, indeed, in his sleep, he would utter little yells, as from pain, but that occurred, no doubt, when in his dreams he encountered huge flaming dogs who threatened him direfully.

His devotion to the child grew until it was a sublime thing. He wagged at his approach; he sank down in despair at his departure. He could detect the sound of the child's step among all the noises of the neighborhood. It was like a calling voice to him.

The scene of their companionship was a kingdom governed by this terrible potentate, the child; but neither criticism nor rebellion ever lived for an instant in the heart of the one subject. Down in the mystic, hidden fields of his little dog-soul bloomed flowers of love and fidelity and perfect faith.

The child was in the habit of going on many expeditions to observe strange things in the vicinity. On these occasions his friend usually jogged aimfully along behind. Perhaps, though, he went ahead. This necessitated his turning around every quarter minute to make sure the child was coming. He was filled with a large idea of the importance of these journeys. He would carry himself with such an air! He was proud to be the retainer of so great a monarch.

One day, however, the father of the family got quite exceptionally drunk. He came home and held carnival with the cooking utensils, the furniture, and his wife. He was in the midst of this recreation when the child, followed by the dark brown dog, entered the room. They were returning from their voyages.

The child's practiced eye instantly noted his father's state. He dived under the table, which experience had taught him was a rather safe place. The dog, lacking skill in such matters, was, of course, unaware of the true condition of affairs. He looked with interested eyes at his friend's sudden dive. He interpreted it to mean: Joyous gambol. He started to patter across the floor to join him. He was the picture of a little dark brown dog en route to a friend.

The head of the family saw him at this moment. He gave a huge howl of joy, and knocked the dog down with a heavy coffeepot. The dog, yelling in supreme astonishment and fear, writhed to his feet and ran for cover. The man kicked out with a ponderous foot. It caused the dog to swerve as if caught in a tide. A second blow of the coffeepot laid him upon the floor.

Here the child, uttering loud cries, came valiantly forth like a knight. The father of the family paid no attention to these calls of the child, but advanced with glee upon the dog. Upon being knocked down twice in swift succession, the latter apparently gave up all hope of escape. He rolled over on his back and held his paws in a peculiar manner. At the same time with his eyes and his ears he offered up a small prayer.

But the father was in a mood for having fun, and it occurred to him that it would be a fine thing to throw the dog out of the window. So he reached down and, grabbing the animal by a leg, lifted him, squirming, up. He swung him two or three times hilariously about his head, and then flung him with great accuracy through the window.

The soaring dog created a surprise in the block. A woman watering plants in an opposite window gave an involuntary shout and dropped a flowerpot. A man in another window leaned perilously out to watch the flight of the dog. A woman who had been hanging out clothes in a yard began to caper wildly. Her mouth was filled with clothespins, but her arms gave vent to a sort of exclamation. In appearance she was like a gagged prisoner. Children ran whooping.

The dark brown body crashed in a heap on the roof of a shed five stories below. From thence it rolled to the pavement of an alleyway.

The child in the room far above burst into a long, dirge-like cry, and toddled hastily out of the room. It took him a long time to reach the alley, because his size compelled him to go downstairs backward, one step at a time, and holding with both hands to the step above.

When they came for him later, they found him seated by the body of his dark brown friend.

1894?

[*The Cosmopolitan*, Vol. 30 (March, 1901), pp. 481–486.]

BILLIE ATKINS WENT TO OMAHA

[An American Tramp's Excursion]

Billie Atkins is a traveler. He has seen the cold blue gleam of the northern lakes, the tangled green thickets of Florida and the white peaks of the Rockies. All this has he seen and much more, for he has been a tramp for sixteen years.

One winter evening when the "sitting room" of a lodging house just off the Bowery was thronged with loungers Billie came in, mellow with drink and in the eloquent stage. He chose to charm them with a description of a journey from Denver to Omaha. They all listened with appreciation, for when Billie is quite drunk he tells a tale with indescribable gestures and humorous emotions that makes one feel that, after all, the buffets of fate are rather more comic than otherwise.

It seems that when Billie was in Denver last winter it suddenly occurred to him that he wished to be in Omaha. He did not deem it necessary to explain this fancy: he merely announced that he happened to be in Denver last winter and that then it occurred to him that he wished to be in Omaha. Apparently these ideas come to his class like bolts of compelling lightning. After that swift thought of Omaha it was impossible for Denver to contain him; he must away. When the night express on the Union Pacific pulled out Billie "made a great sneak" behind some freight cars and climbed onto the "blind" end of the baggage car.

It was a very dark night and Billie congratulated himself that he had not been discovered. He huddled to a little heap on the car platform and thought, with a woman's longing, of Omaha.

However, it was not long before an icy stream of water struck Billie a startling blow in the face, and as he raised his eyes he saw in the red glare from the engine a very jocular fireman crouching on the coal and holding the nozzle of a small hose in his hand. And at frequent intervals during the night this jocular fireman would climb up on the coal and play the hose on Billie. The drenched tramp changed his position and curled himself up into a little ball and swore graphically, all to no purpose. The fireman persisted with his hose and when he thought that Billie was getting too comfortable he came back to the rear of the tender and doused him with a pailful of very cold water.

But Billie stuck to his position. For one reason, the express went too fast for him to get safely off, and for another reason he wished to go to Omaha.

The train rushed out of the shadow of the mountains and into the cold gray of dawn on the prairies. The biting chill of the morning made Billie shake in his wet clothes. He adjusted himself on the edge of the rocking car platform where he could catch the first rays of the sun. And it was this change of position that got him into certain difficulties. At about eight o'clock the express went roaring through a little village. Billie, sunning himself on the edge of the steps, espied three old farmers seated on the porch of the village store. They grinned at him and waved their arms.

"I taut they was jest givin' me er jolly," said Billie, "so I waved me hand at 'em an' gives 'em er laugh, an' th' train went on. But it turned out they wasn't motionin' t' me at all, but was all th' while givin' er tip t' th' brakey that I was on th' blind. An' 'fore I knew it th' brakey came over th' top, or aroun' th' side, or somehow, an' I was a-gittin' kicked in th' neck."

" 'Gitoffahere! gitoffahere!'

"I was dead escared b'cause th' train was goin' hell bentin'.

"'Gitoffahere! gitoffahere'

"'Oh, please, mister,' I sez, 'I can't git off—th' train's goin' too fast.'"

But he kept on kickin' me fer a while til finally he got tired an' stopped th' train b'cause I could a-never got off th' way she was runnin'. By this time th' passengers in all th' cars got onto it that they was puttin' er bum off th' blind, an' when I got down off th' step, I see every winder in th' train was fuller heads, an' they gimme er great laugh until I had t' turn me back an' walk off."

As it happened, the nearest station to where Billie then found himself was eighteen miles distant. He dried his clothes as best he could and then swore along the tracks for a mile or two. But it was weary business—tramping along in the vast vacancy of the plains. Billie got tired and lay down to wait for a freight train. After a time one came and as the long string of boxcars thundered past him, he made another "great sneak" and a carefully calculated run and grab. He got safely on the little step and then he began to do what he called "ridin' th' ladder." That is to say, he clung to the little iron ladder that is fastened to the end of each car. He remained hanging there while the long train crept slowly over the plains.

He did not dare to show himself above the top of the car for fear of the brakeman. He considered himself safe down between the ends of the jolting cars, but once, as he chanced to look toward the sky, he saw a burly brakeman leaning on the brakewheel and regarding him.

"Come up here," said the brakeman.

Billie climbed painfully to the top of the car.

"Got any money?" said the brakeman.

"No," replied Billie.

"Well, then, gitoffahere," said the brakeman, and Billie received another installment of kicks. He went down the ladder and puckered his mouth and drew in his breath, preparatory to getting off the car, but the train had arrived at a small grade and Billie became frightened. The little wheels were all a-humming and the cars lurched like boats on the sea.

"Oh, please, mister," said Billie, "I can't git off. It's a-goin' too fast."

The brakeman swore and began the interesting operation of treading, with his brass toed boots, on Billie's fingers. Billie hung hard. He cast glances of despair at the rapid fleeting ground and shifted his grip often. But presently the brakeman's heels came down with extraordinary force and Billie involuntarily released his hold.

He fell in a heap and rolled over and over. His face and body were scratched and bruised, and on the top of his head there was a contusion that fitted like a new derby. His clothes had been rags, but they were now exaggerated out of all semblance of clothes. He sat up and looked at the departing train. "Gawd-dernit," he said, "I'll never git t' Omaha at this rate."

Presently Billie developed a most superhuman hunger. He saw the houses of a village some distance away, and he made for them, resolved to have something to eat if it cost a life. But still he knew he would be arrested if he appeared on the streets of any well organized, respectable town in the trousers he was then obliged to wear. He was in a quandary until by good fortune he perceived a pair of brown overalls hanging on a line in the rear of an isolated house.

He "made a great sneak on 'em." This sort of thing requires patience, but not more than an hour later, he bore off a large square of cloth which he had torn from one leg of the overalls. At another house he knocked at the door and when a woman came he stood very carefully facing her and requested a needle and thread. She gave them to him, and he waited until she had shut the door before he turned and went away.

He retired then into a thick growing patch of sunflowers on the outskirts of the town and started in to sew the piece of overall to his trousers. He had not been engaged long at his task before "two hundred kids" accumulated in front of the sunflower patch and began to throw stones at him. For some time the sky was darkened by a shower of missiles of all sizes. Occasionally Billie, without his trousers, would make little forays, yelling savage threats. These would compel the boys to retire some distance, but they always returned again with renewed ardor. Billie thought he would never get his trousers mended.

But this adventure was the cause of his again meeting Black John Randolph, who Billie said was "th' whitest pardner" he ever had. While he was engaged in conflict with the horde of boys a negro came running down the road and began to belabor them with a boot blacking kit. The boys ran off, and Billie saw with delight that his rescuer was Black John Randolph, whom he had known in Memphis.

Billie, unmolested, sewed his trousers. Then he told Black John that he was hungry, and the two swooped down on the town. Black John shined shoes until dark. He shined for all the available citizens of the place. Billie stood around and watched. The earnings were sixty cents. They spent it all for gingerbread, for it seems that Billie had developed a sudden marvelous longing for gingerbread.

Having feasted, Billie decided to make another attempt for Omaha. He and Black John went to the railroad yard and there they discovered an eastbound freight car that was empty save for one tramp and seven cans of peaches. They parleyed with the tramp and induced him to give up his claim on two-thirds of the car. They settled very comfortably, and that night Billie was again on his way to Omaha. The three of them lived for twenty-four hours on canned peaches, and would have been happy ever after no doubt if it had not happened that their freight car was presently switched off to a side line, and sent careering off in the wrong direction.

When Billie discovered this he gave a whoop and fell out of the car, for he was very particular about walking, and he did not wish to be dragged far from the main line. He trudged back to it, and there discovered a lumber car that contained about forty tramps.

This force managed to overawe the trainmen for a time and compel a free ride for a few miles, but presently the engine was stopped, and the trainmen formed in war array and advanced with clubs.

Billie had had experience in such matters. He "made a sneak." He repaired to a coal car and cuddled among the coal. He buried his body completely, and of his head only his nose and his eyes could have been seen.

The trainmen spread the tramps out over the prairie in a wide fleeing circle, as when a stone is hurled into a placid creek. They remained cursing in their beards, and the train went on.

Billie, snug in his bed, smiled without disarranging the coal that covered his mouth, and thought of Omaha.

But in an hour or two he got impatient, and upreared his head to look at the scenery. An eagle-eyed brakeman espied him.

"Got any money?"

"No."

"Well, then, gitoffahere."

Billie got off. The brakeman continued to throw coal at him until the train had hauled him beyond range.

"Hully mack'rel," said Billie, "I'll never git t' Omaha."

He was quite discouraged. He lay down on a bank beside the track to think, and while there he went to sleep. When he awoke a freight train was thundering past him. Still half asleep, he made a dash and a grab. He was up the ladder and on top of the car before he had recovered all of his faculties. A brakeman charged on him. "Got any money?"

"No, but, please, mister, won't yeh please let me stay on yer train fer a little ways? I'm awful tired, and I wanta git t' Omaha."

The brakeman reflected. Then he searched Billie's pockets, and finding half a plug of tobacco, took possession of it. He decided to let Billie ride for a time.

Billie perched on top of the car and admired the changing scenery while the train went twenty miles. Then the brakeman induced him to get off, considering no doubt that a twenty mile ride was sufficient in exchange for a half plug of tobacco.

The rest of the trip is incoherent, like the detailed accounts of great battles. Billie boarded trains and got thrown off on his head, on his left shoulder, on his right shoulder, on his hands and knees. He struck the ground slanting, straight, from above, and full sideways. His clothes were shredded and torn like the sails of a gale blown brig. His skin was tattooed with bloody lines, crosses, triangles, and all the devices known to geometry. But he wouldn't walk, and he was bound to reach Omaha. So he let the trainmen use him as a projectile with which to bombard the picturesque Western landscape.

And eventually he reached Omaha. One night, when it was snowing and cold winds whistled among the city's chimneys, he arrived in a coal car. He was filled with glee that he had reached the place of his endeavor. He could not repress his pride when he thought of the conquered miles. He went forth from the coal car with a blithe step.

The police would not let him stand on a corner nor sit down anywhere. They drove him about for two or three hours, until he happened to think of the railroad station. He went there, and was just getting into a nice doze by the warm red stove in the waiting room, when an official of some kind took him by the collar, and leading him calmly to the door, kicked him out into the snow. After that he was ejected from four saloons in rapid succession.

"Hully mack'rel!" he said, as he stood in the snow and quavered and trembled.

Until three o'clock in the morning various industrious policemen kept him moving from place to place as if he were pawn in a game of chess, until finally Billie became desperate and approached an officer in this fashion: "Say, mister, won't yeh please arrest me? I wanta go t' jail so's I can sleep."

"What?"

"I say, won't yer please arrest me? I wanta go t' jail so I kin sleep."

The policeman studied Billie for a moment. Then he made an impatient gesture. "Oh, can't yeh arrest yerself? The jail's a long ways from here, an' I don't wanta take yeh way up there."

"Sure—I kin," said Billie. "Where is it?"

The policeman gave him directions, and Billie started for the jail.

He had considerable difficulty in finding it. He was often obliged to accost people in the street. "Please, mister, can yeh tell me where the jail is?"

At last he found it, and after a short parley, they admitted him. They gave him permission to sleep on a sort of an iron slab swung by four chains from the ceiling. Billie sank down upon this couch and arrayed his meager rags about his form. Before he was completely in the arms of the slumber god, however, he made a remark expressive of a new desire, a sudden born longing. "Huly mack'rel, I mus' start back for Denver in th' mornin'."

May 20, 1894

[New York *Press*, part 4, p. 3.]

MR. BINKS' DAY OFF:
A STUDY OF A CLERK'S HOLIDAY

When Binks was coming uptown in a Broadway cable car one afternoon he caught some superficial glimpses of Madison Square as he ducked his head to peek through between a young woman's bonnet and a young man's newspaper. The green of the little park vaguely astonished Binks. He had grown accustomed to a white and brown park; now, all at once, it was radiant green. The grass, the leaves, had come swiftly, silently, as if a great green light from the sky had shone suddenly upon the little desolate-hued place.

The vision cheered the mind of Binks. It cried to him that nature was still supreme; he had begun to think the banking business to be the pivot on which the universe turned. Produced by this wealth of young green, faint, faraway voices called to him. Certain subtle memories swept over him. The million leaves looked into his soul and said something sweet and pure in an unforgotten song, the melody of his past. Binks began to dream.

When he arrived at the little Harlem flat he sat down to dinner with an air of profound dejection, which Mrs. Binks promptly construed into an insult to her cooking, and to the time and thought she had expended in preparing the meal. She promptly resented it. "Will, what's the matter now?" she demanded. Apparently she had asked this question ten thousand times.

"Nothin'," said Binks, shortly, filled with gloom. He meant by this remark that his ailment was so subtle that her feminine mind would not be enlightened by any explanation.

The head of the family was in an ugly mood. The little Binkses suddenly paused in their uproar and became very wary children. They knew that it would be dangerous to do anything irrelevant to their father's bad temper. They studied his face with their large eyes, filled with childish seriousness and speculation. Meanwhile they ate with the most extraordinary caution. They handled their little forks with such care that there was

barely a sound. At each slight movement of their father they looked apprehensively at him, expecting the explosion.

The meal continued amid a somber silence. At last, however, Binks
spoke, clearing his throat of the indefinite rage that was in it and looking
over at his wife. The little Binkses seemed to inwardly dodge, but he
merely said: "I wish I could get away into the country for a while!"

His wife bristled with that brave anger which agitates a woman when
she sees fit to assume that her husband is weak spirited. "If I worked as
hard as you do, if I slaved over those old books the way you do, I'd have a
vacation once in awhile or I'd tear their old office down." Upon her face
was a Roman determination. She was a personification of all manner of
courages and rebellions and powers.

Binks felt the falsity of her emotion in a vague way, but at that time he
only made a sullen gesture. Later, however, he cried out in a voice of sudden violence: "Look at Tommie's dress! Why the dickens don't you put a
bib on that child?"

His wife glared over Tommie's head at her husband, as she leaned
around in her chair to tie on the demanded bib. The two looked as hostile
as warring redskins. In the wife's eyes there was an intense opposition and
defiance, an assertion that she now considered the man she had married to
be beneath her in intellect, industry, valor. There was in this glance a jeer
at the failures of his life. And Binks, filled with an inexpressible rebellion
at what was to him a lack of womanly perception and sympathy in her,
replied with a look that called his wife a drag, an uncomprehending thing
of vain ambitions, the weight of his existence.

The baby meanwhile began to weep because his mother, in her exasperation, had yanked him and hurt his neck. Her anger, groping for an outlet,
had expressed itself in the nervous strength of her fingers. "Keep still,
Tommie," she said to him. "I didn't hurt you. You needn't cry the minute
anybody touches you!" He made a great struggle and repressed his loud
sobs, but the tears continued to fall down his cheeks and his underlip
quivered from a baby sense of injury, the anger of an impotent child who
seems as he weeps to be planning revenges.

"I don't see why you don't keep that child from eternally crying," said
Binks, as a final remark. He then arose and went away to smoke, leaving
Mrs. Binks with the children and the disheveled table.

Later that night, when the children were in bed, Binks said to his wife:
"We ought to get away from the city for a while at least this spring. I can
stand it in the summer, but in the spring—". He made a motion with his
hand that represented the new things that are born in the heart when spring
comes into the eyes.

"It will cost something, Phil," said Mrs. Binks.

"That's true," said Binks. They both began to reflect, contemplating the shackles of their poverty. "And besides, I don't believe I could get off," said Binks after a time.

Nothing more was said of it that night. In fact, it was two or three days afterward that Binks came home and said: "Margaret, you get the children ready on Saturday noon and we'll all go out and spend Sunday with your Aunt Sarah!"

When he came home on Saturday his hat was far back on the back of his head from the speed he was in. Mrs. Binks was putting on her bonnet before the glass, turning about occasionally to admonish the little Binkses, who, in their new clothes, were wandering around, stiffly, and getting into all sorts of small difficulties. They had been ready since eleven o'clock. Mrs. Binks had been obliged to scold them continually, one after the other, and sometimes three at once.

"Hurry up," said Binks, immediately, "ain't got much time. Say, you ain't going to let Jim wear that hat, are you? Where's his best one? Good heavens, look at Margaret's dress! It's soiled already! Tommie, stop that, do you hear? Well, are you ready?"

Indeed, it was not until the Binkses had left the city far behind and were careering into New Jersey that they recovered their balances. Then something of the fresh quality of the country stole over them and cooled their nerves. Horse cars and ferryboats were maddening to Binks when he was obliged to convoy a wife and three children. He appreciated the vast expanses of green, through which ran golden hued roads. The scene accented his leisure and his lack of responsibility.

Near the track a little river jostled over the stones. At times the cool thunder of its roar came faintly to the ear. The Ramapo Hills were in the background, faintly purple, and surmounted with little peaks that shone with the luster of the sun. Binks began to joke heavily with the children. The little Binkses, for their part, asked the most superhuman questions about details of the scenery. Mrs. Binks leaned contentedly back in her seat and seemed to be at rest, which was a most extraordinary thing.

When they got off the train at the little rural station they created considerable interest. Two or three loungers began to view them in a sort of concentrated excitement. They were apparently fascinated by the Binkses and seemed to be indulging in all manner of wild and intense speculation. The agent, as he walked into his station, kept his head turned. Across the dusty street, wide at this place, a group of men upon the porch of a battered grocery store shaded their eyes with their hands. The Binkses felt dimly like a circus and were a trifle bewildered by it. Binks gazed up and down, this way and that; he tried to be unaware of the stare of the citizens.

Finally, he approached the loungers, who straightened their forms suddenly and looked very expectant.

"Can you tell me where Miss Pattison lives?"

The loungers arose as one man. "It's th' third house up that road there."

"It's a white house with green shutters!"

"There, that's it—yeh can see it through th' trees!" Binks discerned that his wife's aunt was a well known personage, and also that the coming of the Binkses was an event of vast importance. When he marched off at the head of his flock, he felt like a drum major. His course was followed by the unwavering, intent eyes of the loungers.

The street was lined with two rows of austere and solemn trees. In one way it was like parading between the plumes on an immense hearse. These trees, lowly sighing in a breath-like wind, oppressed one with a sense of melancholy and dreariness. Back from the road, behind flower beds, controlled by boxwood borders, the houses were asleep in the drowsy air. Between them one could get views of the fields lying in a splendor of gold and green. A monotonous humming song of insects came from the regions of sunshine, and from some hidden barnyard a hen suddenly burst forth in a sustained cackle of alarm. The tranquillity of the scene contained a meaning of peace and virtue that was incredibly monotonous to the warriors from the metropolis. The sense of a city is battle. The Binkses were vaguely irritated and astonished at the placidity of this little town. This life spoke to them of no absorbing nor even interesting thing. There was something unbearable about it. "I should go crazy if I had to live here," said Mrs. Binks. A warrior in the flood tide of his blood, going from the hot business of war to a place of utter quiet, might have felt that there was an insipidity in peace. And thus felt the Binkses from New York. They had always named the clash of the swords of commerce as sin, crime, but now they began to imagine something admirable in it. It was high wisdom. They put aside their favorite expressions: "The curse of gold," "A mad passion to get rich," "The rush for the spoils." In the light of their contempt for this stillness, the conflicts of the city were exalted. They were at any rate wondrously clever.

But what they did feel was the fragrance of the air, the radiance of the sunshine, the glory of the fields and the hills. With their ears still clogged by the tempest and fury of city uproars, they heard the song of the universal religion, the mighty and mystic hymn of nature, whose melody is in each landscape. It appealed to their elemental selves. It was as if the earth had called recreant and heedless children and the mother word, of vast might and significance, brought them to sudden meekness. It was the universal thing whose power no one escapes. When a man hears it he usually remains silent. He understands then the sacrilege of speech.

When they came to the third house, the white one, with the green blinds, they perceived a woman, in a plaid sunbonnet, walking slowly down a path. Around her was a riot of shrubbery and flowers. From the long and tangled grass of the lawn grew a number of cherry trees. Their dark green foliage was thickly sprinkled with bright red fruit. Some sparrows were scuffling among the branches. The little Binkses began to whoop at sight of the woman in the plaid sunbonnet.

"Hay-oh, Aunt Sarah, hay-oh!" they shouted.

The woman shaded her eyes with her hand. "Well, good gracious, if it ain't Marg'ret Binks! An' Phil, too! Well, I am surprised!"

She came jovially to meet them. "Why, how are yeh all? I'm awful glad t' see yeh!"

The children, filled with great excitement, babbled questions and ejaculations while she greeted the others.

"Say, Aunt Sarah, gimme some cherries!"

"Look at th' man over there!"

"Look at th' flowers!"

"Gimme some flowers, Aunt Sarah!"

And little Tommie, red faced from the value of his information, bawled out: "Aunt Sah-wee, dey have horse tars where I live!" Later he shouted: "We come on a twain of steam tars!"

Aunt Sarah fairly bristled with the most enthusiastic hospitality. She beamed upon them like a sun. She made desperate attempts to gain possession of everybody's bundles that she might carry them to the house. There was a sort of a little fight over the baggage. The children clamored questions at her; she tried heroically to answer them. Tommie, at times, deluged her with news.

The curtains of the dining room were pulled down to keep out the flies. This made a deep, cool gloom in which corners of the old furniture caught wandering rays of light and shone with a mild luster. Everything was arranged with an unspeakable neatness that was the opposite of comfort. A branch of an apple tree, moved by the gentle wind, brushed softly against the closed blinds.

"Take off yer things," said Aunt Sarah.

Binks and his wife remained talking to Aunt Sarah, but the children speedily swarmed out over the farm, raiding in countless directions. It was only a matter of seconds before Jimmie discovered the brook behind the barn. Little Margaret roamed among the flowers, bursting into little cries at sight of new blossoms, new glories. Tommie gazed at the cherry trees for a few moments in profound silence. Then he went and procured a pole. It was very heavy, relatively. He could hardly stagger under it, but with infinite toil he dragged it to the proper place and somehow managed to push it erect. Then with a deep earnestness of demeanor he began a little onslaught upon the trees. Very often his blow missed the entire tree and the pole thumped on the ground. This necessitated the most extraordinary labor. But then at other times he would get two or three cherries at one wild swing of his weapon.

Binks and his wife spent the larger part of the afternoon out under the apple trees at the side of the house. Binks lay down on his back, with his head in the long lush grass. Mrs. Binks moved lazily to and fro in a rocking chair that had been brought from the house. Aunt Sarah, sometimes appearing, was strenuous in an account of relatives, and the Binkses had only to listen. They were glad of it, for this warm, sleepy air, pulsating with the sounds of insects, had enchained them in a great indolence.

It was to this place that Jimmie ran after he had fallen into the brook and scrambled out again. Holding his arms out carefully from his dripping person, he was roaring tremendously. His new sailor suit was a sight. Little Margaret came often to describe the wonders of her journeys, and Tommie, after a frightful struggle with the cherry trees, toddled over and went to sleep in the midst of a long explanation of his operations. The breeze stirred the locks on his baby forehead. His breath came in long sighs of content. Presently he turned his head to cuddle deeper into the grass. One arm was thrown in childish abandon over his head. Mrs. Binks stopped rocking to gaze at him. Presently she bent and noiselessly brushed away a spear of grass that was troubling the baby's temple. When she straightened up she saw that Binks, too, was absorbed in a contemplation of Tommie. They looked at each other presently, exchanging a vague smile. Through the silence came the voice of a plowing farmer berating his horses in a distant field.

The peace of the hills and the fields came upon the Binkses. They allowed Jimmie to sit up in bed and eat cake while his clothes were drying. Uncle Daniel returned from a wagon journey and recited them a ponderous tale of a pig that he had sold to a man with a red beard. They had no difficulty in feeling much interest in the story.

Binks began to expand with enormous appreciations. He would not go into the house until they compelled him. And as soon as the evening meal was finished he dragged his wife forth on a trip to the top of the hill behind the house. There was a great view from there, Uncle Daniel said.

The path, gray with little stones in the dusk, extended above them like a pillar. The pines were beginning to croon in a mournful key, inspired by the evening winds. Mrs. Binks had great difficulty in climbing this upright road. Binks was obliged to assist her, which he did with a considerable care and tenderness. In it there was a sort of a reminiscence of their courtship. It was a repetition of old days. Both enjoyed it because of this fact, although they subtly gave each other to understand that they disdained this emotion as an altogether unAmerican thing, for she, as a woman, was proud, and he had great esteem for himself as a man.

At the summit they seated themselves upon a fallen tree, near the edge of a cliff. The evening silence was upon the earth below them. Far in the west the sun lay behind masses of corn-colored clouds, tumbled and heaved into crags, peaks and canyons. On either hand stood the purple hills in motionless array. The valley lay wreathed in somber shadows. Slowly there went on the mystic process of the closing of the day. The corn-colored clouds faded to yellow and finally to a faint luminous green, inexpressibly vague. The rim of the hills was then an edge of crimson. The mountains became a profound blue. From the night, approaching in the east, came a wind. The trees of the mountain raised plaintive voices, bending toward the faded splendors of the day.

This song of the trees arose in low, sighing melody into the still air. It was filled with an infinite sorrow—a sorrow for birth, slavery, death. It was a wall telling the griefs, the pains of all ages. It was the symbol of agonies. It celebrated all suffering. Each man finds in this sound the expression of his own grief. It is the universal voice raised in lamentations.

As the trees huddled and bent, as if to hide from their eyes a certain sight, the green tints became blue. A faint suggestion of yellow replaced the crimson. The sun was dead.

The Binkses had been silent. These songs of the trees awe. They had remained motionless during this ceremony, their eyes fixed upon the mighty and indefinable changes which spoke to them of the final thing—the inevitable end. Their eyes had an impersonal expression. They were purified, chastened by this sermon, this voice calling to them from the sky. The hills had spoken and the trees had crooned their song. Binks finally stretched forth his arm in a wondering gesture.

"I wonder why," he said; "I wonder why the dickens it—why it—why—"

Tangled in his tongue was the unformulated question of the centuries, but Mrs. Binks had stolen forth her arm and linked it with his. Her head leaned softly against his shoulder.

July 8, 1894
[New York *Press*, part 4, p. 2.]

THE MEN IN THE STORM*

The blizzard began to swirl great clouds of snow along the streets, sweeping it down from the roofs, and up from the pavements, until the faces of pedestrians tingled and burned as from a thousand needle-prickings. Those on the walks huddled their necks closely in the collars of their coats, and went along stooping like a race of aged people. The drivers of vehicles hurried their horses furiously on their way. They were made more cruel by the exposure of their position, aloft on high seats. The street cars, bound uptown, went slowly, the horses slipping and straining in the spongy brown mass that lay between the rails. The drivers, muffled to the eyes, stood erect, facing the wind, models of grim philosophy. Overhead trains rumbled and roared, and the dark structure of the elevated railroad, stretching over the avenue, dripped little streams and drops of water upon the mud and snow beneath.

All the clatter of the street was softened by the masses that lay upon the cobbles, until, even to one who looked from a window, it became important music, a melody of life made necessary to the ear by the dreariness of the pitiless beat and sweep of the storm. Occasionally one could see black figures of men busily shoveling the white drifts from the walks. The sounds from their labor created new recollections of rural experiences which every man manages to have in a measure. Later, the immense windows of the shops became aglow with light, throwing great beams of orange and yellow upon the pavement. They were infinitely cheerful, yet in a way they accentuated the force and discomfort of the storm, and gave a meaning to the pace of the people and the vehicles, scores of pedestrians and drivers, wretched with cold faces, necks, and feet, speeding for scores of unknown doors and entrances, scattering to an infinite variety of shelters, to places which the imagination made warm with the familiar colors of home.

There was an absolute expression of hot dinners in the pace of the people. If one dared to speculate upon the destination of those who came trooping, he lost himself in a maze of social calculation; he might fling a handful of sand and attempt to follow the flight of each particular grain. But as to the suggestion of hot dinners, he was in firm lines of thought, for it was upon every hurrying face. It is a matter of tradition; it is from the tales of childhood. It comes forth with every storm.

However, in a certain part of a dark west-side street, there was a collection of men to whom these things were as if they were not. In this street

* *Midnight Sketches.*

was located a charitable house where for five cents the homeless of the city could get a bed at night, and in the morning coffee and bread.

During the afternoon of the storm, the whirling snows acted as drivers, as men with whips, and at half-past three the walk before the closed doors of the house was covered with wanderers of the street, waiting. For some distance on either side of the place they could be seen lurking in the doorways and behind projecting parts of buildings, gathering in close bunches in an effort to get warm. A covered wagon drawn up near the curb sheltered a dozen of them. Under the stairs that led to the elevated railway station, there were six or eight, their hands stuffed deep in their pockets, their shoulders stooped, jiggling their feet. Others always could be seen coming, a strange procession, some slouching along with the characteristic hopeless gait of professional strays, some coming with hesitating steps, wearing the air of men to whom this sort of thing was new.

It was an afternoon of incredible length. The snow, blowing in twisting clouds, sought out the men in their meager hiding places, and skillfully beat in among them, drenching their persons with showers of fine stinging flakes. They crowded together, muttering, and fumbling in their pockets to get their red inflamed wrists covered by the cloth.

Newcomers usually halted at one end of the groups and addressed a question, perhaps much as a matter of form, "Is it open yet?"

Those who had been waiting inclined to take the questioner seriously and became contemptuous. "No; do yeh think we'd be standin' here?"

The gathering swelled in numbers steadily and persistently. One could always see them coming, trudging slowly through the storm.

Finally, the little snow plains in the street began to assume a leaden hue from the shadows of evening. The buildings upreared gloomily save where various windows became brilliant figures of light, that made shimmers and splashes of yellow on the snow. A street lamp on the curb struggled to illuminate, but it was reduced to impotent blindness by the swift gusts of sleet crusting its panes.

In this half-darkness, the men began to come from their shelter-places and mass in front of the doors of charity. They were of all types, but the nationalities were mostly American, German, and Irish. Many were strong, healthy, clear-skinned fellows, with that stamp of countenance which is not frequently seen upon seekers after charity. There were men of undoubted patience, industry, and temperance, who, in time of ill-fortune, do not habitually turn to rail at the state of society, snarling at the arrogance of the rich, and bemoaning the cowardice of the poor, but who at these times are apt to wear a sudden and singular meekness, as if they saw the world's progress marching from them, and were trying to perceive where they had failed, what they had lacked, to be thus vanquished in the race.

Then there were others, of the shifting Bowery element, who were used to paying ten cents for a place to sleep, but who now came here because it was cheaper.

But they were all mixed in one mass so thoroughly that one could not have discerned the different elements, but for the fact that the laboring men, for the most part, remained silent and impassive in the blizzard, their eyes fixed on the windows of the house, statues of patience.

The sidewalk soon became completely blocked by the bodies of the men. They pressed close to one another like sheep in a winter's gale, keeping one another warm by the heat of their bodies. The snow came upon this compressed group of men until, directly from above, it might have appeared like a heap of snow-covered merchandise, if it were not for the fact that the crowd swayed gently with a unanimous rhythmical motion. It was wonderful to see how the snow lay upon the heads and shoulders of these men, in little ridges an inch thick perhaps in places, the flakes steadily adding drop and drop, precisely as they fall upon the unresisting grass of the fields. The feet of the men were all wet and cold, and the wish to warm them accounted for the slow, gentle rhythmical motion. Occasionally some man whose ear or nose tingled acutely from the cold winds would wriggle down until his head was protected by the shoulders of his companions.

There was a continuous murmuring discussion as to the probability of the doors being speedily opened. They persistently lifted their eyes toward the windows. One could hear little combats of opinion.

"There's a light in th' winder!"

"Naw; it's a reflection f'm across th' way."

"Well, didn't I see 'em light it?"

"You did?"

"I did!"

"Well, then, that settles it!"

As the time approached when they expected to be allowed to enter, the men crowded to the doors in an unspeakable crush, jamming and wedging in a way that it seemed would crack bones. They surged heavily against the building in a powerful wave of pushing shoulders. Once a rumor flitted among all the tossing heads.

"They can't open th' door! Th' fellers er smack up agin 'em."

Then a dull roar of rage came from the men on the outskirts; but all the time they strained and pushed until it appeared to be impossible for those that they cried out against to do anything but be crushed to pulp.

"Ah, git away f'm th' door!"

"Git outa that!"

"Throw 'em out!"

"Kill 'em!"

"Say, fellers, now, what th' 'ell? G've 'em a chance t' open th' door!"

"Yeh damn pigs, give 'em a chance t' open th' door!"

Men in the outskirts of the crowd occasionally yelled when a boot-heel of one of the trampling feet crushed on their freezing extremities.

"Git off me feet, yeh clumsy tarrier!"

"Say, don't stand on me feet! Walk on th' ground!"

A man near the doors suddenly shouted: "O-o-oh! Le' me out—le' me out!" And another, a man of infinite valor, once twisted his head so as to half face those who were pushing behind him. "Quit yer shovin', yeh"— and he delivered a volley of the most powerful and singular invective, straight into the faces of the men behind him. It was as if he was hammering the noses of them with curses of triple brass. His face, red with rage, could be seen, upon it an expression of sublime disregard of consequences. But nobody cared to reply to his imprecations; it was too cold. Many of them snickered, and all continued to push.

In occasional pauses of the crowd's movement the men had opportunities to make jokes; usually grim things, and no doubt very uncouth. Nevertheless, they were notable—one does not expect to find the quality of humor in a heap of old clothes under a snowdrift.

The winds seemed to grow fiercer as time wore on. Some of the gusts of snow that came down on the close collection of heads cut like knives and needles, and the men huddled, and swore, not like dark assassins, but in a sort of American fashion, grimly and desperately, it is true, but yet with a wondrous under-effect, indefinable and mystic, as if there was some kind of humor in this catastrophe, in this situation in a night of snow-laden winds.

Once the window of the huge dry-goods shop across the street furnished material for a few moments of forgetfulness. In the brilliantly lighted space appeared the figure of a man. He was rather stout and very well clothed. His beard was fashioned charmingly after that of the Prince of Wales. He stood in an attitude of magnificent reflection. He slowly stroked his mustache with a certain grandeur of manner, and looked down at the snow-encrusted mob. From below, there was denoted a supreme complacence in him. It seemed that the sight operated inversely, and enabled him to more clearly regard his own delightful environment.

One of the mob chanced to turn his head, and perceived the figure in the window. "Hello, look-it 'is whiskers," he said genially.

Many of the men turned then, and a shout went up. They called to him in all strange keys. They addressed him in every manner, from familiar and cordial greetings to carefully-worded advice concerning changes in his personal appearance. The man presently fled, and the mob chuckled ferociously, like ogres who had just devoured something.

They turned then to serious business. Often they addressed the stolid front of the house.

"Oh, let us in fer Gawd's sake!"

"Let us in, or we'll all drop dead!"

"Say, what's th' use o' keepin' us poor Indians out in th' cold?"

And always some one was saying, "Keep off my feet."

The crushing of the crowd grew terrific toward the last. The men, in keen pain from the blasts, began almost to fight. With the pitiless whirl of snow upon them, the battle for shelter was going to the strong. It became known that the basement door at the foot of a little steep flight of stairs was the one to be opened, and they jostled and heaved in this direction like laboring fiends. One could hear them panting and groaning in their fierce exertion.

Usually some one in the front ranks was protesting to those in the rear— "O-o-ow! Oh, say now, fellers, let up, will yeh? Do yeh wanta kill somebody?"

A policeman arrived and went into the midst of them, scolding and berating, occasionally threatening, but using no force but that of his hands and shoulders against these men who were only struggling to get in out of the storm. His decisive tones rang out sharply—"Stop that pushin' back there! Come, boys, don't push! Stop that! Here you, quit yer shovin'! Cheese that!"

When the door below was opened, a thick stream of men forced a way down the stairs, which were of an extraordinary narrowness, and seemed only wide enough for one at a time. Yet they somehow went down almost three abreast. It was a difficult and painful operation. The crowd was like a turbulent water forcing itself through one tiny outlet. The men in the rear, excited by the success of the others, made frantic exertions, for it seemed that this large band would more than fill the quarters, and that many would be left upon the pavements. It would be disastrous to be of the last, and accordingly men with the snow biting their faces writhed and twisted with their might. One expected that, from the tremendous pressure, the narrow passage to the basement door would be so choked and clogged with human limbs and bodies that movement would be impossible. Once indeed the crowd was forced to stop, and a cry went along that a man had been injured at the foot of the stairs. But presently the slow movement began again, and the policeman fought at the top of the flight to ease the pressure of those that were going down.

A reddish light from a window fell upon the faces of the men when they, in turn, arrived at the last three steps and were about to enter. One could then note a change of expression that had come over their features. As they stood thus upon the threshold of their hopes, they looked suddenly contented and complacent. The fire had passed from their eyes and the snarl had vanished from their lips. The very force of the crowd in the rear, which had previously vexed them, was regarded from another point of view, for it now made it inevitable that they should go through the little doors into the place that was cheery and warm with light.

The tossing crowd on the sidewalk grew smaller and smaller. The snow beat with merciless persistence upon the bowed heads of those who waited. The wind drove it up from the pavements in frantic forms of winding white, and it seethed in circles about the huddled forms passing in one by one, three by three, out of the storm.

October, 1894
[The Arena, Vol. 10, pp. 662–667.]

CONEY ISLAND'S FAILING DAYS

"Down here at your Coney Island, toward the end of the season, I am made to feel very sad," said the stranger to me. "The great mournfulness that settles upon a summer resort at this time always depresses me exceedingly. The mammoth empty buildings, planned by extraordinarily optimistic architects, remind me in an unpleasant manner of my youthful dreams. In those days of visions I erected huge castles for the reception of my friends and admirers, and discovered later that I could have entertained them more comfortably in a small two story frame structure. There is a mighty pathos in these gaunt and hollow buildings, impassively and stolidly suffering from an enormous hunger for the public. And the unchangeable, ever imperturbable sea pursues its quaint devices blithely at the feet of these mournful wooden animals, gabbling and frolicking, with no thought for absent man nor maid!"

As the stranger spoke, he gazed with considerable scorn at the emotions of the sea; and the breeze from the far Navesink hills gently stirred the tangled, philosophic hair upon his forehead. Presently he went on: "The buildings are in effect more sad than the men, but I assure you that some of the men look very sad. I watched a talented and persuasive individual who was operating in front of a tintype gallery, and he had only the most marvelously infrequent opportunities to display his oratory and finesse. The occasional stragglers always managed to free themselves before he could drag them into the gallery and take their pictures. In the long intervals he gazed about him with a bewildered air, as if he felt his world dropping from under his feet. Once I saw him spy a promising youth afar off. He lurked with muscles at a tension, and then at the proper moment he swooped. 'Look-a-here,' he said, with tears of enthusiasm in his eyes, 'the best picture in the world! An' on'y four fer a quarter. O'ny jest try it, an' you'll go away perfectly satisfied!'

" 'I'll go away perfectly satisfied without trying it,' replied the promising youth, and he did. The tintype man wanted to dash his samples to the ground and whip the promising youth. He controlled himself, however, and went to watch the approach of two women and a little boy who were nothing more than three dots, away down the boardwalk.

"At one place I heard the voice of a popcorn man raised in a dreadful note, as if he were chanting a death hymn. It made me shiver as I felt all the tragedy of the collapsed popcorn market. I began to see that it was an insult to the pain and suffering of these men to go near to them without buying anything. I took new and devious routes sometimes.

"As for the railroad guards and station men, they were so tolerant of the presence of passengers that I felt it to be an indication of their sense of relief from the summer's battle. They did not seem so greatly irritated by patrons of the railroad as I have seen them at other times. And in all the beer gardens the waiters had opportunity to indulge that delight in each other's society and conversation which forms so important a part in a waiter's idea of happiness. Sometimes the people in a sparsely occupied place will fare more strange than those in a crowded one. At one time I waited twenty minutes for a bottle of the worst beer in Christendom while my waiter told a charmingly naive story to a group of his compatriots. I protested sotto voce at the time that such beer might at least have the merit of being brought quickly.

"The restaurants, however, I think to be quite delicious, being in a large part thoroughly disreputable and always provided with huge piles of red boiled crabs. These huge piles of provision around on the floor and on the oyster counters always give me the opinion that I am dining on the freshest food in the world, and I appreciate the sensation. If need be, it also allows a man to revel in dreams of unlimited quantity.

"I found countless restaurants where I could get things almost to my taste, and, as I ate, watch the grand, eternal motion of the sea and have the waiter come up and put the pepper castor on the menu card to keep the salt breeze from interfering with my order for dinner.

"And yet I have an occasional objection to the sea, when dining in sight of it; for a man with a really artistic dining sense always feels important as a duke when he is indulging in his favorite pastime, and, as the sea always makes me feel that I am a trivial object, I cannot dine with absolute comfort in its presence. The conflict of the two perceptions disturbs me. This is why I have grown to prefer the restaurants down among the narrow board streets. I tell you this because I think an explanation is due to you."

As we walked away from the beach and around one of those huge buildings whose pathos had so aroused the stranger's interest, we came into view of two acres of merry-go-rounds, circular swings, roller coasters, observation wheels and the like. The stranger paused and regarded them.

"Do you know," he said, "I am deeply fascinated by all these toys. For, of course, you perceive that they are really enlarged toys. They reinforce me in my old opinion that humanity only needs to be provided for ten minutes with a few whirligigs and things of the sort, and it can forget at least four centuries of misery. I rejoice in these whirligigs," continued the stranger, eloquently, "and as I watch here and there a person going around and around or up and down, or over and over, I say to myself that whirligigs must be made in heaven.

"It is a mystery to me why some man does not provide a large number of wooden rocking horses and let the people sit and dreamfully rock themselves into temporary forgetfulness. There could be intense quiet enforced by special policemen, who, however, should allow subdued conversation on the part of the patrons of the establishment. Deaf mutes should patrol to and fro selling slumberous drinks. These things are none of them insane. They are particularly rational. A man needs a little nerve quiver, and he gets it by being flopped around in the air like a tailless kite. He needs the introduction of a reposeful element, and he procures it upon a swing that makes him feel like thirty-five emotional actresses all trying to swoon upon one rug. There are some people who stand apart and deride these machines. If you could procure a dark night for them and the total absence of their friends they would smile, many of them. I assure you that I myself would indulge in these forms of intoxication if I were not a very great philosopher."

We strolled to the music hall district, where the skylines of the rows of buildings are wondrously near to each other, and the crowded little thoroughfares resemble the eternal "Street Scene in Cairo." There was an endless strumming and tooting and shrill piping in clamor and chaos, while at all times there were interspersed the sharp cracking sounds from the shooting galleries and the coaxing calls of innumerable fakirs. At the stand where one can throw at wooden cats and negro heads and be in danger of winning cigars, a self-reliant youth bought a whole armful of baseballs, and missed with each one. Everybody grinned. A heavily built man openly jeered. "You couldn't hit a church!" "Couldn't I?" retorted the young man, bitterly. Near them three bad men were engaged in an intense conversation. The fragment of a sentence suddenly dominated the noises. "He's got money to burn." The sun, meanwhile, was muffled in the clouds back of Staten Island and the Narrows. Softened tones of sapphire and carmine touched slantingly the sides of the buildings. A view of the sea, to be caught between two of the houses, showed it to be of a pale, shimmering green. The lamps began to be lighted, and shed a strong orange radiance. In one restaurant the only occupants were a little music hall singer and a youth. She was laughing and chatting in a light-hearted way not peculiar to music hall girls. The youth looked as if he desired to be at some other place. He was singularly wretched and uncomfortable. The stranger said he judged from appearances that the little music hall girl must think a great deal of that one youth. His sympathies seemed to be for the music hall girl. Finally there was a sea of salt meadow, with a black train shooting across it.

"I have made a discovery in one of these concert halls," said the stranger, as we retraced our way. "It is an old gray-haired woman, who occupies proudly the position of chief pianist. I like to go and sit and wonder by what mighty process of fighting and drinking she achieved her position. To see her, you would think she was leading an orchestra of seventy pieces, although she alone composes it. It is great reflection to watch that gray head. At those moments I am willing to concede that I must be relatively happy, and that is a great admission from a philosopher of my attainments.

"How seriously all these men out in front of the dens take their vocations. They regard people with a voracious air, as if they contemplated any moment making a rush and a grab and mercilessly compelling a great expenditure. This scant and feeble crowd must madden them. When I first came to this part of the town I was astonished and delighted, for it was the nearest approach to a den of wolves that I had encountered since leaving the West. Oh, no, of course the Coney Island of today is not the Coney Island of the ancient days. I believe you were about to impale me upon that sentence, were you not?"

We walked along for some time in silence until the stranger went to buy a frankfurter. As he returned, he said: "When a man is respectable he is fettered to certain wheels, and when the chariot of fashion moves, he is dragged along at the rear. For his agony, he can console himself with the law that if a certain thing has not yet been respectable, he need only wait a sufficient time and it will eventually be so. The only disadvantage is that he is obliged to wait until other people wish to do it, and he is likely to lose his own craving. Now I have a great passion for eating frankfurters on the street, and if I were respectable I would be obliged to wait until the year 3365 when men will be able to hold their positions in society only by consuming immense quantities of frankfurters on the street. And by that time I would have undoubtedly developed some new pastime.

But I am not respectable. I am a philosopher. I eat frankfurters on the street with the same equanimity that you might employ toward a cigarette.

"See those three young men enjoying themselves. With what rakish, daredevil airs they smoke those cigars. Do you know, the spectacle of three modern young men enjoying themselves is something that I find vastly interesting and instructive. I see revealed more clearly the purpose of the inexorable universe which plans to amuse us occasionally to keep us from the rebellion of suicide. And I see how simply and drolly it accomplishes its end. The insertion of a mild quantity of the egotism of sin into the minds of these young men causes them to wildly enjoy themselves. It is necessary to encourage them, you see, at this early day. After all, it is only great philosophers who have the wisdom to be utterly miserable."

As we walked toward the station the stranger stopped often to observe types which interested him. He did it with an unconscious calm insolence as if the people were bugs. Once a bug threatened to beat him. "What 'cher lookin' at?" he asked of him. "My friend," said the stranger. "If any one displays real interest in you in this world, you should take it as an occasion for serious study and reflection. You should be supremely amazed to find that a man can be interested in anybody but himself!" The belligerent seemed quite abashed. He explained to a friend: "He ain't right! What? I dunno. Something 'bout 'study' er something. He's got wheels in his head!"

On the train the cold night wind blew transversely across the reeling cars, and in the dim light of the lamps one could see the close rows of heads swaying and jolting with the motion. From directly in front of us peanut shells fell to the floor amid a regular and interminable crackling. A stout man, who slept with his head forward upon his breast, crunched them often beneath his uneasy feet. From some unknown place a drunken voice was raised in song.

"This return of the people to their battles always has a stupendous effect upon me," said the stranger. "The gayety which arises upon these Sunday night occasions is different from all other gayeties. There is an unspeakable air of recklessness and bravado and grief about it. This trainload is going toward that inevitable, overhanging, devastating Monday. That singer there tomorrow will be a truckman, perhaps, and swearing ingeniously at his horses and other truckmen. He feels the approach of this implacable Monday. Two hours ago he was engulfed in whirligigs and beer and had forgotten that there were Mondays. Now he is confronting it, and as he can't battle it, he scorns it. You can hear the undercurrent of it in that song, which is really as grievous as the cry of a child.

If he had no vanity—well, it is fortunate for the world that we are not all great thinkers."

We sat on the lower deck of the Bay Ridge boat and watched the marvelous lights of New York looming through the purple mist. The little Italian band situated up one stairway, through two doors and around three corners from us, sounded in beautiful, faint and slumberous rhythm. The breeze fluttered again in the stranger's locks. We could hear the splash of the waves against the bow. The sleepy lights looked at us with hue of red and green and orange. Overhead some dust-colored clouds scudded across the deep indigo sky. "Thunderation," said the stranger, "if I did not know of so many yesterdays and have such full knowledge of tomorrows, I should be perfectly happy at this moment, and that would create a sensation among philosophers all over the world."

October 14, 1894
[New York *Press*, part 5, p. 2.]

IN A PARK ROW RESTAURANT

"Whenever I come into a place of this sort, I am reminded of the battle of Gettysburg," remarked the stranger. To make me hear him he had to raise his voice considerably, for we were seated in one of the Park Row restaurants during the noon hour rush. "I think that if a squadron of Napoleon's dragoons charged into this place they would be trampled under foot before they could get a biscuit. They were great soldiers, no doubt, but they would at once perceive that there were many things about sweep and dash and fire of war of which they were totally ignorant.

"I come in here for the excitement. You know, when I was Sheriff, long ago, of one of the gayest counties of Nevada, I lived a life that was full of thrills, for the citizens could not quite comprehend the uses of a sheriff, and did not like to see him busy himself in other people's affairs continually. One man originated a popular philosophy, in which he asserted that if a man required pastime, it was really better to shoot the sheriff than any other person, for then it would be quite impossible for the sheriff to organize a posse and pursue the assassin. The period which followed the promulgation of this theory gave me habits which I fear I can never outwear. I require fever and exhilaration in life, and when I come in here it carries me back to the old days."

I was obliged to put my head far forward, or I could never have heard the stranger's remarks. Crowds of men were swarming in from streets and invading the comfort of seated men in order that they might hang their hats and overcoats upon the long rows of hooks that lined the sides of the room. The finding of vacant chairs became a serious business. Men dashed to and fro in swift searches. Some of those already seated were eating with terrible speed, or else casting impatient or tempestuous glances at the waiters.

Meanwhile the waiters dashed about the room as if a monster pursued them, and they sought escape wildly through the walls. It was like the scattering and scampering of a lot of water bugs, when one splashes the surface of the brook with a pebble. Withal, they carried incredible masses of dishes and threaded their swift ways with rare skill. Perspiration stood upon their foreheads, and their breaths came strainedly. They served customers with such speed and violence that it often resembled a personal assault. The crumbs from the previous diner were swept off with one fierce motion of a napkin. A waiter struck two blows at the table and left there a knife and a fork. And then came the viands in a volley, thumped down in haste, causing men to look sharp to see if their trousers were safe.

There was in the air an endless clatter of dishes, loud and bewilderingly rapid, like the gallop of a thousand horses. From afar back, at the places of communication to the kitchen, there came the sound of a continual roaring altercation, hoarse and vehement, like the cries of the officers of a regiment under attack. A mist of steam fluttered where the waiters crowded and jostled about the huge copper coffee urns. Over in one corner a man who toiled there like a foundryman was continually assailed by sharp cries. "Brown th' wheat!" An endless string of men were already filing past the cashier, and, even in these moments, this latter was a marvel of self-possession and deftness. As the spring doors clashed to and fro, one heard the interminable thunder of the street, and through the window, partially obscured by displayed vegetables and roasts and pies, could be seen the great avenue, a picture in gray tones, save where a bit of green park gleamed, the foreground occupied by this great typical turmoil of car and cab, truck and mail van, wedging their way through an opposing army of the same kind and surrounded on all sides by the mobs of hurrying people.

"A man might come in here with a very creditable stomach and lose his head and get indigestion," resumed the stranger, thoughtfully. "It is astonishing how fast a man can eat when he tries. This air is surcharged with appetites. I have seen very orderly, slow-moving men become possessed with the spirit of this rush, lose control of themselves and all at once begin to dine like madmen. It is impossible not to feel the effect of this impetuous atmosphere.

"When consommé grows popular in these places all breweries will have to begin turning out soups. I am reminded of the introduction of canned soup into my town in the West. When the boys found that they could not get full on it they wanted to lynch the proprietor of the supply store for selling an inferior article, but a drummer who happened to be in town explained to them that it was a temperance drink.

"It is plain that if the waiters here could only be put upon a raised platform and provided with repeating rifles that would shoot corn muffins, butter cakes, Irish stews or any delicacy of the season, the strain of this strife would be greatly lessened. As long as the waiters were competent marksmen the meals here would be conducted with great expedition. The only difficulty would be when, for instance, a waiter made an error and gave an Irish stew to the wrong man. The latter would have considerable difficulty in passing it along to the right one. Of course the system would cause awkward blunders for a time. You can imagine an important gentleman in a white waistcoat getting up to procure the bill of fare from an adjacent table and by chance intercepting a hamburger steak bound for a man down by the door. The man down by the door would refuse to pay for a steak that had never come into his possession.

"In some such manner thousands of people could be accommodated in restaurants that at present during the noon hour can feed only a few hundred. Of course eloquent pickets would have to be stationed in the distance to intercept any unsuspecting gentlemen from the West who might consider the gunnery of the waiters in a personal way and resent what would look to them like an assault. I remember that my old friend Jim Wilkinson, the ex-sheriff of Tin Can, Nevada, got very drunk one night and wandered into the business end of the bowling alley there. Of course he thought that they were shooting at him, and in reply he killed three of the best bowlers in Tin Can."

October 28, 1894
[New York *Press,* part 5, p. 3.]

STORIES TOLD BY AN ARTIST

A TALE ABOUT HOW "GREAT GRIEF" GOT HIS HOLIDAY DINNER

[Great Grief's Holiday Dinner]

Wrinkles had been peering into the little dry-goods box that acted as a cupboard.

"There are only two eggs and a half of a loaf of bread left," he announced brutally.

"Heavens!" said Warwickson, from where he lay smoking on the bed. He spoke in his usual dismal voice. By it he had earned his popular name of Great Grief.

Wrinkles was a thrifty soul. A sight of an almost bare cupboard maddened him. Even when he was not hungry, the ghosts of his careful ancestors caused him to rebel against it. He sat down with a virtuous air. "Well, what are we going to do?" he demanded of the others. It is good to be the thrifty man in a crowd of unsuccessful artists, for then you can keep the others from starving peacefully. "What are we going to do?"

"Oh, shut up, Wrinkles," said Grief from the bed. "You make me think."

Little Pennoyer, with head bent afar down, had been busily scratching away at a pen and ink drawing. He looked up from his board to utter his plaintive optimism.

"The *Monthly Amazement* may pay me tomorrow. They ought to. I've waited over three months now. I'm going down there tomorrow, and perhaps I'll get it."

His friends listened to him tolerantly, but at last Wrinkles could not omit a scornful giggle. He was such an old man, almost twenty-eight, and he had seen so many little boys be brave. "Oh, no doubt, Penny, old man." Over on the bed, Grief croaked deep down in his throat. Nothing was said for a long time thereafter.

The crash of the New York streets came faintly. Occasionally one could hear the tramp of feet in the intricate corridors of this begrimed building that squatted, slumbering and aged, between two exalted commercial structures that would have had to bend afar down to perceive it. The light snow beat pattering into the window corners, and made vague and gray the vista of chimneys and roofs. Often, the wind scurried swiftly and raised a long cry.

Great Grief leaned upon his elbow. "See to the fire, will you, Wrinkles?"

Wrinkles pulled the coal box out from under the bed and threw open the stove door preparatory to shoveling some fuel. A red glare plunged at the first faint shadows of dusk. Little Pennoyer threw down his pen and tossed his drawing over on the wonderful heap of stuff that hid the table. "It's too dark to work." He lit his pipe and walked about, stretching his shoulders like a man whose labor was valuable.

When dusk came it saddened these youths. The solemnity of darkness always caused them to ponder. "Light the gas, Wrinkles," said Grief.

The flood of orange light showed clearly the dull walls lined with scratches, the tousled bed in one corner, the mass of boxes and trunks in another, the little fierce stove, and the wonderful table. Moreover, there were some wine-colored draperies flung in some places, and on a shelf, high up, there was a plaster cast dark with dust in the creases. A long stovepipe wandered off in the wrong direction, and then twined impulsively toward a hole in the wall. There were some extensive cobwebs on the ceiling.

"Well, let's eat," said Grief.

Later, there came a sad knock at the door. Wrinkles, arranging a tin pail on the stove; little Pennoyer busy at slicing the bread; and Great Grief, affixing the rubber tube to the gas stove, yelled: "Come in!"

The door opened and Corinson entered dejectedly. His overcoat was very new. Wrinkles flashed an envious glance at it, but almost immediately he cried: "Hello, Corrie, old boy!"

Corinson sat down and felt around among the pipes until he found a good one. Great Grief had fixed the coffee to boil on the gas stove, but he had to watch it closely, for the rubber tube was short, and a chair was balanced on a trunk, and then the gas stove was balanced on the chair. Coffee making was a feat.

"Well," said Grief, with his back turned, "how goes it, Corrie? How's Art, hey?" He fastened a terrible emphasis upon the word.

"Crayon portraits," said Corinson.

"What?" They turned towards him with one movement, as if from a lever connection. Little Pennoyer dropped his knife.

"Crayon portraits," repeated Corinson. He smoked away in profound cynicism. "Fifteen dollars a week or more, this time of year, you know." He smiled at them like a man of courage.

Little Pennoyer picked up his knife again. "Well, I'll be blowed," said Wrinkles. Feeling it incumbent upon him to think, he dropped into a chair and began to play serenades on his guitar and watch to see when the water for the eggs would boil. It was a habitual pose.

Great Grief, however, seemed to observe something bitter in the affair. "When did you discover that you couldn't draw?" he said stiffly.

"I haven't discovered it yet," replied Corinson, with a serene air. "I merely discovered that I would rather eat."

"Oh!" said Grief.

"Hand me the eggs, Grief," said Wrinkles. "The water's boiling."

Little Pennoyer burst into the conversation. "We'd ask you to dinner, Corrie, but there's only three of us and there's two eggs. I dropped a piece of bread on the floor, too. I'm shy one."

"That's all right, Penny," said the other; "don't trouble yourself. You artists should never be hospitable. I'm going, anyway. I've got to make a call. Well, good night, boys. I've got to make a call. Drop in and see me."

When the door closed upon him, Grief said: "The coffee's done. I hate that fellow. That overcoat cost thirty dollars, if it cost a red. His egotism is so tranquil. It isn't like yours, Wrinkles. He—"

The door opened again and Corinson thrust in his head. "Say, you fellows, you know it's Thanksgiving tomorrow."

"Well, what of it?" demanded Grief.

Little Pennoyer said: "Yes, I know it is, Corrie, I thought of it this morning."

"Well, come out and have a table d'hote with me tomorrow night. I'll blow you off in good style."

While Wrinkles played an exuberant air on his guitar, little Pennoyer did part of a ballet. They cried ecstatically: "Will we? Well, I guess yes!"

When they were alone again, Grief said: "I'm not going, anyhow. I hate that fellow."

"Oh, fiddle," said Wrinkles. "You're an infernal crank. And besides, where's your dinner coming from tomorrow night if you don't go? Tell me that."

Little Pennoyer said: "Yes, that's so, Grief. Where's your dinner coming from if you don't go?"

Grief said: "Well, I hate him, anyhow."

Little Pennoyer's four dollars could not last for ever. When he received it he and Wrinkles and Great Grief went to a table d'hote. Afterwards little Pennoyer discovered that only two dollars and a half remained. A small magazine away down town had accepted one out of the six drawings that he had taken them, and later had given him four dollars for it. Penny was so disheartened when he saw that his money was not going to last for ever that, even with two dollars and a half in his pockets, he felt much worse than when he was penniless, for at that time he anticipated twenty-four. Wrinkles lectured upon "Finance."

Great Grief said nothing, for it was established that when he received six dollar checks from comic weeklies he dreamed of renting studios at seventy-five dollars per month, and was likely to go out and buy five dollars' worth of second-hand curtains and plaster casts.

When he had money Penny always hated the cluttered den in the old building. He desired then to go out and breathe boastfully like a man. But he obeyed Wrinkles, the elder and the wise, and if you had visited that room about ten o'clock of a morning or about seven of an evening you would have thought that rye bread, frankfurters, and potato salad from Second Avenue were the only foods in the world.

Purple Sanderson lived there too, but then he really ate. He had learned parts of the gas fitter's trade before he came to be such a great artist, and when his opinions disagreed with that of every art manager in New York, he went to see a plumber, a friend of his, for whose opinion he had a great respect. In consequence, he frequented a very neat restaurant on Twenty-third Street, and sometimes on Saturday nights he openly scorned his companions.

Purple was a good fellow, Grief said, but one of his singularly bad traits was that he always remembered everything. One night, not long after little Pennoyer's great discovery, Purple came in, and as he was neatly hanging up his coat, said: "Well, the rent will be due in four days."

"Will it?" demanded Penny, astounded. Penny was always astounded when the rent came due. It seemed to him the most extraordinary occurrence.

"Certainly it will," said Purple, with the irritated air of a superior financial man.

"My soul!" said Wrinkles.

Great Grief lay on the bed smoking a pipe and waiting for fame. "Oh, go home, Purple. You resent something. It wasn't me—it was the calendar."

"Try and be serious a moment, Grief."

"You're a fool, Purple."

Penny spoke from where he was at work. "Well, if those *Amazement* people pay me when they said they would I'll have money then."

"So you will, dear," said Grief, satirically. "You'll have money to burn. Did the *Amazement* people ever pay you when they said they would? You're wonderfully important all of a sudden, it seems to me. You talk like an artist."

Wrinkles, too, smiled at little Pennoyer. "The *Established Magazine* people wanted Penny to hire models and make a try for them too. It will only cost him a big blue chip. By the time he has invested all the money he hasn't got and the rent is two weeks overdue, he will be able to tell the landlord to wait seven months until the Monday morning after the day of publication. Go ahead, Penny."

It was the habit to make game of little Pennoyer. He was always having gorgeous opportunities, with no opportunity to take advantage of his opportunities.

Penny smiled at them, his tiny, tiny smile of courage.

"You're a confident little cuss," observed Grief, irrelevantly.

"Well, the world has no objection to your being confident also, Grief," said Purple.

"Hasn't it?" said Grief. "Well, I want to know!"

Wrinkles could not be light-spirited long. He was obliged to despair when occasion offered. At last he sank down in a chair and seized his guitar. "Well, what's to be done?" he said. He began to play mournfully.

"Throw Purple out," mumbled Grief from the bed.

"Are you fairly certain that you will have money then, Penny?" asked Purple.

Little Pennoyer looked apprehensive. "Well, I don't know," he said.

And then began that memorable discussion, great in four minds. The tobacco was of the "Long John" brand. It smelled like burning mummies.

Once Purple Sanderson went to his home in St. Lawrence county to enjoy some country air, and, incidentally, to explain his life failure to his people. Previously, Great Grief had given him odds that he would return sooner than he had planned, and everybody said that Grief had a good bet. It is not a glorious pastime, this explaining of life failures.

Later, Great Grief and Wrinkles went to Haverstraw to visit Grief's cousin and sketch. Little Pennoyer was disheartened, for it is bad to be imprisoned in brick and dust and cobbles when your ear can hear in the distance the harmony of the summer sunlight upon leaf and blade of green. Besides, he did not hear Wrinkles and Grief discoursing and quarreling in the den, and Purple coming in at six o'clock with contempt.

On Friday afternoon he discovered that he only had fifty cents to last until Saturday morning, when he was to get his check from the *Gamin*. He was an artful little man by this time, however, and it is as true as the sky that when he walked toward the *Gamin* office on Saturday he had twenty cents remaining.

The cashier nodded his regrets. "Very sorry, Mr.—er—Pennoyer, but our payday, you know, is on Monday. Come around any time after ten."

"Oh, it don't matter," said Penny. As he walked along on his return he reflected deeply how he could invest his twenty cents in food to last until Monday morning any time after ten. He bought two coffee cakes in a Third Avenue bakery. They were very beautiful. Each had a hole in the center and a handsome scallop all around the edges.

Penny took great care of those cakes. At odd times he would rise from his work and go to see that no escape had been made. On Sunday he got up at noon and compressed breakfast and noon into one meal. Afterwards he had almost three-quarters of a cake still left to him. He congratulated himself that with strategy he could make it endure until Monday morning, any time after ten.

At three in the afternoon there came a faint-hearted knock. "Come in," said Penny. The door opened and old Tim Connegan, who was trying to be a model, looked in apprehensively. "I beg pardon, sir," he said at once.

"Come in, Tim, you old thief," said Penny. Tim entered, slowly and bashfully. "Sit down," said Penny. Tim sat down and began to rub his knees, for rheumatism had a mighty hold upon him.

Penny lit his pipe and crossed his legs. "Well, how goes it?"

Tim moved his square jaw upward and flashed Penny a little glance.

"Bad?" said Penny.

The old man raised his hand impressively. "I've been to every studio in the hull city and I never see such absences in my life. What with the seashore and the mountains, and this and that resort, I think all the models will be starved by fall. I found one man in up on Fifty-seventh Street. He ses to me: 'Come around Tuesday—I may want yez and I may not.' That was last week. You know, I live down on the Bowery, Mr. Pennoyer, and when I got up there on Tuesday, he ses: 'Confound you, are you here again?' ses he. I went and sat down in the park, for I was too tired for the walk back. And there you are, Mr. Pennoyer. What with tramping around to look for men that are thousand miles away, I'm near dead."

"It's hard," said Penny.

"It is, sir. I hope they'll come back soon. The summer is the death of us all, sir; it is. Sure, I never know where my next meal is coming until I get it. That's true."

"Had anything today?"

"Yes, sir—a little."

"How much?"

"Well, sir, a lady gave me a cup of coffee this morning. It was good, too, I'm telling you."

Penny went to his cupboard. When he returned, he said: "Here's some cake."

Tim thrust forward his hands, palms erect. "Oh, now, Mr. Pennoyer, I couldn't. You—"

"Go ahead. What's the odds?"

"Oh, now—"

"Go ahead, you old bat."

Penny smoked.

When Tim was going out, he turned to grow eloquent again. "Well, I can't tell you how much I'm obliged to you, Mr. Pennoyer. You—"

"Don't mention it, old man."

Penny smoked.

October 28, 1894
[New York *Press,* part 4, p. 6.]

THE SILVER PAGEANT

"It's rotten," said Grief.

"Oh, it's fair, old man. Still, I would not call it a great contribution to American art," said Wrinkles.

"You've got a good thing, Gaunt, if you go at it right," said little Pennoyer.

These were all volunteer orations. The boys had come in one by one and spoken their opinions. Gaunt listened to them no more than if they had been so many match peddlers. He never heard anything close at hand, and he never saw anything excepting that which transpired across a mystic wide sea. The shadow of his thoughts was in his eyes, a little gray mist, and, when what you said to him had passed out of your mind, he asked: "Wha—a—at?" It was understood that Gaunt was very good to tolerate the presence of the universe, which was noisy and interested in itself. All the younger men, moved by an instinct of faith, declared that he would one day be a great artist if he would only move faster than a pyramid. In the meantime he did not hear their voices. Occasionally when he saw a man take vivid pleasure in life, he faintly evinced an admiration. It seemed to strike him as a feat. As for him, he was watching that silver pageant across a sea.

When he came from Paris to New York somebody told him that he must make his living. He went to see some book publishers, and talked to them in his manner—as if he had just been stunned. At last one of them gave him drawings to do, and it did not surprise him. It was merely as if rain had come down.

Great Grief went to see him in his studio, and returned to the den to say: "Gaunt is working in his sleep. Somebody ought to set fire to him."

It was then that the others went over and smoked, and gave their opinions of a drawing. Wrinkles said: "Are you really looking at it, Gaunt? I don't think you've seen it yet, Gaunt."

"What?"

"Why don't you look at it?"

When Wrinkles departed, the model, who was resting at that time, followed him into the hall and waved his arms in rage. "That feller's crazy. Yeh ought t' see—" and he recited lists of all the wrongs that can come to models.

It was a superstitious little band over in the den. They talked often of Gaunt. "He's got pictures in his eyes," said Wrinkles. They had expected genius to blindly stumble at the preface and ceremonies of the world, and each new flounder by Gaunt made a stir in the den. It awed them, and they waited.

At last one morning Gaunt burst into the room. They were all as dead men.

"I'm going to paint a picture." The mist in his eyes was pierced by a Coverian gleam. His gestures were wild and extravagant. Grief, stretched out smoking on the bed, Wrinkles and little Pennoyer working at their drawing boards tilted against the table, were suddenly frozen. If bronze statues had come and danced heavily before them, they could not have been thrilled further.

Gaunt tried to tell them of something, but it became knotted in his throat, and then suddenly he dashed out again.

Later they went earnestly over to Gaunt's studio. Perhaps he would tell them of what he saw across the sea.

He lay dead upon the floor. There was a little gray mist before his eyes.

When they finally arrived home that night they took a long time to undress for bed, and then came the moment when they waited for some one to put out the gas. Grief said at last, with the air of a man whose brain is desperately driven: "I wonder—I—what do you suppose he was going to paint?"

Wrinkles reached and turned out the gas, and from the sudden profound darkness, he said: "There is a mistake. He couldn't have had pictures in his eyes."

1894?

[*Last Words*. London: Digby, Long & Co.
(March, 1902), pp. 145–148.]

WHEN EVERY ONE IS PANIC STRICKEN
[The Fire]

We were walking on one of the shadowy side streets, west of Sixth Avenue. The midnight silence and darkness was upon it save where at the point of intersection with the great avenue, there was a broad span of yellow light. From there came the steady monotonous jingle of streetcar bells and the weary clatter of hoofs on the cobbles. While the houses in this street turned black and mystically silent with the night, the avenue continued its eternal movement and life, a great vein that never slept nor paused. The gorgeous orange-hued lamps of a saloon flared plainly, and the figures of some loungers could be seen as they stood on the corner. Passing to and fro, the tiny black figures of people made an ornamental border on this fabric of yellow light.

The stranger was imparting to me some grim midnight reflections upon existence, and in the heavy shadows and in the great stillness pierced only by the dull thunder of the avenue, they were very impressive.

Suddenly the muffled cry of a woman came from one of those dark, impassive houses near us. There was the sound of the splinter and crash of broken glass, falling to the pavement. "What's that?" gasped the stranger. The scream contained that ominous quality, that weird timber which denotes fear of imminent death.

A policeman, huge and panting, ran past us with glitter of buttons and shield in the darkness. He flung himself upon the fire alarm box at the corner where the lamp shed a flicker of carmine tints upon the pavement. "Come on," shouted the stranger. He dragged me excitedly down the street. We came upon an old four story structure, with a long sign of a bakery over the basement windows, and the region about the quaint front door plastered with other signs. It was one of those ancient dwellings which the churning process of the city had changed into a hive of little industries.

At this time some dull gray smoke, faintly luminous in the night, writhed out from the tops of the second story windows, and from the basement there glared a deep and terrible hue of red, the color of satanic wrath, the color of murder. "Look! Look!" shouted the stranger.

It was extraordinary how the street awakened. It seemed but an instant before the pavements were studded with people. They swarmed from all directions, and from the dark mass arose countless exclamations, eager and swift.

"Where is it? Where is it?"

"No. 135."

"It's that old bakery."

"Is everybody out?"

"Look—gee—say, lookut 'er burn, would yeh?"

The windows of almost every house became crowded with people, clothed and partially clothed, many having rushed from their beds. Here were many women, and as their eyes fastened upon that terrible growing mass of red light one could hear their little cries, quavering with fear and dread. The smoke oozed in greater clouds from the spaces between the sashes of the windows, and urged by the fervor of the heat within, ascended in more rapid streaks and curves.

Upon the sidewalk there had been a woman who was fumbling mechanically with the buttons at the neck of her dress. Her features were lined in anguish; she seemed to be frantically searching her memory— her memory, that poor feeble contrivance that had deserted her at the first of the crisis, at the momentous time. She really struggled and tore hideously at some frightful mental wall that upreared between her and her senses, her very instincts. The policeman, running back from the fire alarm box, grabbed her, intending to haul her away from danger of falling things. Then something came to her like a bolt from the sky. The creature turned all gray, like an ape. A loud shriek rang out that made the spectators bend their bodies, twisting as if they were receiving sword thrusts.

"My baby! My baby! My baby!"

The policeman simply turned and plunged into the house. As the woman tossed her arms in maniacal gestures about her head, it could then be seen that she waved in one hand a little bamboo easel, of the kind which people sometimes place in corners of their parlors. It appeared that she had with great difficulty saved it from the flames. Its cost should have been about thirty cents.

A long groaning sigh came from the crowd in the street, and from all the thronged windows. It was full of distress and pity, and a sort of cynical scorn for their impotency. Occasionally the woman screamed again. Another policeman was fending her off from the house, which she wished to enter in the frenzy of her motherhood, regardless of the flames. These people of the neighborhood, aroused from their beds, looked at the spectacle in a half-dazed fashion at times, as if they were contemplating the ravings of a red beast in a cage. The flames grew as if fanned by tempests, a sweeping, inexorable appetite of a thing, shining, with fierce, pitiless brilliancy, gleaming in the eyes of the crowd that were upturned to it in an ecstasy of awe, fear and, too, half-barbaric admiration. They felt the human helplessness that comes when nature breaks forth in passion, overturning the obstacles, emerging at a leap from the position of a slave to that of a master, a giant. There became audible a humming noise, the buzzing of curious machinery. It was the voices of the demons of the flame. The house, in manifest heroic indifference to the fury that raged in its entrails, maintained a stolid and imperturbable exterior, looming black and immovable against the turmoil of crimson.

Eager questions were flying to and fro in the street.

"Say, did a copper go in there?"

"Yeh! He come out again, though."

"He did not! He's in there yet!"

"Well, didn't I see 'im?"

"How long ago was the alarm sent in?"

" 'Bout a minute."

A woman leaned perilously from a window of a nearby apartment house and spoke querulously into the shadowy, jostling crowd beneath her, "Jack!"

And the voice of an unknown man in an unknown place answered her gruffly and short in the tones of a certain kind of downtrodden husband who rebels upon occasion, "What?"

"Will you come up here," cried the woman, shrilly irritable. "Supposin' this house should get afire—" It came to pass that during the progress of the conflagration these two held a terse and bitter domestic combat, infinitely commonplace in language and mental maneuvers.

The blaze had increased with a frightful vehemence and swiftness. Unconsciously, at times, the crowd dully moaned, their eyes fascinated by this exhibition of the strength of nature, their master after all, that ate them and their devices at will whenever it chose to fling down their little restrictions. The flames changed in color from crimson to lurid orange as glass was shattered by the heat, and fell crackling to the pavement. The baker, whose shop had been in the basement, was running about, weeping. A policeman had fought interminably to keep the crowd away from the front of the structure.

"Thunderation!" yelled the stranger, clutching my arm in a frenzy of excitement, "did you ever see anything burn so? Why, it's like an explosion. It's only been a matter of seconds since it started."

In the street, men had already begun to turn toward each other in that indefinite regret and sorrow, as if they were not quite sure of the reason of their mourning.

"Well, she's a goner!"

"Sure—went up like a box of matches!"

"Great Scott, lookut 'er burn!"

Some individual among them furnished the inevitable grumble. "Well, these—" It was a half-coherent growling at conditions, men, fate, law.

Then, from the direction of the avenue there suddenly came a tempestuous roar, a clattering, rolling rush and thunder, as from the headlong sweep of a battery of artillery. Wild and shrill, like a clangorous noise of war, arose the voice of a gong.

One could see a sort of a delirium of excitement, of ardorous affection, go in a wave of emotion over this New York crowd, usually so stoical. Men looked at each other. "Quick work, eh?" They crushed back upon the pavements, leaving the street almost clear. All eyes were turned toward the corner, where the lights of the avenue glowed.

The roar grew and grew until it was as the sound of an army, charging. That policeman's hurried fingers sending the alarm from the box at the corner had aroused a tornado, a storm of horses, machinery, men. And now they were coming in clamor and riot of hoofs and wheels, while over all rang the piercing cry of the gong, tocsin-like, a noise of barbaric fights.

It thrilled the blood, this thunder. The stranger jerked his shoulders nervously and kept up a swift muttering. "Hear 'em come!" he said, breathlessly.

Then in an instant a fire patrol wagon, as if apparitional, flashed into view at the corner. The lights of the avenue gleamed for an instant upon the red and brass of the wagon, the helmets of the crew and the glossy sides of the galloping horses. Then it swung into the dark street and thundered down upon its journey, with but a half-view of a driver making his reins to be steel ribbons over the backs of his horses, mad from the fervor of their business.

The stranger's hand tightened convulsively upon my arm. His enthusiasm was like the ardor of one who looks upon the pageantry of battles. "Ah, look at 'em! Look at 'em! Ain't that great? Why it hasn't been any time at all since the alarm was sent in, and now look!" As this clanging, rolling thing, drawn swiftly by the beautiful might of the horses, clamored through the street, one could feel the cheers, wild and valorous, at the very lips of these people habitually so calm, cynical, impassive. The crew tumbled from their wagon and ran toward the house. A hoarse shout arose high above the medley of noises.

Other roars, other clangings, were to be heard from all directions. It was extraordinary, the loud rumblings of wheels and the pealings of gongs aroused by a movement of the policeman's fingers.

Of a sudden, three white horses dashed down the street with their engine, a magnificent thing of silver-like glitter, that sent a storm of red sparks high into the air and smote the heart with the wail of its whistle.

A hosecart swept around the corner and into the narrow lane, whose close walls made the reverberations like the crash of infantry volleys. There was shine of lanterns, of helmets, of rubber coats, of the bright, strong trappings of the horses. The driver had been confronted by a dreadful little problem in streetcars and elevated railway pillars just as he was about to turn into the street, but there had been no pause, no hesitation. A clever dodge, a shrill grinding of the wheels in the streetcar tracks, a miss of this and an escape of that by a beautifully narrow margin, and the hosecart went on its headlong way. When the gleam-white and gold of the cart stopped in the shadowy street, it was but a moment before a stream of water, of a cold steel color, was plunging through a window into the yellow glare, into this house which was now a den of fire wolves, lashing, carousing, leaping, straining. A wet snake-like hose trailed underfoot to where the steamer was making the air pulsate with its swift vibrations.

From another direction had come another thunder that developed into a crash of sounds, as a hook-and-ladder truck, with long and graceful curves, spun around the other corner, with the horses running with steady leaps toward the place of the battle. It was always obvious that these men who drove were drivers in blood and fiber, charioteers incarnate.

When the ladders were placed against the side of the house, firemen went slowly up them, dragging their hose. They became outlined like black beetles against the red and yellow expanses of flames. A vast cloud of smoke, sprinkled thickly with sparks, went coiling heavily toward the black sky. Touched by the shine of the blaze, the smoke sometimes glowed dull red, the color of bricks. A crowd that, it seemed, had sprang from the cobbles, born at the sound of the wheels rushing through the night, thickly thronged the walks, pushed here and there by the policemen who scolded them roundly, evidently in an eternal state of injured surprise at their persistent desire to get a view of things.

As we walked to the corner we looked back and watched the red glimmer from the fire shine on the dark surging crowd over which towered at times the helmets of police. A billow of smoke swept away from the structure. Occasionally, burned out sparks, like fragments of dark tissue, fluttered in the air. At the corner a steamer was throbbing, churning, shaking in its power as if overcome with rage. A fireman was walking tranquilly about it scrutinizing the mechanism. He wore a blasé air. They all, in fact, seemed to look at fires with the calm, unexcited vision of veterans. It was only the populace with their new nerves, it seemed, who could feel the thrill and dash of these attacks, these furious charges made in the dead of night, at high noon, at any time, upon the common enemy, the loosened flame.

November 25, 1894
[New York *Press*, part 4, p. 6.]

WHEN A MAN FALLS A CROWD GATHERS

[A Street Scene in New York]

The man and the boy conversed in Italian, mumbling the soft syllables and making little, quick egotistical gestures. Suddenly the man glared and wavered on his limbs for a moment as if some blinding light had flashed before his vision; then he swayed like a drunken man and fell. The boy grasped his arm convulsively and made an attempt to support his companion, so that the body slid to the sidewalk with an easy motion like a corpse sinking into the sea. The boy screamed.

Instantly people from all directions turned their gaze upon that figure prone upon the sidewalk. In a moment there was a dodging, peering, pushing crowd about the man. A volley of questions, replies, speculations flew to and fro among all the bobbing heads.

"What's th' matter? what's th' matter?"

"Oh, a jag, I guess!"

"Aw, he's got a fit!"

"What's th' matter? what's th' matter?"

Two streams of people coming from different directions met at this point to form a great crowd. Others came from across the street.

Down under their feet, almost lost under this mass of people, lay a man, hidden in the shadows caused by their forms, which, in fact, barely allowed a particle of light to pass between them. Those in the foremost rank bent down eagerly, anxious to see everything. Others behind them crowded savagely like starving men fighting for bread. Always the question could be heard flying in the air: "What's th' matter?" Some, near to the body, and perhaps feeling the danger of being forced over upon it, twisted their heads and protested violently to those unheeding ones who were scuffling in the rear: "Say, quit yer shovin', can't yeh? What do yeh want, anyhow? Quit!"

Somebody back in the throng suddenly said: "Say, young feller, cheese that pushin'! I ain't no peach!"

Another voice said: "Well, dat's all right—"

The boy who had been with the Italian was standing helplessly, a frightened look in his eyes, and holding the man's hand. Sometimes he looked about him dumbly, with indefinite hope, as if he expected sudden assistance to come from the clouds. The men about him frequently jostled him until he was obliged to put his hand upon the breast of the body to maintain his balance. Those nearest the man upon the sidewalk at first saw his body go through a singular contortion. It was as if an invisible hand had reached up from the earth and had seized him by the hair. He seemed dragged slowly, pitilessly backward, while his body stiffened convulsively, his hands clenched, and his arms swung rigidly upward. Through his pallid, half-closed lids one could see the steel-colored, as-sassin-like gleam of his eye, that shone with a mystic light as a corpse might glare at those live ones who seemed about to trample it under foot. As for the men near, they hung back, appearing as if they expected it might spring erect and grab them. Their eyes, however, were held in a spell of fascination. They scarce seemed to breathe. They were contemplating a depth into which a human being had sunk, and the marvel of this mys-

tery of life or death held them chained. Occasionally from the rear a man
came thrusting his way impetuously, satisfied that there was a horror to
be seen, and apparently insane to get a view of it. More self-contained
men swore at these persons when they tread upon their toes.

The streetcars jingled past this scene in endless parade. Occasionally,
down where the elevated road crossed the street, one could hear sometimes
a thunder, suddenly begun and suddenly ended. Over the heads of the
crowd hung an immovable canvas sign: "Regular Dinner twenty cents."

The body on the pave seemed like a bit of debris sunk in this human
ocean.

But after the first spasm of curiosity had passed away, there were those
in the crowd who began to bethink themselves of some way to help. A
voice called out: "Rub his wrists." The boy and a man on the other side
of the body began to rub the wrists and slap the palms of the man. A tall
German suddenly appeared, and resolutely began to push the crowd back.
"Get back there—get back," he repeated continually while he pushed at
them. He seemed to have authority; the crowd obeyed him. He and
another man knelt down by the man in the darkness and loosened his
shirt at the throat. Once they struck a match and held it close to the man's
face. This livid visage, suddenly appearing under their feet in the light
of the match's yellow glare, made the crowd shudder. Half articulate
exclamations could be heard. There were men who nearly created a
riot in the madness of their desire to see the thing.

Meanwhile others had been questioning the boy. "What's his name?
Where does he live?"

Then a policeman appeared. The first part of this little drama had
gone on without his assistance, but now he came, striding swiftly, his
helmet towering over the crowd and shading that impenetrable police
face. He charged the crowd as if he were a squadron of Irish Lancers.
The people fairly withered before this onslaught. Occasionally he shouted:
"Come, make way there. Come, now!" He was evidently a man whose
life was half-pestered out of him by people who were sufficiently unreasonable and stupid as to insist on walking in the streets. He felt the
rage toward them that a placid cow feels toward the flies that hover in
clouds and disturb its repose. When he arrived at the center of the crowd
he first said, threateningly: "What's th' matter here?" And then, when he
saw that human bit of wreckage at the bottom of the sea of men, he said
to it: "Come, git up out a' that! Git out a' here!"

Whereupon hands were raised in the crowd and a volley of decorated
information was blazed at the officer.

"Ah, he's got a fit, can't yeh see?"

"He's got a fit!"

"What th' 'ell yeh doin'? Leave 'im be!"

The policeman menaced with a glance the crowd from whose safe precincts the defiant voices had emerged.

A doctor had come. He and the policeman bent down at the man's side. Occasionally the officer reared up to create room. The crowd fell away before his admonitions, his threats, his sarcastic questions, and before the sweep of those two huge buckskin gloves.

At last the peering ones saw the man on the sidewalk begin to breathe heavily, strainedly, as if he had just come to the surface from some deep water. He uttered a low cry in his foreign way. It was like a baby's squeal or the sad wail of a little storm-tossed kitten. As this cry went forth to all those eager ears the jostling, crowding recommenced again furiously, until the doctor was obliged to yell warningly a dozen times. The policeman had gone to send the ambulance call.

Then a man struck another match, and in its meager light the doctor felt the skull of the prostrate man carefully to discover if any wound had been caused by his fall to the stone sidewalk. The crowd pressed and crushed again. It was as if they fully expected to see blood by the light of the match, and the desire made them appear almost insane. The policeman returned and fought with them. The doctor looked up occasionally to scold and demand room.

At last, out of the faint haze of light far up the street, there came the sound of a gong beating rapidly. A monstrous truck loaded to the sky with barrels scurried to one side with marvelous agility. And then the black wagon, with its gleam of gold lettering and bright brass gong, clattered into view, the horse galloping. A young man, as imperturbable almost as if he were at a picnic, sat upon the rear seat. When they picked up the limp body, from which came little moans and howls, the crowd almost turned into a mob. When the ambulance started on its banging and clanging return, they stood and gazed until it was quite out of sight. Some resumed their way with an air of relief. Others still continued to stare after the vanished ambulance and its burden as if they had been cheated, as if the curtain had been rung down on a tragedy that was but half completed; and this impenetrable blanket intervening between a sufferer and their curiosity seemed to make them feel an injustice.

December 2, 1894
[New York *Press*, part 3, p. 5.]

THE DUEL THAT WAS NOT FOUGHT*

Patsy Tulligan was not as wise as seven owls, but his courage could throw a shadow as long as the steeple of a cathedral. There were men on Cherry Street who had whipped him five times, but they all knew that Patsy would be as ready for the sixth time as if nothing had happened.

Once he and two friends had been away up on Eighth Avenue, far out of their country, and upon their return journey that evening they stopped frequently in saloons until they were as independent of their surroundings as eagles, and cared much less about thirty days on Blackwell's.

On Lower Sixth Avenue they paused in a saloon where there was a good deal of lamp glare and polished wood to be seen from the outside, and within the mellow light shone on much furbished brass and more polished wood. It was a better saloon than they were in the habit of seeing, but they did not mind it. They sat down at one of the little tables that were in a row parallel to the bar and ordered beer. They blinked stolidly at the decorations, the bartender, and the other customers. When anything transpired they discussed it with dazzling frankness, and what they said of it was as free as air to the other people in the place.

At midnight there were few people in the saloon. Patsy and his friends still sat drinking. Two well-dressed men were at another table, smoking cigars slowly and swinging back in their chairs. They occupied themselves with themselves in the usual manner, never betraying by a wink of an eyelid that they knew that other folk existed. At another table directly behind Patsy and his companions was a slim little Cuban, with miraculously small feet and hands, and with a youthful touch of down upon his lip. As he lifted his cigarette from time to time his little finger was bent in dainty fashion, and there was a green flash when a huge emerald ring caught the light. The bartender came often with his little brass tray. Occasionally Patsy and his two friends quarreled.

Once this little Cuban happened to make some slight noise and Patsy turned his head to observe him. Then Patsy made a careless and rather loud comment to his two friends. He used a word which is no more than passing the time of day down in Cherry Street, but to the Cuban it was a dagger point. There was a harsh scraping sound as a chair was pushed swiftly back.

The little Cuban was upon his feet. His eyes were shining with a rage that flashed there like sparks as he glared at Patsy. His olive face had

* Midnight Sketches.

turned a shade of gray from his anger. Withal his chest was thrust out in portentous dignity, and his hand, still grasping his wineglass, was cool and steady, the little finger still bent, the great emerald gleaming upon it. The others, motionless, stared at him.

"Sir," he began ceremoniously. He spoke gravely and in a slow way, his tone coming in a marvel of self-possessed cadences from between those lips which quivered with wrath. "You have insult me. You are a dog, a hound, a cur. I spit upon you. I must have some of your blood."

Patsy looked at him over his shoulder.

"What's th' matter wi'che?" he demanded. He did not quite understand the words of this little man who glared at him steadily, but he knew that it was something about fighting. He snarled with the readiness of his class and heaved his shoulders contemptuously. "Ah, what's eatin' yeh? Take a walk! You hain't got nothin' t' do with me, have yeh? Well, den, go sit on yerself."

And his companions leaned back valorously in their chairs and scrutinized this slim young fellow who was addressing Patsy.

"What's de little Dago chewin' about?"

"He wants t' scrap!"

"What!"

The Cuban listened with apparent composure. It was only when they laughed that his body cringed as if he was receiving lashes. Presently he put down his glass and walked over to their table. He proceeded always with the most impressive deliberation.

"Sir," he began again. "You have insult me. I must have s-s-satisfac-shone. I must have your body upon the point of my sword. In my country you would already be dead. I must have s-s-satisfac-shone."

Patsy had looked at the Cuban with a trifle of bewilderment. But at last his face began to grow dark with belligerency, his mouth curve in that wide sneer with which he would confront an angel of darkness. He arose suddenly in his seat and came toward the little Cuban. He was going to be impressive too.

"Say, young feller, if yeh go shootin' off yer face at me, I'll wipe d'joint wid yeh. What'cher gaffin' about, hey? Are yeh givin' me er jolly? Say, if yeh pick me up fer a cinch, I'll fool yeh. Dat's what! Don't take me fer no dead easy mug." And as he glowered at the little Cuban, he ended his oration with one eloquent word, "Nit!"

The bartender nervously polished his bar with a towel, and kept his eyes fastened upon the men. Occasionally he became transfixed with interest, leaning forward with one hand upon the edge of the bar and the other holding the towel grabbed in a lump, as if he had been turned into bronze when in the very act of polishing.

The Cuban did not move when Patsy came toward him and delivered his oration. At its conclusion he turned his livid face toward where, above him, Patsy was swaggering and heaving his shoulders in a consummate display of bravery and readiness. The Cuban, in his clear, tense tones, spoke one word. It was the bitter insult. It seemed to fairly spin from his lips and crackle in the air like breaking glass.

Every man save the little Cuban made an electric movement. Patsy roared a black oath and thrust himself forward until he towered almost directly above the other man. His fists were doubled into knots of bone and hard flesh. The Cuban had raised a steady finger.

"If you touch me wis your hand, I will keel you."

The two well-dressed men had come swiftly, uttering protesting cries. They suddenly intervened in this second of time in which Patsy had sprung forward and the Cuban had uttered his threat. The four men were now a tossing, arguing, violent group, one well-dressed man lecturing the Cuban, and the other holding off Patsy, who was now wild with rage, loudly repeating the Cuban's threat, and maneuvering and struggling to get at him for revenge's sake.

The bartender, feverishly scouring away with his towel, and at times pacing to and fro with nervous and excited tread, shouted out: "Say, for heaven's sake, don't fight in here. If yeh wanta fight, go out in the street and fight all yeh please. But don't fight in here."

Patsy knew only one thing, and this he kept repeating: "Well, he wants t' scrap! I didn't begin dis! He wants t' scrap."

The well-dressed man confronting him continually replied: "Oh, well, now, look here, he's only a lad. He don't know what he's doing. He's crazy mad. You wouldn't slug a kid like that."

Patsy and his aroused companions, who cursed and growled, were persistent with their argument. "Well, he wants t' scrap!" The whole affair was as plain as daylight when one saw this great fact. The interference and intolerable discussion brought the three of them forward, battleful and fierce.

"What's eatin' you, anyhow?" they demanded. "Dis ain't your business, is it? What business you got shootin' off your face?"

The other peacemaker was trying to restrain the little Cuban, who had grown shrill and violent.

"If he touch me wis his hand I will keel him. We must fight like gentlemen or else I keel him when he touch me wis his hand."

The man who was fending off Patsy comprehended these sentences that were screamed behind his back, and he explained to Patsy: "But he wants to fight you with swords. With swords, you know."

The Cuban, dodging around the peacemakers, yelled in Patsy's face:

"Ah, if I could get you before me wis my sword! Ah! Ah! A-a-ah!" Patsy made a furious blow with a swift fist, but the peacemakers bucked against his body suddenly like football players.

Patsy was greatly puzzled. He continued doggedly to try to get near enough to the Cuban to punch him. To these attempts the Cuban replied savagely: "If you touch me wis your hand, I will cut your heart in two piece."

At last Patsy said: "Well, if he's so dead stuck on fightin' wid swords, I'll fight 'im. Soitenly! I'll fight 'im." All this palaver had evidently tired him, and he now puffed out his lips with the air of a man who is willing to submit to any conditions if he can only bring on the row soon enough. He swaggered. "I'll fight 'im wid swords. Let 'im bring on his swords, an' I'll fight 'im till he's ready t' quit."

The two well-dressed men grinned. "Why, look here," they said to Patsy, "he'd punch you full of holes. Why, he's a fencer. You can't fight him with swords. He'd kill you in 'bout a minute."

"Well, I'll giv' 'im a go at it, anyhow," said Patsy, stouthearted and resolute. "I'll giv' 'im a go at it, anyhow, an' I'll stay wid 'im long as I kin."

As for the Cuban, his lithe little body was quivering in an ecstasy of the muscles. His face radiant with a savage joy, he fastened his glance upon Patsy, his eyes gleaming with a gloating, murderous light. A most unspeakable, animal-like rage was in his expression. "Ah! ah! He will fight me! Ah!" He bent unconsciously in the posture of a fencer. He had all the quick, springy movements of a skillful swordsman. "Ah, the b-r-r-rute! The b-r-r-rute! I will stick him like a pig!"

The two peacemakers, still grinning broadly, were having a great time with Patsy. "Why, you infernal idiot, this man would slice you all up. You better jump off the bridge if you want to commit suicide. You wouldn't stand a ghost of a chance to live ten seconds."

Patsy was as unshaken as granite. "Well, if he wants t' fight wid swords, he'll get it. I'll giv' 'im a go at it, anyhow."

One man said: "Well, have you got a sword? Do you know what a sword is? Have you got a sword?"

"No, I ain't got none," said Patsy honestly, "but I kin git one." Then he added valiantly: "An' quick too."

The two men laughed. "Why, can't you understand it would be sure death to fight a sword duel with this fellow?"

"Dat's all right! See? I know me own business. If he wants t' fight one of dees damn duels, I'm in it, understan'?"

"Have you ever fought one, you fool?"

"No, I ain't. But I will fight one, dough! I ain't no muff. If he wants t' fight a duel, by Gawd, I'm wid 'im! D'yeh understan' dat?" Patsy cocked his hat and swaggered. He was getting very serious.

The little Cuban burst out: "Ah, come on, sirs: come on! We can take cab. Ah, you big cow, I will stick you, I will stick you. Ah, you will look very beautiful, very beautiful. Ah, come on, sirs. We will stop at hotel— my hotel. I there have weapons."

"Yeh will, will yeh? Yeh bloomin' little black Dago," cried Patsy in hoarse and maddened reply to the personal part of the Cuban's speech. He stepped forward. "Git yer damn swords," he commanded. "Git yer swords. Git 'em quick! I'll fight wi'che! I'll fight wid anyting, too! See? I'll fight yeh wid a knife an' fork if yeh say so! I'll fight yeh standin' up er sittin' down!" Patsy delivered this intense oration with sweeping, intensely emphatic gestures, his hands stretched out eloquently, his jaw thrust forward, his eyes glaring.

"Ah," cried the little Cuban joyously. "Ah, you are in very pretty temper. Ah, how I will cut your heart in two piece, my dear, d-e-a-r friend." His eyes, too, shone like carbuncles, with a swift, changing glitter, always fastened upon Patsy's face.

The two peacemakers were perspiring and in despair. One of them blurted out: "Well, I'll be blamed if this ain't the most ridiculous thing I ever saw." The other said: "For ten dollars I'd be tempted to let these two infernal blockheads have their duel."

Patsy was strutting to and fro, and conferring grandly with his friends. "He took me for a muff. He tought he was goin' t' bluff me out, talkin' 'bout swords. He'll get fooled." He addressed the Cuban: "You're a fine little dirty picter of a scrapper, ain'che? I'll chew yez up, dat's what I will."

There began then some rapid action. The patience of well-dressed men is not an eternal thing. It began to look as if it would at last be a fight with six corners to it. The faces of the men were shining red with anger. They jostled each other defiantly, and almost every one blazed out at three or four of the others. The bartender had given up protesting. He swore for a time, and banged his glasses. Then he jumped the bar and ran out of the saloon, cursing sullenly.

When he came back with a policeman, Patsy and the Cuban were preparing to depart together. Patsy was delivering his last oration: "I'll fight yeh wid swords! Sure I will! Come ahead, Dago! I'll fight yeh anywheres wid anyting! We'll have a large, juicy scrap, an' don't yeh forgit dat! I'm right wid yez. I ain't no muff! I scrap wid a man jest as soon as he ses scrap, an' if yeh wanta scrap, I'm yer kitten. Understan' dat?"

The policeman said sharply: "Come, now; what's all this?" He had a distinctly business air.

The little Cuban stepped forward calmly. "It is none of your business."

The policeman flushed to his ears. "What?"

One well-dressed man touched the other on the sleeve. "Here's the time to skip," he whispered. They halted a block away from the saloon and watched the policeman pull the Cuban through the door. There was a minute of scuffle on the sidewalk, and into this deserted street at midnight fifty people appeared at once as if from the sky to watch it.

At last the three Cherry Hill men came from the saloon, and swaggered with all their old valor toward the peacemakers. "Ah," said Patsy to them, "he was so hot talkin' about this duel business, but I would a-givin 'im a great scrap, an' don't yeh forgit it."

For Patsy was not as wise as seven owls, but his courage could throw a shadow as long as the steeple of a cathedral.

December 9, 1894
[New York *Press*, part 3, p. 2.]

A CHRISTMAS DINNER WON IN BATTLE

Tom had set up a plumbing shop in the prairie town of Levelville as soon as the people learned to care more about sanitary conditions than they did about the brand of tobacco smoked by the inhabitants of Mars. Nevertheless he was a wise young man, for he was only one week ahead of the surveyors. A railroad, like a magic wand, was going to touch Levelville and change it to a great city. In an incredibly short time, the town had a hotel, a mayor, a board of aldermen and more than a hundred real estate agents, besides a blueprint of the plans for a street railway three miles long. When the cowboys rode in with their customary noise to celebrate the fact that they had been paid, their efforts were discouraged by new policemen in uniform. Levelville had become a dignified city.

As the town expanded in marvelous circles out over the prairies, Tom bestrode the froth of the wave of progress. He was soon one of the first citizens. These waves carry men to fortune with sudden sweeping movements, and Tom had the courage, the temerity, and the assurance to hold his seat like a knight-errant.

In the democratic and genial atmosphere of this primary boom, he became an intimate acquaintance of Colonel Fortman, the president of the railroad, and with more courage, temerity, and assurance, had already fallen violently in love with his daughter, the incomparable Mildred. He carried his intimacy with the colonel so far as to once save his life from the flying might of the 5:30 express. It seems that the colonel had ordered the engineer of the 5:30 to make his time under all circumstances; to make his time if he had to run through fire, blood, and earthquake. The engineer decided that the usual rule relating to the speed of trains when passing through freight yards could not concern an express that was ordered to slow down for nothing but the wrath of heaven and in consequence, at the time of this incident, the 5:30 was shrieking through the Levelville freight yard at fifty miles an hour, roaring over the switches and screaming along the lines of boxcars. The colonel and Tom were coming from the shops. They had just rounded the corner of a car and stepped out upon the main track when this whirring, boiling, howling demon of an express came down upon them. Tom had an instant in which to drag his companion off the rails; the train whistled past them like an enormous projectile. "Damn that fellow—he's making his time," panted the old colonel gazing after the long speeding shadow with its two green lights. Later he said very soberly: "I'm much obliged to you for that Tom, old boy."

When Tom went to him a year later, however, to ask for the hand of Mildred, the colonel replied: "My dear man, I think you are insane. Mildred will have over a million dollars at my death, and while I don't mean to push the money part of it too far forward, yet Mildred with her beauty, her family name and her wealth, can marry the finest in the land. There isn't anyone too great for her. So you see, my dear man, it is impossible that she could consider you for a moment."

Whereupon Tom lost his temper. He had the indignation of a good, sound-minded, fearless-eyed young fellow who is assured of his love and assured almost of the love of the girl. Moreover, it filled him with unspeakable rage to be called: "My dear man."

They then accused each other of motives of which neither were guilty, and Tom went away. It was a serious quarrel. The colonel told Tom never to dare to cross his threshold. They passed each other on the street without a wink of an eye to disclose the fact that one knew that the other existed. As time went on the colonel became more massively aristocratic and more impenetrably stern. Levelville had developed about five grades of society, and the Fortmans mingled warily with the dozen families that formed the highest and iciest grades. Once when the colonel and Mildred were driving through town, the girl bowed to a young man who passed them.

"Who the deuce was that?" said the colonel airily. "Seems to me I ought to know that fellow."

"That's the man that saved your life from the 5:30," replied Mildred.

"See here, young lady," cried the colonel angrily, "don't you take his part against me."

About a year later came the great railway strike. The papers of the city foreshadowed it vaguely from time to time, but no one apparently took the matter in a serious way. There had been threats and rumors of threats but the general public had seemed to view them as idle bombast. At last, however, the true situation displayed itself suddenly and vividly. Almost the entire force of the great P.C.C. and W.U. system went on strike. The people of the city awoke one morning to find the gray sky of dawn splashed with a bright crimson color. The strikers had set ablaze one of the company's shops in the suburbs and the light from it flashed out a red ominous signal of warning foretelling the woe and despair of the struggle that was to ensue. Rumors came that the men usually so sober, industrious, and imperturbable were running in a wild mob, raving and destroying. Whereupon, the people who had laughed to scorn any idea of being prepared for this upheaval began to assiduously abuse the authorities for not being ready to meet it.

That morning Tom, in his shirt sleeves, went into the back part of his shop to direct some of his workmen about a certain job, and when he came out he was well covered by as honest a coating of grime and soot as was ever worn by journeyman. He went to the sink to dispose of this adornment and while there he heard his men talking of the strike. One was saying: "Yes, sir; sure as th' dickens! They say they're goin' t' burn th' president's house an' everybody in it." Tom's body stiffened at these words. He felt himself turn cold. A moment later he left the shop forgetting his coat, forgetting his covering of soot and grime.

In the main streets of the city there was no evident change. The horses of the jangling streetcars still slipped and strained in the deep mud into which the snow had been churned. The store windows were gay with the color of Christmas. Innumerable turkeys hung before each butcher's shop. Upon the walks the businessmen had formed into little eager groups discussing the domestic calamity. Against the leaden-hued sky, over the tops of the buildings, arose a great leaning pillar of smoke marking the spot upon which stood the burning shop.

Tom hurried on through that part of town which was composed of little narrow streets with tiny gray houses on either side. There he saw a concourse of Slavs, Polacks, Italians and Hungarians, laborers of the company, floundering about in the mud and raving, conducting a riot in their own inimitable way. They seemed as bloodthirsty, pitiless, mad, as starved wolves. And Tom presented a figure no less grim as he ran through the crowd, coatless and now indeed hatless, with pale skin showing through the grime. He went until he came to a stretch of commons across which he could see the Fortmans' house standing serenely with no evidences of riot about it. He moderated his pace then.

When he had gone about halfway across this little snow-covered common, he looked back, for he heard cries. Across the white fields, winding along the muddy road, there came a strange procession. It resembled a parade of Parisians at the time of the first revolution. Fists were wildly waving and at times hoarse voices rang out. It was as if this crowd was delirious from drink. As it came nearer Tom could see women—gaunt and ragged creatures with inflamed visages and rolling eyes. There were men with dark, sinister faces whom Tom had never before seen. They had emerged from the earth, so to speak, to engage in this carousal of violence. And from this procession there came continual threatening ejaculations, shrill cries for revenge, and querulous voices of hate, that made a sort of barbaric hymn, a pagan chant of savage battle and death.

Tom waited for them. Those in the lead evidently considered him to be one of their number since his face was grimed and his garments disheveled. One gigantic man, with bare and brawny arms and throat, gave him invitation with a fierce smile. "Come ahn, Swipsey, while we go roast 'em."

A raving gray-haired woman, struggling in the mud, sang a song which consisted of one endless line:

"We'll burn th' foxes out,
We'll burn th' foxes out
We'll burn th' foxes out."

As for the others, they babbled and screamed in a vast variety of foreign tongues. Tom walked along with them listening to the cries that came from the terrible little army, marching with clenched fists and with gleaming eyes fastened upon the mansion that upreared so calmly before them.

When they arrived, they hesitated a moment, as if awed by the impassive silence of the structure with closed shutters and barred doors, which stolidly and indifferently confronted them.

Then from the center of the crowd came the voice of the gray-headed old woman: "Break in th' door! Break in th' door!" And then it was that Tom displayed the desperation born of his devotion to the girl within the house. Although he was perhaps braver than most men, he had none of that magnificent fortitude, that gorgeous tranquillity amid upheavals and perils which is the attribute of people in plays; but he stepped up on the porch and faced the throng. His face was wondrously pallid and his hands trembled but he said: "You fellows can't come in here."

There came a great sarcastic howl from the crowd. "Can't we?" They broke into laughter at this wildly ridiculous thing. The brawny, bare-armed giant seized Tom by the arm, "Get outa th' way, you yap," he said between his teeth. In an instant Tom was punched and pulled and knocked this way and that way, and amid the pain of these moments he was conscious that members of the mob were delivering thunderous blows upon the huge doors. Directly indeed they crashed down and he felt the crowd sweep past him and into the house. He clung to a railing; he had no more sense of balance than a feather. A blow in the head had made him feel that the ground swirled and heaved around him. He had no further interest in rioting, and such scenes of excitement. Gazing out over the common he saw two patrol wagons, loaded with policemen, and the lashed horses galloping in the mud. He wondered dimly why they were in such a hurry.

But at that moment a scream rang from the house out through the open doors. He knew the voice and, like an electric shock, it aroused him from his semi-stupor. Once more alive, he turned and charged into the house as valiant and as full of rage as a Roman. Pandemonium reigned within. There came yells and roars, splinterings, cracklings, crashes. The scream of Mildred again rang out; this time he knew it came from the dining room before whose closed door four men were as busy as miners with improvised pick and drill.

Tom grasped a heavy oaken chair that stood ornamentally in the hall and, elevating it above his head, ran madly at the four men. When he was almost upon them, he let the chair fly. It seemed to strike all of them. A heavy oak chair of the old English type is one of the most destructive of weapons. Still, there seemed to be enough of the men left, for they flew at him from all sides like dragons. In the dark of the hallway, Tom put down his head and half-closed his eyes and plied his fists. He knew he had but a moment in which to stand up, but there was a sort of grim joy in knowing that the most terrific din of this affray was going straight through the dining room door, and into the heart of Mildred and when she knew that her deliverer was— He saw a stretch of blood-red sky flame under his lids and then sank to the floor, blind, deaf, and nerveless.

When the old colonel arrived in one of the patrol wagons, he did not wait to see the police attack in front but ran around to the rear. As he passed the dining room windows he saw his wife's face. He shouted, and when they opened a window he clambered with great agility into the room. For a minute they deluged each other with shouts of joy and tears. Then finally the old colonel said: "But they did not get in here. How was that?"

"Oh, papa," said Mildred, "they were trying to break in when somebody came and fought dreadfully with them and made them stop."

"Heavens, who could it have been?" said the colonel. He went to the door and opened it. A group of police became visible, hurrying about the wide hall, but near the colonel's feet lay a body with a white still face.

"Why, it's—it's—" ejaculated the colonel in great agitation.

"It's Tom," cried Mildred.

When Tom came to his senses he found that his fingers were clasped tightly by a soft white hand which by some occult power of lovers he knew at once.

"Tom," said Mildred.

And the old colonel from further away said: "Tom, my boy!"

But Tom was something of an obstinate young man. So as soon as he felt himself recovered sufficiently, he arose and went unsteadily toward the door.

"Tom, where are you going?" cried Mildred.

"Where are you going, Tom?" called the colonel.

"I'm going home," said Tom doggedly. "I didn't intend to cross this threshold—I—" He swayed unsteadily and seemed almost about to fall. Mildred screamed and ran toward him. She made a prisoner of him. "You shall not go home," she told him.

"Well," began Tom weakly yet persistently, "I—"

"No, no, Tom," said the colonel, "you are to eat a Christmas dinner with us tomorrow and then I wish to talk with you about—about—"

"About what?" said Tom.

"About—about—damnitall, about marrying my daughter," cried the colonel.

January 1, 1895
[*The Plumbers' Trade Journal*, Vol. 17, pp. 26–27.]

A LOVELY JAG IN A CROWDED CAR

The crosstown car was bound for the great shopping district, and one side of it was lined with women who sat in austere silence regarding each other in occasional furtive glances and preserving their respectability with fierce vigilance. A solitary man sat in a corner meekly pretending that he was interested in his newspaper. The conductor came and went without discussion, like a well-bred servant. The atmosphere of the car was as decorous as that of the most frigid of drawing rooms.

However, the decorous atmosphere was doomed to be destroyed by a wild red demon of drink and destruction. He was standing on a street corner, swaying gently on his wavering legs and blinking at the cobbles. Frequently he regarded the passing people with an expression of the most benign amiability.

As the car came near to him he tottered greatly in his excitement. He waved his umbrella and shouted: "Stop sh' car! Stop sh' car!"

The driver pulled stoutly at the reins with his gloved left hand, and with his right one swung the polished brass of the brake lever. The car halted and, upon the rear platform, the conductor reached down to help the wild, red demon of drink and destruction aboard the car. He climbed up the steps with an important and serious air, as if he were boarding a frigate; then he went smiling in jovial satisfaction into the car. As he was about to sit down there were two sharp, clanging notes on the bell, the driver released his brake and again tightened his reins, and the car started with a sudden jerk that caused the man to be precipitated violently into a seat as if some one had struck him. He seemed to feel a keen humor in the situation for, upon recovering himself, he looked at the other passengers and laughed.

As for the women bound for the shopping district, they had suddenly turned into so many statues of ice. They stared out of the little windows which cut the street scenes in half and allowed but the upper parts of people to be seen, moving curiously without any legs. Whenever the eyes of the women were obliged to encounter the man they assumed at once an expression of the most heroic disgust and disdain. The man over in the corner grinned, urchinlike.

The drunken man put his hands on his knees and beamed about him in absolute unalloyed happiness. He seemed to believe that he was engaged in carousing with a convivial party and these friends were represented to his mind by the silent row of women who were going shopping. He had not the air of a man who was on a solitary spree; he was conducting a great celebration. The universe was engaged with him in a vast rakish song to flagon and cup, the sun had its hat over its eye, all of humanity staggered and smiled.

Presently his excited spirits overflowed to such an extent that he was obliged to sing. He began to beat time with his forefinger as if he was leading a grand chorus.

> "But th' younger shon was er shon-of-a-gun,
>   He was! He was!
> 'E shuffle' cards an' 'e play fer mon,
>   He did! He did!
> He wore shilk hat an' er high stannin' collar.
> He'd go out with'er boys an' gi' full an' then
>   holler.
> Oh, he was er—"

He was interrupted by the conductor, who came in and said in a heavy undertone: "Close that trap now or I'll put'che off!"

The injustice of the conductor was both an astonishment and a grief to the man. He had been on the best of terms with each single atom in space, and now here suddenly appeared a creature who gruffly stated a dampening fact. He spoke very loudly in his pain and disappointment: "Pu' me off? What 'che go pu' me off fer? We ain't doin' er shing! G'wan way! Go shtand on er end z'car! Thash where you b'long! You ain' got no business talk me."

The conductor returned scowling to the rear platform. He turned and looked at the man with a glance that was full of menace.

Meanwhile, within the car, the inebriated passenger continued to conduct the grand celebration. "Hurray!" he said, at the conclusion of one of his little ballads. "Le's all haver drink! Le's all haver noz' drink! Shay! Shay, look here a minute." He began to pound on the floor with his umbrella and make earnest gestures at the conductor. "Shay, look here!"

The conductor, watchful-eyed but self-contained, came forward. "Well," he said.

"Bringesh noz' round drinkshs," said the man. "Bringesh noz' round drinkshs."

"Say, you'll have to cool down some or I'll put'che off th' car. What d'yeh think?" said the conductor.

But the man was busy trying to find out the preference of each of the passengers. "What'll yeh take?" he demanded of each one, smiling genially. Whereupon the women opposite to him stared at the floor, at the ceiling, at the forward end of the car and at the rear end of the car, their lips set in stern lines.

Notwithstanding all these icy expressions, his face remained lit with a sunny grin, as if he were convinced that every one regarded him affectionately. He insisted that they should all take something.

"What'll yeh take? What? Ain'che drinkin'? What? Shay, yeh mus' take somethin'. What? Well, all ri'. I'll order Manhattan fer yeh! Shay, Jim," he called loudly to the conductor, "bringesh noz' Manhattan."

With infinite pains and thoroughness he canvassed the passengers, putting to each one the formidable question, "What'll yeh drink?" The faces of the women were set in lines of horror, dismay, and disgust. No one uttered a syllable in reply save the man over in the corner, who said indulgently: "Oh, I guess I'll take a beer."

At the conclusion of his canvass the man spent some anxious moments in reflection, calculating carefully upon his fingers. Then he triumphantly ordered one beer and nine Manhattan cocktails of the conductor.

The latter, who was collecting fares at the time, turned and said: "Say, lookahere, now, you've got t' quit this thing. Just close your face or I'll throw yeh out in th' street."

"Tha's all ri'," said the other, nodding his head portentously and wisely. "Tha's all ri'. You ain't go' throw me out. I ain't doin' er shing. Wha' you throw me out fer? Tha's all ri'." Then he returned to his demeanor of command. "Come. Hur' up! Bringesh nine Manhattans an'—an'—le's see—somebody order beer, didn' they? Who order beer?" He gazed inquiringly at the imperturbable faces. Finally he addressed the man over in the corner. "Shay, didn' you order beer?"

The man in the corner grinned. "Well, yes, I guess it was me."

"Look here, bringesh nine Manhattans an' er beer," called the celebrating man to the conductor. "Hur' up! Bringesh 'em quick."

The conductor looked scornfully away.

As the car passed through the region of the great stores the group of women gradually diminished until finally they disappeared altogether, and, as the car went on its way toward a distant ferry, there remained within only the celebrating individual and the man over in the corner. The celebrator became more jovial as time went forward. He rejoiced that the world was to him one vast landscape of pure rose color. The humming of the wheels and the clatter of the horses' hoofs did not drown the sound of this high quavering voice that sang of the pearl-hued joys of life as seen through a pair of strange, oblique, temporary spectacles. The conductor, musing upon the rear platform, had grown indifferent.

At last the celebrator seemed overcome by the wild thought that the car had passed the point where he had intended to leave it. He broke off in the midst of a ballad and scrambled for the door. "Stop sh' car," he yelled. The conductor reached for the bell strap, but before the car stopped the celebrator sprawled out upon the cobbles. He arose instantly and began a hurried and unsteady journey back up the street, retracing the way over which the car had just brought him. He seemed overwhelmed with anxiety.

The man in the corner came to the rear platform and gazed after the form of the celebrator. "Well, he was a peach," he said.

"That's what he was," said the conductor.

They both turned to watch him and they remained there deep in reflection, absorbed in contemplation of this wavering figure in the distance, until observation was no longer possible.

January 6, 1895
[New York Press, part 5, p. 6.]

A MYSTERY OF HEROISM*

The dark uniforms of the men were so coated with dust from the incessant wrestling of the two armies that the regiment almost seemed a part of the clay bank which shielded them from the shells. On the top of the hill a battery was arguing in tremendous roars with some other guns, and to the eye of the infantry the artillerymen, the guns, the caissons, the horses, were distinctly outlined upon the blue sky. When a piece was fired, a red streak as round as a log flashed low in the heavens, like a monstrous bolt of lightning. The men of the battery wore white duck trousers, which somehow emphasized their legs; and when they ran and crowded in little groups at the bidding of the shouting officers, it was more impressive than usual to the infantry.

Fred Collins, of A Company, was saying: "Thunder! I wisht I had a drink. Ain't there any water round here?" Then somebody yelled: "There goes th' bugler!"

As the eyes of half the regiment swept in one machinelike movement, there was an instant's picture of a horse in a great convulsive leap of a death wound and a rider leaning back with a crooked arm and spread fingers before his face. On the ground was the crimson terror of an exploding shell, with fibers of flame that seemed like lances. A glittering bugle swung clear of the rider's back as fell headlong the horse and the man. In the air was an odor as from a conflagration.

Sometimes they of the infantry looked down at a fair little meadow which spread at their feet. Its long green grass was rippling gently in a breeze. Beyond it was the gray form of a house half torn to pieces by shells and by the busy axes of soldiers who had pursued firewood. The line of an old fence was now dimly marked by long weeds and by an occasional post. A shell had blown the well-house to fragments. Little lines of gray smoke ribboning upward from some embers indicated the place where had stood the barn.

From beyond a curtain of green woods there came the sound of some stupendous scuffle, as if two animals of the size of islands were fighting. At a distance there were occasional appearances of swift-moving men, horses, batteries, flags, and with the crashing of infantry volleys were heard, often, wild and frenzied cheers. In the midst of it all Smith and Ferguson, two privates of A Company, were engaged in a heated discussion which involved the greatest questions of the national existence.

* *The Little Regiment.*

The battery on the hill presently engaged in a frightful duel. The white legs of the gunners scampered this way and that way, and the officers redoubled their shouts. The guns, with their demeanors of stolidity and courage, were typical of something infinitely self-possessed in this clamor of death that swirled around the hill.

One of a "swing" team was suddenly smitten quivering to the ground, and his maddened brethren dragged his torn body in their struggle to escape from this turmoil and danger. A young soldier astride one of the leaders swore and fumed in his saddle and furiously jerked at the bridle. An officer screamed out an order so violently that his voice broke and ended the sentence in a falsetto shriek.

The leading company of the infantry regiment was somewhat exposed, and the colonel ordered it moved more fully under the shelter of the hill. There was the clank of steel against steel.

A lieutenant of the battery rode down and passed them, holding his right arm carefully in his left hand. And it was as if this arm was not at all a part of him, but belonged to another man. His sober and reflective charger went slowly. The officer's face was grimy and perspiring, and his uniform was tousled as if he had been in direct grapple with an enemy. He smiled grimly when the men stared at him. He turned his horse toward the meadow.

Collins, of A Company, said: "I wisht I had a drink. I bet there's water in that there ol' well yonder!"

"Yes; but how you goin' to git it?"

For the little meadow which intervened was now suffering a terrible onslaught of shells. Its green and beautiful calm had vanished utterly. Brown earth was being flung in monstrous handfuls. And there was a massacre of the young blades of grass. They were being torn, burned, obliterated. Some curious fortune of the battle had made this gentle little meadow the object of the red hate of the shells, and each one as it exploded seemed like an imprecation in the face of a maiden.

The wounded officer who was riding across this expanse said to himself: "Why, they couldn't shoot any harder if the whole army was massed here!"

A shell struck the gray ruins of the house, and as, after the roar, the shattered wall fell in fragments, there was a noise which resembled the flapping of shutters during a wild gale of winter. Indeed, the infantry paused in the shelter of the bank appeared as men standing upon a shore contemplating a madness of the sea. The angel of calamity had under its glance the battery upon the hill. Fewer white-legged men labored about the guns. A shell had smitten one of the pieces, and after the flare, the smoke, the dust, the wrath of this blow were gone, it was possible to see white legs stretched horizontally upon the ground. And at that interval to the rear where it is the business of battery horses to stand with their noses to the fight, awaiting the command to drag their guns out of the destruction, or into it, or wheresoever these incomprehensible humans demanded with whip and spur—in this line of passive and dumb spectators, whose fluttering hearts yet would not let them forget the iron laws of man's control of them—in this rank of brute soldiers there had been relentless and hideous carnage. From the ruck of bleeding and prostrate horses, the men of the infantry could see one animal raising its stricken body with its forelegs and turning its nose with mystic and profound eloquence toward the sky.

Some comrades joked Collins about his thirst. "Well, if yeh want a drink so bad, why don't yeh go git it?"

"Well, I will in a minnet, if yeh don't shut up!"

A lieutenant of artillery floundered his horse straight down the hill with as little concern as if it were level ground. As he galloped past the colonel of the infantry, he threw up his hand in swift salute. "We've got to get out of that," he roared angrily. He was a black-bearded officer, and his eyes, which resembled beads, sparkled like those of an insane man. His jumping horse sped along the column of infantry.

The fat major, standing carelessly with his sword held horizontally behind him and with his legs far apart, looked after the receding horseman and laughed. "He wants to get back with orders pretty quick, or there'll be no batt'ry left," he observed.

The wise young captain of the second company hazarded to the lieutenant colonel that the enemy's infantry would probably soon attack the hill, and the lieutenant colonel snubbed him.

A private in one of the rear companies looked out over the meadow, and then turned to a companion and said, "Look there, Jim!" It was the wounded officer from the battery, who some time before had started to ride across the meadow, supporting his right arm carefully with his left hand. This man had encountered a shell apparently at a time when no one perceived him, and he could now be seen lying face downward with a stirruped foot stretched across the body of his dead horse. A leg of the charger extended slantingly upward, precisely as stiff as a stake. Around this motionless pair the shells still howled.

There was a quarrel in A Company. Collins was shaking his fist in the faces of some laughing comrades. "Dern yeh! I ain't afraid t' go. If yeh say much, I will go!"

"Of course, yeh will! You'll run through that there medder, won't yeh?"

Collins said, in a terrible voice: "You see now!" At this ominous threat his comrades broke into renewed jeers.

Collins gave them a dark scowl, and went to find his captain. The latter was conversing with the colonel of the regiment.

"Captain," said Collins, saluting and standing at attention—in those days all trousers bagged at the knees—"Captain, I want t' git permission to go git some water from that there well over yonder!"

The colonel and the captain swung about simultaneously and stared across the meadow. The captain laughed. "You must be pretty thirsty, Collins?"

"Yes, sir, I am."

"Well—ah," said the captain. After a moment, he asked, "Can't you wait?"

"No, sir."

The colonel was watching Collins's face. "Look here, my lad," he said, in a pious sort of voice—"look here, my lad"—Collins was not a lad—"don't you think that's taking pretty big risks for a little drink of water?"

"I dunno," said Collins uncomfortably. Some of the resentment toward his companions, which perhaps had forced him into this affair, was beginning to fade. "I dunno wether 'tis."

The colonel and the captain contemplated him for a time.

"Well," said the captain finally.

"Well," said the colonel, "if you want to go, why, go."

Collins saluted. "Much obliged t' yeh."

As he moved away the colonel called after him. "Take some of the other boys' canteens with you, an' hurry back, now."

"Yes, sir, I will."

The colonel and the captain looked at each other then, for it had suddenly occurred that they could not for the life of them tell whether Collins wanted to go or whether he did not.

They turned to regard Collins, and as they perceived him surrounded by gesticulating comrades, the colonel said: "Well, by thunder! I guess he's going."

Collins appeared as a man dreaming. In the midst of the questions, the advice, the warnings, all the excited talk of his company mates, he maintained a curious silence.

They were very busy in preparing him for his ordeal. When they inspected him carefully, it was somewhat like the examination that grooms give a horse before a race; and they were amazed, staggered, by the whole affair. Their astonishment found vent in strange repetitions.

"Are yeh sure a-goin'?" they demanded again and again.

"Certainly I am," cried Collins at last, furiously.

He strode sullenly away from them. He was swinging five or six canteens by their cords. It seemed that his cap would not remain firmly on his head, and often he reached and pulled it down over his brow.

There was a general movement in the compact column. The long animal-like thing moved slightly. Its four hundred eyes were turned upon the figure of Collins.

"Well, sir, if that ain't th' derndest thing! I never thought Fred Collins had the blood in him for that kind of business."

"What's he goin' to do, anyhow?"

"He's goin' to that well there after water."

"We ain't dyin' of thirst, are we? That's foolishness."

"Well, somebody put him up to it, an' he's doin' it."

"Say, he must be a desperate cuss."

When Collins faced the meadow and walked away from the regiment, he was vaguely conscious that a chasm, the deep valley of all prides, was suddenly between him and his comrades. It was provisional, but the provision was that he return as a victor. He had blindly been led by quaint emotions, and laid himself under an obligation to walk squarely up to the face of death.

But he was not sure that he wished to make a retraction, even if he could do so without shame. As a matter of truth, he was sure of very little. He was mainly surprised.

It seemed to him supernaturally strange that he had allowed his mind to maneuver his body into such a situation. He understood that it might be called dramatically great.

However, he had no full appreciation of anything, excepting that he was actually conscious of being dazed. He could feel his dulled mind groping after the form and color of this incident. He wondered why he did not feel some keen agony of fear cutting his sense like a knife. He wondered at this, because human expression had said loudly for centuries that men should feel afraid of certain things, and that all men who did not feel this fear were phenomena—heroes.

He was, then, a hero. He suffered that disappointment which we would all have if we discovered that we were ourselves capable of those deeds which we most admire in history and legend. This, then, was a hero. After all, heroes were not much.

No, it could not be true. He was not a hero. Heroes had no shames in their lives, and, as for him, he remembered borrowing fifteen dollars from a friend and promising to pay it back the next day, and then avoiding that friend for ten months. When, at home, his mother had aroused him for the early labor of his life on the farm, it had often been his fashion to be irritable, childish, diabolical; and his mother had died since he had come to the war.

He saw that, in this matter of the well, the canteens, the shells, he was an intruder in the land of fine deeds.

He was now about thirty paces from his comrades. The regiment had just turned its many faces toward him.

From the forest of terrific noises there suddenly emerged a little uneven line of men. They fired fiercely and rapidly at distant foliage on which appeared little puffs of white smoke. The spatter of skirmish firing was added to the thunder of the guns on the hill. The little line of men ran forward. A color sergeant fell flat with his flag as if he had slipped on ice. There was hoarse cheering from this distant field.

Collins suddenly felt that two demon fingers were pressed into his ears. He could see nothing but flying arrows, flaming red. He lurched from the shock of this explosion, but he made a mad rush for the house, which he viewed as a man submerged to the neck in a boiling surf might view the shore. In the air little pieces of shell howled, and the earthquake explosions drove him insane with the menace of their roar. As he ran the canteens knocked together with a rhythmical tinkling.

As he neared the house, each detail of the scene became vivid to him. He was aware of some bricks of the vanished chimney lying on the sod. There was a door which hung by one hinge.

Rifle bullets called forth by the insistent skirmishers came from the far-off bank of foliage. They mingled with the shells and the pieces of shells until the air was torn in all directions by hootings, yells, howls. The sky was full of fiends who directed all their wild rage at his head.

When he came to the well, he flung himself face downward and peered into its darkness. There were furtive silver glintings some feet from the surface. He grabbed one of the canteens and, unfastening its cap, swung it down by the cord. The water flowed slowly in with an indolent gurgle.

And now, as he lay with his face turned away, he was suddenly smitten with the terror. It came upon his heart like the grasp of claws. All the power faded from his muscles. For an instant he was no more than a dead man.

The canteen filled with a maddening slowness, in the manner of all bottles. Presently he recovered his strength and addressed a screaming oath to it. He leaned over until it seemed as if he intended to try to push water into it with his hands. His eyes as he gazed down into the well shone like two pieces of metal, and in their expression was a great appeal and a great curse. The stupid water derided him.

There was the blaring thunder of a shell. Crimson light shone through the swift-boiling smoke, and made a pink reflection on part of the wall of the well. Collins jerked out his arm and canteen with the same motion that a man would use in withdrawing his head from a furnace.

He scrambled erect and glared and hesitated. On the ground near him lay the old well bucket, with a length of rusty chain. He lowered it swiftly into the well. The bucket struck the water and then, turning lazily over, sank. When, with hand reaching tremblingly over hand, he hauled it out, it knocked often against the walls of the well and spilled some of its contents.

In running with a filled bucket, a man can adopt but one kind of gait. So, through this terrible field over which screamed practical angels of death, Collins ran in the manner of a farmer chased out of a dairy by a bull.

His face went staring white with anticipating—anticipation of a blow that would whirl him around and down. He would fall as he had seen other men fall, the life knocked out of them so suddenly that their knees were no more quick to touch the ground than their heads. He saw the long blue line of the regiment, but his comrades were standing looking at him from the edge of an impossible star. He was aware of some deep wheelruts and hoofprints in the sod beneath his feet.

The artillery officer who had fallen in this meadow had been making groans in the teeth of the tempest of sound. These futile cries, wrenched from him by his agony, were heard only by shells, bullets. When wild-eyed Collins came running, this officer raised himself. His face contorted and blanched from pain, he was about to utter some great beseeching cry. But suddenly his face straightened, and he called: "Say, young man, give me a drink of water, will you?"

Collins had no room amid his emotions for surprise. He was mad from the threats of destruction.

"I can't!" he screamed, and in his reply was a full description of his quaking apprehension. His cap was gone and his hair was riotous. His clothes made it appear that he had been dragged over the ground by the heels. He ran on.

The officer's head sank down, and one elbow crooked. His foot in its brass-bound stirrup still stretched over the body of his horse, and the other leg was under the steed.

But Collins turned. He came dashing back. His face had now turned gray, and in his eyes was all terror. "Here it is! here it is!"

The officer was as a man gone in drink. His arm bent like a twig. His head drooped as if his neck were of willow. He was sinking to the ground, to lie face downward.

Collins grabbed him by the shoulder. "Here it is. Here's your drink. Turn over. Turn over, man, for God's sake!"

With Collins hauling at his shoulder, the officer twisted his body and fell with his face turned toward that region where lived the unspeakable noises of the swirling missiles. There was the faintest shadow of a smile on his lips as he looked at Collins. He gave a sigh, a little primitive breath like that from a child.

Collins tried to hold the bucket steadily, but his shaking hands caused the water to splash all over the face of the dying man. Then he jerked it away and ran on.

The regiment gave him a welcoming roar. The grimed faces were wrinkled in laughter.

His captain waved the bucket away. "Give it to the men!"

The two genial, skylarking young lieutenants were the first to gain possession of it. They played over it in their fashion.

When one tried to drink, the other teasingly knocked his elbow. "Don't Billie! You'll make me spill it," said the one. The other laughed.

Suddenly there was an oath, the thud of wood on the ground, and a swift murmur of astonishment among the ranks. The two lieutenants glared at each other. The bucket lay on the ground empty.

August 1 and 2, 1895
[Philadelphia Press, August 1, p. 11; August 2, p. 9.]

A GRAY SLEEVE*

I

"It looks as if it might rain this afternoon," remarked the lieutenant of artillery.

"So it does," the infantry captain assented. He glanced casually at the sky. When his eyes had lowered to the green-shadowed landscape before him, he said fretfully: "I wish those fellows out yonder would quit pelting at us. They've been at it since noon."

At the edge of a grove of maples, across wide fields, there occasionally appeared little puffs of smoke of a dull hue in this gloom of sky which expressed an impending rain. The long wave of blue and steel in the field moved uneasily at the eternal barking of the faraway sharpshooters, and the men, leaning upon their rifles, stared at the grove of maples. Once a private turned to borrow some tobacco from a comrade in the rear rank, but, with his hand still stretched out, he continued to twist his head and glance at the distant trees. He was afraid the enemy would shoot him at a time when he was not looking.

Suddenly the artillery officer said, "See what's coming!"

Along the rear of the brigade of infantry a column of cavalry was sweeping at a hard gallop. A lieutenant, riding some yards to the right of the column, bawled furiously at the four troopers just at the rear of the colors. They had lost distance and made a little gap, but at the shouts of the lieu-

* *The Little Regiment.*

tenant they urged their horses forward. The bugler, careering along behind the captain of the troop, fought and tugged like a wrestler to keep his frantic animal from bolting far ahead of the column.

On the springy turf the innumerable hoofs thundered in a swift storm of sound. In the brown faces of the troopers their eyes were set like bits of flashing steel.

The long line of the infantry regiments standing at ease underwent a sudden movement at the rush of the passing squadron. The foot soldiers turned their heads to gaze at the torrent of horses and men.

The yellow folds of the flag fluttered back in silken, shuddering waves, as if it were a reluctant thing. Occasionally a giant spring of a charger would rear the firm and sturdy figure of a soldier suddenly head and shoulders above his comrades. Over the noise of the scudding hoofs could be heard the creaking of leather trappings, the jingle and clank of steel, and the tense, low-toned commands or appeals of the men to their horses. And the horses were mad with the headlong sweep of this movement. Powerful underjaws bent back and straightened so that the bits were clamped as rigidly as vises upon the teeth, and glistening necks arched in desperate resistance to the hands at the bridles. Swinging their heads in rage at the granite laws of their lives, which compelled even their angers and their ardors to chosen directions and chosen paces, their flight was as a flight of harnessed demons.

The captain's bay kept its pace at the head of the squadron with the lithe bounds of a thoroughbred, and this horse was proud as a chief at the roaring trample of his fellows behind him. The captain's glance was calmly upon the grove of maples whence the sharpshooters of the enemy had been picking at the blue line. He seemed to be reflecting. He stolidly rose and fell with the plunges of his horse in all the indifference of a deacon's figure seated plumply in church. And it occurred to many of the watching infantry to wonder why this officer could remain imperturbable and reflective when his squadron was thundering and swarming behind him like the rushing of a flood.

The column swung in a saber-curve toward a break in a fence, and dashed into a roadway. Once a little plank bridge was encountered, and the sound of the hoofs upon it was like the long roll of many drums. An old captain in the infantry turned to his first lieutenant and made a remark which was a compound of bitter disparagement of cavalry in general and soldierly admiration of this particular troop.

Suddenly the bugle sounded, and the column halted with a jolting upheaval amid sharp, brief cries. A moment later the men had tumbled from their horses and, carbines in hand, were running in a swarm toward the

grove of maples. In the road one of every four of the troopers was standing
with braced legs, and pulling and hauling at the bridles of four frenzied
horses.

The captain was running awkwardly in his boots. He held his saber
low, so that the point often threatened to catch in the turf. His yellow hair
ruffled out from under his faded cap. "Go in hard now!" he roared, in a
voice of hoarse fury. His face was violently red.

The troopers threw themselves upon the grove like wolves upon a great
animal. Along the whole front of woods there was the dry crackling of
musketry, with bitter, swift flashes and smoke that writhed like stung phantoms. The troopers yelled shrilly and spanged bullets low into the foliage.

For a moment, when near the woods, the line almost halted. The men
struggled and fought for a time like swimmers encountering a powerful
current. Then with a supreme effort they went on again. They dashed
madly at the grove, whose foliage, from the high light of the field, was as
inscrutable as a wall.

Then suddenly each detail of the calm trees became apparent, and with
a few more frantic leaps the men were in the cool gloom of the woods.
There was a heavy odor as from burned paper. Wisps of gray smoke
wound upward. The men halted; and, grimy, perspiring, and puffing, they
searched the recesses of the woods with eager, fierce glances. Figures could
be seen flitting afar off. A dozen carbines rattled at them in an angry volley.

During this pause the captain strode along the line, his face lit with a
broad smile of contentment. "When he sends this crowd to do anything, I
guess he'll find we do it pretty sharp," he said to the grinning lieutenant.

"Say, they didn't stand that rush a minute, did they?" said the subaltern.
Both officers were profoundly dusty in their uniforms, and their faces were
soiled like those of two urchins.

Out in the grass behind them were three tumbled and silent forms.

Presently the line moved forward again. The men went from tree to
tree like hunters stalking game. Some at the left of the line fired occasionally, and those at the right gazed curiously in that direction. The men still
breathed heavily from their scramble across the field.

Of a sudden a trooper halted and said: "Hello! there's a house!" Every
one paused. The men turned to look at their leader.

The captain stretched his neck and swung his head from side to side.
"By George, it is a house!" he said.

Through the wealth of leaves there vaguely loomed the form of a large
white house. These troopers, brown-faced from many days of campaign-
ing, each feature of them telling of their placid confidence and courage,
were stopped abruptly by the appearance of this house. There was some

subtle suggestion—some tale of an unknown thing—which watched them from they knew not what part of it.

A rail fence girded a wide lawn of tangled grass. Seven pines stood along a driveway which led from two distant posts of a vanished gate. The blue-clothed troopers moved forward until they stood at the fence, peering over it.

The captain put one hand on the top rail and seemed to be about to climb the fence, when suddenly he hesitated and said in a low voice: "Watson, what do you think of it?"

The lieutenant stared at the house. "Derned if I know!" he replied.

The captain pondered. It happened that the whole company had turned a gaze of profound awe and doubt upon this edifice which confronted them. The men were very silent.

At last the captain swore and said: "We are certainly a pack of fools. Derned old deserted house halting a company of Union cavalry, and making us gape like babies!"

"Yes, but there's something—something—" insisted the subaltern in a half stammer.

"Well, if there's 'something—something' in there, I'll get it out," said the captain. "Send Sharpe clean around to the other side with about twelve men, so we will sure bag your 'something—something,' and I'll take a few of the boys and find out what's in the damned old thing!"

He chose the nearest eight men for his "storming party," as the lieutenant called it. After he had waited some minutes for the others to get into position, he said "Come ahead" to his eight men, and climbed the fence.

The brighter light of the tangled lawn made him suddenly feel tremendously apparent, and he wondered if there could be some mystic thing in the house which was regarding this approach. His men trudged silently at his back. They stared at the windows and lost themselves in deep speculations as to the probability of there being, perhaps, eyes behind the blinds—malignant eyes, piercing eyes.

Suddenly a corporal in the party gave vent to a startled exclamation and half threw his carbine into position. The captain turned quickly, and the corporal said: "I saw an arm move the blinds. An arm with a gray sleeve!"

"Don't be a fool, Jones, now!" said the captain sharply.

"I swear t'—" began the corporal, but the captain silenced him.

When they arrived at the front of the house, the troopers paused, while the captain went softly up the front steps. He stood before the large front door and studied it. Some crickets chirped in the long grass, and the nearest pine could be heard in its endless sighs. One of the privates moved uneasily, and his foot crunched the gravel. Suddenly the captain swore angrily and kicked the door with a loud crash. It flew open.

II

The bright lights of the day flashed into the old house when the captain angrily kicked open the door. He was aware of a wide hallway carpeted with matting and extending deep into the dwelling. There was also an old walnut hat rack and a little marble-topped table with a vase and two books upon it. Farther back was a great venerable fireplace containing dreary ashes.

But directly in front of the captain was a young girl. The flying open of the door had obviously been an utter astonishment to her, and she remained transfixed there in the middle of the floor, staring at the captain with wide eyes.

She was like a child caught at the time of a raid upon the cake. She wavered to and fro upon her feet, and held her hands behind her. There were two little points of terror in her eyes, as she gazed up at the young captain in dusty blue, with his reddish, bronze complexion, his yellow hair, his bright saber held threateningly.

These two remained motionless and silent, simply staring at each other for some moments.

The captain felt his rage fade out of him and leave his mind limp. He had been violently angry, because this house had made him feel hesitant, wary. He did not like to be wary. He liked to feel confident, sure. So he had kicked the door open, and had been prepared to march in like a soldier of wrath.

But now he began, for one thing, to wonder if his uniform was so dusty and old in appearance. Moreover, he had a feeling that his face was covered with a compound of dust, grime, and perspiration. He took a step forward and said, "I didn't mean to frighten you." But his voice was coarse from his battle-howling. It seemed to him to have hempen fibers in it.

The girl's breath came in little, quick gasps, and she looked at him as she would have looked at a serpent.

"I didn't mean to frighten you," he said again.

The girl, still with her hands behind her, began to back away.

"Is there any one else in the house?" he went on, while slowly following her. "I don't wish to disturb you, but we had a fight with some rebel skirmishers in the woods, and I thought maybe some of them might have come in here. In fact, I was pretty sure of it. Are there any of them here?"

The girl looked at him and said, "No!" He wondered why extreme agitation made the eyes of some women so limpid and bright.

"Who is here besides yourself?"

By this time his pursuit had driven her to the end of the hall, and she remained there with her back to the wall and her hands still behind her.

When she answered this question, she did not look at him, but down at the floor. She cleared her voice and then said, "There is no one here."

"No one?"

She lifted her eyes to him in that appeal that the human being must make even to falling trees, crashing boulders, the sea in a storm, and said, "No, no, there is no one here." He could plainly see her tremble.

Of a sudden he bethought him that she continually kept her hands behind her. As he recalled her air when first discovered, he remembered she appeared precisely as a child detected at one of the crimes of childhood. Moreover, she had always backed away from him. He thought now that she was concealing something which was an evidence of the presence of the enemy in the house.

"What are you holding behind you?" he said suddenly.

She gave a little quick moan, as if some grim hand had throttled her.

"What are you holding behind you?"

"Oh, nothing—please. I am not holding anything behind me; indeed I'm not."

"Very well. Hold your hands out in front of you, then."

"Oh, indeed, I'm not holding anything behind me. Indeed I'm not."

"Well," he began. Then he paused, and remained for a moment dubious. Finally, he laughed. "Well, I shall have my men search the house, anyhow. I'm sorry to trouble you, but I feel sure that there is some one here whom we want." He turned to the corporal, who, with the other men, was gaping quietly in at the door, and said: "Jones, go through the house."

As for himself, he remained planted in front of the girl, for she evidently did not dare to move and allow him to see what she held so carefully behind her back. So she was his prisoner.

The men rummaged around on the ground floor of the house. Sometimes the captain called to them. "Try that closet," "Is there any cellar?" But they found no one, and at last they went trooping toward the stairs which led to the second floor.

But at this movement on the part of the men the girl uttered a cry—a cry of such fright and appeal that the men paused. "Oh, don't go up there! Please don't go up there! —ple—ease! There is no one there! Indeed—indeed there is not! Oh, ple—ease!"

"Go on, Jones," said the captain calmly.

The obedient corporal made a preliminary step, and the girl bounded toward the stairs with another cry.

As she passed him, the captain caught sight of that which she had concealed behind her back, and which she had forgotten in this supreme moment. It was a pistol.

She ran to the first step and, standing there, faced the men, one hand extended with perpendicular palm, and the other holding the pistol at her side. "Oh, please, don't go up there! Nobody is there—indeed, there is not! P-l-e-a-s-e!" Then suddenly she sank swiftly down upon the step and, huddling forlornly, began to weep in the agony and with the convulsive tremors of an infant. The pistol fell from her fingers and rattled down to the floor.

The astonished troopers looked at their astonished captain. There was a short silence.

Finally, the captain stooped and picked up the pistol. It was a heavy weapon of the army pattern. He ascertained that it was empty.

He leaned toward the shaking girl and said gently, "Will you tell me what you were going to do with this pistol?"

He had to repeat the question a number of times, but at last a muffled voice said, "Nothing."

"Nothing!" He insisted quietly upon a further answer. At the tender tones of the captain's voice, the phlegmatic corporal turned and winked gravely at the man next to him.

"Won't you tell me?"

The girl shook her head.

"Please tell me!"

The silent privates were moving their feet uneasily and wondering how long they were to wait.

The captain said: "Please, won't you tell me?"

Then this girl's voice began in stricken tones, half coherent, and amid violent sobbing: "It was grandpa's. He—he—he said he was going to shoot anybody who came in here—he didn't care if there were thousands of 'em. And—and I know he would, and I was afraid they'd kill him. And so—and—so I stole away his pistol—and I was going to hide it when you—you—you kicked open the door."

The men straightened up and looked at each other. The girl began to weep again.

The captain mopped his brow. He peered down at the girl. He mopped his brow again. Suddenly he said: "Ah, don't cry like that."

He moved restlessly and looked down at his boots. He mopped his brow again.

Then he gripped the corporal by the arm and dragged him some yards back from the others. "Jones," he said, in an intensely earnest voice, "will you tell me what in the devil I am going to do?"

The corporal's countenance became illuminated with satisfaction at being thus requested to advise his superior officer. He adopted an air of great thought, and finally said: "Well, of course, the feller with the gray sleeve must be upstairs, and we must get past the girl and up there somehow. Suppose I take her by the arm and lead her—"

"What!" interrupted the captain from between his clenched teeth. As he turned away from the corporal, he said fiercely over his shoulder: "You touch that girl and I'll split your skull!"

III

The corporal looked after his captain with an expression of mingled amazement, grief, and philosophy. He seemed to be saying to himself that there unfortunately were times, after all, when one could not rely upon the most reliable of men. When he returned to the group he found the captain bending over the girl and saying: "Why is it that you don't want us to search upstairs?"

The girl's head was buried in her crossed arms. Locks of her hair had escaped from their fastenings, and these fell upon her shoulder.

"Won't you tell me?"

The corporal here winked again at the man next to him.

"Because," the girl moaned—"because—there isn't anybody up there."

The captain at last said timidly: "Well, I'm afraid—I'm afraid we'll have to—"

The girl sprang to her feet again, and implored him with her hands. She looked deep into his eyes with her glance, which was at this time like that of the fawn when it says to the hunter, "Have mercy upon me!"

These two stood regarding each other. The captain's foot was on the bottom step, but he seemed to be shrinking. He wore an air of being deeply wretched and ashamed. There was a silence.

Suddenly the corporal said in a quick, low tone: "Look out, captain!"

All turned their eyes swiftly toward the head of the stairs. There had appeared there a youth in a gray uniform. He stood looking coolly down at them. No word was said by the troopers. The girl gave vent to a little wail of desolation, "Oh, Harry!"

He began slowly to descend the stairs. His right arm was in a white sling, and there were some fresh bloodstains upon the cloth. His face was rigid and deathly pale, but his eyes flashed like lights. The girl was again moaning in an utterly dreary fashion, as the youth came slowly down toward the silent men in blue.

Six steps from the bottom of the flight he halted and said, "I reckon it's me you're looking for."

The troopers had crowded forward a trifle and, posed in lithe, nervous attitudes, were watching him like cats. The captain remained unmoved. At the youth's question he merely nodded his head and said, "Yes."

The young man in gray looked down at the girl, and then, in the same even tone, which now, however, seemed to vibrate with suppressed fury, he said: "And is that any reason why you should insult my sister?"

At this sentence, the girl intervened, desperately, between the young man in gray and the officer in blue. "Oh, don't, Harry, don't! He was good to me! He was good to me, Harry—indeed he was!"

The youth came on in his quiet, erect fashion until the girl could have touched either of the men with her hand, for the captain still remained with his foot upon the first step. She continually repeated: "Oh, Harry! Oh, Harry!"

The youth in gray maneuvered to glare into the captain's face, first over one shoulder of the girl and then over the other. In a voice that rang like metal, he said: "You are armed and unwounded, while I have no weapons and am wounded; but—"

The captain had stepped back and sheathed his saber. The eyes of these two men were gleaming fire, but otherwise the captain's countenance was imperturbable. He said: "You are mistaken. You have no reason to—"

"You lie!"

All save the captain and the youth in gray started in an electric movement. These two words crackled in the air like shattered glass. There was a breathless silence.

The captain cleared his throat. His look at the youth contained a quality of singular and terrible ferocity, but he said in his stolid tone: "I don't suppose you mean what you say now."

Upon his arm he had felt the pressure of some unconscious little fingers. The girl was leaning against the wall as if she no longer knew how to keep her balance, but those fingers—he held his arm very still. She murmured: "Oh, Harry, don't! He was good to me—indeed he was!"

The corporal had come forward until he in a measure confronted the youth in gray, for he saw those fingers upon the captain's arm, and he knew that sometimes very strong men were not able to move hand nor foot under such conditions.

The youth had suddenly seemed to become weak. He breathed heavily and clung to the rail. He was glaring at the captain, and apparently summoning all his will power to combat his weakness. The corporal addressed him with profound straightforwardness: "Don't you be a derned fool!" The youth turned toward him so fiercely that the corporal threw up a knee and an elbow like a boy who expects to be cuffed.

The girl pleaded with the captain. "You won't hurt him, will you? He don't know what he's saying. He's wounded, you know. Please don't mind him!"

"I won't touch him," said the captain, with rather extraordinary earnestness; "don't you worry about him at all. I won't touch him!"

Then he looked at her, and the girl suddenly withdrew her fingers from his arm.

The corporal contemplated the top of the stairs, and remarked without surprise: "There's another of 'em coming!"

An old man was clambering down the stairs with much speed. He waved a cane wildly. "Get out of my house, you thieves! Get out! I won't have you cross my threshold! Get out!" He mumbled and wagged his head in an old man's fury. It was plainly his intention to assault them.

And so it occurred that a young girl became engaged in protecting a stalwart captain, fully armed, and with eight grim troopers at his back, from the attack of an old man with a walking stick!

A blush passed over the temples and brow of the captain, and he looked particularly savage and weary. Despite the girl's efforts, he suddenly faced the old man.

"Look here," he said distinctly, "we came in because we had been fighting in the woods yonder, and we concluded that some of the enemy were in this house, especially when we saw a gray sleeve at the window. But this young man is wounded, and I have nothing to say to him. I will even take it for granted that there are no others like him upstairs. We will go away, leaving your damned old house just as we found it! And we are no more thieves and rascals than you are!"

The old man simply roared: "I haven't got a cow nor a pig nor a chicken on the place! Your soldiers have stolen everything they could carry away. They have torn down half my fences for firewood. This afternoon some of your accursed bullets even broke my windowpanes!"

The girl had been faltering: "Grandpa! Oh, grandpa!"

The captain looked at the girl. She returned his glance from the shadow of the old man's shoulder. After studying her face a moment, he said: "Well, we will go now." He strode toward the door, and his men clanked docilely after him.

At this time there was the sound of harsh cries and rushing footsteps from without. The door flew open, and a whirlwind composed of blue-coated troopers came in with a swoop. It was headed by the lieutenant. "Oh, here you are!" he cried, catching his breath. "We thought—Oh, look at the girl!"

The captain said intensely: "Shut up, you fool!"

The men settled to a halt with a clash and a bang. There could be heard the dulled sound of many hoofs outside the house.

"Did you order up the horses?" inquired the captain.

"Yes. We thought—"

"Well, then, let's get out of here," interrupted the captain morosely.

The men began to filter out into the open air. The youth in gray had been hanging dismally to the railing of the stairway. He now was climbing slowly up to the second floor. The old man was addressing himself directly to the serene corporal.

"Not a chicken on the place!" he cried.

"Well, I didn't take your chickens, did I?"

"No, maybe you didn't but—"

The captain crossed the hall and stood before the girl in rather a culprit's fashion. "You are not angry at me, are you?" he asked timidly.

"No," she said. She hesitated a moment, and then suddenly held out her hand. "You were good to me—and I'm—much obliged."

The captain took her hand, and then he blushed, for he found himself unable to formulate a sentence that applied in any way to the situation.

She did not seem to heed that hand for a time.

He loosened his grasp presently, for he was ashamed to hold it so long without saying anything clever. At last, with an air of charging an entrenched brigade, he contrived to say: "I would rather do anything than frighten or trouble you."

His brow was warmly perspiring. He had a sense of being hideous in his dusty uniform and with his grimy face.

She said, "Oh, I'm so glad it was you instead of somebody who might have—might have hurt brother Harry and grandpa!"

He told her, "I wouldn't have hurt 'em for anything!"

There was a little silence.

"Well, good-bye!" he said at last.

"Good-bye!"

He walked toward the door past the old man, who was scolding at the vanishing figure of the corporal. The captain looked back. She had remained there watching him.

At the bugle's order, the troopers standing beside their horses swung briskly into the saddle. The lieutenant said to the first sergeant: "Williams, did they ever meet before?"

"Hanged if I know!"

"Well, say—"

The captain saw a curtain move at one of the windows. He cantered from his position at the head of the column and steered his horse between two flower beds.

"Well, good-bye!"

The squadron trampled slowly past.

"Good-bye!"

They shook hands.

He evidently had something enormously important to say to her, but it seemed that he could not manage it. He struggled heroically. The bay charger, with his great mystically solemn eyes, looked around the corner of his shoulder at the girl.

The captain studied a pine tree. The girl inspected the grass beneath the window. The captain said hoarsely: "I don't suppose—I don't suppose—I'll ever see you again!"

She looked at him affrightedly and shrank back from the window. He seemed to have woefully expected a reception of this kind for his question. He gave her instantly a glance of appeal.

She said: "Why, no, I don't suppose we will."

"Never?"

"Why, no, 'tain't possible. You—you are a—Yankee!"

"Oh, I know it, but—" Eventually he continued: "Well, some day, you know, when there's no more fighting, we might—" He observed that she had again withdrawn suddenly into the shadow, so he said: "Well, goodbye!"

When he held her fingers she bowed her head, and he saw a pink blush steal over the curves of her cheek and neck.

"Am I never going to see you again?"

She made no reply.

"Never?" he repeated.

After a long time, he bent over to hear a faint reply: "Sometimes—when there are no troops in the neighborhood—grandpa don't mind if I —walk over as far as that old oak tree yonder—in the afternoons."

It appeared that the captain's grip was very strong, for she uttered an exclamation and looked at her fingers as if she expected to find them mere fragments. He rode away.

The bay horse leaped a flower bed. They were almost to the drive, when the girl uttered a panic-stricken cry.

The captain wheeled his horse violently, and upon his return journey went straight through a flower bed.

The girl had clasped her hands. She beseeched him wildly with her eyes. "Oh, please, don't believe it! I never walk to the old oak tree. Indeed I don't! I never—never—never walk there."

The bridle drooped on the bay charger's neck. The captain's figure seemed limp. With an expression of profound dejection and gloom he stared off at where the leaden sky met the dark green line of the woods. The long-impending rain began to fall with a mournful patter, drop and drop. There was a silence.

At last a low voice said, "Well—I might—sometimes I might—perhaps—

but only once in a great while—I might walk to the old tree—in the afternoons."

October 12, 14, and 15, 1895
[Philadelphia *Press*, p. 11, each issue.]

THE JUDGMENT OF THE SAGE

A beggar crept wailing through the streets of a city. A certain man came to him there and gave him bread, saying: "I give you this loaf, because of God's word." Another came to the beggar and gave him bread, saying: "Take this loaf; I give it because you are hungry."

Now there was a continual rivalry among the citizens of this town as to who should appear to be the most pious man, and the event of the gifts to the beggar made discussion. People gathered in knots and argued furiously to no particular purpose. They appealed to the beggar, but he bowed humbly to the ground, as befitted one of his condition, and answered: "It is a singular circumstance that the loaves were of one size and of the same quality. How, then, can I decide which of these men gave bread more piously?"

The people heard of a philosopher who traveled through their country, and one said: "Behold, we who give not bread to beggars are not capable of judging those who have given bread to beggars. Let us, then, consult this wise man."

"But," said some, "mayhap this philosopher, according to your rule that one must have given bread before judging they who give bread, will not be capable."

"That is an indifferent matter to all truly great philosophers." So they made search for the wise man, and in time they came upon him, strolling along at his ease in the manner of philosophers.

"Oh, most illustrious sage," they cried.

"Yes," said the philosopher promptly.

"Oh, most illustrious sage, there are two men in our city, and one gave bread to a beggar, saying: 'Because of God's word.' And the other gave bread to the beggar, saying: 'Because you are hungry.' Now, which of these, oh, most illustrious sage, is the more pious man?"

"Eh?" said the philosopher.

"Which of these, oh, most illustrious sage, is the more pious man?"

"My friends," said the philosopher suavely addressing the concourse, "I see that you mistake me for an illustrious sage. I am not he whom you seek.

However, I saw a man answering my description pass here some time ago. With speed you may overtake him. Adieu."

January, 1896
[*The Bookman*, Vol. 2, p. 412.]

ONE DASH—HORSES
[Horses—One Dash]

Richardson pulled up his horse and looked back over the trail, where the crimson serape of his servant flamed amid the dusk of the mesquite. The hills in the west were carved into peaks, and were painted the most profound blue. Above them, the sky was of that marvelous tone of green—like still, sun-shot water—which people denounce in pictures.

José was muffled deep in his blanket, and his great toppling sombrero was drawn low over his brow. He shadowed his master along the dimming trail in the fashion of an assassin. A cold wind of the impending night swept over the wilderness of mesquite.

"Man," said Richardson, in lame Mexican, as the servant drew near, "I want eat! I want sleep! Understand—no? Quickly! Understand?"

"Si, señor," said José, nodding. He stretched one arm out of his blanket, and pointed a yellow finger into the gloom. "Over there, small village! Si, señor."

They rode forward again. Once the American's horse shied and breathed quiveringly at something which he saw or imagined in the darkness, and the rider drew a steady, patient rein and leaned over to speak tenderly, as if he were addressing a frightened woman. The sky had faded to white over the mountains, and the plain was a vast, pointless ocean of black.

Suddenly some low houses appeared squatting amid the bushes. The horsemen rode into a hollow until the houses rose against the somber sundown sky, and then up a small hillock, causing these habitations to sink like boats in the sea of shadow.

A beam of red firelight fell across the trail. Richardson sat sleepily on his horse while the servant quarreled with somebody—a mere voice in the gloom—over the price of bed and board. The houses about him were for the most part like tombs in their whiteness and silence, but there were scudding black figures that seemed interested in his arrival.

José came at last to the horses' heads, and the American slid stiffly from his seat. He muttered a greeting, as with his spurred feet he clicked into the adobe house that confronted him. The brown, stolid face of a woman shone in the light of the fire. He seated himself on the earthen floor, and blinked drowsily at the blaze. He was aware that the woman was clinking earthenware, and hieing here and everywhere in the maneuvers of the housewife. From a dark corner of the room there came the sound of two or three snores twining together.

The woman handed him a bowl of tortillas. She was a submissive creature, timid and large-eyed. She gazed at his enormous silver spurs, his large and impressive revolver, with the interest and admiration of the highly privileged cat of the adage. When he ate, she seemed transfixed off there in the gloom, her white teeth shining.

José entered, staggering under two Mexican saddles large enough for building sites. Richardson decided to smoke a cigarette, and then changed his mind. It would be much finer to go to sleep. His blanket hung over his left shoulder, furled into a long pipe of cloth, according to a Mexican fashion. By doffing his sombrero, unfastening his spurs and his revolver belt, he made himself ready for the slow, blissful twist into the blanket. Like a cautious man, he lay close to the wall, and all his property was very near his hand.

The mesquite brush burned long. José threw two gigantic wings of shadow as he flapped his blanket about him—first across his chest under his arms, and then around his neck and across his chest again, this time over his arms, with the end tossed on his right shoulder. A Mexican thus snugly enveloped can nevertheless free his fighting arm in a beautifully brisk way, merely shrugging his shoulder as he grabs for the weapon at his belt. They always wear their serapes in this manner.

The firelight smothered the rays which, streaming from a moon as large as a drumhead, were struggling at the open door. Richardson heard from the plain the fine, rhythmical trample of the hoofs of hurried horses. He went to sleep wondering who rode so fast and so late. And in the deep silence the pale rays of the moon must have prevailed against the red spears of the fire until the room was slowly flooded to its middle with a rectangle of silver light.

Richardson was awakened by the sound of a guitar. It was badly played —in this land of Mexico, from which the romance of the instrument ascends to us like a perfume. The guitar was groaning and whining like a badgered soul. A noise of scuffling feet accompanied the music. Sometimes laughter arose, and often the voices of men saying bitter things to each other; but always the guitar cried on, the treble sounding as if some one were beating iron, and the bass humming like bees.

"Damn it! they're having a dance," muttered Richardson, fretfully. He heard two men quarreling in short, sharp words like pistol shots; they were calling each other worse names than common people know in other countries.

He wondered why the noise was so loud. Raising his head from his saddle pillow, he saw, with the help of the valiant moonbeams, a blanket hanging flat against the wall at the farther end of the room. Being of the opinion that it concealed a door, and remembering that Mexican drink made men very drunk, he pulled his revolver closer to him and prepared for sudden disaster.

Richardson was dreaming of his far and beloved North.

"Well, I would kill him, then!"

"No, you must not!"

"Yes, I will kill him! Listen! I will ask this American beast for his beautiful pistol and spurs and money and saddle, and if he will not give them—you will see!"

"But these Americans—they are a strange people. Look out, señor."

Then twenty voices took part in the discussion. They rose in quivering shrillness, as from men badly drunk.

Richardson felt the skin draw tight around his mouth, and his knee joints turned to bread. He slowly came to a sitting posture, glaring at the motionless blanket at the far end of the room. This stiff and mechanical movement, accomplished entirely by the muscles of the wrist, must have looked like the rising of a corpse in the wan moonlight, which gave everything a hue of the grave.

My friend, take my advice, and never be executed by a hangman who doesn't talk the English language. It, or anything that resembles it, is the most difficult of deaths. The tumultuous emotions of Richardson's terror destroyed that slow and careful process of thought by means of which he understood Mexican. Then he used his instinctive comprehension of the first and universal language, which is tone. Still, it is disheartening not to be able to understand the detail of threats against the blood of your body.

Suddenly the clamor of voices ceased. There was a silence—a silence of decision. The blanket was flung aside, and the red light of a torch flared into the room. It was held high by a fat, round-faced Mexican, whose little snake-like mustache was as black as his eyes, and whose eyes were black as jet. He was insane with the wild rage of a man whose liquor is dully burning at his brain. Five or six of his fellows crowded after him. The guitar, which had been thrummed doggedly during the time of the high words, now suddenly stopped.

They contemplated each other. Richardson sat very straight and still, his right hand lost in the folds of his blanket. The Mexicans jostled in the light of the torch, their eyes blinking and glittering.

The fat one posed in the manner of a grandee. Presently his hand dropped to his belt, and from his lips there spun an epithet—a hideous word which often foreshadows knife-blows, a word peculiarly of Mexico, where people have to dig deep to find an insult that has not lost its savor.

The American did not move. He was staring at the fat Mexican with a strange fixedness of gaze, not fearful, not dauntless, not anything that could be interpreted; he simply stared.

The fat Mexican must have been disconcerted, for he continued to pose as a grandee with more and more sublimity, until it would have been easy for him to fall over backward. His companions were swaying in a very drunken manner. They still blinked their beady eyes at Richardson. Ah, well, sirs, here was a mystery. At the approach of their menacing company, why did not this American cry out and turn pale, or run, or pray them mercy? The animal merely sat still, and stared, and waited for them to begin. Well, evidently he was a great fighter; or perhaps he was an idiot. Indeed, this was an embarrassing situation, for who was going forward to discover whether he was a great fighter or an idiot?

To Richardson, whose nerves were tingling and twitching like live wires, and whose heart jolted inside him, this pause was a long horror; and for these men who could so frighten him there began to swell in him a fierce hatred—a hatred that made him long to be capable of fighting all of them, a hatred that made him capable of fighting all of them. A 44-caliber revolver can make a hole large enough for little boys to shoot marbles through, and there was a certain fat Mexican, with a mustache like a snake, who came extremely near to have eaten his last tamale merely because he frightened a man too much.

José had slept the first part of the night in his fashion, his body hunched into a heap, his legs crooked, his head touching his knees. Shadows had obscured him from the sight of the invaders. At this point he arose, and began to prowl quakingly over toward Richardson, as if he meant to hide behind him.

Of a sudden the fat Mexican gave a howl of glee. José had come within the torch's circle of light. With roars of singular ferocity the whole group of Mexicans pounced on the American's servant.

He shrank shuddering away from them, beseeching by every device of word and gesture. They pushed him this way and that. They beat him with their fists. They stung him with their curses. As he groveled on his knees, the fat Mexican took him by the throat and said: "I'm going to kill you!" And continually they turned their eyes to see if they were to succeed in causing the initial demonstration by the American.

Richardson looked on impassively. Under the blanket, however, his fingers were clenched as rigidly as iron upon the handle of his revolver.

Here suddenly two brilliant clashing chords from the guitar were heard, and a woman's voice, full of laughter and confidence, cried from without: "Hello! hello! Where are you?"

The lurching company of Mexicans instantly paused and looked at the ground. One said, as he stood with his legs wide apart in order to balance himself: "It is the girls! They have come!" He screamed in answer to the question of the woman: "Here!" And without waiting he started on a pilgrimage toward the blanket-covered door. One could now hear a number of female voices giggling and chattering.

Two other Mexicans said: "Yes; it is the girls! Yes!" They also started quietly away. Even the fat Mexican's ferocity seemed to be affected. He looked uncertainly at the still immovable American. Two of his friends grasped him gaily. "Come, the girls are here! Come!" He cast another glower at Richardson. "But this——" he began. Laughing, his comrades hustled him toward the door. On its threshold, and holding back the blanket with one hand, he turned his yellow face with a last challenging glare toward the American. José, bewailing his state in little sobs of utter despair and woe, crept to Richardson and huddled near his knee. Then the cries of the Mexicans meeting the girls were heard, and the guitar burst out in joyous humming.

The moon clouded, and but a faint square of light fell through the open main door of the house. The coals of the fire were silent save for occasional sputters. Richardson did not change his position. He remained staring at the blanket which hid the strategic door in the far end. At his knees José was arguing, in a low, aggrieved tone, with the saints. Without, the Mexicans laughed and danced, and—it would appear from the sound—drank more.

In the stillness and night Richardson sat wondering if some serpent-like Mexican was sliding toward him in the darkness, and if the first thing he knew of it would be the deadly sting of the knife. "Sssh," he whispered to José. He drew his revolver from under the blanket and held it on his leg.

The blanket over the door fascinated him. It was a vague form, black and unmoving. Through the opening it shielded was to come, probably, menace, death. Sometimes he thought he saw it move.

As grim white sheets, the black and silver of coffins, all the panoply of death, affect us because of that which they hide, so this blanket, dangling before a hole in an adobe wall, was to Richardson a horrible emblem, and a horrible thing in itself. In his present mood Richardson could not have been brought to touch it with his finger.

The celebrating Mexicans occasionally howled in song. The guitarist played with speed and enthusiasm.

Richardson longed to run. But in this threatening gloom, his terror convinced him that a move on his part would be a signal for the pounce of death. José, crouching abjectly, occasionally mumbled. Slowly and ponderous as stars the minutes went.

Suddenly Richardson thrilled and started. His breath, for a moment, left him. In sleep his nerveless fingers had allowed his revolver to fall and clang upon the hard floor. He grabbed it up hastily, and his glance swept apprehensively over the room.

A chill blue light of dawn was in the place. Every outline was slowly growing; detail was following detail. The dread blanket did not move. The riotous company had gone or become silent.

Richardson felt in his blood the effect of this cold dawn. The candor of breaking day brought his nerve. He touched José. "Come," he said. His servant lifted his lined, yellow face and comprehended. Richardson buckled on his spurs and strode up; José obediently lifted the two great saddles. Richardson held two bridles and a blanket on his left arm; in his right hand he held his revolver. They sneaked toward the door.

The man who said that spurs jingled was insane. Spurs have a mellow clash—clash—clash. Walking in spurs—notably Mexican spurs—you remind yourself vaguely of a telegraphic lineman. Richardson was inexpressibly shocked when he came to walk. He sounded to himself like a pair of cymbals. He would have known of this if he had reflected; but then he was escaping, not reflecting. He made a gesture of despair, and from under the two saddles José tried to make one of hopeless horror. Richardson stooped, and with shaking fingers unfastened the spurs. Taking them in his left hand, he picked up his revolver, and they slunk on toward the door.

On the threshold Richardson looked back. In a corner he saw, watching him with large eyes, the Indian man and woman who had been his hosts. Throughout the night they had made no sign, and now they neither spoke nor moved. Yet Richardson thought he detected meek satisfaction at his departure.

The street was still and deserted. In the eastern sky there was a lemon-colored patch.

José had picketed the horses at the side of the house. As the two men came around the corner, Richardson's animal set up a whinny of welcome. The little horse had evidently heard them coming. He stood facing them, his ears cocked forward, his eyes bright with welcome.

Richardson made a frantic gesture, but the horse, in his happiness at the appearance of his friends, whinnied with enthusiasm.

The American felt at this time that he could have strangled his well-beloved steed. Upon the threshold of safety he was being betrayed by his horse, his friend. He felt the same hate for the horse that he would have felt for a dragon. And yet, as he glanced wildly about him, he could see nothing stirring in the street, nor at the doors of the tomb-like houses.

José had his own saddle girth and both bridles buckled in a moment. He curled the picket ropes with a few sweeps of his arm. The fingers of Richardson, however, were shaking so that he could hardly buckle the girth. His hands were in invisible mittens. He was wondering, calculating, hoping about his horse. He knew the little animal's willingness and courage under all circumstances up to this time, but then—here it was different. Who could tell if some wretched instance of equine perversity was not about to develop? Maybe the little fellow would not feel like smoking over the plain at express speed this morning, and so he would rebel and kick and be wicked. Maybe he would be without feeling of interest, and run listlessly. All men who have had to hurry in the saddle know what it is to be on a horse who does not understand the dramatic situation. Riding a lame sheep is bliss to it. Richardson, fumbling furiously at the girth, thought of these things.

Presently he had it fastened. He swung into the saddle, and as he did so his horse made a mad jump forward. The spurs of José scratched and tore the flanks of his great black animal, and side by side the two horses raced down the village street. The American heard his horse breathe a quivering sigh of excitement.

Those four feet skimmed. They were as light as fairy puffballs. The houses of the village glided past in a moment, and the great, clear, silent plain appeared like a pale blue sea of mist and wet bushes. Above the mountains the colors of the sunlight were like the first tones, the opening chords, of the mighty hymn of the morning.

The American looked down at his horse. He felt in his heart the first thrill of confidence. The little animal, unurged and quite tranquil, moving his ears this way and that way with an air of interest in the scenery, was nevertheless bounding into the eye of the breaking day with the speed of a frightened antelope. Richardson, looking down, saw the long, fine reach of forelimb as steady as steel machinery. As the ground reeled past, the long dried grasses hissed, and cactus plants were dull blurs. A wind whirled the horse's mane over his rider's bridle hand.

José's profile was lined against the pale sky. It was as that of a man who swims alone in an ocean. His eyes glinted like metal fastened on some unknown point ahead of him, some mystic place of safety. Occasionally his mouth puckered in a little unheard cry; and his legs, bent back, worked spasmodically as his spurred heels sliced the flanks of his charger.

Richardson consulted the gloom in the west for signs of a hard-riding, yelling cavalcade. He knew that, whereas his friends the enemy had not attacked him when he had sat still and with apparent calmness confronted them, they would certainly take furiously after him now that he had run from them—now that he had confessed to them that he was the weaker. Their valor would grow like weeds in the spring, and upon discovering his escape they would ride forth dauntless warriors.

Sometimes he was sure he saw them. Sometimes he was sure he heard them. Continually looking backward over his shoulder, he studied the purple expanses where the night was marching away. José rolled and shuddered in his saddle, persistently disturbing the stride of the black horse, fretting and worrying him until the white foam flew and the great shoulders shone like satin from the sweat.

At last Richardson drew his horse carefully down to a walk. José wished to rush insanely on, but the American spoke to him sternly. As the two paced forward side by side, Richardson's little horse thrust over his soft nose and inquired into the black's condition.

Riding with José was like riding with a corpse. His face resembled a cast in lead. Sometimes he swung forward and almost pitched from his seat. Richardson was too frightened himself to do anything but hate this man for his fear. Finally he issued a mandate which nearly caused José's eyes to slide out of his head and fall to the ground like two silver coins.

"Ride behind me—about fifty paces."

"Señor——" stuttered the servant.

"Go!" cried the American, furiously. He glared at the other and laid his hand on his revolver. José looked at his master wildly. He made a piteous gesture. Then slowly he fell back, watching the hard face of the American for a sign of mercy.

Richardson had resolved in his rage that at any rate he was going to use the eyes and ears of extreme fear to detect the approach of danger; and so he established his servant as a sort of outpost.

As they proceeded he was obliged to watch sharply to see that the servant did not slink forward and join him. When José made beseeching circles in the air with his arm he replied by menacingly gripping his revolver.

José had a revolver, too; nevertheless it was very clear in his mind that the revolver was distinctly an American weapon. He had been educated in the Rio Grande country.

Richardson lost the trail once. He was recalled to it by the loud sobs of his servant.

Then at last José came clattering forward, gesticulating and wailing. The little horse sprang to the shoulder of the black. They were off.

Richardson, again looking backward, could see a slanting flare of dust on the whitening plain. He thought that he could detect small moving figures in it.

José's moans and cries amounted to a university course in theology. They broke continually from his quivering lips. His spurs were as motors. They forced the black horse over the plain in great headlong leaps.

But under Richardson there was a little insignificant rat-colored beast who was running apparently with almost as much effort as it requires for a bronze statue to stand still. As a matter of truth, the ground seemed merely something to be touched from time to time with hoofs that were as light as blown leaves. Occasionally Richardson lay back and pulled stoutly at his bridle to keep from abandoning his servant.

José harried at his horse's mouth, flopped around in the saddle, and made his two heels beat like flails. The black ran like a horse in despair.

Crimson serapes in the distance resemble drops of blood on the great cloth of plain.

Richardson began to dream of all possible chances. Although quite a humane man, he did not once think of his servant. José being a Mexican, it was natural that he should be killed in Mexico; but for himself, a New Yorker——

He remembered all the tales of such races for life, and he thought them badly written.

The great black horse was growing indifferent. The jabs of José's spurs no longer caused him to bound forward in wild leaps of pain. José had at last succeeded in teaching him that spurring was to be expected, speed or no speed, and now he took the pain of it dully and stolidly, as an animal who finds that doing his best gains him no respite.

José was turned into a raving maniac. He bellowed and screamed, working his arms and his heels like one in a fit. He resembled a man on a sinking ship, who appeals to the ship. Richardson, too, cried madly to the black horse.

The spirit of the horse responded to these calls, and, quivering and breathing heavily, he made a great effort, a sort of final rush, not for himself apparently, but because he understood that his life's sacrifice, perhaps, had been invoked by these two men who cried to him in the universal tongue. Richardson had no sense of appreciation at this time—he was too frightened—but often now he remembers a certain black horse.

From the rear could be heard a yelling, and once a shot was fired—in the air, evidently. Richardson moaned as he looked back. He kept his hand on his revolver. He tried to imagine the brief tumult of his capture —the flurry of dust from the hoofs of horses pulled suddenly to their haunches, the shrill, biting curses of the men, the ring of the shots, his own last contortion. He wondered, too, if he could not somehow manage to pelt that fat Mexican, just to cure his abominable egotism.

It was José, the terror-stricken, who at last discovered safety. Suddenly he gave a howl of delight, and astonished his horse into a new burst of speed. They were on a little ridge at the time, and the American at the top of it saw his servant gallop down the slope and into the arms, so to speak, of a small column of horsemen in gray and silver clothes. In the dim light of the early morning they were as vague as shadows, but Richardson knew them at once for a detachment of rurales, that crack cavalry corps of the Mexican army which polices the plain so zealously, being of themselves the law and the arm of it—a fierce and swift-moving body that knows little of prevention, but much of vengeance. They drew up suddenly, and the rows of great silver-trimmed sombreros bobbed in surprise.

Richardson saw José throw himself from his horse and begin to jabber at the leader of the party. When he arrived he found that his servant had already outlined the entire situation, and was then engaged in describing him, Richardson, as an American señor of vast wealth, who was the friend of almost every governmental potentate within two hundred miles. This seemed to profoundly impress the officer. He bowed gravely to Richardson and smiled significantly at his men, who unslung their carbines.

The little ridge hid the pursuers from view, but the rapid thud of their horses' feet could be heard. Occasionally they yelled and called to each other.

Then at last they swept over the brow of the hill, a wild mob of almost fifty drunken horsemen. When they discerned the pale-uniformed rurales, they were sailing down the slope at top speed.

If toboggans halfway down a hill should suddenly make up their minds to turn around and go back, there would be an effect somewhat like that now produced by the drunken horsemen. Richardson saw the rurales serenely swing their carbines forward, and, peculiar-minded person that he was, felt his heart leap into his throat at the prospective volley. But the officer rode forward alone.

It appeared that the man who owned the best horse in this astonished company was the fat Mexican with the snaky mustache, and, in consequence, this gentleman was quite a distance in the van. He tried to pull up, wheel his horse, and scuttle back over the hill as some of his companions had done, but the officer called to him in a voice harsh with rage.

"——!" howled the officer. "This señor is my friend, the friend of my friends. Do you dare pursue him,——?——!——!——!——!" These lines represent terrible names, all different, used by the officer.

The fat Mexican simply groveled on his horse's neck. His face was green; it could be seen that he expected death.

The officer stormed with magnificent intensity: "——!——!——!"

Finally he sprang from his saddle and, running to the fat Mexican's side, yelled: "Go!" and kicked the horse in the belly with all his might. The animal gave a mighty leap into the air, and the fat Mexican, with one wretched glance at the contemplative rurales, aimed his steed for the top of the ridge. Richardson again gulped in expectation of a volley, for, it is said, this is one of the favorite methods of the rurales for disposing of objectionable people. The fat, green Mexican also evidently thought that he was to be killed while on the run, from the miserable look he cast at the troops. Nevertheless, he was allowed to vanish in a cloud of yellow dust at the ridgetop.

José was exultant, defiant, and, oh! bristling with courage. The black horse was drooping sadly, his nose to the ground. Richardson's little animal, with his ears bent forward, was staring at the horses of the rurales as if in an intense study. Richardson longed for speech, but he could only bend forward and pat the shining, silken shoulders. The little horse turned his head and looked back gravely.

January 4 and 6, 1896
[Philadelphia *Press*, January 4, p. 11; January 6, p. 10.]

A TALE OF MERE CHANCE

BEING AN ACCOUNT OF THE PURSUIT OF THE TILES, THE STATEMENT OF THE CLOCK, AND THE GRIP OF A COAT OF ORANGE SPOTS, TOGETHER WITH SOME CRITICISM OF A DETECTIVE SAID TO BE CARVED FROM AN OLD TABLE LEG

[The White Tiles]

Yes, my friend, I killed the man, but I would not have been detected in it were it not for some very extraordinary circumstances. I had long considered this deed, but I am a delicate and sensitive person, you understand, and I hesitated over it as the diver hesitates on the brink of a dark and icy mountain pool. A thought of the shock of the contact holds one back.

As I was passing his house one morning, I said to myself, "Well, at any rate, if she loves him it will not be for long." And after that decision I was not myself, but a sort of a machine.

I rang the bell, and the servants admitted me to the drawing room. I waited there while the old tall clock placidly ticked its speech of time. The rigid and austere chairs remained in possession of their singular imperturbability, although, of course, they were aware of my purpose. But the little white tiles of the floor whispered one to another and looked at me. Presently he entered the room, and I, drawing my revolver, shot him. He screamed—you know that scream—mostly amazement—and as he fell forward his blood was upon the little white tiles. They huddled and covered their eyes from this rain. It seemed to me that the old clock stopped ticking as a man may gasp in the middle of a sentence, and a chair threw itself in my way as I sprang toward the door.

A moment later, I was walking down the street, tranquil, you understand, and I said to myself: "It is done. Long years from this day I will say to her that it was I who killed him. After time has eaten the conscience of the thing, she will admire my courage."

I was elated that the affair had gone off so smoothly, and I felt like returning home and taking a long, full sleep, like a tired workingman. When people passed me, I contemplated their stupidity with a sense of satisfaction.

But those accursed little white tiles!

I heard a shrill crying and chattering behind me, and, looking back, I saw them, bloodstained and impassioned, raising their little hands and screaming "Murder! It was he!" I have said that they had little hands. I am not sure of it, but they had some means of indicating me as unerringly as pointing fingers. As for their movement, they swept along as easily as dry, light leaves are carried by the wind. Always they were shrilly piping their song of my guilt.

My friend, may it never be your fortune to be pursued by a crowd of little bloodstained tiles. I used a thousand means to be free from the clash-clash of those tiny feet. I ran through the world at my best speed, but it was no better than that of an ox, while they, my pursuers, were always fresh, eager, relentless.

I am an ingenious person, and I used every trick that a desperate, fertile man can invent. Hundreds of times I had almost evaded them when some smoldering, neglected spark would blaze up and discover me.

I felt that the eye of conviction would have no terrors for me; but the eyes of suspicion which I saw in city after city, on road after road, drove me to the verge of going forward and saying, "Yes, I have murdered."

People would see the following, clamorous troops of bloodstained tiles, and give me piercing glances, so that these swords played continually at my heart. But we are a decorous race, thank God. It is very vulgar to apprehend murderers on the public streets. We have learned correct manners from the English. Besides, who can be sure of the meaning of clamoring tiles? It might be merely a trick in politics.

Detectives? What are detectives? Oh, yes, I have read of them and their deeds, when I come to think of it. The prehistoric races must have been remarkable. I have never been able to understand how the detectives navigated in stone boats. Still, specimens of their pottery excavated in Taumalipas show a remarkable knowledge of mechanics. I remember the little hydraulic—what's that? Well, what you say may be true, my friend, but I think you dream.

The little stained tiles. My friend, I stopped in an inn at the ends of the earth, and in the morning they were there flying like little birds and pecking at my window.

I should have escaped. Heavens, I should have escaped. What was more simple? I murdered, and then walked into the world, which is wide and intricate.

Do you know that my own clock assisted in the hunting of me? They asked what time I left my home that morning, and it replied at once, "Half-past eight." The watch of a man I had chanced to pass near the house of the crime told the people "Seven minutes after nine." And, of course, the tall old clock in the drawing room went about day after day repeating, "Eighteen minutes after nine."

Do you say that the man who caught me was very clever? My friend, I have lived long, and he was the most incredible blockhead of my experience. An enslaved, dust-eating Mexican vaquero wouldn't hitch his pony to such a man. Do you think he deserves credit for my capture? If he had been as pervading as the atmosphere, he would never have caught me. If he was a detective, as you say, I could carve a better one from an old table leg. But the tiles! That is another matter. At night I think they flew in a long high flock, like pigeons. In the day, little mad things, they murmured on my trail like frothy-mouthed weasels.

I see that you note these great, round, vividly orange spots on my coat. Of course, even if the detective were really carved from an old table leg, he could hardly fail to apprehend a man thus badged. As sores come upon one in the plague, so came these spots upon my coat. When I discovered them, I made effort to free myself of this coat. I tore, tugged, wrenched at it, but around my shoulders it was like the grip of a dead man's arms. Do you know that I have plunged into a thousand lakes? I have smeared this coat with a thousand paints. But day and night the spots burn like lights. I might walk from this jail today if I could rid myself of this coat, but it clings—clings—clings.

At any rate, the person you call a detective was not so clever to discover a man in a coat of spotted orange, followed by shrieking, bloodstained tiles. Yes, that noise from the corridor is most peculiar. But they are always there, muttering and watching, clashing and jostling. It sounds as if the dishes of Hades were being washed. Yet I have become used to it. Once, indeed, in the night, I cried out to them: "In God's name, go away, little bloodstained tiles!" But they doggedly answered: "It is the law."

March, 1896

[*The English Illustrated Magazine,* Vol. 14, pp. 569–571.]

THREE MIRACULOUS SOLDIERS*

I

The girl was in the front room on the second floor, peering through the blinds. It was the "best room." There was a very new rag carpet on the floor. The edges of it had been dyed with alternate stripes of red and green. Upon the wooden mantel there were two little puffy figures in clay—a shepherd and a shepherdess probably. A triangle of pink and white wool hung carefully over the edge of this shelf. Upon the bureau there was nothing at all save a spread newspaper, with edges folded to make it into a mat. The quilts and sheets had been removed from the bed and were stacked upon a chair. The pillows and the great feather mattress were muffled and tumbled until they resembled great dumplings. The picture of a man terribly leaden in complexion hung in an oval frame on one white wall and steadily confronted the bureau.

From between the slats of the blinds she had a view of the road as it wended across the meadow to the woods, and again where it reappeared crossing the hill, half a mile away. It lay yellow and warm in the summer sunshine. From the long grasses of the meadow came the rhythmic click of the insects. Occasional frogs in the hidden brook made a peculiar chug-chug sound, as if somebody throttled them. The leaves of the wood swung in gentle winds. Through the dark green branches of the pines that grew in the front yard could be seen the mountains, far to the southeast, and inexpressibly blue.

Mary's eyes were fastened upon the little streak of road that appeared on the distant hill. Her face was flushed with excitement, and the hand which stretched in a strained pose on the sill trembled because of the nervous shaking of the wrist. The pines whisked their green needles with a soft, hissing sound against the house.

At last the girl turned from the window and went to the head of the stairs. "Well, I just know they're coming, anyhow," she cried argumentatively to the depths.

A voice from below called to her angrily: "They ain't. We've never seen one yet. They never come into this neighborhood. You just come down here and 'tend to your work insteader watching for soldiers."

"Well, ma, I just know they're coming."

A voice retorted with the shrillness and mechanical violence of occasional housewives. The girl swished her skirts defiantly and returned to the window.

* The Little Regiment.

Upon the yellow streak of road that lay across the hillside there now was a handful of black dots—horsemen. A cloud of dust floated away. The girl flew to the head of the stairs and whirled down into the kitchen.

"They're coming! They're coming!"

It was as if she had cried "Fire!" Her mother had been peeling potatoes while seated comfortably at the table. She sprang to her feet. "No—it can't be—how you know it's them—where?" The stubby knife fell from her hand, and two or three curls of potato skin dropped from her apron to the floor.

The girl turned and dashed upstairs. Her mother followed, gasping for breath, and yet contriving to fill the air with question, reproach, and remonstrance. The girl was already at the window, eagerly pointing. "There! There! See 'em! See 'em!"

Rushing to the window, the mother scanned for an instant the road on the hill. She crouched back with a groan. "It's them, sure as the world! It's them!" She waved her hands in despairing gestures.

The black dots vanished into the wood. The girl at the window was quivering, and her eyes were shining like water when the sun flashes. "Hush! They're in the woods! They'll be here directly." She bent down and intently watched the green archway whence the road emerged. "Hush! I hear 'em coming," she swiftly whispered to her mother, for the elder woman had dropped dolefully upon the mattress and was sobbing. And indeed the girl could hear the quick, dull trample of horses. She stepped aside with sudden apprehension, but she bent her head forward in order to still scan the road.

"Here they are!"

There was something very theatrical in the sudden appearance of these men to the eyes of the girl. It was as if a scene had been shifted. The forest suddenly disclosed them—a dozen brown-faced troopers in blue—galloping.

"Oh, look!" breathed the girl. Her mouth was puckered into an expression of strange fascination, as if she had expected to see the troopers change into demons and gloat at her. She was at last looking upon those curious beings who rode down from the North—those men of legend and colossal tale—they who were possessed of such marvelous hallucinations.

The little troop rode in silence. At its head was a youthful fellow with some dim yellow stripes upon his arm. In his right hand he held his carbine, slanting upward, with the stock resting upon his knee. He was absorbed in a scrutiny of the country before him.

At the heels of the sergeant the rest of the squad rode in thin column, with creak of leather and tinkle of steel and tin. The girl scanned the faces of the horsemen, seeming astonished vaguely to find them of the type she knew.

The lad at the head of the troop comprehended the house and its environments in two glances. He did not check the long, swinging stride of his horse. The troopers glanced for a moment like casual tourists, and then returned to their study of the region in front. The heavy thudding of the hoofs became a small noise. The dust, hanging in sheets, slowly sank.

The sobs of the woman on the bed took form in words which, while strong in their note of calamity, yet expressed a querulous mental reaching for some near thing to blame. "And it'll be lucky fer us if we ain't both butchered in our sleep—plundering and running off horses—old Santo's gone—you see if he ain't—plundering—"

"But, ma," said the girl, perplexed and terrified in the same moment, "they've gone."

"Oh, but they'll come back!" cried the mother, without pausing her wail. "They'll come back—trust them for that—running off horses. O John, John! why did you, why did you?" She suddenly lifted herself and sat rigid, staring at her daughter. "Mary," she said in a tragic whisper, "the kitchen door isn't locked!" Already she was bent forward to listen, her mouth agape, her eyes fixed upon her daughter.

"Mother," faltered the girl.

Her mother again whispered, "The kitchen door isn't locked."

Motionless and mute, they stared into each other's eyes.

At last the girl quavered, "We better—we better go and lock it." The mother nodded. Hanging arm in arm, they stole across the floor toward the head of the stairs. A board of the floor creaked. They halted and exchanged a look of dumb agony.

At last they reached the head of the stairs. From the kitchen came the bass humming of the kettle and frequent sputterings and cracklings from the fire. These sounds were sinister. The mother and the girl stood incapable of movement. "There's somebody down there!" whispered the elder woman.

Finally, the girl made a gesture of resolution. She twisted her arm from her mother's hands and went two steps downward. She addressed the kitchen: "Who's there?" Her tone was intended to be dauntless. It rang so dramatically in the silence that a sudden new panic seized them, as if the suspected presence in the kitchen had cried out to them. But the girl ventured again: "Is there anybody there?" No reply was made save by the kettle and the fire.

With a stealthy tread the girl continued her journey. As she neared the last step the fire crackled explosively, and the girl screamed. But the mystic presence had not swept around the corner to grab her, so she dropped to a seat on the step and laughed. "It was—was only the—the fire," she said, stammering hysterically.

Then she arose with sudden fortitude and cried: "Why, there isn't anybody there! I know there isn't." She marched down into the kitchen. In her face was dread, as if she half expected to confront something, but the room was empty. She cried joyously: "There's nobody here! Come on down, ma." She ran to the kitchen door and locked it.

The mother came down to the kitchen. "Oh, dear, what a fright I've had! It's given me the sick headache. I know it has."

"Oh, ma," said the girl.

"I know it has—I know it. Oh, if your father was only here! He'd settle those Yankees mighty quick—he'd settle 'em! Two poor helpless women—"

"Why, ma, what makes you act so? The Yankees haven't—"

"Oh, they'll be back—they'll be back. Two poor helpless women! Your father and your uncle Asa and Bill off gallivanting around and fighting when they ought to be protecting their home! That's the kind of men they are. Didn't I say to your father just before he left—?"

"Ma," said the girl, coming suddenly from the window, "the barn door is open. I wonder if they took old Santo?"

"Oh, of course they have—of course—Mary, I don't see what we are going to do—I don't see what we are going to do."

The girl said, "Ma, I'm going to see if they took old Santo."

"Mary," cried the mother, "don't you dare!"

"But think of poor old Sant, ma."

"Never you mind old Santo. We're lucky to be safe ourselves, I tell you. Never mind old Santo. Don't you dare to go out there, Mary—Mary!"

The girl had unlocked the door and stepped out upon the porch. The mother cried in despair, "Mary!"

"Why, there isn't anybody out here," the girl called in response. She stood for a moment with a curious smile upon her face, as of gleeful satisfaction at her daring.

The breeze was waving the boughs of the apple trees. A rooster with an air importantly courteous was conducting three hens upon a foraging tour. On the hillside at the rear of the gray old barn the red leaves of a creeper flamed amid the summer foliage. High in the sky clouds rolled toward the north. The girl swung impulsively from the little stoop and ran toward the barn.

The great door was open, and the carved peg which usually performed the office of a catch lay on the ground. The girl could not see into the barn because of the heavy shadows. She paused in a listening attitude and heard a horse munching placidly. She gave a cry of delight and sprang across the threshold. Then she suddenly shrank back and gasped. She had confronted three men in gray seated upon the floor with their legs stretched out and their backs against Santo's manger. Their dust-covered countenances were expanded in grins.

As Mary sprang backward and screamed, one of the calm men in gray, still grinning, announced, "I knowed you'd holler." Sitting there comfortably, the three surveyed her with amusement.

Mary caught her breath, throwing her hand up to her throat. "Oh!" she said, "you—you frightened me!"

"We're sorry, lady, but couldn't help it no way," cheerfully responded another. "I knowed you'd holler when I seen you coming yere, but I raikoned we couldn't help it no way. We hain't a-troubling this yere barn, I don't guess. We been doing some mighty tall sleeping yere. We done woke when them Yanks loped past."

"Where did you come from? Did—did you escape from the—the Yankees?" The girl still stammered and trembled.

The three soldiers laughed. "No, m'm. No, m'm. They never cotch us. We was in a muss down the road yere about two mile. And Bill yere, they gi'n it to him in the arm, kehplunk. And they pasted me thar, too. Curious. And Sim yere, he didn't get nothing, but they chased us all quite a little piece, and we done lose track of our boys."

"Was it—was it those who passed here just now? Did they chase you?"

The men in gray laughed again. "What—them? No, indeedee! There was a mighty big swarm of Yanks and a mighty big swarm of our boys, too. What—that little passel? No, m'm."

She became calm enough to scan them more attentively. They were much begrimed and very dusty. Their gray clothes were tattered. Splashed mud had dried upon them in reddish spots. It appeared, too, that the men had not shaved in many days. In the hats there was a singular diversity. One soldier wore the little blue cap of the Northern infantry, with corps emblem and regimental number; one wore a great slouch hat with a wide hole in the crown; and the other wore no hat at all. The left sleeve of one man and the right sleeve of another had been slit, and the arms were neatly bandaged with clean cloths. "These hain't no more than two little cuts," explained one. "We stopped up yere to Mis' Leavitt's—she said her name was—and she bind them for us. Bill yere, he had the thirst come on him. And the fever too. We—"

"Did you ever see my father in the army?" asked Mary. "John Hinckson —his name is."

The three soldiers grinned again, but they replied kindly: "No, m'm. No, m'm, we hain't never. What is he—in the cavalry?"

"No," said the girl. "He and my uncle Asa and my cousin—his name is Bill Parker—they are all with Longstreet—they call him."

"Oh," said the soldiers. "Longstreet? Oh, they're a good smart ways from yere. 'Way off up nawtheast. There hain't nothing but cavalry down yere. They're in the infantry, probably."

"We haven't heard anything from them for days and days," said Mary.

"Oh, they're all right in the infantry," said one man, to be consoling. "The infantry don't do much fighting. They go bellering out in a big swarm and only a few of 'em get hurt. But if they was in the cavalry—the cavalry—"

Mary interrupted him without intention. "Are you hungry?" she asked. The soldiers looked at each other, struck by some sudden and singular shame. They hung their heads. "No, m'm," replied one at last.

Santo, in his stall, was tranquilly chewing and chewing. Sometimes he looked benevolently over at them. He was an old horse, and there was something about his eyes and his forelock which created the impression that he wore spectacles. Mary went and patted his nose. "Well, if you are hungry, I can get you something," she told the men. "Or you might come to the house."

"We wouldn't dast go to the house," said one. "That passel of Yanks was only a scouting crowd, most like. Just an advance. More coming, likely."

"Well, I can bring you something," cried the girl eagerly. "Won't you let me bring you something?"

"Well," said the soldier with embarrassment, "we hain't had much. If you could bring us a little snack-like—just a snack—we'd—"

Without waiting for him to cease, the girl turned toward the door. But before she had reached it she stopped abruptly. "Listen!" she whispered. Her form was bent forward, her head turned and lowered, her hand extended toward the men in a command for silence.

They could faintly hear the thudding of many hoofs, the clank of arms, and frequent calling voices.

"By cracky, it's the Yanks!" The soldiers scrambled to their feet and came toward the door. "I knowed that first crowd was only an advance."

The girl and the three men peered from the shadows of the barn. The view of the road was intersected by tree trunks and a little henhouse. However, they could see many horsemen streaming down the road. The horsemen were in blue. "Oh, hide—hide—hide!" cried the girl, with a sob in her voice.

"Wait a minute," whispered a gray soldier excitedly. "Maybe they're going along by. No, by thunder, they hain't! They're halting. Scoot, boys!"

They made a noiseless dash into the dark end of the barn. The girl, standing by the door, heard them break forth an instant later in clamorous whispers. "Where'll we hide? Where'll we hide? There hain't a place to hide!" The girl turned and glanced wildly about the barn. It seemed true. The stock of hay had grown low under Santo's endless munching, and from occasional levyings by passing troopers in gray. The poles of the mow were barely covered, save in one corner where there was a little bunch.

The girl espied the great feedbox. She ran to it and lifted the lid. "Here! here!" she called. "Get in here."

They had been tearing noiselessly around the rear part of the barn. At her low call they came and plunged at the box. They did not all get in at the same moment without a good deal of a tangle. The wounded men gasped and muttered, but they at last were flopped down on the layer of feed which covered the bottom. Swiftly and softly the girl lowered the lid, and then turned like a flash toward the door.

No one appeared there, so she went close to survey the situation. The troopers had dismounted and stood in silence by their horses. A gray-bearded man, whose red cheeks and nose shone vividly above the whiskers, was strolling about with two or three others. They wore double-breasted coats, and faded yellow sashes were wound under their black leather sword belts. The gray-bearded soldier was apparently giving orders, pointing here and there.

Mary tiptoed to the feedbox. "They've all got off their horses," she said to it. A finger projected from a knothole near the top and said to her very plainly, "Come closer." She obeyed, and then a muffled voice could be heard: "Scoot for the house, lady, and if we don't see you again, why, much obliged for what you done."

"Good-bye," she said to the feedbox.

She made two attempts to walk dauntlessly from the barn, but each time she faltered and failed just before she reached the point where she could have been seen by the blue-coated troopers. At last, however, she made a sort of rush forward and went out into the bright sunshine.

The group of men in double-breasted coats wheeled in her direction at the instant. The gray-bearded officer forgot to lower his arm, which had been stretched forth in giving an order.

She felt that her feet were touching the ground in a most unnatural manner. Her bearing, she believed, was suddenly grown awkward and ungainly. Upon her face she thought that this sentence was plainly written: "There are three men hidden in the feedbox."

The gray-bearded soldier came toward her. She stopped; she seemed about to run away. But the soldier doffed his little blue cap and looked amiable. "You live here, I presume?" he said.

"Yes," she answered.

"Well, we are obliged to camp here for the night, and as we've got two wounded men with us I don't suppose you'd mind if we put them in the barn."

"In—in the barn?"

He became aware that she was agitated. He smiled assuringly. "You needn't be frightened. We won't hurt anything around here. You'll all be safe enough."

The girl balanced on one foot and swung the other to and fro in the grass. She was looking down at it. "But—but I don't think ma would like it if—if you took the barn."

The old officer laughed. "Wouldn't she?" said he. "That's so. Maybe she wouldn't." He reflected for a time and then decided cheerfully: "Well, we will have to go ask her, anyhow. Where is she? In the house?"

"Yes," replied the girl, "she's in the house. She—she'll be scared to death when she sees you!"

"Well, you go and ask her then," said the soldier, always wearing a benign smile. "You go ask her and then come and tell me."

When the girl pushed open the door and entered the kitchen, she found it empty. "Ma!" she called softly. There was no answer. The kettle still was humming its low song. The knife and the curl of potato skin lay on the floor.

She went to her mother's room and entered timidly. The new, lonely aspect of the house shook her nerves. Upon the bed was a confusion of coverings. "Ma!" called the girl, quaking in fear that her mother was not there to reply. But there was a sudden turmoil of the quilts, and her mother's head was thrust forth. "Mary!" she cried, in what seemed to be a supreme astonishment, "I thought—I thought—"

"Oh, ma," blurted the girl, "there's over a thousand Yankees in the yard, and I've hidden three of our men in the feedbox!"

The elder woman, however, upon the appearance of her daughter had begun to thrash hysterically about on the bed and wail.

"Ma!" the girl exclaimed, "and now they want to use the barn—and our men in the feedbox! What shall I do, ma? What shall I do?"

Her mother did not seem to hear, so absorbed was she in her grievous flounderings and tears. "Ma!" appealed the girl. "Ma!"

For a moment Mary stood silently debating, her lips apart, her eyes fixed. Then she went to the kitchen window and peeked.

The old officer and the others were staring up the road. She went to another window in order to get a proper view of the road, and saw that they were gazing at a small body of horsemen approaching at a trot and raising much dust. Presently she recognized them as the squad that had passed the house earlier, for the young man with the dim yellow chevron still rode at their head. An unarmed horseman in gray was receiving their close attention.

As they came very near to the house she darted to the first window again. The gray-bearded officer was smiling a fine broad smile of satisfaction. "So you got him?" he called out. The young sergeant sprang from his horse, and his brown hand moved in a salute. The girl could not hear his reply. She saw the unarmed horseman in gray stroking a very black mustache and looking about him coolly and with an interested air. He appeared so indifferent that she did not understand he was a prisoner until she heard the graybeard call out: "Well, put him in the barn. He'll be safe there, I guess." A party of troopers moved with the prisoner toward the barn.

The girl made a sudden gesture of horror, remembering the three men in the feedbox.

III

The busy troopers in blue scurried about the long lines of stamping horses. Men crooked their backs and perspired in order to rub with cloths or bunches of grass these slim equine legs upon whose splendid machinery they depended so greatly. The lips of the horses were still wet and frothy from the steel bars which had wrenched at their mouths all day. Over their backs and about their noses sped the talk of the men.

"Moind where yer plug is steppin', Finerty! Keep 'im aff me!"

"An ould elephant! He shtrides like a schoolhouse."

"Bill's little mar'—she was plum beat when she come in with Crawford's crowd."

"Crawford's the hardest-ridin' cavalryman in the army. An' he don't use up a horse, neither—much. They stay fresh when the others are most a-droppin'."

"Finerty, will yeh moind that cow a' yours?"

Amid a bustle of gossip and banter, the horses retained their air of solemn rumination, twisting their lower jaws from side to side and sometimes rubbing noses dreamfully.

Over in front of the barn three troopers sat talking comfortably. Their carbines were leaned against the wall. At their side and outlined in the black of the open door stood a sentry, his weapon resting in the hollow of his arm. Four horses, saddled and accoutred, were conferring with their heads close together. The four bridle reins were flung over a post.

Upon the calm green of the land, typical in every way of peace, the hues of war brought thither by the troops shone strangely. Mary, gazing curiously, did not feel that she was contemplating a familiar scene. It was no longer the home acres. The new blue, steel, and faded yellow thoroughly dominated the old green and brown. She could hear the voices of the men, and it seemed from their tone that they had camped there for years. Everything with them was usual. They had taken possession of the landscape in such a way that even the old marks appeared strange and formidable to the girl.

Mary had intended to go and tell the commander in blue that her mother did not wish his men to use the barn at all, but she paused when she heard him speak to the sergeant. She thought she perceived then that it mattered little to him what her mother wished, and that an objection by her or by anybody would be futile. She saw the soldiers conduct the prisoner in gray into the barn, and for a long time she watched the three chatting guards and the pondering sentry. Upon her mind in desolate weight was the recollection of the three men in the feedbox.

It seemed to her that in a case of this description it was her duty to be a heroine. In all the stories she had read when at boarding school in Pennsylvania, the girl characters, confronted with such difficulties, invariably did hairbreadth things. True, they were usually bent upon rescuing and recovering their lovers, and neither the calm man in gray nor any of the three in the feedbox was lover of hers; but then, a real heroine would not pause over this minor question. Plainly a heroine would take measures to rescue the four men. If she did not at least make the attempt, she would be false to those carefully constructed ideals which were the accumulation of years of dreaming.

But the situation puzzled her. There was the barn with only one door, and with four armed troopers in front of this door, one of them with his back to the rest of the world, engaged, no doubt, in a steadfast contemplation of the calm man and, incidentally, of the feedbox. She knew, too, that even if she should open the kitchen door, three heads and perhaps four would turn casually in her direction. Their ears were real ears.

Heroines, she knew, conducted these matters with infinite precision and dispatch. They severed the hero's bonds, cried a dramatic sentence, and stood between him and his enemies until he had run far enough away. She saw well, however, that even should she achieve all things up to the point where she might take glorious stand between the escaping and the pursuers, those grim troopers in blue would not pause. They would run around her, make a circuit. One by one she saw the gorgeous contrivances and expedients of fiction fall before the plain, homely difficulties of this situation. They were of no service. Sadly, ruefully, she thought of the calm man and of the contents of the feedbox.

The sum of her invention was that she could sally forth to the commander of the blue cavalry and, confessing to him that there were three of her friends and his enemies secreted in the feedbox, pray him to let them depart unmolested. But she was beginning to believe the old graybeard to be a bear. It was hardly probable that he would give this plan his support. It was more probable that he and some of his men would at once descend upon the feedbox and confiscate her three friends. The difficulty with her idea was that she could not learn its value without trying it, and then in case of failure it would be too late for remedies and other plans. She reflected that war made men very unreasonable.

All that she could do was to stand at the window and mournfully regard the barn. She admitted this to herself with a sense of deep humiliation. She was not, then, made of that fine stuff, that mental satin, which enabled some other beings to be of such mighty service to the distressed. She was defeated by a barn with one door, by four men with eight eyes and eight ears—trivialities that would not impede the real heroine.

The vivid white light of broad day began slowly to fade. Tones of gray came upon the fields, and the shadows were of lead. In this more somber atmosphere the fires built by the troops down in the far end of the orchard grew more brilliant, becoming spots of crimson color in the dark grove.

The girl heard a fretting voice from her mother's room. "Mary!" She hastily obeyed the call. She perceived that she had quite forgotten her mother's existence in this time of excitement.

The elder woman still lay upon the bed. Her face was flushed, and perspiration stood amid new wrinkles upon her forehead. Weaving wild glances from side to side, she began to whimper. "Oh, I'm just sick—I'm just sick! Have those men gone yet? Have they gone?"

The girl smoothed a pillow carefully for her mother's head. "No, ma. They're here yet. But they haven't hurt anything—it doesn't seem. Will I get you something to eat?"

Her mother gestured her away with the impatience of the ill. "No—no —just don't bother me. My head is splitting, and you know very well that nothing can be done for me when I get one of these spells. It's trouble— that's what makes them. When are those men going? Look here, don't you go 'way. You stick close to the house now."

"I'll stay right here," said the girl. She sat in the gloom and listened to her mother's incessant moaning. When she attempted to move, her mother cried out at her. When she desired to ask if she might try to alleviate the pain, she was interrupted shortly. Somehow her sitting in passive silence within hearing of this illness seemed to contribute to her mother's relief. She assumed a posture of submission. Sometimes her mother projected questions concerning the local condition, and although she labored to be graphic and at the same time soothing, unalarming, her form of reply was always displeasing to the sick woman, and brought forth ejaculations of angry impatience.

Eventually the woman slept in the manner of one worn from terrible labor. The girl went slowly and softly to the kitchen. When she looked from the window, she saw the four soldiers still at the barn door. In the west, the sky was yellow. Some tree trunks intersecting it appeared black as streaks of ink. Soldiers hovered in blue clouds about the bright splendor of the fires in the orchard. There were glimmers of steel.

The girl sat in the new gloom of the kitchen and watched. The soldiers lit a lantern and hung it in the barn. Its rays made the form of the sentry seem gigantic. Horses whinnied from the orchard. There was a low hum of human voices. Sometimes small detachments of troopers rode past the front of the house. The girl heard the abrupt calls of sentries. She fetched some food and ate it from her hand, standing by the window. She was so afraid that something would occur that she barely left her post for an instant.

A picture of the interior of the barn hung vividly in her mind. She recalled the knotholes in the boards at the rear, but she admitted that the prisoners could not escape through them. She remembered some inadequacies of the roof, but these also counted for nothing. When confronting the problem, she felt her ambitions, her ideals, tumbling headlong like cottages of straw.

Once she felt that she had decided to reconnoitre at any rate. It was night; the lantern at the barn and the campfires made everything without their circle into masses of heavy mystic blackness. She took two steps toward the door. But there she paused. Innumerable possibilities of danger had assailed her mind. She returned to the window and stood wavering. At last, she went swiftly to the door, opened it, and slid noiselessly into the darkness.

For a moment she regarded the shadows. Down in the orchard the campfires of the troops appeared precisely like a great painting, all in reds upon a black cloth. The voices of the troopers still hummed. The girl started slowly off in the opposite direction. Her eyes were fixed in a stare; she studied the darkness in front for a moment, before she ventured upon a forward step. Unconsciously, her throat was arranged for a sudden shrill scream. High in the tree branches she could hear the voice of the wind, a melody of the night, low and sad, the plaint of an endless, incommunicable sorrow. Her own distress, the plight of the men in gray—these near matters as well as all she had known or imagined of grief—everything was expressed in this soft mourning of the wind in the trees. At first she felt like weeping. This sound told her of human impotency and doom. Then later the trees and the wind breathed strength to her, sang of sacrifice, of dauntless effort, of hard carven faces that did not blanch when Duty came at midnight or at noon.

She turned often to scan the shadowy figures that moved from time to time in the light at the barn door. Once she trod upon a stick, and it flopped, crackling in the intolerable manner of all sticks. At this noise, however, the guards at the barn made no sign. Finally, she was where she could see the knotholes in the rear of the structure gleaming like pieces of

metal from the effect of the light within. Scarcely breathing in her excitement, she glided close and applied an eye to a knothole. She had barely
achieved one glance at the interior before she sprang back shuddering.

For the unconscious and cheerful sentry at the door was swearing away
in flaming sentences, heaping one gorgeous oath upon another, making a
conflagration of his description of his troop horse.

"Why," he was declaring to the calm prisoner in gray, "you ain't got a
horse in your hull damned army that can run forty rod with that there
little mar'!"

As in the outer darkness Mary cautiously returned to the knothole, the
three guards in front suddenly called in low tones: "S-s-s-h!" "Quit, Pete;
here comes the lieutenant." The sentry had apparently been about to resume his declamation, but at these warnings he suddenly posed in a soldierly manner.

A tall and lean officer with a smooth face entered the barn. The sentry
saluted primly. The officer flashed a comprehensive glance about him. "Everything all right?"

"All right, sir."

This officer had eyes like the points of stilettos. The lines from his nose
to the corners of his mouth were deep and gave him a slightly disagreeable
aspect, but somewhere in his face there was a quality of singular thoughtfulness, as of the absorbed student dealing in generalities, which was utterly in opposition to the rapacious keenness of the eyes, which saw
everything.

Suddenly he lifted a long finger and pointed. "What's that?"

"That? That's a feedbox, I suppose."

"What's in it?"

"I don't know. I—"

"You ought to know," said the officer sharply. He walked over to the
feedbox and flung up the lid. With a sweeping gesture he reached down
and scooped a handful of feed. "You ought to know what's in everything
when you have prisoners in your care," he added, scowling.

During the time of this incident, the girl had nearly swooned. Her hands
searched weakly over the boards for something to which to cling. With
the pallor of the dying she had watched the downward sweep of the officer's arm, which after all had only brought forth a handful of feed. The
result was a stupefaction of her mind. She was astonished out of her senses
at this spectacle of three large men metamorphosed into a handful of feed.

IV

It is perhaps a singular thing that this absence of the three men from
the feedbox at the time of the sharp lieutenant's investigation should terrify the girl more than it should joy her. That for which she had prayed

had come to pass. Apparently the escape of these men in the face of every improbability had been granted her, but her dominating emotion was fright. The feedbox was a mystic and terrible machine, like some dark magician's trap. She felt it almost possible that she should see the three weird men floating spectrally away through the air. She glanced with swift apprehension behind her, and, when the dazzle from the lantern's light had left her eyes, saw only the dim hillside stretched in solemn silence.

The interior of the barn possessed for her another fascination because it was now uncanny. It contained that extraordinary feedbox. When she peeped again at the knothole, the calm, gray prisoner was seated upon the feedbox, thumping it with his dangling, careless heels as if it were in no wise his conception of a remarkable feedbox. The sentry also stood facing it. His carbine he held in the hollow of his arm. His legs were spread apart, and he mused. From without came the low mumble of the three other troopers. The sharp lieutenant had vanished.

The trembling yellow light of the lantern caused the figures of the men to cast monstrous wavering shadows. There were spaces of gloom which shrouded ordinary things in impressive garb. The roof presented an inscrutable blackness, save where small rifts in the shingles glowed phosphorescently. Frequently old Santo put down a thunderous hoof. The heels of the prisoner made a sound like the booming of a wild kind of drum. When the men moved their heads, their eyes shone with ghoulish whiteness, and their complexions were always waxen and unreal. And there was that profoundly strange feedbox, imperturbable with its burden of fantastic mystery.

Suddenly from down near her feet the girl heard a crunching sound, a sort of nibbling, as if some silent and very discreet terrier was at work upon the turf. She faltered back; here was, no doubt, another grotesque detail of this most unnatural episode. She did not run, because physically she was in the power of these events. Her feet chained her to the ground in submission to this march of terror after terror. As she stared at the spot from which this sound seemed to come, there floated through her mind a vague, sweet vision—a vision of her safe little room, in which at this hour she usually was sleeping.

The scratching continued faintly and with frequent pauses, as if the terrier was then listening. When the girl first removed her eyes from the knothole the scene appeared of one velvet blackness; then gradually objects loomed with a dim luster. She could see now where the tops of the trees joined the sky, and the form of the barn was before her, dyed in heavy purple. She was ever about to shriek, but no sound came from her constricted throat. She gazed at the ground with the expression of countenance of one who watches the sinister-moving grass where a serpent approaches.

Dimly she saw a piece of sod wrenched free and drawn under the great foundation beam of the barn. Once she imagined that she saw human hands, not outlined at all, but sufficient in color, form, or movement to make subtle suggestion.

Then suddenly a thought that illuminated the entire situation flashed in her mind like a light. The three men, late of the feedbox, were beneath the floor of the barn and were now scraping their way under this beam. She did not consider for a moment how they could come there. They were marvelous creatures. The supernatural was to be expected of them. She no longer trembled, for she was possessed upon this instant of the most unchangeable species of conviction. The evidence before her amounted to no evidence at all, but nevertheless her opinion grew in an instant from an irresponsible acorn to a rooted and immovable tree. It was as if she was on a jury.

She stooped down hastily and scanned the ground. There she indeed saw a pair of hands hauling at the dirt where the sod had been displaced. Softly, in a whisper like a breath, she said, "Hey!"

The dim hands were drawn hastily under the barn. The girl reflected for a moment. Then she stooped and whispered: "Hey! It's me!"

After a time there was a resumption of the digging. The ghostly hands began once more their cautious mining. She waited. In hollow reverberations from the interior of the barn came the frequent sounds of old Santo's lazy movements. The sentry conversed with the prisoner.

At last the girl saw a head thrust slowly from under the beam. She perceived the face of one of the miraculous soldiers from the feedbox. A pair of eyes glintered and wavered, then finally settled upon her, a pale statue of a girl. The eyes became lit with a kind of humorous greeting. An arm gestured at her.

Stooping, she breathed, "All right." The man drew himself silently back under the beam. A moment later the pair of hands resumed their cautious task. Ultimately the head and arms of the man were thrust strangely from the earth. He was lying on his back. The girl thought of the dirt in his hair. Wriggling slowly and pushing at the beam above him, he forced his way out of the curious little passage. He twisted his body and raised himself upon his hands. He grinned at the girl and drew his feet carefully from under the beam. When he at last stood erect beside her, he at once began mechanically to brush the dirt from his clothes with his hands. In the barn the sentry and his prisoner were evidently engaged in an argument.

The girl and the first miraculous soldier signaled warily. It seemed that they feared that their arms would make noises in passing through the air. Their lips moved, conveying dim meanings.

In this sign language the girl described the situation in the barn. With guarded motions, she told him of the importance of absolute stillness. He nodded, and then in the same manner he told her of his two companions under the barn floor. He informed her again of their wounded state, and wagged his head to express his despair. He contorted his face, to tell how sore were their arms; and jabbed the air mournfully, to express their remote geographical position.

This signaling was interrupted by the sound of a body being dragged or dragging itself with slow, swishing sound under the barn. The sound was too loud for safety. They rushed to the hole and began to semaphore until a shaggy head appeared with rolling eyes and quick grin.

With frantic downward motions of their arms they suppressed this grin and with it the swishing noise. In dramatic pantomime they informed this head of the terrible consequences of so much noise. The head nodded, and painfully, but with extreme care, the second man pushed and pulled himself from the hole.

In a faint whisper the first man said, "Where's Sim?"

The second man made low reply: "He's right here." He motioned reassuringly toward the hole.

When the third head appeared, a soft smile of glee came upon each face, and the mute group exchanged expressive glances.

When they all stood together, free from this tragic barn, they breathed a long sigh that was contemporaneous with another smile and another exchange of glances.

One of the men tiptoed to a knothole and peered into the barn. The sentry was at that moment speaking. "Yes, we know 'em all. There isn't a house in this region that we don't know who is in it most of the time. We collar 'em once in a while—like we did you. Now, that house out yonder, we—"

The man suddenly left the knothole and returned to the others. Upon his face, dimly discerned, there was an indication that he had made an astonishing discovery. The others questioned him with their eyes, but he simply waved an arm to express his inability to speak at that spot. He led them back toward the hill, prowling carefully. At a safe distance from the barn he halted, and as they grouped eagerly about him, he exploded in an intense undertone: "Why, that—that's Cap'n Sawyer they got in yonder."

"Cap'n Sawyer!" incredulously whispered the other men.

But the girl had something to ask. "How did you get out of that feedbox?"

He smiled. "Well, when you put us in there, we was just in a minute when we allowed it wasn't a mighty safe place, and we allowed we'd get out. And we did. We skedaddled 'round and 'round until it 'peared like we was going to get cotched, and then we flung ourselves down in the cow stalls where it's low-like—just dirt floor—and then we just naturally went a-whooping under the barn floor when the Yanks come. And we didn't know Cap'n Sawyer by his voice nohow. We heard 'im discoursing, and we allowed it was a mighty pert man, but we didn't know that it was him. No, m'm."

These three men, so recently from a situation of peril, seemed suddenly to have dropped all thought of it. They stood with sad faces looking at the barn. They seemed to be making no plans at all to reach a place of more complete safety. They were halted and stupefied by some unknown calamity.

"How do you raikon they cotch him, Sim?" one whispered mournfully.

"I don't know," replied another in the same tone.

Another with a low snarl expressed in two words his opinion of the methods of Fate: "Oh, hell!"

The three men started then as if simultaneously stung, and gazed at the young girl who stood silently near them. The man who had sworn began to make agitated apology: "Pardon, miss! 'Pon my soul, I clean forgot you was by. 'Deed, and I wouldn't swear like that if I had knowed. 'Deed, I wouldn't."

The girl did not seem to hear him. She was staring at the barn. Suddenly she turned and whispered, "Who is he?"

"He's Cap'n Sawyer, m'm," they told her sorrowfully. "He's our own cap'n. He's been in command of us yere since a long time. He's got folks about yere. Raikon they cotch him while he was a-visiting."

She was still for a time, and then, awed, she said: "Will they—will they hang him?"

"No, m'm. Oh, no, m'm. Don't raikon no such thing. No, m'm."

The group became absorbed in a contemplation of the barn. For a time no one moved or spoke. At last the girl was aroused by slight sounds, and, turning, she perceived that the three men who had so recently escaped from the barn were now advancing toward it.

v

The girl, waiting in the darkness, expected to hear the sudden crash and uproar of a fight as soon as the three creeping men should reach the barn. She reflected in an agony upon the swift disaster that would befall any enterprise so desperate. She had an impulse to beg them to come away. The grass rustled in silken movements as she sped toward the barn.

When she arrived, however, she gazed about her bewildered. The men were gone. She searched with her eyes, trying to detect some moving thing, but she could see nothing.

Left alone again, she began to be afraid of the night. The great stretches of darkness could hide crawling dangers. From sheer desire to see a human, she was obliged to peep again at the knothole. The sentry had apparently wearied of talking. Instead, he was reflecting. The prisoner still sat on the feedbox, moodily staring at the floor. The girl felt in one way that she was looking at a ghastly group in wax. She started when the old horse put down an echoing hoof. She wished the men would speak; their silence reinforced the strange aspect. They might have been two dead men.

The girl felt impelled to look at the corner of the interior where were the cow stalls. There was no light there save the appearance of peculiar gray haze which marked the track of the dimming rays of the lantern. All else was somber shadow. At last she saw something move there. It might have been as small as a rat, or it might have been a part of something as large as a man. At any rate, it proclaimed that something in that spot was alive. At one time she saw it plainly, and at other times it vanished, because her fixture of gaze caused her occasionally to greatly tangle and blur those peculiar shadows and faint lights. At last, however, she perceived a human head. It was monstrously disheveled and wild. It moved slowly forward until its glance could fall upon the prisoner and then upon the sentry. The wandering rays caused the eyes to glitter like silver. The girl's heart pounded so that she put her hand over it.

The sentry and the prisoner remained immovably waxen, and over in the gloom the head thrust from the floor watched them with its silver eyes.

Finally, the prisoner slipped from the feedbox and, raising his arms, yawned at great length. "Oh, well," he remarked, "you boys will get a good licking if you fool around here much longer. That's some satisfaction, anyhow, even if you did bag me. You'll get a good walloping." He reflected for a moment, and decided: "I'm sort of willing to be captured if you fellows only get a damned good licking for being so smart."

The sentry looked up and smiled a superior smile. "Licking, hey? Nixey!" He winked exasperatingly at the prisoner. "You fellows are not fast enough, my boy. Why didn't you lick us at ——? and at ——? and at ——?" He named some of the great battles.

To this the captive officer blurted in angry astonishment: "Why, we did!"

The sentry winked again in profound irony. "Yes—I know you did. Of course. You whipped us, didn't you? Fine kind of whipping that was! Why, we—"

He suddenly ceased, smitten mute by a sound that broke the stillness of the night. It was the sharp crack of a distant shot that made wild echoes among the hills. It was instantly followed by the hoarse cry of a human voice, a faraway yell of warning, singing of surprise, peril, fear of death.

A moment later there was a distant fierce spattering of shots. The sentry and the prisoner stood facing each other, their lips apart, listening.

The orchard at that instant awoke to sudden tumult. There were the thud and scramble and scamper of feet, the mellow, swift clash of arms, men's voices in question, oath, command, hurried and unhurried, resolute and frantic. A horse sped along the road at a raging gallop. A loud voice shouted, "What is it, Ferguson?" Another voice yelled something incoherent. There was a sharp, discordant chorus of command. An uproarious volley suddenly rang from the orchard. The prisoner in gray moved from his intent, listening attitude. Instantly the eyes of the sentry blazed, and he said with a new and terrible sternness: "Stand where you are!"

The prisoner trembled in his excitement. Expressions of delight and triumph bubbled to his lips. "A surprise, by Gawd! Now—now, you'll see!"

The sentry stolidly swung his carbine to his shoulder. He sighted carefully along the barrel until it pointed at the prisoner's head, about at his nose. "Well, I've got you, anyhow. Remember that! Don't move!"

The prisoner could not keep his arms from nervously gesturing. "I won't; but—"

"And shut your mouth!"

The three comrades of the sentry flung themselves into view. "Pete—devil of a row!—can you—"

"I've got him," said the sentry calmly and without moving. It was as if the barrel of the carbine rested on piers of stone. The three comrades turned and plunged into the darkness.

In the orchard it seemed as if two gigantic animals were engaged in a mad, floundering encounter, snarling, howling in a whirling chaos of noise and motion. In the barn the prisoner and his guard faced each other in silence.

As for the girl at the knothole, the sky had fallen at the beginning of this clamor. She would not have been astonished to see the stars swinging from their abodes, and the vegetation, the barn, all blow away. It was the end of everything, the grand universal murder. When two of the three miraculous soldiers who formed the original feedbox corps emerged in detail from the hole under the beam and slid away into the darkness, she did no more than glance at them.

Suddenly she recollected the head with silver eyes. She started forward and again applied her eyes to the knothole. Even with the din resounding from the orchard, from up the road and down the road, from the heavens and from the deep earth, the central fascination was this mystic head. There, to her, was the dark god of the tragedy.

The prisoner in gray at this moment burst into a laugh that was no more than a hysterical gurgle. "Well, you can't hold that gun out for ever! Pretty soon you'll have to lower it."

The sentry's voice sounded slightly muffled, for his cheek was pressed against the weapon. "I won't be tired for some time yet."

The girl saw the head slowly rise, the eyes fixed upon the sentry's face. A tall, black figure slunk across the cow stalls and vanished in back of old Santo's quarters. She knew what was to come to pass. She knew this grim thing was upon a terrible mission, and that it would reappear again at the head of the little passage between Santo's stall and the wall, almost at the sentry's elbow; and yet when she saw a faint indication as of a form crouching there, a scream from an utterly new alarm almost escaped her.

The sentry's arms, after all, were not of granite. He moved restively. At last he spoke in his even, unchanging tone: "Well, I guess you'll have to climb into that feedbox. Step back and lift the lid."

"Why, you don't mean—"

"Step back!"

The girl felt a cry of warning arising to her lips as she gazed at this sentry. She noted every detail of his facial expression. She saw, moreover, his mass of brown hair bunching disgracefully about his ears, his clear eyes lit now with a hard, cold light, his forehead puckered in a mighty scowl, the ring upon the third finger of the left hand. "Oh, they won't kill him! Surely they won't kill him!" The noise of the fight in the orchard was the loud music, the thunder and lightning, the rioting of the tempest which people love during the critical scene of a tragedy.

When the prisoner moved back in reluctant obedience, he faced for an instant the entrance of the little passage, and what he saw there must have been written swiftly, graphically in his eyes. And the sentry read it and knew then that he was upon the threshold of his death. In a fraction of time, certain information went from the grim thing in the passage to the prisoner, and from the prisoner to the sentry. But at that instant the black formidable figure arose, towered, and made its leap. A new shadow flashed across the floor when the blow was struck.

As for the girl at the knothole, when she returned to sense she found herself standing with clenched hands and screaming with her might.

As if her reason had again departed from her, she ran around the barn, in at the door, and flung herself sobbing beside the body of the soldier in blue.

The uproar of the fight became at last coherent, inasmuch as one party was giving shouts of supreme exultation. The firing no longer sounded in crashes; it was now expressed in spiteful crackles, the last words of the combat, spoken with feminine vindictiveness.

Presently there was a thud of flying feet. A grimy, panting, red-faced mob of troopers in blue plunged into the barn, became instantly frozen to attitudes of amazement and rage, and then roared in one great chorus: "He's gone!"

The girl who knelt beside the body upon the floor turned toward them her lamenting eyes and cried: "He's not dead, is he? He can't be dead?"

They thronged forward. The sharp lieutenant who had been so particular about the feedbox knelt by the side of the girl and laid his head against the chest of the prostrate soldier. "Why, no," he said, rising and looking at the man. "He's all right. Some of you boys throw some water on him."

"Are you sure?" demanded the girl, feverishly.

"Of course! He'll be better after a while."

"Oh!" said she softly, and then looked down at the sentry. She started to arise, and the lieutenant reached down and hoisted rather awkwardly at her arm.

"Don't you worry about him. He's all right."

She turned her face with its curving lips and shining eyes once more toward the unconscious soldier upon the floor. The troopers made a lane to the door, the lieutenant bowed, the girl vanished.

"Queer," said a young officer. "Girl very clearly worst kind of rebel, and yet she falls to weeping and wailing like mad over one of her enemies. Be around in the morning with all sorts of doctoring—you see if she ain't. Queer."

The sharp lieutenant shrugged his shoulders. After reflection he shrugged his shoulders again. He said: "War changes many things; but it doesn't change everything, thank God!"

March 15, 1896
[Saint Paul *Pioneer Press*, p. 24.]

A FREIGHT CAR INCIDENT

[A Texas Legend]

"Remember that time, Major?" said the railroad man.

"You bet I do," rejoined the major.

"Go ahead and tell it," said the others.

The major lifted his glass, and carefully scrutinized the bright liquid.

"Well, Tom's line, you see, was just being put through the interior of the State at that time, and one day he asked me to go out with him to some little town which he was going to open up with an auction sale of lots, and free beer and sandwiches for the people, and all that, you know. Well, I went along, and there was a big freight car loaded down with kegs and provisions. Everybody was having a great time. Tom got ill during the sale, so he went into a little shanty to lie down, while I went over to the freight car to get some ice to put on his head. I was in the car scouting around after ice when, all of a sudden, someone slammed the door to, and made the inside of the car as dark as pitch. Then somebody in the darkness began to swear like a pirate, and I heard him swing his revolver loose. I began to see the game then.

It seems that there was a fellow around there that a good many people wanted to kill, and they said they were going to kill him that day at the sale, too. Somebody had pointed him out to me during the morning, and I had heard him brag, so I recognized this voice in the darkness. I think he decided they had slammed the door on him so that when he opened it to come out they could get a good fair chance to make a sieve of him. The way that man swore was positively frightful. He wasn't very good company, either. I stood still so long that I felt the bones in my legs creak like old timbers, and I didn't breathe any harder than a canary bird. He went on swearing at a great rate. I began to think of Tom and his pain, wishing he had died rather than I had come for that ice.

At last I found that I had got to move. There was no help for it. My legs refused to support me in this position any longer. My head was growing dizzy, and if I didn't change my attitude I would fall down. I hadn't remained motionless for so very long either, but in a darkness where a man can't tell whether he is standing on his feet or his ears, the faculty of balance isn't much to be counted on. My heart stopped short when I felt myself sway, but I shifted one foot quickly, and there I was again. But that accursed foot had made a squeak.

The fellow listened for a moment, and then he yelled: "Who th' hell is in here?"

I didn't say a word, but just dropped down to the floor as easy as a sack of oats.

He listened for a time, and then bellowed out again: "Who's in here?" I supposed he figured that it wasn't one of his enemies, or they would have got him while he was swearing to himself over in the corner.

"Who's in here, by Gawd! Com along now, galoot, an' speak up er I'll begin t' bore leetle holes in yeh! Who er yeh, anyhow? Whistle some, naw, by Gawd, er I'll fair eat yeh!"

He was beginning to get mad as a wildcat. I could fairly hear that fellow lashing himself into a rage and getting more crazy every minute. All the kegs were up in his corner, and when I felt around with one hand I couldn't find a thing to get behind. Every second I expected to hear him

begin to work his gun, and if you have ever lain in the darkness and wondered at what precise spot the impending bullet would strike, you know
how I felt. So, when he yelled out again: "Who er yeh?" I spoke up and
said: "It's only me."

"Thunder!" cried he, in a roar like a bull, "Who's me? Give me yer hull
damn name an' pedigree, mister, if yeh ain't fond of a reg'lar howling,
helling row!"

"I'm from Houston," said I.

"Houston," said he, with a snort. "An' what er yeh doin' here, stranger?"

"I came out to the sale," I told him.

"Hum," said he; and then he remained still for some time over in his
end of the car.

I was congratulating myself that I ran no more chance of trouble with
this fiend, and that the whole thing was now a mere matter of waiting
for some merciful fate to let me out, when suddenly the fellow said:
"Mister!"

"Sir?" said I.

"Open that there door!"

"Er—what?"

"Open that there door!"

"Er—the door of the car?"

He began to froth at the mouth, I think. "Sure!" he roared. "Th' door
t' th' car! There hain't fifty doors here, be ther! Slid 'er open, or else,
mister, you be a goner, sure!" And then he cursed my ancestors for fifteen
generations.

"Well—but—look here," said I. "Ain't—look here—ain't they going to
shoot as soon as anybody opens that door? It—"

"None 'a yer damned business, stranger!" the fellow howled. "Open that
there door, er I'll everlastin'ly make er ventilator of yeh. Come on, now!
Step up!" He began to prowl over in my direction. "Where are yeh? Come
on now, galoot! Where are yeh? Oh, jest lemme lay my ol' gun ag'in yeh,
an' I'll fin' out! Step up!"

This cat-like approach in the darkness was too much for me. "Hold
on," said I; "I'll open the door."

He gave a grunt and paused. I got up and went over to the door.

"Now, stranger," the fellow said, "es soon es yeh open the door, jest step
enside an' watch Luke Burnham peel th' skin off er them skunks."

"But, look here—" said I.

"Stranger, this hain't no time t' arger! Open th' door!"

I put my hand on the door and prepared to slide my body along with it.
I had hoped to find it locked, but unfortunately it was not. When I gave

it a preliminary shake it rattled easily, and I could see that there was going to be no trouble in opening the door.

I turned toward the interior of the car for one last remonstrance. "Say, I haven't got anything to do with this thing. I'm just up here from Houston to go to the sale—"

But the fellow howled again: "Stranger, er you makin' a damn fool o' me? By the—"

"Hold on," said I. "I'll open the door."

I got all prepared, and then turned my head. "Are you ready?"

"Let 'er go!"

He was standing back in the car. I could see the dull glint of the revolvers in each hand.

"Let 'er go!" he said again.

I braced myself and put one hand out to reach the end of the door; then, with a groan, I pulled. The door slid open, and I fell on my hands and knees in the end of the car.

"Hell!" said the fellow. I turned my head. There was nothing to be seen but blue sky and green prairie and the little group of yellow board shanties with a red auction flag and a crowd of people in front of one of them.

The fellow swore and flung himself out of the car. He went prowling off toward the crowd, with his guns held barrels down and with his nervous fingers on the triggers. I followed him at a respectful distance.

As he came near to them he began to walk like a cat on wet pavements, lifting each leg a way up. "Where is he? Where is th' white-livered skunk what slammed thet door on me? Where is he? Where is he? Let 'im show hisself! He dassent! Where is he? Where is he?"

He went among them, bellowing in his bull fashion, and not a man moved. "Where's all these galoots what was goin' t' shoot at me? Where be they? Let 'em come! Let 'em show theirselves! Let 'em come at me! Oh, ther's them here as has got guns hangin' to 'em; but let 'em pull 'em! Let 'em pull 'em onc't! Jest let 'em tap 'em with their fingers, an' I'll drive a stove hole through every last one 'a their low-down hides! Lessee a man pull a gun! Lessee! An' lessee th' man what slammed th' door on me! Let 'im projuce hisself, th' —," and he cursed this unknown individual in language that was like black smoke.

But the men with guns remained silent and grave. The crowd for the most part gave him room enough to pitch a circus tent. When the train left, he was still roaring around after the man who had slammed the door.

"And so they didn't kill him, after all," said someone at the end of the narrative.

"Oh, yes; they got him that night," said the major, "in a saloon some-where. They got him all right."

April 12, 1896
[Brooklyn *Daily Eagle*, p. 19.]

THE LITTLE REGIMENT*

I

The fog made the clothes of the men of the column in the roadway seem of a luminous quality. It imparted to the heavy infantry overcoats a new color, a kind of blue which was so pale that a regiment might have been merely a long, low shadow in the mist. However, a muttering, one part grumble, three parts joke, hovered in the air above the thick ranks, and blended in an undertoned roar, which was the voice of the column.

The town on the southern shore of the little river loomed spectrally, a faint etching upon the gray cloud masses which were shifting with oily languor. A long row of guns upon the northern bank had been pitiless in their hatred, but a little battered belfry could be dimly seen still point-ing with invincible resolution toward the heavens.

The enclouded air vibrated with noises made by hidden colossal things. The infantry tramplings, the heavy rumbling of the artillery, made the earth speak of gigantic preparation. Guns on distant heights thundered from time to time with sudden, nervous roar, as if unable to endure in silence a knowledge of hostile troops massing, other guns going to position. These sounds, near and remote, defined an immense battleground, de-scribed the tremendous width of the stage of the prospective drama. The voices of the guns, slightly casual, unexcited in their challenges and warn-ings, could not destroy the unutterable eloquence of the word in the air, a meaning of impending struggle which made the breath halt at the lips.

The column in the roadway was ankle-deep in mud. The men swore piously at the rain which drizzled upon them, compelling them to stand always very erect in fear of the drops that would sweep in under their coat collars. The fog was as cold as wet clothes. The men stuffed their hands deep into their pockets, and huddled their muskets in their arms. The machinery of orders had rooted these soldiers deeply into the mud precisely as almighty nature roots mullein stalks.

They listened and speculated when a tumult of fighting came from the dim town across the river. When the noise lulled for a time they re-sumed their descriptions of the mud and graphically exaggerated the num-

* *The Little Regiment.*

ber of hours they had been kept waiting. The general commanding their division rode along the ranks, and they cheered admiringly, affectionately, crying out to him gleeful prophecies of the coming battle. Each man scanned him with a peculiarly keen personal interest, and afterward spoke of him with unquestioning devotion and confidence, narrating anecdotes which were mainly untrue.

When the jokers lifted the shrill voices which invariably belonged to them, flinging witticisms at their comrades, a loud laugh would sweep from rank to rank, and soldiers who had not heard would lean forward and demand repetition. When were borne past them some wounded men with gray and blood-smeared faces, and eyes that rolled in that helpless beseeching for assistance from the sky which comes with supreme pain, the soldiers in the mud watched intently, and from time to time asked of the bearers an account of the affair. Frequently they bragged of their corps, their division, their brigade, their regiment. Anon they referred to the mud and the cold drizzle. Upon this threshold of a wild scene of death they, in short, defied the proportion of events with that splendor of heedlessness which belongs only to veterans.

"Like a lot of wooden soldiers," swore Billie Dempster, moving his feet in the thick mass, and casting a vindictive glance indefinitely. "Standing in the mud for a hundred years."

"Oh, shut up!" murmured his brother Dan. The manner of his words implied that this fraternal voice near him was an indescribable bore.

"Why should I shut up?" demanded Billie.

"Because you're a fool," cried Dan, taking no time to debate it; "the biggest fool in the regiment."

There was but one man between them, and he was habituated. These insults from brother to brother had swept across his chest, flown past his face, many times during two long campaigns. Upon this occasion he simply grinned first at one, then at the other.

The way of these brothers was not an unknown topic in regimental gossip. They had enlisted simultaneously, with each sneering loudly at the other for doing it. They left their little town, and went forward with the flag, exchanging protestations of undying suspicion. In the camplife they so openly despised each other that, when entertaining quarrels were lacking, their companions often contrived situations calculated to bring forth display of this fraternal dislike.

Both were large-limbed, strong young men, and often fought with friends in camp unless one was near to interfere with the other. This latter happened rather frequently, because Dan, preposterously willing for any manner of combat, had a very great horror of seeing Billie in a fight; and Billie, almost odiously ready himself, simply refused to see Dan stripped to his shirt and with his fists aloft. This sat queerly upon them, and made them the objects of plots.

When Dan jumped through a ring of eager soldiers and dragged forth his raving brother by the arm, a thing often predicted would almost come to pass. When Billie performed the same office for Dan, the prediction would again miss fulfillment by an inch. But indeed they never fought together, although they were perpetually upon the verge.

They expressed longing for such conflict. As a matter of truth, they had at one time made full arrangement for it, but even with the encouragement and interest of half of the regiment they somehow failed to achieve collision.

If Dan became a victim of police duty, no jeering was so destructive to the feelings as Billie's comment. If Billie got a call to appear at the headquarters, none would so genially prophesy his complete undoing as Dan. Small misfortunes to one were, in truth, invariably greeted with hilarity by the other, who seemed to see in them great reinforcement of his opinion.

As soldiers, they expressed each for each a scorn intense and blasting. After a certain battle, Billie was promoted to corporal. When Dan was told of it, he seemed smitten dumb with astonishment and patriotic indignation. He stared in silence, while the dark blood rushed to Billie's forehead, and he shifted his weight from foot to foot. Dan at last found his tongue, and said: "Well, I'm durned!" If he had heard that an army mule had been appointed to the post of corps commander, his tone could not have had more derision in it. Afterward, he adopted a fervid insubordination, an almost religious reluctance to obey the new corporal's orders, which came near to developing the desired strife.

It is here finally to be recorded also that Dan, most ferociously profane in speech, very rarely swore in the presence of his brother; and that Billie, whose oaths came from his lips with the grace of falling pebbles, was seldom known to express himself in this manner when near his brother Dan.

At last the afternoon contained a suggestion of evening. Metallic cries rang suddenly from end to end of the column. They inspired at once a quick, businesslike adjustment. The long thing stirred in the mud. The men had hushed, and were looking across the river. A moment later the shadowy mass of pale blue figures was moving steadily toward the stream. There could be heard from the town a clash of swift fighting and cheering. The noise of the shooting coming through the heavy air had its sharpness taken from it, and sounded in thuds.

There was a halt upon the bank above the pontoons. When the column went winding down the incline, and streamed out upon the bridge, the fog had faded to a great degree, and in the clearer dusk the guns on a distant ridge were enabled to perceive the crossing. The long whirling outcries of the shells came into the air above the men. An occasional solid shot struck the surface of the river, and dashed into view a sudden vertical jet. The distance was subtly illuminated by the lightning from the deep-booming guns. One by one the batteries on the northern shore aroused, the innumerable guns bellowed in angry oration at the distant ridge. The rolling thunder crashed and reverberated as a wild surf sounds on a still night, and to this music the column marched across the pontoons.

The waters of the grim river curled away in a smile from the ends of the great boats, and slid swiftly beneath the planking. The dark, riddled walls of the town upreared before the troops, and from a region hidden by these hammered and tumbled houses came incessantly the yells and firings of a prolonged and close skirmish.

When Dan had called his brother a fool, his voice had been so decisive, so brightly assured, that many men had laughed, considering it to be great humor under the circumstances. The incident happened to rankle deep in Billie. It was not any strange thing that his brother had called him a fool. In fact, he often called him a fool with exactly the same amount of cheerful and prompt conviction, and before large audiences, too. Billie wondered in his own mind why he took such profound offence in this case; but, at any rate, as he slid down the bank and on to the bridge with his regiment, he was searching his knowledge for something that would pierce Dan's blithesome spirit. But he could contrive nothing at this time, and his impotency made the glance which he was once able to give his brother still more malignant.

The guns far and near were roaring a fearful and grand introduction for this column which was marching upon the stage of death. Billie felt it, but only in a numb way. His heart was cased in that curious dissonant metal which covers a man's emotions at such times. The terrible voices from the hills told him that in this wide conflict his life was an insignificant fact, and that his death would be an insignificant fact. They portended the whirlwind to which he would be as necessary as a butterfly's waved wing. The solemnity, the sadness of it came near enough to make him wonder why he was neither solemn nor sad. When his mind vaguely adjusted events according to their importance to him, it appeared that the uppermost thing was the fact that upon the eve of battle, and before many comrades, his brother had called him a fool.

Dan was in a particularly happy mood. "Hurray! Look at 'em shoot," he said, when the long witches' croon of the shells came into the air. It enraged Billie when he felt the little thorn in him, and saw at the same time that his brother had completely forgotten it.

The column went from the bridge into more mud. At this southern end there was a chaos of hoarse directions and commands. Darkness was coming upon the earth, and regiments were being hurried up the slippery bank. As Billie floundered in the black mud, amid the swearing, sliding crowd, he suddenly resolved that, in the absence of other means of hurting Dan, he would avoid looking at him, refrain from speaking to him, pay absolutely no heed to his existence; and this, done skillfully, would, he imagined, soon reduce his brother to a poignant sensitiveness.

At the top of the bank the column again halted and rearranged itself, as a man after a climb rearranges his clothing. Presently the great steel-backed brigade, an infinitely graceful thing in the rhythm and ease of its veteran movement, swung up a little narrow, slanting street.

Evening had come so swiftly that the fighting on the remote borders of the town was indicated by thin flashes of flame. Some building was on fire, and its reflection upon the clouds was an oval of delicate pink.

II

All demeanor of rural serenity had been wrenched violently from the little town by the guns and by the waves of men which had surged through it. The hand of war laid upon this village had in an instant changed it to a thing of remnants. It resembled the place of a monstrous shaking of the earth itself. The windows, now mere unsightly holes, made the tumbled and blackened dwellings seem skeletons. Doors lay splintered to fragments. Chimneys had flung their bricks everywhere. The artillery fire had not neglected the rows of gentle shade trees which had lined the streets. Branches and heavy trunks cluttered the mud in driftwood tangles, while a few shattered forms had contrived to remain dejectedly, mournfully upright. They expressed an innocence, a helplessness, which perforce created a pity for their happening into this cauldron of battle. Furthermore, there was under foot a vast collection of odd things reminiscent of the charge, the fight, the retreat. There were boxes and barrels filled with earth, behind which riflemen had lain snugly, and in these little trenches were the dead in blue with the dead in gray, the poses eloquent of the struggles for possession of the town, until the history of the whole conflict was written plainly in the streets.

And yet the spirit of this little city, its quaint individuality, poised in the air above the ruins, defying the guns, the sweeping volleys; holding in contempt those avaricious blazes which had attacked many dwellings. The hard earthen sidewalks proclaimed the games that had been played there during long lazy days, in the careful shadows of the trees. "General Merchandise," in faint letters upon a long board, had to be read with a slanted glance, for the sign dangled by one end; but the porch of the old store was a palpable legend of wide-hatted men, smoking.

This subtle essence, this soul of the life that had been, brushed like invisible wings the thoughts of the men in the swift columns that came up from the river.

In the darkness a loud and endless humming arose from the great blue crowds bivouacked in the streets. From time to time a sharp spatter of firing from far picket lines entered this bass chorus. The smell from the smoldering ruins floated on the cold night breeze.

Dan, seated ruefully upon the doorstep of a shot-pierced house, was proclaiming the campaign badly managed. Orders had been issued forbidding campfires.

Suddenly he ceased his oration and, scanning the group of his comrades, said: "Where's Billie? Do you know?"

"Gone on picket."

"Get out! Has he?" said Dan. "No business to go on picket. Why don't some of them other corporals take their turn?"

A bearded private was smoking his pipe of confiscated tobacco, seated comfortably upon a horsehair trunk which he had dragged from the house. He observed: "*Was* his turn."

"No such thing," cried Dan. He and the man on the horsehair trunk held discussion in which Dan stoutly maintained that if his brother had been sent on picket it was an injustice. He ceased his argument when another soldier, upon whose arms could faintly be seen the two stripes of a corporal, entered the circle. "Humph," said Dan, "where you been?"

The corporal made no answer. Presently Dan said: "Billie, where you been?"

His brother did not seem to hear these inquiries. He glanced at the house which towered above them, and remarked casually to the man on the horsehair trunk: "Funny, ain't it? After the pelting this town got, you'd think there wouldn't be one brick left on another."

"Oh," said Dan, glowering at his brother's back. "Getting mighty smart, ain't you?"

The absence of campfires allowed the evening to make apparent its quality of faint silver light in which the blue clothes of the throng became black, and the faces became white expanses, void of expression. There was considerable excitement a short distance from the group around the doorstep. A soldier had chanced upon a hoop skirt, and arrayed in it he was performing a dance amid the applause of his companions. Billie and a greater part of the men immediately poured over there to witness the exhibition.

"What's the matter with Billie?" demanded Dan of the man upon the horsehair trunk.

"How do I know?" rejoined the other in mild resentment. He arose and walked away. When he returned he said briefly, in a weather-wise tone, that it would rain during the night.

Dan took a seat upon one end of the horsehair trunk. He was facing the crowd around the dancer, which in its hilarity swung this way and that way. At times he imagined that he could recognize his brother's face.

He and the man on the other end of the trunk thoughtfully talked of the army's position. To their minds, infantry and artillery were in a most precarious jumble in the streets of the town; but they did not grow nervous over it, for they were used to having the army appear in a precarious jumble to their minds. They had learned to accept such puzzling situations as a consequence of their position in the ranks, and were now usually in possession of a simple but perfectly immovable faith that somebody understood the jumble. Even if they had been convinced that the army was a headless monster, they would merely have nodded with the veteran's singular cynicism. It was none of their business as soldiers. Their duty was to grab sleep and food when occasion permitted, and cheerfully fight wherever their feet were planted until more orders came. This was a task sufficiently absorbing.

They spoke of other corps, and, this talk being confidential, their voices dropped to tones of awe. "The Ninth"—"The First"—"The Fifth"—"The Sixth"—"The Third"—the simple numerals rang with eloquence, each having a meaning which was to float through many years as no intangible arithmetical mist, but as pregnant with individuality as the names of cities.

Of their own corps they spoke with a deep veneration, an idolatry, a supreme confidence which apparently would not blanch to see it matched against everything.

It was as if their respect for other corps was due partly to a wonder that organizations not blessed with their own famous numeral could take such an interest in war. They could prove that their division was the best in the corps, and that their brigade was the best in the division. And their regiment—it was plain that no fortune of life was equal to the chance which caused a man to be born, so to speak, into this command, the keystone of the defending arch.

At times Dan covered with insults the character of a vague, unnamed general to whose petulance and busybody spirit he ascribed the order which made hot coffee impossible.

Dan said that victory was certain in the coming battle. The other man seemed rather dubious. He remarked upon the fortified line of hills, which had impressed him even from the other side of the river. "Shucks," said Dan. "Why, we—" He pictured a splendid overflowing of these hills by the sea of men in blue. During the period of this conversation Dan's glance searched the merry throng about the dancer. Above the babble of voices in the street a faraway thunder could sometimes be heard—evidently from the very edge of the horizon—the boom-boom of restless guns.

III

Ultimately the night deepened to the tone of black velvet. The outlines of the fireless camp were like the faint drawings upon ancient tapestry. The glint of a rifle, the shine of a button, might have been of threads of silver and gold sewn upon the fabric of the night. There was little presented to the vision, but to a sense more subtle there was discernible in the atmosphere something like a pulse; a mystic beating which would have told a stranger of the presence of a giant thing—the slumbering mass of regiments and batteries.

With fires forbidden, the floor of a dry old kitchen was thought to be a good exchange for the cold earth of December, even if a shell had exploded in it and knocked it so out of shape that when a man lay curled in his blanket his last waking thought was likely to be of the wall that bellied out above him, as if strongly anxious to topple upon the score of soldiers.

Billie looked at the bricks ever about to descend in a shower upon his face, listened to the industrious pickets plying their rifles on the border of the town, imagined some measure of the din of the coming battle, thought of Dan and Dan's chagrin, and, rolling over in his blanket, went to sleep with satisfaction.

At an unknown hour he was aroused by the creaking of boards. Lifting himself upon his elbow, he saw a sergeant prowling among the sleeping forms. The sergeant carried a candle in an old brass candlestick. He would have resembled some old farmer on an unusual midnight tour if it were not for the significance of his gleaming buttons and striped sleeves.

Billie blinked stupidly at the light until his mind returned from the journeys of slumber. The sergeant stooped among the unconscious soldiers, holding the candle close, and peering into each face.

"Hello, Haines," said Billie. "Relief?"

"Hello, Billie," said the sergeant. "Special duty."

"Dan got to go?"

"Jameson, Hunter, McCormack, D. Dempster. Yes. Where is he?"

"Over there by the winder," said Billie, gesturing. "What is it for, Haines?"

"You don't think I know, do you?" demanded the sergeant. He began to pipe sharply but cheerily at men upon the floor. "Come, Mac, get up here. Here's a special for you. Wake up, Jameson. Come along, Dannie, me boy."

Each man at once took this call to duty as a personal affront. They pulled themselves out of their blankets, rubbed their eyes, and swore at whoever was responsible. "Them's orders," cried the sergeant. "Come! Get out of here." An undetailed head with disheveled hair thrust out from a blanket, and a sleepy voice said: "Shut up, Haines, and go home."

When the detail clanked out of the kitchen, all but one of the remaining men seemed to be again asleep. Billie, leaning on his elbow, was gazing into darkness. When the footsteps died to silence, he curled himself into his blanket.

At the first cool lavender lights of daybreak he aroused again, and scanned his recumbent companions. Seeing a wakeful one he asked: "Is Dan back yet?"

The man said: "Hain't seen 'im."

Billie put both hands behind his head, and scowled into the air. "Can't see the use of these cussed details in the nighttime," he muttered in his most unreasonable tones. "Darn nuisances. Why can't they—?" He grumbled at length and graphically.

When Dan entered with the squad, however, Billie was convincingly asleep.

IV

The regiment trotted in double time along the street, and the colonel seemed to quarrel over the right of way with many artillery officers. Batteries were waiting in the mud, and the men of them, exasperated by the bustle of this ambitious infantry, shook their fists from saddle and caisson, exchanging all manner of taunts and jests. The slanted guns continued to look reflectively at the ground.

On the outskirts of the crumbled town a fringe of blue figures was firing into the fog. The regiment swung out into skirmish lines, and the fringe of blue figures departed, turning their backs and going joyfully around the flank.

The bullets began a low moan off toward a ridge which loomed faintly in the heavy mist. When the swift crescendo had reached its climax, the missiles zipped just overhead, as if piercing an invisible curtain. A battery on the hill was crashing with such tumult that it was as if the guns had quarreled and had fallen pell-mell and snarling upon each other. The shells howled on their journey toward the town. From short range distance there came a spatter of musketry, sweeping along an invisible line and making faint sheets of orange light.

Some in the new skirmish lines were beginning to fire at various shadows discerned in the vapor—forms of men suddenly revealed by some humor of the laggard masses of clouds. The crackle of musketry began to dominate the purring of the hostile bullets. Dan, in the front rank, held his rifle poised, and looked into the fog keenly, coldly, with the air of a sportsman. His nerves were so steady that it was as if they had been drawn from his body, leaving him merely a muscular machine; but his numb heart was somehow beating to the pealing march of the fight.

The waving skirmish line went backward and forward, ran this way and that way. Men got lost in the fog, and men were found again. Once they got too close to the formidable ridge, and the thing burst out as if repulsing a general attack. Once another blue regiment was apprehended on the very edge of firing into them. Once a friendly battery began an elaborate and scientific process of extermination. Always as busy as brokers, the men slid here and there over the plain, fighting their foes, escaping from their friends, leaving a history of many movements in the wet yellow turf, cursing the atmosphere, blazing away every time they could identify the enemy.

In one mystic changing of the fog, as if the fingers of spirits were drawing aside these draperies, a small group of the gray skirmishers, silent, statuesque, was suddenly disclosed to Dan and those about him. So vivid and near were they that there was something uncanny in the revelation.

There might have been a second of mutual staring. Then each rifle in each group was at the shoulder. As Dan's glance flashed along the barrel of his weapon, the figure of a man suddenly loomed as if the musket had been a telescope. The short black beard, the slouch hat, the pose of the man as he sighted to shoot, made a quick picture in Dan's mind. The same moment, it would seem, he pulled his own trigger, and the man, smitten, lurched forward, while his exploding rifle made a slanting crimson streak in the air, and the slouch hat fell before the body. The billows of the fog, governed by singular impulses, rolled between.

"You got that feller sure enough," said a comrade to Dan. Dan looked at him absent-mindedly.

v

When the next morning calmly displayed another fog, the men of the regiment exchanged eloquent comments; but they did not abuse it at length, because the streets of the town now contained enough galloping aides to make three troops of cavalry, and they knew that they had come to the verge of the great fight.

Dan conversed with the man who had once possessed a horsehair trunk; but they did not mention the line of hills which had furnished them in more careless moments with an agreeable topic. They avoided it now as condemned men do the subject of death, and yet the thought of it stayed in their eyes as they looked at each other and talked gravely of other things.

The expectant regiment heaved a long sigh of relief when the sharp

call, "Fall in!" repeated indefinitely, arose in the streets. It was inevitable
that a bloody battle was to be fought, and they wanted to get it off their
minds. They were, however, doomed again to spend a long period planted
firmly in the mud. They craned their necks, and wondered where some
of the other regiments were going.

At last the mists rolled carelessly away. Nature made at this time all
provisions to enable foes to see each other, and immediately the roar of
guns resounded from every hill. The endless cracking of the skirmishers
swelled to rolling crashes of musketry. Shells screamed with panther-like
noises at the houses. Dan looked at the man of the horsehair trunk, and
the man said: "Well, here she comes!"

The tenor voices of younger officers and the deep and hoarse voices
of the older ones rang in the streets. These cries pricked like spurs. The
masses of men vibrated from the suddenness with which they were plunged
into the situation of troops about to fight. That the orders were long expected did not concern the emotion.

Simultaneous movement was imparted to all these thick bodies of men
and horses that lay in the town. Regiment after regiment swung rapidly
into the streets that faced the sinister ridge.

This exodus was theatrical. The little sober-hued village had been like
the cloak which disguises the king of drama. It was now put aside, and
an army, splendid thing of steel and blue, stood forth in the sunlight.

Even the soldiers in the heavy columns drew deep breaths at the sight,
more majestic than they had dreamed. The heights of the enemy's position were crowded with men who resembled people come to witness some
mighty pageant. But as the column moved steadily to their positions, the
guns, matter-of-fact warriors, doubled their number, and shells burst with
red thrilling tumult on the crowded plain. One came into the ranks of the
regiment, and after the smoke and the wrath of it had faded, leaving motionless figures, every one stormed according to the limits of his vocabulary,
for veterans detest being killed when they are not busy.

The regiment sometimes looked sideways at its brigade companions,
composed of men who had never been in battle; but no frozen blood could
withstand the heat of the splendor of this army before the eyes on the
plain, these lines so long that the flanks were little streaks, this mass of
men of one intention. The recruits carried themselves heedlessly. At the
rear was an idle battery, and three artillerymen in a foolish row on
a caisson nudged each other and grinned at the recruits. "You'll catch
it pretty soon," they called out. They were impersonally gleeful, as if they
themselves were not also likely to catch it pretty soon. But with this picture of an army in their hearts, the new men perhaps felt the devotion
which the drops may feel for the wave; they were of its power and glory;

they smiled jauntily at the foolish row of gunners, and told them to go to blazes.

The column trotted across some little bridges, and spread quickly into lines of battle. Before them was a bit of plain, and back of the plain was the ridge. There was no time left for considerations. The men were staring at the plain, mightily wondering how it would feel to be out there, when a brigade in advance yelled and charged. The hill was all gray smoke and firepoints.

That fierce elation in the terrors of war, catching a man's heart and making it burn with such ardor that he becomes capable of dying, flashed in the faces of the men like colored lights, and made them resemble leashed animals, eager, ferocious, daunting at nothing. The line was really in its first leap before the wild, hoarse crying of the orders.

The greed for close quarters which is the emotion of a bayonet charge came then into the minds of the men and developed until it was a madness. The field, with its faded grass of a Southern winter, seemed to this fury miles in width.

High, slow-moving masses of smoke, with an odor of burning cotton, engulfed the line until the men might have been swimmers. Before them the ridge, the shore of this gray sea, was outlined, crossed, and recrossed by sheets of flame. The howl of the battle arose to the noise of innumerable wind demons.

The line, galloping, scrambling, plunging like a herd of wounded horses, went over a field that was sown with corpses, the records of other charges.

Directly in front of the black-faced, whooping Dan, carousing in this onward sweep like a new kind of fiend, a wounded man appeared, raising his shattered body, and staring at this rush of men down upon him. It seemed to occur to him that he was to be trampled; he made a desperate, piteous effort to escape; then finally huddled in a waiting heap. Dan and the soldier near him widened the interval between them without looking down, without appearing to heed the wounded man. This little clump of blue seemed to reel past them as boulders reel past a train.

Bursting through a smoke-wave, the scampering, unformed bunches came upon the wreck of the brigade that had preceded them, a floundering mass stopped afar from the hill by the swirling volleys.

It was as if a necromancer had suddenly shown them a picture of the fate which awaited them; but the line with muscular spasm hurled itself over this wreckage and onward, until men were stumbling amid the relics of other assaults, the point where the fire from the ridge consumed.

The men, panting, perspiring, with crazed faces, tried to push against it; but it was as if they had come to a wall. The wave halted, shuddered in an agony from the quick struggle of its two desires, then toppled, and broke into a fragmentary thing which has no name.

Veterans could now at last be distinguished from recruits. The new regiments were instantly gone, lost, scattered, as if they never had been. But the sweeping failure of the charge, the battle, could not make the veterans forget their business. With a last throe, the band of maniacs drew itself up and blazed a volley at the hill, insignificant to those iron entrenchments, but nevertheless expressing that singular final despair which enables men coolly to defy the walls of a city of death.

After this episode the men renamed their command. They called it the Little Regiment.

VI

"I seen Dan shoot a feller yesterday. Yes sir. I'm sure it was him that done it. And maybe he thinks about that feller now, and wonders if *he* tumbled down just about the same way. Them things come up in a man's mind."

Bivouac fires upon the sidewalks, in the streets, in the yards, threw high their wavering reflections, which examined, like slim, red fingers, the dingy, scarred walls and the piles of tumbled brick. The droning of voices again arose from great blue crowds.

The odor of frying bacon, the fragrance from countless little coffee pails floated among the ruins. The rifles, stacked in the shadows, emitted flashes of steely light. Wherever a flag lay horizontally from one stack to another was the bed of an eagle which had led men into the mystic smoke.

The men about a particular fire were engaged in holding in check their jovial spirits. They moved whispering around the blaze, although they looked at it with a certain fine contentment, like laborers after a day's hard work.

There was one who sat apart. They did not address him save in tones suddenly changed. They did not regard him directly, but always in little sidelong glances.

At last a soldier from a distant fire came into this circle of light. He studied for a time the man who sat apart. Then he hesitatingly stepped closer, and said: "Got any news, Dan?"

"No," said Dan.

The newcomer shifted his feet. He looked at the fire, at the sky, at the other men, at Dan. His face expressed a curious despair; his tongue was plainly in rebellion. Finally, however, he contrived to say: "Well, there's some chance yet, Dan. Lots of the wounded are still lying out there, you know. There's some chance yet."

"Yes," said Dan.

The soldier shifted his feet again, and looked miserably into the air. After another struggle he said: "Well, there's some chance yet, Dan." He moved hastily away.

One of the men of the squad, perhaps encouraged by this example, now approached the still figure. "No news yet, hey?" he said, after coughing behind his hand.

"No," said Dan.

"Well," said the man, "I've been thinking of how he was fretting about you the night you went on special duty. You recollect? Well, sir, I was surprised. He couldn't say enough about it. I swan, I don't believe he slep' a wink after you left, but just lay awake cussing special duty and worrying. I was surprised. But there he lay cussing. He—"

Dan made a curious sound, as if a stone had wedged in his throat. He said: "Shut up, will you?"

Afterward the men would not allow his moody contemplation of the fire to be interrupted.

"Oh, let him alone, can't you?"

"Come away from there, Casey!"

"Say, can't you leave him be?"

They moved with reverence about the immovable figure, with its countenance of mask-like invulnerability.

VII

After the red round eye of the sun had stared long at the little plain and its burden, darkness, a sable mercy, came heavily upon it, and the wan hands of the dead were no longer seen in strange frozen gestures.

The heights in front of the plain shone with tiny campfires, and from the town in the rear, small shimmerings ascended from the blazes of the bivouac. The plain was a black expanse upon which, from time to time, dots of light, lanterns, floated slowly here and there. These fields were long steeped in grim mystery.

Suddenly, upon one dark spot, there was a resurrection. A strange thing had been groaning there, prostrate. Then it suddenly dragged itself to a sitting posture, and became a man.

The man stared stupidly for a moment at the lights on the hill, then turned and contemplated the faint coloring over the town. For some moments he remained thus, staring with dull eyes, his face unemotional, wooden.

Finally he looked around him at the corpses dimly to be seen. No change flashed into his face upon viewing these men. They seemed to suggest merely that his information concerning himself was not too complete. He ran his fingers over his arms and chest, bearing always the air of an idiot upon a bench at an almshouse door.

Finding no wound in his arms nor in his chest, he raised his hand to his head, and the fingers came away with some dark liquid upon them. Holding these fingers close to his eyes, he scanned them in the same stupid fashion, while his body gently swayed.

The soldier rolled his eyes again toward the town. When he arose, his clothing peeled from the frozen ground like wet paper. Hearing the sound of it, he seemed to see reason for deliberation. He paused and looked at the ground, then at his trousers, then at the ground.

Finally he went slowly off toward the faint reflection, holding his hands palm outward before him, and walking in the manner of a blind man.

VIII

The immovable Dan again sat unaddressed in the midst of comrades who did not joke aloud. The dampness of the usual morning fog seemed to make the little campfires furious.

Suddenly a cry arose in the streets, a shout of amazement and delight. The men making breakfast at the fire looked up quickly. They broke forth in clamorous exclamation: "Well! Of all things! Dan! Dan! Look who's coming! Oh, Dan!"

Dan the silent raised his eyes and saw a man, with a bandage of the size of a helmet about his head, receiving a furious demonstration from the company. He was shaking hands, and explaining and haranguing to a high degree.

Dan started. His face of bronze flushed to his temples. He seemed about to leap from the ground, but then suddenly he sank back, and resumed his impassive gazing.

The men were in a flurry. They looked from one to the other. "Dan! Look! See who's coming!" some cried again. "Dan! Look!"

He scowled at last, and moved his shoulders sullenly. "Well, don't I know it?"

But they could not be convinced that his eyes were in service. "Dan! Why can't you look? See who's coming!"

He made a gesture then of irritation and rage. "Curse it! Don't I know it?"

The man with a bandage of the size of a helmet moved forward, always shaking hands and explaining. At times his glance wandered to Dan, who saw with his eyes riveted.

After a series of shiftings, it occurred naturally that the man with the bandage was very near to the man who saw the flames. He paused, and there was a little silence. Finally he said: "Hello, Dan."

"Hello, Billie."

June, 1896
[*McClure's Magazine*, Vol. 7, pp. 12–22.]

THE VETERAN*

Out of the low window could be seen three hickory trees placed irregularly in a meadow that was resplendent in springtime green. Farther away, the old, dismal belfry of the village church loomed over the pines. A horse meditating in the shade of one of the hickories lazily swished his tail. The warm sunshine made an oblong of vivid yellow on the floor of the grocery.

"Could you see the whites of their eyes?" said the man who was seated on a soapbox.

"Nothing of the kind," replied old Henry warmly. "Just a lot of flitting figures, and I let go at where they 'peared to be the thickest. Bang!"

"Mr. Fleming," said the grocer—his deferential voice expressed somehow the old man's exact social weight—"Mr. Fleming, you never was frightened much in them battles, was you?"

The veteran looked down and grinned. Observing his manner, the entire group tittered. "Well, I guess I was," he answered finally. "Pretty well scared, sometimes. Why, in my first battle I thought the sky was falling down. I thought the world was coming to an end. You bet I was scared."

Every one laughed. Perhaps it seemed strange and rather wonderful to them that a man should admit the thing, and in the tone of their laughter there was probably more admiration than if old Fleming had declared that he had always been a lion. Moreover, they knew that he had ranked as an orderly sergeant, and so their opinion of his heroism was fixed. None, to be sure, knew how an orderly sergeant ranked, but then it was understood to be somewhere just shy of a major general's stars. So when old Henry admitted that he had been frightened, there was a laugh.

"The trouble was," said the old man, "I thought they were all shooting at me. Yes, sir, I thought every man in the other army was aiming at me in particular, and only me. And it seemed so darned unreasonable, you know. I wanted to explain to 'em what an almighty good fellow I was, because I thought then they might quit all trying to hit me. But I couldn't explain, and they kept on being unreasonable—blim!—blam!—bang! So I run!"

Two little triangles of wrinkles appeared at the corners of his eyes. Evidently he appreciated some comedy in this recital. Down near his feet, however, little Jim, his grandson, was visibly horror-stricken. His hands were clasped nervously, and his eyes were wide with astonishment at this terrible scandal, his most magnificent grandfather telling such a thing.

The Little Regiment.

"That was at Chancellorsville. Of course, afterward I got kind of used to it. A man does. Lots of men, though, seem to feel all right from the start. I did, as soon as I 'got on to it,' as they say now; but at first I was pretty flustered. Now, there was young Jim Conklin, old Si Conklin's son —that used to keep the tannery—you none of you recollect him—well, he went into it from the start just as if he was born to it. But with me it was different. I had to get used to it."

When little Jim walked with his grandfather he was in the habit of skipping along on the stone pavement in front of the three stores and the hotel of the town and betting that he could avoid the cracks. But upon this day he walked soberly, with his hand gripping two of his grandfather's fingers. Sometimes he kicked abstractedly at dandelions that curved over the walk. Any one could see that he was much troubled.

"There's Sickles's colt over in the medder, Jimmie," said the old man. "Don't you wish you owned one like him?"

"Um," said the boy, with a strange lack of interest. He continued his reflections. Then finally he ventured: "Grandpa—now—was that true what you was telling those men?"

"What?" asked the grandfather. "What was I telling them?"

"Oh, about your running."

"Why, yes, that was true enough, Jimmie. It was my first fight, and there was an awful lot of noise, you know."

Jimmie seemed dazed that this idol, of its own will, should so totter. His stout boyish idealism was injured.

Presently the grandfather said: "Sickles's colt is going for a drink. Don't you wish you owned Sickles's colt, Jimmie?"

The boy merely answered: "He ain't as nice as our'n." He lapsed then into another moody silence.

One of the hired men, a Swede, desired to drive to the county-seat for purposes of his own. The old man loaned a horse and an unwashed buggy. It appeared later that one of the purposes of the Swede was to get drunk.

After quelling some boisterous frolic of the farm hands and boys in the garret, the old man had that night gone peacefully to sleep, when he was aroused by clamoring at the kitchen door. He grabbed his trousers, and they waved out behind as he dashed forward. He could hear the voice of the Swede, screaming and blubbering. He pushed the wooden button, and, as the door flew open, the Swede, a maniac, stumbled inward, chattering, weeping, still screaming. "De barn fire! Fire! Fire! De barn fire! Fire! Fire! Fire!"

There was a swift and indescribable change in the old man. His face ceased instantly to be a face; it became a mask, a gray thing, with horror written about the mouth and eyes. He hoarsely shouted at the foot of the little rickety stairs, and immediately, it seemed, there came down an avalanche of men. No one knew that during this time the old lady had been standing in her night clothes at the bedroom door, yelling: "What's th' matter? What's th' matter? What's th' matter?"

When they dashed toward the barn it presented to their eyes its usual appearance, solemn, rather mystic in the black night. The Swede's lantern was overturned at a point some yards in front of the barn doors. It contained a wild little conflagration of its own, and even in their excitement some of those who ran felt a gentle secondary vibration of the thrifty part of their minds at sight of this overturned lantern. Under ordinary circumstances it would have been a calamity.

But the cattle in the barn were trampling, trampling, trampling, and above this noise could be heard a humming like the song of innumerable bees. The old man hurled aside the great doors, and a yellow flame leaped out at one corner and sped and wavered frantically up the old gray wall. It was glad, terrible, this single flame, like the wild banner of deadly and triumphant foes.

The motley crowd from the garret had come with all the pails of the farm. They flung themselves upon the well. It was a leisurely old machine, long dwelling in indolence. It was in the habit of giving out water with a sort of reluctance. The men stormed at it, cursed it; but it continued to allow the buckets to be filled only after the wheezy windlass had howled many protests at the mad-handed men.

With his opened knife in his hand old Fleming himself had gone headlong into the barn, where the stifling smoke swirled with the air currents, and where could be heard in its fullness the terrible chorus of the flames, laden with tones of hate and death, a hymn of wonderful ferocity.

He flung a blanket over an old mare's head, cut the halter close to the manger, led the mare to the door, and fairly kicked her out to safety. He returned with the same blanket, and rescued one of the workhorses. He took five horses out, and then came out himself, with his clothes bravely on fire. He had no whiskers, and very little hair on his head. They soused five pailfuls of water on him. His eldest son made a clean miss with the sixth pailful, because the old man had turned and was running down the decline and around to the basement of the barn, where were the stanchions of the cows. Some one noticed at the time that he ran very lamely, as if one of the frenzied horses had smashed his hip.

The cows, with their heads held in the heavy stanchions, had thrown themselves, strangled themselves, tangled themselves: done everything which the ingenuity of their exuberant fear could suggest to them.

Here, as at the well, the same thing happened to every man save one.

Their hands went mad. They became incapable of everything save the power to rush into dangerous situations.

The old man released the cow nearest the door, and she, blind drunk with terror, crashed into the Swede. The Swede had been running to and fro babbling. He carried an empty milk pail, to which he clung with an unconscious, fierce enthusiasm. He shrieked like one lost as he went under the cow's hoofs, and the milk pail, rolling across the floor, made a flash of silver in the gloom.

Old Fleming took a fork, beat off the cow, and dragged the paralyzed Swede to the open air. When they had rescued all the cows save one, which had so fastened herself that she could not be moved an inch, they returned to the front of the barn and stood sadly, breathing like men who had reached the final point of human effort.

Many people had come running. Someone had even gone to the church, and now, from the distance, rang the tocsin note of the old bell. There was a long flare of crimson on the sky, which made remote people speculate as to the whereabouts of the fire.

The long flames sang their drumming chorus in voices of the heaviest bass. The wind whirled clouds of smoke and cinders into the faces of the spectators. The form of the old barn was outlined in black amid these masses of orange-hued flames.

And then came this Swede again, crying as one who is the weapon of the sinister fates. "De colts! De colts! You have forgot de colts!"

Old Fleming staggered. It was true; they had forgotten the two colts in the box stalls at the back of the barn. "Boys," he said, "I must try to get 'em out." They clamored about him then, afraid for him, afraid of what they should see. Then they talked wildly each to each. "Why, it's sure death!" "He would never get out!" "Why, it's suicide for a man to go in there!" Old Fleming stared absent-mindedly at the open doors. "The poor little things," he said. He rushed into the barn.

When the roof fell in, a great funnel of smoke swarmed toward the sky, as if the old man's mighty spirit, released from its body—a little bottle—had swelled like the genie of fable. The smoke was tinted rose-hue from the flames, and perhaps the unutterable midnights of the universe will have no power to daunt the color of this soul.

August, 1896

[*McClure's Magazine,* Vol. 7, pp. 222–224.]

THE SNAKE

Where the path wended across the ridge, the bushes of huckleberry and sweet fern swarmed at it in two curling waves until it was a mere winding line traced through a tangle. There was no interference by clouds, and as the rays of the sun fell full upon the ridge, they called into voice innumerable insects which chanted the heat of the summer day in steady, throbbing, unending chorus.

A man and a dog came from the laurel thickets of the valley where the white brook brawled with the rocks. They followed the deep line of the path across the ridge. The dog—a large lemon-and-white setter—walked, tranquilly meditative, at his master's heels.

Suddenly from some unknown and yet near place in advance there came a dry, shrill, whistling rattle that smote motion instantly from the limbs of the man and the dog. Like the fingers of a sudden death, this sound seemed to touch the man at the nape of the neck, at the top of the spine, and change him, as swift as thought, to a statue of listening horror, surprise, rage. The dog, too—the same icy hand was laid upon him, and he stood crouched and quivering, his jaw dropping, the froth of terror upon his lips, the light of hatred in his eyes.

Slowly the man moved his hands toward the bushes, but his glance did not turn from the place made sinister by the warning rattle. His fingers, unguided, sought for a stick of weight and strength. Presently they closed about one that seemed adequate, and holding this weapon poised before him, the man moved slowly forward, glaring. The dog, with his nervous nostrils fairly fluttering, moved warily, one foot at a time, after his master.

But when the man came upon the snake, his body underwent a shock as if from a revelation, as if after all he had been ambushed. With a blanched face, he sprang forward, and his breath came in strained gasps, his chest heaving as if he were in the performance of an extraordinary muscular trial. His arm with the stick made a spasmodic, defensive gesture.

The snake had apparently been crossing the path in some mystic travel when to his sense there came the knowledge of the coming of his foes. The dull vibration perhaps informed him, and he flung his body to face the danger. He had no knowledge of paths; he had no wit to tell him to slink noiselessly into the bushes. He knew that his implacable enemies were approaching; no doubt they were seeking him, hunting him. And so he cried his cry, an incredibly swift jangle of tiny bells, as burdened with pathos as the hammering upon quaint cymbals by the Chinese at war—for, indeed, it was usually his death music.

"Beware! Beware! Beware!"

The man and the snake confronted each other. In the man's eyes were hatred and fear. In the snake's eyes were hatred and fear. These enemies maneuvered, each preparing to kill. It was to be a battle without mercy. Neither knew of mercy for such a situation. In the man was all the wild strength of the terror of his ancestors, of his race, of his kind. A deadly repulsion had been handed from man to man through long dim centuries. This was another detail of a war that had begun evidently when first there were men and snakes. Individuals who do not participate in this strife incur the investigations of scientists. Once there was a man and a snake who were friends, and at the end, the man lay dead with the marks of the snake's caress just over his East Indian heart. In the formation of devices, hideous and horrible, Nature reached her supreme point in the making of the snake, so that priests who really paint hell well fill it with snakes instead of fire. These curving forms, these scintillant colorings create at once, upon sight, more relentless animosities than do shake barbaric tribes. To be born a snake is to be thrust into a place a-swarm with formidable foes. To gain an appreciation of it, view hell as pictured by priests who are really skillful.

As for this snake in the pathway, there was a double curve some inches back of its head, which, merely by the potency of its lines, made the man feel with tenfold eloquence the touch of the death-fingers at the nape of his neck. The reptile's head was waving slowly from side to side and its hot eyes flashed like little murder-lights. Always in the air was the dry, shrill whistling of the rattles.

"Beware! Beware! Beware!"

The man made a preliminary feint with his stick. Instantly the snake's heavy head and neck were bent back on the double curve and instantly the snake's body shot forward in a low, straight, hard spring. The man jumped with a convulsive chatter and swung his stick. The blind, sweeping blow fell upon the snake's head and hurled him so that steel-colored plates were for a moment uppermost. But he rallied swiftly, agilely, and again the head and neck bent back to the double curve, and the steaming, wide-open mouth made its desperate effort to reach its enemy. This attack, it could be seen, was despairing, but it was nevertheless impetuous, gallant, ferocious, of the same quality as the charge of the lone chief when the walls of white faces close upon him in the mountains. The stick swung unerringly again, and the snake, mutilated, torn, whirled himself into the last coil.

And now the man went sheer raving mad from the emotions of his forefathers and from his own. He came to close quarters. He gripped the stick with his two hands and made it speed like a flail. The snake, tumbling in the anguish of final despair, fought, bit, flung itself upon this stick which was taking its life.

At the end, the man clutched his stick and stood watching in silence. The dog came slowly, and with infinite caution stretched his nose forward, sniffing. The hair upon his neck and back moved and ruffled as if a sharp wind was blowing. The last muscular quivers of the snake were causing the rattles to still sound their treble cry, the shrill, ringing war chant and hymn of the grave of the thing that faces foes at once countless, implacable, and superior.

"Well, Rover," said the man, turning to the dog with a grin of victory, "we'll carry Mr. Snake home to show the girls."

His hands still trembled from the strain of the encounter, but he pried with his stick under the body of the snake and hoisted the limp thing upon it. He resumed his march along the path, and the dog walked, tranquilly meditative, at his master's heels.

August, 1896
[The Pocket Magazine, Vol. 2, pp. 125–132.]

RAFT STORY*

Captain William B. Hiller sails the bark *Tillie B.* His ship now lies in Erie Basin and both the captain and the *Tillie B.* are just recovering from a most singular adventure of the sea. When questioned, the captain was reticent; he is a sane and honest captain in the American merchant marine and he objects to gaining reputation as a purveyor of sea yarns. But there are many old salts in his forecastle and no old salt that lives could let slip a chance to tell what they saw when 500 miles off the coast of Labrador on the 1st day of last July.

It seems that the *Tillie B.* was bowling along on her course before a fair wind when the man forward espied something long and black some two points off the starboard bow. It was monstrous in size and lay quietly on the water awaiting the ship. The man at the bow was nonplussed for a moment. The thing was not land. It was not a ship. It was not a whale. It was not anything that enters into the ordinary vocabulary of a man at the bow. It was a mystery; that is all it could be called. Recollecting his business the lookout cried: "Something mysterious, sir, pint off the sta'board!"

The mate went to the rail and looking at the thing said: "It is not land! It is not a ship! It is not a whale! Then what is it?"

* By permission of Alfred A. Knopf, Inc. Hitherto unpublished in book form.

Everybody on deck went to the rail and looking at the thing said: "It is not land! It is not a ship! It is not a whale! Then what is it?"

Meanwhile the *Tillie B.* was sailing nearer and nearer to this formidable object. Finally the mate grew nervous and going to the cabin stairs called down to Captain Hiller.

"We've sighted something, sir, and it's not land, it's not a ship and it's not a whale and we don't know what it is."

The captain came on deck and going to the rail looked at the object and said: "It's not la——" But here he seized his speaking trumpet and an instant later the wild orders roared through the vessel: "Slip the trolley! Throw the ship onto a switch—send a man back with a flag—wire the superintendent—helltopay—this here's a sea serpent!"

Immediately all was panic on board the *Tillie B.* Men rushed to and fro dragging at ropes and blaspheming at their misfortune while the captain roared more orders than nine shiploads of sailors could possibly have obeyed. But before they could stop the ship she had sailed very close to the thing and the captain, going to the rail, said: "It is not land! It is not a ship! It is not a whale! It is NOT a sea serpent but may I have my own mainm'st stuffed down my throat if it is not the famous lumber raft which was lost in the North Atlantic some years ago and for which U.S.S. *Enterprise* and the revenue cutter *Grant* made such painful but useless search."

And so Captain William B. Hiller, of the bark *Tillie B.*, now lying in Erie Basin, solemnly states that on July 1st he discovered the celebrated raft some 500 miles off the coast of Labrador. It was headed southwest, he says, but was not making much more way than a foundry. The raft is larger than any ocean liner and it would be an ugly customer to meet under the conditions of a twenty knot gait and a dark night. The sea serpents do not object to navigation by ships but lumber rafts are more unreasonable.

John Leary, the lumber expert who first conceived the plan of transporting lumber at sea by means of a raft was recently interviewed at his Newton Creek sawmill. "I think Captain Hiller's story to be very probable. I was employed personally in the construction of this raft and I know that it was constructed as strong—if not stronger—than many ocean steamers. Its general compactness and solidity made it almost as inseparable as one great massive log.

"This raft was the largest by some three hundred feet of any ever shipped by sea. In fact it was too large. Nothing like it is now attempted. It was constructed on an improvised dry dock at Two Rivers, Nova Scotia, in the fall of 1890 and launched on the plan of an Atlantic liner's launching. The longest rafts we now undertake are 300 feet long and weigh about 4000 tons. The one we lost was 600 feet in length, longer than any liner. It weighed 10,000 tons. The method we used in constructing the monster was new and has been patented in this country, Canada and Europe. We now use it on a smaller scale. It took us just one day over six months to build the great raft and we required the steady employment of 55 men. The distinguishing feature of the system now patented——and what makes me feel positive that wherever the raft is, it is whole——is the method of fastening the structure together with chains. It is not a matter of merely bunching the logs and then binding them, as many might conclude. The method in fact is quite ingenious. For instance the strength is all concentrated in one long and powerful center chain. The raft may be towed by either termination of this chain. Side chains placed diagonally to the center are added at the ends so that the greater the force applied to the towline, the stronger the logs are drawn together and at every yard or so along the body, chains leading from the center line are brought through to the surface and after being carried over a distance of about six feet return to the center chain.

"The great 600 feet raft was 62 feet beam at its widest part. It was constructed like a monstrous cigar as this form seemed to us most seaworthy. The necessary tapering to accomplish this design was mainly secured by arranging the timbers with the butts toward the center.

"When completed the structure contained 25,000 sticks of spruce and pine timber from 35 to 95 feet in length and a great quantity of beech, birch, and maple, making a total of 4,500,000 feet of timber. The diameters of the logs ran from twelve inches to thirty-five at the butts and from six inches to ten at the tips. At the time it was launched and ready to be towed the raft had cost us about thirty-two thousand dollars and the contract price for towing it to our Long Island yards was thirty-five hundred dollars.

"The launching of the raft was a most interesting event. A vast crowd came to see it. The ways upon which it was slid into the sea were twelve hundred feet in length. The raft at first moved slowly but its speed naturally increased until it cleared the 1000 feet between it and the water in about thirty seconds without straining a chain or showing the slightest change in its form.

"When the cradle was removed, the raft was found to draw only 19½ feet of water.

"The object of bringing lumber to New York in this manner is to get the longest logs here since vessels trading to Nova Scotia cannot handle sticks over sixty feet long. In the general market those of greater length come from Michigan and Ohio by rail, which is very expensive.

"Having such full knowledge of the strength of the raft's structure I make little doubt of the truth of Captain Hiller's report."

At the offices of the various trans-Atlantic lines word had been received of the *Tillie B.'s* discovery and the report seemed to be generally credited.

Collector Kilbreth, however, is really the man who keeps tabs on the sea serpents and other ocean mysteries for the United States government and he was openly and shamelessly bored when the story was brought to his ears. "It's all right, my boy," he said, waving his hand wearily, "it's all right. Don't get excited. It is only another Menace to Navigation. Listen; have you ever heard of the phantom stove factory which prowls the sea at midnight looking for unwary ships? No? Do you know that last April the ship *Actoronhisuppers* from Khartum heard the weird chortle of many frogs when seven hundred miles from land? Do you know that every possible combination of inventive imagination is worked on me every day? Talk about the wonders of the deep! Why I—well, as a matter of brevity I do not believe the raft story. Common sense tells me that by this time the celebrated monster is torn to pieces."

August 2, 1896?
[*Bulletin of the New York Public Library,*
Vol. 60 (October, 1956), pp. 479–482.]

AN INDIANA CAMPAIGN*

I

When the able-bodied citizens of the village formed a company and marched away to the war, Major Tom Boldin assumed in a manner the burden of the village cares. Everybody ran to him when they felt obliged to discuss their affairs. The sorrows of the town were dragged before him. His little bench at the sunny side of Migglesville tavern became a sort of open court where people came to speak resentfully of their grievances. He accepted his position and struggled manfully under the load. It behooved him, as a man who had seen the sky red over the quaint, low cities of Mexico, and the compact Northern bayonets gleaming on the narrow roads.

One warm summer day the major sat asleep on his little bench. There was a lull in the tempest of discussion which usually enveloped him. His cane, by use of which he could make the most tremendous and impressive gestures, reposed beside him. His hat lay upon the bench, and his old bald head had swung far forward until his nose actually touched the first button of his waistcoat.

The sparrows wrangled desperately in the road, defying perspiration. Once a team went jangling and creaking past, raising a yellow blur of dust

* *The Little Regiment.*

before the soft tones of the field and sky. In the long grass of the meadow across the road the insects chirped and clacked eternally.

Suddenly a frowzy-headed boy appeared in the roadway, his bare feet pattering rapidly. He was extremely excited. He gave a shrill whoop as he discovered the sleeping major, and rushed toward him. He created a terrific panic among some chickens which had been scratching intently near the major's feet. They clamored in an insanity of fear, and rushed hither and thither seeking a way of escape, whereas in reality all ways lay plainly open to them.

This tumult caused the major to arouse with a sudden little jump of amazement and apprehension. He rubbed his eyes and gazed about him. Meanwhile, some clever chicken had discovered a passage to safety and led the flock into the garden, where they squawked in sustained alarm.

Panting from his run and choked with terror, the little boy stood before the major, struggling with a tale that was ever upon the tip of his tongue.

"Major—now—major—"

The old man, roused from a delicious slumber, glared impatiently at the little boy. "Come, come! What's th' matter with yeh?" he demanded. "What's th' matter? Don't stand there shaking! Speak up!"

"Lots is th' matter!" the little boy shouted valiantly, with a courage born of the importance of his tale. "My ma's chickens 'uz all stole, an'—now—he's over in th' woods!"

"Who is? Who is over in the woods? Go ahead!"

"Now—th' rebel is!"

"What?" roared the major.

"Th' rebel!" cried the little boy, with the last of his breath.

The major pounced from his bench in tempestuous excitement. He seized the little boy by the collar and gave him a great jerk. "Where? Are yeh sure? Who saw 'im? How long ago? Where is he now? Did you see 'im?"

The little boy, frightened at the major's fury, began to sob. After a moment he managed to stammer: "He—now—he's in the woods. I saw 'im. He looks uglier'n anythin'."

The major released his hold upon the boy, and, pausing for a time, indulged in a glorious dream. Then he said: "By thunder! we'll ketch th' cuss. You wait here," he told the boy, "an' don't say a word t' anybody. Do yeh hear?"

The boy, still weeping, nodded, and the major hurriedly entered the inn. He took down from its pegs an awkward, smooth-bore rifle and carefully examined the enormous percussion cap that was fitted over the nipple. Mistrusting the cap, he removed it and replaced it with a new one. He scrutinized the gun keenly, as if he could judge in this manner the condition of the load. All his movements were deliberate and deadly.

When he arrived upon the porch of the tavern he beheld the yard filled with people. Peter Witheby, sooty-faced and grinning, was in the van. He looked at the major. "Well?" he said.

"Well?" returned the major, bridling.

"Well, what's 'che got?" said old Peter.

" 'Got?' Got a rebel over in th' woods!" roared the major.

At this sentence the women and boys, who had gathered eagerly about him, gave vent to startled cries. The women had come from adjacent houses, but the little boys represented the entire village. They had miraculously heard the first whisper of rumor, and they performed wonders in getting to the spot. They clustered around the important figure of the major and gazed in silent awe. The women, however, burst forth. At the word "rebel," which represented to them all terrible things, they deluged the major with questions which were obviously unanswerable.

He shook them off with violent impatience. Meanwhile Peter Witheby was trying to force exasperating interrogations through the tumult to the major's ears. "What? No! Yes! How d' I know?" the maddened veteran snarled as he struggled with his friends. "No! Yes! What? How in thunder d' I know?" Upon the steps of the tavern the landlady sat, weeping forlornly.

At last the major burst through the crowd and went to the roadway. There, as they all streamed after him, he turned and faced them. "Now, look a' here, I don't know any more about this than you do," he told them forcibly. "All that I know is that there's a rebel over in Smith's woods, an' all I know is that I'm a-goin' after 'im."

"But hol' on a minnet," said old Peter. "How do yeh know he's a rebel?"

"I know he is!" cried the major. "Don't yeh think I know what a rebel is?"

Then, with a gesture of disdain at the babbling crowd, he marched determinedly away, his rifle held in the hollow of his arm. At this heroic moment a new clamor arose, half admiration, half dismay. Old Peter hobbled after the major, continually repeating, "Hol' on a minnet."

The little boy who had given the alarm was the center of a throng of lads who gazed with envy and awe, discovering in him a new quality. He held forth to them eloquently. The women stared after the figure of the major and old Peter, his pursuer. Jerozel Bronson, a half-witted lad who comprehended nothing save an occasional genial word, leaned against the fence and grinned like a skull. The major and the pursuer passed out of view around the turn in the road where the great maples lazily shook the dust that lay on their leaves.

For a moment the little group of women listened intently, as if they expected to hear a sudden shot and cries from the distance. They looked at each other, their lips a little ways apart. The trees sighed softly in the heat of the summer sun. The insects in the meadow continued their monotonous humming, and, somewhere, a hen had been stricken with fear and was cackling loudly.

Finally, Mrs. Goodwin said: "Well, I'm goin' up to th' turn a' th' road, anyhow." Mrs. Willets and Mrs. Joe Peterson, her particular friends, cried out at this temerity, but she said: "Well, I'm goin', anyhow."

She called Bronson. "Come on, Jerozel. You're a man, an' if he should chase us, why, you mus' pitch inteh 'im. Hey?"

Bronson always obeyed everybody. He grinned an assent, and went with her down the road.

A little boy attempted to follow them, but a shrill scream from his mother made him halt.

The remaining women stood motionless, their eyes fixed upon Mrs. Goodwin and Jerozel. Then at last one gave a laugh of triumph at her conquest of caution and fear, and cried: "Well, I'm goin' too!"

Another instantly said, "So am I." There began a general movement. Some of the little boys had already ventured a hundred feet away from the main body, and at this unanimous advance they spread out ahead in little groups. Some recounted terrible stories of rebel ferocity. Their eyes were large with excitement. The whole thing, with its possible dangers, had for them a delicious element. Johnnie Peterson, who could whip any boy present, explained what he would do in case the enemy should happen to pounce out at him.

The familiar scene suddenly assumed a new aspect. The field of corn which met the road upon the left was no longer a mere field of corn. It was a darkly mystic place whose recesses could contain all manner of dangers. The long green leaves, waving in the breeze, rustled from the passing of men. In the song of the insects there were now omens, threats.

There was a warning in the enamel blue of the sky, in the stretch of yellow road, in the very atmosphere. Above the tops of the corn loomed the distant foliage of Smith's woods, curtaining the silent action of a tragedy whose horrors they imagined.

The women and the little boys came to a halt, overwhelmed by the impressiveness of the landscape. They waited silently.

Mrs. Goodwin suddenly said: "I'm goin' back."

The others, who all wished to return, cried at once disdainfully: "Well, go back, if yeh want to!"

A cricket at the roadside exploded suddenly in his shrill song, and a woman who had been standing near shrieked in startled terror. An electric movement went through the group of women. They jumped and gave vent to sudden screams. With the fears still upon their agitated faces, they turned to berate the one who had shrieked. "My! what a goose you are, Sallie! Why, it took my breath away. Goodness sakes, don't holler like that again!"

II

"Hol' on a minnet!" Peter Witheby was crying to the major, as the latter, full of the importance and dignity of his position as protector of Migglesville, paced forward swiftly. The veteran already felt upon his brow a wreath formed of the flowers of gratitude, and as he strode he was absorbed in planning a calm and self-contained manner of wearing it. "Hol' on a minnet!" piped old Peter in the rear.

At last the major, aroused from his dream of triumph, turned about wrathfully. "Well, what?"

"Now, look a' here," said Peter. "What 'che goin' t' do?"

The major, with a gesture of supreme exasperation, wheeled again and went on. When he arrived at the cornfield he halted and waited for Peter. He had suddenly felt that indefinable menace in the landscape. "Well?" demanded Peter, panting.

The major's eyes wavered a trifle. "Well," he repeated—"well, I'm goin' in there an' bring out that there rebel."

They both paused and studied the gently swaying masses of corn and, behind them, the looming woods, sinister with possible secrets.

"Well," said old Peter.

The major moved uneasily and put his hand to his brow. Peter waited in obvious expectation.

The major crossed through the grass at the roadside and climbed the fence. He put both legs over the topmost rail and then sat perched there, facing the woods. Once he turned his head and asked, "What?"

"I hain't said anythin'," answered Peter.

The major clambered down from the fence and went slowly into the corn, his gun held in readiness. Peter stood in the road.

Presently the major returned and said in a cautious whisper: "If yeh hear anythin', you come a-runnin', will yeh?"

"Well, I hain't got no gun nor nuthin'," said Peter, in the same low tone; "what good 'ud I do?"

"Well, yeh might come along with me an' watch," said the major. "Four eyes is better'n two."

"If I had a gun—" began Peter.

"Oh, yeh don't need no gun," interrupted the major, waving his hand. "All I'm afraid of is that I won't find 'im. My eyes ain't so good as they was."

"Well—"

"Come along," whispered the major. "Yeh hain't afraid, are yeh?"

"No, but—"

"Well, come along, then. What's th' matter with yeh?"

Peter climbed the fence. He paused on the top rail and took a prolonged stare at the inscrutable woods. When he joined the major in the cornfield he said, with a touch of anger: "Well, you got the gun. Remember that. If he comes for me, I hain't got a blame thing!"

"Shucks!" answered the major. "He ain't a-goin' t' come for yeh."

The two then began a wary journey through the corn. One by one the long aisles between the rows appeared. As they glanced along each of them it seemed as if some gruesome thing had just previously vacated it. Old Peter halted once and whispered: "Say, look a' here; supposin'—supposin'—"

"Supposin' what?" demanded the major.

"Supposin'—" said Peter. "Well, remember you got th' gun, an' I hain't got anythin'."

"Thunder!" said the major.

When they got to where the stalks were very short because of the shade cast by the trees of the wood, they halted again. The leaves were gently swishing in the breeze. Before them stretched the mystic green wall of the forest, and there seemed to be in it eyes which followed each of their movements.

Peter at last said, "I don't believe there's anybody in there."

"Yes, there is, too," said the major. "I'll bet anythin' he's in there."

"How d' yeh know?" asked Peter. "I'll bet he ain't within a mile o' here."

The major suddenly ejaculated, "Listen!"

They bent forward, scarce breathing, their mouths agape, their eyes glinting. Finally, the major turned his head. "Did yeh hear that?" he said hoarsely.

"No," said Peter in a low voice. "What was it?"

The major listened for a moment. Then he turned again. "I thought I heerd somebody holler!" he explained cautiously.

They both bent forward and listened once more. Peter, in the intentness of his attitude, lost his balance and was obliged to lift his foot hastily and with noise.

"S-s-sh!" hissed the major.

After a minute Peter spoke quite loudly: "Oh, shucks! I don't believe yeh heerd anythin'."

The major made a frantic downward gesture with his hand. "Shet up, will yeh!" he said in an angry undertone.

Peter became silent for a moment, but presently he said again: "Oh, yeh didn't hear anythin'."

The major turned to glare at his companion in despair and wrath. "What's th' matter with yeh? Can't yeh shet up?"

"Oh, this here ain't no use. If you're goin' in after 'im, why don't yeh go in after 'im?"

"Well, gimme time, can't yeh?" said the major, in a growl. And, as if to add more to this reproach, he climbed the fence that compassed the woods, looking resentfully back at his companion.

"Well?" said Peter, when the major paused.

The major stepped down upon the thick carpet of brown leaves that stretched under the trees. He turned then to whisper: "You wait here, will yeh?" His face was red with determination.

"Well, hol' on a minnet!" said Peter. "You—I—we'd better—"

"No," said the major. "You wait here."

He went stealthily into the thickets. Peter watched him until he grew to be a vague, slow-moving shadow. From time to time he could hear the leaves crackle and twigs snap under the major's awkward tread. Peter, intent, breathless, waited for the peal of sudden tragedy. Finally, the woods grew silent in a solemn and impressive hush that caused Peter to feel the thumping of his heart. He began to look about him to make sure that nothing should spring upon him from the somber shadows. He scrutinized this cool gloom before him, and at times he thought he could perceive the moving of swift silent shapes. He concluded that he had better go back and try to muster some assistance to the major.

As Peter came through the corn, the women in the road caught sight of the glittering figure and screamed. Many of them began to run. The little boys, with all their valor, scurried away in clouds. Mrs. Joe Peterson, however, cast a glance over her shoulders as she, with her skirts gathered up, was running as best she could. She instantly stopped and, in tones of deepest scorn, called out to the others, "Why, it's on'y Pete Witheby!" They came faltering back then, those who had been naturally swiftest in the race avoiding the eyes of those whose limbs had enabled them to flee a short distance.

Peter came rapidly, appreciating the glances of vivid interest in the eyes of the women. To their lightning-like questions, which hit all sides of the episode, he opposed a new tranquillity gained from his sudden ascent in importance. He made no answer to their clamor. When he had reached the top of the fence, he called out commandingly: "Here you, Johnnie, you and George, run an' git my gun! It's hangin' on th' pegs over th' bench in th' shop."

At this terrible sentence, a shuddering cry broke from the women. The boys named sped down the road, accompanied by a retinue of envious companions.

Peter swung his legs over the rail and faced the woods again. He twisted his head once to say: "Keep still, can't yeh? Quit scufflin' aroun'!" They could see by his manner that this was a supreme moment. The group became motionless and still. Later, Peter turned to say, "S-s-sh!" to a restless boy, and the air with which he said it smote them all with awe.

The little boys who had gone after the gun came pattering along hurriedly, the weapon borne in the midst of them. Each was anxious to share in the honor. The one who had been delegated to bring it was bullying and directing his comrades.

Peter said, "S-s-sh!" He took the gun and poised it in readiness to sweep the cornfield. He scowled at the boys and whispered angrily: "Why didn't yeh bring th' powder horn an' th' thing with th' bullets in? I told yeh t' bring 'em. I'll send somebody else next time."

"Yeh didn't tell us!" cried the two boys shrilly.

"S-s-sh! Quit yeh noise," said Peter, with a violent gesture.

However, this reproof enabled other boys to recover that peace of mind which they had lost when seeing their friends loaded with honors.

The women had cautiously approached the fence and, from time to time, whispered feverish questions; but Peter repulsed them savagely, with an air of being infinitely bothered by their interference in his intent watch. They were forced to listen again in silence to the weird and prophetic chanting of the insects and the mystic silken rustling of the corn.

At last the thud of hurrying feet in the soft soil of the field came to their ears. A dark form sped toward them. A wave of a mighty fear swept over the group, and the screams of the women came hoarsely from their choked throats. Peter swung madly from his perch, and turned to use the fence as a rampart.

But it was the major. His face was inflamed and his eyes were glaring. He clutched his rifle by the middle and swung it wildly. He was bounding at a great speed for his fat, short body.

"It's all right! it's all right!" he began to yell, some distance away. "It's all right! It's on'y ol' Milt' Jacoby!"

When he arrived at the top of the fence, he paused and mopped his brow.

"What?" they thundered, in an agony of sudden unreasoning disappointment.

Mrs. Joe Peterson, who was a distant connection of Milton Jacoby, thought to forestall any damage to her social position by saying at once, disdainfully, "Drunk, I s'pose!"

"Yep," said the major, still on the fence, and mopped his brow. "Drunk as a fool. Thunder! I was surprised. I—I—thought it was a rebel, sure."

The thoughts of all these women wavered for a time. They were at a loss for precise expression of their emotion. At last, however, they hurled this superior sentence at the major:

"Well, yeh might have known."

September, 1896

[*The Pocket Magazine,* Vol. 2, pp. 92–114.]

IN THE TENDERLOIN:
A DUEL BETWEEN AN ALARM CLOCK AND
A SUICIDAL PURPOSE

Everybody knows all about the Tenderloin district of New York. There is no man that has the slightest claim to citizenship that does not know all there is to know concerning the Tenderloin. It is wonderful—this amount of truth which the world's clergy and police forces have collected concerning the Tenderloin. My friends from the stars obtain all this information, if possible, and then go into this wilderness and apply it. Upon observing you, certain spirits of the jungle will term you a wise guy, but there is no gentle humor in the Tenderloin, so you need not fear that this remark is anything but a tribute to your knowledge.

Once upon a time there was fought in the Tenderloin a duel between an Alarm Clock and a Suicidal Purpose. That such a duel was fought is a matter of no consequence, but it may be worth a telling, because it may be the single Tenderloin incident about which every man in the world has not exhaustive information.

It seems that Swift Doyer and his girl quarreled. Swift was jealous in the strange and devious way of his kind, and at midnight, his voice burdened with admonition, grief and deadly menace, roared through the little flat and conveyed news of the strife up the air shaft and down the air shaft.

"Lied to me, didn't you?" he cried. "Told me a lie and thought I wouldn't get onto you. Lied to me! Lied to me! There's where I get crazy. If you hadn't lied to me in one thing, and I hadn't collared you flat in it, I might believe all the rest, but now—how do I know you ever tell the truth? How do I know I ain't always getting a game? Hey? How do I know?"

To the indifferent people whose windows opened on the air shaft there came the sound of a girl's low sobbing, while into it at times burst wildly the hoarse bitterness and rage of the man's tone. A grim thing is a Tenderloin air shaft.

Swift arose and paused his harangue for a moment while he lit a cigarette. He puffed at it vehemently and scowled, black as a storm-god, in the direction of the sobbing.

"Come! Get up out of that," he said, with ferocity. "Get up and look at me and let me see you lie!"

There was a flurry of white in the darkness, which was no more definite to the man than the ice floes which your reeling ship passes in the night. Then, when the gas glared out suddenly, the girl stood before him. She was a wondrous white figure in her vestal-like robe. She resembled the priestess in paintings of long-gone Mediterranean religions. Her hair fell wildly on her shoulder. She threw out her arms and cried to Swift in a woe that seemed almost as real as the woe of good people.

"Oh, oh, my heart is broken! My heart is broken!"

But Swift knew as well as the rest of mankind that these girls have no hearts to be broken, and this acting filled him with a new rage. He grabbed an alarm clock from the dresser and banged her heroically on the head with it.

She fell and quivered for a moment. Then she arose, and, calm and dry-eyed, walked to the mirror. Swift thought she was taking an account of the bruises, but when he resumed his cyclonic tirade, she said: "I've taken morphine, Swift!"

Swift leaped at a little red pillbox. It was empty. Eight quarter-grain pills make two grains. The Suicidal Purpose was distinctly ahead of the Alarm Clock. With great presence of mind Swift now took the empty pillbox and flung it through the window.

At this time a great battle was begun in the dining room of the little flat. Swift dragged the girl to the sideboard, and in forcing her to drink whiskey he almost stuffed the bottle down her throat. When the girl still sank to the depths of an infinite drowsiness, sliding limply in her chair like a cloth figure, he dealt her furious blows, and our decorous philosophy knows little of the love and despair that was in those caresses. With his voice he called the light into her eyes, called her from the sinister slumber which her senses welcomed, called her soul back from the verge.

He propped the girl in a chair and ran to the kitchen to make coffee. His fingers might have been from a dead man's hands, and his senses confused the coffee, the water, the coffee pot, the gas stove, but by some fortune he managed to arrange them correctly. When he lifted the girlish figure and carried her to the kitchen, he was as wild, haggard, gibbering, as a man of midnight murders, and it is only because he was not engaged in the respectable and literary assassination of a royal juke that almost any sensible writer would be ashamed of this story. Let it suffice, then, that when the steel-blue dawn came and distant chimneys were black against a rose sky, the girl sat at the dining room table chattering insanely and gesturing. Swift, with his hands pressed to his temples, watched her from the other side of the table, with all his mind in his eyes, for each gesture was still a reminiscence, and each tone of her voice a ballad to him. And yet he could not half measure his misery. The tragedy was made of homeliest details. He had to repeat to himself that he, worn-out, stupefied from his struggle, was sitting there awaiting the moment when the unseen hand should whirl this soul into the abyss, and that then he should be alone.

The girl saw a fly alight on a picture. "Oh," she said, "there's a little fly." She arose and thrust out her finger. "Hello, little fly," she said, and touched the fly. The insect was perhaps too cold to be alert, for it fell at the touch of her finger. The girl gave a cry of remorse, and, sinking to her knees, searched the floor, meanwhile uttering tender apologies.

At last she found the fly, and, taking it, her palm went to the gas jet which still burned weirdly in the dawning. She held her hand close to the flame. "Poor little fly," she said, "I didn't mean to hurt you. I wouldn't hurt you for anything. There now—p'r'aps when you get warm you can fly away again. Did I crush the poor little bit of fly? I'm awful sorry—honest, I am. Poor little thing! Why I wouldn't hurt you for the world, poor little fly"—

Swift was woefully pale and so nerve-weak that his whole body felt a singular coolness. Strange things invariably come into a man's head at the wrong time, and Swift was aware that this scene was defying his preconceptions. His instruction had been that people when dying behaved in a certain manner. Why did this girl occupy herself with an accursed fly? Why in the name of the gods of the drama did she not refer to her past? Why, by the shelves of the saints of literature, did she not clutch her brow and say: "Ah, once I was an innocent girl?" What was wrong with this death scene? At one time he thought that his sense of propriety was so scandalized that he was upon the point of interrupting the girl's babble.

But here a new thought struck him. The girl was not going to die. How could she under these circumstances? The form was not correct.

All this was not relevant to the man's love and despair, but, behold, my friend, at the tragic, the terrible point in life there comes an irrelevancy to the human heart direct from the Wise God. And this is why Swift Doyer thought those peculiar thoughts.

The girl chattered to the fly minute after minute, and Swift's anxiety grew dim and more dim until his head fell forward on the table and he slept as a man who has moved mountains, altered rivers, caused snow to come because he wished it to come, and done his duty.

For an hour the girl talked to the fly, the gas jet, the walls, the distant chimneys. Finally she sat opposite the slumbering Swift and talked softly to herself.

When broad day came they were both asleep, and the girl's fingers had gone across the table until they had found the locks on the man's forehead. They were asleep, and this after all is a human action, which may safely be done by characters in the fiction of our time.

October 1, 1896
[*Town Topics*, Vol. 36, p. 14.]

A DETAIL*

The tiny old lady in the black dress and curious little black bonnet had at first seemed alarmed at the sound made by her feet upon the stone pavements. But later she forgot about it, for she suddenly came into the tempest of the Sixth Avenue shopping district, where from the streams of people and vehicles went up a roar like that from headlong mountain torrents.

She seemed then like a chip that catches, recoils, turns, and wheels, a reluctant thing in the clutch of the impetuous river. She hesitated, faltered, debated with herself. Frequently she seemed about to address people; then of a sudden she would evidently lose her courage. Meanwhile the torrent jostled her, swung her this and that way.

At last, however, she saw two young women gazing in at a shop window. They were well-dressed girls; they wore gowns with enormous sleeves that made them look like full-rigged ships with all sails set. They seemed to have plenty of time; they leisurely scanned the goods in the window. Other people had made the tiny old woman much afraid because obviously they were speeding to keep such tremendously important engagements. She went close to the girls and peered in at the same window. She watched them furtively for a time. Then finally she said: "Excuse me!"

The girls looked down at this old face with its two large eyes turned toward them.

"Excuse me: can you tell me where I can get any work?"

For an instant the two girls stared. Then they seemed about to exchange a smile, but, at the last moment, they checked it. The tiny old lady's eyes were upon them. She was quaintly serious, silently expectant. She made one marvel that in that face the wrinkles showed no trace of experience, knowledge; they were simply little soft, innocent creases. As for her glance, it had the trustfulness of ignorance and the candor of babyhood.

"I want to get something to do, because I need the money," she continued, since, in their astonishment, they had not replied to her first question. "Of course I'm not strong and I couldn't do very much, but I can sew

* *Midnight Sketches.*

well; and in a house where there was a good many menfolks, I could do all the mending. Do you know any place where they would like me to come?"

The young women did then exchange a smile, but it was a subtle tender smile, the edge of personal grief.

"Well, no, madam," hesitatingly said one of them at last; "I don't think I know any one."

A shade passed over the tiny old lady's face, a shadow of the wing of disappointment. "Don't you?" she said, with a little struggle to be brave in her voice.

Then the girl hastily continued: "But if you will give me your address, I may find some one, and if I do, I will surely let you know of it."

The tiny old lady dictated her address, bending over to watch the girl write on a visiting card with a little silver pencil. Then she said: "I thank you very much." She bowed to them, smiling, and went on down the avenue.

As for the two girls, they walked to the curb and watched this aged figure, small and frail, in its black gown and curious black bonnet. At last, the crowd, the innumerable wagons, intermingling and changing with uproar and riot, suddenly engulfed it.

October, 1896
[*The Pocket Magazine*, Vol. 2, pp. 145–148.]

THE VOICE OF THE MOUNTAIN

The old man Popocatepetl was seated on a high rock with his white mantle about his shoulders. He looked at the sky, he looked at the sea, he looked at the land—nowhere could he see any food. And he was very hungry, too.

Who can understand the agony of a creature whose stomach is as large as a thousand churches, when this same stomach is as empty as a broken water jar?

He looked longingly at some islands in the sea. "Ah, those flat cakes! If I had them." He stared at storm clouds in the sky. "Ah, what a drink is there." But the King of Everything, you know, had forbidden the old man Popocatepetl to move at all, because he feared that every footprint would make a great hole in the land. So the old fellow was obliged to sit still and wait for his food to come within reach. Any one who has tried this plan knows what intervals lie between meals.

Once his friend, the little eagle, flew near, and Popocatepetl called to him. "Ho, tiny bird, come and consider with me as to how I shall be fed."

The little eagle came and spread his legs apart and considered manfully, but he could do nothing with the situation. "You see," he said, "this is no ordinary hunger which one goat will suffice—"

Popocatepetl groaned an assent.

"—but it is an enormous affair," continued the little eagle, "which requires something like a dozen stars. I don't see what can be done unless we get that little creature of the earth—that little animal with two arms, two legs, one head, and a very brave air, to invent something. He is said to be very wise."

"Who claims it for him?" asked Popocatepetl.

"He claims it for himself," responded the eagle.

"Well, summon him. Let us see. He is doubtless a kind little animal, and when he sees my distress he will invent something."

"Good!" The eagle flew until he discovered one of these small creatures. "Oh, tiny animal, the great chief Popocatepetl summons you!"

"Does he, indeed!"

"Popocatepetl, the great chief," said the eagle again, thinking that the little animal had not heard rightly.

"Well, and why does he summon me?"

"Because he is in distress, and he needs your assistance."

The little animal reflected for a time, and then said, "I will go."

When Popocatepetl perceived the little animal and the eagle he stretched forth his great, solemn arms. "Oh, blessed little animal with two arms, two legs, a head, and a very brave air, help me in my agony. Behold I, Popocatepetl, who saw the King of Everything fashioning the stars, I, who knew the sun in his childhood, I, Popocatepetl, appeal to you, little animal. I am hungry."

After a while the little animal asked: "How much will you pay?"

"Pay?" said Popocatepetl.

"Pay?" said the eagle.

"Assuredly," quoth the little animal. "Pay!"

"But," demanded Popocatepetl, "were you never hungry? I tell you I am hungry, and is your first word then 'pay'?"

The little animal turned coldly away. "Oh, Popocatepetl, how much wisdom has flown past you since you saw the King of Everything fashioning the stars and since you knew the sun in his childhood? I said 'pay,' and, moreover, your distress measures my price. It is our law. Yet it is true that we did not see the King of Everything fashioning the stars. Nor did we know the sun in his childhood."

Then did Popocatepetl roar and shake in his rage. "Oh, louse—louse—louse! Let us bargain then! How much for your blood?" Over the head of the little animal hung death.

But he instantly bowed himself and prayed: "Popocatepetl, the great, you who saw the King of Everything fashioning the stars, and who knew the sun in his childhood, forgive this poor little animal. Your sacred hunger shall be my care. I am your servant."

"It is well," said Popocatepetl at once, for his spirit was ever kindly. "And now, what will you do?"

The little animal put his hand upon his chin and reflected. "Well, it seems you are hungry, and the King of Everything has forbidden you to go for food in fear that your monstrous feet will riddle the earth with holes. What you need is a pair of wings."

"A pair of wings!" cried Popocatepetl delightedly.

"A pair of wings!" screamed the eagle in joy.

"How very simple, after all."

"And yet how wise!"

"But," said Popocatepetl, after the first outburst, "who can make me these wings?"

The little animal replied: "I and my kind are great, because at times we can make one mind control a hundred thousand bodies. This is the secret of our performance. It will be nothing for us to make wings for even you, great Popocatepetl. I and my kind will come"—continued the crafty little animal—"we will come and dwell on this beautiful plain that stretches from the sea to the sea, and we will make wings for you."

Popocatepetl wished to embrace the little animal. "Oh, glorious! Oh, best of little brutes! Run! run! run! Summon your kind, dwell in the plain and make me wings. Ah, when once Popocatepetl can soar on his wings from star to star, then, indeed—"

Poor old stupid Popocatepetl! The little animal summoned his kind, they dwelt on the plains, they made this and they made that, but they made no wings for Popocatepetl.

And sometimes when the thunderous voice of the old peak rolls and rolls, if you know that tongue, you can hear him say: "Oh, traitor! Traitor! Traitor! Where are my wings? My wings, traitor! I am hungry! Where are my wings?"

But the little animal merely places his finger beside his nose and winks. "Your wings, indeed, fool! Sit still and howl for them! Old idiot!"

November, 1896

[*The Pocket Magazine*, Vol. 3, pp. 136–142.]

YEN-NOCK BILL
AND
HIS SWEETHEART

They called him Yen-Nock Bill. He had been a book agent, a confidence man, a member of a celebrated minstrel troupe, a shoplifter, a waiter in a Bowery restaurant and other things. But he had never been guilty of a dishonest act in his life. He used to say so, solemnly.

"No, sir," he often remarked, "I've lived at a pretty hot gait all my life, but I've always been on the level. Never did a crooked thing since I was born. No, sir!"

He did not stick at an occupation because he was fond of a certain delicate amusement of the Chinese. A most peculiar truth of life is the fact that, when a man gets to be an opium smoker, he has ill-fortune. Disaster comes upon his business schemes, and his valuable friends slide unaccountably away from him. And so it happened that, when Bill fell deadly ill with pneumonia, there was nobody to come to him and bid him a good journey through the skyland.

On the contrary, his dragon of a landlady paced the halls and wondered who was going to provide the four dollars Bill owed for lodging. She was a woman with business principles, and she wanted her four dollars. She did not give three hurrahs in Hades whether Bill lived or died, so long as he did not put her to pecuniary loss. She was a just woman; her life had been a hard struggle for daily bread, and when anybody owed her four dollars, it was no more than fair that she should be paid.

Bill was a small man. He had a way of pulling the sheet up to his throat with one thin hand, and then coughing until his whole body jumped and writhed. When he was not coughing, he simply lay and rolled his eyes. In the days of his prosperity, when his particular confidence game was paying him a great deal of money, Bill had a sweetheart, and it becomes a most painful obligation to introduce her into this story.

When Julie heard of Bill's plight, she went there post haste. She flung herself down at the bedside and cried: "Oh, Billie!"

Bill raised himself and scanned her with a cold eye. "Why th'ell didn't you come before?" he demanded. "You're a nice one, you are. Leaving me here to die—leaving me here to die all alone—all alone—without a friend in the world." He shed tears.

Julie soothed him and flattered the man in the manner of woman, even in the face of his arrant injustice, and by the way the irritation in his voice was of a quality worse than knife blades. "I'll take you right to the flat, dear," cried Julie, sobbing. "There I can take care of you and 'tend you until you get well; poor, poor boy!"

But when she put out her hand to smooth his brow, he brushed her away savagely. "Oh, you make me tired, you fool! Tell me how I'm going to get around there, will you? You are an ass."

Thereupon Julie pleaded with him. "I'll call a cab, dear, and have it right here at the door, and the coachman can help you downstairs. I'll go around now and borrow Swift Doyer's winter overcoat, and then I'll go home and have Mary fix everything ready for you. And then I'll have the doctor come right over. Won't you come, dear? Won't you?"

Bill turned his stern face toward the wall. "No," he answered. To one who had no interest in the proceedings it would have been plain that Bill lied, but since this woman loved this man, she could never tell when he lied to her. So she continued to beseech him. Always he answered: "No."

At last she went into the hall to beg the landlady to use her influence, but the door was no sooner closed behind her than Bill cried out, in a wild spasm of sick man's rage: "Julie, Julie!"

Julie returned in a flurry. "What, dear? What is it?"

"Why don't you order the cab?" he cried, shrilly. "Get a gait on you, will you! Think I want to lie here forever?"

"All right, Billie—all right," answered Julie. She kissed him and hurried away. Bill scowled at the wall and muttered sullenly to himself. Suddenly he had seemed possessed of some great grievance.

Julie returned, out of breath, and with Swift Doyer's winter overcoat over her arm. "It's all right!" she cried. "The cab's at the door, and everything is all fixed."

But here the landlady appeared as a factor. Previously she had been concerned chiefly about her four dollars, but now her ideas of respectability were concerned. She evidently had concluded that it would be better for Bill to die alone in the hall bedroom. "He shan't be taken from my house until I know where he is going," she said, coldly and significantly to Julie.

The girl flashed upon her one of those tearful glances into which a woman can put scorn, rage, and at the same time entreaty. Julie hesitated a moment, and the landlady never knew how near she came to a time of fire and the sword, whirlwind and sudden death. Better ask a ravenous wolf to sleep under your pillow than to stand between a woman who loves so completely and the man.

But Julie went calmly away with no word. Later a four-wheeler drew up before the house, and Swift Doyer and Jimmie the Mole emerged from it. "We want that sick man," said Swift to the landlady. "I'm his friend, and I'm going to take him home." The landlady gracefully accepted four dollars from Swift, and led the way to the hall bedroom.

"Let 'er go easy, boys," said Bill, with a wan smile, as they carried him around the curve of the stairs. In daylight Bill was a sad figure. Two weeks' growth of red beard was on his leaden face, and his eyes swung and turned in a way that was at once childish and insane. But when they bundled him into the cab, Julie put her arms about his neck and cooed and murmured. The instant they were alone in Julie's flat he began to howl at her. Swift Doyer was a good fellow, but he used to remark that Bill's voice made him wish that he was a horse, so that he could spring upon the bed and trample him to death. And for many days thereafter Bill bullied and abused, rated and raged at the girl, until people whose windows opened on the air shaft often remarked: "Say, why don't she kill him!"

Julie arrived at a point where she threw out her hands and said: "Oh, be good to me; won't you, Billie, dear?"

"No! Why should I?"

November 29, 1896
[New York *Journal*, p. 35.]

DIAMONDS AND DIAMONDS*

Jimmie the Mole derived his name from a certain way he would look at you when you lied to him. Lie to Jimmie in those days and he would shrug down his shoulders and squint at you most horribly and steadfastly until you grew nervous, probably, and went away. But when he was lying to you, he was a polished and courtly gentleman with no shadow of facial deformity about him.

Once Jimmie was smitten with a financial famine. He was about to take a trip to Boston, too, where some confiding man had offered him work in a concert hall as a sweet singer of ballads. Jimmie had a Tenderloin voice. This means a tenor well-suited to the air: "She has fallen by the wayside." Sometimes he went forth into the great wide world and made money with this voice.

Jimmie, being penniless and anxious to go to Boston, went to see the Flasher. "You better go over to Nellie Doyer's and borrow enough money for my ticket to Boston and then let me take your ring along with me. I'll see if I can't cop out a small bundle." The obedient Flasher borrowed money for the ticket and the obedient Flasher gave her ring to Jimmie.

* By permission of Alfred A. Knopf, Inc. Hitherto unpublished in book form.

Jimmie went to Boston and for two weeks made glad the rafters with his Tenderloin voice.

While standing in a corner saloon one morning, he espied a large fat personage in black clothing and with a large diamond stuck in a shirt emphatically soiled. This man seemed to strike Jimmie with considerable interest. He hung near and furtively watched this fat person drink whiskey.

Once he found himself at the bar elbow to elbow with this man. As has been said, Jimmie was often a courtly and polished gentleman. "I beg your pardon," he said, "but would you like to buy a ring?"

The fat person had not been a Boston alderman for nothing. He turned sharply and said: "No."

"I'm in hard luck just now and I need a hundred bad or I wouldn't think of selling it. If you happen to know of anybody who might like a nice diamond, I hope you won't mind telling me."

The fat person relented at this point because Jimmie's voice was obviously that of a courtly and polished gentleman. "Well, no I don't remember anybody just now. Let's look at the ring."

Jimmie held forth a graceful hand.

"Fine stone," said the ex-alderman.

"Yes," replied Jimmie. "A present from my girl in Chicago. She'll be crazy when she finds out that I've blown it in. Can't help it though. Hard luck is hard luck. I came here looking for a theatrical job—that's my business—but I don't get a thing but a frost from every manager I strike. Hard luck is hard luck."

"Sure," said the fat person. "How much do you want for the ring?"

"Well, I'll take a hundred," answered Jimmie candidly, "and the ring is worth that to anybody. It'll stand me a hundred in any pawnshop but I don't want to get up against the pawnshops anymore and when I've got anything to sell I'd rather have it go outright to some good fellow."

The fat person again gazed down at the ring. "Let me see it off your finger, will you?"

"Sure," said Jimmie.

The other looked at the ring close both inside and outside. "Looks like a good ring."

"It is a good ring. I'd like to see a man prove there was anything fake about that ring."

"Dan," called the fat person to the bartender. "How's that for a giglamp?" He pushed the trinket over the bar.

"Gee," cried the bartender, holding it high. "Say, that's a peach."

The fat person said to Jimmie: "Young feller, I'm almost coming around to giving up a hundred for it myself."

Jimmie shrugged his shoulders. "A hundred and it's yours."

The other again examined the ring. Finally he said: "Well—you bring it around to a jeweler's with me and if he says it's worth the money you say it is, why, I'll throw down a hundred for it." Whereupon he cast a keen eye at Jimmie.

But Jimmie promptly cried: "Certainly. Come ahead."

When they walked into the street, the fat person rather shied away from Jimmie and with singular intentness he kept his eyes straight to the front. "You say"—he observed. "You say your girl in Chicago gave you this ring?"

"Oh, that's on the level all right," answered the Mole. "But"—he added and he looked squarely at the fat person, "I've heard people say that they saw it on the finger of a ranchman from Montana just a little while before he came to Chicago on a skate."

"Um," said the fat person with a quick sidelong glance. He whistled indifferently.

When they had entered the jeweler's shop, the fat person crowded his great form against the showcase and said: "My friend, would you mind telling us what this ring is worth?"

When the jeweler appeared he seemed bored. Evidently he was bored because he thought somebody was going to be swindled, but why this should bore him more than it should enrage him or make him weep, none can tell.

"Let's see it." Jimmie gave him the ring and he went away. When he returned, he drummed on the counter and stared at the ceiling. "It's worth about two hundred dollars."

"It is, is it?" said the fat person.

"Yes."

"Would you give two hundred for it?"

"If I was buying diamonds for myself I might. But as a dealer, I might give a hundred. Or maybe a hundred and fifty."

"You would, would you?" said the fat person. Jimmie took the ring again and the two marched away.

The fat person led swiftly some distance down the sidewalk. When he stopped he said: "Well, I'll take the ring at a hundred."

"All right," said the Mole. "I'll keep to my bargain although it seems as if I might have struck higher."

"A hundred dollars is a good deal of money," said the fat person. "The Montana—"

"Take the ring," said Jimmie.

The other counted out the hundred in bills. "Here's your money— gimme the ring." At this point they eyed each other warily but the transfer was made in safety. This ornament of politics had the ring and the polished and courtly gentleman had the bills.

"Well, good-bye, old boy," cried the fat person.

"Good luck to you," rejoined Jimmie. "I'd come and break a cold bottle with you only I must light out for Chicago to see my girl. Say," he said facing around again, "I almost wish I hadn't—"

But the fat person waved his hand gaily and walked rapidly away. "Ta-ta, old boy," he cried. Jimmie the Mole gazed after him wistfully.

The next morning Jimmie was in New York. When he arrived at Flasher's flat she was at breakfast. He took from his jacket one hundred dollars in bills and from his finger he took her ring. He laid them on the table before her.

"There," he said with a tired sigh.

"Same old game, Jimmie?"

"Same old game."

"You always were so smooth, Jimmie," murmured Flasher.

This money would have endured some time if the Mole had not fallen in love with his luck and gone to the races. In consequence he was again obliged to borrow the two hundred dollar diamond from Flasher.

The next day he appeared in a jewelry shop in a remote eastside street. "Fred," he said to the proprietor, "I want you to make me a ringer for this again." He handed the man the diamond ring. "And, look here, I won't pay more than three dollars either. A guy in Boston the other day charged me four dollars and a half for the same fake you make."

If you are a politician and you allow a man to substitute a ring of paste and gold plate for a two-hundred-dollar diamond ring and sell it to you for a hundred dollars merely because you have had a jeweler appraise the real diamond—if you are this kind of an ass and dwell in a live ward, let your idiocy be known. It will make you friends. People will laugh and vote for you out of a sense of humor. If you don't believe it, look at the returns and see who was elected last year to the board of aldermen from the 204th ward of the city of Boston.

1896?

[*Bulletin of the New York Public Library,*
Vol. 60 (October, 1956), pp. 483–486.]

AN ELOQUENCE OF GRIEF*

The windows were high and saintly, of the shape that is found in churches. From time to time a policeman at the door spoke sharply to some incoming person. "Take your hat off!" He displayed in his voice the horror of a priest when the sanctity of a chapel is defied or forgotten. The courtroom was crowded with people who sloped back comfortably in their chairs, regarding with undeviating glances the procession, and its attendant and guardian policemen, that moved slowly inside the spear-topped railing. All persons connected with a case went close to the magistrate's desk before a word was spoken in the matter, and then their voices were toned to the ordinary talking strength. The crowd in the courtroom could not hear a sentence; they could merely see shifting figures, men that gestured quietly, women that sometimes raised an eager eloquent arm. They could not always see the judge, although they were able to estimate his location by the tall stands surmounted by white globes that were at either hand of him. And so those who had come for curiosity's sweet sake wore an air of being in wait for a cry of anguish, some loud painful protestation that would bring the proper thrill to their jaded, world-weary nerves—wires that refused to vibrate for ordinary affairs.

Inside the railing the court officers shuffled the various groups with speed and skill; and behind the desk the magistrate patiently toiled his way through mazes of wonderful testimony.

In a corner of this space devoted to those who had business before the judge, an officer in plain clothes stood with a girl that wept constantly. None seemed to notice the girl, and there was no reason why she should be noticed, if the curious in the body of the courtroom were not interested in the devastation which tears bring upon some complexions. Her tears seemed to burn like acid, and they left fierce pink marks on her face. Occasionally the girl looked across the room, where two well-dressed young women and a man stood waiting with the serenity of people who are not concerned as to the interior fittings of a jail.

The business of the court progressed, and presently the girl, the officer, and the well-dressed contingent stood before the judge. Thereupon two lawyers engaged in some preliminary firewheels, which were endured generally in silence. The girl, it appeared, was accused of stealing fifty dollars' worth of silk clothing from the room of one of the well-dressed women. She had been a servant in the house.

In a clear way, and with none of the ferocity that an accuser often

* *Midnight Sketches.*

exhibits in a police court, calmly and moderately, the two young women gave their testimony. Behind them stood their escort, always mute. His part, evidently, was to furnish the dignity, and he furnished it heavily, almost massively.

When they had finished, the girl told her part. She had full, almost Afric lips, and they had turned quite white. The lawyer for the others asked some questions, which he did—be it said, in passing—with the air of a man throwing flowerpots at a stone house.

It was a short case and soon finished. At the end of it the judge said that, considering the evidence, he would have to commit the girl for trial. Instantly the quick-eyed court officer began to clear the way for the next case. The well-dressed women and their escort turned one way and the girl turned another, toward a door with an austere arch leading into a stone-paved passage. Then it was that a great cry rang through the court-room, the cry of this girl who believed that she was lost.

The loungers, many of them, underwent a spasmodic movement as if they had been knifed. The court officers rallied quickly. The girl fell back opportunely for the arms of one of them, and her wild heels clicked twice on the floor. "I am innocent! Oh, I am innocent!"

People pity those who need none, and the guilty sob alone; but, innocent or guilty, this girl's scream described such a profound depth of woe, it was so graphic of grief, that it slit with a dagger's sweep the curtain of commonplace, and disclosed the gloom-shrouded specter that sat in the young girl's heart so plainly, in so universal a tone of the mind, that a man heard expressed some far-off midnight terror of his own thought.

The cries died away down the stone-paved passage. A patrolman leaned one arm composedly on the railing, and down below him stood an aged, almost toothless wanderer, tottering and grinning.

"Plase, yer honor," said the old man as the time arrived for him to speak, "if ye'll lave me go this time, I've niver been dhrunk befoor, sir."

A court officer lifted his hand to hide a smile.

1896?

[*The Open Boat and Other Stories*. London:
William Heinemann (April 18, 1898), pp. 267–270.]

THE AUCTION*

Some said that Ferguson gave up sailoring because he was tired of the sea. Some said that it was because he loved a woman. In truth it was because he was tired of the sea and because he loved a woman.

He saw the woman once, and immediately she became for him the symbol of all things unconnected with the sea. He did not trouble to look again at the gray old goddess, the muttering slave of the moon. Her splendors, her treacheries, her smiles, her rages, her vanities were no longer on his mind. He took heels after a little human being, and the woman made his thought spin at all times like a top; whereas the ocean had only made him think when he was on watch.

He developed a grin for the power of the sea, and, in derision, he wanted to sell the red-and-green parrot which had sailed four voyages with him. The woman, however, had a sentiment concerning the bird's plumage, and she commanded Ferguson to keep it, in order, as it happened, that she might forget to put food in its cage.

The parrot did not attend the wedding. It stayed at home and blasphemed at a stock of furniture, bought on the installment plan, and arrayed for the reception of the bride and groom.

As a sailor, Ferguson had suffered the acute hankering for port; and being now always in port, he tried to force life to become an endless picnic. He was not an example of diligent and peaceful citizenship. Ablution became difficult in the little apartment, because Ferguson kept the washbasin filled with ice and bottles of beer: and so, finally, the dealer in second-hand furniture agreed to auction the household goods on commission. Owing to an exceedingly liberal definition of a term, the parrot and cage were included. "On the level?" cried the parrot. "On the level? On the level? On the level?"

On the way to the sale, Ferguson's wife spoke hopefully. "You can't tell, Jim," she said. "Perhaps some of 'em will get to biddin', and we might get almost as much as we paid for the things."

The auction room was in a cellar. It was crowded with people and with house furniture; so that as the auctioneer's assistant moved from one piece to another he caused a great shuffling. There was an astounding number of old women in curious bonnets. The rickety stairway was thronged with men who wished to smoke and be free from the old women.

* *Midnight Sketches.*

Two lamps made all the faces appear yellow as parchment. Incidentally they could impart a luster of value to very poor furniture.

The auctioneer was a fat, shrewd-looking individual who seemed also to be a great bully. The assistant was the most imperturbable of beings, moving with the dignity of an image on rollers. As the Fergusons forced their way down the stairway, the assistant roared: "Number twenty-one!"

"Number twenty-one!" cried the auctioneer. "Number twenty-one! A fine new handsome bureau! Two dollars? Two dollars is bid! Two and a half! Two and a half! Three? Three is bid. Four! Four dollars! A fine new handsome bureau at four dollars! Four dollars! Four dollars! F-o-u-r d-o-l-l-a-r-s! Sold at four dollars."

"On the level?" cried the parrot, muffled somewhere among furniture and carpets. "On the level? On the level?" Every one tittered.

Mrs. Ferguson had turned pale, and gripped her husband's arm. "Jim! Did you hear? The bureau—four dollars—"

Ferguson glowered at her with the swift brutality of a man afraid of a scene. "Shut up, can't you!"

Mrs. Ferguson took a seat upon the steps; and hidden there by the thick ranks of men, she began to softly sob. Through her tears appeared the yellowish mist of the lamplight, streaming about the monstrous shadows of the spectators. From time to time these latter whispered eagerly: "See, that went cheap!" In fact when anything was bought at a particularly low price, a murmur of admiration arose for the successful bidder.

The bedstead was sold for two dollars, the mattresses and springs for one dollar and sixty cents. This figure seemed to go through the woman's heart. There was derision in the sound of it. She bowed her head in her hands. "Oh, God, a dollar sixty! Oh, God, a dollar sixty!"

The parrot was evidently under heaps of carpet, but the dauntless bird still raised the cry, "On the level?"

Some of the men near Mrs. Ferguson moved timidly away upon hearing her low sobs. They perfectly understood that a woman in tears is formidable.

The shrill voice went like a hammer, beat and beat, upon the woman's heart. An odor of varnish, of the dust of old carpets, assailed her and seemed to possess a sinister meaning. The golden haze from the two lamps was an atmosphere of shame, sorrow, greed. But it was when the parrot called that a terror of the place and of the eyes of the people arose in her so strongly that she could not have lifted her head any more than if her neck had been of iron.

At last came the parrot's turn. The assistant fumbled until he found the ring of the cage, and the bird was drawn into view. It adjusted its feathers calmly and cast a rolling wicked eye over the crowd.

"Oh, the good ship Sarah sailed the seas,
And the wind it blew all day—"

This was part of a ballad which Ferguson had tried to teach it. With a singular audacity and scorn, the parrot bawled these lines at the auctioneer as if it considered them to bear some particular insult.

The throng in the cellar burst into laughter. The auctioneer attempted to start the bidding, and the parrot interrupted with a repetition of the lines. It swaggered to and fro on its perch, and gazed at the faces of the crowd, with so much rowdy understanding and derision that even the auctioneer could not confront it. The auction was brought to a halt; a wild hilarity developed, and every one gave jeering advice.

Ferguson looked down at his wife and groaned. She had cowered against the wall, hiding her face. He touched her shoulder, and she arose. They sneaked softly up the stairs with heads bowed.

Out in the street, Ferguson gripped his fists and said: "Oh, but wouldn't I like to strangle it!"

His wife cried in a voice of wild grief: "It—it m-made us a laughingstock in—in front of all that crowd!"

For the auctioning of their household goods, the sale of their home— this financial calamity lost its power in the presence of the social shame contained in a crowd's laughter.

1896?
[*The Open Boat and Other Stories.* London:
William Heinemann (April 18, 1898), pp. 273–277.]

A POKER GAME

Usually a poker game is a picture of peace. There is no drama so low-voiced and serene and monotonous. If an amateur loser does not softly curse, there is no orchestral support. Here is one of the most exciting and absorbing occupations known to intelligent American manhood; here a year's reflection is compressed into a moment of thought; here the nerves may stand on end and scream to themselves, but a tranquillity as from heaven is only interrupted by the click of chips. The higher the stakes the more quiet the scene; this is a law that applies everywhere save on the stage.

And yet sometimes in a poker game things happen. Everybody remembers the celebrated corner on bay rum that was triumphantly consummated by Robert F. Cinch, of Chicago, assisted by the United States courts and whatever other federal power he needed. Robert F. Cinch enjoyed his victory four months. Then he died, and young Bobbie Cinch came to New York in order to more clearly demonstrate that there was a good deal of fun in twenty-two million dollars.

Old Henry Spuytendyvil owns all the real estate in New York save that previously appropriated by the hospitals and Central Park. He had been a friend of Bob's father. When Bob appeared in New York, Spuytendyvil entertained him correctly. It came to pass that they just naturally played poker.

One night they were having a small game in an uptown hotel. There were five of them, including two lawyers and a politician. The stakes depended on the ability of the individual fortune.

Bobbie Cinch had won rather heavily. He was as generous as sunshine, and when luck chases a generous man it chases him hard, even though he cannot bet with all the skill of his opponents.

Old Spuytendyvil had lost a considerable amount. One of the lawyers from time to time smiled quietly, because he knew Spuytendyvil well, and he knew that anything with the name of loss attached to it sliced the old man's heart into sections.

At midnight Archie Bracketts, the actor, came into the room. "How you holding 'em, Bob?" said he.

"Pretty well," said Bob.

"Having any luck, Mr. Spuytendyvil?"

"Blooming bad," grunted the old man.

Bracketts laughed and put his foot on the round of Spuytendyvil's chair. "There," said he, "I'll queer your luck for you." Spuytendyvil sat at the end of the table. "Bobbie," said the actor, presently, as young Cinch won another pot, "I guess I better knock your luck." So he took his foot from the old man's chair and placed it on Bob's chair. The lad grinned good-naturedly and said he didn't care.

Bracketts was in a position to scan both of the hands. It was Bob's ante, and old Spuytendyvil threw in a red chip. Everybody passed out up to Bobbie. He filled in the pot and drew a card.

Spuytendyvil drew a card. Bracketts, looking over his shoulder, saw him holding the ten, nine, eight, and seven of diamonds. Theatrically speaking, straight flushes are as frequent as berries on a juniper tree, but as a matter of truth the reason that straight flushes are so admired is because they are not as common as berries on a juniper tree. Bracketts stared; drew a cigar slowly from his pocket, and, placing it between his teeth, forgot its existence.

Bobbie was the only other stayer. Bracketts flashed an eye for the lad's hand and saw the nine, eight, six, and five of hearts. Now, there are but six hundred and forty-five emotions possible to the human mind, and Bracketts immediately had them all. Under the impression that he had finished his cigar, he took it from his mouth and tossed it toward the grate without turning his eyes to follow its flight.

There happened to be a complete silence around the green-clothed table. Spuytendyvil was studying his hand with a kind of contemptuous smile, but in his eyes there perhaps was to be seen a cold, stern light expressing something sinister and relentless.

Young Bob sat as he had sat. As the pause grew longer, he looked up once inquiringly at Spuytendyvil.

The old man reached for a white chip. "Well, mine are worth about that much," said he, tossing it into the pot. Thereupon he leaned back comfortably in his chair and renewed his stare at the five straight diamonds. Young Bob extended his hand leisurely toward his stack. It occurred to Bracketts that he was smoking, but he found no cigar in his mouth.

The lad fingered his chips and looked pensively at his hand. The silence of those moments oppressed Bracketts like the smoke from a conflagration.

Bobbie Cinch continued for some moments to coolly observe his cards. At last he breathed a little sigh and said, "Well, Mr. Spuytendyvil, I can't play a sure thing against you." He threw in a white chip. "I'll just call you. I've got a straight flush." He faced down his cards.

Old Spuytendyvil's fear, horror, and rage could only be equaled in volume to a small explosion of gasoline. He dashed his cards upon the table. "There!" he shouted, glaring frightfully at Bobbie. "I've got a straight flush, too! And mine is Jack high!"

Bobbie was at first paralyzed with amazement, but in a moment he recovered, and, apparently observing something amusing in the situation, he grinned.

Archie Bracketts, having burst his bond of silence, yelled for joy and relief. He smote Bobbie on the shoulder. "Bob, my boy," he cried exuberantly, "you're no gambler, but you're a mighty good fellow, and if you hadn't been you would be losing a good many dollars this minute."

Old Spuytendyvil glowered at Bracketts. "Stop making such an infernal din, will you, Archie," he said morosely. His throat seemed filled with pounded glass. "Pass the whiskey."

1896?

[*Last Words*. London: Digby, Long & Co.
(March, 1902), pp. 263–267.]

A MAN AND SOME OTHERS

Dark mesquite spread from horizon to horizon. There was no house or horseman from which a mind could evolve a city or a crowd. The world was declared to be a desert and unpeopled. Sometimes, however, on days when no heat mist arose, a blue shape, dim, of the substance of a specter's veil, appeared in the southwest, and a pondering sheepherder might remember that there were mountains.

In the silence of these plains the sudden and childish banging of a tin pan could have made an iron-nerved man leap into the air. The sky was ever flawless; the maneuvering of clouds was an unknown pageant; but at times a sheepherder could see, miles away, the long white streamers of dust rising from the feet of another's flock, and the interest became intense.

Bill was arduously cooking his dinner, bending over the fire and toiling like a blacksmith. A movement, a flash of strange color perhaps, off in the bushes, caused him to suddenly turn his head. Presently he arose, and, shading his eyes with his hand, stood motionless and gazing. He perceived at last a Mexican sheepherder winding through the brush toward his camp.

"Hello!" shouted Bill.

The Mexican made no answer, but came steadily forward until he was within some twenty yards. There he paused and, folding his arms, drew himself up in the manner affected by the villain in the play. His serape muffled the lower part of his face, and his great sombrero shaded his brow. Being unexpected and also silent, he had something of the quality of an apparition; moreover, it was clearly his intention to be mystic and sinister.

The American's pipe, sticking carelessly in the corner of his mouth, was twisted until the wrong side was uppermost, and he held his frying pan poised in the air. He surveyed with evident surprise this apparition in the mesquite. "Hello, José!" he said. "What's the matter?"

The Mexican spoke with the solemnity of funeral tollings: "Beel, you mus' geet off range. We want you geet off range. We no like. Un'erstan'? We no like."

"What you talking about?" said Bill. "No like what?"

"We no like you here. Un'erstan'? Too mooch. You mus' geet out. We no like. Un'erstan'?"

"Understand? No; I don't know what the blazes you're gittin' at." Bill's eyes wavered in bewilderment, and his jaw fell. "I must git out? I must git off the range? What you givin' us?"

The Mexican unfolded his serape with his small yellow hand. Upon his face was then to be seen a smile that was gently, almost caressingly murderous. "Beel," he said, "git out!"

Bill's arm dropped until the frying pan was at his knee. Finally he turned again toward the fire. "Go on, you doggone little yaller rat!" he said over his shoulder. "You fellers can't chase me off this range. I got as much right here as anybody."

"Beel," answered the other in a vibrant tone, thrusting his head forward and moving one foot, "you geet out or we keel you."

"Who will?" said Bill.

"I—and the others." The Mexican tapped his breast gracefully.

Bill reflected for a time, and then he said: "You ain't got no manner of licence to warn me off'n this range, and I won't move a rod. Understand? I've got rights, and I suppose if I don't see 'em through, no one is likely to give me a good hand and help me lick you fellers, since I'm the only white man in half a day's ride. Now, look; if you fellers try to rush this camp, I'm goin' to plug about fifty per cent of the gentlemen present, sure. I'm goin' in for trouble, an' I'll git a lot of you. 'Nuther thing: if I was a fine valuable caballero like you, I'd stay in the rear till the shootin' was done, because I'm goin' to make a particular p'int of shootin' you through the chest." He grinned affably, and made a gesture of dismissal.

As for the Mexican, he waved his hands in a consummate expression of indifference. "Oh, all right," he said. Then, in a tone of deep menace and glee, he added: "We will keel you eef you no geet. They have decide'."

"They have, have they?" said Bill. "Well, you tell them to go to the devil!"

II

Bill had been a mine owner in Wyoming, a great man, an aristocrat, one who possessed unlimited credit in the saloons down the gulch. He had the social weight that could interrupt a lynching or advise a bad man of the particular merits of a remote geographical point. However, the fates exploded the toy balloon with which they had amused Bill, and on the evening of the same day he was a professional gambler with ill fortune dealing him unspeakable irritation in the shape of three big cards whenever another fellow stood pat. It is well here to inform the world that Bill considered his calamities of life all dwarfs in comparison with the excitement of one particular evening when three kings came to him with criminal regularity against a man who always filled a straight. Later he became a cowboy, more weirdly abandoned than if he had never been an aristocrat. By this time all that remained of his former splendor was his pride, or his vanity, which was one thing which need not have remained. He killed the foreman of the ranch over an inconsequent matter as to which of them was a liar, and the midnight train carried him eastward. He became a brakeman on the Union Pacific, and really gained high honors in the hobo war that for many years has devastated the beautiful railroads of our country. A creature of ill fortune himself, he practised all the ordinary cruelties upon these other creatures of ill fortune. He was of so fierce a mien that tramps usually surrendered at once whatever coin or tobacco they had in their possession; and if afterward he kicked them from the train, it was only because this was a recognized treachery of the war upon the hoboes. In a famous battle fought in Nebraska in 1879, he would have achieved a lasting distinction if it had not been for a deserter from the United States army. He was at the head of a heroic and sweeping charge which really broke the power of the hoboes in that county for three months; he had already worsted four tramps with his own coupling stick, when a stone thrown by the ex-third-baseman of F Troop's nine laid him flat on the prairie, and later enforced a stay in the hospital in Omaha. After his recovery he engaged with other railroads, and shuffled cars in countless yards. An order to strike came upon him in Michigan, and afterward the vengeance of the railroad pursued him until he assumed a name. This mask is like the darkness in which the burglar chooses to move. It destroys many of the healthy fears. It is a small thing, but it eats that which we call our conscience. The conductor of No. 419 stood in the caboose within two feet of Bill's nose and called him a liar. Bill requested him to use a milder term. He had not bored the foreman of Tin Can Ranch with any such request, but had killed him with expedition. The conductor seemed to insist, and so Bill let the matter drop.

He became the bouncer of a saloon on the Bowery in New York. Here most of his fights were as successful as had been his brushes with the hoboes in the West. He gained the complete admiration of the four clean bartenders who stood behind the great and glittering bar. He was an honored man. He nearly killed Bad Hennessy, who, as a matter of fact, had more reputation than ability, and his fame moved up the Bowery and down the Bowery.

But let a man adopt fighting as his business, and the thought grows constantly within him that it is his business to fight. These phrases became mixed in Bill's mind precisely as they are here mixed; and let a man get this idea in his mind, and defeat begins to move toward him over the unknown ways of circumstance. One summer night three sailors from the U.S.S. *Seattle* sat in the saloon drinking and attending to other people's affairs in an amiable fashion. Bill was a proud man since he had thrashed so many citizens, and it suddenly occurred to him that the loud talk of the sailors was very offensive. So he swaggered upon their attention and warned them that the saloon was the flowery abode of peace and gentle silence. They glanced at him in surprise, and without a moment's pause consigned him to a worse place than any stoker of them knew. Whereupon he flung one of them through the side door before the others could prevent it. On the sidewalk there was a short struggle, with many hoarse epithets in the air, and then Bill slid into the saloon again. A frown of false rage was upon his brow, and he strutted like a savage king. He took a long yellow night stick from behind the lunch counter and started importantly toward the main doors to see that the incensed seamen did not again enter.

The ways of sailormen are without speech, and, together in the street, the three sailors exchanged no word, but they moved at once. Landsmen would have required three years of discussion to gain such unanimity. In silence, and immediately, they seized a long piece of scantling that lay handy. With one forward to guide the battering ram and with two behind him to furnish the power, they made a beautiful curve and came down like the Assyrians on the front door of that saloon.

Strange and still strange are the laws of fate. Bill, with his kingly frown and his long night stick, appeared at precisely that moment in the doorway. He stood like a statue of victory; his pride was at its zenith; and in the same second this atrocious piece of scantling punched him in the bulwarks of his stomach, and he vanished like a mist. Opinions differed as to where the end of the scantling landed him, but it was ultimately clear that it landed him in southwestern Texas, where he became a sheepherder.

The sailors charged three times upon the plate glass front of the saloon, and when they had finished, it looked as if it had been the victim of a rural fire company's success in saving it from the flames. As the proprietor of the place surveyed the ruins, he remarked that Bill was a very zealous guardian of property. As the ambulance surgeon surveyed Bill, he remarked that the wound was really an excavation.

III

As his Mexican friend tripped blithely away, Bill turned with a thoughtful face to his frying pan and his fire. After dinner he drew his revolver from its scarred old holster and examined every part of it. It was the revolver that had dealt death to the foreman, and it had also been in free fights in which it had dealt death to several or none. Bill loved it because its allegiance was more than that of man, horse, or dog. It questioned neither social nor moral position; it obeyed alike the saint and the assassin. It was the claw of the eagle, the tooth of the lion, the poison of the snake; and when he swept it from its holster, this minion smote where he listed, even to the battering of a far penny. Wherefore it was his dearest possession, and was not to be exchanged in southwestern Texas for a handful of rubies, nor even the shame and homage of the conductor of No. 419.

During the afternoon he moved through his monotony of work and leisure with the same air of deep meditation. The smoke of his supper-time fire was curling across the shadowy sea of mesquite when the instinct of the plainsman warned him that the stillness, the desolation, was again invaded. He saw a motionless horseman in black outline against the pallid sky. The silhouette displayed serape and sombrero, and even the Mexican spurs as large as pies. When this black figure began to move toward the camp, Bill's hand dropped to his revolver.

The horseman approached until Bill was enabled to see pronounced American features and a skin too red to grow on a Mexican face. Bill released his grip on his revolver.

"Hello!" called the horseman.

"Hello!" answered Bill.

The horseman cantered forward. "Good evening," he said, as he again drew rein.

"Good evenin'," answered Bill, without committing himself by too much courtesy.

For a moment the two men scanned each other in a way that is not ill-mannered on the plains, where one is in danger of meeting horsethieves or tourists.

Bill saw a type which did not belong in the mesquite. The young fellow had invested in some Mexican trappings of an expensive kind. Bill's eyes searched the outfit for some sign of craft, but there was none. Even with his local regalia, it was clear that the young man was of a far, black Northern city. He had discarded the enormous stirrups of his Mexican saddle; he used the small English stirrup, and his feet were thrust forward until the steel tightly gripped his ankles. As Bill's eyes traveled over the stranger, they lighted suddenly upon the stirrups and the thrust feet, and immediately he smiled in a friendly way. No dark purpose could dwell in the innocent heart of a man who rode thus on the plains.

As for the stranger, he saw a tattered individual with a tangle of hair and beard, and with a complexion turned brick-color from the sun and whiskey. He saw a pair of eyes that at first looked at him as the wolf looks at the wolf, and then became childlike, almost timid, in their glance. Here was evidently a man who had often stormed the iron walls of the city of success, and who now sometimes valued himself as the rabbit values his prowess.

The stranger smiled genially and sprang from his horse. "Well, sir, I suppose you will let me camp here with you tonight?"

"Eh?" said Bill.

"I suppose you will let me camp here with you tonight?"

Bill for a time seemed too astonished for words. "Well," he answered, scowling in inhospitable annoyance, "well, I don't believe this here is a good place to camp tonight, mister."

The stranger turned quickly from his saddle girth.

"What?" he said in surprise. "You don't want me here? You don't want me to camp here?"

Bill's feet scuffled awkwardly, and he looked steadily at a cactus plant. "Well, you see, mister," he said, "I'd like your company well enough, but —you see, some of these here greasers are goin' to chase me off the range tonight; and while I might like a man's company all right, I couldn't let him in for no such game when he ain't got nothin' to do with the trouble."

"Going to chase you off the range?" cried the stranger.

"Well, they said they were goin' to do it," said Bill.

"And—great heavens!—will they kill you, do you think?"

"Don't know. Can't tell till afterwards. You see, they take some feller that's alone like me, and then they rush his camp when he ain't quite ready for 'em, and ginerally plug 'im with a sawed-off shotgun load before he has a chance to git at 'em. They lay around and wait for their chance, and it comes soon enough. Of course a feller alone like me has got to let up watching some time. Maybe they ketch 'im asleep. Maybe the feller gits tired waiting, and goes out in broad day, and kills two or three just to make the whole crowd pile on him and settle the thing. I heard of a case like that once. It's awful hard on a man's mind—to git a gang after him."

"And so they're going to rush your camp tonight?" cried the stranger. "How do you know? Who told you?"

"Feller come and told me."

"And what are you going to do? Fight?"

"Don't see nothin' else to do," answered Bill, gloomily, still staring at the cactus plant.

There was a silence. Finally the stranger burst out in an amazed cry. "Well, I never heard of such a thing in my life! How many of them are there?"

"Eight," answered Bill. "And now look-a here: you ain't got no manner of business foolin' around here just now, and you might better lope off before dark. I don't ask no help in this here row. I know your happening along here just now don't give me no call on you, and you'd better hit the trail."

"Well, why in the name of wonder don't you go get the sheriff?" cried the stranger.

"Oh, hell!" said Bill.

IV

Long, smoldering clouds spread in the western sky, and to the east silver mists lay on the purple gloom of the wilderness.

Finally, when the great moon climbed the heavens and cast its ghastly radiance upon the bushes, it made a new and more brilliant crimson of the campfire, where the flames capered merrily through its mesquite branches, filling the silence with the fire chorus, an ancient melody which surely bears a message of the inconsequence of individual tragedy—a message that is in the boom of the sea, the sliver of the wind through the grass-blades, the silken clash of hemlock boughs.

No figures moved in the rosy space of the camp, and the search of the moonbeams failed to disclose a living thing in the bushes. There was no owl-faced clock to chant the weariness of the long silence that brooded upon the plain.

The dew gave the darkness under the mesquite a velvet quality that made air seem nearer to water, and no eye could have seen through it the black things that moved like monster lizards toward the camp. The branches, the leaves, that are fain to cry out when death approaches in the wilds, were frustrated by these mystic bodies gliding with the finesse of the escaping serpent. They crept forward to the last point where assuredly no frantic attempt of the fire could discover them, and there they paused to locate the prey. A romance relates the tale of the black cell hidden deep in the earth, where, upon entering, one sees only the little eyes of snakes fixing him in menaces. If a man could have approached a certain spot in the bushes, he would not have found it romantically necessary to have his hair rise. There would have been a sufficient expression of horror in the feeling of the death-hand at the nape of his neck and in his rubber knee joints.

Two of these bodies finally moved toward each other until for each there grew out of the darkness a face placidly smiling with tender dreams of assassination. "The fool is asleep by the fire, God be praised!" The lips of the other widened in a grin of affectionate appreciation of the fool and his plight. There was some signaling in the gloom, and then began a series of subtle rustlings, interjected often with pauses during which no sound arose but the sound of faint breathing.

A bush stood like a rock in the stream of firelight, sending its long shadow backward. With painful caution the little company traveled along this shadow, and finally arrived at the rear of the bush. Through its branches they surveyed for a moment of comfortable satisfaction a form in a gray blanket extended on the ground near the fire. The smile of joyful anticipation fled quickly, to give place to a quiet air of business. Two men lifted shotguns with much of the barrels gone, and, sighting these weapons through the branches, pulled trigger together.

The noise of the explosions roared over the lonely mesquite as if these guns wished to inform the entire world; and as the gray smoke fled, the dodging company in back of the bush saw the blanketed form twitching. Whereupon they burst out in chorus in a laugh, and arose as merry as a lot of banqueters. They gleefully gestured congratulations, and strode bravely into the light of the fire.

Then suddenly a new laugh rang from some unknown spot in the darkness. It was a fearsome laugh of ridicule, hatred, ferocity. It might have been demoniac. It smote them motionless in their gleeful prowl, as the stern voice from the sky smites the legendary malefactor. They might have been a weird group in wax, the light of the dying fire on their yellow faces and shining athwart their eyes turned toward the darkness whence might come the unknown and the terrible.

The thing in the gray blanket no longer twitched; but if the knives in their hands had been thrust toward it, each knife was now drawn back, and its owner's elbow was thrown upward, as if he expected death from the clouds.

This laugh had so chained their reason that for a moment they had no wit to flee. They were prisoners to their terror. Then suddenly the belated decision arrived, and with bubbling cries they turned to run; but at that instant there was a long flash of red in the darkness, and with the report one of the men shouted a bitter shout, spun once, and tumbled headlong. The thick bushes failed to impede the rout of the others.

The silence returned to the wilderness. The tired flames faintly illumined the blanketed thing and the flung corpse of the marauder, and sang the fire chorus, the ancient melody which bears the message of the inconsequence of human tragedy.

v

"Now you are worse off than ever," said the young man, dry-voiced and awed.

"No, I ain't," said Bill, rebelliously. "I'm one ahead."

After reflection, the stranger remarked, "Well, there's seven more."

They were cautiously and slowly approaching the camp. The sun was flaring its first warming rays over the gray wilderness. Upreared twigs, prominent branches, shone with golden light, while the shadows under the mesquite were heavily blue.

Suddenly the stranger uttered a frightened cry. He had arrived at a point whence he had, through openings in the thicket, a clear view of a dead face.

"Gosh!" said Bill, who at the next instant had seen the thing; "I thought at first it was that there José. That would have been queer, after what I told 'im yesterday."

They continued their way, the stranger wincing in his walk, and Bill exhibiting considerable curiosity.

The yellow beams of the new sun were touching the grim hues of the dead Mexican's face, and creating there an inhuman effect which made his countenance more like a mask of dulled brass. One hand, grown curiously thinner, had been flung out regardlessly to a cactus bush.

Bill walked forward and stood looking respectfully at the body. "I know that feller; his name is Miguel. He——"

The stranger's nerves might have been in that condition when there is no backbone to the body, only a long groove. "Good heavens!" he exclaimed, much agitated; "don't speak that way!"

"What way?" said Bill. "I only said his name was Miguel."

After a pause the stranger said: "Oh, I know; but——" He waved his hand. "Lower your voice, or something. I don't know. This part of the business rattles me, don't you see?"

"Oh, all right," replied Bill, bowing to the other's mysterious mood. But in a moment he burst out violently and loud in the most extraordinary profanity, the oaths winging from him as the sparks go from the funnel.

He had been examining the contents of the bundled gray blanket, and he had brought forth, among other things, his frying pan. It was now only a rim with a handle; the Mexican volley had centered upon it. A Mexican shotgun of the abbreviated description is ordinarily loaded with flatirons, stove-lids, lead pipe, old horseshoes, sections of chain, window weights, railroad sleepers and spikes, dumbbells, and any other junk which may be at hand. When one of these loads encounters a man vitally, it is likely to make an impression upon him, and a cooking utensil may be supposed to subside before such an assault of curiosities.

Bill held high his desecrated frying pan, turning it this way and that way. He swore until he happened to note the absence of the stranger. A moment later he saw him leading his horse from the bushes. In silence and sullenly the young man went about saddling the animal. Bill said, "Well, goin' to pull out?"

The stranger's hands fumbled uncertainly at the throat-latch. Once he exclaimed irritably, blaming the buckle for the trembling of his fingers. Once he turned to look at the dead face with the light of the morning sun upon it. At last he cried, "Oh, I know the whole thing was all square enough—couldn't be squarer—but—somehow or other, that man there takes the heart out of me." He turned his troubled face for another look. "He seems to be all the time calling me a—he makes me feel like a murderer."

"But," said Bill, puzzling, "you didn't shoot him, mister; I shot him."

"I know; but I feel that way, somehow. I can't get rid of it."

Bill considered for a time; then he said diffidently, "Mister, you're an eddycated man, ain't you?"

"What?"

"You're what they call a—a eddycated man, ain't you?"

The young man, perplexed, evidently had a question upon his lips, when there was a roar of guns, bright flashes, and in the air such hooting and whistling as would come from a swift flock of steam boilers. The stranger's horse gave a mighty, convulsive spring, snorting wildly in its sudden anguish, fell upon its knees, scrambled afoot again, and was away in the uncanny death-run known to men who have seen the finish of brave horses.

"This comes from discussin' things," cried Bill, angrily.

He had thrown himself flat on the ground facing the thicket whence had come the firing. He could see the smoke winding over the bush tops. He lifted his revolver, and the weapon came slowly up from the ground and poised like the glittering crest of a snake. Somewhere on his face there was a kind of a smile, cynical, wicked, deadly, of a ferocity which at the same time had brought a deep flush to his face, and had caused two upright lines to glow in his eyes.

"Hello, José!" he called, amiable for satire's sake. "Got your old blunderbusses loaded up again yet?"

The stillness had returned to the plain. The sun's brilliant rays swept over the sea of mesquite, painting the far mists of the west with faint rosy light, and high in the air some great bird fled toward the south.

"You come out here," called Bill, again addressing the landscape, "and I'll give you some shootin' lessons. That ain't the way to shoot." Receiving no reply, he began to invent epithets and yell them at the thicket. He was something of a master of insult, and, moreover, he dived into his memory to bring forth imprecations tarnished with age, unused since fluent Bowery days. The occupation amused him, and sometimes he laughed so that it was uncomfortable for his chest to be against the ground.

Finally the stranger, prostrate near him, said wearily, "Oh, they've gone."

"Don't you believe it," replied Bill, sobering swiftly. "They're there yet—every man of 'em."

"How do you know?"

"Because I do. They won't shake us so soon. Don't put your head up, or they'll get you, sure."

Bill's eyes, meanwhile, had not wavered from their scrutiny of the thicket in front. "They're there, all right; don't you forget it. Now you listen." So he called out: "José! Ojo, José! Speak up, *hombre!* I want have talk. Speak up, you yaller cuss, you!"

Whereupon a mocking voice from off in the bushes said, "Señor?"

"There," said Bill to his ally; "didn't I tell you? The whole batch." Again he lifted his voice. "José—look—ain't you gittin' kinder tired? You better go home, you fellers, and git some rest."

The answer was a sudden furious chatter of Spanish, eloquent with hatred, calling down upon Bill all the calamities which life holds. It was as if some one had suddenly enraged a cageful of wildcats. The spirits of all the revenges which they had imagined were loosened at this time, and filled the air.

"They're in a holler," said Bill, chuckling, "or there'd be shootin'."

Presently he began to grow angry. His hidden enemies called him nine kinds of coward, a man who could fight only in the dark, a baby who would run from the shadows of such noble Mexican gentlemen, a dog that sneaked. They described the affair of the previous night, and informed him of the base advantage he had taken of their friend. In fact, they in all sincerity endowed him with every quality which he no less earnestly believed them to possess. One could have seen the phrases bite him as he lay there on the ground fingering his revolver.

VI

It is sometimes taught that men do the furious and desperate thing from an emotion that is as even and placid as the thoughts of a village clergyman on Sunday afternoon. Usually, however, it is to be believed that a panther is at the time born in the heart, and that the subject does not resemble a man picking mulberries.

"B' Gawd!" said Bill, speaking as from a throat filled with dust, "I'll go after 'em in a minute."

"Don't you budge an inch!" cried the stranger, sternly. "Don't you budge!"

"Well," said Bill, glaring at the bushes—"well——"

"Put your head down!" suddenly screamed the stranger, in white alarm. As the guns roared, Bill uttered a loud grunt, and for a moment leaned panting on his elbow, while his arm shook like a twig. Then he upreared like a great and bloody spirit of vengeance, his face lighted with the blaze of his last passion. The Mexicans came swiftly and in silence.

The lightning action of the next few moments was of the fabric of dreams to the stranger. The muscular struggle may not be real to the drowning man. His mind may be fixed on the far, straight shadows in back of the stars, and the terror of them. And so the fight, and his part in it, had to the stranger only the quality of a picture half drawn. The rush of feet, the spatter of shots, the cries, the swollen faces seen like masks on the smoke, resembled a happening of the night.

And yet afterward certain lines, forms, lived out so strongly from the incoherence that they were always in his memory.

He killed a man, and the thought went swiftly by him, like the feather on the gale, that it was easy to kill a man.

Moreover, he suddenly felt for Bill, this grimy sheepherder, some deep form of idolatry. Bill was dying, and the dignity of last defeat, the superiority of him who stands in his grave, was in the pose of the lost sheepherder.

The stranger sat on the ground idly mopping the sweat and powder stain from his brow. He wore the gentle idiot smile of an aged beggar as he watched three Mexicans limping and staggering in the distance. He noted at this time that one who still possessed a serape had from it none of the grandeur of the cloaked Spaniard, but that against the sky the silhouette resembled a cornucopia of childhood's Christmas.

They turned to look at him, and he lifted his weary arm to menace them with his revolver. They stood for a moment banded together, and hooted curses at him.

Finally he arose and, walking some paces, stooped to loosen Bill's gray hands from a throat. Swaying as if slightly drunk, he stood looking down into the still face.

Struck suddenly with a thought, he went about with dulled eyes on the ground, until he plucked his gaudy blanket from where it lay, dirty from trampling feet. He dusted it carefully, and then returned and laid it over Bill's form. There he again stood motionless, his mouth just agape and the same stupid glance in his eyes, when all at once he made a gesture of fright and looked wildly about him.

He had almost reached the thicket when he stopped, smitten with alarm. A body contorted, with one arm stiff in the air, lay in his path. Slowly and warily he moved around it, and in a moment the bushes, nodding and whispering, their leaf-faces turned toward the scene behind him, swung and swung again into stillness and the peace of the wilderness.

February, 1897

[*The Century Magazine*, Vol. 53, pp. 601–607.]

THE OPEN BOAT

A Tale Intended to be after the Fact: Being
the Experience of Four Men from the
Sunk Steamer *Commodore*

I

None of them knew the color of the sky. Their eyes glanced level, and were fastened upon the waves that swept toward them. These waves were of the hue of slate, save for the tops, which were of foaming white, and all of the men knew the colors of the sea. The horizon narrowed and widened, and dipped and rose, and at all times its edge was jagged with waves that seemed thrust up in points like rocks.

Many a man ought to have a bathtub larger than the boat which here rode upon the sea. These waves were most wrongfully and barbarously abrupt and tall, and each froth-top was a problem in small-boat navigation.

The cook squatted in the bottom, and looked with both eyes at the six inches of gunwale which separated him from the ocean. His sleeves were rolled over his fat forearms, and the two flaps of his unbuttoned vest dangled as he bent to bail out the boat. Often he said, "Gawd! that was a narrow clip." As he remarked it he invariably gazed eastward over the broken sea.

The oiler, steering with one of the two oars in the boat, sometimes raised himself suddenly to keep clear of water that swirled in over the stern. It was a thin little oar, and it seemed often ready to snap.

The correspondent, pulling at the other oar, watched the waves and wondered why he was there.

The injured captain, lying in the bow, was at this time buried in that profound dejection and indifference which comes, temporarily at least, to even the bravest and most enduring when, willy-nilly, the firm fails, the army loses, the ship goes down. The mind of the master of a vessel is rooted deep in the timbers of her, though he command for a day or a decade; and this captain had on him the stern impression of a scene in the grays of dawn of seven turned faces, and later a stump of a topmast with a white ball on it, that slashed to and fro at the waves, went low and lower, and down. Thereafter there was something strange in his voice. Although steady, it was deep with mourning, and of a quality beyond oration or tears.

"Keep'er a little more south, Billie," said he.

"A little more south, sir," said the oiler in the stern.

A seat in this boat was not unlike a seat upon a bucking broncho, and by the same token a broncho is not much smaller. The craft pranced and reared and plunged like an animal. As each wave came, and she rose for it, she seemed like a horse making at a fence outrageously high. The manner of her scramble over these walls of water is a mystic thing, and, moreover, at the top of them were ordinarily these problems in white water, the foam racing down from the summit of each wave requiring a new leap, and a leap from the air. Then, after scornfully bumping a crest, she would slide and race and splash down a long incline, and arrive bobbing and nodding in front of the next menace.

A singular disadvantage of the sea lies in the fact that after successfully surmounting one wave you discover that there is another behind it just as important and just as nervously anxious to do something effective in the way of swamping boats. In a ten-foot dinghy one can get an idea of the resources of the sea in the line of waves that is not probable to the average experience, which is never at sea in a dinghy. As each slaty wall of water approached, it shut all else from the view of the men in the boat, and it was not difficult to imagine that this particular wave was the final outburst of the ocean, the last effort of the grim water. There was a terrible grace in the move of the waves, and they came in silence, save for the snarling of the crests.

In the wan light the faces of the men must have been gray. Their eyes must have glinted in strange ways as they gazed steadily astern. Viewed from a balcony, the whole thing would doubtless have been weirdly picturesque. But the men in the boat had no time to see it, and if they had had leisure, there were other things to occupy their minds. The sun swung steadily up the sky, and they knew it was broad day because the color of the sea changed from slate to emerald-green streaked with amber lights, and the foam was like tumbling snow. The process of the breaking day was unknown to them. They were aware only of this effect upon the color of the waves that rolled toward them.

In disjointed sentences the cook and the correspondent argued as to the difference between a life-saving station and a house of refuge. The cook had said: "There's a house of refuge just north of the Mosquito Inlet Light, and as soon as they see us they'll come off in their boat and pick us up."

"As soon as who see us?" said the correspondent.

"The crew," said the cook.

"Houses of refuge don't have crews," said the correspondent. "As I understand them, they are only places where clothes and grub are stored for the benefit of shipwrecked people. They don't carry crews."

"Oh, yes, they do," said the cook.

"No, they don't," said the correspondent.

"Well, we're not there yet, anyhow," said the oiler, in the stern.

"Well," said the cook, "perhaps it's not a house of refuge that I'm thinking of as being near Mosquito Inlet Light; perhaps it's a lifesaving station."

"We're not there yet," said the oiler in the stern.

II

As the boat bounced from the top of each wave the wind tore through the hair of the hatless men, and as the craft plopped her stern down again the spray slashed past them. The crest of each of these waves was a hill, from the top of which the men surveyed for a moment a broad tumultuous expanse, shining and wind-riven. It was probably splendid, it was probably glorious, this play of the free sea, wild with lights of emerald and white and amber.

"Bully good thing it's an onshore wind," said the cook. "If not, where would we be? Wouldn't have a show."

"That's right," said the correspondent.

The busy oiler nodded his assent.

Then the captain, in the bow, chuckled in a way that expressed humor, contempt, tragedy, all in one. "Do you think we've got much of a show now, boys?" said he.

Whereupon the three were silent, save for a trifle of hemming and hawing. To express any particular optimism at this time they felt to be childish and stupid, but they all doubtless possessed this sense of the situation in their minds. A young man thinks doggedly at such times. On the other hand, the ethics of their condition was decidedly against any open suggestion of hopelessness. So they were silent.

"Oh, well," said the captain, soothing his children, "we'll get ashore all right."

But there was that in his tone which made them think; so the oiler quoth, "Yes! if this wind holds."

The cook was bailing. "Yes! if we don't catch hell in the surf."

Canton-flannel gulls flew near and far. Sometimes they sat down on the sea, near patches of brown seaweed that rolled over the waves with a movement like carpets on a line in a gale. The birds sat comfortably in groups, and they were envied by some in the dinghy, for the wrath of the sea was no more to them than it was to a covey of prairie chickens a thousand miles inland. Often they came very close and stared at the men with black bead-like eyes. At these times they were uncanny and sinister in their unblinking scrutiny, and the men hooted angrily at them, telling them to be gone. One came, and evidently decided to alight on the top of the captain's head. The bird flew parallel to the boat and did not circle, but made short sidelong jumps in the air in chicken fashion. His black eyes were wistfully fixed upon the captain's head. "Ugly brute," said the oiler to the bird. "You look as if you were made with a jackknife." The cook and the correspondent swore darkly at the creature. The captain naturally wished to knock it away with the end of the heavy painter, but he did not dare do it, because anything resembling an emphatic gesture would have capsized this freighted boat; and so, with his open hand, the captain gently and carefully waved the gull away. After it had been discouraged from the pursuit the captain breathed easier on account of his hair, and others breathed easier because the bird struck their minds at this time as being somehow gruesome and ominous.

In the meantime the oiler and the correspondent rowed. And also they rowed. They sat together in the same seat, and each rowed an oar. Then the oiler took both oars; then the correspondent took both oars; then the oiler; then the correspondent. They rowed and they rowed. The very ticklish part of the business was when the time came for the reclining one in the stern to take his turn at the oars. By the very last star of truth, it is easier to steal eggs from under a hen than it was to change seats in the dinghy. First the man in the stern slid his hand along the thwart and moved with care, as if he were of Sèvres. Then the man in the rowing-seat slid his hand along the other thwart. It was all done with the most extraordinary care. As the two sidled past each other, the whole party kept watchful eyes on the coming wave, and the captain cried: "Look out, now! Steady, there!"

The brown mats of seaweed that appeared from time to time were like islands, bits of earth. They were traveling, apparently, neither one way nor the other. They were, to all intents, stationary. They informed the men in the boat that it was making progress slowly toward the land.

The captain, rearing cautiously in the bow after the dinghy soared on a great swell, said that he had seen the lighthouse at Mosquito Inlet. Presently the cook remarked that he had seen it. The correspondent was at the oars then, and for some reason he too wished to look at the lighthouse; but his back was toward the far shore, and the waves were important, and for some time he could not seize an opportunity to turn his head. But at last there came a wave more gentle than the others, and when at the crest of it he swiftly scoured the western horizon.

"See it?" said the captain.

"No," said the correspondent, slowly; "I didn't see anything."

"Look again," said the captain. He pointed. "It's exactly in that direction."

At the top of another wave the correspondent did as he was bid, and this time his eyes chanced on a small, still thing on the edge of the swaying horizon. It was precisely like the point of a pin. It took an anxious eye to find a lighthouse so tiny.

"Think we'll make it, Captain?"

"If this wind holds and the boat don't swamp, we can't do much else," said the captain.

The little boat, lifted by each towering sea and splashed viciously by the crests, made progress that in the absence of seaweed was not apparent to those in her. She seemed just a wee thing wallowing, miraculously top up, at the mercy of five oceans. Occasionally a great spread of water, like white flames, swarmed into her.

"Bail her, cook," said the captain, serenely.

"All right, Captain," said the cheerful cook.

III

It would be difficult to describe the subtle brotherhood of men that was here established on the seas. No one said that it was so. No one mentioned it. But it dwelt in the boat, and each man felt it warm him. They were a captain, an oiler, a cook, and a correspondent, and they were friends— friends in a more curiously ironbound degree than may be common. The hurt captain, lying against the water jar in the bow, spoke always in a low voice and calmly; but he could never command a more ready and swiftly obedient crew than the motley three of the dinghy. It was more than a mere recognition of what was best for the common safety. There was surely in it a quality that was personal and heartfelt. And after this devotion to the commander of the boat, there was this comradeship, that the correspondent, for instance, who had been taught to be cynical of men, knew even at the time was the best experience of his life. But no one said that it was so. No one mentioned it.

"I wish we had a sail," remarked the captain. "We might try my overcoat on the end of an oar, and give you two boys a chance to rest." So the cook and the correspondent held the mast and spread wide the overcoat; the oiler steered; and the little boat made good way with her new rig. Sometimes the oiler had to scull sharply to keep a sea from breaking into the boat, but otherwise sailing was a success.

Meanwhile the lighthouse had been growing slowly larger. It had now almost assumed color, and appeared like a little gray shadow on the sky. The man at the oars could not be prevented from turning his head rather often to try for a glimpse of this little gray shadow.

At last, from the top of each wave, the men in the tossing boat could see land. Even as the lighthouse was an upright shadow on the sky, this land seemed but a long black shadow on the sea. It certainly was thinner than paper. "We must be about opposite New Smyrna," said the cook, who had coasted this shore often in schooners. "Captain, by the way, I believe they abandoned that lifesaving station there about a year ago."

"Did they?" said the captain.

The wind slowly died away. The cook and the correspondent were not now obliged to slave in order to hold high the oar. But the waves continued their old impetuous swooping at the dinghy, and the little craft, no longer under way, struggled woundily over them. The oiler or the correspondent took the oars again.

Shipwrecks are *apropos* of nothing. If men could only train for them and have them occur when the men had reached pink condition, there would be less drowning at sea. Of the four in the dinghy none had slept any time worth mentioning for two days and two nights previous to embarking in the dinghy, and in the excitement of clambering about the deck of a foundering ship they had also forgotten to eat heartily.

For these reasons, and for others, neither the oiler nor the correspondent was fond of rowing at this time. The correspondent wondered ingenuously how in the name of all that was sane could there be people who thought it amusing to row a boat. It was not an amusement; it was a diabolical punishment, and even a genius of mental aberrations could never conclude that it was anything but a horror to the muscles and a crime against the back.

He mentioned to the boat in general how the amusement of rowing struck him, and the weary-faced oiler smiled in full sympathy. Previously to the foundering, by the way, the oiler had worked a double watch in the engine room of the ship.

"Take her easy now, boys," said the captain. "Don't spend yourselves. If we have to run a surf you'll need all your strength, because we'll sure have to swim for it. Take your time."

Slowly the land arose from the sea. From a black line it became a line of black and a line of white—trees and sand. Finally the captain said that he could make out a house on the shore. "That's the house of refuge, sure," said the cook. "They'll see us before long, and come out after us."

The distant lighthouse reared high. "The keeper ought to be able to make us out now, if he's looking through a glass," said the captain. "He'll notify the lifesaving people."

"None of those other boats could have got ashore to give word of this wreck," said the oiler, in a low voice, "else the lifeboat would be out hunting us."

Slowly and beautifully the land loomed out of the sea. The wind came again. It had veered from the northeast to the southeast. Finally a new sound struck the ears of the men in the boat. It was the low thunder of the surf on the shore. "We'll never be able to make the lighthouse now," said the captain. "Swing her head a little more north, Billie."

"A little more north, sir," said the oiler.

Whereupon the little boat turned her nose once more down the wind, and all but the oarsman watched the shore grow. Under the influence of this expansion doubt and direful apprehension were leaving the minds of the men. The management of the boat was still most absorbing, but it could not prevent a quiet cheerfulness. In an hour, perhaps, they would be ashore.

Their backbones had become thoroughly used to balancing in the boat, and they now rode this wild colt of a dinghy like circus men. The correspondent thought that he had been drenched to the skin, but happening to feel in the top pocket of his coat, he found therein eight cigars. Four of them were soaked with seawater; four were perfectly scatheless. After a search, somebody produced three dry matches; and thereupon the four waifs rode impudently in their little boat and, with an assurance of an impending rescue shining in their eyes, puffed at the big cigars, and judged well and ill of all men. Everybody took a drink of water.

IV

"Cook," remarked the captain, "there don't seem to be any signs of life about your house of refuge."

"No," replied the cook. "Funny they don't see us!"

A broad stretch of lowly coast lay before the eyes of the men. It was of low dunes topped with dark vegetation. The roar of the surf was plain, and sometimes they could see the white lip of a wave as it spun up the beach. A tiny house was blocked out black upon the sky. Southward, the slim lighthouse lifted its little gray length.

Tide, wind, and waves were swinging the dinghy northward. "Funny they don't see us," said the men.

The surf's roar was here dulled, but its tone was nevertheless thunderous and mighty. As the boat swam over the great rollers the men sat listening to this roar. "We'll swamp sure," said everybody.

It is fair to say here that there was not a lifesaving station within twenty miles in either direction; but the men did not know this fact, and in consequence they made dark and opprobrious remarks concerning the eyesight of the nation's lifesavers. Four scowling men sat in the dinghy and surpassed records in the invention of epithets.

"Funny they don't see us."

The light-heartedness of a former time had completely faded. To their sharpened minds it was easy to conjure pictures of all kinds of incompetency and blindness and, indeed, cowardice. There was the shore of the populous land, and it was bitter and bitter to them that from it came no sign.

"Well," said the captain, ultimately, "I suppose we'll have to make a try for ourselves. If we stay out here too long, we'll none of us have strength left to swim after the boat swamps."

And so the oiler, who was at the oars, turned the boat straight for the shore. There was a sudden tightening of muscles. There was some thinking.

"If we don't all get ashore," said the captain—"if we don't all get ashore, I suppose you fellows know where to send news of my finish?"

They then briefly exchanged some addresses and admonitions. As for the reflections of the men, there was a great deal of rage in them. Perchance they might be formulated thus: "If I am going to be drowned—if I am going to be drowned—if I am going to be drowned, why, in the name of the seven mad gods who rule the sea, was I allowed to come thus far and contemplate sand and trees? Was I brought here merely to have my nose dragged away as I was about to nibble the sacred cheese of life? It is preposterous. If this old ninny-woman, Fate, cannot do better than this, she should be deprived of the management of men's fortunes. She is an old hen who knows not her intention. If she has decided to drown me, why did she not do it in the beginning and save me all this trouble? The whole affair is absurd. . . . But no; she cannot mean to drown me. She dare not drown me. She cannot drown me. Not after all this work." Afterward the man might have had an impulse to shake his fist at the clouds. "Just you drown me, now, and then hear what I call you!"

The billows that came at this time were more formidable. They seemed always just about to break and roll over the little boat in a turmoil of foam. There was a preparatory and long growl in the speech of them. No mind unused to the sea would have concluded that the dinghy could ascend these sheer heights in time. The shore was still afar. The oiler was a wily surf-man. "Boys," he said swiftly, "she won't live three minutes more, and we're too far out to swim. Shall I take her to sea again, Captain?"

"Yes; go ahead!" said the captain.

This oiler, by a series of quick miracles and fast and steady oarsmanship, turned the boat in the middle of the surf and took her safely to sea again.

There was a considerable silence as the boat bumped over the furrowed sea to deeper water. Then somebody in gloom spoke: "Well, anyhow, they must have seen us from the shore by now."

The gulls went in slanting flight up the wind toward the gray, desolate east. A squall, marked by dingy clouds and clouds brick-red, like smoke from a burning building, appeared from the southeast.

"What do you think of those lifesaving people? Ain't they peaches?"

"Funny they haven't seen us."

"Maybe they think we're out here for sport! Maybe they think we're fishin'. Maybe they think we're damned fools."

It was a long afternoon. A changed tide tried to force them southward, but wind and wave said northward. Far ahead, where coastline, sea, and sky formed their mighty angle, there were little dots which seemed to indicate a city on the shore.

"St. Augustine?"

The captain shook his head. "Too near Mosquito Inlet."

And the oiler rowed, and then the correspondent rowed; then the oiler rowed. It was a weary business. The human back can become the seat of more aches and pains than are registered in books for the composite anatomy of a regiment. It is a limited area, but it can become the theater of innumerable muscular conflicts, tangles, wrenches, knots, and other comforts.

"Did you ever like to row, Billie?" asked the correspondent.

"No," said the oiler; "hang it!"

When one exchanged the rowing-seat for a place in the bottom of the boat, he suffered a bodily depression that caused him to be careless of everything save an obligation to wiggle one finger. There was cold seawater swashing to and fro in the boat, and he lay in it. His head, pillowed on a thwart, was within an inch of the swirl of a wave-crest, and sometimes a particularly obstreperous sea came inboard and drenched him once more. But these matters did not annoy him. It is almost certain that if the boat had capsized he would have tumbled comfortably out upon the ocean as if he felt sure that it was a great soft mattress.

"Look! There's a man on the shore!"

"Where?"

"There! See 'im? See 'im?"

"Yes, sure! He's walking along."

"Now he's stopped. Look! He's facing us!"

"He's waving at us!"

"So he is! By thunder!"

"Ah, now we're all right! Now we're all right! There'll be a boat out here for us in half an hour."

"He's going on. He's running. He's going up to that house there."

The remote beach seemed lower than the sea, and it required a searching glance to discern the little black figure. The captain saw a floating stick, and they rowed to it. A bath towel was by some weird chance in the boat, and, tying this on the stick, the captain waved it. The oarsman did not dare turn his head, so he was obliged to ask questions.

"What's he doing now?"

"He's standing still again. He's looking, I think. . . . There he goes again—toward the house. . . . Now he's stopped again."

"Is he waving at us?"

"No, not now; he was, though."

"Look! There comes another man!"

"He's running."

"Look at him go, would you!"

"Why, he's on a bicycle. Now he's met the other man. They're both waving at us. Look!"

"There comes something up the beach."

"What the devil is that thing?"

"Why, it looks like a boat."

"Why, certainly, it's a boat."

"No; it's on wheels."

"Yes, so it is. Well, that must be the lifeboat. They drag them along shore on a wagon."

"That's the lifeboat, sure."

"No, by God, it's—it's an omnibus."

"I tell you it's a lifeboat."

"It is not! It's an omnibus. I can see it plain. See? One of these big hotel omnibuses."

"By thunder, you're right. It's an omnibus, sure as fate. What do you suppose they are doing with an omnibus? Maybe they are going around collecting the life-crew, hey?"

"That's it, likely. Look! There's a fellow waving a little black flag. He's standing on the steps of the omnibus. There come those other two fellows.

Now they're all talking together. Look at the fellow with the flag. Maybe he ain't waving it!"

"That ain't a flag, is it? That's his coat. Why, certainly, that's his coat."

"So it is; it's his coat. He's taken it off and is waving it around his head. But would you look at him swing it!"

"Oh, say, there isn't any lifesaving station there. That's just a winter-resort hotel omnibus that has brought over some of the boarders to see us drown."

"What's that idiot with the coat mean? What's he signaling, anyhow?"

"It looks as if he were trying to tell us to go north. There must be a lifesaving station up there."

"No; he thinks we're fishing. Just giving us a merry hand. See? Ah, there, Willie!"

"Well, I wish I could make something out of those signals. What do you suppose he means?"

"He don't mean anything; he's just playing."

"Well, if he'd just signal us to try the surf again, or to go to sea and wait, or go north, or go south, or go to hell, there would be some reason in it. But look at him! He just stands there and keeps his coat revolving like a wheel. The ass!"

"There come more people."

"Now there's quite a mob. Look! Isn't that a boat?"

"Where? Oh, I see where you mean. No, that's no boat."

"That fellow is still waving his coat."

"He must think we like to see him do that. Why don't he quit it? It don't mean anything."

"I don't know. I think he is trying to make us go north. It must be that there's a lifesaving station there somewhere."

"Say, he ain't tired yet. Look at 'im wave!"

"Wonder how long he can keep that up. He's been revolving his coat ever since he caught sight of us. He's an idiot. Why aren't they getting men to bring a boat out? A fishing boat—one of those big yawls—could come out here all right. Why don't he do something?"

"Oh, it's all right now."

"They'll have a boat out here for us in less than no time, now that they've seen us."

A faint yellow tone came into the sky over the low land. The shadows on the sea slowly deepened. The wind bore coldness with it, and the men began to shiver.

"Holy smoke!" said one, allowing his voice to express his impious mood, "if we keep on monkeying out here! If we've got to flounder out here all night!"

"Oh, we'll never have to stay here all night! Don't you worry. They've seen us now, and it won't be long before they'll come chasing out after us."

The shore grew dusky. The man waving a coat blended gradually into this gloom, and it swallowed in the same manner the omnibus and the group of people. The spray, when it dashed uproariously over the side, made the voyagers shrink and swear like men who were being branded.

"I'd like to catch the chump who waved the coat. I feel like socking him one, just for luck."

"Why? What did he do?"

"Oh, nothing, but then he seemed so damned cheerful."

In the meantime the oiler rowed, and then the correspondent rowed, and then the oiler rowed. Gray-faced and bowed forward, they mechanically, turn by turn, plied the leaden oars. The form of the lighthouse had vanished from the southern horizon, but finally a pale star appeared, just lifting from the sea. The streaked saffron in the west passed before the all-merging darkness, and the sea to the east was black. The land had vanished, and was expressed only by the low and drear thunder of the surf.

"If I am going to be drowned—if I am going to be drowned—if I am going to be drowned, why, in the name of the seven mad gods who rule the sea, was I allowed to come thus far and contemplate sand and trees? Was I brought here merely to have my nose dragged away as I was about to nibble the sacred cheese of life?"

The patient captain, drooped over the water jar, was sometimes obliged to speak to the oarsman.

"Keep her head up! Keep her head up!"

"Keep her head up, sir." The voices were weary and low.

This was surely a quiet evening. All save the oarsman lay heavily and listlessly in the boat's bottom. As for him, his eyes were just capable of noting the tall black waves that swept forward in a most sinister silence, save for an occasional subdued growl of a crest.

The cook's head was on a thwart, and he looked without interest at the water under his nose. He was deep in other scenes. Finally he spoke. "Billie," he murmured, dreamfully, "what kind of pie do you like best?"

V

"Pie!" said the oiler and the correspondent, agitatedly. "Don't talk about those things, blast you!"

"Well," said the cook, "I was just thinking about ham sandwiches, and—"

A night on the sea in an open boat is a long night. As darkness settled finally, the shine of the light, lifting from the sea in the south, changed to full gold. On the northern horizon a new light appeared, a small bluish gleam on the edge of the waters. These two lights were the furniture of the world. Otherwise there was nothing but waves.

Two men huddled in the stern, and distances were so magnificent in the dinghy that the rower was enabled to keep his feet partly warm by thrusting them under his companions. Their legs indeed extended far under the rowing-seat until they touched the feet of the captain forward. Sometimes, despite the efforts of the tired oarsman, a wave came piling into the boat, an icy wave of the night, and the chilling water soaked them anew. They would twist their bodies for a moment and groan, and sleep the dead sleep once more, while the water in the boat gurgled about them as the craft rocked.

The plan of the oiler and the correspondent was for one to row until he lost the ability, and then arouse the other from his sea-water couch in the bottom of the boat.

The oiler plied the oars until his head drooped forward and the overpowering sleep blinded him; and he rowed yet afterward. Then he touched a man in the bottom of the boat, and called his name. "Will you spell me for a little while?" he said meekly.

"Sure, Billie," said the correspondent, awaking and dragging himself to a sitting position. They exchanged places carefully, and the oiler, cuddling down in the seawater at the cook's side, seemed to go to sleep instantly.

The particular violence of the sea had ceased. The waves came without snarling. The obligation of the man at the oars was to keep the boat headed so that the tilt of the rollers would not capsize her, and to preserve her from filling when the crests rushed past. The black waves were silent and hard to be seen in the darkness. Often one was almost upon the boat before the oarsman was aware.

In a low voice the correspondent addressed the captain. He was not sure that the captain was awake, although this iron man seemed to be always awake. "Captain, shall I keep her making for that light north, sir?"

The same steady voice answered him. "Yes. Keep it about two points off the port bow."

The cook had tied a lifebelt around himself in order to get even the warmth which this clumsy cork contrivance could donate, and he seemed almost stove-like when a rower, whose teeth invariably chattered wildly as soon as he ceased his labor, dropped down to sleep.

The correspondent, as he rowed, looked down at the two men sleeping underfoot. The cook's arm was around the oiler's shoulders, and, with their fragmentary clothing and haggard faces, they were the babes of the sea—a grotesque rendering of the old babes in the wood.

Later he must have grown stupid at his work, for suddenly there was a growling of water, and a crest came with a roar and a swash into the boat, and it was a wonder that it did not set the cook afloat in his lifebelt. The cook continued to sleep, but the oiler sat up, blinking his eyes and shaking with the new cold.

"Oh, I'm awful sorry, Billie," said the correspondent, contritely.

"That's all right, old boy," said the oiler, and lay down again and was asleep.

Presently it seemed that even the captain dozed, and the correspondent thought that he was the one man afloat on all the oceans. The wind had a voice as it came over the waves, and it was sadder than the end.

There was a long, loud swishing astern of the boat, and a gleaming trail of phosphorescence, like blue flame, was furrowed on the black waters. It might have been made by a monstrous knife.

Then there came a stillness, while the correspondent breathed with open mouth and looked at the sea.

Suddenly there was another swish and another long flash of bluish light, and this time it was alongside the boat, and might almost have been reached with an oar. The correspondent saw an enormous fin speed like a shadow through the water, hurling the crystalline spray and leaving the long glowing trail.

The correspondent looked over his shoulder at the captain. His face was hidden, and he seemed to be asleep. He looked at the babes of the sea. They certainly were asleep. So, being bereft of sympathy, he leaned a little way to one side and swore softly into the sea.

But the thing did not then leave the vicinity of the boat. Ahead or astern, on one side or the other, at intervals long or short, fled the long sparkling streak, and there was to be heard the *whirroo* of the dark fin. The speed and power of the thing was greatly to be admired. It cut the water like a gigantic and keen projectile.

The presence of this biding thing did not affect the man with the same horror that it would if he had been a picnicker. He simply looked at the sea dully and swore in an undertone.

Nevertheless, it is true that he did not wish to be alone with the thing. He wished one of his companions to awake by chance and keep him company with it. But the captain hung motionless over the water jar, and the oiler and the cook in the bottom of the boat were plunged in slumber.

VI

"If I am going to be drowned—if I am going to be drowned—if I am going to be drowned, why, in the name of the seven mad gods who rule the sea, was I allowed to come thus far and contemplate sand and trees?"

During this dismal night, it may be remarked that a man would conclude that it was really the intention of the seven mad gods to drown him, despite the abominable injustice of it. For it was certainly an abominable injustice to drown a man who had worked so hard, so hard. The man felt it would be a crime most unnatural. Other people had drowned at sea since galleys swarmed with painted sails, but still—

When it occurs to a man that nature does not regard him as important, and that she feels she would not maim the universe by disposing of him, he at first wishes to throw bricks at the temple, and he hates deeply the fact that there are no bricks and no temples. Any visible expression of nature would surely be pelleted with his jeers.

Then, if there be no tangible thing to hoot, he feels, perhaps, the desire to confront a personification and indulge in pleas, bowed to one knee, and with hands supplicant, saying, "Yes, but I love myself."

A high cold star on a winter's night is the word he feels that she says to him. Thereafter he knows the pathos of his situation.

The men in the dinghy had not discussed these matters, but each had, no doubt, reflected upon them in silence and according to his mind. There was seldom any expression upon their faces save the general one of complete weariness. Speech was devoted to the business of the boat.

To chime the notes of his emotion, a verse mysteriously entered the correspondent's head. He had even forgotten that he had forgotten this verse, but it suddenly was in his mind.

A soldier of the Legion lay dying in Algiers;
There was lack of woman's nursing, there was dearth of woman's tears;
But a comrade stood beside him, and he took that comrade's hand,
And he said, "I never more shall see my own, my native land."

In his childhood the correspondent had been made acquainted with the fact that a soldier of the Legion lay dying in Algiers, but he had never regarded the fact as important. Myriads of his schoolfellows had informed him of the soldier's plight, but the dinning had naturally ended by making him perfectly indifferent. He had never considered it his affair that a soldier of the Legion lay dying in Algiers, nor had it appeared to him as a matter for sorrow. It was less to him than the breaking of a pencil's point.

Now, however, it quaintly came to him as a human, living thing. It was no longer merely a picture of a few throes in the breast of a poet, meanwhile drinking tea and warming his feet at the grate; it was an actuality —stern, mournful, and fine.

The correspondent plainly saw the soldier. He lay on the sand with his feet out straight and still. While his pale left hand was upon his chest in an attempt to thwart the going of his life, the blood came between his fingers. In the far Algerian distance, a city of low square forms was set against a sky that was faint with the last sunset hues. The correspondent, plying the oars and dreaming of the slow and slower movements of the lips of the soldier, was moved by a profound and perfectly impersonal comprehension. He was sorry for the soldier of the Legion who lay dying in Algiers.

The thing which had followed the boat and waited had evidently grown bored at the delay. There was no longer to be heard the slash of the cutwater, and there was no longer the flame of the long trail. The light in the north still glimmered, but it was apparently no nearer to the boat. Sometimes the boom of the surf rang in the correspondent's ears, and he turned the craft seaward then and rowed harder. Southward, some one had evidently built a watch fire on the beach. It was too low and too far to be seen, but it made a shimmering, roseate reflection upon the bluff in back of it, and this could be discerned from the boat. The wind came stronger, and sometimes a wave suddenly raged out like a mountain cat, and there was to be seen the sheen and sparkle of a broken crest.

The captain, in the bow, moved on his water jar and sat erect. "Pretty long night," he observed to the correspondent. He looked at the shore. "Those lifesaving people take their time."

"Did you see that shark playing around?"

"Yes, I saw him. He was a big fellow, all right."

"Wish I had known you were awake."

Later the correspondent spoke into the bottom of the boat. "Billie!" There was a slow and gradual disentanglement. "Billie, will you spell me?"

"Sure," said the oiler.

As soon as the correspondent touched the cold, comfortable seawater in the bottom of the boat and had huddled close to the cook's lifebelt he was deep in sleep, despite the fact that his teeth played all the popular airs. This sleep was so good to him that it was but a moment before he heard a voice call his name in a tone that demonstrated the last stages of exhaustion. "Will you spell me?"

"Sure, Billie."

The light in the north had mysteriously vanished, but the correspondent took his course from the wide-awake captain.

Later in the night they took the boat farther out to sea, and the captain directed the cook to take one oar at the stern and keep the boat facing the seas. He was to call out if he should hear the thunder of the surf. This plan enabled the oiler and the correspondent to get respite together. "We'll give those boys a chance to get into shape again," said the captain. They curled down and, after a few preliminary chatterings and trembles, slept once more the dead sleep. Neither knew they had bequeathed to the cook the company of another shark, or perhaps the same shark.

As the boat caroused on the waves, spray occasionally bumped over the side and gave them a fresh soaking, but this had no power to break their repose. The ominous slash of the wind and the water affected them as it would have affected mummies.

"Boys," said the cook, with the notes of every reluctance in his voice, "she's drifted in pretty close. I guess one of you had better take her to sea again." The correspondent, aroused, heard the crash of the toppled crests.

As he was rowing, the captain gave him some whiskey-and-water, and this steadied the chills out of him. "If I ever get ashore and anybody shows me even a photograph of an oar—"

At last there was a short conversation.

"Billie! . . . Billie, will you spell me?"

"Sure," said the oiler.

VII

When the correspondent again opened his eyes, the sea and the sky were each of the gray hue of the dawning. Later, carmine and gold was painted upon the waters. The morning appeared finally, in its splendor, with a sky of pure blue, and the sunlight flamed on the tips of the waves.

On the distant dunes were set many little black cottages, and a tall white windmill reared above them. No man, nor dog, nor bicycle appeared on the beach. The cottages might have formed a deserted village.

The voyagers scanned the shore. A conference was held in the boat. "Well," said the captain, "if no help is coming, we might better try a run through the surf right away. If we stay out here much longer we will be too weak to do anything for ourselves at all." The others silently acquiesced in this reasoning. The boat was headed for the beach. The correspondent wondered if none ever ascended the tall wind-tower, and if then they never looked seaward. This tower was a giant, standing with its back to the plight of the ants. It represented in a degree, to the correspondent, the serenity of nature amid the struggles of the individual—nature in the wind, and nature in the vision of men. She did not seem cruel to him then, nor beneficent, nor treacherous, nor wise. But she was indifferent, flatly indifferent. It is, perhaps, plausible that a man in this situation, impressed with the unconcern of the universe, should see the innumerable flaws of his life, and have them taste wickedly in his mind, and wish for another chance. A distinction between right and wrong seems absurdly clear to him, then, in this new ignorance of the grave-edge, and he understands that if he were given another opportunity he would mend his conduct and his words, and be better and brighter during an introduction or at a tea.

"Now, boys," said the captain, "she is going to swamp sure. All we can do is to work her in as far as possible, and then when she swamps, pile out and scramble for the beach. Keep cool now, and don't jump until she swamps sure."

The oiler took the oars. Over his shoulders he scanned the surf. "Captain," he said, "I think I'd better bring her about and keep her head-on to the seas and back her in."

"All right, Billie," said the captain. "Back her in." The oiler swung the boat then, and, seated in the stern, the cook and the correspondent were obliged to look over their shoulders to contemplate the lonely and indifferent shore.

The monstrous inshore rollers heaved the boat high until the men were again enabled to see the white sheets of water scudding up the slanted beach. "We won't get in very close," said the captain. Each time a man could wrest his attention from the rollers, he turned his glance toward the shore, and in the expression of the eyes during this contemplation there was a singular quality. The correspondent, observing the others, knew that they were not afraid, but the full meaning of their glances was shrouded.

As for himself, he was too tired to grapple fundamentally with the fact. He tried to coerce his mind into thinking of it, but the mind was dominated at this time by the muscles, and the muscles said they did not care. It merely occurred to him that if he should drown it would be a shame.

There were no hurried words, no pallor, no plain agitation. The men simply looked at the shore. "Now, remember to get well clear of the boat when you jump," said the captain.

Seaward the crest of a roller suddenly fell with a thunderous crash, and the long white comber came roaring down upon the boat.

"Steady now," said the captain. The men were silent. They turned their eyes from the shore to the comber and waited. The boat slid up the incline, leaped at the furious top, bounced over it, and swung down the long back of the wave. Some water had been shipped, and the cook bailed it out.

But the next crest crashed also. The tumbling, boiling flood of white water caught the boat and whirled it almost perpendicular. Water swarmed in from all sides. The correspondent had his hands on the gunwale at this time, and when the water entered at that place he swiftly withdrew his fingers, as if he objected to wetting them.

The little boat, drunken with this weight of water, reeled and snuggled deeper into the sea.

"Bail her out, cook! Bail her out!" said the captain.

"All right, Captain," said the cook.

"Now, boys, the next one will do for us sure," said the oiler. "Mind to jump clear of the boat."

The third wave moved forward, huge, furious, implacable. It fairly swallowed the dinghy, and almost simultaneously the men tumbled into the sea. A piece of lifebelt had lain in the bottom of the boat, and as the correspondent went overboard he held this to his chest with his left hand.

The January water was icy, and he reflected immediately that it was colder than he had expected to find it off the coast of Florida. This appeared to his dazed mind as a fact important enough to be noted at the time. The coldness of the water was sad; it was tragic. This fact was somehow mixed and confused with his opinion of his own situation, so that it seemed almost a proper reason for tears. The water was cold.

When he came to the surface he was conscious of little but the noisy water. Afterward he saw his companions in the sea. The oiler was ahead in the race. He was swimming strongly and rapidly. Off to the correspondent's left, the cook's great white and corked back bulged out of the water; and in the rear the captain was hanging with his one good hand to the keel of the overturned dinghy.

There is a certain immovable quality to a shore, and the correspondent wondered at it amid the confusion of the sea.

It seemed also very attractive; but the correspondent knew that it was a long journey, and he paddled leisurely. The piece of life preserver lay under him, and sometimes he whirled down the incline of a wave as if he were on a hand-sled.

But finally he arrived at a place in the sea where travel was beset with difficulty. He did not pause swimming to inquire what manner of current had caught him, but there his progress ceased. The shore was set before him like a bit of scenery on a stage, and he looked at it and understood with his eyes each detail of it.

As the cook passed, much farther to the left, the captain was calling to him, "Turn over on your back, cook! Turn over on your back and use the oar."

"All right, sir." The cook turned on his back, and, paddling with an oar, went ahead as if he were a canoe.

Presently the boat also passed to the left of the correspondent, with the captain clinging with one hand to the keel. He would have appeared like a man raising himself to look over a board fence if it were not for the extraordinary gymnastics of the boat. The correspondent marveled that the captain could still hold to it.

They passed on nearer to shore—the oiler, the cook, the captain—and following them went the water jar, bouncing gaily over the seas.

The correspondent remained in the grip of this strange new enemy—a current. The shore, with its white slope of sand and its green bluff topped with little silent cottages, was spread like a picture before him. It was very near to him then, but he was impressed as one who, in a gallery, looks at a scene from Brittany or Algiers.

He thought: "I am going to drown? Can it be possible? Can it be possible? Can it be possible?" Perhaps an individual must consider his own death to be the final phenomenon of nature.

But later a wave perhaps whirled him out of this small deadly current, for he found suddenly that he could again make progress toward the shore. Later still he was aware that the captain, clinging with one hand to the keel of the dinghy, had his face turned away from the shore and toward him, and was calling his name. "Come to the boat! Come to the boat!"

In his struggle to reach the captain and the boat, he reflected that when one gets properly wearied drowning must really be a comfortable arrangement—a cessation of hostilities accompanied by a large degree of relief; and he was glad of it, for the main thing in his mind for some moments had been horror of the temporary agony. He did not wish to be hurt.

Presently he saw a man running along the shore. He was undressing with most remarkable speed. Coat, trousers, shirt, everything flew magically off him.

"Come to the boat!" called the captain.

"All right, Captain." As the correspondent paddled, he saw the captain let himself down to bottom and leave the boat. Then the correspondent performed his one little marvel of the voyage. A large wave caught him and flung him with ease and supreme speed completely over the boat and far beyond it. It struck him even then as an event in gymnastics and a true miracle of the sea. An overturned boat in the surf is not a plaything to a swimming man.

The correspondent arrived in water that reached only to his waist, but his condition did not enable him to stand for more than a moment. Each wave knocked him into a heap, and the undertow pulled at him.

Then he saw the man who had been running and undressing, and undressing and running, come bounding into the water. He dragged ashore the cook, and then waded toward the captain; but the captain waved him away and sent him to the correspondent. He was naked—naked as a tree in winter; but a halo was about his head, and he shone like a saint. He gave a strong pull, and a long drag, and a bully heave at the correspondent's hand. The correspondent, schooled in the minor formulae, said, "Thanks, old man." But suddenly the man cried, "What's that?" He pointed a swift finger. The correspondent said, "Go."

In the shallows, face downward, lay the oiler. His forehead touched sand that was periodically, between each wave, clear of the sea.

The correspondent did not know all that transpired afterward. When he achieved safe ground he fell, striking the sand with each particular part of his body. It was as if he had dropped from a roof, but the thud was grateful to him.

It seems that instantly the beach was populated with men with blankets, clothes, and flasks, and women with coffeepots and all the remedies sacred to their minds. The welcome of the land to the men from the sea was warm and generous; but a still and dripping shape was carried slowly up the beach, and the land's welcome for it could only be the different and sinister hospitality of the grave.

When it came night, the white waves paced to and fro in the moonlight, and the wind brought the sound of the great sea's voice to the men on the shore, and they felt that they could then be interpreters.

June, 1897

[*Scribner's Magazine*, Vol. 21, pp. 728–740.]

HOW THE DONKEY LIFTED THE HILLS

Many people suppose that the donkey is lazy. This is a great mistake. It is his pride.

Years ago, there was nobody quite so fine as the donkey. He was a great swell in those times. No one could express an opinion of anything without the donkey showing where he was in it. No one could mention the name of an important personage without the donkey declaring how well he knew him.

The donkey was, above all things, a proud and aristocratic beast.

One day a party of animals were discussing one thing and another, until finally the conversation drifted around to mythology.

"I have always admired that giant, Atlas," observed the ox in the course of the conversation. "It was amazing how he could carry things."

"Oh yes, Atlas," said the donkey. "I knew him very well. I once met a man and we got talking of Atlas. I expressed my admiration for the giant and my desire to meet him some day, if possible. Whereupon the man said there was nothing quite so easy. He was sure that his dear friend, Atlas, would be happy to meet so charming a donkey. Was I at leisure next Monday? Well, then, could I dine with him upon that date? So, you see, it was all arranged. I found Atlas to be a very pleasant fellow."

"It has always been a wonder to me how he could have carried the earth on his back," said the horse.

"Oh, my dear sir, nothing is more simple," cried the donkey. "One has only to make up one's mind to it, and then—do it. That is all. I am quite sure that if I wished I could carry a range of mountains upon my back."

All the others said, "Oh, my!"

"Yes, I could," asserted the donkey, stoutly. "It is merely a question of making up one's mind. I will bet."

"I will wager also," said the horse. "I will wager my ears that you can't carry a range of mountains upon your back."

"Done," cried the donkey.

Forthwith the party of animals set out for the mountains. Suddenly, however, the donkey paused and said, "Oh, but look here. Who will place this range of mountains upon my back? Surely I can not be expected to do the loading also."

Here was a great question. The party consulted. At length the ox said, "We will have to ask some men to shovel the mountain upon the donkey's back."

Most of the others clapped their hoofs or their paws and cried, "Ah, that is the thing."

The horse, however, shook his head doubtfully. "I don't know about these men. They are very sly. They will introduce some deviltry into the affair."

"Why, how silly," said the donkey. "Apparently you do not understand men. They are the most gentle, guileless creatures."

"Well," retorted the horse, "I will doubtless be able to escape, since I am not to be encumbered with any mountains. Proceed."

The donkey smiled in derision at these observations by the horse.

Presently they came upon some men who were laboring away like mad, digging ditches, felling trees, gathering fruits, carrying water, building huts.

"Look at these men, would you," said the horse. "Can you trust them after this exhibition of their depravity? See how each one selfishly—"

The donkey interrupted with a loud laugh.

"What nonsense!"

And then he cried out to the men, "Ho, my friends, will you please come and shovel a range of mountains upon my back?"

"What?"

"Will you please come and shovel a range of mountains upon my back?"

The men were silent for a time. Then they went apart and debated. They gesticulated a great deal.

Some apparently said one thing and some another. At last they paused, and one of their number came forward.

"Why do you wish a range of mountains shoveled upon your back?"

"It is a wager," cried the donkey.

The men consulted again. And as the discussion became older, their heads went closer and closer together, until they merely whispered, and did not gesticulate at all. Ultimately they cried, "Yes, certainly we will shovel a range of mountains upon your back for you."

"Ah, thanks," said the donkey.

"Here is surely some deviltry," said the horse behind his hoof to the ox.

The entire party proceeded then to the mountains. The donkey drew a long breath and braced his legs.

"Are you ready?" asked the men.

"All ready," cried the donkey.

The men began to shovel.

The dirt and stones flew over the donkey's back in showers. It was not long before his legs were hidden. Presently only his neck and head remained in view. Then at last this wise donkey vanished. There had been made no great effect upon the range of mountains. They still towered toward the sky.

The watching crowd saw a heap of dirt and stones make a little movement, and then was heard a muffled cry. "Enough! Enough! It was not two ranges of mountains! It is not fair! It is not fair!"

But the men only laughed as they shoveled on.

"Enough! Enough! Oh, woe is me—thirty snow-capped peaks upon my little back. Ah, these false, false men! Oh, virtuous, wise, and holy men, desist."

The men again laughed. They were as busy as fiends with their shovels.

"Ah, brutal, cowardly, accursed men; ah, good, gentle, and holy men, please remove some of those damnable peaks. I will adore your beautiful shovels forever. I will be slave to the beckoning of your little fingers. I will no longer be my own donkey—I will be your donkey."

The men burst into a triumphant shout and ceased shoveling.

"Swear it, mountain-carrier!"

"I swear! I swear! I swear!"

The other animals scampered away then, for these men in their plots and plans were very terrible. "Poor old foolish fellow," cried the horse; "he may keep his ears. He will need them to hear and count the blows that are now to fall upon him."

The men unearthed the donkey. They beat him with their shovels. "Ho, come on, slave." Encrusted with earth, yellow-eyed from fright, the donkey limped toward his prison. His ears hung down like leaves of the plantain during the great rain.

So, now, when you see a donkey with a church, a palace, and three villages upon his back, and he goes with infinite slowness, moving but one leg at a time, do not think him lazy. It is his pride.

June, 1897

[*The Pocket Magazine*, Vol. 4, pp. 144–151.]

THE VICTORY OF THE MOON

The Strong Man of the Hills lost his wife. Immediately he went abroad, calling aloud. The people all crouched afar in the dark of their huts, and cried to him when he was yet a long distance away: "No, no, great chief, we have not even seen the imprint of your wife's sandal in the sand. If we had seen it, you would have found us bowed down in worship before the marks of her ten glorious brown toes, for we are but poor devils of Indians, and the grandeur of the sun rays on her hair would have turned our eyes to dust."

"Her toes are not brown. They are pink," said the Strong Man from the Hills. "Therefore do I believe that you speak the truth when you say you have not seen her, good little men of the valley. In this matter of her great loveliness, however, you speak a little too strongly. As she is no longer among my possessions, I have no mind to hear her praised. Whereabouts is the best man of you?"

None of them had stomach for this honor at the time. They surmised that the Strong Man of the Hills had some plan for combat, and they knew that the best of them would have in this encounter only the strength of the meat in the grip of the fire. "Great King," they said, in one voice, "there is no best man here."

"How is this?" roared the Strong Man. "There must be one who excels. It is a law. Let him step forward, then."

But they solemnly shook their heads. "There is no best man here."

The Strong Man turned upon them so furiously that many fell to the ground. "There must be one. Let him step forward." Shivering, they huddled together and tried, in their fear, to thrust each other toward the Strong Man.

At this time a young philosopher approached the throng slowly. The philosophers of that age were all young men in the full heat of life. The old graybeards were, for the most part, very stupid, and were so accounted.

"Strong Man from the Hills," said the young philosopher, "go to yonder brook and bathe. Then come and eat of this fruit. Then gaze for a time at the blue sky and the green earth. Afterward I have something to say to you."

"You are not so wise that I am obliged to bathe before listening to you?" demanded the Strong Man, insolently.

"No," said the young philosopher. All the people thought this reply very strange.

"Why, then, must I bathe and eat of fruit and gaze at the earth and the sky?"

"Because they are pleasant things to do."

"Have I, do you think, any thirst at this time for pleasant things?"

"Bathe, eat, gaze," said the young philosopher with a gesture.

The Strong Man did, indeed, whirl his bronzed and terrible limbs in the silver water. Then he lay in the shadow of a tree and ate the cool fruit and gazed at the sky and the earth. "This is a fine comfort," he said. After a time he suddenly struck his forehead with his finger. "By the way, did I tell you that my wife had fled from me?"

"I know it," said the young philosopher.

Later the Strong Man slept peacefully. The young philosopher smiled.

But in the night the little men of the valley came clamoring: "O, Strong Man of the Hills, the moon derides you!"

The philosopher went to them in the darkness. "Be still, little people. It is nothing. The derision of the moon is nothing."

But the little men of the valley would not cease their uproar. "O, Strong Man! Strong Man, awake! Awake! The moon derides you!"

Then the Strong Man aroused and shook his locks away from his eyes. "What is it, good little men of the valley?"

"O, Strong Man, the moon derides you! O, Strong Man!"

The Strong Man looked, and there, indeed, was the moon laughing down at him. He sprang to his feet and roared. "Ah, old, fat lump of moon, you laugh! Have you seen my wife?"

The moon said no word, but merely smiled in a way that was like a flash of silver bars.

"Well, then, moon, take this home to her," thundered the Strong Man, and he hurled his spear.

The moon clapped both hands to its eye, and cried: "Oh! Oh!"

The little people of the valley cried: "Oh, this terrible Strong Man! He has smitten our sacred moon in the eye!"

The young philosopher cried nothing at all.

The Strong Man threw his coat of crimson feathers upon the ground. He took his knife and felt its edge. "Look you, philosopher," he said. "I have lost my wife; and the bath, the meal of fruit in the shade, the sight of sky and earth are still good to me. But when this false moon derides me, there must be a killing."

"I understand you," said the young philosopher.

The Strong Man ran off into the night. The little men of the valley clapped their hands in ecstasy and terror. "Ah! ah! what a battle will there be!"

The Strong Man went into his own hills and gathered there many great rocks and trunks of trees. It was strange to see him erect upon a peak of the mountains and hurling these things at the moon. He kept the air full of them.

"Fat moon, come closer," he shouted. "Come closer, and let it be my knife against your knife. Oh, to think that we are obliged to tolerate such an old, fat, stupid, lazy, good-for-nothing moon. You are ugly as death, while I— Oh, moon, you stole my beloved, and it was nothing, but when you stole my beloved and laughed at me, it became another matter. And yet you are so ugly, so fat, so stupid, so lazy, so good-for-nothing. Ah, I shall go mad! Come closer, moon, and let me examine your round, gray skull with this club."

And he always kept the air full of great missiles.

The moon merely laughed, and said: "Why should I come closer?"

Wildly did the Strong Man pile rock upon rock. He built him a tower that was the father of all towers. It made the mountains appear to be babes. Upon the summit of it he swung his great club and flourished his knife.

The little men in the valley far below beheld a great storm, and at the end of it they said: "Look, the moon is dead." The cry went to and fro on the earth: "The moon is dead!"

The Strong Man went to the home of the moon. She, the sought one, lay upon a cloud, and her little foot dangled over the side of it. The Strong Man took this little foot in his two hands and kissed it. "Ah, beloved!" he moaned, "I would rather this little foot was upon my dead neck than that the moon should ever have the privilege of seeing it."

She leaned over the edge of the cloud and gazed at him. "How dusty you are! Why do you puff so? Veritably, you are an ordinary person. Why did I ever find you interesting?"

The Strong Man flung his knife into the air and turned back toward the earth. "If the young philosopher had been at my elbow," he reflected, bitterly, "I would doubtless have gone at the matter in another way. What does my strength avail me in this contest?"

The battered moon, limping homeward, replied to the Strong Man from the Hills: "Aye, surely. My weakness is in this thing as strong as your strength. I am victor with my ugliness, my age, my stoutness, my laziness, my good-for-nothingness. Woman is woman. Men are equal in everything save good fortune. I envy you not."

July, 1897

[*The Pocket Magazine*, Vol. 4, pp. 144–152.]

FLANAGAN AND HIS SHORT
FILIBUSTERING ADVENTURE

"I have got twenty men at me back who will fight to the death," said the warrior to the old filibuster.

"And they can be blowed, for all me," replied the old filibuster. "Common as sparrows—cheap as cigarettes. Show me twenty men with steel clamps on their mouths, with holes in their heads where memory ought to be, and I want 'em. But twenty brave men merely? I'd rather have twenty brave onions."

Thereupon the warrior removed sadly, feeling that no salaams were paid to valor in these days of mechanical excellence.

Valor, in truth, is no bad thing to have when filibustering; but many medals are to be won by the man who knows not the meaning of "pow-wow," before or afterward. Twenty brave men with tongues hung lightly may make trouble rise from the ground like smoke from grass because of their subsequent fiery pride, whereas twenty cow-eyed villains who accept unrighteous and far-compelling kicks as they do the rain of heaven may halo the ultimate history of an expedition with gold, and plentifully bedeck their names, winning forty years of gratitude from patriots, simply by remaining silent. As for the cause, it may be only that they have no friends or other credulous furniture.

If it were not for the curse of the swinging tongue, it is surely to be said that the filibustering industry, flourishing now in the United States, would be pie. Under correct conditions, it is merely a matter of dealing with some little detectives whose skill at search is rated by those who pay them at a value of twelve or twenty dollars each week. It is nearly axiomatic that normally a twelve-dollar-per-week detective cannot defeat a one-hundred-thousand-dollar filibustering excursion. Against the criminal, the detective represents the commonwealth; but in this other case he represents his desire to show cause why his salary should be paid. He represents himself merely, and he counts no more than a grocer's clerk.

But the pride of the successful filibuster often smites him and his cause like an axe, and men who have not confided in their mothers go prone with him. It can make the dome of the Capitol tremble, and incite the senators to overturning benches. It can increase the salaries of detectives who could not detect the location of a pain in the chest. It is a wonderful thing, this pride.

Filibustering was once such a simple game. It was managed blandly by gentle captains and smooth and undisturbed gentlemen who at other times dealt in law, soap, medicine, and bananas. It was a great pity that the little cote of doves in Washington was obliged to rustle officially, and naval men were kept from their berths at night, and sundry custom house people got wiggings, all because the returned adventurer powwowed in his pride. A yellow-and-red banner would have been long since smothered in a shame of defeat if a contract to filibuster had been let to some admirable organization like one of our trusts.

And yet the game is not obsolete; it is still played by the wise and the silent—men whose names are not display-typed and blathered from one end of the country to the other.

There is in mind now a man who knew one side of a fence from the other side when he looked sharply. They were hunting for captains then to command the first vessels of what has since become a famous little fleet. One was recommended to this man, and he said: "Send him down to my office, and I'll look him over." He was an attorney, and he liked to lean back in his chair, twirl a paper knife, and let the other fellow talk.

The seafaring man came, and stood, and appeared confounded. The attorney asked the terrible first question of the filibuster to the applicant. He said, "Why do you want to go?"

The captain reflected, changed his attitude three times, and decided ultimately that he didn't know. He seemed greatly ashamed. The attorney, looking at him, saw that he had eyes that resembled a lambkin's eyes.

"Glory?" said the attorney at last.

"No-o," said the captain.

"Pay?"

"No-o; not that so much."

"Think they'll give you a land grant when they win out?"

"No; never thought."

"No glory. No immense pay. No land grant. What are you going for, then?"

"Well, I don't know," said the captain, with his glance on the floor, and shifting his position again. "I don't know. I guess it's just for fun, mostly." The attorney asked him out to have a drink.

When he stood on the bridge of his outgoing steamer, the attorney saw him again. His shore meekness and uncertainty were gone. He was clear-eyed and strong, aroused like a mastiff at night. He took his cigar out of his mouth, and yelled some sudden language at the deck.

This steamer had about her a quality of unholy medieval disrepair which is usually accounted the principal prerogative of the United States revenue marine. There is many a seaworthy icehouse if she was a good ship. She swashed through the seas as genially as an old wooden clock, burying her head under waves that came only like children at play, and on board it cost a ducking to go from anywhere to anywhere.

The captain had commanded vessels that shore people thought were liners; but when a man gets the ant of desire-to-see-what-it's-like stirring in his heart, he will wallow out to sea in a pail. The thing surpasses a man's love for his sweetheart. The great tank steamer *Thunder Voice* had long been Flanagan's sweetheart, but he was far happier off Hatteras watching this wretched little portmanteau boom down the slant of a wave.

The crew scraped acquaintance, one with another, gradually. Each man came ultimately to ask his neighbor what particular turn of ill fortune or inherited deviltry caused him to try this voyage. When one frank, bold man saw another frank, bold man aboard, he smiled, and they became friends. There was not a mind on board the ship that was not fastened to the dangers of the coast of Cuba, and taking wonder at this prospect and delight in it. Still, in jovial moments they termed each other accursed idiots.

At first there was some trouble in the engine room, where there were many steel animals, for the most part painted red and in other places very shiny, bewildering, complex, incomprehensible to any one who don't care, usually thumping, thumping, thumping, with the monotony of a snore.

It seems that this engine was as whimsical as a gas-meter. The chief engineer was a fine old fellow with a gray mustache; but the engine told him that it didn't intend to budge until it felt better. He came to the bridge and said: "The blamed old thing has laid down on us, sir."

"Who was on duty?" roared the captain.

"The second, sir."

"Why didn't he call you?"

"Don't know, sir." Later the stokers had occasion to thank the stars that they were not second engineers.

The *Foundling* was soundly thrashed by the waves for loitering, while the captain and the engineers fought the obstinate machinery. During this wait on the sea, the first gloom came to the faces of the company. The ocean is wide, and a ship is a small place for the feet, and an ill ship is worriment. Even when she was again under way, the gloom was still upon the crew. From time to time men went to the engine room doors and, looking down, wanted to ask questions of the chief engineer, who slowly prowled to and fro and watched with careful eye his red-painted mysteries. No man wished to have a companion know that he was anxious, and so questions were caught at the lips. Perhaps none commented save the first mate, who remarked to the captain, "Wonder what the bally old thing will do, sir, when we're chased by a Spanish cruiser?"

The captain merely grinned. Later he looked over the side and said to himself with scorn: "Sixteen knots! sixteen knots!—sixteen hinges on the inner gates of Hades! Sixteen knots! Seven is her gait, and nine if you crack her up to it."

There may never be a captain whose crew can't sniff his misgivings. They scent it as a herd scents the menace far through the trees and over the ridges. A captain that does not know that he is on a foundering ship sometimes can take his men to tea and buttered toast twelve minutes before the disaster; but let him fret for a moment in the loneliness of his cabin, and in no time it affects the liver of a distant and sensitive seaman. Even as Flanagan reflected on the *Foundling,* viewing her as a filibuster, word arrived that a winter of discontent had come to the stokeroom.

The captain knew that it requires sky to give a man courage. He sent for a stoker, and talked to him on the bridge. The man, standing under the sky, instantly and shamefacedly denied all knowledge of the business. Nevertheless, a jaw had presently to be broken by a fist because the *Foundling* could only steam nine knots and because the stokeroom has no sky, no wind, no bright horizon.

When the *Foundling* was somewhere off Savannah a blow came from the northeast, and the steamer, headed southeast, rolled like a boiling potato. The first mate was a fine officer, and so a wave crashed him into the deckhouse and broke his arm. The cook was a good cook, and so the heave of the ship flung him heels over head with a pot of boiling water and caused him to lose interest in everything save his legs. "By the piper!" said Flanagan to himself, "this filibustering is no trick with cards."

Later there was more trouble in the stokeroom. All the stokers participated save the one with a broken jaw, who had become discouraged. The captain had an excellent chest development. When he went aft roaring, it was plain that a man could beat carpets with a voice like that one.

II

One night the *Foundling* was off the southern coast of Florida and running at half-speed toward the shore. The captain was on the bridge. "Four flashes at intervals of one minute," he said to himself, gazing steadfastly toward the beach. Suddenly a yellow eye opened in the black face of the night, and looked at the *Foundling,* and closed again. The captain studied his watch and the shore. Three times more the eye opened, and looked at the *Foundling,* and closed again. The captain called to the vague figures on the deck below him. "Answer it." The flash of a light from the bow of the steamer displayed for a moment in golden color the crests of the in-riding waves.

The *Foundling* lay to, and waited. The long swells rolled her gracefully, and her two stub masts, reaching into the darkness, swung with the solemnity of batons timing a dirge. When the ship had left Boston she had been as encrusted with ice as a Dakota stagedriver's beard; but now the gentle wind of Florida softly swayed the lock on the forehead of the coatless Flanagan, and he lit a new cigar without troubling to make a shield of his hands.

Finally a dark boat came plashing over the waves. As it came very near, the captain leaned forward, and perceived that the men in her rowed like seamstresses, and at the same time a voice hailed him in bad English. "It's a dead sure connection," said he to himself.

At sea, to load two hundred thousand rounds of rifle ammunition, seven hundred and fifty rifles, two rapid-fire field guns with a hundred shells, forty bundles of machetes, and a hundred pounds of dynamite, from yawls, and by men who are not born stevedores, and in a heavy ground swell, and with the searchlight of a United States cruiser sometimes flashing like lightning in the sky to the southward, is no business for a Sunday school class. When at last the *Foundling* was steaming for the open, over the gray sea, at dawn, there was not a man of the forty come aboard from the Florida shore, nor of the fifteen sailed from Boston, who was not glad, standing with his hair matted to his forehead with sweat, smiling at the broad wake of the *Foundling* and the dim streak on the horizon which was Florida.

But there is a point of the compass in these waters which men call the northeast. When the strong winds come from that direction they kick up a turmoil that is not good for a *Foundling* stuffed with coal and war stores. In the gale which came, this ship was no more than a drunken soldier.

The Cuban leader, standing on the bridge with the captain, was presently informed that of his men thirty-nine out of a possible thirty-nine were seasick. And in truth they were seasick. There are degrees in this complaint, but that matter was waived between them. They were all sick to the limits. They strewed the deck in every posture of human anguish; and when the *Foundling* ducked and water came sluicing down from the bows, they let it sluice. They were satisfied if they could keep their heads clear of the wash; and if they could not keep their heads clear of the wash, they didn't care. Presently the *Foundling* swung her course to the southeast, and the waves pounded her broadside. The patriots were all ordered below decks, and there they howled and measured their misery one against another. All day the *Foundling* plopped and foundered over a blazing bright meadow of an ocean whereon the white foam was like flowers.

The captain on the bridge mused and studied the bare horizon. "Hell!" said he to himself, and the word was more in amazement than in indignation or sorrow. "Thirty-nine seasick passengers, the mate with a broken arm, a stoker with a broken jaw, the cook with a pair of scalded legs, and an engine likely to be taken with all these diseases, if not more! If I get back to a home port with a spoke of the wheel gripped in my hands, it'll be fair luck!"

There is a kind of corn whiskey bred in Florida which the natives declare is potent in the proportion of seven fights to a drink. Some of the Cuban volunteers had had the forethought to bring a small quantity of this whiskey aboard with them; and being now in the fireroom and seasick, and feeling that they would not care to drink liquor for two or three years to come, they gracefully tendered their portions to the stokers. The stokers accepted these gifts without avidity, but with a certain earnestness of manner.

As they were stokers and toiling, the whirl of emotion was delayed, but it arrived ultimately and with emphasis. One stoker called another stoker a weird name; and the latter, righteously inflamed at it, smote his mate with an iron shovel, and the man fell headlong over a heap of coal, which crashed gently, while piece after piece rattled down upon the deck.

A third stoker was providentially enraged at the scene, and assailed the second stoker. They fought for some moments, while the seasick Cubans sprawled on the deck watched with languid, rolling glances the ferocity of the scuffle. One was so indifferent to the strategic importance of the space he occupied that he was kicked in the shins.

When the second engineer came to separate the combatants, he was sincere in his efforts, and he came near to disabling them for life.

The captain said, "I'll go down there and——"

But the leader of the Cubans restrained him. "No, no," he cried; "you must not. We must treat them like children, very gently, all the time, you see, or else when we get back to a United States port they will—what you call—spring?—yes, spring the whole business. We must—jolly them. You see?"

"You mean," said the captain, thoughtfully, "they are likely to get mad and give the expedition dead away when we reach port again, unless we blarney them now?"

"Yes, yes," cried the Cuban leader; "unless we are so very gentle with them they will make many troubles afterward for us in the newspapers, and then in court."

"Well, but I won't have my crew——" began the captain.

"But you must," interrupted the Cuban. "You must. It is the only thing. You are like the captain of a pirate ship. You see? Only you can't throw them overboard like him. You see?"

"Hum," said the captain, "this here filibustering business has got a lot to it when you come to look it over."

He called the fighting stokers to the bridge, and the three came, meek and considerably battered. He was lecturing them soundly, but sensibly, when he suddenly tripped a sentence and cried: "Here! Where's that other fellow? How does it come he wasn't in the fight?"

The row of stokers cried at once, eagerly: "He's hurt, sir. He's got a broken jaw, sir."

"So he has, so he has," murmured the captain, much embarrassed.

And because of all these affairs, the *Foundling* steamed toward Cuba with its crew in a sling, if one may be allowed to speak in that way.

III

At night the *Foundling* approached the coast like a thief. Her lights were muffled so that from the deck the sea shone with its own radiance, like the faint shimmer of some kinds of silk. The men on deck spoke in whispers, and even down in the fireroom the hidden stokers, working before the blood-red furnace doors, used no words, and walked tiptoe. The stars were out in the blue velvet sky, and their light, with the soft shine of the sea, caused the coast to appear black as the side of a coffin. The surf boomed in low thunder on the distant beach.

The *Foundling's* engines ceased their thumping for a time. She glided quietly forward until a bell chimed faintly in the engine room. Then she paused, with a flourish of phosphorescent waters.

"Give the signal," said the captain. Three times a flash of light went from the bow. There was a moment of waiting. Then an eye like the one on the coast of Florida opened and closed, opened and closed, opened and closed. The Cubans, grouped in a great shadow on deck, burst into a low chatter of delight. A hiss from their leader silenced them.

"Well?" said the captain.

"All right," said the leader.

At the giving of the word it was not apparent that any one on board the *Foundling* had ever been seasick. The boats were lowered swiftly—too swiftly. Boxes of cartridges were dragged from the hold and passed over the side with a rapidity that made men in the boats exclaim against it. They were being bombarded. When a boat headed for shore, its rowers pulled like madmen. The captain paced slowly to and fro on the bridge. In the engine room the engineers stood at their station, and in the stokehole the firemen fidgeted silently around the furnace doors.

On the bridge Flanagan reflected. "Oh, I don't know," he observed; "this filibustering business isn't so bad. Pretty soon I'll be off to sea again, with nothing to do but some big lying when I get into port."

In one of the boats returning from shore came twelve Cuban officers, the greater number of them convalescing from wounds, while two or three of them had been ordered to America on commissions from the insurgents. The captain welcomed them, and assured them of a speedy and safe voyage.

Presently he went again to the bridge and scanned the horizon. The sea was lonely, like the spaces amid the suns. The captain grinned, and softly smote his chest. "It's dead easy," said he. It was near the end of the cargo, and the men were breathing like spent horses, although their elation grew with each moment, when suddenly a voice spoke from the sky. It was not a loud voice, but the quality of it brought every man on deck to full stop and motionless, as if they had all been changed to wax. "Captain," said the man at the masthead, "there's a light to the west'ard, sir. Think it's a steamer, sir."

There was a still moment until the captain called, "Well, keep your eye on it now." Speaking to the deck, he said, "Go ahead with your unloading."

The second engineer went to the galley to borrow a tin cup. "Hear the news, second?" asked the cook. "Steamer coming up from the west'ard."

"Gee!" said the second engineer. In the engine room he said to the chief: "Steamer coming up to the west'ard, sir."

The chief engineer began to test various little machines with which his domain was decorated. Finally he addressed the stokeroom: "Boys, I want you to look sharp now. There's a steamer coming up to the west'ard."

"All right, sir," said the stokeroom.

From time to time the captain hailed the masthead. "How is she now?"

"Seems to be coming down on us pretty fast, sir."

The Cuban leader came anxiously to the captain. "Do you think we can save all the cargo? It is rather delicate business. No?"

"Go ahead," said Flanagan. "Fire away. I'll wait for you."

There continued the hurried shuffling of feet on deck, and the low cries of the men unloading the cargo. In the engine room the chief and his assistant were staring at the gong. In the stokeroom the firemen breathed through their teeth. A shovel slipped from where it leaned against the side, and banged on the floor. The stokers started, and looked around quickly.

Climbing to the rail and holding on to a stay, the captain gazed westward. A light had raised out of the deep. After watching this light for a time, he called to the Cuban leader, "Well, as soon as you're ready now, we might as well be skipping out."

Finally the Cuban leader told him: "Well, this is the last load. As soon as the boats come back you can be off."

"Shan't wait for the boats," said the captain. "That fellow is too close." As the last boat went shoreward the *Foundling* turned, and like a black shadow stole seaward to cross the bows of the oncoming steamer. "Waited about ten minutes too long," said the captain to himself.

Suddenly the light in the west vanished. "Hum," said Flanagan; "he's up to some meanness."

Every one outside the engine rooms was set on watch. The *Foundling*, going at full speed into the northeast, slashed a wonderful trail of blue silver on the dark bosom of the sea.

A man on deck cried out hurriedly, "There she is, sir!" Many eyes searched the western gloom, and one after another the glances of the men found a tiny black shadow on the deep, with a line of white beneath it.

"He couldn't be heading better if he had a line to us," said Flanagan.

There was a thin flash of red in the darkness. It was long and keen, like a crimson rapier. A short, sharp report sounded, and then a shot whined swiftly in the air and blipped into the sea. The captain had been about to take a bite of plug tobacco at the beginning of this incident, and his arm was raised. He remained like a frozen figure while the shot whined, and then, as it blipped into the sea, his hand went to his mouth, and he bit the plug. He looked wide-eyed at the shadow with its line of white.

The senior Cuban officer came hurriedly to the bridge. "It is no good to surrender," he cried; "they would only shoot or hang all of us."

There was another thin red flash and a report. A loud whirring noise passed over the ship.

"I'm not going to surrender," said the captain, hanging with both hands to the rail. He appeared like a man whose traditions of peace are clenched in his heart. He was as astonished as if his hat had turned into a dog. Presently he wheeled quickly, and said: "What kind of a gun is that?"

"It is a one-pounder," cried the Cuban officer. "The boat is one of those little gunboats made from a yacht. You see?"

"Well, if it's only a yawl, he'll sink us in five more minutes," said Flanagan. For a moment he looked helplessly off at the horizon. His under jaw hung low. But a moment later something touched him like a stiletto-point of inspiration. He leaped to the pilothouse, and roared at the man at the wheel. The *Foundling* sheered suddenly to starboard, made a clumsy turn, and Flanagan was bellowing through the tube to the engine room before anybody discovered that the old basket was heading straight for the Spanish gunboat. The ship lunged forward like a draught horse on the gallop.

This strange maneuver by the *Foundling* first dealt consternation on board. Men instinctively crouched on the instant, and then swore their supreme oath, which was unheard by their own ears.

Later the maneuver of the *Foundling* dealt consternation on board the gunboat. She had been going victoriously forward, dim-eyed from the fury of her pursuit. Then this tall, threatening shape had suddenly loomed over her like a giant apparition.

The people on board the *Foundling* heard panic shouts, hoarse orders. The little gunboat was paralyzed with astonishment.

Suddenly Flanagan yelled with rage, and sprang for the wheel. The helmsman had turned his eyes away. As the captain whirled the wheel far to starboard, he heard a crunch, as the *Foundling,* lifted on a wave, smashed her shoulder against the gunboat, and he saw, shooting past, a little launch sort of a thing with men on her that ran this way and that way. The Cuban officers, joined by the cook and a seaman, emptied their revolvers into the surprised terror of the seas.

There was naturally no pursuit. Under comfortable speed the *Foundling* stood to the northward.

The captain went to his berth chuckling. "There, by God!" he said. "There, now!"

IV

When Flanagan came again on deck, the first mate, his arm in a sling, walked the bridge. Flanagan was smiling a wide smile. The bridge of the *Foundling* was dipping afar and then afar. With each lunge of the little steamer the water seethed and boomed alongside, and the spray dashed high and swiftly.

"Well," said Flanagan, inflating himself, "we've had a great deal of a time, and we've come through it all right, and thank Heaven it is all over."

The sky in the northeast was of a dull brick-red in tone, shaded here and there by black masses that billowed out in some fashion from the flat heavens.

"Look there," said the mate.

"Hum," said the captain. "Looks like a blow, don't it?"

Later the surface of the water rippled and flickered in the preliminary wind. The sea had become the color of lead. The swashing sound of the waves on the sides of the *Foundling* was now provided with some manner of ominous significance. The men's shouts were hoarse.

A squall struck the *Foundling* on her starboard quarter, and she leaned under the force of it as if she were never to return to the even keel. "I'll be glad when we get in," said the mate. "I'm going to quit then. I've got enough."

"Hell!" said the beaming Flanagan.

The steamer crawled on into the northwest. The white water sweeping out from her deadened the chug-chug-chug of the tired old engines.

Once, when the boat careened, she laid her shoulder flat on the sea and rested in that manner. The mate, looking down the bridge, which slanted more than a coal chute, whistled softly to himself. Slowly, heavily, the *Foundling* arose to meet another sea.

At night waves thundered mightily on the bows of the steamer, and water, lighted with the beautiful phosphorescent glamor, went boiling and howling along the deck.

By good fortune the chief engineer crawled safely, but utterly drenched, to the galley for coffee. "Well, how goes it, chief?" said the cook, standing with his fat arms folded, in order to prove that he could balance himself under any condition.

The engineer shook his head slowly. "This old biscuit-box will never see port again. Why, she'll fall to pieces."

Finally, at night, the captain said, "Launch the boats." The Cubans hovered about him. "Is the ship going to sink?" The captain addressed them politely: "Gentlemen, we are in trouble; but all I ask of you is that you do just what I tell you, and no harm will come to anybody."

The mate directed the lowering of the first boat, and the men performed this task with all decency, like people at the side of a grave.

A young oiler came to the captain. "The chief sends word, sir, that the water is almost up to the fires."

"Keep at it as long as you can."

"Keep at it as long as we can, sir."

Flanagan took the senior Cuban officer to the rail, and, as the steamer sheered high on a great sea, showed him a yellow dot on the horizon. It was smaller than a needle when its point is toward you.

"There," said the captain. The wind-driven spray was lashing his face. "That's Jupiter Light on the Florida coast. Put your men in the boat we've just launched, and the mate will take you to that light."

Afterward Flanagan turned to the chief engineer. "We can never beach her," said the old man. "The stokers have got to quit in a minute." Tears were in his eyes.

The *Foundling* was a wounded thing. She lay on the water with gasping engines, and each wave resembled her death blow.

Now the way of a good ship on the sea is finer than swordplay; but this is when she is alive. If a time comes that the ship dies, then her way is the way of a floating old glove, and she has that much vim, spirit, buoyancy. At this time many men on the *Foundling* suddenly came to know that they were clinging to a corpse.

The captain went to the stokeroom, and what he saw as he swung down the companion suddenly turned him hesitant and dumb. He had served the sea for many years, but this fireroom said something to him which he had not heard in his other voyages. Water was swirling to and fro with the roll of the ship, fuming greasily around half-strangled machinery that still attempted to perform its duty. Steam arose from the water, and through its clouds shone the red glare of the dying fires. As for the stokers, death might have been with silence in this room. One lay in his berth, his hands under his head, staring moodily at the wall. One sat near the foot of the companion, his face hidden in his arms. One leaned against the side, and gazed at the snarling water as it rose, and its mad eddies among the machinery. In the unholy red light and gray mist of this stifling, dim inferno they were strange figures with their silence and their immobility. The wretched *Foundling* groaned deeply as she lifted, and groaned deeply as she sank into the trough, while hurried waves then thundered over her with the noise of landslides.

But Flanagan took control of himself suddenly, and then he stirred the fireroom. The stillness had been so unearthly that he was not altogether inapprehensive of strange and grim deeds when he charged into them; but precisely as they had submitted to the sea, so they submitted to Flanagan. For a moment they rolled their eyes like hurt cows, but they obeyed the voice. The situation simply required a voice.

When the captain returned to the deck the hue of this fireroom was in his mind, and then he understood doom and its weight and complexion.

When finally the *Foundling* sank, she shifted and settled as calmly as an animal curls down in the bush-grass. Away over the waves three bobbing boats paused to witness this quiet death. It was a slow maneuver, altogether without the pageantry of uproar; but it flashed pallor into the faces of all men who saw it, and they groaned when they said, "There she goes!" Suddenly the captain whirled and knocked his head on the gunwale. He sobbed for a time, and then he sobbed and swore also.

v

There was a dance at the Imperial Inn. During the evening some irresponsible young men came from the beach, bringing the statement that several boatloads of people had been perceived offshore. It was a charming dance, and none cared to take time to believe this tale. The fountain in the courtyard plashed softly, and couple after couple paraded through the aisles of palms, where lamps with red shades threw a rose light upon the gleaming leaves. High on some balcony a mockingbird called into the evening. The band played its waltzes slumbrously, and its music to the people among the palms came faintly and like the melodies in dreams.

Sometimes a woman said, "Oh, it is not really true, is it, that there was a wreck out at sea?"

A man usually said, "No; of course not."

At last, however, a youth came violently from the beach. He was triumphant in manner. "They're out there," he cried—"a whole boatload!" He received eager attention, and he told all that he supposed. His news destroyed the dance. After a time the band was playing delightfully to space. The guests had donned wraps and hurried to the beach. One little girl cried, "Oh, mama, may I go too?" Being refused permission, she pouted.

As they came from the shelter of the great hotel, the wind was blowing swiftly from the sea, and at intervals a breaker shone livid. The women shuddered, and their bending companions seized the opportunity to draw the cloaks closer. The sand of the beach was wet, and dainty slippers made imprints in it clear and deep.

"Oh dear," said a girl; "supposin' they were out there drowning while we were dancing!"

"Oh, nonsense!" said her younger brother; "that don't happen."

"Well, it might, you know, Roger. How can you tell?"

A man who was not her brother gazed at her then with profound admiration. Later she complained of the damp sand and, drawing back her skirts, looked ruefully at her little feet.

A mother's son was venturing too near to the water in his interest and excitement. Occasionally she cautioned and reproached him from the background.

Save for the white glare of the breakers, the sea was a great wind-crossed void. From the throng of charming women floated the perfume of many flowers. Later there floated to them a body with a calm face of an Irish type. The expedition of the *Foundling* will never be historic.

August 28, 1897

[*The Illustrated London News,* Vol. 111, pp. 279–282.]

AN OLD MAN GOES WOOING

The melancholy fisherman made his way through a street that was mainly as dark as a tunnel. Sometimes an open door threw a rectangle of light upon the pavement, and within the cottages were scenes of working women and men, who comfortably smoked and talked. From them came the sounds of laughter and the babble of children. Each time the old man passed through one of these radiant zones the light etched his face in profile with touches flaming and somber, until there was a resemblance to a stern and mournful Dante portrait.

Once a whistling lad came through the darkness. He peered intently for purposes of recognition. "Good avenin', Mickey," he cried cheerfully. The old man responded with a groan, which intimated that the lamentable reckless optimism of the youth had forced from him an expression of an emotion that he had been enduring in saintly patience and silence. He continued his pilgrimage toward the kitchen of the village inn.

The kitchen is a great and worthy place. The long range with its lurid heat continually emits the fragrance of broiling fish, roasting mutton, joints, and fowl. The high black ceiling is ornamented with hams and flitches of bacon. There is a long, dark bench against one wall, and it is fronted by a dark table, handy for glasses of stout. On an old mahogany dresser rows of plates face the distant range, and reflect the red shine of the peat. Smoke which has in it the odor of an American forest fire eddies through the air. The great stones of the floor are scarred by the black mud from the inn yard. And here the gossip of a countryside goes on amid the sizzle of broiling fish and the loud protesting splutter of joints taken from the oven.

When the old man reached the door of this paradise, he stopped for a moment with his finger on the latch. He sighed deeply; evidently he was undergoing some lachrymose reflection. For somewhere overhead in the inn he could hear the wild clamor of dining pig-buyers, men who were come for the pig fair to be held on the morrow. Evidently in the little parlor of the inn these men were dining amid an uproar of shouted jests and laughter. The revelry sounded like the fighting of two mobs amid a rain of missiles and the crash of shop windows. The old man raised his hand as if, unseen there in the darkness, he was going to solemnly damn the dinner of the pig-buyers.

Within the kitchen Nora, tall, strong, intrepid, approached the fiery stove in the manner of a boxer. Her left arm was held high to guard her face, which was already crimson from the blaze. With a flourish of her apron she achieved a great brown humming joint from the oven, and, emerging a glowing and triumphant figure from the steam and smoke and rapid play of heat, she slid the pan upon the table, even as she saw the old man standing within the room and lugubriously cleaning the mud from his boots. " 'Tis you, Mickey?" she said.

He made no reply until he had found his way to the long bench. "It is," he said then. It was clear that in the girl's opinion he had gained some kind of strategic advantage. The sanctity of her kitchen was successfully violated, but the old man betrayed no elation. Lifting one knee and placing it over the other, he grunted in the blissful weariness of a venerable laborer returned to his own fireside. He coughed dismally. "Ah, 'tis no good a man gits from fishin' these days. I moind the toimes whin they would be hoppin' up clear o' the wather, there was that little room fur thim. I would be likin' a bottle o' stout."

"Niver fear you, Mickey," answered the girl. Swinging here and there in the glare of the fire, Nora, with her towering figure and bare brawny arms, was like a feminine blacksmith at a forge. The old man, pallid, emaciated, watched her from the shadows of the other side of the room. The lines from the sides of his nose to the corners of his mouth sank low to an expression of despair deeper than any moans. He should have been painted upon the door of a tomb with weeping willows arched above him and men in gray robes slowly booming the drums of death. Finally he spoke. "I would be likin' a bottle o' stout, Nora, me girrl," he said.

"Niver fear you, Mickey," again she replied with cheerful obstinacy.

She was admiring her famous roast, which now sat in its platter on the rack over the range. There was a lull in her tumultuous duties. The old man coughed and moved his foot with a scraping sound on the stones. The noise of dining pig-buyers, now heard through doors and winding corridors of the inn, was a roll of a faraway storm.

A woman in a dark dress entered the kitchen and keenly examined the roast and Nora's other feats. "Mickey here would be wantin' a bottle o' stout," said the girl to her mistress. The woman turned toward the spectral figure in the gloom, and regarded it quietly with a clear eye. "Have yez the money, Mickey?" she said. This question seemed to strike the old man as the final point in human brutality. "A-ah," he said, stricken to the heart. He rolled his eyes toward the throne of heaven.

"Have yez the money, Mickey?" repeated the woman of the house.

Profoundly embittered, he replied in short terms, "I have."

"There now," cried Nora, in astonishment and admiration. Poising a large iron spoon, she was motionless, staring with open mouth at the old man. He searched his pockets slowly during a complete silence in the kitchen. He brought forth two coppers and laid them sadly, reproachfully, and yet defiantly on the table.

"There now," cried Nora, stupefied.

They brought him a bottle of the black brew, and Nora poured it out for him with her own red hand, which looked to be as broad as his chest. A collar of brown foam curled at the top of the glass. With measured movements the old man filled a short pipe. There came a sudden howl from another part of the inn. One of the pig-buyers was at the head of the stairs bawling for the mistress. The two women hurriedly freighted themselves with the roast and the vegetables, and sprang with them to placate the pig-buyers. Alone, the old man studied the gleam of the fire on the floor. It faded and brightened in the way of lightning at the horizon's edge.

When Nora returned, the strapping grenadier of a girl was blushing and giggling. The pig-buyers had been humorous. "I moind the toime—" began the old man sorrowfully, "I moind the toime whin yez was a wee bit of a girrl, Nora, an' wouldn't be havin' words wid min loike thim buyers."

"I moind the toime whin yez could attind to your own affairs, ye ould skileton," said the girl promptly. He made a gesture which may have expressed his stirring grief at the levity of the new generation, and then lapsed into another stillness.

The girl, a giantess, carrying, lifting, pushing, an incarnation of dauntless labor, changing the look of the whole kitchen with a moment's manipulation of her great arms, did not heed the old man for a long time. When she finally glanced toward him, she saw that he was sunk forward with his gray face on his arms. A growl of heavy breathing ascended. He was asleep.

She marched to him and put both hands to his collar. Despite his feeble and dreamy protestations, she dragged him out from behind the table and across the floor. She opened the door and thrust him out into the night.

October 19, 1897

[*The Philistine*, Vol. 9 (July, 1899), pp. 44–50.]

A FISHING VILLAGE

The brook curved down over the rocks, innocent and white, until it faced a little strand of smooth gravel and flat stones. It turned then to the left, and thereafter its guilty current was tinged with the pink of diluted blood. Boulders standing neck-deep in the water were rimmed with red; they wore bloody collars whose tops marked the supreme instant of some tragic movement of the stream. In the pale green shallows of the bay's edge, the outward flow from the criminal little brook was as eloquently marked as if a long crimson carpet had been laid upon the waters. The scene of the carnage was the strand of smooth gravel and flat stones, and the fruit of the carnage was cleaned mackerel.

Far to the south, where the slate of the sea and the gray of the sky wove together, could be seen Fastnet Rock, a mere button on the moving, shimmering cloth, while a liner, no larger than a needle, spun a thread of smoke aslant. The gulls swept screaming along the dull line of the other shore of Roaring Water Bay, and near the mouth of the brook circled among the fishing boats that lay at anchor, their brown, leathery sails idle and straight. The wheeling, shrieking, tumultuous birds stared with their hideous unblinking eyes at the Capers—men from Cape Clear—who prowled to and fro on the decks amid shouts and the creak of the tackle. Shoreward, a little shriveled man, overcome by a profound melancholy, fished hopelessly from the end of the pier. Behind him, on a hillside, sat a white village, nestled among more trees than is common in this part of Southern Ireland.

A dinghy sculled by a youth in a blue jersey wobbled rapidly past the pier-head and stopped at the foot of the moss-green, dank, stone steps, where the waves were making slow but regular leaps to mount higher, and then falling back gurgling, choking, and waving the long, dark seaweeds. The melancholy fisherman walked over to the top of the steps. The young man was fastening the painter of his boat in an iron ring. In the dinghy were three round baskets heaped high with mackerel. They glittered like masses of new silver coin at times, and then other lights of faint carmine and peacock blue would chase across the sides of the fish in a radiance that was finer than silver.

The melancholy fisherman looked at this wealth. He shook his head mournfully. "Ah, now, Denny. This would not be a very good kill."

The young man snorted indignantly at his fellow-townsman. "This will be th' bist kill th' year, Mickey. Go along now."

The melancholy old man became immersed in deeper gloom. "Shure I have been in th' way of seein' miny a grand day whin th' fish was runnin' sthrong in these wathers, but there will be no more big kills here. No more. No more." At the last his voice was only a dismal croak.

"Come along outa that now, Mickey," cried the youth impatiently. "Come away wid you."

"All gone now. A-ll go-o-ne now!" The old man wagged his gray head, and, standing over the baskets of fishes, groaned as Mordecai groaned for his people.

"'Tis you would be cryin' out, Mickey, whativer," said the youth with scorn. He was giving his basket into the hands of five incompetent but jovial little boys to carry to a waiting donkey cart.

"An' why should I not?" said the old man sternly. "Me—in want—"

As the youth swung his boat swiftly out toward an anchored smack, he made answer in a softer tone. "Shure, if yez got for th' askin', 'tis you, Mickey, that would niver be in want." The melancholy old man returned to his line. And the only moral in this incident is that the young man is the type that America procures from Ireland, and the old man is one of the home types, bent, pallid, hungry, disheartened, with a vision that magnifies with a microscope glance any fly-wing of misfortune, and heroically and conscientiously invents disasters for the future. Usually the thing that remains to one of this type is a sympathy as quick and acute for others as is his pity for himself.

The donkey with his cartload of gleaming fish, and escorted by the whooping and laughing boys, galloped along the quay and up a street of the village until he was turned off at the gravelly strand, at the point where the color of the brook was changing. Here twenty people of both sexes and all ages were preparing the fish for market. The mackerel, beautiful as fire-etched salvers, first were passed to a long table, around which worked as many women as could have elbow room. Each one could clean a fish with two motions of the knife. Then the washers, men who stood over the troughs filled with running water from the brook, soused the fish until the outlet became a sinister element that in an instant changed the brook from a happy thing of gorse and heather of the hills to an evil stream, sullen and reddened. After being washed, the fish were carried to a group of girls with knives, who made the cuts that enabled each fish to flatten out in the manner known of the breakfast table. And after the girls came the men and boys, who rubbed each fish thoroughly with great handfuls of coarse salt, which was whiter than snow, and shone in the daylight from a multitude of gleaming points, diamond-like. Last came the packers, drilled in the art of getting neither too few nor too many mackerel into a barrel, sprinkling constantly prodigal layers of brilliant salt. There were many intermediate corps of boys and girls carrying fish from point to point, and sometimes building them in stacks convenient to the hands of the more important laborers.

A vast tree hung its branches over the place. The leaves made a shadow that was religious in its effect, as if the spot was a chapel consecrated to labor. There was a hush upon the devotees. The women at the large table worked intently, steadfastly, with bowed heads. Their old petticoats were tucked high, showing the coarse brogans which they wore—and the visible ankles were proportioned to the brogans as the diameter of a straw is to that of a half-crown. The national red under-petticoat was a fundamental part of the scene.

Just over the wall, in the sloping street, could be seen the be-jerseyed Capers, brawny, and with shocks of yellow beard. They paced slowly to and fro amid the geese and children. They, too, spoke little, even to each other; they smoked short pipes in saturnine dignity and silence. It was the fish. They who go with nets upon the reeling sea grow still with the mystery and solemnity of the trade. It was Brittany; the first respectable catch of the year had changed this garrulous Irish hamlet into a hamlet of Brittany.

The Capers were waiting for high tide. It had seemed for a long time that, for the south of Ireland, the mackerel had fled in company with potato; but here, at any rate, was a temporary success, and the occasion was momentous. A strolling Caper took his pipe and pointed with the stem out upon the bay. There was little wind, but an ambitious skipper had raised his anchor, and the craft, her strained brown sails idly swinging, was drifting away on the first oily turn of the tide.

On the top of the pier the figure of the melancholy old man was portrayed upon the polished water. He was still dangling his line hopelessly. He gazed down into the misty water. Once he stirred and murmured: "Bad luck to thim." Otherwise he seemed to remain motionless for hours. One by one the fishing boats floated away. The brook changed its color, and in the dusk showed a tumble of pearly white among the rocks.

A cold night wind, sweeping transversely across the pier, awakened perhaps the rheumatism in the old man's bones. He arose and, mumbling

The Bride Comes to Yellow Sky 383

and grumbling, began to wind his line. The waves were lashing the stones.
He moved off toward the intense darkness of the village streets.

November 19, 1897
[*The Westminster Budget*, Vol. 10, p. 13.]

THE BRIDE COMES TO YELLOW SKY

I

The great Pullman was whirling onward with such dignity of motion that
a glance from the window seemed simply to prove that the plains of Texas
were pouring eastward. Vast flats of green grass, dull-hued spaces of mesquite and cactus, little groups of frame houses, woods of light and tender
trees, all were sweeping into the east, sweeping over the horizon, a precipice.

A newly married pair had boarded this coach at San Antonio. The man's
face was reddened from many days in the wind and sun, and a direct
result of his new black clothes was that his brick-colored hands were constantly performing in a most conscious fashion. From time to time he looked
down respectfully at his attire. He sat with a hand on each knee, like a
man waiting in a barber's shop. The glances he devoted to other passengers were furtive and shy.

The bride was not pretty, nor was she very young. She wore a dress of
blue cashmere, with small reservations of velvet here and there, and with
steel buttons abounding. She continually twisted her head to regard her
puff sleeves, very stiff, straight, and high. They embarrassed her. It was
quite apparent that she had cooked, and that she expected to cook, dutifully. The blushes caused by the careless scrutiny of some passengers as she
had entered the car were strange to see upon this plain, underclass countenance, which was drawn in placid, almost emotionless lines.

They were evidently very happy. "Ever been in a parlor car before?" he
asked, smiling with delight.

"No," she answered. "I never was. It's fine, ain't it?"

"Great! And then after a while we'll go forward to the diner, and get
a big layout. Finest meal in the world. Charge a dollar."

"Oh, do they?" cried the bride. "Charge a dollar? Why, that's too much—
for us—ain't it, Jack?"

"Not this trip, anyhow," he answered bravely. "We're going to go the
whole thing."

Later, he explained to her about the trains. "You see, it's a thousand
miles from one end of Texas to the other; and this train runs right across

it, and never stops but four times." He had the pride of an owner. He pointed out to her the dazzling fittings of the coach; and in truth her eyes opened wider as she contemplated the sea-green figured velvet, the shining brass, silver, and glass, the wood that gleamed as darkly brilliant as the surface of a pool of oil. At one end a bronze figure sturdily held a support for a separated chamber, and at convenient places on the ceiling were frescoes in olive and silver.

To the minds of the pair, their surroundings reflected the glory of their marriage that morning in San Antonio. This was the environment of their new estate, and the man's face in particular beamed with an elation that made him appear ridiculous to the negro porter. This individual at times surveyed them from afar with an amused and superior grin. On other occasions he bullied them with skill in ways that did not make it exactly plain to them that they were being bullied. He subtly used all the manners of the most unconquerable kind of snobbery. He oppressed them; but of this oppression they had small knowledge, and they speedily forgot that infrequently a number of travelers covered them with stares of derisive enjoyment. Historically there was supposed to be something infinitely humorous in their situation.

"We are due in Yellow Sky at 3:42," he said, looking tenderly into her eyes.

"Oh, are we?" she said, as if she had not been aware of it. To evince surprise at her husband's statement was part of her wifely amiability. She took from a pocket a little silver watch; and as she held it before her, and stared at it with a frown of attention, the new husband's face shone.

"I bought it in San Anton' from a friend of mine," he told her gleefully.

"It's seventeen minutes past twelve," she said, looking up at him with a kind of shy and clumsy coquetry. A passenger, noting this play, grew excessively sardonic, and winked at himself in one of the numerous mirrors.

At last they went to the dining car. Two rows of negro waiters, in glowing white suits, surveyed their entrance with the interest, and also the equanimity, of men who had been forewarned. The pair fell to the lot of a waiter who happened to feel pleasure in steering them through their meal. He viewed them with the manner of a fatherly pilot, his countenance radiant with benevolence. The patronage, entwined with the ordinary deference, was not plain to them. And yet, as they returned to their coach, they showed in their faces a sense of escape.

To the left, miles down a long purple slope, was a little ribbon of mist where moved the keening Rio Grande. The train was approaching it at an angle, and the apex was Yellow Sky. Presently it was apparent that, as the distance from Yellow Sky grew shorter, the husband became commensurately restless. His brick-red hands were more insistent in their prominence. Occasionally he was even rather absent-minded and faraway when the bride leaned forward and addressed him.

As a matter of truth, Jack Potter was beginning to find the shadow of a deed weigh upon him like a leaden slab. He, the town marshal of Yellow Sky, a man known, liked, and feared in his corner, a prominent person, had gone to San Antonio to meet a girl he believed he loved, and there, after the usual prayers, had actually induced her to marry him, without consulting Yellow Sky for any part of the transaction. He was now bringing his bride before an innocent and unsuspecting community.

Of course people in Yellow Sky married as it pleased them, in accordance with a general custom; but such was Potter's thought of his duty to his friends, or of their idea of his duty, or of an unspoken form which does not control men in these matters, that he felt he was heinous. He had committed an extraordinary crime. Face to face with this girl in San Antonio, and spurred by his sharp impulse, he had gone headlong over all the social hedges. At San Antonio he was like a man hidden in the dark. A knife to sever any friendly duty, any form, was easy to his hand in that remote city. But the hour of Yellow Sky—the hour of daylight—was approaching.

He knew full well that his marriage was an important thing to his town. It could only be exceeded by the burning of the new hotel. His friends could not forgive him. Frequently he had reflected on the advisability of telling them by telegraph, but a new cowardice had been upon him. He feared to do it. And now the train was hurrying him toward a scene of amazement, glee, and reproach. He glanced out of the window at the line of haze swinging slowly in toward the train.

Yellow Sky had a kind of brass band, which played painfully, to the delight of the populace. He laughed without heart as he thought of it. If the citizens could dream of his prospective arrival with his bride, they would parade the band at the station and escort them, amid cheers and laughing congratulations, to his adobe home.

He resolved that he would use all the devices of speed and plains-craft in making the journey from the station to his house. Once within that safe citadel, he could issue some sort of a vocal bulletin, and then not go among the citizens until they had time to wear off a little of their enthusiasm.

The bride looked anxiously at him. "What's worrying you, Jack?"

He laughed again. "I'm not worrying, girl. I'm only thinking of Yellow Sky."

She flushed in comprehension.

A sense of mutual guilt invaded their minds and developed a finer tenderness. They looked at each other with eyes softly aglow. But Potter often laughed the same nervous laugh. The flush upon the bride's face seemed quite permanent.

The traitor to the feelings of Yellow Sky narrowly watched the speeding landscape. "We're nearly there," he said.

Presently the porter came and announced the proximity of Potter's home. He held a brush in his hand, and, with all his airy superiority gone, he brushed Potter's new clothes as the latter slowly turned this way and that way. Potter fumbled out a coin and gave it to the porter, as he had seen others do. It was a heavy and muscle-bound business, as that of a man shoeing his first horse.

The porter took their bag, and as the train began to slow they moved forward to the hooded platform of the car. Presently the two engines and their long string of coaches rushed into the station of Yellow Sky.

"They have to take water here," said Potter, from a constricted throat and in mournful cadence, as one announcing death. Before the train stopped, his eye had swept the length of the platform, and he was glad and astonished to see there was none upon it but the station-agent, who, with a slightly hurried and anxious air, was walking toward the water tanks. When the train had halted, the porter alighted first, and placed in position a little temporary step.

"Come on, girl," said Potter, hoarsely. As he helped her down they each laughed on a false note. He took the bag from the negro, and bade his wife cling to his arm. As they slunk rapidly away, his hangdog glance perceived that they were unloading the two trunks, and also that the station-agent, far ahead near the baggage car, had turned and was running toward him, making gestures. He laughed, and groaned as he laughed, when he noted the first effect of his marital bliss upon Yellow Sky. He gripped his wife's arm firmly to his side, and they fled. Behind them the porter stood, chuckling fatuously.

II

The California express on the Southern Railway was due at Yellow Sky in twenty-one minutes. There were six men at the bar of the Weary Gentleman saloon. One was a drummer who talked a great deal and rapidly; three were Texans who did not care to talk at that time; and two were Mexican sheepherders, who did not talk as a general practice in the Weary Gentleman saloon. The barkeeper's dog lay on the boardwalk that crossed in front of the door. His head was on his paws, and he glanced drowsily here and there with the constant vigilance of a dog that is kicked on occasion. Across the sandy street were some vivid green grass-plots, so wonderful in appearance, amid the sands that burned near them in a blazing sun, that they caused a doubt in the mind. They exactly resembled the grass mats used to represent lawns on the stage. At the cooler end of the railway station, a man without a coat sat in a tilted chair and smoked his pipe. The fresh-cut bank of the Rio Grande circled near the town, and there could be seen beyond it a great plum-colored plain of mesquite.

Save for the busy drummer and his companions in the saloon, Yellow Sky was dozing. The newcomer leaned gracefully upon the bar, and recited many tales with the confidence of a bard who has come upon a new field.

"—and at the moment that the old man fell downstairs with the bureau in his arms, the old woman was coming up with two scuttles of coal, and of course—"

The drummer's tale was interrupted by a young man who suddenly appeared in the open door. He cried: "Scratchy Wilson's drunk, and has turned loose with both hands." The two Mexicans at once set down their glasses and faded out of the rear entrance of the saloon.

The drummer, innocent and jocular, answered: "All right, old man. S'pose he has? Come in and have a drink, anyhow."

But the information had made such an obvious cleft in every skull in the room that the drummer was obliged to see its importance. All had become instantly solemn. "Say," said he, mystified, "what is this?" His three companions made the introductory gesture of eloquent speech, but the young man at the door forestalled them.

"It means, my friend," he answered, as he came into the saloon, "that for the next two hours this town won't be a health resort."

The barkeeper went to the door and locked and barred it. Reaching out of the window, he pulled in heavy wooden shutters and barred them. Immediately a solemn, chapel-like gloom was upon the place. The drummer was looking from one to another.

"But say," he cried, "what is this, anyhow? You don't mean there is going to be a gunfight?"

"Don't know whether there'll be a fight or not," answered one man, grimly. "But there'll be some shootin'—some good shootin'."

The young man who had warned them waved his hand. "Oh, there'll be a fight fast enough, if any one wants it. Anybody can get a fight out there in the street. There's a fight just waiting."

The drummer seemed to be swayed between the interest of a foreigner and a perception of personal danger.

"What did you say his name was?" he asked.

"Scratchy Wilson," they answered in chorus.

"And will he kill anybody? What are you going to do? Does this happen often? Does he rampage around like this once a week or so? Can he break in that door?"

"No; he can't break down that door," replied the barkeeper. "He's tried it three times. But when he comes you'd better lay down on the floor, stranger. He's dead sure to shoot at it, and a bullet may come through."

Thereafter the drummer kept a strict eye upon the door. The time had not yet been called for him to hug the floor, but, as a minor precaution, he sidled near to the wall. "Will he kill anybody?" he said again.

The men laughed low and scornfully at the question.

"He's out to shoot, and he's out for trouble. Don't see any good in experimentin' with him."

"But what do you do in a case like this? What do you do?"

A man responded: "Why, he and Jack Potter—"

"But," in chorus the other men interrupted, "Jack Potter's in San Anton'."

"Well, who is he? What's he got to do with it?"

"Oh, he's the town marshal. He goes out and fights Scratchy when he gets on one of these tears."

"Wow!" said the drummer, mopping his brow. "Nice job he's got."

The voices had toned away to mere whisperings. The drummer wished to ask further questions, which were born of an increasing anxiety and bewilderment; but when he attempted them, the men merely looked at him in irritation and motioned him to remain silent. A tense waiting hush was upon them. In the deep shadows of the room their eyes shone as they listened for sounds from the street. One man made three gestures at the barkeeper; and the latter, moving like a ghost, handed him a glass and a bottle. The man poured a full glass of whiskey, and set down the bottle noiselessly. He gulped the whiskey in a swallow, and turned again toward the door in immovable silence. The drummer saw that the barkeeper, without a sound, had taken a Winchester from beneath the bar. Later he saw this individual beckoning to him, so he tiptoed across the room.

"You better come with me back of the bar."

"No, thanks," said the drummer, perspiring. "I'd rather be where I can make a break for the back door."

Whereupon the man of bottles made a kindly but peremptory gesture. The drummer obeyed it, and, finding himself seated on a box with his head below the level of the bar, balm was laid upon his soul at sight of various zinc and copper fittings that bore a resemblance to armor plate. The barkeeper took a seat comfortably upon an adjacent box.

"You see," he whispered, "this here Scratchy Wilson is a wonder with a gun—a perfect wonder—and when he goes on the war trail, we hunt our holes—naturally. He's about the last one of the old gang that used to hang out along the river here. He's a terror when he's drunk. When he's sober he's all right—kind of simple—wouldn't hurt a fly—nicest fellow in town. But when he's drunk—whoo!"

There were periods of stillness. "I wish Jack Potter was back from San

Anton'," said the barkeeper. "He shot Wilson up once—in the leg—and he would sail in and pull out the kinks in this thing."

Presently they heard from a distance the sound of a shot, followed by three wild yowls. It instantly removed a bond from the men in the darkened saloon. There was a shuffling of feet. They looked at each other. "Here he comes," they said.

III

A man in a maroon-colored flannel shirt, which had been purchased for purposes of decoration, and made principally by some Jewish women on the East Side of New York, rounded a corner and walked into the middle of the main street of Yellow Sky. In either hand the man held a long, heavy, blue-black revolver. Often he yelled, and these cries rang through a semblance of a deserted village, shrilly flying over the roofs in a volume that seemed to have no relation to the ordinary vocal strength of a man. It was as if the surrounding stillness formed the arch of a tomb over him. These cries of ferocious challenge rang against walls of silence. And his boots had red tops with gilded imprints, of the kind beloved in winter by little sledding boys on the hillsides of New England.

The man's face flamed in a rage begot of whiskey. His eyes, rolling, and yet keen for ambush, hunted the still doorways and windows. He walked with the creeping movement of the midnight cat. As it occurred to him, he roared menacing information. The long revolvers in his hands were as easy as straws; they were moved with an electric swiftness. The little fingers of each hand played sometimes in a musician's way. Plain from the low collar of the shirt, the cords of his neck straightened and sank, straightened and sank, as passion moved him. The only sounds were his terrible invitations. The calm adobes preserved their demeanor at the passing of this small thing in the middle of the street.

There was no offer of fight—no offer of fight. The man called to the sky. There were no attractions. He bellowed and fumed and swayed his revolvers here and everywhere.

The dog of the barkeeper of the Weary Gentleman saloon had not appreciated the advance of events. He yet lay dozing in front of his master's door. At sight of the dog, the man paused and raised his revolver humorously. At sight of the man, the dog sprang up and walked diagonally away, with a sullen head, and growling. The man yelled, and the dog broke into a gallop. As it was about to enter an alley, there was a loud noise, a whistling, and something spat the ground directly before it. The dog screamed, and, wheeling in terror, galloped headlong in a new direction. Again there was a noise, a whistling, and sand was kicked viciously before it. Fear-stricken, the dog turned and flurried like an animal in a pen. The man stood laughing, his weapons at his hips.

Ultimately the man was attracted by the closed door of the Weary Gentleman saloon. He went to it and, hammering with a revolver, demanded drink.

The door remaining imperturbable, he picked a bit of paper from the walk, and nailed it to the framework with a knife. He then turned his back contemptuously upon this popular resort and, walking to the opposite side of the street and spinning there on his heel quickly and lithely, fired at the bit of paper. He missed it by a half-inch. He swore at himself, and went away. Later, he comfortably fusilladed the windows of his most intimate friend. The man was playing with this town. It was a toy for him.

But still there was no offer of fight. The name of Jack Potter, his ancient antagonist, entered his mind, and he concluded that it would be a glad thing if he should go to Potter's house, and by bombardment induce him to come out and fight. He moved in the direction of his desire, chanting Apache scalp-music.

When he arrived at it, Potter's house presented the same still front as had the other adobes. Taking up a strategic position, the man howled a challenge. But this house regarded him as might a great stone god. It gave no sign. After a decent wait, the man howled further challenges, mingling with them wonderful epithets.

Presently there came the spectacle of a man churning himself into deepest rage over the immobility of a house. He fumed at it as the winter wind attacks a prairie cabin in the North. To the distance there should have gone the sound of a tumult like the fighting of two hundred Mexicans. As necessity bade him, he paused for breath or to reload his revolvers.

IV

Potter and his bride walked sheepishly and with speed. Sometimes they laughed together shamefacedly and low.

"Next corner, dear," he said finally.

They put forth the efforts of a pair walking bowed against a strong wind. Potter was about to raise a finger to point the first appearance of the new home when, as they circled the corner, they came face to face with a man in a maroon-colored shirt, who was feverishly pushing cartridges into a large revolver. Upon the instant the man dropped his revolver to the ground, and, like lightning, whipped another from its holster. The second weapon was aimed at the bridegroom's chest.

There was a silence. Potter's mouth seemed to be merely a grave for his tongue. He exhibited an instinct to at once loosen his arm from the woman's grip, and he dropped the bag to the sand. As for the bride, her face had gone as yellow as old cloth. She was a slave to hideous rites, gazing at the apparitional snake.

The two men faced each other at a distance of three paces. He of the revolver smiled with a new and quiet ferocity.

"Tried to sneak up on me," he said. "Tried to sneak up on me!" His eyes grew more baleful. As Potter made a slight movement, the man thrust his revolver venomously forward. "No; don't you do it, Jack Potter. Don't you move a finger toward a gun just yet. Don't you move an eyelash. The time has come for me to settle with you, and I'm goin' to do it my own way, and loaf along with no interferin'. So if you don't want a gun bent on you, just mind what I tell you."

Potter looked at his enemy. "I ain't got a gun on me, Scratchy," he said. "Honest, I ain't." He was stiffening and steadying, but yet somewhere at the back of his mind a vision of the Pullman floated: the sea-green figured velvet, the shining brass, silver, and glass, the wood that gleamed as darkly brilliant as the surface of a pool of oil—all the glory of the marriage, the environment of the new estate. "You know I fight when it comes to fighting, Scratchy Wilson; but I ain't got a gun on me. You'll have to do all the shootin' yourself."

His enemy's face went livid. He stepped forward, and lashed his weapon to and fro before Potter's chest. "Don't you tell me you ain't got no gun on you, you whelp. Don't tell me no lie like that. There ain't a man in Texas ever seen you without no gun. Don't take me for no kid." His eyes blazed with light, and his throat worked like a pump.

"I ain't takin' you for no kid," answered Potter. His heels had not moved an inch backward. "I'm takin' you for a damn fool. I tell you I ain't got a gun, and I ain't. If you're goin' to shoot me up, you better begin now. You'll never get a chance like this again."

So much enforced reasoning had told on Wilson's rage. He was calmer. "If you ain't got a gun, why ain't you got a gun?" he sneered. "Been to Sunday school?"

"I ain't got a gun because I've just come from San Anton' with my wife. I'm married," said Potter. "And if I'd thought there was going to be any galoots like you prowling around when I brought my wife home, I'd had a gun, and don't you forget it."

"Married!" said Scratchy, not at all comprehending.

"Yes, married. I'm married," said Potter, distinctly.

"Married?" said Scratchy. Seemingly for the first time, he saw the drooping, drowning woman at the other man's side. "No!" he said. He was like a creature allowed a glimpse of another world. He moved a pace backward, and his arm, with the revolver, dropped to his side. "Is this the lady?" he asked.

"Yes; this is the lady," answered Potter.

There was another period of silence.

"Well," said Wilson at last, slowly, "I s'pose it's all off now."

"It's all off if you say so, Scratchy. You know I didn't make the trouble." Potter lifted his valise.

"Well, I 'low it's off, Jack," said Wilson. He was looking at the ground. "Married!" He was not a student of chivalry; it was merely that in the presence of this foreign condition he was a simple child of the earlier plains. He picked up his starboard revolver, and, placing both weapons in their holsters, he went away. His feet made funnel-shaped tracks in the heavy sand.

February, 1898

[*McClure's Magazine*, Vol. 10, pp. 377–384.]

DEATH AND THE CHILD

I

The peasants who were streaming down the mountain trail had, in their sharp terror, evidently lost their ability to count. The cattle and the huge round bundles seemed to suffice to the minds of the crowd if there were now two in each case where there had been three. This brown stream poured on with a constant wastage of goods and beasts. A goat fell behind to scout the dried grass, and its owner, howling, flogging his donkeys, passed far ahead. A colt, suddenly frightened, made a stumbling charge up the hillside. The expenditure was always profligate, and always unnamed, unnoted. It was as if fear was a river, and this horde had simply been caught in the torrent, man tumbling over beast, beast over man, as helpless in it as the logs that fall and shoulder grindingly through the gorges of a lumber country. It was a freshet that might sear the face of the tall, quiet mountain; it might draw a livid line across the land, this downpour of fear with a thousand homes adrift in the current—men, women, babes, animals. From it there arose a constant babble of tongues, shrill, broken, and sometimes choking, as from men drowning. Many made gestures, painting their agonies on the air with fingers that twirled swiftly.

The blue bay, with its pointed ships, and the white town lay below them, distant, flat, serene. There was upon this vista a peace that a bird knows when, high in air, it surveys the world, a great, calm thing rolling noiselessly toward the end of the mystery. Here on the height one felt the existence of the universe scornfully defining the pain in ten thousand minds. The sky was an arch of stolid sapphire. Even to the mountains, raising their mighty shapes from the valley, this headlong rush of the fugitives was too minute. The sea, the sky, and the hills combined in their grandeur to term this misery inconsequent. Then, too, it sometimes happened that a face seen as it passed on the flood reflected curiously the spirit of them all, and still more. One saw then a woman of the opinion of the vaults above the clouds. When a child cried, it cried always because of some adjacent misfortune—some discomfort of a packsaddle or rudeness of an encircling arm. In the dismal melody of this flight there were often sounding chords of apathy. Into these preoccupied countenances one felt that needles could be thrust without purchasing a scream. The trail wound here and there, as the sheep had willed in the making of it.

Although this throng seemed to prove that the whole of humanity was fleeing in one direction—with every tie severed that binds us to the soil— a young man was walking rapidly up the mountain, hastening to a side of the path from time to time to avoid some particularly wide rush of people and cattle. He looked at everything in agitation and pity. Frequently he called admonitions to maniacal fugitives, and at other times he exchanged strange stares with the imperturbable ones. They seemed to him to wear merely the expressions of so many boulders rolling down the hill. He exhibited wonder and awe with his pitying glances.

Turning once toward the rear, he saw a man in the uniform of a lieutenant of infantry marching the same way. He waited then, subconsciously elate at a prospect of being able to make into words the emotion which heretofore had been expressed only in the flash of eyes and sensitive movements of his flexible mouth. He spoke to the officer in rapid French, waving his arms wildly, and often pointing with a dramatic finger. "Ah, this is too cruel, too cruel, too cruel! Is it not? I did not think it would be as bad as this. I did not think—God's mercy!—I did not think at all. And yet, I am a Greek. Or, at least, my father was a Greek. I did not come here to fight. I am really a correspondent, you see? I was to write for an Italian paper. I have been educated in Italy. I have spent nearly all my life in Italy. At the schools and universities. I knew nothing of war! I was a student—a student. I came here merely because my father was a Greek, and for his sake I thought of Greece—I loved Greece. But I did not dream——"

He paused, breathing heavily. His eyes glistened from that soft overflow which comes on occasion to the glance of a young woman. Eager, passionate, profoundly moved, his first words while facing the procession of fugitives had been an active definition of his own dimension, his personal relation to men, geography, life. Throughout he had preserved the fiery dignity of a tragedian.

The officer's manner at once deferred to this outburst. "Yes," he said, polite, but mournful; "these poor people—these poor people! I do not know what is to become of these poor people."

The young man declaimed again: "I had no dream—I had no dream that it would be like this! This is too cruel—too cruel! Now I want to be a soldier. Now I want to fight. Now I want to do battle for the land of my father." He made a sweeping gesture into the northwest.

The officer was also a young man, but he was bronzed and steady. Above his high military collar of crimson cloth with one silver star upon it appeared a profile stern, quiet, and confident, respecting fate, fearing only opinion. His clothes were covered with dust; the only bright spot was the flame of the crimson collar. At the violent cries of his companion he smiled as if to himself, meanwhile keeping his eyes fixed in a glance ahead.

From a land toward which their faces were bent came a continuous boom of artillery fire. It was sounding in regular measures, like the beating of a colossal clock—a clock that was counting the seconds in the lives of the stars, and men had time to die between the ticks. Solemn, oracular, inexorable, the great seconds tolled over the hills as if God fronted this dial rimmed by the horizon. The soldier and the correspondent found themselves silent. The latter in particular was sunk in a great mournfulness, as if he had resolved willy-nilly to swing to the bottom of the abyss where dwelt secrets of this kind, and had learned beforehand that all to be met there was cruelty and hopelessness. A strap of his bright new leather leggings came unfastened, and he bowed over it slowly, impressively, as one bending over the grave of a child.

Then, suddenly, the reverberations mingled until one could not separate one explosion from another, and into the hubbub came the drawling sound of a leisurely musketry fire. Instantly, for some reason of cadence, the noise was irritating, silly, infantile. This uproar was childish. It forced the nerves to object, to protest against this racket, which was as idle as the din of a lad with a drum.

The lieutenant lifted his finger and pointed. He spoke in vexed tones, as if he held the other man personally responsible for the noise. "Well, there!" he said. "If you wish for war, you now have an opportunity magnificent."

The correspondent raised himself upon his toes. He tapped his chest with gloomy pride. "Yes! There is war! There is the war I wish to enter. I fling myself in. I am a Greek—a Greek, you understand. I wish to fight for my country. You know the way. Lead me! I offer myself." Struck with a sudden thought, he brought a case from his pocket, and, extracting a card, handed it to the officer with a bow. "My name is Peza," he said simply.

A strange smile passed over the soldier's face. There was pity and pride— the vanity of experience—and contempt in it. "Very well," he said, returning the bow. "If my company is in the middle of the fight, I shall be glad for the honor of your companionship. If my company is not in the middle of the fight, I will make other arrangements for you."

Peza bowed once more, very stiffly, and correctly spoke his thanks. On the edge of what he took to be a great venture toward death, he discovered that he was annoyed at something in the lieutenant's tone. Things immediately assumed new and extraordinary proportions. The battle, the great carnival of woe, was sunk at once to an equation with a vexation by a stranger. He wanted to ask the lieutenant what was his meaning. He bowed again majestically. The lieutenant bowed. They flung a shadow of manners, of capering tinsel ceremony, across a land that groaned, and it satisfied something within themselves completely.

In the meantime the river of fleeing villagers was changed to simply a last dropping of belated creatures who fled past stammering and flinging their hands high. The two men had come to the top of the great hill. Before them was a green plain as level as an inland sea. It swept northward, and merged finally into a length of silvery mist. Upon the near part of this plain, and upon two gray, treeless mountains at the sides of it, were little black lines from which floated slanting sheets of smoke. It was not a battle, to the nerves; one could survey it with equanimity, as if it were a tea-table. But upon Peza's mind it struck a loud, clanging blow. It was war. Edified, aghast, triumphant, he paused suddenly, his lips apart. He remembered the pageants of carnage that had marched through the dreams of his childhood. Love he knew; that he had confronted alone, isolated, wondering, an individual, an atom taking the hand of a titanic principle. Like the faintest breeze on his forehead, he felt here the vibration from the hearts of forty thousand men.

The lieutenant's nostrils were moving. "I must go at once," he said. "I must go at once."

"I will go with you, wherever you go," shouted Peza, loudly.

A primitive track wound down the side of the mountain, and in their rush they bounded from here to there, choosing risks which in the ordinary caution of man would surely have seemed of remarkable danger. The ardor of the correspondent surpassed the full energy of the soldier. Several times he turned and shouted: "Come on! Come on!"

At the foot of the path they came to a wide road which extended toward the battle in a yellow and straight line. Some men were trudging wearily to the rear. They were without rifles; their clumsy uniforms were dirty and all awry. They turned eyes dully aglow with fever upon the pair striding toward the battle. Others were bandaged with the triangular kerchief, upon which one could still see, through bloodstains, the little explanatory pictures illustrating the ways to bind various wounds—"Fig. 1," "Fig. 2," "Fig. 7." Mingled with the pacing soldiers were peasants, in-

different, capable of smiling, gibbering about the battle, which was to
them an ulterior drama. A man was leading a string of three donkeys to
the rear, and at intervals he was accosted by wounded or fevered soldiers,
from whom he defended his animals with ape-like cries and mad gesticula-
tions. After much chattering they usually subsided gloomily, and allowed
him to go with his sleek little beasts unburdened. Finally he encountered
a soldier who walked slowly, with the assistance of a staff. His head was
bound with a wide bandage, grimy from blood and mud. He made application to the peasant, and immediately they were involved in a hideous
Levantine discussion. The peasant whined and clamored, sometimes spitting like a kitten. The wounded soldier jawed on thunderously, his great
hands stretched in claw-like graspings over the peasant's head. Once he
raised his staff and made threat with it. Then suddenly the row was at an
end. The other sick men saw their comrade mount the leading donkey,
and at once begin to drum with his heels. None attempted to gain the backs
of the remaining animals. They gazed after him dully. Finally they saw
the caravan outlined for a moment against the sky. The soldier was still
waving his arms passionately, having it out with the peasant.

Peza was alive with despair for these men who looked at him with such
doleful, quiet eyes. "Ah, my God!" he cried to the lieutenant, "these poor
souls!—these poor souls!"

The officer faced about angrily. "If you are coming with me, there is no
time for this." Peza obeyed instantly and with a sudden meekness. In the
moment some portion of egotism left him, and he modestly wondered if
the universe took cognizance of him to an important degree. This theater
for slaughter, built by the inscrutable needs of the earth, was an enormous
affair, and he reflected that the accidental destruction of an individual,
Peza by name, would perhaps be nothing at all.

With the lieutenant, he was soon walking along behind a series of little
crescent-shaped trenches, in which were soldiers tranquilly interested,
gossiping with the hum of a tea-party. Although these men were not at
this time under fire, he concluded that they were fabulously brave, else
they would not be so comfortable, so at home, in their sticky brown
trenches. They were certain to be heavily attacked before the day was old.
The universities had not taught him to understand this attitude. At the
passing of the young man in very nice tweed, with his new leggings, his
new white helmet, his new field-glass case, his new revolver holster, the
soiled soldiers turned with the same curiosity which a being in strange
garb meets at the corners of streets. He might as well have been prome-
nading a populous avenue. The soldiers volubly discussed his identity.

To Peza there was something awful in the absolute familiarity of each
tone, expression, gesture. These men, menaced with battle, displayed the

curiosity of the café. Then, on the verge of his great encounter toward death, he found himself extremely embarrassed, composing his face with difficulty, wondering what to do with his hands, like a gawk at a levee.

He felt ridiculous, and also he felt awed, aghast at these men who could turn their faces from the ominous front and debate his clothes, his business. There was an element which was newborn into his theory of war.

He was not averse to the brisk pace at which the lieutenant moved along the line. The roar of fighting was always in Peza's ears. It came from some short hills ahead and to the left. The road curved suddenly and entered a wood. The trees stretched their luxuriant and graceful branches over grassy slopes. A breeze made all this verdure gently rustle and speak in long silken sighs. Absorbed in listening to the hurricane racket from the front, he still remembered that these trees were growing, the grass-blades were extending, according to their process. He inhaled a deep breath of moisture and fragrance from the grove, a wet odor which expressed the opulent fecundity of unmoved nature, marching on with her million plans for multiple life, multiple death.

Farther on, they came to a place where the Turkish shells were landing. There was a long, hurtling sound in the air, and then one had sight of a shell. To Peza it was of the conical missiles which friendly officers had displayed to him on board warships. Curiously enough, too, this first shell smacked of the foundry—of men with smudged faces, of the blare of furnace fires. It brought machinery immediately into his mind. He thought that if he was killed there at that time, it would be as romantic to the old standards as death by a bit of falling iron in a factory.

II

A child was playing on a mountain, and disregarding a battle that was waging on the plain. Behind him was the little cobbled hut of his fled parents. It was now occupied by a pearl-colored cow, that stared out from the darkness, thoughtful and tender-eyed. The child ran to and fro, fumbling with sticks, and making great machinations with pebbles. By a striking exercise of artistic licence, the sticks were ponies, cows, and dogs, and the pebbles were sheep. He was managing large agricultural and herding affairs. He was too intent on them to pay much heed to the fight four miles away, which at that distance resembled in sound the beating of surf upon rocks. However, there were occasions when some louder outbreak of that thunder stirred him from his serious occupation, and he turned then a questioning eye upon the battle, a small stick poised in his hand, interrupted in the act of sending his dog after his sheep. His tranquillity in regard to the death on the plain was as invincible as that of the mountain on which he stood.

It was evident that fear had swept the parents away from their home in a manner that could make them forget this child, the first-born. Nevertheless, the hut was cleaned bare. The cow had committed no impropriety in billeting herself at the domicile of her masters. This smoke-colored and odorous interior contained nothing as large as a hummingbird. Terror had operated on these runaway people in its sinister fashion—elevating details to enormous heights, causing a man to remember a button while he forgot a coat, overpowering every one with recollections of a broken coffee cup, deluging them with fears for the safety of an old pipe, and causing them to forget their first-born. Meanwhile the child played soberly with his trinkets.

He was solitary. Engrossed in his own pursuits, it was seldom that he lifted his head to inquire of the world why it made so much noise. The stick in his hand was much larger to him than was an army corps of the distance. It was too childish for the mind of the child. He was dealing with sticks.

The battlelines writhed at times in the agony of a sea creature on the sands. These tentacles flung and waved in a supreme excitement of pain, and the struggles of the great outlined body brought it near and nearer to the child. Once he looked at the plain, and saw some men running wildly across a field. He had seen people chasing obdurate beasts in such fashion, and it struck him immediately that it was a manly thing, which he would incorporate in his game. Consequently he raced furiously at his stone sheep, flourishing a cudgel, crying the shepherd calls. He paused frequently to get a cue of manner from the soldiers fighting on the plain. He reproduced, to a degree, any movements which he accounted rational to his theory of sheepherding, the business of men, the traditional and exalted living of his father.

III

It was as if Peza was a corpse walking on the bottom of the sea, and finding there fields of grain, groves, weeds, the faces of men, voices. War, a strange employment of the race, presented to him a scene crowded with familiar objects which wore the livery of their commonness placidly, undauntedly. He was smitten with keen astonishment; a spread of green grass, lit with the flames of poppies, was too old for the company of this new ogre. If he had been devoting the full lens of his mind to this phase, he would have known that he was amazed that the trees, the flowers, the grass, all tender and peaceful nature, had not taken to heels at once upon the outbreak of battle. He venerated the immovable poppies.

The road seemed to lead into the apex of an angle formed by the two defensive lines of the Greeks. There was a struggle of wounded men, and of gunless and jaded men. These latter did not seem to be frightened. They remained very cool, walking with unhurried steps, and busy in gossip. Peza tried to define them. Perhaps during the fight they had reached the limit of their mental storage, their capacity for excitement, for tragedy, and had then simply come away. Peza remembered his visit to a certain place of pictures, where he had found himself amid heavenly skies and diabolic midnights—the sunshine beating red upon desert sands, nude bodies flung to the shore in the green moonglow, ghastly and starving men clawing at a wall in darkness, a girl at her bath, with screened rays falling upon her pearly shoulders, a dance, a funeral, a review, an execution—all the strength of Argus-eyed art; and he had whirled and whirled amid this universe, with cries of woe and joy, sin and beauty, piercing his ears until he had been obliged to simply come away. He remembered that as he had emerged he had lit a cigarette with unction, and advanced promptly to a café. A great hollow quiet seemed to be upon the earth.

This was a different case, but in his thoughts he conceded the same causes to many of these gunless wanderers. They, too, may have dreamed at lightning speed, until the capacity for it was overwhelmed. As he watched them, he again saw himself walking toward the café, puffing upon his cigarette. As if to reinforce his theory, a soldier stopped him with an eager but polite inquiry for a match. He watched the man light his little roll of tobacco and paper and begin to smoke ravenously.

Peza no longer was torn with sorrow at the sight of wounded men. Evidently he found that pity had a numerical limit, and when this was passed the emotion became another thing. Now, as he viewed them, he merely felt himself very lucky, and beseeched the continuance of his superior fortune. At the passing of these slouched and stained figures he now heard a reiteration of warning. A part of himself was appealing through the medium of these grim shapes. It was plucking at his sleeve and pointing, telling him to beware of these soldiers only as he would have cared for the harms of broken dolls. His whole vision was focused upon his own chance.

The lieutenant suddenly halted. "Look," he said; "I find that my duty is in another direction; I must go another way. But if you wish to fight, you have only to go forward, and any officer of the fighting line will give you opportunity." He raised his cap ceremoniously. Peza raised his new white helmet. The stranger to battles uttered thanks to his chaperon, the one who had presented him. They bowed punctiliously, staring at each other with civil eyes.

The lieutenant moved quietly away through a field. In an instant it flashed upon Peza's mind that this desertion was perfidious. He had been subjected to a criminal discourtesy. The officer fetched him into the middle of the thing, and then left him to wander helplessly toward death. At one time he was upon the point of shouting at the officer.

In the vale there was an effect as if one was then beneath the battle. It was going on above, somewhere. Alone, unguided, Peza felt like a man groping in a cellar. He reflected, too, that one should always see the beginning of a fight. It was too difficult to thus approach it when the affair was in full swing. The trees hid all the movements of troops from him, and he thought he might be walking out to the very spot which chance had provided for the reception of a fool. He asked eager questions of passing soldiers. Some paid no heed to him; others shook their heads mournfully. They knew nothing, save that war was hard work. If they talked at all, it was in testimony of having fought well, savagely. They did not know if the army was going to advance, hold its ground, or retreat. They were weary.

A long, pointed shell flashed through the air, and struck near the base of a tree with a fierce upheaval, compounded of earth and flames. Looking back, Peza could see the shattered tree quivering from head to foot. Its whole being underwent a convulsive tremor which was an exhibition of pain and, furthermore, deep amazement. As he advanced through the vale, the shells continued to hiss and hurtle in long, low flights, and the bullets purred in the air. The missiles were flying into the breast of an astounded nature. The landscape, bewildered, agonized, was suffering a rain of infamous shots, and Peza imagined a million eyes gazing at him with the gaze of startled antelopes.

There was a resolute crashing of musketry from the tall hill on the left, and from directly in front there was a mingled din of artillery and musketry firing. Peza felt that his pride was playing a great trick in forcing him forward in this manner under conditions of strangeness, isolation, and ignorance. But he recalled the manner of the lieutenant, the smile on the hilltop among the flying peasants. Peza blushed, and pulled the peak of his helmet down on his forehead. He strode on firmly. Nevertheless, he hated the lieutenant, and he resolved that on some future occasion he would take much trouble to arrange a stinging social revenge upon that grinning jackanapes. It did not occur to him, until later, that he was now going to battle mainly because at a previous time a certain man had smiled.

IV

The road moved around the base of a little hill, and on this hill a battery of mountain guns was leisurely shelling something unseen. In the lee of the height, the mules, contented under their heavy saddles, were quietly browsing the long grass. Peza ascended the hill by a slanting path. He felt his heart beat swiftly. Once at the top of the hill, he would be obliged to look this phenomenon in the face. He hurried with a mysterious idea of preventing by this strategy the battle from making his appearance a signal for some tremendous renewal. This vague thought seemed logical at the time. Certainly this living thing had knowledge of his coming. He endowed it with the intelligence of a barbaric deity. And so he hurried. He wished to surprise war, this terrible emperor, when it was only growling on its throne. The ferocious and horrible sovereign was not to be allowed to make the arrival a pretext for some fit of smoky rage and blood. In this half-lull, Peza had distinctly the sense of stealing upon the battle unawares.

The soldiers watching the mules did not seem to be impressed by anything august. Two of them sat side by side and talked comfortably; another lay flat upon his back, staring dreamily at the sky; another cursed a mule for certain refractions. Despite their uniforms, their bandoleers and rifles, they were dwelling in the peace of hostlers. However, the long shells were whooping from time to time over the brow of the hill, and swirling in almost straight lines toward the vale of trees, flowers, and grass. Peza, hearing and seeing the shells, and seeing the pensive guardians of the mules, felt reassured. They were accepting the conditions of war as easily as an old sailor accepts the chair behind the counter of a tobacco shop. Or it was merely that the farm boy had gone to sea, and he had adjusted himself to the circumstances immediately, and with only the usual first misadventures in conduct. Peza was proud and ashamed that he was not of them—these stupid peasants who, throughout the world, hold potentates on their thrones, make statesmen illustrious, provide generals with lasting victories, all with ignorance, indifference, or half-witted hatred, moving the world with the strength of their arms, and getting their heads knocked together, in the name of God, the king, or the stock exchange—immortal, dreaming, hopeless asses who surrender their reason to the care of a shining puppet, and persuade some toy to carry their lives in his purse. Peza mentally abased himself before them, and wished to stir them with furious kicks.

As his eyes ranged above the rim of the plateau, he saw a group of artillery officers talking busily. They turned at once, and regarded his ascent. A moment later a row of infantry soldiers, in a trench beyond the little guns, all faced him. Peza bowed to the officers. He understood at the time that he had made a good and cool bow, and he wondered at it; for his breath was coming in gasps—he was stifling from sheer excitement. He felt like a tipsy man trying to conceal his muscular uncertainty from the people in the street. But the officers did not display any knowledge. They bowed. Behind them Peza saw the plain, glittering green, with three lines of black marked upon it heavily. The front of the first of these lines was frothy with smoke. To the left of this hill was a craggy mountain, from which came a continual dull rattle of musketry. Its summit was ringed with the white smoke. The black lines on the plain slowly moved. The shells that came from there passed overhead, with the sound of great birds frantically flapping their wings. Peza thought of the first sight of the sea during a storm. He seemed to feel against his face the wind that races over the tops of cold and tumultuous billows.

He heard a voice afar off: "Sir, what would you?" He turned, and saw the dapper captain of the battery standing beside him. Only a moment had elapsed.

"Pardon me, sir," said Peza, bowing again.

The officer was evidently reserving his bows. He scanned the new-comer attentively. "Are you a correspondent?" he asked.

Peza produced a card. "Yes; I came as a correspondent," he replied. "But now, sir, I have other thoughts. I wish to help. You see? I wish to help."

"What do you mean?" said the captain. "Are you a Greek? Do you wish to fight?"

"Yes; I am a Greek; I wish to fight." Peza's voice surprised him by coming from his lips in even and deliberate tones. He thought with grati-fication that he was behaving rather well. Another shell, traveling from some unknown point on the plain, whirled close and furiously in the air, pursuing an apparently horizontal course, as if it were never going to touch the earth. The dark shape swished across the sky.

"Ah," cried the captain, now smiling, "I am not sure that we will be able to accommodate you with a fierce affair here just at this time, but——" He walked gaily to and fro behind the guns with Peza, pointing out to him the lines of the Greeks, and describing his opinion of the general plan of defence. He wore the air of an amiable host. Other officers ques-tioned Peza in regard to the politics of the war. The king, the ministry, Germany, England, Russia—all these huge words were continually upon their tongues. "And the people in Athens, were they——?" Amid this vivacious babble, Peza, seated upon an ammunition box, kept his glance high, watching the appearance of shell after shell. These officers were like men who had been lost for days in the forest. They were thirsty for any scrap of news. Nevertheless, one of them would occasionally dispute their informant courteously. What would Servia have to say to that? No, no; France and Russia could never allow it. Peza was elated. The shells killed no one. War was not so bad! He was simply having coffee in the smoking room of some embassy where reverberate the names of nations.

A rumor had passed along the motley line of privates in the trench. The new arrival with the clean white helmet was a famous English cavalry officer, come to assist the army with his counsel. They stared at the figure of him, surrounded by officers. Peza, gaining sense of the glances and whispers, felt that his coming was an event.

Later, he resolved that he could, with temerity, do something finer. He contemplated the mountain where the Greek infantry was engaged, and announced leisurely to the captain of the battery that he thought presently of going in that direction and getting into the fight. He re-affirmed the sentiments of a patriot. The captain seemed surprised. "Oh, there will be fighting here at this knoll in a few minutes," he said orientally. "That will be sufficient. You had better stay with us. Besides, I have been ordered to resume fire." The officers all tried to dissuade him from departing. It was really not worth the trouble. The battery would begin again directly; then it would be amusing for him.

Peza felt that he was wandering, with his protestations of high patriotism, through a desert of sensible men. These officers gave no heed to his exalted declarations. They seemed too jaded. They were fighting the men who were fighting them. Palaver of the particular kind had subsided before their intense preoccupation in war as a craft. Moreover, many men had talked in that manner, and only talked.

Peza believed at first that they were treating him delicately; they were considerate of his inexperience. War had turned out to be such a gentle business that Peza concluded that he could scorn this idea. He bade them an heroic farewell, despite their objections.

However, when he reflected upon their ways afterward, he saw dimly that they were actuated principally by some universal childish desire for a spectator of their fine things. They were going into action, and they wished to be seen at war, precise and fearless.

V

Climbing slowly to the high infantry position, Peza was amazed to meet a soldier whose jaw had been half shot away, and who was being helped down the steep track by two tearful comrades. The man's breast was drenched with blood, and from a cloth which he held to the wound drops were splashing wildly upon the stones of the path. He gazed at Peza for a moment. It was a mystic gaze, which Peza withstood with difficulty. He was exchanging looks with a specter; all aspect of the man was somehow gone from this victim. As Peza went on, one of the un-wounded soldiers loudly shouted to him to return and assist in this tragic march. But even Peza's fingers revolted. He was afraid of the specter; he would not have dared to touch it. He was surely craven in the movement of refusal he made to them. He scrambled hastily on up the path. He was running away!

At the top of the hill he came immediately upon a part of the line that was in action. Another battery of mountain guns was here, firing at the streaks of black on the plain. There were trenches filled with men lining parts of the crest, and near the base were other trenches, all crashing away mightily. The plain stretched as far as the eye could see, and from where silver mist ended this emerald ocean of grass, a great ridge of snow-topped mountains poised against a fleckless blue sky. Two knolls, green and yellow with grain, sat on the prairie, confronting the dark hills of the Greek position. Between them were the lines of the enemy. A row of trees, a village, a stretch of road showed faintly on this great canvas, this tremendous picture; but men, the Turkish battalions, were emphasized startlingly upon it. The ranks of troops between the knolls and the Greek position were as black as ink. The first line, of course, was muffled in smoke; but at the rear of it, battalions crawled up, and to and fro, plainer than beetles on a plate. Peza had never understood that masses of men were so declarative, so unmistakable, as if nature makes every arrangement to give information of the coming and the presence of destruction, the end, oblivion. The firing was full, complete, a roar of cataracts, and this pealing of concerted volleys was adjusted to the grandeur of the far-off range of snowy mountains. Peza, breathless, pale, felt that he had been set upon a pillar, and was surveying mankind, the world. In the mean-time dust had got in his eye. He took his handkerchief and mechanically administered to it.

An officer with a double stripe of purple on his trousers paced in the rear of the battery of howitzers. He waved a little cane. Sometimes he paused in his promenade to study the field through his glasses. "A fine scene, sir," he cried airily, upon the approach of Peza. It was like a blow in the chest to the wide-eyed volunteer. It revealed to him a point of view.

"Yes, sir; it is a fine scene," he answered.

They spoke in French. "I am happy to be able to entertain monsieur with a little fine practice," continued the officer. "I am firing upon that mass of troops you see there, a little to the right. They are probably form-ing for another attack."

Peza smiled. Here again appeared manners—manners erect by the side of death.

The right-flank gun of the battery thundered; there was a belch of fire and smoke; the shell, flung swiftly and afar, was known only to the ear, in which rang a broadening, hooting wake of sound. The howitzer had thrown itself backward convulsively, and lay with its wheels moving in the air as a squad of men rushed toward it; and later, it seemed as if each little gun had made the supreme effort of its being in each par-ticular shot. They roared with voices far too loud, and the thunderous effort caused a gun to bound as in a dying convulsion. And then occasion-ally one was hurled with wheels in air. These shuddering howitzers pre-sented an appearance of so many cowards, always longing to bolt to the rear, but being implacably held up to their business by this throng of soldiers who ran in squads to drag them up again to their obligation. The guns were herded and cajoled and bullied interminably. One by one, in relentless program, they were dragged forward to contribute a profound vibration of steel and wood, a flash and a roar, to the important happiness of men.

The adjacent infantry celebrated a good shot with smiles and an outburst of gleeful talk.

"Look, sir," cried an officer once to Peza. Thin smoke was drifting lazily before Peza, and, dodging impatiently, he brought his eyes to bear upon that part of the plain indicated by the officer's finger. The enemy's infantry was advancing to attack. From the black lines had come forth an inky mass which was shaped much like a human tongue. It advanced slowly, casually, without apparent spirit, but with an insolent confidence that was like a proclamation of the inevitable.

The impetuous part was all played by the defensive side.

Officers called; men plucked each other by the sleeve. There were shouts—motion. All eyes were turned upon the inky mass which was flowing toward the base of the hills, heavily, languorously, as oily and thick as one of the streams that ooze through a swamp.

Peza was chattering a question at every one. In the way, pushed aside, or in the way again, he continued to repeat it: "Can they take the position? Can they take the position? Can they take the position?" He was apparently addressing an assemblage of deaf men. Every eye was busy watching every hand. The soldiers did not even seem to see the interesting stranger in the white helmet, who was crying out so feverishly.

Finally, however, the hurried captain of the battery espied him, and heeded his question. "No, sir! No, sir! It is impossible!" he shouted angrily. His manner seemed to denote that if he had had sufficient time he would have completely insulted Peza. The latter swallowed the crumb of news without regard to the coating of scorn, and, waving his hand in adieu, he began to run along the crest of the hill toward the part of the Greek line against which the attack was directed.

VI

Peza, as he ran along the crest of the mountain, believed that his action was receiving the wrathful attention of the hosts of the foe. To him, then, it was incredible foolhardiness thus to call to himself the stares of thousands of hateful eyes. He was like a lad induced by playmates to commit some indiscretion in a cathedral. He was abashed; perhaps he even blushed as he ran. It seemed to him that the whole solemn ceremony of war had paused during this commission. So he scrambled wildly over the rocks in his haste to end the embarrassing ordeal. When he came among the crowning rifle pits, filled with eager soldiers, he wanted to yell with joy.

None noticed him, save a young officer of infantry, who said: "Sir, what do you want?" It was obvious that people had devoted some attention to their own affairs.

Peza asserted, in Greek, that he wished above everything to battle for the fatherland. The officer nodded. With a smile he pointed to some dead men, covered with blankets, from which were thrust upturned dusty shoes.

"Yes; I know, I know," cried Peza. He thought the officer was poetically alluding to the danger.

"No," said the officer, at once. "I mean cartridges—a bandoleer. Take a bandoleer from one of them."

Peza went cautiously toward a body. He moved a hand toward a corner of a blanket. There he hesitated, stuck, as if his arm had turned to plaster. Hearing a rustle behind him, he spun quickly. Three soldiers of the close rank in the trench were regarding him. The officer came again, and tapped him on the shoulder. "Have you any tobacco?" Peza looked at him in bewilderment. His hand was still extended toward the blanket which covered the dead soldier.

"Yes," he said; "I have some tobacco." He gave the officer his pouch. As if in compensation, the other directed a soldier to strip the bandoleer from the corpse. Peza, having crossed the long cartridge belt on his breast, felt that the dead man had flung his two arms around him.

A soldier, with a polite nod and smile, gave Peza a rifle—a relic of another dead man. Thus he felt, besides the clutch of a corpse about his neck, that the rifle was as unhumanly horrible as a snake that lives in a tomb. He heard at his ear something that was in effect like the voices of those two dead men, their low voices speaking to him of bloody death, mutilation. The bandoleer gripped him tighter; he wished to raise his hands to his throat, like a man who is choking. The rifle was clumsy; upon his palms he felt the movement of the sluggish currents of a serpent's life; it was crawling and frightful.

All about him were these peasants, with their interested countenances, gibbering of the fight. From time to time a soldier cried out in semi-humorous lamentations descriptive of his thirst. One bearded man sat munching a great bit of hard bread. Fat, greasy, squat, he was like an idol made of tallow. Peza felt dimly that there was a distinction between this man and a young student who could write sonnets and play the piano quite well. This old blockhead was coolly gnawing at the bread, while he—Peza—was being throttled by a dead man's arms.

He looked behind him, and saw that a head, by some chance, had been uncovered from its blanket. Two liquid-like eyes were staring into his face. The head was turned a little sideways, as if to get better opportunity for the scrutiny. Peza could feel himself blanch. He was being drawn and drawn by these dead men, slowly, firmly down, as to some mystic chamber under the earth, where they could walk, dreadful figures, swollen and blood-marked. He was bidden; they had commanded him; he was going, going, going.

When the man in the new white helmet bolted for the rear, many of the soldiers in the trench thought that he had been struck. But those who had been nearest to him knew better. Otherwise they would have heard the silken, sliding, tender noise of the bullet, and the thud of its impact. They bawled after him curses, and also outbursts of self-congratulation and vanity. Despite the prominence of the cowardly part, they were enabled to see in this exhibition a fine comment upon their own fortitude. The other soldiers thought that Peza had been wounded somewhere in the neck, because, as he ran, he was tearing madly at the bandoleer— the dead man's arms. The soldier with the bread paused in his eating, and cynically remarked upon the speed of the runaway.

An officer's voice was suddenly heard calling out the calculation of the distance to the enemy, the readjustment of the sights. There was a stirring rattle along the line. The men turned their eyes to the front. Other trenches, beneath them, to the right, were already heavily in action. The smoke was lifting toward the blue sky. The soldier with the bread placed it carefully on a bit of paper beside him as he turned to kneel in the trench.

VII

In the late afternoon the child ceased his play on the mountain with his flocks and his dogs. Part of the battle had whirled very near to the base of his hill, and the noise was great. Sometimes he could see fantastic, smoky shapes, which resembled the curious figures in foam which one sees on the slant of a rough sea. The plain, indeed, was etched in white circles and whirligigs, like the slope of a colossal wave. The child took seat on a stone, and contemplated the fight. He was beginning to be astonished. He had never before seen cattle herded with such uproar. Lines of flame flashed out here and there. It was mystery.

Finally, without any preliminary indication, he began to weep. If the men struggling on the plain had had time, and greater vision, they could have seen this strange, tiny figure seated on a boulder, surveying them while the tears streamed. It was as simple as some powerful symbol.

As the magic clear light of day amid the mountains dimmed the distances, and the plain shone as a pallid blue cloth marked by the red threads of the firing, the child arose and moved off to the unwelcoming door of his home. He called softly for his mother, and complained of his hunger in the familiar formulae. The pearl-colored cow, grinding her jaws thoughtfully, stared at him with her large eyes. The peaceful gloom of evening was slowly draping the hills.

The child heard a rattle of loose stones on the hillside, and, facing the sound, saw, a moment later, a man drag himself up to the crest of the hill and fall panting. Forgetting his mother and his hunger, filled with calm interest, the child walked forward, and stood over the heaving form. His eyes, too, were now large and inscrutably wise and sad, like those of the animal in the house.

After a silence, he spoke inquiringly: "Are you a man?"

Peza rolled over quickly, and gazed up into the fearless and cherubic countenance. He did not attempt to reply. He breathed as if life was about to leave his body. He was covered with dust; his face had been cut in some way, and his cheek was ribboned with blood. All the spick of his former appearance had vanished in a general dishevelment, in which he resembled a creature that had been flung to and fro, up and down, by cliffs and prairies during an earthquake. He rolled his eye glassily at the child.

They remained thus until the child repeated his words: "Are you a man?"

Peza gasped in the manner of a fish. Palsied, windless, and abject, he confronted the primitive courage, the sovereign child, the brother of the mountains, the sky, and the sea, and he knew that the definition of his misery could be written on a wee grass-blade.

March 19 and 26, 1898
[*Harper's Weekly*, Vol. 42, March 19, pp. 281–282;
March 26, pp. 297–298.]

THE FIVE WHITE MICE

Freddie was mixing a cocktail. His hand with the long spoon was whirling swiftly, and the ice in the glass hummed and rattled like a cheap watch. Over by the window, a gambler, a millionaire, a railway conductor, and the agent of a vast American syndicate were playing seven-up. Freddie surveyed them with the ironical glance of a man who is mixing a cocktail.

From time to time a swarthy Mexican waiter came with his tray from the rooms at the rear, and called his orders across the bar. The sounds of the indolent stir of the city, awakening from its siesta, floated over the screens which barred the sun and the inquisitive eye. From the far-away kitchen could be heard the roar of the old French *chef,* driving, herding, and abusing his Mexican helpers.

A string of men came suddenly in from the street. They stormed up to the bar. There were impatient shouts. "Come, now, Freddie, don't stand there like a portrait of yourself. Wiggle!" Drinks of many kinds and colors —amber, green, mahogany, strong and mild—began to swarm upon the bar, with all the attendants of lemon, sugar, mint, and ice. Freddie, with Mexican support, worked like a sailor in the provision of them, sometimes talking with that scorn for drink and admiration for those who drink which is the attribute of a good barkeeper.

At last a man was afflicted with a stroke of dice-shaking. A herculean discussion was waging, and he was deeply engaged in it, but at the same time he lazily flirted the dice. Occasionally he made great combinations. "Look at that, would you?" he cried proudly. The others paid little heed. Then violently the craving took them. It went along the line like an epidemic, and involved them all. In a moment they had arranged a carnival of dice-shaking, with money penalties and liquid prizes. They clamorously made it a point of honor with Freddie that he too should play, and take his chance of sometimes providing this large group with free refreshment. With bent heads, like football players, they surged over the tinkling dice, jostling, cheering, and bitterly arguing. One of the quiet company playing seven-up at the corner table said profanely that the row reminded him of a bowling contest at a picnic.

After the regular shower, many carriages rolled over the smooth *calle*, and sent a musical thunder through the Casa Verde. The shop windows became aglow with light, and the walks were crowded with youths, callow and ogling, dressed vainly according to supposititious fashions. The policemen had muffled themselves in their gnome-like cloaks and placed their lanterns as obstacles for the carriages in the middle of the street. The City of Mexico gave forth the deep, mellow organ-tones of its evening resurrection.

But still the group at the bar of the Casa Verde were shaking dice. They had passed beyond shaking for drinks for the crowd, for Mexican dollars, for dinner, for the wine at dinner. They had even gone to the trouble of separating the cigars and cigarettes from the dinner's bill, and causing a distinct man to be responsible for them. Finally they were aghast. Nothing remained within sight of their minds which even remotely suggested further gambling. There was a pause for deep consideration.

"Well—"

"Well—"

A man called out in the exuberance of creation. "I know! Let's stake for a box tonight at the circus! A box at the circus!" The group was profoundly edified. "That's it! That's it! Come on, now! Box at the circus!" A dominating voice cried: "Three dashes—high man out!" An American, tall, and with a face of copper red from the rays that flash among the Sierra Madres and burn on the cactus deserts, took the little leathern cup, and spun the dice out upon the polished wood. A fascinated assemblage hung upon the bar rail. Three kings turned their pink faces upward. The tall man flourished the cup, burlesquing, and flung the two other dice. From them he ultimately extracted one more pink king. "There," he said. "Now, let's see! Four kings!" He began to swagger in a sort of provisional way.

The next man took the cup, and blew softly on the top of it. Poising it in his hand, he then surveyed the company with a stony eye, and paused. They knew perfectly well that he was applying the magic of deliberation and ostentatious indifference, but they could not wait in tranquillity during the performance of all these rites. They began to call out impatiently: "Come, now—hurry up!" At last the man, with a gesture that was singularly impressive, threw the dice. The others set up a howl of joy. "Not a pair!" There was another solemn pause. The men moved restlessly. "Come, now, go ahead!" In the end, the man, induced and abused, achieved something that was nothing in the presence of four kings. The tall man climbed on the footrail and leaned hazardously forward. "Four kings! My four kings are good to go out," he bellowed into the middle of the mob; and although in a moment he did pass into the radiant region of exemption, he continued to bawl advice and scorn.

The mirrors and oiled woods of the Casa Verde were now dancing with blue flashes from a great buzzing electric lamp. A host of quiet members of the Anglo-Saxon colony had come in for their pre-dinner cocktails. An amiable person was exhibiting to some tourists this popular American saloon. It was a very sober and respectable time of day. Freddie reproved courageously the dice-shaking brawlers, and, in return, he received the choicest advice in a tumult of seven combined vocabularies. He laughed. He had been compelled to retire from the game, but he was keeping an interested, if furtive, eye upon it.

Down at the end of the line there was a youth at whom everybody railed for his flaming ill luck. At each disaster, Freddie swore from behind the bar in a sort of affectionate contempt. "Why this Kid has had no luck for two days. Did you ever see such throwin'?"

The contest narrowed eventually to the New York Kid and an individual who swung about placidly on legs that moved in nefarious circles. He had a grin that resembled a bit of carving. He was obliged to lean down and blink rapidly to ascertain the facts of his venture, but fate presented him with five queens. His smile did not change, but he puffed gently, like a man who has been running.

The others, having emerged unscathed from this part of the conflict, waxed hilarious with the Kid. They smote him on either shoulder. "We've got you stuck for it, Kid! You can't beat that game! Five queens!"

Up to this time the Kid had displayed only the temper of the gambler; but the cheerful hoots of the players, supplemented now by a ring of guying noncombatants, caused him to feel profoundly that it would be fine to beat the five queens. He addressed a gambler's slogan to the interior of the cup:

> Oh, five white mice of chance,
> Shirts of wool and corduroy pants,
> Gold and wine, women and sin,
> All for you if you let me come in—
> Into the house of chance.

Flashing the dice sardonically out upon the bar, he displayed three aces. From two dice in the next throw he achieved one more ace. For his last throw, he rattled the single dice for a long time. He already had four aces; if he accomplished another one, the five queens were vanquished, and the box at the circus came from the drunken man's pocket. All of the Kid's movements were slow and elaborate. For his last throw he planted the cup bottom up on the bar, with the one dice hidden under it. Then he turned and faced the crowd with the air of a conjuror or a cheat.

"Oh, maybe it's an ace," he said in boastful calm. "Maybe it's an ace."

Instantly he was presiding over a little drama in which every man was absorbed. The Kid leaned with his back against the bar rail and with his elbows upon it.

"Maybe it's an ace," he repeated.

A jeering voice in the background said: "Yes; maybe it is, Kid!"

The Kid's eyes searched for a moment among the men. "I'll bet fifty dollars it is an ace," he said.

Another voice asked: "American money?"

"Yes," answered the Kid.

"Oh!" There was a general laugh at this discomfiture. However, no one came forward at the Kid's challenge, and presently he turned to the cup. "Now, I'll show you." With the manner of a mayor unveiling a statue, he lifted the cup. There was revealed naught but a ten-spot. In the roar which arose could be heard each man ridiculing the cowardice of his neighbor, and above all the din rang the voice of Freddie berating every one.

"Why, there isn't one liver to every five men in the outfit. That was the greatest cold bluff I ever saw worked. He wouldn't know how to cheat with dice if he wanted to. Don't know the first thing about it. I could hardly keep from laughin' when I seen him drillin' you around. Why,

I tell you I had that fifty dollars right in my pocket, if I wanted to be a chump. You're an easy lot!"

Nevertheless, the group who had won in the circus-box game did not relinquish their triumph. They burst like a storm about the head of the Kid, swinging at him with their fists. "'Five white mice'!" they quoted, choking. "'Five white mice'!"

"Oh, they are not so bad," said the Kid.

Afterward it often occurred that a man would suddenly jeer a finger at the Kid and derisively say: "'Five white mice'!"

On the route from the dinner to the circus, others of the party often asked the Kid if he had really intended to make his appeal to mice. They suggested other animals—rabbits, dogs, hedgehogs, snakes, opossums. To this banter the Kid replied with a serious expression of his belief in the fidelity and wisdom of the five white mice. He presented a most eloquent case, decorated with fine language and insults, in which he proved that, if one was going to believe in anything at all, one might as well choose the five white mice. His companions, however, at once and unanimously pointed out to him that his recent exploit did not place him in the light of a convincing advocate.

The Kid discerned two figures in the street. They were making imperious signs at him. He waited for them to approach, for he recognized one as the other Kid—the 'Frisco Kid: there were two Kids. With the 'Frisco Kid was Benson. They arrived almost breathless. "Where you been?" cried the 'Frisco Kid. It was an arrangement that, upon meeting, the one that could first ask this question was entitled to use a tone of limitless injury. "What you been doing? Where you going? Come on with us. Benson and I have got a little scheme."

The New York Kid pulled his arm from the grapple of the other. "I can't. I've got to take these sutlers to the circus. They stuck me for it, shaking dice at Freddie's. I can't, I tell you."

The two did not at first attend to his remarks. "Come on; we've got a little scheme."

"I can't. They've stuck me. I've got to take 'm to the circus."

At this time it did not suit the men with the scheme to recognize these objections as important. "Oh, take 'm some other time." "Well, can't you take 'm some other time?" "Let 'm go." "Damn the circus." "Get cold feet!" "What did you get stuck for?" "Get cold feet!"

But despite their fighting, the New York Kid broke away from them. "I can't, I tell you. They stuck me."

As he left them, they yelled with rage. "Well, meet us, now, do you hear? In the Casa Verde, as soon as the circus quits! Hear?" They threw maledictions after him.

In the City of Mexico, a man goes to the circus without descending in any way to infant amusements, because the Circo Teatro Orrin is one of the best in the world, and too easily surpasses anything of the kind in the United States, where it is merely a matter of a number of rings, if possible, and a great professional agreement to lie to the public. Moreover, the American clown who in the Mexican arena prances and gabbles is the clown to whom writers refer as the delight of their childhood and lament that he is dead. At this circus the Kid was not debased by the sight of mournful prisoner elephants and caged animals, forlorn and sickly. He sat in his box until late, and laughed, and swore, when past laughing at the comic, foolish, wise clown.

When he returned to the Casa Verde, there was no display of the 'Frisco Kid and Benson. Freddie was leaning upon the bar, listening to four men terribly discuss a question that was not plain. There was a card-game in the corner, of course. Sounds of revelry pealed from the rear rooms.

When the Kid asked Freddie if he had seen his friend and Benson, Freddie looked bored. "Oh, yes, they were in here just a minute ago, but I don't know where they went. They've got their skates on. Where've they been? Came in here rolling across the floor like two little gilt gods. They wobbled around for a time, and then 'Frisco wanted me to send six bottles of wine around to Benson's rooms; but I didn't have anybody to send this time of night, and so they got mad and went out. Where did they get their loads?"

In the first deep gloom of the street the Kid paused a moment, debating. But presently he heard quavering voices: "Oh, Kid! Kid! Come 'ere!" Peering, he recognized two vague figures against the opposite wall. He crossed the street, and they said: "Hello Kid."

"Say, where did you get it?" he demanded sternly. "You Indians better go home. What did you want to get scragged for?" His face was luminous with virtue.

As they swung to and fro they made angry denials. "We ain' load'. We ain' load'. Big chump! Comonangetadrink."

The sober youth turned then to his friend. "Hadn't you better go home, Kid? Come on, it's late. You'd better break away."

The 'Frisco Kid wagged his head decisively. "Got take Benson home first. He'll be wallowing round in a minute. Don't mind me. I'm all right."

"Ce'r'ly he's all right," said Benson, arousing from deep thought. "He's all right. But better take 'm home, though. That's ri-right. He's load'. But he's all right. No need go home any more 'n you. But better take 'm home. He's load'." He looked at his companion with compassion. "Kid, you're load'."

The sober Kid spoke abruptly to his friend from San Francisco. "Kid, pull yourself together, now. Don't fool. We've got to brace this ass of a Benson all the way home. Get hold of his other arm."

The 'Frisco Kid immediately obeyed his comrade, without a word or a glower. He seized Benson, and came to attention like a soldier. Later, indeed, he meekly ventured: "Can't we take cab?" But when the New York Kid snapped out that there were no convenient cabs, he subsided to an impassive silence. He seemed to be reflecting upon his state without astonishment, dismay, or any particular emotion. He submitted himself woodenly to the direction of his friend.

Benson had protested when they had grasped his arms. "W'asha doing?" he said in a new and guttural voice. "W'asha doing? I ain' load'. Comonangetadrink. I—"

"Oh, come along, you idiot," said the New York Kid. The 'Frisco Kid merely presented the mien of a stoic to the appeal of Benson, and in silence dragged away at one of his arms. Benson's feet came from that particular spot on the pavement with the reluctance of roots, and also with the ultimate suddenness of roots. The three of them lurched out into the street in the abandon of tumbling chimneys. Benson was meanwhile noisily challenging the others to produce any reasons for his being taken home. His toes clashed into the curb when they reached the other side of the *calle*, and for a moment the Kids hauled him along, with the points of his shoes scraping musically on the pavement. He balked formidably as they were about to pass the Casa Verde. "No, no! Leshavanothdrink! Anothdrink! Onemore!"

But the 'Frisco Kid obeyed the voice of his partner in a manner that was blind, but absolute, and they scummed Benson on past the door. Locked together, the three swung into a dark street. The sober Kid's flank was continually careering ahead of the other wing. He harshly admonished the 'Frisco child, and the latter promptly improved in the same manner of unthinking, complete obedience. Benson began to recite the tale of a love affair—a tale that didn't even have a middle. Occasionally the New York Kid swore. They toppled on their way like three comedians playing at it on the stage.

At midnight a little Mexican street burrowing among the walls of the city is as dark as a whale's throat at deep sea. Upon this occasion heavy clouds hung over the capital, and the sky was a pall. The projecting balconies could make no shadows.

"Shay," said Benson, breaking away from his escort suddenly, "what want g'ome for? I ain' load'. You got reg'lar spool-fact'ry in your head— you N' York Kid, there. Thish oth' Kid, he's mos' proper—mos' proper shober. He's drunk, but—but he's shober."

"Ah, shut up, Benson," said the New York Kid. "Come along, now. We can't stay here all night." Benson refused to be corralled, but spread his legs and twirled like a dervish, meanwhile under the evident impression that he was conducting himself most handsomely. It was not long before he gained the opinion that he was laughing at the others. "Eight purple dogsh—dogs! Eight purple dogs! Tha's what Kid'll see in the morn'. Look ou' for 'em. They—"

As Benson, describing the canine phenomena, swung wildly across the sidewalk, it chanced that three other pedestrians were passing in shadowy rank. Benson's shoulder jostled one of them.

A Mexican wheeled upon the instant. His hand flashed to his hip. There was a moment of silence, during which Benson's voice was not heard raised in apology. Then an indescribable comment, one burning word, came from between the Mexican's teeth.

Benson, rolling about in a semidetached manner, stared vacantly at the Mexican, who thrust his lean yellow face forward, while his fingers played nervously at his hip. The New York Kid could not follow Spanish well, but he understood when the Mexican breathed softly: "Does the señor want to fight?"

Benson simply gazed in gentle surprise. The woman next to him at dinner had said something inventive. His tailor had presented his bill. Something had occurred which was mildly out of the ordinary, and his surcharged brain refused to cope with it. He displayed only the agitation of a smoker temporarily without a light.

The New York Kid had almost instantly grasped Benson's arm, and was about to jerk him away when the other Kid, who up to this time had been an automaton, suddenly projected himself forward, thrust the rubber Benson aside, and said: "Yes."

There was no sound nor light in the world. The wall at the left happened to be of the common prison-like construction—no door, no window, no opening at all. Humanity was enclosed and asleep. Into the mouth of the sober Kid came a wretched, bitter taste, as if it had filled with blood. He was transfixed, as if he was already seeing the lightning ripples on the knife blade.

But the Mexican's hand did not move at that time. His face went still further forward, and he whispered: "So?" The sober Kid saw this face as if he and it were alone in space—a yellow mask, smiling in eager cruelty, in satisfaction, and, above all, it was lit with sinister decision. As for the features, they were reminiscent of an unplaced, a forgotten type, which really resembled with precision those of a man who had shaved him three times in Boston in 1888. But the expression burned his mind as sealing wax burns the palm, and, fascinated, stupefied, he actually watched the progress of the man's thought toward the point where a knife would be wrenched from its sheath. The emotion, a sort of mechanical fury, a breeze made by electric fans, a rage made by vanity, smote the dark countenance in wave after wave.

Then the New York Kid took a sudden step forward. His hand was also at his hip. He was gripping there a revolver of robust size. He recalled that upon its black handle was stamped a hunting scene in which a sportsman in fine leggings and a peaked cap was taking aim at a stag less than one-eighth of an inch away.

His pace forward caused instant movement of the Mexicans. One immediately took two steps to face him squarely. There was a general adjustment, pair and pair. The opponent of the New York Kid was a tall man and quite stout. His sombrero was drawn low over his eyes; his serape was flung on his left shoulder; his back was bent in the supposed manner of a Spanish grandee. This concave gentleman cut a fine and terrible figure. The lad, moved by the spirits of his modest and perpendicular ancestors, had time to feel his blood roar at sight of the pose.

He was aware that the third Mexican was over on the left, fronting Benson; and he was aware that Benson was leaning against the wall, sleepily and peacefully eyeing the convention. So it happened that these six men stood, side fronting side, five of them with their right hands at their hips, and with their bodies lifted nervously, while the central pair exchanged a crescendo of provocations. The meaning of their words rose and rose. They were traveling in a straight line toward collision.

The New York Kid contemplated his Spanish grandee. He drew his revolver upward until the hammer was surely free of the holster. He waited, immovable and watchful, while the garrulous 'Frisco Kid expended two and a half lexicons on the middle Mexican.

The Eastern lad suddenly decided that he was going to be killed. His mind leaped forward and studied the aftermath. The story would be a marvel of brevity when first it reached the far New York home, written in a careful hand on a bit of cheap paper, topped and footed and backed by the printed fortifications of the cable company. But they are often as stones flung into mirrors, these bits of paper upon which are laconically written all the most terrible chronicles of the times. He witnessed the uprising of his mother and sister, and the invincible calm of his hard-mouthed old father, who would probably shut himself in his library and smoke alone. Then his father would come, and they would bring him here, and say: "This is the place." Then, very likely, each would remove his hat. They would stand quietly with their hats in their hands for a decent minute. He pitied his old financing father, unyielding and millioned, a man who commonly spoke twenty-two words a year to his beloved son. The Kid understood it at this time. If his fate was not impregnable, he might have turned out to be a man and have been liked by his father.

The other Kid would mourn his death. He would be preternaturally correct for some weeks, and recite the tale without swearing. But it would not bore him. For the sake of his dead comrade he would be glad to be preternaturally correct and to recite the tale without swearing.

These views were perfectly stereopticon, flashing in and away from his thought with an inconceivable rapidity, until, after all, they were simply one quick, dismal impression. And now, here is the unreal real: into this Kid's nostrils, at the expectant moment of slaughter, had come the scent of new-mown hay, a fragrance from a field of prostrate grass, a fragrance which contained the sunshine, the bees, the peace of meadows, and the wonder of a distant crooning stream. It had no right to be supreme, but it was supreme, and he breathed it as he waited for pain and a sight of the unknown.

But in the same instant, it may be, his thought flew to the 'Frisco Kid, and it came upon him like a flicker of lightning that the 'Frisco Kid was not going to be there to perform, for instance, the extraordinary office of respectable mourner. The other Kid's head was muddled, his hand was unsteady, his agility was gone. This other Kid was facing the determined and most ferocious gentleman of the enemy. The New York Kid became convinced that his friend was lost. There was going to be a screaming murder. He was so certain of it that he wanted to shield his eyes from sight of the leaping arm and the knife. It was sickening—utterly sickening. The New York Kid might have been taking his first sea voyage. A combination of honorable manhood and inability prevented him from running away.

He suddenly knew that it was possible to draw his own revolver, and by a swift maneuver face down all three Mexicans. If he was quick enough he would probably be victor. If any hitch occurred in the draw he would undoubtedly be dead with his friends. It was a new game. He had never been obliged to face a situation of this kind in the Beacon Club in New York. In this test the lungs of the Kid still continued to perform their duty:

> Oh, five white mice of chance,
> Shirts of wool and corduroy pants
> Gold and wine, women and sin,
> All for you if you let me come in—
> Into the house of chance.

He thought of the weight and size of his revolver, and dismay pierced him. He feared that in his hands it would be as unwieldy as a sewing machine for this quick work. He imagined, too, that some singular providence might cause him to lose his grip as he raised his weapon; or it might get fatally entangled in the tails of his coat. Some of the eels of despair lay wet and cold against his back.

But at the supreme moment the revolver came forth as if it were greased, and it arose like a feather. This somnolent machine, after months of repose, was finally looking at the breasts of men.

Perhaps in this one series of movements the Kid had unconsciously used nervous force sufficient to raise a bale of hay. Before he comprehended it, he was standing behind his revolver, glaring over the barrel at the Mexicans, menacing first one and then another. His finger was tremoring on the trigger. The revolver gleamed in the darkness with a fine silver light.

The fulsome grandee sprang backward with a low cry. The man who had been facing the 'Frisco Kid took a quick step away. The beautiful array of Mexicans was suddenly disorganized.

The cry and the backward steps revealed something of great importance to the New York Kid. He had never dreamed that he did not have a complete monopoly of all possible trepidations. The cry of the grandee was that of a man who suddenly sees a poisonous snake. Thus the Kid was able to understand swiftly that they were all human beings. They were unanimous in not wishing for too bloody a combat. There was a sudden expression of the equality. He had vaguely believed that they were not going to evince much consideration for his dramatic development as an active factor. They even might be exasperated into an onslaught by it. Instead, they had respected his movement with a respect as great even as an ejaculation of fear and backward steps. Upon the instant he pounced forward, and began to swear, unreeling great English oaths as thick as ropes, and lashing the faces of the Mexicans with them. He was bursting with rage because these men had not previously confided to him that they were vulnerable. The whole thing had been an absurd imposition. He had been seduced into respectful alarm by the concave attitude of the grandee. And after all there had been an equality of emotion—an equality! He was furious. He wanted to take the serape of the grandee and swaddle him in it.

The Mexicans slunk back, their eyes burning wistfully. The Kid took aim first at one and then at another. After they had achieved a certain distance, they paused and drew up in a rank. They then resumed some of their old splendor of manner. A voice hailed him in a tone of cynical bravado, as if it had come from between high lips of smiling mockery: "Well, señor, it is finished?"

The Kid scowled into the darkness, his revolver drooping at his side.

After a moment he answered: "I am willing." He found it strange that he should be able to speak after this silence of years.

"Good night, señor."

"Good night."

When he turned to look at the 'Frisco Kid, he found him in his original position, his hand upon his hip. He was blinking in perplexity at the point where the Mexicans had vanished.

"Well," said the sober Kid, crossly, "are you ready to go home now?"

The 'Frisco Kid said: "Where they gone?" His voice was undisturbed, but inquisitive.

Benson suddenly propelled himself from his dreamful position against the wall. " 'Frisco Kid's all right. He's drunk's fool, and he's all right. But you New York Kid, you're shober." He passed into a state of profound investigation. "Kid shober 'cause didn't go with us. Didn't go with us 'cause went to damn circus. Went to damn circus 'cause lose shakin' dice. Lose shakin' dice 'cause—what make lose shakin' dice, Kid?"

The New York Kid eyed the senile youth. "I don't know. The five white mice, maybe."

Benson puzzled so over this reply that he had to be held erect by his friends. Finally the 'Frisco Kid said: "Let's go home."

Nothing had happened.

April 10, 1898
[New York *World*, p. 32.]

THE WISE MEN

They were youths of subtle mind. They were very wicked, according to report, and yet they managed to have it reflect credit upon them. They often had the well-informed and the great talkers of the American colony engaged in reciting their misdeeds, and facts relating to their sins were usually told with a flourish of awe and fine admiration.

One was from San Francisco, and one was from New York; but they resembled each other in appearance. This is an idiosyncrasy of geography.

They were never apart in the City of Mexico, at any rate, excepting, perhaps, when one had retired to his hotel for a respite; and then the other was usually camped down at the office, sending up servants with clamorous messages: "Oh, get up, and come on down."

They were two lads—they were called the Kids—and far from their mothers. Occasionally some wise man pitied them, but he usually was alone in his wisdom; the other folk frankly were transfixed at the splendor of the audacity and endurance of these Kids.

"When do those two boys ever sleep?" murmured a man, as he viewed them entering a café about eight o'clock one morning. Their smooth, infantile faces looked bright and fresh enough, at any rate. "Jim told me he saw them still at it about four-thirty this morning."

"Sleep?" ejaculated a companion, in a glowing voice. "They never sleep! They go to bed once in every two weeks." His boast of it seemed almost a personal pride.

"They'll end with a crash, though, if they keep it up at this pace," said a gloomy voice from behind a newspaper.

The Café Colorado has a front of white and gold, in which are set larger plate glass windows than are commonly to be found in Mexico. Two little wings of willow, flip-flapping incessantly, serve as doors. Under them small stray dogs go furtively into the café, and are shied into the street again by the waiters. On the sidewalk there is always a decorative effect in loungers, ranging from the newly arrived and superior tourist to the old veteran of the silver mines, bronzed by violent suns. They contemplate, with various shades of interest, the show of the street—the red, purple, dusty white, glaring forth against the walls in the furious sunshine.

One afternoon the Kids strolled into the Café Colorado. A half-dozen of the men who sat smoking and reading with a sort of Parisian effect at the little tables which lined two sides of the room looked up, and bowed, smiling; and although this coming of the Kids was anything but an unusual event, at least a dozen men wheeled in their seats to stare after them. Three waiters polished tables, and moved chairs noisily, and appeared to be eager. Distinctly these Kids were of importance.

Behind the distant bar the tall form of old Pop himself awaited them, smiling with broad geniality. "Well, my boys, how are you?" he cried in a voice of profound solicitude. He allowed five or six of his customers to languish in the care of Mexican bartenders, while he himself gave his eloquent attention to the Kids, lending all the dignity of a great event to their arrival. "How are the boys today, eh?"

"You're a smooth old guy," said one, eyeing him. "Are you giving us this welcome so we won't notice it when you push your worst whiskey at us?"

Pop turned in appeal from one Kid to the other Kid. "There, now! Hear that, will you?" He assumed an oratorical pose. "Why, my boys, you always get the best—the very best—that this house has got."

"Yes, we do!" The Kids laughed. "Well, bring it out, anyhow; and if it's the same you sold us last night, we'll grab your cash register and run."

Pop whirled a bottle along the bar, and then gazed at it with a rapt expression. "Fine as silk," he murmured. "Now just taste that, and if it isn't the finest whiskey you ever put in your face, why, I'm a liar, that's all."

The Kids surveyed him with scorn, and poured out their allowances. Then they stood for a time, insulting Pop about his whiskey. "Usually it tastes exactly like new parlor furniture," said the San Francisco Kid. "Well, here goes; and you want to look out for your cash register."

"Your health, gentlemen," said Pop, with a grand air; and as he wiped his bristling gray mustache he wagged his head with reference to the cash register question. "I could catch you before you got very far."

"Why, are you a runner?" said one, derisively.

"You just bank on me, my boy," said Pop, with deep emphasis. "I'm a flier."

The Kids set down their glasses suddenly, and looked at him. "You must be," they said. Pop was tall and graceful, and magnificent in manner, but he did not display those qualities of form which mean speed in the animal. His hair was gray; his face was round and fat from much living. The buttons of his glittering white vest formed a fine curve, so that if the concave surface of a piece of barrel-hoop had been laid against Pop it would have touched each button. "You must be," observed the Kids again.

"Well, you can laugh all you like, but—no jolly, now, boys—I tell you I'm a winner. Why, I bet you I can skin anything in this town on a square go. When I kept my place in Eagle Pass, there wasn't anybody who could touch me. One of these sure things came down from San Anton'. Oh, he was a runner, he was—one of these people with wings. Well, I skinned 'im. What? Certainly I did. Never touched me."

The Kids had been regarding him in grave silence, but at this moment they grinned, and said, quite in chorus: "Oh, you old liar!"

Pop's voice took on a whining tone of earnestness: "Boys, I'm telling it to you straight. I'm a flier."

One of the Kids had had a dreamy cloud in his eye, and he cried out suddenly: "Say, what a joke to play this on Freddie!"

The other jumped ecstatically. "Oh, wouldn't it be, though? Say, he wouldn't do a thing but howl! He'd go crazy!"

They looked at Pop as if they longed to be certain that he was, after all, a runner. "Say, now, Pop—on the level," said one of them, wistfully, "can you run?"

"Boys," swore Pop, "I'm a peach! On the dead level, I'm a peach."

"By golly, I believe the old Indian can run," said one to the other, as if they were alone in conference.

"That's what I can," cried Pop.

The Kids said: "Well, so long, old man." They went to a table, and sat down. They ordered a salad. They were always ordering salads. This was because one Kid had a wild passion for salads, and the other did not care much. So at any hour of the day or night they might be seen ordering a salad. When this one came, they went into a sort of executive session. It was a very long consultation. Some of the men noted it; they said there was deviltry afoot. Occasionally the Kids laughed in supreme enjoyment of something unknown. The low rumble of wheels came from the street. Often could be heard the parrot-like cries of distant vendors. The sunlight streamed through the green curtains and made some little amber-colored flitterings on the marble floor. High up among the severe decorations of the ceiling—reminiscent of the days when the great building was a palace —a small white butterfly was wending through the cool air spaces. The long billiard hall stretched back to a vague gloom. The balls were always clicking, and one could see endless elbows crooking. Beggars slunk through the wicker doors, and were ejected by the nearest waiter.

At last the Kids called Pop to them. "Sit down, Pop! Have a drink!" They scanned him carefully. "Say, now, Pop, on your solemn oath, can you run?"

"Boys," said Pop, piously, and raising his hand, "I can run like a rabbit."

"On your oath?"

"On my oath."

"Can you beat Freddie?"

Pop appeared to look at the matter from all sides. "Well, boys, I'll tell you: no man is cocksure of anything in this world, and I don't want to say that I can best any man; but I've seen Freddie run, and I'm ready to swear I can beat 'im. In a hundred yards I'd just about skin 'im neat—you un-derstand—just about neat. Freddie is a good average runner, but I—you understand—I'm just—a little—bit—better."

The Kids had been listening with the utmost attention. Pop spoke the latter part slowly and meaningly. They thought that he intended them to see his great confidence.

One said: "Pop, if you throw us in this thing, we'll come here and drink for two weeks without paying. We'll back you, and work a josh on Freddie! But oh—if you throw us!"

To this menace Pop cried: "Boys, I'll make the run of my life! On my oath!"

The salad having vanished, the Kids arose. "All right, now," they warned him. "If you play us for duffers, we'll get square. Don't you for-get it!"

"Boys, I'll give you a race for your money. Bank on that. I may lose—understand, I may lose—no man can help meeting a better man, but I think I can skin 'im, and I'll give you a run for your money, you bet."

"All right, then. But look here," they told him. "You keep your face closed. Nobody but us gets in on this. Understand?"

"Not a soul," Pop declared.

They left him, gesturing a last warning from the wicker doors.

In the street they saw Benson, his cane gripped in the middle, strolling among the white-clothed, jabbering natives on the shady side. They semaphored to him eagerly, their faces a-shine with a plot. He came across cautiously, like a man who ventures into dangerous company.

"We're going to get up a race—Pop and Fred. Pop swears he can skin 'im. This is a tip; keep it dark, now. Say, won't Freddie be hot?"

Benson looked as if he had been compelled to endure these exhibitions of insanity for a century. "Oh, you fellows are off. Pop can't beat Freddie. He's an old bat. Why, it's impossible. Pop can't beat Freddie."

"Can't he? Want to bet he can't?" said the Kids. "There, now; let's see—you're talking so large."

"Well, you——"

"Oh, bet! Bet, or else close your trap. That's the way!"

"How do you know you can pull off the race? Seen Freddie?"

"No; but——"

"Well, see him, then. Can't bet now, with no race arranged. I'll bet with you all right, all right. I'll give you fellows a tip, though—you're a pair of asses. Pop can't run any faster than a brick schoolhouse."

The Kids scowled at him, and defiantly said: "Can't he?"

They left him, and went to the Casa Verde. Freddie, beautiful in his white jacket, was holding one of his innumerable conversations across the bar. He smiled when he saw them. "Where you boys been?" he demanded in a paternal tone. Almost all the proprietors of American cafés in the city used to adopt a paternal tone when they spoke to the Kids.

"Oh, been 'round," they replied.

"Have a drink," said the proprietor of the Casa Verde, forgetting his other social obligations.

During the course of this ceremony one of the Kids remarked: "Freddie, Pop says he can beat you running."

"Does he?" observed Freddie, without excitement. He was used to various snares of the Kids.

"That's what. He says he can leave you at the wire, and not see you again."

"Well, he lies," replied Freddie, placidly.

"And I'll bet you a bottle of wine that he can do it, too."

"Rats!" said Freddie.

"Oh, that's all right," pursued a Kid. "You can throw bluffs all you like; but he can lose you in a hundred yard dash, you bet."

Freddie drank his whiskey, and then settled his elbows on the bar. "Say, now, what do you boys keep coming in here with some pipe-story all the time for? You can't josh me. Do you think you can scare me about Pop? Why, I know I can beat 'im. He's an old man. He can't run with me; certainly not. Why, you fellows are just jollying me."

"Are we, though?" said the Kids. "You daresn't bet the bottle of wine."

"Oh, of course I can bet you a bottle of wine," said Freddie, disdainfully. "Nobody cares about a bottle of wine, but——"

"Well, make it five, then," advised one of the Kids.

Freddie hunched his shoulders. "Why, certainly I will. Make it ten if you like, but——"

"We do," they said.

"Ten, is it? All right; that goes." A look of weariness came over Freddie's face. "But you boys are foolish. I tell you, Pop is an old man. How can you expect him to run? Of course I'm no great runner, but, then, I'm young and healthy, and—and a pretty smooth runner, too. Pop is old and fat, and, then, he doesn't do a thing but tank all day. It's a cinch."

The Kids looked at him, and laughed rapturously. They waved their fingers at him. "Ah, there!" they cried. They meant that they had made a victim of him.

But Freddie continued to expostulate: "I tell you, he couldn't win—an old man like him. You're crazy! Of course I know that you don't care about ten bottles of wine, but then—to make such bets as that! You're twisted."

"Are we, though?" cried the Kids, in mockery. They had precipitated Freddie into a long and thoughtful treatise on every possible chance of the thing as he saw it. They disputed with him from time to time, and jeered at him. He labored on through his argument. Their childish faces were bright with glee.

In the midst of it Wilburson entered. Wilburson worked—not too much, though. He had hold of the Mexican end of a great importing house of New York, and, as he was a junior partner, he worked—but not too much, though. "What's the howl?" he said.

The Kids giggled. "We've got Freddie rattled."

"Why," said Freddie, turning to him, "these two Indians are trying to tell me that Pop can beat me running."

"Like the devil!" said Wilburson, incredulously.

"Well, can't he?" demanded a Kid.

"Why, certainly not," said Wilburson, dismissing every possibility of it with a gesture. "That old bat? Certainly not! I'll bet fifty dollars that Freddie——"

"Take you," said a Kid.

"What?" said Wilburson. "That Freddie won't beat Pop?"

The Kid that had spoken now nodded his head.

"That Freddie won't beat Pop?" repeated Wilburson.

"Yes; is it a go?"

"Why, certainly," retorted Wilburson. "Fifty? All right."

"Bet you five bottles on the side," ventured the other Kid.

"Why, certainly," exploded Wilburson, wrathfully. "You fellows must take me for something easy. I'll take all those kind of bets that I can get. Cer-tain-ly."

They settled the details. The course was to be paced off on the asphalt of one of the adjacent side streets; and then, at about eleven o'clock in the evening, the match would be run. Usually in Mexico the streets of a city grow lonely and dark but a little time after nine o'clock. There are occasional lurking figures, perhaps, but no crowds, lights, noise. The course would doubtless be undisturbed. As for the policemen in the vicinity, they—well, they were conditionally amiable.

The Kids went to see Pop. They told him of the arrangements; and then in deep tones they said: "Oh, Pop, if you throw us!"

Pop appeared to be a trifle shaken by the weight of responsibility thrust upon him, but he spoke out bravely: "Boys, I'll pinch that race. Now you watch me. I'll pinch it!"

The Kids went then on some business of their own, for they were not seen again until evening. When they returned to the neighborhood of the Café Colorado, the usual evening stream of carriages was whirling along the *calle*. The wheels hummed on the asphalt, and the coachmen towered in their great sombreros. On the sidewalk a gazing crowd sauntered, the better classes self-satisfied and proud in their derby hats and cutaway coats, the lower classes muffling their dark faces in their blankets, slipping along in leather sandals. An electric light sputtered and fumed over the throng. The afternoon shower had left the pave wet and glittering; the air was still laden with the odor of rain on flowers, grass, leaves.

In the Café Colorado a cosmopolitan crowd ate, drank, played billiards, gossiped, or read in the glaring yellow light. When the Kids entered, a large circle of men that had been gesticulating near the bar greeted them with a roar:

"Here they are now!"

"Oh, you pair of peaches!"

"Say, got any more money to bet with?"

The Kids smiled complacently. Old Colonel Hammigan, grinning, pushed his way to them. "Say, boys, we'll all have a drink on you now, because you won't have any money after eleven o'clock. You'll be going down the backstairs in your stocking feet."

Although the Kids remained unnaturally serene and quiet, argument in the Café Colorado became tumultuous. Here and there a man who did not intend to bet ventured meekly that perchance Pop might win; and the others swarmed upon him in a whirlwind of angry denial and ridicule.

Pop, enthroned behind the bar, looked over at this storm with a shadow of anxiety upon his face; this widespread flouting affected him; but the Kids looked blissfully satisfied with the tumult they had stirred.

Blanco, honest man, ever worrying for his friends, came to them. "Say, you fellows, you aren't betting too much? This thing looks kind of shaky, don't it?"

The faces of the Kids grew sober, and after consideration one said: "No; I guess we've got a good thing, Blanco. Pop is going to surprise them, I think."

"Well, don't——"

"All right, old boy. We'll watch out."

From time to time the Kids had much business with certain orange, red, blue, purple, and green bills. They were making little memoranda on the backs of visiting cards. Pop watched them closely, the shadow still upon his face. Once he called to them; and when they came, he leaned over the bar, and said intensely: "Say, boys, remember, now—I might lose this race. Nobody can ever say for sure, and if I do—why——"

"Oh, that's all right, Pop," said the Kids, reassuringly. "Don't mind it. Do your durnedest, and let it go at that."

When they had left him, however, they went to a corner to consult. "Say, this is getting interesting. Are you in deep?" asked one, anxiously, of his friend.

"Yes; pretty deep," said the other, stolidly. "Are you?"

"Deep as the devil," replied the other, in the same tone.

They looked at each other stonily, and went back to the crowd. Benson had just entered the café. He approached them with a gloating smile of victory. "Well, where's all that money you were going to bet?"

"Right here," said the Kids, thrusting into their vest pockets.

At eleven o'clock a curious thing was learned. When Pop and Freddie, the Kids, and all, came to the little side street, it was thick with people. It seems that the news of this great race had spread like the wind among the Americans, and they had come to witness the event. In the darkness the crowd moved, gesticulating and mumbling in argument.

The principals, the Kids, and those with them surveyed this scene with some dismay. "Say, here's a go." Even then a policeman might be seen approaching, the light from his little lantern flickering on his white cap, gloves, brass buttons, and on the butt of the old-fashioned Colt's revolver which hung at his belt. He addressed Freddie in swift Mexican. Freddie listened, nodding from time to time. Finally Freddie turned to the others to translate: "He says he'll get into trouble if he allows this race when all this crowd is here."

There was a murmur of discontent. The policeman looked at them with an expression of anxiety on his broad brown face.

"Oh, come on. We'll go hold it on some other fellow's beat," said one of the Kids.

The group moved slowly away, debating.

Suddenly the other Kid cried: "I know! The Paseo!"

"By jiminy!" said Freddie, "just the thing. We'll get a cab, and go out to the Paseo. S-s-sh! Keep it quiet. We don't want all this mob."

Later they tumbled into a cab—Pop, Freddie, the Kids, old Colonel Hammigan, and Benson. They whispered to the men who had wagered: "The Paseo." The cab whirled away up the back street. There were occasional grunts and groans—cries of "Oh, get off me feet!" and of "Quit! You're killing me!" Six people do not have fun in one cab. The principals spoke to each other with the respect and friendliness which comes to good men at such times.

Once a Kid put his head out of the window and looked backward. He pulled it in again, and cried: "Great Scott! Look at that, would you!"

The others struggled to do as they were bid, and afterward shouted: "Holy smoke!" "Well, I'll be blowed!" "Thunder and turf!"

Galloping after them came innumerable other cabs, their lights twinkling, streaming in a great procession through the night. "The street is full of them," ejaculated the old colonel.

The Paseo de la Reforma is the famous drive of the City of Mexico, leading to the castle of Chapultepec, which last ought to be well known in the United States.

It is a broad, fine avenue of macadam, with a much greater quality of dignity than anything of the kind we possess in our own land. It seems of the Old World, where to the beauty of the thing itself is added the solemnity of tradition and history, the knowledge that feet in buskins trod the same stones, that cavalcades of steel thundered there before the coming of carriages.

When the Americans tumbled out of their cabs, the giant bronzes of Aztec and Spaniard loomed dimly above them like towers. The four rows of poplar trees rustled weirdly off there in the darkness. Pop took out his watch, and struck a match. "Well, hurry up this thing. It's almost midnight."

The other cabs came swarming, the drivers lashing their horses; for these Americans, who did all manner of strange things, nevertheless always paid well for it. There was a mighty hubbub then in the darkness.

Five or six men began to pace off the distance and quarrel. Others knotted their handkerchiefs together to make a tape. Men were swearing over bets, fussing and fuming about the odds. Benson came to the Kids, swaggering. "You're a pair of asses." The cabs waited in a solid block down the avenue. Above the crowd, the tall statues hid their visages in the night.

At last a voice floated through the darkness: "Are you ready, there?" Everybody yelled excitedly. The men at the tape pulled it out straight. "Hold it higher, Jim, you fool!" A silence fell then upon the throng. Men bent down, trying to pierce the darkness with their eyes. From out at the starting point came muffled voices. The crowd swayed and jostled.

The racers did not come. The crowd began to fret, its nerves burning. "Oh, hurry up!" shrilled some one.

The voice called again: "Ready, there?"

Everybody replied: "Yes; all ready! Hurry up!"

There was more muffled discussion at the starting point. In the crowd a man began to make a proposition: "I'll bet twenty——" But the throng interrupted with a howl: "Here they come!" The thickly packed body of men swung as if the ground had moved. The men at the tape shouldered madly at their fellows, bawling: "Keep back! Keep back!"

From the profound gloom came the noise of feet pattering furiously. Vague forms flashed into view for an instant. A hoarse roar broke from the crowd. Men bent and swayed and fought. The Kids, back near the tape, exchanged another stolid look. A white form shone forth. It grew like a specter. Always could be heard the wild patter. A barbaric scream broke from the crowd: "By Gawd, it's Pop! Pop! Pop's ahead!"

The old man spun toward the tape like a madman, his chin thrown back, his gray hair flying. His legs moved like maniac machinery. And as he shot forward a howl as from forty cages of wild animals went toward the imperturbable chieftains in bronze. The crowd flung themselves forward. "Oh, you old Indian! You savage! You cuss, you! Durn my buttons, did you ever see such running?"

"Ain't he a peach? Well!"

"Say, this beats anything!"

"Where's the Kids? H-e-y, Kids!"

"Look at 'im, would you? Did you ever think?"

These cries flew in the air, blended in a vast shout of astonishment and laughter.

For an instant the whole great tragedy was in view. Freddie, desperate, his teeth shining, his face contorted, whirling along in deadly effort, was twenty feet behind the tall form of old Pop, who, dressed only in his— only in his underclothes—gained with each stride. One grand, insane moment, and then Pop had hurled himself against the tape—victor!

Freddie, falling into the arms of some men, struggled with his breath, and at last managed to stammer: "Say—can't—can't that old—old man run!"

Pop, puffing and heaving, could only gasp: "Where's my shoes? Who's got my shoes?"

Later Freddie scrambled, panting, through the crowd, and held out his hand. "Good man, Pop!" And then he looked up and down the tall, stout form. "Hell! Who would think you could run like that?"

The Kids were surrounded by a crowd, laughing tempestuously.

"How did you know he could run?"

"Why didn't you give me a line on him?"

"Say—great snakes!—you fellows had a nerve to bet on Pop."

"Why, I was cocksure he couldn't win."

"Oh, you fellows must have seen him run before!"

"Who would ever think it!"

Benson came by, filling the midnight air with curses. They turned to jeer him. "What's the matter, Benson?"

"Somebody pinched my handkerchief. I tied it up in that string. Damn it!"

The Kids laughed blithely. "Why, hullo, Benson!" they said.

There was a great rush for cabs. Shouting, laughing, wondering, the crowd hustled into their conveyances, and the drivers flogged their horses toward the city again.

"Won't Freddie be crazy! Say, he'll be guyed about this for years."

"But who would ever think that old tank could run so?"

One cab had to wait while Pop and Freddie resumed various parts of their clothing.

As they drove home, Freddie said: "Well, Pop, you beat me!"

Pop said: "That's all right, old man."

The Kids, grinning, said: "How much did you lose, Benson?"

Benson said defiantly: "Oh, not so much. How much did you win?"

"Oh, not so much!"

Old Colonel Hammigan, squeezed down in a corner, had apparently been reviewing the event in his mind, for he suddenly remarked: "Well, I'm damned!"

They were late in reaching the Café Colorado; but when they did, the bottles were on the bar as thick as pickets on a fence.

April 18, 1898
[*The Open Boat and Other Stories.*
London: William Heinemann, pp. 87–105.]

THE MONSTER

I

Little Jim was, for the time, engine Number 36, and he was making the run between Syracuse and Rochester. He was fourteen minutes behind time, and the throttle was wide open. In consequence, when he swung around the curve at the flower bed, a wheel of his cart destroyed a peony. Number 36 slowed down at once and looked guiltily at his father, who was mowing the lawn. The doctor had his back to this accident, and he continued to pace slowly to and fro, pushing the mower.

Jim dropped the tongue of the cart. He looked at his father and at the broken flower. Finally he went to the peony and tried to stand it on its pins, resuscitated, but the spine of it was hurt, and it would only hang limply from his hand. Jim could do no reparation. He looked again toward his father.

He went on to the lawn, very slowly, and kicking wretchedly at the turf. Presently his father came along with the whirring machine, while the sweet, new grass blades spun from the knives. In a low voice, Jim said, "Pa!"

The doctor was shaving this lawn as if it were a priest's chin. All during the season he had worked at it in the coolness and peace of the evenings after supper. Even in the shadow of the cherry trees the grass was strong and healthy. Jim raised his voice a trifle. "Pa!"

The doctor paused, and with the howl of the machine no longer occupying the sense, one could hear the robins in the cherry trees arranging their affairs. Jim's hands were behind his back, and sometimes his fingers clasped and unclasped. Again he said, "Pa!" The child's fresh and rosy lip was lowered.

The doctor stared down at his son, thrusting his head forward and frowning attentively. "What is it, Jimmie?"

"Pa!" repeated the child at length. Then he raised his finger and pointed at the flower bed. "There!"

"What?" said the doctor, frowning more. "What is it, Jim?"

After a period of silence, during which the child may have undergone a severe mental tumult, he raised his finger and repeated his former word—"There!" The father had respected this silence with perfect courtesy. Afterward his glance carefully followed the direction indicated by the child's finger, but he could see nothing which explained to him. "I don't understand what you mean, Jimmie," he said.

It seemed that the importance of the whole thing had taken away the boy's vocabulary. He could only reiterate, "There!"

The doctor mused upon the situation, but he could make nothing of it. At last he said, "Come, show me."

Together they crossed the lawn toward the flower bed. At some yards from the broken peony Jimmie began to lag. "There!" The word came almost breathlessly.

"Where?" said the doctor.

Jimmie kicked at the grass. "There!" he replied.

The doctor was obliged to go forward alone. After some trouble he found the subject of the incident, the broken flower. Turning then, he saw the child lurking at the rear and scanning his countenance.

The father reflected. After a time he said, "Jimmie, come here." With an infinite modesty of demeanor the child came forward. "Jimmie, how did this happen?"

The child answered, "Now—I was playin' train—and—now—I runned over it."

"You were doing what?"

"I was playin' train."

The father reflected again. "Well, Jimmie," he said, slowly, "I guess you had better not play train any more today. Do you think you had better?"

"No, sir," said Jimmie.

During the delivery of the judgment the child had not faced his father, and afterwards he went away, with his head lowered, shuffling his feet.

II

It was apparent from Jimmie's manner that he felt some kind of desire to efface himself. He went down to the stable. Henry Johnson, the negro who cared for the doctor's horses, was sponging the buggy. He grinned fraternally when he saw Jimmie coming. These two were pals. In regard to almost everything in life they seemed to have minds precisely alike. Of course there were points of emphatic divergence. For instance, it was plain from Henry's talk that he was a very handsome negro, and he was known to be a light, a weight, and an eminence in the suburb of the town, where lived the larger number of the negroes, and obviously this glory was over Jimmie's horizon; but he vaguely appreciated it and paid deference to Henry for it mainly because Henry appreciated it and deferred to himself. However, on all points of conduct as related to the doctor, who was the moon, they were in complete but unexpressed understanding. Whenever Jimmie became the vicitim of an eclipse he went to the stable to solace himself with Henry's crimes. Henry, with the elasticity of his race, could usually provide a sin to place himself on a footing with the disgraced one. Perhaps he would remember that he had forgotten to put the hitching strap

in the back of the buggy on some recent occasion, and had been reprimanded by the doctor. Then these two would commune subtly and without words concerning their moon, holding themselves sympathetically as
people who had committed similar treasons. On the other hand, Henry
would sometimes choose to absolutely repudiate this idea, and when Jimmie appeared in his shame would bully him most virtuously, preaching
with assurance the precepts of the doctor's creed, and pointing out to Jimmie all his abominations. Jimmie did not discover that this was odious
in his comrade. He accepted it and lived in its shadow with humility,
merely trying to conciliate the saintly Henry with acts of deference. Won
by this attitude, Henry would sometimes allow the child to enjoy the felicity of squeezing the sponge over a buggy wheel, even when Jimmie was
still gory from unspeakable deeds.

Whenever Henry dwelt for a time in sackcloth, Jimmie did not patronize
him at all. This was a justice of his age, his condition. He did not know.
Besides, Henry could drive a horse, and Jimmie had a full sense of this
sublimity. Henry personally conducted the moon during the splendid
journeys through the country roads, where farms spread on all sides, with
sheep, cows, and other marvels abounding.

"Hello, Jim!" said Henry, poising his sponge. Water was dripping from
the buggy. Sometimes the horses in the stalls stamped thunderingly on the
pine floor. There was an atmosphere of hay and of harness.

For a minute Jimmie refused to take an interest in anything. He was
very downcast. He could not even feel the wonders of wagon-washing.
Henry, while at work, narrowly observed him.

"Your pop done wallop yer, didn't he?" he said at last.

"No," said Jimmie, defensively; "he didn't."

After this casual remark Henry continued his labor, with a scowl of
occupation. Presently he said: "I done tol' yer many's th' time not to go
a-foolin' an' a-projjeckin' with them flowers. Yer pop don' like it nohow."
As a matter of fact, Henry had never mentioned flowers to the boy.

Jimmie preserved a gloomy silence, so Henry began to use seductive wiles
in this affair of washing a wagon. It was not until he began to spin a
wheel on the tree, and the sprinkling water flew everywhere, that the boy
was visibly moved. He had been seated on the sill of the carriage-house
door, but at the beginning of this ceremony he arose and circled toward
the buggy, with an interest that slowly consumed the remembrance of a
late disgrace.

Johnson could then display all the dignity of a man whose duty it was
to protect Jimmie from a splashing. "Look out, boy! look out! You done
gwi' spile yer pants. I raikon your mommer don' 'low this foolishness,

she know it. I ain't gwi' have you round yere spilin' yer pants, an' have Mis' Trescott light on me pressen'ly. 'Deed I ain't."

He spoke with an air of great irritation, but he was not annoyed at all. This tone was merely a part of his importance. In reality he was always delighted to have the child there to witness the business of the stable. For one thing, Jimmie was invariably overcome with reverence when he was told how beautifully a harness was polished or a horse groomed. Henry explained each detail of this kind with unction, procuring great joy from the child's admiration.

III

After Johnson had taken his supper in the kitchen, he went to his loft in the carriage-house and dressed himself with much care. No belle of a court circle could bestow more mind on a toilet than did Johnson. On second thought, he was more like a priest arraying himself for some parade of the church. As he emerged from his room and sauntered down the carriage-drive, no one would have suspected him of ever having washed a buggy.

It was not altogether a matter of the lavender trousers, nor yet the straw hat with its bright silk band. The change was somewhere far in the interior of Henry. But there was no cakewalk hyperbole in it. He was simply a quiet, well-bred gentleman of position, wealth, and other necessary achievements out for an evening stroll, and he had never washed a wagon in his life.

In the morning, when in his working clothes, he had met a friend— "Hello, Pete!" "Hello, Henry!" Now, in his effulgence, he encountered this same friend. His bow was not at all haughty. If it expressed anything, it expressed consummate generosity—"Good-evenin', Misteh Washington." Pete, who was very dirty, being at work in a potato-patch, responded in a mixture of abasement and appreciation—"Good-evenin', Misteh Johnsing."

The shimmering blue of the electric arc lamps was strong in the main street of the town. At numerous points it was conquered by the orange glare of the outnumbering gaslights in the windows of shops. Through this radiant lane moved a crowd, which culminated in a throng before the post office, awaiting the distribution of the evening mails. Occasionally there came into it a shrill electric streetcar, the motor singing like a cageful of grasshoppers, and possessing a great gong that clanged forth both warnings and simple noise. At the little theater, which was a varnish and red-plush miniature of one of the famous New York theaters, a company of strollers was to play *East Lynne*. The young men of the town were mainly gathered at the corners, in distinctive groups which expressed various shades and lines of chumship, and had little to do with any social gradations. There they discussed everything with critical insight, passing the whole town in review as it swarmed in the street. When the gongs of the electric cars ceased for a moment to harry the ears, there could be heard the sound of the feet of the leisurely crowd on the bluestone pavement, and it was like the peaceful evening lashing at the shore of a lake. At the foot of the hill, where two lines of maples sentineled the way, an electric lamp glowed high among the embowering branches and made most wonderful shadow-etchings on the road below it.

When Johnson appeared amid the throng a member of one of the profane groups at a corner instantly telegraphed news of this extraordinary arrival to his companions. They hailed him. "Hello, Henry! Going to walk for a cake tonight?"

"Ain't he smooth?"

"Why, you've got that cake right in your pocket, Henry!"

"Throw out your chest a little more."

Henry was not ruffled in any way by these quiet admonitions and compliments. In reply he laughed a supremely good-natured, chuckling laugh, which nevertheless expressed an underground complacency of superior metal.

Young Griscom, the lawyer, was just emerging from Reifsnyder's barber shop, rubbing his chin contentedly. On the steps he dropped his hand and looked with wide eyes into the crowd. Suddenly he bolted back into the shop. "Wow!" he cried to the parliament; "you ought to see the coon that's coming!"

Reifsnyder and his assistant instantly poised their razors high and turned toward the window. Two belathered heads reared from the chairs. The electric shine in the street caused an effect like water to them who looked through the glass from the yellow glamor of Reifsnyder's shop. In fact, the people without resembled the inhabitants of a great aquarium that here had a square pane in it. Presently into this frame swam the graceful form of Henry Johnson.

"Chee!" said Reifsnyder. He and his assistant with one accord threw their obligations to the winds and, leaving their lathered victims helpless, advanced to the window. "Ain't he a taisy?" said Reifsnyder, marveling.

But the man in the first chair, with a grievance in his mind, had found a weapon. "Why, that's only Henry Johnson, you blamed idiots! Come on now, Reif, and shave me. What do you think I am—a mummy?"

Reifsnyder turned, in a great excitement. "I bait you any money that vas not Henry Johnson! Henry Johnson! Rats!" The scorn put into this last word made it an explosion. "That man vas a Pullman-car porter or someding. How could that be Henry Johnson?" he demanded, turbulently. "You vas crazy."

The man in the first chair faced the barber in a storm of indignation. "Didn't I give him those lavender trousers?" he roared.

And young Griscom, who had remained attentively at the window, said: "Yes, I guess that was Henry. It looked like him."

"Oh, vell," said Reifsnyder, returning to his business, "if you think so! Oh, vell!" He implied that he was submitting for the sake of amiability.

Finally the man in the second chair, mumbling from a mouth made timid by adjacent lather, said: "That was Henry Johnson all right. Why, he always dresses like that when he wants to make a front! He's the biggest dude in town—anybody knows that."

"Chinger!" said Reifsnyder.

Henry was not at all oblivious of the wake of wondering ejaculation that streamed out behind him. On other occasions he had reaped this same joy, and he always had an eye for the demonstration. With a face beaming with happiness he turned away from the scene of his victories into a narrow side street, where the electric light still hung high, but only to exhibit a row of tumble-down houses leaning together like paralytics.

The saffron Miss Bella Farragut, in a calico frock, had been crouched on the front stoop, gossiping at long range, but she espied her approaching caller at a distance. She dashed around the corner of the house, galloping like a horse. Henry saw it all, but he preserved the polite demeanor of a guest when a waiter spills claret down his cuff. In this awkward situation he was simply perfect.

The duty of receiving Mr. Johnson fell upon Mrs. Farragut, because Bella, in another room, was scrambling wildly into her best gown. The fat old woman met him with a great ivory smile, sweeping back with the door, and bowing low. "Walk in, Misteh Johnson, walk in. How is you dis ebenin', Misteh Johnson—how is you?"

Henry's face showed like a reflector as he bowed and bowed, bending almost from his head to his ankles. "Good-evenin', Mis' Fa'gut; good-evenin'. How is you dis evenin'? Is all you' folks well, Mis' Fa'gut?"

After a great deal of kowtow, they were planted in two chairs opposite each other in the living room. Here they exchanged the most tremendous civilities, until Miss Bella swept into the room, when there was more kowtow on all sides, and a smiling show of teeth that was like an illumination.

The cooking-stove was of course in this drawing room, and on the fire was some kind of a long-winded stew. Mrs. Farragut was obliged to arise and attend to it from time to time. Also young Sim came in and went to bed on his pallet in the corner. But to all these domesticities the three maintained an absolute dumbness. They bowed and smiled and ignored and imitated until a late hour, and if they had been the occupants of the most gorgeous salon in the world they could not have been more like three monkeys.

After Henry had gone, Bella, who encouraged herself in the appropriation of phrases, said, "Oh, ma, isn't he divine?"

IV

A Saturday evening was a sign always for a larger crowd to parade the thoroughfare. In summer the band played until ten o'clock in the little park. Most of the young men of the town affected to be superior to this band, even to despise it; but in the still and fragrant evenings they invariably turned out in force, because the girls were sure to attend this concert, strolling slowly over the grass, linked closely in pairs, or preferably in threes, in the curious public dependence upon one another which was their inheritance. There was no particular social aspect to this gathering, save that group regarded group with interest, but mainly in silence. Perhaps one girl would nudge another girl and suddenly say, "Look! there goes Gertie Hodgson and her sister!" And they would appear to regard this as an event of importance.

On a particular evening a rather large company of young men were gathered on the sidewalk that edged the park. They remained thus beyond the borders of the festivities because of their dignity, which would not exactly allow them to appear in anything which was so much fun for the younger lads. These latter were careering madly through the crowd, precipitating minor accidents from time to time, but usually fleeing like mist swept by the wind before retribution could lay hands upon them.

The band played a waltz which involved a gift of prominence to the bass horn, and one of the young men on the sidewalk said that the music reminded him of the new engines on the hill pumping water into the reservoir. A similarity of this kind was not inconceivable, but the young man did not say it because he disliked the band's playing. He said it because it was fashionable to say that manner of thing concerning the band. However, over in the stand, Billie Harris, who played the snare drum, was always surrounded by a throng of boys, who adored his every whack.

After the mails from New York and Rochester had been finally distributed, the crowd from the post office added to the mass already in the park. The wind waved the leaves of the maples, and, high in the air, the blue-burning globes of the arc lamps caused the wonderful traceries of leaf shadows on the ground. When the light fell upon the upturned face of a girl, it caused it to glow with a wonderful pallor. A policeman came suddenly from the darkness and chased a gang of obstreperous little boys. They hooted him from a distance. The leader of the band had some of the mannerisms of the great musicians, and during a period of silence the crowd smiled when they saw him raise his hand to his brow, stroke it sentimentally, and glance upward with a look of poetic anguish. In the shivering light, which gave to the park an effect like a great vaulted hall, the throng swarmed, with a gentle murmur of dresses switching the turf, and with a steady hum of voices.

Suddenly, without preliminary bars, there arose from afar the great hoarse roar of a factory whistle. It raised and swelled to a sinister note, and then it sang on the night wind one long call that held the crowd in the park immovable, speechless. The bandmaster had been about to vehemently let fall his hand to start the band on a thundering career through a popular march, but, smitten by this giant voice from the night, his hand dropped slowly to his knee, and, his mouth agape, he looked at his men in silence. The cry died away to a wail, and then to stillness. It released the muscles of the company of young men on the sidewalk, who had been like statues, posed eagerly, lithely, their ears turned. And then they wheeled upon each other simultaneously, and, in a single explosion, they shouted, "One!"

Again the sound swelled in the night and roared its long ominous cry, and as it died away the crowd of young men wheeled upon each other and, in chorus, yelled, "Two!"

There was a moment of breathless waiting. Then they bawled, "Second district!" In a flash the company of indolent and cynical young men had vanished like a snowball disrupted by dynamite.

v

Jake Rogers was the first man to reach the home of Tuscarora Hose Company Number Six. He had wrenched his key from his pocket as he tore down the street, and he jumped at the springlock like a demon. As the doors flew back before his hands he leaped and kicked the wedges from a pair of wheels, loosened a tongue from its clasp, and in the glare of the electric light which the town placed before each of its hose-houses the next comers beheld the spectacle of Jake Rogers bent like hickory in the manfulness of his pulling, and the heavy cart was moving slowly toward the doors. Four men joined him at the time, and as they swung with the cart out into the street, dark figures sped toward them from the ponderous shadows in back of the electric lamps. Some set up the inevitable question, "What district?"

"Second," was replied to them in a compact howl. Tuscarora Hose Company Number Six swept on a perilous wheel into Niagara Avenue, and as the men, attached to the cart by the rope which had been paid out from the windlass under the tongue, pulled madly in their fervor and abandon, the gong under the axle clanged incitingly. And sometimes the same cry was heard, "What district?"

"Second."

On a grade Johnnie Thorpe fell and, exercising a singular muscular ability, rolled out in time for the track of the oncoming wheel, and arose, disheveled and aggrieved, casting a look of mournful disenchantment upon the black crowd that poured after the machine. The cart seemed to be the apex of a dark wave that was whirling as if it had been a broken dam. Behind the lad were stretches of lawn, and in that direction front doors were banged by men who hoarsely shouted out into the clamorous avenue, "What district?"

At one of these houses a woman came to the door bearing a lamp, shielding her face from its rays with her hands. Across the cropped grass the avenue represented to her a kind of black torrent, upon which, nevertheless, fled numerous miraculous figures upon bicycles. She did not know that the towering light at the corner was continuing its nightly whine.

Suddenly a little boy somersaulted around the corner of the house as if he had been projected down a flight of stairs by a catapultian boot. He halted himself in front of the house by dint of a rather extraordinary evolution with his legs. "Oh, ma," he gasped, "can I go? Can I, ma?"

She straightened with the coldness of the exterior mother-judgment, although the hand that held the lamp trembled slightly. "No, Willie; you had better come to bed."

Instantly he began to buck and fume like a mustang. "Oh, ma," he cried, contorting himself—"oh, ma, can't I go? Please, ma, can't I go? Can't I go, ma?"

"It's half-past nine now, Willie."

He ended by wailing out a compromise: "Well, just down to the corner, ma? Just down to the corner?"

From the avenue came the sound of rushing men who wildly shouted. Somebody had grappled the bell-rope in the Methodist church, and now over the town rang this solemn and terrible voice, speaking from the clouds. Moved from its peaceful business, this bell gained a new spirit in the portentous night, and it swung the heart to and fro, up and down, with each peal of it.

"Just down to the corner, ma?"

"Willie, it's half-past nine now."

VI

The outlines of the house of Dr. Trescott had faded quietly into the evening, hiding a shape such as we call Queen Anne against the pall of the blackened sky. The neighborhood was at this time so quiet, and seemed so devoid of obstructions, that Hannigan's dog thought it a good opportunity to prowl in forbidden precincts, and so came and pawed Trescott's lawn, growling, and considering himself a formidable beast. Later, Peter Washington strolled past the house and whistled, but there was no dim light shining from Henry's loft, and presently Peter went his way. The rays from the street, creeping in silvery waves over the grass, caused the row of shrubs along the drive to throw a clear, bold shade.

A wisp of smoke came from one of the windows at the end of the house and drifted quietly into the branches of a cherry tree. Its companions followed it in slowly increasing numbers, and finally there was a current controlled by invisible banks which poured into the fruit-laden boughs of the cherry tree. It was no more to be noted than if a troop of dim and silent gray monkeys had been climbing a grapevine into the clouds.

After a moment the window brightened as if the four panes of it had been stained with blood, and a quick ear might have been led to imagine the fire-imps calling and calling, clan joining clan, gathering to the colors. From the street, however, the house maintained its dark quiet, insisting to a passer-by that it was the safe dwelling of people who chose to retire early to tranquil dreams. No one could have heard this low droning of the gathering clans.

Suddenly the panes of the red window tinkled and crashed to the ground, and at other windows there suddenly reared other flames, like bloody specters at the apertures of a haunted house. This outbreak had been well planned, as if by professional revolutionists.

A man's voice suddenly shouted: "Fire! Fire! Fire!" Hannigan had flung his pipe frenziedly from him because his lungs demanded room. He tumbled down from his perch, swung over the fence, and ran shouting towards the front door of the Trescotts'. Then he hammered on the door, using his fists as if they were mallets. Mrs. Trescott instantly came to one of the windows on the second floor. Afterward she knew she had been about to say, "The doctor is not at home, but if you will leave your name, I will let him know as soon as he comes."

Hannigan's bawling was for a minute incoherent, but she understood that it was not about croup.

"What?" she said, raising the window swiftly.

"Your house is on fire! You're all ablaze! Move quick if—" His cries were resounding in the street as if it were a cave of echoes. Many feet pattered swiftly on the stones. There was one man who ran with an almost fabulous speed. He wore lavender trousers. A straw hat with a bright silk band was held half crumpled in his hand.

As Henry reached the front door, Hannigan had just broken the lock with a kick. A thick cloud of smoke poured over them, and Henry, ducking his head, rushed into it. From Hannigan's clamor he knew only one thing, but it turned him blue with horror. In the hall a lick of flame had found the cord that supported "Signing the Declaration." The engraving slumped suddenly down at one end, and then dropped to the floor, where it burst with the sound of a bomb. The fire was already roaring like a winter wind among the pines.

At the head of the stairs Mrs. Trescott was waving her arms as if they were two reeds. "Jimmie! Save Jimmie!" she screamed in Henry's face. He plunged past her and disappeared, taking the long-familiar routes among these upper chambers, where he had once held office as a sort of second assistant housemaid.

Hannigan had followed him up the stairs, and grappled the arm of the maniacal woman there. His face was black with rage. "You must come down," he bellowed.

She would only scream at him in reply: "Jimmie! Jimmie! Save Jimmie!" But he dragged her forth while she babbled at him.

As they swung out into the open air a man ran across the lawn and, seizing a shutter, pulled it from its hinges and flung it far out upon the grass. Then he frantically attacked the other shutters one by one. It was a kind of temporary insanity.

"Here, you," howled Hannigan, "hold Mrs. Trescott—And stop—"

The news had been telegraphed by a twist of the wrist of a neighbor who had gone to the fire box at the corner, and the time when Hannigan and his charge struggled out of the house was the time when the whistle roared its hoarse night call, smiting the crowd in the park, causing the leader of the band, who was about to order the first triumphal clang of a military march, to let his hand drop slowly to his knees.

VII

Henry pawed awkwardly through the smoke in the upper halls. He had attempted to guide himself by the walls, but they were too hot. The paper was crimpling, and he expected at any moment to have a flame burst from under his hands.

"Jimmie!"

He did not call very loud, as if in fear that the humming flames below would overhear him.

"Jimmie! Oh, Jimmie!"

Stumbling and panting, he speedily reached the entrance to Jimmie's room and flung open the door. The little chamber had no smoke in it at all. It was faintly illuminated by a beautiful rosy light reflected circuitously from the flames that were consuming the house. The boy had apparently just been aroused by the noise. He sat in his bed, his lips apart, his eyes wide, while upon his little white-robed figure played caressingly the light from the fire. As the door flew open he had before him this apparition of his pal, a terror-stricken negro, all tousled and with wool scorching, who leaped upon him and bore him up in a blanket as if the whole affair were a case of kidnapping by a dreadful robber chief. Without waiting to go

The Monster 441

through the usual short but complete process of wrinkling up his face, Jimmie let out a gorgeous bawl, which resembled the expression of a calf's deepest terror. As Johnson, bearing him, reeled into the smoke of the hall, he flung his arms about his neck and buried his face in the blanket. He called twice in muffled tones: "Mam-ma! Mam-ma!"

When Johnson came to the top of the stairs with his burden, he took a quick step backward. Through the smoke that rolled to him he could see that the lower hall was all ablaze. He cried out then in a howl that resembled Jimmie's former achievement. His legs gained a frightful faculty of bending sideways. Swinging about precariously on these reedy legs, he made his way back slowly, back along the upper hall. From the way of him then, he had given up almost all idea of escaping from the burning house, and with it the desire. He was submitting, submitting because of his fathers, bending his mind in a most perfect slavery to this conflagration.

He now clutched Jimmie as unconsciously as when, running toward the house, he had clutched the hat with the bright silk band.

Suddenly he remembered a little private staircase which led from a bedroom to an apartment which the doctor had fitted up as a laboratory and workhouse, where he used some of his leisure, and also hours when he might have been sleeping, in devoting himself to experiments which came in the way of his study and interest.

When Johnson recalled this stairway the submission to the blaze departed instantly. He had been perfectly familiar with it, but his confusion had destroyed the memory of it.

In his sudden momentary apathy there had been little that resembled fear, but now, as a way of safety came to him, the old frantic terror caught him. He was no longer creature to the flames, and he was afraid of the battle with them. It was a singular and swift set of alternations in which he feared twice without submission, and submitted once without fear.

"Jimmie!" he wailed, as he staggered on his way. He wished this little inanimate body at his breast to participate in his tremblings. But the child had lain limp and still during these headlong charges and countercharges, and no sign came from him.

Johnson passed through two rooms and came to the head of the stairs. As he opened the door great billows of smoke poured out, but, gripping Jimmie closer, he plunged down through them. All manner of odors assailed him during this flight. They seemed to be alive with envy, hatred, and malice. At the entrance to the laboratory he confronted a strange spectacle. The room was like a garden in the region where might be burning flowers. Flames of violet, crimson, green, blue, orange, and purple were blooming everywhere. There was one blaze that was precisely the hue of a delicate coral. In another place was a mass that lay merely in phosphorescent inaction like a pile of emeralds. But all these marvels were to be seen dimly through clouds of heaving, turning, deadly smoke.

Johnson halted for a moment on the threshold. He cried out again in the negro wail that had in it the sadness of the swamps. Then he rushed across the room. An orange-colored flame leaped like a panther at the lavender trousers. This animal bit deeply into Johnson. There was an explosion at one side, and suddenly before him there reared a delicate, trembling sapphire shape like a fairy lady. With a quiet smile she blocked his path and doomed him and Jimmie. Johnson shrieked, and then ducked in the manner of his race in fights. He aimed to pass under the left guard of the sapphire lady. But she was swifter than eagles, and her talons caught in him as he plunged past her. Bowing his head as if his neck had been struck, Johnson lurched forward, twisting this way and that way. He fell on his back. The still form in the blanket flung from his arms, rolled to the edge of the floor and beneath the window.

Johnson had fallen with his head at the base of an old-fashioned desk. There was a row of jars upon the top of this desk. For the most part, they were silent amid this rioting, but there was one which seemed to hold a scintillant and writhing serpent.

Suddenly the glass splintered, and a ruby-red snake-like thing poured its thick length out upon the top of the old desk. It coiled and hesitated, and then began to swim a languorous way down the mahogany slant. At the angle it waved its sizzling molten head to and fro over the closed eyes of the man beneath it. Then, in a moment, with a mystic impulse, it moved again, and the red snake flowed directly down into Johnson's upturned face.

Afterward the trail of this creature seemed to reek, and amid flames and low explosions drops like red-hot jewels pattered softly down it at leisurely intervals.

VIII

Suddenly all roads led to Dr. Trescott's. The whole town flowed toward one point. Chippeway Hose Company Number One toiled desperately up Bridge Street Hill even as the Tuscaroras came in an impetuous sweep down Niagara Avenue. Meanwhile the machine of the hook-and-ladder experts from across the creek was spinning on its way. The chief of the fire department had been playing poker in the rear room of Whiteley's cigar store, but at the first breath of the alarm he sprang through the door like a man escaping with the kitty.

In Whilomville, on these occasions, there was always a number of people who instantly turned their attention to the bells in the churches and schoolhouses. The bells not only emphasized the alarm, but it was the habit to send these sounds rolling across the sky in a stirring brazen uproar until the flames were practically vanquished. There was also a kind of rivalry as to which bell should be made to produce the greatest din. Even the Valley Church, four miles away among the farms, had heard the voices of its brethren, and immediately added a quaint little yelp.

Dr. Trescott had been driving homeward, slowly smoking a cigar, and feeling glad that this last case was now in complete obedience to him, like a wild animal that he had subdued, when he heard the long whistle, and chirped to his horse under the unlicensed but perfectly distinct impression that a fire had broken out in Oakhurst, a new and rather high-flying suburb of the town which was at least two miles from his own home. But in the second blast and in the ensuing silence he read the designation of his own district. He was then only a few blocks from his house. He took out the whip and laid it lightly on the mare. Surprised and frightened at this extraordinary action, she leaped forward, and as the reins straightened like steel bands, the doctor leaned backward a trifle. When the mare whirled him up to the closed gate he was wondering whose house could be afire. The man who had rung the signal-box yelled something at him, but he already knew. He left the mare to her will.

In front of his door was a maniacal woman in a wrapper. "Ned!" she screamed at sight of him. "Jimmie! Save Jimmie!"

Trescott had grown hard and chill. "Where?" he said. "Where?"

Mrs. Trescott's voice began to bubble. "Up—up—up—" She pointed at the second-story windows.

Hannigan was already shouting: "Don't go in that way! You can't go in that way!"

Trescott ran around the corner of the house and disappeared from them. He knew from the view he had taken of the main hall that it would be impossible to ascend from there. His hopes were fastened now to the stairway which led from the laboratory. The door which opened from this room out upon the lawn was fastened with a bolt and lock, but he kicked close to the lock and then close to the bolt. The door with a loud crash flew back. The doctor recoiled from the roll of smoke, and then bending low, he stepped into the garden of burning flowers. On the floor his stinging eyes could make out a form in a smoldering blanket near the window. Then, as he carried his son toward the door, he saw that the whole lawn seemed now alive with men and boys, the leaders in the great charge that the whole town was making. They seized him and his burden, and overpowered him in wet blankets and water.

But Hannigan was howling: "Johnson is in there yet! Henry Johnson is in there yet! He went in after the kid! Johnson is in there yet!"

These cries penetrated to the sleepy senses of Trescott, and he struggled with his captors, swearing, unknown to him and to them, all the deep blasphemies of his medical-student days. He rose to his feet and went again toward the door of the laboratory. They endeavored to restrain him, although they were much affrighted at him.

But a young man who was a brakeman on the railway, and lived in one of the rear streets near the Trescotts, had gone into the laboratory and brought forth a thing which he laid on the grass.

IX

There were hoarse commands from in front of the house. "Turn on your water, Five!" "Let 'er go, One!" The gathering crowd swayed this way and that way. The flames, towering high, cast a wild red light on their faces. There came the clangor of a gong from along some adjacent street. The crowd exclaimed at it. "Here comes Number Three!" "That's Three a-comin'!" A panting and irregular mob dashed into view, dragging a hose cart. A cry of exultation arose from the little boys. "Here's Three!" The lads welcomed Never-Die Hose Company Number Three as if it was composed of a chariot dragged by a band of gods. The perspiring citizens flung themselves into the fray. The boys danced in impish joy at the displays of prowess. They acclaimed the approach of Number Two. They welcomed Number Four with cheers. They were so deeply moved by this whole affair that they bitterly guyed the late appearance of the hook-and-ladder company, whose heavy apparatus had almost stalled them on the Bridge Street hill. The lads hated and feared a fire, of course. They did not particularly want to have anybody's house burn, but still it was fine to see the gathering of the companies, and amid a great noise to watch their heroes perform all manner of prodigies.

They were divided into parties over the worth of different companies, and supported their creeds with no small violence. For instance, in that part of the little city where Number Four had its home it would be most daring for a boy to contend the superiority of any other company. Likewise, in another quarter, when a strange boy was asked which fire company was the best in Whilomville, he was expected to answer "Number One." Feuds, which the boys forgot and remembered according to chance or the importance of some recent event, existed all through the town.

They did not care much for John Shipley, the chief of the department. It was true that he went to a fire with the speed of a falling angel, but when there he invariably lapsed into a certain still mood, which was almost a preoccupation, moving leisurely around the burning structure and surveying it, puffing meanwhile at a cigar. This quiet man, who even when life was in danger seldom raised his voice, was not much to their fancy. Now old Sykes Huntington, when he was chief, used to bellow continually like a bull and gesticulate in a sort of delirium. He was much finer as a spectacle than this Shipley, who viewed a fire with the same steadiness that he viewed a raise in a large jack pot. The greater number of the boys could never understand why the members of these companies persisted in reelecting Shipley, although they often pretended to understand it, because "My father says" was a very formidable phrase in argument, and the fathers seemed almost unanimous in advocating Shipley.

At this time there was considerable discussion as to which company had got the first stream of water on the fire. Most of the boys claimed that Number Five owned that distinction, but there was a determined minority who contended for Number One. Boys who were the blood adherents of other companies were obliged to choose between the two on this occasion, and the talk waxed warm.

But a great rumor went among the crowds. It was told with hushed voices. Afterward a reverent silence fell even upon the boys. Jimmie Trescott and Henry Johnson had been burned to death, and Dr. Trescott himself had been most savagely hurt. The crowd did not even feel the police pushing at them. They raised their eyes, shining now with awe, toward the high flames.

The man who had information was at his best. In low tones he described the whole affair. "That was the kid's room—in the corner there. He had measles or somethin', and this coon—Johnson—was a-settin' up with 'im, and Johnson got sleepy or somethin' and upset the lamp, and the doctor he was down in his office, and he came running up, and they all got burned together till they dragged 'em out."

Another man, always preserved for the deliverance of the final judgment, was saying: "Oh, they'll die sure. Burned to flinders. No chance. Hull lot of 'em. Anybody can see." The crowd concentrated its gaze still more closely upon these flags of fire which waved joyfully against the black sky. The bells of the town were clashing unceasingly.

A little procession moved across the lawn and toward the street. There were three cots, borne by twelve of the firemen. The police moved sternly, but it needed no effort of theirs to open a lane for this slow cortège. The men who bore the cots were well known to the crowd, but in this solemn parade during the ringing of the bells and the shouting, and with the red glare upon the sky, they seemed utterly foreign, and Whilomville paid them a deep respect. Each man in this stretcher party had gained a reflected majesty. They were footmen to death, and the crowd made subtle obeisance to this august dignity derived from three prospective graves. One woman turned away with a shriek at sight of the covered body on the first stretcher, and people faced her suddenly in silent and mournful indignation. Otherwise there was barely a sound as these twelve important men with measured tread carried their burdens through the throng.

The little boys no longer discussed the merits of the different fire companies. For the greater part they had been routed. Only the more coura-geous viewed closely the three figures veiled in yellow blankets.

x

Old Judge Denning Hagenthorpe, who lived nearly opposite the Tres-cotts, had thrown his door wide open to receive the afflicted family. When it was publicly learned that the doctor and his son and the negro were still alive, it required a specially detailed policeman to prevent people from scaling the front porch and interviewing these sorely wounded. One old lady appeared with a miraculous poultice, and she quoted most damning Scripture to the officer when he said that she could not pass him. Through-out the night some lads old enough to be given privileges or to compel them from their mothers remained vigilantly upon the curb in anticipation of a death or some such event. The reporter of the *Morning Tribune* rode thither on his bicycle every hour until three o'clock.

Six of the ten doctors in Whilomville attended at Judge Hagenthorpe's house.

Almost at once they were able to know that Trescott's burns were not vitally important. The child would possibly be scarred badly, but his life was undoubtedly safe. As for the negro Henry Johnson, he could not live. His body was frightfully seared, but more than that, he now had no face. His face had simply been burned away.

Trescott was always asking news of the two other patients. In the morn-ing he seemed fresh and strong, so they told him that Johnson was doomed. They then saw him stir on the bed, and sprang quickly to see if the band-ages needed readjusting. In the sudden glance he threw from one to an-other he impressed them as being both leonine and impracticable.

The morning paper announced the death of Henry Johnson. It contained a long interview with Edward J. Hannigan, in which the latter described in full the performance of Johnson at the fire. There was also an editorial built from all the best words in the vocabulary of the staff. The town halted in its accustomed road of thought, and turned a reverent attention to the memory of this hostler. In the breasts of many people was the regret that they had not known enough to give him a hand and a lift when he was alive, and they judged themselves stupid and ungenerous for this failure.

The name of Henry Johnson became suddenly the title of a saint to the little boys. The one who thought of it first could, by quoting it in an argu-ment, at once overthrow his antagonist, whether it applied to the subject or whether it did not.

> "Nigger, nigger, never die,
> Black face and shiny eye."

Boys who had called this odious couplet in the rear of Johnson's march buried the fact at the bottom of their hearts.

Later in the day Miss Bella Farragut, of No. 7 Watermelon Alley, announced that she had been engaged to marry Mr. Henry Johnson.

XI

The old judge had a cane with an ivory head. He could never think at his best until he was leaning slightly on this stick and smoothing the white top with slow movements of his hands. It was also to him a kind of narcotic. If by any chance he mislaid it, he grew at once very irritable, and was likely to speak sharply to his sister, whose mental incapacity he had patiently endured for thirty years in the old mansion on Ontario Street. She was not at all aware of her brother's opinion of her endowments, and so it might be said that the judge had successfully dissembled for more than a quarter of a century, only risking the truth at the times when his cane was lost.

On a particular day the judge sat in his armchair on the porch. The sunshine sprinkled through the lilac bushes and poured great coins on the boards. The sparrows disputed in the trees that lined the pavements. The judge mused deeply, while his hands gently caressed the ivory head of his cane.

Finally he arose and entered the house, his brow still furrowed in a thoughtful frown. His stick thumped solemnly in regular beats. On the second floor he entered a room where Dr. Trescott was working about the bedside of Henry Johnson. The bandages on the negro's head allowed only one thing to appear, an eye, which unwinkingly stared at the judge. The latter spoke to Trescott on the condition of the patient. Afterward he evidently had something further to say, but he seemed to be kept from it by the scrutiny of the unwinking eye, at which he furtively glanced from time to time.

When Jimmie Trescott was sufficiently recovered, his mother had taken him to pay a visit to his grandparents in Connecticut. The doctor had remained to take care of his patients, but as a matter of truth he spent most of his time at Judge Hagenthorpe's house, where lay Henry Johnson. Here he slept and ate almost every meal in the long nights and days of his vigil.

At dinner, and away from the magic of the unwinking eye, the judge said, suddenly, "Trescott, do you think it is—" As Trescott paused expectantly, the judge fingered his knife. He said, thoughtfully, "No one wants to advance such ideas, but somehow I think that that poor fellow ought to die."

There was in Trescott's face at once a look of recognition, as if in this tangent of the judge he saw an old problem. He merely sighed and answered, "Who knows?" The words were spoken in a deep tone that gave them an elusive kind of significance.

The judge retreated to the cold manner of the bench. "Perhaps we may not talk with propriety of this kind of action, but I am induced to say that you are performing a questionable charity in preserving this negro's life. As near as I can understand, he will hereafter be a monster, a perfect monster, and probably with an affected brain. No man can observe you as I have observed you and not know that it was a matter of conscience with you, but I am afraid, my friend, that it is one of the blunders of virtue." The judge had delivered his views with his habitual oratory. The last three words he spoke with a particular emphasis, as if the phrase was his discovery.

The doctor made a weary gesture. "He saved my boy's life."

"Yes," said the judge, swiftly—"yes, I know!"

"And what am I to do?" said Trescott, his eyes suddenly lighting like an outburst from smoldering peat. "What am I to do? He gave himself for—for Jimmie. What am I to do for him?"

The judge abased himself completely before these words. He lowered his eyes for a moment. He picked at his cucumbers.

Presently he braced himself straightly in his chair. "He will be your creation, you understand. He is purely your creation. Nature has very evidently given him up. He is dead. You are restoring him to life. You are making him, and he will be a monster, and with no mind."

"He will be what you like, Judge," cried Trescott, in sudden polite fury. "He will be anything, but, by God! he saved my boy."

The judge interrupted in a voice trembling with emotion: "Trescott! Trescott! Don't I know?"

Trescott had subsided to a sullen mood. "Yes, you know," he answered, acidly; "but you don't know all about your own boy being saved from death." This was a perfectly childish allusion to the judge's bachelorhood. Trescott knew that the remark was infantile, but he seemed to take desperate delight in it.

But it passed the judge completely. It was not his spot.

"I am puzzled," said he, in profound thought. "I don't know what to say."

Trescott had become repentant. "Don't think I don't appreciate what you say, Judge. But—"

"Of course!" responded the judge, quickly. "Of course."

"It—" began Trescott.

"Of course," said the judge.

In silence they resumed their dinner.

"Well," said the judge, ultimately, "it is hard for a man to know what to do."

"It is," said the doctor, fervidly.

There was another silence. It was broken by the judge: "Look here, Trescott; I don't want you to think—"

"No, certainly not," answered the doctor, earnestly.

"Well, I don't want you to think I would say anything to—It was only that I thought that I might be able to suggest to you that—perhaps—the affair was a little dubious."

With an appearance of suddenly disclosing his real mental perturbation, the doctor said: "Well, what would you do? Would you kill him?" he asked, abruptly and sternly.

"Trescott, you fool," said the old man, gently.

"Oh, well, I know, Judge, but then—" He turned red, and spoke with new violence: "Say, he saved my boy—do you see? He saved my boy."

"You bet he did," cried the judge, with enthusiasm. "You bet he did." And they remained for a time gazing at each other, their faces illuminated with memories of a certain deed.

After another silence, the judge said, "It is hard for a man to know what to do."

XII

Late one evening Trescott, returning from a professional call, paused his buggy at the Hagenthorpe gate. He tied the mare to the old tin-covered post, and entered the house. Ultimately he appeared with a companion—a man who walked slowly and carefully, as if he were learning. He was wrapped to the heels in an old-fashioned ulster. They entered the buggy and drove away.

After a silence only broken by the swift and musical humming of the wheels on the smooth road, Trescott spoke. "Henry," he said, "I've got you a home here with old Alek Williams. You will have everything you want to eat and a good place to sleep, and I hope you will get along there all right. I will pay all your expenses, and come to see you as often as I can. If you don't get along, I want you to let me know as soon as possible, and then we will do what we can to make it better."

The dark figure at the doctor's side answered with a cheerful laugh. "These buggy wheels don' look like I washed 'em yesterday, docteh," he said.

Trescott hesitated for a moment, and then went on insistently, "I am taking you to Alek Williams, Henry, and I—"

The figure chuckled again. "No, 'deed! No, seh! Alek Williams don' know a hoss! 'Deed he don't. He don' know a hoss from a pig." The laugh that followed was like the rattle of pebbles.

Trescott turned and looked sternly and coldly at the dim form in the gloom from the buggy-top. "Henry," he said, "I didn't say anything about horses. I was saying—"

"Hoss? Hoss?" said the quavering voice from these near shadows. "Hoss? 'Deed I don' know all erbout a hoss! 'Deed I don't." There was a satirical chuckle.

At the end of three miles the mare slackened and the doctor leaned forward, peering, while holding tight reins. The wheels of the buggy bumped often over outcropping boulders. A window shone forth, a simple square of topaz on a great black hillside. Four dogs charged the buggy with ferocity, and when it did not promptly retreat, they circled courageously around the flanks, baying. A door opened near the window in the hillside, and a man came and stood on a beach of yellow light.

"Yah! yah! You Roveh! You Susie! Come yah! Come yah this minit!"

Trescott called across the dark sea of grass, "Hello, Alek!"

"Hello!"

"Come down here and show me where to drive."

The man plunged from the beach into the surf, and Trescott could then only trace his course by the fervid and polite ejaculations of a host who was somewhere approaching. Presently Williams took the mare by the head and, uttering cries of welcome and scolding the swarming dogs, led the equipage toward the lights. When they halted at the door and Trescott was climbing out, Williams cried, "Will she stand, docteh?"

"She'll stand all right, but you better hold her for a minute. Now, Henry." The doctor turned and held both arms to the dark figure. It crawled to him painfully like a man going down a ladder. Williams took the mare away to be tied to a little tree, and when he returned he found them awaiting him in the gloom beyond the rays from the door.

He burst out then like a siphon pressed by a nervous thumb. "Hennery! Hennery, ma ol' frien'. Well, if I ain' glade. If I ain' glade!"

Trescott had taken the silent shape by the arm and led it forward into the full revelation of the light. "Well, now, Alek, you can take Henry and put him to bed, and in the morning I will—"

Near the end of this sentence old Williams had come front to front with Johnson. He gasped for a second, and then yelled the yell of a man stabbed in the heart.

For a fraction of a moment Trescott seemed to be looking for epithets. Then he roared: "You old black chump! You old black—Shut up! Shut up! Do you hear?"

Williams obeyed instantly in the matter of his screams, but he continued in a lowered voice: "Ma Lode a' massy! Who'd ever think? Ma Lode a' massy!"

Trescott spoke again in the manner of a commander of a battalion. "Alek!"

The old negro again surrendered, but to himself he repeated in a whisper, "Ma Lode!" He was aghast and trembling.

As these three points of widening shadows approached the golden doorway a hale old negress appeared there, bowing. "Good-evenin', docteh! Good-evenin'! Come in! come in!" She had evidently just retired from a tempestuous struggle to place the room in order, but she was now bowing rapidly. She made the effort of a person swimming.

"Don't trouble yourself, Mary," said Trescott, entering. "I've brought Henry for you to take care of, and all you've got to do is to carry out what I tell you." Learning that he was not followed, he faced the door, and said, "Come in, Henry."

Johnson entered. "Whee!" shrieked Mrs. Williams. She almost achieved a back somersault. Six young members of the tribe of Williams made a simultaneous plunge for a position behind the stove, and formed a wailing heap.

XIII

"You know very well that you and your family lived usually on less than three dollars a week, and now that Dr. Trescott pays you five dollars a week for Johnson's board, you live like millionaires. You haven't done a stroke of work since Johnson began to board with you—everybody knows that—and so what are you kicking about?"

The judge sat in his chair on the porch, fondling his cane, and gazing down at old Williams, who stood under the lilac bushes. "Yes, I know, Jedge," said the negro, wagging his head in a puzzled manner. "'Tain't like as if I didn't 'preciate what the docteh done, but—but—well, yeh see, Jedge," he added, gaining a new impetus, "it's—it's hard wuk. This ol' man nev' did wuk so hard. Lode, no."

"Don't talk such nonsense, Alek," spoke the judge, sharply. "You have never really worked in your life—anyhow, enough to support a family of sparrows—and now when you are in a more prosperous condition than ever before, you come around talking like an old fool."

The negro began to scratch his head. "Yeh see, Jedge," he said at last, "my ol' 'ooman she cain't 'ceive no lady callahs, nohow."

"Hang lady callers!" said the judge, irascibly. "If you have flour in the barrel and meat in the pot, your wife can get along without receiving lady callers, can't she?"

"But they won't come ainyhow, Jedge," replied Williams, with an air of still deeper stupefaction. "Noner ma wife's frien's ner noner ma frien's 'ill come near ma res'dence."

"Well, let them stay home if they are such silly people."

The old negro seemed to be seeking a way to elude this argument, but, evidently finding none, he was about to shuffle meekly off. He halted, however. "Jedge," said he, "ma ol' 'ooman's near driv' abstracted."

"Your old woman is an idiot," responded the judge.

Williams came very close and peered solemnly through a branch of lilac. "Jedge," he whispered, "the chillens."

"What about them?"

Dropping his voice to funereal depths, Williams said, "They—they cain't eat."

"Can't eat!" scoffed the judge, loudly. "Can't eat! You must think I am as big an old fool as you are. Can't eat—the little rascals! What's to prevent them from eating?"

In answer, Williams said, with mournful emphasis, "Hennery." Moved with a kind of satisfaction at his tragic use of the name, he remained staring at the judge for a sign of its effect.

The judge made a gesture of irritation. "Come, now, you old scoundrel, don't beat around the bush any more. What are you up to? What do you want? Speak out like a man, and don't give me any more of this tiresome rigamarole."

"I ain't er-beatin' round 'bout nuffin, Jedge," replied Williams, indignantly. "No, seh; I say whatter got to say right out. 'Deed I do."

"Well, say it, then."

"Jedge," began the negro, taking off his hat and switching his knee with it, "Lode knows I'd do jes' 'bout as much fer five dollehs er week as ainy cul'd man, but—but this yere business is awful, Jedge. I raikon 'ain't been no sleep in—in my house sence docteh done fetch 'im."

"Well, what do you propose to do about it?"

Williams lifted his eyes from the ground and gazed off through the trees. "Raikon I got good appetite, an' sleep jes' like er dog, but he—he's done broke me all up. 'Tain't no good, nohow. I wake up in the night; I hear 'im, mebbe, er-whimperin' an' er-whimperin', an' I sneak an' I sneak until I try th' do' to see if he locked in. An' he keep me er-puzzlin' an' er-quakin' all night long. Don't know how'll do in th' winter. Can't let 'im out where th' chillen is. He'll done freeze where he is now." Williams spoke these sentences as if he were talking to himself. After a silence of deep reflection he continued: "Folks go round sayin' he ain't Hennery Johnson at all. They say he's er devil!"

"What?" cried the judge.

"Yesseh," repeated Williams, in tones of injury, as if his veracity had been challenged. "Yesseh. I'm er-tellin' it to yeh straight, Jedge. Plenty cul'd people folks up my way say it is a devil."

"Well, you don't think so yourself, do you?"

"No. 'Tain't no devil. It's Hennery Johnson."

"Well, then, what is the matter with you? You don't care what a lot of foolish people say. Go on 'tending to your business, and pay no attention to such idle nonsense."

" 'Tis nonsense, Jedge; but he *looks* like er devil."

"What do you care what he looks like?" demanded the judge.

"Ma rent is two dollehs and er half er month," said Williams, slowly.

"It might just as well be ten thousand dollars a month," responded the judge. "You never pay it, anyhow."

"Then, anoth' thing," continued Williams, in his reflective tone. "If he was all right in his haid I could stan' it; but, Jedge, he's crazier 'n er loon. Then when he looks like er devil, an' done skears all ma frien's away, an' ma chillens cain't eat, an' ma ole 'ooman jes' raisin' Cain all the time, an' ma rent two dollehs an' er half er month, an' him not right in his haid, it seems like five dollehs er week—"

The judge's stick came down sharply and suddenly upon the floor of the porch. "There," he said, "I thought that was what you were driving at."

Williams began swinging his head from side to side in the strange racial mannerism. "Now hol' on a minnet, Jedge," he said, defensively. " 'Tain't like as if I didn't 'preciate what the docteh done. 'Tain't that. Docteh Trescott is er kind man, an' 'tain't like as if I didn't 'preciate what he done; but—but—"

"But what? You are getting painful, Alek. Now tell me this: did you ever have five dollars a week regularly before in your life?"

Williams at once drew himself up with great dignity, but in the pause after that question he drooped gradually to another attitude. In the end he answered, heroically: "No, Jedge, I 'ain't. An' 'tain't like as if I was er-sayin' five dollehs wasn't er lot er money for a man like me. But, Jedge, what er man oughter git fer this kinder wuk is er salary. Yesseh, Jedge," he repeated, with a great impressive gesture; "fer this kinder wuk er man oughter git er Salary." He laid a terrible emphasis upon the final word.

The judge laughed. "I know Dr. Trescott's mind concerning this affair, Alek; and if you are dissatisfied with your boarder, he is quite ready to move him to some other place; so, if you care to leave word with me that you are tired of the arrangement and wish it changed, he will come and take Johnson away."

Williams scratched his head again in deep perplexity. "Five dollehs is er big price fer bo'd, but 'tain't no big price fer the bo'd of er crazy man," he said, finally.

"What do you think you ought to get?" asked the judge.

"Well," answered Alek, in the manner of one deep in a balancing of the scales, "he looks like er devil, an' done skears e'rybody, an' ma chillens cain't eat, an' I cain't sleep, an' he ain't right in his haid, an'—"

"You told me all those things."

After scratching his wool, and beating his knee with his hat, and gazing off through the trees and down at the ground, Williams said, as he kicked nervously at the gravel, "Well, Jedge, I think it is wuth—" He stuttered.

"Worth what?"

"Six dollehs," answered Williams, in a desperate outburst.

The judge lay back in his great armchair and went through all the motions of a man laughing heartily, but he made no sound save a slight cough. Williams had been watching him with apprehension.

"Well," said the judge, "do you call six dollars a salary?"

"No, seh," promptly responded Williams. "'Tain't a salary. No, 'deed! 'Tain't a salary." He looked with some anger upon the man who questioned his intelligence in this way.

"Well, supposing your children can't eat?"

"I—"

"And supposing he looks like a devil? And supposing all those things continue? Would you be satisfied with six dollars a week?"

Recollections seemed to throng in Williams's mind at these interrogations, and he answered dubiously. "Of co'se a man who ain't right in his haid, an' looks like er devil—But six dollehs—" After these two attempts at a sentence Williams suddenly appeared as an orator, with a great shiny palm waving in the air. "I tell yeh, Jedge, six dollehs is six dollehs, but if I git six dollehs for bo'ding Hennery Johnson, I uhns it! I uhns it!"

"I don't doubt that you earn six dollars for every week's work you do," said the judge.

"Well, if I bo'd Hennery Johnson fer six dollehs er week, I uhns it! I uhns it!" cried Williams, wildly.

XIV

Reifsnyder's assistant had gone to his supper, and the owner of the shop was trying to placate four men who wished to be shaved at once. Reifsnyder was very garrulous—a fact which made him rather remarkable among barbers, who, as a class, are austerely speechless, having been taught silence by the hammering reiteration of a tradition. It is the customers who talk in the ordinary event.

As Reifsnyder waved his razor down the cheek of a man in the chair, he turned often to cool the impatience of the others with pleasant talk, which they did not particularly heed.

"Oh, he should have let him die," said Bainbridge, a railway engineer, finally replying to one of the barber's orations. "Shut up, Reif, and go on with your business!"

Instead, Reifsnyder paused shaving entirely, and turned to front the speaker. "Let him die?" he demanded. "How vas that? How can you let a man die?"

"By letting him die, you chump," said the engineer. The others laughed a little, and Reifsnyder turned at once to his work, sullenly, as a man overwhelmed by the derision of numbers.

"How vas that?" he grumbled later. "How can you let a man die when he vas done so much for you?"

"'When he vas done so much for you?'" repeated Bainbridge. "You better shave some people. How vas that? Maybe this ain't a barber shop?"

A man hitherto silent now said, "If I had been the doctor, I would have done the same thing."

"Of course," said Reifsnyder. "Any man vould do it. Any man that vas not like you, you—old—flint-hearted—fish." He had sought the final words with painful care, and he delivered the collection triumphantly at Bainbridge. The engineer laughed.

The man in the chair now lifted himself higher, while Reifsnyder began an elaborate ceremony of anointing and combing his hair. Now free to join comfortably in the talk, the man said: "They say he is the most terrible thing in the world. Young Johnnie Bernard—that drives the grocery wagon —saw him up at Alek Williams's shanty, and he says he couldn't eat anything for two days."

"Chee!" said Reifsnyder.

"Well, what makes him so terrible?" asked another.

"Because he hasn't got any face," replied the barber and the engineer in duet.

"Hasn't got any face!" repeated the man. "How can he do without any face?"

> "He has no face in the front of his head,
> In the place where his face ought to grow."

Bainbridge sang these lines pathetically as he arose and hung his hat on a hook. The man in the chair was about to abdicate in his favor. "Get a gait on you now," he said to Reifsnyder. "I go out at 7:31."

As the barber foamed the lather on the cheeks of the engineer he seemed to be thinking heavily. Then suddenly he burst out. "How would you like to be with no face?" he cried to the assemblage.

"Oh, if I had to have a face like yours—" answered one customer.

Bainbridge's voice came from a sea of lather. "You're kicking because if losing faces became popular, you'd have to go out of business."

"I don't think it will become so much popular," said Reifsnyder.

"Not if it's got to be taken off in the way his was taken off," said another man. "I'd rather keep mine, if you don't mind."

"I guess so!" cried the barber. "Just think!"

The shaving of Bainbridge had arrived at a time of comparative liberty for him. "I wonder what the doctor says to himself?" he observed. "He may be sorry he made him live."

"It was the only thing he could do," replied a man. The others seemed to agree with him.

"Supposing you were in his place," said one, "and Johnson had saved your kid. What would you do?"

"Certainly!"

"Of course! You would do anything on earth for him. You'd take all the trouble in the world for him. And spend your last dollar on him. Well, then?"

"I wonder how it feels to be without any face?" said Reifsnyder, musingly.

The man who had previously spoken, feeling that he had expressed himself well, repeated the whole thing. "You would do anything on earth for him. You'd take all the trouble in the world for him. And spend your last dollar on him. Well, then?"

"No, but look," said Reifsnyder; "supposing you don't got a face!"

XV

As soon as Williams was hidden from the view of the old judge he began to gesture and talk to himself. An elation had evidently penetrated to his vitals, and caused him to dilate as if he had been filled with gas. He snapped his fingers in the air, and whistled fragments of triumphal music. At times, in his progress toward his shanty, he indulged in a shuffling movement that was really a dance. It was to be learned from the intermediate monologue that he had emerged from his trials laureled and proud. He was the unconquerable Alexander Williams. Nothing could exceed the bold self-reliance of his manner. His kingly stride, his heroic song, the derisive flourish of his hands—all betokened a man who had successfully defied the world.

On his way he saw Zeke Paterson coming to town. They hailed each other at a distance of fifty yards.

"How do, Broth' Paterson?"

"How do, Broth' Williams?"

They were both deacons.

"Is you' folks well, Broth' Paterson?"

"Middlin', middlin'. How's you' folks, Broth' Williams?"

Neither of them had slowed his pace in the smallest degree. They had simply begun this talk when a considerable space separated them, continued it as they passed, and added polite questions as they drifted steadily apart. Williams's mind seemed to be a balloon. He had been so inflated that he had not noticed that Paterson had definitely shied into the dry ditch as they came to the point of ordinary contact.

Afterward, as he went a lonely way, he burst out again in song and pantomimic celebration of his estate. His feet moved in prancing steps.

When he came in sight of his cabin, the fields were bathed in a blue dusk, and the light in the window was pale. Cavorting and gesticulating, he gazed joyfully for some moments upon this light. Then suddenly another idea seemed to attack his mind, and he stopped, with an air of being suddenly dampened. In the end he approached his home as if it were the fortress of an enemy.

Some dogs disputed his advance for a loud moment, and then discovering their lord, slunk away embarrassed. His reproaches were addressed to them in muffled tones.

Arriving at the door, he pushed it open with the timidity of a new thief. He thrust his head cautiously sideways, and his eyes met the eyes of his wife, who sat by the table, the lamplight defining a half of her face. "Sh!" he said, uselessly. His glance traveled swiftly to the inner door which shielded the one bed-chamber. The pickaninnies, strewn upon the floor of the living room, were softly snoring. After a hearty meal they had promptly dispersed themselves about the place and gone to sleep. "Sh!" said Williams again to his motionless and silent wife. He had allowed only his head to appear. His wife, with one hand upon the edge of the table and the other at her knee, was regarding him with wide eyes and parted lips as if he were a specter. She looked to be one who was living in terror, and even the familiar face at the door had thrilled her because it had come suddenly.

Williams broke the tense silence. "Is he all right?" he whispered, waving his eyes towards the inner door. Following his glance timorously, his wife nodded, and in a low tone answered: "I raikon he's done gone t' sleep."

Williams then slunk noiselessly across his threshold.

He lifted a chair, and with infinite care placed it so that it faced the dreaded inner door. His wife moved slightly, so as to also squarely face it. A silence came upon them in which they seemed to be waiting for a calamity, pealing and deadly.

Williams finally coughed behind his hand. His wife started, and looked upon him in alarm. "'Pears like he done gwine keep quiet ter-night," he breathed. They continually pointed their speech and their looks at the inner door, paying it the homage due to a corpse or a phantom. Another long stillness followed this sentence. Their eyes shone white and wide. A wagon rattled down the distant road. From their chairs they looked at the window, and the effect of the light in the cabin was a presentation of an intensely black and solemn night. The old woman adopted the attitude used always in church at funerals. At times she seemed to be upon the point of breaking out in prayer.

"He mighty quiet ter-night," whispered Williams. "Was he good ter-day?" For answer his wife raised her eyes to the ceiling in the supplication of Job. Williams moved restlessly. Finally he tiptoed to the door. He knelt slowly and without a sound, and placed his ear near the keyhole. Hearing a noise behind him, he turned quickly. His wife was staring at him aghast. She stood in front of the stove, and her arms were spread out in the natural movement to protect all her sleeping ducklings.

But Williams arose without having touched the door. "I raikon he er-sleep," he said, fingering his wool. He debated with himself for some time. During this interval his wife remained, a great fat statue of a mother shielding her children.

It was plain that his mind was swept suddenly by a wave of temerity. With a sounding step he moved toward the door. His fingers were almost upon the knob when he swiftly ducked and dodged away, clapping his hands to the back of his head. It was as if the portal had threatened him. There was a little tumult near the stove, where Mrs. Williams's desperate retreat had involved her feet with the prostrate children.

After the panic Williams bore traces of a feeling of shame. He returned to the charge. He firmly grasped the knob with his left hand, and with his other hand turned the key in the lock. He pushed the door, and as it swung portentously open he sprang nimbly to one side like the fearful slave liberating the lion. Near the stove a group had formed, the terror-stricken mother, with her arms stretched, and the aroused children clinging frenziedly to her skirts.

The light streamed after the swinging door, and disclosed a room six feet one way and six feet the other way. It was small enough to enable the radiance to lay it plain. Williams peered warily around the corner made by the doorpost.

Suddenly he advanced, retired, and advanced again with a howl. His palsied family had expected him to spring backward, and at his howl they heaped themselves wondrously. But Williams simply stood in the little room emitting his howls before an open window. "He's gone! He's gone! He's gone!" His eye and his hand had speedily proved the fact. He had even thrown open a little cupboard.

Presently he came flying out. He grabbed his hat, and hurled the outer door back upon its hinges. Then he tumbled headlong into the night. He was yelling: "Docteh Trescott! Docteh Trescott!" He ran wildly through the fields and galloped in the direction of town. He continued to call to Trescott, as if the latter was within easy hearing. It was as if Trescott was poised in the contemplative sky over the running negro, and could heed this reaching voice—"Docteh Trescott!"

In the cabin, Mrs. Williams, supported by relays from the battalion of children, stood quaking watch until the truth of daylight came as a reinforcement and made them arrogant, strutting, swashbuckler children and a mother who proclaimed her illimitable courage.

XVI

Theresa Page was giving a party. It was the outcome of a long series of arguments addressed to her mother, which had been overheard in part by her father. He had at last said five words, "Oh, let her have it." The mother had then gladly capitulated.

Theresa had written nineteen invitations, and distributed them at recess to her schoolmates. Later her mother had composed five large cakes, and still later a vast amount of lemonade.

So the nine little girls and the ten little boys sat quite primly in the dining room, while Theresa and her mother plied them with cake and lemonade, and also with ice cream. This primness sat now quite strangely upon them. It was owing to the presence of Mrs. Page. Previously in the parlor alone with their games they had overturned a chair; the boys had let more or less of their hoodlum spirit shine forth. But when circumstances could be possibly magnified to warrant it, the girls made the boys victims of an insufferable pride, snubbing them mercilessly. So in the dining room they resembled a class at Sunday school, if it were not for the subterranean smiles, gestures, rebuffs, and poutings which stamped the affair as a children's party.

Two little girls of this subdued gathering were planted in a settle with their backs to the broad window. They were beaming lovingly upon each other with an effect of scorning the boys.

Hearing a noise behind her at the window, one little girl turned to face it. Instantly she screamed and sprang away, covering her face with her hands. "What was it? What was it?" cried every one in a roar. Some slight movement of the eyes of the weeping and shuddering child informed the company that she had been frightened by an appearance at the window. At once they all faced the imperturbable window, and for a moment there was a silence. An astute lad made an immediate census of the other lads. The prank of slipping out and looming spectrally at a window was too venerable. But the little boys were all present and astonished.

As they recovered their minds they uttered warlike cries, and through a side door sallied rapidly out against the terror. They vied with each other in daring.

None wished particularly to encounter a dragon in the darkness of the garden, but there could be no faltering when the fair ones in the dining room were present. Calling to each other in stern voices, they went dragooning over the lawn, attacking the shadows with ferocity, but still with the caution of reasonable beings. They found, however, nothing new to the peace of the night. Of course there was a lad who told a great lie. He described a grim figure, bending low and slinking off along the fence. He gave a number of details, rendering his lie more splendid by a repetition of certain forms which he recalled from romances. For instance, he insisted that he had heard the creature emit a hollow laugh.

Inside the house the little girl who had raised the alarm was still shuddering and weeping. With the utmost difficulty was she brought to a state approximating calmness by Mrs. Page. Then she wanted to go home at once.

Page entered the house at this time. He had exiled himself until he concluded that this children's party was finished and gone. He was obliged to escort the little girl home because she screamed again when they opened the door and she saw the night.

She was not coherent even to her mother. Was it a man? She didn't know. It was simply a thing, a dreadful thing.

XVII

In Watermelon Alley the Farraguts were spending their evening as usual on the little rickety porch. Sometimes they howled gossip to other people on other rickety porches. The thin wail of a baby arose from a near house. A man had a terrific altercation with his wife, to which the alley paid no attention at all.

There appeared suddenly before the Farraguts a monster making a low and sweeping bow. There was an instant's pause, and then occurred something that resembled the effect of an upheaval of the earth's surface. The old woman hurled herself backward with a dreadful cry. Young Sim had been perched gracefully on a railing. At sight of the monster he simply fell over it to the ground. He made no sound, his eyes stuck out, his nerveless hands tried to grapple the rail to prevent a tumble, and then he vanished. Bella, blubbering, and with her hair suddenly and mysteriously disheveled, was crawling on her hands and knees fearsomely up the steps.

Standing before this wreck of a family gathering, the monster continued to bow. It even raised a deprecatory claw. "Don' make no botheration 'bout me, Miss Fa'gut," it said, politely. "No, 'deed. I jes' drap in ter ax if yer well this evenin', Miss Fa'gut. Don' make no botheration. No, 'deed. I gwine ax you to go to er daince with me, Mis Fa'gut. I ax you if I can have the magnifercent gratitude of you' company on that 'casion, Miss Fa'gut."

The girl cast a miserable glance behind her. She was still crawling away. On the ground beside the porch young Sim raised a strange bleat, which expressed both his fright and his lack of wind. Presently the monster, with a fashionable amble, ascended the steps after the girl.

She groveled in a corner of the room as the creature took a chair. It seated itself very elegantly on the edge. It held an old cap in both hands. "Don' make no botheration, Miss Fa'gut. Don' make no botheration. No, 'deed. I jes' drap in ter ax you if you won' do me the proud of acceptin' ma humble invitation to er daince, Miss Fa'gut."

She shielded her eyes with her arms and tried to crawl past it, but the genial monster blocked the way. "I jes' drap in ter ax you 'bout er daince, Miss Fa'gut. I ax you if I kin have the magnifercent gratitude of you' company on that 'casion, Miss Fa'gut."

In a last outbreak of despair, the girl, shuddering and wailing, threw herself face downward on the floor, while the monster sat on the edge of the chair gabbling courteous invitations, and holding the old hat daintily to his stomach.

At the back of the house, Mrs. Farragut, who was of enormous weight, and who for eight years had done little more than sit in an armchair and describe her various ailments, had with speed and agility scaled a high board fence.

XVIII

The black mass in the middle of Trescott's property was hardly allowed to cool before the builders were at work on another house. It had sprung upward at a fabulous rate. It was like a magical composition born of the ashes. The doctor's office was the first part to be completed, and he had already moved in his new books and instruments and medicines.

Trescott sat before his desk when the chief of police arrived. "Well, we found him," said the latter.

"Did you?" cried the doctor. "Where?"

"Shambling around the streets at daylight this morning. I'll be blamed if I can figure on where he passed the night."

"Where is he now?"

"Oh, we jugged him. I didn't know what else to do with him. That's what I want you to tell me. Of course we can't keep him. No charge could be made, you know."

"I'll come down and get him."

The official grinned retrospectively. "Must say he had a fine career while he was out. First thing he did was to break up a children's party at Page's. Then he went to Watermelon Alley. Whoo! He stampeded the whole outfit. Men, women, and children running pell-mell, and yelling. They say one old woman broke her leg, or something, shinning over a fence. Then he went right out on the main street, and an Irish girl threw a fit, and there was a sort of a riot. He began to run, and a big crowd chased him, firing rocks. But he gave them the slip somehow down there by the foundry and in the railroad yard. We looked for him all night, but couldn't find him."

"Was he hurt any? Did anybody hit him with a stone?"

"Guess there isn't much of him to hurt anymore, is there? Guess he's been hurt up to the limit. No. They never touched him. Of course nobody really wanted to hit him, but you know how a crowd gets. It's like—it's like—"

"Yes, I know."

For a moment the chief of the police looked reflectively at the floor. Then he spoke hesitatingly. "You know Jake Winter's little girl was the one that he scared at the party. She is pretty sick, they say."

"Is she? Why, they didn't call me. I always attend the Winter family."

"No? Didn't they?" asked the chief, slowly. "Well—you know—Winter is—well, Winter has gone clean crazy over this business. He wanted—he wanted to have you arrested."

"Have me arrested? The idiot! What in the name of wonder could he have me arrested for?"

"Of course. He is a fool. I told him to keep his trap shut. But then you know how he'll go all over town yapping about the thing. I thought I'd better tip you."

"Oh, he is of no consequence; but then, of course, I'm obliged to you, Sam."

"That's all right. Well, you'll be down tonight and take him out, eh? You'll get a good welcome from the jailer. He don't like his job for a cent. He says you can have your man whenever you want him. He's got no use for him."

"But what is this business of Winter's about having me arrested?"

"Oh, it's a lot of chin about your having no right to allow this—this—this man to be at large. But I told him to tend to his own business. Only I thought I'd better let you know. And I might as well say right now, doctor, that there is a good deal of talk about this thing. If I were you, I'd come to the jail pretty late at night, because there is likely to be a crowd around the door, and I'd bring a—er—mask, or some kind of a veil, anyhow."

XIX

Martha Goodwin was single, and well along into the thin years. She lived with her married sister in Whilomville. She performed nearly all the housework in exchange for the privilege of existence. Every one tacitly recognized her labor as a form of penance for the early end of her be-trothed, who had died of smallpox, which he had not caught from her.

But despite the strenuous and unceasing workaday of her life, she was a woman of great mind. She had adamantine opinions upon the situation in Armenia, the condition of women in China, the flirtation between Mrs.

Minster of Niagara Avenue and young Griscom, the conflict in the Bible class of the Baptist Sunday school, the duty of the United States toward the Cuban insurgents, and many other colossal matters. Her fullest experience of violence was gained on an occasion when she had seen a hound clubbed, but in the plan which she had made for the reform of the world she advocated drastic measures. For instance, she contended that all the Turks should be pushed into the sea and drowned, and that Mrs. Minster and young Griscom should be hanged side by side on twin gallows. In fact, this woman of peace, who had seen only peace, argued constantly for a creed of illimitable ferocity. She was invulnerable on these questions, because eventually she overrode all opponents with a sniff. This sniff was an active force. It was to her antagonists like a bang over the head, and none was known to recover from this expression of exalted contempt. It left them windless and conquered. They never again came forward as candidates for suppression. And Martha walked her kitchen with a stern brow, an invincible being like Napoleon.

Nevertheless her acquaintances, from the pain of their defeats, had been long in secret revolt. It was in no wise a conspiracy, because they did not care to state their open rebellion, but nevertheless it was understood that any woman who could not coincide with one of Martha's contentions was entitled to the support of others in the small circle. It amounted to an arrangement by which all were required to disbelieve any theory for which Martha fought. This, however, did not prevent them from speaking of her mind with profound respect.

Two people bore the brunt of her ability. Her sister Kate was visibly afraid of her, while Carrie Dungen sailed across from her kitchen to sit respectfully at Martha's feet and learn the business of the world. To be sure, afterward, under another sun, she always laughed at Martha and pretended to deride her ideas, but in the presence of the sovereign she always remained silent or admiring. Kate, the sister, was of no consequence at all. Her principal delusion was that she did all the work in the upstairs rooms of the house, while Martha did it downstairs. The truth was seen only by the husband, who treated Martha with a kindness that was half banter, half deference. Martha herself had no suspicion that she was the only pillar of the domestic edifice. The situation was without definitions. Martha made definitions, but she devoted them entirely to the Armenians and Griscom and the Chinese and other subjects. Her dreams, which in early days had been of love, of meadows and the shade of trees, of the face of a man, were now involved otherwise, and they were companioned in the kitchen curiously, Cuba, the hot-water kettle, Armenia, the washing of the dishes, and the whole thing being jumbled. In regard to social misdemeanors, she who was simply the mausoleum of a dead passion was probably the most savage critic in town. This unknown woman, hidden in a kitchen as in a well, was sure to have a considerable effect of the one kind or the other in the life of the town. Every time it moved a yard, she had personally contributed an inch. She could hammer so stoutly upon the door of a proposition that it would break from its hinges and fall upon her, but at any rate it moved. She was an engine, and the fact that she did not know that she was an engine contributed largely to the effect. One reason that she was formidable was that she did not even imagine that she was formidable. She remained a weak, innocent, and pig-headed creature, who alone would defy the universe if she thought the universe merited this proceeding.

One day Carrie Dungen came across from her kitchen with speed. She had a great deal of grist. "Oh," she cried, "Henry Johnson got away from where they was keeping him, and came to town last night, and scared everybody almost to death."

Martha was shining a dishpan, polishing madly. No reasonable person could see cause for this operation, because the pan already glistened like silver. "Well!" she ejaculated. She imparted to the word a deep meaning. "This, my prophecy, has come to pass." It was a habit.

The overplus of information was choking Carrie. Before she could go on she was obliged to struggle for a moment. "And, oh, little Sadie Winter is awful sick, and they say Jake Winter was around this morning trying to get Doctor Trescott arrested. And poor old Mrs. Farragut sprained her ankle in trying to climb a fence. And there's a crowd around the jail all the time. They put Henry in jail because they didn't know what else to do with him, I guess. They say he is perfectly terrible."

Martha finally released the dishpan and confronted the headlong speaker. "Well!" she said again, poising a great brown rag. Kate had heard the excited newcomer, and drifted down from the novel in her room. She was a shivery little woman. Her shoulder blades seemed to be two panes of ice, for she was constantly shrugging and shrugging. "Serves him right if he was to lose all his patients," she said suddenly, in bloodthirsty tones. She snipped her words out as if her lips were scissors.

"Well, he's likely to," shouted Carrie Dungen. "Don't a lot of people say that they won't have him any more? If you're sick and nervous, Doctor Trescott would scare the life out of you, wouldn't he? He would me. I'd keep thinking."

Martha, stalking to and fro, sometimes surveyed the two other women with a contemplative frown.

XX

After the return from Connecticut, little Jimmie was at first much afraid of the monster who lived in the room over the carriage-house. He could not identify it in any way. Gradually, however, his fear dwindled under the influence of a weird fascination. He sidled into closer and closer relations with it.

One time the monster was seated on a box behind the stable basking in the rays of the afternoon sun. A heavy crêpe veil was swathed about its head.

Little Jimmie and many companions came around the corner of the stable. They were all in what was popularly known as the baby class, and consequently escaped from school a half-hour before the other children. They halted abruptly at sight of the figure on the box. Jimmie waved his hand with the air of a proprietor.

"There he is," he said.

"O-o-o!" murmured all the little boys—"o-oo-!" They shrank back and grouped according to courage or experience, as at the sound the monster slowly turned its head. Jimmie had remained in the van alone. "Don't be afraid! I won't let him hurt you," he said, delighted.

"Huh!" they replied, contemptuously. "We ain't afraid."

Jimmie seemed to reap all the joys of the owner and exhibitor of one of the world's marvels, while his audience remained at a distance—awed and entranced, fearful and envious.

One of them addressed Jimmie gloomily. "Bet you dassent walk right up to him." He was an older boy than Jimmie, and habitually oppressed him to a small degree. This new social elevation of the smaller lad probably seemed revolutionary to him.

"Huh!" said Jimmie, with deep scorn. "Dassent I? Dassent I, hey? Dassent I?"

The group was immensely excited. It turned its eyes upon the boy that Jimmie addressed. "No, you dassent," he said, stolidly, facing a moral defeat. He could see that Jimmie was resolved. "No, you dassent," he repeated, doggedly.

"Ho?" cried Jimmie. "You just watch!—you just watch!"

Amid a silence he turned and marched toward the monster. But possibly the palpable wariness of his companions had an effect upon him that weighed more than his previous experience, for suddenly, when near to the monster, he halted dubiously. But his playmates immediately uttered a derisive shout, and it seemed to force him forward. He went to the monster and laid his hand delicately on its shoulder. "Hello, Henry," he said, in a voice that trembled a trifle. The monster was crooning a weird line of negro melody that was scarcely more than a thread of sound, and it paid no heed to the boy.

Jimmie strutted back to his companions. They acclaimed him and hooted his opponent. Amid this clamor the larger boy with difficulty preserved a dignified attitude.

"I dassent, dassent I?" said Jimmie to him. "Now, you're so smart, let's see you do it!"

This challenge brought forth renewed taunts from the others. The larger boy puffed out his cheeks. "Well, I ain't afraid," he explained, sullenly. He had made a mistake in diplomacy, and now his small enemies were tumbling his prestige all about his ears. They crowed like roosters and bleated like lambs, and made many other noises which were supposed to bury him in ridicule and dishonor. "Well, I ain't afraid," he continued to explain through the din.

Jimmie, the hero of the mob, was pitiless. "You ain't afraid, hey?" he sneered. "If you ain't afraid, go do it, then."

"Well, I would if I wanted to," the other retorted. His eyes wore an expression of profound misery, but he preserved steadily other portions of a pot-valiant air. He suddenly faced one of his persecutors. "If you're so smart, why don't you go do it?" This persecutor sank promptly through the group to the rear. The incident gave the badgered one a breathing spell, and for a moment even turned the derision in another direction. He took advantage of his interval. "I'll do it if anybody else will," he announced, swaggering to and fro.

Candidates for the adventure did not come forward. To defend themselves from this countercharge, the other boys again set up their crowing and bleating. For a while they would hear nothing from him. Each time he opened his lips their chorus of noises made oratory impossible. But at last he was able to repeat that he would volunteer to dare as much in the affair as any other boy.

"Well, you go first," they shouted.

But Jimmie intervened to once more lead the populace against the large boy. "You're mighty brave, ain't you?" he said to him. "You dared me to do it, and I did—didn't I? Now who's afraid?" The others cheered this view loudly, and they instantly resumed the baiting of the large boy.

He shamefacedly scratched his left shin with his right foot. "Well, I ain't afraid." He cast an eye at the monster. "Well, I ain't afraid." With a glare of hatred at his squalling tormentors, he finally announced a grim intention. "Well, I'll do it, then, since you're so fresh. Now!"

The mob subsided as with a formidable countenance he turned toward the impassive figure on the box. The advance was also a regular progression from high daring to craven hesitation. At last, when some yards from the monster, the lad came to a full halt, as if he had encountered a stone wall. The observant little boys in the distance promptly hooted. Stung again by these cries, the lad sneaked two yards forward. He was crouched like a young cat ready for a backward spring. The crowd at the rear, beginning to respect this display, uttered some encouraging cries. Suddenly the lad gathered himself together, made a white and desperate rush forward, touched the monster's shoulder with a far-outstretched finger, and sped away, while his laughter rang out wild, shrill, and exultant.

The crowd of boys reverenced him at once, and began to throng into his camp, and look at him, and be his admirers. Jimmie was discomfited for a moment, but he and the larger boy, without agreement or word of any kind, seemed to recognize a truce, and they swiftly combined and began to parade before the others.

"Why, it's just as easy as nothing," puffed the larger boy. "Ain't it, Jim?"

"Course," blew Jimmie. "Why, it's as e-e-easy."

They were people of another class. If they had been decorated for courage on twelve battlefields, they could not have made the other boys more ashamed of the situation.

Meanwhile they condescended to explain the emotions of the excursion, expressing unqualified contempt for any one who could hang back. "Why, it ain't nothin'. He won't do nothin' to you," they told the others, in tones of exasperation.

One of the very smallest boys in the party showed signs of a wistful desire to distinguish himself, and they turned their attention to him, pushing at his shoulders while he swung away from them, and hesitated dreamily. He was eventually induced to make furtive expedition, but it was only for a few yards. Then he paused, motionless, gazing with open mouth. The vociferous entreaties of Jimmie and the large boy had no power over him.

Mrs. Hannigan had come out on her back porch with a pail of water. From this coign she had a view of the secluded portion of the Trescott grounds that was behind the stable. She perceived the group of boys, and the monster on the box. She shaded her eyes with her hand to benefit her vision. She screeched then as if she was being murdered. "Eddie! Eddie! You come home this minute!"

Her son querulously demanded, "Aw, what for?"

"You come home this minute. Do you hear?"

The other boys seemed to think this visitation upon one of their number required them to preserve for a time the hang-dog air of a collection of culprits, and they remained in guilty silence until the little Hannigan, wrathfully protesting, was pushed through the door of his home. Mrs. Hannigan cast a piercing glance over the group, stared with a bitter face at the Trescott house, as if this new and handsome edifice was insulting her, and then followed her son.

There was wavering in the party. An inroad by one mother always caused them to carefully sweep the horizon to see if there were more coming. "This is my yard," said Jimmie, proudly. "We don't have to go home."

The monster on the box had turned its black crêpe countenance toward the sky, and was waving its arms in time to a religious chant. "Look at him now," cried a little boy. They turned, and were transfixed by the solemnity and mystery of the indefinable gestures. The wail of the melody was mournful and slow. They drew back. It seemed to spellbind them with the power of a funeral. They were so absorbed that they did not hear the doctor's buggy drive up to the stable. Trescott got out, tied his horse, and approached the group. Jimmie saw him first, and at his look of dismay the others wheeled.

"What's all this, Jimmie?" asked Trescott, in surprise.

The lad advanced to the front of his companions, halted, and said nothing. Trescott's face gloomed slightly as he scanned the scene.

"What were you doing, Jimmie?"

"We was playin'," answered Jimmie, huskily.

"Playing at what?"

"Just playin'."

Trescott looked gravely at the other boys, and asked them to please go home. They proceeded to the street much in the manner of frustrated and revealed assassins. The crime of trespass on another boy's place was still a crime when they had only accepted the other boy's cordial invitation, and they were used to being sent out of all manner of gardens upon the sudden appearance of a father or a mother. Jimmie had wretchedly watched the departure of his companions. It involved the loss of his position as a lad who controlled the privileges of his father's grounds, but then he knew that in the beginning he had no right to ask so many boys to be his guests.

Once on the sidewalk, however, they speedily forgot their shame as trespassers, and the large boy launched forth in a description of his success in the late trial of courage. As they went rapidly up the street, the little boy who had made the furtive expedition cried out confidently from the rear, "Yes, and I went almost up to him, didn't I, Willie?"

The large boy crushed him in a few words. "Huh!" he scoffed. "You only went a little way. I went clear up to him."

The pace of the other boys was so manly that the tiny thing had to trot, and he remained at the rear, getting entangled in their legs in his attempts to reach the front rank and become of some importance, dodging this way and that way, and always piping out his little claim to glory.

XXI

"By the way, Grace," said Trescott, looking into the dining room from his office door, "I wish you would send Jimmie to me before school-time."

When Jimmie came, he advanced so quietly that Trescott did not at first note him. "Oh," he said, wheeling from a cabinet, "here you are, young man."

"Yes, sir."

Trescott dropped into his chair and tapped the desk with a thoughtful finger. "Jimmie, what were you doing in the back garden yesterday—you and the other boys—to Henry?"

"We weren't doing anything, pa."

Trescott looked sternly into the raised eyes of his son. "Are you sure you were not annoying him in any way? Now what were you doing, exactly?"

"Why, we—why, we—now—Willie Dalzel said I dassent go right up to him, and I did; and then he did; and then—the other boys were 'fraid; and then—you comed."

Trescott groaned deeply. His countenance was so clouded in sorrow that the lad, bewildered by the mystery of it, burst suddenly forth in dismal lamentations. "There, there. Don't cry, Jim," said Trescott, going round the desk. "Only—" He sat in a great leather reading-chair, and took the boy on his knee. "Only I want to explain to you—"

After Jimmie had gone to school, and as Trescott was about to start on his round of morning calls, a message arrived from Doctor Moser. It set forth that the latter's sister was dying in the old homestead, twenty miles away up the valley, and asked Trescott to care for his patients for the day at least. There was also in the envelope a little history of each case and of what had already been done. Trescott replied to the messenger that he would gladly assent to the arrangement.

He noted that the first name on Moser's list was Winter, but this did not seem to strike him as an important fact. When its turn came, he rang the Winter bell. "Good morning, Mrs. Winter," he said, cheerfully, as the door was opened. "Doctor Moser has been obliged to leave town today, and he has asked me to come in his stead. How is the little girl this morning?"

Mrs. Winter had regarded him in stony surprise. At last she said: "Come in! I'll see my husband." She bolted into the house. Trescott entered the hall, and turned to the left into the sitting room.

Presently Winter shuffled through the door. His eyes flashed toward Trescott. He did not betray any desire to advance far into the room. "What do you want?" he said.

"What do I want? What do I want?" repeated Trescott, lifting his head suddenly. He had heard an utterly new challenge in the night of the jungle.

"Yes, that's what I want to know," snapped Winter. "What do you want?"

Trescott was silent for a moment. He consulted Moser's memoranda. "I see that your little girl's case is a trifle serious," he remarked. "I would advise you to call a physician soon. I will leave you a copy of Dr. Moser's record to give to any one you may call." He paused to transcribe the record on a page of his notebook. Tearing out the leaf, he extended it to Winter as he moved toward the door. The latter shrunk against the wall. His head was hanging as he reached for the paper. This caused him to grasp air, and so Trescott simply let the paper flutter to the feet of the other man.

"Good morning," said Trescott from the hall. This placid retreat seemed to suddenly arouse Winter to ferocity. It was as if he had then recalled all the truths which he had formulated to hurl at Trescott. So he followed him into the hall, and down the hall to the door, and through the door to the porch, barking in fiery rage from a respectful distance. As Trescott imperturbably turned the mare's head down the road, Winter stood on the porch, still yelping. He was like a little dog.

XXII

"Have you heard the news?" cried Carrie Dungen, as she sped toward Martha's kitchen. "Have you heard the news?" Her eyes were shining with delight.

"No," answered Martha's sister Kate, bending forward eagerly. "What was it? What was it?"

Carrie appeared triumphantly in the open door. "Oh, there's been an awful scene between Doctor Trescott and Jake Winter. I never thought that Jake Winter had any pluck at all, but this morning he told the doctor just what he thought of him."

"Well, what did he think of him?" asked Martha.

"Oh, he called him everything. Mrs. Howarth heard it through her front blinds. It was terrible, she says. It's all over town now. Everybody knows it."

"Didn't the doctor answer back?"

"No! Mrs. Howarth—she says he never said a word. He just walked down to his buggy and got in, and drove off as co-o-o-l. But Jake gave him jinks, by all accounts."

"But what did he say?" cried Kate, shrill and excited. She was evidently at some kind of a feast.

"Oh, he told him that Sadie had never been well since that night Henry Johnson frightened her at Theresa Page's party, and he held him responsible, and how dared he cross his threshold—and—and—and—"

"And what?" said Martha.

"Did he swear at him?" said Kate, in fearsome glee.

"No—not much. He did swear at him a little, but not more than a man does anyhow when he is real mad, Mrs. Howarth says."

"O-oh!" breathed Kate. "And did he call him any names?"

Martha, at her work, had been for a time in deep thought. She now interrupted the other. "It don't seem as if Sadie Winter had been sick since that time Henry Johnson got loose. She's been to school almost the whole time since then, hasn't she?"

They combined upon her in immediate indignation. "School? School? I should say not. Don't think for a moment. School!"

Martha wheeled from the sink. She held an iron spoon, and it seemed as if she was going to attack them. "Sadie Winter has passed here many a morning since then carrying her school bag. Where was she going? To a wedding?"

The others, long accustomed to a mental tyranny, speedily surrendered.

"Did she?" stammered Kate. "I never saw her."

Carrie Dungen made a weak gesture.

"If I had been Doctor Trescott," exclaimed Martha, loudly, "I'd have knocked that miserable Jake Winter's head off."

Kate and Carrie, exchanging glances, made an alliance in the air. "I don't see why you say that, Martha," replied Carrie, with considerable boldness, gaining support and sympathy from Kate's smile. "I don't see how anybody can be blamed for getting angry when their little girl gets almost scared to death and gets sick from it, and all that. Besides, everybody says—"

"Oh, I don't care what everybody says," said Martha.

"Well, you can't go against the whole town," answered Carrie, in sudden sharp defiance.

"No, Martha, you can't go against the whole town," piped Kate, following her leader rapidly.

" 'The whole town,' " cried Martha. "I'd like to know what you call 'the whole town.' Do you call these silly people who are scared of Henry Johnson 'the whole town'?"

"Why, Martha," said Carrie, in a reasoning tone, "you talk as if you wouldn't be scared of him!"

"No more would I," retorted Martha.

"O-oh, Martha, how you talk!" said Kate. "Why, the idea! Everybody's afraid of him."

Carrie was grinning. "You've never seen him, have you?" she asked, seductively.

"No," admitted Martha.

"Well, then, how do you know that you wouldn't be scared?"

Martha confronted her. "Have you ever seen him? No? Well, then, how do you know you *would* be scared?"

The allied forces broke out in chorus: "But, Martha, everybody says so. Everybody says so."

"Everybody says what?"

"Everybody that's seen him say they were frightened almost to death. 'Tisn't only women, but it's men too. It's awful."

Martha wagged her head solemnly. "I'd try not to be afraid of him."

"But supposing you could not help it?" said Kate.

"Yes, and look here," cried Carrie. "I'll tell you another thing. The Hannigans are going to move out of the house next door."

"On account of him?" demanded Martha.

Carrie nodded. "Mrs. Hannigan says so herself."

"Well, of all things!" ejaculated Martha. "Going to move, eh? You don't say so! Where they going to move to?"

"Down on Orchard Avenue."

"Well, of all things! Nice house?"

"I don't know about that. I haven't heard. But there's lots of nice houses on Orchard."

"Yes, but they're all taken," said Kate. "There isn't a vacant house on Orchard Avenue."

"Oh yes, there is," said Martha. "The old Hampstead house is vacant."

"Oh, of course," said Kate. "But then I don't believe Mrs. Hannigan would like it there. I wonder where they can be going to move to?"

"I'm sure I don't know," sighed Martha. "It must be to some place we don't know about."

"Well," said Carrie Dungen, after a general reflective silence, "it's easy enough to find out, anyhow."

"Who knows—around here?" asked Kate.

"Why, Mrs. Smith, and there she is in her garden," said Carrie, jumping to her feet. As she dashed out of the door, Kate and Martha crowded at the window. Carrie's voice rang out from near the steps. "Mrs. Smith! Mrs. Smith! Do you know where the Hannigans are going to move to?"

XXIII

The autumn smote the leaves, and the trees of Whilomville were panoplied in crimson and yellow. The winds grew stronger, and in the melancholy purple of the nights the home shine of a window became a finer thing. The little boys, watching the sear and sorrowful leaves drifting down from the maples, dreamed of the near time when they could heap bushels in the streets and burn them during the abrupt evenings.

Three men walked down Niagara Avenue. As they approached Judge Hagenthorpe's house he came down his walk to meet them in the manner of one who has been waiting.

"Are you ready, Judge?" one said.

"All ready," he answered.

The four then walked to Trescott's house. He received them in his office, where he had been reading. He seemed surprised at this visit of four very active and influential citizens, but he had nothing to say of it.

After they were all seated, Trescott looked expectantly from one face to another. There was a little silence. It was broken by John Twelve, the wholesale grocer, who was worth $400,000, and reported to be worth over a million.

"Well, doctor," he said, with a short laugh, "I suppose we might as well admit at once that we've come to interfere in something which is none of our business."

"Why, what is it?" asked Trescott, again looking from one face to another. He seemed to appeal particularly to Judge Hagenthorpe, but the old man had his chin lowered musingly to his cane, and would not look at him.

"It's about what nobody talks of—much," said Twelve. "It's about Henry Johnson."

Trescott squared himself in his chair. "Yes?" he said.

Having delivered himself of the title, Twelve seemed to become more easy. "Yes," he answered, blandly, "we wanted to talk to you about it."

"Yes?" said Trescott.

Twelve abruptly advanced on the main attack. "Now see here, Trescott, we like you, and we have come to talk right out about this business. It may be none of our affairs and all that, and as for me, I don't mind if you tell me so; but I am not going to keep quiet and see you ruin yourself. And that's how we all feel."

"I am not ruining myself," answered Trescott.

"No, maybe you are not exactly ruining yourself," said Twelve, slowly, "but you are doing yourself a great deal of harm. You have changed from being the leading doctor in town to about the last one. It is mainly because there are always a large number of people who are very thoughtless fools, of course, but then that doesn't change the condition."

A man who had not heretofore spoken said, solemnly, "It's the women."

"Well, what I want to say is this," resumed Twelve: "Even if there are a lot of fools in the world, we can't see any reason why you should ruin yourself by opposing them. You can't teach them anything, you know."

"I am not trying to teach them anything." Trescott smiled wearily. "I—it is a matter of—well—"

"And there are a good many of us that admire you for it immensely," interrupted Twelve; "but that isn't going to change the minds of all those ninnies."

"It's the women," stated the advocate of this view again.

"Well, what I want to say is this," said Twelve. "We want you to get out of this trouble and strike your old gait again. You are simply killing your practice through your infernal pig-headedness. Now this thing is out of the ordinary, but there must be ways to—to beat the game somehow, you see. So we've talked it over—about a dozen of us—and, as I say, if you want to tell us to mind our own business, why, go ahead; but we've talked it over, and we've come to the conclusion that the only way to do is to get Johnson a place somewhere off up the valley, and—"

Trescott wearily gestured. "You don't know, my friend. Everybody is so afraid of him, they can't even give him good care. Nobody can attend to him as I do myself."

"But I have a little no-good farm up beyond Clarence Mountain that I was going to give to Henry," cried Twelve, aggrieved. "And if you— and if you—if you—through your house burning down, or anything—why, all the boys were prepared to take him right off your hands, and—and—"

Trescott arose and went to the window. He turned his back upon them. They sat waiting in silence. When he returned he kept his face in the shadow. "No, John Twelve," he said, "it can't be done."

There was another stillness. Suddenly a man stirred on his chair.

"Well, then, a public institution—" he began.

"No," said Trescott; "public institutions are all very good, but he is not going to one."

In the background of the group old Judge Hagenthorpe was thought-fully smoothing the polished ivory head of his cane.

XXIV

Trescott loudly stamped the snow from his feet and shook the flakes from his shoulders. When he entered the house he went at once to the dining room, and then to the sitting room. Jimmie was there, reading painfully in a large book concerning giraffes and tigers and crocodiles.

"Where is your mother, Jimmie?" asked Trescott.

"I don't know, pa," answered the boy. "I think she is upstairs."

Trescott went to the foot of the stairs and called, but there came no answer. Seeing that the door of the little drawing room was open, he entered. The room was bathed in the half-light that came from the four dull panes of mica in the front of the great stove. As his eyes grew used to the shadows he saw his wife curled in an armchair. He went to her. "Why, Grace," he said, "didn't you hear me calling you?"

She made no answer, and as he bent over the chair he heard her trying to smother a sob in the cushion.

"Grace!" he cried. "You're crying!"

She raised her face. "I've got a headache, a dreadful headache, Ned."

"A headache?" he repeated, in surprise and incredulity.

He pulled a chair close to hers. Later, as he cast his eye over the zone of light shed by the dull red panes, he saw that a low table had been drawn close to the stove, and that it was burdened with many small cups and plates of uncut tea-cake. He remembered that the day was Wednesday, and that his wife received on Wednesday.

"Who was here today, Gracie?" he asked.

From his shoulder there came a mumble, "Mrs. Twelve."

"Was she—um," he said. "Why—didn't Anna Hagenthorpe come over?" The mumble from his shoulder continued, "She wasn't well enough."

Glancing down at the cups, Trescott mechanically counted them. There were fifteen of them. "There, there," he said. "Don't cry, Grace. Don't cry."

The wind was whining round the house, and the snow beat aslant upon the windows. Sometimes the coal in the stove settled with a crumbling sound, and the four panes of mica flashed a sudden new crimson. As he sat holding her head on his shoulder, Trescott found himself occasionally trying to count the cups. There were fifteen of them.

August, 1898
[*Harper's Magazine*, Vol. 97, pp. 343–376.]

HIS NEW MITTENS*

Little Horace was walking home from school, brilliantly decorated by a pair of new red mittens. A number of boys were snowballing gleefully in a field. They hailed him. "Come on, Horace! We're having a battle."

Horace was sad. "No," he said, "I can't, I've got to go home." At noon his mother had admonished him: "Now, Horace, you come straight home as soon as school is out. Do you hear? And don't you get them nice new mittens all wet, either. Do you hear?" Also his aunt had said: "I declare, Emily, it's a shame the way you allow that child to ruin his things." She had meant mittens. To his mother, Horace had dutifully replied, "Yes'm." But he now loitered in the vicinity of the group of uproarious boys, who were yelling like hawks as the white balls flew.

Some of them immediately analyzed this extraordinary hesitancy. "Hah!" they paused to scoff, "afraid of your new mittens, ain't you?" Some smaller boys, who were not yet so wise in discerning motives, applauded this attack with unreasonable vehemence. "A-fray-ed of his mit-tens! A-fray-ed of his mit-tens." They sang these lines to cruel and monotonous music which is as old perhaps as American childhood, and which it is the privi-

* A part of *Whilomville Stories*, though not included in the original edition.

lege of the emancipated adult to completely forget. "A-fray-ed of his mittens!"

Horace cast a tortured glance toward his playmates, and then dropped
his eyes to the snow at his feet. Presently he turned to the trunk of one
of the great maple trees that lined the curb. He made a pretense of closely
examining the rough and virile bark. To his mind, this familiar street of
Whilomville seemed to grow dark in the thick shadow of shame. The trees
and the houses were now palled in purple.

"A-fray-ed of his mit-tens!" The terrible music had in it a meaning from
the moonlit war drums of chanting cannibals.

At last Horace, with supreme effort, raised his head. " 'Tain't them I
care about," he said, gruffly. "I've got to go home. That's all."

Whereupon each boy held his left forefinger as if it were a pencil and
began to sharpen it derisively with his right forefinger. They came closer,
and sang like a trained chorus, "A-fray-ed of his mit-tens!"

When he raised his voice to deny the charge it was simply lost in the
screams of the mob. He was alone, fronting all the traditions of boyhood
held before him by inexorable representatives. To such a low state had
he fallen that one lad, a mere baby, outflanked him and then struck him
in the cheek with a heavy snowball. The act was acclaimed with loud
jeers. Horace turned to dart at his assailant, but there was an immediate
demonstration on the other flank, and he found himself obliged to keep
his face toward the hilarious crew of tormentors. The baby retreated in
safety to the rear of the crowd, where he was received with fulsome compliments upon his daring. Horace retreated slowly up the walk. He continually tried to make them heed him, but the only sound was the chant,
"A-fray-ed of his mit-tens!" In this desperate withdrawal the beset and
haggard boy suffered more than is the common lot of man.

Being a boy himself, he did not understand boys at all. He had, of
course, the dismal conviction that they were going to dog him to his
grave. But near the corner of the field they suddenly seemed to forget all
about it. Indeed, they possessed only the malevolence of so many flitter-
headed sparrows. The interest had swung capriciously to some other matter. In a moment they were off in the field again, carousing amid the snow.
Some authoritative boy had probably said, "Aw, come on!"

As the pursuit ceased, Horace ceased his retreat. He spent some time
in what was evidently an attempt to adjust his self-respect, and then began
to wander furtively down toward the group. He, too, had undergone an
important change. Perhaps his sharp agony was only as durable as the
malevolence of the others. In this boyish life obedience to some unformulated creed of manners was enforced with capricious but merciless
rigor. However, they were, after all, his comrades, his friends.

They did not heed his return. They were engaged in an altercation. It had evidently been planned that this battle was between Indians and soldiers. The smaller and weaker boys had been induced to appear as Indians in the initial skirmish, but they were now very sick of it, and were reluctantly but steadfastly affirming their desire for a change of caste. The larger boys had all won great distinction, devastating Indians materially, and they wished the war to go on as planned. They explained vociferously that it was proper for the soldiers always to thrash the Indians. The little boys did not pretend to deny the truth of this argument; they confined themselves to the simple statement that, in that case, they wished to be soldiers. Each little boy willingly appealed to the others to remain Indians, but as for himself he reiterated his desire to enlist as a soldier. The larger boys were in despair over this dearth of enthusiasm in the small Indians. They alternately wheedled and bullied, but they could not persuade the little boys, who were really suffering dreadful humiliation rather than submit to another onslaught of soldiers. They were called all the baby names that had the power of stinging deep into their pride, but they remained firm.

Then a formidable lad, a leader of reputation, one who could whip many boys that wore long trousers, suddenly blew out his cheeks and shouted, "Well, all right then. I'll be an Indian myself. Now." The little boys greeted with cheers this addition to their wearied ranks, and seemed then content. But matters were not mended in the least, because all of the personal following of the formidable lad, with the addition of every outsider, spontaneously forsook the flag and declared themselves Indians. There were now no soldiers. The Indians had carried everything unanimously. The formidable lad used his influence, but his influence could not shake the loyalty of his friends, who refused to fight under any colors but his colors.

Plainly there was nothing for it but to coerce the little ones. The formidable lad again became a soldier, and then graciously permitted to join him all the real fighting strength of the crowd, leaving behind a most forlorn band of little Indians. Then the soldiers attacked the Indians, exhorting them to opposition at the same time.

The Indians at first adopted a policy of hurried surrender, but this had no success, as none of the surrenders were accepted. They then turned to flee, bawling out protests. The ferocious soldiers pursued them amid shouts. The battle widened, developing all manner of marvelous detail.

Horace had turned toward home several times, but, as a matter of fact, this scene held him in a spell. It was fascinating beyond anything which the grown man understands. He had always in the back of his head a sense of guilt, even a sense of impending punishment for disobedience, but they could not weigh with the delirium of this snow battle.

II

One of the raiding soldiers, espying Horace, called out in passing, "A-fray-ed of his mit-tens!" Horace flinched at this renewal, and the other lad paused to taunt him again. Horace scooped some snow, molded it into a ball, and flung it at the other. "Ho!" cried the boy, "you're an Indian, are you? Hey, fellers, here's an Indian that ain't been killed yet." He and Horace engaged in a duel in which both were in such haste to mold snowballs that they had little time for aiming.

Horace once struck his opponent squarely in the chest. "Hey," he shouted, "you're dead. You can't fight any more, Pete. I killed you. You're dead."

The other boy flushed red, but he continued frantically to make ammunition. "You never touched me!" he retorted, glowering. "You never touched me! Where, now?" he added, defiantly. "Where did you hit me?"

"On the coat! Right on your breast! You can't fight any more! You're dead!"

"You never!"

"I did, too! Hey, fellers, ain't he dead? I hit 'im square!"

"He never!"

Nobody had seen the affair, but some of the boys took sides in absolute accordance with their friendship for one of the concerned parties. Horace's opponent went about contending, "He never touched me! He never came near me! He never came near me!"

The formidable leader now came forward and accosted Horace. "What was you? An Indian? Well, then, you're dead—that's all. He hit you. I saw him."

"Me?" shrieked Horace. "He never came within a mile of me——"

At that moment he heard his name called in a certain familiar tune of two notes, with the last note shrill and prolonged. He looked toward the sidewalk, and saw his mother standing there in her widow's weeds, with two brown paper parcels under her arm. A silence had fallen upon all the boys. Horace moved slowly toward his mother. She did not seem to note his approach; she was gazing austerely off through the naked branches of the maples where two crimson sunset bars lay on the deep blue sky.

At a distance of ten paces Horace made a desperate venture. "Oh, ma," he whined, "can't I stay out for a while?"

"No," she answered solemnly, "you come with me." Horace knew that profile; it was the inexorable profile. But he continued to plead, because it was not beyond his mind that a great show of suffering now might diminish his suffering later.

He did not dare to look back at his playmates. It was already a public scandal that he could not stay out as late as other boys, and he could imagine his standing now that he had been again dragged off by his mother in sight of the whole world. He was a profoundly miserable human being.

Aunt Martha opened the door for them. Light streamed about her straight skirt. "Oh," she said, "so you found him on the road, eh? Well, I declare! It was about time!"

Horace slunk into the kitchen. The stove, straddling out on its four iron legs, was gently humming. Aunt Martha had evidently just lighted the lamp, for she went to it and began to twist the wick experimentally.

"Now," said the mother, "let's see them mittens."

Horace's chin sank. The aspiration of the criminal, the passionate desire for an asylum from retribution, from justice, was aflame in his heart. "I—I—don't—don't know where they are," he gasped finally, as he passed his hand over his pockets.

"Horace," intoned his mother, "you are tellin' me a story!"

" 'Tain't a story," he answered, just above his breath. He looked like a sheep-stealer.

His mother held him by the arm, and began to search his pockets. Almost at once she was able to bring forth a pair of very wet mittens. "Well, I declare!" cried Aunt Martha. The two women went close to the lamp, and minutely examined the mittens, turning them over and over. Afterward, when Horace looked up, his mother's sad-lined, homely face was turned toward him. He burst into tears.

His mother drew a chair near the stove. "Just you sit there now, until I tell you to git off." He sidled meekly into the chair. His mother and his aunt went briskly about the business of preparing supper. They did not display a knowledge of his existence; they carried an effect of oblivion so far that they even did not speak to each other. Presently they went into the dining and living room; Horace could hear the dishes rattling. His Aunt Martha brought a plate of food, placed it on a chair near him, and went away without a word.

Horace instantly decided that he would not touch a morsel of the food. He had often used this ruse in dealing with his mother. He did not know why it brought her to terms, but certainly it sometimes did.

The mother looked up when the aunt returned to the other room. "Is he eatin' his supper?" she asked.

The maiden aunt, fortified in ignorance, gazed with pity and contempt upon this interest. "Well, now, Emily, how do I know?" she queried. "Was I goin' to stand over 'im? Of all the worryin' you do about that child! It's a shame the way you're bringin' up that child."

"Well, he ought to eat somethin'. It won't do fer him to go without eatin'," the mother retorted weakly.

Aunt Martha, profoundly scorning the policy of concession which these words meant, uttered a long, contemptuous sigh.

III

Alone in the kitchen, Horace stared with somber eyes at the plate of food. For a long time he betrayed no sign of yielding. His mood was adamantine. He was resolved not to sell his vengeance for bread, cold ham, and a pickle, and yet it must be known that the sight of them affected him powerfully. The pickle in particular was notable for its seductive charm. He surveyed it darkly.

But at last, unable to longer endure his state, his attitude in the presence of the pickle, he put out an inquisitive finger and touched it, and it was cool and green and plump. Then a full conception of the cruel woe of his situation swept upon him suddenly, and his eyes filled with tears, which began to move down his cheeks. He sniffled. His heart was black with hatred. He painted in his mind scenes of deadly retribution. His mother would be taught that he was not one to endure persecution meekly, without raising an arm in his defense. And so his dreams were of a slaughter of feelings, and near the end of them his mother was pictured as coming, bowed with pain, to his feet. Weeping, she implored his charity. Would he forgive her? No; his once tender heart had been turned to stone by her injustice. He could not forgive her. She must pay the inexorable penalty.

The first item in this horrible plan was the refusal of the food. This he knew by experience would work havoc in his mother's heart. And so he grimly waited.

But suddenly it occurred to him that the first part of his revenge was in danger of failing. The thought struck him that his mother might not capitulate in the usual way. According to his recollection, the time was more than due when she should come in, worried, sadly affectionate, and ask him if he was ill. It had then been his custom to hint in a resigned voice that he was the victim of secret disease, but that he preferred to suffer in silence and alone. If she was obdurate in her anxiety, he always asked her in a gloomy, low voice to go away and leave him to suffer in silence and alone in the darkness without food. He had known this maneuvering to result even in pie.

But what was the meaning of the long pause and the stillness? Had his old and valued ruse betrayed him? As the truth sank into his mind, he supremely loathed life, the world, his mother. Her heart was beating back the besiegers; he was a defeated child.

He wept for a time before deciding upon the final stroke. He would run away. In a remote corner of the world he would become some sort of bloody-handed person driven to a life of crime by the barbarity of his mother. She should never know his fate. He would torture her for years with doubts and doubts, and drive her implacably to a repentant grave. Nor would his Aunt Martha escape. Some day, a century hence, when his mother was dead, he would write to his Aunt Martha, and point out her part in the blighting of his life. For one blow against him now he would, in time, deal back a thousand—aye, ten thousand.

He arose and took his coat and cap. As he moved stealthily toward the door he cast a glance backward at the pickle. He was tempted to take it, but he knew that if he left the plate inviolate his mother would feel even worse.

A blue snow was falling. People, bowed forward, were moving briskly along the walks. The electric lamps hummed amid showers of flakes. As Horace emerged from the kitchen, a shrill squall drove the flakes around the corner of the house. He cowered away from it, and its violence illumined his mind vaguely in new directions. He deliberated upon a choice of remote corners of the globe. He found that he had no plans which were definite enough in a geographical way, but without much loss of time he decided upon California. He moved briskly as far as his mother's front gate on the road to California. He was off at last. His success was a trifle dreadful; his throat choked.

But at the gate he paused. He did not know if his journey to California would be shorter if he went down Niagara Avenue or off through Hogan Street. As the storm was very cold and the point was very important, he decided to withdraw for reflection to the woodshed. He entered the dark shanty, and took seat upon the old chopping-block upon which he was supposed to perform for a few minutes every afternoon when he returned from school. The wind screamed and shouted at the loose boards, and there was a rift of snow on the floor to leeward of a crack.

Here the idea of starting for California on such a night departed from his mind, leaving him ruminating miserably upon his martyrdom. He saw nothing for it but to sleep all night in the woodshed and start for California in the morning bright and early. Thinking of his bed, he kicked over the floor and found that the innumerable chips were all frozen tightly, bedded in ice.

Later he viewed with joy some signs of excitement in the house. The flare of a lamp moved rapidly from window to window. Then the kitchen door slammed loudly and a shawled figure sped toward the gate. At last he was making them feel his power. The shivering child's face was lit with saturnine glee as in the darkness of the woodshed he gloated over the evi-

dences of consternation in his home. The shawled figure had been his
Aunt Martha dashing with the alarm to the neighbors.

The cold of the woodshed was tormenting him. He endured only because of the terror he was causing. But then it occurred to him that, if
they instituted a search for him, they would probably examine the woodshed. He knew that it would not be manful to be caught so soon. He was
not positive now that he was going to remain away for ever, but at any
rate he was bound to inflict some more damage before allowing himself
to be captured. If he merely succeeded in making his mother angry, she
would thrash him on sight. He must prolong the time in order to be safe.
If he held out properly, he was sure of a welcome of love, even though
he should drip with crimes.

Evidently the storm had increased, for when he went out it swung him
violently with its rough and merciless strength. Panting, stung, half-
blinded with the driving flakes, he was now a waif, exiled, friendless,
and poor. With a bursting heart, he thought of his home and his mother.
To his forlorn vision they were as far away as heaven.

IV

Horace was undergoing changes of feeling so rapidly that he was merely
moved hither and then thither like a kite. He was now aghast at the
merciless ferocity of his mother. It was she who had thrust him into this
wild storm, and she was perfectly indifferent to his fate, perfectly indifferent. The forlorn wanderer could no longer weep. The strong sobs caught
at his throat, making his breath come in short, quick snuffles. All in him
was conquered save the enigmatical childish ideal of form, manner. This
principle still held out, and it was the only thing between him and submission. When he surrendered, he must surrender in a way that deferred to the undefined code. He longed simply to go to the kitchen and
stumble in, but his unfathomable sense of fitness forbade him.

Presently he found himself at the head of Niagara Avenue, staring
through the snow into the blazing windows of Stickney's butcher shop.
Stickney was the family butcher, not so much because of a superiority to
other Whilomville butchers as because he lived next door and had been an
intimate friend of the father of Horace. Rows of glowing pigs hung head
downward behind the tables, which bore huge pieces of red beef. Clumps
of attenuated turkeys were suspended here and there. Stickney, hale and
smiling, was bantering with a woman in a cloak, who, with a monster
basket on her arm, was dickering for eight cents' worth of something.
Horace watched them through a crusted pane. When the woman came
out and passed him, he went toward the door. He touched the latch with
his finger, but withdrew again suddenly to the sidewalk. Inside Stickney
was whistling cheerily and assorting his knives.

Finally Horace went desperately forward, opened the door, and entered the shop. His head hung low. Stickney stopped whistling. "Hello, young man," he cried; "what brings you here?"

Horace halted, but said nothing. He swung one foot to and fro over the sawdust floor.

Stickney had placed his two fat hands palms downward and wide apart on the table, in the attitude of a butcher facing a customer, but now he straightened. "Here," he said, "what's wrong? What's wrong, kid?"

"Nothin'," answered Horace, huskily. He labored for a moment with something in his throat, and afterwards added, "O'ny—I've—I've run away, and——"

"Run away!" shouted Stickney. "Run away from what? Who?"

"From—home," answered Horace. "I don't like it there any more. I——" He had arranged an oration to win the sympathy of the butcher; he had prepared a table setting forth the merits of his case in the most logical fashion, but it was as if the wind had been knocked out of his mind. "I've run away. I——"

Stickney reached an enormous hand over the array of beef, and firmly grappled the emigrant. Then he swung himself to Horace's side. His face was stretched with laughter, and he playfully shook his prisoner. "Come —come—come. What dashed nonsense is this? Run away, hey? Run away?" Whereupon the child's long-tried spirit found vent in howls.

"Come, come," said Stickney, busily. "Never mind now, never mind. You just come along with me. It'll be all right. I'll fix it. Never you mind."

Five minutes later the butcher, with a great ulster over his apron, was leading the boy homeward.

At the very threshold, Horace raised his last flag of pride. "No—no," he sobbed. "I don't want to. I don't want to go in there." He braced his foot against the step and made a very respectable resistance.

"Now Horace," cried the butcher. He thrust open the door with a bang. "Hello there!" Across the dark kitchen the door to the living room opened and Aunt Martha appeared. "You've found him!" she screamed.

"We've come to make a call," roared the butcher. At the entrance to the living room a silence fell upon them all. Upon a couch Horace saw his mother lying limp, pale as death, her eyes gleaming with pain. There was an electric pause before she swung a waxen hand toward Horace. "My child," she murmured, tremulously. Whereupon the sinister person addressed, with a prolonged wail of grief and joy, ran to her with speed. "Mam-ma! Mam-ma! Oh, mam-ma!" She was not able to speak in a known tongue as she folded him in her weak arms.

Aunt Martha turned defiantly upon the butcher, because her face betrayed her. She was crying. She made a gesture half military, half feminine.

"Won't you have a glass of our root beer, Mr. Stickney? We make it ourselves."

November, 1898
[*McClure's Magazine*, Vol. 12, pp. 54–61.]

THE BLUE HOTEL

I

The Palace Hotel at Fort Romper was painted a light blue, a shade that is on the legs of a kind of heron, causing the bird to declare its position against any background. The Palace Hotel, then, was always screaming and howling in a way that made the dazzling winter landscape of Nebraska seem only a gray swampish hush. It stood alone on the prairie, and when the snow was falling the town two hundred yards away was not visible. But when the traveler alighted at the railway station he was obliged to pass the Palace Hotel before he could come upon the company of low clapboard houses which composed Fort Romper, and it was not to be thought that any traveler could pass the Palace Hotel without looking at it. Pat Scully, the proprietor, had proved himself a master of strategy when he chose his paints. It is true that on clear days, when the great transcontinental expresses, long lines of swaying Pullmans, swept through Fort Romper, passengers were overcome at the sight, and the cult that knows the brown-reds and the subdivisions of the dark greens of the East expressed shame, pity, horror, in a laugh. But to the citizens of this prairie town and to the people who would naturally stop there, Pat Scully had performed a feat. With this opulence and splendor, these creeds, classes, egotisms, that streamed through Romper on the rails day after day, they had no color in common.

As if the displayed delights of such a blue hotel were not sufficiently enticing, it was Scully's habit to go every morning and evening to meet the leisurely trains that stopped at Romper and work his seductions upon any man that he might see wavering, gripsack in hand.

One morning, when a snow-crusted engine dragged its long string of freight cars and its one passenger coach to the station, Scully performed the marvel of catching three men. One was a shaky and quick-eyed Swede, with a great shining cheap valise; one was a tall bronzed cowboy, who was on his way to a ranch near the Dakota line; one was a little silent man from the East, who didn't look it, and didn't announce it. Scully practically made them prisoners. He was so nimble and merry and kindly that each probably felt it would be the height of brutality to try to escape.

They trudged off over the creaking board sidewalks in the wake of the eager little Irishman. He wore a heavy fur cap squeezed tightly down on his head. It caused his two red ears to stick out stiffly, as if they were made of tin.

At last, Scully, elaborately, with boisterous hospitality, conducted them through the portals of the blue hotel. The room which they entered was small. It seemed to be merely a proper temple for an enormous stove, which, in the center, was humming with godlike violence. At various points on its surface the iron had become luminous and glowed yellow from the heat. Beside the stove Scully's son Johnnie was playing High-Five with an old farmer who had whiskers both gray and sandy. They were quarreling. Frequently the old farmer turned his face toward a box of sawdust —colored brown from tobacco juice—that was behind the stove, and spat with an air of great impatience and irritation. With a loud flourish of words Scully destroyed the game of cards, and bustled his son upstairs with part of the baggage of the new guests. He himself conducted them to three basins of the coldest water in the world. The cowboy and the Easterner burnished themselves fiery red with this water, until it seemed to be some kind of metal polish. The Swede, however, merely dipped his fingers gingerly and with trepidation. It was notable that throughout this series of small ceremonies the three travelers were made to feel that Scully was very benevolent. He was conferring great favors upon them. He handed the towel from one to another with an air of philanthropic impulse.

Afterward they went to the first room, and, sitting about the stove, listened to Scully's officious clamor at his daughters, who were preparing the midday meal. They reflected in the silence of experienced men who tread carefully amid new people. Nevertheless, the old farmer, stationary, invincible in his chair near the warmest part of the stove, turned his face from the sawdust box frequently and addressed a glowing commonplace to the strangers. Usually he was answered in short but adequate sentences by either the cowboy or the Easterner. The Swede said nothing. He seemed to be occupied in making furtive estimates of each man in the room. One might have thought that he had the sense of silly suspicion which comes to guilt. He resembled a badly frightened man.

Later, at dinner, he spoke a little, addressing his conversation entirely to Scully. He volunteered that he had come from New York, where for ten years he had worked as a tailor. These facts seemed to strike Scully as fascinating, and afterward he volunteered that he had lived at Romper for fourteen years. The Swede asked about the crops and the price of labor. He seemed barely to listen to Scully's extended replies. His eyes continued to rove from man to man.

Finally, with a laugh and a wink, he said that some of these Western communities were very dangerous; and after his statement he straightened his legs under the table, tilted his head, and laughed again, loudly. It was plain that the demonstration had no meaning to the others. They looked at him wondering and in silence.

II

As the men trooped heavily back into the front room, the two little windows presented views of a turmoiling sea of snow. The huge arms of the wind were making attempts—mighty, circular, futile—to embrace the flakes as they sped. A gatepost like a still man with a blanched face stood aghast amid this profligate fury. In a hearty voice Scully announced the presence of a blizzard. The guests of the blue hotel, lighting their pipes, assented with grunts of lazy masculine contentment. No island of the sea could be exempt in the degree of this little room with its humming stove. Johnnie, son of Scully, in a tone which defined his opinion of his ability as a card player, challenged the old farmer of both gray and sandy whiskers to a game of High-Five. The farmer agreed with a contemptuous and bitter scoff. They sat close to the stove, and squared their knees under a wide board. The cowboy and the Easterner watched the game with interest. The Swede remained near the window, aloof, but with a countenance that showed signs of an inexplicable excitement.

The play of Johnnie and the graybeard was suddenly ended by another quarrel. The old man arose while casting a look of heated scorn at his adversary. He slowly buttoned his coat, and then stalked with fabulous dignity from the room. In the discreet silence of all other men the Swede laughed. His laughter rang somehow childish. Men by this time had begun to look at him askance, as if they wished to inquire what ailed him.

A new game was formed jocosely. The cowboy volunteered to become the partner of Johnnie, and they all then turned to ask the Swede to throw in his lot with the little Easterner. He asked some questions about the game, and, learning that it wore many names, and that he had played it when it was under an alias, he accepted the invitation. He strode toward the men nervously, as if he expected to be assaulted. Finally, seated, he gazed from face to face and laughed shrilly. This laugh was so strange that the Easterner looked up quickly, the cowboy sat intent and with his mouth open, and Johnnie paused, holding the cards with still fingers.

Afterward there was a short silence. Then Johnnie said, "Well, let's get at it. Come on now!" They pulled their chairs forward until their knees were bunched under the board. They began to play, and their interest in the game caused the others to forget the manner of the Swede.

The cowboy was a board-whacker. Each time that he held superior cards he whanged them, one by one, with exceeding force, down upon

the improvised table, and took the tricks with a glowing air of prowess
and pride that sent thrills of indignation into the hearts of his opponents.
A game with a board-whacker in it is sure to become intense. The countenances of the Easterner and the Swede were miserable whenever the cowboy thundered down his aces and kings, while Johnnie, his eyes gleaming
with joy, chuckled and chuckled.

Because of the absorbing play none considered the strange ways of the
Swede. They paid strict heed to the game. Finally, during a lull caused
by a new deal, the Swede suddenly addressed Johnnie: "I suppose there
have been a good many men killed in this room." The jaws of the others
dropped and they looked at him.

"What in hell are you talking about?" said Johnnie.

The Swede laughed again his blatant laugh, full of a kind of false
courage and defiance. "Oh, you know what I mean all right," he answered.

"I'm a liar if I do!" Johnnie protested. The card was halted, and the
men stared at the Swede. Johnnie evidently felt that as the son of the proprietor he should make a direct inquiry. "Now, what might you be drivin'
at, mister?" he asked. The Swede winked at him. It was a wink full of cunning. His fingers shook on the edge of the board. "Oh, maybe you think I
have been to nowheres. Maybe you think I'm a tenderfoot?"

"I don't know nothin' about you," answered Johnnie, "and I don't give
a damn where you've been. All I got to say is that I don't know what you're
driving at. There hain't never been nobody killed in this room."

The cowboy, who had been steadily gazing at the Swede, then spoke:
"What's wrong with you, mister?"

Apparently it seemed to the Swede that he was formidably menaced.
He shivered and turned white near the corners of his mouth. He sent
an appealing glance in the direction of the little Easterner. During these
moments he did not forget to wear his air of advanced pot-valor. "They
say they don't know what I mean," he remarked mockingly to the
Easterner.

The latter answered after prolonged and cautious reflection. "I don't
understand you," he said, impassively.

The Swede made a movement then which announced that he thought
he had encountered treachery from the only quarter where he had expected sympathy, if not help. "Oh, I see you are all against me. I see—"

The cowboy was in a state of deep stupefaction. "Say," he cried, as he
tumbled the deck violently down upon the board, "say, what are you
gittin' at, hey?"

The Swede sprang up with the celerity of a man escaping from a snake
on the floor. "I don't want to fight!" he shouted. "I don't want to fight!"

The cowboy stretched his long legs indolently and deliberately. His hands were in his pockets. He spat into the sawdust box. "Well, who the hell thought you did?" he inquired.

The Swede backed rapidly toward a corner of the room. His hands were out protectingly in front of his chest, but he was making an obvious struggle to control his fright. "Gentlemen," he quavered, "I suppose I am going to be killed before I can leave this house! I suppose I am going to be killed before I can leave this house!" In his eyes was the dying-swan look. Through the windows could be seen the snow turning blue in the shadow of dusk. The wind tore at the house, and some loose thing beat regularly against the clapboards like a spirit tapping.

A door opened, and Scully himself entered. He paused in surprise as he noted the tragic attitude of the Swede. Then he said, "What's the matter here?"

The Swede answered him swiftly and eagerly: "These men are going to kill me."

"Kill you!" ejaculated Scully. "Kill you! What are you talkin'?"

The Swede made the gesture of a martyr.

Scully wheeled sternly upon his son. "What is this, Johnnie?"

The lad had grown sullen. "Damned if I know," he answered. "I can't make no sense to it." He began to shuffle the cards, fluttering them together with an angry snap. "He says a good many men have been killed in this room, or something like that. And he says he's goin' to be killed here too. I don't know what ails him. He's crazy, I shouldn't wonder."

Scully then looked for explanation to the cowboy, but the cowboy simply shrugged his shoulders.

"Kill you?" said Scully again to the Swede. "Kill you? Man, you're off your nut."

"Oh, I know," burst out the Swede. "I know what will happen. Yes, I'm crazy—yes. Yes, of course, I'm crazy—yes. But I know one thing—" There was a sort of sweat of misery and terror upon his face. "I know I won't get out of here alive."

The cowboy drew a deep breath, as if his mind was passing into the last stages of dissolution. "Well, I'm doggoned," he whispered to himself.

Scully wheeled suddenly and faced his son. "You've been troublin' this man!"

Johnnie's voice was loud with its burden of grievance. "Why, good Gawd, I ain't done nothin' to 'im."

The Swede broke in. "Gentlemen, do not disturb yourselves. I will leave this house. I will go away, because"—he accused them dramatically with his glance—"because I do not want to be killed."

Scully was furious with his son. "Will you tell me what is the matter, you young divil? What's the matter, anyhow? Speak out!"

"Blame it!" cried Johnnie in despair, "don't I tell you I don't know? He —he says we want to kill him, and that's all I know. I can't tell what ails him."

The Swede continued to repeat: "Never mind, Mr. Scully; never mind. I will leave this house. I will go away, because I do not wish to be killed. Yes, of course, I am crazy—yes. But I know one thing! I will go away. I will leave this house. Never mind, Mr. Scully; never mind. I will go away."

"You will not go 'way," said Scully. "You will not go 'way until I hear the reason of this business. If anybody has troubled you I will take care of him. This is my house. You are under my roof, and I will not allow any peaceable man to be troubled here." He cast a terrible eye upon Johnnie, the cowboy, and the Easterner.

"Never mind, Mr. Scully; never mind. I will go away. I do not wish to be killed." The Swede moved toward the door which opened upon the stairs. It was evidently his intention to go at once for his baggage.

"No, no," shouted Scully peremptorily; but the white-faced man slid by him and disappeared. "Now," said Scully severely, "what does this mane?"

Johnnie and the cowboy cried together: "Why, we didn't do nothin' to 'im!"

Scully's eyes were cold. "No," he said, "you didn't?"

Johnnie swore a deep oath. "Why, this is the wildest loon I ever see. We didn't do nothin' at all. We were jest sittin' here playin' cards, and he—"

The father suddenly spoke to the Easterner. "Mr. Blanc," he asked, "what has these boys been doin'?"

The Easterner reflected again. "I didn't see anything wrong at all," he said at last, slowly.

Scully began to howl. "But what does it mane?" He stared ferociously at his son. "I have a mind to lather you for this, me boy."

Johnnie was frantic. "Well, what have I done?" he bawled at his father.

III

"I think you are tongue-tied," said Scully finally to his son, the cowboy, and the Easterner; and at the end of this scornful sentence he left the room.

Upstairs the Swede was swiftly fastening the straps of his great valise. Once his back happened to be half turned toward the door, and, hearing a noise there, he wheeled and sprang up, uttering a loud cry. Scully's wrinkled visage showed grimly in the light of the small lamp he carried. This yellow effulgence, streaming upward, colored only his prominent features, and left his eyes, for instance, in mysterious shadow. He resembled a murderer.

"Man! man!" he exclaimed, "have you gone daffy?"

"Oh, no! Oh, no!" rejoined the other. "There are people in this world who know pretty nearly as much as you do—understand?"

For a moment they stood gazing at each other. Upon the Swede's deathly pale cheeks were two spots brightly crimson and sharply edged, as if they had been carefully painted. Scully placed the light on the table and sat himself on the edge of the bed. He spoke ruminatively. "By cracky, I never heard of such a thing in my life. It's a complete muddle. I can't, for the soul of me, think how you ever got this idea into your head." Presently he lifted his eyes and asked: "And did you sure think they were going to kill you?"

The Swede scanned the old man as if he wished to see into his mind. "I did," he said at last. He obviously suspected that this answer might precipitate an outbreak. As he pulled on a strap his whole arm shook, the elbow wavering like a bit of paper.

Scully banged his hand impressively on the footboard of the bed. "Why, man, we're goin' to have a line of ilictric streetcars in this town next spring."

"'A line of electric streetcars,'" repeated the Swede, stupidly.

"And," said Scully, "there's a new railroad goin' to be built down from Broken Arm to here. Not to mintion the four churches and the smashin' big brick schoolhouse. Then there's the big factory, too. Why, in two years Romper'll be a met-tro-*pol*-is."

Having finished the preparation of his baggage, the Swede straightened himself. "Mr. Scully," he said, with sudden hardihood, "how much do I owe you?"

"You don't owe me anythin'," said the old man, angrily.

"Yes, I do," retorted the Swede. He took seventy-five cents from his pocket and tendered it to Scully; but the latter snapped his fingers in disdainful refusal. However, it happened that they both stood gazing in a strange fashion at three silver pieces on the Swede's open palm.

"I'll not take your money," said Scully at last. "Not after what's been goin' on here." Then a plan seemed to strike him. "Here," he cried, picking up his lamp and moving toward the door. "Here! Come with me a minute."

"No," said the Swede, in overwhelming alarm.

"Yes," urged the old man. "Come on! I want you to come and see a picter —just across the hall—in my room."

The Swede must have concluded that his hour was come. His jaw dropped and his teeth showed like a dead man's. He ultimately followed Scully across the corridor, but he had the step of one hung in chains.

Scully flashed the light high on the wall of his own chamber. There was revealed a ridiculous photograph of a little girl. She was leaning against a balustrade of gorgeous decoration, and the formidable bang to her hair was prominent. The figure was as graceful as an upright sled-stake, and, withal, it was of the hue of lead. "There," said Scully, tenderly, "that's the picter of my little girl that died. Her name was Carrie. She had the purtiest hair you ever saw! I was that fond of her, she—"

Turning then, he saw that the Swede was not contemplating the picture at all, but, instead, was keeping keen watch on the gloom in the rear.

"Look, man!" cried Scully, heartily. "That's the picter of my little gal that died. Her name was Carrie. And then here's the picter of my oldest boy, Michael. He's a lawyer in Lincoln, an' doin' well. I gave that boy a grand eddication, and I'm glad for it now. He's a fine boy. Look at 'im now. Ain't he bold as blazes, him there in Lincoln, an honored an' respicted gintleman! An honored and respicted gintleman," concluded Scully with a flourish. And, so saying, he smote the Swede jovially on the back.

The Swede faintly smiled.

"Now," said the old man, "there's only one more thing." He dropped suddenly to the floor and thrust his head beneath the bed. The Swede could hear his muffled voice. "I'd keep it under me piller if it wasn't for that boy Johnnie. Then there's the old woman— Where is it now? I never put it twice in the same place. Ah, now come out with you!"

Presently he backed clumsily from under the bed, dragging with him an old coat rolled into a bundle. "I've fetched him," he muttered. Kneeling on the floor, he unrolled the coat and extracted from its heart a large yellow-brown whiskey bottle.

His first maneuver was to hold the bottle up to the light. Reassured, apparently, that nobody had been tampering with it, he thrust it with a generous movement toward the Swede.

The weak-kneed Swede was about to eagerly clutch this element of strength, but he suddenly jerked his hand away and cast a look of horror upon Scully.

"Drink," said the old man affectionately. He had risen to his feet, and now stood facing the Swede.

There was a silence. Then again Scully said: "Drink!"

The Swede laughed wildly. He grabbed the bottle, put it to his mouth; and as his lips curled absurdly around the opening and his throat worked, he kept his glance, burning with hatred, upon the old man's face.

IV

After the departure of Scully the three men, with the cardboard still upon their knees, preserved for a long time an astounded silence. Then Johnnie said: "That's the doddangedest Swede I ever see."

"He ain't no Swede," said the cowboy, scornfully.

"Well, what is he then?" cried Johnnie. "What is he then?"

"It's my opinion," replied the cowboy deliberately, "he's some kind of a Dutchman." It was a venerable custom of the country to entitle as Swedes all light-haired men who spoke with a heavy tongue. In consequence the idea of the cowboy was not without its daring. "Yes, sir," he repeated. "It's my opinion this feller is some kind of a Dutchman."

"Well, he says he's a Swede, anyhow," muttered Johnnie, sulkily. He turned to the Easterner: "What do you think, Mr. Blanc?"

"Oh, I don't know," replied the Easterner.

"Well, what do you think makes him act that way?" asked the cowboy.

"Why, he's frightened." The Easterner knocked his pipe against a rim of the stove. "He's clear frightened out of his boots."

"What at?" cried Johnnie and the cowboy together.

The Easterner reflected over his answer.

"What at?" cried the others again.

"Oh, I don't know, but it seems to me this man has been reading dime novels, and he thinks he's right out in the middle of it—the shootin' and stabbin' and all."

"But," said the cowboy, deeply scandalized, "this ain't Wyoming, ner none of them places. This is Nebrasker."

"Yes," added Johnnie, "an' why don't he wait till he gits *out West?*"

The traveled Easterner laughed. "It isn't different there even—not in these days. But he thinks he's right in the middle of hell."

Johnnie and the cowboy mused long.

"It's awful funny," remarked Johnnie at last.

"Yes," said the cowboy. "This is a queer game. I hope we don't git snowed in, because then we'd have to stand this here man bein' around with us all the time. That wouldn't be no good."

"I wish pop would throw him out," said Johnnie.

Presently they heard a loud stamping on the stairs, accompanied by ringing jokes in the voice of old Scully, and laughter, evidently from the Swede. The men around the stove stared vacantly at each other. "Gosh!" said the cowboy. The door flew open, and old Scully, flushed and anecdotal, came into the room. He was jabbering at the Swede, who followed him, laughing bravely. It was the entry of two roisterers from a banquet hall.

"Come now," said Scully sharply to the three seated men, "move up and give us a chance at the stove." The cowboy and the Easterner obediently sidled their chairs to make room for the newcomers. Johnnie, however, simply arranged himself in a more indolent attitude, and then remained motionless.

"Come! Git over, there," said Scully.

"Plenty of room on the other side of the stove," said Johnnie.

"Do you think we want to sit in the draught?" roared the father.

But the Swede here interposed with a grandeur of confidence. "No, no. Let the boy sit where he likes," he cried in a bullying voice to the father.

"All right! All right!" said Scully, deferentially. The cowboy and the Easterner exchanged glances of wonder.

The five chairs were formed in a crescent about one side of the stove. The Swede began to talk; he talked arrogantly, profanely, angrily. Johnnie, the cowboy, and the Easterner maintained a morose silence, while old Scully appeared to be receptive and eager, breaking in constantly with sympathetic ejaculations.

Finally the Swede announced that he was thirsty. He moved in his chair, and said that he would go for a drink of water.

"I'll git it for you," cried Scully at once.

"No," said the Swede, contemptuously. "I'll get it for myself." He arose and stalked with the air of an owner off into the executive parts of the hotel.

As soon as the Swede was out of hearing Scully sprang to his feet and whispered intensely to the others: "Upstairs he thought I was tryin' to poison 'im."

"Say," said Johnnie, "this makes me sick. Why don't you throw 'im out in the snow?"

"Why, he's all right now," declared Scully. "It was only that he was from the East, and he thought this was a tough place. That's all. He's all right now."

The cowboy looked with admiration upon the Easterner. "You were straight," he said. "You were on to that there Dutchman."

"Well," said Johnnie to his father, "he may be all right now, but I don't see it. Other time he was scared, but now he's too fresh."

Scully's speech was always a combination of Irish brogue and idiom, Western twang and idiom, and scraps of curiously formal diction taken from the story-books and newspapers. He now hurled a strange mass of language at the head of his son. "What do I keep? What do I keep? What do I keep?" he demanded, in a voice of thunder. He slapped his knee impressively, to indicate that he himself was going to make reply, and that all should heed. "I keep a hotel," he shouted. "A hotel, do you mind? A guest under my roof has sacred privileges. He is to be intimidated by none. Not one word shall he hear that would prijudice him in favor of goin' away. I'll not have it. There's no place in this here town where they can say they iver took in a guest of mine because he was afraid to stay here." He wheeled suddenly upon the cowboy and the Easterner. "Am I right?"

"Yes, Mr. Scully," said the cowboy, "I think you're right."

"Yes, Mr. Scully," said the Easterner, "I think you're right."

V

At six-o'clock supper, the Swede fizzed like a fire-wheel. He sometimes seemed on the point of bursting into riotous song, and in all his madness he was encouraged by old Scully. The Easterner was encased in reserve; the cowboy sat in wide-mouthed amazement, forgetting to eat, while Johnnie wrathily demolished great plates of food. The daughters of the house, when they were obliged to replenish the biscuits, approached as warily as Indians, and, having succeeded in their purpose, fled with ill-concealed trepidation. The Swede domineered the whole feast, and he gave it the appearance of a cruel bacchanal. He seemed to have grown suddenly taller; he gazed, brutally disdainful, into every face. His voice rang through the room. Once when he jabbed out harpoon-fashion with his fork to pinion a biscuit, the weapon nearly impaled the hand of the Easterner, which had been stretched quietly out for the same biscuit.

After supper, as the men filed toward the other room, the Swede smote Scully ruthlessly on the shoulder. "Well, old boy, that was a good, square meal." Johnnie looked hopefully at his father; he knew that shoulder was tender from an old fall; and, indeed, it appeared for a moment as if Scully was going to flame out over the matter, but in the end he smiled a sickly smile and remained silent. The others understood from his manner that he was admitting his responsibility for the Swede's new viewpoint.

Johnnie, however, addressed his parent in an aside. "Why don't you license somebody to kick you downstairs?" Scully scowled darkly by way of reply.

When they were gathered about the stove, the Swede insisted on another game of High-Five. Scully gently deprecated the plan at first, but the Swede turned a wolfish glare upon him. The old man subsided, and the Swede canvassed the others. In his tone there was always a great threat. The cowboy and the Easterner both remarked indifferently that they would play. Scully said that he would presently have to go to meet the 6:58 train, and so the Swede turned menacingly upon Johnnie. For a moment their glances crossed like blades, and then Johnnie smiled and said, "Yes, I'll play."

They formed a square, with the little board on their knees. The Easterner and the Swede were again partners. As the play went on, it was noticeable that the cowboy was not board-whacking as usual. Meanwhile, Scully, near the lamp, had put on his spectacles and, with an appearance curiously like an old priest, was reading a newspaper. In time he went out to meet the 6:58 train, and, despite his precautions, a gust of polar wind whirled into the room as he opened the door. Besides scattering the cards, it chilled the players to the marrow. The Swede cursed frightfully. When Scully returned, his entrance disturbed a cozy and friendly scene. The Swede again cursed. But presently they were once more intent, their heads bent forward and their hands moving swiftly. The Swede had adopted the fashion of board-whacking.

Scully took up his paper and for a long time remained immersed in matters which were extraordinarily remote from him. The lamp burned badly, and once he stopped to adjust the wick. The newspaper, as he turned from page to page, rustled with a slow and comfortable sound. Then suddenly he heard three terrible words: "You are cheatin'!"

Such scenes often prove that there can be little of dramatic import in environment. Any room can present a tragic front; any room can be comic. This little den was now hideous as a torture chamber. The new faces of the men themselves had changed it upon the instant. The Swede held a huge fist in front of Johnnie's face, while the latter looked steadily over it into the blazing orbs of his accuser. The Easterner had grown pallid; the cowboy's jaw had dropped in that expression of bovine amazement which was one of his important mannerisms. After the three words, the first sound in the room was made by Scully's paper as it floated forgotten to his feet. His spectacles had also fallen from his nose, but by a clutch he had saved them in air. His hand, grasping the spectacles, now remained poised awkwardly and near his shoulder. He stared at the card-players.

Probably the silence was while a second elapsed. Then, if the floor had been suddenly twitched out from under the men they could not have moved quicker. The five had projected themselves headlong toward a common point. It happened that Johnnie, in rising to hurl himself upon the Swede, had stumbled slightly because of his curiously instinctive care for the cards and the board. The loss of the moment allowed time for the arrival of Scully, and also allowed the cowboy time to give the Swede a great push which sent him staggering back. The men found tongue together, and hoarse shouts of rage, appeal, or fear burst from every throat. The cowboy pushed and jostled feverishly at the Swede, and the Easterner and Scully clung wildly to Johnnie; but through the smoky air, above the swaying bodies of the peace-compellers, the eyes of the two warriors ever sought each other in glances of challenge that were at once hot and steely.

Of course the board had been overturned, and now the whole company of cards was scattered over the floor, where the boots of the men trampled the fat and painted kings and queens as they gazed with their silly eyes at the war that was waging above them.

Scully's voice was dominating the yells. "Stop now! Stop, I say! Stop, now—"

Johnnie, as he struggled to burst through the rank formed by Scully and the Easterner, was crying, "Well, he says I cheated! He says I cheated! I won't allow no man to say I cheated! If he says I cheated, he's a —— ——!"

The cowboy was telling the Swede, "Quit, now! Quit, d'ye hear—"

The screams of the Swede never ceased: "He did cheat! I saw him! I saw him—"

As for the Easterner, he was importuning in a voice that was not heeded: "Wait a moment, can't you? Oh, wait a moment. What's the good of a fight over a game of cards? Wait a moment—"

In this tumult no complete sentences were clear. "Cheat"—"Quit"—"He says"—these fragments pierced the uproar and rang out sharply. It was remarkable that, whereas Scully undoubtedly made the most noise, he was the least heard of any of the riotous band.

Then suddenly there was a great cessation. It was as if each man had paused for breath; and although the room was still lighted with the anger of men, it could be seen that there was no danger of immediate conflict, and at once Johnnie, shouldering his way forward, almost succeeded in confronting the Swede. "What did you say I cheated for? What did you say I cheated for? I don't cheat, and I won't let no man say I do!"

The Swede said, "I saw you! I saw you!"

"Well," cried Johnnie, "I'll fight any man what says I cheat!"

"No, you won't," said the cowboy. "Not here."

"Ah, be still, can't you?" said Scully, coming between them.

The quiet was sufficient to allow the Easterner's voice to be heard. He was repeating, "Oh, wait a moment, can't you? What's the good of a fight over a game of cards? Wait a moment!"

Johnnie, his red face appearing above his father's shoulder, hailed the Swede again. "Did you say I cheated?"

The Swede showed his teeth. "Yes."

"Then," said Johnnie, "we must fight."

"Yes, fight," roared the Swede. He was like a demoniac. "Yes, fight! I'll show you what kind of a man I am! I'll show you who you want to fight! Maybe you think I can't fight! Maybe you think I can't! I'll show you, you skin, you card-sharp! Yes, you cheated! You cheated! You cheated!"

"Well, let's go at it, then, mister," said Johnnie, coolly.

The cowboy's brow was beaded with sweat from his efforts in intercepting all sorts of raids. He turned in despair to Scully. "What are you goin' to do now?"

A change had come over the Celtic visage of the old man. He now seemed all eagerness; his eyes glowed.

"We'll let them fight," he answered, stalwartly. "I can't put up with it any longer. I've stood this damned Swede till I'm sick. We'll let them fight."

<h2 style="text-align:center">VI</h2>

The men prepared to go out-of-doors. The Easterner was so nervous that he had great difficulty in getting his arms into the sleeves of his new leather coat. As the cowboy drew his fur cap down over his ears his hands trembled. In fact, Johnnie and old Scully were the only ones who displayed no agitation. These preliminaries were conducted without words.

Scully threw open the door. "Well, come on," he said. Instantly a terrific wind caused the flame of the lamp to struggle at its wick, while a puff of black smoke sprang from the chimney-top. The stove was in mid-current of the blast, and its voice swelled to equal the roar of the storm. Some of the scarred and bedabbled cards were caught up from the floor and dashed helplessly against the farther wall. The men lowered their heads and plunged into the tempest as into a sea.

No snow was falling, but great whirls and clouds of flakes, swept up from the ground by the frantic winds, were streaming southward with the speed of bullets. The covered land was blue with the sheen of an unearthly satin, and there was no other hue save where, at the low, black railway station—which seemed incredibly distant—one light gleamed like a tiny jewel. As the men floundered into a thigh-deep drift, it was known that the Swede was bawling out something. Scully went to him, put a hand on his shoulder, and projected an ear. "What's that you say?" he shouted.

"I say," bawled the Swede again, "I won't stand much show against this gang. I know you'll all pitch on me."

Scully smote him reproachfully on the arm. "Tut, man!" he yelled. The wind tore the words from Scully's lips and scattered them far alee.

"You are all a gang of—" boomed the Swede, but the storm also seized the remainder of this sentence.

Immediately turning their backs upon the wind, the men had swung around a corner to the sheltered side of the hotel. It was the function of the little house to preserve here, amid this great devastation of snow, an irregular V-shape of heavily encrusted grass, which crackled beneath the feet. One could imagine the great drifts piled against the windward side. When the party reached the comparative peace of this spot it was found that the Swede was still bellowing.

"Oh, I know what kind of a thing this is! I know you'll all pitch on me. I can't lick you all!"

Scully turned upon him panther-fashion. "You'll not have to whip all of us. You'll have to whip my son Johnnie. An' the man what troubles you durin' that time will have me to dale with."

The arrangements were swiftly made. The two men faced each other, obedient to the harsh commands of Scully, whose face, in the subtly luminous gloom, could be seen set in the austere impersonal lines that are pictured on the countenances of the Roman veterans. The Easterner's teeth were chattering, and he was hopping up and down like a mechanical toy. The cowboy stood rock-like.

The contestants had not stripped off any clothing. Each was in his ordinary attire. Their fists were up, and they eyed each other in a calm that had the elements of leonine cruelty in it.

During this pause, the Easterner's mind, like a film, took lasting impressions of three men—the iron-nerved master of the ceremony; the Swede, pale, motionless, terrible; and Johnnie, serene yet ferocious, brutish yet heroic. The entire prelude had in it a tragedy greater than the tragedy of action, and this aspect was accentuated by the long, mellow cry of the blizzard, as it sped the tumbling and wailing flakes into the black abyss of the south.

"Now!" said Scully.

The two combatants leaped forward and crashed together like bullocks. There was heard the cushioned sound of blows, and of a curse squeezing out from between the tight teeth of one.

As for the spectators, the Easterner's pent-up breath exploded from him with a pop of relief, absolute relief from the tension of the preliminaries. The cowboy bounded into the air with a yowl. Scully was immovable as from supreme amazement and fear at the fury of the fight which he himself had permitted and arranged.

For a time the encounter in the darkness was such a perplexity of flying arms that it presented no more detail than would a swiftly revolving wheel. Occasionally a face, as if illumined by a flash of light, would shine out, ghastly and marked with pink spots. A moment later, the men might have been known as shadows, if it were not for the involuntary utterance of oaths that came from them in whispers.

Suddenly a holocaust of warlike desire caught the cowboy, and he bolted forward with the speed of a broncho. "Go it, Johnnie! go it! Kill him! Kill him!"

Scully confronted him. "Kape back," he said; and by his glance the cowboy could tell that this man was Johnnie's father.

To the Easterner there was a monotony of unchangeable fighting that was an abomination. This confused mingling was eternal to his sense, which was concentrated in a longing for the end, the priceless end. Once the fighters lurched near him, and as he scrambled hastily backward he heard them breathe like men on the rack.

"Kill him, Johnnie! Kill him! Kill him! Kill him!" The cowboy's face was contorted like one of those agony masks in museums.

"Keep still," said Scully, icily.

Then there was a sudden loud grunt, incomplete, cut short, and Johnnie's body swung away from the Swede and fell with sickening heaviness to the grass. The cowboy was barely in time to prevent the mad Swede from flinging himself upon his prone adversary. "No, you don't," said the cowboy, interposing an arm. "Wait a second."

Scully was at his son's side. "Johnnie! Johnnie, me boy!" His voice had a quality of melancholy tenderness. "Johnnie! Can you go on with it?" He looked anxiously down into the bloody, pulpy face of his son.

There was a moment of silence, and then Johnnie answered in his ordinary voice, "Yes, I—it—yes."

Assisted by his father he struggled to his feet. "Wait a bit now till you git your wind," said the old man.

A few paces away the cowboy was lecturing the Swede. "No, you don't! Wait a second!"

The Easterner was plucking at Scully's sleeve. "Oh, this is enough," he pleaded. "This is enough! Let it go as it stands. This is enough!"

"Bill," said Scully, "git out of the road." The cowboy stepped aside. "Now." The combatants were actuated by a new caution as they advanced toward collision. They glared at each other, and then the Swede aimed a lightning blow that carried with it his entire weight. Johnnie was evidently half stupid from weakness, but he miraculously dodged, and his fist sent the overbalanced Swede sprawling.

The cowboy, Scully, and the Easterner burst into a cheer that was like a chorus of triumphant soldiery, but before its conclusion the Swede had scuffled agilely to his feet and come in berserk abandon at his foe. There was another perplexity of flying arms, and Johnnie's body again swung away and fell, even as a bundle might fall from a roof. The Swede instantly staggered to a little wind-waved tree and leaned upon it, breathing like an engine, while his savage and flame-lit eyes roamed from face to face as the men bent over Johnnie. There was a splendor of isolation in his situation at this time which the Easterner felt once when, lifting his eyes from the man on the ground, he beheld that mysterious and lonely figure, waiting.

"Are you any good yet, Johnnie?" asked Scully in a broken voice.

The son gasped and opened his eyes languidly. After a moment he answered, "No—I ain't—any good—any—more." Then, from shame and bodily ill, he began to weep, the tears furrowing down through the blood-stains on his face. "He was too—too—too heavy for me."

Scully straightened and addressed the waiting figure. "Stranger," he said, evenly, "it's all up with our side." Then his voice changed into that vibrant huskiness which is commonly the tone of the most simple and deadly announcements. "Johnnie is whipped."

Without replying, the victor moved off on the route to the front door of the hotel.

The cowboy was formulating new and unspellable blasphemies. The Easterner was startled to find that they were out in a wind that seemed to come direct from the shadowed arctic floes. He heard again the wail of the snow as it was flung to its grave in the south. He knew now that all this time the cold had been sinking into him deeper and deeper, and he wondered that he had not perished. He felt indifferent to the condition of the vanquished man.

"Johnnie, can you walk?" asked Scully.

"Did I hurt—hurt him any?" asked the son.

"Can you walk, boy? Can you walk?"

Johnnie's voice was suddenly strong. There was a robust impatience in it. "I asked you whether I hurt him any!"

"Yes, yes, Johnnie," answered the cowboy, consolingly; "he's hurt a good deal."

They raised him from the ground, and as soon as he was on his feet he went tottering off, rebuffing all attempts at assistance. When the party rounded the corner they were fairly blinded by the pelting of the snow. It burned their faces like fire. The cowboy carried Johnnie through the drift to the door. As they entered, some cards again rose from the floor and beat against the wall.

The Easterner rushed to the stove. He was so profoundly chilled that he almost dared to embrace the glowing iron. The Swede was not in the room. Johnnie sank into a chair and, folding his arms on his knees, buried his face in them. Scully, warming one foot and then the other at a rim of the stove, muttered to himself with Celtic mournfulness. The cowboy had removed his fur cap, and with a dazed and rueful air he was running one hand through his tousled locks. From overhead they could hear the creaking of boards, as the Swede tramped here and there in his room.

The sad quiet was broken by the sudden flinging open of a door that led toward the kitchen. It was instantly followed by an inrush of women. They precipitated themselves upon Johnnie amid a chorus of lamentation. Before they carried their prey off to the kitchen, there to be bathed and harangued with that mixture of sympathy and abuse which is a feat of their sex, the mother straightened herself and fixed old Scully with an eye of stern reproach. "Shame be upon you, Patrick Scully!" she cried. "Your own son, too. Shame be upon you!"

"There, now! Be quiet, now!" said the old man, weakly.

"Shame be upon you, Patrick Scully!" The girls, rallying to this slogan, sniffed disdainfully in the direction of those trembling accomplices, the cowboy and the Easterner. Presently they bore Johnnie away, and left the three men to dismal reflection.

VII

"I'd like to fight this here Dutchman myself," said the cowboy, breaking a long silence.

Scully wagged his head sadly. "No, that wouldn't do. It wouldn't be right. It wouldn't be right."

"Well, why wouldn't it?" argued the cowboy. "I don't see no harm in it."

"No," answered Scully, with mournful heroism. "It wouldn't be right. It was Johnnie's fight, and now we mustn't whip the man just because he whipped Johnnie."

"Yes, that's true enough," said the cowboy; "but—he better not get fresh with me, because I couldn't stand no more of it."

"You'll not say a word to him," commanded Scully, and even then they heard the tread of the Swede on the stairs. His entrance was made theatric. He swept the door back with a bang and swaggered to the middle of the room. No one looked at him. "Well," he cried, insolently, at Scully, "I s'pose you'll tell me now how much I owe you?"

The old man remained stolid. "You don't owe me nothin'."

"Huh!" said the Swede, "huh! Don't owe 'im nothin'."

The cowboy addressed the Swede. "Stranger, I don't see how you come to be so gay around here."

Old Scully was instantly alert. "Stop!" he shouted, holding his hand forth, fingers upward. "Bill, you shut up!"

The cowboy spat carelessly into the sawdust box. "I didn't say a word, did I?" he asked.

"Mr. Scully," called the Swede, "how much do I owe you?" It was seen that he was attired for departure, and that he had his valise in his hand.

"You don't owe me nothin'," repeated Scully in the same imperturbable way.

"Huh!" said the Swede. "I guess you're right. I guess if it was any way at all, you'd owe me somethin'. That's what I guess." He turned to the cowboy. " 'Kill him! Kill him! Kill him!' " he mimicked, and then guffawed victoriously. " 'Kill him!' " He was convulsed with ironical humor.

But he might have been jeering the dead. The three men were immovable and silent, staring with glassy eyes at the stove.

The Swede opened the door and passed into the storm, giving one derisive glance backward at the still group.

As soon as the door was closed, Scully and the cowboy leaped to their feet and began to curse. They trampled to and fro, waving their arms and smashing into the air with their fists. "Oh, but that was a hard min-ute!" wailed Scully. "That was a hard minute! Him there leerin' and scoffin'! One bang at his nose was worth forty dollars to me that minute! How did you stand it, Bill?"

"How did I stand it?" cried the cowboy in a quivering voice. "How did I stand it? Oh!"

The old man burst into sudden brogue. "I'd loike to take that Swade," he wailed, "and hould 'im down on a shtone flure and bate 'im to a jelly wid a shtick!"

The cowboy groaned in sympathy. "I'd like to git him by the neck and ha-ammer him"—he brought his hand down on a chair with a noise like a pistol-shot—"hammer that there Dutchman until he couldn't tell himself from a dead coyote!"

"I'd bate 'im until he—"

"I'd show *him* some things—"

And then together they raised a yearning, fanatic cry—"Oh-o-oh! if we only could—"

"Yes!"

"Yes!"

"And then I'd—"

"O-o-oh!"

VIII

The Swede, tightly gripping his valise, tacked across the face of the storm as if he carried sails. He was following a line of little naked, gasping trees which, he knew, must mark the way of the road. His face, fresh from the pounding of Johnnie's fists, felt more pleasure than pain in the wind and the driving snow. A number of square shapes loomed upon him fi-nally, and he knew them as the houses of the main body of the town. He found a street and made travel along it, leaning heavily upon the wind whenever, at a corner, a terrific blast caught him.

He might have been in a deserted village. We picture the world as thick with conquering and elate humanity, but here, with the bugles of the tempest pealing, it was hard to imagine a peopled earth. One viewed the existence of man then as a marvel, and conceded a glamor of wonder to these lice which were caused to cling to a whirling, fire-smitten, ice-locked, disease-stricken, space-lost bulb. The conceit of man was explained by this storm to be the very engine of life. One was a coxcomb not to die in it. However, the Swede found a saloon.

In front of it an indomitable red light was burning, and the snowflakes were made blood-color as they flew through the circumscribed territory of the lamp's shining. The Swede pushed open the door of the saloon and entered. A sanded expanse was before him, and at the end of it four men sat about a table drinking. Down one side of the room extended a radiant bar, and its guardian was leaning upon his elbows listening to the talk of the men at the table. The Swede dropped his valise upon the floor and, smiling fraternally upon the barkeeper, said, "Gimme some whiskey, will you?" The man placed a bottle, a whiskey glass, and a glass of ice-thick water upon the bar. The Swede poured himself an abnormal portion of whiskey and drank it in three gulps. "Pretty bad night," remarked the bartender, indifferently. He was making the pretension of blindness which is usually a distinction of his class; but it could have been seen that he was furtively studying the half-erased bloodstains on the face of the Swede. "Bad night," he said again.

"Oh, it's good enough for me," replied the Swede, hardily, as he poured himself some more whiskey. The barkeeper took his coin and maneuvered it through its reception by the highly nickeled cash-machine. A bell rang; a card labeled "20 cts." had appeared.

"No," continued the Swede, "this isn't too bad weather. It's good enough for me."

"So?" murmured the barkeeper, languidly.

The copious drams made the Swede's eyes swim, and he breathed a trifle heavier. "Yes, I like this weather. I like it. It suits me." It was apparently his design to impart a deep significance to these words.

"So?" murmured the bartender again. He turned to gaze dreamily at the scroll-like birds and bird-like scrolls which had been drawn with soap upon the mirrors in back of the bar.

"Well, I guess I'll take another drink," said the Swede, presently. "Have something?"

"No, thanks; I'm not drinkin'," answered the bartender. Afterward he asked, "How did you hurt your face?"

The Swede immediately began to boast loudly. "Why, in a fight. I thumped the soul out of a man down here at Scully's hotel."

The interest of the four men at the table was at last aroused.

"Who was it?" said one.

"Johnnie Scully," blustered the Swede. "Son of the man what runs it. He will be pretty near dead for some weeks, I can tell you. I made a nice thing of him, I did. He couldn't get up. They carried him in the house. Have a drink?"

Instantly the men in some subtle way encased themselves in reserve. "No, thanks," said one. The group was of curious formation. Two were prominent local businessmen; one was the district attorney; and one was a professional gambler of the kind known as "square." But a scrutiny of the group would not have enabled an observer to pick the gambler from the men of more reputable pursuits. He was, in fact, a man so delicate in manner, when among people of fair class, and so judicious in his choice of victims, that in the strictly masculine part of the town's life he had come to be explicitly trusted and admired. People called him a thoroughbred. The fear and contempt with which his craft was regarded were undoubtedly the reason why his quiet dignity shone conspicuous above the quiet dignity of men who might be merely hatters, billiard-markers, or grocery clerks. Beyond an occasional unwary traveler who came by rail, this gambler was supposed to prey solely upon reckless and senile farmers, who, when flush with good crops, drove into town in all the pride and confidence of an absolutely invulnerable stupidity. Hearing at times in circuitous fashion of the despoilment of such a farmer, the important men of Romper invariably laughed in contempt of the victim, and if they thought of the wolf at all, it was with a kind of pride at the knowledge that he would never dare think of attacking their wisdom and courage. Besides, it was popular that this gambler had a real wife and two real children in a neat cottage in a suburb, where he led an exemplary home life; and when any one even suggested a discrepancy in his character, the crowd immediately vociferated descriptions of this virtuous family circle. Then men who led exemplary home lives, and men who did not lead exemplary home lives, all subsided in a bunch, remarking that there was nothing more to be said.

However, when a restriction was placed upon him—as, for instance, when a strong clique of members of the new Pollywog Club refused to permit him, even as a spectator, to appear in the rooms of the organization—the candor and gentleness with which he accepted the judgment disarmed many of his foes and made his friends more desperately partisan. He invariably distinguished between himself and a respectable Romper man so quickly and frankly that his manner actually appeared to be a continual broadcast compliment.

And one must not forget to declare the fundamental fact of his entire position in Romper. It is irrefutable that in all affairs outside his business, in all matters that occur eternally and commonly between man and man, this thieving card-player was so generous, so just, so moral, that, in a contest, he could have put to flight the consciences of nine tenths of the citizens of Romper.

And so it happened that he was seated in this saloon with the two prominent local merchants and the district attorney.

The Swede continued to drink raw whiskey, meanwhile babbling at the barkeeper and trying to induce him to indulge in potations. "Come on. Have a drink. Come on. What—no? Well, have a little one, then. By gawd, I've whipped a man tonight, and I want to celebrate. I whipped him good, too. Gentlemen," the Swede cried to the men at the table, "have a drink?"

"Ssh!" said the barkeeper.

The group at the table, although furtively attentive, had been pretending to be deep in talk, but now a man lifted his eyes toward the Swede and said, shortly, "Thanks. We don't want any more."

At this reply the Swede ruffled out his chest like a rooster. "Well," he exploded, "it seems I can't get anybody to drink with me in this town. Seems so, don't it? Well!"

"Ssh!" said the barkeeper.

"Say," snarled the Swede, "don't you try to shut me up. I won't have it. I'm a gentleman, and I want people to drink with me. And I want 'em to drink with me now. *Now*—do you understand?" He rapped the bar with his knuckles.

Years of experience had calloused the bartender. He merely grew sulky. "I hear you," he answered.

"Well," cried the Swede, "listen hard then. See those men over there? Well, they're going to drink with me, and don't you forget it. Now you watch."

"Hi!" yelled the barkeeper, "this won't do!"

"Why won't it?" demanded the Swede. He stalked over to the table, and by chance laid his hand upon the shoulder of the gambler. "How about this?" he asked wrathfully. "I asked you to drink with me."

The gambler simply twisted his head and spoke over his shoulder. "My friend, I don't know you."

"Oh, hell!" answered the Swede, "come and have a drink."

"Now, my boy," advised the gambler, kindly, "take your hand off my shoulder and go 'way and mind your own business." He was a little, slim man, and it seemed strange to hear him use this tone of heroic patronage to the burly Swede. The other men at the table said nothing.

"What! You won't drink with me, you little dude? I'll make you, then! I'll make you!" The Swede had grasped the gambler frenziedly at the throat, and was dragging him from his chair. The other men sprang up. The barkeeper dashed around the corner of his bar. There was a great tumult, and then was seen a long blade in the hand of the gambler. It shot forward, and a human body, this citadel of virtue, wisdom, power, was pierced as easily as if it had been a melon. The Swede fell with a cry of supreme astonishment.

The prominent merchants and the district attorney must have at once tumbled out of the place backward. The bartender found himself hanging limply to the arm of a chair and gazing into the eyes of a murderer.

"Henry," said the latter, as he wiped his knife on one of the towels that hung beneath the bar rail, "you tell 'em where to find me. I'll be home, waiting for 'em." Then he vanished. A moment afterward the barkeeper was in the street dinning through the storm for help and, moreover, companionship.

The corpse of the Swede, alone in the saloon, had its eyes fixed upon a dreadful legend that dwelt atop of the cash-machine: "This registers the amount of your purchase."

IX

Months later, the cowboy was frying pork over the stove of a little ranch near the Dakota line, when there was a quick thud of hoofs outside, and presently the Easterner entered with the letters and the papers.

"Well," said the Easterner at once, "the chap that killed the Swede has got three years. Wasn't much, was it?"

"He has? Three years?" The cowboy poised his pan of pork, while he ruminated upon the news. "Three years. That ain't much."

"No. It was a light sentence," replied the Easterner as he unbuckled his spurs. "Seems there was a good deal of sympathy for him in Romper."

"If the bartender had been any good," observed the cowboy, thoughtfully, "he would have gone in and cracked that there Dutchman on the head with a bottle in the beginnin' of it and stopped all this here murderin'."

"Yes, a thousand things might have happened," said the Easterner, tartly.

The cowboy returned his pan of pork to the fire, but his philosophy continued. "It's funny, ain't it? If he hadn't said Johnnie was cheatin' he'd be alive this minute. He was an awful fool. Game played for fun, too. Not for money. I believe he was crazy."

"I feel sorry for that gambler," said the Easterner.

"Oh, so do I," said the cowboy. "He don't deserve none of it for killin' who he did."

"The Swede might not have been killed if everything had been square."

"Might not have been killed?" exclaimed the cowboy. "Everythin' square? Why, when he said that Johnnie was cheatin' and acted like such a jackass? And then in the saloon he fairly walked up to git hurt?" With these arguments the cowboy browbeat the Easterner and reduced him to rage.

"You're a fool!" cried the Easterner, viciously. "You're a bigger jackass than the Swede by a million majority. Now let me tell you one thing. Let me tell you something. Listen! Johnnie *was* cheating!"

" 'Johnnie,' " said the cowboy, blankly. There was a minute of silence, and then he said, robustly, "Why, no. The game was only for fun."

"Fun or not," said the Easterner, "Johnnie was cheating. I saw him. I know it. I saw him. And I refused to stand up and be a man. I let the Swede fight it out alone. And you—you were simply puffing around the place and wanting to fight. And then old Scully himself! We are all in it! This poor gambler isn't even a noun. He is kind of an adverb. Every sin is the result of a collaboration. We, five of us, have collaborated in the murder of this Swede. Usually there are from a dozen to forty women really involved in every murder, but in this case it seems to be only five men—you, I, Johnnie, old Scully; and that fool of an unfortunate gambler came merely as a culmination, the apex of a human movement, and gets all the punishment."

The cowboy, injured and rebellious, cried out blindly into this fog of mysterious theory: "Well, I didn't do anythin', did I?"

November 26 and December 3, 1898
[*Collier's Weekly*, Vol. 22, pp. 14–16, each issue.]

THE PRICE OF THE HARNESS*
[The Woof of Thin Red Threds]

I

Twenty-five men were making a road out of a path up the hillside. The light batteries in the rear were impatient to advance, but first must be done all that digging and smoothing which gains no encrusted medals from war. The men worked like gardeners, and a road was growing from the old pack-animal trail.

Trees arched from a field of guinea-grass, which resembled young wild corn. The day was still and dry. The men working were dressed in the consistent blue of the United States regulars. They looked indifferent, almost stolid, despite the heat and the labor. There was little talking. From time to time a Government pack-train, led by a sleek-sided tender bell-mare, came from one way or the other, and the men stood aside as the strong, hard, black-and-tan animals crowded eagerly after their curious feminine leader.

A volunteer staff officer appeared, and, sitting his horse in the middle of the work, asked the sergeant in command some questions which were apparently not relevant to any military business.

Men straggling along on various duties almost invariably spun some kind of joke as they passed.

A corporal and four men were guarding boxes of spare ammunition at the top of the hill, and one of the number often went to the foot of the hill, swinging canteens.

The day wore down to the Cuban dusk in which the shadows are all grim and of ghastly shape. The men began to lift their eyes from the

* *Wounds in the Rain.*

shovels and picks, and glance in the direction of their camp. The sun
threw his last lance through the foliage. The steep mountain range on the
right turned blue, and as without detail as a curtain. The tiny ruby of
light ahead meant that the ammunition guard were cooking their supper.
From somewhere in the world came a single rifle-shot.

Figures appeared, dim in the shadow of the trees. A murmur, a sigh of
quiet relief, arose from the working party. Later, they swung up the hill
in an unformed formation, being always like soldiers, and unable even to
carry a spade save like United States regular soldiers. As they passed
through some fields, the bland white light of the end of the day feebly
touched each hard bronze profile.

"Wonder if we'll git anythin' to eat," said Watkins, in a low voice.

"Should think so," said Nolan, in the same tone. They betrayed no impatience; they seemed to feel a kind of awe of the situation.

The sergeant turned. One could see the cool gray eye flashing under
the brim of the campaign hat. "What in hell you fellers kickin' about?" he
asked. They made no reply, understanding that they were being suppressed.

As they moved on, a murmur arose from the tall grass on either hand.
It was the noise from the bivouac of ten thousand men, although one saw
practically nothing from the low-cut roadway. The sergeant led his party
up a wet clay bank and into a trampled field. Here were scattered tiny
white shelter tents, and in the darkness they were luminous like the rearing
stones in a graveyard. A few fires burned blood-red, and the shadowy
figures of men moved with no more expression of detail than there is in the
swaying of foliage on a windy night.

The working party felt their way to where their tents were pitched. A
man suddenly cursed; he had mislaid something and he knew he was not
going to find it that night. Watkins spoke again with the monotony of a
clock: "Wonder if we'll git anythin' to eat."

Martin, with eyes turned pensively to the stars, began a treatise. "Them
Spaniards—"

"Oh, quit it," cried Nolan. "What th' piper do you know about th'
Spaniards, you fat-head Dutchman? Better think of your belly, you blunderin' swine, an' what you're goin' to put in it, grass or dirt."

A laugh, a sort of deep growl, arose from the prostrate men. In the
meantime the sergeant had reappeared and was standing over them. "No
rations tonight," he said gruffly, and, turning on his heel, walked away.

This announcement was received in silence. But Watkins had flung himself face downward, and putting his lips close to a tuft of grass, he formulated oaths. Martin arose and, going to his shelter, crawled in sulkily.

After a long interval Nolan said aloud, "Hell!" Grierson, enlisted for the war, raised a querulous voice. "Well, I wonder when we *will* git fed?"

From the ground about him came a low chuckle full of ironical comment upon Grierson's lack of certain qualities which the other men felt themselves to possess.

II

In the cold light of dawn the men were on their knees, packing, strapping, and buckling. The comic toy hamlet of shelter tents had been wiped out as if by a cyclone. Through the trees could be seen the crimson of a light battery's blankets, and the wheels creaked like the sound of a musketry fight. Nolan, well gripped by his shelter tent, his blanket, and his cartridge belt, and bearing his rifle, advanced upon a small group of men who were hastily finishing a can of coffee.

"Say, give us a drink, will yeh?" he asked, wistfully. He was as sad-eyed as an orphan beggar.

Every man in the group turned to look him straight in the face. He had asked for the principal ruby out of each one's crown. There was a grim silence. Then one said, "What fer?" Nolan cast his glance to the ground and went away abashed.

But he espied Watkins and Martin surrounding Grierson, who had gained three pieces of hardtack by mere force of his audacious inexperience. Grierson was fending his comrades off tearfully.

"Now, don't be damn pigs," he cried. "Hold on a minute." Here Nolan asserted a claim. Grierson groaned. Kneeling piously, he divided the hardtack with minute care into four portions. The men, who had had their heads together like players watching a wheel of fortune, arose suddenly, each chewing. Nolan interpolated a drink of water and sighed contentedly.

The whole forest seemed to be moving. From the field on the other side of the road a column of men in blue was slowly pouring; the battery had creaked on ahead; from the rear came a hum of advancing regiments. Then from a mile away rang the noise of a shot, then another shot; in a moment the rifles there were drumming, drumming, drumming. The artillery boomed out suddenly. A day of battle was begun.

The men made no exclamations. They rolled their eyes in the direction of the sound, and then swept with a calm glance the forests and the hills which surrounded them, implacably mysterious forests and hills which lent to every rifle-shot the ominous quality which belongs to secret assassination. The whole scene would have spoken to the private soldiers of ambushes, sudden flank attacks, terrible disasters if it were not for those cool gentlemen with shoulder straps and swords, who, the private soldiers knew, were of another world and omnipotent for the business.

The battalions moved out into the mud and began a leisurely march in the damp shade of the trees. The advance of two batteries had churned the black soil into a formidable paste. The brown leggings of the men, stained with the mud of other days, took on a deeper color. Perspiration broke gently out on the reddish faces. With his heavy roll of blanket and the half of a shelter tent crossing his right shoulder and under his left arm, each man presented the appearance of being clasped from behind, wrestler fashion, by a pair of thick white arms.

There was something distinctive in the way they carried their rifles. There was the grace of an old hunter somewhere in it, the grace of a man whose rifle has become absolutely a part of himself. Furthermore, almost every blue shirtsleeve was rolled to the elbow, disclosing forearms of almost incredible brawn. The rifles seemed light, almost fragile, in the hands that were at the end of these arms, never fat, but always with rolling muscles and veins that seemed on the point of bursting. And another thing was the silence and the marvelous impassivity of the faces as the column made its slow way toward where the whole forest spluttered and fluttered with battle.

Opportunely, the battalion was halted astraddle of a stream, and before it again moved most of the men had filled their canteens. The firing increased. Ahead and to the left, a battery was booming at methodical intervals, while the infantry racket was that continual drumming which, after all, often sounds like rain on a roof. Directly ahead one could hear the deep voices of fieldpieces.

Some wounded Cubans were carried by in litters improvised from hammocks swung on poles. One had a ghastly cut in the throat, probably from a fragment of shell, and his head was turned as if Providence particularly wished to display this wide and lapping gash to the long column that was winding toward the front. And another Cuban, shot through the groin, kept up a continual wail as he swung from the tread of his bearers. "Ay—ee! Ay—ee! Madre mia! Madre mia!" He sang this bitter ballad into the ears of at least three thousand men as they slowly made way for his bearers on the narrow wood-path. These wounded insurgents were, then, to a large part of the advancing army, the visible messengers of bloodshed, death, and the men regarded them with thoughtful awe. This doleful sobbing cry, "Madre mia," was a tangible consequent misery of all that firing on in front, into which the men knew they were soon to be plunged. Some of them wished to inquire of the bearers the details of what had happened, but they could not speak Spanish, and so it was as if fate had intentionally sealed the lips of all in order that even meager information might not leak out concerning this mystery—battle. On the other hand, many unversed private soldiers looked upon the unfortunate as men who had seen thousands maimed and bleeding, and absolutely could not conjure any further interest in such scenes.

A young staff officer passed on horseback. The vocal Cuban was always wailing, but the officer wheeled past the bearers without heeding anything. And yet he never before had seen such a sight. His case was different from that of the private soldiers. He heeded nothing because he was busy, immensely busy, and hurried with a multitude of reasons and desires for doing his duty perfectly. His whole life had been a mere period of preliminary reflection for this situation, and he had no clear idea of anything save his obligation as an officer. A man of this kind might be stupid; it is conceivable that in remote cases certain bumps on his head might be composed entirely of wood; but those traditions of fidelity and courage which have been handed to him from generation to generation, and which he has tenaciously preserved despite the persecution of legislators and the indifference of his country, make it incredible that in battle he should ever fail to give his best blood and his best thought for his general, for his men, and for himself.

And so this young officer in the shapeless hat and the torn and dirty shirt failed to heed the wails of the wounded man, even as the pilgrim fails to heed the world as he raises his illumined face toward his purpose—rightly or wrongly his purpose—his sky of the ideal of duty; and the wonderful part of it is, that he is guided by an ideal which he has himself created, and has alone protected from attack. The young man was merely an officer in the United States regular army.

The column swung across a shallow ford and took a road which passed the right flank of one of the American batteries.

On a hill it was booming and belching great clouds of white smoke. The infantry looked up with interest. Arrayed below the hill and behind the battery were the horses and limbers, the riders checking their pawing mounts, and behind each rider a red blanket flamed against the fervent green of the bushes. As the infantry moved along the road, some of the battery horses turned at the noise of the trampling feet and surveyed the men with eyes deep as wells, serene, mournful, generous eyes, lit heartbreakingly with something that was akin to a philosophy, a religion of self-sacrifice—oh, gallant, gallant horses!

"I know a feller in that battery," said Nolan, musingly. "A driver."

"Damn sight rather be a gunner," said Martin.

"Why would ye?" said Nolan, opposingly.

"Well, I'd take my chances as a gunner b'fore I'd sit way up in th' air on a raw-boned plug an' git shot at."

"Aw—" began Nolan.

"They've had some losses t'-day all right," interrupted Grierson.

"Horses?" asked Watkins.

"Horses, an' men too," said Grierson.

"How d'yeh know?"

"A feller told me there by the ford."

They kept only a part of their minds bearing on this discussion, because they could already hear high in the air the wire-string note of the enemy's bullets.

III

The road taken by this battalion, as it followed other battalions, is something less than a mile long in its journey across a heavily wooded plain. It is greatly changed now; in fact, it was metamorphosed in two days; but at that time it was a mere track through dense shrubbery from which rose great, dignified arching trees. It was, in fact, a path through a jungle.

The battalion had no sooner left the battery in the rear than bullets began to drive overhead. They made several different sounds, but as they were mainly high shots, it was usual for them to make the faint note of a vibrant string touched elusively, half-dreamily.

The military balloon, a fat, wavering yellow thing, was leading the advance like some new conception of war-god. Its bloated mass shone above the trees, and served incidentally to indicate to the men at the rear that comrades were in advance. The track itself exhibited, for all its visible length, a closely knit procession of soldiers in blue, with breasts crossed with white shelter tents. The first ominous order of battle came down the line. "Use the cut-off. Don't use the magazine until you're ordered." Noncommissioned officers repeated the command gruffly. A sound of clicking locks rattled along the columns. All men knew that the time had come.

The front had burst out with a roar like a brush fire. The balloon was dying, dying a gigantic and public death before the eyes of two armies. It quivered, sank, faded into the trees amid the flurry of a battle that was suddenly and tremendously like a storm.

The American battery thundered behind the men with a shock that seemed likely to tear the backs of their heads off. The Spanish shrapnel fled on a line to their left, swirling and swishing in supernatural velocity. The noise of the rifle bullets broke in their faces like the noise of so many lamp chimneys or sped overhead in swift, cruel spitting. And at the front, the battle sound, as if it were simply music, was beginning to swell and swell until the volleys rolled like a surf.

The officers shouted hoarsely.

"Come on, men! Hurry up, boys! Come on, now! Hurry up!" The soldiers, running heavily in their accouterments, dashed forward. A baggage guard was swiftly detailed; the men tore their rolls from their shoulders as if the things were afire. The battalion, stripped for action, again dashed forward.

"Come on, men! Come on!"

To them the battle was as yet merely a road through the woods crowded with troops who lowered their heads anxiously as the bullets fled high. But a moment later the column wheeled abruptly to the left and entered a field of tall green grass. The line scattered to a skirmish formation. In front was a series of knolls, treed sparsely like orchards, and although no enemy was visible, these knolls were all popping and spitting with rifle fire. In some places there were to be seen long gray lines of dirt entrenchments. The American shells were kicking up reddish clouds of dust from the brow of one of the knolls where stood a pagoda-like house. It was not much like a battle with men; it was a battle with a bit of charming scenery, enigmatically potent for death.

Nolan knew that Martin had suddenly fallen. "What—" he began.

"They've hit me," said Martin.

"Jesus!" said Nolan.

Martin lay on the ground, clutching his left forearm just below the elbow with all the strength of his right hand. His lips were pursed ruefully. He did not seem to know what to do. He continued to stare at his arm.

Then suddenly the bullets drove at them low and hard. The men flung themselves face down in the grass. Nolan lost all thought of his friend. Oddly enough, he felt somewhat like a man hiding under a bed, and he was just as sure that he could not raise his head high without being shot as a man hiding under a bed is sure that he cannot raise his head without bumping it.

A lieutenant was seated in the grass just behind him. He was in the careless and yet rigid pose of a man balancing a loaded plate on his knee at a picnic. He was talking in soothing, paternal tones.

"Now, don't get rattled. We're all right here. Just as safe as being in church. . . . They're all going high. Don't mind them. . . . Don't mind them. . . . They're all going high. We've got them rattled and they can't shoot straight. Don't mind them."

The sun burned down steadily from a pale blue sky upon the crackling woods and knolls and fields. From the roar of musketry, it might have been that the celestial heat was frying this part of the world.

Nolan snuggled close to the grass.

He watched a gray line of entrenchments, above which floated the veriest gossamer of smoke. A flag lolled on a staff behind it. The men in the trench volleyed whenever an American shell exploded near them. It was some kind of infantile defiance. Frequently a bullet came from the woods directly behind Nolan and his comrades. They thought at the time that these bullets were from the rifle of some incompetent soldier of their own side.

There was no cheering. The men would have looked about them wondering where the army was if it were not that the crash of the fighting for the distance of a mile denoted plainly enough where that army was.

Officially, the battalion had not yet fired a shot; there had been merely some irresponsible popping by men on the extreme left flank. But it was known that the lieutenant colonel who had been in command was dead, shot through the heart, and that the captains were thinned down to two. At the rear went on a long tragedy in which men, bent and hasty, hurried to shelter with other men, helpless, dazed, and bloody. Nolan knew of it all from the hoarse and affrighted voices which he heard as he lay flattened in the grass. There came to him a sense of exultation. Here, then, was one of those dread and lurid situations which in a nation's history stand out in crimson letters, becoming tales of blood to stir generation after generation. And he was in it and unharmed. If he lived through the battle, he would be a hero of the desperate fight at—and here he wondered for a second what fate would be pleased to bestow as a name for this battle.

But it is quite sure that hardly another man in the battalion was engaged in any thoughts concerning the historic. On the contrary, they deemed it ill that they were being badly cut up on a most unimportant occasion. It would have benefited the conduct of whoever were weak if they had known that they were engaged in a battle that would be famous for ever.

IV

Martin had picked himself up from where the bullet had knocked him, and addressed the lieutenant. "I'm hit, sir," he said.

The lieutenant was very busy. "All right, all right," he said, heeding the man just enough to learn where he was wounded. "Go over that way. You ought to see a dressing station under those trees."

Martin found himself dizzy and sick. The sensation in his arm was distinctly galvanic. The feeling was so strange that he could wonder at times if a wound was really what ailed him. Once, in this dazed way, he examined his arm; he saw the hole. Yes, he was shot; that was it. And more than in any other way it affected him with a profound sadness.

As directed by the lieutenant, he went to the clump of trees, but he found no dressing station there. He found only a dead soldier lying with his face buried in his arms and with his shoulders humped high as if he were convulsively sobbing. Martin decided to make his way to the road, deeming that he thus would better his chances of getting to a surgeon. But he suddenly found his way blocked by a fence of barbed wire. Such was his mental condition that he brought up at a rigid halt before this fence and stared stupidly at it. It did not seem to him possible that this obstacle could be defeated by any means. The fence was there and it stopped his progress. He could not go in that direction.

But as he turned he espied that procession of wounded men, strange pilgrims, which had already worn a path in the tall grass. They were passing through a gap in the fence. Martin joined them. The bullets were flying over them in sheets, but many of them bore themselves as men who had now exacted from fate a singular immunity. Generally there were no outcries, no kicking, no talk at all. They too, like Martin, seemed buried in a vague but profound melancholy.

But there was one who cried out loudly. A man shot in the head was being carried arduously by four comrades, and he continually yelled one word that was terrible in its primitive strength. "Bread! Bread! Bread!"

Following him and his bearers were a limping crowd of men, less cruelly wounded, who kept their eyes always fixed on him, as if they gained from his extreme agony some balm for their own sufferings.

"Bread! Give me bread!"

Martin plucked a man by the sleeve. The man had been shot in the foot, and was making his way with the help of a curved, incompetent stick. It is an axiom of war that wounded men can never find straight sticks.

"What's the matter with that feller?" asked Martin.

"Nutty," said the man.

"Why is he?"

"Shot in th' head," answered the other, impatiently.

The wail of the sufferer arose in the field amid the swift rasp of bullets and the boom and shatter of shrapnel. "Bread! Bread! Oh, God, can't you give me bread? Bread!" The bearers of him were suffering exquisite agony, and often they exchanged glances which exhibited their despair of ever getting free of this tragedy. It seemed endless.

"Bread! Bread! Bread!"

But despite the fact that there was always in the way of this crowd a wistful melancholy, one must know that there were plenty of men who laughed, laughed at their wounds whimsically, quaintly, inventing odd humors concerning bicycles and cabs, extracting from this shedding of their blood a wonderful amount of material for cheerful badinage, and with their faces twisted from pain as they stepped, they often joked like music hall stars. And perhaps this was the most tearful part of all.

They trudged along a road until they reached a ford. Here under the eave of the bank lay a dismal company. In the mud and in the damp shade of some bushes were a half-hundred pale-faced men prostrate. Two or three surgeons were working there. Also there was a chaplain, grim-

mouthed, resolute, his surtout discarded. Overhead always was that incessant maddening wail of bullets.

Martin was standing gazing drowsily at the scene when a surgeon
grabbed him. "Here, what's the matter with you?" Martin was daunted.
He wondered what he had done that the surgeon should be so angry
with him.

"In the arm," he muttered, half shamefacedly.

After the surgeon had hastily and irritably bandaged the injured member, he glared at Martin and said, "You can walk all right, can't you?"

"Yes, sir," said Martin.

"Well, now, you just make tracks down that road."

"Yes, sir." Martin went meekly off. The doctor had seemed exasperated
almost to the point of madness.

The road was at this time swept with the fire of a body of Spanish
sharpshooters who had come cunningly around the flanks of the American
army, and were now hidden in the dense foliage that lined both sides of
the road. They were shooting at everything. The road was as crowded as a
street in a city, and at an absurdly short range they emptied their rifles
at the passing people. They were aided always by the over-sweep from the
regular Spanish line of battle.

Martin was sleepy from his wound. He saw tragedy follow tragedy, but
they created in him no feeling of horror.

A man with a red cross on his arm was leaning against a great tree.
Suddenly he tumbled to the ground, and writhed for a moment in the way
of a child oppressed with colic. A comrade immediately began to bustle
importantly. "Here," he called to Martin, "help me carry this man, will
you?"

Martin looked at him with dull scorn. "I'll be damned if I do," he said.
"Can't carry myself, let alone somebody else."

This answer, which rings now so inhuman, pitiless, did not affect the
other man. "Well, all right," he said; "here comes some other fellers." The
wounded man had now turned blue-gray; his eyes were closed; his body
shook in a gentle, persistent chill.

Occasionally Martin came upon dead horses, their limbs sticking out
and up like stakes. One beast, mortally shot, was besieged by three or four
men who were trying to push it into the bushes, where it could live its
brief time of anguish without thrashing to death any of the wounded men
in the gloomy procession.

The mule train, with extra ammunition, charged toward the front, still
led by the tinkling bell-mare.

An ambulance was stuck momentarily in the mud, and above the crack of battle one could hear the familiar objurgations of the driver as he whirled his lash.

Two privates were having a hard time with a wounded captain whom they were supporting to the rear. He was half cursing, half wailing out the information that he not only would not go another step toward the rear, but was certainly going to return at once to the front. They begged, pleaded, at great length, as they continually headed him off. They were not unlike two nurses with an exceptionally bad and headstrong little duke.

The wounded soldiers paused to look impassively upon this struggle. They were always like men who could not be aroused by anything further.

The visible hospital was mainly straggling thickets intersected with narrow paths, the ground being covered with men. Martin saw a busy person with a book and a pencil, but he did not approach him to become officially a member of the hospital. All he desired was rest and immunity from nagging. He took seat painfully under a bush and leaned his back upon the trunk. There he remained thinking, his face wooden.

V

"My gawd," said Nolan, squirming on his belly in the grass, "I can't stand this much longer."

Then suddenly every rifle in the firing line seemed to go off of its own accord. It was the result of an order, but few men heard the order; in the main they had fired because they heard others fire, and their sense was so quick that the volley did not sound too ragged. These marksmen had been lying for nearly an hour in stony silence, their sights adjusted, their fingers fondling their rifles, their eyes staring at the entrenchments of the enemy. The battalion had suffered heavy losses, and these losses had been hard to bear, for a soldier always reasons that men lost during a period of in-action are men badly lost.

The line now sounded like a great machine set to running frantically in the open air, the bright sunshine of a green field. To the *prut* of the magazine rifles was added the under-chorus of the clicking mechanism, steady and swift, as if the hand of one operator was controlling it all. It reminds one always of a loom, a great, grand steel loom, clinking, clanking, plunking, plinking, to weave a woof of thin red threads, the cloth of death. By the men's shoulders, under their eager hands dropped continually the yellow empty shells, spinning into the crushed grass-blades, to remain there and mark for the belated eye the line of a battalion's fight.

All impatience, all rebellious feeling, had passed out of the men as soon as they had been allowed to use their weapons against the enemy. They now were absorbed in this business of hitting something, and all the long training at the rifle ranges, all the pride of the marksman which had been so long alive in them, made them forget for the time everything but shooting. They were as deliberate and exact as so many watchmakers.

A new sense of safety was rightfully upon them. They knew that those mysterious men in the high far trenches in front were having the bullets sping in their faces with relentless and remarkable precision; they knew, in fact, that they were now doing the thing which they had been trained endlessly to do, and they knew they were doing it well. Nolan, for instance, was overjoyed. "Plug 'em," he said. "Plug 'em." He laid his face to his rifle as if it were his mistress. He was aiming under the shadow of a certain portico of a fortified house; there he could faintly see a long black line which he knew to be a loophole cut for riflemen, and he knew that every shot of his was going there under the portico, mayhap through the loophole to the brain of another man like himself. He loaded the awkward magazine of his rifle again and again. He was so intent that he did not know of new orders until he saw the men about him scrambling to their feet and running forward, crouching low as they ran.

He heard a shout. "Come on, boys! We can't be last! We're going up! We're going up." He sprang to his feet and, stooping, ran with the others. Something fine, soft, gentle, touched his heart as he ran. He had loved the regiment, the army, because the regiment, the army, was his life. He had no other outlook; and now these men, his comrades, were performing his dream-scenes for him. They were doing as he had ordained in his visions. It is curious that in this charge he considered himself as rather unworthy. Although he himself was in the assault with the rest of them, it seemed to him that his comrades were dazzlingly courageous. His part, to his mind, was merely that of a man who was going along with the crowd.

He saw Grierson biting madly with his pincers at a barbed wire fence. They were half-way up the beautiful sylvan slope; there was no enemy to be seen, and yet the landscape rained bullets. Somebody punched him violently in the stomach. He thought dully to lie down and rest, but instead he fell with a crash.

The sparse line of men in blue shirts and dirty slouch hats swept on up the hill. He decided to shut his eyes for a moment because he felt very dreamy and peaceful. It seemed only a minute before he heard a voice say, "There he is." Grierson and Watkins had come to look for him. He searched their faces at once and keenly, for he had a thought that the line might be driven down the hill and leave him in Spanish hands. But he saw that everything was secure, and he prepared no questions.

"Nolan," said Grierson clumsily, "do you know me?"

The man on the ground smiled softly. "Of course I know you, you chowder-faced monkey. Why wouldn't I know you?"

Watkins knelt beside him. "Where did they plug you, boy?"

Nolan was somewhat dubious. "It ain't much, I don't think, but it's somewheres there." He laid a finger on the pit of his stomach. They lifted his shirt, and then privately they exchanged a glance of horror.

"Does it hurt, Jimmie?" said Grierson, hoarsely.

"No," said Nolan, "it don't hurt any, but I feel sort of dead-to-the-world and numb all over. I don't think it's very bad."

"Oh, it's all right," said Watkins.

"What I need is a drink," said Nolan, grinning at them. "I'm chilly—lyin' on this damp ground."

"It ain't very damp, Jimmie," said Grierson.

"Well, it is damp," said Nolan, with sudden irritability. "I can feel it. I'm wet, I tell you—wet through—just from lyin' here."

They answered hastily. "Yes, that's so, Jimmie. It is damp. That's so."

"Just put your hand under my back and see how wet the ground is," he said.

"No," they answered. "That's all right, Jimmie. We know it's wet."

"Well, put your hand under and see," he cried, stubbornly.

"Oh, never mind, Jimmie."

"No," he said, in a temper. "See for yourself."

Grierson seemed to be afraid of Nolan's agitation, and so he slipped a hand under the prostrate man, and presently withdrew it covered with blood. "Yes," he said, hiding his hand carefully from Nolan's eyes, "you were right, Jimmie."

"Of course I was," said Nolan, contentedly closing his eyes. "This hillside holds water like a swamp." After a moment he said, "Guess I ought to know. I'm flat here on it, and you fellers are standing up."

He did not know he was dying. He thought he was holding an argument on the condition of the turf.

VI

"Cover his face," said Grierson, in a low and husky voice afterwards.

"What'll I cover it with?" said Watkins.

They looked at themselves. They stood in their shirts, trousers, leggings, shoes; they had nothing.

"Oh," said Grierson, "here's his hat." He brought it and laid it on the face of the dead man. They stood for a time. It was apparent that they thought it essential and decent to say or do something. Finally Watkins said in a broken voice, "Aw, it's a damn shame."

They moved slowly off toward the firing line.

In the blue gloom of evening, in one of the fever tents, the two rows of still figures became hideous, charnel. The languid movement of a hand was surrounded with spectral mystery, and the occasional painful twisting of a body under a blanket was terrifying, as if dead men were moving in their graves under the sod. A heavy odor of sickness and medicine hung in the air.

"What regiment are you in?" said a feeble voice.

"Twenty-ninth Infantry," answered another voice.

"Twenty-ninth! Why, the man on the other side of me is in the Twenty-ninth."

"He is? . . . Hey there, partner, are you in the Twenty-ninth?"

A third voice merely answered wearily: "Martin, of C Company."

"What? Jack, is that you?"

"It's part of me. . . . Who are you?"

"Grierson, you fathead. I thought you were wounded."

There was the noise of a man gulping a great drink of water, and at its conclusion Martin said, "I am."

"Well, what you doin' in the fever place, then?"

Martin replied with drowsy impatience. "Got the fever too."

"Gee!" said Grierson.

Thereafter there was silence in the fever tent, save for the noise made by a man over in a corner, a kind of man always found in an American crowd, a heroic, implacable comedian and patriot, of a humor that has bitterness and ferocity and love in it, and he was wringing from the situation a grim meaning by singing "The Star-Spangled Banner" with all the ardor which could be procured from his fever-stricken body.

"Billie," called Martin in a low voice, "where's Jimmie Nolan?"

"He's dead," said Grierson.

A triangle of raw gold light shone on a side of the tent. Somewhere in the valley an engine's bell was ringing, and it sounded of peace and home as if it hung on a cow's neck.

"An' where's Ike Watkins?"

"Well, he ain't dead, but he got shot through the lungs. They say he ain't got much show."

Through the clouded odors of sickness and medicine rang the dauntless voice of the man in the corner.

December, 1898

[*The Cosmopolitan*, Vol. 26, pp. 164–172.]

A SELF-MADE MAN

AN EXAMPLE OF SUCCESS THAT ANY ONE CAN FOLLOW

Tom had a hole in his shoe. It was very round and very uncomfortable, particularly when he went on wet pavements. Rainy days made him feel that he was walking on frozen dollars, although he had only to think for a moment to discover he was not.

He used up almost two packs of playing cards by means of putting four cards at a time inside his shoe as a sort of temporary sole, which usually lasted about half a day. Once he put in four aces for luck. He went downtown that morning and got refused work. He thought it wasn't a very extraordinary performance for a young man of ability, and he was not sorry that night to find his packs were entirely out of aces.

One day Tom was strolling down Broadway. He was in pursuit of work, although his pace was slow. He had found that he must take the matter coolly. So he puffed tenderly at a cigarette and walked as if he owned stock. He imitated success so successfully, that if it wasn't for the constant reminder (king, queen, deuce, and trey) in his shoe, he would have gone into a store and bought something.

He had borrowed five cents that morning off his landlady, for his mouth craved tobacco. Although he owed her much for board, she had unlimited confidence in him, because his stock of self-assurance was very large indeed. And as it increased in a proper ratio with the amount of his bills, his relations with her seemed on a firm basis. So he strolled along and smoked with his confidence in fortune in nowise impaired by his financial condition.

Of a sudden he perceived an old man seated upon a railing and smoking a clay pipe.

He stopped to look, because he wasn't in a hurry, and because it was an unusual thing on Broadway to see old men seated upon railings and smoking clay pipes.

And to his surprise the old man regarded him very intently in return. He stared, with a wistful expression, into Tom's face, and he clasped his hands in trembling excitement.

Tom was filled with astonishment at the old man's strange demeanor. He stood puffing at his cigarette, and tried to understand matters. Failing, he threw his cigarette away, took a fresh one from his pocket, and approached the old man.

"Got a match?" he inquired, pleasantly.

The old man, much agitated, nearly fell from the railing as he leaned dangerously forward.

"Sonny, can you read?" he demanded in a quavering voice.

"Certainly, I can," said Tom, encouragingly. He waived the affair of the match.

The old man fumbled in his pocket. "You look honest, sonny. I've been lookin' fer an honest feller fer a'most a week. I've set on this railing fer six days," he cried, plaintively.

He drew forth a letter and handed it to Tom. "Read it fer me, sonny, read it," he said, coaxingly.

Tom took the letter and leaned back against the railings. As he opened it and prepared to read, the old man wriggled like a child at a forbidden feast.

Thundering trucks made frequent interruptions, and seven men in a hurry jogged Tom's elbow, but he succeeded in reading what follows:

> Office of Ketchum R. Jones, Attorney-at-Law,
> Tin Can, Nevada, May 19, 18—.

Rufus Wilkins, Esq.

Dear Sir,—I have as yet received no acknowledgment of the draft from the sale of the north section lots, which I forwarded to you on 25th June. I would request an immediate reply concerning it.

Since my last I have sold the three corner lots at five thousand each. The city grew so rapidly in that direction that they were surrounded by brick stores almost before you would know it. I have also sold for four thousand dollars the ten acres of outlying sagebrush, which you once foolishly tried to give away. Mr. Simpson, of Boston, bought the tract. He is very shrewd, no doubt, but he hasn't been in the West long. Still, I think if he holds it for about a thousand years, he may come out all right.

I worked him with the projected-horse-car-line gag.

Inform me of the address of your New York attorneys, and I will send on the papers. Pray do not neglect to write me concerning the draft sent on 25th June.

In conclusion, I might say that if you have any eastern friends who are after good western investments inform them of the glorious future of Tin Can. We now have three railroads, a bank, an electric light plant, a projected horse-car line, and an art society. Also, a saw manufactory, a patent car-wheel mill, and a Methodist Church. Tin Can is marching forward to take her proud stand as the metropolis of the West. The rose-hued future holds no glories to which Tin Can does not—

Tom stopped abruptly. "I guess the important part of the letter came first," he said.

"Yes," cried the old man, "I've heard enough. It is just as I thought. George has robbed his dad." The old man's frail body quivered with grief. Two tears trickled slowly down the furrows of his face.

"Come, come, now," said Tom, patting him tenderly on the back. "Brace up, old feller. What you want to do is to get a lawyer and go put the screws on George."

"Is it really?" asked the old man, eagerly.

"Certainly, it is," said Tom.

"All right," cried the old man, with enthusiasm. "Tell me where to get one." He slid down from the railing and prepared to start off.

Tom reflected. "Well," he said, finally, "I might do for one myself."

"What!" shouted the old man in a voice of admiration. "Are you a lawyer as well as a reader?"

"Well," said Tom again, "I might appear to advantage as one. All you need is a big front," he added, slowly. He was a profane young man.

The old man seized him by the arm. "Come on, then," he cried, "and we'll go put the screws on George."

Tom permitted himself to be dragged by the weak arms of his companion around a corner and along a side street. As they proceeded, he was internally bracing himself for a struggle, and putting large bales of self-assurance around where they would be likely to obstruct the advance of discovery and defeat.

By the time they reached a brownstone house, hidden away in a street of shops and warehouses, his mental balance was so admirable that he seemed to be in possession of enough information and brains to ruin half of the city, and he was no more concerned about the king, queen, deuce, and trey than if they had been discards that didn't fit his draw. He infused so much confidence and courage into his companion that the old man went along the street breathing war, like a decrepit hound on the scent of new blood.

He ambled up the steps of the brownstone house as if he were charging earthworks. He unlocked the door, and they passed along a dark hallway. In a rear room they found a man seated at table engaged with a very late breakfast. He had a diamond in his shirt front and a bit of egg on his cuff.

"George," said the old man in a fierce voice that came from his aged throat with a sound like the crackle of burning twigs, "here's my lawyer, Mr. er—ah—Smith, and we want to know what you did with the draft that was sent on 25th June."

The old man delivered the words as if each one was a musket shot. George's coffee spilled softly upon the tablecover, and his fingers worked convulsively upon a slice of bread. He turned a white, astonished face toward the old man and the intrepid Thomas.

The latter, straight and tall, with a highly legal air, stood at the old man's side. His glowing eyes were fixed upon the face of the man at the table. They seemed like two little detective cameras taking pictures of the other man's thoughts.

"Father, what d—do you mean?" faltered George, totally unable to withstand the two cameras and the highly legal air.

"What do I mean?" said the old man with a feeble roar, as from an ancient lion. "I mean that draft—that's what I mean. Give it up or we'll—we'll"—he paused to gain courage by a glance at the formidable figure at his side—"we'll put the screws on you."

"Well, I was—I was only borrowin' it for 'bout a month," said George.

"Ah," said Tom.

George started, glared at Tom, and then began to shiver like an animal with a broken back. There were a few moments of silence. The old man was fumbling about in his mind for more imprecations. George was wilting and turning limp before the glittering orbs of the valiant attorney. The latter, content with the exalted advantage he had gained by the use of the expression "Ah," spoke no more, but continued to stare.

"Well," said George, finally, in a weak voice, "I s'pose I can give you a check for it, 'though I was only borrowin' it for 'bout a month. I don't think you have treated me fairly, father, with your lawyers and your threats, and all that. But I'll give you the check."

The old man turned to his attorney. "Well?" he asked.

Tom looked at the son and held an impressive debate with himself. "I think we may accept the check," he said coldly after a time.

George arose and tottered across the room. He drew a check that made the attorney's heart come privately into his mouth. As he and his client passed triumphantly out, he turned a last highly legal glare upon George that reduced that individual to a mere paste.

On the sidewalk the old man went into a spasm of delight and called his attorney all the admiring and endearing names there were to be had. "Lord, how you settled him!" he cried ecstatically.

They walked slowly back toward Broadway. "The scoundrel," murmured the old man. "I'll never see 'im again. I'll desert 'im. I'll find a nice quiet boarding place and—"

"That's all right," said Tom. "I know one. I'll take you right up"—which he did.

He came near being happy ever after. The old man lived at advanced rates in the front room at Tom's boarding house. And the latter basked in the proprietress's smiles, which had a commercial value, and were a great improvement on many we see.

The old man, with his quantities of sagebrush, thought Thomas owned all the virtues mentioned in high class literature, and his opinion, too, was of commercial value. Also, he knew a man who knew another man who received an impetus which made him engage Thomas on terms that were highly satisfactory. Then it was that the latter learned he had not succeeded sooner because he did not know a man who knew another man.

So it came to pass that Tom grew to be Thomas G. Somebody. He achieved that position in life from which he could hold out for good wines when he went to poor restaurants. His name became entangled with the name of Wilkins in the ownership of vast and valuable tracts of sagebrush in Tin Can, Nevada.

At the present day he is so great that he lunches frugally at high prices. His fame has spread through the land as a man who carved his way to fortune with no help but his undaunted pluck, his tireless energy, and his sterling integrity.

Newspapers apply to him now, and he writes long signed articles to struggling young men, in which he gives the best possible advice as to how to become wealthy. In these articles, he, in a burst of glorification, cites the king, queen, deuce, and trey, the four aces, and all that. He alludes tenderly to the nickel he borrowed and spent for cigarettes as the foundation of his fortune.

"To succeed in life," he writes, "the youth of America have only to see an old man seated upon a railing and smoking a clay pipe. Then go up and ask him for a match."

March, 1899
[*The Cornhill Magazine*, Vol. 79, pp. 324–329.]

THE CLAN OF NO-NAME*

Unwind my riddle.
Cruel as hawks the hours fly;
Wounded men seldom come home to die;
The hard waves see an arm flung high;
Scorn hits strong because of a lie;
Yet there exists a mystic tie.
Unwind my riddle.

I

She was out in the garden. Her mother came to her rapidly. "Margharita! Margharita, Mister Smith is here! Come!" Her mother was fat and commercially excited. Mister Smith was a matter of some importance to all Tampa people, and since he was really in love with Margharita he was distinctly of more importance to this particular household.

Palm trees tossed their sprays over the fence toward the rutted sand of the street. A little foolish fishpond in the center of the garden emitted a sound of redfins flipping, flipping. "No, mamma," said the girl; "let Mr. Smith wait. I like the garden in the moonlight."

Her mother threw herself into that state of virtuous astonishment which is the weapon of her kind. "Margharita!"

The girl evidently considered herself to be a privileged belle, for she answered quite carelessly, "Oh, let him wait."

The mother threw abroad her arms with a semblance of great high-minded suffering and withdrew. Margharita walked alone in the moonlit garden. Also an electric light threw its shivering gleam over part of her parade.

There was peace for a time. Then, suddenly, through the faint brown palings was stuck an envelope white and square. Margharita approached this envelope with an indifferent stride. She hummed a silly air, she bore herself casually, but there was something that made her grasp it hard, a peculiar muscular exhibition, not discernible to indifferent eyes. She did not clutch it, but she took it—simply took it in a way that meant everything and, to measure it by vision, it was a picture of the most complete disregard.

She stood straight for a moment; then she drew from her bosom a photograph and thrust it through the palings. She walked rapidly into the house.

* *Wounds in the Rain.*

II

A man in garb of blue and white—something related to what we call bed-ticking—was seated in a curious little cupola on the top of a Spanish blockhouse. The blockhouse sided a white military road that curved away from the man's sight into a blur of trees. On all sides of him were fields of tall grass, studded with palms and lined with fences of barbed wire. The sun beat aslant through the trees, and the man sped his eyes deep into the dark tropical shadows, that seemed velvet with coolness. These tranquil vistas resembled painted scenery in a theater, and, moreover, a hot, heavy silence lay upon the land.

The soldier in the watching place leaned an unclean Mauser rifle in a corner and, reaching down, took a glowing coal on a bit of palm bark handed up to him by a comrade. The men below were mainly asleep. The sergeant in command drowsed near the open door, the arm above his head showing his long keen-angled chevrons, attached carelessly with safety pins. The sentry lit his cigarette and puffed languorously.

Suddenly he heard from the air around him the querulous, deadly swift spit of rifle bullets; and an instant later the poppety-pop of a small volley sounded in his face, close, as if it were fired only ten feet away. Involuntarily he threw back his head quickly, as if he were protecting his nose from a falling tile. He screamed an alarm and fell into the blockhouse. In the gloom of it, men with their breaths coming sharply between their teeth were tumbling wildly for positions at the loopholes. The door had been slammed, but the sergeant lay just within, propped up as when he drowsed, but now with blood flowing steadily over the hand that he pressed flatly to his chest. His face was in stark yellow agony; he chokingly repeated: "Fuego! Por Dios, hombres!"

The men's ill-conditioned weapons were jammed through the loopholes, and they began to fire from all four sides of the blockhouse, from the simple datum, apparently, that the enemy were in the vicinity. The fumes of burnt powder grew stronger and stronger in the little square fortress. The rattling of the magazine locks was incessant, and the interior might have been that of a gloomy manufactory if it were not for the sergeant down under the feet of the men, coughing out: "Por Dios, hombres! Por Dios! Fuego!"

III

A string of five Cubans, in linen that had turned earthy brown in color, slid through the woods at a pace that was neither a walk nor a run. It was a kind of rack. In fact, the whole manner of the men, as they thus moved, bore a rather comic resemblance to the American pacing horse. But they had come many miles since sunup over mountainous and half-marked paths, and were plainly still fresh. The men were all practicos—guides.

They made no sound in their swift travel, but moved their half-shod feet with the skill of cats. The woods lay around them in a deep silence, such as one might find at the bottom of a lake.

Suddenly the leading practico raised his hand. The others pulled up short and dropped the butts of their weapons calmly and noiselessly to the ground. The leader whistled a low note, and immediately another practico appeared from the bushes. He moved close to the leader without a word, and then they spoke in whispers.

"There are twenty men and a sergeant in the blockhouse."

"And the road?"

"One company of cavalry passed to the east this morning at seven o'clock. They were escorting four carts. An hour later, one horseman rode swiftly to the westward. About noon, ten infantry soldiers with a corporal were taken from the big fort and put in the first blockhouse, to the east of the fort. There were already twelve men there. We saw a Spanish column moving off toward Mariel."

"No more?"

"No more."

"Good. But the cavalry?"

"It is all right. They were going a long march."

"The expedition is a half league behind. Go and tell the general."

The scout disappeared. The five other men lifted their guns and resumed their rapid and noiseless progress. A moment later no sound broke the stillness save the thump of a mango, as it dropped lazily from its tree to the grass. So strange had been the apparition of these men, their dress had been so allied in color to the soil, their passing had so little disturbed the solemn rumination of the forest, and their going had been so like a spectral dissolution, that a witness could have wondered if he dreamed.

IV

A small expedition had landed with arms from the United States, and had now come out of the hills and to the edge of a wood. Before them was a long-grassed rolling prairie marked with palms. A half mile away was the military road, and they could see the top of a blockhouse. The insurgent scouts were moving somewhere off in the grass. The general sat comfortably under a tree, while his staff of three young officers stood about him chatting. Their linen clothing was notable from being distinctly whiter than that of the men who, one hundred and fifty in number, lay on the ground in a long brown fringe, ragged—indeed, bare in many places—but singularly reposeful, unworried, veteran-like.

The general, however, was thoughtful. He pulled continually at his little thin mustache. As far as the heavily patrolled and guarded military road was concerned, the insurgents had been in the habit of dashing across it in small bodies whenever they pleased, but to safely scoot over it with a valuable convoy of arms was decidedly a more important thing. So the general awaited the return of his practicos with anxiety. The still pampas betrayed no sign of their existence.

The general gave some orders, and an officer counted off twenty men to go with him and delay any attempt of the troop of cavalry to return from the eastward. It was not an easy task, but it was a familiar task—checking the advance of a greatly superior force by a very hard fire from concealment. A few rifles had often bayed a strong column for sufficient length of time for all strategic purposes. The twenty men pulled themselves together tranquilly. They looked quite indifferent. Indeed, they had the supremely casual manner of old soldiers, hardened to battle as a condition of existence.

Thirty men were then told off, whose function it was to worry and rag at the blockhouse and check any advance from the westward. A hundred men, carrying precious burdens—besides their own equipment—were to pass in as much of a rush as possible between these two wings, cross the road, and skip for the hills, their retreat being covered by a combination of the two firing parties. It was a trick that needed both luck and neat arrangement. Spanish columns were for ever prowling through this province in all directions and at all times. Insurgent bands—the lightest of light infantry—were kept on the jump, even when they were not incommoded by fifty boxes, each one large enough for the coffin of a little man, and heavier than if the little man were in it, and fifty small but formidable boxes of ammunition.

The carriers stood to their boxes, and the firing parties leaned on their rifles. The general arose and strolled to and fro, his hands behind him. Two of his staff were jesting at the third, a young man with a face less bronzed, and with very new accoutrements. On the strap of his cartouche were a gold star and a silver star, placed in a horizontal line, denoting that he was a second lieutenant. He seemed very happy; he laughed at all their jests, although his eye roved continually over the sunny grasslands, where was going to happen his first fight. One of his stars was bright, like his hopes; the other was pale, like death.

Two practicos came racking out of the grass. They spoke rapidly to the general; he turned and nodded to his officers. The two firing parties filed out and diverged toward their positions. The general watched them through his glasses. It was strange to note how soon they were dim to the unaided eye. The little patches of brown in the green grass did not look like men at all.

Practicos continually ambled up to the general. Finally he turned and made a sign to the bearers. The first twenty men in line picked up their boxes, and this movement rapidly spread to the tail of the line. The weighted procession moved painfully out upon the sunny prairie. The general, marching at the head of it, glanced continually back, as if he were compelled to drag behind him some ponderous iron chain. Besides the obvious mental worry, his face bore an expression of intense physical strain, and he even bent his shoulders, unconsciously tugging at the chain to hurry it through this enemy-crowded valley.

v

The fight was opened by eight men who, snuggling in the grass within three hundred yards of the blockhouse, suddenly blazed away at the bedticking figure in the cupola and at the open door, where they could see vague outlines. Then they laughed and yelled insulting language, for they knew that, as far as the Spaniards were concerned, the surprise was as much as having a diamond bracelet turn to soap. It was this volley that smote the sergeant and caused the man in the cupola to scream and tumble from his perch.

The eight men, as well as all other insurgents within fair range, had chosen good positions for lying close, and for a time they let the blockhouse rage, although the soldiers therein could occasionally hear, above the clamor of their weapons, shrill and almost wolfish calls coming from men whose lips were laid against the ground. But it is not in the nature of them of Spanish blood, and armed with rifles, to long endure the sight of anything so tangible as an enemy's blockhouse without shooting at it—other conditions being partly favorable. Presently the steaming soldiers in the little fort could hear the sping and shiver of bullets striking the wood that guarded their bodies.

A perfectly white smoke floated up over each firing Cuban, the penalty of the Remington rifle, but about the blockhouse there was only the lightest gossamer of blue. The blockhouse stood always for some big, clumsy, and rather incompetent animal, while the insurgents, scattered on two sides of it, were little enterprising creatures of another species, too wise to come too near, but joyously raging at its easiest flanks and dirling the lead into its sides in a way to make it fume and spit and rave like the tomcat when the glad free-band foxhound pups catch him in the lane.

The men, outlying in the grass, chuckled deliriously at the fury of the Spanish fire. They howled opprobrium to encourage the Spaniards to fire more ill-used, incapable bullets. Whenever an insurgent was about to fire, he ordinarily prefixed the affair with a speech. "Do you want something to eat? Yes? All right." Bang! "Eat that." The more common expressions of the incredibly foul Spanish tongue were trifles light as air in this badinage, which was shrieked out from the grass during the spin of bullets and the dull rattle of the shooting.

But at some time there came a series of sounds from the east, that began in a few disconnected pruts and ended as if an amateur was trying to play the long roll upon a muffled drum. Those of the insurgents in the blockhouse-attacking party who had neighbors in the grass turned and looked at them seriously. They knew what the new sound meant. It meant that the twenty men who had gone to the eastward were now engaged. A column of some kind was approaching from that direction, and they knew by the clatter that it was a solemn occasion.

In the first place, they were now on the wrong side of the road. They were obliged to cross it to rejoin the main body, provided, of course, that the main body succeeded itself in crossing it. To accomplish this, the party at the blockhouse would have to move to the eastward until out of sight or good range of the maddened little fort. But, judging from the heaviness of the firing, the party of twenty who protected the east were almost sure to be driven immediately back. Hence travel in that direction would become exceedingly hazardous. Hence a man looked seriously at his neighbor. It might easily be that in a moment they were to become an isolated force and woefully on the wrong side of the road.

Any retreat to the westward was absurd, since primarily they would have to widely circle the blockhouse, and, more than that, they could hear even now, in that direction, Spanish bugle calling to Spanish bugle far and near, until one would think that every man in Cuba was a trumpeter and had come forth to parade his talent.

VI

The insurgent general stood in the middle of the road gnawing his lips. Occasionally, he stamped a foot and beat his hands passionately together. The carriers were streaming past him, patient, sweating fellows, bowed under their burdens, but they could not move fast enough for him when others of his men were engaged both to the east and to the west, and he, too, knew from the sound that those to the east were in a sore way. Moreover, he could hear that accursed bugling, bugling, bugling in the west.

He turned suddenly to the new lieutenant, who stood behind him, pale and quiet. "Did you ever think a hundred men were so many?" he cried, incensed to the point of beating them. Then he said longingly: "Oh, for a half an hour! Or even twenty minutes!"

A practico racked violently up from the east. It is characteristic of these men that, although they take a certain roadster gait and hold it for ever, they cannot really run, sprint, race. "Captain Rodriguez is attacked by two hundred men, señor, and the cavalry is behind them. He wishes to know—"

The general was furious; he pointed. "Go! Tell Rodriguez to hold his place for twenty minutes, even if he leaves every man dead."

The practico shambled hastily off.

The last of the carriers were swarming across the road. The rifle-drumming in the east was swelling out and out, evidently coming slowly nearer. The general bit his nails. He wheeled suddenly upon the young lieutenant. "Go to Bas at the blockhouse. Tell him to hold the devil himself for ten minutes and then bring his men out of that place."

The long line of bearers was crawling like a dun worm toward the safety of the foothills. High bullets sang a faint song over the aide as he saluted. The bugles had in the west ceased, and that was more ominous than bugling. It meant that the Spanish troops were about to march, or perhaps that they had marched.

The young lieutenant ran along the road until he came to the bend which marked the range of sight from the blockhouse. He drew his machete, his stunning new machete, and hacked feverishly at the barbed wire fence which lined the north side of the road at that point. The first wire was obdurate, because it was too high for his stroke, but two more cut like candy, and he stepped over the remaining one, tearing his trousers in passing on the lively serpentine ends of the severed wires. Once out in the field, and bullets seemed to know him and call for him and speak their wish to kill him. But he ran on, because it was his duty, and because he would be shamed before men if he did not do his duty, and because he was desolate out there all alone in the fields with death.

A man running in this manner from the rear was in immensely greater danger than those who lay snug and close. But he did not know it. He thought, because he was five hundred—four hundred and fifty—four hundred yards away from the enemy and the others were only three hundred yards away, that they were in far more peril. He ran to join them because of his opinion. He did not care to do it, but he thought that was what men of his kind would do in such a case. There was a standard, and he must follow it, obey it, because it was a monarch, the Prince of Conduct.

A bewildered and alarmed face raised itself from the grass, and a voice cried to him: "Drop, Manolo! Drop! Drop!" He recognized Bas and flung himself to the earth beside him.

"Why," he said panting, "what's the matter?"

"Matter?" said Bas. "You are one of the most desperate and careless officers I know. When I saw you coming I wouldn't have given a peseta for your life."

"Oh, no," said the young aide. Then he repeated his orders rapidly. But he was hugely delighted. He knew Bas well; Bas was a pupil of Maceo; Bas invariably led his men; he never was a mere spectator of their battle; he was known for it throughout the western end of the island. The new officer had early achieved a part of his ambition—to be called a brave man by established brave men.

"Well, if we get away from here quickly it will be better for us," said Bas, bitterly. "I've lost six men killed, and more wounded. Rodriguez can't hold his position there, and in a little time more than a thousand men will come from the other direction."

He hissed a low call, and later the young aide saw some of the men sneaking off with the wounded, lugging them on their backs as porters carry sacks. The fire from the blockhouse had become aweary, and as the insurgent fire also slackened, Bas and the young lieutenant lay in the weeds listening to the approach of the eastern fight, which was sliding toward them like a door to shut them off.

Bas groaned. "I leave my dead. Look there." He swung his hand in a gesture, and the lieutenant, looking, saw a corpse. He was not stricken as he expected; there was very little blood; it was a mere thing.

"Time to travel," said Bas suddenly. His imperative hissing brought his men near him; there were a few hurried questions and answers; then, characteristically, the men turned in the grass, lifted their rifles, and fired a last volley into the blockhouse, accompanying it with their shrill cries. Scrambling low to the ground, they were off in a winding line for safety. Breathing hard, the lieutenant stumbled his way forward. Behind him he could hear the men calling each to each: "Segue! Segue! Segue! Go on! Get out! Git!" Everybody understood that the peril of crossing the road was compounding from minute to minute.

VII

When they reached the gap through which the expedition had passed, they fled out upon the road like scared wild fowl tracking along a sea-beach. A cloud of blue figures far up this dignified shaded avenue fired at once. The men already had begun to laugh as they shied one by one across the road. "Segue! Segue!" The hard part for the nerves had been the lack of information of the amount of danger. Now that they could see it, they accounted it all the more lightly for their previous anxiety.

Over in the other field, Bas and the young lieutenant found Rodriguez, his machete in one hand, his revolver in the other, smoky, dirty, sweating. He shrugged his shoulders when he saw them and pointed disconsolately to the brown thread of carriers moving toward the foothills. His own men were crouched in line just in front of him, blazing like a prairie fire.

Now began the fight of a scant rear guard to hold back the pressing Spaniards until the carriers could reach the top of the ridge, a mile away. This ridge, by the way, was more steep than any roof; it conformed more to the sides of a French warship. Trees grew vertically from it, however, and a man burdened only with his rifle usually pulled himself wheezingly up in a sort of ladder-climbing process, grabbing the slim trunks above him. How the loaded carriers were to conquer it in a hurry, no one knew. Rodriguez shrugged his shoulders as one who would say with philosophy, smiles, tears, courage: "Isn't this a mess!"

At an order, the men scattered back for four hundred yards with the rapidity and mystery of a handful of pebbles flung in the night. They left one behind who cried out, but it was now a game in which some were sure to be left behind to cry out.

The Spaniards deployed on the road and for twenty minutes remained there, pouring into the field such a fire from their magazines as was hardly heard at Gettysburg. As a matter of truth the insurgents were at this time doing very little shooting, being chary of ammunition. But it is possible for the soldier to confuse himself with his own noise, and undoubtedly the Spanish troops thought throughout their din that they were being fiercely engaged. Moreover, a firing line—particularly at night or when opposed to a hidden foe—is nothing less than an emotional chord, a chord of a harp that sings because a puff of air arrives or when a bit of down touches it. This is always true of new troops or stupid troops, and these troops were rather stupid troops. But the way in which they mowed the verdure in the distance was a sight for a farmer.

Presently the insurgents slunk back to another position, where they fired enough shots to stir again the Spaniards into an opinion that they were in a heavy fight. But such a misconception could only endure for a number of minutes. Presently it was plain that the Spaniards were about to advance, and, moreover, word was brought to Rodriguez that a small band of guerillas were already making an attempt to worm around the right flank. Rodriguez cursed despairingly; he sent both Bas and the young lieutenant to that end of the line to hold the men to their work as long as possible.

In reality the men barely needed the presence of their officers. The kind of fighting left practically everything to the discretion of the individual, and they arrived at concert of action mainly because of the equality of experience in the wisdoms of bushwhacking.

The yells of the guerillas could plainly be heard, and the insurgents answered in kind. The young lieutenant found desperate work on the right flank. The men were raving mad with it, babbling, tearful, almost frothing at the mouth. Two terrible bloody creatures passed him, creeping on all fours, and one in a whimper was calling upon God, his mother, and a saint. The guerillas, as effectually concealed as the insurgents, were driving their bullets low through the smoke at sight of a flame, a movement of the grass, or sight of a patch of dirty brown coat. They were no column-o'-four soldiers; they were as slinky and snaky and quick as so many Indians. They were, moreover, native Cubans, and because of their treachery to the one-star flag they never by any chance received quarter if they fell into the hands of the insurgents. Nor, if the case was reversed, did they ever give quarter. It was life and life, death and death; there was no middle ground, no compromise. If a man's crowd was rapidly retreating and he was tumbled over by a slight hit, he should curse the sacred graves that the wound was not through the precise center of his heart. The machete is a fine broad blade, but it is not so nice as a drilled hole in the chest; no man wants his deathbed to be a shambles. The men fighting on the insurgents' right knew that if they fell they were lost.

On the extreme right, the young lieutenant found five men in a little saucer-like hollow. Two were dead, one was wounded and staring blankly at the sky, and two were emptying hot rifles furiously. Some of the guerillas had snaked into positions only a hundred yards away.

The young man rolled in among the men in the saucer. He could hear the barking of the guerillas and the screams of the two insurgents. The rifles were popping and spitting in his face, it seemed, while the whole land was alive with a noise of rolling and drumming. Men could have gone drunken in all this flashing and flying and snarling and din, but at this time he was very deliberate. He knew that he was thrusting himself into a trap whose door, once closed, opened only when the black hand knocked; and every part of him seemed to be in panic-stricken revolt. But something controlled him; something moved him inexorably in one direction; he perfectly understood, but he was only sad, sad with a serene dignity, with the countenance of a mournful young prince. He was of a kind—that seemed to be it; and the men of his kind, on peak or plain, from the dark northern ice fields to the hot wet jungles, through all wine and want, through all lies and unfamiliar truth, dark or light—the men of his kind were governed by their gods, and each man knew the law and yet could not give tongue to it, but it was the law; and if the spirits of the men of his kind were all sitting in critical judgment upon him even then in the sky, he could not have bettered his conduct; he needs must obey the law, and always with the law there is only one way. But from peak and plain, from dark northern ice fields and hot wet jungles, through wine and want, through all lies and unfamiliar truth, dark or light, he heard breathed to him the approval and the benediction of his brethren.

He stooped and gently took a dead man's rifle and some cartridges. The battle was hurrying, hurrying, hurrying, but he was in no haste. His glance caught the staring eye of the wounded soldier, and he smiled at him quietly. The man—simple doomed peasant—was not of his kind, but the law on fidelity was clear.

He thrust a cartridge into the Remington and crept up beside the two unhurt men. Even as he did so, three or four bullets cut so close to him that all his flesh tingled. He fired carefully into the smoke. The guerillas were certainly not now more than fifty yards away.

He raised him coolly for his second shot, and almost instantly it was as if some giant had struck him in the chest with a beam. It whirled him in a great spasm back into the saucer. As he put his two hands to his breast, he could hear the guerillas screeching exultantly, every throat vomiting forth all the infamy of a language prolific in the phrasing of infamy.

One of the other men came rolling slowly down the slope, while his rifle followed him and, striking another rifle, clanged out. Almost immediately the survivor howled and fled wildly. A whole volley missed him, and then one or more shots caught him as a bird is caught on the wing.

The young lieutenant's body seemed galvanized from head to foot. He concluded that he was not hurt very badly, but when he tried to move he found that he could not lift his hands from his breast. He had turned to lead. He had had a plan of taking a photograph from his pocket and looking at it.

There was a stir in the grass at the edge of the saucer, and a man appeared there, looking where lay the four insurgents. His negro face was not an eminently ferocious one in its lines, but now it was lit with an illimitable blood-greed. He and the young lieutenant exchanged a singular glance; then he came stepping eagerly down. The young lieutenant closed his eyes, for he did not want to see the flash of the machete.

VIII

The Spanish colonel was in a rage, and yet immensely proud; immensely proud, and yet in a rage of disappointment. There had been a fight, and the insurgents had retreated, leaving their dead; but still a valuable expedition had broken through his lines and escaped to the mountains. As a matter of truth, he was not sure whether to be wholly delighted or wholly angry, for well he knew that the importance lay not so much in the truthful account of the action as it did in the heroic prose of the official report, and in the fight itself lay material for a purple splendid poem. The insurgents had run away; no one could deny it; it was plain even to whatever privates had fired with their eyes shut. This was worth a loud blow and splutter. However, when all was said and done, he could not help but reflect that if he had captured this expedition he would have been a brigadier general, if not more.

He was a short, heavy man with a beard, who walked in a manner common to all elderly Spanish officers, and to many young ones; that is to say, he walked as if his spine was a stick and a little longer than his body; as if he suffered from some disease of the backbone which allowed him but scant use of his legs. He toddled along the road, gesticulating disdainfully and muttering: "Ca! Ca! Ca!"

He berated some soldiers for an immaterial thing, and as he approached, the men stepped precipitately back, as if he were a fire engine. They were most of them young fellows who displayed, when under orders, the manner of so many faithful dogs. At present they were black, tongue-hanging, thirsty boys, bathed in the nervous weariness of the after-battle time.

Whatever he may truly have been in character, the colonel closely resembled a gluttonous and libidinous old pig, filled from head to foot with the pollution of a sinful life. "Ca!" he snarled, as he toddled. "Ca! Ca!" The soldiers saluted as they backed to the side of the road. The air was full of the odor of burnt rags. Over on the prairie guerillas and regulars were rummaging the grass. A few unimportant shots sounded from near the base of the hills.

A guerilla, glad with plunder, came to a Spanish captain. He held in his hand a photograph. "Mira, señor. I took this from the body of an officer whom I killed machete to machete."

The captain shot from the corner of his eye a cynical glance at the guerilla, a glance which commented upon the last part of the statement. "M-m-m," he said. He took the photograph and gazed with a slow faint smile, the smile of a man who knows bloodshed and homes and love, at the face of a girl. He turned the photograph presently, and on the back of it was written: "One lesson in English I will give you—this: I love you. Margharita." The photograph had been taken in Tampa.

The officer was silent for a half minute, while his face still wore the slow faint smile. "Pobrecito," he murmured finally, with a philosophic sigh which was brother to a shrug. Without deigning a word to the guerilla he thrust the photograph in his pocket and walked away.

High over the green earth, in the dizzy blue heights, some great birds were slowly circling with down-turned beaks.

IX

Margharita was in the gardens. The blue electric rays shone through the plumes of the palm and shivered in feathery images on the walk. In the little foolish fishpond some stalwart fish was apparently bullying the others, for often there sounded a frantic splashing.

Her mother came to her rapidly. "Margharita! Mister Smith is here! Come!"

"Oh, is he?" cried the girl. She followed her mother to the house. She swept into the little parlor with a grand air, the egotism of a savage. Smith had heard the whirl of her skirts in the hall, and his heart, as usual, thumped hard enough to make him gasp. Every time he called, he would sit waiting with the dull fear in his breast that her mother would enter and indifferently announce that she had gone up to heaven or off to New

York with one of his dream rivals, and he would never see her again in this wide world. And he would conjure up tricks to then escape from the house without any one observing his face break up into furrows. It was part of his love to believe in the absolute treachery of his adored one. So whenever he heard the whirl of her skirts in the hall he felt that he had again leased happiness from a dark fate.

She was rosily beaming and all in white. "Why, Mister Smith," she exclaimed, as if he was the last man in the world she expected to see.

"Good-evenin'," he said, shaking hands nervously. He was always awkward and unlike himself at the beginning of one of these calls. It took him some time to get into form.

She posed her figure in operatic style on a chair before him, and immediately galloped off a mile of questions, information of herself, gossip and general outcries which left him no obligation but to look beamingly intelligent and from time to time say "Yes?" His personal joy, however, was to stare at her beauty.

When she stopped and wandered as if uncertain which way to talk, there was a minute of silence, which each of them had been educated to feel was very incorrect; very incorrect indeed. Polite people always babbled at each other like two brooks.

He knew that the responsibility was upon him, and, although his mind was mainly upon the form of the proposal of marriage which he intended to make later, it was necessary that he should maintain his reputation as a well-bred man by saying something at once. It flashed upon him to ask: "Won't you please play?" But the time for the piano ruse was not yet; it was too early. So he said the first thing that came into his head: "Too bad about young Manolo Prat being killed over there in Cuba, wasn't it?"

"Wasn't it a pity?" she answered.

"They say his mother is heartbroken," he continued. "They're afraid she's goin' to die."

"And wasn't it queer that we didn't hear about it for almost two months?"

"Well, it's no use tryin' to git quick news from there."

Presently they advanced to matters more personal, and she used upon him a series of star-like glances which crumpled him at once to squalid slavery. He gloated upon her, afraid, afraid, yet more avaricious than a thousand misers. She fully comprehended; she laughed and taunted him with her eyes. She impressed upon him that she was like a will-o'-the-wisp, beautiful beyond compare, but impossible, almost impossible, at least very difficult; then again, suddenly, impossible—impossible—impossible. He was glum; he would never dare propose to this radiance; it was like asking to be pope.

A moment later, there chimed into the room something that he knew to be a more tender note. The girl became dreamy as she looked at him; her voice lowered to a delicious intimacy of tone. He leaned forward; he was about to outpour his bully-ragged soul in fine words, when—presto—she was the most casual person he had ever laid eyes upon, and was asking him about the route of the proposed trolley line.

But nothing short of a fire could stop him now. He grabbed her hand. "Margharita," he murmured gutturally, "I want you to marry me."

She glared at him in the most perfect lie of astonishment. "What do you say?"

He arose, and she thereupon arose also and fled back a step. He could only stammer out her name. And thus they stood, defying the principles of the dramatic art.

"I love you," he said at last.

"How—how do I know you really—truly love me?" she said, raising her eyes timorously to his face; and this timorous glance, this one timorous glance, made him the superior person in an instant. He went forward as confident as a grenadier, and, taking both her hands, kissed her.

That night she took a stained photograph from her dressing table and, holding it over the candle, burned it to nothing, her red lips meanwhile parted with the intentness of her occupation. On the back of the photograph was written: "One lesson in English I will give you—this: I love you."

For the word is clear only to the kind who on peak or plain, from dark northern ice fields to the hot wet jungles, through all wine and want, through lies and unfamiliar truth, dark or light, are governed by the unknown gods; and, though each man knows the law, no man may give tongue to it.

March, 1899?
[*Wounds in the Rain*. New York: Frederick A.
Stokes Co. (September, 1900), pp. 42–73.]

GOD REST YE, MERRY GENTLEMEN*

Little Nell, sometimes called the Blessed Damosel, was a war correspondent for the New York *Eclipse,* and at sea on the dispatch boats he wore pajamas, and on shore he wore whatever fate allowed him, which clothing was in the main unsuitable to the climate. He had been cruising in the Caribbean on a small tug, awash always, habitable never, wildly looking for Cervera's fleet; although what he was going to do with four armored

---

* *Wounds in the Rain.*

cruisers and two destroyers in the event of his really finding them had not been explained by the managing editor. The cable instructions read: "Take tug; go find Cervera's fleet." If his unfortunate nine-knot craft should happen to find these great twenty-knot ships, with their two spiteful and faster attendants, Little Nell had wondered how he was going to lose them again. He had marveled, both publicly and in secret, on the uncompromising asininity of managing editors at odd moments, but he had wasted little time. The *Jefferson G. Johnson* was already coaled, so he passed the word to his skipper, bought some tinned meats, cigars, and beer, and soon the *Johnson* sailed on her mission, tooting her whistle in graceful farewell to some friends of hers in the bay.

So the *Johnson* crawled giddily to one wave-height after another, and fell, aslant, into one valley after another for a longer period than was good for the hearts of the men, because the *Johnson* was merely a harbor tug, with no architectural intention of parading the high seas, and the crew had never seen the decks all white water like a mere sunken reef. As for the cook, he blasphemed hopelessly hour in and hour out, meanwhile pursuing the equipment of his trade frantically from side to side of the galley. Little Nell dealt with a great deal of grumbling, but he knew it was not the real evil grumbling. It was merely the unhappy words of men who wished expression of comradeship for their wet, forlorn, half-starved lives, to which, they explained, they were not accustomed, and for which, they explained, they were not properly paid. Little Nell condoled and condoled without difficulty. He laid words of gentle sympathy before them, and smothered his own misery behind the face of a reporter of the New York *Eclipse*. But they tossed themselves in their cockleshell even as far as Martinique; they knew many races and many flags, but they did not find Cervera's fleet. If they had found that elusive squadron this timid story would never have been written; there would probably have been a lyric. The *Johnson* limped one morning into the Mole St. Nicholas, and there Little Nell received this dispatch: "Can't understand your inaction. What are you doing with the boat? Report immediately. Fleet transports already left Tampa. Expected destination near Santiago. Proceed there immediately. Place yourself under orders.—Rogers, *Eclipse*."

One day, steaming along the high, luminous blue coast of Santiago province, they fetched into view the fleets, a knot of masts and funnels, looking incredibly inshore, as if they were glued to the mountains. Then mast left mast, and funnel left funnel, slowly, slowly, and the shore remained still, but the fleets seemed to move out toward the eager *Johnson*. At the speed of nine knots an hour the scene separated into its parts. On an easily rolling sea, under a crystal sky, black-hulled transports—erstwhile packets—lay waiting, while gray cruisers and gunboats lay near shore, shelling the beach and some woods. From their gray sides came thin red flashes, belches of white smoke, and then over the waters sounded boom—boom—boom-boom. The crew of the *Jefferson G. Johnson* forgave Little Nell all the suffering of a previous fortnight.

To the westward, about the mouth of Santiago harbor, sat a row of castellated gray battleships, their eyes turned another way, waiting.

The *Johnson* swung past a transport whose decks and rigging were aswarm with black figures, as if a tribe of bees had alighted upon a log. She swung past a cruiser indignant at being left out of the game, her deck thick with white-clothed tars watching the play of their luckier brethren. The cold blue lifting seas tilted the big ships easily, slowly, and heaved the little ones in the usual sinful way, as if very little babes had surreptitiously mounted sixteen-hand trotting hunters. The *Johnson* leered and tumbled her way through a community of ships. The bombardment ceased, and some of the troopships edged in near the land. Soon boats black with men and towed by launches were almost lost to view in the scintillant mystery of light which appeared where the sea met the land. A disembarkation had begun. The *Johnson* sped on at her nine knots, and Little Nell chafed exceedingly, gloating upon the shore through his glasses, anon glancing irritably over the side to note the efforts of the excited tug. Then at last they were in a sort of cove, with troopships, newspaper boats, and cruisers on all sides of them, and over the water came a great hum of human voices, punctuated frequently by the clang of engine-room gongs as the steamers maneuvered to avoid jostling.

In reality it was the great moment—the moment for which men, ships, islands, and continents had been waiting for months; but somehow it did not look it. It was very calm; a certain strip of high, green, rocky shore was being rapidly populated from boat after boat; that was all. Like many preconceived moments, it refused to be supreme.

But nothing lessened Little Nell's frenzy. He knew that the army was landing—he could see it; and little did he care if the great moment did not look its part—it was his virtue as a correspondent to recognize the great moment in any disguise. The *Johnson* lowered a boat for him, and he dropped into it swiftly, forgetting everything. However, the mate, a bearded philanthropist, flung after him a mackintosh and a bottle of whiskey. Little Nell's face was turned toward those other boats filled with men, all eyes upon the placid, gentle, noiseless shore. Little Nell saw many soldiers seated stiffly beside upright rifle barrels, their blue breasts crossed with white shelter tents and blanket rolls. Launches screeched; jack-tars pushed or pulled with their boathooks; a beach was alive with working soldiers, some of them stark naked. Little Nell's boat touched the shore amid a babble of tongues, dominated at that time by a single stern voice, which was repeating, "Fall in, B Company!"

He took his mackintosh and his bottle of whiskey and invaded Cuba. It was a trifle bewildering. Companies of those same men in blue and brown were being rapidly formed and marched off across a little open space—near a pool—near some palm trees—near a house—into the hills. At one side, a mulatto in dirty linen and an old straw hat was hospitably using a machete to cut open some green cocoanuts for a group of idle invaders. At the other side, up a bank, a blockhouse was burning furiously; while near it some railway sheds were smoldering, with a little Rogers engine standing amid the ruins, gray, almost white, with ashes until it resembled a ghost. Little Nell dodged the encrimsoned blockhouse, and proceeded where he saw a little village street lined with flimsy wooden cottages. Some ragged Cuban cavalrymen were tranquilly tending their horses in a shed which had not yet grown cold of the Spanish occupation. Three American soldiers were trying to explain to a Cuban that they wished to buy drinks. A native rode by, clubbing his pony, as always. The sky was blue; the sea talked with a gravelly accent at the feet of some rocks; upon its bosom the ships sat quiet as gulls. There was no mention, directly, of invasion—invasion for war—save in the roar of the flames at the blockhouse; but none even heeded this conflagration, excepting to note that it threw out a great heat. It was warm, very warm. It was really hard for Little Nell to keep from thinking of his own affairs: his debts, other misfortunes, loves, prospects of happiness. Nobody was in a flurry; the Cubans were not tearfully grateful; the American troops were visibly glad of being released from those ill transports, and the men often asked, with interest, "Where's the Spaniards?" And yet it must have been a great moment! It was a *great* moment!

It seemed made to prove that the emphatic time of history is not the emphatic time of the common man, who throughout the change of nations feels an itch on his shin, a pain in his head, hunger, thirst, a lack of sleep; the influence of his memory of past firesides, glasses of beer, girls, theaters, ideals, religions, parents, faces, hurts, joys.

Little Nell was hailed from a comfortable veranda, and, looking up, saw Walkley of the *Eclipse,* stretched in a yellow-and-green hammock, smoking his pipe with an air of having always lived in that house, in that village. "Oh, dear little Nell, how glad I am to see your angel face again! There! don't try to hide it; I can see it. Did you bring a corkscrew too? You're superseded as master of the slaves. Did you know it? And by Rogers, too! Rogers is a Sadducee, a cadaver, and a pelican, appointed to the post of chief correspondent, no doubt, because of his rare gift of incapacity. Never mind."

"Where is he now?" asked Little Nell, taking seat on the steps.

"He is down interfering with the landing of the troops," answered Walkley, swinging a leg. "I hope you have the *Johnson* well stocked with food as well as with cigars, cigarettes, and tobaccos, ales, wines, and liquors. We shall need them. There is already famine in the house of Walkley. I have discovered that the system of transportation for our gallant soldiery does not strike in me the admiration which I have often felt when viewing the management of an ordinary bun-shop. A hunger, stifling, jammed together amid odors, and everybody irritable—ye gods, how irritable! And so I—— Look! look!"

The *Jefferson G. Johnson,* well known to them at an incredible distance, could be seen striding the broad sea, the smoke belching from her funnel, headed for Jamaica. "The Army Lands in Cuba!" shrieked Walkley. "Shafter's Army Lands near Santiago! Special type! Half the front page! Oh, the Sadducee! The cadaver! The pelican!"

Little Nell was dumb with astonishment and fear. Walkley, however, was at least not dumb. "That's the pelican! That's Mr. Rogers making his first impression upon the situation. He has engraved himself upon us. We are tattooed with him. There will be a fight tomorrow, sure, and we will cover it even as you found Cervera's fleet. No food, no horses, no money. I am transport-lame; you are sea-weak. We will never see our salaries again. Whereby Rogers is a fool."

"Anybody else here?" asked Little Nell wearily.

"Only young Point." Point was an artist on the *Eclipse.* "But he has nothing. Pity there wasn't an almshouse in this God-forsaken country. Here comes Point now." A sad-faced man came along carrying much luggage. "Hello, Point! lithographer *and* genius, have you food? Food. Well, then, you had better return yourself to Tampa by wire. You are no good here. Only one more little mouth to feed."

Point seated himself near Little Nell. "I haven't had anything to eat since daybreak," he said gloomily, "and I don't care much, for I am simply dog-tired."

"Don't tell *me* you are dog-tired, my talented friend," cried Walkley from his hammock. "Think of me. And now what's to be done?"

They stared for a time disconsolately at where, over the rim of the sea, trailed black smoke from the *Johnson.* From the landing-place below and to the right came the howls of a man who was superintending the disembarkation of some mules. The burning blockhouse still rendered its hollow roar. Suddenly the men-crowded landing set up its cheer, and the steamers all whistled long and raucously. Tiny black figures were raising an American flag over a blockhouse on the top of a great hill.

"That's mighty fine Sunday stuff," said Little Nell. "Well, I'll go and get the order in which the regiments landed, and who was first ashore, and all that. Then I'll go and try to find General Lawton's headquarters. His division has got the advance, I think."

"And, lo! I will write a burning description of the raising of the flag," said Walkley. "While the brilliant Point buskies for food—and makes damn sure he gets it," he added fiercely.

Little Nell thereupon wandered over the face of the earth, threading out the story of the landing of the regiments. He only found about fifty men who had been the first American soldier to set foot on Cuba, and of these he took the most probable. The army was going forward in detail, as soon as the pieces were landed. There was a house something like a crude country tavern—the soldiers in it were looking over their rifles and talking. There was a well of water quite hot—more palm trees—an inscrutable background.

When he arrived again at Walkley's mansion he found the veranda crowded with correspondents in khaki, duck, dungaree, and flannel. They wore riding breeches, but that was mainly forethought. They could see now that fate intended them to walk. Some were writing copy, while Walkley discoursed from his hammock. Rhodes—doomed to be shot in action some days later—was trying to borrow a canteen from men who had one, and from men who had none. Young Point, wan, utterly worn out, was asleep on the floor. Walkley pointed to him. "That is how he appears after his foraging journey, during which he ran all Cuba through a sieve. Oh, yes; a can of corn and a half-bottle of lime juice."

"Say, does anybody know the name of the commander of the 26th Infantry?"

"Who commands the first brigade of Kent's Division?"

"What was the name of the chap that raised the flag?"

"What time is it?"

And a woeful man was wandering here and there with a cold pipe, saying plaintively, "Who's got a match? Anybody here got a match?"

Little Nell's left boot hurt him at the heel, and so he removed it, taking great care and whistling through his teeth. The heated dust was upon them all, making everybody feel that bathing was unknown and shattering their tempers. Young Point developed a snore which brought grim sarcasm from all quarters. Always, below, hummed the traffic of the landing-place.

When night came Little Nell thought best not to go to bed until late, because he recognized the mackintosh as but a feeble comfort. The evening was a glory. A breeze came from the sea, fanning spurts of flame out of the ashes and charred remains of the sheds, while overhead lay a splendid summer night sky, aflash with great tranquil stars. In the streets of the village were two or three fires, frequently and suddenly reddening with their glare the figures of low-voiced men who moved here and there. The lights of the transports blinked on the murmuring plain in front of the village; and far to the westward Little Nell could sometimes note a subtle indication of a playing searchlight, which alone marked the presence of the invisible battleships, half-mooned about the entrance of Santiago harbor, waiting—waiting—waiting.

When Little Nell returned to the veranda he stumbled along a man-strewn place, until he came to the spot where he left his mackintosh; but he found it gone. His curses mingled then with those of the men upon whose bodies he had trodden. Two English correspondents, lying awake to smoke a last pipe, reared and looked at him lazily. "What's wrong, old chap?" murmured one. "Eh? Lost it, eh? Well, look here; come here and take a bit of my blanket. It's a jolly big one. Oh, no trouble at all, man. There you are. Got enough? Comfy? Good night."

A sleepy voice arose in the darkness. "If this hammock breaks, I shall hit at least ten of those Indians down there. Never mind. This is war."

The men slept. Once the sound of three or four shots rang across the windy night, and one head uprose swiftly from the veranda, two eyes looked dazedly at nothing, and the head as swiftly sank. Again a sleepy voice was heard. "Usual thing! Nervous sentries!" The men slept. Before dawn a pulseless, penetrating chill came into the air, and the correspondents awakened, shivering, into a blue world. Some of the fires still smoldered. Walkley and Little Nell kicked vigorously into Point's framework. "Come on, brilliance! Wake up, talent! Don't be sodgering. It's too cold to sleep, but it's not too cold to hustle." Point sat up dolefully. Upon his face was a childish expression. "Where are we going to get breakfast?" he asked, sulking.

"There's no breakfast for you, you hound! Get up and hustle." Accordingly they hustled. With exceeding difficulty they learned that nothing emotional had happened during the night, save the killing of two Cubans who were so secure in ignorance that they could not understand the challenge of two American sentries. Then Walkley ran a gamut of commanding officers, and Little Nell pumped privates for their impressions of Cuba. When his indignation at the absence of breakfast allowed him, Point made sketches. At the full break of day the *Adolphus,* an *Eclipse* dispatch boat, sent a boat ashore with Tailor and Shackles in it, and Walkley departed tearlessly for Jamaica, soon after he had bestowed upon his friends much tinned goods and blankets.

"Well, we've got our stuff off," said Little Nell. "Now Point and I must breakfast."

Shackles, for some reason, carried a great hunting knife, and with it Little Nell opened a tin of beans. "Fall to," he said amiably to Point.

There were some hard biscuits. Afterwards they—the four of them—marched off on the route of the troops. They were well loaded with luggage, particularly young Point, who had somehow made a great gathering of unnecessary things. Hills covered with verdure soon enclosed them. They heard that the army had advanced some nine miles with no fighting. Evidences of the rapid advance were here and there—coats, gauntlets, blanket rolls on the ground. Mule-trains came herding back along the narrow trail to the sound of a little tinkling bell. Cubans were appropriating the coats and blanket rolls.

The four correspondents hurried onward. The surety of impending battle weighed upon them always, but there was a score of minor things more intimate. Little Nell's left heel had chafed until it must have been quite raw, and every moment he wished to take seat by the roadside and console himself from pain. Shackles and Point disliked each other extremely, and often they foolishly quarreled over something, or nothing. The blanket rolls and packages for the hand oppressed everybody. It was like being burned out of a boarding house, and having to carry one's trunk eight miles to the nearest neighbor. Moreover, Point, since he had stupidly overloaded, with great wisdom placed various cameras and other trifles in the hands of his three less burdened and more sensible friends. This made them fume and gnash, but in complete silence, since he was hideously youthful and innocent and unaware. They all wished to rebel, but none of them saw their way clear, because—they did not understand. But somehow it seemed a barbarous project—no one wanted to say anything—cursed him privately for a little ass, but—said nothing. For instance, Little Nell wished to remark, "Point, you are not a thoroughbred in a half of a way. You are an inconsiderate, thoughtless little swine." But, in truth, he said, "Point, when you started out you looked like a Christmas tree. If we keep on robbing you of your bundles there soon won't be anything left for the children." Point asked dubiously, "What do you mean?" Little Nell merely laughed with deceptive good nature.

They were always very thirsty. There was always a howl for the half-bottle of lime juice. Five or six drops from it were simply heavenly in the warm water from the canteens. Point seemed to try to keep the lime juice in his possession, in order that he might get more benefit of it. Before the war was ended the others found themselves declaring vehemently that they loathed Point, and yet when men asked them the reason they grew quite inarticulate. The reasons seemed then so small, as childish as the reasons of a lot of women. And yet at the time his offences loomed enormous.

The surety of impending battle still weighed upon them. Then it came that Shackles turned seriously ill. Suddenly he dropped his own and much of Point's traps upon the trail, wriggled out of his blanket roll, flung it away, and took seat heavily at the roadside. They saw with surprise that his face was pale as death, and yet streaming with sweat.

"Boys," he said in his ordinary voice, "I'm clean played out. I can't go another step. You fellows go on, and leave me to come as soon as I am able."

"Oh, no, that wouldn't do at all," said Little Nell and Tailor together.

Point moved over to a soft place, and dropped amid whatever traps he was himself carrying.

"Don't know whether it's ancestral or merely from the—sun—but I've got a stroke," said Shackles, and gently slumped over to a prostrate position before either Little Nell or Tailor could reach him.

Thereafter Shackles was parental; it was Little Nell and Tailor who were really suffering from a stroke, either ancestral or from the sun.

"Put my blanket roll under my head, Nell, me son," he said gently. "There now! That is very nice. It is delicious. Why, I'm all right, only—only tired." He closed his eyes, and something like an easy slumber came over him. Once he opened his eyes. "Don't trouble about me," he remarked.

But the two fussed about him, nervous, worried, discussing this plan and that plan. It was Point who first made a businesslike statement. Seated carelessly and indifferently upon his soft place, he finally blurted out:

"Say! Look here! Some of us have got to go on. We can't all stay here. Some of us have got to go on."

It was quite true; the *Eclipse* could take no account of strokes. In the end Point and Tailor went on, leaving Little Nell to bring on Shackles as soon as possible. The latter two spent many hours in the grass by the roadside. They made numerous abrupt acquaintances with passing staff officers, privates, muleteers, many stopping to inquire the wherefore of the death-faced figure on the ground. Favors were done often and often, by peer and peasant—small things, of no consequence, and yet warming.

It was dark when Shackles and Little Nell had come slowly to where they could hear the murmur of the army's bivouac.

"Shack," gasped Little Nell to the man leaning forlornly upon him, "I guess we'd better bunk down here where we stand."

"All right, old boy. Anything you say," replied Shackles, in the bass and hollow voice which arrives with such condition.

They crawled into some bushes, and distributed their belongings upon the ground. Little Nell spread out the blankets, and generally played housemaid. Then they lay down, supperless, being too weary to eat. The men slept.

At dawn Little Nell awakened and looked wildly for Shackles, whose empty blanket was pressed flat like a wet newspaper on the ground. But at nearly the same moment Shackles appeared, elate.

"Come on," he cried; "I've rustled an invitation for breakfast."

Little Nell came on with celerity.

"Where? Who?" he said.

"Oh! some officers," replied Shackles airily. If he had been ill the previous day, he showed it now only in some curious kind of deference he paid to Little Nell.

Shackles conducted his comrade, and soon they arrived at where a captain and his one subaltern arose courteously from where they were squatting near a fire of little sticks. They wore the wide white trouser-stripes of infantry officers, and upon the shoulders of their blue campaign shirts were the little marks of their rank; but otherwise there was little beyond their manners to render them different from the men who were busy with breakfast near them. The captain was old, grizzled—a common type of captain in the tiny American army—overjoyed at the active service, confident of his business, and yet breathing out in some way a note of pathos. The war was come too late. Age was grappling him, and honors were only for his widow and his children—merely a better life insurance policy. He had spent his life policing Indians with much labor, cold, and heat, but with no glory for him or his fellows. All he now could do was to die at the head of his men. If he had youthfully dreamed of a general's stars, they were now impossible to him, and he knew it. He was too old to leap so far; his sole honor was a new invitation to face death. And yet, with his ambitions lying half-strangled, he was going to take his men into any sort of holocaust, because his traditions were of gentlemen and soldiers, and because—he loved it for itself—the thing itself—the whirl, the unknown. If he had been degraded at that moment to be a pot-wrestler, no power could have starved him from going through the campaign as a spectator. Why, the army! It was in each drop of his blood.

The lieutenant was very young. Perhaps he had been hurried out of West Point at the last moment, upon a shortage of officers appearing. To him, all was opportunity. He was, in fact, in great luck. Instead of going off in 1898 to grill for an indefinite period on some God-forgotten heap of red-hot sand in New Mexico, he was here in Cuba, on real business, with his regiment. When the big engagement came he was sure to emerge from it either horizontally or at the head of a company, and what more could a boy ask? He was a very modest lad, and talked nothing of his frame of mind, but an expression of blissful contentment was ever upon his face. He really accounted himself the most fortunate boy of his time; and he felt almost certain that he would do well. It was necessary to do well. He would do well.

And yet in many ways these two were alike; the grizzled captain with his gently mournful countenance—"Too late"—and the elate young second lieutenant, his commission hardly dry. Here again it was the influence of the army. After all they were both children of the army.

It is possible to spring into the future here and chronicle what happened later. The captain, after thirty-five years of waiting for his chance, took his Mauser bullet through the brain at the foot of San Juan Hill in the very beginning of the battle, and the boy arrived on the crest panting, sweating, but unscratched, and not sure whether he commanded one company or a whole battalion. Thus fate dealt to the hosts of Shackles and Little Nell.

The breakfast was of canned tomatoes stewed with hard bread, more hard bread, and coffee. It was very good fare, almost royal. Shackles and Little Nell were absurdly grateful as they felt the hot bitter coffee tingle in them. But they departed joyfully before the sun was fairly up, and passed into Siboney. They never saw the captain again.

The beach at Siboney was furious with traffic, even as had been the beach at Daiquiri. Launches shouted, jack-tars prodded with their boat-hooks, and load of men followed load of men. Straight, parade-like, on the shore stood a trumpeter playing familiar calls to the troop-horses who swam toward him eagerly through the salt seas. Crowding closely into the cove were transports of all sizes and ages. To the left and to the right of the little landing-beach green hills shot upward like the wings in a theater. They were scarred here and there with blockhouses and rifle pits. Up one hill a regiment was crawling, seemingly inch by inch. Shackles and Little Nell walked among palms and scrubby bushes, near pools, over spaces of sand holding little monuments of biscuit boxes, ammunition boxes, and supplies of all kinds. Some regiment was just collecting itself from the ships, and the men made great patches of blue on the brown sand.

Shackles asked a question of a man accidently: "Where's that regiment going to?" He pointed to the force that was crawling up the hill. The man grinned, and said, "They're going to look for a fight!"

"Looking for a fight!" said Shackles and Little Nell together. They stared into each other's eyes. Then they set off for the foot of the hill. The hill was long and toilsome. Below them spread wider and wider a vista of ships quiet on a gray sea; a busy, black disembarkation place; tall, still, green hills; a village of well separated cottages; palms; a bit of road; soldiers marching. They passed vacant Spanish trenches; little twelve-foot blockhouses. Soon they were on a fine upland near the sea. The path, under ordinary conditions, must have been a beautiful wooded way. It wound in the shade of thickets of fine trees, then through rank growths of bushes with revealed and fantastic roots, then through a grassy space which had all the beauty of a neglected orchard. But always from under their feet scuttled noisy land crabs, demons to the nerves, which in some way possessed a semblance of moon-like faces upon their blue or red bodies, and these faces were turned with expressions of deepest horror upon Shackles and Little Nell as they sped to overtake the pugnacious regiment. The route was paved with coats, hats, tent-and-blanket-rolls, ration-tins, haversacks—everything but ammunition belts, rifles and canteens.

They heard a dull noise of voices in front of them—men talking too loud for the etiquette of the forest—and presently they came upon two or three soldiers lying by the roadside, flame-faced, utterly spent from the hurried march in the heat. One man came limping back along the path. He looked to them anxiously for sympathy and comprehension. "Hurt m' knee. I swear I couldn't keep up with th' boys. I had to leave 'm. Wasn't that tough luck?" His collar rolled away from a red, muscular neck, and his bare forearms were better than stanchions. Yet he was almost babyishly tearful in his attempt to make the two correspondents feel that he had not turned back because he was afraid. They gave him scant courtesy, tinctured with one drop of sympathetic yet cynical understanding. Soon they overtook the hospital squad; men addressing chaste language to some pack-mules; a talkative sergeant; two amiable, cool-eyed young surgeons. Soon they were amid the rear troops of the dismounted volunteer cavalry regiment which was moving to attack. The men strode easily along, arguing one to another on ulterior matters. If they were going into battle, they either did not know it or they concealed it well. They were more like men going into a bar at one o'clock in the morning. Their laughter rang through the Cuban woods. And in the meantime, soft, mellow, sweet, sang the voice of the Cuban wood dove, the Spanish guerilla calling to his mate—forest music; on the flanks, deep back on both flanks, the adorable wood dove, singing only of love. Some of the advancing Americans said it was beautiful. It *was* beautiful. The Spanish guerilla calling to his mate. What could be more beautiful?

Shackles and Little Nell rushed precariously through waist-high bushes until they reached the center of the single-filed regiment. The firing then broke out in front. All the woods set up a hot sputtering; the bullets sped along the path and across it from both sides. The thickets presented nothing but dense masses of light green foliage, out of which these swift steel things were born supernaturally.

It was a volunteer regiment going into its first action, against an enemy of unknown force, in a country where the vegetation was thicker than fur on a cat. There might have been a dreadful mess; but in military matters the only way to deal with a situation of this kind is to take it frankly by the throat and squeeze it to death. Shackles and Little Nell felt the thrill of the orders. "Come ahead, men! Keep right ahead, men!

Come on!" The volunteer cavalry regiment, with all the willingness in the world, went ahead into the angle of a V-shaped Spanish formation.

It seemed that every leaf had turned into a soda bottle and was popping its cork. Some of the explosions seemed to be against the men's very faces, others against the backs of their necks. "Now, men! Keep goin' ahead. Keep on goin'." The forward troops were already engaged. They, at least, had something at which to shoot. "Now, captain, if you're ready." "Stop that swearing there." "Got a match?" "Steady, now, men."

A gate appeared in a barbed wire fence. Within were billowy fields of long grass, dotted with palms and luxuriant mango trees. It was Elysian—a place for lovers, fair as Eden in its radiance of sun, under its blue sky. One might have expected to see white-robed figures walking slowly in the shadows. A dead man, with a bloody face, lay twisted in a curious contortion at the waist. Some one was shot in the leg, his pins knocked cleanly from under him.

"Keep goin', men." The air roared, and the ground fled reelingly under their feet. Light, shadow, trees, grass. Bullets spat from every side. Once they were in a thicket, and the men, blanched and bewildered, turned one way and then another, not knowing which way to turn. "Keep goin', men." Soon they were in the sunlight again. They could see the long scant line, which was being drained man by man—one might say drop by drop. The musketry rolled forth in great full measure from the magazine carbines. "Keep goin', men." "Christ, I'm shot!" "They're flankin' us, sir." "We're bein' fired into by our own crowd, sir." "Keep goin', men." A low ridge before them was a bottling establishment blowing up in detail. From the right—it seemed at that time to be the far right—they could hear steady, crashing volleys—the United States regulars in action.

Then suddenly—to use a phrase of the street—the whole bottom of the thing fell out. It was suddenly and mysteriously ended. The Spaniards had run away, and some of the regulars were chasing them. It was a victory.

When the wounded men dropped in the tall grass they quite disappeared, as if they had sunk in water. Little Nell and Shackles were walking along through the fields, disputing.

"Well, damn it, man!" cried Shackles, "we *must* get a list of the killed and wounded."

"That is not nearly so important," quoth Little Nell, academically, "as to get the first account to New York of the first action of the army in Cuba."

They came upon Tailor, lying with a bared torso and a small red hole through his left lung. He was calm, but evidently out of temper. "Good

God, Tailor!" they cried, dropping to their knees like two pagans; "are you hurt, old boy?"

"Hurt?" he said gently. "No, 'tis not so deep as a well nor so wide as a church door, but it's enough, d' you see? You understand, do you? Idiots!"

Then he became very official. "Shackles, feel and see what's under my leg. It's a small stone, or a burr, or something. Don't be clumsy now! Be careful! Be careful!" Then he said, angrily, "Oh, you didn't find it at all. Damn it!"

In reality there was nothing there, and so Shackles could not have removed it. "Sorry, old boy," he said meekly.

"Well, you may observe that I can't stay here more than a year," said Tailor, with some oratory, "and the hospital people have their own work in hand. It behooves you, Nell, to fly to Siboney, arrest a dispatch boat, get a cot and some other things, and some minions to carry me. If I get once down to the base I'm all right, but if I stay here I'm dead. Meantime Shackles can stay here and try to look as if he liked it."

There was no disobeying the man. Lying there with a little red hole in his left lung, he dominated them through his helplessness, and through their fear that if they angered him he would move and—bleed.

"Well?" said Little Nell.

"Yes," said Shackles, nodding.

Little Nell departed.

"That blanket you lent me," Tailor called after him, "is back there somewhere with Point."

Little Nell noted that many of the men who were wandering among the wounded seemed so spent with the toil and excitement of their first action that they could hardly drag one leg after the other. He found himself suddenly in the same condition. His face, his neck, even his mouth, felt dry as sunbaked bricks, and his legs were foreign to him. But he swung desperately into his five mile task. On the way he passed many things: bleeding men carried by comrades; others making their way grimly, with encrimsoned arms; then the little settlement of the hospital squad; men on the ground everywhere, many in the path; one young captain dying, with great gasps, his body pale blue, and glistening, like the inside of a rabbit's skin. But the voice of the Cuban wood dove, soft, mellow, sweet, singing only of love, was no longer heard from the wealth of foliage.

Presently the hurrying correspondent met another regiment coming to assist—a line of a thousand men in single file through the jungle. "Well, how is it going, old man?" "How is it coming on?" "Are we doin' 'em?" Then, after an interval, came other regiments, moving out. He had to take to the bush to let these long lines pass him, and he was delayed, and had to flounder amid brambles. But at last, like a successful pilgrim, he arrived at the brow of the great hill overlooking Siboney. His practised eye scanned the fine broad brow of the sea with its clustering ships, but he saw thereon no *Eclipse* dispatch boats. He zigzagged heavily down the hill, and arrived finally amid the dust and outcries of the base. He seemed to ask a thousand men if they had seen an *Eclipse* boat on the water, or an *Eclipse* correspondent on the shore. They all answered, "No."

He was like a poverty-stricken and unknown suppliant at a foreign Court. Even his plea got only ill hearings. He had expected the news of the serious wounding of Tailor to appall the other correspondents, but they took it quite calmly. It was as if their sense of an impending great battle between two large armies had quite got them out of focus for these minor tragedies. Tailor was hurt—yes? They looked at Little Nell, dazed. How curious that Tailor should be almost the first—how *very* curious—yes. But, as far as arousing them to any enthusiasm of active pity, it seemed impossible. He was lying up there in the grass, was he? Too bad, too bad, too bad!

Little Nell went alone and lay down in the sand with his back against a rock. Tailor was prostrate up there in the grass. Never mind. Nothing was to be done. The whole situation was too colossal. Then into his zone came Walkley the invincible.

"Walkley!" yelled Little Nell. Walkley came quickly, and Little Nell lay weakly against his rock and talked. In thirty seconds Walkley understood everything, had hurled a drink of whiskey into Little Nell, had admonished him to lie quiet, and had gone to organize and manipulate. When he returned he was a trifle dubious and backward. Behind him was a singular squad of volunteers from the *Adolphus*, carrying among them a wire-woven bed.

"Look here, Nell!" said Walkley, in bashful accents; "I've collected a battalion here which is willing to go bring Tailor; but—they say—you—can't you show them where he is?"

"Yes," said Little Nell, arising.

When the party arrived at Siboney, and deposited Tailor in the best place, Walkley had found a house and stocked it with canned soups. Therein Shackles and Little Nell reveled for a time, and then rolled on the floor in their blankets. Little Nell tossed a great deal. "Oh, I'm so tired. Good God, I'm tired. I'm—tired."

In the morning a voice aroused them. It was a swollen, important, circus voice saying, "Where is Mr. Nell? I wish to see him immediately."

"Here I am, Rogers," cried Little Nell.

"Oh, Nell," said Rogers, "here's a dispatch to me which I thought you had better read."

Little Nell took the dispatch. It was: "Tell Nell can't understand his inaction; tell him come home first steamer from Port Antonio, Jamaica."

May, 1899

[*The Cornhill Magazine,* Vol. 79, pp. 577–592.]

THE LONE CHARGE OF WILLIAM B. PERKINS*

He could not distinguish between a five-inch quick-firing gun and a nickel-plated ice pick, and so, naturally, he had been elected to fill the position of war correspondent. The responsible party was the editor of the Minnesota *Herald*. Perkins had no information of war, and no particular rapidity of mind for acquiring it, but he had that rank and fibrous quality of courage which springs from the thick soil of Western America.

It was morning in Guantanamo Bay. If the marines encamped on the hill had had time to turn their gaze seaward, they might have seen a small newspaper dispatch boat wending its way toward the entrance of the harbor over the blue, sunlit waters of the Caribbean. In the stern of this tug Perkins was seated upon some coal bags, while the breeze gently ruffled his greasy pajamas. He was staring at a brown line of entrenchments surmounted by a flag, which was Camp McCalla. In the harbor were anchored two or three grim, gray cruisers and a transport. As the tug steamed up the radiant channel, Perkins could see men moving on shore near the charred ruins of a village. Perkins was deeply moved; here already was more war than he had ever known in Minnesota. Presently he, clothed in the essential garments of a war correspondent, was rowed to the sandy beach. Marines in yellow linen were handling an ammunition supply. They paid no attention to the visitor, being morose from the inconveniences of two days and nights of fighting. Perkins toiled up the zigzag path to the top of the hill, and looked with eager eyes at the trenches, the field pieces, the funny little Colts, the flag, the grim marines lying wearily on their arms. And still more he looked through the clear air over 1,000 yards of mysterious woods from which emanated at inopportune times repeated flocks of Mauser bullets.

Perkins was delighted. He was filled with admiration for these jaded and smoky men who lay so quietly in the trenches waiting for a resumption of guerilla enterprise. But he wished they would heed him. He wanted to

* *Wounds in the Rain.*

talk about it. Save for sharp inquiring glances, no one acknowledged his existence.

Finally he approached two young lieutenants, and in his innocent Western way he asked them if they would like a drink. The effect on the two young lieutenants was immediate and astonishing. With one voice they answered, "Yes, we would." Perkins almost wept with joy at this amiable response, and he exclaimed that he would immediately board the tug and bring off a bottle of Scotch. This attracted the officers, and in a burst of confidence one explained that there had not been a drop in camp. Perkins lunged down the hill, and fled to his boat, where in his exuberance he engaged in the preliminary altercation with some whiskey. Consequently he toiled again up the hill in the blasting sun with his enthusiasm in no wise abated. The parched officers were very gracious, and such was the state of mind of Perkins that he did not note properly how serious and solemn was his engagement with the whiskey. And because of this fact, and because of his antecedents, there happened the lone charge of William B. Perkins.

Now, as Perkins went down the hill, something happened. A private in those high trenches found that a cartridge was clogged in his rifle. It then becomes necessary with most kinds of rifles to explode the cartridge. The private took the rifle to his captain, and explained the case. But it would not do in that camp to fire a rifle for mechanical purposes and without warning, because the eloquent sound would bring six hundred tired marines to tension and high expectancy. So the captain turned, and in a loud voice announced to the camp that he found it necessary to shoot into the air. The communication rang sharply from voice to voice. Then the captain raised the weapon and fired. Whereupon—and whereupon—a large line of guerillas lying in the bushes decided swiftly that their presence and position were discovered, and swiftly they volleyed.

In a moment the woods and the hills were alive with the crack and sputter of rifles. Men on the warships in the harbor heard the old familiar flut-flut-fluttery-fluttery-flut-flut-flut from the entrenchments. Incidentally the launch of the *Marblehead*, commanded by one of our headlong American ensigns, streaked for the strategic woods like a galloping marine dragoon, peppering away with its blunderbuss in the bow.

Perkins had arrived at the foot of the hill, where began the arrangement of 150 marines that protected the short line of communication between the main body and the beach. These men had all swarmed into line behind fortifications improvised from the boxes of provisions. And to them were gathering naked men who had been bathing, naked men who arrayed themselves speedily in cartridge belts and rifles. The woods and the hills went flut-flut-flut-fluttery-fluttery-flut-flllluttery-flut. Under the boughs of a beautiful tree lay five wounded men thinking vividly.

And now it befell Perkins to discover a Spaniard in the bush. The distance was some five hundred yards. In a loud voice he announced his perception. He also declared hoarsely that if he only had a rifle he would go and possess himself of this particular enemy. Immediately an amiable lad shot in the arm said: "Well, take mine." Perkins thus acquired a rifle and a clip of five cartridges.

"Come on!" he shouted. This part of the battalion was lying very tight, not yet being engaged, but not knowing when the business would swirl around to them.

To Perkins they replied with a roar. "Come back here, you damned fool. Do you want to get shot by your own crowd? Come back, —— ——!" As a detail, it might be mentioned that the fire from a part of the hill swept the journey upon which Perkins had started.

Now behold the solitary Perkins adrift in the storm of fighting, even as a champagne jacket of straw is lost in a great surf. He found it out quickly. Four seconds elapsed before he discovered that he was an alms-house idiot plunging through hot, crackling thickets on a June morning in Cuba. Sss-s-swing-sing-ing-pop went the lightning-swift metal grass-hoppers over him and beside him. The beauties of rural Minnesota illuminated his conscience with the gold of lazy corn, with the sleeping green of meadows, with the cathedral gloom of pine forests. Sshsh-swing-pop! Perkins decided that if he cared to extricate himself from a tangle of imbecility he must shoot. The entire situation was that he must shoot. It was necessary that he should shoot. Nothing would save him but shooting. It is a law that men thus decide when the waters of battle close over their minds. So with a prayer that the Americans would not hit him in the back nor the left side, and that the Spaniards would not hit him in the front, he knelt like a supplicant alone in the desert of chaparral, and emptied his magazine at his Spaniard before he discovered that his Spaniard was a bit of dried palm branch.

Then Perkins flurried like a fish. His reason for being was a Spaniard in the bush. When the Spaniard turned into a dried palm branch, he could no longer furnish himself with one adequate reason.

Then did he dream frantically of some anthracite hiding-place, some profound dungeon of peace where blind mules live placidly chewing the far-gathered hay.

"Sss-swing-wing-pop! Prut-prut-prrrut!" Then a field gun spoke. "*Boom-*ra-swow-ow-ow-ow-*pum.*" Then a Colt automatic began to bark. "Crack-crk-crk-crk-crk-crk," endlessly. Raked, enfiladed, flanked, surrounded, and overwhelmed, what hope was there for William B. Perkins of the Minnesota *Herald?*

But war is a spirit. War provides for those that it loves. It provides sometimes death and sometimes a singular and incredible safety. There were few ways in which it was possible to preserve Perkins. One way was by means of a steam boiler.

Perkins espied near him an old, rusty steam boiler lying in the bushes. War only knows how it was there, but there it was, a temple shining resplendent with safety. With a moan of haste, Perkins flung himself through that hole which expressed the absence of the steam pipe.

Then, ensconced in his boiler, Perkins comfortably listened to the ring of a fight which seemed to be in the air above him. Sometimes bullets struck their strong, swift blow against the boiler's sides, but none entered to interfere with Perkins's rest.

Time passed. The fight, short anyhow, dwindled to prut . . . prut . . . prut-prut . . . prut. And when the silence came, Perkins might have been seen cautiously protruding from the boiler. Presently he strolled back toward the marine lines with his hat not able to fit his head for the new bumps of wisdom that were on it.

The marines, with an annoyed air, were settling down again when an apparitional figure came from the bushes. There was great excitement. "It's that crazy man," they shouted, and as he drew near they gathered tumultuously about him and demanded to know how he had accomplished it.

Perkins made a gesture, the gesture of a man escaping from an unintentional mudbath, the gesture of a man coming out of battle, and then he told them.

The incredulity was immediate and general. "Yes, you did! What? In an old boiler? An old boiler? Out in that brush? Well, we guess not." They did not believe him until two days later, when a patrol happened to find the rusty boiler, relic of some curious transaction in the ruin of the Cuban sugar industry. The patrol then marveled at the truthfulness of war correspondents until they were almost blind.

Soon after his adventure Perkins boarded the tug, wearing a countenance of poignant thoughtfulness.

July, 1899
[McClure's Magazine, Vol. 13, pp. 279–282.]

THE ANGEL CHILD*

I

Although Whilomville was in no sense a summer resort, the advent of the warm season meant much to it, for then came visitors from the city—people of considerable confidence—alighting upon their country cousins. Moreover, many citizens who could afford to do so escaped at this time to the seaside. The town, with the commerical life quite taken out of it, drawled and drowsed through long months, during which nothing was worse than the white dust which arose behind every vehicle at blinding noon, and nothing was finer than the cool sheen of the hose sprays over the cropped lawns under the many maples in the twilight.

One summer the Trescotts had a visitation. Mrs. Trescott owned a cousin who was a painter of high degree. I had almost said that he was of national reputation, but, come to think of it, it is better to say that almost everybody in the United States who knew about art and its travail knew about him. He had picked out a wife, and naturally, looking at him, one wondered how he had done it. She was quick, beautiful, imperious, while he was quiet, slow, and misty. She was a veritable queen of health, while he, apparently, was of a most brittle constitution. When he played tennis, particularly, he looked every minute as if he were going to break.

They lived in New York, in awesome apartments wherein Japan and Persia, and indeed all the world, confounded the observer. At the end was a cathedral-like studio. They had one child. Perhaps it would be better to say that they had one CHILD. It was a girl. When she came to Whilomville with her parents, it was patent that she had an inexhaustible store of white frocks, and that her voice was high and commanding. These things the town knew quickly. Other things it was doomed to discover by a process.

Her effect upon the children of the Trescott neighborhood was singular. They at first feared, then admired, then embraced. In two days she was a Begum. All day long her voice could be heard directing, drilling, and compelling those freeborn children; and to say that they felt oppression would be wrong, for they really fought for records of loyal obedience.

All went well until one day was her birthday.

On the morning of this day she walked out into the Trescott garden and said to her father, confidently, "Papa, give me some money, because this is my birthday."

* Whilomville Stories.

He looked dreamily up from his easel. "Your birthday?" he murmured. Her envisioned father was never energetic enough to be irritable unless some one broke through into that place where he lived with the desires of his life. But neither wife nor child ever heeded or even understood the temperamental values, and so some part of him had grown hardened to their inroads. "Money?" he said. "Here." He handed her a five-dollar bill. It was that he did not at all understand the nature of a five-dollar bill. He was deaf to it. He had it; he gave it; that was all.

She sallied forth to a waiting people—Jimmie Trescott, Dan Earl, Ella Earl, the Margate twins, the three Phelps children, and others. "I've got some pennies now," she cried, waving the bill, "and I am going to buy some candy." They were deeply stirred by this announcement. Most children are penniless three hundred days in the year, and to another possessing five pennies they pay deference. To little Cora waving a bright green note these children paid heathenish homage. In some disorder they thronged after her to a small shop on Bridge Street hill. First of all came ice cream. Seated in the comic little back parlor, they clamored shrilly over plates of various flavors, and the shopkeeper marveled that cream could vanish so quickly down throats that seemed wide open, always, for the making of excited screams.

These children represented the families of most excellent people. They were all born in whatever purple there was to be had in the vicinity of Whilomville. The Margate twins, for example, were out-and-out prize-winners. With their long golden curls and their countenances of similar vacuity, they shone upon the front bench of all Sunday school functions, hand in hand, while their uplifted mother felt about her the envy of a hundred other parents, and less heavenly children scoffed from near the door.

Then there was little Dan Earl, probably the nicest boy in the world, gentle, fine-grained, obedient to the point where he obeyed anybody. Jimmie Trescott himself was, indeed, the only child who was at all versed in villainy, but in these particular days he was on his very good behavior. As a matter of fact, he was in love. The beauty of his regal little cousin had stolen his manly heart.

Yes, they were all most excellent children, but, loosened upon this candy shop with five dollars, they resembled, in a tiny way, drunken reveling soldiers within the walls of a stormed city. Upon the heels of ice cream and cake came chocolate mice, butterscotch, "everlastings," chocolate cigars, taffy-on-a-stick, taffy-on-a-slate-pencil, and many semi-transparent devices resembling lions, tigers, elephants, horses, cats, dogs, cows, sheep, tables, chairs, engines (both railway and for the fighting of fire), soldiers, fine ladies, odd-looking men, clocks, watches, revolvers, rabbits, and bedsteads. A cent was the price of a single wonder.

Some of the children, going quite daft, soon had thought to make fight over the spoils, but their queen ruled with an iron grip. Her first inspiration was to satisfy her own fancies, but as soon as that was done she mingled prodigality with a fine justice, dividing, balancing, bestowing, and sometimes taking away from somebody even that which he had.

It was an orgy. In thirty-five minutes those respectable children looked as if they had been dragged at the tail of a chariot. The sacred Margate twins, blinking and grunting, wished to take seat upon the floor, and even the most durable Jimmie Trescott found occasion to lean against the counter, wearing at the time a solemn and abstracted air, as if he expected something to happen to him shortly.

Of course their belief had been in an unlimited capacity, but they found there was an end. The shopkeeper handed the queen her change.

"Two seventy-three from five leaves two twenty-seven, Miss Cora," he said, looking upon her with admiration.

She turned swiftly to her clan. "O-oh!" she cried, in amazement. "Look how much I have left!" They gazed at the coins in her palm. They knew then that it was not their capacities which were endless; it was the five dollars.

The queen led the way to the street. "We must think up some way of spending more money," she said, frowning. They stood in silence, awaiting her further speech.

Suddenly she clapped her hands and screamed with delight. "Come on!" she cried. "I know what let's do." Now behold, she had discovered the red-and-white pole in front of the shop of one William Neeltje, a barber by trade.

It becomes necessary to say a few words concerning Neeltje. He was new to the town. He had come and opened a dusty little shop on dusty Bridge Street hill, and although the neighborhood knew from the courier winds that his diet was mainly cabbage, they were satisfied with that meager datum. Of course Reifsnyder came to investigate him for the local Barbers' Union, but he found in him only sweetness and light, with a willingness to charge any price at all for a shave or a haircut. In fact, the advent of Neeltje would have made barely a ripple upon the placid bosom of Whilomville if it were not that his name was Neeltje.

At first the people looked at his signboard out of the eye corner, and wondered lazily why any one should bear the name of Neeltje; but as time went on, men spoke to other men, saying, "How do you pronounce the name of that barber up there on Bridge Street hill?" And then, before any could prevent it, the best minds of the town were splintering their lances against William Neeltje's signboard. If a man had a mental superior, he guided him seductively to this name, and watched with glee his wrecking. The clergy of the town even entered the lists. There was one among them who had taken a collegiate prize in Syriac, as well as in several less opaque languages, and the other clergymen—at one of their weekly meetings—sought to betray him into this ambush. He pronounced the name correctly, but that mattered little, since none of them knew whether he did or did not; and so they took triumph according to their ignorance. Under these arduous circumstances it was certain that the town should look for a nickname, and at this time the nickname was in process of formation. So William Neeltje lived on with his secret, smiling foolishly toward the world.

"Come on," cried little Cora. "Let's all get our hair cut. That's what let's do. Let's all get our hair cut! Come on! Come on! Come on!"

The others were carried off their feet by the fury of this assault. To get their hair cut! What joy! Little did they know if this were fun; they only knew that their small leader said it was fun. Chocolate-stained but confident, the band marched into William Neeltje's barber shop.

"We wish to get our hair cut," said little Cora, haughtily.

Neeltje, in his shirt sleeves, stood looking at them with his half-idiot smile.

"Hurry, now!" commanded the queen. A dray horse toiled step by step, step by step, up Bridge Street hill; a far woman's voice arose; there could be heard the ceaseless hammers of shingling carpenters; all was summer peace. "Come on, now. Who's goin' first? Come on, Ella; you go first. Gettin' our hair cut! Oh what fun!"

Little Ella Earl would not, however, be first in the chair. She was drawn toward it by a singular fascination, but at the same time she was afraid of it, and so she hung back, saying: "No! You go first! No! You go first!" The question was precipitated by the twins and one of the Phelps children. They made simultaneous rush for the chair, and screamed and kicked, each pair preventing the third child. The queen entered this mêlée, and decided in favor of the Phelps boy. He ascended the chair. Thereat an awed silence fell upon the band. And always William Neeltje smiled fatuously.

He tucked a cloth in the neck of the Phelps boy and, taking scissors, began to cut his hair. The group of children came closer and closer. Even the queen was deeply moved. "Does it hurt any?" she asked, in a wee voice.

"Naw," said the Phelps boy, with dignity. "Anyhow, I've had m' hair cut afore."

When he appeared to them looking very soldierly with his cropped little head, there was a tumult over the chair. The Margate twins howled; Jimmie Trescott was kicking them on the shins. It was a fight.

But the twins could not prevail, being the smallest of all the children. The queen herself took the chair, and ordered Neeltje as if he were a lady's maid. To the floor there fell proud ringlets, blazing even there in their humiliation with a full fine bronze light. Then Jimmie Trescott, then Ella Earl (two long ash-colored plaits), then a Phelps girl, then another Phelps girl; and so on from head to head. The ceremony received unexpected check when the turn came to Dan Earl. This lad, usually docile to any rein, had suddenly grown mulishly obstinate. No, he would not, he would not. He himself did not seem to know why he refused to have his hair cut, but, despite the shrill derision of the company, he remained obdurate. Anyhow, the twins, long held in check and now feverishly eager, were already struggling for the chair.

And so to the floor at last came the golden Margate curls, the heart treasure and glory of a mother, three aunts, and some feminine cousins.

All having been finished, the children, highly elate, thronged out into the street. They crowed and cackled with pride and joy, anon turning to scorn the cowardly Dan Earl.

Ella Earl was an exception. She had been pensive for some time, and now the shorn little maiden began vaguely to weep. In the door of his shop William Neeltje stood watching them, upon his face a grin of almost inhuman idiocy.

II

It now becomes the duty of the unfortunate writer to exhibit these children to their fond parents. "Come on, Jimmie," cried little Cora, "let's go show mamma." And they hurried off, these happy children, to show mamma.

The Trescotts and their guests were assembled, indolently awaiting the luncheon bell. Jimmie and the angel child burst in upon them. "Oh, mamma," shrieked little Cora, "see how fine I am! I've had my hair cut! Isn't it splendid? And Jimmie too!"

The wretched mother took one sight, emitted one yell, and fell into a chair. Mrs. Trescott dropped a large lady's journal and made a nerveless mechanical clutch at it. The painter gripped the arms of his chair and leaned forward, staring until his eyes were like two little clock faces. Dr. Trescott did not move or speak.

To the children the next moments were chaotic. There were a loudly wailing mother and a pale-faced, aghast mother; a stammering father and a grim and terrible father. The angel child did not understand anything of it save the voice of calamity, and in a moment all her little imperialism went to the winds. She ran sobbing to her mother. "Oh, mamma! mamma! mamma!"

The desolate Jimmie heard out of this inexplicable situation a voice which he knew well, a sort of colonel's voice, and he obeyed like any good soldier. "Jimmie!"

He stepped three paces to the front. "Yes, sir."

"How did this—how did this happen?" said Trescott.

Now Jimmie could have explained how had happened anything which had happened, but he did not know what had happened, so he said, "I—I—nothin'."

"And, oh, look at her frock!" said Mrs. Trescott, brokenly.

The words turned the mind of the mother of the angel child. She looked up, her eyes blazing. "Frock!" she repeated. "Frock! What do I care for her frock? Frock!" she choked out again from the depths of her bitterness. Then she arose suddenly, and whirled tragically upon her husband. "Look!" she declaimed. "All—her lovely—hair—all her lovely hair—gone—gone!" The painter was apparently in a fit; his jaw was set, his eyes were glazed, his body was stiff and straight. "All gone—all—her lovely hair—all gone—my poor little darlin'—my—poor—little—darlin'!" And the angel child added her heartbroken voice to her mother's wail as they fled into each other's arms.

In the meantime Trescott was patiently unraveling some skeins of Jimmie's tangled intellect. "And then you went to this barber's on the hill. Yes. And where did you get the money? Yes. I see. And who besides you and Cora had their hair cut? The Margate twi— Oh, Lord!"

Over at the Margate place old Eldridge Margate, the grandfather of the twins, was in the back garden picking peas and smoking ruminatively to himself. Suddenly he heard from the house great noises. Doors slammed, women rushed upstairs and downstairs calling to each other in voices of agony. And then full and mellow upon the still air arose the roar of the twins in pain.

Old Eldridge stepped out of the pea patch and moved toward the house, puzzled, staring, not yet having decided that it was his duty to rush forward. Then around the corner of the house shot his daughter Mollie, her face pale with horror.

"What's the matter?" he cried.

"Oh, father," she gasped, "the children! They—"

Then around the corner of the house came the twins, howling at the top of their power, their faces flowing with tears. They were still hand in hand, the ruling passion being strong even in this suffering. At sight of them old Eldridge took his pipe hastily out of his mouth. "Good God!" he said.

The Angel Child

And now what befell one William Neeltje, a barber by trade? And what was said by angry parents of the mother of such an angel child? And what was the fate of the angel child herself?

There was surely a tempest. With the exception of the Margate twins, the boys could well be eliminated from the affair. Of course it didn't matter if their hair was cut. Also the two little Phelps girls had had very short hair, anyhow, and their parents were not too greatly incensed. In the case of Ella Earl, it was mainly the pathos of the little girl's own grieving; but her mother played a most generous part, and called upon Mrs. Trescott, and condoled with the mother of the angel child over their equivalent losses. But the Margate contingent! They simply screeched.

Trescott, composed and cool-blooded, was in the middle of a giddy whirl. He was not going to allow the mobbing of his wife's cousins, nor was he going to pretend that the spoliation of the Margate twins was a virtuous and beautiful act. He was elected, gratuitously, to the position of a buffer.

But, curiously enough, the one who achieved the bulk of the misery was old Eldridge Margate, who had been picking peas at the time. The feminine Margates stormed his position as individuals, in pairs, in teams, and *en masse*. In two days they may have aged him seven years. He must destroy the utter Neeltje. He must midnightly massacre the angel child and her mother. He must dip his arms in blood to the elbows.

Trescott took the first opportunity to express to him his concern over the affair, but when the subject of the disaster was mentioned, old Eldridge, to the doctor's great surprise, actually chuckled long and deeply. "Oh, well, look-a-here," he said. "I never was so much in love with them there damn curls. The curls was purty—yes—but then I'd a darn sight rather see boys look more like boys than like two little wax figgers. An', ye know, the little cusses like it themselves. *They* never took no stock in all this washin' an' combin' an' fixin' an' goin' to church an' paradin' an' showin' off. They stood it because they were told to. That's all. Of course this here Neel-te-gee, er whatever his name is, is a plumb dumb ijit, but I don't see what's to be done, now that the kids is full well cropped. I might go and burn his shop over his head, but that wouldn't bring no hair back on to the kids. They're even kicking on sashes now, an' that's all right, 'cause what fer does a boy want a sash?"

Whereupon Trescott perceived that the old man wore his brains above his shoulders, and Trescott departed from him rejoicing greatly that it was only women who could not know that there was finality to most disasters, and that when a thing was fully done, no amount of door-slammings, rushings upstairs and downstairs, calls, lamentations, tears, could bring back a single hair to the heads of twins.

But the rains came and the winds blew in the most biblical way when a certain fact came to light in the Trescott household. Little Cora, corroborated by Jimmie, innocently remarked that five dollars had been given her by her father on her birthday, and with this money the evil had been wrought. Trescott had known it, but he—thoughtful man—had said nothing. For her part, the mother of the angel child had up to that moment never reflected that the consummation of the wickedness must have cost a small sum of money. But now it was all clear to her. He was the guilty one—he! "My angel child!"

The scene which ensued was inspiriting. A few days later, loungers at the railway station saw a lady leading a shorn and still undaunted lamb. Attached to them was a husband and father who was plainly bewildered, but still more plainly vexed, as if he would be saying: "Damn 'em! Why can't they leave me alone?"

August, 1899
[*Harper's Magazine*, Vol. 99, pp. 358-364.]

LYNX-HUNTING*

Jimmie lounged about the dining room and watched his mother with large, serious eyes. Suddenly he said, "Ma—now—can I borrow pa's gun?"

She was overcome with the feminine horror which is able to mistake preliminary words for the full accomplishment of the dread thing. "Why, Jimmie!" she cried. "Of al-l wonders! Your father's gun! No indeed you can't!"

He was fairly well crushed, but he managed to mutter, sullenly, "Well, Willie Dalzel, he's got a gun." In reality his heart had previously been beating with such tumult—he had himself been so impressed with the daring and sin of his request—that he was glad that all was over now, and his mother could do very little further harm to his sensibilities. He had been influenced into the venture by the larger boys.

"Huh!" the Dalzel urchin had said; "your father's got a gun, hasn't he? Well, why don't you bring that?"

Puffing himself, Jimmie had replied, "Well, I can, if I want to." It was a black lie, but really the Dalzel boy was too outrageous with his eternal bill-posting about the gun which a beaming uncle had entrusted to him. Its possession made him superior in manfulness to most boys in the neighborhood—or at least they enviously conceded him such position—but he was so overbearing, and stuffed the fact of his treasure so relentlessly down

* *Whilomville Stories.*

their throats, that on this occasion the miserable Jimmie had lied as naturally as most animals swim.

Willie Dalzel had not been checkmated, for he had instantly retorted,
"Why don't you get it, then?"

"Well, I can, if I want to."

"Well, get it, then!"

"Well, I can, if I want to."

Thereupon Jimmie had paced away with great airs of surety as far as
the door of his home, where his manner changed to one of tremulous mis-
giving as it came upon him to address his mother in the dining room.
There had happened that which had happened.

When Jimmie returned to his two distinguished companions he was
blown out with a singular pomposity. He spoke these noble words: "Oh,
well, I guess I don't want to take the gun out today."

They had been watching him with gleaming ferret eyes, and they detected his falsity at once. They challenged him with shouted gibes, but it
was not in the rules for the conduct of boys that one should admit anything whatsoever, and so Jimmie, backed into an ethical corner, lied as
stupidly, as desperately, as hopelessly as ever lone savage fights when surrounded at last in his jungle.

Such accusations were never known to come to any point, for the reason
that the number and kind of denials always equaled or exceeded the number of accusations, and no boy was ever brought really to book for these
misdeeds.

In the end they went off together, Willie Dalzel with his gun being a
trifle in advance and discoursing upon his various works. They passed along
a maple-lined avenue, a highway common to boys bound for that free land
of hills and woods in which they lived in some part their romance of the
moment, whether it was of Indians, miners, smugglers, soldiers, or outlaws.
The paths were their paths, and much was known to them of the secrets
of the dark green hemlock thickets, the wastes of sweet fern and huckleberry, the cliffs of gaunt bluestone with the sumach burning red at their
feet. Each boy had, I am sure, a conviction that some day the wilderness
was to give forth to him a marvelous secret. They felt that the hills and the
forest knew much, and they heard a voice of it in the silence. It was vague,
thrilling, fearful, and altogether fabulous. The grown folk seemed to regard these wastes merely as so much distance between one place and another place, or as a rabbit-cover, or as a district to be judged according
to the value of the timber; but to the boys it spoke some great inspiring
word, which they knew even as those who pace the shore know the enigmatic speech of the surf. In the meantime they lived there, in season, lives
of ringing adventure—by dint of imagination.

The boys left the avenue, skirted hastily through some private grounds, climbed a fence, and entered the thickets. It happened that at school the previous day Willie Dalzel had been forced to read and acquire in some part a solemn description of a lynx. The meager information thrust upon him had caused him grimaces of suffering, but now he said, suddenly, "I'm goin' to shoot a lynx."

The other boys admired this statement, but they were silent for a time. Finally Jimmie said, meekly, "What's a lynx?" He had endured his ignorance as long as he was able.

The Dalzel boy mocked him. "Why, don't you know what a lynx is? A lynx? Why, a lynx is a animal somethin' like a cat, an' it's got great big green eyes, and it sits on the limb of a tree an' jus' glares at you. It's a pretty bad animal, I tell you. Why, when I—"

"Huh!" said the third boy. "Where'd you ever see a lynx?"

"Oh, I've seen 'em—plenty of 'em. I bet you'd be scared if you seen one once."

Jimmie and the other boy each demanded, "How do you know I would?"

They penetrated deeper into the wood. They climbed a rocky zigzag path which led them at times where with their hands they could almost touch the tops of giant pines. The gray cliffs sprang sheer toward the sky. Willie Dalzel babbled about his impossible lynx, and they stalked the mountain-side like chamois-hunters, although no noise of bird or beast broke the stillness of the hills. Below them Whilomville was spread out somewhat like the cheap green-and-black lithograph of the time— "A Bird's-eye View of Whilomville, N. Y."

In the end the boys reached the top of the mountain and scouted off among wild and desolate ridges. They were burning with the desire to slay large animals. They thought continually of elephants, lions, tigers, crocodiles. They discoursed upon their immaculate conduct in case such monsters confronted them, and they all lied carefully about their courage.

The breeze was heavy with the smell of sweet fern. The pines and hemlocks sighed as they waved their branches. In the hollows the leaves of the laurels were lacquered where the sunlight found them. No matter the weather, it would be impossible to long continue an expedition of this kind without a fire, and presently they built one, snapping down for fuel the brittle under branches of the pines. About this fire they were willed to conduct a sort of play, the Dalzel boy taking the part of a bandit chief, and the other boys being his trusty lieutenants. They stalked to and fro, long-strided, stern yet devil-may-care, three terrible little figures.

Jimmie had an uncle who made game of him whenever he caught him in this kind of play, and often this uncle quoted derisively the following classic: "Once aboard the lugger, Bill, and the girl is mine. Now to burn the château and destroy all evidence of our crime. But, hark 'e, Bill, no wiolence." Wheeling abruptly, he addressed these dramatic words to his comrades. They were impressed; they decided at once to be smugglers, and in the most ribald fashion they talked about carrying off young women.

At last they continued their march through the woods. The smuggling *motif* was now grafted fantastically upon the original lynx idea, which Willie Dalzel refused to abandon at any price.

Once they came upon an innocent bird which happened to be looking another way at the time. After a great deal of maneuvering and big words, Willie Dalzel reared his fowling piece and blew this poor thing into a mere rag of wet feathers, of which he was proud.

Afterward the other big boy had a turn at another bird. Then it was plainly Jimmie's chance. The two others had, of course, some thought of cheating him out of this chance, but of a truth he was timid to explode such a thunderous weapon, and as soon as they detected this fear they simply overbore him, and made it clearly understood that if he refused to shoot he would lose his caste, his scalp-lock, his girdle, his honor.

They had reached the old death-colored snake-fence which marked the limits of the upper pasture of the Fleming farm. Under some hickory trees the path ran parallel to the fence. Behold! a small priestly chipmunk came to a rail and, folding his hands on his abdomen, addressed them in his own tongue. It was Jimmie's shot. Adjured by the others, he took the gun. His face was stiff with apprehension. The Dalzel boy was giving forth fine words. "Go ahead. Aw, don't be afraid. It's nothin' to do. Why, I've done it a million times. Don't shut both your eyes, now. Jus' keep one open and shut the other one. He'll get away if you don't watch out. Now you're all right. Why don't you let 'er go? Go ahead."

Jimmie, with his legs braced apart, was in the center of the path. His back was greatly bent, owing to the mechanics of supporting the heavy gun. His companions were screeching in the rear. There was a wait.

Then he pulled trigger. To him there was a frightful roar, his cheek and his shoulder took a stunning blow, his face felt a hot flush of fire, and, opening his two eyes, he found that he was still alive. He was not too dazed to instantly adopt a becoming egotism. It had been the first shot of his life.

But directly after the well-mannered celebration of this victory a certain cow, which had been grazing in the line of fire, was seen to break wildly across the pasture, bellowing and bucking. The three smugglers and lynx-hunters looked at each other out of blanched faces. Jimmie had hit the cow. The first evidence of his comprehension of this fact was in the celerity with which he returned the discharged gun to Willie Dalzel.

They turned to flee. The land was black, as if it had been overshadowed suddenly with thick storm-clouds, and even as they fled in their horror a gigantic Swedish farm hand came from the heavens and fell upon them, shrieking in eerie triumph. In a twinkle they were clouted prostrate. The Swede was elate and ferocious in a foreign and fulsome way. He continued to beat them and yell.

From the ground they raised their dismal appeal. "Oh, please, mister, we didn't do it! He did it! I didn't do it! We didn't do it! We didn't mean to do it! Oh, please, mister!"

In these moments of childish terror little lads go half blind, and it is possible that few moments of their after life made them suffer as they did when the Swede flung them over the fence and marched them toward the farmhouse. They begged like cowards on the scaffold, and each one was for himself. "Oh, please let me go, mister! I didn't do it, mister! He did it! Oh, p-l-ease let me go, mister!"

The boyish view belongs to boys alone, and if this tall and knotted laborer was needlessly without charity, none of the three lads questioned it. Usually when they were punished they decided that they deserved it, and the more they were punished the more they were convinced that they were criminals of a most subterranean type. As to the hitting of the cow being a pure accident, and therefore not of necessity a criminal matter, such reading never entered their heads. When things happened and they were caught, they commonly paid dire consequences, and they were accustomed to measure the probabilities of woe utterly by the damage done, and not in any way by the culpability. The shooting of the cow was plainly heinous, and undoubtedly their dungeons would be knee-deep in water.

"He did it, mister!" This was a general outcry. Jimmie used it as often as did the others. As for them, it is certain that they had no direct thought of betraying their comrade for their own salvation. They thought themselves guilty because they were caught; when boys were not caught they might possibly be innocent. But captured boys were guilty. When they cried out that Jimmie was the culprit, it was principally a simple expression of terror.

Old Henry Fleming, the owner of the farm, strode across the pasture toward them. He had in his hand a most cruel whip. This whip he flourished. At his approach the boys suffered the agonies of the fire regions. And yet anybody with half an eye could see that the whip in his hand was a mere accident, and that he was a kind old man—when he cared.

When he had come near he spoke crisply. "What you boys ben doin' to my cow?" The tone had deep threat in it. They all answered by saying that none of them had shot the cow. Their denials were tearful and clamorous, and they crawled knee by knee. The vision of it was like three martyrs being dragged toward the stake. Old Fleming stood there, grim, tight-lipped. After a time he said, "Which boy done it?"

There was some confusion, and then Jimmie spake. "I done it, mister."

Fleming looked at him. Then he asked, "Well, what did you shoot 'er fer?"

Jimmie thought, hesitated, decided, faltered, and then formulated this: "I thought she was a lynx."

Old Fleming and his Swede at once lay down in the grass and laughed themselves helpless.

September, 1899
[*Harper's Magazine,* Vol. 99, pp. 552–557.]

THE REVENGE OF THE *ADOLPHUS**

I

"Stand by."

Shackles had come down from the bridge of the *Adolphus* and flung this command at three fellow correspondents who in the galley were busy with pencils trying to write something exciting and interesting from four days' quiet cruising. They looked up casually. "What for?" They did not intend to arouse for nothing. Ever since Shackles had heard the men of the navy directing each other to stand by for this thing and that thing, he had used the two words as his pet phrase and was continually telling his friends to stand by. Sometimes its portentous and emphatic reiteration became highly exasperating, and men were apt to retort sharply. "Well, I *am* standing by, ain't I?" On this occasion they detected that he was serious. "Well, what for?" they repeated. In his answer Shackles was reproachful as well as impressive. "Stand by? Stand by for a Spanish gunboat. A Spanish gunboat in chase! Stand by for *two* Spanish gunboats—*both* of them in chase!"

The others looked at him for a brief space and were almost certain that they saw truth written upon his countenance. Whereupon they tumbled out of the galley and galloped up to the bridge. The cook, with a mere ink-ling of tragedy, was now out on deck bawling, "What's the matter? What's the matter? What's the matter?" Aft, the grimy head of a stoker was thrust suddenly up through the deck, so to speak. The eyes flashed in a quick look astern, and then the head vanished. The correspondents were scram-bling on the bridge. "Where's my glasses, damn it? Here—let me take a look. Are they Spaniards, Captain? Are you sure?"

The skipper of the *Adolphus* was at the wheel. The pilothouse was so

* *Wounds in the Rain.*

arranged that he could not see astern without hanging forth from one of the side windows, but apparently he had made early investigation. He did not reply at once. At sea, he never replied at once to questions. At the very first, Shackles had discovered the merits of this deliberate manner and had taken delight in it. He invariably detailed his talk with the captain to the other correspondents. "Look here. I've just been to see the skipper. I said: 'I would like to put into Cape Haytien.' Then he took a little think. Finally he said: 'All right.' Then I said: 'I suppose we'll need to take on more coal there?' He took another little think. I said: 'Ever ran into that port before?' He took another little think. Finally he said: 'Yes.' I said: 'Have a cigar?' He took another little think. See? There's where I fooled 'im——"

While the correspondents spun the hurried questions at him, the captain of the *Adolphus* stood with his brown hands on the wheel and his cold glance aligned straight over the bow of his ship.

"Are they Spanish gunboats, Captain? Are they, Captain?"

After a profound pause, he said: "Yes." The four correspondents hastily and in perfect time presented their backs to him and fastened their gaze on the pursuing foe. They saw a dull gray curve of sea going to the feet of the high green-and-blue coast-line of northeastern Cuba, and on this sea were two miniature ships with clouds of iron-colored smoke pouring from their funnels.

One of the correspondents strolled elaborately to the pilothouse. "Aw—Captain," he drawled, "do you think they can catch us?"

The captain's glance was still aligned over the bow of his ship. Ultimately he answered: "I don't know."

From the top of the little *Adolphus's* stack, thick dark smoke swept level for a few yards and then went rolling to leeward in great hot obscuring clouds. From time to time the grimy head was thrust through the deck, the eyes took the quick look astern, and then the head vanished. The cook was trying to get somebody to listen to him. "Well, you know, damn it all, it won't be no fun to be ketched by them Spaniards. Be Gawd, it won't. Look here, what do you think they'll do to us, hey? Say, I don't like this, you know. I'm damned if I do." The sea, cut by the hurried bow of the *Adolphus,* flung its waters astern in the formation of a wide angle, and the lines of the angle ruffled and hissed as they fled, while the thumping screw tormented the water at the stern. The frame of the steamer underwent regular convulsions as in the strenuous sobbing of a child.

The mate was standing near the pilothouse. Without looking at him, the captain spoke his name. "Ed!"

"Yes, sir," cried the mate with alacrity.

The captain reflected for a moment. Then he said: "Are they gainin' on us?"

The mate took another anxious survey of the race. "No-o-yes, I think they are—a little."

After a pause the captain said: "Tell the chief to shake her up more."

The mate, glad of an occupation in these tense minutes, flew down to the engine-room door. "Skipper says shake 'er up more!" he bawled. The head of the chief engineer appeared, a grizzly head now wet with oil and sweat. "What?" he shouted angrily. It was as if he had been propelling the ship with his own arms. Now he was told that his best was not good enough. "What? shake 'er up more? Why, she can't carry another pound, I tell you! Not another ounce! We——" Suddenly he ran forward and climbed to the bridge. "Captain," he cried in the loud, harsh voice of one who lived usually amid the thunder of machinery, "she can't do it, sir! Be Gawd, she can't! She's turning over now faster than she ever did in her life, and we'll all blow to hell——"

The low-toned, impassive voice of the captain suddenly checked the chief's clamor. "I'll blow her up," he said, "but I won't git ketched if I kin help it." Even then the listening correspondents found a second in which to marvel that the captain had actually explained his point of view to another human being.

The engineer stood blank. Then suddenly he cried: "All right, sir!" He threw a hurried look of despair at the correspondents, the deck of the *Adolphus,* the pursuing enemy, Cuba, the sky and the sea; he vanished in the direction of his post.

A correspondent was suddenly re-gifted with the power of prolonged speech. "Well, you see, the game is up, damn it. See? We can't get out of it. The skipper will blow up the whole bunch before he'll let his ship be taken, and the Spaniards are gaining. Well, that's what comes from going to war in an eight-knot tub." He bitterly accused himself, the others, and the dark, sightless, indifferent world.

This certainty of coming evil affected each one differently. One was made garrulous; one kept absent-mindedly snapping his fingers and gazing at the sea; another stepped nervously to and fro, looking everywhere as if for employment for his mind. As for Shackles, he was silent and smiling, but it was a new smile that caused the lines about his mouth to betray quivering weakness. And each man looked at the others to discover their degree of fear and did his best to conceal his own, holding his crackling nerves with all his strength.

As the *Adolphus* rushed on, the sun suddenly emerged from behind gray clouds, and its rays dealt titanic blows, so that in a few minutes the sea was a glowing blue plain with the golden shine dancing at the tips of the waves. The coast of Cuba glowed with light. The pursuers displayed detail after detail in the new atmosphere. The voice of the cook was heard in high vexation. "Am I to git dinner as usual? How do I know? Nobody tells me what to do! Am I to git dinner as usual?"

The mate answered ferociously. "Of course you are! What do you s'pose? Ain't you the cook, you damn fool?"

The cook retorted in a mutinous scream. "Well, how would I know? If this ship is goin' to blow up——"

II

The captain called from the pilothouse. "Mr. Shackles! Oh, Mr. Shackles!" The correspondent moved hastily to a window. "What is it, Captain?" The skipper of the *Adolphus* raised a battered finger and pointed over the bows. "See 'er?" he asked, laconic but quietly jubilant. Another steamer was smoking at full speed over the sunlit seas. A great billow of pure white was on her bows. "Great Scott!" cried Shackles. "Another Spaniard?"

"No," said the captain, "that there is a United States cruiser!"

"What?" Shackles was dumbfounded into muscular paralysis. "No! Are you *sure?*"

The captain nodded. "Sure, take the glass. See her ensign? Two funnels, two masts with fighting tops. She ought to be the *Chancellorville.*"

Shackles choked. "Well, I'm blowed!"

"Ed!" said the captain.

"Yessir!"

"Tell the chief there is no hurry."

Shackles suddenly bethought him of his companions. He dashed to them and was full of quick scorn of their gloomy faces. "Hi, brace up there! Are you blind? Can't you see her?"

"See what?"

"Why, the *Chancellorville,* you blind mice!" roared Shackles. "See 'er? See 'er? See 'er?"

The others sprang, saw, and collapsed. Shackles was a madman for the purpose of distributing the news. "Cook!" he shrieked. "Don't you see 'er, cook? Good Gawd, man, don't you see 'er?" He ran to the lower deck and howled his information everywhere. Suddenly the whole ship smiled. Men clapped each other on the shoulder and joyously shouted. The captain thrust his head from the pilothouse to look back at the Spanish ships. Then he looked at the American cruiser. "Now, we'll see," he said grimly and vindictively to the mate. "Guess somebody else will do some running," the mate chuckled.

The two gunboats were still headed hard for the *Adolphus,* and she kept on her way. The American cruiser was coming swiftly. "It's the *Chancellor-*

ville!" cried Shackles. "I know her! We'll see a fight at sea, my boys! A fight
at sea!" The enthusiastic correspondents pranced in Indian revels.

The *Chancellorville*—2000 tons—18.6 knots—ten five-inch guns—came on
tempestuously, sheering the water high with her sharp bow. From her
funnels the smoke raced away in driven sheets. She loomed with extraordinary rapidity like a ship bulging and growing out of the sea. She swept
by the *Adolphus* so close that one could have thrown a walnut on board.
She was a glistening gray apparition with a blood-red waterline, with
brown gun muzzles and white-clothed motionless jack-tars; and in her rush
she was silent, deadly silent. Probably there entered the mind of every man
on board the *Adolphus* a feeling almost of idolatry for this living thing,
stern but, to their thought, incomparably beautiful. They would have
cheered but that each man seemed to feel that a cheer would be too puny
a tribute.

It was at first as if she did not see the *Adolphus*. She was going to pass
without heeding this little vagabond of the high seas. But suddenly a megaphone gaped over the rail of her bridge, and a voice was heard measuredly,
calmly intoning. "Hello—there! Keep—well—to—the—north'ard—and—out
of   my—way—and   I'll—go—in—and—see—what—those—people—want——"
Then nothing was heard but the swirl of water. In a moment the *Adolphus*
was looking at a high gray stern. On the quarterdeck, sailors were poised
about the breach of the after-pivot-gun.

The correspondents were reveling. "Captain," yelled Shackles, "we can't
miss this! We must see it!" But the skipper had already flung over the wheel.
"Sure," he answered almost at once. "We can't miss it."

The cook was arrogantly, grossly triumphant. His voice rang along the
deck. "There, now! How will the Spinachers like that? Now, it's *our* turn!
We've been doin' the runnin' away, but now we'll do the chasin'!" Apparently feeling some twinge of nerves from the former strain, he suddenly
demanded: "Say, who's got any whiskey? I'm near dead for a drink."

When the *Adolphus* came about, she laid her course for a position to the
northward of a coming battle, but the situation suddenly became complicated. When the Spanish ships discovered the identity of the ship that
was steaming toward them, they did not hesitate over their plan of action.
With one accord they turned and ran for port. Laughter arose from the
Adolphus. The captain broke his orders, and, instead of keeping to the
northward, he headed in the wake of the impetuous *Chancellorville*. The
correspondents crowded on the bow.

The Spaniards, when their broadsides became visible, were seen to be
ships of no importance, mere little gunboats for work in the shallows back
of the reefs; and it was certainly discreet to refuse encounter with the five-
inch guns of the *Chancellorville*. But the joyful *Adolphus* took no account

of this discretion. The pursuit of the Spaniards had been so ferocious that the quick change to heels-over-head flight filled that corner of the mind which is devoted to the spirit of revenge. It was this that moved Shackles to yell taunts futilely at the far-away ships. "Well, how do you like it, eh? How do you like it?" The *Adolphus* was drinking compensation for her previous agony.

The mountains of the shore now shadowed high into the sky, and the square white houses of a town could be seen near a vague cleft which seemed to mark the entrance to a port. The gunboats were now near to it.

Suddenly white smoke streamed from the bow of the *Chancellorville* and developed swiftly into a great bulb which drifted in fragments down the wind. Presently the deep-throated boom of the gun came to the ears on board the *Adolphus*. The shot kicked up a high jet of water into the air astern of the last gunboat. The black smoke from the funnels of the cruiser made her look like a collier on fire, and in her desperation she tried many more long shots, but presently the *Adolphus,* murmuring disappointment, saw the *Chancellorville* sheer from the chase.

In time they came up with her, and she was an indignant ship. Gloom and wrath was on the forecastle, and wrath and gloom was on the quarter-deck. A sad voice from the bridge said: "Just missed 'em." Shackles gained permission to board the cruiser, and in the cabin he talked to Lieutenant Commander Surrey, tall, baldheaded, and angry. "Shoals," said the captain of the *Chancellorville.* "I can't go any nearer, and those gunboats could steam along a stone sidewalk if only it was wet." Then his bright eyes became brighter. "I tell you what! The *Chicken,* the *Holy Moses,* and the *Mongolian* are on station off Nuevitas. If you will do me a favor—why, tomorrow I will give those people a game!"

III

The *Chancellorville* lay all night watching off the port of the two gunboats. Soon after daylight, the lookout descried three smokes to the westward, and they were later made out to be the *Chicken,* the *Holy Moses,* and the *Aldolphus,* the latter tagging hurriedly after the United States vessels.

The *Chicken* had been a harbor tug, but she was now the U.S.S. *Chicken,* by your leave. She carried a six-pounder forward and a six-pounder aft, and her main point was her conspicuous vulnerability. The *Holy Moses* had been the private yacht of a Philadelphia millionaire. She carried six six-pounders, and her main point was the chaste beauty of the officers' quarters.

On the bridge of the *Chancellorville,* Lieutenant Commander Surrey surveyed his squadron with considerable satisfaction. Presently he signaled to the lieutenant who commanded the *Holy Moses* and to the boatswain who commanded the *Chicken* to come aboard the flagship. This was all very well for the captain of the yacht, but it was not so easy for the captain of the tugboat, who had two heavy lifeboats swung fifteen feet above the water. He had been accustomed to talking with senior officers from his own pilothouse through the intercession of the blessed megaphone. However, he got a lifeboat overside and was pulled to the *Chancellorville* by three men—which cut his crew almost into halves.

In the cabin of the *Chancellorville,* Surrey disclosed to his two captains his desires concerning the Spanish gunboats, and they were glad for being ordered down from the Nuevitas station, where life was very dull. He also announced that there was a shore battery, containing, he believed, four field guns—three-point-two's. His draught—he spoke of it as *his* draught— would enable him to go in close enough to engage the battery at moderate range, but he pointed out that the main parts of the attempt to destroy the Spanish gunboats must be left to the *Holy Moses* and the *Chicken.* His business, he thought, could only be to keep the air so singing about the ears of the battery that the men at the guns would be unable to take an interest in the dash of the smaller American craft into the bay.

The officers spoke in their turns. The captain of the *Chicken* announced that he saw no difficulties. The squadron would follow the senior officer in line ahead, the S.O. would engage the batteries as soon as possible, she would turn to starboard when the depth of water forced her to do so, and the *Holy Moses* and the *Chicken* would run past her into the bay and fight the Spanish ships wherever they were to be found. The captain of the *Holy Moses,* after some moments of dignified thought, said that he had no suggestions to make that would better this plan.

Surrey pressed an electric bell; a marine orderly appeared; he was sent with a message. The message brought the navigating officer of the *Chancellorville* to the cabin, and the four men nosed over a chart.

In the end Surrey declared that he had made up his mind, and the juniors remained in expectant silence for three minutes while he stared at the bulkhead. Then he said that the plan of the *Chicken's* captain seemed to him correct in the main. He would make one change. It was that he should first steam in and engage the battery and the other vessels should remain in their present positions until he signaled them to run into the bay. If the squadron steamed ahead in line, the battery could, if it chose, divide its fire between the cruiser and the gunboats constituting the more important attack. He had no doubt, he said, that he could soon silence the battery by tumbling the earth-works on to the guns and driving away the men, even if he did not succeed in hitting the pieces. Of course he had no doubt of being able to silence the battery in twenty minutes. Then he would signal for the *Holy Moses* and the *Chicken* to make their rush, and of course he would support them with his fire as much as conditions enabled him. He arose then, indicating that the conference was at an end. In the few moments more that all four men remained in the cabin, the talk changed its character completely. It was now unofficial, and the sharp badinage concealed furtive affections, Academy friendships, the feelings of old-time shipmates hiding everything under a veil of jokes. "Well, good luck to you, old boy! Don't get that valuable packet of yours sunk under you. Think how it would weaken the navy. Would you mind buying me three pairs of pajamas in the town yonder? If your engines get disabled, tote her under your arm. You can do it. Good-bye, old man; don't forget to come out all right——"

When the captains of the *Holy Moses* and the *Chicken* emerged from the cabin, they strode the deck with a new step. They were proud men. The marine on duty above their boats looked at them curiously and with awe. He detected something which meant action, conflict. The boats' crews saw it also. As they pulled their steady stroke, they studied fleetingly the face of the officer in the stern sheets. In both cases they perceived a glad man and yet a man filled with a profound consideration of the future.

IV

A bird-like whistle stirred the decks of the *Chancellorville*. It was followed by the hoarse bellowing of the boatswain's mate. As the cruiser turned her bow toward the shore, she happened to steam near the *Adolphus*. The usual calm voice hailed the dispatch boat. "Keep—that—gauze undershirt of yours—well—out of the—line of fire."

"Ay, ay, sir!"

The cruiser then moved slowly toward the shore, watched by every eye in the smaller American vessels. She was deliberate and steady, and this was reasonable even to the impatience of the other craft, because the wooded shore was likely to suddenly develop new factors. Slowly she swung to starboard; smoke belched over her, and the roar of a gun came along the water.

The battery was indicated by a long thin streak of yellow earth. The first shot went high, plowing the chaparral on the hillside. The *Chancellorville* wore an air for a moment of being deep in meditation. She flung another shell, which landed squarely on the earth-work, making a great dun cloud. Before the smoke had settled, there was a crimson flash from the battery. To the watchers at sea, it was smaller than a needle. The shot made a geyser of crystal water, four hundred yards from the *Chancellorville*.

The cruiser, having made up her mind, suddenly went at the battery, hammer and tongs. She moved to and fro casually, but the thunder of her guns was gruff and angry. Sometimes she was quite hidden in her own smoke, but with exceeding regularity the earth of the battery spurted into the air. The Spanish shells, for the most part, went high and wide of the cruiser, jetting the water far away.

Once a Spanish gunner took a festive side show chance at the waiting group of the three nondescripts. It went like a flash over the *Adolphus*, singing a wistful metallic note. Whereupon the *Adolphus* broke hurriedly for the open sea, and men on the *Holy Moses* and the *Chicken* laughed hoarsely and cruelly. The correspondents had been standing excitedly on top of the pilothouse, but at the passing of the shell they promptly eliminated themselves by dropping with a thud to the deck below. The cook again was giving tongue. "Oh, say, this won't do! I'm damned if it will! We ain't no armored cruiser, you know. If one of them shells hits us—well, we finish right there. 'Tain't like as if it was our *business*, foolin' 'round within the range of them guns. There's no sense in it. Them other fellows don't seem to mind it, but it's their *business*. If it's your *business*, you go ahead and do it, but if it ain't, you—look at that, would you!"

The *Chancellorville* had sent up a spread of flags, and the *Holy Moses* and the *Chicken* were steaming in.

v

They on the *Chancellorville* sometimes could see into the bay, and they perceived the enemy's gunboats moving out as if to give battle. Surrey feared that this impulse would not endure or that it was some mere pretense for the edification of the townspeople and the garrison, so he hastily signaled the *Holy Moses* and the *Chicken* to go in. Thankful for small favors, they came on like charging bantams. The battery had ceased firing. As the two auxiliaries passed under the stern of the cruiser, the megaphone hailed them. "You—will—see—the—en-em-y—soon—as—you—round—the—point. A—fine—chance. Good—luck."

As a matter of fact, the Spanish gunboats had not been informed of the presence of the *Holy Moses* and the *Chicken* off the bar, and they were just blustering down the bay over the protective shoals to make it appear that they scorned the *Chancellorville*. But suddenly, from around the point, there burst into view a steam yacht, closely followed by a harbor tug. The gunboats took one swift look at this horrible sight and fled screaming.

Lieutenant Reigate, commanding the *Holy Moses,* had under his feet a craft that was capable of some speed, although before a solemn tribunal one would have to admit that she conscientiously belied almost everything that the contractors had said of her originally. Boatswain Pent, commanding the *Chicken,* was in possession of an utterly different kind. The *Holy Moses* was an antelope; the *Chicken* was a man who could carry a piano on his back. In this race Pent had the mortification of seeing his vessel outstripped badly.

The entrance of the two American craft had had a curious effect upon the shores of the bay. Apparently every one had slept in the assurance that the *Chancellorville* could not cross the bar, and that the *Chancellorville* was the only hostile ship. Consequently, the appearance of the *Holy Moses* and the *Chicken* created a curious and complete emotion. Reigate, on the bridge of the *Holy Moses,* laughed when he heard the bugles shrilling and saw through his glasses the wee figures of men running hither and thither on the shore. It was the panic of the china when the bull entered the shop. The whole bay was bright with sun. Every detail of the shore was plain. From a brown hut abeam of the *Holy Moses,* some little men ran out waving their arms and turning their tiny faces to look at the enemy. Directly ahead, some four miles, appeared the scattered white houses of a town with a wharf and some schooners in front of it. The gunboats were making for the town. There was a stone fort on the hill overshadowing, but Reigate conjectured that there was no artillery in it.

There was a sense of something intimate and impudent in the minds of the Americans. It was like climbing over a wall and fighting a man in his own garden. It was not that they could be in any wise shaken in their resolve; it was simply that the overwhelmingly Spanish aspect of things made them feel like gruff intruders. Like many of the emotions of wartime, this emotion had nothing at all to do with war.

Reigate's only commissioned subordinate called up from the bow gun. "May I open fire, sir? I think I can fetch that last one."

"Yes." Immediately the six-pounder crashed, and in the air was the spinning-wire noise of the flying shot. It struck so close to the last gunboat that it appeared that the spray went aboard. The swift-handed men at the gun spoke of it. "Gave 'm a bath that time anyhow. First one they've ever had. Dry 'em off this time, Jim." The young ensign said: "Steady." And so the *Holy Moses* raced in, firing, until the whole town, fort, water front, and shipping were as plain as if they had been done on paper by a mechanical draftsman. The gunboats were trying to hide in the bosom of the town. One was frantically tying up to the wharf and the other was anchoring within a hundred yards of the shore. The Spanish infantry, of course, had dug trenches along the beach, and suddenly the air over the *Holy Moses* sang with bullets. The shoreline thrummed with musketry. Also some antique shells screamed.

VI

The *Chicken* was doing her best. Pent's posture at the wheel seemed to indicate that her best was about thirty-four knots. In his eagerness he was braced as if he alone was taking in a 10,000-ton battleship through Hell Gate.

But the *Chicken* was not too far in the rear, and Pent could see clearly that he was to have no minor part to play. Some of the antique shells had struck the *Holy Moses,* and he could see the escaped steam shooting up from her. She lay close inshore and was lashing out with four six-pounders as if this was the last opportunity she would have to fire them. She had made the Spanish gunboats very sick. A solitary gun on the one moored to the wharf was from time to time firing wildly; otherwise the gunboats were silent. But the beach in front of the town was a line of fire. The *Chicken* headed for the *Holy Moses* and, as soon as possible, the six-pounder in her bow began to crack at the gunboat moored to the wharf.

In the meantime, the *Chancellorville* prowled off the bar, listening to the firing, anxious, acutely anxious, and feeling her impotency in every inch of her smart steel frame. And in the meantime, the *Adolphus* squatted on the waves and brazenly waited for news. One could thoughtfully count the seconds and reckon that, in this second and that second, a man had died—if one chose. But no one did it. Undoubtedly, the spirit was that the flag should come away with honor, honor complete, perfect, leaving no loose unfinished end over which the Spaniards could erect a monument of satisfaction, glorification. The distant guns boomed to the ears of the silent bluejackets at their stations on the cruiser.

The *Chicken* steamed up to the *Holy Moses* and took into her nostrils the odor of steam, gunpowder, and burnt things. Rifle bullets simply streamed over them both. In the merest flash of time, Pent took into his remembrance the body of a dead quartermaster on the bridge of his consort. The two megaphones uplifted together, but Pent's eager voice cried out first.

"Are you injured, sir?"

"No, not completely. My engines can get me out after—after we have sunk those gunboats." The voice had been utterly conventional but it changed to sharpness. "Go in and sink that gunboat at anchor."

As the *Chicken* rounded the *Holy Moses* and started inshore, a man called to him from the depths of finished disgust. "They're takin' to their boats, sir." Pent looked and saw the men of the anchored gunboat lower their boats and pull like mad for shore.

The *Chicken,* assisted by the *Holy Moses,* began a methodical killing of the anchored gunboat. The Spanish infantry on shore fired frenziedly at the *Chicken.* Pent, giving the wheel to a waiting sailor, stepped out to a point where he could see the men at the guns. One bullet spanged past him and into the pilothouse. He ducked his head into the window. "That hit you, Murry?" he inquired with interest.

"No, sir," cheerfully responded the man at the wheel.

Pent became very busy superintending the fire of his absurd battery. The anchored gunboat simply would not sink. It evinced that unnatural stubbornness which is sometimes displayed by inanimate objects. The gunboat at the wharf had sunk as if she had been scuttled, but this riddled thing at anchor would not even take fire. Pent began to grow flurried—privately. He could not stay there for ever. Why didn't the damned gunboat admit its destruction? Why——

He was at the forward gun when one of his engine-room force came to him and, after saluting, said serenely: "The men at the after gun are all down, sir."

It was one of those curious lifts which an enlisted man, without in any way knowing it, can give his officer. The impudent tranquillity of the man at once set Pent to rights, and the stoker departed admiring the extraordinary coolness of his captain.

The next few moments contained little but heat, an odor, applied mechanics, and an expectation of death. Pent developed a fervid and amazed appreciation of the men, his men, men he knew very well, but strange men. What explained them? He was doing his best because he was captain of the *Chicken,* and he lived or died by the *Chicken.* But what could move these men to watch his eye in bright anticipation of his orders and then obey them with enthusiastic rapidity? What caused them to speak of the action as some kind of joke—particularly when they knew he could overhear them? What manner of men? And he anointed them secretly with his fullest affection.

Perhaps Pent did not think all this during the battle. Perhaps he thought it so soon after the battle that his full mind became confused as to the time. At any rate, it stands as an expression of his feeling.

The enemy had gotten a field gun down to the shore, and with it they began to throw three-inch shells at the *Chicken.* In this war it was usual that the downtrodden Spaniards in their ignorance should use smokeless powder, while the Americans, by the power of the consistent, everlasting three-ply, wire-woven, double back-action imbecility of a hayseed government, used powder which on sea and on land cried their position to heaven, and, accordingly, good men got killed without reason. At first, Pent could not locate the field gun at all, but as soon as he found it, he ran aft with one man and brought the after six-pounder again into action. He paid little heed to the old gun crew. One was lying on his face apparently dead; another was prone, with a wound in the chest; while the third sat with his back to the deckhouse holding a smitten arm. This last one called out huskily, "Give 'm hell, sir."

The minutes of the battle were either days, years, or they were flashes of a second. Once Pent, looking up, was astonished to see three shell holes in the *Chicken's* funnel—made surreptitiously, so to speak.—"If we don't silence that field gun, she'll sink us, boys."—The eyes of the man sitting with his back against the deckhouse were looking from out his ghastly face at the new gun crew. He spoke with the supreme laziness of a wounded man. "Give 'm hell."—Pent felt a sudden twist of his shoulder. He was wounded—slightly.—The anchored gunboat was in flames.

VII

Pent took his little bloodstained towboat out to the *Holy Moses*. The yacht was already under way for the bay entrance. As they were passing out of range the Spaniards heroically redoubled their fire—which is their custom. Pent, moving busily about the decks, stopped suddenly at the door of the engine room. His face was set and his eyes were steely. He spoke to one of the engineers. "During the action I saw you firing at the enemy with a rifle. I told you once to stop, and then I saw you at it again. Pegging away with a rifle is no part of your business. I want you to understand that you are in trouble." The humbled man did not raise his eyes from the deck. Presently the *Holy Moses* displayed an anxiety for the *Chicken's* health.

"One killed and four wounded, sir."

"Have you enough men left to work your ship?"

After deliberation, Pent answered: "No, sir."

"Shall I send you assistance?"

"No, sir. I can get to sea all right."

As they neared the point they were edified by the sudden appearance of a serio-comic ally. The *Chancellorville* at last had been unable to stand the strain, and had sent in her launch with an ensign, five seamen, and a number of marksmen marines. She swept hotfoot around the point, bent on terrible slaughter; the one-pounder of her bow presented a formidable appearance. The *Holy Moses* and the *Chicken* laughed until they brought indignation to the brow of the young ensign. But he forgot it when with some of his men he boarded the *Chicken* to do what was possible for the wounded. The nearest surgeon was aboard the *Chancellorville*. There was absolute silence on board the cruiser as the *Holy Moses* steamed up to report. The bluejackets listened with all their ears. The commander of the yacht spoke slowly into his megaphone: "We have—destroyed—the two —gunboats—sir." There was a burst of confused cheering on the forecastle of the *Chancellorville*, but an officer's cry quelled it.

"Very—good. Will—you—come aboard?"

Two correspondents were already on the deck of the cruiser. Before the last of the wounded were hoisted aboard the cruiser the *Adolphus* was on her way to Key West. When she arrived at that port of desolation Shackles fled to file the telegrams, and the other correspondents fled to the hotel for clothes, good clothes, clean clothes; and food, good food, much food; and drink, much drink, any kind of drink.

Days afterward, when the officers of the noble squadron received the newspapers containing an account of their performance, they looked at each other somewhat dejectedly: "Heroic assault—grand daring of Boatswain Pent—superb accuracy of the *Holy Moses'* fire—gallant tars of the *Chicken*—their names should be remembered as long as America stands—terrible losses of the enemy——"

When the Secretary of the Navy ultimately read the report of Commander Surrey, S. O. P., he had to prick himself with a dagger in order to remember that anything at all out of the ordinary had occurred.

September, 1899
[*Strand Magazine,* Vol. 18, pp. 724–733.]

THE SERGEANT'S PRIVATE MADHOUSE*

The moonlight was almost steady blue flame, and all this radiance was lavished out upon a still, lifeless wilderness of stunted trees and cactus plants. The shadows lay upon the ground, pools of black and sharply outlined, resembling substances, fabrics, and not shadows at all. From afar came the sound of the sea coughing among the hollows in the coral rock.

The land was very empty; one could easily imagine that Cuba was a simple vast solitude; one could wonder at the moon taking all the trouble of this splendid illumination. There was no wind; nothing seemed to live.

But in a particular large group of shadows lay an outpost of some forty United States marines. If it had been possible to approach them from any direction without encountering one of their sentries, one could have gone stumbling among sleeping men and men who sat waiting, their blankets tented over their heads; one would have been in among them before one's mind could have decided whether they were men or devils. If a marine moved, he took the care and the time of one who walks across a death-chamber. The lieutenant in command reached for his watch, and the nickel chain gave forth the faintest tinkling sound. He could see the glistening five or six pairs of eyes that slowly turned to regard him. His sergeant lay near him, and he bent his face down to whisper. "Who's on post behind the big cactus plant?"

"Dryden," rejoined the sergeant just over his breath.

After a pause the lieutenant murmured: "He's got too many nerves. I shouldn't have put him there." The sergeant asked if he should crawl down and look into affairs at Dryden's post. The young officer nodded assent, and the sergeant, softly cocking his rifle, went away on his hands and knees. The lieutenant, with his back to a dwarf tree, sat watching the

---

* *Wounds in the Rain.*

sergeant's progress for the few moments that he could see him moving from one shadow to another. Afterward, the officer waited to hear Dryden's quick but low-voiced challenge, but time passed and no sound came from the direction of the post behind the cactus bush.

The sergeant, as he came nearer and nearer to this cactus bush—a number of peculiarly dignified columns throwing shadows of inky darkness— had slowed his pace, for he did not wish to trifle with the feelings of the sentry, and he was expecting the stern hail and was ready with the immediate answer which turns away wrath. He was not made anxious by the fact that he could not yet see Dryden, for he knew that the man would be hidden in a way practiced by sentry marines since the time when two men had been killed by a disease of excessive confidence on picket. Indeed, as the sergeant went still nearer he became more and more angry. Dryden was evidently a most proper sentry.

Finally he arrived at a point where he could see Dryden seated in the shadow, staring into the bushes ahead of him, his rifle ready on his knee. The sergeant in his rage longed for the peaceful precincts of the Washington Marine Barracks, where there would have been no situation to prevent the most complete non-commissioned oratory. He felt indecent in his capacity of a man able to creep up to the back of a G Company member on guard duty. Never mind; in the morning back at camp——

But, suddenly, he felt afraid. There was something wrong with Dryden. He remembered old tales of comrades creeping out to find a picket, seated against a tree perhaps, upright enough, but stone dead. The sergeant paused and gave the inscrutable back of the sentry a long stare. Dubious, he again moved forward. At three paces, he hissed like a little snake. Dryden did not show a sign of hearing. At last, the sergeant was in a position from which he was able to reach out and touch Dryden on the arm. Whereupon was turned to him the face of a man livid with mad fright. The sergeant grabbed him by the wrist and with discreet fury shook him. "Here! Pull yourself together!"

Dryden paid no heed, but turned his wild face from the newcomer to the ground in front. "Don't you see 'em, sergeant? Don't you see 'em?"

"Where?" whispered the sergeant.

"Ahead, and a little on the right flank. A reg'lar skirmish line. Don't you see 'em?"

"Naw," whispered the sergeant. Dryden began to shake. He began moving one hand from his head to his knee and from his knee to his head rapidly, in a way that is without explanation. "I don't dare fire," he wept. "If I do they'll see me, and oh, how they'll pepper me!"

The sergeant, lying on his belly, understood one thing. Dryden had gone mad. Dryden was the March Hare. The old man gulped down his uproarious emotions as well as he was able and used the most simple device. "Go," he said, "and tell the lieutenant while I cover your post for you." "No! They'd see me! They'd see me! And then they'd pepper me! Oh, how they'd pepper me!"

The sergeant was face to face with the biggest situation of his life. In the first place he knew that at night a large or small force of Spanish guerillas was never more than easy rifle range from any marine outpost, both sides maintaining a secrecy as absolute as possible in regard to their real position and strength. Everything was on a watch-spring foundation. A loud word might be paid for by a night attack which would involve five hundred men who needed their earned sleep, not to speak of some of them who would need their lives. The slip of a foot and the rolling of a pint of gravel might go from consequence to consequence until various crews went to general quarters on their ships in the harbor, their batteries booming as the swift searchlight flashes tore through the foliage. Men would get killed—notably the sergeant and Dryden—and outposts would be cut off, and the whole night would be one pitiless turmoil. And so Sergeant George H. Peasley began to run his private madhouse behind the cactus bush.

"Dryden," said the sergeant, "you do as I tell you and go tell the lieutenant."

"I don't dare move," shivered the man. "They'll see me if I move. They'll see me. They're almost up now. Let's hide——"

"Well, then, you stay here a moment, and I'll go and——"

Dryden turned upon him a look so tigerish that the old man felt his hair move. "Don't you stir," he hissed. "You want to give me away. You want them to see me. Don't you stir." The sergeant decided not to stir.

He became aware of the slow wheeling of eternity, its majestic incomprehensibility of movement. Seconds, minutes, were quaint little things, tangible as toys, and there were billions of them, all alike. "Dryden," he whispered at the end of a century in which, curiously, he had never joined the marine corps at all but had taken to another walk of life and prospered greatly in it. "Dryden, this is all foolishness." He thought of the expedient of smashing the man over the head with his rifle, but Dryden was so supernaturally alert that there surely would issue some small scuffle, and there could be not even the fraction of a scuffle. The sergeant relapsed into the contemplation of another century.

His patient had one fine virtue. He was in such terror of the phantom skirmish line that his voice never went above a whisper, whereas his delusion might have expressed itself in hyena yells and shots from his rifle. The sergeant, shuddering, had visions of how it might have been—the mad private leaping into the air and howling and shooting at his friends and making them the center of the enemy's eager attention. This, to his mind, would have been conventional conduct for a maniac. The trembling victim of an idea was somewhat puzzling. The sergeant decided that from time to time he would reason with his patient. "Look here, Dryden, you don't see any real Spaniards. You've been drinking or—something. Now——"

But Dryden only glared him into silence. Dryden was inspired with such a profound contempt of him that it was become hatred. "Don't you stir!" And it was clear that if the sergeant did stir, the mad private would introduce calamity. "Now," said Peasley to himself, "if those guerillas *should* take a crack at us tonight, they'd find a lunatic asylum right in the front, and it would be astonishing."

The silence of the night was broken by the quick low voice of a sentry to the left some distance. The breathless stillness brought an effect to the words as if they had been spoken in one's ear.

"*Halt—who's there?—halt or I'll fire!*" Bang!

At the moment of sudden attack, particularly at night, it is improbable that a man registers much detail of either thought or action. He may afterward say: "I was here." He may say: "I was there." "I did this." "I did that." But there remains a great incoherency because of the tumultuous thought which seethes through the head. "Is this defeat?" At night in a wilderness and against skillful foes half seen, one does not trouble to ask if it is also Death. Defeat is Death, then, save for the miraculous. But the exaggerating, magnifying first thought subsides in the ordered mind of the soldier, and he knows, soon, what he is doing and how much of it. The sergeant's immediate impulse had been to squeeze close to the ground and listen— listen—above all else, listen. But the next moment he grabbed his private asylum by the scruff of its neck, jerked it to its feet, and started to retreat upon the main outpost.

To the left, rifle flashes were bursting from the shadows. To the rear, the lieutenant was giving some hoarse order or admonition. Through the air swept some Spanish bullets, very high, as if they had been fired at a man in a tree. The private asylum came on so hastily that the sergeant found he could remove his grip, and soon they were in the midst of the men of the outpost. Here there was no occasion for enlightening the lieutenant. In the first place such surprises required statement, question, and answer. It is impossible to get a grossly original and fantastic idea through a man's head in less than one minute of rapid talk, and the sergeant knew the lieutenant could not spare the minute. He himself had no minutes to devote to anything but the business of the outpost. And the madman disappeared from his pen, and he forgot about him.

It was a long night, and the little fight was as long as the night. It was a heartbreaking work. The forty marines lay in an irregular oval. From all sides, the Mauser bullets sang low and hard. Their occupation was to prevent a rush, and to this end they potted carefully at the flash of a Mauser—save when they got excited for a moment, in which case their magazines rattled like a great Waterbury watch. Then they settled again to a systematic potting.

The enemy were not of the regular Spanish forces. They were of a corps of guerillas, native-born Cubans who preferred the flag of Spain. They were all men who knew the craft of the woods and were all recruited from the district. They fought more like red Indians than any people but the red Indians themselves. Each seemed to possess an individuality, a fighting individuality, which is only found in the highest order of irregular soldiers. Personally they were as distinct as possible, but through equality of knowledge and experience they arrived at concert of action. So long as they operated in the wilderness, they were formidable troops. It mattered little whether it was daylight or dark; they were mainly invisible. They had schooled from the Cubans insurgent to Spain. As the Cubans fought the Spanish troops, so would these particular Spanish troops fight the Americans. It was wisdom.

The marines thoroughly understood the game. They must lie close and fight until daylight, when the guerillas promptly would go away. They had withstood other nights of this kind, and now their principal emotion was probably a sort of frantic annoyance.

Back at the main camp, whenever the roaring volleys lulled, the men in the trenches could hear their comrades of the outpost, and the guerillas pattering away interminably. The moonlight faded and left an equal darkness upon the wilderness. A man could barely see the comrade at his side. Sometimes guerillas crept so close that the flame from their rifles seemed to scorch the faces of the marines, and the reports sounded as if from within two or three inches of their very noses. If a pause came, one could hear the guerillas gabbling to each other in a kind of drunken delirium. The lieutenant was praying that the ammunition would last. Everybody was praying for daybreak.

A black hour came finally, when the men were not fit to have their troubles increased. The enemy made a wild attack on one portion of the oval which was held by about fifteen men. The remainder of the force was busy enough, and the fifteen were naturally left to their devices. Amid the whirl of it, a loud voice suddenly broke out in song:

> "While shepherds watched their flocks by night,
>   All seated on the ground,
>   An angel of the Lord came down,
>   And glory shone around."

"Who the hell is that?" demanded the lieutenant from a throat full of smoke. There was almost a full stop of the firing. The Americans were somewhat puzzled. Practical ones muttered that the fool should have a bayonet-hilt shoved down his throat. Others felt a thrill at the strangeness of the thing. Perhaps it was a sign!

> "The minstrel boy to the war has gone,
>   In the ranks of death you'll find him,
>   His father's sword he has girded on
> And his wild harp slung behind him."

This croak was as lugubrious as a coffin. "Who is it? Who is it?" snapped the lieutenant. "Stop him, somebody."

"It's Dryden, sir," said old Sergeant Peasley, as he felt around in the darkness for his madhouse. "I can't find him—yet."

> "Please, oh, please, oh, do not let me fall;
>   You're—gurgh-ugh——"

The sergeant had pounced upon him.

This singing had had an effect upon the Spaniards. At first they had fired frenziedly at the voice, but they soon ceased, perhaps from sheer amazement. Both sides took a spell of meditation.

The sergeant was having some difficulty with his charge. "Here, you, grab 'im. Take 'im by the throat. Be quiet, you devil."

One of the fifteen men, who had been hard pressed, called out, "We've only got about one clip apiece, Lieutenant. If they come again——"

The lieutenant crawled to and fro among his men, taking clips of cartridges from those who had many. He came upon the sergeant and his madhouse. He felt Dryden's belt and found it simply stuffed with ammunition. He examined Dryden's rifle and found in it a full clip. The madhouse had not fired a shot. The lieutenant distributed these valuable prizes among the fifteen men. As the men gratefully took them, one said: "If they had come again hard enough, they would have had us, sir—maybe."

But the Spaniards did not come again. At the first indication of daybreak, they fired their customary good-bye volley. The marines lay tight while the slow dawn crept over the land. Finally the lieutenant arose among them, and he was a bewildered man, but very angry. "Now where is that idiot, Sergeant?"

"Here he is, sir," said the old man cheerfully. He was seated on the ground beside the recumbent Dryden, who, with an innocent smile on his face, was sound asleep.

"Wake him up," said the lieutenant briefly.

The sergeant shook the sleeper. "Here, Minstrel Boy, turn out. The lieutenant wants you."

Dryden climbed to his feet and saluted the officer with a dazed and childish air. "Yes, sir."

The lieutenant was obviously having difficulty in governing his feelings, but he managed to say with calmness, "You seem to be fond of singing, Dryden? Sergeant, see if he has any whiskey on him."

"Sir?" said the madhouse, stupefied. "Singing—fond of singing?"

Here the sergeant interposed gently, and he and the lieutenant held palaver apart from the others. The marines, hitching more comfortably their almost empty belts, spoke with grins of the madhouse. "Well, the Minstrel Boy made 'em clear out. They couldn't stand it. But—I wouldn't want to be in his boots. He'll see fireworks when the old man interviews him on the uses of grand opera in modern warfare. How do you think he managed to smuggle a bottle along without us finding it out?"

When the weary outpost was relieved and marched back to camp, the men could not rest until they had told a tale of the voice in the wilderness. In the meantime the sergeant took Dryden aboard a ship, and to those who took charge of the man, he defined him as "the most useful goddam crazy man in the service of the United States."

September 30, 1899
[*The Saturday Evening Post*, Vol. 172, pp. 214–215.]

THE BATTLE OF FORTY FORT*

The Congress, sitting at Philadelphia, had voted our Wyoming country two companies of infantry for its protection against the Indians, with the single provision that we raise the men and arm them ourselves. This was not too brave a gift, but no one could blame the poor Congress, and indeed one could wonder that they found occasion to think of us at all, since at the time every gentleman of them had his coat tails gathered high in his hands in readiness for flight to Baltimore. But our two companies of foot were no sooner drilled, equipped, and in readiness to defend the colony when they were ordered off down to the Jerseys to join General Washington. So it can be seen what service Congress did us in the way of protection. Thus the Wyoming Valley, sixty miles deep in the wilderness, held its log houses full of little besides mothers, maids, and children. To the clamor against this situation the badgered Congress could only reply

---

* *Wyoming Valley Tales.*

by the issue of another generous order, directing that one full company of foot be raised in the town of Westmoreland for the defense of said town, and that the said company find their own arms, ammunition, and blankets. Even people with our sense of humor could not laugh at this joke.

When the first two companies were forming, I had thought to join one, but my father forbade me, saying that I was too young, although I was full sixteen, tall, and very strong. So it turned out that I was not off fighting with Washington's army when Butler with his rangers and Indians raided Wyoming. Perhaps I was in the better place to do my duty, if I could.

When wandering Indians visited the settlements, their drunkenness and insolence were extreme, but the few white men remained calm, and often enough pretended oblivion to insults which, because of their wives and families, they dared not attempt to avenge. In my own family, my father's imperturbability was scarce superior to my mother's coolness, and such was our faith in them that we twelve children also seemed to be fearless. Neighbor after neighbor came to my father in despair of the defenseless condition of the valley, declaring that they were about to leave everything and flee over the mountains to Stroudsberg. My father always wished them Godspeed and said no more. If they urged him to fly also, he usually walked away from them.

Finally there came a time when all the Indians vanished. We rather would have had them tipsy and impudent in the settlements; we knew what their disappearance portended. It was the serious sign. Too soon the news came that "Indian Butler" was on his way.

The valley was vastly excited. People with their smaller possessions flocked into the blockhouses, and militia officers rode everywhere to rally every man. A small force of Continentals—regulars of the line—had joined our people, and the little army was now under the command of the Continental officer, Major Zebulon Butler.

I had thought that with all this hubbub of an impending life-and-death struggle in the valley my father would allow the work of our farm to slacken. But in this I was notably mistaken. The milking and the feeding and the work in the fields went on as if there never had been an Indian south of the Canadas. My mother and my sisters continued to cook, to wash, to churn, to spin, to dye, to mend, to make soap, to make maple sugar. Just before the break of each day, my younger brother Andrew and myself tumbled out for some eighteen hours' work, and woe to us if we departed the length of a dog's tail from the laws which our father had laid down. It was a life with which I was familiar, but it did seem to me that with the Indians almost upon us he might have allowed me, at least, to go to the Fort and see our men drilling.

But one morning we aroused as usual at his call at the foot of the ladder, and, dressing more quickly than Andrew, I climbed down from the loft to find my father seated by a blazing fire reading by its light in his Bible.

"Son," said he.

"Yes, father?"

"Go and fight."

Without a word more I made hasty preparation. It was the first time in my life that I had a feeling that my father would change his mind. So strong was this fear that I did not even risk a good-bye to my mother and sisters. At the end of the clearing I looked back. The door of the house was open, and in the blazing light of the fire I saw my father seated as I had left him.

At Forty Fort I found between three and four hundred under arms, while the stockade itself was crowded with old men, and women and children. Many of my acquaintances welcomed me; indeed, I seemed to know everybody save a number of the Continental officers. Colonel Zebulon Butler was in chief command, while directly under him was Colonel Denison, a man of the valley, and much respected. Colonel Denison asked news of my father, whose temper he well knew. He said to me: "If God spares Nathan Denison I shall tell that obstinate old fool my true opinion of him. He will get himself and all his family butchered and scalped."

I joined Captain Bidlack's company, for the reason that a number of my friends were in it. Every morning we were paraded and drilled in the open ground before the Fort, and I learned to present arms and to keep my heels together, although to this day I have never been able to see any point to these accomplishments, and there was very little of the presenting of arms or of the keeping together of heels in the battle which followed these drills. I may say truly that I would now be much more grateful to Captain Bidlack if he had taught us to run like a wild horse.

There was considerable friction between the officers of our militia and the Continental officers. I believe the Continental officers had stated themselves as being in favor of a cautious policy, whereas the men of the valley were almost unanimous in their desire to meet Indian Butler more than half-way. They knew the country, they said, and they knew the Indians, and they deduced that the proper plan was to march forth and attack the British force near the head of the valley. Some of the more hotheaded ones rather openly taunted the Continentals, but these veterans of Washington's army remained silent and composed amid more or less wildness of talk. My own concealed opinions were that, although our people were brave and determined, they had much better allow the Continental officers to manage the valley's affairs.

At the end of June, we heard the news that Colonel John Butler, with some four hundred British and Colonial troops, which he called the

Rangers, and with about five hundred Indians, had entered the valley at its head and taken Fort Wintermoot after an opposition of a perfunctory character. I could present arms very well, but I do not think that I could yet keep my heels together. But Indian Butler was marching upon us, and even Captain Bidlack refrained from being annoyed at my refractory heels.

The officers held councils of war, but in truth both fort and camp rang with a discussion in which everybody joined with great vigor and endurance. I may except the Continental officers, who told us what they thought we should do, and then, declaring that there was no more to be said, remained in a silence which I thought was rather grim. The result was that on the 3rd of July our force of about 300 men marched away, amid the roll of drums and the proud career of flags, to meet Indian Butler and his two kinds of savages. There yet remains with me a vivid recollection of a close row of faces above the stockade of Forty Fort which viewed our departure with that profound anxiety which only an imminent danger of murder and scalping can produce. I myself was never particularly afraid of the Indians, for to my mind the great and almost the only military virtue of the Indians was that they were silent men in the woods. If they were met squarely on terms approaching equality, they could always be whipped. But it was another matter to a fort filled with women and children and cripples, to whom the coming of the Indians spelled pillage, arson, and massacre. The British sent against us in those days some curious upholders of the honor of the King, and although Indian Butler, who usually led them, afterward contended that everything was performed with decency and care for the rules, we always found that those of our dead whose bodies we recovered invariably lacked hair on the tops of their heads, and if worse wasn't done to them we wouldn't even use the word mutilate.

Colonel Zebulon Butler rode along the column when we halted once for water. I looked at him eagerly, hoping to read in his face some sign of his opinions. But on the soldierly mask I could read nothing, although I am certain now that he felt that the fools among us were going to get us well beaten. But there was no vacillation in the direction of our march. We went straight until we could hear through the woods the infrequent shots of our leading party at retreating Indian scouts.

Our Colonel Butler then sent forward four of his best officers, who reconnoitered the ground in the enemy's front like so many engineers marking the place for a bastion. Then each of the six companies were told their place in the line. We of Captain Bidlack's company were on the extreme right. Then we formed in line and marched into battle, with me burning with the high resolve to kill Indian Butler and bear his sword into Forty Fort, while at the same time I was much shaken lest one of

Indian Butler's Indians might interfere with the noble plan. We moved stealthily among the pine trees, and I could not forbear looking constantly to right and left to make certain that everybody was of the same mind about this advance. With our Captain Bidlack was Captain Durkee of the regulars. He was also a valley man, and it seemed that every time I looked behind me I met the calm eye of this officer, and I came to refrain from looking behind me.

Still, I was very anxious to shoot Indians, and if I had doubted my ability in this direction I would have done myself a great injustice, for I could drive a nail to the head with a rifle ball at respectable range. I contend that I was not at all afraid of the enemy, but I much feared that certain of my comrades would change their minds about the expediency of battle on July 3, 1778.

But our company was as steady and straight as a fence. I do not know who first saw dodging figures in the shadows of the trees in our front. The first fire we received, however, was from our flank, where some hidden Indians were yelling and firing, firing and yelling. We did not mind the war whoops. We had heard too many drunken Indians in the settlements before the war. They wounded the lieutenant of the company next to ours, and a moment later they killed Captain Durkee. But we were steadily advancing and firing regular volleys into the shifting frieze of figures before us. The Indians gave their cries as if the imps of Hades had given tongue to their emotions. They fell back before us so rapidly and so cleverly that one had to watch his chance as the Indians sped from tree to tree. I had a sudden burst of rapture that they were beaten, and this was accentuated when I stepped over the body of an Indian whose forehead had a hole in it as squarely in the middle as if the location had been previously surveyed. In short, we were doing extremely well.

Soon we began to see the slower figures of white men through the trees, and it is only honest to say that they were easier to shoot. I myself caught sight of a fine officer in a uniform that seemed of green and buff. His sword belt was fastened by a great shining brass plate, and, no longer feeling the elegancies of marksmanship, I fired at the brass plate. Such was the conformation of the ground between us that he disappeared as if he had sunk in the sea. We, all of us, were loading behind the trees and then charging ahead with fullest confidence.

But suddenly from our own left came wild cries from our men, while at the same time the yells of Indians redoubled in that direction. Our rush checked itself instinctively. The cries rolled toward us. Once I heard a word that sounded like "Quarte." Then, to be truthful, our line wavered. I heard Captain Bidlack give an angry and despairing shout, and I think he was killed before he finished it.

In a word, our left wing had gone to pieces. It was in complete rout. I know not the truth of the matter; but it seems that Colonel Denison had given an order which was misinterpreted for the order to retreat. At any rate, there can be no doubt of how fast the left wing ran away.

We ran away too. The company on our immediate left was the company of regulars, and I remember some red-faced and powder-stained men bellowing at me contemptuously. That company stayed, and, for the most part, died. I don't know what they mustered when we left the Fort, but from the battle eleven worn and ragged men emerged. In my running was wisdom. The country was suddenly full of fleet Indians, upon us with the tomahawk. Behind me as I ran I could hear the screams of men cleaved to the earth. I think the first things that most of us discarded were our rifles. Afterward, upon serious reflection, I could not recall where I gave my rifle to the grass.

I ran for the river. I saw some of our own men running ahead of me, and I envied them. My point of contact with the river was the top of a high bank. But I did not hesitate to leap for the water with all my ounces of muscle. I struck out strongly for the other shore. I expected to be shot in the water. Upstream, and downstream, I could hear the crack of rifles, but none of the enemy seemed to be paying direct heed to me. I swam so well that I soon able to put my feet on the slippery round stones and wade. When I reached a certain sandy beach, I lay down and puffed and blew my exhaustion. I watched the scene on the river. Indians appeared in groups on the opposite bank, firing at various heads of my comrades, who, like me, had chosen the Susquehanna as their refuge. I saw more than one hand fling up and the head turn sideways and sink.

I set out for home. I set out for home in that perfect spirit of dependence which I had always felt toward my father and my mother. When I arrived I found nobody in the living room but my father, seated in his great chair and reading his Bible, even as I had left him.

The whole shame of the business came upon me suddenly. "Father," I choked out, "we have been beaten."

"Ay," said he, "I expected it."

October, 1899

[*Cassell's Magazine,* Vol. 31, New Series (April, 1901), pp. 591–594.]

THE SURRENDER OF FORTY FORT*

Immediately after the battle of July 3, my mother said: "We had best take the children and go into the Fort."

But my father replied: "I will not go. I will not leave my property. All that I have in the world is here, and if the savages destroy it they may as well destroy me also."

My mother said no other word. Our household was ever given to stern silence, and such was my training that it did not occur to me to reflect that if my father cared for his property it was not my property, and I was entitled to care somewhat for my life.

Colonel Denison was true to the word which he had passed to me at the Fort before the battle. He sent a messenger to my father, and this messenger stood in the middle of our living room and spake with a clear, indifferent voice. "Colonel Denison bids me come here and say that John Bennet is a wicked man, and the blood of his own children will be upon his head." As usual, my father said nothing. After the messenger had gone, he remained silent for hours in his chair by the fire, and this stillness was so impressive to his family that even my mother walked on tiptoe as she went about her work. After this long time my father said, "Mary!"

Mother halted and looked at him. Father spoke slowly, and as if every word was wrested from him with violent pangs. "Mary, you take the girls and go to the Fort. I and Solomon and Andrew will go over the mountains to Stroudsberg."

Immediately my mother called us all to set about packing such things as could be taken to the Fort. And by nightfall we had seen them within its palisade, and my father, myself, and my little brother Andrew, who was only eleven years old, were off over the hills on a long march to the Delaware settlements. Father and I had our rifles, but we seldom dared to fire them, because of the roving bands of Indians. We lived as well as we could on blackberries and raspberries. For the most part, poor little Andrew rode first on the back of my father and then on my back. He was a good little man, and only cried when he would wake in the dead of night very cold and very hungry. Then my father would wrap him in an old gray coat that was so famous in the Wyoming country that there was not even an Indian who did not know of it. But this act he did without any direct display of tenderness, for the fear, I suppose, that he would weaken little Andrew's growing manhood. Now, in these days of safety,

* *Wyoming Valley Tales.*

and even luxury, I often marvel at the iron spirit of the people of my young days. My father, without his coat and no doubt very cold, would then sometimes begin to pray to his God in the wilderness, but in low voice, because of the Indians. It was July, but even July nights are cold in the pine mountains, breathing a chill which goes straight to the bones.

But it is not my intention to give in this section the ordinary adventures of the masculine part of my family. As a matter of fact, my mother and the girls were undergoing in Forty Fort trials which made as nothing the happenings on our journey, which ended in safety.

My mother and her small flock were no sooner established in the crude quarters within the palisade than negotiations were opened between Colonel Denison and Colonel Zebulon Butler on the American side, and Indian Butler on the British side, for the capitulation of the Fort with such arms and military stores as it contained, the lives of the settlers to be strictly preserved. But Indian Butler did not seem to feel free to promise safety for the lives of the Continental Butler and the pathetic little fragment of the regular troops. These men always fought so well against the Indians that whenever the Indians could get them at their mercy there was small chance of anything but a massacre. So every regular left before the surrender; and I fancy that Colonel Zebulon Butler considered himself a much abused man, for if we had left ourselves entirely under his direction there is no doubt but what we could have saved the valley. He had taken us out on July 3 because our militia officers had almost threatened him. In the end he had said: "Very well, I can go as far as any of you." I was always on Butler's side of the argument, but owing to the singular arrangement of circumstances, my opinion at the age of sixteen counted upon neither the one side nor the other.

The Fort was left in charge of Colonel Denison. He had stipulated before the surrender that no Indians should be allowed to enter the stockade and molest these poor families of women whose fathers and brothers were either dead or fled over the mountains, unless their physical debility had been such that they were able neither to get killed in the battle nor to take the long trail to the Delaware. Of course, this excepts those men who were with Washington.

For several days the Indians, obedient to the British officers, kept out of the Fort, but soon they began to enter in small bands and went sniffing and poking in every corner to find plunder. Our people had hidden everything as well as they were able, and for a period little was stolen. My mother told me that the first thing of importance to go was Colonel Denison's hunting shirt, made of "fine forty" linen. It had a double cape, and was fringed about the cape and about the wristbands. Colonel Denison at the time was in my mother's cabin. An Indian entered, and, rolling a thieving eye about the place, sighted first of all the remarkable shirt which Colonel Denison was wearing. He seized the shirt and began to tug, while the Colonel backed away, tugging and protesting at the same time. The womenfolk saw at once that the Colonel would be tomahawked if he did not give up his shirt, and they begged him to do it. He finally elected not to be tomahawked, and came out of his shirt. While my mother unbuttoned the wristbands, the Colonel cleverly dropped into the lap of a certain Polly Thornton a large packet of Continental bills, and his money was thus saved for the settlers.

Colonel Denison had several stormy interviews with Indian Butler, and the British commander finally ended in frankly declaring that he could do nothing with the Indians at all. They were beyond control, and the defenseless people in the Fort would have to take the consequence. I do not mean that Colonel Denison was trying to recover his shirt; I mean that he was objecting to a situation which was now almost unendurable. I wish to record also that the Colonel lost a large beaver hat. In both cases he willed to be tomahawked and killed rather than suffer the indignity, but mother prevailed over him. I must confess to this discreet age that my mother engaged in fisticuffs with a squaw. This squaw came into the cabin and, without preliminary discussion, attempted to drag from my mother the petticoat she was wearing. My mother forgot the fine advice she had given to Colonel Denison. She proceeded to beat the squaw out of the cabin, and although the squaw appealed to some warriors who were standing without, the warriors only laughed, and my mother kept her petticoat.

The Indians took the feather beds of the people and, ripping them open, flung the feathers broadcast. Then they stuffed these sacks full of plunder, and flung them across the backs of such of the settlers' horses as they had been able to find. In the old days my mother had had a side-saddle, of which she was very proud when she rode to meeting on it. She had also a brilliant scarlet cloak, which every lady had in those days, and which I can remember as one of the admirations of my childhood. One day my mother had the satisfaction of seeing a squaw ride off from the Fort with this prize saddle reversed on a small nag, and with the proud squaw thus mounted wearing the scarlet cloak, also reversed. My sister Martha told me afterward that they laughed, even in their misfortunes. A little later they had the satisfaction of seeing the smoke from our house and barn arising over the tops of the trees.

When the Indians first began their pillaging, an old Mr. Sutton, who occupied a cabin near my mother's cabin, anticipated them by donning all his best clothes. He had had a theory that the Americans would be free to retain the clothes that they wore. And his best happened to be a suit of

Quaker gray, from beaver to boots, in which he had been married. Not long afterward my mother and my sisters saw passing the door an Indian arrayed in Quaker gray, from beaver to boots. The only odd thing which impressed them was that the Indian had appended to the dress a long string of Yankee scalps. Sutton was a good Quaker, and if he had been wearing the suit there would have been no string of scalps.

They were, in fact, badgered, insulted, robbed by the Indians so openly that the British officers would not come into the Fort at all. They stayed in their camp, affecting to be ignorant of what was happening. It was about all they could do. The Indians had only one idea of war, and it was impossible to reason with them when they were flushed with victory and stolen rum.

The hand of Fate fell heavily upon one rogue whose ambition it was to drink everything that the Fort contained. One day he inadvertently came upon a bottle of spirits of camphor, and in a few hours he was dead.

But it was known that General Washington contemplated sending a strong expedition into the valley, to clear it of the invaders and thrash them. Soon there were no enemies in the country save small roving parties of Indians, who prevented work in the fields and burned whatever cabins the earlier torches had missed.

The first large party to come into the valley was composed mainly of Captain Spaulding's company of regulars, and at its head rode Colonel Zebulon Butler. My father, myself, and little Andrew returned with this party to set to work immediately to build out of nothing a prosperity similar to that which had vanished in the smoke.

October, 1899

[*Last Words.* London: Digby, Long & Co. (March, 1902), pp. 81–88.]

"OL' BENNET" AND THE INDIANS*

My father was so well known of the Indians that, as I was saying, his old gray coat was a sign through the northern country. I know of no reason for this save that he was honest and obstreperously minded his own affairs, and could fling a tomahawk better than the best Indian. I will not declare upon how hard it is for a man to be honest and to mind his own affairs, but I fully know that is is hard to throw a tomahawk as my father threw it, straighter than a bullet from a dueling pistol. He had always dealt fairly with the Indians, and I cannot tell why they hated him so bitterly,

* *Wyoming Valley Tales.*

unless it was that when an Indian went foolishly drunk my father would deplore it with his foot, if it so happened that the drunkenness was done in our cabin. It is true to say that when the war came, a singularly large number of kicked Indians journeyed from the Canadas to revisit with torch and knife the scenes of the kicking.

If people had thoroughly known my father, he would have had no enemies. He was the best of men. He had a code of behavior for himself, and for the whole world as well. If people wished his good opinion they only had to do exactly as he did, and to have his views. I remember that once my sister Martha made me a waistcoat of rabbits' skins, and generally it was considered a great ornament. But one day my father espied me in it, and commanded me to remove it for ever. Its appearance was indecent, he said, and such a garment tainted the soul of him who wore it. In the ensuing fortnight a poor peddler arrived from the Delaware, who had suffered great misfortunes in the snows. My father fed him and warmed him, and when he gratefully departed, gave him the rabbits'-skin waistcoat, and the poor man went off clothed indecently in a garment that would taint his soul. Afterward, in a daring mood, I asked my father why he had so cursed this peddler, and he recommended that I should study my Bible more closely, and there read that my own devious ways should be mended before I sought to judge the enlightened acts of my elders. He set me to plowing the upper twelve acres, and I was hardly allowed to loose my grip of the plow handles until every furrow was drawn.

The Indians called my father "Ol' Bennet," and he was known broadcast as a man whose doom was sealed when the redskins caught him. As I have said, the feeling is inexplicable to me. But Indians who had been ill-used and maltreated by downright ruffians, against whom revenge could with a kind of propriety be directed—many of these Indians avowedly gave up a genuine wrong in order to direct a fuller attention to the getting of my father's scalp. This most unfair disposition of the Indians was a great, deep anxiety to all of us up to the time when General Sullivan and his avenging army marched through the valley and swept our tormentors afar.

And yet great calamities could happen in our valley, even after the coming and passing of General Sullivan. We were partly mistaken in our gladness. The British force of Loyalists and Indians met Sullivan in one battle, and, finding themselves overmatched and beaten, they scattered in all directions. The Loyalists, for the most part, went home, but the Indians cleverly broke up into small bands, and General Sullivan's army had no sooner marched beyond the Wyoming Valley than some of these small bands were back into the valley, plundering outlying cabins and shooting people from the thickets and woods that bordered the fields.

General Sullivan had left a garrison at Wilkes-Barre, and at this time we lived in its strong shadow. It was too formidable for the Indians to attack, and it could protect all who valued protection enough to remain under its wings, but it could do little against the flying small bands. My father chafed in the shelter of the garrison. His best lands lay beyond Forty Fort, and he wanted to be at his plowing. He made several brief references to his plowing that led us to believe that his plowing was the fundamental principle of life. None of us saw any means of contending him. My sister Martha began to weep, but it no more mattered than if she had begun to laugh. My mother said nothing. Ay, my wonderful mother said nothing. My father said he would go plow some of the land above Forty Fort. Immediately this was with us some sort of law. It was like a rain, or a wind, or a drought.

He went, of course. My young brother Andrew went with him, and he took the new span of oxen and a horse. They began to plow a meadow which lay in a bend of the river above Forty Fort. Andrew rode the horse hitched ahead of the oxen. At a certain thicket the horse shied so that little Andrew was almost thrown down. My father seemed to have begun a period of apprehension at this time, but it was of no service. Four Indians suddenly appeared out of the thicket. Swiftly, and in silence, they pounced with tomahawk, rifle, and knife upon my father and my brother, and in a moment they were captives of the redskins—that fate whose very phrasing was a thrill to the heart of every colonist. It spelled death, or that horrible simple absence, vacancy, mystery, which is harder than death.

As for us, he had told my mother that if he and Andrew were not returned at sundown she might construe a calamity. So at sundown we gave the news to the Fort, and directly we heard the alarm gun booming out across the dusk like a salute to the death of my father, a solemn, final declaration. At the sound of this gun my sisters all began newly to weep. It simply defined our misfortune. In the morning a party was sent out, which came upon the deserted plow, the oxen calmly munching, and the horse still excited and affrighted. The soldiers found the trail of four Indians. They followed the trail some distance over the mountains, but the redskins with their captives had a long start, and pursuit was all but useless. The result of this expedition was that we knew at least that father and Andrew had not been massacred immediately. But in those days this was a most meager consolation. It was better to wish them well dead.

My father and Andrew were hurried over the hills at a terrible pace by the four Indians. Andrew told me afterward that he could think sometimes that he was dreaming of being carried off by goblins. The redskins said no word, and their moccasined feet made no sound. They were like evil spirits. But it was as he caught glimpses of father's pale face, every wrinkle in it deepened and hardened, that Andrew saw everything in its light. And Andrew was but thirteen years old. It is a tender age at which to be burned at the stake.

In time the party came upon two more Indians, who had as a prisoner a man named Lebbeus Hammond. He had left Wilkes-Barre in search of a strayed horse. He was riding the animal back to the Fort when the Indians caught him. He and my father knew each other well, and their greeting was like them.

"What! Hammond! You here?"

"Yes, I'm here."

As the march was resumed, the principal Indian bestrode Hammond's horse, but the horse was very high-nerved and scared, and the bridle was only a temporary one made from hickory withes. There was no saddle. And so finally the principal Indian came off with a crash, alighting with exceeding severity upon his head. When he got upon his feet he was in such a rage that the three captives thought to see him dash his tomahawk into the skull of the trembling horse, and, indeed, his arm was raised for the blow, but suddenly he thought better of it. He had been touched by a real point of Indian inspiration. The party was passing a swamp at the time, so he mired the horse almost up to its eyes, and left it to the long death.

I had said that my father was well known of the Indians, and yet I have to announce that none of his six captors knew him. To them he was a complete stranger, for upon camping the first night they left my father unbound. If they had had any idea that he was "Ol' Bennet" they would never have left him unbound. He suggested to Hammond that they try to escape that night, but Hammond seemed not to care to try it yet.

In time they met a party of over forty Indians, commanded by a Loyalist. In that band there were many who knew my father. They cried out with rejoicing when they perceived him. "Ha!" they shouted, "Ol' Bennet!" They danced about him, making gestures expressive of the torture. Later in the day my father accidentally pulled a button from his coat, and an Indian took it from him.

My father asked to be allowed to have it again, for he was a very careful man, and in those days all good husbands were trained to bring home the loose buttons. The Indians laughed, and explained that a man who was to die at Wyalusing—one day's march—need not be particular about a button.

The three prisoners were now sent off in care of seven Indians, while the Loyalist took the remainder of his men down the valley to further harass the settlers. The seven Indians were now very careful of my father, allowing him scarce a wink. Their tomahawks came up at the slightest sign. At the camp that night they bade the prisoners lie down, and then placed poles across them. An Indian lay upon either end of these poles. My father managed, however, to let Hammond know that he was determined to make an attempt to escape. There was only one night between him and the stake, and he was resolved to make what use he could of it. Hammond seems to have been dubious from the start, but the men of that time were not daunted by broad risks. In his opinion the rising would be a failure, but this did not prevent him from agreeing to rise with his friend. My brother Andrew was not considered at all. No one asked him if he wanted to rise against the Indians. He was only a boy, and supposed to obey his elders. So, as none asked his views, he kept them to himself; but I wager you he listened, all ears, to the furtive consultations, consultations which were mere casual phrases at times, and at other times swift, brief sentences shot out in a whisper.

The band of seven Indians relaxed in vigilance as they approached their own country, and on the last night from Wyallusing the Indian part of the camp seemed much inclined to take deep slumber after the long and rapid journey. The prisoners were held to the ground by poles as on the previous night, and then the Indians pulled their blankets over their heads and passed into heavy sleep. One old warrior sat by the fire as guard, but he seems to have been a singularly inefficient man, for he was continually drowsing, and if the captives could have got rid of the poles across their chests and legs they would have made their flight sooner.

The camp was on a mountainside amid a forest of lofty pines. The night was very cold, and the blasts of wind swept down upon the crackling, resinous fire. A few stars peeped through the feathery pine branches. Deep in some gulch could be heard the roar of a mountain stream. At one o'clock in the morning three of the Indians arose, and, releasing the prisoners, commanded them to mend the fire. The prisoners brought dead pine branches; the ancient warrior on watch sleepily picked away with his knife at the deer's head which he had roasted; the other Indians retired again to their blankets, perhaps each depending upon the others for the exercise of precautions. It was a tremendously slack business; the Indians were feeling security because they knew that the prisoners were too wise to try to run away.

The warrior on watch mumbled placidly to himself as he picked at the deer's head. Then he drowsed again, just the short nap of a man who had been up too long. My father stepped quickly to a spear, and backed away from the Indian; then he drove it straight through his chest. The Indian raised himself spasmodically, and then collapsed into that campfire which the captives had made burn so brilliantly, and as he fell he screamed. Instantly his blanket, his hair, he himself began to burn, and over him was my father tugging frantically to get the spear out again.

My father did not recover the spear. It had so gone through the old warrior that it could not readily be withdrawn, and my father left it.

The scream of the watchman instantly aroused the other warriors, who, as they scrambled in their blankets, found over them a terrible white-lipped creature with an axe—an axe, the most appallingly brutal of weapons. Hammond buried his weapon in the head of the leader of the Indians even as the man gave out his first great cry. The second blow missed an agile warrior's head, but caught him in the nape of the neck, and he swung, to bury his face in the red-hot ashes at the edge of the fire.

Meanwhile my brother Andrew had been gallantly snapping empty guns. In fact he snapped three empty guns at the Indians, who were in the purest panic. He did not snap the fourth gun, but took it by the barrel, and, seeing a warrior rush past him, he cracked his skull with the clubbed weapon. He told me, however, that his snapping of the empty guns was very effective, because it made the Indians jump and dodge.

Well, this slaughter continued in the red glare of the fire on the lonely mountainside until two shrieking creatures ran off through the trees, but even then my father hurled a tomahawk with all his strength. It struck one of the fleeing Indians on the shoulder. His blanket dropped from him, and he ran on practically naked.

The three whites looked at each other, breathing deeply. Their work was plain to them in the five dead and dying Indians underfoot. They hastily gathered weapons and moccasins, and in six minutes from the time when my father had hurled the spear through the Indian sentinel they had started to make their way back to the settlements, leaving the campfire to burn out its short career alone amid the dead.

September, 1899

[*Cassell's Magazine*, Vol. 31, New Series (December, 1900), pp. 108–111.]

THE LOVER AND THE TELLTALE*

When the angel child returned with her parents to New York, the fond heart of Jimmie Trescott felt its bruise greatly. For two days he simply moped, becoming a stranger to all former joys. When his old comrades yelled invitation, as they swept off on some interesting quest, he replied with mournful gestures of disillusion.

He thought often of writing to her, but of course the shame of it made him pause. Write a letter to a girl? The mere enormity of the idea caused

* *Whilomville Stories.*

him shudders. Persons of his quality never wrote letters to girls. Such was the occupation of mollycoddles and snivelers. He knew that if his acquaintances and friends found in him evidences of such weakness and general milkiness, they would fling themselves upon him like so many wolves and bait him beyond the borders of sanity.

However, one day at school, in that time of the morning session when children of his age were allowed fifteen minutes of play in the school grounds, he did not as usual rush forth ferociously to his games. Commonly he was of the worst hoodlums, preying upon his weaker brethren with all the cruel disregard of a grown man. On this particular morning he stayed in the schoolroom, and with his tongue stuck from the corner of his mouth, and his head twisting in a painful way, he wrote to little Cora, pouring out to her all the poetry of his hungry soul, as follows: "My dear Cora I love thee with all my hart oh come bac again, bac, bac gain for I love thee best of all oh come bac again When the spring come again we'l fly and we'l fly like a brid."

As for the last word, he knew under normal circumstances perfectly well how to spell "bird," but in this case he had transposed two of the letters through excitement, supreme agitation.

Nor had this letter been composed without fear and furtive glancing. There was always a number of children who, for the time, cared more for the quiet of the schoolroom than for the tempest of the playground, and there was always that dismal company who were being forcibly deprived of their recess—who were being "kept in." More than one curious eye was turned upon the desperate and lawless Jimmie Trescott suddenly taken to ways of peace, and as he felt these eyes he flushed guiltily, with felonious glances from side to side.

It happened that a certain vigilant little girl had a seat directly across the aisle from Jimmie's seat, and she had remained in the room during the intermission, because of her interest in some absurd domestic details concerning her desk. Parenthetically it might be stated that she was in the habit of imagining this desk to be a house, and at this time, with an important little frown, indicative of a proper matron, she was engaged in dramatizing her ideas of a household.

But this small Rose Goldege happened to be of a family which numbered few males. It was, in fact, one of those curious middle-class families that hold much of their ground, retain most of their position, after all their visible means of support have been dropped in the grave. It contained now only a collection of women who existed submissively, defiantly, securely, mysteriously, in a pretentious and often exasperating virtue. It was often too triumphantly clear that they were free of bad habits. However, "bad habits" is a term here used in a commoner meaning, because it is certainly true that the principal and indeed solitary joy which entered their lonely lives was the joy of talking wickedly and busily about their neighbors. It was all done without dream of its being of the vulgarity of the alleys. Indeed it was simply a constitutional but not incredible chastity and honesty expressing itself in its ordinary superior way of the whirling circles of life, and the vehemence of the criticism was not lessened by a further infusion of an acid of worldly defeat, worldly suffering, and worldly hopelessness.

Out of this family circle had sprung the typical little girl who discovered Jimmie Trescott agonizingly writing a letter to his sweetheart. Of course all the children were the most abandoned gossips, but she was peculiarly adapted to the purpose of making Jimmie miserable over this particular point. It was her life to sit of evenings about the stove and hearken to her mother and a lot of spinsters talk of many things. During these evenings she was never licensed to utter an opinion either one way or the other way. She was then simply a very little girl sitting open-eyed in the gloom, and listening to many things which she often interpreted wrongly. They on their part kept up a kind of smug-faced pretense of concealing from her information in detail of the widespread crime, which pretense may have been more elaborately dangerous than no pretense at all. Thus all her home teaching fitted her to recognize at once in Jimmie Trescott's manner that he was concealing something that would properly interest the world. She set up a scream. "Oh! Oh! Oh! Jimmie Trescott's writing to his girl! Oh! Oh!"

Jimmie cast a miserable glance upon her—a glance in which hatred mingled with despair. Through the open window he could hear the boisterous cries of his friends—his hoodlum friends—who would no more understand the utter poetry of his position than they would understand an ancient tribal sign language. His face was set in a truer expression of horror than any of the romances describe upon the features of a man flung into a moat, a man shot in the breast with an arrow, a man cleft in the neck with a battle-axe. He was succedaneous of the fullest power of childish pain. His one course was to rush upon her and attempt, by an impossible means of strangulation, to keep her important news from the public.

The teacher, a thoughtful young woman at her desk upon the platform, saw a little scuffle which informed her that two of her scholars were larking. She called out sharply. The command penetrated to the middle of an early world struggle. In Jimmie's age there was no particular scruple in the minds of the male sex against laying warrior hands upon their weaker sisters. But, of course, this voice from the throne hindered Jimmie in what might have been a berserk attack.

Even the little girl was retarded by the voice, but, without being unlawful, she managed soon to shy through the door and out upon the playground, yelling, "Oh, Jimmie Trescott's been writing to his girl!"

The unhappy Jimmie was following as closely as he was allowed by his knowledge of the decencies to be preserved under the eye of the teacher.

Jimmie himself was mainly responsible for the scene which ensued on the playground. It is possible that the little girl might have run, shrieking his infamy, without exciting more than a general but unmilitant interest. These barbarians were excited only by the actual appearance of human woe; in that event they cheered and danced. Jimmie made the strategic mistake of pursuing little Rose, and thus exposed his thin skin to the whole school. He had in his cowering mind a vision of a hundred children turning from their play under the maple trees and speeding toward him over the gravel with sudden wild taunts. Upon him drove a yelping demoniac mob, to which his words were futile. He saw in this mob boys that he dimly knew, and his deadly enemies, and his retainers, and his most intimate friends. The virulence of his deadly enemy was no greater than the virulence of his intimate friend. From the outskirts the little informer could be heard still screaming the news, like a toy parrot with clockwork inside it. It broke up all sorts of games, not so much because of the mere fact of the letter-writing as because the children knew that some sufferer was at the last point, and, like little blood-fanged wolves, they thronged to the scene of his destruction. They galloped about him shrilly chanting insults. He turned from one to another, only to meet with howls. He was baited.

Then, in one instant, he changed all this with a blow. Bang! The most pitiless of the boys near him received a punch, fairly and skillfully, which made him bellow out like a walrus, and then Jimmie laid desperately into the whole world, striking out frenziedly in all directions. Boys who could handily whip him, and knew it, backed away from this onslaught. Here was intention—serious intention. They themselves were not in frenzy, and their cooler judgment respected Jimmie's efforts when he ran amuck. They saw that it really was none of their affair. In the meantime the wretched little girl who had caused the bloody riot was away by the fence, weeping because boys were fighting.

Jimmie several times hit the wrong boy—that is to say, he several times hit a wrong boy hard enough to arouse also in him a spirit of strife. Jimmie wore a little shirtwaist. It was passing now rapidly into oblivion. He was sobbing, and there was one bloodstain upon his cheek. The school ground sounded like a pine tree when a hundred crows roost in it at night.

Then upon the situation there pealed a brazen bell. It was a bell that these children obeyed, even as older nations obey the formal law which is printed in calfskin. It smote them into some sort of inaction; even Jimmie was influenced by its potency, although, as a finale, he kicked out lustily into the legs of an intimate friend who had been one of the foremost in the torture.

When they came to form into line for the march into the schoolroom it was curious that Jimmie had many admirers. It was not his prowess; it was the soul he had infused into his gymnastics; and he, still panting, looked about him with a stern and challenging glare.

And yet when the long tramping line had entered the schoolroom his status had again changed. The other children then began to regard him as a boy in disrepair, and boys in disrepair were always accosted ominously from the throne. Jimmie's march toward his seat was a feat. It was composed partly of a most slinking attempt to dodge the perception of the teacher and partly of pure braggadocio erected for the benefit of his observant fellow men.

The teacher looked carefully down at him. "Jimmie Trescott," she said.

"Yes'm," he answered, with businesslike briskness, which really spelled out falsity in all its letters.

"Come up to the desk."

He rose amid the awe of the entire schoolroom.

When he arrived she said, "Jimmie, you've been fighting."

"Yes'm," he answered. This was not so much an admission of the fact as it was a concessional answer to anything she might say.

"Who have you been fighting?" she asked.

"I dunno', 'm."

Whereupon the empress blazed out in wrath. "You don't know who you've been fighting?"

Jimmie looked at her gloomily. "No, 'm."

She seemed about to disintegrate to mere flaming fagots of anger. "You don't know who you've been fighting?" she demanded, blazing. "Well, you stay in after school until you find out."

As he returned to his place all the children knew by his vanquished air that sorrow had fallen upon the house of Trescott. When he took his seat he saw gloating upon him the satanic black eyes of the little Goldege girl.

October, 1899

[*Harper's Magazine*, Vol. 99, pp. 759–763.]

"SHOWIN' OFF"*

Jimmie Trescott's new velocipede had the largest front wheel of any velocipede in Whilomville. When it first arrived from New York he wished to sacrifice school, food, and sleep to it. Evidently he wished to become a sort of perpetual velocipede rider. But the powers of the family laid a number of judicious embargoes upon him, and he was prevented from becoming a fanatic. Of course this caused him to retain a fondness for the three-wheeled thing much longer than if he had been allowed to debauch himself for a span of days. But in the end it was an immaterial machine to him. For long periods he left it idle in the stable.

One day he loitered from school toward home by a very circuitous route. He was accompanied by only one of his retainers. The object of this détour was the wooing of a little girl in a red hood. He had been in love with her for some three weeks. His desk was near her desk in school, but he had never spoken to her. He had been afraid to take such a radical step. It was not customary to speak to girls. Even boys who had school-going sisters seldom addressed them during that part of a day which was devoted to education.

The reasons for this conduct were very plain. First, the more robust boys considered talking with girls an unmanly occupation; second, the greater part of the boys were afraid; third, they had no idea of what to say, because they esteemed the proper sentences should be supernaturally incisive and eloquent. In consequence, a small contingent of blue-eyed weaklings were the sole intimates of the frail sex, and for it they were boisterously and disdainfully called "girl-boys."

But this situation did not prevent serious and ardent wooing. For instance, Jimmie and the little girl who wore the red hood must have exchanged glances at least two hundred times in every school hour, and this exchange of glances accomplished everything. In them the two children renewed their curious inarticulate vows.

Jimmie had developed a devotion to school which was the admiration of his father and mother. In the mornings he was so impatient to have it made known to him that no misfortune had befallen his romance during the night that he was actually detected at times feverishly listening for the "first bell." Dr. Trescott was exceedingly complacent of the change, and as for Mrs. Trescott, she had ecstatic visions of a white-haired Jimmie leading the nations in knowledge, comprehending all from bugs to comets. It was merely the doing of the little girl in the red hood.

* *Whilomville Stories.*

When Jimmie made up his mind to follow his sweetheart home from school, the project seemed such an arbitrary and shameless innovation that he hastily lied to himself about it. No, he was not following Abbie. He was merely making his way homeward through the new and rather longer route of Bryant Street and Oakland Park. It had nothing at all to do with a girl. It was a mere eccentric notion.

"Come on," said Jimmie, gruffly, to his retainer. "Let's go home this way."

"What fer?" demanded the retainer.

"Oh, b'cause."

"Huh?"

"Oh, it's more fun—goin' this way."

The retainer was bored and loath, but that mattered very little. He did not know how to disobey his chief. Together they followed the trail of red-hooded Abbie and another small girl. These latter at once understood the object of the chase, and looking back giggling, they pretended to quicken their pace. But they were always looking back. Jimmie now began his courtship in earnest. The first thing to do was to prove his strength in battle. This was transacted by means of the retainer. He took that devoted boy and flung him heavily to the ground, meanwhile mouthing a preposterous ferocity.

The retainer accepted this behavior with a sort of bland resignation. After his overthrow he raised himself, coolly brushed some dust and dead leaves from his clothes, and then seemed to forget the incident.

"I can jump farther'n you can," said Jimmie, in a loud voice.

"I know it," responded the retainer, simply.

But this would not do. There must be a contest.

"Come on," shouted Jimmie, imperiously. "Let's see you jump."

The retainer selected a footing on the curb, balanced and calculated a moment, and jumped without enthusiasm. Jimmie's leap of course was longer.

"There!" he cried, blowing out his lips. "I beat you, didn't I? Easy. I beat you." He made a great hubbub, as if the affair was unprecedented.

"Yes," admitted the other, emotionless.

Later, Jimmie forced his retainer to run a race with him, held more jumping matches, flung him twice to earth, and generally behaved as if a retainer was indestructible. If the retainer had been in the plot, it is conceivable that he would have endured this treatment with mere whispered, half-laughing protests. But he was not in the plot at all, and so he became enigmatic. One cannot often sound the profound well in which lie the meanings of boyhood.

Following the two little girls, Jimmie eventually passed into that suburb of Whilomville which is called Oakland Park. At his heels came a badly battered retainer. Oakland Park was a somewhat strange country to the boys. They were dubious of the manners and customs, and of course they would have to meet the local chieftains, who might look askance upon this invasion.

Jimmie's girl departed into her home with a last backward glance that almost blinded the thrilling boy. On this pretext and that pretext, he kept his retainer in play before the house. He had hopes that she would emerge as soon as she had deposited her schoolbag.

A boy came along the walk. Jimmie knew him at school. He was Tommie Semple, one of the weaklings who made friends with the fair sex. "Hello, Tom," said Jimmie. "You live round here?"

"Yeh," said Tom, with composed pride. At school he was afraid of Jimmie, but he did not evince any of this fear as he strolled well inside his own frontiers. Jimmie and his retainer had not expected this boy to display the manners of a minor chief, and they contemplated him attentively. There was a silence.

Finally Jimmie said: "I can put you down." He moved forward briskly. "Can't I?" he demanded.

The challenged boy backed away. "I know you can," he declared, frankly and promptly.

The little girl in the red hood had come out with a hoop. She looked at Jimmie with an air of insolent surprise in the fact that he still existed, and began to trundle her hoop off toward some other little girls who were shrilly playing near a nursemaid and a perambulator.

Jimmie adroitly shifted his position until he too was playing near the perambulator, pretentiously making mincemeat out of his retainer and Tommie Semple.

Of course little Abbie had defined the meaning of Jimmie's appearance in Oakland Park. Despite this nonchalance and grand air of accident, nothing could have been more plain. Whereupon she of course became insufferably vain in manner, and whenever Jimmie came near her she tossed her head and turned away her face, and daintily swished her skirts as if he were contagion itself. But Jimmie was happy. His soul was satisfied with the mere presence of the beloved object so long as he could feel that she furtively gazed upon him from time to time and noted his extraordinary prowess, which he was proving upon the persons of his retainer and Tommie Semple. And he was making an impression. There could be no doubt of it. He had many times caught her eye fixed admiringly upon him as he mauled the retainer. Indeed, all the little girls gave attention to his deeds, and he was the hero of the hour.

Presently a boy on a velocipede was seen to be tooling down toward them. "Who's this comin'?" said Jimmie, bluntly, to the Semple boy.

"That's Horace Glenn," said Tommie, "an' he's got a new velocipede, an' he can ride it like anything."

"Can you lick him?" asked Jimmie.

"I don't—I never fought with 'im," answered the other. He bravely tried to appear as a man of respectable achievement, but with Horace coming toward them the risk was too great. However, he added, *"Maybe* I could."

The advent of Horace on his new velocipede created a sensation which he haughtily accepted as a familiar thing. Only Jimmie and his retainer remained silent and impassive. Horace eyed the two invaders.

"Hello, Jimmie!"

"Hello, Horace!"

After the typical silence Jimmie said, pompously, "I got a velocipede."

"Have you?" asked Horace, anxiously. He did not wish anybody in the world but himself to possess a velocipede.

"Yes," sang Jimmie. "An' it's a bigger one than that, too! A good deal bigger! An' it's a better one, too!"

"Huh!" retorted Horace, sceptically.

"'Ain't I, Clarence? 'Ain't I? 'Ain't I got one bigger'n that?"

The retainer answered with alacrity: "Yes, he has! A good deal bigger! An' it's a dandy, too!"

This corroboration rather disconcerted Horace, but he continued to scoff at any statement that Jimmie also owned a velocipede. As for the contention that this supposed velocipede could be larger than his own, he simply wouldn't hear of it.

Jimmie had been a very gallant figure before the coming of Horace, but the new velocipede had relegated him to a squalid secondary position. So he affected to look with contempt upon it. Voluminously he bragged of the velocipede in the stable at home. He painted its virtues and beauty in loud and extravagant words, flaming words. And the retainer stood by, glibly endorsing everything.

The little company heeded him, and he passed on vociferously from extravagance to utter impossibility. Horace was very sick of it. His defense was reduced to a mere mechanical grumbling: "Don't believe you got one 'tall. Don't believe you got one 'tall."

Jimmie turned upon him suddenly. "How fast can you go? How fast can you go?" he demanded. "Let's see. I bet you can't go fast."

Horace lifted his spirits and answered with proper defiance. "Can't I?" he mocked. "Can't I?"

"No, you can't," said Jimmie. "You can't go fast."

Horace cried: "Well, you see me now! I'll show you! I'll show you if I can't go fast!" Taking a firm seat on his vermilion machine, he pedaled furiously up the walk, turned, and pedaled back again. "There, now!" he shouted, triumphantly. "Ain't that fast? There, now!" There was a low murmur of appreciation from the little girls. Jimmie saw with pain that even his divinity was smiling upon his rival. "There! Ain't that fast? Ain't that fast?" He strove to pin Jimmie down to an admission. He was exuberant with victory.

Notwithstanding a feeling of discomfiture, Jimmie did not lose a moment of time. "Why," he yelled, "that ain't goin' fast 'tall! That ain't goin' fast 'tall! Why, I can go almost *twice* as fast as that! Almost *twice* as fast! Can't I, Clarence?"

The loyal retainer nodded solemnly at the wide-eyed group. "Course you can!"

"Why," spouted Jimmie, "you just ought to see me ride once! You just ought to see me! Why, I can go like the wind! Can't I, Clarence? And I can ride far, too—oh, awful far! Can't I, Clarence? Why, I wouldn't have that one! 'Tain't any good! You just ought to see mine once!"

The overwhelmed Horace attempted to reconstruct his battered glories. "I can ride right over the curbstone—at some of the crossin's," he announced, brightly.

Jimmie's derision was a splendid sight. " '*Right over the curbstone*'! Why, that wouldn't be *nothin'* for me to do! I've rode mine down Bridge Street Hill. Yessir! 'Ain't I, Clarence? Why, it ain't nothin' to ride over a curbstone—not for *me*! Is it, Clarence?"

"Down Bridge Street hill? You never!" said Horace, hopelessly.

"Well, didn't I, Clarence? Didn't I, now?"

The faithful retainer again nodded solemnly at the assemblage.

At last Horace, having fallen as low as was possible, began to display a spirit for climbing up again. "Oh, you can do wonders!" he said laughing. "You can do wonders! I s'pose you could ride down that bank there?" he asked, with art. He had indicated a grassy terrace some six feet in height which bounded one side of the walk. At the bottom was a small ravine in which the reckless had flung ashes and tins. "I s'pose you could ride down that bank?"

All eyes now turned upon Jimmie to detect a sign of his weakening, but he instantly and sublimely arose to the occasion. "That bank?" he asked, scornfully. "Why, I've ridden down banks like that many a time. 'Ain't I, Clarence?"

This was too much for the company. A sound like the wind in the leaves arose; it was the song of incredulity and ridicule. "O—o—o—o—o!" And on the outskirts a little girl suddenly shrieked out, "Storyteller!"

Horace had certainly won a skirmish. He was gleeful. "Oh, you can do wonders!" he gurgled. "You can do wonders!" The neighborhood's super-ficial hostility to foreigners arose like magic under the influence of his sudden success, and Horace had the delight of seeing Jimmie persecuted in that manner known only to children and insects.

Jimmie called angrily to the boy on the velocipede, "If you'll lend me yours, I'll show you whether I can or not."

Horace turned his superior nose in the air. "Oh no! I don't ever lend it." Then he thought of a blow which would make Jimmie's humiliation com-plete. "Besides," he said, airily, "'tain't really anything hard to do. I could do it—easy—if I wanted to."

But his supposed adherents, instead of receiving this boast with cheers, looked upon him in a sudden blank silence. Jimmie and his retainer pounced like cats upon their advantage.

"Oh," they yelled, "you *could*, eh? Well, let's see you do it, then! Let's see you do it! Let's see you do it! Now!" In a moment the crew of little spectators were gibing at Horace.

The blow that would make Jimmie's humiliation complete! Instead, it had boomeranged Horace into the mud. He kept up a sullen muttering: "'Tain't really anything! I could if I wanted to!"

"Dare you to!" screeched Jimmie and his partisans. "Dare you to! Dare you to! Dare you to!"

There were two things to be done—to make gallant effort or to retreat. Somewhat to their amazement, the children at last found Horace moving through their clamor to the edge of the bank. Sitting on the velocipede, he looked at the ravine, and then, with gloomy pride, at the other children. A hush came upon them, for it was seen that he was intending to make some kind of ante-mortem statement.

"I—" he began. Then he vanished from the edge of the walk. The start had been unintentional—an accident.

The stupefied Jimmie saw the calamity through a haze. His first clear vision was when Horace, with a face as red as a red flag, arose bawling from his tangled velocipede. He and his retainer exchanged a glance of horror and fled the neighborhood. They did not look back until they had reached the top of the hill near the lake. They could see Horace walking slowly under the maples toward his home, pushing his shattered velocipede before him. His chin was thrown high, and the breeze bore them the sound of his howls.

November, 1899

[*Harper's Magazine*, Vol. 99, pp. 855–860.]

VIRTUE IN WAR*

[West Pointer and Volunteer; or, Virtue in War]

I

Gates had left the regular army in 1890, those parts of him which had not been frozen having been well fried. He took with him nothing but an oaken constitution and a knowledge of the plains and the best wishes of his fellow officers. The Standard Oil Company differs from the United States Government in that it understands the value of the loyal and intelligent services of good men and is almost certain to reward them at the expense of incapable men. This curious practice emanates from no beneficent emotion of the Standard Oil Company, on whose feelings you could not make a scar with a hammer and chisel. It is simply that the Standard Oil Company knows more than the United States Government and makes use of virtue whenever virtue is to its advantage. In 1890 Gates really felt in his bones that, if he lived a rigorously correct life and several score of his classmates and intimate friends died off, he would get command of a troop of horse by the time he was unfitted by age to be an active cavalry leader. He left the service of the United States and entered the service of the Standard Oil Company. In the course of time he knew that, if he lived a rigorously correct life, his position and income would develop strictly in parallel with the worth of his wisdom and experience, and he would not have to walk on the corpses of his friends.

But he was not happier. Part of his heart was in a barrack, and it was not enough to discourse of the old regiment over the port and cigars to ears which were polite enough to betray a languid ignorance. Finally came the year 1898, and Gates dropped the Standard Oil Company as if it were hot. He hit the steel trail to Washington and there fought the first serious action of the war. Like most Americans, he had a native State, and one morning he found himself major in a volunteer infantry regiment whose voice had a peculiar sharp twang to it which he could remember from childhood. The colonel welcomed the West Pointer with loud cries of joy; the lieutenant colonel looked at him with the pebbly eye of distrust; and the senior major, having had up to this time the best battalion in the regiment, strongly disapproved of him. There were only two majors, so the lieutenant colonel commanded the first battalion, which gave him an occupation. Lieutenant colonels under the new rules do not always have occupations. Gates got the third battalion—four companies commanded by

* *Wounds in the Rain.*

intelligent officers who could gauge the opinions of their men at two thousand yards and govern themselves accordingly. The battalion was immensely interested in the new major. It thought it ought to develop views about him. It thought it was its blankety-blank business to find out immediately if it liked him personally. In the company streets the talk was nothing else. Among the non-commissioned officers there were eleven old soldiers of the regular army, and they knew—and cared—that Gates had held commission in the "Sixteenth Cavalry"—as *Harper's Weekly* says. Over this fact they rejoiced and were glad, and they stood by to jump lively when he took command. He would know his work and he would know *their* work, and then in battle there would be killed only what men were absolutely necessary, and the sick list would be comparatively free of fools.

The commander of the second battalion had been called by an Atlanta paper "Major Rickets C. Carmony, the commander of the second battalion of the 307th——, when at home one of the biggest wholesale hardware dealers in his State. Last evening he had ice cream, at his own expense, served out at the regular mess of the battalion, and after dinner the men gathered about his tent, where three hearty cheers for the popular major were given." Carmony had bought twelve copies of this newspaper and mailed them home to his friends.

In Gates's battalion there were more kicks than ice cream, and there was no ice cream at all. Indignation ran high at the rapid manner in which he proceeded to make soldiers of them. Some of his officers hinted finally that the men wouldn't stand it. They were saying that they had enlisted to fight for their country—yes, but they weren't going to be bullied day in and day out by a perfect stranger. They were patriots, they were, and just as good men as ever stepped—just as good as Gates or anybody like him. But, gradually, despite itself, the battalion progressed. The men were not altogether conscious of it. They evolved rather blindly. Presently there were fights with Carmony's crowd as to which was the better battalion at drills, and at last there was no argument. It was generally admitted that Gates commanded the crack battalion. The men, believing that the beginning and the end of all soldiering was in these drills of precision, were somewhat reconciled to their major when they began to understand more of what he was trying to do for them, but they were still fiery untamed patriots of lofty pride, and they resented his manner toward them. It was abrupt and sharp.

The time came when everybody knew that the Fifth Army Corps was the corps designated for the first active service in Cuba. The officers and men of the 307th observed with despair that their regiment was not in the Fifth Army Corps. The colonel was a strategist. He understood everything in a flash. Without a moment's hesitation he obtained leave and mounted the night express for Washington. There he drove Senators and Congressmen in span, tandem and four-in-hand. With the telegraph he stirred so deeply the governor, the people, and the newspapers of his State that whenever on a quiet night the President put his head out of the White House he could hear the distant vast commonwealth humming with indignation. And as it is well known that the Chief Executive listens to the voice of the people, the 307th was transferred to the Fifth Army Corps. It was sent at once to Tampa, where it was brigaded with two dusty regiments of regulars, who looked at it calmly and said nothing. The brigade commander happened to be no less a person than Gates's old colonel in the "Sixteenth Cavalry"—as *Harper's Weekly* says—and Gates was cheered. The old man's rather solemn look brightened when he saw Gates in the 307th. There was a great deal of battering and pounding and banging for the 307th at Tampa, but the men stood it, more in wonder than in anger. The two regular regiments carried them along when they could, and when they couldn't waited impatiently for them to come up. Undoubtedly the regulars wished the volunteers were in garrison at Sitka, but they said practically nothing. They minded their own regiments. The colonel was an invaluable man in a telegraph office. When came the scramble for transports the colonel retired to a telegraph office and talked so ably to Washington that the authorities pushed a number of corps aside and made way for the 307th, as if on it depended everything. The regiment got one of the best transports, and after a series of delays and some starts and an equal number of returns, they finally sailed for Cuba.

II

Now Gates had a singular adventure on the second morning after his arrival at Atlanta to take his post as a major in the 307th.

He was in his tent, writing, when suddenly the flap was flung away and a tall young private stepped inside.

"Well, Maje," said the newcomer, genially, "how goes it?"

The major's head flashed up, but he spoke without heat.

"Come to attention and salute."

"Huh!" said the private.

"Come to attention and salute."

The private looked at him in resentful amazement, and then inquired: "Ye ain't mad, are ye? Ain't nothin' to get huffy about, is there?"

"I— Come to attention and salute."

"Well," drawled the private, as he stared, "seein' as ye are so darn perticular, I don't care if I do—if it'll make yer meals set on yer stummick any better."

Drawing a long breath and grinning ironically, he lazily pulled his heels together and saluted with a flourish.

"There," he said, with a return to his earlier genial manner. "How's that suit ye, Maje?"

There was a silence which to an impartial observer would have seemed pregnant with dynamite and bloody death. Then the major cleared his throat and coldly said: "And now, what is your business?"

"Who—me?" asked the private. "Oh, I just sorter dropped in." With a deeper meaning he added: "Sorter dropped in in a friendly way, thinkin' ye was mebbe a different kind of a feller from what ye be."

The inference was clearly marked.

It was now Gates's turn to stare, and stare he unfeignedly did.

"Go back to your quarters," he said at length.

The volunteer became very angry.

"Oh, ye needn't be so up-in-th'-air, need ye? Don't know's I'm dead anxious to inflict my company on yer since I've had a good look at ye. There may be men in this here battalion what's had just as much edjewcation as you have, and I'm damned if they ain't got better *manners*. Good-mornin'," he said, with dignity; and, passing out of the tent, he flung the flap back in place with an air of slamming it as if it had been a door. He made his way back to his company street, striding high. He was furious. He met a large crowd of his comrades.

"What's the matter, Lige?" asked one, who noted his temper.

"Oh, nothin'," answered Lige, with terrible feeling. "Nothin'. I jest been lookin' over the new major—that's all."

"What's he like?" asked another.

"Like?" cried Lige. "He's like nothin'. He ain't out'n the same kittle as us. No. Gawd made him all by himself—sep'rate. He's a speshul produc', he is, an' he won't have no truck with jest common—*men*, like you be."

He made a venomous gesture which included them all.

"Did he set on ye?" asked a soldier.

"Set on me? No," replied Lige, with contempt. "I set on *him*. I sized 'im up in a minute. 'Oh, I don't know,' I says, as I was comin' out; 'guess you ain't the only man in the world,' I says."

For a time Lige Wigram was quite a hero. He endlessly repeated the tale of his adventure, and men admired him for so soon taking the conceit out of the new officer. Lige was proud to think of himself as a plain and simple patriot who had refused to endure any high-soaring nonsense.

But he came to believe that he had not disturbed the singular composure of the major, and this concreted his hatred. He hated Gates, not as a soldier sometimes hates an officer, a hatred half of fear. Lige hated as man to man. And he was enraged to see that, so far from gaining any hatred in return, he seemed incapable of making Gates have any thought of him save as a unit in a body of three hundred men. Lige might just as well have gone and grimaced at the obelisk in Central Park.

When the battalion became the best in the regiment he had no part in the pride of the companies. He was sorry when men began to speak well of Gates. He was really a very consistent hater.

III

The transport occupied by the 307th was commanded by some sort of Scandinavian who was afraid of the shadows of his own topmasts. He would have run his steamer away from a floating Gainsborough hat, and, in fact, he ran her away from less on some occasions. The officers, wishing to arrive with the other transports, sometimes remonstrated, and to them he talked of his owners. Every officer in the convoying warships loathed him, for in case any hostile vessel should appear they did not see how they were going to protect this rabbit, who would probably manage during a fight to be in about a hundred places on the broad, broad sea, and all of them offensive to the navy's plan. When he was not talking of his owners he was remarking to the officers of the regiment that a steamer really was not like a valise, and that he was unable to take his ship under his arm and climb trees with it. He further said that "them naval fellows" were not near so smart as they thought they were.

From an indigo sea arose the lonely shore of Cuba. Ultimately, the fleet was near Santiago, and most of the transports were bidden to wait a minute while the leaders found out their minds. The skipper to whom the 307th were prisoners waited for thirty hours halfway between Jamaica and Cuba. He explained that the Spanish fleet might emerge from Santiago harbor at any time, and he did not propose to be caught. His owners— Whereupon the colonel arose as one having nine hundred men at his back, and he passed up to the bridge and he spake with the captain. He explained indirectly that each individual of his nine hundred men had decided to be the first American soldier to land for this campaign, and that in order to accomplish the marvel it was necessary for the transport to be nearer than forty-five miles from the Cuban coast. If the skipper would only land the regiment the colonel would consent to his then taking his interesting old ship and going to hell with it. And the skipper spake with the colonel. He pointed out that, as far as he officially was concerned, the United States Government did not exist. He was responsible solely to his owners. The colonel pondered these sayings. He perceived that the skipper meant that he was running his ship as he deemed best, in consideration of the capital invested by his owners, and that he was not at all concerned with the feelings of a certain American military expedition to Cuba. He was a free son of the sea—he was a sovereign citizen of the republic of the waves. He was like Lige.

However, the skipper ultimately incurred the danger of taking his ship under the terrible guns of the *New York, Iowa, Oregon, Massachusetts, Indiana, Brooklyn, Texas,* and a score of cruisers and gunboats. It was a brave act for the captain of a United States transport, and he was visibly nervous until he could again get to sea, where he offered praises that the accursed 307th was no longer sitting on his head. For almost a week he rambled at his cheerful will over the adjacent high seas, having in his hold a great quantity of military stores as successfully secreted as if they had been buried in a copper box in the cornerstone of a new public building in Boston. He had had his master's certificate for twenty-one years, and those people couldn't tell a marlinespike from the starboard side of the ship.

The 307th was landed in Cuba, but to their disgust they found that about ten thousand regulars were ahead of them. They got immediate orders to move out from the base on the road to Santiago. Gates was interested to note that the only delay was caused by the fact that many men of the other battalions strayed off sightseeing. In time the long regiment wound slowly among hills that shut them from sight of the sea.

For the men to admire, there were palm trees, little brown huts, passive, uninterested Cuban soldiers much worn from carrying American rations inside and outside. The weather was not oppressively warm, and the journey was said to be only about seven miles. There were no rumors save that there had been one short fight, and the army had advanced to within sight of Santiago. Having a peculiar faculty for the derision of the romantic, the 307th began to laugh. Actually there was not *anything* in the world which turned out to be as books describe it. Here they had landed from the transport expecting to be at once flung into line of battle and sent on some kind of furious charge, and now they were trudging along a quiet trail lined with somnolent trees and grass. The whole business so far struck them as being a highly tedious burlesque.

After a time they came to where the camps of regular regiments marked the sides of the road—little villages of tents no higher than a man's waist. The colonel found his brigade commander, and the 307th was sent off into a field of long grass, where the men grew suddenly solemn with the importance of getting their supper.

In the early evening some regulars told one of Gates's companies that at daybreak this division would move to an attack upon something.

"How d' you know?" said the company, deeply awed.

"Heard it."

"Well, what are we to attack?"

"Dunno."

The 307th was not at all afraid, but each man began to imagine the morrow. The regulars seemed to have as much interest in the morrow as they did in the last Christmas. It was none of their affair, apparently.

"Look here," said Lige Wigram, to a man in the 17th Regular Infantry, "whereabouts are we goin' ter-morrow an' who do we run up against—do ye know?"

The 17th soldier replied, truculently: "If I ketch th' —— —— —— what stole my terbaccer, I'll whirl in an' break every —— —— bone in his body."

Gates's friends in the regular regiments asked him numerous questions as to the reliability of his organization. Would the 307th stand the racket? They were certainly not contemptuous; they simply did not seem to consider it important whether the 307th would or whether it would not.

"Well," said Gates, "they won't run the length of a tentpeg if they can gain any idea of what they're fighting; they won't bunch if they've about six acres of open ground to move in; they won't get rattled at all if they see you fellows taking it easy, and they'll fight like the devil as long as they thoroughly, completely, absolutely, satisfactorily, exhaustively understand what the business is. They're lawyers. All excepting my battalion."

IV

Lige awakened into a world obscured by blue fog. Somebody was gently shaking him. "Git up; we're going to move." The regiment was buckling up itself. From the trail came the loud creak of a light battery moving ahead. The tones of all men were low; the faces of the officers were composed, serious. The regiment found itself moving along behind the battery before it had time to ask itself more than a hundred questions. The trail wound through a dense tall jungle, dark, heavy with dew.

The battle broke with a snap—far ahead. Presently Lige heard from the air above him a faint low note as if somebody were blowing softly in the mouth of a bottle. It was a stray bullet which had wandered a mile to tell him that war was before him. He nearly broke his neck looking upward. "Did ye hear that?" But the men were fretting to get out of this gloomy jungle. They wanted to see something. The faint rup-rup-rrrrup-rup on in the front told them that the fight had begun; death was abroad, and so the mystery of this wilderness excited them. This wilderness was portentously still and dark.

They passed the battery aligned on a hill above the trail, and they had not gone far when the gruff guns began to roar and they could hear the rocket-like swish of the flying shells. Presently everybody must have called out for the assistance of the 307th. Aides and couriers came flying back to them.

"Is this the 307th? Hurry up your men, please, Colonel. You're needed more every minute."

Oh, they were, were they? Then the regulars were not going to do *all* the fighting? The old 307th was bitterly proud or proudly bitter. They left their blanket rolls under the guard of God and pushed on, which is one of the reasons why the Cubans of that part of the country were, later, so well equipped. There began to appear fields, hot, golden-green in the sun. On some palm-dotted knolls before them they could see little lines of black dots—the American advance. A few men fell, struck down by other men who, perhaps half a mile away, were aiming at somebody else. The loss was wholly in Carmony's battalion, which immediately bunched and backed away, coming with a shock against Gates's advance company. This shock sent a tremor through all of Gates's battalion, until men in the very last files cried out nervously, "Well, what in hell is up now?" There came an order to deploy and advance. An occasional hoarse yell from the regulars could be heard. The deploying made Gates's heart bleed for the colonel. The old man stood there directing the movement, straight, fearless, somberly defiant of—everything. Carmony's four companies were like four herds. And all the time the bullets, from no living man knows where, kept pecking at them and pecking at them. Gates, the excellent Gates, the highly educated and strictly military Gates, grew rankly insubordinate. He knew that the regiment was suffering from nothing but the deadly range and oversweep of the modern rifle, of which many proud and confident nations know nothing save that they have killed savages with it, which is the least of all informations.

Gates rushed upon Carmony.

"God damn it, man, if you can't get your people to deploy, for God's sake give me a chance! I'm stuck in the woods!"

Carmony gave nothing, but Gates took all he could get, and his battalion deployed and advanced like men. The old colonel almost burst into tears, and he cast one quick glance of gratitude at Gates, which the younger officer wore on his heart like a secret decoration.

There was a wild scramble up hill, down dale, through thorny thickets. Death smote them with a kind of slow rhythm, leisurely taking a man now here, now there, but the cat-spit sound of the bullets was always. A large number of the men of Carmony's battalion came on with Gates. They were willing to do anything, anything. They had no real fault, unless it was that early conclusion that any brave high-minded youth was necessarily a good soldier immediately, from the beginning. In them had been born a swift feeling that the unpopular Gates knew everything, and they followed the trained soldier.

If they followed him, he certainly took them into it. As they swung heavily up one steep hill, like so many wind-blown horses, they came suddenly out into the real advance. Little blue groups of men were making frantic rushes forward and then flopping down on their bellies to fire volleys while other groups made rushes. Ahead they could see a heavy house-like fort which was inadequate to explain from whence came the myriad bullets. The remainder of the scene was landscape. Pale men, yellow men, blue men came out of this landscape quiet and sad-eyed with wounds. Often they were grimly facetious. There is nothing in the American regular so amazing as his conduct when he is wounded—his apologetic limp, his deprecatory arm-sling, his embarrassed and ashamed shot-hole through the lungs. The men of the 307th looked at calm creatures who had divers punctures, and they were made better. These men told them that it was only necessary to keep a-going. They of the 307th lay on their bellies, red, sweating, and panting, and heeded the voice of the elder brother.

Gates walked in back of his line, very white of face, but hard and stern past anything his men knew of him. After they had violently adjured him to lie down and he had given weak backs a cold, stiff touch, the 307th charged by rushes. The hatless colonel made frenzied speech, but the man of the time was Gates. The men seemed to feel that this was his business. Some of the regular officers said afterward that the advance of the 307th was very respectable indeed. They were rather surprised, they said. At least five of the crack regiments of the regular army were in this division, and the 307th could win no more than a feeling of kindly appreciation.

Yes, it was very good, very good indeed, but did you notice what was being done at the same moment by the 12th, the 17th, the 7th, the 8th, the 25th, the——?

Gates felt that his charge was being a success. He was carrying out a successful function. Two captains fell bang on the grass, and a lieutenant slumped quietly down with a death wound. Many men sprawled suddenly. Gates was keeping his men almost even with the regulars, who were charging on his flanks. Suddenly he thought that he must have come close to the fort and that a Spaniard had tumbled a great stone block down upon his leg. Twelve hands reached out to help him, but he cried:

"No damn your souls—go on—go on!"

He closed his eyes for a moment, and it really was only for a moment. When he opened them he found himself alone with Lige Wigram, who lay on the ground near him.

"Maje," said Lige, "yer a good man. I've been a-follerin' ye all day, an' I want to say yer a good man."

The major turned a coldly scornful eye upon the private.

"Where are you wounded? Can you walk? Well, if you can, go to the rear and leave me alone. I'm bleeding to death, and you bother me."

Lige, despite the pain in his wounded shoulder, grew indignant.

"Well," he mumbled, "you and me have been on th' outs fer a long time, an' I only wanted to tell ye that what I seen of ye t'day has made me feel mighty different."

"Go to the rear—if you can walk," said the major.

"Now, Maje, look here. A little thing like that—"

"Go to the rear."

Lige gulped with sobs.

"Maje, I know I didn't understand ye at first, but ruther'n let a little thing like that come between us, I'd—I'd——"

"Go to the rear."

In this reiteration Lige discovered a resemblance to that first old offensive phrase, "Come to attention and salute." He pondered over the resemblance, and he saw that nothing had changed. The man bleeding to death was the same man to whom he had once paid a friendly visit with unfriendly results. He thought now that he perceived a certain hopeless gulf, a gulf which is real or unreal, according to circumstances. Sometimes all men are equal; occasionally they are not. If Gates had ever criticized Lige's manipulation of a hay fork on the farm at home, Lige would have furiously disdained his hate or blame. He saw now that he must not openly approve the major's conduct in war. The major's pride was in his business, and his, Lige's, congratulations were beyond all enduring.

The place where they were lying suddenly fell under a new heavy rain of bullets. They sputtered about the men, making the noise of large grasshoppers.

"Major!" cried Lige. "Major Gates! It won't do for ye to be left here, sir. Ye'll be killed."

"But you can't help it, lad. You take care of yourself."

"I'm damned if I do," said the private, vehemently. "If I can't git *you* out, I'll stay and wait."

The officer gazed at his man with that same icy, contemptuous gaze.

"I'm—I'm a dead man anyhow. You go to the rear, do you hear?"

"No."

The dying major drew his revolver, cocked it, and aimed it unsteadily at Lige's head.

"Will you obey orders?"

"No."

"One?"

"No."

"Two?"

"No."

Gates weakly dropped his revolver.

"Go to the devil, then. You're no soldier, but—" He tried to add something. "But—" He heaved a long moan. "But—you—you— Oh, I'm so-o-o tired."

v

After the battle, three correspondents happened to meet on the trail. They were hot, dusty, weary, hungry, and thirsty, and they repaired to the shade of a mango tree and sprawled luxuriously. Among them they mustered two score friends who on that day had gone to the far shore of the hereafter, but their senses were no longer resonant. Shackles was babbling plaintively about mint juleps, and the others were bidding him to have done.

"By the way," said one, at last, "it's too bad about poor old Gates of the 307th. He bled to death. His men were crazy. They were blubbering and cursing around there like wild people. It seems that when they got back there to look for him they found him just about gone, and another wounded man was trying to stop the flow with his hat! His hat, mind you. Poor old Gatesie!"

"Oh, no, Shackles!" said the third man of the party. "Oh, no, you're wrong. The best mint juleps in the world are made right in New York, Philadelphia, or Boston. That Kentucky idea is only a tradition."

A wounded man approached them. He had been shot through the shoulder, and his shirt had been diagonally cut away, leaving much bare skin. Over the bullet's point of entry there was a kind of white spider, shaped from pieces of adhesive plaster. Over the point of departure there was a bloody bulb of cotton strapped to the flesh by other pieces of adhesive plaster. His eyes were dreamy, wistful, sad. "Say, gents, have any of ye got a bottle?" he asked.

A correspondent raised himself suddenly and looked with bright eyes at the soldier.

"Well, you have got a nerve," he said grinning. "Have we got a bottle, eh! Who in hell do you think we are? If we had a bottle of good licker, do you suppose we could let the whole army drink out of it? You have too much faith in the generosity of men, my friend!"

The soldier stared, ox-like, and finally said, "Huh?"

"I say," continued the correspondent, somewhat more loudly, "that if we had had a bottle we would have probably finished it ourselves by this time."

"But," said the other, dazed, "I *meant* an empty bottle. I didn't mean no *full* bottle."

The correspondent was humorously irascible. "An empty bottle! You must be crazy! Who ever heard of a man looking for an empty bottle? It isn't sense! I've seen a million men looking for full bottles, but you're the first man I ever saw who insisted on the bottle's being empty. What in the world do you want it for?"

"Well, ye see, mister," explained Lige, slowly, "our major, he was killed this mornin' an' we're jes' goin' to bury him, an' I thought I'd jest take a look 'round an' see if I couldn't borry an empty bottle, an' then I'd take an' write his name an' reg'ment on a paper an' put it in th' bottle an' bury it with him, so's when they come fer to dig him up some time an' take him home, there sure wouldn't be no mistake."

"Oh!"

November, 1899
[*Frank Leslie's Popular Monthly,* Vol. 49, pp. 88–101.]

MAKING AN ORATOR*

In the school at Whilomville it was the habit, when children had progressed to a certain class, to have them devote Friday afternoon to what was called elocution. This was in the piteously ignorant belief that orators were thus made. By process of school law, unfortunate boys and girls were dragged up to address their fellow scholars in the literature of the midcentury. Probably the children who were most capable of expressing themselves, the children who were most sensitive to the power of speech, suffered the most wrong. Little blockheads who could learn eight lines of conventional poetry, and could get up and spin it rapidly at their classmates, did not undergo a single pang. The plan operated mainly to agonize many children permanently against arising to speak their thought to fellow creatures.

Jimmie Trescott had an idea that by exhibition of undue ignorance he could escape from being promoted into the first classroom which exacted such penalty from its inmates. He preferred to dwell in a less classic shade rather than venture into a domain where he was obliged to perform a certain duty which struck him as being worse than death. However, willy-nilly, he was somehow sent ahead into the place of torture.

Every Friday at least ten of the little children had to mount the stage beside the teacher's desk and babble something which none of them understood. This was to make them orators. If it had been ordered that they should croak like frogs, it would have advanced most of them just as far toward oratory.

Alphabetically Jimmie Trescott was near the end of the list of victims, but his time was none the less inevitable. "Tanner, Timmens, Trass, Trescott—" He saw his downfall approaching.

* *Whilomville Stories.*

He was passive to the teacher while she drove into his mind the incomprehensible lines of "The Charge of the Light Brigade":

> Half a league, half a league,
> Half a league onward—

He had no conception of a league. If in the ordinary course of life somebody had told him that he was half a league from home, he might have been frightened that half a league was fifty miles; but he struggled manfully with the valley of death and a mystic six hundred, who were performing something there which was very fine, he had been told. He learned all the verses.

But as his own Friday afternoon approached he was moved to make known to his family that a dreadful disease was upon him, and was likely at any time to prevent him from going to his beloved school.

On the great Friday when the children of his initials were to speak their pieces Dr. Trescott was away from home, and the mother of the boy was alarmed beyond measure at Jimmie's curious illness, which caused him to lie on the rug in front of the fire and groan cavernously.

She bathed his feet in hot mustard water until they were lobster-red. She also placed a mustard plaster on his chest.

He announced that these remedies did him no good at all—no good at all. With an air of martyrdom he endured a perfect downpour of motherly attention all that day. Thus the first Friday was passed in safety.

With singular patience he sat before the fire in the dining room and looked at picture books, only complaining of pain when he suspected his mother of thinking that he was getting better.

The next day being Saturday and a holiday, he was miraculously delivered from the arms of disease, and went forth to play, a blatantly healthy boy.

He had no further attack until Thursday night of the next week, when he announced that he felt very, very poorly. The mother was already chronically alarmed over the condition of her son, but Dr. Trescott asked him questions which denoted some incredulity. On the third Friday Jimmie was dropped at the door of the school from the doctor's buggy. The other children, notably those who had already passed over the mountain of distress, looked at him with glee, seeing in him another lamb brought to butchery. Seated at his desk in the schoolroom, Jimmie sometimes remembered with dreadful distinctness every line of "The Charge of the Light Brigade," and at other times his mind was utterly empty of it. Geography, arithmetic, and spelling—usually great tasks—quite rolled off him. His mind was dwelling with terror upon the time when his name should be called and he was obliged to go up to the platform, turn, bow, and recite his message to his fellow men.

Desperate expedients for delay came to him. If he could have engaged the services of a real pain, he would have been glad. But steadily, inexorably, the minutes marched on toward his great crisis, and all his plans for escape blended into a mere panic fear.

The maples outside were defeating the weakening rays of the afternoon sun, and in the shadowed schoolroom had come a stillness, in which, nevertheless, one could feel the complacence of the little pupils who had already passed through the flames. They were calmly prepared to recognize as a spectacle the torture of others.

Little Johnnie Tanner opened the ceremony. He stamped heavily up to the platform, and bowed in such a manner that he almost fell down. He blurted out that it would ill befit him to sit silent while the name of his fair Ireland was being reproached, and he appealed to the gallant soldier before him if every British battlefield was not sown with the bones of sons of the Emerald Isle. He was also heard to say that he had listened with deepening surprise and scorn to the insinuation of the honorable member from North Glenmorganshire that the loyalty of the Irish regiments in her Majesty's service could be questioned. To what purpose, then, he asked, had the blood of Irishmen flowed on a hundred fields? To what purpose had Irishmen gone to their death with bravery and devotion in every part of the world where the victorious flag of England had been carried? If the honorable member for North Glenmorganshire insisted upon construing a mere pothouse row between soldiers in Dublin into a grand treachery to the colors and to her Majesty's uniform, then it was time for Ireland to think bitterly of her dead sons, whose graves now marked every step of England's progress, and yet who could have their honors stripped from them so easily by the honorable member for North Glenmorganshire. Furthermore, the honorable member for North Glenmorganshire—

It is needless to say that little Johnnie Tanner's language made it exceedingly hot for the honorable member for North Glenmorganshire. But Johnnie was not angry. He was only in haste. He finished the honorable member for North Glenmorganshire in what might be called a gallop.

Susie Timmens then went to the platform, and with a face as pale as death whisperingly reiterated that she would be Queen of the May. The child represented there a perfect picture of unnecessary suffering. Her small lips were quite blue, and her eyes, opened wide, stared with a look of horror at nothing.

The phlegmatic Trass boy, with his moon face only expressing peasant parentage, calmly spoke some undeniably true words concerning destiny.

In his seat Jimmie Trescott was going half blind with fear of his approaching doom. He wished that the Trass boy would talk for ever about destiny. If the schoolhouse had taken fire he thought that he would have felt simply relief. Anything was better. Death amid the flames was preferable to a recital of "The Charge of the Light Brigade."

But the Trass boy finished his remarks about destiny in a very short time. Jimmie heard the teacher call his name, and he felt the whole world look at him. He did not know how he made his way to the stage. Parts of him seemed to be of lead, and at the same time parts of him seemed to be light as air, detached. His face had gone as pale as had been the face of Susie Timmens. He was simply a child in torment; that is all there is to be said specifically about it; and to intelligent people the exhibition would have been not more edifying than a dogfight.

He bowed precariously, choked, made an inarticulate sound, and then he suddenly said,

"Half a leg—"

"*League*," said the teacher, coolly.

"Half a leg—"

"*League*," said the teacher.
"*League*," repeated Jimmie, wildly.

"Half a league, half a league, half a league onward."

He paused here and looked wretchedly at the teacher.
"Half a league," he muttered—"half a league—"
He seemed likely to keep continuing this phrase indefinitely, so after a time the teacher said, "Well, go on."
"Half a league," responded Jimmie.
The teacher had the opened book before her, and she read from it:

"'All in the valley of Death
Rode the—'

Go on," she concluded.
Jimmie said,

"All in the valley of Death
Rode the—the—the—"

He cast a glance of supreme appeal upon the teacher, and breathlessly whispered, "Rode the what?"

The young woman flushed with indignation to the roots of her hair.

"Rode the six hundred,"

she snapped at him.

The class was a-rustle with delight at this cruel display. They were no better than a Roman populace in Nero's time.

Jimmie started off again:

"Half a leg—league, half a league, half a league onward,
All in the valley of death rode the six hundred.
Forward—forward—forward—"

"The Light Brigade," suggested the teacher, sharply.

"The Light Brigade," said Jimmie. He was about to die of the ignoble pain of his position.

As for Tennyson's lines, they had all gone grandly out of his mind, leaving it a whited wall.

The teacher's indignation was still rampant. She looked at the miserable wretch before her with an angry stare.

"You stay in after school and learn that all over again," she commanded. "And be prepared to speak it next Friday. I am astonished at you, Jimmie. Go to your seat."

If she had suddenly and magically made a spirit of him and left him free to soar high above all the travail of our earthly lives she could not have overjoyed him more. He fled back to his seat without hearing the low-toned gibes of his schoolmates. He gave no thought to the terrors of the next Friday. The evils of the day had been sufficient, and to a childish mind a week is a great space of time.

With the delightful inconsistency of his age he sat in blissful calm and watched the sufferings of an unfortunate boy named Zimmerman, who was the next victim of education. Jimmie, of course, did not know that on this day there had been laid for him the foundation of a finished incapacity for public speaking which would be his until he died.

December, 1899

[*Harper's Magazine,* Vol. 100, pp. 25–28.]

TWELVE O'CLOCK

"Where were you at twelve o'clock, noon, on the 9th of June, 1875?"—
Question on intelligent cross-examination.

I

"Excuse *me*," said Ben Roddle with graphic gestures to a group of citizens in Nantucket's store. "Excuse *me!* When them fellers in leather pants an' six-shooters ride in, I go home an' set in th' cellar. That's what I do. When you see me pirooting through the streets at th' same time an' occasion as them punchers, you kin put me down fer bein' crazy. Excuse *me!*"

"Why, Ben," drawled old Nantucket, "you ain't never really seen 'em turned loose. Why, I kin remember—in th' old days—when——"

"Oh, damn yer old days!" retorted Roddle. Fixing Nantucket with the eye of scorn and contempt, he said, "I suppose you'll be sayin' in a minute that in th' old days you used to kill Injuns, won't you?"

There was some laughter, and Roddle was left free to expand his ideas on the periodic visits of cowboys to the town. "Mason Rickets, he had ten big punkins a-sittin' in front of his store, an' them fellers from the Upside-down-P ranch shot 'em—shot 'em all—an' Rickets lyin' on his belly in th' store a-callin' fer 'em to quit it. An' what did they do? Why, they *laughed* at 'im—just *laughed* at 'im! That don't do a town no good. Now, how would an eastern capiterlist"—(it was the town's humor to be always gassing of phantom investors who were likely to come any moment and pay a thousand prices for everything)—"how would an eastern capiterlist like that? Why, you couldn't see 'im fer th' dust on his trail. Then he'd tell all his friends: 'That there town may be all right, but ther's too much loose-handed shootin' fer my money.' An' he'd be right, too. Them rich fellers, they don't make no bad breaks with their money. They watch it all th' time b'cause they know blame well there ain't hardly room fer their feet fer th' pikers an' tinhorns an' thimble-riggers what are layin' fer 'em. I tell you, one puncher racin' his cow-pony hell-bent-fer-election down Main Street an' yellin' an' shootin', an' nothin' at all done about it, would scare away a whole herd of capiterlists. An' it ain't right. It oughter be stopped."

A pessimistic voice asked: "How you goin' to stop it, Ben?"

"Organize," replied Roddle, pompously. "Organize. That's the only way to make these fellers lay down. I——"

From the street sounded a quick scudding of pony hoofs, and a party of cowboys swept past the door. One man, however, was seen to draw rein and dismount. He came clanking into the store. "Mornin', gentlemen," he said civilly.

"Mornin'," they answered in subdued voices.

He stepped to the counter and said, "Give me a paper of fine cut, please." The group of citizens contemplated him in silence. He certainly did not look threatening. He appeared to be a young man of twenty-five years, with a tan from wind and sun, with a remarkably clear eye from perhaps a period of enforced temperance, a quiet young man who wanted to buy some tobacco. A six-shooter swung low on his hip, but at the moment it looked more decorative than warlike; it seemed merely a part of his old gala dress—his sombrero with its band of rattlesnake-skin, his great flaming neckerchief, his belt of embroidered Mexican leather, his high-heeled boots, his huge spurs. And, above all, his hair had been watered and brushed until it lay as close to his head as the fur lies to a wet cat. Paying for his tobacco, he withdrew.

Ben Roddle resumed his harangue. "Well, there you are! Looks like a calm man now, but in less 'n half an hour he'll be as drunk as three bucks an' a squaw, an' then—excuse *me!*"

II

On this day the men of two outfits had come into town, but Ben Roddle's ominous words were not justified at once. The punchers spent most of the morning in an attack on whiskey which was too earnest to be noisy.

At five minutes of eleven, a tall, lank, brick-colored cowboy strode over to Placer's Hotel. Placer's Hotel was a notable place. It was the best hotel within two hundred miles. Its office was filled with armchairs and brown papier-maché spittoons. At one end of the room was a wooden counter painted a bright pink, and on this morning a man was behind the counter writing in a ledger. He was the proprietor of the hotel, but his customary humor was so sullen that all strangers immediately wondered why in life he had chosen to play the part of mine host. Near his left hand, double doors opened into the dining room, which in warm weather was always kept darkened in order to discourage the flies, which was not compassed at all.

Placer, writing in his ledger, did not look up when the tall cowboy entered.

"Mornin', mister," said the latter. "I've come to see if you kin grub-stake th' hull crowd of us fer dinner t'day."

Placer did not then raise his eyes, but with a certain churlishness, as if it annoyed him that his hotel was patronized, he asked: "How many?"

"Oh, about thirty," replied the cowboy. "An' we want th' best dinner you kin raise an' scrape. Everything th' best. We don't care what it costs s' long as we git a good square meal. We'll pay a dollar a head: by God, we will! We won't kick on nothin' in th' bill if you do it up fine. If you ain't got it in the house, rustle th' hull town fer it. That's our gait. So you just tear loose, an' we'll——"

At this moment the machinery of a cuckoo clock on the wall began to whirr, little doors flew open, and a wooden bird appeared and cried "Cuckoo!" And this was repeated until eleven o'clock had been announced, while the cowboy, stupefied, glass-eyed, stood with his red throat gulping. At the end he wheeled upon Placer and demanded: *"What in hell is that?"*

Placer revealed by his manner that he had been asked this question too many times. "It's a clock," he answered shortly.

"I know it's a clock," gasped the cowboy; "but what *kind* of a clock?"

"A cuckoo clock. Can't you see?"

The cowboy, recovering his self-possession by a violent effort, suddenly went shouting into the street. "Boys! Say, boys! Come 'ere a minute!"

His comrades, comfortably inhabiting a nearby saloon, heard his stentorian calls, but they merely said one to another: "What's th' matter with Jake?—he's off his nut again."

But Jake burst in upon them with violence. "Boys," he yelled, "come over to th' hotel! They got a clock with a bird inside it, an' when it's eleven o'clock or anything like that, th' bird comes out and says 'Toot-toot, toot-toot!' that way, as many times as whatever time of day it is. It's immense! Come on over!"

The roars of laughter which greeted his proclamation were of two qualities; some men laughing because they knew all about cuckoo clocks, and other men laughing because they had concluded that the eccentric Jake had been victimized by some wise child of civilization.

Old Man Crumford, a venerable ruffian who probably had been born in a corral, was particularly offensive with his loud guffaws of contempt. "Bird a-comin' out of a clock an' a-tellin' ye th' time! Haw-haw-haw!" He swallowed his whiskey. "A bird! a-tellin' ye th' time! Haw-haw! Jake, you ben up agin some new drink. You ben drinkin' lonely an' got up agin some snake-medicine licker. A bird a-tellin' ye th' time! Haw-haw!"

The shrill voice of one of the younger cowboys piped from the background. "Brace up, Jake. Don't let 'em laugh at ye. Bring 'em that salt codfish of yourn what kin pick out th' ace."

"Oh, he's only kiddin' us. Don't pay no 'tention to 'im. He thinks he's smart."

A cowboy whose mother had a cuckoo clock in her house in Philadelphia spoke with solemnity. "Jake's a liar. There's no such clock in the world. What? a bird inside a clock to tell the time? Change your drink, Jake."

Jake was furious, but his fury took a very icy form. He bent a withering glance upon the last speaker. "I don't mean a *live* bird," he said, with terrible dignity. "It's a wooden bird, an'——"

"A wooden bird!" shouted Old Man Crumford. "Wooden bird a-tellin' ye th' time! Haw-haw!"

But Jake still paid his frigid attention to the Philadelphian. "An' if yer sober enough to walk, it ain't such a blame long ways from here to th' hotel, an' I'll bet my pile agin yours if you only got two bits."

"I don't want your money, Jake," said the Philadelphian. "Somebody's been stringin' you—that's all. I wouldn't take your money." He cleverly appeared to pity the other's innocence.

"You couldn't *git* my money," cried Jake, in sudden hot anger. "You couldn't git it. Now—since yer so fresh—let's see how much you got." He clattered some large gold pieces noisily upon the bar.

The Philadelphian shrugged his shoulders and walked away. Jake was triumphant. "Any more bluffers round here?" he demanded. "Any more? Any more bluffers? Where's all these here hot sports? Let 'em step up. Here's my money—come an' git it."

But they had ended by being afraid. To some of them his tale was absurd, but still one must be circumspect when a man throws forty-five dollars in gold upon the bar and bids the world come and win it. The general feeling was expressed by Old Man Crumford, when with deference he asked: "Well, this here bird, Jake—what kinder lookin' bird is it?"

"It's a little brown thing," said Jake, briefly. Apparently he almost disdained to answer.

"Well—how does it work?" asked the old man, meekly.

"Why in blazes don't you go an' look at it?" yelled Jake. "Want me to paint it in iles fer you? Go an' look!"

III

Placer was writing in his ledger. He heard a great trample of feet and clink of spurs on the porch, and there entered quietly the band of cowboys, some of them swaying a trifle, and these last being the most painfully decorous of all. Jake was in advance. He waved his hand toward the clock. "There she is," he said laconically. The cowboys drew up and stared. There was some giggling, but a serious voice said half-audibly, "I don't see no bird."

Jake politely addressed the landlord. "Mister, I've fetched these here friends of mine in here to see yer clock——"

Placer looked up suddenly. "Well, they can see it, can't they?" he asked in sarcasm. Jake, abashed, retreated to his fellows.

There was a period of silence. From time to time the men shifted their feet. Finally, Old Man Crumford leaned toward Jake, and in a penetrating whisper demanded, "Where's th' bird?" Some frolicsome spirits on the outskirts began to call "Bird! Bird!" as men at a political meeting call for a particular speaker.

Jake removed his big hat and nervously mopped his brow.

The young cowboy with the shrill voice again spoke from the skirts of the crowd. "Jake, is ther' sure 'nough a bird in that thing?"

"Yes. Didn't I tell you once?"

"Then," said the shrill-voiced man, in a tone of conviction, "it ain't a clock at all. It's a bird cage."

"I tell you it's a clock," cried the maddened Jake, but his retort could hardly be heard above the howls of glee and derision which greeted the words of him of the shrill voice.

Old Man Crumford was again rampant. "Wooden bird a-tellin' ye th' time! Haw-haw!"

Amid the confusion Jake went again to Placer. He spoke almost in supplication. "Say, mister, what time does this here thing go off ag'in?"

Placer lifted his head, looked at the clock, and said, "Noon."

There was a stir near the door, and Big Watson of the Square-X outfit, at this time very drunk indeed, came shouldering his way through the crowd and cursing everybody. The men gave him much room, for he was notorious as a quarrelsome person when drunk. He paused in front of Jake, and spoke as through a wet blanket. "What's all this Goddamn monkeyin' about?"

Jake was already wild at being made a butt for everybody, and he did not give backward. "None a' your damn business, Watson."

"Huh?" growled Watson, with the surprise of a challenged bull.

"I said," repeated Jake, distinctly, "it's none a' your damn business."

Watson whipped his revolver half out of its holster. "I'll make it m' business, then, you——"

But Jake had backed a step away, and was holding his left hand palm outward toward Watson, while in his right he held his six-shooter, its muzzle pointing at the floor. He was shouting in a frenzy, "No—don't you try it, Watson! Don't you dare try it, or, by Gawd, I'll kill you, sure—*sure!*"

He was aware of a torment of cries about him from fearful men; from men who protested, from men who cried out because they cried out. But he kept his eyes on Watson, and those two glared murder at each other, neither seeming to breathe, fixed like two statues.

A loud new voice suddenly rang out: "Hol' on a minute!" All spectators who had not stampeded turned quickly, and saw Placer standing behind his bright pink counter, with an aimed revolver in each hand.

"Cheese it!" he said. "I won't have no fightin' here. If you want to fight, git out in the street."

Big Watson laughed, and speeding up his six-shooter like a flash of blue light, he shot Placer through the throat—shot the man as he stood behind his absurd pink counter with his two aimed revolvers in his incompetent hands. With a yell of rage and despair, Jake smote Watson on the pate with his heavy weapon, and knocked him sprawling and bloody. Somewhere a woman shrieked like windy, midnight death. Placer fell behind the counter, and down upon him came his ledger and his inkstand, so that one could not have told blood from ink.

The cowboys did not seem to hear, see, nor feel, until they saw numbers of citizens with Winchesters running wildly upon them. Old Man Crumford threw high a passionate hand. "Don't shoot! We'll not fight ye fer 'im."

Nevertheless two or three shots rang, and a cowboy who had been about to gallop off suddenly slumped over on his pony's neck, where he held for a moment like an old sack, and then slid to the ground, while his pony, with flapping rein, fled to the prairie.

"In God's name, don't shoot!" trumpeted Old Man Crumford. "We'll not fight ye fer 'im!"

"It's murder," bawled Ben Roddle.

In the chaotic street it seemed for a moment as if everybody would kill everybody. "Where's the man what done it?" These hot cries seemed to declare a war which would result in an absolute annihilation of one side. But the cowboys were singing out against it. They would fight for nothing —yes—they often fought for nothing—but they would not fight for this dark something.

At last, when a flimsy truce had been made between the inflamed men, all parties went to the hotel. Placer, in some dying whim, had made his way out from behind the pink counter, and, leaving a horrible trail, had traveled to the center of the room, where he had pitched headlong over the body of Big Watson.

The men lifted the corpse and laid it at the side.

"Who done it?" asked a white, stern man.

A cowboy pointed at Big Watson. "That's him," he said huskily.

There was a curious grim silence, and then suddenly, in the death chamber, there sounded the loud whirring of the clock's works, little doors flew open, a tiny wooden bird appeared and cried "Cuckoo"—twelve times.

December, 1899

[*The Pall Mall Magazine*, Vol. 19, pp. 462–468.]

THE SECOND GENERATION*

I

Caspar Cadogan resolved to go to the tropic wars and do something. The air was blue and gold with the pomp of soldiering, and in every ear rang the music of military glory. Caspar's father was a United States Senator from the great State of Skowmulligan, where the war fever ran very high. Chill is the blood of many of the sons of millionaires, but Caspar took the fever and posted to Washington. His father had never denied him anything, and this time all that Caspar wanted was a little captaincy in the Army—just a simple little captaincy.

The old man had been entertaining a delegation of respectable bunco-steerers from Skowmulligan who had come to him on a matter which is none of the public's business.

Bottles of whiskey and boxes of cigars were still on the table in the sumptuous private parlor. The Senator had said, "Well, gentlemen, I'll do what I can for you." By this sentence he meant whatever he meant.

Then he turned to his eager son. "Well, Caspar?" The youth poured out his modest desires. It was not altogether his fault. Life had taught him a generous faith in his own abilities. If any one had told him that he was simply an ordinary damned fool he would have opened his eyes wide at the person's lack of judgment. All his life people had admired him.

The Skowmulligan war horse looked with quick disapproval into the eyes of his son. "Well, Caspar," he said slowly, "I am of the opinion that they've got all the golf experts and tennis champions and cotillion leaders and piano tuners and billiard markers that they really need as officers. Now, if you were a soldier—"

"I know," said the young man with a gesture, "but I'm not exactly a fool, I hope, and I think if I get a chance I can do something. I'd like to try. I would, indeed."

The Senator lit a cigar. He assumed an attitude of ponderous reflection. "Y-yes, but this country is full of young men who are not fools. Full of 'em."

Caspar fidgeted in the desire to answer that, while he admitted the profusion of young men who were not fools, he felt that he himself possessed interesting and peculiar qualifications which would allow him to make his mark in any field of effort which he seriously challenged. But he did not make this graceful statement, for he sometimes detected something ironic in his father's temperament. The Skowmulligan war horse had not thought of

* *Wounds in the Rain.*

expressing an opinion of his own ability since the year 1865, when he was young, like Caspar.

"Well, well," said the Senator finally. "I'll see about it. I'll see about it." The young man was obliged to await the end of his father's characteristic method of thought. The war horse never gave a quick answer, and if people tried to hurry him they seemed able to arouse only a feeling of irritation against making a decision at all. His mind moved like the wind, but practice had placed a Mexican bit in the mouth of his judgment. This old man of light, quick thought had taught himself to move like an ox cart. Caspar said, "Yes, sir." He withdrew to his club, where, to the affectionate inquiries of some envious friends, he replied, "The old man is letting the idea soak."

The mind of the war horse was decided far sooner than Caspar expected. In Washington a large number of well-bred, handsome young men were receiving appointments as lieutenants, as captains, and occasionally as majors. They were a strong, healthy, clean-eyed, educated collection. They were a prime lot. A German field marshal would have beamed with joy if he could have had them—to send to school. Anywhere in the world they would have made a grand show as material, but intrinsically they were not lieutenants, captains, and majors. They were fine men, though manhood is only an essential part of a lieutenant, a captain, or a major. But, at any rate, this arrangement had all the logic of going to sea in a bathing-machine.

The Senator found himself reasoning that Caspar was as good as any of them, and better than many. Presently he was bleating here and there that his boy should have a chance. "The boy's all right, I tell you, Henry. He's wild to go, and I don't see why they shouldn't give him a show. He's got plenty of nerve, and he's keen as a whiplash. I'm going to get him an appointment, and if you can do anything to help it along I wish you would."

Then he betook himself to the White House and the War Department and made a stir. People think that Administrations are always slavishly, abominably anxious to please the Machine. They are not; they wish the Machine sunk in red fire, for, by the power of ten thousand past words, looks, gestures, writings, the Machine comes along and takes the Administration by the nose and twists it, and the Administration dare not even yell. The huge force which carries an election to success looks reproachfully at the Administration and says, "Give me a bun." That is a very small thing with which to reward a Colossus.

The Skowmulligan war horse got his bun and took it to his hotel, where Caspar was moodily reading war rumors. "Well, my boy, here you are." Caspar was a captain and commissary on the staff of Brigadier General

Reilly, commander of the Second Brigade of the First Division of the Thirtieth Army Corps.

"I had to work for it," said the Senator grimly. "They talked to me as if they thought you were some sort of empty-headed idiot. None of 'em seemed to know you personally. They just sort of took it for granted. Finally I got pretty hot in the collar." He paused a moment; his heavy, grooved face set hard; his blue eyes shone. He clapped a hand down upon the handle of his chair.

"Caspar, I've got you into this thing, and I believe you'll do all right, and I'm not saying this because I distrust either your sense or your grit. But I want you to understand you've *got to make a go of it.* I'm not going to talk any twaddle about your country and your country's flag. You understand all about that. But now you're a soldier, and there'll be this to do and that to do, and fighting to do, and you've got to do *every damned one of 'em* right up to the handle. I don't know how much of a shindy this thing is going to be, but any shindy is enough to show how much there is in a man. You've got your appointment, and that's all I can do for you; but I'll thrash you with my own hands if, when the Army gets back, the other fellows say my son is 'nothing but a good-looking dude.'"

He ceased, breathing heavily. Caspar looked bravely and frankly at his father, and answered in a voice which was not very tremulous. "I'll do my best. This is my chance. I'll do my best with it."

The Senator had a marvelous ability of transition from one manner to another. Suddenly he seemed very kind. "Well, that's all right, then. I guess you'll get along all right with Reilly. I know him well, and he'll see you through. I helped him along once. And now about this commissary business. As I understand it, a commissary is a sort of caterer in a big way —that is, he looks out for a good many more things than a caterer has to bother his head about. Reilly's brigade has probably from two to three thousand men in it, and in regard to certain things you've got to look out for every man of 'em every day. I know perfectly well you couldn't successfully run a boarding house in Ocean Grove. How are you going to manage for all these soldiers, hey? Thought about it?"

"No," said Caspar, injured. "I didn't want to be a commissary. I wanted to be a captain in the line."

"They wouldn't hear of it. They said you would have to take a staff appointment, where people could look after you."

"Well, let them look after me," cried Caspar resentfully; "but when there's any fighting to be done I guess I won't necessarily be the last man."

"That's it," responded the Senator. "That's the spirit." They both thought that the problem of war would eliminate to an equation of actual battle.

Ultimately Caspar departed into the South to an encampment in salty grass under pine trees. Here lay an Army corps twenty thousand strong. Caspar passed into the dusty sunshine of it, and for many weeks he was lost to view.

II

"Of course I don't know a blamed thing about it," said Caspar frankly and modestly to a circle of his fellow staff officers. He was referring to the duties of his office.

Their faces became expressionless; they looked at him with eyes in which he could fathom nothing. After a pause one politely said, "Don't you?" It was the inevitable two words of convention.

"Why," cried Caspar, "I didn't know what a commissary officer was until I *was* one. My old Guv'nor told me. He'd looked it up in a book somewhere, I suppose; but *I* didn't know."

"Didn't you?"

The young man's face glowed with sudden humor. "Do you know, the word was intimately associated in my mind with camels. Funny, eh? I think it came from reading that rhyme of Kipling's about the commissariat camel."

"Did it?"

"Yes. Funny, isn't it? Camels!"

The brigade was ultimately landed at Siboney as part of an army to attack Santiago. The scene at the landing sometimes resembled the inspiriting daily drama at the approach to the Brooklyn Bridge. There was a great bustle, during which the wise man kept his property gripped in his hands lest it might march off into the wilderness in the pocket of one of the striding regiments. Truthfully, Caspar should have had frantic occupation, but men saw him wandering bootlessly here and there, crying, "Has any one seen my saddlebags? Why, if I lose them I'm ruined. I've got everything packed away in 'em. Everything!"

They looked at him gloomily and without attention. "No," they said. It was to intimate that they would not give a rip if he had lost his nose, his teeth, and his self-respect. Reilly's brigade collected itself from the boats and went off, each regiment's soul burning with anger because some other regiment was in advance of it. Moving along through the scrub and under the palms, men talked mostly of things that did not pertain to the business in hand.

General Reilly finally planted his headquarters in some tall grass under a mango tree. "Where's Cadogan?" he said suddenly as he took off his hat and smoothed the wet gray hair from his brow. Nobody knew. "I saw him looking for his saddlebags down at the landing," said an officer dubiously. "Bother him," said the General contemptuously. "Let him stay there."

Three venerable regimental commanders came, saluted stiffly, and sat in the grass. There was a powwow, during which Reilly explained much that the division commander had told him. The venerable colonels nodded; they understood. Everything was smooth and clear to their minds. But still, the colonel of the Forty-fourth Regular Infantry murmured about the commissariat. His men—and then he launched forth in a sentiment concerning the privations of his men in which you were confronted with his feeling that his men—his men were the only creatures of importance in the universe, which feeling was entirely correct for him. Reilly grunted. He did what most commanders did. He set the competent line to doing the work of the incompetent part of the staff.

In time Caspar came trudging along the road merrily swinging his saddlebags. "Well, General," he cried as he saluted, "I found 'em."

"Did you?" said Reilly. Later an officer rushed to him tragically: "General, Cadogan is off there in the bushes eatin' potted ham and crackers all by himself." The officer was sent back into the bushes for Caspar, and the General sent Caspar with an order. Then Reilly and the three venerable colonels, grinning, partook of potted ham and crackers. "Tashe a' right," said Reilly, with his mouth full. "Dorsey, see if 'e got some'n else."

"Mush be selfish young pig," said one of the colonels, with his mouth full. "Who's he, General?"

"Son—Sen'tor Cad'gan—ol' frien' mine—dash 'im."

Caspar wrote a letter:

"Dear Father: I am sitting under a tree using the flattest part of my canteen for a desk. Even as I write the division ahead of us is moving forward and we don't know what moment the storm of battle may break out. I don't know what the plans are. General Reilly knows, but he is so good as to give me very little of his confidence. In fact, I might be part of a forlorn hope from all to the contrary I've heard from him. I understood you to say in Washington that you at one time had been of some service to him, but if that is true I can assure you he has completely forgotten it. At times his manner to me is little short of being offensive, but of course I understand that it is only the way of a crusty old soldier who has been made boorish and bearish by a long life among the Indians. I dare say I shall manage it all right without a row.

"When you hear that we have captured Santiago, please send me by first steamer a box of provisions and clothing, particularly sardines, pickles, and lightweight underwear. The other men on the staff are nice quiet chaps, but they seem a bit crude. There has been no fighting yet save the skirmish by Young's brigade. Reilly was furious because we couldn't get in it. I met General Peel yesterday. He was very nice. He said he knew you well when he was in Congress. Young Jack May is on Peel's staff. I knew him well in college. We spent an hour talking over old times. Give my love to all at home."

The march was leisurely. Reilly and his staff strolled out to the head of the long, sinuous column and entered the sultry gloom of the forest. Some less fortunate regiments had to wait among the trees at the side of the trail, and as Reilly's brigade passed them, officer called to officer, classmate to classmate, and in these greetings rang a note of everything from West Point to Alaska. They were going into an action in which they, the officers, would lose over a hundred in killed and wounded—officers alone—and these greetings, in which many nicknames occurred, were in many cases farewells such as one pictures being given with ostentation, solemnity, fervor. "There goes Gory Widgeon! Hello, Gory! Where you starting for? Hey, Gory!"

Caspar communed with himself and decided that he was not frightened. He was eager and alert; he thought that now his obligation to his country, or himself, was to be faced, and he was mad to prove to old Reilly and the others that after all he was a very capable soldier.

III

Old Reilly was stumping along the line of his brigade and mumbling like a man with a mouthful of grass. The fire from the enemy's position was incredible in its swift fury, and Reilly's brigade was getting its share of a very bad ordeal. The old man's face was of the color of the tomato, and in his rage he mouthed and sputtered strangely. As he pranced along his thin line, scornfully erect, voices arose from the grass beseeching him to take care of himself. At his heels scrambled a bugler with pallid skin and clenched teeth, a chalky, trembling youth, who kept his eye on old Reilly's back and followed it.

The old gentleman was quite mad. Apparently he thought the whole thing a dreadful mess, but now that his brigade was irrevocably in it he was full-tilting here and everywhere to establish some irreproachable, immaculate kind of behavior on the part of every man-jack in his brigade. The intentions of the three venerable colonels were the same. They stood behind their lines, quiet, stern, courteous old fellows, admonishing their regiments to be very pretty in the face of such a hail of magazine-rifle and machine-gun fire as had never in this world been confronted save by beardless savages when the white man had found occasion to take his burden to some new place.

And the regiments were pretty. The men lay on their little stomachs, and got peppered according to the law, and said nothing as the good blood pumped out into the grass; and even if a solitary rookie tried to get a decent reason to move to some haven of rational men, the cold voice of an officer made him look criminal with a shame that was a credit to his regimental education. Behind Reilly's command was a bullet-torn jungle through which it could not move as a brigade; ahead of it were Spanish trenches on hills. Reilly considered that he was in a fix, no doubt; but he said this only to himself. Suddenly he saw on the right a little point of blue-shirted men already halfway up the hill. It was some pathetic fragment of the Sixth United States Infantry. Chagrined, shocked, horrified, Reilly bellowed to his bugler, and the chalk-faced youth unlocked his teeth and sounded the charge by rushes.

The men formed hastily and grimly, and rushed. Apparently there awaited them only the fate of respectable soldiers. But they went because— of the opinions of others, perhaps. They went because—no loud-mouthed lot of jailbirds such as the Twenty-seventh Infantry could do anything that they could not do better. They went because Reilly ordered it. They went because they went.

And yet not a man of them to this day has made a public speech explaining precisely how he did the whole thing and detailing with what initiative and ability he comprehended and defeated a situation which he did not comprehend at all.

Reilly never saw the top of the hill. He was heroically striving to keep up with his men when a bullet ripped quietly through his left lung, and he fell back into the arms of the bugler, who received him as he would have received a Christmas present. The three venerable colonels inherited the brigade in swift succession. The senior commanded for about fifty seconds, at the end of which he was mortally shot. Before they could get the news to the next in rank he, too, was shot. The junior colonel ultimately arrived with a lean and puffing little brigade at the top of the hill. The men lay down and fired volleys at whatever was practicable.

In and out of the ditch-like trenches lay the Spanish dead, lemon-faced corpses dressed in shabby blue-and-white ticking. Some were huddled down comfortably like sleeping children; one had died in the attitude of a man flung back in a dentist's chair; one sat in the trench with his chin sunk despondently to his breast; few preserved a record of the agitation of battle. With the greater number it was as if death had touched them so gently, so lightly, that they had not known of it. Death had come to them rather in the form of an opiate than of a bloody blow.

But the arrived men in the blue shirts had no thought of the sallow corpses. They were eagerly exchanging a hail of shots with the Spanish second line, whose ash-colored entrenchments barred the way to a city white amid trees. In the pauses the men talked.

"We done the best. Old E Company got there. Why, one time the hull of B Company was *behind* us."

"Jones, he was the first man up. I saw 'im."

"Which Jones?"

"Did you see ol' Two-bars runnin' like a land crab? Made good time, too. He hit only in the high places. He's all right."

"The lootenant is all right, too. He was a good ten yards ahead of the best of us. I hated him at the post, but for this here active service there's none of 'em can touch him."

"This is mighty different from being at the post."

"Well, we done it, an' it wasn't b'cause *I* thought it could be done. When we started, I ses to m'self: 'Well, here goes a lot o' damned fools.'"

"'Tain't over yet."

"Oh, they'll never git us back from here. If they start to chase us back from here we'll pile 'em up so high the last ones can't climb over. We've come this far, an' we'll stay here. I ain't done pantin'."

"Anything is better than packin' through that jungle an' gettin' blistered from front, rear, an' both flanks. I'd rather tackle another hill than go trailin' in them woods, so thick you can't tell whether you are one man or a division of cav'lry."

"Where's that young kitchen-soldier, Cadogan, or whatever his name is? Ain't seen him today."

"Well, *I* seen him. He was right in with it. He got shot, too, about half up the hill, in the leg. I seen it. He's all right. Don't worry about him. He's all right."

"I seen 'im, too. He done his stunt. As soon as I can git this piece of barbed wire entanglement out o' me throat I'll give 'm a cheer."

"He ain't shot at all, b'cause there he stands, there. See 'im?"

Rearward, the grassy slope was populous with little groups of men searching for the wounded. Reilly's brigade began to dig with its bayonets and shovel with its meat-ration cans.

IV

Senator Cadogan paced to and fro in his private parlor and smoked small brown, weak cigars. These little wisps seemed utterly inadequate to console such a ponderous satrap.

It was the evening of the 1st of July, 1898, and the Senator was immensely excited, as could be seen from the superlatively calm way in which he called out to his private secretary, who was in an adjoining room. The voice was serene, gentle, affectionate, low.

"Baker, I wish you'd go over again to the War Department and see if they've heard anything about Caspar."

A very bright-eyed, hatchet-faced young man appeared in a doorway, pen still in hand. He was hiding a nettle-like irritation behind all the finished audacity of a smirking, sharp, lying, trustworthy young politician. "I've just got back from there, sir," he suggested.

The Skowmulligan war horse lifted his eyes and looked for a short second into the eyes of his private secretary. It was not a glare or an eagle glance; it was something beyond the practice of an actor; it was simply meaning. The clever private secretary grabbed his hat and was at once enthusiastically away. "All right, sir," he cried. "I'll find out."

The War Department was ablaze with light, and messengers were running. With the assurance of a retainer of an old house Baker made his way through much small-caliber vociferation. There was rumor of a big victory; there was rumor of a big defeat. In the corridors various watchdogs arose from their armchairs and asked him of his business in tones of uncertainty which in no wise compared with their previous habitual deference to the private secretary of the war horse of Skowmulligan.

Ultimately Baker arrived in a room where some kind of head clerk sat writing feverishly at a roll-top desk. Baker asked a question, and the head clerk mumbled profanely without lifting his head. Apparently he said: "How in the blankety-blank blazes do I know?"

The private secretary let his jaw fall. Surely some new spirit had come suddenly upon the heart of Washington—a spirit which Baker understood to be almost defiantly indifferent to the wishes of Senator Cadogan, a spirit which was not courteously oily. What could it mean? Baker's foxlike mind sprang wildly to a conception of overturned factions, changed friends, new combinations. The assurance which had come from experience of a broad political situation suddenly left him, and he would not have been amazed if some one had told him that Senator Cadogan now controlled only six votes in the State of Skowmulligan. "Well," he stammered in his bewilderment, "well—there isn't any news of the old man's son, hey?" Again the head clerk replied blasphemously.

Eventually Baker retreated in disorder from the presence of this head clerk, having learned that the latter did not give a damn if Caspar Cadogan were sailing through Hades on an ice yacht.

Baker stormed other and more formidable officials. In fact, he struck as high as he dared. They one and all flung him short, hard words, even as men pelt an annoying cur with pebbles. He emerged from the brilliant light, from the groups of men with anxious, puzzled faces, and as he walked back to the hotel he did not know if his name were Baker or Cholmondeley.

However, as he walked up the stairs to the Senator's rooms he contrived to concentrate his intellect upon a manner of speaking.

The war horse was still pacing his parlor and smoking. He paused at Baker's entrance. "Well?"

"Mr. Cadogan," said the private secretary coolly, "they told me at the

Department that they did not give a cuss whether your son was alive or dead."

The Senator looked at Baker and smiled gently. "What's that, my boy?" he asked in a soft and considerate voice.

"They said—" gulped Baker, with a certain tenacity. "They said that they didn't give a cuss whether your son was alive or dead."

There was a silence for the space of three seconds. Baker stood like an image; he had no machinery for balancing the issues of this kind of situation, and he seemed to feel that if he stood as still as a stone frog he would escape the ravages of a terrible Senatorial wrath which was about to break forth in a hurricane speech which would snap off trees and sweep away barns. "Well," drawled the Senator lazily, "who did you see, Baker?"

The private secretary resumed a certain usual manner of breathing. He told the names of the men whom he had seen.

"Ye-e-es," remarked the Senator. He took another little brown cigar and held it with a thumb and first finger, staring at it with the calm and steady scrutiny of a scientist investigating a new thing. "So they don't care whether Caspar is alive or dead, eh? Well . . . maybe they don't. . . . That's all right. . . . However . . . I think I'll just look in on 'em and state my views."

When the Senator had gone, the private secretary ran to the window and leaned afar out. Pennsylvania Avenue was gleaming silver blue in the light of many arc-lamps; the cable trains groaned along to the clangor of gongs; from the window, the walks presented a hardly diversified aspect of shirt-waists and straw hats. Sometimes a newsboy screeched.

Baker watched the tall, heavy figure of the Senator moving out to intercept a cable train. "Great Scott!" cried the private secretary to himself, "there'll be three distinct kinds of grand, plain practical fireworks. The old man is going for 'em. I wouldn't be in Lascum's boots. Ye gods, what a row there'll be."

In due time the Senator was closeted with some kind of deputy third assistant battery-horse in the offices of the War Department. The official obviously had been told off to make a supreme effort to pacify Cadogan, and he certainly was acting according to his instructions. He was almost in tears; he spread out his hands in supplication, and his voice whined and wheedled.

"Why, really, you know, Senator, we can only beg you to look at the circumstances. Two scant divisions at the top of that hill; over a thousand men killed and wounded; the line so thin that any strong attack would smash our Army to flinders. The Spaniards have probably received reinforcements under Pando; Shafter seems to be too ill to be actively in command of our troops; Lawton can't get up with his division before tomorrow.

We are actually expecting . . . no, I won't say expecting . . . but we would not be surprised . . . nobody in the department would be surprised if before daybreak we were compelled to give to the country the news of a disaster which would be the worst blow the National pride has ever suffered. Don't you see? Can't you see our position, Senator?"

The Senator, with a pale but composed face, contemplated the official with eyes that gleamed in a way not usual with the big, self-controlled politician.

"I'll tell you frankly, sir," continued the other, "I'll tell you frankly that at this moment we don't know whether we are afoot or a-horseback. Everything is in the air. We don't know whether we have won a glorious victory or simply got ourselves in a deuce of a fix."

The Senator coughed. "I suppose my boy is with the two divisions at the top of that hill? He's with Reilly."

"Yes; Reilly's brigade is up there."

"And when do you suppose the War Department can tell me if he is all right? I want to know."

"My dear Senator, frankly, I don't know. Again I beg you to think of our position. The Army is in a muddle; it's a general thinking that he must fall back, and yet not sure that he *can* fall back without losing the Army. Why, we're worrying about the lives of sixteen thousand men and the self-respect of the nation, Senator."

"I see," observed the Senator, nodding his head slowly. "And naturally the welfare of one man's son doesn't—how do they say it?—doesn't cut any ice."

v

And in Cuba it rained. In a few days Reilly's brigade discovered that by their successful charge they had gained the inestimable privilege of sitting in a wet trench and slowly but surely starving to death. Men's tempers crumbled like dry bread. The soldiers who so cheerfully, quietly, and decently had captured positions which the foreign experts had said were impregnable, now in turn underwent an attack which was furious as well as insidious. The heat of the sun alternated with rains which boomed and roared in their falling like mountain cataracts. It seemed as if men took the fever through sheer lack of other occupation. During the days of battle none had had time to get even a tropic headache, but no sooner was that brisk period over than men began to shiver and shudder by squads and platoons. Rations were scarce enough to make a little fat strip of bacon seem of the size of a corner lot, and coffee grains were pearls. There would have been godless quarreling over fragments if it were not that with these fevers came a great listlessness, so that men were almost content to die if death required no exertion.

It was an occasion which distinctly separated the sheep from the goats. The goats were few enough, but their qualities glared out like crimson spots.

One morning Jameson and Ripley, two captains in the Forty-fourth Foot, lay under a flimsy shelter of sticks and palm branches. Their dreamy, dull eyes contemplated the men in the trench which went to left and right. To them came Caspar Cadogan, moaning. "By Jove," he said, as he flung himself wearily on the ground, "I can't stand much more of this, you know. It's killing me." A bristly beard sprouted through the grime on his face; his eyelids were crimson; an indescribably dirty shirt fell away from his roughened neck; and at the same time various lines of evil and greed were deepened on his face, until he practically stood forth as a revelation, a confession. "I can't stand it. By Jove, I can't."

Stanford, a lieutenant under Jameson, came stumbling along toward them. He was a lad of the class of '98 at West Point. It could be seen that he was flaming with fever. He rolled a calm eye at them. "Have you any water, sir?" he said to his captain. Jameson got upon his feet and helped Stanford to lay his shaking length under the shelter. "No, boy," he answered gloomily. "Not a drop. You got any, Rip?"

"No," answered Ripley, looking with anxiety upon the young officer. "Not a drop."

"You, Cadogan?"

Here Caspar hesitated oddly for a second, and then in a tone of deep regret made answer, "No, Captain; not a mouthful."

Jameson moved off weakly. "You lay quietly, Stanford, and I'll see what I can rustle."

Presently Caspar felt that Ripley was steadily regarding him. He returned the look with one of half-guilty questioning.

"God forgive you, Cadogan," said Ripley, "but you are a damned beast. Your canteen is full of water."

Even then the apathy in their veins prevented the scene from becoming as sharp as the words sounded. Caspar sputtered like a child, and at length merely said: "No, it isn't." Stanford lifted his head to shoot a keen, proud glance at Caspar, and then turned away his face.

"You lie," said Ripley. "I can tell the sound of a full canteen as far as I can hear it."

"Well, if it is, I—I must have forgotten it."

"You lie; no man in this Army just now forgets whether his canteen is full or empty. Hand it over."

Fever is the physical counterpart of shame, and when a man has the one he accepts the other with an ease which would revolt his healthy self. However, Caspar made a desperate struggle to preserve the forms. He

arose and, taking the string from his shoulder, passed the canteen to Ripley. But after all there was a whine in his voice, and the assumption of
dignity was really a farce. "I think I had better go, Captain. You can have
the water if you want it, I'm sure. But—but I fail to see—I fail to see what
reason you have for insulting me."

"Do you?" said Ripley stolidly. "That's all right."

Caspar stood for a terrible moment. He simply did not have the strength
to turn his back on this—this affair. It seemed to him that he must stand
for ever and face it. But when he found the audacity to look again at Ripley
he saw the latter was not at all concerned with the situation. Ripley, too,
had the fever. The fever changes all laws of proportion. Caspar went away.

"Here, youngster; here is your drink."

Stanford made a weak gesture. "I wouldn't touch a drop from his
blamed canteen if it was the last water in the world," he murmured in his
high, boyish voice.

"Don't you be a young jackass," quoth Ripley tenderly.

The boy stole a glance at the canteen. He felt the propriety of arising
and hurling it after Caspar, but—he, too, had the fever.

"Don't you be a young jackass," said Ripley again.

VI

Senator Cadogan was happy. His son had returned from Cuba, and the
8:30 train that evening would bring him to the station nearest to the stone
and red shingle villa which the Senator and his family occupied on the
shores of Long Island Sound. The Senator's steam yacht lay some hundred
yards from the beach. She had just returned from a trip to Montauk Point,
where the Senator had made a gallant attempt to gain his son from the
transport on which he was coming from Cuba. He had fought a brave
sea fight with sundry petty little doctors and ship's officers, who had raked
him with broadsides, describing the laws of quarantine, and had used
inelegant speech to a United States Senator as he stood on the bridge of
his own steam yacht. These men had grimly asked him to tell exactly how
much better was Caspar than any other returning soldier.

But the Senator had not given them a long fight. In fact, the truth came
to him quickly, and with almost a blush he had ordered the yacht back
to her anchorage off the villa. As a matter of fact, the trip to Montauk
Point had been undertaken largely from impulse. Long ago the Senator had
decided that when his boy returned the greeting should have something
Spartan in it. He would make a welcome such as most soldiers get. There
should be no flowers and carriages when the other poor fellows got none.
He should consider Caspar as a soldier. That was the way to treat a man.
But in the end a sharp acid of anxiety had worked upon the iron old man,
until he had ordered the yacht to take him out and make a fool of him.

The result filled him with a chagrin which caused him to delegate to the mother and sisters the entire business of succoring Caspar at Montauk Point Camp. He had remained at home conducting the huge correspondence of an active national politician and waiting for this son whom he so loved and whom he so wished to be a man of a certain strong, taciturn, shrewd ideal. The recent yacht voyage he now looked upon as a kind of confession of his weakness, and he was resolved that no more signs should escape him.

But yet his boy had been down there against the enemy and among the fevers. There had been grave perils, and his boy must have faced them. And he could not prevent himself from dreaming through the poetry of fine actions, in which visions his son's face shone out manly and generous. During these periods the people about him, accustomed as they were to his silence and calm in time of stress, considered that affairs in Skowmulligan might be most critical. In no other way could they account for this exaggerated phlegm.

On the night of Caspar's return he did not go to dinner, but had a tray sent to his library, where he remained writing. At last he heard the spin of the dogcart's wheels on the gravel of the drive, and a moment later there penetrated to him the sound of joyful feminine cries. He lit another cigar; he knew that it was now his part to bide with dignity the moment when his son should shake off that other welcome and come to him. He could still hear them; in their exuberance they seemed to be capering like schoolchildren. He was impatient, but this impatience took the form of a polar stolidity.

Presently there were quick steps and a jubilant knock at his door. "Come in," he said.

In came Caspar, thin, yellow, and in soiled khaki. "They almost tore me to pieces," he cried, laughing. "They danced around like wild things." Then as they shook hands he dutifully said: "How are you, sir?"

"How are you, my boy?" answered the Senator, casually but kindly.

"Better than I might expect, sir," cried Caspar cheerfully. "We had a pretty hard time, you know."

"You look as if they'd given you a hard run," observed the father in a tone of slight interest.

Caspar was eager to tell. "Yes, sir," he said rapidly. "We did, indeed. Why, it was awful. We—any of us—were lucky to get out of it alive. It wasn't so much the Spaniards, you know. The Army took care of them all right. It was the fever and the—you know, we couldn't get anything to eat. And the mismanagement. Why, it was frightful."

"Yes, I've heard," said the Senator. A certain wistful look came into his eyes, but he did not allow it to become prominent. Indeed, he suppressed it. "And you, Caspar? I suppose you did your duty?"

Caspar answered with becoming modesty. "Well, I didn't do more than anybody else, I don't suppose, but—well, I got along all right, I guess."

"And this great charge up San Juan Hill?" asked the father slowly. "Were you in that?"

"Well—yes; I was in it," replied the son.

The Senator brightened a trifle. "You were, eh? In the front of it? or just sort of going along?"

"Well—I don't know. I couldn't tell exactly. Sometimes I was in front of a lot of them, and sometimes I was—just sort of going along."

This time the Senator emphatically brightened. "That's all right, then. And of course—of course you performed your commissary duties correctly?"

The question seemed to make Caspar uncommunicative and sulky. "I did when there was anything to do," he answered. "But the whole thing was on the most unbusinesslike basis you can imagine. And they wouldn't tell you anything. Nobody would take time to instruct you in your duties, and of course if you didn't know a thing your superior officer would swoop down on you and ask you why in the deuce such and such a thing wasn't done in such and such a way. Of course I did the best I could."

The Senator's countenance had again become somberly indifferent. "I see. But you weren't directly rebuked for incapacity, were you? No; of course you weren't. But—I mean—did any of your superior officers suggest that you were 'no good,' or anything of that sort? I mean—did you come off with a clean slate?"

Caspar took a small time to digest his father's meaning. "Oh, yes, sir," he cried at the end of his reflection. "The commissary was in such a hopeless mess anyhow that nobody thought of doing anything but curse Washington."

"Of course," rejoined the Senator harshly. "But supposing that you had been a competent and well-trained commissary officer. What then?"

Again the son took time for consideration, and in the end deliberately replied: "Well, if I had been a competent and well-trained commissary I would have sat there and eaten up my heart and cursed Washington."

"Well, then, that's all right. And now, about this charge up San Juan. Did any of the generals speak to you afterward and say that you had done well? Didn't any of them see you?"

"Why, n-n-no, I don't suppose they did . . . any more than I did them. You see, this charge was a big thing and covered lots of ground, and I hardly saw anybody excepting a lot of the men."

"Well, but didn't any of the men see you? Weren't you ahead some of the time leading them on and waving your sword?"

Caspar burst into laughter. "Why, no. I had all I could do to scramble along and try to keep up. And I didn't want to go up at all."

"Why?" demanded the Senator.

"Because—because the Spaniards were shooting so much. And you could see men falling, and the bullets rushed around you in—by the bushel. And then at last it seemed that if we once drove them away from the top of the hill there would be less danger. So we all went up."

The Senator chuckled over this description. "And you didn't flinch at all?"

"Well," rejoined Caspar humorously, "I won't say I wasn't frightened."

"No, of course not. But then, you did not let anybody know it?"

"Of course not."

"You understand, naturally, that I am bothering you with all these questions because I desire to hear how my only son behaved in the crisis. I don't want to worry you with it. But if you went through the San Juan charge with credit I'll have you made a major."

"Well," said Caspar, "I wouldn't say I went through that charge with credit. I went through it all good enough, but the enlisted men around went through in the same way."

"But weren't you encouraging them and leading them on by your example?"

Caspar smirked. He began to see a point. "Well, sir," he said with a charming hesitation, "aw—er—I—well, I dare say I was doing my share of it."

The perfect form of the reply delighted the father. He could not endure blatancy; his admiration was to be won only by a bashful hero. Now he beat his hand impulsively down upon the table. "That's what I wanted to know. That's it exactly. I'll have you made a major next week. You've found your proper field at last. You stick to the Army, Caspar, and I'll back you up. That's the thing. In a few years it will be a great career. The United States is pretty sure to have an Army of about a hundred and fifty thousand men. And, starting in when you did and with me to back you up —why, we'll make you a General in seven or eight years. That's the ticket. You stay in the Army." The Senator's cheek was flushed with enthusiasm, and he looked eagerly and confidently at his son.

But Caspar had pulled a long face. "The Army?" he said. "Stay in the Army?"

The Senator continued to outline quite rapturously his idea of the future. "The Army, evidently, is just the place for you. You know as well as I do that you have not been a howling success, exactly, in anything else which you have tried. But now the Army just suits you. It is the kind of career which especially suits you. Well, then, go in, and go at it hard. Go in to win. Go at it."

"But—" began Caspar.

The Senator interrupted swiftly. "Oh, don't worry about that part of it. I'll take care of all that. You won't get jailed in some Arizona adobe for the rest of your natural life. There won't be much more of that, anyhow; and besides, as I say, I'll look after all that end of it. The chance is splendid. A young, healthy, and intelligent man, with the start you've already got, and with my backing, can do anything—anything! There will be a lot of active service—oh, yes, I'm sure of it—and everybody who—"

"But," said Caspar, wan, desperate, heroic, "father, I don't care to stay in the Army."

The Senator lifted his eyes and darkened. "What?" he said. "What's that?" He looked at Caspar.

The son became tightened and wizened like an old miser trying to withhold gold. He replied with a sort of idiot obstinacy, "I don't care to stay in the Army."

The Senator's jaw clenched down, and he was dangerous. But, after all, there was something mournful somewhere. "Why, what do you mean?" he asked gruffly.

"Why, I couldn't get along, you know. The—the—"

"The what?" demanded the father, suddenly uplifted with thunderous anger. "The what?"

Caspar's pain found a sort of outlet in mere irresponsible talk. "Well, you know—the other men, you know. I couldn't get along with them, you know. They're peculiar, somehow; odd; I didn't understand them, and they didn't understand me. We—we didn't hitch, somehow. They're a queer lot. They've got funny ideas. I don't know how to explain it exactly, but—somehow—I don't like 'em. That's all there is to it. They're good fellows enough, I know, but—"

"Oh, well, Caspar," interrupted the Senator. Then he seemed to weigh a great fact in his mind. "I guess—" He paused again in profound consideration. "I guess—" He lit a small brown cigar. "I guess you are no damn good."

December 2, 1899

[*The Saturday Evening Post*, Vol. 172, pp. 449–452.]

AN EPISODE OF WAR

The lieutenant's rubber blanket lay on the ground, and upon it he had poured the company's supply of coffee. Corporals and other representatives of the grimy and hot-throated men who lined the breastwork had come for each squad's portion.

The lieutenant was frowning and serious at this task of division. His lips pursed as he drew with his sword various crevices in the heap, until brown squares of coffee, astoundingly equal in size, appeared on the blanket. He was on the verge of a great triumph in mathematics, and the corporals were thronging forward, each to reap a little square, when suddenly the lieutenant cried out and looked quickly at a man near him as if he suspected it was a case of personal assault. The others cried out also when they saw blood upon the lieutenant's sleeve.

He had winced like a man stung, swayed dangerously, and then straightened. The sound of his hoarse breathing was plainly audible. He looked sadly, mystically, over the breastwork at the green face of a wood, where now were many little puffs of white smoke. During this moment the men about him gazed statue-like and silent, astonished and awed by this catastrophe which happened when catastrophes were not expected—when they had leisure to observe it.

As the lieutenant stared at the wood, they too swung their heads, so that for another instant all hands, still silent, contemplated the distant forest as if their minds were fixed upon the mystery of a bullet's journey.

The officer had, of course, been compelled to take his sword into his left hand. He did not hold it by the hilt. He gripped it at the middle of the blade, awkwardly. Turning his eyes from the hostile wood, he looked at the sword as he held it there, and seemed puzzled as to what to do with it, where to put it. In short, this weapon had of a sudden become a strange thing to him. He looked at it in a kind of stupefaction, as if he had been endowed with a trident, a scepter, or a spade.

Finally he tried to sheathe it. To sheathe a sword held by the left hand, at the middle of the blade, in a scabbard hung at the left hip, is a feat worthy of a sawdust ring. This wounded officer engaged in a desperate struggle with the sword and the wobbling scabbard, and during the time of it he breathed like a wrestler.

But at this instant the men, the spectators, awoke from their stone-like poses and crowded forward sympathetically. The orderly-sergeant took the sword and tenderly placed it in the scabbard. At the time, he leaned nervously backward, and did not allow even his finger to brush the body of the lieutenant. A wound gives strange dignity to him who bears it. Well men shy from this new and terrible majesty. It is as if the wounded man's hand is upon the curtain which hangs before the revelations of all existence —the meaning of ants, potentates, wars, cities, sunshine, snow, a feather dropped from a bird's wing; and the power of it sheds radiance upon a bloody form, and makes the other men understand sometimes that they are little. His comrades look at him with large eyes thoughtfully. Moreover, they fear vaguely that the weight of a finger upon him might send him headlong, precipitate the tragedy, hurl him at once into the dim, gray unknown. And so the orderly-sergeant, while sheathing the sword, leaned nervously backward.

There were others who proffered assistance. One timidly presented his shoulder and asked the lieutenant if he cared to lean upon it, but the latter waved him away mournfully. He wore the look of one who knows he is the victim of a terrible disease and understands his helplessness. He again stared over the breastwork at the forest, and then, turning, went slowly rearward. He held his right wrist tenderly in his left hand as if the wounded arm was made of very brittle glass.

And the men in silence stared at the wood, then at the departing lieutenant; then at the wood, then at the lieutenant.

As the wounded officer passed from the line of battle, he was enabled to see many things which as a participant in the fight were unknown to him. He saw a general on a black horse gazing over the lines of blue infantry at the green woods which veiled his problems. An aide galloped furiously, dragged his horse suddenly to a halt, saluted, and presented a paper. It was, for a wonder, precisely like a historical painting.

To the rear of the general and his staff a group, composed of a bugler, two or three orderlies, and the bearer of the corps standard, all upon maniacal horses, were working like slaves to hold their ground, preserve their respectful interval, while the shells boomed in the air about them, and caused their chargers to make furious quivering leaps.

A battery, a tumultuous and shining mass, was swirling toward the right. The wild thud of hoofs, the cries of the riders shouting blame and praise, menace and encouragement, and, last, the roar of the wheels, the slant of the glistening guns, brought the lieutenant to an intent pause. The battery swept in curves that stirred the heart; it made halts as dramatic as the crash of a wave on the rocks, and when it fled onward this aggregation of wheels, levers, motors had a beautiful unity, as if it were a missile. The sound of it was a war chorus that reached into the depths of man's emotion.

The lieutenant, still holding his arm as if it were of glass, stood watching this battery until all detail of it was lost, save the figures of the riders, which rose and fell and waved lashes over the black mass.

Later, he turned his eyes toward the battle, where the shooting some-times crackled like bush-fires, sometimes sputtered with exasperating ir-regularity, and sometimes reverberated like the thunder. He saw the smoke rolling upward and saw crowds of men who ran and cheered, or stood and blazed away at the inscrutable distance.

He came upon some stragglers, and they told him how to find the field hospital. They described its exact location. In fact, these men, no longer having part in the battle, knew more of it than others. They told the per-formance of every corps, every division, the opinion of every general. The lieutenant, carrying his wounded arm rearward, looked upon them with wonder.

At the roadside a brigade was making coffee and buzzing with talk like a girls' boarding school. Several officers came out to him and inquired con-cerning things of which he knew nothing. One, seeing his arm, began to scold. "Why, man, that's no way to do. You want to fix that thing." He appropriated the lieutenant and the lieutenant's wound. He cut the sleeve and laid bare the arm, every nerve of which softly fluttered under his touch. He bound his handkerchief over the wound, scolding away in the meantime. His tone allowed one to think that he was in the habit of being wounded every day. The lieutenant hung his head, feeling, in this pres-ence, that he did not know how to be correctly wounded.

The low white tents of the hospital were grouped around an old school-house. There was here a singular commotion. In the foreground two am-bulances interlocked wheels in the deep mud. The drivers were tossing the blame of it back and forth, gesticulating and berating, while from the am-bulances, both crammed with wounded, there came an occasional groan. An interminable crowd of bandaged men were coming and going. Great numbers sat under the trees nursing heads or arms or legs. There was a dispute of some kind raging on the steps of the schoolhouse. Sitting with his back against a tree a man with a face as gray as a new army blanket was serenely smoking a corncob pipe. The lieutenant wished to rush for-ward and inform him that he was dying.

A busy surgeon was passing near the lieutenant. "Good morning," he said, with a friendly smile. Then he caught sight of the lieutenant's arm, and his face at once changed. "Well, let's have a look at it." He seemed possessed suddenly of a great contempt for the lieutenant. This wound evidently placed the latter on a very low social plane. The doctor cried out impatiently: "What mutton-head had tied it up that way anyhow?" The lieutenant answered, "Oh, a man."

When the wound was disclosed the doctor fingered it disdainfully. "Humph," he said. "You come along with me and I'll 'tend to you." His voice contained the same scorn as if he were saying: "You will have to go to jail."

The lieutenant had been very meek, but now his face flushed, and he looked into the doctor's eyes. "I guess I won't have it amputated," he said.

"Nonsense, man! Nonsense! Nonsense!" cried the doctor. "Come along, now. I won't amputate it. Come along. Don't be a baby."

"Let go of me," said the lieutenant, holding back wrathfully, his glance fixed upon the door of the old schoolhouse, as sinister to him as the portals of death.

And this is the story of how the lieutenant lost his arm. When he reached home, his sisters, his mother, his wife, sobbed for a long time at the sight of the flat sleeve. "Oh, well," he said, standing shamefaced amid these tears, "I don't suppose it matters so much as all that."

Christmas, 1899
[*The Gentlewoman*, London, pp. 24, XIV.]

SHAME*

"Don't come in here botherin' me," said the cook, intolerantly. "What with your mother bein' away on a visit, an' your father comin' home soon to lunch, I have enough on my mind—and that without bein' bothered with *you*. The kitchen is no place for little boys, anyhow. Run away, and don't be interferin' with my work." She frowned and made a grand pretense of being deep in herculean labors; but Jimmie did not run away.

"Now—they're goin' to have a picnic," he said, half audibly.

"What?"

"Now—they're goin' to have a picnic."

"Who's goin' to have a picnic?" demanded the cook, loudly. Her accent could have led one to suppose that if the projectors did not turn out to be the proper parties, she immediately would forbid this picnic.

Jimmie looked at her with more hopefulness. After twenty minutes of futile skirmishing, he had at least succeeded in introducing the subject. To her question he answered, eagerly: "Oh, everybody! Lots and lots of boys and girls. Everybody."

"Who's everybody?"

According to custom, Jimmie began to singsong through his nose in a quite indescribable fashion an enumeration of the prospective picnickers: "Willie Dalzel an' Dan Earl an' Ella Earl an' Wolcott Margate an' Reeves Margate an' Walter Phelps an' Homer Phelps an' Minnie Phelps an'—oh—

* *Whilomville Stories.*

lots more girls an'—everybody. An' their mothers an' big sisters too." Then he announced a new bit of information: "They're goin' to have a picnic."

"Well, let them," said the cook, blandly.

Jimmie fidgeted for a time in silence. At last he murmured, "I—now—I thought maybe you'd let me go."

The cook turned from her work with an air of irritation and amazement that Jimmie should still be in the kitchen. "Who's stoppin' you?" she asked, sharply. "I ain't stoppin' you, am I?"

"No," admitted Jimmie, in a low voice.

"Well, why don't you go, then? Nobody's stoppin' you."

"But," said Jimmie, "I—you—now—each fellow has got to take somethin' to eat with 'm."

"Oh ho!" cried the cook, triumphantly. "So that's it, is it? So that's what you've been shyin' round here fer, eh? Well, you may as well take yourself off without more words. What with your mother bein' away on a visit, an' your father comin' home soon to his lunch, I have enough on my mind—an' that without being bothered with *you*."

Jimmie made no reply, but moved in grief toward the door. The cook continued: "Some people in this house seem to think there's 'bout a thousand cooks in this kitchen. Where I used to work b'fore, there was some reason in 'em. I ain't a horse. A picnic!"

Jimmie said nothing, but he loitered.

"Seems as if I had enough to do, without havin' *you* come round talkin' about picnics. Nobody ever seems to think of the work I have to do. Nobody ever seems to think of it. Then they come and talk to me about picnics! What do I care about picnics?"

Jimmie loitered.

"Where I used to work b'fore, there was some reason in 'em. I never heard tell of no picnics right on top of your mother bein' away on a visit an' your father comin' home soon to his lunch. It's all foolishness."

Little Jimmie leaned his head flat against the wall and began to weep. She stared at him scornfully. "Cryin', eh? Cryin'? What are you cryin' fer?"

"N-n-nothin'," sobbed Jimmie.

There was a silence, save for Jimmie's convulsive breathing. At length the cook said: "Stop that blubberin', now. Stop it! This kitchen ain't no place fer it. Stop it!— Very well! If you don't stop, I won't give you nothin' to go to the picnic with—there!"

For the moment he could not end his tears. "You never said," he sputtered—"you never said you'd give me anything."

"An' why would I?" she cried, angrily. "Why would I—with you in here a-cryin' an' a-blubberin' an' a-bleatin' round? Enough to drive a woman crazy! I don't see how you could expect me to! The idea!"

Suddenly Jimmie announced: "I've stopped cryin'. I ain't goin' to cry no more 'tall."

"Well, then," grumbled the cook—"well, then, stop it. I've got enough on my mind." It chanced that she was making for luncheon some salmon croquettes. A tin still half full of pinky prepared fish was beside her on the table. Still grumbling, she seized a loaf of bread and, wielding a knife, she cut from this loaf four slices, each of which was as big as a six-shilling novel. She profligately spread them with butter, and jabbing the point of her knife into the salmon tin she brought up bits of salmon, which she flung and flattened upon the bread. Then she crashed the pieces of bread together in pairs, much as one would clash cymbals. There was no doubt in her own mind but that she had created two sandwiches.

"There," she cried. "That'll do you all right. Lemme see. What'll I put 'em in? There—I've got it." She thrust the sandwiches into a small pail and jammed on the lid.

Jimmie was ready for the picnic. "Oh, thank you, Mary!" he cried, joyfully, and in a moment he was off, running swiftly.

The picnickers had started nearly half an hour earlier, owing to his inability to quickly attack and subdue the cook, but he knew that the rendezvous was in the grove of tall, pillarlike hemlocks and pines that grew on a rocky knoll at the lake shore. His heart was very light as he sped, swinging his pail. But a few minutes previously his soul had been gloomed in despair; now he was happy. He was going to the picnic, where privilege of participation was to be bought by the contents of the little tin pail.

When he arrived in the outskirts of the grove he heard a merry clamor, and when he reached the top of the knoll he looked down the slope upon a scene which almost made his little breast burst with joy. They actually had two campfires! Two campfires! At one of them Mrs. Earl was making something—chocolate, no doubt—and at the other a young lady in white duck and a sailor hat was dropping eggs into boiling water. Other grown-up people had spread a white cloth and were laying upon it things from baskets. In the deep cool shadow of the trees the children scurried, laughing. Jimmie hastened forward to join his friends.

Homer Phelps caught first sight of him. "Ho!" he shouted; "here comes Jimmie Trescott! Come on, Jimmie; you be on our side!" The children had divided themselves into two bands for some purpose of play. The others of Homer Phelps's party loudly endorsed his plan. "Yes, Jimmie, you be on *our* side." Then arose the usual dispute. "Well, we got the weakest side."

" 'Tain't any weaker'n ours."

Homer Phelps suddenly started and, looking hard, said, "What you got in the pail, Jim?"

Jimmie answered, somewhat uneasily, "Got m' lunch in it."

Instantly that brat of a Minnie Phelps simply tore down the sky with her shrieks of derision. "Got his *lunch* in it! In a *pail!*" She ran screaming to her mother. "Oh, mamma! Oh, mamma! Jimmie Trescott's got his picnic in a pail!"

Now there was nothing in the nature of this fact to particularly move the others—notably the boys, who were not competent to care if he had brought his luncheon in a coal bin; but such is the instinct of childish society that they all immediately moved away from him. In a moment he had been made a social leper. All old intimacies were flung into the lake, so to speak. They dared not compromise themselves. At safe distances the boys shouted, scornfully: "Huh! Got his picnic in a pail!" Never again during that picnic did the little girls speak of him as Jimmie Trescott. His name now was Him.

His mind was dark with pain as he stood, the hang-dog, kicking the gravel, and muttering as defiantly as he was able, "Well, I can have it in a pail if I want to." This statement of freedom was of no importance, and he knew it, but it was the only idea in his head.

He had been baited at school for being detected in writing a letter to little Cora, the angel child, and he had known how to defend himself, but this situation was in no way similar. This was a social affair, with grown people on all sides. It would be sweet to catch the Margate twins, for instance, and hammer them into a state of bleating respect for his pail; but that was a matter for the jungles of childhood, where grown folk seldom penetrated. He could only glower.

The amiable voice of Mrs. Earl suddenly called: "Come, children! Everything's ready!" They scampered away, glancing back for one last gloat at Jimmie standing there with his pail.

He did not know what to do. He knew that the grown folk expected him at the spread, but if he approached he would be greeted by a shameful chorus from the children—more especially from some of those damnable little girls. Still, luxuries beyond all dreaming were heaped on that cloth. One could not forget them. Perhaps if he crept up modestly, and was very gentle and very nice to the little girls, they would allow him peace. Of course it had been dreadful to come with a pail to such a grand picnic, but they might forgive him.

Oh no, they would not! He knew them better. And then suddenly he remembered with what delightful expectations he had raced to this grove, and self-pity overwhelmed him, and he thought he wanted to die and make every one feel sorry.

The young lady in white duck and a sailor hat looked at him, and then spoke to her sister, Mrs. Earl. "Who's that hovering in the distance, Emily?"

Mrs. Earl peered. "Why, it's Jimmie Trescott! Jimmie, come to the picnic! Why don't you come to the picnic, Jimmie?" He began to sidle toward the cloth.

But at Mrs. Earl's call there was another outburst from many of the children. "He's got his picnic in a pail! In a *pail!* Got it in a pail!"

Minnie Phelps was a shrill fiend. "Oh, mamma, he's got it in that pail! See! Isn't it funny? Isn't it dreadful funny?"

"What ghastly prigs children are, Emily!" said the young lady. "They are spoiling that boy's whole day, breaking his heart, the little cats! I think I'll go over and talk to him."

"Maybe you had better not," answered Mrs. Earl, dubiously. "Somehow these things arrange themselves. If you interfere, you are likely to prolong everything."

"Well, I'll try, at least," said the young lady.

At the second outburst against him Jimmie had crouched down by a tree, half hiding behind it, half pretending that he was not hiding behind it. He turned his sad gaze toward the lake. The bit of water seen through the shadows seemed perpendicular, a slate-colored wall. He heard a noise near him, and turning he perceived the young lady looking down at him. In her hand she held plates. "May I sit near you?" she asked, coolly.

Jimmie could hardly believe his ears. After disposing herself and the plates upon the pine needles, she made brief explanation. "They're rather crowded, you see, over there. I don't like to be crowded at a picnic, so I thought I'd come here. I hope you don't mind."

Jimmie made haste to find his tongue. "Oh, I don't mind! I *like* to have you here." The ingenuous emphasis made it appear that the fact of his liking to have her there was in the nature of a law-dispelling phenomenon, but she did not smile.

"How large is that lake?" she asked.

Jimmie, falling into the snare, at once began to talk in the manner of a proprietor of the lake. "Oh, it's almost twenty miles long, an' in one place it's almost four miles wide! an' it's *deep* too—awful deep—an' it's got real steamboats on it, an'—oh—lots of other boats, an'—an'—an'—"

"Do you go out on it sometimes?"

"Oh, lots of times! My father's got a boat," he said, eyeing her to note the effect of his words.

She was correctly pleased and struck with wonder. "Oh, has he?" she cried, as if she never before had heard of a man owning a boat.

Jimmie continued: "Yes, an' it's a grea' big boat, too, with sails, real sails; an' sometimes he takes me out in her too; an' once he took me fishin', an' we had sandwiches, plenty of 'em, an' my father he drank beer right out of the bottle—*right out of the bottle!*"

The young lady was properly overwhelmed by this amazing intelligence.

Jimmie saw the impression he had created, and he enthusiastically resumed his narrative: "An' after, he let me throw the bottles in the water, and I throwed 'em 'way, 'way, 'way out. An' they sank, an'—never comed up," he concluded, dramatically.

His face was glorified; he had forgotten all about the pail; he was absorbed in this communion with a beautiful lady who was so interested in what he had to say.

She indicated one of the plates, and said, indifferently: "Perhaps you would like some of those sandwiches. I made them. Do you like olives? And there's a deviled egg. I made that also."

"Did you really?" said Jimmie, politely. His face gloomed for a moment because the pail was recalled to his mind, but he timidly possessed himself of a sandwich.

"Hope you are not going to scorn my deviled egg," said his goddess. "I am very proud of it." He did not; he scorned little that was on the plate.

Their gentle intimacy was ineffable to the boy. He thought he had a friend, a beautiful lady, who liked him more than she did anybody at the picnic, to say the least. This was proved by the fact that she had flung aside the luxuries of the spread cloth to sit with him, the exile. Thus early did he fall a victim to woman's wiles.

"Where do you live?" he asked, suddenly.

"Oh, a long way from here! In New York."

His next question was put very bluntly. "Are you married?"

"Oh, no!" she answered, gravely.

Jimmie was silent for a time, during which he glanced shyly and furtively up at her face. It was evident that he was somewhat embarrassed. Finally he said, "When I grow up to be a man—"

"Oh, that is some time yet!" said the beautiful lady.

"But when I *do*, I—I should like to marry you."

"Well, I will remember it," she answered; "but don't talk of it now, because it's such a long time; and—I wouldn't wish you to consider yourself bound." She smiled at him.

He began to brag. "When I grow up to be a man, I'm goin' to have lots an' lots of money, an' I'm goin' to have a grea' big house, an' a horse an' a shotgun, an' lots an' lots of books 'bout elephants an' tigers, an' lots an' lots of ice cream an' pie an'—caramels." As before, she was impressed; he could see it. "An' I'm goin' to have lots an' lots of children—'bout three hundred, I guess—an' there won't none of 'em be girls. They'll all be boys—like me."

"Oh, my!" she said.

His garment of shame was gone from him. The pail was dead and well buried. It seemed to him that months elapsed as he dwelt in happiness near the beautiful lady and trumpeted his vanity.

At last there was a shout. "Come on! we're going home." The picnickers trooped out of the grove. The children wished to resume their jeering, for Jimmie still gripped his pail, but they were restrained by the circumstances. He was walking at the side of the beautiful lady.

During this journey he abandoned many of his habits. For instance, he never traveled without skipping gracefully from crack to crack between the stones, or without pretending that he was a train of cars, or without some mumming device of childhood. But now he behaved with dignity. He made no more noise than a little mouse. He escorted the beautiful lady to the gate of the Earl home, where he awkwardly, solemnly, and wistfully shook hands in good-bye. He watched her go up the walk; the door clanged.

On his way home he dreamed. One of these dreams was fascinating. Supposing the beautiful lady was his teacher in school! Oh, my! wouldn't he be a good boy, sitting like a statuette all day long, and knowing every lesson to perfection, and—everything. And then supposing that a boy should sass her. Jimmie painted himself waylaying that boy on the homeward road, and the fate of the boy was a thing to make strong men cover their eyes with their hands. And she would like him more and more—more and more. And he—he would be a little god.

But as he was entering his father's grounds an appalling recollection came to him. He was returning with the bread-and-butter and the salmon untouched in the pail! He could imagine the cook, nine feet tall, waving her fist. "An' so that's what I took trouble for, is it? So's you could bring it back? So's you could bring it back?" He skulked toward the house like a marauding bushranger. When he neared the kitchen door he made a desperate rush past it, aiming to gain the stables and there secrete his guilt. He was nearing them, when a thunderous voice hailed him from the rear: "Jimmie Trescott, where you goin' with that pail?"

It was the cook. He made no reply, but plunged into the shelter of the stables. He whirled the lid from the pail and dashed its contents beneath a heap of blankets. Then he stood panting, his eyes on the door. The cook did not pursue, but she was bawling: "Jimmie Trescott, what you doin' with that pail?"

He came forth, swinging it. "Nothin'," he said, in virtuous protest.

"I know better," she said, sharply, as she relieved him of his curse.

In the morning Jimmie was playing near the stable, when he heard a shout from Peter Washington, who attended Dr. Trescott's horse: "Jim! Oh, Jim!"

"What?"

"Come yah."

Jimmie went reluctantly to the door of the stable, and Peter Washington asked: "Wut's dish yer fish an' brade doin' unner dese yer blankups?"

"I don't know. I didn't have nothin' to do with it," answered Jimmie, indignantly.

"Don' tell *me!*" cried Peter Washington, as he flung it all away—"don' tell *me!* When I fin' fish an' brade unner dese yer blankups, I don' go an' think dese yer ho'ses er yer pop's put 'em. I *know*. An' if I caitch enny more dish yer fish an' brade in dish yer stable, *I'll* tell yer pop."

January, 1900
[*Harper's Magazine*, Vol. 100, pp. 320–324.]

THE CARRIAGE-LAMPS*

It was the fault of a small nickel-plated revolver, a most incompetent weapon, which, wherever one aimed, would fling the bullet as the devil willed, and no man, when about to use it, could tell exactly what was in store for the surrounding country. This treasure had been acquired by Jimmie Trescott after arduous bargaining with another small boy. Jimmie wended homeward, patting his hip pocket at every three paces.

Peter Washington, working in the carriage-house, looked out upon him with a shrewd eye. "Oh, Jim," he called, "wut you got in yer hind pocket?"

"Nothin'," said Jimmie, feeling carefully under his jacket to make sure that the revolver wouldn't fall out.

Peter chuckled. "S'more foolishness, I raikon. You gwine be hung one day, Jim, you keep up all dish yer nonsense."

Jimmie made no reply, but went into the back garden, where he hid the revolver in a box under a lilac bush. Then he returned to the vicinity of Peter, and began to cruise to and fro in the offing, showing all the signals of one wishing to open treaty. "Pete," he said, "how much does a box of cartridges cost?"

Peter raised himself violently, holding in one hand a piece of harness, and in the other an old rag. "Ca'tridgers! *Ca'tridgers!* Lan' sake! wut the kid want with ca'tridgers? Knew it! Knew it! Come home er-holdin' on to his hind pocket like he got money in it. An' now he want ca'tridgers."

Jimmie, after viewing with dismay the excitement caused by his question, began to move warily out of the reach of a possible hostile movement.

"Ca'tridgers!" continued Peter, in scorn and horror. "Kid like you! No bigger'n er minute! Look yah, Jim, you done been swappin' round, an' you done got hol' of er pistol!" The charge was dramatic.

The wind was almost knocked out of Jimmie by this display of Peter's

* *Whilomville Stories.*

terrible miraculous power, and as he backed away his feeble denials were more convincing than a confession.

"I'll tell yer pop!" cried Peter, in virtuous grandeur. "I'll tell yer pop!"

In the distance Jimmie stood appalled. He knew not what to do. The dread adult wisdom of Peter Washington had laid bare the sin, and disgrace stared at Jimmie.

There was a whirl of wheels, and a high, lean trotting-mare spun Doctor Trescott's buggy toward Peter, who ran forward busily. As the doctor climbed out, Peter, holding the mare's head, began his denunciation: "Docteh, I gwine tell on Jim. He come home er-holdin' on to his hind pocket, an' proud like he won a tuhkey-raffle, an' I sure know what he been up to, an' I done challenge him, an' he nev' say he didn't."

"Why, what do you mean?" said the doctor. "What's this, Jimmie?"

The boy came forward, glaring wrathfully at Peter. In fact, he suddenly was so filled with rage at Peter that he forgot all precautions. "It's about a pistol," he said, bluntly. "I've got a pistol. I swapped for it."

"I done tol' 'im his pop wouldn' stand no fiah-awms, an' him a kid like he is. I done tol' 'im. Lan' sake! he strut like he was a soldier! Come in yere proud, an' er-holdin' on to his hind pocket. He think he was Jesse James, I raikon. But I done tol' 'im his pop stan' no sech foolishness. First thing—*blam*—he shoot his haid off. No, seh, he too tinety t' come in yere er-struttin' like he jest bought Main Street. I tol' 'im. I done tol' 'im—shawp. I don' wanter be loafin' round dis yer stable if Jim he gwine go shootin' round an' shootin' round—*blim—blam—blim—blam!* No, seh. I retiahs. I retiahs. It's all right if er grown man got er gun, but ain't no kids come foolishin' round *me* with fiah-awms. No, seh. I retiahs."

"Oh, be quiet, Peter!" said the doctor. "Where is this thing, Jimmie?"

The boy went sulkily to the box under the lilac bush and returned with the revolver. "Here 'tis," he said, with a glare over his shoulder at Peter. The doctor looked at the silly weapon in critical contempt.

"It's not much of a thing, Jimmie, but I don't think you are quite old enough for it yet. I'll keep it for you in one of the drawers of my desk."

Peter Washington burst out proudly: "I done tol' 'im th' docteh wouldn' stan' no traffickin' round yere with fiah-awms. I done tol' 'im."

Jimmie and his father went together into the house, and as Peter unharnessed the mare he continued his comments on the boy and the revolver. He was not cast down by the absence of hearers. In fact, he usually talked better when there was no one to listen save the horses. But now his observations bore small resemblance to his earlier and public statements. Admiration and the keen family pride of a Southern negro who has been long in one place were now in his tone.

"That boy! He's er devil! When he get to be er man—wow! He'll jes' take an' make things whirl round yere. Raikon we'll all take er back seat when he come erlong er-raisin' Cain."

He had unharnessed the mare, and with his back bent was pushing the buggy into the carriage-house.

"Er pistol! An' him no bigger than er minute!"

A small stone whizzed past Peter's head and clattered on the stable. He hastily dropped all occupation and struck a curious attitude. His right knee was almost up to his chin, and his arms were wreathed protectingly about his head. He had not looked in the direction from which the stone had come, but he had begun immediately to yell: "You Jim! Quit! Quit, I tell yer, Jim! Watch out! You gwine break somethin', Jim!"

"Yah!" taunted the boy, as with the speed and ease of a light-cavalry-man he maneuvered in the distance. "Yah! Told on me, did you! Told on me, hey! There! How do you like that?" The missiles resounded against the stable.

"Watch out, Jim! You gwine break something, Jim, I tell yer! Quit yer foolishness, Jim! Ow! Watch out, boy! I—"

There was a crash. With diabolic ingenuity, one of Jimmie's pebbles had entered the carriage-house and had landed among a row of carriage-lamps on a shelf, creating havoc which was apparently beyond all reason of physical law. It seemed to Jimmie that the racket of falling glass could have been heard in an adjacent county.

Peter was a prophet who after persecution was suffered to recall every-thing to the mind of the persecutor. "*There!* Knew it! Knew it! *Now* I raikon you'll quit. Hi! jes' look ut dese yer lamps! Fer lan' sake! Oh, now yer pop jes' break ev'ry bone in yer body!"

In the doorway of the kitchen the cook appeared with a startled face. Jimmie's father and mother came suddenly out on the front veranda. "What was that noise?" called the doctor.

Peter went forward to explain. "Jim he was er-heavin' rocks at me, doc-teh, an' erlong come one rock an' go *blam* inter all th' lamps an' jes' skitter 'em t' bits. I declayah—"

Jimmie, half blinded with emotion, was nevertheless aware of a light-ning glance from his father, a glance which cowed and frightened him to the ends of his toes. He heard the steady but deadly tones of his father in a fury: "Go into the house and wait until I come."

Bowed in anguish, the boy moved across the lawn and up the steps. His mother was standing on the veranda still gazing toward the stable. He loitered in the faint hope that she might take some small pity on his state. But she could have heeded him no less if he had been invisible. He entered the house.

When the doctor returned from his investigation of the harm done by

Jimmie's hand, Mrs. Trescott looked at him anxiously, for she knew that he was concealing some volcanic impulses. "Well?" she asked.

"It isn't the lamps," he said at first. He seated himself on the rail. "I don't know what we are going to do with that boy. It isn't so much the lamps as it is the other thing. He was throwing stones at Peter because Peter told me about the revolver. What are we going to do with him?"

"I'm sure I don't know," replied the mother. "We've tried almost everything. Of course much of it is pure animal spirits. Jimmie is not naturally vicious—"

"Oh, I know," interrupted the doctor, impatiently. "Do you suppose, when the stones were singing about Peter's ears, he cared whether they were flung by a boy who was naturally vicious or a boy who was not? The question might interest him afterward, but at the time he was mainly occupied in dodging these effects of pure animal spirits."

"Don't be too hard on the boy, Ned. There's lots of time yet. He's so young yet, and—I believe he gets most of his naughtiness from that wretched Dalzel boy. That Dalzel boy—well, he's simply awful!" Then, with true motherly instinct to shift blame from her own boy's shoulders, she proceeded to sketch the character of the Dalzel boy in lines that would have made that talented young vagabond stare. It was not admittedly her feeling that the doctor's attention should be diverted from the main issue and his indignation divided among the camps, but presently the doctor felt himself burn with wrath for the Dalzel boy.

"Why don't you keep Jimmie away from him?" he demanded. "Jimmie has no business consorting with abandoned little predestined jailbirds like him. If I catch him on the place I'll box his ears."

"It is simply impossible, unless we kept Jimmie shut up all the time," said Mrs. Trescott. "I can't watch him every minute of the day, and the moment my back is turned, he's off."

"I should think those Dalzel people would hire somebody to bring up their child for them," said the doctor. "They don't seem to know how to do it themselves."

Presently you would have thought from the talk that one Willie Dalzel had been throwing stones at Peter Washington because Peter Washington had told Doctor Trescott that Willie Dalzel had come into possession of a revolver.

In the meantime Jimmie had gone into the house to await the coming of his father. He was in a rebellious mood. He had not intended to destroy the carriage-lamps. He had been merely hurling stones at a creature whose perfidy deserved such action, and the hitting of the lamps had been merely another move of the great conspirator Fate to force one Jimmie Trescott into dark and troublous ways. The boy was beginning to find the world a bitter place. He couldn't win appreciation for a single virtue; he could only achieve quick, rigorous punishment for his misdemeanors. Everything was an enemy. Now there were those silly old lamps—what were they doing up on that shelf, anyhow? It would have been just as easy for them at the time to have been in some other place. But no; there they had been, like the crowd that is passing under the wall when the mason for the first time in twenty years lets fall a brick. Furthermore, the flight of that stone had been perfectly unreasonable. It had been a sort of freak in physical law. Jimmie understood that he might have thrown stones from the same fatal spot for an hour without hurting a single lamp. He was a victim—that was it. Fate had conspired with the detail of his environment to simply hound him into a grave or into a cell.

But who would understand? Who would understand? And here the boy turned his mental glance in every direction, and found nothing but what was to him the black of cruel ignorance. Very well; some day they would—

From somewhere out in the street he heard a peculiar whistle of two notes. It was the common signal of the boys in the neighborhood, and, judging from the direction of the sound, it was apparently intended to summon him. He moved immediately to one of the windows of the sitting room. It opened upon a part of the grounds remote from the stables and cut off from the veranda by a wing. He perceived Willie Dalzel loitering in the street. Jimmie whistled the signal after having pushed up the window sash some inches. He saw the Dalzel boy turn and regard him, and then call several other boys. They stood in a group and gestured. These gestures plainly said: "Come out. We've got something on hand." Jimmie sadly shook his head.

But they did not go away. They held a long consultation. Presently Jimmie saw the intrepid Dalzel boy climb the fence and begin to creep among the shrubbery, in elaborate imitation of an Indian scout. In time he arrived under Jimmie's window, and raised his face to whisper: "Come on out! We're going on a bear-hunt."

A bear-hunt! Of course Jimmie knew that it would not be a real bear-hunt, but would be a sort of carouse of pretension and big talking and preposterous lying and valor, wherein each boy would strive to have himself called Kit Carson by the others. He was profoundly affected. However, the parental word was upon him, and he could not move. "No," he answered, "I can't. I've got to stay in."

"Are you a prisoner?" demanded the Dalzel boy, eagerly.

"No-o—yes—I s'pose I am."

The other lad became much excited, but he did not lose his wariness. "Don't you want to be rescued?"

"Why—no—I dun'no'," replied Jimmie, dubiously.

Willie Dalzel was indignant. "Why, of course you want to be rescued! We'll rescue you. I'll go and get my men." And thinking this a good sentence, he repeated, pompously, "I'll go and get my men." He began to crawl away, but when he was distant some ten paces he turned to say: "Keep up a stout heart. Remember that you have friends who will be faithful unto death. The time is not now far off when you will again view the blessed sunlight."

The poetry of these remarks filled Jimmie with ecstasy, and he watched eagerly for the coming of the friends who would be faithful unto death. They delayed some time, for the reason that Willie Dalzel was making a speech.

"Now, men," he said, "our comrade is a prisoner in yon—in yond—in that there fortress. We must to the rescue. Who volunteers to go with me?" He fixed them with a stern eye.

There was a silence, and then one of the smaller boys remarked, "If Doc Trescott ketches us trackin' over his lawn—"

Willie Dalzel pounced upon the speaker and took him by the throat. The two presented a sort of burlesque of the woodcut on the cover of a dime novel which Willie had just been reading—*The Red Captain: A Tale of the Pirates of the Spanish Main.*

"You are a coward!" said Willie, through his clenched teeth.

"No, I ain't, Willie," piped the other, as best he could.

"I say you are," cried the great chieftain, indignantly. "Don't tell *me* I'm a liar." He relinquished his hold upon the coward and resumed his speech. "You know me, men. Many of you have been my followers for long years. You saw me slay Six-handed Dick with my own hand. You know I never falter. Our comrade is a prisoner in the cruel hands of our enemies. Aw, Pete Washington? He dassen't. My pa says if Pete ever troubles me he'll brain 'im. Come on! To the rescue! Who will go with me to the rescue? Aw, come on! What are you afraid of?"

It was another instance of the power of eloquence upon the human mind. There was only one boy who was not thrilled by this oration, and he was a boy whose favorite reading had been of the road agents and gunfighters of the great West, and he thought the whole thing should be conducted in the Deadwood Dick manner. This talk of a "comrade" was silly; "pard" was the proper word. He resolved that he would make a show of being a pirate, and keep secret the fact that he really was Hold-up Harry, the Terror of the Sierras.

But the others were knit close in piratical bonds. One by one they climbed the fence at a point hidden from the house by tall shrubs. With many a low-breathed caution they went upon their perilous adventure.

Jimmie was grown tired of waiting for his friends who would be faithful unto death. Finally he decided that he would rescue himself. It would be a gross breach of rule, but he couldn't sit there all the rest of the day waiting for his faithful-unto-death friends. The window was only five feet from the ground. He softly raised the sash and threw one leg over the sill. But at the same time he perceived his friends snaking among the bushes. He withdrew his leg and waited, seeing that he was now to be rescued in an orthodox way. The brave pirates came nearer and nearer.

Jimmie heard a noise of a closing door, and turning he saw his father in the room, looking at him and the open window in angry surprise. Boys never faint, but Jimmie probably came as near to it as may the average boy.

"What's all this?" asked the doctor, staring. Involuntarily Jimmie glanced over his shoulder through the window. His father saw the creeping figures. "What are those boys doing?" he said, sharply, and he knit his brows.

"Nothin'."

"Nothing! Don't tell me that. Are they coming here to the window?"

"Y-e-s, sir."

"What for?"

"To—to see me."

"What about?"

"About—about nothin'."

"What about?"

Jimmie knew that he could conceal nothing. He said, "They're comin' to—to—to rescue me." He began to whimper.

The doctor sat down heavily.

"What? To rescue you?" he gasped.

"Y-yes, sir."

The doctor's eyes began to twinkle. "Very well," he said presently. "I will sit here and observe this rescue. And on no account do you warn them that I am here. Understand?"

Of course Jimmie understood. He had been mad to warn his friends, but his father's mere presence had frightened him from doing it. He stood trembling at the window, while the doctor stretched in an easy-chair near at hand. They waited. The doctor could tell by his son's increasing agitation that the great moment was near. Suddenly he heard Willie Dalzel's voice hiss out a word: "S-s-silence!" Then the same voice addressed Jimmie at the window: "Good cheer, my comrade. The time is now at hand. I have come. Never did the Red Captain turn his back on a friend. One minute more and you will be free. Once aboard my gallant craft and you can bid defiance to your haughty enemies. Why don't you hurry up? What are you standin' there lookin' like a cow for?"

"I—er—now—you—" stammered Jimmie.

Here Hold-up Harry, the Terror of the Sierras, evidently concluded that Willie Dalzel had had enough of the premier part, so he said: "Brace up, pard. Don't ye turn white-livered now, fer ye know that Hold-up Harry, the Terrar of the Sarahs, ain't the man ter—"

"Oh, stop it!" said Willie Dalzel. "He won't understand that, you know. He's a pirate. Now, Jimmie, come on. Be of light heart, my comrade. Soon you—"

"I 'low arter all this here long time in jail ye thought ye had no friends mebbe, but I tell ye Hold-up Harry, the Terrar of the Sarahs—"

"A boat is waitin'—"

"I have ready a trusty horse—"

Willie Dalzel could endure his rival no longer.

"Look here, Henry, you're spoilin' the whole thing. We're all pirates, don't you see, and you're a pirate too."

"I ain't a pirate. I'm Hold-up Harry, the Terrar of the Sarahs."

"You ain't, I say," said Willie, in despair. "You're spoilin' everything, you are. All right, now. You wait. I'll fix you for this, see if I don't! Oh, come on, Jimmie. A boat awaits us at the foot of the rocks. In one short hour you'll be free for ever from your ex—excwable enemies, and their vile plots. Hasten, for the dawn approaches."

The suffering Jimmie looked at his father, and was surprised at what he saw. The doctor was doubled up like a man with the colic. He was breathing heavily. The boy turned again to his friends. "I—now—look here," he began, stumbling among the words. "You—I—I don't think I'll be rescued today."

The pirates were scandalized. "What?" they whispered, angrily. "Ain't you goin' to be rescued? Well, all right for you, Jimmie Trescott. That's a nice way to act, that is!" Their upturned eyes glowered at Jimmie.

Suddenly Doctor Trescott appeared at the window with Jimmie. "Oh, go home, boys!" he gasped, but they did not hear him. Upon the instant they had whirled and scampered away like deer. The first lad to reach the fence was the Red Captain, but Hold-up Harry, the Terror of the Sierras, was so close that there was little to choose between them.

Doctor Trescott lowered the window, and then spoke to his son in his usual quiet way. "Jimmie, I wish you would go and tell Peter to have the buggy ready at seven o'clock."

"Yes, sir," said Jimmie, and he swaggered out to the stables. "Pete, father wants the buggy ready at seven o'clock."

Peter paid no heed to this order, but with the tender sympathy of a true friend he inquired, "Hu't?"

"Hurt? Did what hurt?"

"Yer trouncin'."

"Trouncin!" said Jimmie, contemptuously. "I didn't get any trouncin'."

"No?" said Peter. He gave Jimmie a quick shrewd glance, and saw that he was telling the truth. He began to mutter and mumble over his work. "Ump! Ump! Dese yer white folks act like they think er boy's made er glass. No trouncin'! Ump!" He was consumed with curiosity to learn why Jimmie had not felt a heavy parental hand, but he did not care to lower his dignity by asking questions about it. At last, however, he reached the limits of his endurance, and in a voice pretentiously careless he asked, "Didn' yer pop take on like mad erbout des yer cay'ge-lamps?"

"Carriage-lamps?" inquired Jimmie.

"Ump."

"No, he didn't say anything about carriage-lamps—not that I remember. Maybe he did, though. Lemme see.—No, he never mentioned 'em."

February, 1900

[*Harper's Magazine*, Vol. 100, pp. 366–372.]

THE KICKING TWELFTH*

["Kim up, the Kickers!"]

The Spitzbergen army was backed by tradition of centuries of victory. In its chronicles, occasional defeats were not printed in italics, but were likely to appear as glorious stands against overwhelming odds. A favorite way to dispose of them was frankly to attribute them to the blunders of the civilian heads of government. This was very good for the army, and probably no army had more self-confidence. When it was announced that an expeditionary force was to be sent to Rostina to chastise an impudent people, a hundred barrack squares filled with excited men, and a hundred sergeant majors hurried silently through the groups, and succeeded in looking as if they were the repositories of the secrets of empire. Officers on leave sped joyfully back to their harness, and recruits were abused with unflagging devotion by every man, from colonels to privates of experience.

The Twelfth Regiment of the Line—the Kicking Twelfth—was consumed with a dread that it was not to be included in the expedition, and the regiment formed itself into an informal indignation meeting. Just as they had proved that a great outrage was about to be perpetrated, warning orders arrived to hold themselves in readiness for active service abroad—in Rostina. The barrack yard was in a flash transferred into a blue-and-buff

* *Spitzbergen Tales.*

pandemonium, and the official bugle itself hardly had power to quell the glad disturbance.

Thus it was that early in the spring the Kicking Twelfth—sixteen hundred men in service equipment—found itself crawling along a road in Rostina. They did not form part of the main force, but belonged to a column of four regiments of foot, two batteries of field guns, a battery of mountain howitzers, a regiment of horse, and a company of engineers. Nothing had happened. The long column had crawled without amusement of any kind through a broad green valley. Big white farmhouses dotted the slopes; but there was no sign of man or beast, and no smoke from the chimneys. The column was operating from its own base, and its general was expected to form a junction with the main body at a given point.

A squadron of the cavalry was fanned out ahead, scouting, and day by day the trudging infantry watched the blue uniforms of the horsemen as they came and went. Sometimes there would sound the faint thuds of a few shots, but the cavalry was unable to find anything to engage.

The Twelfth had no record of foreign service, and it could hardly be said that it had served as a unit in the great civil war, when His Majesty the King had whipped the Pretender. At that time the regiment had suffered from two opinions, so that it was impossible for either side to depend upon it. Many men had deserted to the standard of the Pretender, and a number of officers had drawn their swords for him. When the King, a thorough soldier, looked at the remnant, he saw that they lacked the spirit to be of great help to him in the tremendous battles which he was waging for his throne. And so this emaciated Twelfth was sent off to a corner of the kingdom to guard a dockyard, where some of the officers so plainly expressed their disapproval of this policy that the regiment received its steadfast name, the Kicking Twelfth.

At the time of which I am writing the Twelfth had a few veteran officers and well-bitten sergeants; but the body of the regiment was composed of men who had never heard a shot fired excepting on the rifle range. But it was an experience for which they longed, and when the moment came for the corps' cry—"Kim up, the Kickers"—there was not likely to be a man who would not go tumbling after his leaders.

Young Timothy Lean was a second lieutenant in the first company of the third battalion, and just at this time he was pattering along at the flank of the men, keeping a fatherly lookout for boots that hurt and packs that sagged. He was extremely bored. The mere faraway sound of desultory shooting was not war as he had been led to believe it.

It did not appear that behind that freckled face and under that red hair there was a mind which dreamed of blood. He was not extremely anxious to kill somebody, but he was very fond of soldiering—it had been the career of his father and of his grandfather—and he understood that the profession of arms lost much of its point unless a man shot at people and had people shoot at him. Strolling in the sun through a practically deserted country might be a proper occupation for a divinity student on a vacation, but the soul of Timothy Lean was in revolt at it. Sometimes at night he would go morosely to the camp of the cavalry and hear the infant subalterns laughingly exaggerate the comedy side of the adventures which they had had out with small patrols far ahead. Lean would sit and listen in glum silence to these tales, and dislike the young officers—many of them old military school friends—for having had experience in modern warfare.

"Anyhow," he said savagely, "presently you'll be getting into a lot of trouble, and then the Foot will have to come along and pull you out. We always do. That's history."

"Oh, we can take care of ourselves," said the Cavalry, with good-natured understanding of his mood.

But the next day even Lean blessed the cavalry, for excited troopers came whirling back from the front, bending over their speeding horses, and shouting wildly and hoarsely for the infantry to clear the way. Men yelled at them from the roadside as courier followed courier, and from the distance ahead sounded in quick succession six booms from field guns. The information possessed by the couriers was no longer precious. Everybody knew what a battery meant when it spoke. The bugles cried out, and the long column jolted into a halt. Old Colonel Sponge went bouncing in his saddle back to see the general, and the regiment sat down in the grass by the roadside and waited in silence. Presently the second squadron of the cavalry trotted off along the road in a cloud of dust, and in due time old Colonel Sponge came bouncing back and palavered his three majors and his adjutant. Then there was more talk by the majors, and gradually through the correct channels spread information which in due time reached Timothy Lean.

The enemy, 5000 strong, occupied a pass at the head of the valley some four miles beyond. They had three batteries well posted. Their infantry was entrenched. The ground in their front was crossed and lined with many ditches and hedges; but the enemy's batteries were so posted that it was doubtful if a ditch would ever prove convenient as shelter for the Spitzbergen infantry.

There was a fair position for the Spitzbergen artillery 2300 yards from the enemy. The cavalry had succeeded in driving the enemy's skirmishers back upon the main body, but, of course, had only tried to worry them a little. The position was almost inaccessible on the enemy's right, owing to steep hills which had been crowned by small parties of infantry. The enemy's left, although guarded by a much larger force, was approachable, and might be flanked. This was what the cavalry had to say, and it added briefly a report of two troopers killed and five wounded.

Whereupon Major General Richie, commanding a force of 7500 men of His Majesty of Spitzbergen, set in motion, with a few simple words, the machinery which would launch his army at the enemy. The Twelfth understood the orders when they saw the smart young aide approaching old Colonel Sponge, and they rose as one man, apparently afraid that they would be late. There was a clank of accoutrements. Men shrugged their shoulders tighter against their packs, and thrusting their thumbs between their belts and their tunics, they wriggled into a closer fit with regard to the heavy ammunition equipment. It is curious to note that almost every man took off his cap, and looked contemplatively into it as if to read a maker's name. Then they replaced their caps with great care. There was little talking, and it was not observable that a single soldier handed a token or left a comrade with a message to be delivered in case he should be killed. They did not seem to think of being killed; they seemed absorbed in a desire to know what would happen, and how it would look when it was happening. Men glanced continually at their officers in a plain desire to be quick to understand the very first order that would be given; and officers looked gravely at their men, measuring them, feeling their temper, worrying about them.

A bugle called; there were sharp cries; and the Kicking Twelfth was off to battle.

The regiment had the right of line in the infantry brigade, and as the men tramped noisily along the white road, every eye was strained ahead; but, after all, there was nothing to be seen but a dozen farms—in short, a countryside. It resembled the scenery in Spitzbergen; every man in the Kicking Twelfth had often confronted a dozen such farms with a composure which amounted to indifference. But still down the road came galloping troopers, who delivered information to Colonel Sponge and then galloped on. In time the Twelfth came to the top of a rise, and below them on the plain was the heavy black streak of a Spitzbergen squadron, and behind the squadron loomed the gray bare hill of the Rostina position.

There was a little of skirmish firing. The Twelfth reached a knoll, which the officers easily recognized as the place described by the cavalry as suitable for the Spitzbergen guns. The men swarmed up it in a peculiar formation. They resembled a crowd coming off a race track; but, nevertheless, there were no stray sheep. It was simply that the ground on which actual battles are fought is not like a chessboard. And after them came swinging a six-gun battery, the guns wagging from side to side as the long line turned out of the road, and the drivers using their whips as the leading horses scrambled at the hill. The halted Twelfth lifted its voice and spoke amiably, but with point, to the battery.

"Go on, Guns! We'll take care of you. Don't be afraid. Give it to them!" The teams—lead, swing and wheel—struggled and slipped over the steep and uneven ground; and the gunners, as they clung to their springless positions, wore their usual and natural airs of unhappiness. They made no reply to the infantry. Once upon the top of the hill, however, these guns were unlimbered in a flash, and directly the infantry could hear the loud voice of an officer drawling out the time for fuses. A moment later the first 3.2 bellowed out, and there could be heard the swish and the snarl of a fleeting shell.

Colonel Sponge and a number of officers climbed to the battery's position; but the men of the regiment sat in the shelter of the hill, like so many blindfolded people, and wondered what they would have been able to see if they had been officers. Sometimes the shells of the enemy came sweeping over the top of the hill and burst in great brown explosions in the fields to the rear. The men looked after them and laughed. To the rear could be seen also the mountain battery coming at a comic trot, with every man obviously in a deep rage with every mule. If a man can put in long service with a mule battery and come out of it with an amiable disposition, he should be presented with a medal weighing many ounces. After the mule battery came a long black winding thing, which was three regiments of Spitzbergen infantry; and at the backs of them and to the right was an inky square, which was the remaining Spitzbergen guns. General Richie and his staff clattered up the hill. The blindfolded Twelfth sat still. The inky square suddenly became a long racing line. The howitzers joined their little bark to the thunder of the guns on the hill, and the three regiments of infantry came on. The Twelfth sat still.

Of a sudden a bugle rang its warning, and the officers shouted. Some used the old cry, "Attention! Kim up, the Kickers!"—and the Twelfth knew that it had been told to go on. The majority of the men expected to see great things as soon as they rounded the shoulder of the hill; but there was nothing to be seen save a complicated plain and the gray knolls occupied by the enemy. Many company commanders in low voices worked at their men, and said things which do not appear in the written reports. They talked soothingly; they talked indignantly; and they talked always like fathers. And the men heard no sentences completely; they heard no specific direction, these wide-eyed men. They understood that there was being delivered some kind of exhortation to do as they had been taught, and they also understood that a superior intelligence was anxious over their behavior and welfare.

There was a great deal of floundering through hedges, climbing of walls, and jumping of ditches. Curiously original privates tried to find new and easier ways for themselves, instead of following the men in front of them. Officers had short fits of fury over these people. The more originality they possessed, the more likely they were to become separated from their companies. Colonel Sponge was making an exciting progress on a big charger. When the first song of the bullets came from above, the men wondered why he sat so high; the charger seemed as tall as the Eiffel Tower. But if he was high in the air, he had a fine view, and that supposedly is why people ascend the Eiffel Tower. Very often he had been a joke to them, but when they saw this fat old gentleman so coolly treating the strange new missiles which hummed in the air, it struck them suddenly that they had wronged him seriously, and that a man who could attain the command of a Spitzbergen regiment was entitled to general respect. And they gave him a sudden, quick affection—an affection that would make them follow him heartily, trustfully, grandly—this fat old gentleman, seated on a too-big horse. In a flash his tousled gray head, his short, thick legs, even his paunch, had become specially and humorously endeared to them. And this is the way of soldiers.

But still the Twelfth had not yet come to the place where tumbling bodies begin their test of the very heart of a regiment. They backed through more hedges, jumped more ditches, slid over more walls. The Rostina artillery had seemed to be asleep; but suddenly the guns aroused like dogs from their kennels, and around the Twelfth there began a wild, swift screeching. There arose cries to hurry, to come on; and, as the rifle bullets began to plunge into them, the men saw the high, formidable hills of the enemy's right, and perfectly understood that they were doomed to storm them. The cheering thing was the sudden beginning of a tremendous uproar on the enemy's left.

Every man ran, hard, tense, breathless. When they reached the foot of the hills, they thought they had won the charge already; but they were electrified to see officers above them waving their swords and yelling with anger, surprise, and shame. With a long murmurous outcry the Twelfth began to climb the hill; and as they went and fell, they could hear frenzied shouts—"Kim up, the Kickers!" The pace was slow. It was like the rising of a tide; it was determined, almost relentless in its appearance, but it was slow. If a man fell there was a chance that he would land twenty yards below the point where he was hit. The Kickers crawled, their rifles in their left hands as they pulled and tugged themselves up with their right hands. Ever arose the shout, "Kim up, the Kickers!" Timothy Lean, his face flaming, his eyes wild, yelled it back as if he were delivering the gospel.

The Kickers came up. The enemy—they had been in small force, thinking the hills safe enough from attack—retreated quickly from this preposterous advance, and not a bayonet in the Twelfth saw blood; bayonets very seldom do.

The homing of this successful charge wore an unromantic aspect. About twenty windless men suddenly arrived, and threw themselves upon the crest of the hill, and breathed. And these twenty were joined by others, and still others, until almost 1100 men of the Twelfth lay upon the hilltop, while the regiment's track was marked by body after body, in groups and singly. The first officer—perchance the first man; one never can be certain —the first officer to gain the top of the hill was Timothy Lean, and such was the situation that he had the honor to receive his colonel with a bashful salute.

The regiment knew exactly what it had done; it did not have to wait to be told by the Spitzbergen newspapers. It had taken a formidable position with the loss of about five hundred men, and it knew it. It knew, too, that it was great glory for the Kicking Twelfth; and as the men lay rolling on their bellies, they expressed their joy in a wild cry—"Kim up, the Kickers!" For a moment there was nothing but joy, and then suddenly company commanders were besieged by men who wished to go down the path of the charge and look for their mates. The answers were without the quality of mercy; they were short, snapped, quick words, "No; you can't."

The attack on the enemy's left was sounding in great rolling crashes. The shells in their flight through the air made a noise as of red-hot iron plunged into water, and stray bullets nipped near the ears of the Kickers.

The Kickers looked and saw. The battle was below them. The enemy were indicated by a long, noisy line of gossamer smoke, although there could be seen a toy battery with tiny men employed at the guns. All over the field the shrapnel was bursting, making quick bulbs of white smoke. Far away, two regiments of Spitzbergen infantry were charging, and at the distance this charge looked like a casual stroll. It appeared that small black groups of men were walking meditatively toward the Rostina entrenchments.

There would have orders been given sooner to the Twelfth, but unfortunately Colonel Sponge arrived on top of the hill without a breath of wind in his body. He could not have given an order to save the regiment from being wiped off the earth. Finally he was able to gasp out something and point at the enemy. Timothy Lean ran along the line yelling to the men to sight at 800 yards; and like a slow and ponderous machine the regiment again went to work. The fire flanked a great part of the enemy's trenches.

It could be said that there were only two prominent points of view expressed by the men after their victorious arrival on the crest. One was defined in the exulting use of the corps' cry. The other was a grief-stricken murmur which is invariably heard after a fight—"My God, we're all cut to pieces!"

Colonel Sponge sat on the ground and impatiently waited for his wind to return. As soon as it did, he arose and cried out, "Form up, and we'll charge again! We will win this battle as soon as we can hit them!" The shouts of the officers sounded wild, like men yelling on shipboard in a gale. And the obedient Kickers arose for their task. It was running downhill this time. The mob of panting men poured over the stones.

But the enemy had not been blind to the great advantage gained by the Twelfth, and they now turned upon them a desperate fire of small arms. Men fell in every imaginable way, and their accoutrements rattled on the rocky ground. Some landed with a crash, floored by some tremendous blows; others dropped gently down like sacks of meal; with others, it would positively appear that some spirit had suddenly seized them by their ankles and jerked their legs from under them. Many officers were down, but Colonel Sponge, stuttering and blowing, was still upright. He was almost the last man in the charge, but not to his shame—rather to his stumpy legs. At one time it seemed that the assault would be lost. The effect of the fire was somewhat as if a terrible cyclone were blowing in the men's faces. They wavered, lowering their heads and shouldering weakly, as if it were impossible to make headway against the wind of battle. It was the moment of despair, the moment of the heroism which comes to the chosen of the war-god.

The colonel's cry broke and screeched absolute hatred; other officers simply howled; and the men, silent, debased, seemed to tighten their muscles for one last effort. Again they pushed against this mysterious power of the air, and once more the regiment was charging. Timothy Lean, agile and strong, was well in advance; and afterward he reflected that the men who had been nearest to him were an old grizzled sergeant who would have gone to hell for the honor of the regiment, and a pie-faced lad who had been obliged to lie about his age in order to get into the army.

There was no shock of meeting. The Twelfth came down on a corner of the trenches, and as soon as the enemy had ascertained that the Twelfth was certain to arrive, they scuttled out, running close to the earth and spending no time in glances backward. In these days it is not discreet to wait for a charge to come home. You observe the charge, you attempt to stop it, and if you find that you can't, it is better to retire immediately to some other place. The Rostina soldiers were not heroes, perhaps, but they were men of sense. A maddened and badly frightened mob of Kickers came tumbling into the trench, and shot at the backs of fleeing men. And at that very moment the action was won, and won by the Kickers. The enemy's flank was entirely crippled, and, knowing this, he did not await further and more disastrous information. The Twelfth looked at themselves and knew that they had a record. They sat down and grinned patronizingly as they saw the batteries galloping to advance position to shell the retreat, and they really laughed as the cavalry swept tumultuously forward.

The Twelfth had no more concern with the battle. They had won it, and the subsequent proceedings were only amusing.

There was a call from the flank, and the men wearily adjusted themselves as General Richie, stern and grim as a Roman, looked with his straight glance at a hammered and thin and dirty line of figures which was His Majesty's Twelfth Regiment of the Line. When opposite old Colonel Sponge, a podgy figure standing at attention, the general's face set in still more grim and stern lines. He took off his helmet. "Kim up, the Kickers!" said he. He replaced his helmet and rode off. Down the cheeks of the little fat colonel rolled tears. He stood like a stone for a long moment, and wheeled in supreme wrath upon his surprised adjutant. "Delahaye, you damned fool, don't stand there staring like a monkey! Go, tell young Lean I want to see him." The adjutant jumped as if he were on springs, and went after Lean. That young officer presented himself directly, his face covered wih disgraceful smudges, and he had also torn his breeches. He had never seen the colonel in such a rage. "Lean, you young whelp! you— you're a good boy." And even as the general had turned away from the colonel, the colonel turned away from the lieutenant.

February, 1900

[*The Pall Mall Magazine*, Vol. 20, pp. 173–179.]

THE SHRAPNEL OF THEIR FRIENDS*

From over the knolls came the tiny sound of a cavalry bugle singing out the recall, and later, detached parties of His Majesty's Second Hussars came trotting back to where the Spitzbergen infantry sat complacently on the captured Rostina position. The horsemen were well pleased, and they told how they had ridden thrice through the helter-skelter of the fleeing enemy. They had ultimately been checked by the great truth that when a good enemy runs away in daylight he sooner or later finds a place where he fetches up with a jolt and turns to face the pursuit—notably if it is a cavalry pursuit. The Hussars had discreetly withdrawn, displaying no foolish pride of corps at that time.

There was a general admission that the Kicking Twelfth had taken the chief honors of the day, but the artillery added that if the guns had not

* *Spitzbergen Tales.*

shelled so accurately the Twelfth's charge could not have been made so
successfully, and the three other regiments of infantry, of course, did not
conceal their feeling that their attack on the enemy's left had withdrawn
many rifles that would have been pelting at the Twelfth. The cavalry
simply said that but for them the victory would not have been complete.

Corps' prides met each other face to face at every step, but the Kickers
smiled easily and indulgently. A few recruits bragged, but they bragged
because they were recruits. The older men did not wish it to appear that
they were surprised and rejoicing at the performance of the regiment. If
they were congratulated they simply smirked, suggesting that the ability of
the Twelfth had been long known to them, and that the charge had been
a little thing, you know, just turned off in the way of an afternoon's work.

Major General Richie encamped his troops on the position which they
had taken from the enemy. Old Colonel Sponge of the Twelfth redistributed his officers, and the losses had been so great that Timothy Lean
got command of a company. It was not much of a company. Fifty-three
smudged and sweating men faced their new commander. The company
had gone into action with a strength of eighty-six. The heart of Timothy
Lean beat high with pride. He intended to be some day a general, and if
he ever became a general, that moment of promotion was not equal in joy
to the moment when he looked at his new possession of fifty-three vagabonds. He scanned the faces, and recognized with satisfaction one old
sergeant and two bright young corporals. "Now," said he to himself, "I
have here a snug little body of men with which I can do something." In
him burned the usual fierce fire to make them the best company in the
regiment. He had adopted them; they were his men. "I will do what I can
for you," he said. "Do you the same for me."

The Twelfth bivouacked on the ridge. Little fires were built, and there
appeared among the men innumerable blackened tin cups, which were so
treasured that a faint suspicion in connection with the loss of one could
bring on the grimmest of fights. Meantime certain of the privates silently
readjusted their kits as their names were called out by the sergeants. These
were the men condemned to picket duty after a hard day of marching and
fighting. The dusk came slowly, and the color of the countless fires, spot-
ting the ridge and the plain, grew in the falling darkness. Faraway pickets
fired at something.

One by one the men's heads were lowered to the earth until the ridge
was marked by two long shadowy rows of men. Here and there an officer
sat musing in his dark cloak with a ray of a weakening fire gleaming on
his sword hilt. From the plain there came at times the sound of battery
horses moving restlessly at their tethers, and one could imagine he heard

the throaty, grumbling curse of the drivers. The moon died swiftly through flying light clouds. Faraway pickets fired at something.

In the morning the infantry and guns breakfasted to the music of a racket between the cavalry and the enemy which was taking place some miles up the valley.

The ambitious Hussars had apparently stirred some kind of a hornet's nest, and they were having a good fight with no officious friends near enough to interfere. The remainder of the army looked toward the fight musingly over the tops of tin cups. In time the column crawled lazily forward to see.

The Twelfth, as it crawled, saw a regiment deploy to the right, and saw a battery dash to take position. The cavalry jingled back grinning with pride and expecting to be greatly admired. Presently the Twelfth was bidden to take seat by the roadside and await its turn. Instantly the wise men—and there were more than three—came out of the east and announced that they had divined the whole plan. The Kicking Twelfth was to be held in reserve until the critical moment of the fight, and then they were to be sent forward to win a victory. In corroboration, they pointed to the fact that the general in command was sticking close to them, in order, they said, to give the word quickly at the proper moment. And in truth, on a small hill to the right, Major General Richie sat on his horse and used his glasses, while back of him his staff and the orderlies bestrode their champing, dancing mounts.

It is always good to look hard at a general, and the Kickers were transfixed with interest. The wise men again came out of the east and told what was inside the Richie head, but even the wise men wondered what was inside the Richie head.

Suddenly an exciting thing happened. To the left and ahead was a pounding Spitzbergen battery, and a toy suddenly appeared on the slope behind the guns. The toy was a man with a flag—the flag was white save for a square of red in the center. And this toy began to wigwag, wagwig, and it spoke to General Richie under the authority of the captain of the battery. It said: "The Eighty-eighth are being driven on my center and right."

Now, when the Kicking Twelfth had left Spitzbergen there was an average of six signalmen in each company. A proportion of these signalers had been destroyed in the first engagement, but enough remained so that the Kicking Twelfth read, as a unit, the news of the Eighty-eighth. The word ran quickly. "The Eighty-eighth are being driven on my center and right."

Richie rode to where Colonel Sponge sat aloft on his big horse, and a moment later a cry ran along the column: "Kim up, the Kickers." A large number of the men were already in the road, hitching and twisting at their belts and packs. The Kickers moved forward.

They deployed and passed in a straggling line through the battery, and to the left and right of it. The gunners called out to them carefully, telling them not to be afraid.

The scene before them was startling. They were facing a country cut up by many steep-sided ravines, and over the resultant hills were retreating little squads of the Eighty-eighth. The Twelfth laughed in its exultation. The men could now tell by the volume of fire that the Eighty-eighth were retreating for reasons which were not sufficiently expressed in the noise of the Rostina shooting. Held together by the bugle, the Kickers swarmed up the first hill and lay on the crest. Parties of the Eighty-eighth went through their lines, and the Twelfth told them coarsely its several opinions. The sights were clicked up to 600 yards, and, with a crashing volley, the regiment entered its second battle.

A thousand yards away on the right the cavalry and a regiment of infantry were creeping onward. Sponge decided not to be backward, and the bugle told the Twelfth to go ahead once more. The Twelfth charged, followed by a rabble of rallied men of the Eighty-eighth, who were crying aloud that it had been all a mistake.

A charge in these days is not a running match. Those splendid pictures of leveled bayonets dashing a headlong pace toward the closed ranks of the enemy are absurd as soon as they are mistaken for the actuality of the present. In these days charges are likely to cover at least the half of a mile, and to go at the pace exhibited in the pictures a man would be obliged to have a little steam engine inside of him.

The charge of the Kicking Twelfth somewhat resembled the advance of a great crowd of beaters who, for some reason, passionately desired to start the game. Men stumbled; men fell; men swore. There were cries: "This way!" "Come this way!" "Don't go that way!" "You can't get up that way!" Over the rocks the Twelfth scrambled, red in the face, sweating and angry. Soldiers fell because they were struck by bullets and because they had not an ounce of strength left in them. Colonel Sponge, with a face like a red cushion, was being dragged windless up the steeps by devoted and athletic men. Three of the older captains lay afar back, and swearing with their eyes because their tongues were temporarily out of service.

And yet—and yet, the speed of the charge was slow. From the position of the battery, it looked as if the Kickers were taking a walk over some extremely difficult country.

The regiment ascended a superior height, and found trenches and dead men. They took seat with the dead, satisfied with this company until they could get their wind. For thirty minutes purple-faced stragglers rejoined from the rear. Colonel Sponge looked behind him, and saw that Richie, with his staff, had approached by another route, and had evidently been near enough to see the full extent of the Kickers' exertions. Presently Richie began to pick a way for his horse toward the captured position. He disappeared in a gully between two hills.

Now it came to pass that a Spitzbergen battery on the far right took occasion to mistake the identity of the Kicking Twelfth, and the captain of these guns, not having anything to occupy him in front, directed his six 3.2's upon the ridge where the tired Kickers lay side by side with the Rostina dead. A shrapnel came swinging over the Kickers, seething and fuming. It burst directly over the trenches, and the shrapnel, of course, scattered forward, hurting nobody. But a man screamed out to his officer: "By God, sir, that is one of our own batteries!" The whole line quivered with fright. Five more shells streaked overhead, and one flung its hail into the middle of the third battalion's line, and the Kicking Twelfth shuddered to the very center of its heart and arose like one man and fled.

Colonel Sponge, fighting, frothing at the mouth, dealing blows with his fist right and left, found himself confronting a fury on horseback. Richie was as pale as death, and his eyes sent out sparks. "What does this conduct mean?" he flashed out between his fastened teeth.

Sponge could only gurgle: "The battery—the battery—the battery!"

"The battery?" cried Richie, in a voice which sounded like pistol shots. "Are you afraid of the guns you almost took yesterday? Go back there, you white-livered cowards! You swine! You dogs! Curs! Curs! Curs! Go back there!"

Most of the men halted and crouched under the lashing tongue of their maddened general. But one man found desperate speech, and yelled: "General, it is our own battery that is firing on us!"

Many say that the General's face tightened until it looked like a mask. The Kicking Twelfth retired to a comfortable place, where they were only under the fire of the Rostina artillery. The men saw a staff officer riding over the obstructions in a manner calculated to break his neck directly.

The Kickers were aggrieved, but the heart of the colonel was cut in twain. He even babbled to his majors, talking like a man who is about to die of simple rage. "Did you hear what he said to me? Did you hear what he called us? *Did you hear what he called us?*"

The majors searched their minds for words to heal a deep wound.

The Twelfth received orders to go into camp upon the hill where they had been insulted. Old Sponge looked as if he were about to knock the aide out of the saddle, but he saluted and took the regiment back to the temporary companionship of the Rostina dead.

Major General Richie never apologized to Colonel Sponge. When you are a commanding officer you do not adopt the custom of apologizing for the wrong done to your subordinates. You ride away; and they understand, and are confident of the restitution to honor. Richie never opened his stern young lips to Sponge in reference to the scene near the hill of the Rostina dead, but in time there was a general order No. 20, which spoke definitely of the gallantry of His Majesty's Twelfth regiment of the line and its colonel. In the end Sponge was given a high decoration, because he had been badly used by Richie on that day. Richie knew that it is hard for men to withstand the shrapnel of their friends.

A few days later the Kickers, marching in column on the road, came upon their friend the battery, halted in a field; and they addressed the battery, and the captain of the battery blanched to the tips of his ears. But the men of the battery told the Kickers to go to the devil—frankly, freely, placidly, told the Kickers to go to the devil.

And this story proves that it is sometimes better to be a private.

May, 1900

[*Ainslee's Magazine*, Vol. 5, pp. 303–305.]

"AND IF HE WILLS, WE MUST DIE"*
[The End of the Battle]

A sergeant, a corporal, and fourteen men of the Twelfth Regiment of the Line had been sent out to occupy a house on the main highway. They would be at least a half of a mile in advance of any other picket of their own people. Sergeant Morton was deeply angry at being sent on this duty. He said that he was overworked. There were at least two sergeants, he claimed furiously, whose turn it should have been to go on this arduous mission. He was treated unfairly; he was abused by his superiors; why did any damned fool ever join the army? As for him he would get out of it as soon as possible; he was sick of it; the life of a dog. All this he said to the corporal, who listened attentively, giving grunts of respectful assent.

On the way to this post two privates took occasion to drop to the rear and pilfer in the orchard of a deserted plantation. When the sergeant discovered this absence, he grew black with a rage which was an accumulation of all his irritations. "Run, you!" he howled. "Bring them here! I'll show them—" A private ran swiftly to the rear. The remainder of the squad began to shout nervously at the two delinquents, whose figures

* *Spitzbergen Tales.*

they could see in the deep shade of the orchard, hurriedly picking fruit from the ground and cramming it within their shirts, next to their skins. The beseeching cries of their comrades stirred the criminals more than did the barking of the sergeant. They ran to rejoin the squad, while holding their loaded bosoms, their mouths open with aggrieved explanations.

Jones faced the sergeant with a horrible cancer marked in bumps on his left side. The disease of Patterson showed quite around the front of his waist in many protuberances. "A nice pair!" said the sergeant, with sudden frigidity. "You're the kind of soldiers a man wants to choose for a dangerous outpost duty, ain't you?"

The two privates stood at attention, still looking much aggrieved. "We only—" began Jones huskily.

"Oh, you 'only'!" cried the sergeant. "Yes, you 'only.' I know all about that. But if you think you are going to trifle with me—"

A moment later the squad moved on toward its station. Behind the sergeant's back Jones and Patterson were slyly passing apples and pears to their friends while the sergeant expounded eloquently to the corporal. "You see what kind of men are in the army now. Why, when I joined the regiment it was a very different thing, I can tell you. Then a sergeant had some authority, and if a man disobeyed orders, he had a very small chance of escaping something extremely serious. But now! Good God! If I report these men, the captain will look over a lot of beastly orderly sheets and say: 'Haw, eh, well, Sergeant Morton, these men seem to have very good records; very good records, indeed. I can't be too hard on them; no, not too hard.'" Continued the sergeant: "I tell you, Flagler, the army is no place for a decent man."

Flagler, the corporal, answered with a sincerity of appreciation which with him had become a science. "I think you are right, sergeant," he answered.

Behind them the privates mumbled discreetly. "Damn this sergeant of ours! He thinks we are made of wood. I don't see any reason for all this strictness when we are on active service. It isn't like being at home in barracks! There is no great harm in a couple of men dropping out to raid an orchard of the enemy when all the world knows that we haven't had a decent meal in twenty days."

The reddened face of Sergeant Morton suddenly showed to the rear. "A little more marching and less talking," he said.

When he came to the house he had been ordered to occupy, the sergeant sniffed with disdain. "These people must have lived like cattle," he said angrily. To be sure, the place was not alluring. The ground floor had been used for the housing of cattle, and it was dark and terrible. A flight of steps led to the lofty first floor, which was denuded but respectable. The sergeant's visage lightened when he saw the strong walls of stone and cement. "Unless they turn guns on us, they will never get us out of here," he said cheerfully to the squad. The men, anxious to keep him in an amiable mood, all hurriedly grinned and seemed very appreciative and pleased. "I'll make this into a fortress," he announced. He sent Jones and Patterson, the two orchard thieves, out on sentry duty. He worked the others, then, until he could think of no more things to tell them to do. Afterward he went forth, with a major general's serious scowl, and examined the ground in front of his position. In returning he came upon a sentry, Jones, munching an apple. He sternly commanded him to throw it away.

The men spread their blankets on the floors of the bare rooms, and, putting their packs under their heads and lighting their pipes, they lived in easy peace. Bees hummed in the garden, and a scent of flowers came through the open window. A great fan-shaped bit of sunshine smote the face of one man, and he indolently cursed as he moved his primitive bed to a shadier place.

Another private explained to a comrade: "This is all nonsense anyhow. No sense in occupying this post. They—"

"But, of course," said the corporal, "when she told me herself that she cared more for me than she did for him, I wasn't going to stand any of his talk—" The corporal's listener was so sleepy that he could only grunt his sympathy.

There was a sudden little spatter of shooting. A cry from Jones rang out. With no intermediate scrambling, the sergeant leaped straight to his feet. "Now," he cried, "let us see what you are made of! If," he added bitterly, "you are made of anything!"

A man yelled, "Good God, can't you see you're all tangled up in my cartridge belt?"

Another man yelled: "Keep off my legs! Can't you walk on the floor?"

To the windows there was a blind rush of slumberous men who brushed hair from their eyes even as they made ready their rifles. Jones and Patterson came stumbling up the steps, crying dreadful information. Already the enemy's bullets were spitting and singing over the house.

The sergeant suddenly was stiff and cold with a sense of the importance of the thing. "Wait until you see one," he drawled loudly and calmly, "then shoot."

For some moments the enemy's bullets swung swifter than lightning over the house without anybody being able to discover a target. In this interval a man was shot in the throat. He gurgled, and then lay down on the floor. The blood slowly waved down the brown skin of his neck while he looked meekly at his comrades.

There was a howl. "There they are! There they come!" The rifles crack-led. A light smoke drifted idly through the rooms. There was a strong odor as if from burnt paper and the powder of firecrackers. The men were silent. Through the windows and about the house the bullets of an en-tirely invisible enemy moaned, hummed, spat, burst, and sang.

The men began to curse. "Why can't we see them?" they muttered through their teeth. The sergeant was still frigid. He answered soothingly, as if he were directly reprehensible for this behavior of the enemy. "Wait a moment. You will soon be able to see them. There! Give it to them." A little skirt of black figures had appeared in a field. It was really like shoot-ing at an upright needle from the full length of a ballroom. But the men's spirits improved as soon as the enemy—this mysterious enemy—became a tangible thing, and far off. They had believed the foe to be shooting at them from the adjacent garden.

"Now," said the sergeant ambitiously, "we can beat them off easily if you men are good enough."

A man called out in a tone of quick, great interest. "See that fellow on horseback, Bill? Isn't he on horseback? I thought he was on horseback."

There was a fusillade against another side of the house. The sergeant dashed into the room which commanded that situation. He found a dead soldier on the floor. He rushed out howling: "When was Knowles killed? When was Knowles killed? Damn it, when was Knowles killed?" It was absolutely essential to find out the exact moment this man died. A black-ened private turned upon his sergeant and demanded: "How in hell do I know?" Sergeant Morton had a sense of anger so brief that in the next second he cried: "Patterson!" He had even forgotten his vital interest in the time of Knowles's death.

"Yes?" said Patterson, his face set with some deep-rooted quality of determination. Still, he was a mere farm boy.

"Go in to Knowles's window and shoot at those people," said the sergeant hoarsely. Afterward he coughed. Some of the fumes of the fight had made way to his lungs.

Patterson looked at the door into this other room. He looked at it as if he suspected it was to be his death chamber. Then he entered and stood across the body of Knowles and fired vigorously into a group of plum trees.

"They can't take this house," declared the sergeant in a contemptuous and argumentative tone. He was apparently replying to somebody. The man who had been shot in the throat looked up at him. Eight men were firing from the windows. The sergeant detected in a corner three wounded men talking together feebly. "Don't you think there is anything to do?" he bawled. "Go and get Knowles's cartridges and give them to somebody who can use them! Take Simpson's too." The man who had been shot in the throat looked at him. Of the three wounded men who had been talking, one said: "My leg is all doubled up under me, sergeant." He spoke apologetically.

Meantime the sergeant was reloading his rifle. His foot slipped in the blood of the man who had been shot in the throat, and the military boot made a greasy red streak on the floor.

"Why, we can hold this place," shouted the sergeant jubilantly. "Who says we can't?"

Corporal Flagler suddenly spun away from his window and fell in a heap.

"Sergeant," murmured a man as he dropped to a seat on the floor out of danger, "I can't stand this. I swear I can't. I think we should run away."

Morton, with the kindly eyes of a good shepherd, looked at the man. "You are afraid, Johnston, you are afraid," he said softly. The man struggled to his feet, cast upon the sergeant a gaze full of admiration, reproach, and despair, and returned to his post. A moment later he pitched forward, and thereafter his body hung out of the window, his arms straight and the fists clenched. Incidentally this corpse was pierced afterward by chance three times by bullets of the enemy.

The sergeant laid his rifle against the stonework of the window frame and shot with care until his magazine was empty. Behind him a man, simply grazed on the elbow, was wildly sobbing like a girl. "Damn it, shut up!" said Morton, without turning his head. Before him was a vista of a garden, fields, clumps of trees, woods, populated at the time with little fleeting figures.

He grew furious. "Why didn't he send me orders?" he cried aloud. The emphasis on the word "he" was impressive. A mile back on the road a galloper of the Hussars lay dead beside his dead horse.

The man who had been grazed on the elbow still set up his bleat. Morton's fury veered to this soldier. "Can't you shut up? Can't you shut up? Can't you shut up? Fight! That's the thing to do. Fight!"

A bullet struck Morton, and he fell upon the man who had been shot in the throat. There was a sickening moment. Then the sergeant rolled off to a position upon the bloody floor. He turned himself with a last effort until he could look at the wounded who were able to look at him.

"Kim up, the Kickers," he said thickly. His arms weakened, and he dropped on his face.

After an interval a young subaltern of the enemy's infantry, followed by his eager men, burst into this reeking interior. But just over the threshold he halted before the scene of blood and death. He turned with a shrug to his sergeant. "God, I should have estimated them at least one hundred strong."

July 28, 1900
[*The Illustrated London News*, Vol. 117, pp. 121–122.]

THE UPTURNED FACE*

"What will we do now?" said the adjutant, troubled and excited.

"Bury him," said Timothy Lean.

The two officers looked down close to their toes where lay the body of their comrade. The face was chalk-blue; gleaming eyes stared at the sky. Over the two upright figures was a windy sound of bullets, and on the top of the hill Lean's prostrate company of Spitzbergen infantry was firing measured volleys.

"Don't you think it would be better—" began the adjutant. "We might leave him until tomorrow."

"No," said Lean. "I can't hold that post an hour longer. I've got to fall back, and we've got to bury old Bill."

"Of course," said the adjutant, at once. "Your men got entrenching tools?"

Lean shouted back to his little line, and two men came slowly, one with a pick, one with a shovel. They started in the direction of the Rostina sharpshooters. Bullets cracked near their ears. "Dig here," said Lean gruffly. The men, thus caused to lower their glances to the turf, became hurried and frightened, merely because they could not look to see whence the bullets came. The dull beat of the pick striking the earth sounded amid the swift snap of close bullets. Presently the other private began to shovel.

"I suppose," said the adjutant, slowly, "we'd better search his clothes for —things."

Lean nodded. Together in curious abstraction they looked at the body. Then Lean stirred his shoulders suddenly, arousing himself.

"Yes," he said, "we'd better see what he's got." He dropped to his knees, and his hands approached the body of the dead officer. But his hands wavered over the buttons of the tunic. The first button was brick-red with drying blood, and he did not seem to dare touch it.

"Go on," said the adjutant, hoarsely.

Lean stretched his wooden hand, and his fingers fumbled the blood-stained buttons. At last he rose with ghastly face. He had gathered a watch,

* *Spitzbergen Tales.*

a whistle, a pipe, a tobacco pouch, a handkerchief, a little case of cards and papers. He looked at the adjutant. There was a silence. The adjutant was feeling that he had been a coward to make Lean do all the grisly business.

"Well," said Lean, "that's all, I think. You have his sword and revolver?"

"Yes," said the adjutant, his face working, and then he burst out in a sudden strange fury at the two privates. "Why don't you hurry up with that grave? What are you doing, anyhow? Hurry, do you hear? I never saw such stupid—"

Even as he cried out in his passion the two men were laboring for their lives. Ever overhead the bullets were spitting.

The grave was finished. It was not a masterpiece—a poor little shallow thing. Lean and the adjutant again looked at each other in a curious silent communication.

Suddenly the adjutant croaked out a weird laugh. It was a terrible laugh, which had its origin in that part of the mind which is first moved by the singing of the nerves. "Well," he said, humorously to Lean, "I suppose we had best tumble him in."

"Yes," said Lean. The two privates stood waiting, bent over their implements. "I suppose," said Lean, "it would be better if we laid him in ourselves."

"Yes," said the adjutant. Then, apparently remembering that he had made Lean search the body, he stooped with great fortitude and took hold of the dead officer's clothing. Lean joined him. Both were particular that their fingers should not feel the corpse. They tugged away; the corpse lifted, heaved, toppled, flopped into the grave, and the two officers, straightening, looked again at each other—they were always looking at each other. They sighed with relief.

The adjutant said, "I suppose we should—we should say something. Do you know the service, Tim?"

"They don't read the service until the grave is filled in," said Lean, pressing his lips to an academic expression.

"Don't they?" said the adjutant, shocked that he had made the mistake. "Oh, well," he cried, suddenly, "let us—let us say something—while he can hear us."

"All right," said Lean. "Do you know the service?"

"I can't remember a line of it," said the adjutant.

Lean was extremely dubious. "I can repeat two lines, but—"

"Well, do it," said the adjutant. "Go as far as you can. That's better than nothing. And the beasts have got our range exactly."

Lean looked at his two men. "Attention!" he barked. The privates came to attention with a click, looking much aggrieved. The adjutant lowered his helmet to his knee. Lean, bareheaded, stood over the grave. The Rostina sharpshooters fired briskly.

"O Father, our friend has sunk in the deep waters of death, but his spirit has leaped toward Thee as the bubble arises from the lips of the drowning. Perceive, we beseech, O Father, the little flying bubble, and—"

Lean, although husky and ashamed, had suffered no hesitation up to this point, but he stopped with a hopeless feeling and looked at the corpse.

The adjutant moved uneasily. "And from Thy superb heights—" he began, and then he too came to an end.

"And from Thy superb heights," said Lean.

The adjutant suddenly remembered a phrase in the back part of the Spitzbergen burial service, and he exploited it with the triumphant manner of a man who has recalled everything, and can go on.

"Oh God, have mercy—"

"Oh God, have mercy—" said Lean.

"Mercy," repeated the adjutant, in quick failure.

"Mercy," said Lean. And then he was moved by some violence of feeling, for he turned suddenly upon his two men and tigerishly said, "Throw the dirt in."

The fire of the Rostina sharpshooters was accurate and continuous.

One of the aggrieved privates came forward with his shovel. He lifted his first shovel load of earth, and for a moment of inexplicable hesitation it was held poised above this corpse, which from its chalk-blue face looked keenly out from the grave. Then the soldier emptied his shovel on—on the feet.

Timothy Lean felt as if tons had been swiftly lifted from off his forehead. He had felt that perhaps the private might empty the shovel on—on the face. It had been emptied on the feet. There was a great point gained there—ha, ha!—the first shovelful had been emptied on the feet. How satisfactory!

The adjutant began to babble. "Well, of course—a man we've messed with all these years—impossible—you can't, you know, leave your intimate friends rotting on the field. Go on, for God's sake, and shovel, you."

The man with the shovel suddenly ducked, grabbed his left arm with his right hand, and looked at his officer for orders. Lean picked the shovel from the ground. "Go to the rear," he said to the wounded man. He also addressed the other private. "You get under cover, too; I'll finish this business."

The wounded man scrambled hard still for the top of the ridge without devoting any glances to the direction from whence the bullets came, and the other man followed at an equal pace; but he was different, in that he looked back anxiously three times.

This is merely the way—often—of the hit and unhit.

Timothy Lean filled the shovel, hesitated, and then, in a movement which was like a gesture of abhorrence, he flung the dirt into the grave, and as it landed it made a sound—plop. Lean suddenly stopped and mopped his brow—a tired laborer.

"Perhaps we have been wrong," said the adjutant. His glance wavered stupidly. "It might have been better if we hadn't buried him just at this time. Of course, if we advance tomorrow the body would have been—"

"Damn you," said Lean, "shut your mouth." He was not the senior officer.

He again filled the shovel and flung the earth. Always the earth made that sound—plop. For a space Lean worked frantically, like a man digging himself out of danger.

Soon there was nothing to be seen but the chalk-blue face. Lean filled the shovel. "Good God," he cried to the adjutant. "Why didn't you turn him somehow when you put him in? This—" Then Lean began to stutter.

The adjutant understood. He was pale to the lips. "Go on, man," he cried, beseechingly, almost in a shout.

Lean swung back the shovel. It went forward in a pendulum curve. When the earth landed it made a sound—plop.

March, 1900

[*Ainslee's Magazine*, Vol. 5, pp. 108–110.]

THE KNIFE*

I

Si Bryant's place was on the shore of the lake, and his garden patch, shielded from the north by a bold little promontory and a higher ridge inland, was accounted the most successful and surprising in all Whilomville township. One afternoon Si was working in the garden patch, when Doctor Trescott's man, Peter Washington, came trudging slowly along the road, observing nature. He scanned the white man's fine agricultural results. "Take your eye off them there melons, you rascal," said Si, placidly.

The negro's face widened in a grin of delight. "Well, Mist' Bryant, I

* *Whilomville Stories.*

raikon I ain't on'y make m'se'f covertous er-lookin' at dem yere mellums, sure 'nough. Dey suhtainly is grand."

"That's all right," responded Si, with affected bitterness of spirit. "That's all right. Just don't you admire 'em too much, that's all."

Peter chuckled and chuckled. "Ma Lode! Mist' Bryant, y-y-you don' think I'm gwine come prowlin' in dish yer gawden?"

"No, I know you hain't," said Si, with solemnity. "B'cause, if you did, I'd shoot you so full of holes you couldn't tell yourself from a sponge."

"Um—no, seh! No, seh! I don' raikon you'll get chance at Pete, Mist' Bryant. No, seh. I'll take an' run 'long an' rob er bank 'fore I'll come foolishin' 'round *your* gawden, Mist' Bryant."

Bryant, gnarled and strong as an old tree, leaned on his hoe and laughed a Yankee laugh. His mouth remained tightly closed, but the sinister lines which ran from the sides of his nose to the meetings of his lips developed to form a comic oval, and he emitted a series of grunts, while his eyes gleamed merrily and his shoulders shook. Pete, on the contrary, threw back his head and guffawed thunderously. The effete joke in regard to an American negro's fondness for watermelons was still an admirable pleasantry to them, and this was not the first time they had engaged in badinage over it. In fact, this venerable survival had formed between them a friendship of casual roadside quality.

Afterward Peter went on up the road. He continued to chuckle until he was far away. He was going to pay a visit to old Alek Williams, a negro who lived with a large family in a hut clinging to the side of a mountain. The scattered colony of negroes which hovered near Whilomville was of interesting origin, being the result of some contrabands who had drifted as far north as Whilomville during the great civil war. The descendants of these adventurers were mainly conspicuous for their bewildering number and the facility which they possessed for adding even to this number. Speaking, for example, of the Jacksons—one couldn't hurl a stone into the hills about Whilomville without having it land on the roof of a hut full of Jacksons. The town reaped little in labor from these curious suburbs. There were a few men who came in regularly to work in gardens, to drive teams, to care for horses, and there were a few women who came in to cook or to wash. These latter had usually drunken husbands. In the main the colony loafed in high spirits, and the industrious minority gained no direct honor from their fellows, unless they spent their earnings on raiment, in which case they were naturally treated with distinction. On the whole, the hardships of these people were the wind, the rain, the snow, and any other physical difficulties which they could cultivate. About twice a year the lady philanthropists of Whilomville went up against them, and came away poorer in goods but rich in complacence.

After one of these attacks the colony would preserve a comic air of rectitude for two days, and then relapse again to the genial irresponsibility of a crew of monkeys.

Peter Washington was one of the industrious class who occupied a position of distinction, for he surely spent his money on personal decoration. On occasion he could dress better than the Mayor of Whilomville himself, or at least in more colors, which was the main thing to the minds of his admirers. His ideal had been the late gallant Henry Johnson, whose conquests in Watermelon Alley, as well as in the hill shanties, had proved him the equal if not the superior of any Pullman car porter in the country. Perhaps Peter had too much Virginia laziness and humor in him to be a wholly adequate successor to the fastidious Henry Johnson, but, at any rate, he admired his memory so attentively as to be openly termed a dude by envious people.

On this afternoon he was going to call on old Alek Williams because Alek's eldest girl was just turned seventeen and, to Peter's mind, was a triumph of beauty. He was not wearing his best clothes, because on his last visit Alek's half-breed hound Susie had taken occasion to forcefully extract a quite large and valuable part of the visitor's trousers. When Peter arrived at the end of the rocky field which contained old Alek's shanty he stooped and provided himself with several large stones, weighing them carefully in his hand, and finally continuing his journey with three stones of about eight ounces each. When he was near the house, three gaunt hounds, Rover and Carlo and Susie, came sweeping down upon him. His impression was that they were going to climb him as if he were a tree, but at the critical moment they swerved and went growling and snapping around him, their heads low, their eyes malignant. The afternoon caller waited until Susie presented her side to him; then he heaved one of his eight-ounce rocks. When it landed, her hollow ribs gave forth a drumlike sound, and she was knocked sprawling, her legs in the air. The other hounds at once fled in horror, and she followed as soon as she was able, yelping at the top of her lungs. The afternoon caller resumed his march.

At the wild expressions of Susie's anguish old Alek had flung open the door and come hastily into the sunshine. "Yah, you Suse, come erlong outa dat now. What fer you—Oh, how do, how do, Mist' Wash'ton—how do?"

"How do, Mist' Willums? I done foun' it necessa'y fer ter damnearkill dish yer dawg a' yourn, Mist' Willums."

"Come in, come in, Mist' Wash'ton. Dawg no 'count, Mist' Wash'ton." Then he turned to address the unfortunate animal. "Hu't, did it? Hu't? 'Pears like you gwine lun some saince by time somebody brek yer back. 'Pears like I gwine club yer inter er frazzle 'fore you fin' out some saince. G'w'on 'way f'm yah!"

As the old man and his guest entered the shanty a body of black children spread out in crescent-shape formation and observed Peter with awe. Fat old Mrs. Williams greeted him turbulently, while the eldest girl, Mollie, lurked in a corner and giggled with finished imbecility, gazing at the visitor with eyes that were shy and bold by turns. She seemed at times absurdly overconfident, at times foolishly afraid; but her giggle consistently endured. It was a giggle on which an irascible but right-minded judge would have ordered her forthwith to be buried alive.

Amid a great deal of hospitable gabbling, Peter was conducted to the best chair out of the three that the house contained. Enthroned therein, he made himself charming in talk to the old people, who beamed upon him joyously. As for Mollie, he affected to be unaware of her existence. This may have been a method for entrapping the sentimental interest of that young gazelle, or it may be that the giggle had worked upon him.

He was absolutely fascinating to the old people. They could talk like rotary snowplows, and he gave them every chance, while his face was illumined with appreciation. They pressed him to stay for supper, and he consented, after a glance at the pot on the stove which was too furtive to be noted.

During the meal old Alek recounted the high state of Judge Hagenthorpe's kitchen garden, which Alek said was due to his unremitting industry and fine intelligence. Alek was a gardener, whenever impending starvation forced him to cease temporarily from being a lily of the field.

"Mist' Bryant he suhtainly got er grand gawden," observed Peter.

"Dat so, dat so, Mist' Wash'ton," assented Alek. "He got fine gawden."

"Seems like I nev' *did* see sech mellums, big as er bar'l, layin' dere. I don't raikon an'body in dish yer county kin hol' it with Mist' Bryant when comes ter mellums."

"Dat so, Mist' Wash'ton."

They did not talk of watermelons until their heads held nothing else, as the phrase goes. But they talked of watermelons until, when Peter started for home that night over a lonely road, they held a certain dominant position in his mind. Alek had come with him as far as the fence, in order to protect him from a possible attack by the mongrels. There they had cheerfully parted, two honest men.

The night was dark, and heavy with moisture. Peter found it uncomfortable to walk rapidly. He merely loitered on the road. When opposite Si Bryant's place he paused and looked over the fence into the garden. He imagined he could see the form of a huge melon lying in dim stateliness not ten yards away. He looked at the Bryant house. Two windows, downstairs, were lighted. The Bryants kept no dog, old Si's favorite child having once been bitten by a dog, and having since died, within that year, of pneumonia.

Peering over the fence, Peter fancied that if any low-minded night prowler should happen to note the melon, he would not find it difficult to possess himself of it. This person would merely wait until the lights were out in the house, and the people presumably asleep. Then he would climb the fence, reach the melon in a few strides, sever the stem with his ready knife, and in a trice be back in the road with his prize. There need be no noise, and, after all, the house was some distance.

Selecting a smooth bit of turf, Peter took a seat by the roadside. From time to time he glanced at the lighted windows.

II

When Peter and Alek had said good-bye, the old man turned back in the rocky field and shaped a slow course toward that high dim light which marked the little window of his shanty. It would be incorrect to say that Alek could think of nothing but watermelons. But it was true that Si Bryant's watermelon patch occupied a certain conspicuous position in his thoughts.

He sighed; he almost wished that he was again a conscienceless pickaninny, instead of being one of the most ornate, solemn, and look-at-me-sinner deacons that ever graced the handle of a collection basket. At this time it made him quite sad to reflect upon his granite integrity. A weaker man might perhaps bow his moral head to the temptation, but for him such a fall was impossible. He was a prince of the church, and if he had been nine princes of the church he could not have been more proud. In fact, religion was to the old man a sort of personal dignity. And he was on Sundays so obtrusively good that you could see his sanctity through a door. He forced it on you until you would have felt its influence even in a forecastle.

It was clear in his mind that he must put watermelon thoughts from him, and after a moment he told himself, with much ostentation, that he had done so. But it was cooler under the sky than in the shanty, and as he was not sleepy, he decided to take a stroll down to Si Bryant's place and look at the melons from a pinnacle of spotless innocence. Reaching the road, he paused to listen. It would not do to let Peter hear him, because that graceless rapscallion would probably misunderstand him. But, assuring himself that Peter was well on his way, he set out, walking briskly until he was within four hundred yards of Bryant's place. Here he went to the side of the road, and walked thereafter on the damp, yielding turf. He made no sound.

He did not go on to that point in the main road which was directly opposite the watermelon patch. He did not wish to have his ascetic contemplation disturbed by some chance wayfarer. He turned off along a short lane which led to Si Bryant's barn. Here he reached a place where he could see, over the fence, the faint shapes of the melons.

Alek was affected. The house was some distance away, there was no dog, and doubtless the Bryants would soon extinguish their lights and go to bed. Then some poor lost lamb of sin might come and scale the fence, reach a melon in a moment, sever the stem with his ready knife, and in a trice be back in the road with his prize. And this poor lost lamb of sin might even be a bishop, but no one would ever know it. Alek singled out with his eye a very large melon, and thought that the lamb would prove his judgment if he took that one.

He found a soft place in the grass, and arranged himself comfortably. He watched the lights in the windows.

III

It seemed to Peter Washington that the Bryants absolutely consulted their own wishes in regard to the time for retiring; but at last he saw the lighted windows fade briskly from left to right, and after a moment a window on the second floor blazed out against the darkness. Si was going to bed. In five minutes this window abruptly vanished, and all the world was night.

Peter spent the ensuing quarter-hour in no mental debate. His mind was fixed. He was here, and the melon was there. He would have it. But an idea of being caught appalled him. He thought of his position. He was the beau of his community, honored right and left. He pictured the consternation of his friends and the cheers of his enemies if the hands of the redoubtable Si Bryant should grip him in his shame.

He arose and, going to the fence, listened. No sound broke the stillness, save the rhythmical incessant clicking of myriad insects and the guttural chanting of the frogs in the reeds at the lakeside. Moved by sudden decision, he climbed the fence and crept silently and swiftly down upon the melon. His open knife was in his hand. There was the melon, cool, fair to see, as pompous in its fatness as the cook in a monastery.

Peter put out a hand to steady it while he cut the stem. But at the instant he was aware that a black form had dropped over the fence lining the lane in front of him and was coming stealthily toward him. In a palsy of terror he dropped flat upon the ground, not having strength enough to run away. The next moment he was looking into the amazed and agonized face of old Alek Williams.

There was a moment of loaded silence, and then Peter was overcome by a mad inspiration. He suddenly dropped his knife and leaped upon Alek. "I got che!" he hissed. "I got che! I got che!" The old man sank down as limp as rags. "I got che! I got che! Steal Mist' Bryant's mellums, hey?"

Alek, in a low voice, began to beg. "Oh, Mist' Peter Wash'ton, don' go fer ter be too ha'd on er ole man! I nev' come yere fer ter steal 'em. 'Deed I didn't, Mist' Wash'ton! I come yere jes fer ter *feel* 'em. Oh, please, Mist' Wash'ton—"

"Come erlong outa yere, you ol' rip," said Peter, "an' don' trumple on dese yer baids. I gwine put you w'ah you won' ketch col'."

Without difficulty he tumbled the whining Alek over the fence to the roadway and followed him with sheriff-like expedition. He took him by the scruff. "Come erlong, deacon. I raikon I gwine put you w'ah you kin pray, deacon. Come erlong, deacon."

The emphasis and reiteration of his layman's title in the church produced a deadly effect upon Alek. He felt to his marrow the heinous crime into which this treacherous night had betrayed him. As Peter marched his prisoner up the road toward the mouth of the lane, he continued his remarks: "Come erlong, deacon. Nev' see er man so anxious-like erbout er mellum-paitch, deacon. Seem like you jes' must see 'em er-growin' an' *feel* 'em, deacon. Mist' Bryant he'll be s'prised, deacon, findin' out you come fer ter *feel* his mellums. Come erlong, deacon. Mist' Bryant he expectin' some ole rip like you come soon."

They had almost reached the lane when Alek's cur Susie, who had followed her master, approached in the silence which attends dangerous dogs; and seeing indications of what she took to be war, she appended herself swiftly but firmly to the calf of Peter's left leg. The mêlée was short, but spirited. Alek had no wish to have his dog complicate his already serious misfortunes, and went manfully to the defense of his captor. He procured a large stone, and by beating this with both hands down upon the resounding skull of the animal, he induced her to quit her grip. Breathing heavily, Peter dropped into the long grass at the roadside. He said nothing.

"Mist' Wash'ton," said Alek at last, in a quavering voice, "I raikon I gwine wait yere see what you gwine do ter me."

Whereupon Peter passed into a spasmodic state, in which he rolled to and fro and shook.

"Mist' Wash'ton, I hope dish yer dog 'ain't gone an' give you fitses?"

Peter sat up suddenly. "No, she 'ain't," he answered; "but she gin me er big skeer; an' fer yer 'sistance with er cobblestone, Mist' Willums, I tell you what I gwine do—I tell you what I gwine do." He waited an impressive moment. "I gwine 'lease you!"

Old Alek trembled like a little bush in a wind. "Mist' Wash'ton?"

Quoth Peter, deliberately, "I gwine 'lease you."

The old man was filled with a desire to negotiate this statement at once, but he felt the necessity of carrying off the event without an appearance of haste. "Yes, seh; thank'e, seh; thank'e, Mist' Wash'ton. I raikon I ramble home pressenly." He waited an interval, and then dubiously said, "Good-evenin', Mist' Wash'ton."

"Good-evenin', deacon. Don' come foolin' roun' *feelin'* no mellums, and I say troof. Good-evenin', deacon."

Alek took off his hat and made three profound bows. "Thank 'e seh. Thank 'e, seh. Thank 'e, seh."

Peter underwent another severe spasm, but the old man walked off toward his home with a humble and contrite heart.

IV

The next morning Alek proceeded from his shanty under the complete but customary illusion that he was going to work. He trudged manfully along until he reached the vicinity of Si Bryant's place. Then, by stages, he relapsed into a slink. He was passing the garden patch under full steam when, at some distance ahead of him, he saw Si Bryant leaning casually on the garden fence.

"Good-mornin', Alek."

"Good-mawnin', Mist' Bryant," answered Alek, with a new deference. He was marching on, when he was halted by a word—"Alek!"

He stopped. "Yes, seh."

"I found a knife this mornin' in th' road," drawled Si, "an' I thought maybe it was yourn."

Improved in mind by this divergence from the direct line of attack, Alek stepped up easily to look at the knife. "No, seh," he said, scanning it as it lay in Si's palm, while the cold steel-blue eyes of the white man looked down into his stomach, "'tain't no knife er mine." But he knew the knife. He knew it as if it had been his mother. And at the same moment a spark flashed through his head and made wise his understanding. He knew everything. "'Tain't much of er knife, Mist' Bryant," he said, deprecatingly.

"'Tain't much of a knife, I know that," cried Si, in sudden heat, "but I found it this mornin' in my watermelon patch—hear?"

"Watahmellum paitch?" yelled Alek, not astounded.

"Yes, in my watermelon patch," sneered Si, "an' I think you know something about it, too!"

"Me?" cried Alek. "Me?"

"Yes—you!" said Si, with icy ferocity. "Yes—you!" He had become convinced that Alek was not in any way guilty, but he was certain that the old man knew the owner of the knife, and so he pressed him at first on criminal lines. "Alek, you might as well own up now. You've been meddlin' with my watermelons!"

"Me?" cried Alek again. "Yah's *ma* knife. I done cah'e it foh yeahs."

Bryant changed his ways. "Look here, Alek," he said, confidentially: "I know you and you know me, and there ain't no use in any more skirmishin'. I know that *you* know whose knife that is. Now whose is it?"

This challenge was so formidable in character that Alek temporarily quailed and began to stammer. "Er—now—Mist' Bryant—you—you—frien' er mine—"

"I know I'm a friend of yours, but," said Bryant, inexorably, "who owns this knife?"

Alek gathered unto himself some remnants of dignity and spoke with reproach: "Mist' Bryant, dish yer knife ain' mine."

"No," said Bryant, "it ain't. But you know who it belongs to, an' I want you to tell me—quick."

"Well, Mist' Bryant," answered Alek, scratching his wool, "I won't say's I *do* know who b'longs ter dish yer knife, an' I won't say's I *don't*."

Bryant again laughed his Yankee laugh, but this time there was little humor in it. It was dangerous.

Alek, seeing that he had got himself into hot water by the fine diplomacy of his last sentence, immediately began to flounder and totally submerge himself. "No, Mist' Bryant," he repeated, "I won't say's I *do* know who b'longs ter dish yer knife, an' I won't say's I *don't*." And he began to parrot this fatal sentence again and again. It seemed wound about his tongue. He could not rid himself of it. Its very power to make trouble for him seemed to originate the mysterious Afric reason for its repetition.

"Is he a very close friend of yourn?" said Bryant, softly.

"F-frien'?" stuttered Alek. He appeared to weigh this question with much care. "Well, seems like he *was* er frien', an' then agin, it seems like he—"

"It seems like he *wasn't*?" asked Bryant.

"Yes, seh, jest so, jest so," cried Alek. "Sometimes it seems like he *wasn't*. Then agin—" He stopped for profound meditation.

The patience of the white man seemed inexhaustible. At length his low and oily voice broke the stillness. "Oh, well, of course if he's a friend of yourn Alek! You know I wouldn't want to make no trouble for a friend of yourn."

"Yes, seh," cried the negro at once. "He's er frien' er mine. He is dat."

"Well, then, it seems as if about the only thing to do is for you to tell me his name so's I can send him his knife, and that's all there is to it."

Alek took off his hat, and in perplexity ran his hand over his wool. He studied the ground. But several times he raised his eyes to take a sly peep at the imperturbable visage of the white man. "Y-y-yes, Mist' Bryant.—I raikon dat's erbout all what kin be done. I gwine tell you who b'longs ter dish yer knife."

"Of course," said the smooth Bryant, "it ain't a very nice thing to have to do, but—"

"No, seh," cried Alek, brightly; "I'm gwine tell you, Mist' Bryant. I gwine tell you erbout dat knife. Mist' Bryant," he asked, solemnly, "does you know who b'longs ter dat knife?"

"No, I—"

"Well, I gwine tell. I gwine tell who. Mist' Bryant—" The old man drew himself to a stately pose and held forth his arm. "I gwine tell who. Mist' Bryant, *dish yer knife b'longs ter Sam Jackson!*"

Bryant was startled into indignation. "Who in hell is Sam Jackson?" he growled.

"He's er nigger," said Alek, impressively, "and he wuks in er lumber-yawd up yere in Hoswego."

March, 1900
[*Harper's Magazine*, Vol. 100, pp. 591–598.]

THE STOVE*

I

"They'll bring her," said Mrs. Trescott, dubiously. Her cousin, the painter, the bewildered father of the angel child, had written to say that if they were asked, he and his wife would come to the Trescotts' for the Christmas holidays. But he had not officially stated that the angel child would form part of the expedition. "But of course they'll bring her," said Mrs. Trescott to her husband.

The doctor assented. "Yes, they'll have to bring her. They wouldn't dare leave New York at her mercy."

"Well," sighed Mrs. Trescott, after a pause, "the neighbors will be pleased. When they see her they'll immediately lock up their children for safety."

"Anyhow," said Trescott, "the devastation of the Margate twins was complete. She can't do that particular thing again. I shall be interested to note what form her energy will take this time."

"Oh yes! that's it!" cried the wife. "You'll be *interested*. You've hit it exactly. You'll be interested to note what form her energy will take this time. And then, when the real crisis comes, you'll put on your hat and walk out of the house and leave *me* to straighten things out. This is not a scientific question; this is a practical matter."

"Well, as a practical man, I advocate chaining her out in the stable," answered the doctor.

When Jimmie Trescott was told that his old flame was again to appear,

* *Whilomville Stories.*

he remained calm. In fact, time had so mended his youthful heart that it was a regular apple of oblivion and peace. Her image in his thought was as the track of a bird on deep snow—it was an impression, but it did not concern the depths. However, he did what befitted his state. He went out and bragged in the street: "My cousin is comin' next week f'om New York." —"My cousin is comin' tomorrow f'om New York."

"Girl or boy?" said the populace, bluntly; but, when enlightened, they speedily cried, "Oh, we remember *her!*" They were charmed, for they thought of her as an outlaw, and they surmised that she could lead them into a very ecstasy of sin. They thought of her as a brave bandit, because they had been whipped for various pranks into which she had led them. When Jimmie made his declaration, they fell into a state of pleased and shuddering expectancy.

Mrs. Trescott pronounced her point of view: "The child is a nice child, if only Caroline had some sense. But she hasn't. And Willis is like a wax figure. I don't see what can be done, unless—unless you simply go to Willis and put the whole thing right at him." Then, for purposes of indication, she improvised a speech: "Look here, Willis, you've got a little daughter, haven't you? But, confound it, man, she is not the only girl child ever brought into the sunlight. There are a lot of children. Children are an ordinary phenomenon. In China they drown girl babies. If you wish to submit to this frightful impostor and tyrant, that is all very well, but why in the name of humanity do you make us submit to it?"

Doctor Trescott laughed. "I wouldn't dare say it to him."

"Anyhow," said Mrs. Trescott, determinedly, "that is what you *should* say to him."

"It wouldn't do the slightest good. It would only make him very angry, and I would lay myself perfectly open to a suggestion that I had better attend to my own affairs with more rigor."

"Well, I suppose you are right," Mrs. Trescott again said.

"Why don't you speak to Caroline?" asked the doctor, humorously.

"Speak to Caroline! Why, I wouldn't for the *world!* She'd fly through the roof. She'd snap my head off! Speak to Caroline! You must be mad!"

One afternoon the doctor went to await his visitors on the platform of the railway station. He was thoughtfully smiling. For some quaint reason he was convinced that he was to be treated to a quick manifestation of little Cora's peculiar and interesting powers. And yet, when the train paused at the station, there appeared to him only a pretty little girl in a fur-lined hood, and with her nose reddening from the sudden cold, and— attended respectfully by her parents. He smiled again, reflecting that he had comically exaggerated the dangers of dear little Cora. It amused his philosophy to note that he had really been perturbed.

As the big sleigh sped homeward there was a sudden shrill outcry from the angel child: "Oh, mamma! mamma! They've forgotten my stove!"

"Hush, dear; hush!" said the mother. "It's all right."

"Oh, but, mamma, they've forgotten my stove!"

The doctor thrust his chin suddenly out of his topcoat collar. "Stove?" he said. "Stove? What stove?"

"Oh, just a toy of the child's," explained the mother. "She's grown so fond of it, she loves it so, that if we didn't take it everywhere with her she'd suffer dreadfully. So we always bring it."

"Oh!" said the doctor. He pictured a little tin trinket. But when the stove was really unmasked, it turned out to be an affair of cast iron, as big as a portmanteau, and, as the stage people say, practicable. There was some trouble that evening when came the hour of children's bedtime. Little Cora burst into a wild declaration that she could not retire for the night unless the stove was carried upstairs and placed at her bedside. While the mother was trying to dissuade the child, the Trescotts held their peace and gazed with awe. The incident closed when the lamb-eyed father gathered the stove in his arms and preceded the angel child to her chamber.

In the morning, Trescott was standing with his back to the dining room fire, awaiting breakfast, when he heard a noise of descending guests. Presently the door opened, and the party entered in regular order. First came the angel child, then the cooing mother, and last the great painter with his arm full of the stove. He deposited it gently in a corner and sighed. Trescott wore a wide grin.

"What are you carting that thing all over the house for?" he said, brutally. "Why don't you put it some place where she can play with it, and leave it there?"

The mother rebuked him with a look. "Well, if it gives her pleasure, Ned?" she expostulated, softly. "If it makes the child happy to have the stove with her, why shouldn't she have it?"

"Just so," said the doctor, with calmness.

Jimmie's idea was the roaring fireplace in the cabin of the lone mountaineer. At first he was not able to admire a girl's stove built on well-known domestic lines. He eyed it and thought it was very pretty, but it did not move him immediately. But a certain respect grew to an interest, and he became the angel child's accomplice. And even if he had not had an interest grow upon him, he was certain to have been implicated sooner or later, because of the imperious way of little Cora, who made a serf of him in a few swift sentences. Together they carried the stove out into the desolate garden and squatted it in the snow. Jimmie's snug little muscles had been pitted against the sheer nervous vigor of this little golden-haired girl, and he had not won great honors. When the mind blazed inside the small body, the angel child was pure force. She began to speak: "Now, Jim, get some paper. Get some wood—little sticks at first. Now we want a match. You got a match? Well, go get a match. Get some more wood. Hurry up, now! No. *No!* I'll light it my own self. You get some more wood. There! Isn't that splendid? You get a whole lot of wood an' pile it up here by the stove. An' now what'll we cook? We must have somethin' to cook, you know, else it ain't like the real."

"Potatoes," said Jimmie, at once.

The day was clear, cold, bright. An icy wind sped from over the waters of the lake. A grown person would hardly have been abroad save on compulsion of a kind, and yet, when they were called to luncheon, the two little simpletons protested with great cries.

II

The ladies of Whilomville were somewhat given to the pagan habit of tea parties. When a tea party was to befall a certain house one could read it in the manner of the prospective hostess, who for some previous days would go about twitching this and twisting that, and dusting here and polishing there; the ordinary habits of the household began then to disagree with her, and her unfortunate husband and children fled to the lengths of their tethers. Then there was a hush. Then there was a tea party. On the fatal afternoon a small picked company of latent enemies would meet. There would be a fanfare of affectionate greetings, during which everybody would measure to an inch the importance of what everybody else was wearing. Those who wore old dresses would wish then that they had not come; and those who saw that, in the company, they were well clad, would be pleased or exalted, or filled with the joys of cruelty. Then they had tea, which was a habit and a delight with none of them, their usual beverage being coffee with milk.

Usually the party jerked horribly in the beginning, while the hostess strove and pulled and pushed to make its progress smooth. Then suddenly it would be off like the wind, eight, fifteen, or twenty-five tongues clattering, with a noise like a cotton mill combined with the noise of a few penny whistles. Then the hostess had nothing to do but to look glad and see that everybody had enough tea and cake. When the door was closed behind the last guest, the hostess would usually drop into a chair and say: "Thank Heaven! They're gone!" There would be no malice in this expression. It simply would be that, womanlike, she had flung herself headlong at the accomplishment of a pleasure which she could not even define, and at the end she felt only weariness.

The value and beauty, or oddity, of the teacups was another element which entered largely into the spirit of these terrible enterprises. The quality of the tea was an element which did not enter at all. Uniformly it was rather bad. But the cups! Some of the more ambitious people aspired to have cups each of a different pattern, possessing, in fact, the sole similarity that with their odd curves and dips of form they each resembled anything but a teacup. Others of the more ambitious aspired to a quite severe and godly "set," which, when viewed, appalled one with its austere and rigid family resemblances, and made one desire to ask the hostess if the teapot was not the father of all the little cups, and at the same time protesting gallantly that such a young and charming cream jug surely could not be their mother.

But of course the serious part is that these collections so differed in style and the obvious amount paid for them that nobody could be happy. The poorer ones envied; the richer ones feared—the poorer ones continually striving to overtake the leaders, the leaders always with their heads turned back to hear overtaking footsteps. And none of these things here written did they know. Instead of seeing that they were very stupid, they thought they were very fine. And they gave and took heart-bruises—fierce, deep heart-bruises—under the clear impression that of such kind of rubbish was the kingdom of nice people. The characteristics of outsiders of course emerged in shreds from these tea parties, and it is doubtful if the characteristics of insiders escaped entirely. In fact, these tea parties were in the large way the result of a conspiracy of certain unenlightened people to make life still more uncomfortable.

Mrs. Trescott was in the circle of tea-fighters largely through a sort of artificial necessity—a necessity, in short, which she had herself created in a spirit of femininity.

When the painter and his family came for the holidays, Mrs. Trescott had for some time been feeling that it was her turn to give a tea party, and she was resolved upon it now that she was reinforced by the beautiful wife of the painter, whose charms would make all the other women feel badly. And Mrs. Trescott further resolved that the affair should be notable in more than one way. The painter's wife suggested that, as an innovation, they give the people good tea; but Mrs. Trescott shook her head; she was quite sure they would not like it.

It was an impressive gathering. A few came to see if they could not find out the faults of the painter's wife, and these, added to those who would have attended even without that attractive prospect, swelled the company to a number quite large for Whilomville. There were the usual preliminary jolts, and then suddenly the tea party was in full swing and looked like an unprecedented success.

Mrs. Trescott exchanged a glance with the painter's wife. They felt proud and superior. This tea party was almost perfection.

III

Jimmie and the angel child, after being oppressed by innumerable admonitions to behave correctly during the afternoon, succeeded in reaching the garden, where the stove awaited them. They were enjoying themselves grandly, when snow began to fall so heavily that it gradually dampened their ardor as well as extinguished the fire in the stove. They stood ruefully until the angel child devised the plan of carrying the stove into the stable, and there, safe from the storm, continuing the festivities. But they were met at the door of the stable by Peter Washington.

"What you 'bout, Jim?"

"Now—it's snowin' so hard, we thought we'd take the stove into the stable."

"An' have er fiah in it? No, seh! G'w'on 'way f'm heh!—g'w'on! Don' 'low no sech foolishin' round yer. No, seh!"

"Well, we ain't goin' to hurt your old stable, are we?" asked Jimmie, ironically.

"Dat you ain't, Jim! Not so long's I keep my two eyes right plumb squaah p'inted at ol' Jim. No, seh!" Peter began to chuckle in derision.

The two vagabonds stood before him while he informed them of their iniquities as well as their absurdities, and further made clear his own masterly grasp of the spirit of their devices. Nothing affects children so much as rhetoric. It may not involve any definite presentation of common sense, but if it is picturesque they surrender decently to its influence. Peter was by all means a rhetorician, and it was not long before the two children had dismally succumbed to him. They went away.

Depositing the stove in the snow, they straightened to look at each other. It did not enter either head to relinquish the idea of continuing the game. But the situation seemed invulnerable.

The angel child went on a scouting tour. Presently she returned, flying. "I know! Let's have it in the cellar! In the cellar! Oh, it'll be lovely!"

The outer door of the cellar was open, and they proceeded down some steps with their treasure. There was plenty of light; the cellar was highwalled, warm, and dry. They named it an ideal place. Two huge cylindrical furnaces were humming away, one at either end. Overhead the beams detonated with the different emotions which agitated the tea party.

Jimmie worked like a stoker, and soon there was a fine bright fire in the stove. The fuel was of small brittle sticks which did not make a great deal of smoke.

"Now what'll we cook?" cried little Cora. "What'll we cook, Jim? We must have something to cook, you know."

"Potatoes?" said Jimmie.

But the angel child made a scornful gesture. "No. I've cooked 'bout a million potatoes, I guess. Potatoes aren't nice any more."

Jimmie's mind was all said and done when the question of potatoes had been passed, and he looked weakly at his companion.

"Haven't you got any turnips in your house?" she inquired, contemptuously. "In *my* house we have *turnips.*"

"Oh, turnips!" exclaimed Jimmie, immensely relieved to find that the honor of his family was safe. "Turnips? Oh, bushels an' bushels an' bushels! Out in the shed."

"Well, go an' get a whole lot," commanded the angel child. "Go an' get a whole lot. Grea' big ones. *We* always have grea' big ones."

Jimmie went to the shed and kicked gently at a company of turnips which the frost had amalgamated. He made three journeys to and from the cellar, carrying always the very largest types from his father's store. Four of them filled the oven of little Cora's stove. This fact did not please her, so they placed three rows of turnips on the hot top. Then the angel child, profoundly moved by an inspiration, suddenly cried out, "Oh, Jimmie, let's play we're keepin' a hotel, an' have got to cook for 'bout a thousand people, an' those two furnaces will be the ovens, an' I'll be the chief cook—"

"No; I want to be chief cook some of the time," interrupted Jimmie.

"No; I'll be chief cook my own self. You must be my 'sistant. Now I'll prepare 'em—see? An' then you put 'em in the ovens. Get the shovel. We'll play that's the pan. I'll fix 'em, an' then you put 'em in the ovens. Hold it still, now."

Jim held the coal shovel while little Cora, with a frown of importance, arranged turnips in rows upon it. She patted each one daintily, and then backed away to view it, with her head critically sideways.

"There!" she shouted at last. "That'll do, I guess. Put 'em in the oven."

Jimmie marched with his shovelful of turnips to one of the furnaces. The door was already open, and he slid the shovel in upon the red coals.

"Come on," cried little Cora. "I've got another batch nearly ready."

"But what am I goin' to do with these?" asked Jimmie. "There ain't only one shovel."

"Leave 'm in there," retorted the girl, passionately. "Leave 'm in there, an' then play you're comin' with another pan. 'Tain't right to stand there an' *hold* the pan, you goose."

So Jimmie expelled all his turnips from his shovel out upon the furnace fire, and returned obediently for another batch.

"These are puddings," yelled the angel child, gleefully. "Dozens an' dozens of puddings for the thousand people at our grea' big hotel."

IV

At the first alarm the painter had fled to the doctor's office, where he hid his face behind a book and pretended that he did not hear the noise of feminine reveling. When the doctor came from a round of calls, he too retreated upon the office, and the men consoled each other as well as they were able. Once Mrs. Trescott dashed in to say delightedly that her tea party was not only the success of the season, but it was probably the very nicest tea party that had ever been held in Whilomville. After vainly beseeching them to return with her, she dashed away again, her face bright with happiness.

The doctor and the painter remained for a long time in silence, Trescott tapping reflectively upon the windowpane. Finally he turned to the painter and, sniffing, said: "What is that, Willis? Don't you smell something?"

The painter also sniffed. "Why, yes! It's like—it's like turnips."

"Turnips? No; it can't be."

"Well, it's very much like it."

The puzzled doctor opened the door into the hall, and at first it appeared that he was going to give back two paces. A result of frizzling turnips, which was almost as tangible as mist, had blown in upon his face and made him gasp. "Good God! Willis, what can this be?" he cried.

"Whee!" said the painter. "It's awful, isn't it?"

The doctor made his way hurriedly to his wife, but before he could speak with her he had to endure the business of greeting a score of women. Then he whispered, "Out in the hall there's an awful—"

But at that moment it came to them on the wings of a sudden draught. The solemn odor of burning turnips rolled in like a sea fog and fell upon that dainty, perfumed tea party. It was almost a personality; if some unbidden and extremely odious guest had entered the room, the effect would have been much the same. The sprightly talk stopped with a jolt, and people looked at each other. Then a few brave and considerate persons made the usual attempt to talk away as if nothing had happened. They all looked at their hostess, who wore an air of stupefaction.

The odor of burning turnips grew and grew. To Trescott it seemed to make a noise. He thought he could hear the dull roar of this outrage. Under some circumstances he might have been able to take the situation from a point of view of comedy, but the agony of his wife was too acute and, for him, too visible. She was saying: "Yes, we saw the play the last time we were in New York. I liked it very much. That scene in the second act—the gloomy church, you know, and all that—and the organ playing—and then when the four singing little girls came in—" But Trescott comprehended that she did not know if she was talking of a play or a parachute.

He had not been in the room twenty seconds before his brow suddenly flushed with an angry inspiration. He left the room hastily, leaving behind him an incoherent phrase of apology, and charged upon his office, where he found the painter somnolent.

"Willis!" he cried, sternly, "come with me. It's that damn kid of yours!"

The painter was immediately agitated. He always seemed to feel more than any one else in the world the peculiar ability of his child to create resounding excitement, but he seemed always to exhibit his feelings very late. He arose hastily, and hurried after Trescott to the top of the inside cellar stairway. Trescott motioned him to pause, and for an instant they listened.

"Hurry up, Jim," cried the busy little Cora. "Here's another whole batch of lovely puddings. Hurry up now, an' put 'em in the oven."

Trescott looked at the painter; the painter groaned. Then they appeared violently in the middle of the great kitchen of the hotel with the thousand people in it. "Jimmie, go upstairs!" said Trescott, and then he turned to watch the painter deal with the angel child.

With some imitation of wrath, the painter stalked to his daughter's side and grasped her by the arm.

"Oh, papa! papa!" she screamed. "You're pinching me! You're pinching me! You're pinching me, papa!"

At first the painter had seemed resolved to keep his grip, but suddenly he let go her arm in a panic. "I've hurt her," he said, turning to Trescott.

Trescott had swiftly done much toward the obliteration of the hotel kitchen, but he looked up now and spoke, after a short period of reflection. "You've hurt her, have you? Well, hurt her again. Spank her!" he cried, enthusiastically. "Spank her, confound you, man! She needs it. Here's your chance. Spank her, and spank her good. Spank her!"

The painter naturally wavered over this incendiary proposition, but at last, in one supreme burst of daring, he shut his eyes and again grabbed his precious offspring.

The spanking was lamentably the work of a perfect bungler. It couldn't have hurt at all; but the angel child raised to heaven a loud, clear soprano howl that expressed the last word in even medieval anguish. Soon the painter was aghast. "Stop it, darling! I didn't mean—I didn't mean to—to hurt you so much, you know." He danced nervously. Trescott sat on a box, and devilishly smiled.

But the pasture-call of suffering motherhood came down to them, and a moment later a splendid apparition appeared on the cellar stairs. She understood the scene at a glance. "Willis! What have you been doing?"

Trescott sat on his box, the painter guiltily moved from foot to foot, and the angel child advanced to her mother with arms outstretched, making a piteous wail of amazed and pained pride that would have moved Peter the Great. Regardless of her frock, the panting mother knelt on the stone floor and took her child to her bosom, and looked, then, bitterly, scornfully, at the cowering father and husband.

The painter, for his part, at once looked reproachfully at Trescott, as if to say: "There! You see?"

Trescott arose and extended his hands in a quiet but magnificent gesture of despair and weariness. He seemed about to say something classic, and, quite instinctively, they waited. The stillness was deep, and the wait was longer than a moment. "Well," he said, "we can't live in the cellar. Let's go upstairs."

April, 1900

[*Harper's Magazine*, Vol. 100, pp. 798–804.]

MOONLIGHT ON THE SNOW

I

The town of Warpost had an evil name for three hundred miles in every direction. It radiated like the shine from some stupendous light. The citizens of the place had been for years grotesquely proud of their fame as a collection of hard-shooting gentlemen who invariably "got" the men who came up against them. When a citizen went abroad in the land, he said, "I'm f'm Warpost." And it was as if he had said, "I am the devil himself."

But ultimately it became known to Warpost that the serene-browed angel of peace was in the vicinity. The angel was full of projects for taking comparatively useless bits of prairie, and sawing them up into town lots, and making chaste and beautiful maps of his handiwork, which shook the souls of people who had never been in the West. He commonly traveled here and there in a light wagon, from the tailboard of which he made orations which soared into the empyrean regions of true hydrogen gas. Towns far and near listened to his voice, and followed him singing, until in all that territory you could not throw a stone at a jackrabbit without hitting the site of a projected mammoth hotel, estimated cost fifteen thousand dollars. The stern and lonely buttes were given titles like grim veterans awarded tawdry patents of nobility: Cedar Mountain, Red Cliffs, Lookout Peak. And from the East came both the sane and the insane with hope, with courage, with hoarded savings, with cold decks, with Bibles, with knives in boots, with humility and fear, with bland impudence. Most came with their own money; some came with money gained during a moment of inattention on the part of somebody in the East. And high in the air was the serene-browed angel of peace, with his endless gabble and his pretty maps. It was curious to walk out of an evening to the edge of a vast silent sea of prairie, and to reflect that the angel had parceled this infinity into building lots.

But no change had come to Warpost. Warpost sat with her reputation for bloodshed pressed proudly to her bosom, and saw her mean neighbors leap into being as cities. She saw drunken old reprobates selling acres of red-hot dust, and becoming wealthy men of affairs who congratulated themselves on their shrewdness in holding land which, before the boom, they would have sold for enough to buy a treat all round in the Straight Flush Saloon—only nobody would have given it.

Warpost saw dollars rolling into the coffers of a lot of contemptible men who couldn't shoot straight. She was amazed and indignant. She saw her standard of excellence, her creed, her reason for being great, all tumbling about her ears, and after the preliminary gasps she sat down to think it out.

The first man to voice a conclusion was Bob Hether, the popular barkeeper in Stevenson's Crystal Palace.

"It's this here gunfighter business," he said, leaning on his bar and, with the gentle, serious eyes of a child, surveying a group of prominent citizens who had come in to drink at the expense of Tom Larpent, a gambler. They solemnly nodded assent. They stood in silence, holding their glasses and thinking.

Larpent was chief factor in the life of the town. His gambling house was the biggest institution in Warpost. Moreover, he had been educated somewhere, and his slow speech had a certain mordant quality which was apt to puzzle Warpost, and men heeded him for the reason that they were not always certain as to what he was saying.

"Yes, Bob," he drawled, "I think you are right. The value of human life has to be established before there can be theaters, waterworks, streetcars, women, and babies."

The other men were rather aghast at this cryptic speech, but somebody managed to snigger appreciatively, and the tension was eased.

Smith Hanham, who whirled roulette for Larpent, then gave his opinion.

"Well, when all this here coin is floatin' 'round, it 'pears to me we orter git our hooks on some of it. Them little tin horns over at Crowdger's Corner are up to their necks in it, an' we ain't yit seen a centavo—not a centavetto. That ain't right. It's all well enough to sit 'round takin' money away from innercent cowpunchers s'long's ther's nothin' better; but when these here speculators come 'long flashin' rolls as big as waterbuckets, it's up to us to whirl in an' git some of it."

This became the view of the town, and, since the main stipulation was virtue, Warpost resolved to be virtuous. A great meeting was held, at which it was decreed that no man should kill another man, under penalty of being at once hanged by the populace. All the influential citizens were present, and asserted their determination to deal out a swift punishment which would take no note of an acquaintance or friendship with the guilty man. Bob Hether made a loud, long speech, in which he declared that he, for one, would help hang his "own brother," if his "own brother" transgressed this law which now, for the good of the community, must be for ever held sacred. Everybody was enthusiastic, save a few Mexicans, who did not quite understand; but as they were more than likely to be the victims of any affray in which they engaged, their silence was not considered ominous.

At half-past ten on the next morning Larpent shot and killed a man who had accused him of cheating at a game. Larpent had then taken a chair by the window.

II

Larpent grew tired of sitting in the chair by the window. He went to his bedroom, which opened off the gambling hall. On the table was a bottle of rye whiskey, of a brand which he specially and secretly imported from the East. He took a long drink; he changed his coat, after laving his hands and brushing his hair. He sat down to read, his hand falling familiarly upon an old copy of Scott's *Fair Maid of Perth*.

In time, he heard the slow trample of many men coming up the stairs. The sound certainly did not indicate haste; in fact, it declared all kinds of hesitation. The crowd poured into the gambling hall; there was low talk; a silence; more low talk. Ultimately somebody rapped diffidently on the door of the bedroom.

"Come in," said Larpent. The door swung back and disclosed Warpost, with a delegation of its best men in the front, and at the rear men who stood on their toes and craned their necks. There was no noise. Larpent looked up casually into the eyes of Bob Hether. "So you've come up to the scratch all right, eh, Bobbie?" he asked kindly. "I was wondering if you would weaken on the bloodcurdling speech you made yesterday."

Hether first turned deadly pale, and then flushed beet-red. His six-shooter was in his hand, and it appeared for a moment as if his weak fingers would drop it to the floor.

"Oh, never mind," said Larpent in the same tone of kindly patronage. "The community must and shall hold this law for ever sacred, and your own brother lives in Connecticut, doesn't he?" He laid down his book and arose. He unbuckled his revolver belt and tossed it on the bed. A look of

impatience had come suddenly upon his face. "Well, you don't want me
to be master of ceremonies at my own hanging, do you? Why don't somebody say something or do something? You stand around like a lot of bottles.
Where's your tree, for instance? You know there isn't a tree between here
and the river. Damned little jack-rabbit town hasn't even got a tree for its
hanging. Hello, Coats, you live in Crowdger's Corner, don't you? Well,
you keep out of this thing, then. The Corner has had its boom, and this
is a speculation in real estate which is the business solely of the citizens of
Warpost."

The behavior of the crowd became extraordinary. Men began to back
away; eye did not meet eye; they were victims of an inexplicable influence;
it was as if they had heard sinister laughter from a gloom.

"I know," said Larpent considerately, "that this isn't as if you were going
to hang a comparative stranger. In a sense, this is an intimate affair. I know
full well you could go out and jerk a comparative stranger into kingdom-
come and make a sort of festal occasion of it. But when it comes to performing the same office for an old friend, even the ferocious Bobbie Hether
stands around on one leg like a damned white-livered coward. In short, my
milk-fed patriots, you seem fat-headed enough to believe that I am going
to hang myself if you wait long enough; but unfortunately I am going to
allow you to conduct your own real estate speculations. It seems to me
there should be enough men here who understand the value of corner lots
in a safe and godly town, and hence should be anxious to hurry this business."

The icy tones had ceased, and the crowd breathed a great sigh, as if it
had been freed of a physical pain. But still no one seemed to know where
to reach for the scruff of this weird situation. Finally there was some jostling
on the outskirts of the crowd, and some men were seen to be pushing old
Billie Simpson forward amid some protests. Simpson was on state occasions
the voice of the town. Somewhere in his past he had been a Baptist
preacher. He had fallen far, very far, and the only remnant of his former
dignity was a fatal facility of speech when half drunk. Warpost used him
on those state occasions when it became bitten with a desire to "do the
thing up in style." So the citizens pushed the blear-eyed old ruffian forward
until he stood hemming and hawing in front of Larpent. It was evident at once that he was brutally sober, and hence wholly unfitted for whatever task had been planned for him. A dozen times he croaked like a frog,
meanwhile wiping the back of his hand rapidly across his mouth. At last
he managed to stammer:

"Mister Larpent——"

In some indescribable manner, Larpent made his attitude of respectful
attention to be grossly contemptuous and insulting.

"Yes, Mister Simpson?"

"Er—now—Mister Larpent," began the old man hoarsely, "we wanted to know——" Then, obviously feeling that there was a detail which he had forgotten, he turned to the crowd and whispered, "Where is it?" Many men precipitately cleared themselves out of the way, and down this lane Larpent had an unobstructed view of the body of the man he had slain. Old Simpson again began to croak like a frog.

"Mister Larpent."

"Yes, Mister Simpson."

"Do you—er—do you—admit——"

"Oh, certainly," said the gambler, good-humoredly. "There can be no doubt of it, Mister Simpson, although, with your well-known ability to fog things, you may later possibly prove that you did it yourself. I shot him because he was too officious. Not quite enough men are shot on that account, Mister Simpson. As one fitted by nature to be consummately officious, I hope you will agree with me, Mister Simpson."

Men were plucking old Simpson by the sleeve, and giving him directions. One could hear him say, "What? Yes. All right. What? All right." In the end he turned hurriedly upon Larpent and blurted out:

"Well, I guess we're goin' to hang you."

Larpent bowed. "I had a suspicion that you would," he said, in a pleasant voice. "There has been an air of determination about the entire proceeding, Mister Simpson."

There was an awkward moment.

"Well—well—well, come ahead——"

Larpent courteously relieved a general embarrassment. "Why, of course. We must be moving. Clergy first, Mister Simpson. I'll take my old friend, Bobbie Hether, on my right hand, and we'll march soberly to the business, thus lending a certain dignity to this outing of real estate speculators."

"Tom," quavered Bob Hether, "for Gawd sake, keep your mouth shut."

"He invokes the deity," remarked Larpent, placidly. "But no; my last few minutes I am resolved to devote to inquiries as to the welfare of my friends. Now, you, for instance, my dear Bobbie, present today the lamentable appearance of a rattlesnake that has been four times killed and then left in the sun to rot. It is the effect of friendship upon a highly delicate system. You suffer? It is cruel. Never mind; you will feel better presently."

III

Warpost had always risen superior to her lack of a tree by making use of a fixed wooden crane which appeared over a second story window on the front of Pigrim's general store. This crane had a long tackle always ready for hoisting merchandise to the store's loft. Larpent, coming in the midst of a slow-moving throng, cocked a bright bird-like eye at this crane.

"Mm—yes," he said.

Men began to work frantically. They called each to each in voices strenuous but low. They were in a panic to have the thing finished. Larpent's cold ironical survey drove them mad, and it entered the minds of some that it would be felicitous to hang him before he could talk more. But he occupied the time in pleasant discourse.

"I see that Smith Hanham is not here. Perhaps some undue tenderness of sentiment keeps him away. Such feelings are entirely unnecessary. Don't you think so, Bobbie? Note the feverish industry with which the renegade parson works at the rope. You will never be hung, Simpson. You will be shot for fooling too near a petticoat which doesn't belong to you—the same old habit which got you flung out of the church, you red-eyed old satyr. Ah, the Cross Trail coach approaches. What a situation."

The crowd turned uneasily to follow his glance, and saw, truly enough, the dusty rickety old vehicle coming at the gallop of four lean horses. Ike Boston was driving the coach, and far away he had seen and defined the throng in front of Pigrim's store. First calling out excited information to his passengers, who were all inside, he began to lash his horses and yell. As a result, he rattled wildly up to the scene just as they were arranging the rope around Larpent's neck.

"Whoa," said he to his horses.

The inhabitants of Warpost peered at the windows of the coach, and saw therein six pale, horror-stricken faces. The men at the rope stood hesitating. Larpent smiled blandly. There was a silence. At last a broken voice cried from the coach: "Driver! driver! What is it? What is it?"

Ike Boston spat between the wheel horses and mumbled that he s'posed anybody could see, less'n they were blind. The door of the coach opened, and out stepped a beautiful young lady. She was followed by two little girls, hand clasped in hand, and a white-haired old gentleman with a venerable and peaceful face. And the rough West stood in naked immorality before the eyes of the gentle East. The leatherfaced men of Warpost had never imagined such perfection of feminine charm, such radiance; and as the illumined eyes of the girl wandered doubtfully, fearfully, toward the man with the rope around his neck, a certain majority of practiced ruffians tried to look as if they were having nothing to do with the proceedings.

"Oh," she said, in a low voice, "what are you going to do?"

At first none made reply, but ultimately a hero managed to break the harrowing stillness by stammering out, "Nothin'!" And then, as if aghast at his own prominence, he shied behind the shoulders of a big neighbor.

"Oh, I know," she said. "But it's wicked. Don't you see how wicked it is? Papa, do say something to them."

The clear, deliberate tones of Tom Larpent suddenly made every one stiffen. During the early part of the interruption he had seated himself upon the steps of Pigrim's store, in which position he had maintained a slightly bored air. He now was standing with the rope around his neck and bowing. He looked handsome and distinguished and—a devil, a devil as cold as moonlight upon the ice.

"You are quite right, miss. They are going to hang me; but I can give you my word that the affair is perfectly regular. I killed a man this morning, and, you see, these people here, who look like a fine collection of premier scoundrels, are really engaged in forcing a real estate boom. In short, they are speculators, land barons, and not the children of infamy which you no doubt took them for at first."

"O—oh!" she said, and shuddered.

Her father now spoke haughtily. "What has this man done? Why do you hang him without a trial, even if you have fair proofs?"

The crowd had been afraid to speak to the young lady, but a dozen voices answered her father. "Why, he admits it." "Didn't ye hear?" "There ain't no doubt about it." "No!" "He *sez* he did."

The old man looked at the smiling gambler. "Do you admit that you committed murder?"

Larpent answered slowly. "For the first question in a temporary acquaintance that is a fairly strong beginning. Do you wish me to speak as man to man, or to one who has some kind of official authority to meddle in a thing that is none of his affair?"

"I—ah—I," stuttered the other. "Ah—man to man."

"Then," said Larpent, "I have to inform you that this morning, at about 10:30, a man was shot and killed in my gambling house. He was engaged in the exciting business of trying to grab some money out of which he claimed I had swindled him. The details are not interesting."

The old gentleman waved his arm in a gesture of terror and despair, and tottered toward the coach; the young lady fainted; the two little girls wailed. Larpent sat on the steps with the rope around his neck.

IV

The chief function of Warpost was to prey upon the bands of cowboys who, when they were paid, rode gaily into town to look for sin. To this end there were in Warpost many thugs and thieves. There was treachery and obscenity and merciless greed in every direction. Even Mexico was levied upon to furnish a kind of ruffian which appears infrequently in the northern races. Warpost was not good; it was not tender; it was not chivalrous, but——

But——

There was a quality to the situation in front of Pilgrim's store which made Warpost wish to stampede. There were the two children, their an-

gelic faces turned toward the sky, weeping in the last anguish of fear; there
was the beautiful form of the young lady prostrate in the dust of the road,
with her trembling father bending over her; on the steps sat Larpent, waiting, with a derisive smile, while from time to time he turned his head in the
rope to make a forked-tongued remark as to the character and bearing of
some acquaintance. All the simplicity of a mere lynching was gone from
this thing. Through some bewildering inner power of its own, it was carried
out of the hands of its inaugurators, and was marching along like a great
drama, and they were only spectators. To them it was ungovernable; they
could do no more than stand on one foot and wonder.

Some were heartily sick of everything, and wished to run away. Some
were so interested in the new aspect that they had forgotten why they had
originally come to the front of Pilgrim's store. These were the poets. A
large practical class wished to establish at once the identity of the newcomers. Who were they? Where did they come from? Where were they
going to? It was truthfully argued that they were the parson for the new
church at Crowdger's Corner, with his family.

And a fourth class—a dark-browed, muttering class—wished to go at once
to the root of all disturbance by killing Ike Boston for trundling up in his
old omnibus, and dumping out upon their ordinary lynching party such a
load of tears and inexperience and sentimental argument. In low tones they
addressed vitriolic reproaches.

"But how'd I know?" he protested, almost with tears—"how'd I know
ther'd be all this here kick-up?"

But Larpent suddenly created a great stir. He stood up, and his face
was inspired with new, strong resolution.

"Look here, boys," he said decisively, "you hang me tomorrow—or, anyhow, later on today. We can't keep frightening the young lady and these
two poor babies out of their wits. Ease off on the rope, Simpson, you black-
guard. Frightening women and children is your game, but I'm not going to
stand it. Ike Boston, take your passengers on to Crowdger's Corner, and
tell the young lady that, owing to her influence, the boys changed their
minds about making me swing. Somebody lift the rope where it's caught
under my ear, will you? Boys, when you want me, you'll find me in the
Crystal Palace."

His tone was so authoritative that some obeyed him at once, involuntarily; but, as a matter of fact, his plan met with general approval. Warpost
heaved a great sigh of relief. Why had nobody thought earlier of so easy a
way out of all these here tears?

v

Larpent went to the Crystal Palace, where he took his comfort like a
gentleman, conversing with his friends and drinking. At nightfall two men

rode into town, flung their bridles over a convenient post, and clanked into the Crystal Palace. Warpost knew them in a glance. Talk ceased, and there was a watchful squaring aback.

The foremost was Jack Potter, a famous town marshal of Yellow Sky, but now the sheriff of the county. The other was Scratchy Wilson, once a no less famous desperado. They were both two-handed men of terrific prowess and courage, but Warpost could hardly believe her eyes at view of this daring invasion. It was unprecedented.

Potter went straight to the bar, behind which frowned Bobbie Hether. "You know a man by the name of Larpent?"

"Supposin' I do?" said Bobbie, sourly.

"Well, I want him. Is he in the saloon?"

"Maybe he is, an' maybe he isn't," said Bobbie.

Potter went back among the glinting eyes of the citizens. "Gentlemen, I want a man named Larpent. Is he here?"

Warpost was sullen, but Larpent answered lazily for himself. "Why, you must mean me. My name is Larpent. What do you want?"

"I've got a warrant for your arrest."

There was a movement all over the room as if a puff of wind had come. The swing of a hand would have brought on a murderous mêlée. But after an instant the rigidity was broken by Larpent's laughter.

"Why, you're sold, sheriff," he cried. "I've got a previous engagement. The boys are going to hang me tonight."

If Potter was surprised, he betrayed nothing. "The boys won't hang you tonight, Larpent," he said calmly, "because I'm goin' to take you in to Yellow Sky."

Larpent was looking at the warrant. "Only grand larceny," he observed. "But still, you know, I've promised these people to appear at their performance."

"You're goin' in with me," said the impassive sheriff.

"You bet he is, sheriff," cried an enthusiastic voice; and it belonged to Bobbie Hether. The barkeeper moved down inside his rail, and, inspired like a prophet, he began a harangue to the citizens of Warpost. "Now, look here, boys, that's jest what we want, ain't it? Here we were goin' to hang Tom Larpent jest for the reputation of the town, like. 'Long comes Sheriff Potter, the reg-u-lerly con-sti-tuted officer of the law, an' he says, 'No; the man's mine.' Now, we want to make the reputation of the town as a law-abidin' place; so what do we say to Sheriff Potter? We says, 'A-a-ll right, sheriff; you're reg'lar; we ain't; he's your man.' But supposin' we go to fightin' over it; then what becomes of the reputation of the town, which we was goin' to swing Tom Larpent for?"

The immediate opposition to these views came from a source which a stranger might have difficulty in imagining. Men's foreheads grew thick with lines of obstinacy and disapproval. They were perfectly willing to hang Larpent yesterday, today, or tomorrow as a detail in a set of circumstances at Warpost; but when some outsiders from the alien town of Yellow Sky came into the sacred precincts of Warpost, and proclaimed their intention of extracting a citizen for cause, any citizen for any cause, the stomach of Warpost was fed with a clan's blood, and her children gathered under one invisible banner, prepared to fight as few people in few ages were enabled to fight for their points of view. There was a guttural murmuring.

"No; hold on!" screamed Bobbie, flinging up his hands. "He'll come clear all right. Tom," he appealed wildly to Larpent, "you never committed no Gawd-damn low-down grand larceny?"

"No," said Larpent, coldly.

"But how was it? Can't you tell us how it was?"

Larpent answered with plain reluctance. He waved his hand to indicate that it was all of little consequence.

"Well, he was a tenderfoot, and he played poker with me, and he couldn't play quite good enough. But he thought he could: he could play extremely well, he thought. So he lost his money. I thought he'd squeal."

"Boys," begged Bobbie, "let the sheriff take him."

Some answered at once, "Yes." Others continued to mutter. The sheriff had held his hand because, like all quiet and honest men, he did not wish to perturb any progress toward a peaceful solution, but now he decided to take the scene by the nose and make it obey him.

"Gentlemen," he said formally, "this man is comin' with me. Larpent, get up and come along."

This might have been the beginning, but it was practically the end. The two opinions in the minds of Warpost fought in the air and, like a snow-squall, discouraged all action. Amid general confusion Jack Potter and Scratchy Wilson moved to the door with their prisoner. The last thing seen by the men in the Crystal Palace was the bronze countenance of Jack Potter as he backed from the place.

A man, filled with belated thought, suddenly cried out: "Well, they'll hang him fer this here shootin' game anyhow."

Bobbie Hether looked disdain upon the speaker.

"Will they? An' where'll they get their witnesses? From here, do y' think? No; not a single one. All he's up against is a case of grand larceny, and—even supposin' he done it—what in hell does grand larceny amount to?"

April, 1900

[*Frank Leslie's Popular Monthly*, Vol. 49, pp. 606–618.]

THE TRIAL, EXECUTION, AND BURIAL
OF HOMER PHELPS*

From time to time an enwearied pine bough let fall to the earth its load of melting snow, and the branch swung back glistening in the faint wintry sunlight. Down the gulch a brook clattered amid its ice with the sound of a perpetual breaking of glass. All the forest looked drenched and forlorn.

The skyline was a ragged enclosure of gray cliffs and hemlocks and pines. If one had been miraculously set down in this gulch one could have imagined easily that the nearest human habitation was hundreds of miles away, if it were not for an old half-discernible wood-road that led toward the brook.

"Halt! Who's there?"

This low and gruff cry suddenly dispelled the stillness which lay upon the lonely gulch, but the hush which followed it seemed even more profound. The hush endured for some seconds, and then the voice of the challenger was again raised, this time with a distinctly querulous note in it.

"Halt! Who's there? Why don't you answer when I holler? Don't you know you're likely to get shot?"

A second voice answered, "Oh, you knew who I was easy enough."

"That don't make no diff'rence." One of the Margate twins stepped from a thicket and confronted Homer Phelps on the old wood-road. The majestic scowl of official wrath was upon the brow of Reeves Margate, a long stick was held in the hollow of his arm as one would hold a rifle, and he strode grimly to the other boy. "That don't make no diff'rence. You've got to answer when I holler, anyhow. Willie says so."

At the mention of the dread chieftain's name the Phelps boy daunted a trifle, but he still sulkily murmured, "Well, you knew it was me."

He started on his way through the snow, but the twin sturdily blocked the path. "You can't pass less'n you give the countersign."

"Huh?" said the Phelps boy. "Countersign?"

"Yes—countersign," sneered the twin, strong in his sense of virtue.

But the Phelps boy became very angry. "Can't I, hey? Can't I, hey? I'll show you whether I can or not! I'll show you, Reeves Margate!"

There was a short scuffle, and then arose the anguished clamor of the sentry: "Hey, fellers! Here's a man tryin' to run a-past the guard. Hey, fellers! Hey!"

There was a great noise in the adjacent underbrush. The voice of Willie

* *Whilomville Stories.*

could be heard exhorting his followers to charge swiftly and bravely. Then they appeared—Willie Dalzel, Jimmie Trescott, the other Margate twin, and Dan Earl. The chieftain's face was dark with wrath. "What's the matter? Can't you play it right? 'Ain't you got any sense?" he asked the Phelps boy.

The sentry was yelling out his grievance. "Now—he came along an' I hollered at 'im, an' he didn't pay no 'tention, an' when I ast 'im for the countersign, he wouldn't say nothin'. That ain't no way."

"Can't you play it right?" asked the chief again, with gloomy scorn.

"He knew it was me easy enough," said the Phelps boy.

"That 'ain't got nothin' to do with it," cried the chief, furiously. "That 'ain't got nothin' to do with it. If you're goin' to play, you've got to play it right. It ain't no fun if you go spoilin' the whole thing this way. Can't you play it right?"

"I forgot the countersign," lied the culprit, weakly.

Whereupon the remainder of the band yelled out, with one triumphant voice: "War to the knife! War to the knife! I remember it, Willie. Don't I, Willie?"

The leader was puzzled. Evidently he was trying to develop in his mind a plan for dealing correctly with this unusual incident. He felt, no doubt, that he must proceed according to the books, but unfortunately the books did not cover the point precisely. However, he finally said to Homer Phelps, "You are under arrest." Then with a stentorian voice he shouted, "Seize him!"

His loyal followers looked startled for a brief moment, but directly they began to move upon the Phelps boy. The latter clearly did not intend to be seized. He backed away, expostulating wildly. He even seemed somewhat frightened. "No, no; don't you touch me, I tell you; don't you dare touch me."

The others did not seem anxious to engage. They moved slowly, watching the desperate light in his eyes. The chieftain stood with folded arms, his face growing darker and darker with impatience. At length he burst out: "Oh, seize him, I tell you! Why don't you seize him? Grab him by the leg, Dannie! Hurry up, all of you! Seize him, I keep a-sayin'!"

Thus adjured, the Margate twins and Dan Earl made another pained effort, while Jimmie Trescott maneuvered to cut off a retreat. But, to tell the truth, there was a boyish law which held them back from laying hands of violence upon little Phelps under these conditions. Perhaps it was because they were only playing, whereas he was now undeniably serious. At any rate, they looked very sick of their occupation.

"Don't you dare!" snarled the Phelps boy, facing first one and then another; he was almost in tears—"don't you dare touch me!"

The chieftain was now hopping with exasperation. "Oh, seize him, can't you? You're no good at all!" Then he loosed his wrath upon the Phelps boy: "Stand still, Homer, can't you? You've got to be seized, you know. That ain't the way. It ain't any fun if you keep a-dodgin' that way. Stand still, can't you! You've got to be seized."

"I don't *want* to be seized," retorted the Phelps boy, obstinate and bitter. "But you've *got* to be seized!" yelled the maddened chief. "Don't you see? That's the way to play it."

The Phelps boy answered, promptly, "But I don't want to play that way."

"But that's the *right* way to play it. Don't you see? You've got to play it the right way. You've got to be seized, an' then we'll hold a trial on you, an'—an' all sorts of things."

But this prospect held no illusions for the Phelps boy. He continued doggedly to repeat, "I don't want to play that way!"

Of course in the end the chief stooped to beg and beseech this unreasonable lad. "Oh, come on, Homer! Don't be so mean. You're a-spoilin' everything. We won't hurt you any. Not the tintiest bit. It's all just playin'. What's the matter with you?"

The different tone of the leader made an immediate impression upon the other. He showed some signs of the beginning of weakness. "Well," he asked, "what you goin' to do?"

"Why, first we're goin' to put you in a dungeon, or tie you to a stake, or something like that—just pertend, you know," added the chief, hurriedly. "An' then we'll hold a trial, awful solemn, but there won't be anything what'll hurt you. Not a thing."

And so the game was readjusted. The Phelps boy was marched off between Dan Earl and a Margate twin. The party proceeded to their camp, which was hidden some hundred feet back in the thickets. There was a miserable little hut with a pine-bark roof, which so frankly and constantly leaked that existence in the open air was always preferable. At present it was noisily dripping melted snow into the black moldy interior. In front of this hut a feeble fire was flickering through its unhappy career. Underfoot, the watery snow was of the color of lead.

The party having arrived at the camp, the chief leaned against a tree and, balancing on one foot, drew off a rubber boot. From this boot he emptied about a quart of snow. He squeezed his stocking, which had a hole from which protruded a lobster-red toe. He resumed his boot. "Bring up the prisoner," said he. They did it. "Guilty or not guilty?" he asked.

"Huh?" said the Phelps boy.

"Guilty or not guilty?" demanded the chief, peremptorily. "Guilty or not guilty? Don't you understand?"

Homer Phelps looked profoundly puzzled. "Guilty or not guilty?" he asked, slowly and weakly.

The chief made a swift gesture, and turned in despair to the others. "Oh, he don't do it right! He does it all wrong!" He again faced the prisoner with an air of making a last attempt. "Now look-a-here, Homer, when I say, 'Guilty or not guilty?' you want to up an' say, 'Not guilty.' Don't you see?"

"Not guilty," said Homer, at once.

"No, no, no. Wait till I ask you. Now wait." He called out, pompously, "Pards, if this prisoner before us is guilty, what shall be his fate?"

All those well-trained little infants with one voice sang out, "*Death!*"

"Prisoner," continued the chief, "are you guilty or not guilty?"

"But look-a-here," argued Homer, "you said it wouldn't be nothin' that would hurt. I—"

"Thunder an' lightnin'!" roared the wretched chief. "Keep your mouth shut, can't ye? What in the mischief—"

But there was an interruption from Jimmie Trescott, who shouldered a twin aside and stepped to the front. "Here," he said, very contemptuously, "let me be the prisoner. I'll show 'im how to do it."

"All right, Jim," cried the chief, delighted; "you be the prisoner, then. Now all you fellers with guns stand there in a row! Get out of the way, Homer!" He cleared his throat, and addressed Jimmie. "Prisoner, are you guilty or not guilty?"

"Not guilty," answered Jimmie, firmly. Standing there before his judge— unarmed, slim, quiet, modest—he was ideal.

The chief beamed upon him, and looked aside to cast a triumphant and withering glance upon Homer Phelps. He said: "There! That's the way to do it."

The twins and Dan Earl also much admired Jimmie.

"That's all right so far, anyhow," said the satisfied chief. "An' now we'll —now we'll—we'll perceed with the execution."

"That ain't right," said the new prisoner, suddenly. "That ain't the next thing. You've got to have a trial first. You've got to fetch up a lot of people first who'll say I done it."

"That's so," said the chief. "I didn't think. Here, Reeves, you be first witness. Did the prisoner do it?"

The twin gulped for a moment in his anxiety to make the proper reply. He was at the point where the roads forked. Finally he hazarded, "Yes."

"There," said the chief, "that's one of 'em. Now, Dan, you be a witness. Did he do it?"

Dan Earl, having before him the twin's example, did not hesitate. "Yes," he said.

"Well, then, pards, what shall be his fate?"

Again came the ringing answer, *"Death!"*

With Jimmie in the principal role, this drama, hidden deep in the hemlock thicket, neared a kind of perfection. "You must blindfold me," cried the condemned lad, briskly, "an' then I'll go off an' stand, an' you must all get in a row an' shoot me."

The chief gave this plan his urbane countenance, and the twins and Dan Earl were greatly pleased. They blindfolded Jimmie under his careful directions. He waded a few paces into snow, and then turned and stood with quiet dignity, awaiting his fate. The chief marshaled the twins and Dan Earl in line with their sticks. He gave the necessary commands: "Load! Ready! Aim! Fire!" At the last command the firing party all together yelled, "Bang!"

Jimmie threw his hands high, tottered in agony for a moment, and then crashed full length into the snow—into, one would think, a serious case of pneumonia. It was beautiful.

He arose almost immediately and came back to them, wondrously pleased with himself. They acclaimed him joyously.

The chief was particularly grateful. He was always trying to bring off these little romantic affairs, and it seemed, after all, that the only boy who could ever really help him was Jimmie Trescott. "There," he said to the others, "that's the way it ought to be done."

They were touched to the heart by the whole thing, and they looked at Jimmie with big, smiling eyes. Jimmie, blown out like a balloon-fish with pride of his performance, swaggered to the fire and took seat on some wet hemlock boughs. "Fetch some more wood, one of you kids," he murmured, negligently. One of the twins came fortunately upon a small cedar tree the lower branches of which were dead and dry. An armful of these branches flung upon the sick fire soon made a high, ruddy, warm blaze, which was like an illumination in honor of Jimmie's success.

The boys sprawled about the fire and talked the regular language of the game. "Waal, pards," remarked the chief, "it's many a night we've had together here in the Rockies among the b'ars an' the Indyuns, hey?"

"Yes, pard," replied Jimmie Trescott, "I reckon you're right. Our wild, free life is—there ain't nothin' to compare with our wild, free life."

Whereupon the two lads arose and magnificently shook hands, while the others watched them in an ecstasy. "I'll allus stick by ye, pard," said Jimmie, earnestly. "When yer in trouble, don't forget that Lightnin' Lou is at yer back."

"Thanky, pard," quoth Willie Dalzel, deeply affected. "I'll not forget it, pard. An' don't you forget, either, that Deadshot Demon, the leader of the Red Raiders, never forgets a friend."

But Homer Phelps was having none of this great fun. Since his disgraceful refusal to be seized and executed he had been hovering unheeded on the outskirts of the band. He seemed very sorry; he cast a wistful eye at the romantic scene. He knew too well that if he went near at that particular time he would be certain to encounter a pitiless snubbing. So he vacillated modestly in the background.

At last the moment came when he dared venture near enough to the fire to gain some warmth, for he was now bitterly suffering with the cold. He sidled close to Willie Dalzel. No one heeded him. Eventually he looked at his chief, and with a bright face said, "Now—if I was seized now to be executed, I could do it as well as Jimmie Trescott, I could."

The chief gave a crow of scorn, in which he was followed by the other boys. "Ho!" he cried, "why didn't you do it, then? Why didn't you do it?" Homer Phelps felt upon him many pairs of disdainful eyes. He wagged his shoulders in misery.

"You're dead," said the chief, frankly. "That's what you are. We executed you, we did."

"When?" demanded the Phelps boy, with some spirit.

"Just a little while ago. Didn't we, fellers? Hey, fellers, didn't we?"

The trained chorus cried: "Yes, of course we did. You're dead, Homer. You can't play any more. You're dead."

"That wasn't me. It was Jimmie Trescott," he said, in a low and bitter voice, his eyes on the ground. He would have given the world if he could have retracted his mad refusals of the early part of the drama.

"No," said the chief, "it was you. We're playin' it was you, an' it *was* you. You're dead, you are." And seeing the cruel effect of his words, he did not refrain from administering some advice: "The next time, don't be such a chucklehead."

Presently the camp imagined that it was attacked by Indians, and the boys dodged behind trees with their stick-rifles, shouting out "Bang!" and encouraging each other to resist until the last. In the meantime the dead lad hovered near the fire, looking moodily at the gay and exciting scene. After the fight the gallant defenders returned one by one to the fire, where they grandly clasped hands, calling each other "old pard," and boasting of their deeds.

Parenthetically, one of the twins had an unfortunate inspiration. "I killed the Indy-un chief, fellers. Did you see me kill the Indy-un chief?"

But Willie Dalzel, his own chief, turned upon him wrathfully: "*You* didn't kill no chief. *I* killed 'im with me own hand."

"Oh!" said the twin, apologetically, at once. "It must have been some other Indy-un."

"Who's wounded?" cried Willie Dalzel. "Ain't anybody wounded?" The party professed themselves well and sound. The roving and inventive eye of the chief chanced upon Homer Phelps. "Ho! Here's a dead man! Come on, fellers, here's a dead man! We've got to bury him, you know." And at his bidding they pounced upon the dead Phelps lad. The unhappy boy saw clearly his road to rehabilitation, but mind and body revolted at the idea of burial, even as they had revolted at the thought of execution. "No!" he said, stubbornly. "No! I don't want to be buried! I don't want to be buried!"

"You've *got* to be buried!" yelled the chief, passionately. "'Tain't goin' to hurt ye, is it? Think you're made of glass? Come on, fellers, get the grave ready!"

They scattered hemlock boughs upon the snow in the form of a rectangle, and piled other boughs near at hand. The victim surveyed these preparations with a glassy eye. When all was ready, the chief turned determinedly to him: "Come on now, Homer. We've got to carry you to the grave. Get him by the legs, Jim!"

Little Phelps had now passed into that state which may be described as a curious and temporary childish fatalism. He still objected, but it was only feeble muttering, as if he did not know what he spoke. In some confusion they carried him to the rectangle of hemlock boughs and dropped him. Then they piled other boughs upon him until he was not to be seen. The chief stepped forward to make a short address, but before proceeding with it he thought it expedient, from certain indications, to speak to the grave itself. "Lie still, can't ye? Lie still until I get through." There was a faint movement of the boughs, and then a perfect silence.

The chief took off his hat. Those who watched him could see that his face was harrowed with emotion. "Pards," he began, brokenly—"pards, we've got one more debt to pay them murderin' redskins. Bowie-knife Joe was a brave man an' a good pard, but—he's gone now—gone." He paused for a moment, overcome, and the stillness was only broken by the deep manly grief of Jimmie Trescott.

May, 1900
[*Harper's Magazine*, Vol. 100, pp. 963-968.]

AN ILLUSION IN RED AND WHITE

Nights on the Cuban blockade were long, at times exciting, often dull. The men on the small leaping dispatch boats became as intimate as if they had all been buried in the same coffin. Correspondents who, in New York, had passed as fairly good fellows sometimes turned out to be perfect rogues of vanity and selfishness, but still more often the conceited chumps of

Park Row became the kindly and thoughtful men of the Cuban blockade. Also each correspondent told all he knew, and sometimes more. For this gentle tale I am indebted to one of the brightening stars of New York journalism.

"Now, this is how I imagine it happened. I don't say it happened this way, but this is how I imagine it happened. And it always struck me as being a very interesting story. I hadn't been on the paper very long, but just about long enough to get a good show, when the city editor suddenly gave me this sparkling murder assignment.

"It seems that up in one of the back counties of New York State a farmer had taken a dislike to his wife; and so he went into the kitchen with an axe, and in the presence of their four little children he just casually rapped his wife on the nape of the neck with the head of this axe. It was early in the morning, but he told the children they had better go to bed. Then he took his wife's body out in the woods and buried it.

"This farmer's name was Jones. The widower's eldest child was named Freddy. A week after the murder, one of the long-distance neighbors was rattling past the house in his buckboard when he saw Freddy playing in the road. He pulled up, and asked the boy about the welfare of the Jones family.

" 'Oh, we're all right,' said Freddy, 'only ma—she ain't—she's dead.'

" 'Why, when did she die?' cried the startled farmer. 'What did she die of?'

" 'Oh,' answered Freddy, 'last week a man with red hair and big white teeth and real white hands came into the kitchen, and killed ma with an axe.'

"The farmer was indignant with the boy for telling him this strange childish nonsense, and drove off much disgruntled. But he recited the incident at a tavern that evening, and when people began to miss the familiar figure of Mrs. Jones at the Methodist Church on Sunday mornings, they ended by having an investigation. The calm Jones was arrested for murder, and his wife's body was lifted from its grave in the woods and buried by her own family.

"The chief interest now centered upon the children. All four declared that they were in the kitchen at the time of the crime, and that the murderer had red hair. The hair of the virtuous Jones was gray. They said that the murderer's teeth were large and white. Jones only had about eight teeth, and these were small and brown. They said the murderer's hands were white. Jones's hands were the color of black walnuts. They lifted their dazed, innocent faces, and crying, simply because the mysterious excitement and their new quarters frightened them, they repeated their

heroic legend without important deviation, and without the parrotry same-
ness which would excite suspicion.

"Women came to the jail and wept over them, and made little frocks
for the girls, and little breeches for the boys, and idiotic detectives questioned them at length. Always they upheld the theory of the murderer
with red hair, big white teeth, and white hands. Jones sat in his cell, his
chin sullenly on his first vest-button. He knew nothing about any murder,
he said. He thought his wife had gone on a visit to some relatives. He
had had a quarrel with her, and she had said that she was going to leave
him for a time, so that he might have proper opportunities for cooling
down. Had he seen the blood on the floor? Yes, he had seen the blood on
the floor. But he had been cleaning and skinning a rabbit at that spot on
the day of his wife's disappearance. He had thought nothing of it. What
had his children said when he returned from the fields? They had told
him that their mother had been killed by an axe in the hands of a man
with red hair, big white teeth, and white hands. To questions as to why he
had not informed the police of the county, he answered that he had not
thought it a matter of sufficient importance. He had cordially hated his
wife, anyhow, and he was glad to be rid of her. He decided afterward
that she had run off; and he had never credited the fantastic tale of the
children.

"Of course, there was very little doubt in the minds of the majority
that Jones was guilty, but there was a fairly strong following who insisted
that Jones was a coarse and brutal man, and perhaps weak in his head—
yes—but not a murderer. They pointed to the children and declared that
children could never lie, and these kids, when asked, said that the murder
had been committed by a man with red hair, large white teeth, and white
hands. I myself had a number of interviews with the children, and I was
amazed at the convincing power of their little story. Shining in the depths
of the limpid upturned eyes, one could fairly see tiny mirrored images of
men with red hair, big white teeth, and white hands.

"Now, I'll tell you how it happened—how I imagine it was done. Some
time after burying his wife in the woods Jones strolled back into the house.
Seeing nobody, he called out in the familiar fashion, 'Mother!' Then the
kids came out whimpering. 'Where is your mother?' said Jones. The children looked at him blankly. 'Why, pa,' said Freddy, 'you came in here, and
hit ma with the axe; and then you sent us to bed.' 'Me?' cried Jones. 'I
haven't been near the house since breakfast-time.'

"The children did not know how to reply. Their meager little sense informed them that their father had been the man with the axe, but he
denied it, and to their minds everything was a mere great puzzle with no

meaning whatever, save that it was mysteriously sad and made them cry.

"'What kind of a looking man was it?' said Jones.

"Freddy hesitated. 'Now—he looked a good deal like you, pa.'

"'Like me?' said Jones. 'Why, I thought you said he had red hair?'

"'No, I didn't,' replied Freddy. 'I thought he had gray hair, like yours.'

"'Well,' said Jones, 'I saw a man with kind of red hair going along the road up yonder, and I thought maybe that might have been him.'

"Little Lucy, the second child, here piped up with intense conviction. 'His hair was a little teeny bit red. I saw it.'

"'No,' said Jones. 'The man I saw had very red hair. And what did his teeth look like? Were they big and white?'

"'Yes,' answered Lucy, 'they were.'

"Even Freddy seemed to incline to think it. 'His teeth may have been big and white.'

"Jones said little more at that time. Later he intimated to the children that their mother had gone off on a visit, and although they were full of wonder, and sometimes wept because of the oppression of an incomprehensible feeling in the air, they said nothing. Jones did his chores. Everything was smooth.

"The morning after the day of the murder, Jones and his children had a breakfast of hominy and milk.

"'Well, this man with red hair and big white teeth, Lucy,' said Jones. 'Did you notice anything else about him?'

"Lucy straightened in her chair, and showed the childish desire to come out with brilliant information which would gain her father's approval. 'He had white hands—hands all white——'

"'How about you, Freddy?'

"'I didn't look at them much, but I think they were white,' answered the boy.

"'And what did little Martha notice?' cried the tender parent. 'Did she see the big bad man?'

"'Martha, aged four, replied solemnly, 'His hair was all yed, and his hand was white—all white.'

"'That's the man I saw up the road,' said Jones to Freddy.

"'Yes, sir, it seems like it must have been him,' said the boy, his brain now completely muddled.

"Again Jones allowed the subject of his wife's murder to lapse. The children did not know that it was a murder, of course. Adults were always performing in a way to make children's heads swim. For instance, what could be more incomprehensible than that a man with two horses, dragging a queer thing, should walk all day, making the grass turn down and the earth turn up? And why did they cut the long grass and put it in a barn? And what was a cow for? Did the water in the well like to be there? All these actions and things were grand, because they were associated with the high estate of grown-up people, but they were deeply mysterious. If, then, a man with red hair, big white teeth, and white hands should hit their mother on the nape of the neck with an axe, it was merely a phenomenon of grown-up life. Little Henry, the baby, when he had a want, howled and pounded the table with his spoon. That was all of life to him. He was not concerned with the fact that his mother had been murdered.

"One day Jones said to his children suddenly, 'Look here: I wonder if you could have made a mistake. Are you absolutely sure that the man you saw had red hair, big white teeth, and white hands?'

"The children were indignant with their father. 'Why, of course, pa, we ain't made no mistake. We saw him as plain as day.'

"Later young Freddy's mind began to work like ketchup. His nights were haunted with terrible memories of the man with the red hair, big white teeth, and white hands, and the prolonged absence of his mother made him wonder and wonder. Presently he quite gratuitously developed the theory that his mother was dead. He knew about death. He had once seen a dead dog; also dead chickens, rabbits, and mice. One day he asked his father, 'Pa, is ma ever coming back?'

"Jones said: 'Well, no; I don't think she is.' This answer confirmed the boy in this theory. He knew that dead people did not come back.

"The attitude of Jones toward this descriptive legend of the man with the axe was very peculiar. He came to be in opposition to it. He protested against the convictions of the children, but he could not move them. It was the one thing in their lives of which they were stonily and absolutely positive.

"Now that really ends the story. But I will continue for your amusement. The jury hung Jones as high as they could, and they were quite right: because Jones confessed before he died. Freddy is now a highly respected driver of a grocery wagon in Ogdensburg. When I was up there a good many years afterwards people told me that when he ever spoke of the tragedy at all he was certain to denounce the alleged confession as a lie. He considered his father a victim to the stupidity of juries, and some day he hopes to meet the man with the red hair, big white teeth, and white hands, whose image still remains so distinct in his memory that he could pick him out in a crowd of ten thousand."

May 20, 1900

[New York *World*, supplement, p. 2.]

THE FIGHT*

The child life of the neighborhood was sometimes moved in its deeps at the sight of wagonloads of furniture arriving in front of some house which, with closed blinds and barred doors, had been for a time a mystery, or even a fear. The boys often expressed this fear by stamping bravely and noisily on the porch of the house, and then suddenly darting away with screams of nervous laughter, as if they expected to be pursued by something uncanny. There was a group who held that the cellar of a vacant house was certainly the abode of robbers, smugglers, assassins, mysterious masked men in council about the dim rays of a candle, and possessing skulls, emblematic bloody daggers, and owls. Then, near the first of April, would come along a wagonload of furniture, and children would assemble on the walk by the gate and make serious examination of everything that passed into the house, and taking no thought whatever of masked men.

One day it was announced in the neighborhood that a family was actually moving into the Hannigan house, next door to Dr. Trescott's. Jimmie was one of the first to be informed, and by the time some of his friends came dashing up he was versed in much.

"Any boys?" they demanded, eagerly.

"Yes," answered Jimmie, proudly. "One's a little feller, and one's most as big as me. I saw 'em, I did."

"Where are they?" asked Willie Dalzel, as if under the circumstances he could not take Jimmie's word, but must have the evidence of his senses.

"Oh, they're in there," said Jimmie, carelessly. It was evident he owned these new boys.

Willie Dalzel resented Jimmie's proprietary way. "Ho!" he cried, scornfully. "Why don't they come out, then? Why don't they come out?"

"How d' I know?" said Jimmie.

"Well," retorted Willie Dalzel, "you seemed to know so thundering much about 'em."

At the moment a boy came strolling down the gravel walk which led from the front door to the gate. He was about the height and age of Jimmie Trescott, but he was thick through the chest and had fat legs. His face was round and rosy and plump, but his hair was curly black, and his brows were naturally darkling, so that he resembled both a pudding and a young bull.

He approached slowly the group of older inhabitants, and they had

* *Whilomville Stories.*

grown profoundly silent. They looked him over; he looked them over. They might have been savages observing the first white man, or white men observing the first savage. The silence held steady.

As he neared the gate the strange boy wandered off to the left in a definite way, which proved his instinct to make a circular voyage when in doubt. The motionless group stared at him. In time this unsmiling scrutiny worked upon him somewhat, and he leaned against the fence and fastidiously examined one shoe.

In the end Willie Dalzel authoritatively broke the stillness. "What's your name?" said he, gruffly.

"Johnnie Hedge 'tis," answered the new boy. Then came another great silence while Whilomville pondered this intelligence.

Again came the voice of authority—"Where'd you live b'fore?"

"Jersey City."

These two sentences completed the first section of the formal code. The second section concerned itself with the establishment of the newcomer's exact position in the neighborhood.

"I kin lick you," announced Willie Dalzel, and awaited the answer.

The Hedge boy had stared at Willie Dalzel, but he stared at him again. After a pause he said, "I know you kin."

"Well," demanded Willie, "kin *he* lick you?" And he indicated Jimmie Trescott with a sweep which announced plainly that Jimmie was the next in prowess.

Whereupon the new boy looked at Jimmie respectfully but carefully, and at length said, "I dun'no."

This was the signal for an outburst of shrill screaming, and everybody pushed Jimmie forward. He knew what he had to say, and, as befitted the occasion, he said it fiercely: "Kin you lick me?"

The new boy also understood what he had to say, and, despite his unhappy and lonely state, he said it bravely: "Yes."

"Well," retorted Jimmie, bluntly, "come out and do it, then! Jest come out and do it!" And these words were greeted with cheers. These little rascals yelled that there should be a fight at once. They were in bliss over the prospect. "Go on, Jim! Make 'im come out. He said he could lick you. Aw-aw-aw! He said he could lick you!" There probably never was a fight among this class in Whilomville which was not the result of the goading and guying of two proud lads by a populace of urchins who simply wished to see a show.

Willie Dalzel was very busy. He turned first to the one and then to the other. "You said you could lick him. Well, why don't you come out and do it, then? You said you could lick him, didn't you?"

"Yes," answered the new boy, dogged and dubious.

Willie tried to drag Jimmie by the arm. "Aw, go on, Jimmie! You ain't afraid, are you?"

"No," said Jimmie.

The two victims opened wide eyes at each other. The fence separated them, and so it was impossible for them to immediately engage; but they seemed to understand that they were ultimately to be sacrificed to the ferocious aspirations of the other boys, and each scanned the other to learn something of his spirit. They were not angry at all. They were merely two little gladiators who were being clamorously told to hurt each other. Each displayed hesitation and doubt without displaying fear. They did not exactly understand what were their feelings, and they moodily kicked the ground and made low and sullen answers to Willie Dalzel, who worked like a circus manager.

"Aw, go on, Jim! What's the matter with you? You ain't afraid, are you? Well, then, say something." This sentiment received more cheering from the abandoned little wretches who wished to be entertained, and in this cheering there could be heard notes of derision of Jimmie Trescott. The latter had a position to sustain; he was well known; he often bragged of his willingness and ability to thrash other boys; well, then, here was a boy of his size who said that he could not thrash him. What was he going to do about it? The crowd made these arguments very clear, and repeated them again and again.

Finally Jimmie, driven to aggression, walked close to the fence and said to the new boy, "The first time I catch you out of your own yard I'll lam the head off'n you!" This was received with wild plaudits by the Whilomville urchins.

But the new boy stepped back from the fence. He was awed by Jimmie's formidable mien. But he managed to get out a semi-defiant sentence. "Maybe you will, and maybe you won't," said he.

However, his short retreat was taken as a practical victory for Jimmie, and the boys hooted him bitterly. He remained inside the fence, swinging one foot and scowling, while Jimmie was escorted off down the street amid acclamations. The new boy turned and walked back toward the house, his face gloomy, lined deep with discouragement, as if he felt that the new environment's antagonism and palpable cruelty were sure to prove too much for him.

II

The mother of Johnnie Hedge was a widow, and the chief theory of her life was that her boy should be in school on the greatest possible number of days. He himself had no sympathy with this ambition, but she detected the truth of his diseases with an unerring eye, and he was required to be really ill before he could win the right to disregard the first bell, morning and noon. The chicken pox and the mumps had given him vacations—vacations of misery, wherein he nearly died between pain and nursing. But bad colds in the head did nothing for him, and he was not able to invent a satisfactory hacking cough. His mother was not consistently a Tartar. In most things he swayed her to his will. He was allowed to have more jam, pickles, and pie than most boys; she respected his profound loathing of Sunday school; on summer evenings he could remain out-of-doors until 8:30; but in this matter of school she was inexorable. This single point in her character was of steel.

The Hedges arrived in Whilomville on a Saturday, and on the following Monday Johnnie wended his way to school with a note to the principal and his Jersey City school books. He knew perfectly well that he would be told to buy new and different books, but in those days mothers always had an idea that old books would "do," and they invariably sent boys off to a new school with books which would not meet the selected and unchangeable views of the new administration. The old books never would "do." Then the boys brought them home to annoyed mothers and asked for ninety cents or sixty cents or eighty-five cents or some number of cents for another outfit. In the garret of every house holding a large family there was a collection of effete school books, with mother rebellious because James could not inherit his books from Paul, who should properly be Peter's heir, while Peter should be a beneficiary under Henry's will.

But the matter of the books was not the measure of Johnnie Hedge's unhappiness. This whole business of changing schools was a complete torture. Alone he had to go among a new people, a new tribe, and he apprehended his serious time. There were only two fates for him. One meant victory. One meant a kind of serfdom in which he would subscribe to every word of some superior boy and support his every word. It was not anything like an English system of fagging, because boys invariably drifted into the figurative service of other boys whom they devotedly admired, and if they were obliged to subscribe to everything, it is true that they would have done so freely in any case. One means to suggest that Johnnie Hedge had to find his place. Willie Dalzel was a type of the little chieftain, and Willie was a master, but he was not a bully in a special physical sense. He did not drag little boys by the ears until they cried, nor make them tearfully fetch and carry for him. They fetched and carried, but it was because of their worship of his prowess and genius. And so all through the strata of boy life were chieftains and sub-chieftains and assistant sub-chieftains. There was no question of little Hedge being towed about by the nose; it was, as one has said, that he had to find his place in a new school. And this in itself was a problem which awed his boyish heart. He was a stranger cast away upon the moon. None knew him, understood him, felt for him. He would be surrounded for this initiative time by a horde of jackal creatures who might turn out in the end to be little boys like himself, but this last point his philosophy could not understand in its fulness.

He came to a white meeting house sort of place, in the squat tower of which a great bell was clanging impressively. He passed through an iron gate into a playground worn bare as the bed of a mountain brook by the endless runnings and scufflings of little children. There was still a half-hour before the final clangor in the squat tower, but the playground held a number of frolicsome imps. A loitering boy espied Johnnie Hedge, and he howled: "Oh! oh! Here's a new feller! Here's a new feller!" He advanced upon the strange arrival. "What's your name?" he demanded, belligerently, like a particularly offensive customhouse officer.

"Johnnie Hedge," responded the newcomer shyly.

This name struck the other boy as being very comic. All new names strike boys as being comic. He laughed noisily.

"Oh, fellers, he says his name is Johnnie Hedge! Haw! haw! haw!"

The new boy felt that his name was the most disgraceful thing which had ever been attached to a human being.

"Johnnie Hedge! Haw! haw! What room you in?" said the other lad.

"I dun'no," said Johnnie. In the meantime a small flock of interested vultures had gathered about him. The main thing was his absolute strangeness. He even would have welcomed the sight of his tormentors of Saturday; he had seen them before at least. These creatures were only so many incomprehensible problems. He diffidently began to make his way toward the main door of the school, and the other boys followed him. They demanded information.

"Are you through subtraction yet? We study jogerfre—did you, ever? You live here now? You goin' to school here now?"

To many questions he made answer as well as the clamor would permit, and at length he reached the main door and went quaking unto his new kings. As befitted them, the rabble stopped at the door. A teacher strolling along a corridor found a small boy holding in his hand a note. The boy palpably did not know what to do with the note, but the teacher knew, and took it. Thereafter this little boy was in harness.

A splendid lady in gorgeous robes gave him a seat at a double desk, at the end of which sat a hoodlum with grimy fingernails, who eyed the inauguration with an extreme and personal curiosity. The other desks were gradually occupied by children, who first were told of the new boy, and then turned upon him a speculative and somewhat derisive eye. The school opened; little classes went forward to a position in front of the teacher's platform and tried to explain that they knew something. The new boy was not requisitioned a great deal; he was allowed to lie dormant until he became used to the scenes and until the teacher found, approximately, his mental position. In the meantime he suffered a shower of stares and whispers and giggles, as if he were a man-ape, whereas he was precisely like other children. From time to time he made funny and pathetic little overtures to other boys, but these overtures could not yet be received; he was not known; he was a foreigner. The village school was like a nation. It was tight. Its amiability or friendship must be won in certain ways.

At recess he hovered in the schoolroom around the weak lights of society and around the teacher, in the hope that somebody might be good to him, but none considered him save as some sort of specimen. The teacher of course had a secondary interest in the fact that he was an additional one to a class of sixty-three.

At twelve o'clock, when the ordered files of boys and girls marched toward the door, he exhibited—to no eye—the tremblings of a coward in a charge. He exaggerated the lawlessness of the playground and the street.

But the reality was hard enough. A shout greeted him: "Oh, here's the new feller! Here's the new feller!"

Small and utterly obscure boys teased him. He had a hard time of it to get to the gate. There never was any actual hurt, but everything was competent to smite the lad with shame. It was a curious, groundless shame, but nevertheless it was shame. He was a newcomer, and he definitely felt the disgrace of the fact.

In the street he was seen and recognized by some lads who had formed part of the group of Saturday. They shouted: "Oh, Jimmie! Jimmie! Here he is! Here's that new feller!"

Jimmie Trescott was going virtuously toward his luncheon when he heard these cries behind him. He pretended not to hear, and in this deception he was assisted by the fact that he was engaged at the time in a furious argument with a friend over the relative merits of two *Uncle Tom's Cabin* companies. It appeared that one company had only two bloodhounds, while the other had ten. On the other hand, the first company had two Topsys and two Uncle Toms, while the second had only one Topsy and one Uncle Tom.

But the shouting little boys were hard after him. Finally they were even pulling at his arms. "Jimmie—"

"What?" he demanded, turning with a snarl. "What d'you want? Leggo my arm!"

"Here he is! Here's the new feller! Here's the new feller! Now!"

"I don't care if he is," said Jimmie, with grand impatience. He tilted his chin. "I don't care if he is."

Then they reviled him. "Thought you was goin' to lick him first time you caught him! Yah! You're a 'fraid-cat!" They began to sing: "'Fraid-cat! 'Fraid-cat! 'Fraid-cat!" He expostulated hotly, turning from one to another, but they would not listen. In the meantime the Hedge boy slunk on his way, looking with deep anxiety upon this attempt to send Jimmie against him. But Jimmie would have none of the plan.

III

When the children met again on the playground, Jimmie was openly challenged with cowardice. He had made a big threat in the hearing of comrades, and when invited by them to take advantage of an opportunity, he had refused. They had been fairly sure of their amusement, and they were indignant. Jimmie was finally driven to declare that as soon as school was out for the day, he would thrash the Hedge boy. When finally the children came rushing out of the iron gate, filled with the delights of freedom, a hundred boys surrounded Jimmie in high spirits, for he had said that he was determined. They waited for the lone lad from Jersey City. When he appeared, Jimmie wasted no time. He walked straight to him and said, "Did you say you kin lick me?"

Johnnie Hedge was cowed, shrinking, affrighted, and the roars of a hundred boys thundered in his ears, but again he knew what he had to say. "Yes," he gasped, in anguish.

"Then," said Jimmie, resolutely, "you've got to fight." There was a joyous clamor by the mob. The beleaguered lad looked this way and that way for succor, as Willie Dalzel and other officious youngsters policed an irregular circle in the crowd. He saw Jimmie facing him; there was no help for it; he dropped his books—the old books which would not "do."

Now it was the fashion among tiny Whilomville belligerents to fight much in the manner of little bear cubs. Two boys would rush upon each other, immediately grapple, and—the best boy having probably succeeded in getting the coveted "under hold"—there would presently be a crash to earth of the inferior boy, and he would probably be mopped around in the dust, or the mud, or the snow, or whatever the material happened to be, until the engagement was over. Whatever havoc was dealt out to him was ordinarily the result of his wild endeavors to throw off his opponent and arise. Both infants wept during the fight, as a common thing, and if they wept very hard, the fight was a harder fight. The result was never very bloody, but the complete dishevelment of both victor and vanquished was extraordinary. As for the spectacle, it more resembled a collision of boys in a fog than it did the manly art of hammering another human being into speechless inability.

The fight began when Jimmie made a mad, bear-cub rush at the new boy, amid savage cries of encouragement. Willie Dalzel, for instance, almost howled his head off. Very timid boys on the outskirts of the throng felt their hearts leap to their throats. It was a time when certain natures were impressed that only man is vile.

But it appeared that bear-cub rushing was no part of the instruction received by boys in Jersey City. Boys in Jersey City were apparently schooled curiously. Upon the onslaught of Jimmie, the stranger had gone wild with rage—boylike. Some spark had touched his fighting blood, and in a moment he was a cornered, desperate, fire-eyed little man. He began to swing his arms, to revolve them so swiftly that one might have considered him a small working model of an extra-fine patented windmill which was caught in a gale. For a moment this defense surprised Jimmie more than it damaged him, but two moments later a small, knotty fist caught him squarely in the eye, and with a shriek he went down in defeat. He lay on the ground so stunned that he could not even cry; but if he had been able to cry, he would have cried over his prestige—or something —not over his eye.

There was a dreadful tumult. The boys cast glances of amazement and terror upon the victor, and thronged upon the beaten Jimmie Trescott. It was a moment of excitement so intense that one cannot say what happened. Never before had Whilomville seen such a thing—not the little tots. They were aghast, dumbfounded, and they glanced often over their shoulders at the new boy, who stood alone, his clenched fists at his side, his face crimson, his lips still working with the fury of battle.

But there was another surprise for Whilomville. It might have been seen that the little victor was silently debating against an impulse.

But the impulse won, for the lone lad from Jersey City suddenly wheeled, sprang like a demon, and struck another boy.

A curtain should be drawn before this deed. A knowledge of it is really too much for the heart to bear. The other boy was Willie Dalzel. The lone lad from Jersey City had smitten him full sore.

There is little to say of it. It must have been that a feeling worked gradually to the top of the little stranger's wrath that Jimmie Trescott had been a mere tool, that the front and center of his persecutors had been Willie Dalzel; and, being rendered temporarily lawless by his fighting blood, he raised his hand and smote for revenge.

Willie Dalzel had been in the middle of a vandal's cry, which screeched out over the voices of everybody. The new boy's fist cut it in half, so to say. And then arose the howl of an amazed and terrorized walrus.

One wishes to draw a second curtain. Without discussion or inquiry or brief retort, Willie Dalzel ran away. He ran like a hare straight for home, this redoubtable chieftain. Following him at a heavy and slow pace ran the impassioned new boy. The scene was long remembered.

Willie Dalzel was no coward; he had been panic-stricken into running away from a new thing. He ran as a man might run from the sudden appearance of a vampire or a ghoul or a gorilla. This was no time for academics—he ran.

Jimmie slowly gathered himself and came to his feet. "Where's Willie?" said he, first of all. The crowd sniggered. "Where's Willie?" said Jimmie again.

"Why, he licked him *too!*" answered a boy suddenly.

"He did?" said Jimmie. He sat weakly down on the roadway. "He did?" After allowing a moment for the fact to sink into him, he looked up at the crowd with his one good eye and his one bunged eye, and smiled cheerfully.

June, 1900
[*Harper's Magazine*, Vol. 101, pp. 56–63.]

THIS MAJESTIC LIE*

I

In the twilight, a great crowd was streaming up the Prado in Havana. The people had been down to the shore to laugh and twiddle their fingers at the American blockading fleet—mere colorless shapes on the edge of the sea. Gorgeous challenges had been issued to the faraway ships by little children and women while the men laughed. Havana was happy, for it was known that the illustrious sailor Don Patricio de Montojo had with his fleet met the decaying ships of one Dewey and smitten them into stuffing for a baby's pillow. Of course the American sailors were drunk at the time, but the American sailors were always drunk. Newsboys galloped among the crowd crying *La Lucha* and *La Marina*. The papers said: "This is as we foretold. How could it be otherwise when the cowardly Yankees met our brave sailors?" But the tongues of the exuberant people ran more at large. One man said in a loud voice: "How unfortunate it is that we still have to buy meat in Havana, when so much pork is floating in Manila Bay!" Amid the consequent laughter, another man retorted: "Oh, never mind! That pork in Manila is rotten. It always was rotten." Still another man said: "But, little friend, it would make good manure for our fields if only we had it." And still another man said: "Ah, wait until our soldiers get with the wives of the Americans, and there will be many little Yankees to serve hot on our tables. The men of the *Maine* simply made our appetites good. Never mind the pork in Manila. There

* *Wounds in the Rain.*

will be plenty." Women laughed; children laughed because their mothers laughed; everybody laughed. And—a word with you—these people were cackling and chuckling and insulting their own dead, their own dead men of Spain, for if the poor green corpses floated then in Manila Bay, they were not American corpses.

The newsboys came charging with an extra. The inhabitants of Philadelphia had fled to the forests because of a Spanish bombardment, and also Boston was besieged by the Apaches, who had totally invested the town. The Apache artillery had proved singularly effective, and an American garrison had been unable to face it. In Chicago, millionaires were giving away their palaces for two or three loaves of bread. These dispatches were from Madrid, and every word was truth, but they added little to the enthusiasm, because the crowd—God help mankind—was greatly occupied with visions of Yankee pork floating in Manila Bay. This will be thought to be embittered writing. Very well; the writer admits its untruthfulness in one particular. It is untruthful in that it fails to reproduce one hundredth part of the grossness and indecency of popular expression in Havana up to the time when the people knew they were beaten.

There were no lights on the Prado or in other streets, because of a military order. In the slow-moving crowd, there were a young man and an old woman. Suddenly the young man laughed a strange metallic laugh and spoke in English, not cautiously. "That's damned hard to listen to."

The woman spoke quickly. "Hush, you little idiot. Do you want to be walkin' across that grass-plot in Cabanas with your arms tied behind you?" Then she murmured sadly: "Johnnie, I wonder if that's true—what they say about Manila?"

"I don't know," said Johnnie, "but I think they're lying."

As they crossed the Plaza, they could see that the Café Tacón was crowded with Spanish officers in blue and white pajama uniforms. Wine and brandy were being wildly consumed in honor of the victory at Manila. "Let's hear what they say," said Johnnie to his companion, and they moved across the street and in under the *portales*. The owner of the Café Tacón was standing on a table making a speech amid cheers. He was advocating the crucifixion of such Americans as fell into Spanish hands, and—it was all very sweet and white and tender, but above all it was chivalrous, because it is well known that the Spaniards are a chivalrous people. It has been remarked both by the English newspapers and by the bulls that are bred for the red death. And secretly the corpses in Manila Bay mocked this jubilee; the mocking, mocking corpses in Manila Bay.

II

To be blunt, Johnnie was an American spy. Once he had been the manager of a sugar plantation in Pinar del Rio, and during the insurrection it had been his distinguished function to pay tribute money, food, and forage alike to Spanish columns and insurgent bands. He was performing this straddle with benefit to his crops and with mildew to his conscience when Spain and the United States agreed to skirmish, both in the name of honor. It then became a military necessity that he should change his base. Whatever of the province was still alive was sorry to see him go, for he had been a very dexterous man, and food and wine had been in his house even when a man with a mango could gain the envy of an entire Spanish battalion. Without doubt he had been a mere trimmer, but it was because of his crop—and he always wrote the word thus: C R O P. In those days a man of peace and commerce was in a position parallel to the watchmaker who essayed a task in the midst of a drunken brawl, with oaths, bottles, and bullets flying about his intent bowed head. So many of them—or all of them—were trimmers, and to any armed force they fervently said: "God assist you." And behold, the trimmers dwelt safely in a tumultuous land, and without effort save that their little machines for trimming ran night and day. So, many a plantation became covered with a maze of lies, as if thick-webbing spiders had run from stalk to stalk in the cane. So, sometimes a planter incurred an equal hatred from both sides, and, when in trouble, there was no camp to which he could flee save, straight in air, the camp of the heavenly host.

If Johnnie had not had a crop, he would have been plainly on the side of the insurgents, but his crop staked him down to the soil at a point where the Spaniards could always be sure of finding him—him or his crop; it is the same thing. But when war came between Spain and the United States he could no longer be the cleverest trimmer in Pinar del Rio. And he retreated upon Key West, losing much of his baggage train, not because of panic, but because of wisdom. In Key West he was no longer the manager of a big Cuban plantation; he was a little tan-faced refugee without much money. Mainly he listened; there was nought else to do. In the first place he was a young man of extremely slow speech, and in the Key West Hotel tongues ran like pinwheels. If he had projected his methodic way of thought and speech upon this hurricane, he would have been as effective as the man who tries to smoke against the gale. This truth did not impress him. Really, he was impressed with the fact that, although he knew much of Cuba, he could not talk so rapidly and wisely of it as many war correspondents who had not yet seen the island. Usually he brooded in silence over a bottle of beer and the loss of his crop. He received no sympathy, although there was a plenitude of tender souls. War's first step is to make expectation so high that all present things are fogged and darkened in a tense wonder of the future. None cared about the collapse of Johnnie's plantation when all were thinking of the probable collapse of cities and fleets.

In the meantime battleships, monitors, cruisers, gunboats, and torpedo craft arrived, departed, arrived, departed. Rumors sang about the ears of warships hurriedly coaling. Rumors sang about the ears of warships leisurely coming to anchor. This happened and that happened, and if the news arrived at Key West as a mouse, it was often enough cabled north as an elephant. The correspondents at Key West were perfectly capable of adjusting their perspective, but many of the editors in the United States were like deaf men at whom one has to roar. A few quiet words of information were not enough for them; one had to bawl into their ears a whirlwind tale of heroism, blood, death, victory—or defeat; at any rate, a tragedy. The papers should have sent playwrights to the first part of the war. Playwrights are allowed to lower the curtain from time to time and say to the crowd: "Mark ye, now! Three or four months are supposed to elapse." But the poor devils at Key West were obliged to keep the curtain up all the time. "This isn't a continuous performance." "Yes, it is; it's *got* to be a continuous performance. The welfare of the paper demands it. The people want news." Very well: continuous performance. It is strange how men of sense can go aslant at the bidding of other men of sense and combine to contribute to a general mess of exaggeration and bombast. But we did; and in the midst of the furor I remember the still figure of Johnnie, the planter, the ex-trimmer. He looked dazed.

This was in May.

We all liked him. From time to time some of us heard in his words the vibrant note of a thoughtful experience. But it could not be well heard; it was only like the sound of a bell from under the floor. We were too busy with our own clatter. He was taciturn and competent, while we solved the war in a babble of tongues. Soon we went about our peaceful paths saying ironically one to another: "War is hell." Meanwhile, managing editors fought us tooth and nail, and we all were sent boxes of medals inscribed: "Incompetency." We became furious with ourselves. Why couldn't we send hair-raising dispatches? Why couldn't we inflame the wires? All this we did. If a first-class armored cruiser which had once been a towboat fired a six-pounder shot from her forward thirteen-inch gun turret, the world heard of it, you bet. We were not idle men. We had come to report the war, and we did it. Our good names and our salaries depended upon it, and we were urged by our managing editors to remember that the American people were a collection of super-nervous idiots who would immediately have convulsions if we did not throw them some news—any news. It was not true, at all. The American people were anxious for things decisive to happen; they were not anxious to be lulled to satisfaction with a drug. But we lulled them. We told them this and we told them that, and I warrant you our screaming sounded like the noise of a lot of sea birds settling for the night among the black crags.

In the meantime, Johnnie stared and meditated. In his unhurried, unstartled manner he was singularly like another man who was flying the pennant as commander-in-chief of the North Atlantic Squadron. Johnnie was a refugee; the admiral was an admiral. And yet they were much akin, these two. Their brother was the Strategy Board—the only capable political institution of the war. At Key West the naval officers spoke of their business and were devoted to it and were bound to succeed in it, but when the flagship was in port the only two people who were independent and sane were the admiral and Johnnie. The rest of us were lulling the public with drugs.

There was much discussion of the new batteries at Havana. Johnnie was a typical American. In Europe a typical American is a man with a hard eye, chin whiskers, and a habit of speaking through his nose. Johnnie was a young man of great energy, ready to accomplish a colossal thing for the basic reason that he was ignorant of its magnitude. In fact he attacked all obstacles in life in a spirit of contempt, seeing them smaller than they were until he had actually surmounted them—when he was likely to be immensely pleased with himself. Somewhere in him there was a sentimental tenderness, but it was like a light seen afar at night; it came, went, appeared again in a new place, flickered, flared, went out, left you in a void and angry. And if his sentimental tenderness was a light, the darkness in which it puzzled you was his irony of soul. This irony was directed first at himself; then at you; then at the nation and the flag; then at God. It was a midnight in which you searched for the little elusive, ashamed spark of tender sentiment. Sometimes you thought this was all pretext, the manner and the way of fear of the wit of others; sometimes you thought he was a hardened savage; usually you did not think, but waited in the cheerful certainty that in time the little flare of light would appear in the gloom.

Johnnie decided that he would go and spy upon the fortifications of Havana. If any one wished to know of those batteries, it was the admiral of the squadron, but the admiral of the squadron knew much. I feel sure that he knew the size and position of every gun. To be sure, new guns might be mounted at any time, but they would not be big guns, and doubtless he lacked in his cabin less information than would be worth a man's life. Still, Johnnie decided to be a spy. He would go and look. We of the newspapers pinned him fast to the tail of our kite, and he was taken to see the admiral. I judge that the admiral did not display much interest in the plan. But at any rate it seems that he touched Johnnie smartly enough with a brush to make him, officially, a spy. Then Johnnie bowed and left the cabin. There was no other machinery. If Johnnie was to end his life and leave a little book about it, no one cared—least of all, Johnnie and the admiral. When he came aboard the tug, he displayed his usual stalwart and rather selfish zest for fried eggs. It was all some kind of ordinary matter. It was done every day. It was the business of packing pork, sewing shoes, binding hay. It was commonplace. No one could adjust it, get it in proportion, until—afterwards. On a dark night, they heaved him into a small boat and rowed him to the beach.

III

And one day he appeared at the door of a little lodging house in Havana kept by Martha Clancy, born in Ireland, bred in New York, fifteen years married to a Spanish captain, and now a widow, keeping Cuban lodgers who had no money with which to pay her. She opened the door only a little way and looked down over her spectacles at him.

"Good-mornin', Martha," he said.

She looked a moment in silence. Then she made an indescribable gesture of weariness. "Come in," she said. He stepped inside. "And in God's name couldn't you keep your neck out of this rope? And so you had to come here, did you—to Havana? Upon my soul, Johnnie, my son, you are the biggest fool on two legs."

He moved past her into the courtyard and took his old chair at the table, between the winding stairway and the door—near the orange tree. "Why am I?" he demanded stoutly. She made no reply until she had taken seat in her rocking chair and puffed several times upon a cigarette. Then through the smoke she said meditatively: "Everybody knows ye are a damned little mambi." Sometimes she spoke with an Irish accent.

He laughed. "I'm no more of a mambi than *you* are, anyhow."

"I'm no mambi. But your name is poison to half the Spaniards in Havana. That you know. And if you were once safe in Cayo Hueso, 'tis nobody but a born fool who would come blunderin' into Havana again. Have ye had your dinner?"

"What have you got?" he asked before committing himself.

She arose and spoke without confidence as she moved toward the cupboard. "There's some codfish salad."

"*What?*" said he.

"Codfish salad."

"*Codfish what?*"

"Codfish salad. Ain't it good enough for ye? Maybe this is Delmonico's —no? Maybe ye never heard that the Yankees have us blockaded, hey? Maybe ye think food can be picked in the streets here now, hey? I'll tell ye one thing, my son: if you stay here long you'll see the want of it, and so you had best not throw it over your shoulder."

The spy settled determinedly in his chair and delivered himself of his final decision. "That may all be true, but I'm damned if I eat codfish salad."

Old Martha was a picture of quaint despair. "You'll not?"

"No!"

"Then," she sighed piously, "may the Lord have mercy on ye, Johnnie, for you'll never do here. 'Tis not the time for you. You're due after the blockade. Will you do me the favor of translating why you won't eat codfish salad, you skinny little insurrecto?"

"Codfish salad!" he said with a deep sneer. "Who ever heard of it?"

Outside, on the jumbled pavement of the street, an occasional two-wheeled cart passed with deafening thunder, making one think of the over-turning of houses. Down from the pale sky over the patio came a heavy odor of Havana itself, a smell of old straw. The wild cries of vendors could be heard at intervals.

"You'll not?"

"No."

"And why not?"

"Codfish salad? Not by a blame sight!"

"Well—all right, then. You are more of a pig-headed young imbecile than even I thought from seeing you come into Havana here, where half the town knows you and the poorest Spaniard would give a gold piece to see you go into Cabanas and forget to come out. Did I tell you my son Alfred is sick? Yes, poor little fellow, he lies up in the room you used to have. The fever. And did you see Woodham in Key West? Heaven save us, what quick time he made in getting out. I hear Figtree and Button are working in the cable office over there—no? And when is the war going to end? Are the Yankees going to try to take Havana? It will be a hard job, Johnnie. The Spaniards say it is impossible. Everybody is laughing at the Yankees. I hate to go into the street and hear them. Is General Lee going to lead the army? What's become of Springer? I see you've got a new pair of shoes."

In the evening there was a sudden loud knock at the outer door. Martha looked at Johnnie, and Johnnie looked at Martha. He was still sitting in the patio, smoking. She took the lamp and set it on a table in the little parlor. This parlor connected the street door with the patio, and so Johnnie would be protected from the sight of the people who knocked by the broad il-luminated tract. Martha moved in pensive fashion upon the latch. "Who's there?" she asked casually.

"The police." There it was, an old melodramatic incident from the stage, from the romances. One could scarce believe it. It had all the dignity of a classic resurrection. "The police!" One sneers at its probability; it is too venerable. But so it happened.

"Who?" said Martha.

"The police!"

"What do you want here?"

"Open the door and we'll tell you."

Martha drew back the ordinary huge bolts of a Havana house and opened the door a trifle. "Tell me what you want and begone quickly," she said, "for my little boy is ill of the fever—"

She could see four or five dim figures, and now one of these suddenly placed a foot well within the door so that she might not close it. "We have come for Johnnie. We must search your house."

"Johnnie? Johnnie? Who is Johnnie?" said Martha in her best manner. The police inspector grinned with the light upon his face. "Don't you know Señor Johnnie from Pinar del Rio?" he asked.

"Before the war—yes. But now—where is he?—he must be in Key West?"

"He is in your house."

"He? In my house? Do me the favor to think that I have some intelligence. Would I be likely to be harboring a Yankee in these times? You must think I have no more head than an Orden Publico. And I'll not have you search my house, for there is no one here save my son—who is maybe dying of the fever—and the doctor. The doctor is with him because now is the crisis, and any one little thing may kill or cure my boy, and you will do me the favor to consider what may happen if I allow five or six heavy-footed policemen to go tramping all over my house. You may think—"

"Stop it," said the chief police officer at last. He was laughing and weary and angry.

Martha checked her flow of Spanish. "There!" she thought, "I've done my best. He ought to fall in with it." But as the police entered she began on them again. "You will search the house whether I like it or no. Very well; but if anything happens to my boy? It is a nice way of conduct, anyhow—coming into the house of a widow at night and talking much about this Yankee, and—"

"For God's sake, Señora, hold your tongue. We—"

"Oh, yes, the señora can for God's sake very well hold her tongue, but that wouldn't assist you men into the street where you belong. Take care: if my sick boy suffers from this prowling! No, you'll find nothing in that wardrobe. And do you think he would be under the table? Don't overturn all that linen. Look you, when you go upstairs, tread lightly."

Leaving a man on guard at the street door and another in the patio, the chief policeman and the remainder of his men ascended to the gallery from which opened three sleeping-rooms. They were followed by Martha, adjuring them to make no noise. The first room was empty; the second room was empty; as they approached the door of the third room, Martha whispered supplications. "Now, in the name of God, don't disturb my boy."

The inspector motioned his men to pause, and then he pushed open the door. Only one weak candle was burning in the room, and its yellow light fell upon the bed, whereon was stretched the figure of a little curly-headed boy in a white nighty. He was asleep, but his face was pink with fever, and his lips were murmuring some half-coherent childish nonsense. At the head of the bed stood the motionless figure of a man. His back was to the door, but upon hearing a noise he held up a solemn hand. There was an odor of medicine. Out on the balcony, Martha apparently was weeping.

The inspector hesitated for a moment; then he noiselessly entered the room and with his yellow cane prodded under the bed, in the cupboard, and behind the window curtains. Nothing came of it. He shrugged his shoulders and went out to the balcony. He was smiling sheepishly. Evidently he knew that he had been beaten. "Very good, Señora," he said. "You are clever; some day I shall be clever, too." He shook his finger at her. He was threatening her, but he affected to be playful. "Then—beware! Beware!"

Martha replied blandly, "My late husband, El Capitan Señor Don Patricio de Castellon y Valladolid, was a cavalier of Spain, and if he was alive tonight he would now be cutting the ears from the heads of you and your miserable men, who smell frightfully of cognac."

"Por Dios!" muttered the inspector as, followed by his band, he made his way down the spiral staircase. "It is a tongue! One vast tongue!" At the street door they made ironical bows; they departed, they were angry men.

Johnnie came down when he heard Martha bolting the door behind the police. She brought back the lamp to the table in the patio and stood beside it, thinking. Johnnie dropped into his old chair. The expression on the spy's face was curious, it pictured glee, anxiety, self-complacency; above all it pictured self-complacency. Martha said nothing; she was still by the lamp, musing.

The long silence was suddenly broken by a tremendous guffaw from Johnnie. "Did you ever see sich a lot of fools!" He leaned his head far back and roared victorious merriment.

Martha was almost dancing in her apprehension. "Hush! Be quiet, you little demon! Hush! Do me the favor to allow them to get to the corner before you bellow like a walrus. Be quiet."

The spy ceased his laughter and spoke in indignation. "Why?" he demanded. "Aint' I got a right to laugh?"

"Not with a noise like a cow fallin' into a cucumber-frame," she answered sharply. "Do me the favor—" Then she seemed overwhelmed with a sense of the general hopelessness of Johnnie's character. She began to wag her head. "Oh, but you are the boy for gettin' yourself into the tiger's cage without even so much as the thought of a pocketknife in your thick head. You would be a genius of the first water if you only had a little sense. And now you're here, what are you going to do?"

He grinned at her. "I'm goin' to hold an inspection of the land and sea defenses of the city of Havana."

Martha's spectacles dropped low on her nose, and, looking over the rims of them in grave meditation, she said: "If you can't put up with codfish salad, you had better make short work of your inspection of the land and sea defenses of the city of Havana. You are likely to starve in the meantime. A man who is particular about his food has come to the wrong town if he is in Havana now."

"No, but—" asked Johnnie seriously. "Haven't you any bread?"

"Bread!"

"Well, coffee, then? Coffee alone will do."

"Coffee!"

Johnnie arose deliberately and took his hat. Martha eyed him. "And where do you think you are goin'?" she asked cuttingly.

Still deliberate, Johnnie moved in the direction of the street door. "I'm goin' where I can get something to eat."

Martha sank into a chair with a moan which was a finished opinion— almost a definition—of Johnnie's behavior in life. "And where will you go?" she asked faintly.

"Oh, I don't know," he rejoined. "Some café. Guess I'll go to the Café Aguacate. They feed you well there. I remember—"

"*You* remember? *They* remember! They know you as well as if you were the sign over the door."

"Oh, they won't give me away," said Johnnie with stalwart confidence.

"Gi-give you away? Give you a-way?" stammered Martha.

The spy made no answer, but went to the door, unbarred it, and passed into the street. Martha caught her breath and ran after him and came face to face with him as he turned to shut the door. "Johnnie, if ye come back, bring a loaf of bread. I'm dyin' for one good honest bite in a slice of bread."

She heard his peculiar derisive laugh as she bolted the door. She returned to her chair in the patio. "Well, there," she said with affection, admiration, and contempt. "There he goes! The most hard-headed little ignoramus in twenty nations! What does he care? Nothin'! And why is it? Pure bred-in-the-bone ignorance. Just because he can't stand codfish salad he goes out to a café! A café where they know him as if they had made him! Well—I won't see him again, probably.—But if he comes back, I hope he brings some bread. I'm near dead for it."

IV

Johnnie strolled carelessly through dark narrow streets. Near every corner were two orden publicos—a kind of soldier-police—quiet in the shadow of some doorway, their Remingtons ready, their eyes shining. Johnnie walked past as if he owned them, and their eyes followed him with a sort of lazy mechanical suspicion which was militant in none of its moods.

Johnnie was suffering from a desire to be splendidly imprudent. He wanted to make the situation gasp and thrill and tremble. From time to time he tried to conceive the idea of his being caught, but to save his eyes he could not imagine it. Such an event was impossible to his peculiar breed of fatalism, which could not have conceded death until he had moldered seven years.

He arrived at the Café Aguacate and found it much changed. The thick wooden shutters were up to keep light from shining into the street. Inside, there were only a few Spanish officers. Johnnie walked to the private rooms at the rear. He found an empty one and pressed the electric button. When he had passed through the main part of the café no one had noted him. The first to recognize him was the waiter who answered the bell. This worthy man turned to stone before the presence of Johnnie.

"Buenos noche, Francisco," said the spy, enjoying himself. "I have hunger. Bring me bread, butter, eggs, and coffee." There was a silence; the waiter did not move; Johnnie smiled casually at him.

The man's throat moved; then like one suddenly re-endowed with life, he bolted from the room. After a long time, he returned with the proprietor of the place. In the wicked eye of the latter there gleamed the light of a plan. He did not respond to Johnnie's genial greeting, but at once proceeded to develop his position. "Johnnie," he said, "bread is very dear in Havana. It is very dear."

"Is it?" said Johnnie, looking keenly at the speaker. He understood at once that here was some sort of attack upon him.

"Yes," answered the proprietor of the Café Aguacate slowly and softly. "It is very dear. I think tonight one small bit of bread will cost you one centene—in advance." A centene approximates five dollars in gold.

The spy's face did not change. He appeared to reflect. "And how much for the butter?" he asked at last.

The proprietor gestured. "There is no butter. Do you think we can have everything, with those Yankee pigs sitting out there on their ships?"

"And how much for the coffee?" asked Johnnie musingly.

Again the two men surveyed each other during a period of silence. Then the proprietor said gently, "I think your coffee will cost you about two centenes."

"And the eggs?"

"Eggs are very dear. I think eggs would cost you about three centenes for each one."

The new looked at the old; the North Atlantic looked at the Mediterranean; the wooden nutmeg looked at the olive. Johnnie slowly took six centenes from his pocket and laid them on the table. "That's for bread, coffee, and *one* egg. I don't think I could eat more than one egg tonight. I'm not so hungry as I was."

The proprietor held a perpendicular finger and tapped the table with it. "Oh, señor," he said politely, "I think you would like two eggs."

Johnnie saw the finger. He understood it. "Ye-e-es," he drawled. "I would like two eggs." He placed three more centenes on the table.

"And a little thing for the waiter? I am sure his services will be excellent, invaluable."

"Ye-e-es, for the waiter." Another centene was laid on the table.

The proprietor bowed and preceded the waiter out of the room. There was a mirror on the wall and, springing to his feet, the spy thrust his face close to the honest glass. "Well, I'm damned!" he ejaculated. "Is this me or is this the Honorable D. Hayseed Whiskers of Kansas? Who am I, anyhow? Five dollars in gold!—Say, these people are clever. They know their business, they do. Bread, coffee, and two eggs, and not even sure of getting it! Fifty dol—Never mind; wait until the war is over. Fifty dollars gold!" He sat for a long time; nothing happened. "Eh," he said at last, "that's the game." As the front door of the café closed upon him, he heard the proprietor and one of the waiters burst into derisive laughter.

Martha was waiting for him. "And here ye are, safe back," she said with delight as she let him enter. "And did ye bring the bread? Did ye bring the bread?"

But she saw that he was raging like a lunatic. His face was red and swollen with temper; his eyes shot forth gleams. Presently he stood before her in the patio where the light fell on him. "Don't speak to me," he choked out waving his arms. "Don't speak to me! *Damn* your bread! I went to the Café Aguacate! Oh, yes, I went there! Of course, I did! And do you know what they did to me? No! Oh, they didn't do anything to me at all! Not a thing! Fifty dollars! Ten gold pieces!"

"May the saints guard us," cried Martha. "And what was that for?"

"Because they wanted them more than I did," snarled Johnnie. "Don't you see the game? I go into the Café Aguacate. The owner of the place says to himself, 'Hello! Here's that Yankee what they call Johnnie. He's got no right here in Havana. Guess I'll peach on him to the police. They'll put him in Cabanas as a spy.' Then he does a little more thinking, and finally he says, 'No; I guess I won't peach on him just this minute. First, I'll take a small flier myself.' So in he comes and looks me right in the eye and says, 'Excuse me, but it will be a centene for the bread, a centene for the coffee, and eggs are at three centenes each. Besides, there will be a small matter of another gold piece for the waiter.' I think this over. I think it over hard.—He's clever anyhow.—When this cruel war is over, I'll be after him.—I'm a nice secret agent of the United States government, I am. I come here to be too clever for all the Spanish police, and the first thing I do is get buncoed by a rotten little thimblerigger in a café. Oh, yes, I'm all right."

"May the saints guard us!" cried Martha again. "I'm old enough to be your mother, or maybe your grandmother, and I've seen a lot; but it's many a year since I laid eyes on such a ign'rant and wrong-headed little red Indian as ye are! Why didn't ye take my advice and stay here in the house with decency and comfort? But he must be all for doing everything high and mighty. The Café Aguacate, if ye please. No plain food for his highness. He turns up his nose at codfish sal—"

"Thunder and lightnin', are you going to ram that thing down my throat every two minutes? Are you?" And in truth she could see that one more reference to that illustrious viand would break the back of Johnnie's gentle disposition as one breaks a twig on the knee. She shifted with Celtic ease. "Did ye bring the bread?" she asked.

He gazed at her for a moment and suddenly laughed. "I forgot to mention," he informed her impressively, "that they did not take the trouble to give me either the bread, the coffee, or the eggs."

"The powers!" cried Martha.

"But it's all right. I stopped at a shop." From his pockets, he brought a small loaf, some kind of German sausage, and a flask of Jamaica rum. "About all I could get. And they didn't want to sell them, either. They expect presently they can exchange a box of sardines for a grand piano."

" 'We are not blockaded by the Yankee warships; we are blockaded by our grocers,' " said Martha, quoting the epidemic Havana saying. But she did not delay long from the little loaf. She cut a slice from it and sat eagerly munching. Johnnie seemed more interested in the Jamaica rum. He looked up from his second glass, however, because he heard a peculiar sound. The old woman was weeping. "Hey, what's this?" he demanded in distress, but with the manner of a man who thinks gruffness is the only thing that will make people feel better and cease. "What's this, anyhow? What are you cryin' for?"

"It's the bread," sobbed Martha. "It's the—it's—the br-e-a-ddd."

"Huh? What's the matter with it?"

"It's so good, so g-good." The rain of tears did not prevent her from continuing her unusual report. "Oh, it's so good! This is the first in weeks. I didn't know bread could be so l-like heaven."

"Here," said Johnnie seriously. "Take a little mouthful of this rum. It will do you good."

"No; I only want the bub-bub-bread."

"Well, take the bread, too.—There you are. Now you feel better.—By Jove, when I think of that Café Aguacate man! Fifty dollars gold! And then not to get anything, either. Say, after the war, I'm going there, and I'm just going to raze that place to the ground. You see! I'll make him think he can charge ME fifteen dollars for an egg.—And then not give me the egg."

V

Johnnie's subsequent activity in Havana could truthfully be related in part to a certain temporary price of eggs. It is interesting to note how close that famous event got to his eye, so that, according to the law of perspective, it was as big as the Capitol of Washington, where centers the spirit of his nation. Around him, he felt a similar and ferocious expression of life which informed him too plainly that, if he was caught, he was doomed. Neither the garrison nor the citizens of Havana would tolerate any nonsense in regard to him if he was caught. He would have the steel screw against his neck in short order. And what was the main thing to bear him up against the desire to run away before his work was done? A certain temporary price of eggs! It not only hid the Capitol at Washington; it obscured the dangers in Havana.

Something was learned of the Santa Clara battery, because one morning an old lady in black, accompanied by a young man—evidently her son— visited a house which was to rent on the height, in the rear of the battery. The portero was too lazy and sleepy to show them over the premises, but he granted them permission to investigate for themselves. They spent most of their time on the flat parapeted roof of the house. At length they came down and said that the place did not suit them. The portero went to sleep again.

Johnnie was never discouraged by the thought that his operations would be of small benefit to the admiral commanding the fleet in adjacent waters, and to the general commanding the army which was not going to attack Havana from the land side. At that time it was all the world's opinion that the army from Tampa would presently appear on the Cuban beach at some convenient point to the east or west of Havana. It turned out, of course, that the condition of the defenses of Havana was of not the slightest military importance to the United States, since the city was never attacked either by land or sea. But Johnnie could not foresee this. He continued to take his fancy risk, continued his majestic lie, with satisfaction, sometimes with delight, and with pride. And in the psychologic distance was old

Martha, dancing with fear and shouting: "Oh, Johnnie, me son, what a born fool ye are!"

Sometimes she would address him thus: "And when ye learn all this, how are ye goin' to get out with it?" She was contemptuous.

He would reply, as serious as a Cossack in his fatalism: "Oh, I'll get out some way."

His maneuvers in the vicinity of Regla and Guanabacoa were of a brilliant character. He haunted the sunny long grass in the manner of a jack rabbit. Sometimes he slept under a palm, dreaming of the American advance fighting its way along the military road to the foot of Spanish defenses. Even when awake, he often dreamed it and thought of the all-day crash and hot roar of an assault. Without consulting Washington, he had decided that Havana should be attacked from the southeast. An advance from the west could be contested right up to the bar of the Hotel Inglaterra, but when the first ridge in the southeast would be taken, the whole city with most of its defenses would lie under the American siege guns. And the approach to this position was as reasonable as is any approach toward the muzzles of magazine rifles. Johnnie viewed the grassy fields always as a prospective battleground, and one can see him lying there, filling the landscape with visions of slow-crawling black infantry columns, galloping batteries of artillery, streaks of faint blue smoke marking the modern firing lines, clouds of dust, a vision of ten thousand tragedies. And his ears heard the noises.

But he was no idle shepherd boy with a head haunted by somber and glorious fancies. On the contrary, he was much occupied with practical matters. Some months after the close of the war, he asked me: "Were you ever fired at from very near?" I explained some experiences which I had stupidly esteemed as having been rather near. "But did you ever have 'm fire a volley on you from close—very close—say, thirty feet?"

Highly scandalized, I answered, "No; in that case, I would not be the crowning feature of the Smithsonian Institute."

"Well," he said, "it's a funny effect. You feel as if every hair on your head had been snatched out by the roots." Questioned further, he said, "I walked right up on a Spanish outpost at daybreak once, and about twenty men let go at me. Thought I was a Cuban army, I suppose."

"What did you do?"

"I run."

"Did they hit you, at all?"

"Naw."

It had been arranged that some light ship of the squadron should rendezvous with him at a certain lonely spot on the coast on a certain day and hour and pick him up. He was to wave something white. His shirt was not white, but he waved it whenever he could see the signal-tops of a warship. It was a very tattered banner. After a ten-mile scramble through almost pathless thickets, he had very little on him which respectable men would call a shirt, and the less one says about his trousers the better. This naked savage, then, walked all day up and down a small bit of beach waving a brown rag. At night, he slept in the sand. At full daybreak he began to wave his rag; at noon he was waving his rag; at nightfall he donned his rag and strove to think of it as a shirt. Thus passed two days, and nothing had happened. Then he retraced a twenty-five-mile way to the house of old Martha. At first she took him to be one of Havana's terrible beggars and cried, "And do you come here for alms? Look out, that I do not beg of you." The one unchanged thing was his laugh of pure mockery. When she heard it, she dragged him through the door. He paid no heed to her ejaculations, but went straight to where he had hidden some gold. As he was untying a bit of string from the neck of a small bag, he said, "How is little Alfred?" "Recovered, thank Heaven." He handed Martha a piece of gold. "Take this and buy what you can on the corner. I'm hungry." Martha departed with expedition. Upon her return, she was beaming. She had foraged a thin chicken, a bunch of radishes, and two bottles of wine. Johnnie had finished the radishes and one bottle of wine when the chicken was still a long way from the table. He called stoutly for more, and so Martha passed again into the street with another gold piece. She bought more radishes, more wine, and some cheese. They had a grand feast, with Johnnie audibly wondering until a late hour why he had waved his rag in vain.

There was no end to his suspense, no end to his work. He knew everything. He was an animate guidebook. After he knew a thing once, he verified it in several different ways in order to make sure. He fitted himself for a useful career, like a young man in a college—with the difference that the shadow of the garrotte fell ever upon his way, and that he was occasionally shot at, and that he could not get enough to eat, and that his existence was apparently forgotten, and that he contracted the fever. But—

One cannot think of the terms in which to describe a futility so vast, so colossal. He had built a little boat, and the sea had receded and left him and his boat a thousand miles inland on the top of a mountain. The war-fate had left Havana out of its plan and thus isolated Johnnie and his several pounds of useful information. The war-fate left Havana to become the somewhat indignant victim of a peaceful occupation at the close of the conflict, and Johnnie's data were worth as much as a carpenter's lien on the north pole. He had suffered and labored for about as complete a bit of absolute nothing as one could invent. If the company which owned the sugar plantation had not generously continued his salary during the war, he would not have been able to pay his expenses on the amount allowed him by the government, which, by the way, was a more complete bit of absolute nothing than one could possibly invent.

VI

I met Johnnie in Havana in October, 1898. If I remember rightly, the U.S.S. *Resolute* and the U.S.S. *Scorpion* were in the harbor, but beyond these two terrible engines of destruction there were not as yet any of the more stern signs of the American success. Many Americans were to be seen in the streets of Havana, where they were not in any way molested. Among them was Johnnie in white duck and a straw hat, cool, complacent, and with eyes rather more steady than ever. I addressed him upon the subject of his supreme failure, but I could not perturb his philosophy. In reply he simply asked me to dinner. "Come to the Café Aguacate at 7:30 tonight," he said. "I haven't been there in a long time. We shall see if they cook as well as ever." I turned up promptly and found Johnnie in a private room smoking a cigar in the presence of a waiter who was blue in the gills. "I've ordered the dinner," he said cheerfully. "Now I want to see if you won't be surprised how well they can do here in Havana." I was surprised. I was dumbfounded. Rarely in the history of the world have two rational men sat down to such a dinner. It must have taxed the ability and endurance of the entire working force of the establishment to provide it. The variety of dishes was of course related to the markets of Havana, but the abundance and general profligacy was related only to Johnnie's imagination. Neither of us had an appetite. Our fancies fled in confusion before this puzzling luxury. I looked at Johnnie as if he were a native of Tibet. I had thought him to be a most simple man, and here I found him reveling in food like a fat old senator of Rome's decadence. And if the dinner itself put me to open-eyed amazement, the names of the wines finished everything. Apparently Johnnie had had but one standard, and that was the cost. If a wine had been very expensive, he had ordered it. I began to think him probably a maniac. At any rate, I was sure that we were both fools. Seeing my fixed stare, he spoke with affected languor: "I wish peacocks' brains and melted pearls were to be had here in Havana. We'd have 'em." Then he grinned. As a mere skirmisher I said, "In New York, we think we dine well; but really this, you know—well—Havana—"

Johnnie waved his hand pompously. "Oh, I know."

Directly after coffee, Johnnie excused himself for a moment and left the room. When he returned he said briskly, "Well, are you ready to go?" As soon as we were in a cab and safely out of hearing of the Café Aguacate, Johnnie lay back and laughed long and joyously.

But I was very serious. "Look here, Johnnie," I said to him solemnly, "when you invite me to dine with you, don't you ever do *that* again. And I'll tell you one thing—when you dine with me you will probably get the ordinary table d'hôte." I was an older man.

"Oh, that's all right," he cried. And then he too grew serious. "Well, as far as I am concerned—as far as I am concerned," he said, "the war is now over."

June 24 and July 1, 1900

[New York *Herald*, June 24, section 6, p. 10;
July 1, supplement, p. 3.]

THE CITY URCHIN AND THE CHASTE VILLAGERS*

After the brief encounters between the Hedge boy and Jimmie Trescott and the Hedge boy and Willie Dalzel, the neighborhood which contained the homes of the boys was, as far as child life is concerned, in a state resembling anarchy. This was owing to the signal overthrow and shameful retreat of the boy who had for several years led a certain little clan by the nose. The adherence of the little community did not go necessarily to the boy who could whip all the others, but it certainly could not go to a boy who had run away in a manner that made his shame patent to the whole world. Willie Dalzel found himself in a painful position. This tiny tribe which had followed him with such unwavering faith was now largely engaged in whistling and catcalling and hooting. He chased a number of them into the sanctity of their own yards, but from these coigns they continued to ridicule him.

But it must not be supposed that the fickle tribe went over in a body to the new light. They did nothing of the sort. They occupied themselves with avenging all which they had endured—gladly enough, too—for many months. As for the Hedge boy, he maintained a curious timid reserve, minding his own business with extreme care, and going to school with that deadly punctuality of which his mother was the genius. Jimmie Trescott suffered no adverse criticism from his fellows. He was entitled to be beaten by a boy who had made Willie Dalzel bellow like a bull-calf and run away. Indeed, he received some honors. He had confronted a very superior boy and received a bang in the eye which for a time was the wonder of the children, and he had not bellowed like a bull-calf. As a matter of fact, he was often invited to tell how it had felt, and this he did with some pride, claiming arrogantly that he had been superior to any particular pain.

* *Whilomville Stories.*

Early in the episode he and the Hedge boy had patched up a treaty. Living next door to each other, they could not fail to have each other often in sight. One afternoon they wandered together in the strange indefinite diplomacy of boyhood. As they drew close the new boy suddenly said, "Napple?"

"Yes," said Jimmie, and the new boy bestowed upon him an apple. It was one of those green-coated winter apples which lie for many months in safe and dry places, and can at any time be brought forth for the persecution of the unwary and inexperienced. An older age would have fled from this apple, but to the unguided youth of Jimmie Trescott it was a thing to be possessed and cherished. Wherefore this apple was the emblem of something more than a truce, despite the fact that it tasted like wet Indian meal; and Jimmie looked at the Hedge boy out of one good eye and one bunged eye. The long-drawn animosities of men have no place in the life of a boy. The boy's mind is flexible; he readjusts his position with an ease which is derived from the fact—simply—that he is not yet a man.

But there were other and more important matters. Johnnie Hedge's exploits had brought him into such prominence among the schoolboys that it was necessary to settle a number of points once and for all. There was the usual number of boys in the school who were popularly known to be champions in their various classes. Among these Johnnie Hedge now had to thread his way, every boy taking it upon himself to feel anxious that Johnnie's exact position should be soon established. His fame as a fighter had gone forth to the world, but there were other boys who had fame as fighters, and the world was extremely anxious to know where to place the newcomer. Various heroes were urged to attempt this classification. Usually it was not accounted a matter of supreme importance, but in this boy life it was essential.

In all cases the heroes were backward enough. It was their followings who agitated the question. And so Johnnie Hedge was more or less beset.

He maintained his bashfulness. He backed away from altercation. It was plain that to bring matters to a point he must be forced into a quarrel. It was also plain that the proper person for the business was some boy who could whip Willie Dalzel, and these formidable warriors were distinctly averse to undertaking the new contract. It is a kind of law in boy life that a quiet, decent, peace-loving lad is able to thrash a wide-mouthed talker. And so it had come to pass that by a peculiar system of elimination most of the real chiefs were quiet, decent, peace-loving boys, and they had no desire to engage in a fight with a boy on the sole ground that it was not known who could whip. Johnnie Hedge attended his affairs, they attended their affairs, and around them waged this discussion of relative merit. Jimmie Trescott took a prominent part in these arguments. He contended that Johnnie Hedge could thrash any boy in the world. He was certain of it, and to any one who opposed him he said, "You just get one of those smashes in the eye, and then you'll see." In the meantime there was a grand and impressive silence in the direction of Willie Dalzel. He had gathered remnants of his clan, but the main parts of his sovereignty were scattered to the winds. He was an enemy.

Owing to the circumspect behavior of the new boy, the commotions on the school grounds came to nothing. He was often asked, "Kin you lick him?" And he invariably replied, "I dun'no." This idea of waging battle with the entire world appalled him.

A war for complete supremacy of the tribe which had been headed by Willie Dalzel was fought out in the country of the tribe. It came to pass that a certain half-dime blood-and-thunder pamphlet had a great vogue in the tribe at this particular time. This story relates the experience of a lad who began his career as cabin boy on a pirate ship. Throughout the first fifteen chapters he was rope's-ended from one end of the ship to the other end, and very often he was felled to the deck by a heavy fist. He lived through enough hardships to have killed a battalion of Turkish soldiers, but in the end he rose upon them. Yes, he rose upon them. Hordes of pirates fell before his intrepid arm, and in the last chapters of the book he is seen jauntily careering on his own hook as one of the most callous pirate captains that ever sailed the seas.

Naturally, when this tale was thoroughly understood by the tribe, they had to dramatize it, although it was a dramatization that would gain no royalties for the author. Now it was plain that the urchin who was cast for the cabin boy's part would lead a life throughout the first fifteen chapters which would attract few actors. Willie Dalzel developed a scheme by which some small lad would play cabin boy during this period of misfortune and abuse, and then, when the cabin boy came to the part where he slew all his enemies and reached his zenith, he, Willie Dalzel, should take the part.

This fugitive and disconnected rendering of a great play opened in Jimmie Trescott's back garden. The path between the two lines of gooseberry bushes was elected unanimously to be the ship. Then Willie Dalzel insisted that Homer Phelps should be the cabin boy. Homer tried the position for a time, and then elected that he would resign in favor of some other victim. There was no other applicant to succeed him, whereupon it became necessary to press some boy. Jimmie Trescott was a great actor, as is well known, but he steadfastly refused to engage for the part. Ultimately they seized upon little Dan Earl, whose disposition was so milky and docile that he would do whatever anybody asked of him. But Dan Earl made the one firm revolt of his life after trying existence as cabin boy for some ten minutes. Willie Dalzel was in despair. Then he suddenly sighted the little brother of Johnnie Hedge, who had come into the garden and in a poor-little-stranger sort of fashion was looking wistfully at the play. When he was invited to become the cabin boy he accepted joyfully, thinking that it was his initiation into the tribe. Then they proceeded to give him the rope's-end and to punch him with a realism which was not altogether painless. Directly he began to cry out. They exhorted him not to cry out, not to mind it, but still they continued to hurt him.

There was a commotion among the gooseberry bushes, two branches were swept aside, and Johnnie Hedge walked down upon them. Every boy stopped in his tracks. Johnnie was boiling with rage.

"Who hurt him?" he said, ferociously. "Did *you?*" He had looked at Willie Dalzel.

Willie Dalzel began to mumble: "We was on'y playin'. Wasn't nothin' fer him to cry fer."

The new boy had at his command some big phrases, and he used them. "I am goin' to whip you within an inch of your life. I am goin' to tan the hide off'n you." And immediately there was a mixture—an infusion—of two boys which looked as if it had been done by a chemist. The other children stood back, stricken with horror. But out of this whirl they presently perceived the figure of Willie Dalzel seated upon the chest of the Hedge boy.

"Got enough?" asked Willie, hoarsely.

"No," choked out the Hedge boy. Then there was another flapping and floundering, and finally another calm.

"Got enough?" asked Willie.

"No," said the Hedge boy. A sort of war cloud again puzzled the sight of the observers. Both combatants were breathless, bloodless in their faces, and very weak.

"Got enough?" said Willie.

"No," said the Hedge boy. The carnage was again renewed. All the spectators were silent but Johnnie Hedge's little brother, who shrilly exhorted him to continue the struggle. But it was not plain that the Hedge boy needed any encouragement, for he was crying bitterly, and it has been explained that when a boy cried it was a bad time to hope for peace. He had managed to wriggle over upon his hands and knees. But Willie Dalzel was tenaciously gripping him from the back, and it seemed that his strength would spend itself in futility. The bear cub seemed to have the advantage of the working model of the windmill. They heaved, uttered strange words, wept, and the sun looked down upon them with steady, unwinking eye.

Peter Washington came out of the stable and observed this tragedy of the back garden. He stood transfixed for a moment, and then ran toward it, shouting: "Hi! What's all dish yere? Hi! Stopper dat, stopper dat, you two! For lan' sake, what's all dish yere?" He grabbed the struggling boys and pulled them apart. He was stormy and fine in his indignation. "For lan' sake! You two kids act like you gwine mad dogs. Stopper dat!" The whitened, tearful, soiled combatants, their clothing all awry, glared fiercely at each other as Peter stood between them, lecturing. They made several futile attempts to circumvent him and again come to battle. As he fended them off with his open hands he delivered his reproaches at Jimmie. "I's s'prised at *you!* I suhtainly is!"

"Why?" said Jimmie. "I 'ain't done nothin'. What have I done?"

"Y-y-you done 'courage dese yere kids ter scrap," said Peter, virtuously.

"Me?" cried Jimmie. "I 'ain't had nothin' to do with it."

"I raikon you 'ain't," retorted Peter, with heavy sarcasm. "I raikon you been er-prayin', 'ain't you?" Turning to Willie Dalzel, he said, "You jest take an' run erlong outer dish yere or I'll jest nachually take an' dam-nearkill you." Willie Dalzel went. To the new boy Peter said: "You look like you had some saince, but I raikon you don't know no more'n er rabbit. You jest take an' trot erlong off home, an' don' lemme caitch you round yere er-fightin' or I'll break yer back." The Hedge boy moved away with dignity, followed by his little brother. The latter, when he had placed a sufficient distance between himself and Peter, played his fingers at his nose and called out: "Nig-ger-r-r! Nig-ger-r-r!"

Peter Washington's resentment poured out upon Jimmie. "'Pears like you never would understan' you ain't reg'lar common trash. You take an' 'sociate with an'body what done come erlong."

"Aw, go on," retorted Jimmie, profanely. "Go soak your head, Pete."

The remaining boys retired to the street, whereupon they perceived Willie Dalzel in the distance. He ran to them.

"I licked him!" he shouted, exultantly. "I licked him! Didn't I, now?"

From the Whilomville point of view he was entitled to a favorable answer. They made it. "Yes," they said, "you did."

"I run in," cried Willie, "an' I grabbed 'im, an' afore he knew what it was I throwed 'im. An' then it was easy." He puffed out his chest and smiled like an English recruiting-sergeant. "An' now," said he, suddenly facing Jimmie Trescott, "whose side were you on?"

The question was direct and startling. Jimmie gave back two paces. "He licked you once," he explained, haltingly.

"He never saw the day when he could lick one side of me. I could lick him with my left hand tied behind me. Why, I could lick him when I was asleep." Willie Dalzel was magnificent.

A gate clicked, and Johnnie Hedge was seen to be strolling toward them. "You said," he remarked, coldly, "you licked me, didn't you?"

Willie Dalzel stood his ground. "Yes," he said, stoutly.

"Well, you're a liar," said the Hedge boy.

"You're another," retorted Willie.

"No, I ain't, either, but *you're* a liar."

"You're another," retorted Willie.

"Don't you dare tell *me* I'm a liar, or I'll smack your mouth for you," said the Hedge boy.

"Well, I did, didn't I?" barked Willie. "An' wha' che goin' to do about it?"

"I'm goin' to lam you," said the Hedge boy.

He approached to attack warily, and the other boys held their breaths. Willie Dalzel winced back a pace. "Hol' on a minute," he cried, raising his palm. "I'm not——"

But the comic windmill was again in motion, and between gasps from his exertions Johnnie Hedge remarked, "I'll show—you—whether—you kin —lick me—or not."

The first blows did not reach home on Willie, for he backed away with expedition, keeping up his futile cry, "Hol' on a minute." Soon enough a swinging fist landed on his cheek. It did not knock him down, but it hurt him a little and frightened him a great deal. He suddenly opened his mouth to an amazing and startling extent, tilted back his head, and howled, while his eyes, glittering with tears, were fixed upon this scowling butcher of a Johnnie Hedge. The latter was making slow and vicious circles, evidently intending to renew the massacre.

But the spectators really had been desolated and shocked by the terrible thing which had happened to Willie Dalzel. They now cried out: "No, no; don't hit 'im any more! Don't hit 'im any more!"

Jimmie Trescott, in a panic of bravery, yelled, "We'll all jump on you if you do."

The Hedge boy paused, at bay. He breathed angrily, and flashed his glance from lad to lad. They still protested: "No, no; don't hit 'im any more. Don't hit 'im any more."

"I'll hammer him until he can't stand up," said Johnnie, observing that they all feared him. "I'll fix him so he won't know hisself, an' if any of you kids bother with *me*——"

Suddenly he ceased, he trembled, he collapsed. The hand of one approaching from behind had laid hold upon his ear, and it was the hand of one whom he knew.

The other lads heard a loud, iron-filing voice say, "Caught ye at it again, ye brat, ye." They saw a dreadful woman with gray hair, with a sharp red nose, with bare arms, with spectacles of such magnifying quality that her eyes shone through them like two fierce white moons. She was Johnnie Hedge's mother. Still holding Johnnie by the ear, she swung out swiftly and dexterously, and succeeded in boxing the ears of two boys before the crowd regained its presence of mind and stampeded. Yes, the war for supremacy was over, and the question was never again disputed. The supreme power was Mrs. Hedge.

July, 1900
[*Harper's Magazine*, Vol. 101, pp. 216–221.]

MANACLED

In the First Act there had been a farm scene, wherein real horses had drunk real water out of real buckets, afterward dragging a real wagon off stage L. The audience was consumed with admiration of this play, and the great Theater Nouveau rang to its roof with the crowd's plaudits.

The Second Act was now well advanced. The hero, cruelly victimized by his enemies, stood in prison garb, panting with rage, while two brutal warders fastened real handcuffs on his wrists and real anklets on his ankles. And the hovering villain sneered.

" 'Tis well, Aubrey Pettingill," said the prisoner. "You have so far succeeded; but, mark you, there will come a time——"

The villain retorted with a cutting allusion to the young lady whom the hero loved.

"Curse you," cried the hero, and he made as if to spring upon this demon; but, as the pitying audience saw, he could only take steps four inches long.

Drowning the mocking laughter of the villain came cries from both the audience and the people in back of the wings. "Fire! Fire! Fire!" Throughout the great house resounded the roaring crashes of a throng of human beings moving in terror, and even above this noise could be heard the screams of women more shrill than whistles. The building hummed and shook; it was like a glade which holds some bellowing cataract of the mountains. Most of the people who were killed on the stairs still clutched their playbills in their hands as if they had resolved to save them at all costs.

The Theater Nouveau fronted upon a street which was not of the first importance, especially at night, when it only aroused when the people came to the theater, and aroused again when they came out to go home. On the night of the fire, at the time of the scene between the enchained hero and his tormentor, the thoroughfare echoed with only the scraping shovels of some streetcleaners, who were loading carts with blackened snow and mud. The gleam of lights made the shadowed pavement deeply blue, save where lay some yellow plum-like reflection.

Suddenly a policeman came running frantically along the street. He charged upon the firebox on a corner. Its red light touched with flame each of his brass buttons and the municipal shield. He pressed a lever. He had been standing in the entrance of the theater chatting to the lonely man in the box office. To send an alarm was a matter of seconds.

Out of the theater poured the first hundreds of fortunate ones, and some were not altogether fortunate. Women, their bonnets flying, cried out tender names; men, white as death, scratched and bleeding, looked wildly from face to face. There were displays of horrible blind brutality by the strong. Weaker men clutched and clawed like cats. From the theater itself came the howl of a gale.

The policeman's fingers had flashed into instant life and action the most perfect counterattack to the fire. He listened for some seconds, and presently he heard the thunder of a charging engine. She swept around a corner, her three shining enthrilled horses leaping. Her consort, the hose-cart, roared behind her. There were the loud clicks of the steel-shod hoofs, hoarse shouts, men running, the flash of lights, while the crevice-like streets resounded with the charges of other engines.

At the first cry of fire, the two brutal warders had dropped the arms of the hero and run off the stage with the villain. The hero cried after them angrily: "Where are you going? Here, Pete—Tom—you've left me chained up, damn you!"

The body of the theater now resembled a mad surf amid rocks, but the hero did not look at it. He was filled with fury at the stupidity of the two brutal warders, in forgetting that they were leaving him manacled. Calling loudly, he hobbled off stage L., taking steps four inches long.

Behind the scenes he heard the hum of flames. Smoke, filled with sparks sweeping on spiral courses, rolled thickly upon him. Suddenly his face turned chalk-color beneath his skin of manly bronze for the stage. His voice shrieked: "Pete—Tom—damn you—come back—you've left me chained up."

He had played in this theater for seven years, and he could find his way without light through the intricate passages which mazed out behind the stage. He knew that it was a long way to the street door.

The heat was intense. From time to time masses of flaming wood sung down from above him. He began to jump. Each jump advanced him about three feet, but the effort soon became heartbreaking. Once he fell, it took time to get upon his feet again.

There were stairs to descend. From the top of this flight he tried to fall feet first. He precipitated himself in a way that would have broken his hip under common conditions. But every step seemed covered with glue, and on almost every one he stuck for a moment. He could not even succeed in falling downstairs. Ultimately he reached the bottom, windless from the struggle.

There were stairs to climb. At the foot of the flight he lay for an instant with his mouth close to the floor, trying to breathe. Then he tried to scale this frightful precipice up the face of which many an actress had gone at a canter.

Each succeeding step arose eight inches from its fellow. The hero dropped to a seat on the third step, and pulled his feet to the second step. From this position he lifted himself to a seat on the fourth step. He had not gone far in this manner before his frenzy caused him to lose his balance, and he rolled to the foot of the flight. After all, he could fall downstairs.

He lay there whispering. "They all got out but I. All but I." Beautiful flames flashed above him; some were crimson, some were orange, and here and there were tongues of purple, blue, green.

A curiously calm thought came into his head. "What a fool I was not to foresee this! I shall have Rogers furnish manacles of papier-mâché tomorrow."

The thunder of the fire-lions made the theater have a palsy.

Suddenly the hero beat his handcuffs against the wall, cursing them in a loud wail. Blood started from under his fingernails. Soon he began to bite the hot steel, and blood fell from his blistered mouth. He raved like a wolf.

Peace came to him again. There were charming effects amid the flames. . . . He felt very cool, delightfully cool. . . . "They've left me chained up."

August, 1900
[*Argosy*, Vol. 71, pp. 364–366.]

A LITTLE PILGRIMAGE*

[A Little Pilgrim]

One November it became clear to childish minds in certain parts of Whilomville that the Sunday school of the Presbyterian church would not have for the children the usual tree on Christmas eve. The funds free for that ancient festival would be used for the relief of suffering among the victims of the Charleston earthquake.

The plan had been born in the generous head of the superintendent of the Sunday school, and during one session he had made a strong plea that the children should forego the vain pleasures of a tree and, in glorious application of the Golden Rule, refuse a local use of the fund, and will that it be sent where dire pain might be alleviated. At the end of a tearfully eloquent speech the question was put fairly to a vote, and the children in a burst of virtuous abandon carried the question for Charleston. Many of the teachers had been careful to preserve a finely neutral attitude, but even if they had cautioned the children against being too impetuous they could not have checked the wild impulses.

But this was a long time before Christmas.

Very early, boys held important speech together. "Huh! you ain't goin' to have no Christmas tree at the Presbyterian Sunday school."

Sullenly the victim answered, "No, we ain't."

"Huh!" scoffed the other denomination, "we are goin' to have the all-firedest biggest tree that you ever saw in the world."

The little Presbyterians were greatly downcast.

It happened that Jimmie Trescott had regularly attended the Presbyterian Sunday school. The Trescotts were consistently undenominational, but they had sent their lad on Sundays to one of the places where they thought he would receive benefits. However, on one day in December, Jimmie appeared before his father and made a strong spiritual appeal to be forthwith attached to the Sunday school of the Big Progressive church. Doctor Trescott mused this question considerably. "Well, Jim," he said, "why do you conclude that the Big Progressive Sunday school is better for you than the Presbyterian Sunday school?"

"Now—it's nicer," answered Jimmie, looking at his father with an anxious eye.

"How do you mean?"

* *Whilomville Stories.*

"Why—now—some of the boys what go to the Presbyterian place, they ain't very nice," explained the flagrant Jimmie.

Trescott mused the question considerately once more. In the end he said: "Well, you may change if you wish, this one time, but you must not be changing to and fro. You decide now, and then you must abide by your decision."

"Yessir," said Jimmie, brightly. "Big Progressive."

"All right," said the father. "But remember what I've told you."

On the following Sunday morning Jimmie presented himself at the door of the basement of the Big Progressive church. He was conspicuously washed, notably raimented, prominently polished. And, incidentally, he was very uncomfortable because of all these virtues.

A number of acquaintances greeted him contemptuously. "Hello, Jimmie! What you doin' here? Thought you was a Presbyterian?"

Jimmie cast down his eyes and made no reply. He was too cowed by the change. However, Homer Phelps, who was a regular patron of the Big Progressive Sunday school, suddenly appeared and said, "Hello, Jim!" Jimmie seized upon him. Homer Phelps was amenable to Trescott laws, tribal if you like, but iron-bound, almost compulsory.

"Hello, Homer!" said Jimmie, and his manner was so good that Homer felt a great thrill in being able to show his superior a new condition of life.

"You 'ain't never come here afore, have you?" he demanded, with a new arrogance.

"No, I 'ain't," said Jimmie. Then they stared at each other and maneuvered.

"You don't know *my* teacher," said Homer.

"No, I don't know *her*," admitted Jimmie, but in a way which contended, modestly, that he knew countless other Sunday school teachers.

"Better join our class," said Homer, sagely. "She wears spectacles; don't see very well. Sometimes we do almost what we like."

"All right," said Jimmie, glad to place himself in the hands of his friend. In due time they entered the Sunday school room, where a man with benevolent whiskers stood on a platform and said, "We will now sing No. 33—'Pull for the Shore, Sailor, Pull for the Shore.'" And as the obedient throng burst into melody the man on the platform indicated the time with a fat, white, and graceful hand. He was an ideal Sunday school superintendent—one who had never felt hunger or thirst or the wound of the challenge of dishonor; a man, indeed, with beautiful fat hands who waved them in greasy victorious beneficence over a crowd of children.

Jimmie, walking carefully on his toes, followed Homer Phelps. He felt that the kingly superintendent might cry out and blast him to ashes before he could reach a chair. It was a desperate journey. But at last he heard Homer muttering to a young lady, who looked at him through glasses which greatly magnified her eyes. "A new boy," she said, in an oily and deeply religious voice.

"Yes'm," said Jimmie, trembling. The five other boys of the class scanned him keenly and derided his condition.

"We will proceed to the lesson," said the young lady. Then she cried sternly, like a sergeant, "The seventh chapter of Jeremiah!"

There was a swift fluttering of leaflets. Then the name of Jeremiah, a wise man, towered over the feelings of these boys. Homer Phelps was doomed to read the fourth verse. He took a deep breath, he puffed out his lips, he gathered his strength for a great effort. His beginning was childishly explosive. He hurriedly said:

"'Trust ye not in lying words, saying, The temple of the Lord, The temple of the Lord, The temple of the Lord, are these.'"

"Now," said the teacher, "Johnnie Scanlan, tell us what these words mean." The Scanlan boy shamefacedly muttered that he did not know. The teacher's countenance saddened. Her heart was in her work; she wanted to make a success of this Sunday school class. "Perhaps Homer Phelps can tell us," she remarked.

Homer gulped; he looked at Jimmie. Through the great room hummed a steady hum. A little circle, very near, was being told about Daniel in the lion's den. They were deeply moved. At the moment they liked Sunday school.

"Why—now—it means," said Homer, with a grand pomposity born of a sense of hopeless ignorance—"it means—why, it means that they were in the wrong place."

"No," said the teacher, profoundly; "it means that we should be good, very good indeed. That is what it means. It means that we should love the Lord and be good. Love the Lord and be good. That is what it means."

The little boys suddenly had a sense of black wickedness as their teacher looked austerely upon them. They gazed at her with the wide-open eyes of simplicity. They were stirred again. This thing of being good—this great business of life—apparently it was always successful. They knew from the fairy tales. But it was difficult, wasn't it? It was said to be the most heartbreaking task to be generous, wasn't it? One had to pay the price of one's eyes in order to be pacific, didn't one? As for patience, it was tortured martyrdom to be patient, wasn't it? Sin was simple, wasn't it? But virtue was so difficult that it could only be practiced by heavenly beings, wasn't it?

And the angels, the Sunday school superintendent, and the teacher swam in the high visions of the little boys as beings so good that if a boy scratched his shin in the same room he was a profane and sentenced devil.

"And," said the teacher, "'The temple of the Lord'—what does that mean? I'll ask the new boy. What does that mean?"

"I dun'no," said Jimmie, blankly.

But here the professional bright boy of the class suddenly awoke to his obligations. "Teacher," he cried, "it means church, same as this."

"Exactly," said the teacher, deeply satisfied with this reply. "You know your lesson well, Clarence. I am much pleased."

The other boys, instead of being envious, looked with admiration upon Clarence, while he adopted an air of being habituated to perform such feats every day of his life. Still, he was not much of a boy. He had the virtue of being able to walk on very high stilts, but when the season of stilts had passed he possessed no rank save this Sunday school rank, this clever-little-Clarence business of knowing the Bible and the lesson better than the other boys. The other boys, sometimes looking at him meditatively, did not actually decide to thrash him as soon as he cleared the portals of the church, but they certainly decided to molest him in such ways as would reëstablish their self-respect. Behind the superintendent's chair hung a lithograph of the martyrdom of St. Stephen.

Jimmie, feeling stiff and encased in his best clothes, waited for the ordeal to end. A bell pealed: the fat hand of the superintendent had tapped a bell. Slowly the rustling and murmuring dwindled to silence. The benevolent man faced the school. "I have to announce," he began, waving his body from side to side in the conventional bows of his kind, "that——" Bang went the bell. "Give me your attention, please, children. I have to announce that the Board has decided that this year there will be no Christmas tree, but the——"

Instantly the room buzzed with the subdued clamor of the children. Jimmie was speechless. He stood morosely during the singing of the closing hymn. He passed out into the street with the others, pushing no more than was required.

Speedily the whole idea left him. If he remembered Sunday school at all, it was to remember that he did not like it.

August, 1900

[*Harper's Magazine*, Vol. 101, pp. 401–404.]

AT THE PIT DOOR

The long file of people, two abreast, waiting resignedly for the hour of 7:30 P.M., look round sharply at the open space beside them when the girl with the guitar gives a preliminary strum. They are prepared to welcome anything calculated to chase monotony, for even half-penny comic papers after a time cease to amuse, and those reminiscent of past performances develop, when they pass a certain class, into first-class bores. This is why the guitar girl comes opportunely, and when she lifts up her chin and sings in a raucous voice to a tum-tum accompaniment, the two-abreast crowd listens with all its ears. E 243, at the end of the queue, looks on tolerantly, being a man with musical tastes and consequently of a genial disposition. Here singeth one:

> When you meet a nice young person and you feel you've seen a worse
>   one,
>   And you seek a interduction, don't you know,
> You are puzzled how to greet her, tho no lady could be neater,
>   So very shy and strickly comilfo.
> You puzzle all your mind and brains, you take a deuced lot of pains,
>   You ponder and consider, and you think
> It's a foolish, silly waste of time, take this advice, dear boys of mine,
>   For all you've got to do is—give a wink.
> Give a wink, boys—

The long line that reaches to the pit doors finds itself forced to hum the enticing chorus, either in shrill soprano or growling bass, and one young lady by herself, with a pince-nez and opera glasses, screws up her lips to whistle it. The guitar girl gives a second song—a sentimental one this time, with good-byes forever and weeping sweethearts and departing emigrants, and a waltz refrain, and nearly everybody dead and done for in the last verse. Then the guitar girl brings a scarlet plush bag that suggests the offertory, and going down the line, gleans as much as eightpence-half-penny.

A stout man in a tweed cap and loose tweed suit, that cries aloud at elbows and knees for the darning needle; he has a Windsor chair with him, and a slip of carpet, and these he places on the ground with much care and particularity. Throws then his tweed cap on the ground, slips his jacket off, thumps himself on his broad chest, and bows to his audience.

"Lydies and Gentlemen: I propose this evenin' to clime your kind indulgence whilst I submit to your notice a few feats of strength. I don't prefess to do anything that's not done perfectly striteforward, and I invite your attention to watch whether I do anything that can be called trickery. If any one can bowl me out at pretendin' to do something I don't do, why I'll forfeit"—here the stout man slaps an apparently empty pocket—"I will forfeit five golding sovereigns."

The long line has been a little unconcerned at the acrobat's lecture; but the mention of as much as five pounds seems to quicken its interest. The heads turn round and watch the stout man acutely.

"I first take up the chair between my teeth—thus." The Windsor chair is swung to and fro in the air. "I then place the foot of one of its legs on my chin—thus." The Windsor chair turns lazily around on its perilous axis. "I now place my head between my knees, and I 'old the chair in my mouth —thus."

The stout man contorts himself into a preposterous position and does a kind of flag-signaling with the Windsor chair. "I now puts the chair one side, and I venture to trespass on your valuable time for a few minutes whilst I show you some feats equal to those"—(the stout man for the first time speaks with acerbity)—"equal to those that so-called acribats at the music 'alls are getting their thirty pun a week for."

The stout man holds one foot high and dances round on the other foot in the manner of the ladies at the Moulin Rouge; he performs the unattractive "splits," he stands on his head for a few moments; he walks about on his hands; he does nearly everything that nobody else wants to do. After each achievement he blows a quick kiss to the patient crowd. "Thanking you one and all, lydies and gentlemen, for assisting me by your kind attention, I now ast you to remember that a man's got his livin' to make, altho p'raps we may 'ave different ways of doing it. Can you oblige, miss, by starting the subscription list with a copper? If I can only get a good-looking—Thank you kindly, miss. And you, sir."

A melancholy staring boy on the pavement opposite. It is quite clear that he is about to do something; it is by no means clear what that something is to be. When that stout man has put on his coat and shouldered his Windsor chair and lifted his tweed cap to the crowd politely, the melancholy boy moistens his lips and grasps the lamppost with one hand. Then he whistles. He whistles, truth to say, extremely well, and goes stolidly through the overture to "Zampa" and a frivolous polka, closing with "Rule Britannia" in such a spirit as to make every youth in the waiting line feel that unless he gives the melancholy youth at least a penny he is nothing better than a traitor to his country.

A rattling of bones! A banging of tambourines! A ping-pong of banjos! Six men in straw hats and white canvas suits with scarlet stripes and per-

spiring blackened faces are in a semicircle exchanging noisy repartee and—
when they can think of no repartee—shouting loudly "Ooray!"

"D'you 'member that lil song of yours, Bones, that used to make people
cry?"

"Do I 'member?" inquires Bones (in the Ollendorffian manner) "that
lil song of mine that used to make people cry? Yes, sir; I do 'member that
lil song of mine that used to make people cry."

"Will you 'blige me by singing of it now?"

Bones is a short boy with a stubbled sandy mustache showing through
the lamp-black on his face. He steps out of the semicircle, makes a bow
that is almost obsequious, whilst the others clatter and twang through the
symphony. Then Bones looks up at the side of the theater, and with a sort
of ferocious pathos sings:—

> Little Nellie's joined the ingels,
> She has flown to realms above:
> Never more shall we 'ere see her;
> Gorn's the little soul we love.

> But the mem'ry of her features,
> Always wif us will remine,
> And the sound of tiny voices,
> Lingers in our ears agine.

The semicircle joins in, taking its several parts in a strenuous way.

> Gorn, gorn is she, gorn from all earthly strife,
> Free from all sorrer. . . .

The lugubrious purple song has three verses, and the number is enough.
The line of pit patrons becomes quite depressed and sniffs a good deal, and
one lady, borrowing her husband's handkerchief, weeps openly and without restraint.

"Song and dence!" shouts Tambourine, "entitled, 'Hev you seen a colored coon called Pete!'"

Again a noisy prelude. It is Tambourine himself who steps out this time,
and he dances a few steps on the graveled space as earnest of what is to
come, and to a red-faced white-capped servant who is gazing intently out
of the side window of a neighboring hotel he waves affectionate greetings
and hugs his left side as though the sight of the red-faced domestic had
affected his heart.

> I'm a sassy nigger gal, and me front name it is Sal,

Soft chorus from the semicircle:—

> Hev ye seen a colored coon called Pete?

Tambourine continues:—

> And the games we darkies play,
> in the night and in the day,

Soft chorus as before:—

> Hev ye seen a colored coon called Pete?
> But I want to ask you suthin' and—

The long straight crowd is beginning to look at its watches. The hour is 7:30 precisely, and what the crowd asks with much impatience is, that if they don't mean to open the doors at 7:30, what on earth makes them put 7:30 in the paper for? The worst of theaters is that you can never—A sound of moving bolts. A closing up in the ranks of the long line. A warning word from E 243. The song stops and the minstrels hurry forward to the moving crowd with their straw hats outstretched. It is too late. The crowd is so much engaged in feeling for its half-crowns and in keeping a steady eye on the gaping open doorway that it cannot trouble about any more gifts to entertainers.

" 'Pon me bloomin' oath," says Tambourine with much annoyance, "if this ain't jest like me nawsty luck!"

September, 1900
[The Philistine, Vol. 11, pp. 97–104.]

THE SQUIRE'S MADNESS*

Linton was in his study remote from the interference of domestic sounds. He was writing verses. He was not a poet in the strict sense of the word, because he had eight hundred a year and a manor house in Sussex. But he was devoted, at any rate, and no happiness was for him equal to the happiness of an imprisonment in this lonely study. His place had been a semi-fortified house in the good days when every gentleman was either abroad with a bared sword hunting his neighbors or behind oak-and-iron doors and three-foot walls while his neighbors hunted him. But in the life of Linton it may be said that the only part of the house which remained true to the idea of fortification was the study, which was free only to Linton's wife and certain terriers. The necessary appearance from time to time of a servant always grated upon Linton as much as if from time to time some-body had in the most well-bred way flung a brick through the little panes of his window.

* Completed by Cora Crane.

This window looked forth upon a wide valley of hop fields and sheep pastures, dipping and rising this way and that way, but always a valley until it reached a high faraway ridge upon which stood the upright figure of a windmill, usually making rapid gestures as if it were an excited sentry warning the old gray house of coming danger. A little to the right, on a knoll, red chimneys and parts of red-tiled roofs appeared among trees, and the venerable square tower of the village church rose above them.

For ten years Linton had left vacant Oldrestham Hall, and when at last it became known that he and his wife were to return from an incomprehensible wandering, the village, which for four centuries had turned a feudal eye toward the Hall, was wrung with a prospect of change, a proper change. The great family pew in Oldrestham church would be occupied each Sunday morning by a fat, happy-faced, utterly squire-looking man, who would be dutifully at his post when the parish was stirred by a subscription list. Then, for the first time in many years, the hunters would ride in the early morning merrily out through the park, and there would be also shooting parties, and in the summer groups of charming ladies would be seen walking the terrace, laughing on the lawns and in the rose gardens. The village expected to have the perfectly legal and fascinating privilege of discussing the performances of its own gentry.

The first intimation of calamity was in the news that Linton had rented all the shooting. This prepared the people for the blow, and it fell when they sighted the master of Oldrestham Hall. The older villagers remembered then that there had been nothing in the youthful Linton to promise a fat, happy-faced, dignified, hunting, shooting overlord, but still they could not but resent the appearance of the new squire. There was no conceivable reason for his looking like a gaunt ascetic who would surprise nobody if he borrowed a sixpence from the first yokel he met in the lanes.

Linton was in truth three inches more than six feet in height, but he had bowed himself to five feet eleven inches. His hair shocked out in front like hay, and under it were two spectacled eyes which never seemed to regard anything with particular attention. His face was pale and full of hollows, and the mouth apparently had no expression save a chronic pout of the underlip. His hands were large and rawboned but uncannily white. His whole bent body was thin as that of a man from a long sickbed, and all was finished by two feet which for size could not be matched in the county.

He was very awkward, but apparently it was not so much a physical characteristic as it was a mental inability to consider where he was going or what he was doing. For instance, when passing through a gate it was not uncommon for him to knock his side viciously against one of the posts. This was because he dreamed almost always, and if there had been forty gates in a row he would not then have noted them more than he did the one. As far as the villagers and farmers were concerned he never came out of this manner save in wide-apart cases, when he had forced upon him either some great exhibition of stupidity or some faint indication of double-dealing, and then this smoldering man flared out, encrimsoning his immediate surrounding with a brief fire of ancestral anger. But the lapse back to indifference was more surprising. It was far quicker than the flare in the beginning. His feeling was suddenly ashes at the moment when one was certain it would lick the sky.

Some of the villagers asserted that he was mad. They argued it long in the manner of their kind, repeating, repeating, and repeating, and when an opinion confusingly rational appeared they merely shook their heads in pig-like obstinacy. Anyhow, it was historically clear that no such squire had before been in the line of Lintons of Oldrestham Hall, and the present incumbent was a shock.

The servants at the Hall—notably those who lived in the countryside—came in for a lot of questioning, and none were found too backward in explaining many things which they themselves did not understand. The household was most irregular. They all confessed that it was really so un-customary that they did not know but what they would have to give notice. The master was probably the most extraordinary man in the whole world. The butler said that Linton would drink beer with his meals day in and day out like any carrier resting at a pothouse. It didn't matter even if the meal were dinner. Then suddenly he would change his tastes to the most valuable wines, and in ten days would make the wine cellar look as if it had been wrecked at sea. What was to be done with a gentleman of that kind? The butler said for his part he wanted a master with habits, and he protested that Linton did not have a habit to his name; at least, none that could properly be called a habit.

Barring the cook, the entire establishment agreed categorically with the butler. The cook didn't agree because she was a very good cook indeed, which she thought entitled her to be extremely aloof from the other serv-ants'-hall opinions.

As for the squire's lady, they described her as being not much different from the master. At least she gave support to his most unusual manner of life, and evidently believed that whatever he chose to do was quite correct.

II

Linton had written:

> The garlands of her hair are snakes;
> Black and bitter are her hating eyes.
> A cry the windy death-hall makes—
> O, love, deliver us.

The flung cup rolls to her sandal's tip;
His arm—

Whereupon his thought fumed over the next two lines, coursing like greyhounds, after a fugitive vision of a writhing lover, with the foam of poison on his lips, dying at the feet of the woman. Linton arose, lit a cigarette, placed it on the window ledge, took another cigarette, looked blindly for the matches, thrust a spiral of paper into the flame of the log fire, lit the second cigarette, placed it toppling on a book, and began a search among his pipes for one that would draw well. He gazed at his pictures, at the books on the shelves, out at the green spread of countryside, all without taking mental note. At the window ledge he came upon the first cigarette, and in a matter-of-fact way he returned it to his lips, having forgotten that he had forgotten it.

There was a sound of steps on the stone floor of the quaint little passage that led down to his study, and turning from the window he saw that his wife had entered the room and was looking at him strangely.

"Jack," she said in a low voice, "what is the matter?"

His eyes were burning out from under his shock of hair with a fierceness that belied his feeling of simple surprise. "Nothing is the matter," he answered. "Why do you ask?"

She seemed immensely concerned, but she was visibly endeavoring to hide her concern as well as to abate it. "I—I thought you acted queerly."

He answered: "Why no. I'm not acting queerly. On the contrary," he added smiling, "I'm in one of my most rational moods."

Her look of alarm did not subside. She continued to regard him with the same stare. She was silent for a time and did not move. His own thoughts had quite returned to a contemplation of a poisoned lover, and he did not note the manner of his wife. Suddenly she came to him and, laying a hand on his arm, said, "Jack, you are ill?"

"Why no, dear," he said with a first impatience, "I'm not ill at all. I never felt better in my life." And his mind, beleaguered by this pointless talk, strove to break through to its old contemplation of the poisoned lover. "Hear what I have written." Then he read:

"The garlands of her hair are snakes;
Black and bitter are her hating eyes.
A cry the windy death-hall makes—
O, love, deliver us.
The flung cup rolls to her sandal's tip;
His arm—"

Linton said: "I can't seem to get the lines to describe the man who is dying of the poison on the floor before her. Really I'm having a time with it. What a bore. Sometimes I can write like mad, and other times I don't seem to have an intelligent idea in my head."

He felt his wife's hand tighten on his arm, and he looked into her face. It was so alight with horror that it brought him sharply out of his dreams. "Jack," she repeated tremulously, "you are ill."

He opened his eyes in wonder. "Ill! ill? No; not in the least!"

"Yes, you are ill. I can see it in your eyes. You—act so strangely."

"Act strangely? Why, my dear, what have I done? I feel quite well. Indeed, I was never more fit in my life."

As he spoke he threw himself into a large wing chair and looked up at his wife, who stood gazing at him from the other side of the black oak table upon which Linton wrote his verses.

"Jack, dear," she almost whispered, "I have noticed for days," and she leaned across the table to look more intently into his face. "Yes, your eyes grow more fixed every day—you—you—your head, does it ache, dear?"

Linton arose from his chair and came around the big table toward his wife. As he approached her, an expression akin to terror crossed her face, and she drew back as in fear, holding out both hands to ward him off.

He had been smiling in the manner of a man reassuring a frightened child, but at her shrinking from his outstretched hand he stopped in amazement. "Why, Grace, what is it? tell me."

She was glaring at him, her eyes wide with misery. Linton moved his left hand across his face, unconsciously trying to brush from it that which alarmed her.

"Oh, Jack, you must see some one; I am wretched about you. You are ill!"

"Why, my dear wife," he said, "I am quite, quite well; I am anxious to finish these verses, but words won't come somehow; the man dying—"

"Yes, that is it—you cannot remember—you see that you cannot remember. You must see a doctor. We will go up to town at once," she answered quickly.

" 'Tis true," he thought, "that my memory is not as good as it used to be. I cannot remember dates, and words won't fit in, somehow. Perhaps I don't take enough exercise, dear; is that what worries you?" he asked.

"Yes, yes, dear, you do not go out enough," said his wife. "You cling to this room as the ivy clings to the walls—but we must go to London, you *must* see some one; promise me that you will go, that you will go immediately."

Again Linton saw his wife look at him as one looks at a creature of pity. The faint lines from her nose to the corners of her mouth deepened as if she were in physical pain; her eyes, open to their fullest extent, had in them the expression of a mother watching her dying babe. What was this strange wall that had suddenly raised itself between them? Was he ill? No;

he never had been in better health in his life. He found himself vainly searching for aches in his bones. Again he brushed away this thing which seemed to be upon his face. There must be something on my face, he thought; else why does she look at me with such hopeless despair in her eyes? these kindly eyes that had hitherto been so responsive to each glance of his own. *Why* did she think that he was ill, she who knew well his every mood? *Was he mad?* Did this thing of the poisoned cup that rolled to her sandal's tip—and her eyes, her hating eyes—mean that his— No, it could not be. He fumbled among the papers on the table for a cigarette. He could not find one. He walked to the huge fireplace and peered nearsightedly at the ashes on the hearth.

"What, what do you want, Jack? Be careful! The fire!" cried his wife.

"Why, I want a cigarette," he said.

She started, as if he had spoken roughly to her. "I will get you some; wait, sit quietly—I will bring you some," she replied as she hastened through the small passageway up the stone steps that led from his study.

Linton stood with his back still bent, in the posture of a man picking something from the ground. He did not turn from the fireplace until the echo of his wife's footfall on the stone floors had died away. Then he straightened himself and said, "Well, I'm damned!" And Linton was not a man who swore.

III

A month later the squire and his wife were on their way to London to consult the great brain specialist, Doctor Redmond. Linton now believed that "something" was wrong with him. His wife's anxiety, which she could no longer conceal, forced him to this conclusion; "something" was wrong. Until these few last weeks Linton's wife had managed her household with the care and wisdom of a chatelaine of medieval times. Each day was planned for certain duties in house or village. She had theories as to the management and education of the village children, and this work occupied much of her time. She was the antithesis of her husband. He, a weaver of dream-stories, she of that type of woman who has ideas of the emancipation of women and who believe the problem could be solved by training the minds of the next generation of mothers. Linton was not interested in these questions, but he would smile indulgently at his wife as she talked of the equality of mind of the sexes and the public part in the world's history which would be played by the women of the future.

There was no talk of this kind now. The household management fell into the hands of servants. Night and day his wife watched Linton. He would awaken in the night to find her face close to his own, her eyes burning with feverish anxiety.

"What is it, Grace?" he would cry. "Have I said anything? What is the reason you watch me in this fashion, dear?"

And she would sob, "Jack, you are ill, dear, you are ill. We must go to town; we must, indeed."

Then he would soothe her with fond words and promise that he would go to London.

This present journey was the outcome of those weeks of watching and fear in Linton's wife's mind.

Linton's wife was trembling violently as he helped her down from the cab in front of Doctor Redmond's door. They had made an appointment, so that they were sure of little delay before the portentous interview.

A small page in blue livery opened the door and ushered them into a waiting room. Mrs. Linton dropped heavily into a chair, looking with a frightened air from side to side and biting her underlip nervously. She was moaning half under her breath, "Oh, Jack, you are ill, you are ill."

A short stout man with clean-shaven face and scanty black hair entered the room. His nose was huge and misshapen and his mouth was a straight firm line. Overhanging black brows tried in vain to shadow the piercing dark eyes that darted questioning looks at every one, seeming to search for hidden thoughts as a flashlight from the conning tower of a ship searches for the enemy in time of war.

He advanced toward Mrs. Linton with outstretched hand. "Mrs. Linton?" he said. "Ah!"

She almost jumped from her chair as he came near her, crying, "Oh, doctor, my husband is ill, very ill, very ill!"

Again Doctor Redmond, with his eyes fixed upon her face, ejaculated "Ah!" Turning to Linton he said, "Please wait here, Squire; I will first talk to your wife.—Will you step into my study, madam?" he said to Mrs. Linton, bowing courteously.

Linton's wife ran into the room which the doctor pointed toward as his study.

Linton waited. He moved softly about the room looking at the photographs of Greek ruins which adorned the walls. He stopped finally before a large picture of the Gate of Hadrian. He traveled once more into his dream country. His fancy painted in the figures of men and women who had passed through that gate. He had forgotten his fear of the blotting out of his mind that could conjure these glowing colors. He had forgotten himself.

From this dream he was recalled to the present by a hand being placed gently upon his arm. He half turned and saw the doctor regarding him with sympathetic eyes.

"Come, my dear sir, come into my study," said the doctor. "I have asked your wife to await us here." Linton then turned fully toward the center of the room and found that his wife was seated quietly by a table. Doctor Redmond bowed low to Mrs. Linton as he passed her, and Linton waved his hand, smiled, and said, "Only a moment, dear." She did not reply. The door closed behind them.

"Be seated, my dear sir," said the doctor, drawing forward a chair; "be seated. I want to say something to you, but you must drink this first." He handed Linton a small glass of brandy.

Linton sat down, took the glass mechanically, and gulped the brandy in one great swallow. The doctor stood by the mantel and said slowly, "I rejoice to say to you, sir, that I have never met a man more sound mentally than yourself—"

Linton half started from his chair.

"Stop!" said the doctor; "I have not yet finished.—But it is my painful duty to tell you the truth. *It is your Wife who is Mad! Mad as a Hatter!*"

October, 1900

[*Crampton's Magazine*, Vol. 16, pp. 93–99.]

THE MAN FROM DULUTH*

The man from Duluth reproached his companions. "I don't see as we're having much fun," he said. "This is about the dreamiest time I ever run up against."

One of the New York men waved his hand mournfully. "Well, you see, it is Sunday night, for one thing; and besides that, the town is about dead now, anyhow."

"That's what it is," said the others. They began plaintively to deplore the ravages of reform. Their voices filled with pathos, they spoke of the days that had been. It was the wail of the Tenderloin, the lamentation of the "rounders" who have seen their idols of men and places taken from them.

"Why, I can remember when—"

But the man from Duluth interrupted these tales. "Oh, I've no doubt it was all very great," said he, "but what are we going to do now? That's the point."

The five men stood on a street corner and reflected. Occasionally the visitor from the West prodded the others with accounts of the splendors

* Completed by Cora Crane.

of life in his country, and poked at them comments upon their slumbrous environment.

"It's dead slow," he told them, "dead slow. I'll never come East again expecting to play horse. I'll do my flying in Chicago. You fellows have all been turned down. You're buried. Come out and see me in Chicago and I'll show you real dives with electric lights out in front, and whole neighborhoods that get drunk by half-past three in the afternoon."

The others were eager to explain. "Well, you see, we—"

"Oh, I know you can still have fun in New York if you are a nervy spender," interrupted the man from Duluth; "but I guess you could do that in Mecca or Jerusalem, too. That's no sign of a red-hot town. It's the sign of a dead-slow town."

He stared severely at the New York men. They cast down their eyes and pondered in mournful silence.

At last one man suddenly spoke. He wore an air of having arrived at the only real golden suggestion. "Well, let's go and get a drink, anyhow." It was said with great vigor.

The party aroused at this. "All right, come ahead." "Where'll we go?" "Oh, anywhere; what's the matter with the little French concert hall?" "All right, come ahead."

Led by one, they paraded down the avenue. They were presently among the criss-cross streets of Greenwich. The river was in sight before they halted. Once the silence of their tongues had been broken by the voice of the man from Duluth: "This is a derned long ways to go for a drink."

The man who was in advance conducted the party up the steps of a private house. He rang the bell, and the door presently was opened a little way. A woman's head was thrust out warily. She exclaimed in French when she discovered the size of the band of invaders. She was about to slam the door, but two or three of the men burst forth in very bad but voluble French.

There was a rapid parley. The man from Duluth edged forward. If it came to the worst, he could put his foot where it would prevent the door from closing.

The conductor of the party was a painter who had studied in France. He volleyed prayers and entreaties in a way that he learned in that country. Presently the woman let them in quickly and then banged the door upon the form of some stranger who had tried to insinuate himself inside.

They passed down a mutilated hallway. In the rear of the house, where no doubt had once been kitchens and dining room, there was now a little hall. A gallery occupied one end; at the other there was a tiny stage. There was a scenic arrangement in the form of papier-mâché rocks and boulders. They looked indescribably dusty.

The ceiling was high; in it some little transoms were turned to let in the night air. At the tables that filled the floor space sat two score people babbling French. The polish of the surface of these tables had been worn away in spots by the contact of countless beer and wine glasses. There was an air of dilapidation in the room that imparted itself even to the waiters and to the youth over in the corner who thrummed the piano.

But with it all there was in the atmosphere, enwrapped, it may be, in thick clouds of cigarette smoke that hung and hovered overhead, the irresistible spirit of French carelessness. It was an angel that had flown over seas. There was the presence of a memory of Paris. Everything remained local save the thoughts; these were fleeting, reminiscent. There was something retrospective in the very way the men pounded tables with their glasses, the while humming in chorus with the clattering piano. It was a gayety that was inherited, and it recalled in a way that was meager and sad the mother of it—Paris.

And one then could instantly see that little did it matter here if there were dust and suggestions of cobwebs, nor if the linen generally of the company was soiled, nor if the waiter who brought the wine had stains on his apron and only one eye. In blessed security from these things dwelt this assemblage. The environment was made rose-hued by the laughter of girls; the color of wine was a weapon with which to defy cobwebs and dust stains and spots; whole legions of one-eyed waiters would fail to dampen the ardor of these existences.

Three men sat near the youth who played on the piano. At intervals one of them would arise, vanish for a moment in the bosom of the paper mountains, and then suddenly appear upon the little stage. They relieved each other with the regularity of sentries, and sang from the inexhaustible store of French comic songs. One was wretched, one was fair, and one was an artist. Even the man from Duluth, who comprehended less of French than he did of Sanscrit, enjoyed this latter performer. It is not always necessary to understand a language; sometimes one can be glad that he does not. But the man from Duluth reveled in the songs of him who was an artist. There were eloquent gestures and glances of the eyes that were full symbols. The man from Duluth was ignorant of details; that at which he grinned and giggled was the universal part. Good art of this kind cannot be confined to a language; there is something absorbingly intelligent to the thinking Zulu in the exhibition of a master of it.

One could wonder what he of the eloquent hands was paid. Probably he received the merest trifle. Some French customs are transported in completeness to certain portions of New York, and perhaps in France emotions are cheap. It is usually in the colder countries that publics pay fabulous prices for good emotions.

But the man from Duluth was not always satisfied with the universal part of art. When the audience would suddenly laugh he would lean forward and demand translation from the painter who had studied in France. The latter politely struggled with the difficulties of the task, but usually he failed.

"Say, what was that—what did he say then?" demanded once the man from Duluth.

"Oh—er—well," the painter replied. "Er—well—you see—he was going along the street with three chickens in a basket—and then—er—he, you know—he looked up at a window—and there was a girl in the window, you know—and he looked up at her and kissed his hand, and he said, 'Goodday, sweetheart'—and then he—he was walking backward when he said that—'Good-day, sweetheart'—and then, you know, he didn't see where he was going—and he—he fell down and the chickens got away—and flew up to this girl's window, you know—and he began to—to yell at her, 'Oh, I say, sweetheart, return to me my chickens'—and she laughed at him, and then he said—he said—oh, I don't know what he said. It's funny in French, but it don't sound funny in English—I couldn't make you understand."

The man from Duluth seemed strangely puzzled.

Also, later in the evening, he began to grow weary of even the artistic performer. "Say," he demanded, "don't they ever have girls here that sing?" Every one hastened to explain to him: "Well, you know, it's Sunday night—"

However, at frequent intervals after this time he would burst forth: "Say, this is pretty slow, ain't it?" "Ain't this slow, hey?" "Good Gawd, this is slow!"

"They always have a dance afterward—perhaps you will like that better," somebody said, to comfort him.

Presently, indeed, the performers ceased to pop out from behind the paper rocks. The one-eyed waiter and his fellows made a clear space by dragging away chairs and tables and stacking them in an end of the room. Then the young man at the piano suddenly attacked his instrument, and the ball began. Couples emerged from all portions of the hall to go whirling about in reckless fashion. There was nothing uniform or sedate. It was all emotional. Each couple danced according to moods. Some went solemnly, some affectionately, and at all times; a man would swirl his partner about the floor with a mad speed that would threaten to send her head flying. They were having lots of fun; almost every one was laughing.

"It's dead slow," said the man from Duluth.

Then, suddenly, in the middle of the floor there was a fight. The music stopped with a shrill crash; the dancers scurried out of the way. The atmosphere of the place became instantly tense, ominous, battleful. A woman shrieked; another threw her hand up to her throat, as if feeling an agony of strangulation. The man from Duluth stood on a chair.

Two furious men had dropped from the ceiling, or come up through the floor or from somewhere. They appeared suddenly, like apparitions, in the very center of the hall. It was all as quick as an explosion. There had been peace and jollity; in a flash it was changed to lurid war. Violent, red-faced, swift of motion, they were hammering at each other with their fists, and lunging with their feet in the manner of French infantry soldiers. Their eyes flashed tragic hatred. There was prodigal expenditure of the most vast and extraordinary emotions. The blows were delivered with the energy of mad murder. In that instant of silence that followed the first shrieks and exclamations of the women one could hear their breaths come quick and harsh from between their clenched teeth.

But the men were about eight feet apart from each other. Their savage fists cut harmlessly through the air; the terrific deadly lunges of their feet were mere demonstrations of some kind. The man from Duluth climbed down from his chair. "They're a pair of birds," he said with supreme contempt. He regarded them with eyes of reproach. Apparently he considered that they had swindled him out of something, and he was much injured.

The vivid picture was blurred in a few seconds. Everybody had been frozen for a minute; then all rushed forward. Friends of both parties took flying leaps to avert a dreadful tragedy. The floor became a surge of men, tussling, tugging, and gesticulating in tremendous excitement. The principals in the affair were dragged this way and that way. There arose a wild clamor of explanation, condemnation, and reiteration.

The women, left without escorts, stood trying to look in other directions. Some shuddered with fear; some incessantly tapped the floor with the tips of their boots. They turned to each other with little nervous remarks. And over at a table directly opposite the battle sat the man from Duluth and his friends, silent, motionless, absorbed, grinning with wild, strange glee.

It was impossible to look upon the jumble of men, emotions, and swift French oaths without expecting some sort of a deadly riot. There was an impending horror. Men, frenzied with rage, gestured in each other's faces, the quivering fingers threatened eyes. The lightning-blooded spirit of battle hovered over the swaying crowd. The man from Duluth and his friends were carven with interest. There was a great fight coming, and they were on the spot.

But the crowd finally finished their explanations, their condemnations, and their reiterations. Their fury expended itself in the air; the flaming words and gestures had absorbed the energy for war. Generally the men went back to their female friends. Their collars were wilted, from the grandeur of their emotions perhaps, but they had expressed themselves, and they were satisfied. Only a little mob of five or six people was left upon the scene. They still gestured and roared at each other.

"Oh, what a fake!" said the disgusted man from Duluth. "A great big fight in which nobody hits anybody else. It gives me a pain." He leaned back in his chair and stretched out his legs. He thrust his hands into his pockets and stared calmly, contemptuously, and with incredible insolence at the agitated group before him. "What a husky lot of willies!" Gradually he assumed a demeanor of the greatest importance and prowess. He sneered boldly and obviously at the wrangle. "Holy smoke! I could whip about eight hundred pounds of 'em." He was getting just a little bit drunk.

Downstairs from the gallery at that moment came a little, fat, tipsy Frenchman who was fated to play a great part. Evidently he was aware that there had been a difficulty, and he decided, of course, that with his peculiarly lucid intellect he could go over and straighten the whole thing. So he tottered uncertainly to the crowd, and, wedging his fat body among the gesticulators, he began to argue and explain in a slow, aimless, drunken fashion. No one paid attention to him at first, but it was not long before he had inaugurated an entirely new turmoil. He got one of the principals by the lapel and began another slow, distant harangue. This impassioned individual jerked away and swore in intense French.

Then came again the red apparition of war. There were renewed jostlings, gestures, oaths. Another tragedy impended, perhaps, but the man from Duluth stretched himself and said, "Oh, Gawd," in a tone from the profound and absolute depth of scorn.

Suddenly a woman came toward the crowd. Her hands were outstretched like the claws of an eagle. There was an unspeakable rage in her face, but her high and quavering voice held a burden of tears. "Ah, I kin lick you meself," she cried, with an accent that was from the street. She made a furious dive at the little, fat, tipsy Frenchman.

It seemed that this other man, a principal in the previous affair, was something to her. She had waited back there and trembled long enough. Now she was coming forward like a chieftainess of savages. That little, fat, tipsy Frenchman was the final exasperation; he had renewed the peril to her lover. She sprang at him. At last, at last there was war—real, red war. The man from Duluth climbed swiftly to an erect position upon his chair and cheered with valiant enthusiasm.

The little, fat, tipsy Frenchman was like a porpoise caught in a mighty human net. His face wore an expression of utter drunken woe and astonishment. There was one long crimson mark down his cheek. A dozen men held him and hauled him and berated him and fought at him. A half-dozen more beseeched the woman, holding her arms. Her shrill scream rose above the hoarse babble.

Then from an inner room came a large waiter. He was pushed on by the proprietress of the place, a dingy woman in a brown dress. She was giving him hurried directions, and he was nodding his head, "Yes, yes."

He made a violent charge and seized the little Frenchman, who was casting despairing glances at the ceiling, praying for succor or at least explanation of this phenomenon. The large waiter grappled his coat collar. He gave a prodigious jerk. The little Frenchman's collar and necktie came off with a ripping sound. He was in the last agonies of bewilderment.

Two or three men were trying to pacify the woman. She was turning from them always to shriek at the little Frenchman, who was being noisily dragged out by the large waiter.

She replied in screams to her friends who intercepted her: "Well, no man dare call me a name like that, not any man here. I dare any johnnie in this room to call me a name like that."

"Hurrah!" shouted the man from Duluth from on top of his chair. "Hurrah! hurrah for America and 'The Star-Spangled Banner!' No man here dare call the lady anything."

"What's that?" said the woman. She came ominously toward him. Her face was red and fierce. Her hands were held in the same peculiar claw-like manner. "What's that yeh say?"

"Madam," said the man from Duluth, suddenly sober and serious, "I didn't mean to reflect upon you in any way." His chair shook a little as he changed his weight from one leg to the other. His friends, down below at the table, were gazing solemnly at the ceiling. They were in deep thought.

"Well, yeh think yer jollyin' me, don't yeh?" burst out the woman with sudden violence. "I'll let yeh know—"

The man from Duluth looked down at his friends. He bowed swiftly, but with satirical ceremony. "This is too many for me, boys. I've got no further use for this place. Tra-la-loo! I'll see you next year." He made a flying leap and ran for the door. The woman made a grab at his coattails, but she missed him.

February, 1901

[*Metropolitan Magazine,* Vol. 13, pp. 175–181.]

A MAN BY THE NAME OF MUD

Deep in a leather chair, the Kid sat looking out at where the rain slanted
before the dull brown houses and hammered swiftly upon an occasional
lonely cab. The happy crackle from the great and glittering fireplace behind
him had evidently no meaning of content for him. He appeared morose
and unapproachable, and when a man appears morose and unapproachable it is a fine chance for his intimate friends. Three or four of them discovered his mood, and so hastened to be obnoxious.

"What's wrong, Kid? Lost your thirst?"

"He can never be happy again. He has lost his thirst."

"That's right, Kid. When you quarrel with a man who can whip you,
resort to sarcastic reflection and distance."

They cackled away persistently, but the Kid was mute and continued to
stare gloomily at the street.

Once a man who had been writing letters looked up and said, "I saw
your friend at the Comique the other night." He waited a moment and
then added, "In back."

The Kid wheeled about in his chair at this information, and all the others
saw then that it was important. One man said with deep intelligence, "Ho,
ho, a woman, hey? A woman's come between the two Kids. A woman.
Great, eh?" The Kid launched a glare of scorn across the room, and then
turned again to a contemplation of the rain. His friends continued to do
all in their power to worry him, but they fell ultimately before his impregnable silence.

As it happened, he had not been brooding upon his friend's mysterious
absence at all. He had been concerned with himself. Once in a while he
seemed to perceive certain futilities and lapsed them immediately into a
state of voiceless dejection. These moods were not frequent.

An unexplained thing in his mind, however, was greatly enlightened by
the words of the gossip. He turned then from his harrowing scrutiny of
the amount of pleasure he achieved from living, and settled into a comfortable reflection upon the state of his comrade, the other Kid.

Perhaps it could be indicated in this fashion: "Went to Comique, I suppose. Saw girl. Secondary part, probably. Thought her rather natural.
Went to Comique again. Went again. One time happened to meet omnipotent and good-natured friend. Broached subject to him with great caution.
Friend said—'Why, certainly, my boy, come round tonight, and I'll take
you in back. Remember, it's against all rules, but I think that in your case,
etc.' Kid went. Chorus girls winked same old wink. 'Here's another dude on

the prowl.' Kid aware of this, swearing under his breath and looking very stiff. Meets girl. Knew beforehand that the footlights might have sold him, but finds her very charming. Does not say single thing to her which she naturally expected to hear. Makes no reference to her beauty nor her voice— if she has any. Perhaps takes it for granted that she knows. Girl don't exactly love this attitude, but then feels admiration, because after all she can't tell whether he thinks her nice or whether he don't. New scheme this. Worked by occasional guys in Rome and Egypt, but still, new scheme. Kid goes away. Girl thinks. Later, nails omnipotent and good-natured friend. 'Who was that you brought back?' 'Oh, him? Why, he—' Describes the Kid's wealth, feats, and virtues—virtues of disposition. Girl propounds clever question—'Why did he wish to meet me?' Omnipotent person says, 'Damned if I know.' "

Later, Kid asks girl to supper. Not wildly anxious, but very evident that he asks her because he likes her. Girl accepts; goes to supper. Kid very good comrade and kind. Girl begins to think that here at last is a man who understands her. Details ambitions—long, wonderful ambitions. Explains her points of superiority over the other girls of stage. Says their lives disgust her. She wants to work and study and make something of herself. Kid smokes vast number of cigarettes. Displays and feels deep sympathy. Recalls, but faintly, that he has heard it on previous occasions. They have an awfully good time. Part at last in front of apartment house. "Good night, old chap." "Good night." Squeeze hands hard. Kid has no information at all about kissing her good night, but don't even try. Noble youth. Wise youth. Kid goes home and smokes. Feels strong desire to kill people who say intolerable things of the girl in rows. "Narrow, mean, stupid, ignorant, damnable people." Contemplates the broad, fine liberality of his experienced mind.

Kid and girl become very chummy. Kid like a brother. Listens to her troubles. Takes her out to supper regularly and regularly. Chorus girls now tacitly recognize him as the main guy. Sometimes, may be, girl's mother sick. Can't go to supper. Kid always very noble. Understands perfectly the probabilities of there being others. Lays for 'em, but makes no discoveries. Begins to wonder whether he is a winner or whether she is a girl of marvelous cleverness. Can't tell. Maintains himself with dignity, however. Only occasionally inveighs against the men who prey upon the girls of the stage. Still noble.

Time goes on. Kid grows less noble. Perhaps decides not to be noble at all, or as little as he can. Still inveighs against the men who prey upon the girls of the stage. Thinks the girl stunning. Wants to be dead sure there are no others. Once suspects it, and immediately makes the colossal mistake of his life. Takes the girl to task. Girl won't stand it for a minute. Harangues him. Kid surrenders and pleads with her—pleads with her. Kid's name is mud.

March, 1902

[*Last Words*. London: Digby, Long & Co., pp. 258–262.]

STEPHEN CRANE: A CHRONOLOGY

1871   Birth of Stephen Crane on November 1 at 14 Mulberry Place, Newark, New Jersey. The fourteenth and last child of Reverend Jonathan Townley Crane, graduate of the College of New Jersey (later Princeton University) and presiding elder for the Newark district of Methodism; and his wife Mary Helen, graduate of the City College of New York and daughter of a well-known Methodist minister, George Peck.

1876   Family moves to Paterson, New Jersey, where Dr. Crane is appointed to Cross Street Church.

1878   Dr. Crane is appointed pastor at Port Jervis, New York. In September, Stephen begins his public school education here, the locale of his later *Whilomville Stories* and "The Monster."

1880   Death of Dr. Crane in Port Jervis on February 16. Mrs. Crane supports family by writing for Methodist papers and the New York *Tribune* and the Philadelphia *Press*.

1882   Mrs. Crane moves to Asbury Park, New Jersey, where Stephen attends school until 1888.

1885   Stephen writes his first story, "Uncle Jake and the Bell Handle," never published during his lifetime.

1888   In January, Stephen enrolls at Hudson River Institute (Claverack College) in Claverack, New York, and remains here until 1890. Publishes his first sketch, "Henry M. Stanley," in school magazine *Vidette* (February 1890), and is promoted to captain in military drill. Probably hears Civil War tales from history teacher, retired General Van Petten. During the summer months (1888–92), Stephen assists his brother Townley who operates a news bureau at Asbury Park.

1890   Stephen enters Lafayette College in September as engineering student. Poor class attendance.

1891   Transfers to Syracuse University in January. Correspondent for the New York *Tribune* in Syracuse. Presumably sells sketches to the Detroit *Free Press*; publishes his first story, "The King's Favor," in May issue of the Syracuse *University Herald;* and begins writing

Maggie. Spends little time in the classroom; ends college career in June. During the summer, he meets Hamlin Garland at Avon-by-the-Sea and reports his lecture on William Dean Howells (August 18). In love with Helen Trent. Mother dies in Paterson on December 7.

1892 First substantial publication of his short fiction; five of his *Sullivan County Sketches* appear in the New York *Tribune* (July 3, 10, 17, 24, 31). First of his New York City sketches published, "The Broken-Down Van" (July 10). Fired as reporter by *Tribune* for writing sardonic article on parading Junior Order of United American Mechanics at Asbury Park (August 21). In love with Lily Brandon Munroe.

1893 *Maggie: A Girl of the Streets* is rejected by various publishers; Crane publishes it at his own cost under pseudonym Johnston Smith. Receives encouragement from Garland and Howells. Begins writing *The Red Badge of Courage.*

1894 Sells abridged version (18,000 words) of *The Red Badge* to Bacheller-Johnson Syndicate for ninety dollars; it appears first in the Philadelphia *Press* (December 3–8). Short stories and sketches on social issues appear in *The Arena* and New York *Press.*

1895 In January, meets and falls in love with Nellie Crouse. This same month he begins his trip to the American West and Mexico, writing special features for the Bacheller-Johnson Syndicate. Meets Willa Cather in Lincoln, Nebraska. Publishes volume of free verse in May, *The Black Riders,* which influences later Imagist poets. The complete version (50,000 words) of *The Red Badge* is published by Appleton in October and becomes a best seller and wins a large following in England.

1896 *George's Mother* and revised version of *Maggie* published in June. In September, Crane defends Dora Clark, arrested for "soliciting"; this incident makes him continual target of New York City police. Publishes his first collection of stories, *The Little Regiment and Other Episodes of the American Civil War,* in November, his "last thing dealing with battle." Meets Cora Taylor (Howorth) in November in Jacksonville, Florida, at her establishment, Hotel de Dream.

1897 Shipwrecked off Florida coast on January 2 on *Commodore,* carrying contraband to Cuban insurgents; this incident is source of "The Open Boat," which appears in June. With Cora Taylor he covers short-lived Greco-Turkish War (April–May) as war correspondent for New York *Journal* and *Westminster Gazette.* Publishes *The Third Violet* in May (serialized the previous year). Resides at

Ravensbrook House (Oxted, Surrey) in England with Cora; no evidence that they were ever legally married. Friendships with Joseph Conrad, Henry James, Ford Madox Ford, Harold Frederic, and others. Travels to Ireland in September.

1898   To Cuba and the Spanish-American War as correspondent for Pulitzer's New York *World* and later Hearst's New York *Journal*; first dispatches in April, and last in November. Richard Harding Davis names him the best of the war correspondents in Cuba. Publishes *The Open Boat and Other Tales of Adventure* (April). At the peak of his short story craft, with the appearance of "The Bride Comes to Yellow Sky" (February), "Death and the Child" (March), "The Monster" (August), and "The Blue Hotel" (November–December).

1899   Crane returns to England and to Cora in January; resides at Brede Place (Sussex), legend-filled castle. Publishes second book of poems, *War Is Kind; The Monster and Other Stories;* and *Active Service,* a novel based on his Greek experiences. Writes at feverish pace to pay off many debts; plans a novel on the American Revolution, never finished; and starts *The O'Ruddy,* his last novel.

1900   Recurrence of earlier tubercular attacks in January and periodically until his death on June 5 in a sanitorium at Badenweiler, Germany. Buried at Hillside, New Jersey. Appearance of *Whilomville Stories* and Cuban war stories, *Wounds in the Rain.*

1901   Publication of Crane's non-fictional historical sketches (researched by Kate Frederic), *Great Battles of the World.*

1902   Publication of *Last Words,* which included much of Crane's earliest work; at least two stories, "The Squire's Madness" and "The Man from Duluth," were completed by Cora.

1903   Publication of *The O'Ruddy,* completed by Robert Barr.